WILD CARDS

ACES ABROAD

WILD CARDS

ACES ABROAD

A MOSAIC NOVEL

Edited by

George R. R. Martin

And written by

Stephen Leigh

John Jos. Miller

Leanne C. Harper

Kevin Andrew Murphy

Gail Gerstner-Miller

Walton Simons

Edward Bryant

Lewis Shiner

Carrie Vaughn

Victor W. Milan

Melinda M. Snodgrass

Michael Cassutt

First published in Great Britain in 2014
by Gollancz
An imprint of the Orion Publishing Group
Orion House, 5 Upper St Martin's Lane,
London WC2H 9EA
An Hachette UK Company

This edition published in Great Britain in 2014
by Gollancz

1 3 5 7 9 10 8 6 4 2

A CIP catalogue record for this book
is available from the British Library

ISBN 978 1 4732 0513 0

Printed by Clays Ltd, Birkenhead, Merseyside

bound by CPI Group (UK) Ltd,
Croydon, CR0 4YY

The Orion Publishing Group's policy is to use papers that are
natural, renewable and recyclable products and made from wood
grown in sustainable forests. The logging and manufacturing
processes are expected to conform to the environmental
regulations of the country of origin.

www.georgerrmartin.com
www.orionbooks.co.uk

For Terry Matz,
a treasured friend for longer than
I care to think about

Editor's Note

THE TINT OF HATRED

Stephen Leigh

PROLOGUE

Thursday, November 27, 1986, Washington, DC:

The Sony threw flickering light over Sara's Thanksgiving feast: a Swanson turkey dinner steaming in foil on the coffee table. On the television screen a mob of misshapen jokers marched through a sweltering New York summer afternoon, their mouths moving in silent screams and curses. The grainy scene had the jerky look of an old newsreel, and suddenly the picture swung about to show a handsome man in his mid-thirties, his sleeves rolled up, his suit coat slung over a shoulder and his tie loose on his neck – Senator Gregg Hartmann, as he had been in 1976. Hartmann strode through the police lines blockading the jokers, shrugging away the security men who tried to hold him, shouting at the police himself. Alone, he stood between the authorities and the oncoming crowd of jokers, motioning them back.

Then the camera panned toward a disturbance within the ranks of jokers. The images were jumbled and out of focus: at the center was the ace/prostitute known as Succubus, her body seemingly made of quicksilver flesh, her appearance constantly shifting. The wild card had cursed her with sexual empathy. Succubus could take on whatever shape and form most pleased her clients, but that ability was now out of control. Around her, people responded to her power, grasping out for her with a strange lust on their faces. Her mouth was open in an imploring scream as the pursuing crowd, police and jokers both, bore her down. Her arms were stretched out in supplication, and as the camera panned back, there was Hartmann again, his jaw open in surprise as he gaped at Succubus. Her arms were reaching for *him*, her plea was for *him*. Then she was gone under the mob. For several seconds she was buried, lost. But then the crowd drew back in horror. The camera followed Hartmann closer: he shoved through those around Succubus, angrily pushed them away.

Sara reached for the VCR's remote switch. She touched the pause button, freezing the scene, a moment of time that had shaped her life. She could feel the hot tears streaking her face.

Succubus lay twisted in a pool of blood, her body mangled, her face turned upward as Hartmann stared at her, mirroring Sara's horror.

Sara knew the face that Succubus, whoever she might have really been, had found just before death. Those young features had haunted Sara since childhood – Succubus had taken on Andrea Whitman's face.

Sara's older sister's face. Andrea who, at thirteen, had been brutally murdered in 1950.

Sara knew who had kept that pubescent image of Andrea locked away in his mind for so many years. She knew who had placed Andrea's features on the infinitely malleable body of Succubus. She could imagine that face on Succubus as he lay with her, and that thought hurt Sara most of all.

'You bastard,' Sara whispered to Senator Hartmann, her voice choking. 'You goddamn bastard. You killed my sister and you couldn't even let her stay dead.'

FROM *THE JOURNAL*
OF XAVIER DESMOND

November 30/Jokertown:

My name is Xavier Desmond, and I am a joker.

Jokers are always strangers, even on the street where they were born, and this one is about to visit a number of strange lands. In the next five months I will see veldts and mountains, Rio and Cairo, the Khyber Pass and the Straits of Gibraltar, the Outback and the Champs-Élysées – all very far from home for a man who has often been called the mayor of Jokertown. Jokertown, of course, has no mayor. It is a neighborhood, a ghetto neighborhood at that, and not a city. Jokertown is more than a place though. It is a condition, a state of mind. Perhaps in that sense my title is not undeserved.

I have been a joker since the beginning. Forty years ago, when Jetboy died in the skies over Manhattan and loosed the wild card upon the world, I was twenty-nine years of age, an investment banker with a lovely wife, a two-year-old daughter, and a bright future ahead of me. A month later, when I was finally released from the hospital, I was a monstrosity with a pink elephantine trunk growing from the center of my face where my nose had been. There are seven perfectly functional fingers at the end of my trunk, and over the years I have become quite adept with this 'third hand.' Were I suddenly restored to so-called normal humanity, I believe it would be as traumatic as if one of my limbs were amputated. With my trunk I am ironically somewhat more than human ... and infinitely less.

5

My lovely wife left me within two weeks of my release from the hospital, at approximately the same time that Chase Manhattan informed me that my services would no longer be required. I moved to Jokertown nine months later, following my eviction from my Riverside Drive apartment for 'health reasons.' I last saw my daughter in 1948. She was married in June of 1964, divorced in 1969, remarried in June of 1972. She has a fondness for June weddings, it seems. I was invited to neither of them. The private detective I hired informs me that she and her husband now live in Salem, Oregon, and that I have two grandchildren, a boy and a girl, one from each marriage. I sincerely doubt that either knows that their grandfather is the mayor of Jokertown.

I am the founder and president emeritus of the Jokers' Anti-Defamation League, or JADL, the oldest and largest organization dedicated to the preservation of civil rights for the victims of the wild card virus. The JADL has had its failures, but overall it has accomplished great good. I am also a moderately successful businessman. I own one of New York's most storied and elegant night-clubs, the Funhouse, where jokers and nats and aces have enjoyed all the top joker cabaret acts for more than two decades. The Funhouse has been losing money steadily for the last five years, but no one knows that except me and my accountant. I keep it open because it is, after all, the Funhouse, and were it to close, Jokertown would seem a poorer place.

Next month I will be seventy years of age.

My doctor tells me that I will not live to be seventy-one. The cancer had already metastasized before it was diagnosed. Even jokers cling stubbornly to life, and I have been doing the chemotherapy and the radiation treatments for half a year now, but the cancer shows no sign of remission.

My doctor tells me the trip I am about to embark on will probably take months off my life. I have my prescriptions and will dutifully continue to take the pills, but when one is globe-hopping, radiation therapy must be forgone. I have accepted this.

Mary and I often talked of a trip around the world, in those days before the wild card when we were young and in love. I could never have dreamt that I would finally take that trip without her, in the twilight of my life, and at government expense, as a delegate on a fact-finding mission organized and funded by the Senate Committee on Ace Resources and Endeavors, under the official sponsorship of the United Nations and the World Health Organization. We will visit every continent but Antarctica and call upon thirty-nine different countries (some only for a few hours), and our official charge is to investigate the treatment of wild card victims in cultures around the world.

There are twenty-one delegates, only five of whom are jokers. I suppose my selection is a great honor, recognition of my achievements and my status as a community leader. I believe I have my good friend Dr. Tachyon to thank for it.

But then, I have my good friend Dr. Tachyon to thank for a great many things.

THE TINT OF HATRED

PART ONE

Monday, December 1, 1986, Syria:

A chill, arid wind blew from the mountains of the Jabal Alawite across the lava rock and gravel desert of Badiyat Ash-sham. The wind snapped the canvas peaks of the tents huddled around the village. The gale made those in the market pull the sashes of their robes tighter against the cold. Under the beehive roof of the largest of the mud-brick buildings, a stray gust caused the flame to gutter against the bottom of an enameled teapot.

A small woman, swathed in the *chador*, the black Islamic garb, poured tea into two small cups. Except for a row of bright blue beads on the headpiece, she wore no ornamentation. She passed one of the cups to the other person in the room, a raven-haired man of medium height, whose skin glowed a shimmering, lambent emerald under a brocaded robe of azure. She could feel the warmth radiating from him.

'It will be colder for the next several days, Najib,' she said as she sipped the piercingly sweet tea. 'You'll be more comfortable at least.'

Najib shrugged as if her words meant nothing. His lips tightened; his dark, intense gaze snared her. 'It's Allah's presence that gleams,' he said, his voice gruff with habitual arrogance. 'You've never heard me complain, Misha, even in the heat of summer. Do you think me a woman, wailing my futile misery to the sky?'

Above the veils, Misha's eyes narrowed. 'I am *Kahina*, the Seer, Najib,' she answered, allowing a hint of defiance into her voice. 'I know many hidden things. I know that when the heat ripples over the stones, my brother Najib wishes that he were not *Nur al-Allah*, the Light of Allah.'

Najib's sudden backhanded cuff caught his sister across the side of her face. Her head snapped sideways. Scalding hot tea burned her hand and wrist; the cup shattered on the rugs as she sprawled at his feet. His eyes, utter black against the luminescent face, glared at her as she raised her hand to her stinging cheek. She knew she dared say no more. On her knees she gathered up the shards of the teacup in silence, mopping at the puddle of tea with the hem of her robe.

'Sayyid came to me this morning,' Najib said as he watched her. 'He was complaining again. He says you are not a proper wife.'

'Sayyid is a fatted pig,' Misha answered, though she did not look up.

'He says he must force himself on you.'

'He doesn't need to do so for *me*.'

Najib scowled, making a sound of disgust. '*Pah!* Sayyid leads my army. It is his strategy that will sweep the *kafir* back into the sea. Allah has given him the body of a god and the mind of a conqueror, and he is obedient to me. That's why I gave you to him. The Qur'an says it: "Men have authority over women because Allah has made the one superior to the other. Good women are obedient." You make a mockery of Nur al-Allah's gift.'

'Nur al-Allah shouldn't have given away that which completes him.' Now her eyes came up, challenging him as her tiny hands closed over the pottery shards. 'We were together in the womb, Brother. That's the way Allah made us. He touched you with His light and His voice, and He gave me the gift of His sight. You are His mouth, the prophet; I am your vision of the future. Don't be so foolish as to blind yourself. Your pride will defeat you.'

'Then listen to the words of Allah and be humble. Be glad that Sayyid does not insist on *purdah* for you – he knows you're Kahina, so he doesn't force your seclusion. Our father should never have sent you to Damascus to be educated; the infection of the unbelievers is insidious. Misha, make Sayyid content because that will content me. My will is Allah's will.'

'Only sometimes, Brother …' She paused. Her gaze went distant, her fingers clenched. She cried out as porcelain lacerated her palm. Blood drooled bright along the shallow cuts. Misha swayed, moaning, and then her gaze focused once more.

Najib moved a step closer to her. 'What is it? What did you see?'

Misha cradled her injured hand to her breast, her pupils wide with pain. 'All that ever matters is that which touches yourself, Najib. It doesn't matter that I hurt or that I hate my husband or that Najib and his sister Misha have been lost in Allah's roles for them. All that matters is what the Kahina can tell Nur al-Allah.'

'Woman …' Najib began warningly. His voice had a compelling deepness now, a timbre that brought Misha's head up and made her open her mouth to begin to speak, to obey without thinking. She shivered as if the wind outside had touched her.

'Don't use the gift on me, Najib,' she said gratingly. Her voice sounded harsh against that of her brother. 'I'm not a supplicant. Compel me too often with Allah's tongue and you might one day find that Allah's eyes have been taken from you by my own hand.'

'Then *be* Kahina, Sister,' Najib answered, but it was only his own voice now. He watched as she went to an inlaid chest, took out a strip of cloth, and slowly wrapped her hand. 'Tell me what you just saw. Was it the vision of the *jihad*? Did you see me holding the Caliph's scepter again?'

Misha shut her eyes, bringing back the image of the quick waking dream. 'No,' she told him. 'This was new. In the distance I saw a falcon against the sun. As the bird flew closer, I noticed that it held a hundred people squirming in its talons. A giant stood below on a mountain, and the giant held a bow in his hands. He loosed an arrow at the bird, and the wounded falcon screamed in anger. The voices of those it held screamed also. The giant had nocked a second arrow, but now the bow began to twist in his hands, and the arrow instead struck the giant's own breast. I saw the giant fall …' Misha's eyes opened. 'That's all.'

Najib scowled. He passed a glowing hand over his eyes. 'What does it mean?'

'I don't know what it means. Allah gives me the dreams, but not always the understanding. Perhaps the giant is Sayyid—'

'It was only your own dream, not Allah's.' Najib stalked away from her, and she knew that he was angry. 'I'm the falcon, holding the faithful,' he said. 'You are the giant, large because you belong to Sayyid, who is also large. Allah would remind you of the consequence of defiance.' He faced away from Misha, closing the shutters of the window against the brilliant desert sun. Outside the muzzein called from the village mosque: '*A shhadu allaa alaha illa llah*' – Allah is great. I bear witness that there is no God but Allah.

'All you want is your conquest, the dream of the *jihad*. You want to be the new Muhammad,' Misha answered spitefully. 'You won't accept any other interpretation.'

'*In sha'allah,*' Najib answered: if Allah wills. He refused to face her. 'Some people Allah has visited with His dreadful Scourge, showing their sins with their rotting, twisted flesh. Others, like Sayyid, Allah has favored, gifting them. Each has been given his due. He has chosen *me* to lead the faithful. I only do what I *must* do – I have Sayyid, who guides my armies, and I fight also with the hidden ones like al-Muezzin. You lead too. You are Kahina, and you are also *Fqihas*, the one the women look to for guidance.'

The Light of Allah turned back into the room. In the shuttered dimness he was a spectral presence. 'And as I do Allah's will, *you* must do mine.'

Monday, December 1, 1986, New York:
The press reception was chaos.

Senator Gregg Hartmann finally escaped to an empty corner behind one of the Christmas trees, his wife Ellen and his aide John Werthen following. Gregg surveyed the room with a distinct frown. He shook his head toward the Justice Department ace Billy Ray – Carnifex – and the government security man who tried to join them, waving them back.

Gregg had spent the last hour fending off reporters, smiling blankly for video cameras, and blinking into the constant storm lightning of electronic flashes. The room was noisy with shouted questions and the *click-whirr* of high-speed Nikons. Musak played seasonal tunes over the ceiling speakers.

The main press contingent was now gathered around Dr. Tachyon, Chrysalis, and Peregrine. Tachyon's scarlet hair gleamed like a beacon in the crowd; Peregrine and Chrysalis seemed to be competing to see who could pose most provocatively for the cameras. Nearby, Jack Braun – Golden Boy, the Judas Ace – was being pointedly ignored.

The mob had thinned a bit since Hiram Worchester's staff from the Aces High had set up the buffet tables; some of the press had staked permanent claims around the well-freighted trays.

'Sorry, boss,' John said at Gregg's elbow. Even in the cool room the aide was perspiring. Blinking Christmas lights reflected from his beaded forehead: red, then blue, then green. 'Somebody on the airport staff dropped the ball. It wasn't supposed to be this kind of free-for-all. I told them I wanted the press escorted in *after* you guys were settled. They'd ask a few questions, then …' He shrugged. 'I'll take the blame. I should have checked to make sure everything had been done.'

Ellen gave John a withering glance but said nothing.

'If John's apologizing, make him grovel first, Senator. What a mess.' That last was a whisper in Gregg's ear – his other longtime aide, Amy Sorenson, was circulating through the crowd as one of the security personnel. Her two-way radio was linked directly to a wireless receiver in Gregg's ear. She fed him information, gave him names or details concerning the people he met. Gregg's own memory for names and faces was quite good, but Amy was an excellent backup. Between the two of them Gregg rarely missed giving those around him a personal greeting.

John's fear of Gregg's anger was a bright, pulsing purple amidst the jumble of his emotions. Gregg could feel Ellen's placid, dull acceptance, colored slightly with annoyance. 'It's okay, John,' Gregg said softly, though underneath he was seething. That part of him that he thought of as Puppetman squirmed restlessly, begging to be let loose to play with the cascading emotions in the room. *Half of them are our puppets, controllable. Look, there's Father Squid over near the door, trying to get away from that woman reporter. Feel his scarlet distress even as he's smiling? He'd love to slither away and he's too polite to do it. We could fuel that frustration into rage, make him curse the woman. We could feed on that. All it would take is the smallest nudge ...*

But Gregg couldn't do that, not with the aces gathered here, the ones Gregg didn't dare take as puppets because they had mental abilities of their own, or because he simply felt the prospect too risky: Golden Boy, Fantasy, Mistral, Chrysalis. And the one he feared most of all: Tachyon. *If they even had an inkling of Puppetman's existence, if they knew what I've done to feed him, Tachyon'd have them on me in a pack, the way he did with the Masons.*

Gregg took a deep breath. The corner smelled overbearingly of pine. 'Thanks, boss,' John was saying. Already his lilac fear was receding. Across the room, Gregg saw Father Squid finally disengage himself from the reporter and shamble pitifully toward Hiram's buffet on his tentacles. The reporter saw Gregg at the same moment and gave him a strange, piercing glance. She strode toward him.

Amy had seen the movement as well. 'Sara Morgenstern, *Post* correspondent,' she whispered in Gregg's ear. 'Pulitzer,'76, for her work on the Great Jokertown Riot. Cowrote the nasty article on SCARE in July's *Newsweek*. Just had a makeover too. Looks totally different.'

Amy's warning startled Gregg – he hadn't recognized her. Gregg remembered the article; it had stopped just short of libel, intimating that Gregg and the SCARE aces had been involved in government suppression of facts concerning the Swarm Mother attack. He remembered Morgenstern from various press functions, always the one with the hardball questions, with a sharp edge to her voice. He might have taken her for a puppet, just for spite, but she had never come close to him. Whenever they had been at the same affairs, she had stayed well away.

Now, seeing her approach, he froze for an instant. She had indeed changed. Sara had always been slim, boyish. That was accentuated tonight; she wore tight, black slacks and a clinging blouse. She'd dyed her hair blond, and her makeup accentuated her cheekbones and large, faintly blue eyes. She looked distressingly familiar.

Gregg was suddenly cold and afraid.

Inside, Puppetman howled at a remembered loss.

'Gregg, are you all right?' Ellen's hand touched his shoulder. Gregg shivered at his spouse's touch, shaking his head.

'I'm fine,' he said brusquely. He put on his professional smile, moving out from the corner. Alongside him Ellen and John flanked him in practiced choreography. 'Ms. Morgenstern,' Gregg said warmly, extending his hand and forcing his voice into a calmness he didn't feel. 'I think you know John, but my wife Ellen ... ?'

Sara Morgenstern nodded perfunctorily toward Ellen, but her gaze stayed with Gregg. She had an odd, strained smile on her face that seemed half-challenge and half-invitation. 'Senator,' she said, 'I hope you're looking forward to this trip as much as I am.'

She took his proffered hand. Without volition, Puppetman used the moment of contact. As he had done with every new puppet, he traced the neural pathways back to the brain, opening the doors that would, later, allow him access from a distance. He found the locked gates of her emotions, the turbulent colors swirling behind, and he greedily, possessively, touched them. He unfastened the locks and pins, swung open the entrance.

The red-black loathing that spilled out from behind sent him reeling back. The abhorrence was directed toward *him*, all of it. Totally unexpected, the fury of the emotion was like nothing he'd experienced. Its intensity threatened to drown him, it drove him back. Puppetman gasped; Gregg forced himself to show nothing. He let his hand drop as Puppetman moaned in his head, and the fear that had touched him a moment ago redoubled.

She looks like Andrea, like Succubus – the resemblance is startling. And she detests me; God, how she hates.

'Senator?' Sara repeated.

'Yes, I'm very much looking forward to this,' he said automatically. 'Our society's attitudes toward the victims of the wild card virus have changed for the worse in the last year. In some ways people like the Reverend Leo Barnett would have us regress to the oppression of the fifties. For less enlightened countries, the situation is far, far worse. We can offer them understanding, hope, and help. And we'll learn something ourselves. Dr. Tachyon and myself have great optimism for this trip, or we wouldn't have fought so hard to bring it about.'

The words came with rehearsed smoothness while he recovered. He could hear the friendly casualness of his voice, felt his mouth pull into a proud half-smile. But none of it touched him. He could barely avoid staring rudely at Sara. At this woman who reminded him too much of Andrea Whitman, of Succubus.

I loved her. I couldn't save her.

Sara seemed to sense his fascination, for she cocked her head with that same odd challenge. 'It's also an entertaining little junket, a three-month tour of the world at the taxpayer's expense. Your wife goes with you, your good friends like Dr. Tachyon and Hiram Worchester ...'

At his side Gregg felt Ellen's irritation. She was too practiced a politician's wife to respond, but he could feel her sudden alertness, a jungle cat watching for a weakness in her prey. Off balance, Gregg frowned a moment too late. 'I'm surprised a reporter of your experience would believe that, Ms. Morgenstern. This trip also means giving up the holiday season – normally, I go home after the congressional break. It means stops at places that aren't exactly on Fodor's recommended list. It means meetings, briefings, endless press conferences, and a ton of paperwork that I can certainly do without. I guarantee you this isn't a pleasure trip. I'll have more to do than watch the proceedings and cable a thousand words back home every day.'

He felt the black hatred swelling in her, and the power in him ached to be used. *Let me take her. Let me dampen that fire. Take away that hatred and she'll tell you what she knows. Disarm her.*

She's yours, he answered. Puppetman leapt out. Gregg had encountered hatreds before, a hundred times, but none had ever been focused on him. He found control of the emotion elusive and slippery; her loathing pushed at his control like a palpable, living entity, driving Puppetman back.

What the hell is she hiding? What caused this?

'You sound defensive, Senator,' Sara said. 'Still, a reporter can't help but think that the main purpose of the trip, especially for a potential '88 presidential candidate, might be to finally erase the memories of a decade ago.'

Gregg could not help the intake of breath: *Andrea, Succubus.* Sara grinned: a predator's smile. He readied himself to assault her hatred again.

'I'd say the Great Jokertown Riot obsesses both of us, Senator,' she continued, her voice deceivingly light. 'I know it did when I wrote my piece on it. And your behavior after Succubus's death cost you the Democratic nomination that year. After all, she was only a whore – wasn't she, Senator? – and not worth your ... your little *breakdown*.' The reminder made him flush. 'I'll wager we've both thought about that moment every day since then,' Sara continued. 'It's been ten years now, and *I* still remember.'

Puppetman wailed, retreating. Gregg was startled into silence. *My God, what does she know, what is she hinting at?*

He had no time to formulate a reply. Amy's voice spoke in his ear again. 'Digger Downs is heading over at a trot, Senator. He's with *Aces* magazine – covers the entertainment types; a real sleazeball, if you ask me. Guess he saw Morgenstern and figured he'd listen in to a *good* reporter—'

'Hiya, folks,' Downs's voice intruded before Amy had finished speaking. Gregg looked momentarily away from Sara to see a short, pallid young man. Downs fidgeted nervously, sniffing as if he had a head cold. 'Mind another reporter's nosing in, Sara love?'

Downs was a maddening interruption, his manner rude and falsely familiar. He seemed to sense Gregg's turmoil. He grinned and looked from Sara to Gregg, ignoring Ellen and John.

'I think I've said all I want to – for the moment,' Sara answered. Her pale aqua eyes were still locked on Gregg's; her face seemed childlike with feigned innocence. Then, with a lithe turn, she spun away from him, going toward Tachyon. Gregg stared after her.

'Chick's looking damn good these days, ain't she, Senator?' Downs grinned again. 'Begging your pardon, of course, Mrs. Hartmann. Hey, let me introduce myself. I'm Digger Downs, with *Aces* magazine, and I'll be tagging along on this little venture. We'll be seeing a lot of each other.'

Gregg, watching Sara disappear into the crowd around Tachyon, realized that Downs was staring at him strangely. With an effort he forced his attention away from Sara. 'Pleased to meet you,' he said to Downs.

His smile felt wooden. It made his cheeks ache.

FROM *THE JOURNAL*
OF XAVIER DESMOND

December 1/New York City:

The journey is off to an inauspicious start. For the last hour we have been holding on the runway at Tomlin International, waiting for clearance for takeoff. The problem, we are informed, is not here, but down in Havana. So we wait.

Our plane is a custom 747 that the press has dubbed the *Stacked Deck*. The entire central cabin has been converted to our requirements, the seats replaced with a small medical laboratory, a press room for the print journalists, and a miniature television studio for their electronic counterparts. The newsmen themselves have been segregated in the tail. Already they've made it their own. I was back there twenty minutes ago and found a poker game in progress. The business-class cabin is full of aides, assistants, secretaries, publicists, and security personnel. First class is supposedly reserved exclusively for the delegates.

As there are only twenty-one delegates, we rattle around like peas in a pod. Even here the ghettoes persist – jokers tend to sit with jokers, nats with nats, aces with aces.

Hartmann is the only man aboard who seems entirely comfortable with all three groups. He greeted me warmly at the press conference and sat with Howard and myself for a few moments after boarding, talking earnestly about his hopes for the trip. It is difficult not to like the senator. Jokertown has delivered him huge majorities in each of his campaigns as far back as his term as mayor, and no wonder – no other politician has worked so long and hard to defend jokers' rights. Hartmann gives me hope; he's living proof that there can indeed be trust and mutual respect between joker and nat. He's a decent, honorable man, and in these days when fanatics such as Leo Barnett are inflaming the old hatreds and prejudices, jokers need all the friends they can get in the halls of power.

Dr. Tachyon and Senator Hartmann co-chair the delegation. Tachyon arrived dressed like a foreign correspondent from some *film noir* classic, in a trench coat covered with belts, buttons, and epaulettes, a snap-brim fedora rakishly tilted to one side. The fedora sports a foot-long red feather, however, and I cannot begin to imagine where one goes to purchase a powder-blue crushed-velvet trench coat. A pity that those foreign-correspondent films were all in black and white.

Tachyon would like to think that he shares Hartmann's lack of prejudice toward jokers, but that's not strictly true. He labors unceasingly in his clinic, and one cannot doubt that he cares, and cares deeply … many jokers think of him as a saint, a hero … yet, when one has known the doctor as long as I have, deeper truths become apparent. On some unspoken level he thinks of his good works in Jokertown as a penance. He does his best to hide it, but even after all these years you can see the revulsion in his eyes. Dr. Tachyon and I are 'friends,' we have known each other for decades now, and I believe with all my heart that he sincerely cares for me … but not for a second have I ever felt that he considers me an equal, as Hartmann does. The senator treats me like a man, even an important man, courting me as he might any political leader with votes to deliver. To Dr. Tachyon, I will always be a joker.

Is that his tragedy, or mine?

Tachyon knows nothing of the cancer. A symptom that our friendship is as diseased as my body? Perhaps. He has not been my personal physician for many years now. My doctor is a joker, as are my accountant, my attorney, my broker, and even my banker – the world has changed since the Chase dismissed me, and as mayor of Jokertown I am obliged to practice my own personal brand of affirmative action.

We have just been cleared for takeoff. The seat-hopping is over, people are belting themselves in. It seems I carry Jokertown with me wherever I go – Howard Mueller sits closest to me, his seat customized to accommodate his nine-foot tall form and the immense length of his arms. He's better known as Troll, and he works as chief of security at Tachyon's clinic, but I note that he does not sit with Tachyon among the aces. The other three joker delegates – Father Squid, Chrysalis, and the poet Dorian Wilde – are also here in the center section of first class. Is it coincidence, prejudice, or shame that puts us here, in the seats furthest from the windows? Being a joker makes one a tad paranoid about these things, I fear. The politicians, of both the domestic and UN varieties, have clustered to our right, the aces forward of us (aces up front, of course, of course) and to our left. Must stop now, the stewardess has asked me to put my tray table back up.

Airborne. New York and Robert Tomlin International Airport are far behind us, and Cuba waits ahead. From what I've heard, it will be an easy and pleasant first stop. Havana is almost as American as Las Vegas or Miami Beach, albeit considerably more decadent and wicked. I may actually have friends there – some of the top joker entertainers go on to the Havana casinos after getting their starts in the Funhouse and the Chaos Club. I must remind myself to stay away from the gaming tables, however; joker luck is notoriously bad.

As soon as the seat belt sign went off, a number of the aces ascended to the first-class lounge. I can hear their laughter drifting down the spiral stairway – Peregrine, pretty young Mistral – who looks just like the college student she is when not in her flying gear – boisterous Hiram Worchester, and Asta Lenser, the ballerina from the ABT whose ace name is Fantasy. Already they are a tight little clique, a 'fun bunch' for whom nothing could possibly go wrong. The golden people, and Tachyon very much in their midst. Is it the aces or the women that draw him? I wonder? Even my dear friend Angela, who still loves the man deeply after twenty-odd years, admits that Dr. Tachyon thinks mainly with his penis where women are concerned.

Yet even among the aces there are the odd men out. Jones, the black strongman from Harlem (like Troll and Hiram W. and Peregrine, he requires a custom seat, in his case to support his extraordinary weight), is nursing a beer and reading a copy of *Sports Illustrated*. Radha O'Reilly is just as solitary, gazing out the window. She seems very quiet. Billy Ray and Joanne Jefferson, the two Justice Department aces who head up our security contingent, are not delegates and thus are seated back in the second section.

And then there is Jack Braun. The tensions that swirl around him are almost palpable. Most of the other delegates are polite to him, but no one is truly friendly, and he's being openly shunned by some, such as Hiram Worchester. For Dr. Tachyon, clearly Braun does not even exist. I wonder whose idea it was to bring him on this trip? Certainly not Tachyon's, and it seems too politically dangerous for Hartmann to be responsible. A gesture to appease the conservatives on SCARE perhaps? Or are there ramifications that I have not considered?

Braun glances up at the stairway from time to time, as if he would love nothing so much as to join the happy group upstairs, but remains firmly in his seat. It is hard to credit that this smooth-faced, blond-haired boy in the tailored safari jacket is really the notorious Judas Ace of the fifties. He's my age or close to it, but he looks barely twenty … the kind of boy who might have taken pretty young Mistral to her senior prom a few years back and gotten her home well before midnight.

One of the reporters, a man named Downs from *Aces* magazine, was up here earlier, trying to get Braun to consent to an interview. He was persistent, but Braun's refusal was firm, and Downs finally gave up. Instead he handed out copies of the latest issue of *Aces* and then sauntered up to the lounge, no doubt to pester someone else. I am not a regular reader of *Aces*, but I accepted a copy and suggested to Downs that his publisher consider a companion periodical, to be called *Jokers*. He was not overly enthused about the idea.

The issue features a rather striking cover photograph of the Turtle's shell outlined against the oranges and reds of sunset, blurbed with 'The Turtle – Dead or Alive?' The Turtle has not been seen since Wild Card Day, back in September, when he was napalmed and crashed into the Hudson. Twisted and burnt pieces of his shell were found on the riverbed, though no body has ever been recovered. Several hundred people claim to have seen the Turtle near dawn the following day, flying an older shell in the sky over Jokertown, but since he has not reappeared since, some are putting that sighting down to hysteria and wishful thinking.

I have no opinion on the Turtle, though I would hate to think that he was truly dead. Many jokers believe that he is one of us, that his shell conceals some unspeakable joker deformity. Whether that is true or not, he has been a good friend to Jokertown for a long, long time.

There is, however, an aspect to this trip that no one ever speaks of, although Downs's article brings it to mind. Perhaps it falls to me to mention the unmentionable then. The truth is, all that laughter up in the lounge has a slightly nervous ring to it, and it is no coincidence that this junket, under discussion for so many years, was put together so swiftly in the past two months. They want to get us out of town for a while – not just the jokers, the aces too. The aces *especially*, one might even say.

This last Wild Card Day was a catastrophe for the city, and for every victim of the virus everywhere. The level of violence was shocking and made headlines across the nation. The still-unsolved murder of the Howler, the dismemberment of a child ace in the midst of a huge crowd at Jetboy's Tomb, the attack on Aces High, the destruction of the Turtle (or at least his shell), the wholesale slaughter at the Cloisters, where a dozen bodies were brought out in pieces, the predawn aerial battle that lit up the entire East Side … days and even weeks later the authorities were still not certain that they had an accurate death toll.

One old man was found literally embedded in a solid brick wall, and when they began to chip him out, they found they could not tell where his flesh ended and the wall began. The autopsy revealed a ghastly mess inside, where his internal organs were fused with the bricks that penetrated them.

A *Post* photographer snapped a picture of that old man trapped in his wall. He looks so gentle and sweet. The police subsequently announced that the old man was an ace himself, and moreover a notorious criminal, that he was responsible for the murders of Kid Dinosaur and the Howler, the attempted murder of the Turtle, the attack on Aces High, the battle over the East River, the ghastly blood rites performed at the Cloisters, and a whole range of lesser crimes. A number of aces came forward to support this explanation, but the public does not seem convinced. According to the polls, more people believe the conspiracy theory put forward in the *National Informer* – that the killings were independent, caused by powerful aces known and unknown carrying out personal vendettas, using their powers in utter disregard for law and public safety, and that afterward those aces conspired with each other and the police to cover up their atrocities, blaming everything on one crippled old man who happened to be conveniently dead, clearly at the hands of some ace.

Already several books have been announced, each purporting to explain what *really* happened – the immoral opportunism of the publishing industry knows no bounds. Koch, ever aware of the prevailing winds, has ordered several cases re-opened and has instructed the IAD to investigate the police role.

Jokers are pitiful and loathed. Aces have great power, and for the first time in many years a sizable segment of the public has begun to distrust those aces and fear that power. No wonder that demagogues like Leo Barnett have swelled so vastly in the public mind of late.

So I'm convinced that our tour has a hidden agenda; to wash away the blood with some 'good ink,' as they say, to defuse the fear, to win back trust and take everyone's mind off Wild Card Day.

I admit to mixed feelings about aces, some of whom definitely do abuse their power. Nonetheless, as a joker, I find myself desperately hoping that we succeed … and desperately fearing the consequences if we do not.

BEASTS OF BURDEN

John J. Miller

'From envy, hatred, and malice, and all uncharitableness, Good
Lord, deliver us.'

– The Litany, *Book of Common Prayer*

His rudimentary sexual organs were dysfunctional, but his mounts
thought of him as masculine, perhaps because his stunted, wasted
body looked more male than female. What he thought of himself
was an unopened book. He never communicated about matters of
that sort.

He had no name but that borrowed from folklore and given to
him by his mounts – Ti Malice – and he didn't really care what
they called him as long as they addressed him with respect. He
liked the dark because his weak eyes were unduly sensitive to light.
He never ate because he had no teeth to chew or tongue to taste.
He never drank alcohol because the primitive sack that was his
stomach couldn't digest it. Sex was out of the question.

But he still enjoyed gourmet foods and vintage wines and expensive liquors and all possible varieties of sexual experience. He
had his mounts.

And he always was looking for more.

I.

Chrysalis lived in the Jokertown slum where she owned a bar, so she was accustomed to viewing scenes of poverty and misery. But Jokertown was a slum in the most affluent country on the earth, and Bolosse, the slum district of Port-au-Prince, Haiti's sprawling waterfront capital city, was in one of the poorest.

From the outside the hospital looked like a set from a B-grade horror movie about an eighteenth-century insane asylum. The wall around it was crumbling stone, the sidewalk leading to it was rotting concrete, and the building itself was filthy from years of accumulated bird shit and grime. Inside, it was worse.

The walls were abstract designs of peeling paint and mildew. The bare wooden floors creaked ominously and once Mordecai Jones, the four-hundred-and-fifty-pound ace called the Harlem Hammer, stepped on a section that gave way. He would have fallen all the way through the floor if an alert Hiram Worchester hadn't quickly relieved him of nine tenths of his weight. The smell clinging to the corridors was indescribable, but was mostly compounded of the various odors of death.

But the very worst, thought Chrysalis, were the patients, especially the children. They lay uncomplainingly on filthy bare mattresses that reeked of sweat, urine, and mildew, their bodies racked by diseases banished long ago in America and wasted by the bloat of malnutrition. They watched their visitors troop by without curiosity or comprehension, serene hopelessness filling their eyes.

It was better being a joker, she thought, though she loathed what the wild card virus had done to her once-beautiful body.

Chrysalis couldn't stand any more of the unrelievable suffering. She left the hospital after passing through the first ward and returned to the waiting motorcade. The driver of the jeep she'd been assigned to looked at her curiously, but said nothing. He hummed a happy little tune while they waited for the others, occasionally singing a few off key phrases in Haitian Creole.

The tropical sun was hot. Chrysalis, bundled in an all-enveloping hood and cloak to protect her delicate flesh and skin from the sun's burning rays, watched a group of children playing across the street from the run-down hospital. Sweat trickling in tickling rivulets down her back, she almost envied the children in the cool freedom of their near nakedness. They seemed to be fishing for something in the depths of the storm drain that ran under the street. It took Chrysalis a moment to realize what they were doing, but when she did, all thoughts of envy disappeared. They were drawing water out of the drain and pouring it into battered, rusty pots and cans. Sometimes they stopped to drink a mouthful.

She looked away, wondering if joining Tachyon's little traveling show had been a mistake. It had sounded like a good idea when Tachyon had invited her. It was, after all, an opportunity to travel around the world at government expense while rubbing shoulders with a variety of important and influential people. There was no telling what interesting tidbits of information she would be able to pick up. It had seemed like such a good idea at the time ...

'Well, my dear, if I hadn't actually seen it with my own eyes, I'd say you hadn't the stomach for this sort of thing.'

She smiled mirthlessly as Dorian Wilde heaved himself into the backseat of the jeep next to her. She wasn't in the mood for the poet's famous wit.

'I certainly wasn't expecting treatment like this,' she said in her cultured British accent as Dr. Tachyon, Senator Hartmann, Hiram Worchester, and other important and influential politicians and aces streamed toward the limos waiting for them, while Chrysalis, Wilde, and the other obvious jokers on the tour had to make do with the dirty, dented jeeps clustered at the rear of the cavalcade.

'You should've,' Wilde said. He was a large man whose delicate features were loosing their handsomeness to bloat. He wore an Edwardian outfit that was in desperate need of cleaning and pressing, and enough floral-scented body wash to make Chrysalis glad that they were in an open vehicle. He waved his left hand languorously as he talked and kept his right in the pocket of his jacket. 'Jokers, after all, are the niggers of the world.' He pursed his lips and glanced at their driver, who, like ninety-five percent of

27

Haiti's population, was black. 'A statement not without irony on this island.'

Chrysalis grabbed the back of the driver's seat as the jeep jounced away from the curb, following the rest of the cavalcade as it pulled away from the hospital. The air was cool against Chrysalis's face hidden deep within the folds of her hood, but the rest of her body was drenched with sweat. She fantasized about a long, cool drink and a slow, cool bath for the hour it took the motorcade to wend its way through Port-au-Prince's narrow, twisting streets. When they finally reached the Royal Haitian Hotel, she stepped down into the street almost before the jeep stopped, anxious for the waiting coolness of the lobby, and was instantly engulfed by a sea of beseeching faces, all babbling in Haitian Creole. She couldn't understand what the beggars were saying, but she didn't have to speak their language to understand the want and desperation in their eyes, tattered clothing, and brittle, emaciated bodies.

The press of imploring beggars pinned her against the side of the jeep, and the immediate rush of pity she'd felt for their obvious need was submerged in fear fueled by their piteously beseeching voices and the dozens of thin, sticklike arms thrust out at her.

The driver, before she could say or do anything, reached under the jeep's dashboard and grabbed a long, thin wooden rod that looked like a truncated broomstick, stood up, and began swinging it at the beggars while shouting rapid, harsh phrases in Creole.

Chrysalis heard, and saw, the skinny arm of a young boy snap at the first blow. The second opened the scalp of an old man, and the third missed as the intended victim managed to duck away.

The driver drew the weapon back to strike again. Chrysalis, her usually cautious reserve overcome by sudden outrage, turned to him and screamed, 'Stop! Stop that!' and with the sudden movement the hood fell away from her face, revealing her features for the first time. Revealing, that is, what features she had.

Her skin and flesh were as clear as the finest blown glass, without flaw or bubble. Besides the muscles that clung to her skull and jaw, only the meat of her lips was visible. They were dark red pads on the gleaming expanse of her skull. Her eyes, floating in the depths of their naked sockets, were as blue as fragments of sky.

The driver gaped at her. The beggars, whose importunings had turned to wails of fear, all fell silent at once, as if an invisible octopus had simultaneously slapped a tentacle over each one's mouth. The silence dragged on for a half dozen heartbeats, and then one of the beggars whispered a name in a soft, awed voice.

'Madame Brigitte.'

It passed among the beggars like a whispered invocation, until even those who had crowded around the other vehicles in the motorcade were craning their necks to get a glimpse of her. She pressed back against the jeep, the concentrated stares of the beggars, mixed fear and awe and wonder, frightening her. The tableau held for another moment until the driver spoke a harsh phrase and gestured with his stick. The crowd dispersed at once, but not, however, without some of the beggars shooting Chrysalis final glances of mingled awe and dread.

Chrysalis turned to the driver. He was a tall, thin black in a cheap, ill-fitting blue serge suit and an open-necked shirt. He looked back at her sullenly, but Chrysalis couldn't really read his expression because of the dark sunglasses he wore.

'Do you speak English?' she asked him.

'Oui. A little.' Chrysalis could hear the harsh edge of fear in his voice, and she wondered what put it there.

'Why did you strike them?'

He shrugged. 'These beggars are peasants. Scum from the country, come to Port-au-Prince to beg on the generousness of people as yourself. I tell them to go.'

'Speak loudly and carry a big stick,' Wilde said sardonically from his seat in the back of the jeep.

Chrysalis glared at him. 'You were a big help.'

He yawned. 'I make it a habit never to brawl in the streets. It's so vulgar.'

Chrysalis snorted, turned back to the driver. 'Who,' she asked, 'is "Madame Brigitte"?'

The driver shrugged in a particularly Gallic manner, illustrating again the cultural ties Haiti had to the country from which she'd been politically independent for nearly two hundred years. 'She is a loa, the wife of Baron Samedi.'

'Baron Samedi?'

'A most powerful loa. He is the lord and guardian of the cemetery. The keeper of the crossroads.'

'What's a loa?'

He frowned, shrugged almost angrily. 'A loa is a spirit, a part of God, very powerful and divine.'

'And I resemble this Madame Brigitte?'

He said nothing, but continued to stare at her from behind his dark glasses, and despite the afternoon's tropical heat Chrysalis felt a shiver run down her spine. She felt naked, despite the voluminous cloak she wore. It wasn't a bodily nakedness. She was, in fact, accustomed to going half-naked in public as a private obscene gesture to the world, making sure that everyone saw what she had to see every time she looked in a mirror. It was a spiritual nakedness that she felt, as if everyone who was staring at her was trying to discover who she was, was trying to divine the precious secrets that were the only masks that she had. She felt a desperate need to get away from all the staring eyes, but she wouldn't let herself run from them. It took all her nerve, all the cool she could muster, but she managed to walk into the hotel lobby with precise, measured steps.

Inside it was cool and dark. Chrysalis leaned against a high-backed chair that looked as if it'd been made sometime in the last century and dusted sometime in the last decade. She took a deep, calming breath and let it out slowly.

'What was that all about?'

She looked over her shoulder to see Peregrine regarding her with concern. The winged woman had been in one of the limos at the head of the parade, but she'd obviously seen the byplay that had centered around Chrysalis's jeep. Peregrine's beautiful, satin-feathered wings only added a touch of the exotic to her lithe, tanned sensuality. She should be easy to resent, Chrysalis thought. Her affliction had brought her fame, notoriety, even her own television show. But she looked genuinely concerned, genuinely worried, and Chrysalis felt in need of sympathetic company.

But she couldn't explain something to Peregrine that she only half-understood herself. She shrugged. 'Nothing.' She looked around the lobby that was rapidly filling with tour personnel. 'I could use a few moments of peace and quiet. And a drink.'

'So could I,' a masculine voice announced before Peregrine could speak. 'Let's find the bar and I'll tell you some of the facts of Haitian life.'

Both women turned to look at the man who'd spoken. He was six feet tall, give or take, and strongly built. He wore a suit of white, tropical-weight linen that was immaculately clean and sharply creased. There was something odd about his face. His features didn't quite match. His chin was too long, his nose too broad. His eyes were misaligned and too bright. Chrysalis knew him only by reputation. He was a Justice Department ace, part of the security contingent Washington had assigned to Tachyon's tour. His name was Billy Ray. Some wit at JD with a classical education had tagged him with the nickname Carnifex. He liked it. He was an authentic badass.

'What do you mean?' Chrysalis asked.

Ray looked around the lobby, his lips quirking. 'Let's find the bar and talk things over. Privately.'

Chrysalis glanced at Peregrine, and the winged woman read the appeal in her eyes.

'Mind if I tag along?' she asked.

'Hey, not at all.' Ray frankly admired her lithe, tanned form, and the black-and-white-striped sundress that showed it off. He licked his lips as Chrysalis and Peregrine exchanged unbelieving glances.

The hotel lounge was doing desultory afternoon business. They found an empty table surrounded by other empty tables and gave their orders to a red-uniformed waiter who couldn't decide whom to stare at, Peregrine or Chrysalis. They sat in silence until he'd returned with the drinks, and Chrysalis drank down the thimbleful of amaretto that he'd brought.

'The travel brochures all said that Haiti's supposed to be a bloody tropical paradise,' she said in a tone that indicated she felt the brochures all lied.

'I'll take you to paradise, babe,' Ray said.

Chrysalis liked it when men paid attention to her, sometimes too much. Sometimes, she realized, she conducted her affairs for all the wrong reasons. Even Brennan (Yeoman, she reminded herself, Yeoman. She had to remember that she wasn't supposed to know his real name) had become her lover because she'd forced herself on him. It was, she supposed, the sense of power that she liked, the control she had when she made men come to her. But making men make love to her body was also, she recognized with her habit of relentless self-scrutiny, another way to punish a revulsed world. But Brennan (Yeoman, damnit) had never been revulsed. He had never made her turn out the lights before kissing her, and he had always made love with his eyes open and watching her heart beat, her lungs bellow, her breath catch behind tightly clenched teeth …

Ray's foot moved under the table, touching hers, drawing her back from thoughts of the past, of what was over. She smiled a lazy smile at him, gleaming teeth set in a gleaming skull. There was something about Ray that was unsettling. He talked too loud, he smiled too much, and some part of him, his hands or his feet or his mouth, was always in motion. He had a reputation for violence. Not that she had anything against violence – as long as it wasn't directed at her. For goodness's sake, even she'd lost track of all the men Yeoman had sent to their reward since his arrival in the city. But, paradoxically, Brennan wasn't a violent man. Ray, according to his reputation, had a habit of running amuck. Compared to Brennan, he was a self-centered bore. She wondered if she'd be comparing all the men she would know to her archer, and she felt a rush of annoyance, and regret.

'I doubt that you'd have the skill to transport me to the dreariest shithole in the poorest part of Jokertown, dear boy, let alone paradise.'

Peregrine squelched a twitchy smile and looked away. Chrysalis felt Billy's foot move away as he fixed her with a hard, dangerous stare. He was about to say something vicious when Dr. Tachyon interrupted by flopping into the empty chair next to Peregrine. Ray shot Chrysalis a look that told her the remark wouldn't be forgotten.

'My dear.' Tachyon bowed over Peregrine's hand, kissed it, and nodded greetings to everyone else. It was common knowledge that he was hot over the glamorous flyer, but then, Chrysalis reflected, most men were. Tachyon, however, was self-confident enough to be determined in his pursuit, and thickheaded enough not to call it off, even after numerous polite rebuffs on Peregrine's part.

'How was the meeting with Dr. Tessier?' Peregrine asked, removing her hand delicately from Tachyon's grasp when he showed no inclination of letting it go on his own.

Tachyon frowned, whether in disappointment at Peregrine's continuing coolness or in remembrance of his visit to the Haitian hospital, Chrysalis couldn't tell.

'Dreadful,' he murmured, 'simply dreadful.' He caught the eye of a waiter and gestured him over. 'Bring me something cool, with lots of rum in it.' He looked around the table. 'Anyone else?'

Chrysalis tinged a red-painted fingernail – it looked like a rose petal floating on bone – against her empty cordial glass.

'Yes. And more, um?'

'Amaretto.'

'Amaretto for the lady there.'

The waiter sidled up to Chrysalis and slipped the glass out from in front of her without making eye contact. She could feel his fear. It was funny, in a way, that someone could be afraid of her, but it angered her as well, almost as much as the guilt in Tachyon's eyes every time he looked at her.

Tachyon ran his fingers dramatically through his long, curly red hair. 'There wasn't much incidence of wild card virus that I could see.' He fell silent, sighed gustily. 'And Tessier himself wasn't overly concerned about it. But everything else … by the Ideal, everything else …'

'What do you mean?' Peregrine asked.

'You were there. That hospital was as crowded as a Jokertown bar on Saturday night and about as sanitary. Typhus patients were cheek to jowl with tuberculosis patients and elephantiasis patients and AIDS patients and patients suffering from half a hundred other diseases that have been eradicated everywhere else in the civilized world. As I was having a private chat with the hospital administrator, the electricity went out twice. I tried to call the hotel, but the phones weren't working. Dr. Tessier told me that they're low on blood, antibiotics, painkillers, and just about all medicinals. Fortunately, Tessier and many of the other doctors are masters at utilizing the medicinal properties of native Haitian flora. Tessier showed me a thing or two he's done with distillations from common weeds and such that was remarkable. In fact, someone should write an article on the drugs they've concocted. Some of their discoveries deserve widespread attention in the outside world. But for all their efforts, all their dedication, they're still losing the fight.'

The waiter brought Tachyon's drink in a tall slim glass garnished with slices of fresh fruit and a paper umbrella. Tachyon threw out the fruit and paper umbrella and swallowed half his drink in a single gulp. 'I have never seen such misery and suffering.'

'Welcome to the Third World,' Ray said.

'Indeed.' Tachyon finished off his drink and fixed Chrysalis with his lilac-colored eyes.

'Now, what was that disturbance in front of the hotel?'

Chrysalis shrugged. 'The driver started beating the beggars with a stick—'

'A *cocomacaques*.'

'I beg your pardon?' Tachyon said, turning to Ray.

'It's called a *cocomacaques*. It's a walking stick, polished with oil. Hard as an iron bar. A real nasty weapon.' There was approval in Ray's voice. 'The Tonton Macoute carry them.'

'What?' three voices asked simultaneously.

Ray smiled a smile of superior knowledge. 'Tonton Macoute. That's what the peasants call them. Essentially means "bogeyman." Officially they're called the VSN, the *Volontaires de la Securite Nationale*.' Ray had an atrocious accent. 'They're Duvalier's secret police, headed by a man named Charlemagne Calixte. He's black as a coal mine at midnight and ugly as sin. Somebody tried to poison him once. He lived through it, but it scarred his face terribly. He's the only reason Baby Doc's still in power.'

'Duvalier has his secret police acting as our chaffeurs?' Tachyon asked, astonished. 'Whatever for?'

Ray looked at him as if he were a child. 'So they can watch us. They watch everybody. It's their job.' Ray laughed a sudden, barking laugh. 'They're easy enough to spot. They all have dark sun-glasses and wear blue suits. Sort of a badge of office. There's one over there.'

Ray gestured to the far corner of the lounge. The Tonton Macoute sat at an otherwise empty table, a bottle of rum and half-filled glass in front of him. Even though the lounge was dimly lit, he had on dark glasses, and his blue suit was as unkempt as any of Dorian Wilde's.

'I'll see about this,' Tachyon said, outrage in his voice. He started to stand, but settled back in his chair as a large, scowling man came into the lounge and strode straight toward their table.

'It's him,' Ray whispered. 'Charlemagne Calixte.'

He didn't have to tell them. Calixte was a dark-skinned black, bigger and broader than most Haitians Chrysalis had seen so far, and uglier too. His short kinky hair was salted with white, his eyes were hidden behind dark glasses, and shriveled scar tissue crawled up the right side of his face. His manner and bearing radiated power, confidence, and ruthless efficiency.

'*Bon jour.*' He bowed a precise little bow. His voice was a deep, hideous rasp, as if the poison that had eaten away the side of his face had also affected his tongue and palate.

'*Bon jour,*' Tachyon replied for them all, bowing a precise millimeter less than Calixte had.

'My name is Charlemagne Calixte,' he said in gravelly tones barely louder than a whisper. 'President-for-Life Duvalier has charged me with seeing to your safety while you are visiting our island.'

'Join us,' Tachyon offered, indicating the final empty chair.

Calixte shook his head as precisely as he'd bowed. 'Regretfully, *Msie* Tachyon, I cannot. I have an important appointment for the afternoon. I just stopped by to make sure everything is all right after that unfortunate incident in front of the hotel.' As he spoke he looked directly at Chrysalis.

'Everything's fine,' Tachyon assured him before Chrysalis could speak. 'What I want to know, though, is why the Tomtom—'

'Tonton,' Ray said.

Tachyon glanced at him. 'Of course. The Tonton whatevers, your men, that is, are watching us.'

Calixte gave him a look of polite astonishment. 'Why to protect you from that very sort of thing that happened earlier this afternoon.'

'Protect me? He wasn't protecting me,' Chrysalis said. 'He was beating beggars.'

Calixte stared at her. 'They may have looked like beggars, but many undesirable elements have come into the city.' He looked around the almost empty room, then husked in a barely intelligible whisper, 'Communist elements, you know. They are unhappy with the progressive regime of President-for-Life Duvalier and have threatened to topple his government. No doubt these "beggars" were communist agitators trying to provoke an incident.'

Chrysalis kept quiet, realizing nothing she could say would make any difference. Tachyon was also looking unhappy, but decided not to pursue the matter at this time. After all, they would only be in Haiti one more day before traveling to the Dominican Republic on the other side of the island.

'Also,' Calixte said with a smile as ugly as his scar, 'I am to inform you that dinner tonight at the Palais National will be a formal affair.'

'And after dinner?' Ray said, openly gauging Calixte with his frank stare.

'Excuse me?'

'Is anything planned for after dinner?'

'But of course. Several entertainments have been arranged. There is shopping at the Marché de Fer – the Iron Market – for locally produced handicrafts. The Musée National will stay open late for those who wish to explore our cultural heritage. You know,'

Calixte said, 'we have on display the anchor from the *Santa Maria*, which ran aground on our shores during Columbus's first expedition to the New World. Also, of course, galas have been planned in several of our world-famous nightclubs. And for those interested in some of the more exotic local customs, a trip to a *hounfour* has been arranged.'

'*Hounfour?*' Peregrine asked.

'*Oui*. A temple. A church. A voodoo church.'

'Sounds interesting,' Chrysalis said.

'It's got to be more interesting than looking at anchors,' Ray said insouciantly.

Calixte smiled, his good humor going no farther than his lips. 'As you wish, *msie*. I must go now.'

'What about these policemen?' Tachyon asked.

'They will continue to protect you,' Calixte said depreciatingly, and left.

'They're nothing to worry about,' Ray said, 'leastways while I'm around.' He struck a consciously heroic pose and glanced at Peregrine, who looked down at her drink.

Chrysalis wished she could feel as confident as Ray. There was something unsettling about the Tonton Macoute sitting in the corner of the lounge, watching them from behind his dark glasses with the unblinking patience of a snake. Something malevolent. Chrysalis didn't believe that he was there to protect them. Not for one single, solitary second.

Ti Malice particularly liked the sensations associated with sex. When he was in the mood for such a sensation he'd usually mount a female, because, on the whole, females could maintain a state of pleasure, particularly those adept at self-arousal, much longer than his male mounts could. Of course, there were shades and nuances of sexual sensation, some as subtle as silk dragged across a sensitive nipple, some as blatant as an explosive orgasm ripped from a throttled man, and different mounts were adept at different practices.

This afternoon he wasn't in the mood for anything particularly exotic, so he'd attached himself to a young woman who had a particularly sensitive tactile sense and was enjoying it enjoying itself when his mount came in to report.

'They'll all be at the dinner tonight, and then the group will break up to attend various entertainments. It shouldn't be difficult to obtain one of them. Or more.'

He could understand the mount's report well enough. It was, after all, their world, and he'd had to make some accommodations, like learning to associate meaning with the sounds that spilled from their lips. He couldn't reply verbally, of course, even if he'd wanted to. First, his mouth, tongue, and palate weren't shaped for it, and second, his mouth was, and always had to be, fastened to the side of his mount's neck, with the narrow, hollow tube of his tongue plunged into his mount's carotid artery.

But he knew his mounts well and he could read their needs easily. The mount who'd brought the report, for instance, had two. Its eyes were fastened on the lithe nakedness of the female as it pleasured itself, but it also had a need for his kiss.

He flapped a pale, skinny hand and the mount came forward eagerly, dropping its pants and climbing atop the woman. The female let out an explosive grunt as it entered.

He forced a stream of spittle down his tongue and into his mount's carotid artery, sealing the breach in it, then gingerly climbed, like a frail, pallid monkey, to the male's back, gripped it around the shoulders, and plunged his tongue home just below the mass of scar tissue on the side of its neck.

The male grunted with more than sexual pleasure as he drove his tongue in, siphoning some of the mount's blood into his own body for the oxygen and nutrients he needed to live. He rode the man's back as the man rode the woman, and all three were bound in chains of inexpressible pleasure.

And when the carotid of the female mount ruptured unexpectedly, as they sometimes did, spewing all three with pulsing showers of bright, warm, sticky blood, they continued on. It was a most exciting and pleasurable experience. When it was over, he realized that he would miss the female mount – it had had the most incredibly sensitive skin – but his sense of loss was lessened by anticipation.

Anticipation of new mounts, and the extraordinary abilities they would have.

II.

The Palais National dominated the north end of a large open square near the center of Port-au-Prince. Its architect had cribbed its design from the Capitol Building in Washington, D.C., giving it the same colonnaded portico, long white facade, and central dome. Facing it on the south end of the square were what looked like, and in fact were, military barracks.

The inside of the Palais stood out in stark contrast to everything else Chrysalis had seen in Haiti. The only word to describe it was opulent. The carpets were deep-pile shags, the furniture and bric-a-brac along the hallway they were escorted down by ornately uniformed guards were all authentic antiques, the chandeliers hanging from the high vaulted ceilings were the finest cut crystal.

President-for-Life Jean-Claude Duvalier, and his wife, Madame Michele Duvalier, were waiting in a receiving line with other Haitian dignitaries and functionaries. Baby Doc Duvalier, who'd inherited Haiti in 1971 when his father, François 'Papa Doc' Duvalier, had died, looked like a fat boy who'd outgrown his tight-fitting tuxedo. Chrysalis thought him more petulant-looking than intelligent, more greedy than cunning. It was difficult to imagine how he managed to hold power in a country that was obviously on the brink of utter ruin.

Tachyon, wearing an absurd peach-colored crushed-velvet tuxedo, was standing to his right, introducing Duvalier to the members of his tour. When it came Chrysalis's turn, Baby Doc took her hand and stared at her with the fascination of a young boy with a new toy. He murmured to her politely in French and continued to stare at her as Chrysalis moved down the line.

Michele Duvalier stood next to him. She had the cultivated,

brittle look of a high-fashion model. She was tall and thin and very light-skinned. Her makeup was immaculate, her gown was the latest off-the-shoulder designer creation, and she wore lots of costly, gaudy jewelry at her ears, throat, and wrists. Chrysalis admired the expense with which she dressed, if not the taste.

She drew back a little as Chrysalis approached and nodded a cold, precise millimeter, without offering her hand. Chrysalis sketched an abbreviated curtsy and moved on herself, thinking, *Bitch.*

Calixte, showing the high status he enjoyed in the Duvalier regime, was next. He said nothing to her and did nothing to acknowledge her presence, but Chrysalis felt his stare boring into her all the way down the line. It was a most unsettling feeling and was, Chrysalis realized, a further sample of the charisma and power that Calixte wielded. She wondered why he allowed Duvalier to hang around as a figurehead.

The rest of the receiving line was a confused blur of faces and handshakes. It ended at the doorway leading into the cavernous dining room. The tablecloths on the long wooden table were linen, the place settings were silver, the centerpieces were fragrant sprays of orchid and rose. When she was escorted to her seat, Chrysalis found that she and the other jokers, Xavier Desmond, Father Squid, Troll, and Dorian Wilde, were stuck at the end of the table. Word was whispered that Madame Duvalier had had them seated as far away from her as possible so the sight of them wouldn't ruin her appetite.

However, as wine was being served with the fish course (*Pwason rouj,* the waiter had called it, red snapper served with fresh string beans and fried potatoes), Dorian Wilde stood and recited an extemporaneous, calculatedly overblown ode in praise of Madame Duvalier, all the while gesticulating with the twitching, wriggling, dripping mass of tentacles that was his right hand. Madame Duvalier turned a shade of green only slightly less bilious than that of the ooze that dripped from Wilde's tendrils and was seen to eat very little of the following courses. Gregg Hartmann, sitting near the Duvaliers with the other VIPs, dispatched his pet Doberman,

Billy Ray, to escort Wilde back to his seat, and the dinner continued in a more subdued, less interesting manner.

As the last of the after-dinner liquors were served and the party started to break up into small conversational groups, Digger Downs approached Chrysalis and stuck his camera in her face.

'How about a smile, Chrysalis? Or should I say Debra-Jo? Perhaps you'd care to tell my readers why a native of Tulsa, Oklahoma, speaks with a British accent.'

Chrysalis smiled a brittle smile, keeping the shock and anger she felt off her face. He knew who she was! The man had pried into her past, had discovered her deepest, if not most vital, secret. How did he do it? she wondered, and what else did he know? She glanced around, but it seemed that no one else was paying them any attention. Billy Ray and Asta Lenser, the ballerina-ace called Fantasy, were closest to them, but they seemed absorbed in their own little confrontation. Billy had a hand on her skinny flank and was pulling her close. She was smiling a slow, enigmatic smile at him. Chrysalis turned back to Digger, somehow managing to keep the anger she felt out of her voice.

'I have no idea what you're talking about.'

Digger smiled. He was a rumpled, sallow-looking man. Chrysalis had had dealings with him in the past, and she knew that he was an inveterate snooper who wouldn't let go of a story, especially if it had a juicy, sensational angle.

'Come, come, Miss Jory. It's all down in black and white on your passport application.'

She could have sighed with relief, but kept her expression stonily hostile. The application had had her real name on it, but if that was as far as Digger had probed, she'd be safe. Thoughts of her family raced poisonously through her mind. When she was a little girl, she'd been their darling with long blond hair and a naive young smile. Nothing had been too good for her. Ponies and dolls and baton twirling and piano and dancing lessons, her father had bought them all for her with his Oklahoma oil money. Her mother had taken her everywhere, to recitals and to church meetings and to society teas. But when the virus had struck her at puberty and turned her skin and flesh invisible, making her a walking abomination, they shut her up in a wing of the ranch house, for her own good of course, and took away her ponies and her playmates and all contact with the outside world. For seven years she was shut up, seven years ...

Chrysalis shut off the hateful memories rushing through her mind. She was still, she realized, walking on tricky ground with Digger. She had to concentrate fully on him and forget the family that she'd robbed and fled from.

'That information is confidential,' she told Digger coldly.

He laughed aloud. 'That's very funny, coming from you,' he said, then suddenly sobered at her look of uncontainable fury. 'Of course, perhaps the true story of your real past wouldn't be of much interest to my readers.' He put a conciliatory expression on his pale face. 'I know that you know everything that goes on in Jokertown. Maybe you know something interesting about *him*.'

Digger gestured with his chin and let his eyes flicker in the direction of Senator Hartmann.

'What about him?' Hartmann was a powerful and influential politician who felt strongly about jokers' rights. He was one of the few politicians that Chrysalis supported financially because she liked his policies and not because she needed to keep the wheels greased.

'Let's go somewhere private and talk about it.'

Digger was obviously reluctant to discuss Hartmann openly. Intrigued, Chrysalis glanced at the antique brooch watch pinned above the bodice of her gown. 'I have to leave in ten minutes.' She grinned like a Halloween skeleton. 'I'm going to see a voodoo ceremony. Perhaps if you care to come along, we might find time to discuss things and come to a mutual understanding about the newsworthiness of my background.'

Digger smiled. 'Sounds fine to me. Voodoo ceremony, huh? They going to stick pins in dolls and stuff? Maybe have some kind of sacrifice?'

Chrysalis shrugged. 'I don't know. I've never been to one before.'

'Think they'll mind if I take photos?'

Chrysalis smiled blandly, wishing she was on familiar turf, wishing that she had something to use on this gossip-monger, and wondering, underneath it all, why his interest in Gregg Hartmann?

In a fit of sentiment Ti Malice chose one of his oldest mounts, a male with a body almost as frail and withered as his own, to be his steed for the night. Even though the mount's flesh was ancient, the brain encased in it was still sharp, and more strong-willed than any other Ti Malice had ever encountered. It said, in fact, a lot for Ti Malice's own indominatable will that he was able to control the stubborn old steed. The mental fencing that accompanied riding it was a most pleasurable experience.

He chose the dungeon for the meeting place. It was a quiet, comfortable old room, full of pleasurable sights and smells and memories. The lighting was dim, the air was cool and moist. His favorite tools, along with the remains of his last few partners in experience, were scattered about in agreeable disarray. He had his mount pick up a blood-encrusted flaying knife and test it on its callused palm while he drifted in pleasant reminiscence until the snorting bellow in the corridor outside proclaimed Taureau's approach.

Taureau-trois-graines, as he had named this mount, was a huge male with a body that was thick with slabs of muscle. It had a long, bushy beard and tufts of coarse black hair peered through the tears in its sun-faded work shirt. It wore frayed, worn denim pants, and it had a huge, rampant erection pushing visibly at the fabric that covered its crotch. It always had.

'I have a task for you,' Ti Malice told his mount to say, and Taureau bellowed and tossed its head and rubbed its crotch through the fabric of its pants. 'Some new mounts will be awaiting you on the road to Petionville. Take a squad of *zobops* and bring them to me here.'

'Women?' Taureau asked in a slobbering snort.

'Perhaps,' Ti Malice said through his mount, 'but you are not to have them. Later, perhaps.'

Taureau let out a disappointed bellow, but knew better than to argue.

'Be careful,' Ti Malice warned. 'Some of these mounts may have powers. They may be strong.'

Taureau let out a bray that rattled the tattered half-skeleton hanging in the wall niche next to it. 'Not as strong as me!' It thumped its massive chest with a callused, horny hand.

'Maybe, maybe not. Just take care. I want them all.' He paused to let his mount's words sink in. 'Do not fail me. If you do, you will never know my kiss again.'

Taureau howled like a steer being led to the slaughter block, backed out of the room, bowing furiously, and was gone.

Ti Malice and his mount waited.

In a moment a woman came into the room. Its skin was the color of coffee and milk mixed in equal amounts. Its hair, thick and wild, fell to its waist. It was barefooted and obviously wore nothing under its thin white dress. Its arms were slim, its breasts large, and its legs lithely muscled. Its eyes were black irises floating in pools of red. Ti Malice would have smiled at the sight of it, if he could, for it was his favorite steed.

'Ezili-je-rouge,' he crooned through his mount, 'you had to wait until Taureau left, for you couldn't share a room with the bull and live.'

It smiled a smile with even, perfectly white teeth. 'It might be an interesting way to die.'

'It might,' Ti Malice considered. He had never experienced death by means of intercourse before. 'But I have other needs for you. The *blancs* that have come to visit us are rich and important. They live in America and, I'm sure, have access to many interesting sensations that are unavailable on our poor island.'

Ezili nodded, licking red lips.

'I've set plans in motion to make some of these *blancs* mine, but to ensure my success, I want you to go to their hotel, take one of the others, and make it ready for my kiss. Choose one of the strong ones.'

Ezili nodded. 'Will you take me to America with you?' she asked nervously.

Ti Malice had his mount reach out an ancient, withered hand and caress Ezili's large, firm breasts. It shivered with delight at the touch of the mount's hand.

'Of course, my darling, of course.'

III.

'A limousine?' Chrysalis said with an icy smile to the broadly grinning man wearing dark glasses who was holding the door for her. 'How nice. I was expecting something with four-wheel drive.'

She climbed into the backseat of the limo, and Digger followed her. 'I wouldn't complain,' he said. 'They haven't let the press go anywhere. You should've seen what I had to go through to crash the dinner party. I don't think they like reporters much ... here ...'

His voice ran down as he flopped onto the rear seat next to Chrysalis and noted the expression on her face. She was staring at the facing seat, and the two men who occupied it. One was Dorian Wilde. He was looking more than a little tipsy and fondling a *cocomacaques* similar to the one Chrysalis had seen that afternoon. The stick obviously belonged to the man who was sitting next to him and regarding Chrysalis with a horrible frozen grin that contorted his scarred face into a death mask.

'Chrysalis, my dear!' Wilde exclaimed as the limo pulled away into the night. 'And the glorious fourth estate. Dug up any juicy gossip lately?' Digger looked from Chrysalis to Wilde to the man sitting next to him and decided that silence would be his most appropriate response. 'How rude of me,' Wilde continued. 'I haven't introduced our host. This delightful man has the charming name of Charlemagne Calixte. I believe he's a policeman or something. He's going with us to the *hounfour*.'

Digger nodded and Calixte inclined his head in a precise, non-deferential bow.

'Are you a devotee of voodoo, *Monsieur* Calixte?' Chrysalis asked.

'It is the superstition of peasants,' he said in a raspy growl, thoughtfully fingering the scar tissue that crawled up the right side of his face. 'Although seeing you would almost make one a believer.'

'What do you mean?'

'You have the appearance of a loa. You could be Madame Brigitte, the wife of Baron Samedi.'

'You don't believe that, do you?' Chrysalis asked.

Calixte laughed. It was a gravelly, barking laugh that was as pleasant as his smile. 'Not I, but I am an educated man. It was the sickness that caused your appearance. I know. I have seen others.'

'Other jokers?' Digger asked with, Chrysalis thought, his usual tact.

'I don't know what you mean. I have seen other unnatural deformities. A few.'

'Where are they now?'

Calixte only smiled.

No one felt much like talking. Digger kept shooting Chrysalis questioning glances, but she could tell him nothing, and even if she had a inkling of what was going on, she could hardly speak openly in front of Calixte. Wilde played with Calixte's swagger stick and cadged drinks from the bottle of *clairin*, cheap white rum, that the Haitian took frequent swallows from himself. Calixte drank over half the bottle in twenty minutes, and as he drank he stared at Chrysalis with intense, bloodshot eyes.

Chrysalis, in an effort to avoid Calixte's gaze, looked out the window and was astonished to see that they were no longer in the city, but were traveling down a road that seemed to cut through otherwise unbroken forest.

'Just where are we going?' she asked Calixte, striving to keep her voice level and unafraid.

He took the bottle of *clairin* from Wilde, gulped down a mouthful, and shrugged. 'We are going to the *hounfour*. It is in Petionville, a small suburb just outside Port-au-Prince.'

'Port-au-Prince has no *hounfours* of its own?'

Calixte smiled his blasted smile. 'None that put on such a fine show.'

Silence descended again. Chrysalis knew that they were in trouble, but she couldn't figure out exactly what Calixte wanted of them. She felt like a pawn in a game she didn't even know she'd been playing. She glanced at the others. Digger was looking confused as hell, and Wilde was drunk. Damn. She was more sorry than ever that she'd left familiar, comfortable Jokertown behind to follow Tachyon on his mad, worthless journey. As usual, she only had herself to depend on. It had always been like that, and always would. Part of her mind whispered that once there had been Brennan, but she refused to listen to it. Come to the test, he would have proved as untrustworthy as the rest. He would have.

The driver suddenly pulled the limo to the side of the road and killed the engine. She stared out the window, but could see little. It was dark and the roadside was lit only by infrequent glimpses of the half moon as it occasionally peered out from behind banks of thick clouds. It looked as if they had stopped beside a crossroad, a chance meeting of minor roads that ran blindly through the Haitian forest. Calixte opened the door on his side and climbed out of the limo smoothly and steadily in spite of the fact that he'd drunk most of a bottle of raw rum in less than half an hour. The driver got out too, leaned against the side of the limo, and began to beat a swift tattoo on a small, pointed-end drum that he'd produced from somewhere.

'What's going on?' Digger demanded.

'Engine trouble,' Calixte said succinctly, throwing the empty rum bottle into the jungle.

'And the driver is calling the Haitian Automobile Club,' Wilde, sprawled across the backseat, said with a giggle.

Chrysalis poked Digger and gestured to him to move out. He obeyed, looking around bewilderedly, and she followed him. She didn't want to be trapped in the back of the limo during whatever it was that was going to happen. At least outside the car she had a chance to run for it, although she probably wouldn't be able to get very far in a floor-length gown and high heels. Through the jungle. On a dark night.

'Say,' Digger said in sudden comprehension. 'We're being kidnapped. You can't do this. I'm a reporter.'

Calixte reached into his jacket pocket and withdrew a small, snub-nosed revolver. He pointed it negligently at Digger and said, 'Shut up.'

Downs wisely did.

They didn't have long to wait. From the road that intersected the one they'd been driving upon came the cadenced sound of marching feet. Chrysalis turned to stare down the road and saw what looked like a column of fireflies, bobbing up and down, coming in their direction. It took a moment, but she realized that it was actually a troop of marching men. They wore long, white robes whose hems brushed the roadtop. Each carried a long, skinny candle in his left hand and each was also crowned with a candle set on his forehead by a cloth circlet, producing the firefly effect. They wore masks. There were about fifteen of them.

Leading the column was an immense man who had a decidedly bovine look about him. He was dressed in the cheap, tattered clothes of a Haitian peasant. He was one of the largest men that Chrysalis had ever seen, and as soon as he spotted her he headed straight toward her. He stood before her drooling and rubbing his crotch, which, Chrysalis was surprised and not happy to see, was bulging outward and stretching the frayed fabric of his jeans.

'Jesus,' Digger muttered. 'We're in trouble now. He's an ace.'

Chrysalis glanced at the reporter. 'How do you know?'

'Well, ah, he looks like one, doesn't he?'

He looked like someone who'd been touched by the wild card virus, Chrysalis thought, but that didn't necessarily make him an ace. Before she could question Digger further, however, the bull-like man said something in Creole, and Calixte snapped off a guttural 'Non' in answer.

The bull-man seemed momentarily ready to dispute Calixte's apparent order, but decided to back down. He continued to glower at Chrysalis and finger his erection as he spoke in turn to the strangely garbed men who had accompanied him.

Three of them came forward and dragged a protesting Dorian

Wilde from the backseat of the limo. The poet looked around bewilderedly, fixed his bleary eyes on the bull-man, and giggled.

Calixte grimaced. He snatched his *cocomacaques* from Wilde and lashed out with it, spitting the word '*Masisi*' as he struck.

The blow landed where Wilde's neck curved into his shoulder, and the poet moaned and sagged. The three men supporting him couldn't hold him, and he fell to the ground just as all hell broke loose.

The snap, crack, and pop of small-arms fire sounded from the foliage bordering the roadside, and a couple of the men so strangely crowned by candles went down. A few others broke and ran for it, though most held their ground. The bull-man bellowed in rage and hurtled toward the undergrowth. Chrysalis, who'd dropped to the ground at the first sound of gunfire, saw him get hit in the upper body at least twice, but he didn't even stagger. He crashed into the underbrush and in a moment high-pitched screams mixed with his bellowing.

Calixte crouched behind the limo and calmly returned fire. Digger, like Chrysalis, was huddled on the ground, and Wilde just lay there moaning. Chrysalis decided that it was time to exercise the better part of valor. She crawled under the limo, cursing as she felt her expensive gown snag and tear.

Calixte dove after her. He snatched at her left foot, but only grabbed her shoe. She twisted her foot, the shoe came off, and she was free. She scrambled all the way under the limo, came out on the other side, and rolled into the jungle foliage lining the roadside.

She took a few moments to catch her breath, and then was up and running, staying low and keeping to cover as much as she could. Within moments she was away from the conflict, safe, alone, and, she quickly realized, totally, utterly lost.

She should have paralleled the road, she told herself, rather than taking off blindly into the forest. She should have done a lot of things, like spending the winter in New York and not on this insane tour. But it was too late to worry about any of that. Now all she could do was push ahead.

Chrysalis never imagined that a tropical forest, a jungle, could be so desolate. She saw nothing move, other than tree branches in the night wind, and heard nothing other than the sounds made by that same wind. It was a lonely, frightening feeling, especially to someone used to having a city around them.

She'd lost her brooch watch when she'd scrambled under the limo, so she had no way of measuring time other than the increasing soreness in her body and dryness in her throat. Hours, certainly, had passed before, totally by accident, she stumbled upon a trail. It was rough, narrow, and uneven, obviously made by human feet, but finding it filled her with hope. It was a sign of habitation. It led to somewhere. All she had to do was follow it, and somewhere, sometime, she'd find help.

She started down the trail, too consumed by the exigencies of her immediate situation to worry any more about Calixte's motives in bringing her and the others to the crossroads, the identity of the strangely dressed men crowned with candles, or to even wonder about their mysterious rescuers, if, indeed, the band that had ambushed their kidnappers had meant to rescue them.

She walked through the darkness.

It was difficult going. Right at the start of her trek she'd taken off her right shoe to even her stride, and sometime soon afterward she'd lost it. The ground was not without sticks and stones and other sharp objects, and before long her feet hurt like hell. She cataloged her miseries minutely so she'd know exactly how much to take out of Tachyon's hide if she ever got back to Port-au-Prince.

Not if, she told herself repeatedly. When. When. When.

She was chanting the word as a short, snappy little marching song when she suddenly realized that someone was walking toward her on the trail. It was difficult to say for sure in the uncertain light, but it looked like a man, a tall, frail man carrying a hoe or shovel or something over his shoulder. He was headed right toward her.

She stopped, leaned against a nearby tree, and let out a long, relieved sigh. The brief thought flashed through her mind that he might be a member of Calixte's odd gang, but from what she could discern, he was dressed like a peasant, and he was carrying some sort of farm implement. He was probably just a local out on a late errand. She had the sudden fear that her appearance might scare him away before she could ask for help, but quenched it with the realization that he had to have already seen her, and he was still steadily approaching.

'*Bonjour,*' she called out, exhausting most of her French. But the man made no sign that he had heard. He kept on walking past the tree against which she leaned.

'Hey! Are you deaf?' she reached out and tugged at his arm as he passed by, and as she touched him, he stopped, turned, and fixed her with his gaze.

Chrysalis felt as if a slice of night had stabbed into her heart. She went cold and shivery and for a long moment couldn't catch her breath. She couldn't look away from his eyes.

They were open. They moved, they shifted focus, they even blinked slowly and ponderously, but they did not see. The face from which they peered was scarcely less skeletal than her own. The brow ridges, eye sockets, cheekbones, jaw, and chin stood out in minute detail, as if there were no flesh between the bone and the taut black skin that covered them. She could count the ribs underneath the ragged work shirt as easily as anyone could count her own. She stared at him as he looked toward her and her breath caught again when she realized that he wasn't breathing. She would have screamed or run or done something, but as she stared he took a long, shallow breath that barely inflated his sunken chest. She watched him closely, and twenty seconds passed before he took another.

She suddenly realized that she was still holding his ragged sleeve, and she released it. He continued to stare in her direction for a moment or two, then turned back the way he'd been headed and started walking away.

Chrysalis stared at his back for a moment, shivering, despite the warmth of the evening. She had just seen, talked to, and even touched, she realized, a *zombi*. As a resident of Jokertown and a joker herself, she'd thought herself inured to strangeness, accustomed to the bizarre. But apparently she wasn't. She had never been so afraid in her life, not even when, as a girl barely out of her teens, she had broken into her father's safe to finance her escape from the prison that was her home.

She swallowed hard. *Zombi* or not, he had to be going somewhere. Somewhere where there might be other ... real ... people.

Timorously, because there was nothing else she could do, she began to follow him.

They didn't have far to go. He soon turned off onto a smaller, less-traveled side trail that wound down and around a steep hill. As they passed a sharp curve in the trail, Chrysalis noticed a light burning ahead.

He headed toward the light, and she followed him. It was a kerosene lantern, stuck on a pole in front of what looked like a small, ramshackle hut clinging to the lower slopes of the precipitous hillside. A tiny garden was in front of the hut, and in front of the garden a woman was peering into the night.

She was the most prosperous looking Haitian that Chrysalis had yet seen outside of the Palais National. She was actually plump, her calico dress was fresh and new-looking, and she wore a bright orange madras bandanna wrapped around her head. The woman smiled as Chrysalis and the apparition she was following approached.

'Ah, Marcel, who has followed you home?' She chuckled. 'Madame Brigitte herself, if I'm not mistaken.' She sketched a curtsy that, despite her plumpness, was quite graceful. 'Welcome to my home.'

Marcel kept walking right on past her, ignoring her and heading for the rear of the hut. Chrysalis stopped before the woman, who was regarding her with an open, welcoming expression that contained a fair amount of good-natured curiosity in it.

'Thank you,' Chrysalis said hesitantly. There were a thousand things she could have said, but the question burning in the forefront of her mind had to be answered. 'I have to ask you ... that is ... about Marcel.'

'Yes?'

'He's not actually a *zombi*, is he?'

'Of course he is, my child, of course he is. Come, come.' She made gathering motions with her hands. 'I must go inside and tell my man to call off the search.'

Chrysalis hung back. 'Search?'

'For you, my child, for you.' The woman shook her head and made *tsk*ing sounds. 'You shouldn't have run off like that. It caused quite a bit of trouble and worry for us. We thought that the *zobop* column might capture you again.'

'*Zobop*? What's a *zobop*?' It sounded to Chrysalis like a term for some kind of jazz aficionado. It was all she could do to keep from laughing hysterically at the thought.

'*Zobop* are' – the woman gestured vaguely with her hands as if she were trying to describe an enormously complicated subject in simple words – 'the assistants of a *bokor* – an evil sorcerer – who have sold themselves to the *bokor* for material riches. They follow his bidding in all things, often kidnapping victims chosen by the *bokor*.'

'I … see … And who, if you don't mind my asking, are you?'

The woman laughed good-humoredly. 'No, child, I don't mind at all. It shows admirable caution on your part. I am Mambo Julia, priestess and *première reine* of the local Bizango chapter.' She must have correctly read the baffled look on Chrysalis's face, for she laughed aloud. 'You *blancs* are so funny! You think you know everything. You come to Haiti in your great airplane, walk about for one day, and then dispense your magical advice that will cure all our ills. And not once do even one of you leave Port-au-Prince!' Mambo Julia laughed again, this time with some derision. 'You know nothing of Haiti, the real Haiti. Port-au-Prince is a gigantic cancer that shelters the leeches that are sucking the juices from Haiti's body. But the countryside, ah, the countryside is Haiti's heart!

'Well, my child, I shall tell you everything you need to know to begin to understand. Everything, and more, than you want to know. Come to my hut. Rest. Drink. Have a little something to eat. And listen.'

Chrysalis considered the woman's offer. Right now she was more concerned about her own difficulties than Haiti's, but Mambo

Julia's invitation sounded good. She wanted to rest her aching feet and drink something cold. The idea of food also sounded inviting. It seemed as if she'd last eaten years ago.

'All right,' she said, following Mambo Julia toward the hut. Before they reached the door, a middle-aged man, thin, like most Haitians, with a shock of premature white hair, came around from the back.

'Baptiste!' Mambo Julia cried. 'Have you fed the *zombi*?' The man nodded and bobbed a courteous bow in Chrysalis's direction. 'Good. Tell the others that Madame Brigitte has found her own way home.'

He bowed again, and Chrysalis and Mambo Julia went into the hut.

Inside, it was plainly, neatly, comfortably furnished. Mambo Julia ushered Chrysalis to a rough-hewn plank table and served her fresh water and a selection of fresh, succulent tropical fruits, most of which were unfamiliar, but tasty.

Outside, a drum began to beat a complicated rhythm to the night. Inside, Mambo Julia began to talk.

One of Ti Malice's mounts delivered Ezili's message at midnight. It had succeeded in the task he'd given it. A new mount was lying in drugged slumber at the Royal Haitian Hotel, awaiting its first kiss.

Excited as a child on Christmas morning, Ti Malice decided that he couldn't wait at the fortress for the mounts he'd sent Taureau after to be delivered. He wanted new blood, and he wanted it now.

He moved from his old favorite to a different mount, a girl not much bigger than he, that was already waiting in the special box that he'd had built for occasions when he had to move about in public. It was the size of a large suitcase and was cramped and uncomfortable, but it afforded the privacy he needed for his public excursions. It took a bit of caution, but Ti Malice was smuggled unseen to the third floor of the Royal Haitian Hotel where Ezili, naked and hair flying wild, let him into the room and stood back while the mount bearing him opened the lid and stepped from the box as he moved from the girl's chest to the more comfortable position upon its back and shoulders.

Ezili led him into the bedroom where his new mount was sleeping peacefully.

'He wanted me the moment he saw me,' Ezili said. 'It was easy to get him to bring me here, and easier yet to slip the draught into his drink after he had me.' She pouted, fingering the large, dark nipple of her left breast. 'He was a quick lover,' she said with some disappointment.

'Later,' Ti Malice said through his mount, 'you shall be rewarded.'

Ezili smiled happily as Ti Malice ordered his mount to bring him closer to the bed. The mount complied, bending over the sleeping man, and Ti Malice transferred himself quickly. He snuggled against the man's chest, nuzzling its neck. The man stirred, moaned a little in its drugged sleep. Ti Malice found the spot he needed, bit down with his single, sharp tooth, then drove his tongue home.

The new mount groaned and feebly reached for its neck. But Ti Malice was already firmly in place, mixing his saliva with his mount's blood, and the mount subsided like a grumpy child having a slightly bad dream. It settled down into deep sleep while Ti Malice made it his.

It was a splendid mount, powerful and strong. Its blood tasted wonderful.

IV.

'There have always been two Haitis,' Mambo Julia said. 'There is the city, Port-au-Prince, where the government and its law rule. And there is the countryside, where the Bizango rules.'

'You used that word before,' Chrysalis said, wiping the sweet juices of a succulent tropical fruit off her chin. 'What does it mean?'

'As your skeleton, which I can see so clearly, holds your body together, so the Bizango binds the people of the countryside. It is an organization, a society with a network of obligations and order. Not everyone belongs to it, but everyone has a place in it and all abide by its decisions. The Bizango settles disputes that would otherwise rip us apart. Sometimes it is easy. Sometimes, as when someone is sentenced to become a *zombi*, it is difficult.'

'The Bizango sentenced Marcel to become a *zombi*?'

Mambo Julia nodded. 'He was a bad man. We in Haiti are more permissive about certain things than you Americans. Marcel liked girls. There is nothing wrong with that. Many men have several women. It is all right as long as they can support them and their children. But Marcel liked young girls. Very young girls. He couldn't stop, so the Bizango sat in judgment and sentenced him to become a *zombi*.'

'They turned him into a *zombi*?'

'No, my dear. They judged him.' Mambo Julia lost her air of convivial jollity. '*I* made him into what he is today, and keep him that way by the powders I feed him daily.' Chrysalis placed the half-eaten fruit she was holding back upon its plate, having suddenly lost her appetite. 'It is a most sensible solution. Marcel no longer harms young girls. He is instead a tireless worker for the good of the community.'

'And he'll always be a *zombi*?'

'Well, there have been a few *zombi savane*, those who have been buried and brought back as *zombis*, then somehow managed to return to the state of the living.' Mambo Julia plucked her chin thoughtfully. 'But such have always remained somewhat … impaired.'

Chrysalis swallowed hard. 'I appreciate what you've done for me. I … I'm not sure what Calixte intended, but I'm sure he meant me harm. But now that I'm free, I'd like to return to Port-au-Prince.'

'Of course you do, child. And you shall. In fact, we were planning on it.'

Mambo Julia's words were welcome, but Chrysalis wasn't sure that she cared much for her tone. 'What do you mean?'

Mambo Julie looked at her seriously. 'I'm not sure, either, what Calixte planned for you. I do know that he's been collecting people such as yourself. People who've been changed. I don't know what he does to them, but they become his. They do the dirty deeds that even the Tonton Macoute refuse. And he keeps them busy,' she said with a clenched jaw.

'Charlemagne Calixte is our enemy. He is the power in Port-au-Prince. Jean-Claude Duvalier's father, François, was in his own way a great man. He was ruthless and ambitious. He found his way into power and held it for many years. He first organized the Tonton Macoute, and they helped him line his pockets with the wealth of an entire country.

'But Jean-Claude is unlike his father. He is foolish and weak-willed. He has allowed the real power to flow into Calixte's hands, and that devil is so greedy that he threatens to suck the life from us like a *loup garou*.' She shook her head. 'He must be stopped. His stranglehold must be loosened so the blood will flow through Haiti's veins again. But his power runs deeper than the guns of the Tonton Macoute. He is either a powerful *bokor*, or he has one working for him. The magic of this *bokor* is very strong. It has enabled Calixte to survive several assassination attempts. Though one of them, at least,' she said with some satisfaction, 'left its mark on him.'

'What has all this to do with me?' Chrysalis asked. 'You should go to the United Nations or the media. Let your story be known.'

'The world knows our story,' Mambo Julia said, 'and doesn't care. We are beneath their notice, and perhaps it is best that we are left to work out our problems in our own way.'

'How?' Chrysalis asked, not sure that she wanted to know the answer.

'The Bizango is stronger in the country than in the city, but we have our agents even in Port-au-Prince. We've been watching you *blancs* since your arrival, thinking that Calixte might be bold enough to somehow take advantage of your presence, perhaps even try to make one of you his agent. When you publicly defied the Tonton Macoute, we knew that Calixte would be driven to get even with you. We kept close watch over you and so were able to foil his attempt to kidnap you. But he did manage to take your friends.'

'They're not my friends,' Chrysalis said, starting to realize where

Mambo Julia's argument was heading. 'And even if they were, I couldn't help you rescue them.' She held her hand up, a skeleton's hand with a network of cord and sinew and blood vessels woven around it. 'This is what the wild card virus did to me. It didn't give me any special powers or abilities. You need someone like Billy Ray or Lady Black or Golden Boy to help you—'

Mambo Julia shook her head. 'We need you. You are Madame Brigitte, the wife of Baron Samedi—'

'You don't believe that.'

'No,' she said, 'but the *chasseurs* and *soldats* who live in the small, scattered hamlets, who cannot read and who have never seen television, who know nothing of what you call the wild card virus, they may look upon you and take heart for the deeds they must do tonight. They may not totally believe either, but they will want to and will not think upon the impossibility of defeating the *bokor* and his powerful magic.

'Besides,' she said with some finality, 'you are the only one who can bait the trap. You are the only one who escaped the *zobop* column. You will be the only one who will be accepted into their stronghold.'

Mambo Julia's words both chilled and angered Chrysalis. Chilled her, because she never even wanted to see Calixte again. She had no intention of putting herself in his power. Angered her, because she didn't want to become mixed up in their problems, to die for something she knew virtually nothing about. She was a saloon keeper and information broker. She wasn't a meddling ace who stuck her nose in where it didn't belong. She wasn't an ace of any kind.

Chrysalis pushed her chair away from the table and stood up. 'Well, I'm sorry, but I can't help you. Besides, *I* don't know where Calixte took Digger and Wilde any more than you do.'

'But we do know where they are.' Mambo Julia smiled a smile totally devoid of humor. 'Though you eluded the *chasseurs* who were sent to rescue you, several of the *zobop* did not. It took some persuading, but one finally told us that Calixte's stronghold is Fort Mercredi, the ruined fortress overlooking Port-au-Prince.

The center of his magic is there.' Mambo Julia stood herself and went to open the door. A group of men stood in front of the hut. They all had the look of the country about them in their rough farm clothes, callused hands and feet, and lean, muscular bodies. 'Tonight,' Mambo Julia said, 'the *bokor* dies once and for all.'

Their voices rose in a murmur of surprise and awe when they saw Chrysalis. Most bowed in a gesture of respect and obeisance.

Mambo Julia cried out in Creole, gesturing at Chrysalis, and they answered her loudly, happily. After a few moments she closed the door, turned back to Chrysalis, and smiled.

Chrysalis sighed. It was foolish, she decided, to argue with a woman who had the demonstrated ability to create *zombis*. The feeling of helplessness that descended over her was an old feeling, a feeling from her youth. In New York she controlled everything. Here, it seemed, she was always controlled. She didn't like it, but there was nothing she could do but listen to Mambo Julia's plan.

It was a rather simple plan. Two Bizango *chasseurs* – men with the rank of hunter in the Bizango, Mambo Julia explained – would dress in the *zobop* robes and masks that they'd captured earlier that evening, bring Chrysalis to Calixte's fortress, and tell him that they tracked her down in the forest. When the opportunity presented itself (Chrysalis wasn't pleased with the plan's vagueness on this point, but thought it best to keep her mouth shut), they would let their comrades in and proceed to destroy Calixte and his henchmen.

Chrysalis didn't like it, even though Mambo Julia assured her airily that she would be perfectly safe, that the loa would watch over her. For further protection – unnecessary as it was, Mambo Julia said – the priestess gave her a small bundle wrapped in oilskin.

'This is a *paquets congo*,' Mambo Julia told her. 'I made it myself. It contains very strong magic that will protect you from evil. If you are threatened, open it and spread its contents all around you. But *do not let any touch yourself!* It is strong magic, very, very strong, and you can only use it in this simplest way.'

With that, Mambo Julia sent her off with the *chasseurs*. There were ten or twelve of them, young to middle-aged. Baptiste, Mambo Julia's man, was among them. They continually chattered and joked among themselves as if they were going on a picnic, and they treated Chrysalis with the utmost deference and respect, helping her over the rough spots on the trail. Two carried robes they had taken from the *zobop* column earlier that evening.

The foot-trail they followed led to a rough road where an ancient vehicle, a minibus or van of some kind, was parked. It hardly looked capable of moving, but the engine started right up after everyone had piled in. The trip was slow and bumpy, but they made better time when they eventually turned off onto a wider, graded road that eventually led back to Port-au-Prince.

The city was quiet, although they did occasionally pass other vehicles. It struck Chrysalis that they were traveling through familiar scenery, and she suddenly realized that they were in Bolosse, the slum section of Port-au-Prince where the hospital she'd visited that morning – it seemed like a thousand years ago – was located.

The men sang songs, chattered, laughed, and told jokes. It was hard to believe that they were planning to assassinate the most powerful man in the Haitian government, a man who was reputedly an evil sorcerer as well. They were acting more as if they were going to a ball game. It was either a remarkable display of bravado, or the calming effect of her presence as Madame Brigitte. Whatever caused their attitude, Chrysalis didn't share it. She was scared stiff.

The driver suddenly pulled over and silence fell as he parked the minibus on a narrow street of dilapidated buildings, pointed, and said something in Creole. The *chasseurs* began to disembark, and one courteously offered Chrysalis a hand down. For a moment she thought of running, but saw that Baptiste was keeping a wary, if inconspicuous, eye on her. She sighed to herself and joined the line of men as they walked quietly up the street.

It was a strenuous climb up a steep hill. After a moment Chrysalis realized that they were heading toward the ruins of a fort that she had first noticed when they'd passed through the area earlier in the day. Fort Mercredi, Mambo Julia had called it. It had looked picturesque in the morning. Now it was a dark, looming wreck with an aura of brooding menace about it. The column stopped in a small copse of trees clustered in front of the ruins, and two *chasseurs*, one of them Baptiste, changed into the *zobop* robes and masks. Baptiste courteously motioned Chrysalis forward, and she took a deep breath, willed her legs to stop trembling, and went on. Baptiste took her arm above her elbow, ostensibly to show that she was a prisoner, but she was grateful for the warmth of a human touch. The shaft of night had returned to her heart, but it had grown, had spread until it felt like a dark, icy curtain that had totally enveloped her chest.

The fortress was encircled by a dry moat that had a dilapidated wooden bridge spanning it. They were challenged as they reached the bridge by a voice that shouted a question in Creole. Baptiste answered satisfactorily with a curt password – more information, Chrysalis guessed, wrenched from the unfortunate *zobop* who'd fallen into the hands of the Bizango – and they crossed the bridge.

Two men wearing the semiofficial blue suit of the Tonton Macoutes were lounging on the other side, their dark glasses resting in their breast pockets. Baptiste told them some long, involved story, and looking impressed, they passed them on through the outer defenses of the citadel. They were challenged again in the courtyard beyond, and again passed on, this time led into the interior of the decrepit fort by one of the second pair of guards.

Chrysalis found it maddening not to understand what was being said around her. The tension was growing higher, her heart colder, as fear wound her tighter than a compressed spring. There was nothing she could do, though, but endure it, and hope, however hopelessly, for the best.

The interior of the fortress seemed to be in moderately good repair. It was lit, medievally enough, by infrequent torches in wall niches. The walls and flooring were stone, dry and cool to the touch. The corridor ended at a railless spiral staircase of crumbling stone. The Tonton Macoute led them downward.

Images of a dank dungeon began to dance in Chrysalis's mind. The air took on a damp feel and a mildewy smell. The staircase itself was slippery with unidentifiable ooze and difficult to negotiate in the sandals made from bits of old automobile tires that Mambo Julia had given her. Torches were infrequent, and the pools of light they threw didn't overlap, so they often had to pass through patches of total darkness.

The staircase ended in a large open space that had only a few uncomfortable-looking bits of wooden furniture in it. A series of chambers debouched off this area, and it was to one of these that they were led.

The room was twenty feet on a side and lit better than the corridors through which they'd just passed, but the ceiling, corners, and some spots along the back wall were all in darkness. The dancing light thrown by the torches made it difficult to discern details, and after her first glance inside the room, Chrysalis knew that was probably for the best.

It was a torture chamber, lined with antique devices that looked well cared for and recently used. An iron maiden lay half-open against one wall, the spikes in its interior coated by flakes of either rust or blood. A table loaded down with impedimenta such as pokers and cleavers and scalpels and thumb and foot screws stood next to what Chrysalis imagined was a rack. She didn't know for certain because she'd never seen one, never thought she would see one, never, ever, wanted to see one.

She looked away from the instruments of torture and focused on the group of half a dozen men clustered in the rear of the room. Two were Tonton Macoutes, enjoying the proceedings. The others were Digger Downs and Dorian Wilde, the bull-man who had led the *zobop* column, and Charlemagne Calixte. Downs was shackled in a wall niche next to a moldering skeleton. Wilde was the center of everyone's attention.

A stout, thick beam stuck out from the dungeon's rear wall, close to the ceiling, parallel to the floor. A block and tackle hung from the beam and a rope descended from the sharp, wicked-looking metal hook at the bottom of the block and tackle set. Dorian Wilde was dangling from the rope by his arms. He was trying to haul himself up, but lacked the muscular strength to do so. He couldn't even get a proper grip on the coarse hemp with the mass of tentacles that was his right hand. Sweating, wild-eyed, and straining, he swayed desperately while Calixte operated a ratcheted handcrank that lowered the rope until the bottoms of Wilde's naked feet were hanging just above a bed of hot glowing coals burning in a low brazier that had been placed below the gibbet. Wilde would desperately swing his feet away from the searing heat, Calixte would crank him up and give him a brief respite, then lower him again. He stopped when the bull-man glanced toward the front of the room, noticed Chrysalis, and let out a bellow.

Calixte looked at her and their eyes met. His expression was wildly exultant, and he was sweating profusely, though it was damply cool in the dungeon. He smiled and said something in Creole to the men in the background, who sprang forward and removed Wilde from the gibbet. He then spoke to Baptiste and the other *chasseur*. Baptiste must have answered him satisfactorily, for he nodded, then dismissed them with a curt word and a gesture of his head.

They bowed and started to walk away. Chrysalis took a single instinctive step to follow them, and then the bull-man was before her, breathing heavily and eyeing her strangely. His erection, she noted sickly, was still rampant.

'Well,' Calixte growled in English. 'We are all together again.' He came to Chrysalis, put a hand on the bull's shoulder, and pushed him away. 'We were having a bit of amusement. The *blanc* offended me and I was teaching him some manners.' He nodded at Wilde, who was huddled on the damp flagstone paving, heaving great shuddering breaths. Calixte never took his eyes off Chrysalis. They were bright and fevered, burning with unspeakable excitement and pleasure. 'You also have been difficult.' He plucked at the scar tissue that glinted glassily in the torchlight. He seemed deep in mad thought. 'You need, I think, a lesson also.' He seemed to make up his mind. 'He'll have the others. I don't think he'd mind if we used you up. Taureau.' He turned to the bull-man, spoke some words in Creole.

Chrysalis scarcely understood him, even though he spoke

63

English. His words were thick and blurry, even more so than usual. He was either very drunk, very stoned, or very mad. Perhaps, she realized, all three. She was frantic with terror. The *chasseurs* weren't supposed to leave, she thought wildly. They were supposed to kill Calixte! Her heart beat faster than the drums she'd heard sounding through the Haitian night. The dark fear centered in her chest threatened to flow out and overwhelm her entire being. For a moment she teetered on the thin edge of irrationality, and then Taureau came forward, snorting and drooling, one massive hand unbuttoning the fly of his jeans, and Chrysalis knew what she had to do.

She clutched the packet that Mambo Julia had given her and with frantic, shaking fingers pulled off the paper wrapping, exposing a small leather sack closed by a drawstring. She ripped open the mouth of the sack and with trembling hands threw it and its contents at Taureau.

The sack hit him in the face and he walked right into a cloud of fine, grayish powder that billowed out from it. It coated his hands, arms, chest, and face. He stopped for a moment, snorted, shook his head, then kept right on coming.

Chrysalis broke. She turned with a sob and started to run, thinking incoherently that she should have known better, that Mambo Julia was a conniving fraud, that what was about to happen was nothing compared to what she would experience in a lifetime of domination by Calixte, and then she heard a horrible, bellowing scream that froze every nerve, muscle, and sinew in her body.

She turned. Taureau was standing still, but shivering from head to toe as every massive muscle in his body spasmed. His eyes nearly bulged from his head as he stared at Chrysalis and screamed again, a horrible, drawn-out wail that wasn't even remotely human. His hands clenched and unclenched, and then he began to rake at his face, tearing long furrows of meat away from his cheeks with his thick, blunt fingernails, howling all the while like a damned soul burning.

A memory flashed through Chrysalis's mind, a terse recollection of a cool, dark bar, a delightful drink, and a short Tachyon speech on Haitian herbal medicine. Mambo Julia's *paquets congo* contained no magic powder, no concoction compounded during a fearful ritual and consecrated to the dark voodoo loa. It was simply some herbal preparation, a fast acting, topically effective neurotoxin of some kind. At least that's what she told herself, and almost believed.

The awful tableau held for a moment, and then Calixte barked a word to the Tonton Macoutes who were watching Taureau with astonished eyes. One stepped forward, put a hand on the bull-man's shoulder. Taureau turned with the speed of an adrenalized cat, grabbed the man by his wrist and shoulder, and ripped his arm from his body. The Tonton Macoute stared at Taureau for a moment with unbelieving eyes, and then, blood fountaining from his shoulder, he fell weeping to the floor, trying unsuccessfully to stanch the bleeding with his remaining hand.

Taureau brandished the arm above his head like a gory club, shaking it at Chrysalis. Blood splattered across her face and she choked back the bile that rose in her throat.

Calixte roared an order in Creole, whether at Taureau or his other man Chrysalis didn't know, but the Tonton Macoute ran from the chamber as Taureau whirled in a mad circle, trying to watch everyone at once from crazed, fear-distended eyes.

Calixte kept shouting at Taureau, who was shaking and trembling with terrible muscle spasms. His face was the face of a tortured lunatic, and his dark skin was turning darker. His lips were becoming distinctly blue. He shambled toward Calixte, screaming words that Chrysalis, even though she couldn't understand the language they were spoken in, knew were gibberish.

Calixte calmly drew his pistol. He pointed it at Taureau and spoke again. The joker continued to advance. Calixte squeezed off a shot that hit Taureau high in the left side of his chest, but he kept coming. Calixte shot three more times before the maddened bull covered the distance between them, and the last shot hit him right between the eyes.

But Taureau kept coming. He dropped the arm he'd been brandishing, grabbed Calixte, and with a final spasm of incredible strength, threw him at the chamber's rear wall. Calixte screamed. He reached out to grasp the rope hanging from the gibbet, but he missed. He missed the rope, but not the meathook from which it hung.

The hook took him in the stomach, ripped up through his diaphragm, and skewered his right lung. He showered screams and blood as he kicked his legs and swung in counterpoint rhythm to the spasmodic jerking of his body.

Taureau staggered, clutching his shattered forehead, and fell onto the brazier of burning coals. After a moment he stopped bellowing and there came the crisp sizzle and sweet smell of burning flesh.

Chrysalis was violently sick. After she finished wiping her mouth with the back of her hand, she looked up to see Dorian Wilde standing before the limp, swaying form of Charlemagne Calixte. He smiled and recited:

> 'It is sweet to dance to violins
>> When Love and Life are fair:
> To dance to flutes, to dance to lutes
>> Is delicate and rare:
> But it is not sweet with nimble feet
>> To dance upon the air!'

Digger Downs rattled his chains impotently. 'Someone get me out of here,' he pleaded.

Chrysalis heard the snap of small-arms fire in the upper reaches of the fortress, but the Bizango *chasseurs* were too late. The *bokor*, swaying from the meathook above the dungeon floor, was already dead.

It was hushed up, of course.

Senator Hartmann asked Chrysalis to be silent to help diffuse the fear of the wild card virus that was raging back home. He didn't even want there to be a hint of American jokers and aces mixing in foreign politics. She agreed for two reasons: First, she wanted him in her debt, and second, she always avoided personal publicity anyway. Not even Digger filed a story. He was recalcitrant at first, until Senator Hartmann had a private talk with him, a talk from which Downs emerged happy, smiling, and oddly closemouthed.

The death of Charlemagne Calixte was ascribed to a sudden, unexpected illness. The other dozen bodies found in Fort Mercredi were never mentioned, and the two-score odd deaths and suicides among government officials over the next week or so were never even connected to Calixte's death.

Jean-Claude Duvalier, who suddenly found himself with a sullen, poverty-stricken country to run, was grateful for the lack of publicity, but there was something he discovered at the end of the affair, something puzzling and terrifying that he carefully kept secret.

Among the bodies recovered from Fort Mercredi was that of an old, old man. When Jean-Claude saw the body he blanched nearly white and had it interred in the *Cimetière Extérieur* in haste, at night, without ceremony, before anyone else could recognize it and ask how it was that François Duvalier, supposedly dead for fifteen years, was, or had been until very recently, still alive.

The only one who could answer that question was no longer in Haiti. He was on his way to America where he anticipated a long, interesting, and productive search for new and exciting sensations.

FROM *THE JOURNAL*
OF XAVIER DESMOND

December 8, 1986/Mexico City:

Another state dinner this evening, but I've begged off with a plea of illness. A few hours to relax in my hotel room and write in the journal are most welcome. And my regrets were anything but fabricated – the tight schedule and pressures of the trip have begun to take their toll, I fear. I have not been keeping down all of my meals, although I've done my utmost to see that my distress remains unnoticed. If Tachyon suspected, he would insist on an examination, and once the truth was discovered, I might be sent home.

I will not permit that. I wanted to see all the fabled, far-off lands that Mary and I had once dreamed of together, but already it is clear that what we are engaged in here is far more important than any pleasure trip. Cuba was no Miami Beach, not for anyone who cared to look outside Havana; there are more jokers dying in the cane fields than cavorting on cabaret stages. And Haiti and the Dominican Republic were infinitely worse, as I've already noted in these pages.

A joker presence, a strong joker voice – we desperately need these things if we are to accomplish any good at all. I will not allow myself to be disqualified on medical grounds. Already our numbers are down by one – Dorian Wilde returned to New York rather than continue on to Mexico. I confess to mixed feelings about that. When we began, I had little respect for the 'poet laureate of Jokertown,' whose title is as dubious as my own mayoralty, though his Pulitzer is not. He seems to get a perverse glee from waving those wet, slimy tendrils of his in people's faces, flaunting his deformity in a deliberate attempt to draw a reaction. I suspect this aggressive nonchalance is in fact motivated by the same self-loathing that makes so many jokers take to masks, and a few sad cases actually attempt to amputate the deformed parts of their bodies. Also, he dresses almost as badly as Tachyon with his ridiculous Edwardian affectation, and his unstated preference for perfume over baths makes his company a trial to anyone with a sense of smell. Mine, alas, is quite acute.

Were it not for the legitimacy conferred on him by the Pulitzer, I doubt that he would ever have been named for this tour, but there are very few jokers who have achieved that kind of worldly recognition. I find precious little to admire in his poetry either, and much that is repugnant in his endless mincing recitations.

All that being said, I confess to a certain admiration for his impromptu performance before the Duvaliers. I suspect he received a severe dressing down from the politicians. Hartmann had a long private conversation with 'The Divine Wilde' as we were leaving Haiti, and after that Dorian seemed much subdued.

While I don't agree with much that Wilde has to say, I do nonetheless think he ought to have the right to say it. He will be missed. I wish I knew why he was leaving. I asked him that very question and tried to convince him to go on for the benefit of all his fellow jokers. His reply was an offensive suggestion about the sexual uses of my trunk, couched in the form of a vile little poem. A curious man.

With Wilde gone, Father Squid and myself are the only true representatives of the joker point of view, I feel. Howard M. (Troll, to the world) is an imposing presence, nine feet tall, incredibly strong, his green-tinged skin as tough and hard as horn, and I also know him to be a profoundly decent and competent man, and a very intelligent one, but ... he is by nature a follower, not a leader, and there is a shyness in him, a reticence, that prevents him from speaking out. His height makes it impossible for him to blend with the crowd, but sometimes I think that is what he desires most profoundly.

As for Chrysalis, she is none of those things, and she has her own unique charisma. I cannot deny that she is a respected community leader, one of the most visible (no pun intended) and powerful of jokers. Yet I have never much liked Chrysalis. Perhaps this is my own prejudice and self-interest. The rise of the Crystal Palace has had much to do with the decline of the Funhouse. But there are deeper issues. Chrysalis wields considerable power in Jokertown, but she has never used it to benefit anyone but herself. She has been aggressively apolitical, carefully distancing herself from the JADL and all joker rights agitation. When the times called for passion and commitment, she remained cool and uninvolved, hidden behind her cigarette holders, liqueurs, and upper-class. British accent.

Chrysalis speaks only for Chrysalis, and Troll seldom speaks at all, which leaves it to Father Squid and myself to speak for the jokers. I would do it gladly, but I am so tired ...

I fell asleep early and was wakened by the sounds of my fellow delegates returning from the dinner. It went rather well, I understand. Excellent. We need some triumphs. Howard tells me that Hartmann gave a splendid speech and seemed to captivate President de la Madrid Hurtado throughout the meal. Peregrine captivated all the other males in the room, according to reports. I wonder if the other women are envious. Mistral is quite pretty, Fantasy is mesmerizing when she dances, and Radha O'Reilly is arresting, her mixed Irish and Indian heritage giving her features a truly exotic cast. But Peregrine overshadows all of them. What do they make of her?

The male aces certainly approve. The *Stacked Deck* is close quarters, and gossip travels quickly up and down the aisles. Word is that Dr. Tachyon and Jack Braun have both made passes and have been firmly rebuffed. If anything, Peregrine seems closest with her cameraman, a nat who travels back with the rest of the reporters. She's making a documentary of this trip.

Hiram is also close to Peregrine, but while there's a certain flirtatiousness to their constant banter, their friendship is more platonic in nature. Worchester has only one true love, and that's food. To that, his commitment is extraordinary. He seems to know all the best restaurants in every city we visit. His privacy is constantly being invaded by local chefs, who sneak up to his hotel room at all hours, carrying their specialties and begging for just a moment, just a taste, just a little approval. Far from objecting, Hiram delights in it.

In Haiti he found a cook he liked so much that he hired him on the spot and prevailed upon Hartmann to make a few calls to the INS and expedite the visa and work permit. We saw the man briefly at the Port-au-Prince airport, struggling with a huge trunk full of cast-iron cookware. Hiram made the trunk light enough for his new employee (who speaks no English, but Hiram insists that spices are a universal language) to carry on one shoulder. At tonight's dinner, Howard tells me, Worchester insisted on visiting the kitchen to get the chef's recipe for *chicken mole,* but while he was back there he concocted some sort of flaming dessert in honor of our hosts.

By rights I ought to object to Hiram Worchester, who revels in his acedom more than any other man I know, but I find it hard to dislike anyone who enjoys life so much and brings such enjoyment to those around him. Besides, I am well aware of his various anonymous charities in Jokertown, though he does his best to conceal them. Hiram is no more comfortable around my kind than Tachyon is, but his heart is as large as the rest of him.

Tomorrow the group will fragment yet again. Senators Hartmann and Lyons, Congressman Rabinowitz, and Ericsson from WHO will meet with the leaders of the PRI, Mexico's ruling party, while Tachyon and our medical staff visit a clinic that has claimed extraordinary success in treating the virus with laetrile. Our aces are scheduled to lunch with three of their Mexican counterparts. I'm pleased to say that Troll has been invited to join them. In some quarters, at least, his superhuman strength and near invulnerability have qualified him as an ace. A small breakthrough, of course, but a breakthrough nonetheless.

The rest of us will be traveling down to Yucatan and the Quintana Roo to look at Mayan ruins and the sites of several reported anti-joker atrocities. Rural Mexico, it seems, is not as enlightened as Mexico City. The others will join us in Chichén Itzá the following day, and our last day in Mexico will be given over to tourism.

And then it will be on to Guatemala … perhaps. The daily press has been full of reports on an insurrection down there, an Indian uprising against the central government, and several of our journalists have gone ahead already, sensing a bigger story than this tour. If the situation seems too unstable, we may be forced to skip that stop.

THE TINT OF HATRED

PART TWO

Tuesday, December 9, 1986, Mexico:

'I stand in *El Templo de los Jaguares*, the Temple of the Jaguars, in Chichén Itzá. Under the fierce Yucatan sun the archway is impressive, two thick columns carved in the likeness of gigantic snakes, their huge, stylized heads flanking the entrance, their linked tails supporting the lintel.

'A thousand years ago, the guide books tell us, Mayan priests cheered the players in *El Juego de Pelota*, the ball court twenty-five feet below. It was a game that would be familiar to any of us. The players struck a hard rubber ball with their knees, elbows, and hips, scoring as the ball caromed through rings set in the long stone walls flanking the narrow field. A simple game, played for the glory of the god Quetzalcoatl, or Kukulcan, as those here called him.

'As his reward, the captain of the victorious team would be carried to the temple. The losing captain would behead his opponent with an obsidian knife, sending him into a glorious afterlife. A bizarre reward for conquest, by our standards.

'Too different to be comfortable.

'I look out on this ancient place, and the walls are still brown with blood; not of Mayans, but of jokers. The wild card plague struck here late and virulently. Some scientists have hypothesized that the mind-set of the victim influences the virus; thus, from a teenager fascinated by dinosaurs, you get Kid Dinosaur. From an obese

73

master chef such as Hiram Worchester, you get someone who can control gravity. Dr. Tachyon, when asked, has been evasive on the subject, since it suggests that the deformed jokers have somehow punished themselves. That's just the kind of emotional fodder that reactionaries such as fundamentalist preacher Leo Barnett, or a fanatic "prophet" such as Nur al-Allah, would use for their own purposes.

'Still, perhaps it's not surprising that in the ancestral lands of the Mayans, there have been no less than a dozen plumed serpents over the years: images of Kukulcán himself. And here in Mexico, if those of Indian blood had the final say, perhaps even the jokers would be well-treated, for the Mayans considered the deformed blessed by the gods. But those of Mayan descent don't rule.

'In Chichén Itzá, over fifty jokers were killed only a year ago.

'Most of them (but not all) were followers of the new Mayan religion. These ruins were their place of worship. They thought that the virus was a sign to return to the old ways; they didn't think of themselves as victims. The gods had twisted their bodies and rendered them *different* and holy.

'Their religion was a throwback to a violent past. And because they were so different, they were feared. The locals of Spanish and European descent hated them. There was gossip concerning animal and even human sacrifice, of blood rites. It didn't matter if any of it was actually true; it never does. They were *different*. Their own neighbors banded together to rid themselves of this passive threat. They were dragged screaming from the surrounding villages.

'Bound, pleading for mercy, the jokers of Chichén Itzá were laid here. Their throats were slit in brutal parody of Mayan rites – splashing blood stained the carved serpents red. Their bodies were cast into the ball court below. Another atrocity, another "nat vs. joker" incident. Old prejudices amplifying the new.

'Still, what happened here – though horrible – is no worse than what has happened, *is* happening, to jokers at home. You who are reading this: You or someone you know has probably been guilty of the same prejudice that caused this massacre. We're no less susceptible to the fear of the *different*.'

Sara switched off the cassette recorder and laid it atop the serpent's head. Squinting into the brilliant sun, she could see the main group of delegates near the Temple of the Bearded Man; behind, the pyramid of Kukulcán threw a long shadow over the grass.

'A woman of such obvious compassion would keep an open mind, wouldn't she?'

Panic crawled her spine. Sara whirled about to see Senator Hartmann regarding her. It took a long moment to recover her composure. 'You startled me, Senator. Where's the rest of the entourage?'

Hartmann smiled apologetically. 'I'm sorry for sneaking up on you, Ms. Morgenstern. Scaring you wasn't my intention, believe me. As for the others – I told Hiram that I had private business to discuss with you. He's a good friend and helped me escape.' He grinned softly as if at some inner amusement. 'I couldn't quite get away from everyone. Billy Ray's down below, being the dutiful bodyguard.'

Sara frowned into that smile. She picked up her recorder, placed it in her purse. 'I don't think you and I have any "private business," Senator. If you'll excuse me ...'

She started to move past him toward the temple's entrance. She thought for a moment that he might make some move to detain her; she tensed, but he stepped aside politely.

'I meant what I said about compassion,' he commented just before she reached the stairs. 'I know why you dislike me. I know why you look so familiar. Andrea was your sister.'

The words battered Sara like fists. She gasped at the pain.

'I also believe you're a fair person,' Hartmann continued, and each word was another blow. 'I think that if you were finally told the truth, you'd understand.'

Sara gave a cry that was half-sob, unable to hold it back. She placed a hand on cool, rough stone and turned. The sympathy she saw in Hartmann's eyes frightened her.

'Just leave me alone, Senator.'

'We're stuck together on this trip, Ms. Morgenstern. There's no sense in our being enemies, not when there isn't any reason.'

His voice was gentle and persuasive. He sounded kind. It would have been easier if he'd been accusatory, if he'd tried to bribe her or threaten her. Then she could have fought back easily, could have reveled in her fury. But Hartmann stood there, his hands at his sides, looking, of all things, *sad*. She'd imagined Hartmann many ways, but never like this. 'How ...' she began, and found her voice choked. 'When did you find out about Andrea?'

'After our conversation at the press reception, I had my aide Amy run a background check. She found that you'd been born in Cincinnati, that your family name was Whitman. You lived two streets over from me, on Thornview. Andrea was what, seven or eight years older than you? You look a lot like her, like she might have grown up to be.' He steepled his hands to his face, rubbing at the corners of his eyes with his forefingers. 'I'm not very comfortable with lying or evasion, Ms. Morgenstern. That's not my style. I don't think you are either, not from the blunt articles you've written. I think I know why we've been at odds, and I also know it's a mistake.'

'Which means that you think it's my fault.'

'I've never attacked *you* in print.'

'I don't lie in my articles, Senator. They're fair. If you have a problem with any of my facts, let me know and I'll give you verification.'

'Ms. Morgenstern—' Hartmann began, a trace of irritation in his voice. Then, oddly, he leaned his head back and chuckled loudly. 'God, there we go again,' he said, and he sighed. 'Really, I read your articles. I don't always *agree* with you, but I'll be the first to admit that they're well written and researched. I even think that I could like the person who wrote them, if ever we had the chance to talk and know each other.' His gray-blue eyes caught hers. 'What's between us is the ghost of your sister.'

His last words took the breath from her. She couldn't believe that he'd said them; not so casually, not with that innocent smile, not after all those years. 'You killed her,' she breathed, and didn't realize that she'd spoken the words aloud until she saw the shock on Hartmann's face. He went white for an instant. His mouth opened, then clamped shut. He shook his head.

'You can't believe that,' he said. 'Roger Pellman killed her. There was no question at all about that. The poor retarded kid ...' Hartmann shook his head. 'How can I say it gently? He came out of the woods naked and howling like all the demons of hell were after him. Andrea's blood covered him. He *admitted* killing her.'

Hartmann's face was still pale. Sweat beaded on his forehead, and his gaze was withdrawn. 'Damnit, I was *there*, Ms. Morgenstern. I was standing outside in my front yard when Pellman came running up the street, gibbering. He ran into his house, the neighbors all around watching. We all heard his mother scream. Then the cops came, first to the Pellmans', then taking Roger into the woods with them. I saw them carry out the wrapped body. My mom had her arms around your mother. She was hysterical, wailing. It infected all of us. We were *all* crying, all of the kids, even though we really didn't understand what was going on. They handcuffed Roger, hauled him away ...'

Sara stared, bewildered, at Hartmann's haunted face. His hands were clenched into fists at his side. 'How can you say I killed her?' he asked softly. 'Don't you realize that *I* was in love with her, as infatuated as an eleven-year-old kid can be. I would never have done anything to hurt Andrea. I had nightmares for months afterward. I was furious when they assigned Roger Pellman to Longview Psychiatric. I wanted him to *hang* for what he'd done; I wanted to be the one to pull the damn switch on him.'

It can't be. The insistent denial pounded in her head. Yet she looked at Hartmann and knew, somehow, that she was wrong. Doubt had begun to dampen some of the fiery hatred. 'Succubus,' she said, and found her throat dry. She licked her lips. 'You were there, and she had Andrea's face.'

Hartmann took a gulping, deep breath. He looked away from her for a moment, toward the northern temple. Sara followed his gaze and saw that the tour group from the *Stacked Deck* had gone inside. The ball court was deserted, quiet. 'I knew Succubus,' Hartmann said at last, still looking away from her, and she could feel the trembling emotion in his voice. 'I knew her at the end of her public career, and we still saw each other occasionally. I wasn't married then, and Succubus …' He turned around to Sara, and she was surprised to see his eyes bright with moisture. 'Succubus could be *any*one, you know. She was anyone's ideal lover. When she was with you, she was exactly what you wanted.'

In that instant Sara knew what he was going to say. She had already begun to shake her head in denial.

'For me, quite often,' Hartmann continued, 'she was Andrea. You were right, you know, when you said we're both obsessed. We're obsessed by Andrea and her death. If that hadn't happened, I might have forgotten my crush on her six months later, like every pubescent fantasy. But what Roger Pellman did engraved Andrea in my mind. Succubus – she roamed in your head and used what she found there. Inside me, she found Andrea. So when she saw me during the riot, when she wanted me to save her from the violence of the mob, she took the face she had always shown to me: Andrea's.

'I didn't kill your sister, Ms. Morgenstern. I'll plead guilty to thinking of her as my fantasy lover, but that's all. Your sister was an ideal for me. I wouldn't have harmed her at all. I couldn't.'

It can't be.

Sara remembered all the strange links she'd found in the months after she'd first seen the videotape of Succubus's death. Sara had thought that she'd escaped the cloying Andrea-worship of her parents, that she'd left her murdered sister behind her for the rest of her life. Succubus's face had shattered all that. Even after she'd shakily written the article that would eventually win her the Pulitzer, she'd thought it had been a mistake, a cruel trick of fate. But Hartmann had been there. She'd known all along that the Senator was from Ohio. She discovered later that not only was he from Cincinnati, but he'd lived nearby, been a classmate of Andrea's. She'd done more research, suddenly suspicious. Mysterious deaths and violent acts seemed to plague Hartmann: in law school, as a New York City councilman, as mayor, as senator. None of them were ever Hartmann's fault. There was always someone else, someone with motive and desire. But still …

She dug further. She found that five-year-old Hartmann and his parents had been on vacation in New York the day Jetboy died and the virus was loosed on the unsuspecting world. They'd been among the lucky ones. None of them had ever shown any signs of having been infected. Still, if Hartmann were a hidden ace, 'up the sleeve' in the vernacular ...

It was circumstantial. It was flimsy. Her reporter's instinct had screamed 'Objectivity!' at her emotions. That hadn't stopped her from hating him. There was always that gut feeling, the certainty that he was the one. Not Roger Pellman, not the others who had been convicted, but *Hartmann*.

For the last nine years or more she'd believed that.

Yet Hartmann didn't seem dangerous or malign now. He stood there patiently – a plain face, a high forehead threatening to recede and sweating from the fierce sun, a body soft around the waist from years of sitting behind administrative desks. He let her stare, let her search his gaze unflinchingly. Sara found that she couldn't imagine him killing or hurting. A person who enjoyed pain in the way she'd imagined would show it somewhere: in his body language, his eyes, his voice. There was none of it in Hartmann. He had a presence, yes, a charisma, but he didn't feel dangerous.

Would he have told you about Succubus if he hadn't cared? Would a murderer have opened himself that far to someone he didn't know, a hostile reporter? Doesn't violence follow everyone through life? Give him that much credit.

'I ... I have to think about this,' she said.

'That's all I ask,' he answered softly. He took a deep breath, looking around the sun-baked ruins. 'I should get back to the others before everyone starts talking, I suppose. The way Downs is snooping around me, he'll have all sorts of rumors started.' He smiled sadly.

Hartmann moved toward the temple stairs. Sara watched him, frowning at the contradictory thoughts swirling inside her. As the senator passed her, he stopped.

His hand touched her shoulder.

His touch was gentle, warm, and his face was full of sympathy. 'I put Andrea's face on Succubus and I'm sorry that caused you anguish. It's also plagued me.' His hand dropped; her shoulder was cool where he'd been. He glanced at the serpent's heads to either side. 'Pellman killed Andrea. No one else. I'm just a person accidentally caught up in your story. I think we'd make better friends than enemies.'

He seemed to hesitate for a moment, as if waiting for a reply. Sara was looking out to the pyramid, not trusting herself to say anything. All the conflicting emotions that were Andrea surged in her: outrage, an aching loss, bitterness, a thousand others. Sara kept her gaze averted from Hartmann, not wanting him to see.

When she was sure he was gone, she sank down, sitting with her back against a serpent column. Her head on her knees, she let the tears come.

At the bottom of the steps Gregg looked upward at the temple. A grim satisfaction filled him. Toward the end he had felt Sara's hatred dissipate like fog in sunlight, leaving behind only a faint trace of its presence. *I did it without you,* he said to the power inside him. *Her hatred flung you away, but it didn't matter. She's Succubus, she's Andrea; I'll make her come to me by myself. She's mine. I don't need you to force her to me.*

Puppetman was silent.

BLOOD RIGHTS

Leanne C. Harper

The young Lacandon Maya coughed as the smoke followed him across the newly cleared field. Someone had to stay and watch the brush they had cut reduce to the ashes they would use to feed the ground of the *milpa*. The fire was burning evenly so he moved back out of range of the smoke. Everyone else was at home asleep in the afternoon, and the humid warmth made him drowsy too. Smoothing down his long white robe over his bare legs, he ate the cold tamales that were his dinner.

Lying in the shade, he began to blink and fall under his dream's spell once more. His dreams had taken him to the realm of the gods ever since he had been a boy, but it was rare that he remembered what the gods had said or done. José, the old shaman, became so angry when all he could recall were feelings or useless details from his latest vision. The only hope in it all was that the dream became more and more clear each time he had it. He had been denying to José that the dream had returned, waiting for the time when he could remember enough to impress even José, but the shaman knew he lied.

The dream took him to Xibalba, the domain of Ah Puch, the Lord of Death. Xibalba always smelled of smoke and blood. He coughed as the atmosphere of death entered his lungs. The coughing awakened him, and it took him a moment to realize that he was no longer in the underworld. Eyes watering, he backed away from the fire, out of range of the smoke that the wind had sent to follow him. Maybe his ancestors were angry with him too.

He stared at the flames, now slowly dying down, and moved a little closer to the bonfire in the center of the *milpa*. Wild-eyed, he slid into a crouch before the fire and watched it closely. José had told him again and again to trust what he felt and go where his intuition led him. This time, frightened but glad there was no one to see him, he would do it.

With both hands he pushed his black hair back behind his ears and reached forward to pull a short leafy branch from the edge of the brush pile and put it on the ground before him. Slowly, left hand trembling slightly, he drew the machete from its stained leather scabbard at his side. Flexing his right hand, he held it chest-high in front of him. He clenched his jaws and turned his head slightly up and away from looking at his hand. The sweat from his forehead fell into his eyes and dripped off his aristocratic nose as he brought the machete down across the palm of his right hand.

He made no sound. Nor did he move as the bright blood ran down his fingers to fall on the deep green of the leaves. Only his eyes narrowed and his chin lifted. When the branch was covered with his blood, he picked it up with his left hand and threw it into the flames. The air smelled of Xibalba again and of his ancestors' ancient rituals, and he returned to the underworld once more.

As always, a rabbit scribe greeted him, speaking in the ancient language of his people. Clutching the bark paper and brush to its furry chest, it told him in an odd, low voice to follow. Ahau Ah Puch awaited him.

The air was scented by burning blood.

The man and the rabbit had walked through a village of abandoned thatch huts, much like those of his own village. But here patches of thatch were missing from the roofs. The uncovered doorways gaped like the mouths of skulls, while the mud and grass of the walls fell away like the flesh from a decaying body.

The rabbit led him between the high, stone walls of a ball court with carved stone rings set on the walls above his head. He did not remember ever having been in a ball court before, but he knew he could play here, had played here, had scored here. He felt again the hard rubber ball strike the cotton padding on his elbow and arc toward the serpent's coils carved into the stone ring.

He drew his eyes back from the serpent to the face of the Lord of Death, seated on a reed mat on the dais in front of him at the end of the ball court. Ah Puch's eyes were black pits set in the white band across his skull. The Ahau's mouth and nose opened on eternity, and the smells of blood and rotting flesh were strong upon him.

'Hunapu. Ballplayer. You have returned to me.'

The man knelt and put his forehead to the floor before Ah Puch, but he felt no fear. He felt nothing in this dream.

'Hunapu. Son.' The man raised his head at the sound of the old woman's voice to his left. Ix Chel and her even older husband, Itzamna, sat cross-legged on reed mats attended by the rabbit scribe. Their dais was supported by twin, huge turtles whose intermittently blinking eyes were all that showed they lived.

'The cycle ends.' The grandmother continued to speak. 'Change comes for the *hach winik*. The white stickmen have created their own downfall. You, Hunapu, brother to Xbalanque, are the messenger. Go to Kaminaljuyu and meet your brother. Your path will become clear, ballplayer.'

'Do not forget us, ballplayer.' Ah Puch spoke and his voice was vicious and hollow as if he spoke through a mask. 'Your blood is ours. Your enemies' blood is ours.'

For the first time real fear broke through Hunapu's numbness. His hand throbbed in pain to the rhythm of Ah Puch's words, but despite his fear he rose from his kneeling position. His eyes met the endless black of Ah Puch's.

Before he could speak, a ball whose every edge was a razor-sharp blade cut through the air toward him. Then Xibalba was gone and he was back at the dead fire, hearing the old god speak but one word.

'Remember.'

♣

The stocky Mayan worker stood in the shadows of one of the work tents as he watched the last group of archaeological students and professors break up. As they wandered into their sleeping tents, he withdrew even farther into the protection of the tent. His classic Maya profile marked him as a pure-blood Indian, the lowest class in Guatemala's social hierarchy; but here among the blonde students, it marked him as a conquest. It was rare that a student of the past got to sleep with a living example of a race of priest-kings. The worker, dressed in overlarge blue jeans and a filthy University of Pennsylvania T-shirt, saw no reason to discourage this impression. But he made himself as unattractive as possible to watch their simultaneous desire and repulsion. He walked carefully down the short passage between the tents to the sheet-metal storage shed.

The Indian once again assured himself that there were no observers before grasping the padlock and thrusting his pick into the keyhole. Squinting against the flickering firelight, he probed a few times and the lock was open. He flashed bright teeth in a contemptuous look back at the professors' tent. Slipping the lock into a pocket of his jeans, he opened the door and eased himself sideways into the shed. Unlike the archaeologists, he didn't need to stoop.

He waited a moment for his eyes to adjust before tugging a flashlight from his back pocket. The end of the light was covered by a torn piece of cloth secured by a rubber band. The dim circle of light roamed around the room almost at random until it froze on a shelf crowded with objects taken from the tombs and trenches dug around the city. The thief moved sideways along the narrow center aisle, careful not to disturb the pots, statues, and other partially cleaned artifacts on the shelves to either side. The small man pulled half a dozen small pots and miniature statutes off the shelves. None were located at the front of a shelf nor were they the finest examples, but all were intact, if somewhat the worse for their long burial. He put them into a cotton drawstring sack.

Sneering at the rows of ceramics and jade carvings, he wondered why the *norteamericanos* could curse the grave-robbers of the past when they were so efficient at the same thing. He sidled back up the aisle, catching a red-and-black-painted pot as his movement caused it to rock dangerously near the edge. Quick hands picked up a battered jade earplug and he paused, running the flashlight beam around the narrow room once more. Two things caught his eyes, a stingray spine and a bottle of Tanqueray gin kept locked up away from the workers.

Clutching the bottle and the spine against his chest, he listened, head leaned against the door, for any stray noises. All he heard was the muffled sound of lovemaking from a nearby tent. It sounded like the tall redhead. Satisfied that no one would observe him, he slid outside and replaced the lock.

He waited to open the gin until he had climbed up one of the larger hills. The professors said the hills were all temples. He had seen their drawings of what this place had once been. He didn't believe what he had been shown: plazas and tall temples with roof combs, all painted in yellow and red. He especially didn't believe the tall, thin men who presided over the temples. They didn't look like him, anyone he knew, or even much like the murals painted on some of the temple walls, but the professors said that they were his ancestors. It was typical of the *norteamericanos*. But it meant that he was only stealing his inheritance.

Something poked his side as he leaned over to open the bottle. He pulled the stingray spine out of his pocket. One of the blondes, no, the redhead, had told him what the old kings had done. Guh-ross, she had said. He had privately agreed. The *norteamericano* women with whom he slept always asked lots of questions about the ways of the old ones. They seemed to think that he should have the knowledge of a *brujo* just because he was an Indian. *Gringas*. He learned more from them than anyone in his family. They had taught him what was valuable, and more important, what would be immediately missed. He had a nice little collection now. He would be rich after he sold them in Guatemala.

The gin was good. He leaned back against a convenient tree trunk and watched the moon. Ix Chel, the Old Woman, was the moon goddess. The old ones' gods were ugly, not like the Virgin Mary or Jesus or even God in the Church where he had been raised.

He picked up the stingray spine. Someone had brought it long ago up to this city in the Highlands. It was carved with intricate designs along its entire length. He held it beside his leg, measuring it against his thigh. It ran the full length. All those stories. He reached out for the gin bottle, but he missed and fell forward, catching himself with his free hand. He was drunk.

The moonlight shone off his sweating torso as he pulled off his T-shirt and folded it none too neatly into a pad. He put the shirt on his right shoulder. Closing his eyes, he weaved to the left and reopened them, blinking rapidly. He tried to pull his legs up into the position he had seen in so many paintings. It took maneuvering. He had to brace himself against the rock and hold his legs in place with his right hand. He secured the shirt with his jaw and his raised shoulder.

With a sureness that belied his intoxication, he brought up the spine and pierced his right ear.

He gasped and swore at the pain. It swept through him, driving out the alcohol and bringing on a euphoria as the blood flowed from his shredded earlobe and was absorbed by the T-shirt. The high made him tremble. It was better than the gin, better than the marijuana the graduate students had, better than the professor's cocaine he had once stolen and snorted.

Penetrating his shadowed mind was the impression that he was no longer alone on the temple. He opened his eyes, not realizing that he had closed them. For just a moment the temple as it had once stood glowed in the moonlight. The bright reds were muted by the dim light. His wife knelt before him with a rope of thorns drawn through her tongue. Attendants surrounded them. His heavy ornamental head-dress covered his eyes. He blinked.

The temple was a pile of stone covered by the jungle. There was no wife wearing jade, no attendants. He was wearing dirty jeans again. He shook his head sharply to clear away the last of the vision. That hurt, *aiee*, did it hurt. It must have been the gin and listening to those women. According to what they had said, he'd messed up the old rites anyway. The power was supposed to be in the *burning* blood.

The shirt had fallen from his shoulder. It was bright red and sodden with his blood. He thought about it a moment, then pulled out a cigarette lighter he had stolen from one of the professors and tried to burn the shirt. It was too wet; the flames kept going out. Instead he made a fire with some sticks he picked up off the ground. When he finally had a small fire going, he threw on the shirt. The burning blood gave off smoke and a stench that nearly made him sick. Mostly in jest he sat in front of the blaze and aped the cross-legged position he had seen on so many pots, one hand extended toward the flames. He was starting to get very tired and staring at the fire mesmerized him.

What little he knew of Xibalba led him to believe that it was a place of darkness and flames, like the hell the fathers warned him about as a child. It wasn't. It most resembled a remote village where they still lived by the old ways. No television antennas, no radios blaring the latest in rock and roll from Guatemala. All was silent. He saw no one as he walked about the small group of huts. The only movement he saw was a bat flying out of the low doorway of one of the thatch-roofed houses. The roofs were pitched like the ceilings of the temple rooms, high and narrow, rising almost to a point. He felt as if he were walking through a mural on a temple wall. It was all so familiar. He remembered that none of his usual drunken dreams had this clarity.

A rhythmic *ga-pow, ga-pow* brought him through the quiet to a ball court. Three human figures sat on the platform on top of the walls. He recognized them as Ah Puch, Itzamna, and Ix Chel – the Death God, the Old Man, and the Old Woman, supreme in the Mayan pantheon, or as supreme as any of the many deities were. The three were surrounded by animals who assisted them as scribes and servants. Drawing his gaze back down the stone walls to the packed-dirt court itself, he saw the source of the noise. Not deigning to notice him, a creature that was half-human, half-jaguar repeatedly attempted to knock a ball through one of the intricately carved stone hoops high on the walls of the court. The creature never used its paws. Instead it used head, hips, elbows, and knees to send the ball bouncing up the wall toward the ring. The jaguarman and its fangs frightened him. Since the dream had begun, it was the first thing he had felt besides curiosity and wondering how he could steal those stone rings. He watched the muscles beneath the black spots bunch and release as he considered why none of this seemed strange in the least. He lifted his head and stared up at the watchers.

From one corner of his eye he saw the ball coming toward him. Moving in patterns that seemed as familiar as the village, he swung away from it before bringing his elbow up and under the ball and launching it toward the nearest ring. It arched through the goal without touching the stone. The watchers gasped and murmured to each other. He was just as surprised, but he decided that discretion was the best course here.

'Ai! Not bad!' He yelled up at them in Spanish. Lord Death shook his head and glared at the old couple. Itzamna spoke to him in pure Maya. Although he had never spoken the language before in his life, he recognized it and understood it.

'Welcome, Xbalanque, to Xibalba. You are as fine a ballplayer as your namesake.'

'My name's not Xbalanque.'

'From this time, it is.' The black death-mask of Ah Puch glared down at him and he swallowed his next comment.

'Sí, this is a dream and I am Xbalanque.' He spread his hands and nodded. 'Whatever you say.'

Ah Puch looked away.

'You are different; you have always known this.' Ix Chel smiled down at him. It was the smile of a crocodile, not a grandmother. He grinned up at her, wishing he'd wake up. Now.

'You are a thief.'

He began thinking about how he was going to get out of this dream. He had remembered the more troublesome parts of the ancient myths – the decapitations, the houses of multiple horrors …

'You should use your abilities to gain power.'

'Hey, I'll do that. You're right. No problem. Just as soon as I get back.' One of the rabbits who was attending the three gods watched him intently with head canted to one side and nostrils twitching. Occasionally it wrote frantically on an odd, folded piece of paper with a brushlike pen. He was reminded of a comic book he had once read, *Alice in Wonderland*. There had been rabbits in her dream too. And he was getting hungry.

'Go to the city, Xbalanque.' Itzamna's voice was squeaky, pitched even higher than his wife's.

'Hey, isn't there a brother in this somewhere?' He was remembering even more of the myth.

'You'll find him. Go.' The ball court began to quiver in front of his eyes, and the jaguar's paw struck him in the back of the head.

Xbalanque grunted in pain as his head slid off the rock he had apparently been using as a pillow. He pulled himself upright, shoving his bare back against the rough limestone. The dream was still with him, and he couldn't seem to focus on anything. The moon had gone down while he'd been passed out. It was very dark. The uncovered stones of the ruin glowed with their own light, like bones disturbed in a grave. The bones of his people's past glory.

He bent over to pick up his stolen treasures and fell to one knee. Unable to stop himself, he vomited the gin and tortillas he had eaten. *Madre de Dios*, he felt bad. Body empty and shaking, he staggered up again to begin the descent from the pyramid. Maybe that dream was right. He should leave, go to Guatemala City now. Take what he had. It was enough to let him live comfortably for a while.

Christ, his head hurt. Hungover and still drunk. It wasn't fair. The last thing he picked up was the stingray spine. Its barbs were still coated with his blood. Xbalanque reached up to touch his ear gingerly. He fingered the hole in the lobe with pain and disgust. His hand came away bloody. That was definitely not part of the dream. Swaying, he searched through his pockets until he found the earplug. He tried to insert it into his earlobe, but it hurt too much and the torn flesh would not support it. He was almost sick again.

Xbalanque tried to remember the strange dream. It was fading. For the moment all he recalled was that the dream recommended a retreat to the city. It still sounded like a good idea. As he alternately tripped and slid down the side of the hill, he decided to steal a jeep and go in style. Maybe they wouldn't miss it. He couldn't walk all the way with this headache anyway.

Inside the dark, smoke-filled thatch house José listened gravely to Hunapu's tale of his vision. The shaman nodded when Hunapu spoke of his audience with the gods. When he finished, he looked to the old man for interpretation and guidance.

'Your vision is a true one, Hunapu.' He straightened up and slid from his hammock to the dirt floor. Standing before the crouching Hunapu, he threw copal incense on his fire. 'You must do as the gods tell you or bring us all misfortune.'

'But where am I to go? What is Kaminaljuyu?' Hunapu shrugged in his confusion. 'I do not understand. I have no brother, only sisters. I do not play this ball game. Why me?'

'You have been chosen and touched by the gods. They see what we do not.' José put his hand on the young man's shoulder. 'It is very dangerous to question them. They anger easily.

'Kaminaljuyu is Guatemala City. That is where you must go. But first we must prepare you.' The shaman looked past him. 'Sleep tonight. Tomorrow you will go.'

When he returned to the shaman's home in the morning, most of the village was there to share in the magical thing that had happened. When he left them, José walked with him into the rain forest, carrying a package. Out of sight of the village, the shaman wrapped Hunapu's elbows and knees with the cotton padding he had brought with him. The old man told him that this was how he had been dressed in José's dream the night before. It too was a sign that Hunapu's vision was true. José warned him to tell those he met of his quest only if they could be trusted and were Lacandones like himself. The *Ladinos* would try to stop him if they knew.

Xepon was small. Perhaps thirty multicolored houses clustered around the church on the square. Their pink, blue, and yellow paint was faded, and they looked as though they crouched with their backs to the rain that had begun earlier. As Xbalanque bounced down the mountain road into the village, he was happy to see the cantina. He had decided to take the most isolated roads he could find on the worn road map under the driver's seat to get into the city.

He started to park in front of the cantina, but instead decided to park around the side, away from curious eyes. He thought it was strange that he had seen no one since entering town, but the weather was fit for no one, especially him and his hangover. His Reeboks, another gift from the *norteamericanos*, flopped against the wet wood walkway that ran in front of the cantina before he entered the open doorway. It was a disconcerting sound amid a silence broken only by dripping water and the rain on the tin roofs. Even the dimness outside had not prepared him for the darkness within, or the years of tobacco smoke still trapped between the narrow walls. A few tattered and faded *Feliz Navidad* banners hung down from the gray ceiling.

'What do you want?' He was assaulted in Spanish from behind the long bar that lined the wall to his left. The force and hostility behind the question hurt his head. A stooped old Indian woman glared at him from behind the bar.

'*Cerveza.*'

Unconcerned for his preferences, she removed a bottle from the cooler behind the bar and flipped off the cap as he walked toward her. She set it on the stained and pitted wood of the bar. When Xbalanque reached for it, she put a small gnarled hand around the bottle and nodded her chin at him. He pulled some crumpled quetzals from his pocket and laid them on the bar. There was a crash of nearby thunder and they both tensed. He realized for the first time that the reason she was so hostile might not have anything to do with an early customer. She snatched the money off the bar as if to deny her fear and put it into the sash around her stained huipil.

'What do you have to eat?' Whatever was going on certainly had nothing to do with him. The beer tasted good, but it was not what he really needed.

'Black bean soup.' The woman's answer was a statement, definitely not an invitation. It was accompanied by more thunder rolling up the valley.

'What else?' Looking around, Xbalanque belatedly realized that something was extremely wrong. Every cantina he had ever been in, no matter where or how large, had some old drunks sitting around waiting to try to pick up a free drink. And women, even old women such as this one, rarely worked in bars in these small villages.

'Nothing.' Her face was closed to him as he looked for a clue to what was happening.

Another peal of thunder turned into the low growling of truck engines. Both their heads swung toward the door. Xbalanque stepped back from the bar and looked for a back way out. There was none. When he turned again to the old woman, she had her back to him. He ran for the door.

Green-clad soldiers piled off the backs of the two army transports parked in the middle of the square. The paths of the trucks were marked by the broken benches and shrubs they had run over on their way across the tiny park. As the soldiers hit the ground, they pulled their machine guns into firing position. Two-man teams immediately left the central area to search the houses lining the square. Other armed men moved out of the square through the rest of the village.

Palms spread against the plaster, Xbalanque slid along the outside wall of the cantina for the safety of the side street. If he could get to the jeep, he had a chance to escape. He had made it to the corner of the building when one of the soldiers spotted him. At the soldier's order to halt, he jumped for the street, sliding in the mud, and dashed for the jeep.

Shots into the ground in front of him splashed him with mud. Xbalanque threw his hand up to protect his eyes and fell to his knees. Before he could get back up, a sullen-faced soldier grabbed his arm and hauled Xbalanque back to the square, his feet slipping in the thick mud as he scrambled to stand up and walk.

One of the young *Ladino* soldiers stood with his Uzi pointed at

Xbalanque's head while he was shoved facedown in the mud and searched. Xbalanque had hidden the artifacts in the jeep, but the soldiers found the stash of quetzals in his Reeboks. One of them held the wad of money up to the army lieutenant in charge. The lieutenant looked disgusted at the condition of the bills, but he put them in his own pocket anyway. Xbalanque did not protest. Through the excruciating pain in his head that had begun when he fled the soldiers, he was trying to decide what he could say to get out of this. If they knew the jeep was stolen, he was dead.

The sound of more gunfire made him wince into the mud. He raised his head slightly, knocking it into the barrel of the gun above him. The soldier holding it pulled back enough for him to see another man being dragged from inside the dilapidated yellow school on the west side of the square. He heard children crying inside the small building. The second prisoner was also an Indian, tall with eyeglasses knocked askew on his narrow face. The two soldiers escorting him allowed him to regain his feet before presenting him to the lieutenant.

The schoolteacher straightened his glasses before staring directly into the lieutenant's mirrored sunglasses. Xbalanque knew he was in trouble; the schoolteacher was deliberately trying to anger the army officer. It could only result in worse consequences than they already faced.

The lieutenant brought up his swagger stick and knocked the teacher's glasses off his face. When the teacher bent down to pick them up, the officer struck him across the side of the head. With blood dripping down his face onto his white European shirt, the teacher replaced his glasses. The right lens was shattered. Xbalanque began looking for an escape route. He hoped that his guard might be sufficiently distracted. Looking sideways up at the young man with the Uzi, he saw that the boy had not taken his eyes off him.

'You are a communist.' The lieutenant made it a statement, not a question, directed to the teacher. Before the teacher could reply, the officer glanced toward the school-house with annoyance. The children inside were still crying. He swung his swagger stick toward the school and nodded at a soldier to his left. Without aiming, the soldier panned his machine gun across the building, breaking windows and pocking the plaster. A few screams erupted from inside, then silence.

'You are a traitor and an enemy to Guatemala.' He brought the stick up across the other side of the teacher's head. There was more blood, and Xbalanque began to feel sick and somehow *wrong*.

'Where are the other traitors?'

'There are no other traitors.' The teacher shrugged and smiled.

'Fernandez, the church.' The lieutenant spoke to a soldier smoking a cigarette leaning against one of the trucks. Fernandez tossed away the cigarette and picked up the thick tube propped beside him against the truck. While he aimed, another of the men around the trucks shoved a rocket into the launcher.

Turning toward the old colonial church, Xbalanque saw, for the first time, the village priest standing outside arguing with one of the search teams as the soldiers stood there holding silver candlesticks. There was an explosion from the rocket launcher, followed a split second later by the blast as the church fell in on itself. The soldiers standing outside had seen it coming and fallen to the ground. The priest collapsed, from shock or injuries, Xbalanque could not tell. By now he was feeling the pain in every joint and muscle.

The rain mixed with the blood on the teacher's face and, as it dripped down, stained his shirt pink. Xbalanque didn't see any more. The pain had grown until he curled up in the mud, clutching his knees to his chest. Something was happening. It must be because he had never felt such fear before. He knew that he was going to die. The damned old gods had led him to this.

He barely heard the order given to move him up against the school wall with the teacher. The lieutenant didn't even care who he was. For some reason the fact that the officer hadn't even bothered to question him seemed the worst indignity of all.

Xbalanque shook as he stood with his back against the already bullet-marked wall. The soldiers left them there alone and backed off, out of the line of fire. The pain had begun to come in waves, driving out his fear, driving out everything except the enormous weight of the agony in his body. He stared through the soldiers gathering for the firing squad at the rainbow forming between the bright, jade green mountains as the sun finally came out. The teacher patted him on the shoulder.

'Are you all right?' His companion actually looked concerned. Xbalanque was silent as he gathered sufficient energy not to collapse to the ground.

'See, God has a sense of humor.' The madman smiled at him as if at a crying child. Xbalanque cursed him in the language of his Quiche grandmother, a tongue he had not spoken before his dream of Xibalba.

'We die for the lives of our people.' The schoolteacher lifted his head proudly and faced the soldiers' guns as they were raised to aim.

'No. Not again!' Xbalanque rushed the guns as they fired. His force knocked the other man to his knees. As he moved, Xbalanque realized in one small part of his brain that the exquisite agony had gone. As the bullets sped to meet his charge, he felt only stronger, more powerful than he ever had before. The bullets reached him.

Xbalanque hesitated as they struck. He waited an instant for the inevitable pain and final darkness. They didn't come. He looked at the soldiers; they stared back wide-eyed. Some ran for the trucks. Others dropped their guns and simply ran. A few held their ground and kept firing, looking to the lieutenant, who was backing up slowly toward the trucks and calling for Fernandez.

The warrior scooped up a brick from the street and, crying out his name in a mixture of fear and exhilaration, threw it with all his strength at one of the trucks. As it flew, it struck a soldier, crushing his head and splattering blood and brains across his fleeing companions before flying on toward the vehicle. The soldier had slowed its momentum. It was dropping as it streaked toward the truck. The brick struck the gas tank and the transport exploded.

Xbalanque stopped his rush toward the soldiers and stared at the fiery scene. Men in flames – soldiers who had made the shelter of the troop carrier – screamed. The scene was right out of one of the American movies he had watched in the city. But the movies hadn't had the smell of petrol, burning canvas and rubber, and underneath everything else the stench of burning flesh. He began backing away.

Remotely, as if through heavy padding, he felt someone grab his arm. Xbalanque turned to strike his enemy. The teacher was staring down at him through the shattered glasses.

'*Se habla español?*' The taller man was guiding him away from the square up a side street.

'*Sí, sí.*' Xbalanque was beginning to have time to wonder what was happening. He knew he had never before been able to do anything such as this. Something was not right. What had that vision done to him? He was involuntarily relaxing and he felt the strength draining from him. He began to lean against the wall of a peeling pale-red house.

'*Madre de Dios* – we have to keep moving.' The teacher hauled at him. 'They'll bring up the artillery. You're good with bullets, but can you fend off rockets?'

'I don't know …' Xbalanque stopped to think about this for a moment.

'We'll figure it out later. Come *on*.'

Xbalanque realized that the man was right, but it was so difficult. With the fear of death gone, he felt as though he had lost not only the new power but also his regular strength. He looked up the street toward the forested mountainside so far away above the houses. The trees were safety. The soldiers would never follow them into the forest where guerrillas could be waiting to ambush them. The flat sound of a shot brought him back.

The teacher pulled him away from the house and, keeping his hand underneath Xbalanque's arm, steered him toward the green refuge ahead. They cut left between two small houses and moved sideways along the narrow, muddy alley that divided the clapboard and plaster buildings. Xbalanque was moving now, sliding and skidding in the slippery brown mud. Past rear gardens, the alley turned to a path leading up the steep hillside into the trees. The open ground was at least fifteen meters of utter exposure.

He ran into his compatriot as the other man stopped and peered around the corner of the house on the left.

'Clear.' The teacher had not relinquished his grip on Xbalanque's arm. 'Can you run?'

'*Sí.*'

After a frightened dash Xbalanque collapsed a few yards into the forest. The rain forest was thick enough to prevent their being spotted if they stayed still and quiet. They heard the soldiers arguing below until a sergeant came by and ordered them back to the square. Someone in the village would die in their place. The teacher was sweating and nervous. Xbalanque wondered if it was for their unwitting victim or his own unexpected survival. A bullet in the back was not as romantic as a firing squad.

As they trudged deeper into the wet mountains seeking to avoid the soldiers, Xbalanque's companion introduced himself. The teacher was Esteban Akabal, a devoted communist and freedom fighter. Xbalanque listened without comment to a long lecture on the evils of the existing government and the coming revolution. He only wondered at where Akabal found the energy to go on. When Akabal at last slowed down, panting as they worked their way up a difficult trail, Xbalanque asked him why he worked with *Ladinos*.

'It is necessary to work together for the greater good. The divisions between Quiché and *Ladino* are created and encouraged by the repressive regime under which we labor. They are false and, once removed, will no longer hamper the worker's natural desire to join with his fellow worker.' At a level section of the path both men paused to rest.

'The *Ladinos* will use us, but nothing will change their feelings or mine.' Xbalanque shook his head. 'I have no desire to join your workers' army. How do I get a road to the city?'

'You can't take a main road. The soldiers will shoot you on sight.' Akabal looked at the cuts and bruises Xbalanque had incurred on their climb. 'Your talent seems very selective.'

'I don't think it's a talent.' Xbalanque wiped off some of the dried blood on his jeans. 'I had a dream about the gods. They gave me my name and my powers. After the dream I could do – what I did in Xepon.'

'The *norteamericanos* gave you your powers. You are what they call an ace.' Akabal examined him closely. 'I know of few others this far south of the United States.

'It's a disease actually. A red-haired alien from outer space brought it to Earth. Or so they claim, since biological warfare has been outlawed. Most of those who caught it died. Some were changed.'

'I have seen them begging in the city. It was bad sometimes.' Xbalanque shrugged. 'But I'm not like that.'

'A very few become something more than they were. The *norte-americanos* worship these aces.' Akabal shook his head. 'Typical exploitation of the masses by fascist media masters.

'You know, you could be very important to our fight.' The schoolteacher leaned forward. 'The mythic element, a tie to our people's past. It would be good, very good, for us.'

'I don't think so. I'm going to the city.' Chagrined, Xbalanque remembered the treasure he had left in the jeep. 'After I return to Xepon.'

'The people *need* you. You could be a great leader.'

'I've heard this before.' Xbalanque was uncertain. The offer was attractive, but he wanted to be more than the people's-army figurehead. With his power he wanted to *do* something, something with money in it. But first he had to get to Guatemala City.

'Let me help you.' Akabal had that intense look of desire that the graduate students had when they wanted to sleep with the Mayan priest-king, or as one of them had said, a reasonable facsimile thereof. Combined with the blood now caked on his face, it made Akabal appear to be the devil himself. Xbalanque backed off a couple steps.

'No, thank you. I'm just going to go back to Xepon in the morn-ing, get my jeep, and leave.' He started back down the trail. Over his shoulder he spoke to Akabal. 'Thanks for your help.'

'Wait. It's getting dark. You'll never make it back down at night.' The teacher sat back down on a rock beside the trail. 'We're far enough in that, even with more men, they would not dare follow us. We'll stay here tonight, and tomorrow morning we'll start back for the village. It will be safe. It will take the lieutenant at least a day to explain the loss of his truck and get reinforcements.'

Xbalanque stopped and turned back.

'No more talk about armies?'

'No, I promise.' Akabal smiled and gestured for Xbalanque to take another rock.

'Do you have anything to eat? I'm very hungry.' Xbalanque could not remember ever having been this hungry, even in the worst parts of his childhood.

'No. But if we were in New York, you could go to a restaurant called Aces High. It is just for people like you ...'

As Akabal told him about life in the United States for the aces, Xbalanque gathered some branches to protect against the wet ground and lay down on them. He was asleep long before Akabal ended his speech.

In the morning before dawn they were on the trail back down. Akabal had found some nuts and edible plants for food, but Xbalanque remained ravenous and in pain. Still, they made it back to the village in much less time than it had taken them to toil up the trail the day before.

Hunapu found that wearing the heavy cotton padding while he was walking was clumsy and hot, so he wrapped it up and tied it to his back. He had walked a day and a night without sleep when he came to a small Indian village only slightly larger than his own. Hunapu stopped and wrapped the padding around himself as José had done it. The dress of a warrior and a ballplayer, he thought proudly, and held his head high. The people here were not Lacandones and they looked at him suspiciously as he entered with the sunrise.

An old man walked out into the main path that led between the thatched houses. He called out a greeting to Hunapu in a tongue that was similar but not quite the same as that of his people. Hunapu introduced himself to the *t'o'ohil* as he walked up to him.

The village guardian stared at the young man for a full minute of contemplation before inviting him into his home, the largest house Hunapu had ever entered.

While most of the village waited outside for the guardian to tell them about this morning apparition, the two men spoke and drank coffee. It was a difficult conversation at first, but Hunapu soon understood the old man's pronunciations and was able to make himself and his mission known. When Hunapu was finished, the *t'o'ohil* sat back and called his three sons to him. They stood behind him and waited while he spoke to Hunapu.

'I believe that you are Hunapu returned to us. The end of the world comes soon, and the gods have sent messengers to us.' The *t'o'ohil* gestured to one of his sons, a dwarf, to come forward. 'Chan K'in will go with you. As you see, the gods touched him and he speaks to them directly for us. If you are *hach*, true, he will know it. If you are not, he will know that also.'

The dwarf went to stand by Hunapu and looked back at his father and nodded.

'Bol will also go with you.' At this, the youngest son started and glared down at his father. 'He dislikes the old ways and he will not believe you. But he honors me and he will protect his brother in your travels. Bol, get your gun and pack whatever you need. Chan K'in, I will speak to you. Stay.' The old man put down his coffee and stood. 'I will tell the village of your vision and your journey. There may be those who wish to accompany you.'

Hunapu joined him outside and stood silently while the *t'o'ohil* told his people that the young man followed a vision and was to be respected. Most of the people left after that, but a few remained and Hunapu spoke to them of his quest. Although they were Indian, he felt uncomfortable speaking to them because they wore pants and shirts like the *Ladinos*, not the long tunics of the Lacandones.

When Chan K'in and Bol, dressed for travel in the village's traditional clothing and carrying supplies, came for him, only three men were left to hear him. Hunapu rose and the other men walked away, talking among themselves. Chan K'in was calm. His composed face showed nothing of what he felt or if he was reluctant to embark on a journey that would undoubtedly bring his twisted body pain. Bol, though, showed his anger at his father's order. Hunapu wondered if the tall brother would simply shoot him in the back of the head at the first opportunity and return to his life. It did not matter. He had no choice; he had to continue on the path that the gods had chosen for him. He did feel a certain misgiving that the gods would have chosen him to have the company of such garishly dressed men. Used to the simple shifts of his people, he considered the bright red-and-purple embroidery and sashes of these men to be more like the clothing of the *Ladinos* than to be proper dress for real men. No doubt he would see much that he had not seen before on his travels to meet his brother. He hoped that his brother knew how to dress.

It took much less time to get out of the mountains than it had to climb up into them. A few hours walking that began at dawn brought Xbalanque and Akabal back into Xepon. This time the town was crowded with people. Looking at the remains of the truck in the square where most of the activity was centered made Xbalanque proud. Too late he began thinking about the price the town had paid for his escape. Perhaps these people would not be as impressed with him as Akabal. Akabal led him past the angry stares of some of the townsmen and the tearstained hate of many of the women. With so many people and Akabal's firm grip on his arm, he had no chance to make a break for the jeep and escape. They ended up back at the cantina, today the site of a town meeting.

Their entry caused an uproar as some of the men called for his death and others proclaimed him a hero. Xbalanque said nothing. He was afraid to open his mouth. He stood to one side, back against the hard wooden edge of the bar, as Akabal climbed up and began speaking to the groups of men circulating beneath him. It took several moments of mutual shouts and insults in Quiché and Spanish to gain the attention of all the men.

He was so busy watching the men watching him for signs of violence that it took a while for what Akabal was saying to make sense to him. Akabal was again mixing Maya and Spanish in a speech that centered on Xbalanque and his 'mission.' Akabal had taken what Xbalanque had said to him and linked it to a Christian second coming and the end of the world as prophesied by the ancient priests.

Xbalanque, the morning star, was the herald of a new age in which the Indians would take back their lands and become the rulers of their land as they had been centuries before. The coming doom was that of the *Ladinos* and *norteamericanos*, not the Maya, who would inherit the Earth. No longer should the Quiché follow the lead of outsiders, socialist, communist, or democratic. They had to follow their own or lose themselves forever. And Xbalanque was the sign. He had been given his powers by the gods. Confused, Xbalanque remembered Akabal's explanation of his powers as the result of a disease. But even this son of a god could not win alone against the fascist invaders. He was sent here to gain followers, warriors who would fight at his side until they had taken back all that the *Ladinos* and the centuries had stolen from them.

When he had finished, Akabal hauled Xbalanque up onto the bar and jumped down, leaving the stocky man in filthy T-shirt and blue jeans alone above the packed room. Turning to face Xbalanque, Akabal raised his fist into the air and began chanting Xbalanque's name over and over again. Slowly, and then with increasing fervor, every man in the room followed the teacher's lead, many raising their rifles in their fists.

Faced with a chant of his name that shook the room, Xbalanque swallowed nervously, his hunger forgotten. He almost wished that he had only the army to worry about. He was not yet ready to become the leader about which the gods had spoken to him. This was not at all how he had imagined it. He wasn't wearing the splendid uniform he had designed in his mind, and this was not the well trained and directed army that would bring him to power and the presidential palace. They were all staring at him with an expression in their faces that he had never seen before. It was worship and trust. Slowly, trembling, he raised his own fist and saluted them and the gods. He silently prayed to those gods that he would not screw the whole thing up.

A dirty little man, the nightmare of the *Ladinos* come to life, he knew that he was not what these people had seen in their dreams either. But he also knew that he was their only hope now. And whether he was the accidental creation of the *norteamericanos'* sickness or the child of the gods, he swore to all the deities he recognized, Mayan and European, Jesus, Mary, and Itzamna, that he would do everything he could for his people.

But his brother Hunapu had to be having an easier time than he was.

◆

Just outside the village, as Hunapu had been removing his cotton armor, one of the men he had spoken to had joined them. Silently they walked on through the Peten forests, each man with his own thoughts. They moved slowly because of Chan K'in, but not as slowly as Hunapu had expected. The dwarf was clearly used to making his own way with little help from others. There had been no dwarves in Hunapu's village, but they were known to bring good luck and to be the voice of the gods. The little men were revered. José had often said that Hunapu was meant to be a dwarf since he had been touched by the gods. Hunapu looked forward to learning from Chan K'in.

At the height of the sun they took a break. Hunapu was staring at the sun, his namesake, at the center of the sky when Chan K'in hobbled over to him. The dwarf's face still showed nothing. They sat together in silence for some minutes before Chan K'in spoke.

'Tomorrow, at dawn, a sacrifice. The gods wish to make sure that you are worthy.' Chan K'in's huge black eyes were turned on Hunapu, who nodded in agreement. Chan K'in stood up and walked back to sit by his brother. Bol still looked as if he wanted Hunapu dead.

It was a long, hot afternoon for walking. The insects were bad and nothing worked to keep them away. It was nearly dark by the time they had trudged to Yalpina. Chan K'in entered first and spoke to the village elders. When he had gained permission for them to enter, he sent a child out to the waiting party in the forest. Wearing his armor, Hunapu strode into the tiny town square. Everyone had gathered to hear Chan K'in and Hunapu speak. It was plain that they knew Chan K'in, and his reputation gave weight to Hunapu's claims. Until they were hushed by their mothers, the children giggled and made fun of Hunapu's cotton armor and bare legs. But when Hunapu began speaking of his quest to find his brother and join him in a revival of their own Indian culture, the people fell under the spell of his dream. They had their own portents.

Fifteen years earlier a child had been born who had the brilliant feathers of a jungle bird. The girl was thrust forward through the crowd. She was beautiful, and the feathers that replaced her hair only made her more so. She said that she had been waiting for one to come and that Hunapu was surely the one. Hunapu took her hand and she stood at his side.

That night many of the people from the town came to the home of the girl's parents, where Hunapu and Chan K'in were staying, and spoke to them about the future. The girl, Maria, never left Hunapu. When the last villager had left and they curled up by the fire, Maria watched them sleep.

Before dawn Chan K'in woke Hunapu and they trekked out to the forest, leaving Maria behind to get ready to leave. Hunapu had only his machete, but Chan K'in had a slim European knife. Taking the dwarf's knife, Hunapu knelt, holding his hands out in front of him palm up. In the left was the knife. The right, already healed from the machete cut three days before, trembled in anticipation. Without flinching or hesitating Hunapu drove the knife through the palm of his right hand, holding it there while his head dropped back and his body quivered in ecstasy.

With no movement except for a momentary widening of his huge eyes, Chan K'in watched the other man gasping, blood dripping from his hand. He roused himself from his revery to put a piece of hand-loomed cotton cloth on the ground beneath Hunapu's hands. He moved to Hunapu's side and pulled his head over toward him, staring into Hunapu's open, blind eyes as if seeking to peer into his mind itself.

After several minutes Hunapu collapsed to the ground and

Chan K'in snatched up the blood-drenched cloth. Using flint and steel, he lit a small fire. As Hunapu returned to consciousness, he threw the offering onto the fire. Hunapu crawled over and both men watched the smoke rise to heaven to meet the rising sun.

'What did you see?' Chan K'in spoke first, his immobile face giving no clue to his own thoughts.

'The gods are pleased with me, but we must move faster and gather more people. I think ... I saw Xbalanque leading an army of people.' Hunapu nodded to himself and clasped his hands. 'That is what they want.

'It is beginning now. But we still have far to go and much to do before we succeed.' Hunapu looked over at Chan K'in.

The dwarf sat with his stunted legs spread out before him with his chin propped up on his hand.

'For now, we will go back to Yalpina and eat.' He struggled to his feet. 'I saw some trucks. We will take one and travel on the roads from now on.'

Their discussion was interrupted by Maria, who ran into the clearing, panting.

'The cacique, he wants to speak to you now. A runner has come in from another village. The army is sweeping the area looking for rebels. You must leave at once.' Her feathers shone in the early morning light as she looked at him in entreaty.

Hunapu nodded to her.

'I will meet you in the village. Prepare to go with us. You will be a sign to others.' Hunapu turned back toward Chan K'in and closed his eyes in concentration. The trees in the background of the clearing began turning into the houses of Yalpina. The village seemed to grow toward him. The last thing he saw was Chan K'in's surprise and Maria falling to her knees.

By the time Chan K'in and Maria got back to Yalpina, transportation had been arranged. They had time for a quick breakfast, then Hunapu and his companions left in an old Ford pickup truck that carried them south on the road that connected with the capital. Maria joined them as well as half a dozen men from Yalpina. Others who had joined their cause were on their way to the other Indian villages in the Peten and north to Chiapas in Mexico, where tens of thousands of Indians driven from their homes by the *Ladinos* waited.

Xbalanque's army grew larger as he traveled down toward Guatemala City. So did the tales of his feats in Xepon. When he wanted to stop the stories, Akabal explained to him how important it was for his people to believe the fantastic rumors. Reluctantly Xbalanque accepted Akabal's judgment. It seemed to him now that he was constantly accepting Akabal's decisions. Being a leader of his people was not what he had expected.

His jeep and his cache had been intact. He and Akabal rode at the front of the column of old and creaking vehicles of all kinds. By now they had collected several hundred followers, all of whom were armed and ready to fight. In Xepon they had given him the pants and shirt of their village, but each town they rode into had another style and design. When they gave him their own clothes along with their husbands and sons, he felt obligated to wear them.

There were women now. Most had come to follow their men and take care of them, but there were many who had come to fight. Xbalanque was not comfortable with this, but Akabal welcomed them. Most of Xbalanque's time was spent trying to feed his army or worrying about when the government would strike them. Both Xbalanque and Akabal agreed that they had come too far too easily.

Akabal had become obsessed with attempting to get television, radio, and newspaper reporters to join the march. Whenever they entered a town that had a telephone, Akabal began placing calls. As a result, the opposition press was sending out as many people as they could without arousing undue suspicion from the secret police. They counted on a few making it to Xbalanque without being arrested.

Outside Zacualpa that word came. A young boy told them that the army had set up a roadblock with two tanks and five armored troop carriers. Two hundred heavily armed soldiers stood ready to stop their advance with light artillery and rockets.

Xbalanque and Akabal called a meeting with the guerrilla leaders who had had combat experience. Their weapons, old rifles and shotguns, could not compete with the army's M-16's and rockets. Their only chance was to use the guerrilla experience they had to their advantage. Their troops were split up into teams and sent into the hills around Zacualpa. Messengers were sent to the town beyond Zacualpa in an effort to bring fighters in from behind the government army, but that would take time for the runners to take remote paths and circle back. Xbalanque would be the main defense and their inspiration. This would be his true test. If he won, he was suitable to be their leader. If he lost, he had led them only to death.

Xbalanque went back to his jeep and got the stingray spine out of the compartment under the driver's seat. Akabal tried to go with him into the jungle, but Xbalanque told him to stay. The soldiers could have snipers and both of them should not be at risk.

It was mainly an excuse. Xbalanque was terrified that the power would not return. He needed the time to sacrifice again, anything that might help him focus on the strength he had had before and had not felt since. He knew that Akabal would almost certainly have him followed, but he had to be alone.

Xbalanque found a tiny clearing formed by a circle of trees and sat down on the ground. He tried to regain the feeling he had had just before the other dream. He could not find a way to get even a bottle of beer out of the camp. What if being drunk was the key? It had to be the way the graduate students had explained it to him or everyone with him was dead. He had brought with him one of the white cotton shirts he had been given on the way. The intricate designs on it were done solely in bright red thread. It seemed appropriate. He put it on the dirt between his legs.

His ear had healed very quickly and he had been wearing the earplug for a couple of days. Where could he get blood this time? He mentally went through a list of the sacred sites on his body that were traditionally used. Yes, that would do well. He cleaned off the carved spine with the shirt and then pulled out his lower lip. Praying to every sacred name he could remember, he thrust the stingray spine down through his lip, brought it up part way, barbs tearing his flesh, and plunged it through again. Then he leaned over the shirt and let the blood course down the black spine onto the white shirt, making new designs as it flowed.

When only drops of his blood were falling onto the shirt, he pushed the spine all the way through and out of his body. The sickening, copper taste of the blood flooded his mouth and he gagged. Closing his eyes and clenching his fists, he controlled himself and tried to close his throat to the blood in his mouth. Using the same lighter, he set fire to the shirt, starting flames from the four sides of the stained cloth packet.

There weren't any dreams of Xibalba this time. Or any dreams at all that he remembered. But the smoke and the loss of blood made him pass out again. When he awoke, the moon was high above and the night was more than half gone. This time he had no hangover, no pain as his muscles adjusted to forces they were not used to carrying. He felt good, he felt wonderful.

He got up and crossed the clearing to the largest tree and struck the trunk with his bare fist. It exploded, showering the ground with splinters and branches as it fell. He lifted his face to the stars and thanked the gods.

Xbalanque stopped on the trail back to the camp as a man stepped out from behind a tree onto the bare earth. For a moment he was afraid the army had found him, but the man bowed to him. Gun held high, the guard led Xbalanque back down to the others.

For the rest of the night the sounds of the soldiers' preparations kept all but the most experienced of his people awake. Akabal paced beside the jeep, listening to the roaring engines of the tanks as they shifted position or swung their guns to bear on another phantom target. The sounds echoed up into the mountains. Xbalanque watched him in silence for a while.

'I can take them. I feel it.' Xbalanque tried to encourage Akabal. 'All I have to do is hit them with the stones.'

'You can't protect everyone. You probably can't even protect yourself. They've got rockets, lots of them. They have tanks. What are you going to do against a tank?'

'I am told that the treads are the point of weakness. So I will first destroy the treads.' Xbalanque nodded at the teacher.

'Akabal, the gods are with us. I am with you.'

'*You* are with us. Since when are you a god?' Akabal glared at the man leaning on the jeep's steering wheel.

'I think I always have known it. It's just taken some time for others to recognize my power.' Xbalanque looked dreamily up at the sky. 'The morning star. That's me, you know.'

'Mary, Mother of God! You've gone mad!' Akabal stopped pacing long enough to shake his head at Xbalanque.

'I don't think any of us should say that anymore. It's not … proper. All things considered.'

'All things considered? You—' They were interrupted by a runner coming in from the town and the sounds of more activity from below.

There was another quick consultation among the guerrilla leaders. Akabal went over Xbalanque's part in the plan.

'You're going to be followed up to the bridge by the empty trucks. They'll draw the army fire.' The former schoolteacher stared down into the impassive and calm face before him. Xbalanque felt no fear. There was only a euphoria that masked any other emotion. 'But after the first few moments they will need more active opposition. That's you. Your fire will protect our snipers in the hills.'

His stones had been loaded onto rough sledges that he tied to the back of the jeep and the next truck back in line. As the campsite grew lighter, everyone went into position. The guerrilla drivers started their engines. Akabal walked up to the jeep.

'Try not to get yourself killed. We need you.' He put out his hand in farewell.

'Stop worrying. I'll be fine.' Xbalanque touched Akabal's shoulder. 'Get into the hills.'

Xbalanque's move forward was the signal for the column, single-wide on the narrow road, to begin its short journey. Rounding the corner, Xbalanque could see the bridge ahead and the tanks on either side with their guns pointed at him. As they fired, he jumped from the jeep, the increased weight of his body pounding dents into the pavement as he rolled away. The fragments of the jeep exploded toward him. He felt the power in every part of his body and the metal shrapnel bounced off. Still, he kept his head down as he scrambled for the sledge with his ammunition. Grabbing the first stone, he threw it into the air and batted it with his empty hand, sending it screaming through the air and into the hillside above the army. It threw dirt on the soldiers, but that was all. Better aim. The next rock was painstakingly aimed and it broke the tread on the left-hand tank. The one after jammed the turret so that it could not turn. The Indian fighters had started firing now, and the soldiers were beginning to fall. He threw more stones into the ranks of the army and saw men go down. There was blood, more blood than he could ever give by himself. They brought up a rocket and he saw the man shot by an Indian sniper before the soldier could fire. He was throwing as fast and as hard as he could.

Bullets occasionally struck him, but they were stopped by his skin. Xbalanque grew more reckless and stood facing his enemy without taking cover. His missiles were causing some damage, but most of the deaths were from the Indians on the slopes above the soldiers. The men in charge had seen this and were directing most of their fire up the hillsides. Great holes were appearing in the forest where the tanks and rockets had reached. Despite his strength, Xbalanque could not stop the second tank. The angle was wrong. Nothing he threw could reach it.

A new sound entered the battle. A helicopter was coming. Xbalanque realized that it could give the army the aerial spotting advantage that could get his people killed. It came in low and fast above the battle. Xbalanque reached for a stone and found that only a few small pieces of rock were left. He searched the ground frantically for something to throw. Giving up, he tugged a piece of twisted metal from the wreckage of the jeep and sent it flying toward the chopper. The helicopter met the chunk of metal in midair and exploded. Both sides were hit with debris. The fireball that had been a machine fell into the ravine and flames shot up higher than the bridge.

The engine on the remaining tank revved up and it started to back up. Soldiers moved out of the way and began retreating as well. Xbalanque could now get clear aim at the troop carriers. Using more pieces of metal he tore from the jeep, he destroyed two of them. Then he saw something that stopped all his fantasies of being a great warrior. A boy leapt down off the mountain onto the retreating tank. He swung open the hatch from the outside, and before he was shot, dropped a grenade within. There was an instant before the tank blew when the boy's body was draped across the hatch's opening like a flag across a coffin. Then the flames engulfed them both.

As the fighting at the bridge died down with the soldiers' retreat, the Indians began coming down out of the forest and moving toward the bridge. It became quiet. The moaning of the wounded broke the silence and was joined by the sounds of the birds who returned to their nests with the peace.

Akabal leapt down the road cut to join Xbalanque. He was laughing.

'We won! It worked! You were magnificent.' Akabal grabbed Xbalanque and tried to shake him, only to find that the smaller man was immovable.

'Too much blood.' With the boy's death Xbalanque had lost his desire to celebrate their victory.

'But it was *Ladino* blood. That is what matters.' One of their lieutenants had come up to join them.

'Not all of it.'

'But *enough* of it.' The lieutenant looked more closely at Xbalanque. 'You have not seen anything like this before, have you? You must not let our people see you this way. You are a hero. That is your duty.'

'The old gods will feed well today.' Xbalanque stared across the expanse of the bridge to the bodies on the other side. 'Perhaps that is all they were after.'

Xbalanque was caught up in the rush across the bridge. He didn't have time to stop for the body of the boy who really had destroyed a tank. This time his people were taking him along.

♣

The press found them before the army did. Hunapu, Chan K'in, and Bol stood outside their tent in the early morning chill and watched the two helicopters come in over the hills to the south. One landed in the open area where, last night, the dances and speeches had been held. The other set down near the horses. Hunapu had seen the occasional *Ladino* airplane, but never these strange machines. Another *Ladino* perversion of nature in an attempt to gain the level of gods.

Crowds began to gather around the two helicopters. The camp consisted of a few tents and some old and decrepit trucks, but there were now hundreds of people living there. Most slept on the ground. Many of his people were god-touched and had to be helped to the groups by others. It was sad to see so much pain, but it was clear that the gods had begun taking a greater role in the people's lives even before he had been chosen. With so many who were so close to the gods accompanying him, he felt strong and determined. He had to be following the gods' ways.

Maria came up to him and laid her hand on his arm, the tiny feathers covering her brushing lightly against his skin.

'What do they want with us?' Maria was uneasy. She had seen the *Ladino* reaction to the god-touched before.

'They want to make us into one of their circuses, a show for their amusement,' Chan K'in angrily replied. This intrusion into their march toward Kaminaljuyu was unwanted.

'We will find out what they want, Maria. Do not fear them. They are stickmen without strength or true souls.' Hunapu stroked the woman's shoulder. 'Stay here and help keep the people calm.'

Hunapu and Chan K'in began walking toward the helicopter at the center of the encampment. Bol followed, as silent as usual, carrying his rifle and watching the men with cameras as they piled out of the helicopter and stood staring at the quiet mass of people who faced them. When the helicopter's blades swung to a halt, there was almost no noise.

The three men made their way through the crowd slowly. They were careful not to move forward more quickly than someone could get out of their way. Hands, paws, wings, twisted limbs reached out to Hunapu as he passed. He tried to touch them all, but he could not pause to speak or he knew he would never get to the helicopter.

When they reached the machine, painted with a large, hand-lettered PRESS on each side and the bottom, the reporters were huddled against the helicopter. There was fear and revulsion in their eyes. When one of the god-touched moved forward, they all drew back. They did not understand that the god-touched were truer men than themselves. It was typical of the *Ladinos* to be so blind to the truth.

'I am Hunapu. Who are you and why have you come here?' Hunapu spoke first in Maya, then repeated his question in Spanish. He wore the cotton armor as he stood before the reporters and cameramen. The cameras had begun filming as soon as they could pick him out of the crowd.

'Christ, he really does think he's one of those Hero Twins.' The comment in bad Spanish had come from one of the men in front of him. He looked across the huddled group. Not even having the man they wanted in front of them lessened their uneasiness.

'I am Hunapu,' he repeated.

'I'm Tom Peterson from NBC, Central American bureau. We've heard that you have a joker crusade out here. Well, jokers and Indians. That's obviously true.' The tall, blond man looked over Hunapu's shoulder at the crowd. His Spanish had an odd accent. He spoke slowly and drawled in a way Hunapu had never heard before. 'I take it you're in charge. We'd like to talk to you about your plans. Maybe there's someplace where it would be more quiet?'

'We will speak to you here.' Chan K'in stared up at the man dressed in a white cotton European suit. Peterson had ignored the dwarf at Hunapu's side. Their eyes met and it was the blond man who backed down.

'Right. Here is just fine. Joe, make sure you get good sound on this.' Another man moved between Peterson and Hunapu and held a microphone pointed at Peterson, waiting for his next words. But Hunapu's attention had been drawn away.

The reporters from the second helicopter had caught on to what was happening in the center and had begun shoving their way through the people to get to Hunapu. He turned to the men and women holding their equipment up out of the reach of his people as if they were crossing a river.

'Stop.' He spoke in Maya, but his voice caught the attention of the reporters as well as his own people. Everything halted and all eyes turned toward him. 'Bol, bring them here.'

Bol glanced down at his brother before starting for the reporters. The crowd parted for him as he moved forward and again as he brought the journalists to join their fellows. He motioned them to stay put with his rifle before returning to Hunapu and Chan K'in.

Peterson began his questions again.

'What is your destination?'

'We go to Kaminaljuyu.'

'That's right outside Guatemala City, isn't it? Why there?'

'I will meet my brother there.'

'Well, what are you going to do when you meet your brother?'

Before Hunapu could answer the question, one of the women from the second helicopter interrupted.

'Maxine Chen, CBS. What are your feelings about your brother Xbalanque's victory over the soldiers sent to stop him?'

'Xbalanque is fighting the army?'

'You hadn't heard? He's coming through the Highlands and pulling in every Indian revolutionary group that exists. His army has defeated the government every time they've clashed. The Highlands are in a state of emergency and that hasn't even slowed Xbalanque down.' The Oriental woman was no taller than Hunapu. She looked around at his followers.

'There's a rebel behind every tree in the Highlands, has been for years. Down here in the Peten, it's always been quiet. Before now. What's your goal?' Her attention shot back to him.

'When I see my brother Xbalanque, we will decide what we want.'

'In the meantime, what do you plan to do about the army unit sent to stop *you*?'

Hunapu exchanged a glance with Chan K'in.

'Don't you know about that either? Jesus, they're just hours away. Why do you think all of us were so hot to get to you? You may not be here by sundown.'

The dwarf began questioning Maxine Chen.

'How many and how far away?' Chan K'in fixed his impassive black eyes on hers.

'Maybe sixty men, a few more; they don't keep any real forces down here—'

'Maxine!' Peterson had lost his journalistic detachment. 'Stay out of this, for God's sake. You'll get us all arrested.'

'Stuff it, Peterson. You know as well as I do that they've been committing genocide here for years. These people are finally fighting back. Good for them.' She knelt in the dirt and began drawing a map on the ground for Hunapu and Chan K'in.

'I'm getting out of here.' Peterson waved his hand in the air and the helicopter's rotors began turning. The reporters and cameramen climbed back into the helicopter or began running for the one in the horse paddock.

Maxine looked up from the map toward her cameraman.

'Robert, stay with me and we'll have an exclusive.'

The cameraman grabbed sound equipment off a technician ready to bolt and strapped it on.

'Maxine, you're gonna get me killed one day, and I'm gonna come back and haunt you.'

Maxine was already back at the map.

'But not yet, Robert. Did you see any heavy artillery with the government troops?'

It had taken only a little while to get their people organized and to find out what weapons they had. There were some rifles and shotguns, nothing heavier. Most people had machetes, Hunapu called Chan K'in and Bol to him. Together they determined the best course of action. Bol led the discussion, and Hunapu was surprised at his expertise. Although they were facing only a few soldiers, they were at a disadvantage in weapons and experience. Bol recommended attacking the army troops when they came down from the canyons into the savanna. By splitting up their people into two groups, they could best use the terrain. Hunapu had begun to wonder where Bol had gained his knowledge. He suspected the tall, quiet man of having been a rebel.

After instructing his people in the planned defense, Hunapu left the drilling to Bol and made another blood sacrifice. He hoped the sincerity of his prayers would give him the strength he needed to use his god-given power and save his people. The gods would have to be on their side or they would all be destroyed.

When he returned to the camp, Hunapu found it broken down and the half of his warriors who would face the army already mounted. After he climbed up on his own horse, he swung Chan K'in up behind him. He spoke briefly to waiting Indian warriors, encouraging them and enjoining them to fight well for the gods.

Seeing the men on horseback riding toward them, the soldiers had stopped their trucks just outside the mouth of the canyon and unloaded. As the soldiers piled off the troop carrier and the jeeps preceding and following it, they were picked off by the snipers Bol had sent into the bush. Only a ragged line of men faced Hunapu's charge. They were distracted by their fellow soldiers falling to the left and right at the mercy of the snipers. A few of the older men ignored the deaths and stood their ground against the screaming men bearing down on them. The sergeant swore at them to hold ranks and fire at the filthy Indians.

Hunapu's horsemen were unused to firing from the moving animals and were barely able to hold on and shoot. They couldn't aim at the same time. Once the army men realized this, they began taking the horsemen down, one at a time. By now Hunapu was close enough to the soldiers to see the fear and confusion start to evaporate and discipline take over. One man stood up and followed Hunapu with his Uzi aimed squarely at the Lacandon's head. Chan K'in cried out a warning and Hunapu was gone. Chan K'in was alone on the horse, now uncontrolled, and facing the soldier's bullet. As the shot split Chan K'in's skull, Hunapu reappeared behind the soldier and slashed his throat with the obsidian blade, splashing blood over the soldier's companions before vanishing again.

Hunapu brought his rifle butt down on the helmet of a man with a rocket launcher before he could fire into the bush where the snipers hid. Before any of the other soldiers reacted, he reversed the rifle and shot him. Grabbing the rocket launcher, he disappeared and came back almost immediately, without the launcher. This time he killed the sergeant.

Covered with blood and vanishing almost as soon as he appeared, Hunapu was the devil to the soldiers. They could not fight this apparition. No matter where they aimed, he would be somewhere else. They turned their backs on Hunapu's warriors to try to kill Hunapu himself. It was useless. Praying to the Virgin Mary and the saints that they would not be next, the men threw down their guns and knelt on the ground. Not all the kicks and threats of the lieutenant could get them to keep fighting.

Hunapu took thirty-six prisoners, including the lieutenant. Twenty soldiers had been killed. He had lost seventeen men and Chan K'in. The *Ladinos* had been defeated. They were not invincible.

That night while his people celebrated their victory, Hunapu mourned Chan K'in. He was dressed again in the long white tunic of his Lacandon people. Bol had come to him to claim the body of his brother. The tall Indian told him that Chan K'in had seen his death in a vision and knew his fate. Chan K'in's body had been wrapped in white cloth that was now stained by the dwarf's blood. Bol stood holding the small bundle and stared at Hunapu's tired, saddened face across the fire.

'I will see you at Kaminaljuyu.' Hunapu looked up in surprise. 'My brother saw me there, but even if he had not, I would go. May both our journeys go their way in peace, or in death to our enemies.'

Despite the early victories both brothers suffered many losses during the rest of the march to Guatemala City. Xbalanque had been wounded in an assassination attempt, but he had healed with supernatural speed. The attempt had killed two of the guerrilla leaders who had followed and taught him. Word had come down from the north that Guatemalan air force planes were strafing and bombing the lines of Indians who were leaving the refugee camps of Chiapas in Mexico to join their fellows in Guatemala City. Hundreds were reported killed, but thousands kept coming.

The elite, highly trained police and military squads took a constant toll. Xbalanque was slowed, but the mass of people who followed him would not be stopped. At every firefight they took weapons from dead soldiers and armed themselves. Now they had rockets and even a tank, deserted by its frightened crew.

Hunapu fared less well. His people from the Peten had less experience. Many died in each clash with the army. After a battle in which neither side could actually claim a victory and ended only when he finally located the commander and could teleport in to kill him, Hunapu decided that it had become foolish to oppose the army and police directly. He dispersed his followers. They were to make their way singly or in small groups to Kaminaljuyu. Otherwise it seemed inevitable that the government would be able to muster sufficient forces to stop them.

Xbalanque arrived first. A truce had been declared as his army closed in on Guatemala City. Akabal had given interviews over and over again that declared their purpose was not to topple the Guatemalan government. Faced with questioning by the press and the imminent visit from the UN Wild Card tour, the general in charge ordered the army to escort Xbalanque and his followers but not to fire on them unless attacked. Xbalanque and Akabal made sure that the army had no excuses. The country's leader allowed Xbalanque access to Kaminaljuyu.

The ruins of Kaminaljuyu were filled with the followers of the brothers. They had put tents and rough shelters up on the low mounds. Looking over the soldiers, trucks, and tanks that guarded the perimeter of Kaminaljuyu, they could look down on the Guatemala City suburbs that surrounded them. The camp already held five thousand, and more were coming all the time. Besides the Guatemalan Mayas and the refugees from Mexico, others were traveling up from Honduras and El Salvador.

The world was watching to see what would happen in Guatemala City this Christmas. Maxine Chen's coverage of the battle between Hunapu's Indian and joker followers and the Guatemalan army had been an hour-long special report on *60 Minutes*. The meeting between the Hero Twins themselves was to be covered by all the major U.S. networks, cable, and European channels.

Hunapu had never before seen so many people together in one place. As he walked into the camp past the soldiers guarding the perimeter and then past the Maya sentries, he was amazed at the size of the gathering. He and Bol had taken a long and circuitous route to avoid trouble, and it had been a long walk. Unlike the people of the Peten, these followers of Xbalanque dressed in hundreds of different ways, all bright and festive. The atmosphere of celebration didn't seem proper to Hunapu. These people did not appear to be worshiping the gods who had prepared their way and led them here. They looked as though they were at a carnival – some of them looked as though they were the carnival.

Hunapu walked through a third of the crowded camp without being recognized. Sunlight glinting off opalescent feathers caught his eye just as Maria turned and saw him. She called out his name and ran to meet him. At the sound of the name of the other Hero Twin, people began to gather around him.

Maria took his hand and held it for a moment, smiling at him happily.

'I was so worried. I was afraid ...' Maria looked down and away from Hunapu.

'The gods are not finished with us yet.' Hunapu reached out to stroke the down on the side of her face. 'And Bol came most of the way with me after getting back from his village.'

Maria looked down at the hand she was clutching and released it in embarrassment.

'You will wish to see your brother. He has a house at the center of Kaminaljuyu. I would be honored to lead you there.' She stepped back and gestured through the crowd down the rows of tents. Hunapu followed her as she parted the gathered people before him. As he passed, the Indians murmured his name and fell in behind him.

Within a few steps they were accosted by reporters. TV camera lights blazed on, and questions were shouted in English and Spanish. Hunapu glanced up at Bol, who began fending off those who came too close to his charge. They ignored the questions, and the camera crews withdrew after a few minutes of what Maxine called stock shots of Hunapu walking and occasionally greeting someone he recognized.

While most of the structures in Kaminaljuyu were tents or houses built out of whatever scrap material people could find, the large, twin wooden huts built on a plaza at the center of the ruins were impressive, permanent buildings. Their roofs were adorned with vertical roof combs like those on temple ruins, and banners and charms hung from these.

After they reached the open area of the plaza, the crowd stopped following him. Hunapu could hear the cameras and sense the shoving for position as he, Bol, and Maria walked alone to the house on the left. Before they reached it, a man dressed in a mix of red and purple Highland clothing stepped out. He was followed by a tall, thin Highland Maya wearing glasses and dressed in European clothing, except for the sash at his waist.

Hunapu recognized Xbalanque from his dreams of Xibalba, but he had looked younger in them. This man appeared more serious, but he noticed the expensive European watch on his wrist and the *Ladino* leather 'running' shoes on his feet. It seemed a sharp contrast with the jade earplug he wore. Hunapu wondered about the earplug. Had the gods given it to him? Hunapu was caught in his examination of his brother by Xbalanque's companion. The other man took Hunapu by the shoulders and turned him toward the bank of cameras. Xbalanque rested his hand on Hunapu's left shoulder. In the Highland Maya that Hunapu loosely understood, Xbalanque spoke to him softly.

'The first thing we're going to do is get you some real clothes. Wave to the cameras.' Xbalanque followed his own suggestion.

'Then we have to work on ways to get more food into the camp.'

Xbalanque turned him so that they faced each other and then clasped his hand.

'Hold that so they can get our profiles. You know, sun, I was beginning to get worried about you.'

Hunapu looked into the eyes of the man across from him. For the first time since meeting this stranger who was his brother, he saw in Xbalanque's eyes the same shadows of Xibalba that he knew existed in his own. It was obvious that Xbalanque had much to learn about the proper worship of the gods, but it was also clear that he was chosen, like Hunapu, to speak for them.

'Come inside. Akabal will make his statement that *our* statement will be issued later. *Ko'ox.*' The last words Xbalanque spoke were in Lacandon Maya. Hunapu began to think that this Highland quetzal might be a worthy partner. Remembering Maria and Bol, he caught a glimpse of them melting into the crowd as he walked into Xbalanque's house. His brother seemed to catch his thought.

'She's beautiful and very devoted to you, isn't she? She'll take care of your bodyguard and keep the press away until he can get some rest. We've got plans to discuss. Akabal has some wonderful ideas for helping our people.'

For the next several days the brothers held private conferences, lasting long after dark. But on the morning of the third day Esteban Akabal stepped outside to announce that a statement would be read at noon outside the compound where their prisoners were being held.

With the sun directly overhead, Xbalanque, Hunapu, and Akabal walked out of Xbalanque's hut toward the prisoners' compound. As they moved, surrounded by their followers and the reporters, Hunapu's shoulders tensed when he heard the midday army fly-over. The sound of the helicopters always made him nervous. Once there, they waited until the sound equipment was tested. Several of the technicians were wearing Hero Twin T-shirts. Akabal explained that the statement would be read in two parts, the first by Hunapu and the second by Xbalanque. They would speak in Maya and he, Akabal, would translate them into Spanish and English.

Hunapu clutched his piece of paper nervously. Akabal had been aghast to learn that he couldn't read, so he had had to memorize the speech the teacher had written. He thanked the gods for José's training in remembering rituals and spells.

Hunapu stepped closer to his microphone and saw Maxine wave in encouragement. Mentally he asked the gods not to make him look foolish. When he began to speak, his nervousness vanished, drowned in his anger.

'Since the time of your first coming to our lands, you have murdered our children. You have sought to destroy our beliefs. You stole our land and our sacred objects. You enslaved us. You have allowed us no voice in the destruction of our homes. If we spoke out, you kidnapped us, tortured us, and killed us for being men and not the malleable children you wanted.

'It is now that the cycle ends. We *hach winik*, true men, will be free again to live as we wish to live. From the ice of the far north to the fire-lands of the south, we will see the coming of a new world in which all our people can be free.

'The gods are watching us now and they wish to be worshiped in the old, proper ways. In return they will give us the strength we need to overcome those who will try to defeat us again. My brother and I are the signs of this new world to come.'

As he stepped back, Hunapu heard his name being cried out by the thousands of Maya in Kaminaljuyu. He looked over the ruined city in pride, soaking in the strength that his people's worship gave him. Maria had made it to the front of the gathered followers. She raised her arms to him in praise and hundreds of people around her did the same. The gesture spread through the crowd. When it seemed that everyone had lifted their hands to implore his help, Hunapu lifted his face and his arms toward heaven. The noise swelled until he dropped his hands and gazed over the people. Silence fell.

Xbalanque stepped forward.

'We are not *Ladino*. We do not want a war or more death. We seek only what is ours by right: a land, a country, that is ours. This land will be the homeland of any American Indian, no matter where in the Americas he was born. It is our intent to meet the WHO Wild Card delegation while it is in Guatemala City. We will ask for their aid and support in founding a *hach winik* homeland. The god-touched among our people are especially in need of immediate help.

'We do not ask now. We are telling you. *Ko'ox!* Let us go!'

Xbalanque raised his fist in the air and chanted the Lacandon phrase over and over until every Indian in the camp joined him. Hunapu joined the chant and felt the rush of power once again. Watching Xbalanque, he knew his brother felt it as well. It felt right. It was clear that the gods were with them.

Hunapu and Xbalanque flanked Akabal as he translated what they had said. The Hero Twins stood immobile and silent as the teacher refused to answer any other questions. Their people faced them, as silent and stoic now as themselves. When Akabal led the way back to their houses, where they would wait for word from the WHO delegation, their followers parted without a sound to allow them to pass, but closed in before the press could get through.

'Well, one can't accuse them of lacking political savvy.' Senator Gregg Hartmann uncrossed his legs and got up out of the colonial reproduction chair to turn off the hotel room television set.

'A little chutzpah never hurts, Gregg.' Hiram Worchester leaned his head on his hand and looked over at Hartmann. 'But what do you think our response should be?'

'Response! What response can we possibly make?' Senator Lyons interrupted Hartmann's answer. 'We are here to help the victims of the wild card virus. I see no connection whatsoever. These ... revolutionaries or whatever they are are simply trying to use us. We have a responsibility to ignore them. We can hardly afford to become involved in some petty nationalistic squabble!'

Lyons crossed his arms and walked over to the window. Unobtrusively a young Indian maid was let into the room to pick up the remains of their room-service lunch. Head down, she glanced at each of them before silently carrying her heavily loaded tray out the door. Hartmann shook his head at Senator Lyons.

'I understand your point, but did you look at the people out there? A lot of the people who are following these "Hero Twins" are jokers. Don't we have a responsibility toward them?' Hartmann relaxed back into his chair and rolled his back in an attempt to get comfortable. 'Besides, we can't afford to ignore them. It would compromise our own mission if we pretended they, and their problems, didn't exist. The world here is very different from what you're used to seeing, even on the reservations. There are different attitudes. The Indians have been suffering since the Conquest. They take the long view. To them the wild card virus is just another cross to bear.'

''Sides, Senator, you think those boys are aces, like the reporters say?' Mordecai Jones looked across the hotel room at the Wyoming senator. 'Got to say, I've got some sympathy for what they're tryin' to do. Slavery, whatever they call it down here, ain't right.'

'It's obvious that we are involved because of the wild card victims, if nothing else. If meeting with them will help them to get aid, we have a responsibility to do what we can.' Tachyon spoke from his chair. 'On the other hand, I hear lots of talk about homelands and I see very little commitment to working on practical problems. Problems such as the subsistence level of the victims here. You can see that they need medical help. What do you think, Hiram?'

'Gregg's right. We can't avoid a meeting. There's been too much publicity. Beyond that, we are here to see how jokers are treated in other countries. Judging by what we've seen, we could help out down here by leaning on the government a little. This would appear to be a good way to do it. We don't have to endorse their actions, just express our concern.'

'That sounds reasonable. I'll let you deal with the politics. I need to get to that hospital tour.' Tachyon massaged one temple. 'I'm tired of talking to the government. I want to see what's going on.'

The door to the sitting room opened and Billy Ray peered in. 'The phones are ringing off the hooks, and we've got reporters coming up the fire stairs. What are we supposed to tell them?'

Hartmann nodded to Tachyon before answering. 'Those of us

who can spare the time from our carefully timed schedules will see these "Hero Twins." But make it clear that we are doing this in the interests of the wild card victims, not for political reasons.'

'Great. The Father, Chrysalis, and Xavier ought to be back soon. They went out to see the camp and talk to the jokers there.' Anticipating Tachyon's next question, he smiled at the doctor. 'Your car's waiting downstairs. But the sooner you can give me an official statement for the press, the better.'

'I'll have my people start drafting one immediately, Billy.' Hartmann was obviously on familiar ground. 'You'll have it within the hour.'

In the morning everyone gathered, hungover and bleary from the previous night's celebrations, but ready to march off to see the United Nations tour. When Hunapu and Xbalanque came out of their houses, the crowd became quiet. Xbalanque looked out over the people and wished that it were possible to have them follow him into the city. It would look great on film, but Akabal was convinced that it might just be the excuse the government was looking for to open fire. He jumped up onto the hood of the bus that had been chosen to take them into the city. He spoke for almost half an hour before the people appeared to agree that they would stay in Kaminaljuyu.

They arrived at the Camino Real without incident. The only surprise had come from the crowds of Indians lining the streets as they passed. The watchers were silent and impassive, but both Hunapu and Xbalanque were strengthened by their presence. At the Camino Real they jumped down from the truck and were escorted within the building by two of their own guards and almost a score of UN security people.

Xbalanque and Hunapu wore their closest approximation of the dress of the ancient kings. Hair tied up in warrior's knots on top of their heads, they were dressed in cotton tunics and dyed-cotton wrapped skirts. Hunapu was used to wearing only his *xikul*, a knee-length tunic. He felt at home in the ancient style. Xbalanque had spent the early morning tugging on his skirt and feeling self-conscious about his exposed legs. As he looked curiously around the hotel, he saw himself in a wall mirror. He almost stopped in wonder at the vision of a Mayan warrior looking back at him. Xbalanque straightened and raised his head, showing off his jade earplug.

Hunapu's eyes darted from one side of the lobby to the other. He had never seen a building this big with so many strange decorations and oddly dressed people. A fat man in a shiny white shirt and brightly colored, flowered short pants stared at them. The tourist grabbed his wife, who wore a dress that was made on the same loom as the man's pants, by the arm and pointed at them. Catching a glimpse of Xbalanque walking proudly alongside steadied Hunapu.

But it was all he could do not to cry out prayers to the gods when they walked into a room slightly smaller than his family's house and the doors slid shut without a human touch. The room moved under him, and only Xbalanque's calm face kept him from believing he was about to die. He slid his glance toward Akabal. The Maya in Western dress was clenching and releasing his fists rhythmically. Hunapu wondered if he was praying too.

Despite his outward impassivity Xbalanque was the first one out the opening doors when the elevator reached its destination. The entire group walked down the carpeted hall to a door flanked by two more UN soldiers. There were a few moments of discussion before it was agreed that, once the Indian guards had inspected the meeting room, they would retire outside the door until the conference was over. The Hero Twins would be allowed to keep their ceremonial stone knives, however. During this, Xbalanque and Hunapu said nothing, allowing Akabal to make the arrangements. Hunapu watched everything while he attempted to look like a warrior-king. Being in these enclosed spaces made him nervous. He repeatedly looked to his brother for guidance.

Inside the hotel room, the WHO delegates waited for them. Akabal immediately noticed Peregrine's cameraman. 'Out. No cameras, no tapes.' The tall Indian turned to Hartmann. 'It was agreed. At your insistence.'

'Peregrine, the lady with the wings, is one of us. She is only interested in making a historical record—'

'Which you can edit to suit your own purposes. No.'

Hartmann smiled and shrugged at Peregrine. 'Perhaps it would be better if …'

'Sure, no problem.' She flapped her wings lazily and directed her cameraman to leave.

Xbalanque noted that Akabal seemed to be thrown off by the ease at which he had gotten his wish. He turned to look at his brother. Hunapu appeared to be communing directly with the gods. It was clear from looking at him that nothing here was of interest. Xbalanque tried to capture the same assurance.

'Good. Now, we are here to discuss—' Akabal began his prepared introduction, but was interrupted by Hartmann.

'Let's be informal here. Everyone please have a seat. Mr. Akabal, why don't you sit beside me since I believe you'll be doing the translating here?' Hartmann sat down at the head of a table apparently brought into the room for the meeting since the furniture around it had been moved against the walls. 'Do the other gentlemen speak English?'

Xbalanque was about to reply when he caught Akabal's warning glance. Instead he guided Hunapu to a chair.

'No, I'll be translating for them as well.'

Hunapu stared earnestly at the tentacled priest and the man with the nose like Chac, the long-nosed rain god. He was pleased that the god-touched would travel with this group. It was an auspicious sign. But he was also surprised to see a Father who was so blessed by the gods. Perhaps there was more to what the priests had tried to teach him than he had previously believed. He mentioned his thoughts to Akabal, who spoke in English to Hartmann.

'Among our people, the victims of the wild card virus are regarded as being favored by the gods. They are revered, not persecuted.'

'And that's what we're here to talk about, isn't it? Your people.' Hartmann had not stopped smiling since they'd entered the room. Xbalanque did not trust a man who showed his teeth so much.

The man with the elephant's trunk spoke next. 'This new country of yours, would it be open to all jokers?'

Xbalanque pretended to listen to Akabal's translation. He replied in Maya, knowing that Akabal would change his words anyway.

'This homeland takes back only a tiny part of what has been stolen from us. It is for our people, whether god-touched or not. The god-touched of the *Ladinos* have other places to go for help.'

'But why do you feel a separate nation is necessary? It seems to me that your show of political power would impress the Guatemalan government with your strength. They're bound to introduce the reforms you want.' Hartmann brought the conversation back to Akabal, which didn't displease Hunapu. He could feel hostility in this room and a lack of understanding. Whatever else they were, they were also *Ladinos*. He looked over at Akabal as the man replied to one of the *norteamericano*'s questions.

'You aren't listening. We don't want reforms. We want our land back. But only a small part of it, at that. Reforms have come and gone for four hundred years. We are tired of waiting.' Akabal was vehement. 'Do you know that to most Indians this wild card virus is just another smallpox? Another white disease brought to us to kill as many as possible.'

'That's ridiculous!' Senator Lyons was enraged at the accusation. 'Humans had nothing to do with the wild card virus.

'We came here to help you. That is our only purpose. In order to help we feel we have to have the cooperation of the government.' Senator Lyons seemed to be on the defensive. 'We spoke to the general. He's planning to put clinics in the outlying provinces and to bring serious cases of the wild card outbreak here to the city for treatment.'

The brothers exchanged glances. It was clear to each man that these strangers from the north were not about to do anything for them. Hunapu was getting impatient. There were too many things they could be doing in Kaminaljuyu. He wanted to start teaching the uninformed about the old gods and the means of worshiping them.

'We can't change the past. We both know that. So what's the

point? Why are you here?' Hartmann had stopped smiling.

'We are going to form an Indian nation. But we will need help.' Akabal spoke firmly. Xbalanque approved of his lack of tolerance for distraction, even though he wasn't altogether sure about Akabal's plans for a socialist government.

'Do you have no idea of what the United Nations is? Surely you cannot expect us to provide weapons for your war.' Senator Lyons's mouth was ringed with white from his anger.

'No, no weapons. But if you had come out to see our followers, you would have seen how many have been untreated by the *Ladino* doctors in the hope that they would not survive. And yes, I know what the general told you. We will need much medical aid, initially, to care for these people. After that we will need aid for schools, roads, transportation, agriculture. All the things a real country must provide.'

'You understand we're only on a fact-finding tour? We don't have any real authority with the UN or even with the U.S. government, for that matter.' Hartmann leaned back in his seat and spread his hands. 'Sympathy is about all we can offer at this time.'

'We are not about to jeopardize our standing in the international community for your military adventures!' Senator Lyons's eyes swept the three Indians. Hunapu was not impressed. Women should stay out of serious decisions.

'This is a peaceful mission. There is nothing political about suffering, and I don't intend to see you try to make the wild card virus a pawn in your bid for attention,' Lyons said.

'I doubt if the European Jews of the Holocaust would agree that suffering is apolitical, Senator.' Akabal watched Lyons's expression change to chagrin. 'The wild card virus has affected my people. That is a truth. My people face active genocide. That too is truth. If you don't want the wild card virus involved, that's nice, but it's not really possible, is it?

'What do we want from you? Just two things. Humanitarian aid and recognition.' For the first time Akabal looked a little unsure of himself. 'Soon the Guatemalan government is going to try to destroy us. They'll wait until you are gone, you and the reporters following you. We don't intend to allow them to succeed. We have certain ... advantages.'

'They're aces, then?' Hartmann had grown suddenly quiet and introspective.

Some of the reporters had used that term and Akabal had mentioned it, but this was the first time Xbalanque felt that it would fit. He felt like an ace. He and his brother, the little Lacandon, could take anyone. They were the incarnations of the priest-kings of their fathers, favored by the gods or an alien disease. It didn't matter. They would lead their people to victory. He turned to Hunapu and saw that it was as if his brother shared his thoughts.

'To them, they have been called to serve the old gods and be the heralds of the new age, the beginning of the next cycle. By our calendar that will be in your year 2008. They are here to prepare the way over the next *katun*.' Akabal looked back at the *norteamericanos*. 'But yes, I believe that they are aces. The evidence fits. It is hardly unusual for an ace to exhibit powers that appear to be drawn from his cultural heritage, is it?'

There were three short raps on the door. Xbalanque saw the security chief, the one they called Carnifex, look in. He wondered for a moment if this was all an elaborate trap.

'The plane's ready and we need to leave within the next hour.'

'Thanks.' Hartmann put his hand under his chin in thought. 'Speaking simply as a U.S. senator here, I'd like to see what we could work out, Mr. Akabal. Why don't we speak privately for a moment?'

Akabal nodded. 'Perhaps the Father would like to talk to Xbalanque and Hunapu? The brothers speak Spanish, if there is a translator available.'

When Hartmann and Akabal ended their huddle and rejoined them, Xbalanque was ready to leave. Listening to Hunapu, he was becoming afraid that his brother was going to demonstrate calling on the gods right then and there. He knew that wasn't a good idea.

Xbalanque was trying to explain this as Hartmann shook Akabal's hand in farewell. To Xbalanque it seemed as though he held onto the teacher's hand too long. North American customs.

He went back to dissuading Hunapu from pulling his obsidian knife and began leading his brother out.

When they were back in the elevator, escorted again by the UN security people, Xbalanque asked Akabal in Maya what Hartmann had said.

'Nothing. He will "attempt" to set up a "committee" to "study" the matter. He talks like all the Yankees. At least they saw us. It gives us legitimacy in the eyes of the world. That much was useful.'

'They do not believe that we serve the will of the gods, do they?' Hunapu was much more angry than he had allowed himself to show. Xbalanque watched him warily. He looked his brother in the eyes. 'We will show them the power of the gods. They will learn.'

Over the following twenty-four hours they lost half the journalists covering them as the reporters went on with the UN tour. And the army moved more units into place and, more ominously, began to evacuate the surrounding suburbs. Finally all travel into the camp was cut off. The peace from the anthropologists was welcome, but the intent was clear to everyone in Kaminaljuyu. No noncombatants in the camp.

At sunrise and noon for each of the three days since the visit to Hartmann and the tour, Hunapu had sacrificed his own blood on the highest of the temple mounds of the city. Xbalanque had joined him at the last two sunrises. Akabal's pleas for common sense were ignored. As the tension within Kaminaljuyu increased, the brothers grew more insular. Discussing their plans only with each other, they ignored most of the planning sessions held by Akabal and the rebel leaders. Maria spent all her time at Hunapu's side when she was not preparing an altar for a sacrifice. Bol constantly drilled the warriors.

Xbalanque and Hunapu stood atop the ruined temple surrounded by their followers. It was nearly dawn on the fourth day. An ornate decorated bowl was held between them by Maria. Each man held his obsidian blade to the palm of his hand. At the rising of the sun they would cut their flesh and let the blood pour down and mix together in the bowl before they burned it on the altar Maria had arranged with effigies and flowers. The sun was still behind the eastern volcano that loomed over Guatemala City and puffed smoke into the air as if constantly offering sacred tobacco to the gods.

First light. Knives flashed black, shining. Blood flowed, mingled, filled the bowl. Hands, covered with red, lifted to the sun. Thousands of voices raised in a chant welcoming the day with a plea for mercy from the gods. Two thatched huts exploded as the rays of the sun touched them.

The dirt and debris rained down on the people. Those closest to the huts were the first to see that a government rocket had blown the shelters apart. The fighters ran for the perimeter to try to stop the invasion, while those who were unable to defend the camp drew together in a great mass at its center. The government rockets targeted the central plaza where several thousand people knelt and prayed or screamed as the rockets arced overhead to fall nearby.

Maxine Chen was one of the few top journalists left to cover the Hero Twins' crusade. She and her crew had taken shelter behind one of the temple mounds where Maxine taped an introduction to the attack. An Indian girl, seven- or eight-years-old, ran around the side of the mound and in front of Maxine's camera. Her face and her embroidered white huipil were covered with blood, and she was crying out in fear as she ran. Maxine tried to grab her but missed, and the girl was gone.

'Robert ...' Maxine looked across at her cameraman. He ducked out from under his camera and shoved it at the sound man, who barely caught it. Then they were both running into the crowd, getting them up and moving toward the small shelter of the mounds.

On the edge of the ruins the Hero Twins' people were firing down into the soldiers, causing some confusion but not enough damage. The rockets were coming from well behind the front lines of the army. The tank engines rumbled, but they held their ground and fired into the defenders, killing some and destroying the ruins that were their protection.

Struggling against the flow of people into the center of

Kaminaljuyu, Xbalanque and Hunapu managed to make their way to the front lines. They were cheered as their people spotted them. Standing out in the open, Xbalanque began throwing whatever he could get his hands on at the army. It had effect. The troops in front of his attack tried to move back, only to be stopped and ordered forward. Bullets ricocheted off his skin. The defending Indians saw this and drew strength from it. Aiming more carefully, they began to take a toll. But the rockets kept coming, and they could always hear the screams of the people trapped in the center of the camp.

Hunapu flipped back and forth, using his knife to slit the throats of the nearest soldiers before returning to his own place. He targeted officers, as Akabal had warned him to do. But with the press of men behind them, the frontline troops could not flee even when they wanted to escape the demon.

Xbalanque ran out of missiles and retired behind one of the mounds. He was joined by two of the experienced guerrilla leaders. They were frightened by the mass carnage. It was different from a jungle war. When they saw Hunapu shift back, Xbalanque caught him before he could return. Hunapu's cotton armor was soaked with the soldiers' blood. The smell gagged even the rebels. The blood and the smoke from the guns took Xbalanque back to the first time he had experienced it.

'Xibalba.' He spoke only to his brother.

'Yes.' Hunapu nodded. 'The gods have grown hungry. Our blood was not enough. They want more blood, blood with power. A king's blood.'

'Do you think they would accept a general's blood? A war captain's?' Xbalanque looked over his shoulder at the army on the other side of the dirt mound.

The guerrillas were following the exchange closely, looking for a reason to hope for victory. Both nodded at the thought.

'If you can take the general, things will fall apart down the line. They're draftees out there, not volunteers.' The man wiped dusty black hair out of his eyes and shrugged. 'It's the best idea I've heard.'

'Where is the war captain?' Hunapu's eyes fixed on a distant goal. 'I will bring him back. It must be done correctly or the gods will not be pleased.'

'He'll be in the rear. I saw a truck back there with lots of antennas, a communications center. Over to the east.' Xbalanque looked at his brother uneasily. Something felt wrong about him. 'Are you all right?'

'I serve my people and my gods.' Hunapu walked a few steps away and vanished with a soft *clok*.

'I'm not so sure that this was a good idea.' Xbalanque wondered what Hunapu had in mind.

'Got a better one? He'll be okay.' The rebel started to shrug but was stopped with shoulders lifted by the sound of helicopters.

'Xbalanque, you've got to take them. If they can attack from the air, we're dead.' Before the other man had finished, Xbalanque was running back toward the helicopters and the middle of Kaminaljuyu. As the brace of Hueys came into sight, he picked up a rock the size of his head and launched it. The helicopter to the left exploded in flames. Its companion pulled up and away from the camp. But Xbalanque hadn't realized the position of the helicopter he had destroyed. Burning debris fell on his huddled followers, causing as much death and pain as a government rocket.

Xbalanque turned away, cursing himself for being oblivious to his people, and saw Hunapu atop the tallest mound. His brother held a limp figure, half-sprawled on the ground, beside Maria's altar. Xbalanque ran toward the temple.

From the other side Akabal had seen Hunapu appear with his captive. Akabal had been separated from the Twins in the melee following the first mortar strike. Now he turned his back to the mass of followers jammed together around the central dirt mounds. Maxine Chen's tug on his arm stopped him. She joined him, her face filthy and sweating and her two-man crew looking haggard. Robert had reclaimed his camera and filmed everything he could get as he moved around Kaminaljuyu.

'What's going on?' She had to shout to be heard over the crowd and the guns. 'Who's that with Hunapu? Is it Xbalanque?'

Akabal shook his head and kept moving, followed by Chen.

When she saw that Akabal intended to climb the mound in the open, she and Robert hesitated and followed him. The sound man shook his head and crouched at the base of the temple. Xbalanque had been met by Maria, and they scrambled up the other side. The cameraman stepped back and began filming as soon as all six had made it to the top.

Seeing Xbalanque, Hunapu lifted his face and began to chant to the sky. He no longer had his knife, and the dried blood that covered much of his face looked like ceremonial paint. Xbalanque listened for a moment and then shook his head. In an archaic Maya he argued with Hunapu, who continued his chant, oblivious to Xbalanque's interruption. Maxine asked Akabal what was happening, but he shook his head in confusion. Maria had hauled the Guatemalan general onto the earthen altar and began to strip off his uniform.

The guns ceased firing at the same moment Hunapu ended his chant and held out his hand to Xbalanque. In the silence Maxine put her hands to her ears. Maria knelt beside the general, holding the offering bowl in front of her. Xbalanque backed away, shaking his head. Hunapu sharply thrust his arm out at Xbalanque. Looking over Hunapu's shoulder, Xbalanque saw the government tanks roll forward, tearing apart the fence and crushing the Indians under their treads.

As Xbalanque hesitated, the general woke up. Finding himself stretched out on an altar, he cursed and tried to roll off. Maria shoved him back onto it. Noting her feathers, he held himself away from her as if he could be contaminated. He began haranguing Hunapu and Xbalanque in Spanish.

'What the hell do you think you are doing? The Geneva convention clearly states that officer prisoners of war are to be treated with dignity and respect. Give me back my clothes!'

Xbalanque heard the tanks and screams behind him as the Guatemalan army officer cursed him. He tossed his obsidian knife to Hunapu and grabbed the general's flailing arms.

'Let me go. What do you savages think you're doing?' As Hunapu raised the knife, the man's eyes widened. 'You can't do this! Please, this is 1986. You're all mad. Listen, I'll stop them; I'll call them off. Let me up. Please, Jesus, let me up!'

Xbalanque pinned the general back against the altar and looked up as Hunapu brought the knife down.

'Hail, Mary, full of g—'

The obsidian blade cut through flesh and cartilage, spraying the brothers and Maria with blood. Xbalanque watched in horrified fascination as Hunapu decapitated the general, bearing down with the knife against the spine and severing the final connections before lifting the *Ladino*'s head to the sky.

Xbalanque released the dead man's arms and trembling, took the bowl filled with blood from Maria. Shoving the body off the altar, he set fire to the blood as Maria lit copal incense. He threw back his head and called the names of his gods to the sky. His voice was echoed by his people, gathered below with arms thrust into the air toward the temple. Hunapu placed the head, its eyes open and staring into Xibalba, on the altar.

The tanks stopped their advance and began a lumbering retreat. The foot soldiers dropped their guns and ran. A few shot officers that tried to stop them, and the officers joined the flight. The government forces disbanded in chaos, scattering into the city, abandoning their equipment and weapons.

Maxine had vomited at the sight of the sacrifice, but her cameraman had it all on tape. Shaking and pale, she asked Akabal what was happening. He looked down at her with wide eyes.

'It *is* the time of the Fourth Creation. The birth of Huracan, the heart of heaven, our home. The gods have returned to us! Death to the enemies of our people!' Akabal knelt and stretched his hands toward the Hero Twins. 'Lead us to glory, favored of the gods.'

◆

In room 502 of the Camino Real a tourist in flowered shorts and a pale blue polyester shirt stuffed the last souvenir weaving into his suitcase. He looked around the room for his wife and saw her at the window.

'Next time, Martha, don't buy anything that won't fit into your suitcase.' He leaned his considerable weight on the bag and slid the catches closed. 'Where is that boy? We must have called half an hour ago. What's so interesting out there?'

'The people, Simon. It's some kind of procession. I wonder if it's a religious occasion.'

'Is it a riot? With all this unrest we've been hearing about, the sooner we get out of here the better I'm going to feel.'

'No, they just seem to be going somewhere.' His wife continued to peer down at the streets filled with men, women, and children. 'They're all Indians too. You can tell by the costumes.'

'My god, we're going to miss our plane if they don't get a move on.' He glared at his watch as if it was responsible. 'Call again, will you? Where the hell can he be?'

FROM *THE JOURNAL*
OF XAVIER DESMOND

December 15, 1986/en route to Lima, Peru:

I have been dilatory about keeping up my journal – no entry yesterday or the day before. I can only plead exhaustion and a certain
amount of despondence.

Guatemala took its toll on my spirit, I'm afraid. We are, of
course, stringently neutral, but when I saw the televised news
reports of the insurrection and heard some of the rhetoric being
attributed to the Mayan revolutionaries, I dared to hope. When
we actually met with the Indian leaders, I was even briefly elated.
They considered my presence in the room an honor, an auspicious
omen, seemed to treat me with the same sort of respect (or lack
of respect) they gave Hartmann and Tachyon, and the way they
treated their own jokers gave me heart.

Well, I am an old man – an old *joker* in fact – and I tend to
clutch at straws. Now the Mayan revolutionaries have proclaimed
a new nation, an Amerindian homeland, where *their* jokers will be
welcomed and honored. The rest of us need not apply. Not that
I would care much to live in the jungles of Guatemala – even an
autonomous joker homeland down here would scarcely cause a
ripple in Jokertown, let alone any kind of significant exodus. Still,
there are so few places in the world where jokers are welcome,
where we can make our homes in peace … the more we travel on,
the more we see, the more I am forced to conclude that Jokertown

is the best place for us, our only true home. I cannot express how much that conclusion saddens and terrifies me.

Why must we draw these lines, these fine distinctions, these labels and barriers that set us apart? Ace and nat and joker, capitalist and communist, Catholic and Protestant, Arab and Jew, Indian and *Ladino*, and on and on everywhere, and of course true humanity is to be found only on *our* side of the line and we feel free to oppress and rape and kill the 'other,' whoever he might be.

There are those on the *Stacked Deck* who charge that the Guatemalans were engaged in conscious genocide against their own Indian populations, and who see this new nation as a very good thing. But I wonder.

The Mayas think jokers are touched by the gods, specially blessed. No doubt it is better to be honored than reviled for our various handicaps and deformities. No doubt.

But ...

We have the Islamic nations still ahead of us ... a third of the world, someone told me. Some Moslems are more tolerant than others, but virtually all of them consider deformity a sign of Allah's displeasure. The attitudes of the true fanatics such as the Shi'ites in Iran and the Nur sect in Syria are terrifying, Hitlerian. How many jokers were slaughtered when the Ayatollah displaced the Shah? To some Iranians the tolerance he extended to jokers and women was the Shah's greatest sin.

And are we so very much better in the enlightened USA, where fundamentalists like Leo Barnett preach that jokers are being punished for their sins? Oh, yes, there is a distinction, I must remember that. Barnett says he hates the sins but loves the sinners, and if we will only repent and have faith and love Jesus, surely we will be cured.

No, I'm afraid that ultimately Barnett and the Ayatollah and the Mayan priests are all preaching the same creed – that our bodies in some sense reflect our souls, that some divine being has taken a direct hand and twisted us into these shapes to signify his pleasure (the Mayas) or displeasure (Nur al-Allah, the Ayatollah, the Fire-breather). Most of all, each of them is saying that jokers are *different*.

My own creed is distressingly simple – I believe that jokers and aces and nats are all just men and women and ought to be treated as such. During my dark nights of the soul I wonder if I am the only one left who still believes this.

Still brooding about Guatemala and the Mayas. A point I failed to make earlier – I could not help noticing that this glorious idealistic revolution of theirs was led by two aces and a nat. Even down here, where jokers are supposedly kissed by the gods, the aces lead and the jokers follow.

A few days ago – it was during our visit to the Panama Canal, I believe – Digger Downs asked me if I thought the U.S. would ever have a joker president. I told him I'd settle for a joker congressman (I'm afraid Nathan Rabinowitz, whose district includes Jokertown, heard the comment and took it for some sort of criticism of his representation). Then Digger wanted to know if I thought an ace could be elected president. A more interesting question, I must admit. Downs always looks half asleep, but he is sharper than he appears, though not in a class with some of the other reporters aboard the *Stacked Deck*, like Herrmann of AP or Morgenstern of the *Washington Post*.

I told Downs that before this last Wild Card Day it might have been possible ... barely. Certain aces, like the Turtle (still missing, the latest NY papers confirm), Peregrine, Cyclone, and a handful of others are first-rank celebrities, commanding considerable public affection. How much of that could translate to the public arena, and how well it might survive the rough give-and-take of a presidential campaign, that's a more difficult question. Heroism is a perishable commodity.

Jack Braun was standing close enough to hear Digger's question and my reply. Before I could conclude – I wanted to say that the whole equation had changed this September, that among the casualties of Wild Card Day was any faint chance that an ace might be a viable presidential candidate – Braun interrupted. 'They'd tear him apart,' he told us.

What if it was someone they loved? Digger wanted to know.

'They loved the Four Aces,' Braun said.

Braun is no longer quite the exile he was at the beginning of the tour. Tachyon still refuses to acknowledge his existence and Hiram is barely polite, but the other aces don't seem to know or care who he is. In Panama he was often in Fantasy's company, squiring her here and there, and I've heard rumors of a liaison between Golden Boy and Senator Lyons's press secretary, an attractive young blonde. Undoubtedly, of the male aces, Braun is by far the most attractive in the conventional sense, although Mordecai Jones has a certain brooding presence. Downs has been struck by those two also. The next issue of *Aces* will feature a piece comparing Golden Boy and the Harlem Hammer, he informs me.

'WARTS AND ALL'

Kevin Andrew Murphy

December 18, 1986, Lima:

A line of potted plants stood arrayed against the whitewashed walls of the *Museo Larco*. Trailing succulents mingled with shrubby annuals, and spindly vines stretched heavenward on trellis wires, the blossoms displaying all the colors of the old Andrew Lang *Coloured Fairy Books* Howard Mueller had owned as a child: Red, Blue, Yellow, Pink, Orange, Crimson, Lilac, and Violet. The Green were the cacti, most of which were wrinkled and warty.

So was Howard, known to most back in Jokertown simply as Troll.

Tourists took pictures of them, a few angling the shot to get him too.

Howard was used to it. When you grew up a joker, you learned it was hard to avoid the stares. When you reached nine feet tall, it became almost impossible. Fortunately, Howard had also grown an extremely thick skin, at least physically.

He heard the click of shutters behind him, the hushed exclamations in Spanish: '¡Ay, que la chingada! ¡Mira a ese puto!' The Peruvian accent was different from the Puerto Rican he was used to, but there are only so many swear words – and when you worked hospital security, you heard all of them. Especially in Jokertown.

'*Puto*' literally meant 'man whore,' but idiomatically it was

142

whatever insult you wanted. Howard wished his Spanish stretched further than that.

Being nine feet tall, he had also learned to plan his day accordingly. Back home, Howard's favorite spot for his day off was the reading room of the New York Public Library. Bibliophiles tended to be more interested in their books. Plus, Howard had learned to appreciate venues with vaulted ceilings or no ceiling.

He stooped to get a brochure from a wooden stand, selecting one of the English ones, and glanced at the photographic illustrations of various moths and butterflies to be found in the gardens. The text described *Caligo idomeneus*, the owl butterfly, named for the yellow eye spots on its wings that made it look like an owl's face; *Copaxa sapatoza*, a pretty gold Saturn moth with feathery antennae and lunular wing marks; and *Ascalapha odorata* and *Thysania agrippina*, the black witch moth and the white witch moth, two of the largest moths, known by various colorful names throughout Latin America. *Tara bruja*, Spanish for witch moth. Also *la sorcière noire* for the black ones, if you spoke French. Supposedly if one flew over your head, you'd go bald, but if it landed on your hand, you'd win the lottery. Howard had been bald ever since he'd drawn his wild card. But winning the lottery would be nice.

A few specimens of the *Lepidoptera* from the pamphlet fluttered around the museum garden. They were impressive, especially the white witch moths, as big across as a nat's hand.

Howard's hands were more substantial, and green, but that let one mimic a cactus paddle. A moth alit upon it. Howard brought it closer. 'So,' he asked it softly, 'do I win the lottery?' The white witch fanned her wings as coolly as Andersen's Snow Queen might toy with a fan, apparently considering his question, then fluttered off across the lawn.

Howard watched her go and chuckled, taking a moment to adjust the strap of the oversized novelty sunglasses he had purchased back in New York. 'Oversized' was relative. They fit many jokers fine as plain sunglasses, Howard included. The 'novelty' was finding them in his size. Almost everything had to be custom fit.

Howard glanced back to the butterfly guide. The next name for the witch moth was *mariposa de la muerte*, the butterfly of death, though the pamphlet observed that this would be a better name for *Lonomia obliqua*, the giant silkworm moth. Its larval form was known as the assassin caterpillar since it injected an anticoagulant poison through wickedly barbed spines, resulting in several deaths every year. *Megalopyge opercularis*, the flannel moth, was even more dangerous. Nicknamed 'the asp,' its caterpillars, while less poisonous than the assassins, were bewitchingly cute. They looked like fluffy lost toupees in the photograph, but had the poisoned spines hidden beneath silky yellow hair.

Howard wasn't much worried about poison himself. His hard skin was tough as an elephant's hide. But the flannel moth caterpillars looked like they'd be a problem for kids, who'd want to pick them up and pet them.

The witch moths, however, were harmless. From a scientific perspective, at least. But in Peru, in the local Quechua, they were known as *taparaco* and featured prominently in the folktale of '*El Emisario Negro*,' the 'Messenger in Black,' a dark stranger who brought a mysterious box to the Inca Huayna Capac. When he opened it, moths and butterflies flew out like the four and twenty blackbirds. But instead of singing for the king or snipping off maid's noses, they spread a plague. People in folktales were always doing stupid stuff like that. If reading Lang's Coloured Fairy Books had taught Howard anything, it was that if someone gives you a mysterious box, *don't open it.* There was never much good inside. Ask Pandora.

Howard stuffed the brochure in his back pocket and ducked in through the main doors of the museum. He had overheard Fantasy saying that the *Museo Larco* had a world-renowned collection of Pre-Columbian erotic pottery. And it had been ages since he'd gotten laid.

The collection did not disappoint. Howard had to get down on one knee to look in all the cases, but was rewarded with the sight of Pre-Columbian pottery figures getting their freak on as much as nats could. There were even some seeming jokers among them: a bird woman with perky tits; a couple of alpaca jokers, or maybe just pottery alpacas, doing the wild thing; and a skull-faced joker with an oversize dick who looked like Charles Dutton's head on a Pre-Columbian nat's body with, well, Howard's own penis, if less warty, and brown instead of green.

Howard purchased the *Museo Larco*'s coffee table book, then went back out to the gardens to wait for the limo to take him back to the hotel. A purple bougainvillea formed a pleasant bower in one corner, and a giant terra cotta urn tipped on its side served him as a seat. Butterflies and moths fluttered near, still seeming to regard him with their owl eyes and wing spots. He fished a cigar out of his shirt pocket, an extremely fine gift from Fulgencio Batista, the aging president of Cuba, during their brief stop in Havana. He sniffed it to savor it one last time, then bit off the end with his snaggled yellow teeth, which served better than any cigar clipper. Howard spat the end into the bougainvillea and struck a safety match against his skin.

He'd just inhaled a lungful of the sweet smoke when the limousine pulled up, UN flags fluttering prominently. Howard sighed, letting out a cloud of smoke which drove away the butterflies that kept mistaking him for a cactus. He got up, stubbing his cigar out against the urn.

The chauffeur ignored Howard, opening the door instead to let out a tall – relatively speaking – blond man in a linen suit who in turn offered a gallant hand to a petite but stunning woman. The man was Jack Braun, the infamous Golden Boy, the woman Asta Lenser, prima ballerina for the American Ballet Theater, more famed as Fantasy, the ace whose dancing caused all men (and even some women) to desire her.

Howard had a poster of her on the wall of his bedroom, Asta done up as Coppélia, the clockwork doll, from the ballet of the same name – a souvenir of the night Dr. Tachyon had given him his ticket to the Met. Her coiffure for that performance had been tightly wound brassy ringlets that bounced like springs. Today she wore a spiked platinum mullet, like Bowie's Goblin King. A Goblin Queen, and a fetching one at that.

'Oh!' she cried, her hand and arm moving in an elegant yet

theatrical gesture as she pointed to the air above the museum. 'Oh, look, Jack! How beautiful!'

Howard looked as well, watching as a migration of moths and butterflies crested over the roof of the former colonial mansion, chartreuse and crimson, apricot and azure, sulfur and fuchsia, some even translucent, like a cascade of confetti viewed through a Tiffany window, but magically brought to life, their wings all the colors of the rainbow.

Visitors to the garden gaped. Children laughed and pointed. Howard gazed in wonder himself, mystified as to their source. The kaleidoscope of lepidopterans whirled and spun, their patterns tumbling and transforming, a panoply of jeweled fragments.

For a moment, a coven of black witch moths flew together, forming a shape that resembled a hooded figure, like one of Tolkien's ringwraiths, but just as swiftly broke apart, the black moths becoming dark traceries amidst their more colorful companions. Before Howard could follow their progress any further, Fantasy began her dance.

To say she was beautiful was an understatement. To say she was absolutely mesmerizing was the truth. Asta was a dancer, lithe but muscled, supremely agile and in control of her body as she gave herself over to sheer Terpsichorean joy .

Howard did not know all the names for what she did – entrechat, pirouette, cabriole fouette, a graceful arabesque, and a grand jeté – he only knew that he wanted her. She moved like a butterfly, her dress a sheer wrap of delicately peach-tinted silk with full skirts slit to show off her amazing legs. Across her shoulders, trailing from each hand, she wore a gaudy native shawl, doubtless a recent gift from some admirer, woven with threads of cactus fruit pink and cornflower blue.

Asta raised it above her head like moth wings, causing it to flutter as the butterflies swirled around her, drawn half by the colors, half by her movement and magnetism.

All the men watching, Howard included, were held transfixed by her beauty, caught like a lepidopterist's specimens on a pin. There must have been a woman among them, for Howard dimly heard the clicking of a camera shutter. He could do nothing but watch, only able to move what muscles it took to follow her movements, entranced.

Asta's spontaneous dance at last wound to a close as she sank to a spot in the center of the lawn, fluttering her shawl like a butterfly's wings as it comes to rest. She touched her head to her knee, bringing her arms forward to touch her calf so the shawl's colors were fully displayed at the conclusion of her dance's coda.

Applause erupted spontaneously, the noise and the movement causing the moths and butterflies to scatter. Howard shook off the last of his trance and became uncomfortably aware that the front of his jeans was tented by a raging hard-on. This was made even more embarrassing by the fact that it was at an average person's eye level.

Fantasy rose, taking her bows for her impromptu ballet fantasia, surveying her admirers and her audience. She paused with an amused sidelong glance to Howard's crotch. 'And to think,' she remarked impishly, 'we haven't even seen the erotic pottery collection yet, Jack?'

'Of course, Asta.'

Asta simply laughed. While Jack Braun might have been pleased because he knew she would be his tonight, Asta Lenser would never truly belong to anyone but herself.

December 19, 1986, en route to Cuzco:
On board the *Stacked Deck*, people traded seats like Fantasy traded bed partners. All save Howard and Mordecai Jones. The Harlem Hammer required a chair with special reinforcements to withstand his immense weight. Howard required all that plus additional headroom, legroom, and width. He couldn't even stand up in the plane, so spent most of his time stretched out recumbent, staring at the ceiling or chatting with whomever had taken the seats beside him for that leg of the tour.

This morning it was Father Squid and Archbishop Fitzmorris, the tour's representative for Catholic Charities. The Archbishop was a nat in his sixties, with white hair with traces of red and an affable round face offset by silver-rimmed bifocals. He was also exceedingly unflappable, paging through Howard's book of Pre-Columbian erotica with interest. 'Oh my,' he exclaimed, 'some of these remind me of the obscure saints.' He tapped a page and chuckled. 'This gentleman resembles Saint Foutin.'

Howard looked over at the photograph. It was another one of the jokers with a giant dick. 'We've, uh, got a guy sort of like that back at the clinic.'

'Oh?' Father Squid inquired, his tentacles curling with interest. 'Is it Philip, the new janitor? I have told him there's no shame in a joker body, but he does not wish to reveal what he hides beneath that trenchcoat. And, I'm afraid to say, the church ladies have begun to speculate.'

'Uh, no,' Howard said. 'Not Phil. Another guy.'

The Archbishop still marveled at the photograph. 'I hope this poor man's joker is not precisely like Saint Foutin's.'

'Well, more proportional ...' Howard admitted uncomfortably.

'That is good to hear, but still not precisely what I meant,' Archbishop Fitzmorris clarified. 'One of the saint's icons is housed at a little parish in France. When they think the priest isn't looking, women sneak a hand beneath Saint Foutin's robe to touch Him to ensure fertility. Sometimes they even chip off splinters.' He leaned over conspiratorially, whispering, this obviously a favorite scurrilous anecdote. 'You would think the saint's member would be worn away to nothing, and yet it is miraculously restored! Or maybe not so miraculously. Someone in the middle ages was clever enough to drill a hole through the statue and insert a dowel. Every so often, as needed, one of the priests uses a mallet to tap a little more out.'

Howard considered. Like most jokers, he was not entirely pleased with what the wild card had done to him. But at least it hadn't shoved a broomstick up his ass.

'This is an official saint of the church?' asked Father Squid.

'As official as Saint Christopher, if less popular.' Archbishop Fitzmorris reached into his shirt collar and pulled out a silver medallion with the image of a bearded man with a staff giving a child with a halo a piggy-back ride. 'His Holiness took both their days off the universal liturgical calendar, along with those of the rest of the obscure saints, but parishes dedicated to them are still free to celebrate their feast days, as are any who hold a special veneration. "Christopher" is my Christian name, and I am not going to fly anywhere without my patron's protection.' The Archbishop kissed his medallion and tucked it away, then gave Howard an appraising look. 'Do you know, Mr. Mueller, you remind me very much of Saint Christopher. He too was a giant among men – five cubits tall. That, I believe, is about seven and a half feet.'

'I'm taller.'

'I can see,' the Archbishop acceded, 'and if I've heard correctly, quite strong as well. But Saint Christopher was even stronger, for he bore the Christ Child across a river on his back, and with him, the sins of the world. I doubt that even Mr. Braun could bear that burden.'

'Golden Boy has enough of his own sins to bear,' observed Father Squid.

'Truly,' agreed the Archbishop. 'Judas's sin is the greatest of all.'

The conversation was starting to stray into uncomfortable territory, especially considering Golden Boy was seated only a few rows away, still flirting with Fantasy, so Howard asked, 'Did Saint Christopher have warts too?'

'Not that I'm aware of,' said Archbishop Fitzmorris amusedly, 'but the oldest icons of him do give him a dog's head.'

'There's a guy like that over at the Crystal Palace,' Howard mentioned. 'Lupo. Makes a good martini.'

'I shall have to visit,' said the Archbishop. 'I appreciate a good martini.'

'So what happened to the dog's head?' Howard asked.

'After he carried Our Lord across the river, Christopher was rewarded with a human countenance.' The Archbishop swiftly added, 'Mind you, I am simply reciting the hagiography as I learned it as a child, well before the advent of the wild card.'

'Jesus was a joker,' Father Squid stated piously, his tentacles twitching, 'and a hermaphrodite. I do not see why He-She would consider it a reward to make someone into a nat.'

'Who are we to question the ineffable wisdom of the divine?'

'There is that,' agreed Father Squid. 'What I will question, however, is why the Holy Mother Church has still not accepted the Church of Jesus Christ, Joker, as one of Her parishes nor even seen fit to declare a patron saint for wild cards.'

'Father Squid,' the Archbishop sighed, 'you are still a young priest. These matters take time. There are any numbers of patron saints who already deal with plagues – Roch, Sebastian, Godeberta, Camillus de Lillus. And, truth to tell, it has only been forty years. And sadly, there are matters of pride and politics to attend to, societies that wish to have their patron saint named as having dominion over something as important as the wild card virus.'

'The wild card is more than just some plague,' Father Squid stated flatly.

'I agree,' conceded Archbishop Fitzmorris, 'but then it becomes a question of which other saint should have dominion? Saint Jude, who makes all things possible? Eustachius and His Companions, the patrons of difficult situations? Saint Spyridon, the Wonderworker? Personally I advise all those dealing with the wild card to pray to Saint Rita of Cascia, for Rita of the Impossibles would seem the one most suited. That said, Rita's society is small, and Augustinian, and Spyridon dealt in both miracles and plagues, so he's currently the frontrunner. But it would never be wise to count Rita of the Impossibles out.'

Howard considered, trying to remember where he'd heard of Rita of the Impossibles before. 'Didn't Castro say she helped the Dodgers win the pennant a few years back?'

'Heresy!' declared Archbishop Fitzmorris. 'That was the Devil's work!' He unscrewed the cap of an airline bottle of gin, looked for something to mix it with, and failing that, swigged it straight. 'It should have been the Red Sox!'

'I knew you were a Red Sox fan, Christopher,' Father Squid gave the Archbishop a sidelong glance with his cephalopod eyes, 'but a Dominican too?'

'What are you talking about? ' The Archbishop paused, then added, 'But you're quite right. I'm a Franciscan. My primary concerns are charity for the poor and healing for the sick. And annoying the Jesuits. I must leave it to the Dominicans to deal with heresy.' He patted Father Squid on the arm. 'Like you, my good friend. The heretic.'

'I am not a heretic,' huffed Father Squid.

'That's what she said,' laughed Archbishop Fitzmorris.

'Who?'

'Joan of Arc,' said the Archbishop, his blue eyes twinkling, 'and now she's a saint.' He raised the gin in a toast. 'Consider yourself in good company.'

December 19, 1986, Cuzco:

'And here is where the Inca Manco Capac sank his golden rod!' the giant white guinea pig in the rainbow-striped poncho declared, looking like Mr. Rat and Mr. Mole's Peruvian cousin from some unpublished Rackham illustration. She pointed to the cobblestones near an old colonial fountain.

Snickers and repetitions of 'golden rod!' echoed across the *Plaza de Armas*, the old heart of the Incan empire and the new heart of tourism in Cuzco. Howard couldn't figure out whether Peruvians had a thing for dick jokes or were just less uptight than New Yorkers. Probably a little of both.

Two churches and a larger cathedral dominated the plaza, the little *Iglesia del Triunfo*, the larger *Iglesia de la Compania de Jesus*, and the huge brownstone *Cathedral de Santo Domingo*. Howard watched Father Squid and Archbishop Fitzmorris slip inside the gothic façade of the last, still chatting convivially.

Howard wasn't much for church, cathedral ceilings notwithstanding. But the morning walking tour of the plaza had sounded like a good way to stretch his legs after the flight and yet another set of awkwardly pushed together beds back at the last hotel.

Howard missed his bed back home. When he was a teenager, still having his growth spurt and not knowing how tall he was going to get, his old friend Cheetah had helped him cobble it together from a couple brass bedframes.

Cheetah had also gotten him into breaking and entry. Howard

had paid for those bedframes eventually, getting his first honest job as security for Mr. Musso.

Musso's Furniture was long dead and Mr. Musso along with it. Howard didn't know what had happened with Cheetah. They'd grown apart, in more than one sense.

When you passed six and a half feet tall, you started to get used to owning the airspace around your head. Even in Jokertown. At nine feet, the only people Howard was used to seeing at eye level were Tree, Gargantua, and occasionally the Floater, depending on his altitude at the moment. In the Plaza de Armas, what was floating around Howard's head were more butterflies, part of the same seasonal migrations as in Lima. Tourists ran about taking pictures of them, and also, incidentally, of him. Howard tried to be good humored about it.

But walking around the plaza was also a good way to see his fellow jokers. Howard had an eye for security and also had a strong knowledge of the possible jokers folks could draw. While there were a fair number of jokers present, they reminded him of the staff at the Funhouse. The guinea pig tour guide was well groomed, her white hair obviously shampooed and styled, her teeth freshly clipped. A man with jaguar spots, fur, fangs, claws, and a stubby half-grown tail stood in the shade of a tree, giving an expert performance tossing butterfly sticks. A two-headed llama acted as a barker for a stand selling fruit cups, one head crying out in a woman's voice, the other a man's. Both heads wore headbands with red felt reindeer antlers, it being the week before Christmas. And, near the fountain, a group of assorted joker musicians in Santa hats alternated between international holiday tunes and traditional Andean flute muse. Instead of the expected satyr playing the panpipes, they included a golden-skinned wood nymph whose flutes were her own fingers. A bronze-scaled serpent woman danced beside her, her scales chiming like bells. The less-than-presentable local jokers had either been removed by the police or been paid to be elsewhere by local businesses. Howard did not know which.

'*Señors y señoritas!*' the giant guinea pig cried. 'Please turn your attention to the square! The first of our folk dances shall be *La Llamerada!* The dance of the llama herders!'

Excepting the two-headed llama joker, who had a head at each end like the Pushmi-Pullyu from *Doctor Dolittle*, the dancers were all nats, dressed in traditional folk costumes. Their pants and skirts were russet, their shirts and blouses were gold, and their sashes in the gaudy clashing serape colors most Peruvian weavers seemed to favor. Their triangular hats looked somewhere between Masonic ritual headdresses, tea cozies, and Howard's nat grandma Mueller's favorite fringed lampshade. A couple pom-poms decorated the top, a felt llama cut-out was stuck on the front, and for some reason Howard couldn't fathom, a red letter U.

The music was lively and the dance had a lot of hand-clapping, foot-stomping, and skirt-shaking to chase the llamas around the square, or at least the two-headed llama joker. He, she, or they really looked like two llamas when his/her middle was obscured by the dancing nats. Howard wondered how s/he went to the bathroom and hoped it did not involve a catheter. Howard purchased a fruit cup and munched on pineapple and honeydew spears and pieces of an exotic pink fruit called 'mamey.' It tasted sort of pumpkin-cherry-peach flavored, but not really. Like all good fruits, it tasted mostly like itself. Howard ended up buying one of the football-size beige fruits and peeling it with his nails, which were black and sharp and much straighter than his teeth. The mamey had a big pit like an avocado that he tossed in the trash along with the plastic cup full of rinds. More butterflies fluttered around the bin, sipping the spilled nectar with their long tongues, still seeming to regard him with their wingspot eyes.

The next dance was more traditionally Incan, the *Camiles*, the dance of the witch doctors. The pan-pipe-fingered dryad blew a skirling tune on her finger flutes, and the witch doctors twirled around in vicuna ponchos and straw hats decorated with bows, their knapsacks swinging precariously. They unslung them from their backs, making a great show of pulling open the drawstrings and dispensing their wares. Then they ran about the square, rattling gourd maracas, attempting to peddle bundles of herbs, dubious-looking folk charms, and more gourds to those watching, especially to all the jokers present.

Howard didn't know what the gourd cocktails were, but they reeked of licorice and not the good strawberry type. He watched the jaguar-spotted butterfly-stick juggler purchase one with suspiciously loud and quick haggling for a local, giving over all the tips in his hat. Then he drank the brew. One by one his spots disappeared, his fur receded, his claws retracted, his fangs shrank, and even his stubby tail withdrew into his body, leaving a handsome young nat of mestizo heritage.

'I am cured!' the former joker cried. '*¡Estoy curado! ¡Estoy curado!*' The Peruvian accent was thick, but Howard recognized Spanish and what he guessed was Brazilian Portuguese. While he didn't know the words, they were easy enough to guess from context.

He shook his head and sighed. Howard had seen jokers cured of the wild card before. There were a lot of possible reactions. Crying was common. Fainting was another. Freaking out over body parts you no longer had or never had before happened a lot too. But a shapeshifting ace made a great shill for miraculous wild card cures, and many joker tourists bought them. Nothing happened except that one woman with scabby weeping sores and hair that writhed like wire worms had her locks calm down slightly. She began to cry, talking quickly to her companions in Portuguese and repeatedly touch one scabrous hand to her breasts.

Howard supposed the placebo effect was good for something. He ignored the witch doctors' repeated entreaties to buy their snake oil or whatever licorice-scented potion was in their gourds. Instead, he purchased another fruit cup and listened as the band started a new tune.

'Howard, isn't it?' inquired a voice.

'What?' Howard looked down. Coming up to just about his navel was a woman with lustrous raven hair, oversized designer sunglasses, and a rich charcoal alpaca cloak worn like moth wings over a blue watered-silk sundress. One shapely but well muscled white leg stuck out below, poised in a dancer's attitude as she craned her neck up at him, exposing an equally pale throat and a tantalizing glimpse of two small pert breasts.

Though high quality, from Howard's vantage point and experience in Jokertown, he could still spot a wig. He mentally stripped it and the cloak away. 'Fantasy,' he concluded.

'*Shhh*,' she shushed conspiratorially, one coquettish red nail to her lips, 'I'm incognito.' She pulled down her sunglasses, looking at him over the top, exposing eyes a brilliant and vivid heliotrope. 'Just call me "Asta," okay?'

'Didn't you have b—'

'Takisian Lilac,' she answered. 'All the rage. I adore colored contacts.' She pushed her sunglasses back up. 'Did you see that Haitian woman? I'll have to get some in Temptress Red too – though I believe hers are natural.'

Howard tipped down his own sunglasses. 'Same here.'

Asta's scarlet lips pursed in a perfect moue. 'I don't know why you hide them. They're your most striking feature.' She glanced sideways at his crotch. 'One of your most striking features, anyway.'

'I'm a little light sensitive.' Howard pushed his sunglasses back. 'Something I could help you with, Asta?'

'No doubt several things,' she mused flirtatiously, 'but for the moment, could I bother you for a lift? Your height is so much more substantial, and I was wanting to study the *Sijilla*.'

'The *Sijilla*?' Howard repeated.

'The dance of the doctors and lawyers,' Asta explained. 'It's one of the Spanish dances.' She gestured to the square where a new set of folk dancers were taking position and a crowd of onlookers formed a wall of shoulders that would easily block the view of someone Asta's height.

Howard had been to concerts and had girls on his shoulders before, though it had been a while. 'Golden Boy wasn't available?'

'Jack's almost as much of a social butterfly as I am.' Asta waved offhandedly, startling a cloud of the actual butterflies. 'He decided to be elsewhere.' She dimpled. 'Besides, you're taller.'

Howard chuckled. 'I am that.' He reached down, and when Asta didn't resist, placed his hands around her waist and lifted her to his right shoulder.

'Not the most elegant lift I've ever gotten, but certainly the highest,' she observed amusedly. 'We'll make a danseur of you yet.'

'That would be something,' said Howard.

Fantasy watched the dancers taking position. 'I fancy I might bring this *Sijilla* to the world's attention.' Her legs curved tightly but expertly around Howard's shoulder. 'After all, the great Pavlova did the same with the *Jarabe Tapatío*.'

'Don't think I've seen that.'

'Truly?' Asta rested a delicate hand on his opposite shoulder. 'You've never seen the Mexican Hat Dance?'

'Well, yeah….' Howard felt himself blushing, which was always embarrassing, since he blushed a darker green. 'We were just in Mexico.'

'The *Ballet Folklórico*'s was very nice, but it's not what it was under Hernández's direction, and oh, there I go, being catty. I should have said it was wonderful.' She squeezed his shoulder. 'You were there. It was wonderful, wasn't it?'

'Uh, yeah.'

'Good. I trust my secret's safe with you.' Fantasy's legs squeezed like Slither's coils back when Howard had taken her to see the Lizard King and Destiny. 'I shudder to think what would happen if I'd been that candid around Jack….'

Howard chuckled. The *Sijilla* was a lot like the Mexican Hat Dance, meaning one of those Spanish dances with a lot of swishing skirts and flirtation, but instead of charros and girls in poblana dresses, the women had cross-dressed, masked and ponchoed as comical old Spanish doctors and lawyers. The men were costumed like Hispanic devils, with cloven-hoofed spats over their right feet, bird-clawed spats over their left, and leering yellow masks, like the jaundiced love-children of Devil John Darlingfoot and the Chickenfoot Lady.

The music skirled and trilled as the yellow-faced devils pranced in, waggling their masks menacingly, stomping their goat hooves and chicken feet in a lurching gait. The doctors then began waving

bottles of what looked like patent medicines or maybe urine specimens at them. The lawyers brandished papers that looked like lawsuits. Then, after a bit of circling and flirtation, the women began
chasing the men around the plaza. Howard didn't know what Asta
thought, but from his perspective, it began to resemble nothing
half so much as Sadie Hawkin's Day at Jokertown High.

The guinea pig cried out something in Spanish. Asta clapped
her hands in delight, explaining to Howard, 'The dance commemorates the work of the doctors at the ranchos of Qosñipata
and the malaria epidemic there.'

As the doctors and lawyers chased the last of the malaria spirits
away, Howard remarked, 'Tachy would like this. We should...'

The words died on his lips as the men switched masks, coming
back with pinched white elfin faces, manes of copper curls, and
Three Musketeers' hats complete with ostrich plumes. 'Or maybe
not ...'

The doctors and lawyers with their lawsuits and patent medicines
were somewhat less successful dealing with the wild card virus, or
at least that was the interpretation Howard came up with for the
folk ballet. The Takisian devils chased all the other dancers save
the joker MC from the square, the *Sijilla* ended, and the musicians
took a set break.

Asta patted Howard's shoulder. 'Let's keep this our little secret.'

'No trouble there.'

Asta laughed, a sound at once artless and practiced, and she
slipped from his shoulder, sliding down his arm like it was a fire-
man's pole. She landed on her feet, resting one hand against him
for support.

She took it away quickly. 'Oh my,' she said, realizing where
she'd had it, 'that was forward of me.'

Howard shrugged, looking down at her. 'Happens.'

'Let me make it up by buying you lunch. Do you like street
food?'

Howard grinned. 'I'll try anything once.'

'My motto as well.' Asta looked to his crotch, then to his face, then back again. 'Wait here!' She skipped away. 'Back in two shakes of a lamb's tail!'

Butterflies trailed after her, evidently as enchanted as Howard. By the time Asta got back with the food, Howard had a raging boner, but not from her dancing. He waited on the edge of the fountain which had survived a few hundred years and could withstand several hundred pounds of joker.

'They have some wonderful delicacies.' Asta balanced the brown paper sacks and a couple of cups with the practiced ease of a waitress. 'This is mostly for you, but I assume you won't mind if I pick.' She perched next to him, delicate and fairylike, folding the paper bags into neat placemats on the edge of the fountain. '*Pepián de cuy*,' she said, opening the first container. 'Guinea pig with peanut sauce.' She opened the second box, revealing a pile of savory looking meat skewers on a bed of grain. 'And grilled llama with quinoa pilaf. I've never tried either.'

'I've had quinoa,' Howard admitted. 'They've got it in The Cosmic Pumpkin's health food section.'

'An adventurous man,' Asta said admiringly. 'I like that.' She offered him the cup. 'Here's something I doubt they have at The Cosmic Pumpkin.' She grinned. 'Completely herbal and organic, I promise.'

The cup, like almost all cups, was too small in relation to Howard's hand. He had to hold it with his fingertips. The tea was a pleasant greenish yellow, like pale green tea, and had a couple large leaves floating in it about the same color as his skin. He took a sip. It was bittersweet yet pleasant, and sweeter than green tea, what people would be calling an herbal tea these days, but what grandma Mueller had called a tisane.

'It's coca leaf.' Asta smiled impishly and took a sip from her own cup. 'It's what they drink here in the Andes.'

'Coca leaf?' Howard lowered his cup and looked at the leaves. 'Isn't that what cocaine comes from?'

'Not the only place, but the usual one.' Asta laughed. 'The tea is made with the sweet leaves. The bitter ones have more cocaine, but the sweet are what the Andeans prefer for chewing and drinking.' She waved to the tea stand.

Howard saw a couple of native girls dressed in white flamenco-style dresses with more of the same green leaves embroidered around the hems and necklines. Baskets on the counter held heaps of the leaves, both dry and fresh. The styrofoam and tinsel candy canes at the corners of the stand looked almost incongruous.

'They say that the coca bush sprang up where a wanton woman was torn in two by her jealous lovers.' Asta smiled. 'She became Cocamama, the Incan spirit of health and happiness, goddess of the coca plant.' She took another sip of her tea. 'They also say that men are not supposed to chew her leaves before they've satisfied a woman in bed.' She winked at him. 'I think we can bend that rule just this once.'

Howard shifted uncomfortably. 'You like folklore?'

'A professional weakness,' she confessed. 'I love dance, and all the best ballets are based on folktales.' She looked down at the pile of grilled llama. 'I was in my second year at Julliard when my card turned.' She selected a skewer. 'We were rehearsing *Giselle*.' She began to nibble the meat delicately but suggestively. 'I was dancing one of the wilis.'

'The willies?'

'Not that sort of "willie," you naughty boy,' Asta nibbled her meat skewer again, 'or maybe so. "Give you the willies?" Whichever!' She laughed lightly, startling a few curious butterflies. 'Wilis are spirits of jilted maidens who died before their wedding day. They haunt the forest, hoping to find a man to make him dance himself to death. And I had really gotten into my role since my boyfriend had dumped me because while *I* was in the corps de ballet, *he* was soloing as Albrecht.' Asta viciously tore a chunk of llama with her small white teeth. 'I wanted him to want me, I wanted him to suffer, but most of all I wanted him to stop dancing. I got my wish.' She gestured with her half-eaten skewer. 'It's been mostly good since then.' She paused for reflection before admitting with a bemused pout, 'Though if I'm partnered with a danseur, he needs to be a total Kinsey Six – absolutely gay – if I expect any dancing out of him.' She glanced to Howard. 'So what's your story? Liked "The Billy Goats Gruff" a bit much?'

'Yeah, but I don't think it did much with my card.' Howard chuckled. 'When I was a kid, I had warts. Really embarrassed about them. Kids picked on me and called me "Mr. Toad." Then I got the virus. I got really warty, and green too, but no one picked on me after that – though "Mr. Toad" stuck.' He shrugged, picking out a few llama skewers. 'But I'd always liked *The Wind in the Willows*, had a nice copy my grandma gave me for my birthday, and I liked cars too, so I decided I was going to be the first joker NASCAR driver. Helps when you're so tough you can walk away from any crash.' Howard sampled a skewer. He decided that llama tasted halfway between beef and lamb – basically Peruvian shawarma. 'Wild card had other plans. I'd just got my damn driver's license when I got my growth spurt.' Howard tore into the skewers. 'But when I got my growth spurt, I really got my growth spurt. So goodbye "Mr. Toad," hello "Troll."'

'Hello "Troll,"' Asta said flirtatiously. She selected a choice bit of *Pepián de cuy* and nibbled it without comment as the band started tuning up.

Howard finished the rest. He decided that guinea pig was good and tasted like chicken, in the same way that rabbit tasted like chicken, which was basically saying it tasted like rabbit.

He then felt embarrassed as he looked at the giant white guinea pig joker. She announced that the next dance would be the *Chunchos*, the dance of the jungle folk.

Asta stood up next to Howard, leaning on his shoulder as he continued to sit.

Women danced across the plaza bedecked with floral wreaths like you would see at a Renaissance fair and bearing beribboned staves topped with bouquets of silk flowers. The male dancers wore feathered headdresses and were masked with comically mustachioed nat masks. They carried walking sticks which they used to caper like a bunch of Peruvian Bo Jangles.

Then the jungle beasts came out, women in parrot-faced masks and headdresses, the feathers in many colors to match their dresses, nat men got up as bears and monkeys, and animal-like jokers behaving like animals. The werejaguar ace chased the guinea pig into the square, shifting as he did from full man to full jaguar, excepting he was still wearing his poncho and pants, making him look like a South American version of one of the vain tigers from *Little Black Sambo*, tripping over his jeans instead of turning into jaguar butter.

Then the cathedral bell began to toll thunderously, sounding the hour, that being nine in the morning.

Fantasy leaned over. 'Could we go somewhere more private?' she whispered in Howard's ear as the bell tolled. 'I'm being watched.'

The final bell sounded and Howard looked around. There were a number of people watching them, mostly nats and a few jokers with cameras, stealing pictures of the giant joker like they usually did, turning away to pretend they were taking pictures of the cathedral or looking at him sheepishly when he caught them at it. That much was normal and no different for Howard than any given weekend at the Central Park Zoo.

What was different were the butterflies. Clouds still fluttered around the waste bin and the fruit vendors' cart, or perched on the lip of the fountain's upper basin, stealing a drink from the overflowing water. But there were a surprising number of owl butterflies and other lepidopterans with eye-like wingspots who had them pointed at him like camera lenses.

Howard looked directly at one. A moment later, the butterfly fluttered aloft, as if it were nothing more than coincidence and his mind playing tricks on him. But looking out of the corner of his eyes behind his sunglasses, Howard noted a number of others focused on him like a sea of photographers.

He got up and stretched, still watching the butterflies and moths. While some were still focused on him, most of them had their false eyes turned towards Asta.

Howard had been around enough ace powers to know better than to discount something odd as coincidence rather than ascribe it to something more sinister, especially given the hooded figure he'd glimpsed amidst the kaleidoscope of butterflies over the

Museo Larco. The figure who had appeared just as Fantasy arrived.

Howard then recalled the reaction of the butterflies to his cigar. While he did not think he could smoke enough to cover the entire *Plaza de Armas*, there were three churches nearby, and Catholics did like their incense and candles.

'Would you like to go to morning prayers?' Howard asked. 'Archbishop Fitzmorris said he'd be giving a special holiday invocation, and Father Squid should be there too.'

Asta looked like someone who did not usually do church either, but put on her best smile. 'That sounds divine ...'

The *Cathedral de Santo Domingo* had grand doors as befit a cathedral, a holy water font as was to be expected, lines and lines of identically dressed nuns saying rosaries, and a bunch of incense in the air from assorted priests and altar boys swinging censers. A different bishop than Archbishop Fitzmorris stood at the pulpit speaking more Latin than Howard could understand, but that didn't matter. What did matter was that the incense had the desired effect and Asta's retinue of moths and butterflies were driven back.

The cathedral was also connected to the little *Iglesia del Triunfo* which was smaller and stuffier. For some reason probably having to do with politically incorrect history, there was a statue of some saint killing an Inca in it. There was also a whole conflagration of votive candles before an icon of the Virgin Mary.

The air was sweltering as Howard got down on his knees then sank back on his heels to be near the same head height as Asta. She went up on point to embrace him, whispering in his ear, 'Go to the train station. Get tickets for Aguas Calientes. Tell no one. Please, I'll explain everything later!' She kissed him on the cheek. 'A girl's life depends on it!'

Asta then stepped aside, crossed herself, slipped some money in the poor box, and took a match to light a fresh votive.

Howard didn't much like churches, but he liked this one even less once he saw a few dark moths fluttering in the corners out of the range of the candles.

He got up and wandered back through the connection to the

main cathedral, stayed long enough for sake of appearances, as if he'd come to hear Archbishop Fitzmorris and Father Squid give their guest homilies, then he slipped out through the front doors, doing his best to behave like a tourist not certain as to what his next stop should be.

A few new butterflies and moths fluttered after him but seemed nowhere near as interested as they had when he'd had Asta on his shoulders. They became even less interested when he lit his cigar and spent a good amount of time sucking and savoring it.

Fulgencio Batista had excellent taste in cigars. It lasted the stroll to the train station. Howard bought the two tickets, then sat down on the bench, glancing through the tourist brochure for Aguas Calientes and wondering exactly what he was getting himself into. Being nine feet tall and tough as a rhino made him not worry so much about himself – and Asta had the air of a woman whom one shouldn't worry too much about either – but the idea that some kid was in trouble? That was bad.

The old brass station clock showed 10:25, five minutes till the 10:30 train to Aguas Calientes. Howard picked out a few lichen-mottled moths almost camouflaged against the verdigris above the dial. A shadowy robed figure moved silently beside him. Howard started, expecting the hooded apparition he'd glimpsed among the witch moths, but it was just a nun.

The holy sister sat down beside Howard, glanced up at him, smiled pleasantly, then turned back to the platform, humbly counting the beads of her rosary, eyes downcast. Her face was freshly scrubbed, bright and clean without a trace of make-up, and her eyes were large and brown with the tiny pixels in the iris of high quality theatrical contacts.

Howard slipped Fantasy her ticket inside the tourist brochure, but boarded separately.

The train was an old Pullman, all hand-rubbed wood, brass, and antique elegance. Howard found an empty compartment and waited. The whistle blew, the train lurched to a start, then rocked along, wheels clacking in a soothing rhythm that soon faded into the background. Outside the windows, scenery flashed by, rocky hills with rust-colored soil, trees and shrubs in various shades of green as the train wended its way up into the Andes.

The nun joined him a few minutes later, smiled, and drew the windowshades.

After the conductor had taken their tickets, Asta shut the door and checked the compartment for bugs. Literal bugs. Then she sat down.

'So what's up with the butterflies?' Howard asked.

'There's an ace,' Asta explained.

'I guessed that. Which one?'

She threw up her hands in exasperation. 'Hell if I know! The Mothman. The Butterfly Collector. The Lepidopterist. Pick a name!'

'The Messenger in Black?'

'Hortencio said that one, but it didn't make much sense.' She looked puzzled. 'Where the hell did you hear it?'

Howard reached into his back pocket and pulled out the pamphlet from the *Museo Larco*.

'Fucking folklore,' Asta pronounced as she read it over. 'Did everyone have their card turn when they had their nose in a book of fairytales?'

'I didn't.'

'Yeah, right, "Troll."' Asta rolled her eyes and handed the pamphlet back.

'Who's Hortencio?'

'Remember Batista's sons back in Cuba?'

'Yeah. I didn't spend much time with them.'

'Well,' she countered, 'I did. At least with one.' She glared at Howard. 'Don't give me that look. It's not like you weren't hoping to get lucky yourself. And who knows, you just might. I like to blow off steam when I'm bored or curious or scared – and let me tell you, right now I'm fucking terrified.'

The train chugged along, the wheels thrumming with the rhythm of the tracks. 'So what happened with Hortencio Batista?'

'Sex,' she said simply. 'Nothing to brag about from my end, certainly. He probably did. He brags a lot. Bragged about his family's connections with the Mafia, which everyone knows about. About how the Gambiones have cocaine connections to other drug cartels, including ones down here in Peru. And then he bragged about how some drug lord kidnapped another drug lord's little girl and is holding her for ransom, and boo-hoo, the Gambiones are either going to ice the kid or kidnap her themselves to get leverage over the first guy, they're not sure which, but in either case, they know where she is and they're going to do it tomorrow.'

'And he told you all this?'

'No.' She looked incredulous, pausing as if she searching for a suitably catty reply. 'He dropped lots of hints, then passed out from too little sex and too much coke. So I went and read his files.' She shrugged. 'I couldn't go to the cops – they're all corrupt, and even the ones who aren't tend to be "big picture" types who won't give a damn if one little girl gets hurt so long as it screws up the drug trade, so I decided "Fuck it! I'm an ace! I can handle this!" and hatched my own crazy plan. Don't judge – but I'm not too proud to say that I took a page from Alma Spreckles' playbook: I'd rather be an old man's plaything than a young man's slave. So I called this rich old guy I know and told him that I'd bang him twelve ways from Sunday when I get back to New York if he'd just arrange a private helicopter and some guards to fly me and the kid out of Peru before the Gambiones could gank her.' Asta reached under her habit and rummaged around in her dress pocket. 'I mean, look at her.' She handed Howard a photograph. 'She can't be more than seven. Eight at the most.' She bit her lip, blinking back tears. 'I was a little girl like that once. I mean, I was in toe shoes, and I would have killed for a dress that nice, but she's just a little kid. No kid deserves to die.'

Howard looked at the picture. Asta was right. The girl looked six or seven, maybe eight, with chubby cheeks, dark eyes, and native features. She was wearing a foofy white dress with too many crystals and sequins and too much lace, and her smile looked more forced than happy, but she was just a kid. The photographer had also used some tacky glitter effect around her, making it look like a creepy boudoir photo.

Howard flipped it over. On the back was written the name *Lorra* and under that *Cocamama*. 'The goddess of the coca bush?'

'Code name for their operation.' Asta took the photograph. 'Or some sick joke that the kid's going to get ripped in two.'

Howard shook his head. 'You were going to do all this on your own?'

'Oh fuck no!' Asta swore. 'I was going to get Jack to help me. Golden Boy will not shut up about how he once kicked Juan Perón's ass. Trouble is, I was completely blanking on the fact that the man can't keep a secret to save his life, and the drug lord who nabbed Lorra either is an ace or has aces working for him, one of them being this *Emisario Negro* who can spy with butterflies and moths. And what's worse, there's this scary-ass poison dart frog joker-ace assassin they've got called Curare, and that's more than I'd want to tangle with solo, so I've been dancing as fast as I can to find a replacement I can trust.'

'And you picked me.'

'It was either you or the Harlem Hammer.' Asta shrugged. 'And while I've got nothing against bald black guys, so far as I know, Mordecai is a happily married man. I'm not a homewrecker.' She grimaced. 'And even if I were, I know better than to get in the crosshairs of a lady from Harlem.'

'But bald green guys?'

'Howard,' Asta confessed, 'you've been on my radar since I saw you in the audience when I was dancing Coppélia. And I'm scared now, and it's a long train ride to Aguas Calientes.'

'You realize you're wearing a nun's habit.'

'Are you Catholic?'

'No.'

'Good.' She grinned. 'Neither am I.' She began to unbutton his fly. 'Oh my. I see you're not Jewish either.' She paused, then touched him with her small hand.

Howard ached. This was the awful moment. His penis, while green, was proportional. But that meant it was over a foot long, warts and all. It looked more like an English cucumber than something that belonged on a human being. The mere sight had turned nights with women he had liked into 'It's not you, it's me' and another night alone.

'You know,' Asta said the dreaded words, 'I doubt I can take all of this.' She stroked the shaft. 'But I'm certainly willing to try.' She grinned wider. 'Have you ever seen the Dance of the Wilis?'

'No.'

'Philistine,' she chided, 'that needs to be corrected.'

Asta went up on point. Howard already was.

December 19, 1986, Aguas Calientes:

Asta had shed the nun's habit and the alpaca cloak. Her dress underneath was cerulean blue as was her hair, clipped short like Annie Lennox's. Her eyes were the same ultramarine, bright as a Byzantine icon's. While Howard hadn't checked to see if they were contacts, they matched, making her look like a water nymph. This was only appropriate since she had said she was going to be dancing the part of Ondine from the ballet of the same name.

The tape deck of the Jeep began blaring classical music, which was Howard's cue to not look behind himself. Instead, he made some more noise. While Golden Boy could lift a tank over his head and was celebrated for this fact, Troll wasn't quite that strong. But Howard could flip a Chevy on its roof and that still made a hell of a ruckus.

Men ran out of the house holding guns. Then they stopped, gazing in awe and wonder as if beholding a vision of transcendent loveliness who, incidentally, they would also like to bang.

Howard knew how they felt.

Since they were also jamming the main doors and windows, he went around the side and kicked in a side door. It flew off its hinges with a satisfying screech.

The building was two stories and the only snap generalization Howard could make was that it had an ungodly number of butterfly collections displayed on the walls. He clenched the stub of his cigar between his teeth, sucking it just in case any of them spontaneously came to life, but they stayed still: trophies, mummified pets, former associates, or however the Messenger in Black felt about his minions.

Howard loped up the stairs, ducking for the low ceiling at the top and smashing open doors until he was rewarded with one cluttered with a number of dolls and toys, a child's four-poster bed, and a little girl sitting on it behind a woman pointing a gun at him. She pulled the hammer back and he flung the broken door at her, slamming the gun and the woman into the wall. A doll's head exploded and a bullet buried itself with a shower of plaster dust as the woman slumped to the floor.

The girl screamed then continued screaming, saying something in some language that Howard didn't understand. All he knew was that it wasn't Spanish. 'It's okay,' he promised. 'It's going to be okay, Lorra. We're getting you out of here.'

When she wouldn't stop screaming, he just grabbed the bedspread and bundled her in it, pillows and dolls and all. He held the bundle of bed things and squirming kid to his chest and barreled down the stairs and out the side door, then squeezed his eyes tight shut and stumbled towards the strains of Hans Werner Henze's orchestral score, a task made more difficult by the high pitched screams reverberating against his ribcage.

Then his forehead encountered the upper edge of the covered porch. But this was not the first time for that sort of thing by a long shot. Howard smashed through, then bellowed, '*Asta!* Where are you!'

'Over here!' Then, 'Oh fuck, it's the frog!'

'*Lorra!*' croaked a voice. 'Lorra!'

Howard felt like he was playing some warped game of Marco Polo. He felt a hand on his leg, guiding him but still dancing. 'Put her down, here!' Howard heard the slamming of the Jeep's hatch. 'You drive! I still have to dance!'

'How am I going to drive if I can't see?'

'You'll be able to see fine! Just give me a lift and don't look in the rearview mirror!'

Howard did as he was told. He lifted Asta to his shoulders. She locked her legs around his neck like the Old Man of the Sea from

Sinbad, but no doubt his hotter and kinkier Old Lady since she did it in reverse, her ankles locked under Howard's chin, her thighs squeezing his temples, her ass on top of his head, and the back of her skirt falling down over his eyes like a veil.

He suspected this was not the usual choreography of *Ondine,* but Asta was a skilled enough dancer to improvise. Howard opened his eyes. He wasn't transfixed by Fantasy's ace, though he could feel her shifting weight atop his head as she writhed back and forth in interpretive dance, mimicking the motions of a waterfall, the nymph of an Olympia Beer sign.

Howard adjusted the seat by tearing it out. The back seat fit him just fine, his foot reached the gas easily, and for the first time since high school, Mr. Toad's wild ride began in earnest. He tore down the road through the Andean jungle, the ballet score still blaring from the speakers, Asta perched atop his head.

'We're out of sight.' She dismounted by means of the rollbar into the back seat beside him. 'Drive as fast as you can!'

Then something landed on the hood of the Jeep. '*¡Puta fea!*' croaked the giant frog using Howard's limited Spanish vocabulary to call Fantasy some variety of whore. '*¡Monstruo verde! Deja a Lorra!*'

The frog had large gold eyes, black skin with electric blue markings, and was the size of a boy of about nine or so, though there were plenty of undersized adult jokers just like there were oversized ones. He was also wearing electric blue Speedos. He crawled onto the windshield with elongated fingers with enlarged sticky pads, sweating milky slime from his back.

Curare, the poison frog joker assassin.

The joker boy slicked his fingers with frog slime and lunged, grabbing Howard's face, holding onto the windshield with his toes. The poison numbed slightly, but Howard's skin was thick and rough. His only really vulnerable point was his eyes, Howard's analogue to Achilles' heel or Siegfried's shoulder.

The frog must have guessed this, since a sticky tongue shot out and plastered against the right lens of his oversized sunglasses. The tongue retracted. Howard's Croakies fought back, the neoprene strap he'd had custom fit at a New Jersey surf shop to keep mental patients from trying the same trick. Howard considered it a wise investment.

Then the lens popped out. Curare reached for Howard with his poison-slicked fingers.

Howard jammed his knees against the steering wheel and grabbed the sides of the windshield, tearing it off. He threw it beside the road, the frog still on it as they sped away.

'¡Juan!' cried a girl's voice behind Howard followed by the sound of sobbing.

'¡Cállate, pinche putita tonta!' Asta snarled. 'Tu amigo, la rana, se fue. Te estamos tomando a América, y tendras todas las muñecas y cosas que quieres, y todo lo que tienes que hacer es fabricar cocaína para el Sr. Phuc, ¿de acuerdo?'

'¡No lo entiendo!' the girl cried plaintively. '¡No lo entiendo!' Then she said something else in some language that was clearly not Spanish.

'Fuck!' Asta swore. 'She doesn't even speak Spanish!'

'What did she say?' Howard asked, still driving. 'What did you say?'

'She said she doesn't speak Spanish!' Asta viciously popped the tape from the tape deck, abruptly silencing the Ondine concerto. 'I told her we'd take her to America, she wouldn't have to worry about being kidnapped, and a nice old man would give her a place to live.'

'Is that all?' Howard was pretty sure he'd heard Asta call the kid a 'little whore.'

'Yeah!' Asta snapped. 'I skipped the bit about promising Kien blowjobs if he paid for boarding school, but – Oh no you don't!' Asta cried. Next thing there came a stinging slap and more crying. Then Asta produced a pair of handcuffs and cuffed the kid to the rollbar.

Howard was not surprised that Asta had handcuffs. But the rest…. 'Is that really necessary? She's a kid!'

'Would you rather have her jump out of a moving car?'

Howard wasn't certain right now what he would rather have

happen. He gunned the engine and raced up the road through the jungle which Asta had pointed out earlier. 'Why didn't your ace work on frog boy?'

'Doesn't work on boys,' Asta replied automatically. 'Only men. Probably hasn't gone through puberty yet.'

Howard gasped. 'That was another kid?'

'Or he's gay. Or that was a girl frog. I mean, "Curare" could be a girl's name too.'

'Yeah, but "Juan"?'

'Maybe it's like "A Girl Called Johnny"?' Asta speculated plaintively. 'The Waterboys? I've danced to that.'

It was a good song, but a bad lie. 'I just threw a kid from the car?'

'Oh what does it matter!?' Asta screamed, exasperated. 'He's still fucking poisonous! These bastards sell drugs! You think they'd think twice about using a kid as an assassin?'

She had a point, but not one that Howard wanted to concede. He didn't want to hurt a kid and prayed that he hadn't.

Then the girl cried out 'Juan! Juan!'

Rita of the Impossibles or one of Archbishop Fitzsmorris's other potential patron saints of wild cards must have been listening: Howard saw a flashing figure leap from tree to tree, a swatch of black shadows and blue sky, perfectly camouflaged when clinging to the canopy but visible when he crisscrossed over the roadway, the frog boy leaping with the incredible jumping power of a tree frog but scaled to human size. Physically impossible by the square-cube law of course, but like Peregrine's flight, that went out the window when the wild card entered the picture.

Butterflies fluttered through the canopy as well, moths disturbed from the bark as the human tree frog leapt from branch to branch, a gathering army – and visible among that army was its general, a shadowy figure like a wraith that formed for an instant wherever a coven of witch moths gathered together.

The Jeep came out of the jungle into the dazzling brilliance above the treeline and the panoramic view of the valley, climbing up the mountain to Machu Picchu, ancient citadel of the Incas. Howard squinted against the glare, half of his sunglasses missing.

If it were some other time, Howard would have liked to stop and take pictures, admire the grandeur of the long-fallen fortress city, the gray stone of its walls and battlements and the green grass of its squares and avenues. But as it stood, only one sight mattered: a helicopter waited in the central plaza, three figures beside it. 'There!' Asta pointed. 'Phuc sent them!'

Howard was wondering who this Phuc was, since he hadn't asked Asta anything about her patron, only assuming it was some ballet angel she'd met on the casting couch and it's not like he had any call to be judging about that. But the sobbing girl was another matter. '*¡Por favor, déjenme ir!*' she begged as Howard pulled the Jeep to a stop. '*¡Por favor!*'

Asta rolled her eyes. 'Now she speaks Spanish.'

¡No lo entiendo!'

'Give her a break,' Howard said. 'She's been through a lot.' He turned to the girl. 'It's okay, honey,' he told Lorra, wiping the tears from her cheeks as gently as he could with his rough hands. 'It's okay.'

The tears pooled on his finger but refused to go away, crystallizing in an instant. In the cracks between the warts, his finger felt slightly numb. Howard looked down. It wasn't sequins that covered the girl's dress, but frozen tears. The back of the Jeep was awash with them, like the ones cried by the good sister in 'Toads and Diamonds.'

Howard then lifted the tear on his finger and touched it to his tongue. It tasted bittersweet and slightly ethereal, but a numbness spread out from where his tongue touched it.

Not diamonds. Crystals of rock cocaine.

'She's Cocamama,' Howard realized. 'That's not just a code-name, that's her ace.'

'So I lied.' Asta shrugged. 'Most of what I told you is still true. She's not a drug lord's daughter, but she was stolen from the Gambiones' associates, and if they couldn't get her back, they were willing to kill the goose that laid the golden egg. And if they did get her back, they were going to lock her in a dungeon to spin straw into gold, or turn sugar into cocaine, or some other fairytale shit. We still rescued her.'

'Maybe,' Howard allowed, 'but who the fuck's this Mr. Phuc? Another drug lord?'

'He's a wise investor with a diversified portfolio,' Asta explained diplomatically, 'and he takes good care of his people. Lorra won't want for anything and neither will you.' She grinned. 'Kien can be particularly grateful, especially if you have special talents.'

Howard remained unconvinced, so Asta added, 'Listen, when I called Kien from Cuba, he was horrified that the Gambiones were thinking of killing such a talented little girl just because they were pissed that some ace ganked a bunch of their boys to steal her.' Asta uncuffed Lorra from the rollbar. 'And I wasn't making that shit up about *el Emisario Negro* and the assassin frog. Bunch of mafiosos started bleeding out the eyes after getting stung by some damn caterpillars.' Asta clapped the handcuff to her own wrist. 'Hortencio was scared spitless.'

The air about the girl sparkled like a cloud of glitter and she put her hand on Asta. 'None of that!' Asta slapped the child. 'I've done more coke than you can dish out, sugar.'

Lorra began to cry, cocaine diamonds raining to the grass.

'Let her go,' Howard growled.

'What, and leave her here with killers and assassins? I don't think so.' Asta looked bemused. 'I take it you're really not interested in joining Kien's organization?'

'Looks that way.'

'Not even if we're still occasionally fuckbuddies?'

Howard was tempted, if for the barest second, but still felt bad about that. 'No.'

'Your loss,' Asta sighed, 'but I was afraid you'd say that. Jack's a blabbermouth and a boy scout too, but his biggest problem is that he's invulnerable.' Asta smiled bemusedly. 'You're not.' She raised her free hand in a theatrical gesture. 'Ladies?'

There was the sound of guns cocking. Howard looked past Asta to see a trio of Asian women bearing high caliber rifles, elephant guns more than capable of bringing down an elephant and easily able to deal with a rhino. Or a troll.

Sound also issued from the helicopter, an overfamiliar holiday tune: Tchaikovsky's 'Dance of the Sugarplum Fairy' from *The Nutcracker Suite*. Asta went up on point.

'Oh well,' she remarked as Howard became stricken. 'I'd hoped to bring Kien a pet troll for Christmas too. I guess he'll just have to make do with a magic crack whore.' She danced around the girl, pulling Lorra up by the handcuffs, forcing her to stand on tiptoe. 'Practice, dear. Practice! You'll never be a ballerina if you don't do your stretches!'

Lorra cried as she was dragged towards the helicopter, trailing cocaine diamonds like breadcrumbs. Asta paused, letting the girl rest as she demonstrated how to do a dramatic kick.

That was a mistake. Lorra kicked her in the shins. Hard. Asta stumbled.

Howard wrenched his gaze away, hitting the ground behind the Jeep just as the Asian trio let loose with their elephant guns.

Bullets ripped into the side of the car. '*Du ma! Du ma!*' Asta shouted in what Howard guessed was Vietnamese as the tinkling bells of Tchaikovsky's celesta became tripled in volume. He looked under the car seeing five pairs of women's feet getting into the helicopter.

Asta's feet were immediately recognizable and anything but beautiful. They were twisted, as bruised and ugly as her soul.

The *whup-whup-whup* of helicopter rotors began, dirt and cocaine crystals blowing in all directions, moths and butterflies being blown as well as a great migration of dozens of species sacrificed themselves to the blades in a vain attempt to stop the helicopter from ascending. It rose nonetheless and Howard did as well, dodging as one of the gunwomen took another shot.

The grass exploded inches behind him, then a flash of lapis and jet hurtled through the air, Curare landing on the side of the helicopter. The frog boy smeared his elongated fingers across the face of the gunwoman hanging out of the left door.

She froze, as paralyzed as Howard when he'd seen Asta's dance.

Howard saw his chance. Ducking low to avoid the rotors of the rising helicopter, he ran, then jumped, catching the left skid. He hauled himself up, grabbing the paralyzed gunwoman and tossing her aside. This ended up being into the rotors as the helicopter tilted, weighed down by several hundred pounds of joker. An explosion of gore spattered the ground.

He tore open the door, slamming his fist across the cabin into the other gunwoman, smashing her into the far wall. Asta screamed and the girl did as well as Howard grabbed the bench they were buckled into and tore it free, bolts shearing, and pulled them backwards out of the helicopter, falling to the plaza below, holding the bench above himself for the kid's sake at least.

Howard landed like a rhino, flat on his back, the force of the fall knocking the wind out of him, the bench bouncing against his chest as Asta and Lorra screamed. He didn't know how far he'd fallen. Farther than he'd ever fallen before at least.

Above him, whirling in the blue sky, he saw the helicopter, spinning higher, and thousands of moths and butterflies swarming around it as a frog jumped free. The copter was then lost within the kaleidoscope of the lepidopteran migration and tumbled out of his range of vision. A moment later, he heard an explosion, followed a minute later by the smell of burning gasoline and the burnt-hair stench of ten thousand burning insects.

Asta unbuckled herself from the bench, unbuckling Lorra as well, dragging the girl free and limping a few steps away as the bench, now unoccupied, started to tumble away. Howard realized that he was still partially holding it with his right arm.

He pushed it aside as he sat up, watching as Curare crouched on a pile of ancient rubble, clutching the grey stones with his black and electric blue fingers and toes, blinking the nictating membranes of his great golden eyes as he watched the kaleidoscope of butterflies funnel down in a vortex, swirling down and around, taking the shape of a hooded figure. Thousands of colored wings whirled inside, forming a rainbow-colored lining, the world's most lavish living brocade, while the dark outer fabric was a mosaic of a thousand black witch moths with an owl butterfly as the figure's face and two great white witch moths taking the place of hands.

'Forget you, Howard!' Asta raved, staggering painfully. 'Forget you, you fucking frog! Forget you, you, you whatever you are!' she swore, pointing at the Messenger in Black. 'Forget you, crack kid! I'm a fucking diva! I'm a fucking star!' She attempted to go up on point but stumbled, her shins still bleeding from where Lorra had kicked her. 'Forget all of you!'

'*Yes,*' whispered the Messenger in Black in a voice that was not so much a voice as the coordinated rustling of a thousand moth wings. '*Yes.* *Forget.* *That is an excellent suggestion ...*'

It drifted towards her and opened its robes, or its illusion of robes, the black witch moths that formed the sleeves and outer draperies floating aside like the Ghost of Christmas Present revealing Ignorance and Want. Howard could not see what the Messenger in Black revealed because of the angle, but whatever it was must have been terrible to behold for Asta stared aghast, her jaw dropping open. The specter pointed to her and the white witch moth that served it as a hand flew out and into Asta's open mouth.

The ballerina gasped and choked, then fell over, motionless.

The Messenger in Black closed its robes, turning slightly, then buzzed and whispered, the rustling of moth wings seeming to form words again, but not in any language Howard could understand. However, the message was not intended for him. Lorra nodded and began to look through Asta's pockets, producing a handcuff key which she used to free herself.

She gave Fantasy one more kick for good measure, then ran over and embraced Curare. Her aura sparkled with white light as the droplets of milky poison transmuted to clear crystals.

The Messenger in Black turned to Howard, its white witch moth hands multiplying like a magician's cards for it again had two. '*Mr. Mueller,*' the figure whispered, spreading them wide in a gracious gesture, '*I am grateful for your assistance with the recovery of my wards, and while I will not forget your transgressions, I must forgive them, for you were deceived. You acted with the best of intentions,*' Its false owl eyes regarded him, '*for the most part.*'

'Um, thanks.'

'*I have been observing you and your companions during your passage through my demesne, and I must warn you that Fantasy is not the least duplicitous of your fellows. Her motives are base, but human. There is another who does not present the same face to the world as what my pretty ones have seen, and the face behind that face I shudder to describe.*'

'Who?' Howard asked. 'Why?'

'*I dare not say lest the eyes of that monstrous visage be drawn towards me and mine. I only give you a warning, and ask in exchange that you take Fantasy back with you. She will not remember the past day. Use your implicit honesty to weave some plausible lie to cover her misadventures. No one must suspect what has transpired here, for the protection of the children if nothing else.*'

Howard glanced to them, huddled together, clutching each other. 'Tell them I'm sorry.'

The Messenger turned and buzzed in the same language the girl had spoken. She nodded solemnly then walked up, placing her arms around Howard's neck and a kiss on his cheek. His neck numbed slightly where she touched him and his cheek tingled as he rubbed the kiss in.

'*When next we meet, may the circumstances be happier.*'

With that, the Messenger in Black raised its arms, rising up into a kaleidoscope of butterflies and moths, filling the sky in all directions, streaming away in all the colors of Lang's Fairy Books: Red, Blue, Yellow, Pink, Orange, Crimson, Lilac, and Violet. Even Green.

Cocamama embraced Curare, Lorra hugging Juan, and then the frog boy sprang, bearing his playmate away like some Bilbin illustration for a book of Andean folktales.

Howard looked at Asta's unconscious form, still costumed as Ondine except for the cuts on her shins and the bruises on her feet. She looked like the Little Mermaid after suffering the sea hag's curse of each footstep on land feeling like she was walking on knives.

He'd never felt the Little Mermaid deserved that till now.

December 20, 1986, en route to La Paz:

Billy Ray had located a handcuff key that unlocked the handcuffs Asta found herself in when she came to. The official story was that she'd succumbed to altitude sickness.

'So what's the real story?' Digger Downs asked. The reporter had managed it so that he was seated next to Fantasy who was seated beside Howard for this leg of the flight.

'Wasn't Billy going to sit with me?' Asta asked plaintively. 'He was so sympathetic …'

'Yeah, but someone spilled a Bloody Mary on him,' Downs told her. 'Trust me, he's going to be in the restroom for a while.'

Howard grinned. 'Story's exactly what I told you: I ditched the tour to go up to Aguas Calientes to try the hot springs. Hotel beds have been wrecking my back. Came out and found Asta wandering around in a daze with altitude sickness.'

'In handcuffs.'

Fantasy glared at him. 'If any of that hits the papers, I'll sue.'

'Freedom of the press,' Downs countered. 'Bigger question is, were they yours?'

She slapped him.

Downs rubbed his cheek. 'Can I take that as a yes?'

Asta quivered with rage. 'I'm the Prima Ballerina for the American Ballet Company! I know powerful people in New York! And I can have them squash you like a bug!'

She looked a bit troubled as she said the last, then Downs echoed, 'Like a bug?'

Asta looked more troubled, then sneezed. A dusting of iridescent white powder came out her nose, sparkling like the scales of moth wings.

She reached for a tissue and began to wipe it off, mortified. 'Don't you dare …' she threatened. 'One word …'

'One word and I'll be out of a job, because puppies are trained on yesterday's newspapers, and you and your little Studio 54 habit? Old news, sheila. Old news.' Downs laughed. 'Only thing that might make it sell is if you got into some interesting nookie. Did you two….' He waggled his finger between her and Howard.

Asta's expression went from mortified to revolted. 'Me and ... oh now you've gone from vile to simply ridiculous.' She turned to Howard and added, 'No offense meant. You were very kind, and I'm certain you have many stellar qualities, but simple logistics ...' She shook her head, unbuckled her seatbelt, and got up and stalked towards the front of the cabin. 'I'm finding Billy.'

Downs peered after her. 'I smell there's a story here, because I believe her but I don't believe you, mate.' He glanced across the aisle to Howard. 'And that doesn't match up.' He tapped his finger to the side of his nose. 'But I'm probably overthinking it. I'm guessing that Fantasy couldn't resist the all-you-can-snort coke buffet that was Peru and went to Aguas Caliente, and while you were there, you had every guy's Fantasy – and by every guy's Fantasy, I mean every guy. Am I right, mate?'

'Maybe,' Howard chuckled, 'but a gentleman never tells.'

THE TINT OF HATRED

PART THREE

Tuesday, December 23, 1986, Rio:

Sara detested Rio.

From her room in the Luxor Hotel on Atlantica, the city looked like a curving Miami Beach: a display of gleaming, white high-rise hotels arrayed before a wide beach and gentle blue-green surf, all fading into a sun-hazed distance on either side.

The majority of the junket had fulfilled their obligations quickly and were using the Rio stopover for R&R. After all, it was almost the holidays; a month on the tour had worn the idealism off most of them. Hiram Worchester had gone on a binge, eating and drinking his way through the city's myriad *restaurante*. The press had opted for the local *cervezaria* and were sampling the native beers. American dollars exchanged into handfuls of *cruzados* and prices were low. The wealthier of the contingent had invested in the Brazilian gem market – there seemed to be a jewelry stall in every hotel.

And yet Sara was aware of the reality. The standard tourist warnings were indication enough: Don't wear any jewelry on the streets; don't get on the buses, don't trust the taxi drivers; be careful around children or any jokers; don't go out alone, especially if you're a woman; if you want to keep something, lock it up or stay with it. Beware. To Rio's multitudes of poor, any tourist was rich and the rich were fair game.

And reality intruded as, bored and restless, she left the hotel that afternoon, deciding to go see Tachyon at a local clinic. She hailed one of the ubiquitous black-and-yellow VW Beetle cabs. Two blocks in from the ocean, glittering Rio turned dark, mountainous, crowded, and miserable. Through the narrow alleys between buildings she could glimpse the old landmark, Corcovado, the gigantic statue of Christ the Redeemer atop a central peak of the city. Corcovado was a reminder of how the Wild Card had devastated this country. Rio had suffered a major outbreak in 1948. The city had always been wild and poor, with a downtrodden population simmering under the veneer. The virus had let loose months of panic and violence. No one knew which disgruntled ace was responsible for Corcovado. One morning the figure of Christ had simply 'changed,' as if the rising sun were melting a wax figurine. Christ the Redeemer became a joker, a misshapen, hunch-backed *thing*, one of his outstretched arms gone completely, the other twisted around to support the distorted body. Father Squid had celebrated a mass there yesterday; two hundred thousand people had prayed together under the deformed statue.

She'd told the taxi driver to take her to Santa Theresa, the old section of Rio. There, the jokers had gathered as they had gathered in New York's Jokertown, as if taking solace in their mutual afflictions in the shadow of Corcovado. Santa Theresa had been in the warnings too. Near Estrada de Redentor she tapped the driver on the shoulder. 'Stop here,' she said. The driver said something in rapid Portuguese, then shook his head and pulled over.

Sara found that this taxi driver was no different than the rest. She'd forgotten to insist that he turn on his meter when they'd left the hotel. '*Quanto custa?*' It was one of the few phrases she knew: How much? He insisted loudly that the fare was a thousand cruzados, forty dollars. Sara, exasperated and tired of constant small ripoffs, argued back in English. Finally she threw a hundred-cruzado bill at him, still far more than he should have received. He took it, then drove off with a screech of tires. '*Feliz Natal!*' he called sarcastically: Merry Christmas.

Sara flipped him the finger. It gave her little satisfaction. She began looking for the *clínica*.

It had rained that afternoon, the usual rainy-season squall that drenched the city for a few hours and then gave way to sunshine again. Even that hadn't managed to quell the stench of Rio's antiquated sewage system. Walking up the steeply inclined street, she was pursued by fetid odors. Like the others, she walked in the center of the narrow street, moving aside only if she heard a car. She quickly felt conspicuous as the sun began to fall behind the hills. Most of those around her were jokers or those too poor to live anywhere else. She saw none of the police patrols here that routinely swept the tourist streets. A fox-furred snout leered at her as someone jostled past, what looked to be a man-size snail slithered along the sidewalk to her right, a twin-headed prostitute loitered in a doorway. She'd sometimes felt paranoid in Jokertown, but the intensity was nothing like she felt here. In Jokertown she would have at least understood what the voices around her were saying, she would have known that two or three blocks over lay the relative security of Manhattan, she would have been able to call someone from a corner phone booth. Here there was nothing. She had only a vague notion of where she was. If she disappeared, it might be hours before anyone knew she was missing.

It was with distinct relief that she saw the clinic ahead and half ran to its open door.

The place hadn't changed since yesterday when the press corps had visited. It was a crowded, chaotic lunacy. The clinic smelled vile, a combination of antiseptics, disease, and human waste. The floors were filthy, the equipment antiquated, the beds mere cots packed together as closely as possible. Tachyon had howled at the appearance, then had immediately thrown himself into the fray.

He was still there, looking as if he'd never left. '*Boatarde*, Ms. Morgenstern,' he said. His satin jacket missing, his shirt-sleeves rolled halfway up his lanky arms, he was drawing a blood sample from a comatose young girl whose skin was scaled like a lizard's. 'Did you come to work or watch?'

'I thought it was a samba club.'

That gained her a small, weary smile. 'They can use help in back,' he said. '*Felicidades*.' Sara waved to Tachyon and slid between the rows of cots. Near the rear of the clinic she halted in surprise, frowning. Her breath caught.

Gregg Hartmann was crouched beside one of the cots. A joker sat there, bristling with stiff, barbed quills like those of a porcupine. A distinct animal musk came from the man. The Senator, in hospital blues, was carefully cleaning a wound on the joker's upper arm. Despite the odor, despite the patient's appearance, Sara could see only concern on his face as he worked. Hartmann saw Sara and smiled. 'Ms. Morgenstern. Hello.'

'Senator.'

He shook his head. 'You don't need to be so damn formal. It's Gregg. Please.' She could see fatigue in the lines around his eyes, in the huskiness of his voice; he'd evidently been here for some time. Since Mexico, Sara had avoided situations that might leave the two of them alone. But she'd watched him, wishing she could sort out her feelings, wishing that she didn't feel a confused liking for the man. She'd observed how he interacted with others, how he responded to them, and she wondered. Her mind told her that she may have misjudged him; her emotions tore her in two directions at once.

He was looking at her, patient and genial. She ran her hand through her short hair and nodded. 'Gregg, then. And I'm Sara. Tachyon sent me back here.'

'Great. This is Mariu, who was on the wrong end of somebody's knife.' Gregg indicated the joker, who stared at Sara with unblinking, feral intensity. His pupils were reddish, and his lips were drawn back in a snarl. The joker said nothing, either unwilling or unable to talk.

'I guess I should find something to do.' Sara looked around, wanting to leave.

'I could use an extra pair of hands with Mariu here.'

No, she wanted to say. *I don't want to know you. I don't want to have to say I was wrong.* Belatedly Sara shook her head. 'Umm, okay. Sure. What do you want me to do?'

They worked together silently. The wound had been stitched earlier. Gregg cleaned it gently as Sara held the prickly barbs away. He smeared antibiotic ointment on the long wound, pressed gauze to it. Sara noticed most that his touch was gentle, if clumsy. He bound the dressing and stepped back. 'Okay, you're done, Mariu.' Gregg patted the joker carefully on the shoulder. The spiny face nodded slightly, then Mariu padded away without a word. Sara found Gregg looking at her, sweating in the heat of the clinic. 'Thanks.'

'You're welcome.' She took a step back from him, uncomfortable. 'You did a good job with Mariu.'

Gregg laughed. He held out his hands, and Sara saw angry red scratches scattered over them. 'Mariu gave me lots of problems until you showed up. I'm strictly amateur help here. We made a good team, though. Tachyon wanted me to unload supplies; want to give me a hand with that?'

There wasn't a graceful way to say no. They worked in silence for a time, restocking shelves. 'I didn't expect to find you here,' Sara commented as they wrestled a packing crate into a storage room.

Sara saw that he noted her unspoken words and hadn't taken offense. 'Without making sure a video camera was recording my good works, you mean?' he said, smiling. 'Ellen was out shopping with Peregrine. John and Amy had a stack of paperwork this big they wanted me to tackle.' Gregg held his hands two feet apart. 'Coming here seemed a lot more useful. Besides, Tachyon's dedication can give you a guilt complex. I left a note for Security saying I was "going out." I imagine Billy Ray's probably having a fit by now. Promise not to tell on me?'

His face was so innocently mischievous that she had to laugh with him. With the laughter a little more of the brittle hatred flaked away. 'You're a constant surprise, Senator.'

'Gregg, remember?' Softly.

'Sorry.' Her smile faded. For a moment she felt a strong pull to him. She forced the feeling down, denied it. *It's not what you want to feel. It's not real. If anything, it's a backlash reaction for having detested him for so long.* She looked around at the barren, dusty shelves of the storeroom and viciously tore open the carton.

She could feel his eyes watching her. 'You still don't believe what I said about Andrea.' His voice wavered halfway between statement and question. His words, so close to what she'd been thinking, brought sudden heat to her face.

'I'm not sure about anything.'

'And you still hate me.'

'No,' she said. She pulled Styrofoam packing from the box. And then, with sudden, impulsive honesty: 'To me that's probably more scary.'

The admission left her feeling vulnerable and open. Sara was glad that she couldn't see his face. She cursed herself for the confession. It implied attraction for Gregg; it suggested that, far from hating him, she'd come nearly full circle in her feelings, and that was simply something she didn't want him to know. Not yet. Not until she was certain.

The atmosphere between them was charged with tension. She searched for some way to blunt the effect. Gregg could wound her with a word, could make her bleed with a look.

What Gregg did then made Sara wish that she'd never seen Andrea's face on Succubus, that she hadn't spent years loathing the man.

He did nothing.

He reached over her shoulder and handed her a box of sterile bandages. 'I think they go on the top shelf,' he said.

'I think they go on the top shelf.'

Puppetman was screaming inside him, battering at the mind-bars that held him in. The power ached to be loose, to tear into Sara's opened mind and feed there. The hatred that had rebuffed him in New York was gone, and he could *see* Sara's affection; he tasted it, like blood-salt. Radiant, warm vermilion.

So easy, Puppetman moaned. *It would be easy. It's rich, full. We could make that an overwhelming tide. You could take her here. She would beg you for release, she would give you whatever you asked of her – pain, submission, anything, Please ...*

Gregg could barely hold back the power. He'd never felt it so needy, so frantic. He'd known this would be the danger of the trip. Puppetman, that power inside him, would have to feed, and Puppetman only fed on torment and suffering, all the black-red and angry emotions. In New York and Washington it was easy. There were always puppets there, minds he'd found and opened so that he could use them later. Cattle, fodder for the power. There it was easy to slip away unseen, to stalk carefully and then pounce.

Not here. Not on this trip. Absences were conspicuous and needed explanations. He had to be cautious; he had to let the power go hungry. He was used to feeding weekly; since the plane had left New York, he'd managed to feed only once: in Guatemala. Too long ago.

Puppetman was famished. His need could not be held back much longer.

Later, Gregg pleaded. *Remember Mariu? Remember the rich potency we saw in him? We touched him, we opened him. Reach out now – see, you can still feel him, only a block away. A few hours and we feed. But not with Sara. I wouldn't let you have Andrea or Succubus; I won't let you have Sara.*

Do you think she'd love you if she knew? Puppetman mocked. *Do you think she'd still feel affection if you told her? You think she would embrace you, kiss you, let you enter her warmth? If you really want her to love you for yourself, then tell her everything.*

Shut up! Gregg screamed back. *Shut up! You can have Mariu. Sara is mine.*

He forced the power back down. He made himself smile. It was three hours before he found an excuse to leave; he was pleased when Sara decided to stay at the clinic. Shaking from the exertion of keeping Puppetman inside, he went into the night streets.

Santa Theresa, like Jokertown, was alive at night, still vibrant with dark life. Rio herself never seemed to sleep. He could look down into the city and see a deluge of lights flowing in the valleys between the sharp mountains and spilling halfway up the slopes. It was a sight to make one stop for a moment and ponder the small beauties that, unwittingly, a sprawling humanity had made.

Gregg hardly noticed it. The lashing power inside drove him. *Mariu. Feel him. Find him.*

The joker who had brought in the bleeding Mariu had spoken a little English. Gregg overheard the story he'd told Tachyon. Mariu was crazy, he said. Ever since Cara was nice to him, he'd been bothering her. Cara's husband, João, he told Mariu to stay away, told him he was just a fucking joker. Said he'd kill Mariu if Mariu didn't leave Cara alone. Mariu wouldn't listen. He kept following Cara, scaring her. So João cut him.

Gregg had offered to dress Mariu's wound after Tachyon had stitched it up, feeling Puppetman yammering inside. He'd touched the loathsome Mariu, let the power open his mind to feel the raging boil of emotions. He'd known immediately – this would be the one.

He could sense the emanations of the open mind at the edge of his range, perhaps a half mile away. He moved through narrow, twisting streets, still dressed in the blues. Some of his intensity must have shown for he wasn't bothered. Once a crowd of children surrounded him, pulling at his pockets, but he'd looked at them and they'd gone silent, scattering into darkness. He'd moved on, closer to Mariu, until he saw the joker.

Mariu was standing outside a ramshackle, three-story apartment building, watching a window on the second floor. Gregg felt the pulsing, black rage and knew Joõ was there. Mariu's feelings for João were simple, bestial; those for Cara were more complex – a shifting, metallic respect; an azure affection laced through with veins of repressed lust. With his barbed skin Mariu had probably never had a willing lover, Gregg knew, but he could sense the fantasies in his mind. *Now, please.* Gregg took a shuddering breath. He let down the barriers. Puppetman laughed.

He stroked the surface of Mariu's mind possessively, cooing softly to himself. He removed the few restraints an uncaring society and church had put on Mariu. *Yes, be angry*, he whispered to Mariu. *Be full of devout rage. He keeps you from her. He insulted you. He hurt you. Let the fury come, let it blind you until you see nothing but its burning heat.* Mariu was moving restlessly in the street, his arms waving as if to some inner debate. Gregg watched as Puppetman amplified the frustration, the hurt, the anger, until Mariu screamed hoarsely and ran into the building. Gregg closed his eyes, leaning against a shadowed wall. Puppetman rode with Mariu, not seeing with Mariu's eyes but *feeling* with him. He heard shouts in angry Portuguese, the splintering of wood, and suddenly the rage flared up higher than before.

Puppetman was feeding now, taking sustenance from the rampant emotions. Mariu and Joao were struggling, for he could sense, deep underneath, a sensation of pain. He damped the pain down so Mariu would not notice it. The screams of a woman accompanied the shouts now, and from the twisting of Mariu's mind, Gregg knew that Cara was there too. Puppetman increased Mariu's anger until the glare of it nearly blinded him. He knew Mariu could feel nothing else now. The woman screamed louder; there was a distinct dull thud audible even in the street below. Gregg heard the sound of breaking glass and a wail: he opened his eyes to see a body strike the hood of a car and topple into the street. The body was bent at an obscene angle, the spine broken. Mariu was looking down from the window above.

Yes, that was good. That was tasty. This will taste good as well.

Puppetman let the rage slowly fade as Mariu ducked back inside. Now he toyed with the feelings for Cara. He diluted the binding respect, let the affection dim. *You need her. You've always wanted her. You looked at those hidden breasts as she walked by and wondered how they would feel, all silken and warm. You wondered at the hidden place between her legs, how it would taste, how it would feel. You knew it would be hot, slick with desire. You'd stroke yourself at night and think of her writhing underneath you, moaning as you thrust.*

Now Puppetman turned derisive, mocking, modifying passion with the residue of Mariu's anger. *And you knew that she'd never want you, not looking the way you do, not the joker with the needled quills. No. Her body couldn't be for you. She'd laugh about you,*

*making coarse jokes. When João possessed her, he'd laugh and say,
'This would never be Mariu; Mariu would never take pleasure from
me.'*

Cara screamed. Gregg heard cloth tear and felt Mariu's uncontrolled lust. He could imagine it. He could imagine him bearing
her down roughly, uncaring that his barbs gouged her unprotected
skin, looking only for release and imagined vengeance in the violent, agonizing rape.

Enough, he thought, quietly. *Let it be enough.* But Puppetman
only laughed, staying with Mariu until orgasm threw his mind
into chaos. Then Puppetman, sated himself, withdrew. He laughed
hilariously, letting Mariu's emotions drop to normal, let the joker
look in horror at what he'd done.

Already there were more shouts from the building, and Gregg
heard the sirens in the distance. He opened his eyes – gasping,
blinking – and ran.

Inside, Puppetman eased himself into his accustomed place and
quietly let Gregg place the bars around him. Satisfied, he slept.

Friday, December 26, 1986, Syria:

Misha sat bolt upright, sweat-drenched from the dream. She had
evidently cried out in fear, for Sayyid was struggling to sit up in his
own bed.

'*Wallah*, woman! What is it?' Sayyid was hewn from a heroic
mold, fully ten foot tall and muscled like a god. In repose he was
inspiring: a dark, Egyptian giant, a myth given life. Sayyid was the
weapon in Nur al-Allah's hands; terrorists such as al-Muezzin were
the hidden blades. When Sayyid stood before the faithful, towering
over all, they could see in Nur al-Allah's general the visible symbol
of Allah's protection.

In Sayyid's keen mind were the strategies that had defeated the
better-armed and supplied Israeli troops in the Golan Heights,
when the world had thought Nur al-Allah and his followers hopelessly outnumbered. He had orchestrated the rioting in Damascus
when al-Assad's ruling Ba'th Party had tried to move away from
Qu'ranic law, allowing the Nur sect to forge an alliance with the

Sunni and Alawite sects. He craftily advised Nur al-Allah to send the faithful into Beirut when the Christian Druze leaders had threatened to overthrow the reigning Islamic party. When the Swarm Mother had sent her deadly offspring to Earth the year before, it was Sayyid who had protected Nur al-Allah and the faithful. In his mind was victory. For the *jihad* Allah had given Sayyid *hikma*, divine wisdom.

It was a well-kept secret that Sayyid's heroic appearance was also a curse. Nur al-Allah had decreed that jokers were sinners, branded by God. They had fallen from *shari'a*, the true path. They were destined to be slaves of the true faithful at best; at worst they would be exterminated. It would not have been wise for anyone to see that Nur al-Allah's brilliant strategist was nearly a cripple, that Sayyid's mighty, rippling thews could barely support the crushing weight of his body. While his height had doubled, his mass had increased nearly fourfold.

Sayyid was always carefully posed. He moved slowly if at all. When he must go any distance, he rode.

Men who had seen Sayyid in the baths whispered that he was as heroically proportioned everywhere. Misha alone knew that his manhood was as crippled as the rest of him. For the failure of his appearance Sayyid could only blame Allah, and he did not dare. For his inability to stay aroused more than a few moments, he blamed Misha. Tonight, as often, her body bore the livid bruises of his heavy fists. But at least the beatings were quick. There were times when she thought his awful, suffocating weight would never rise from her.

'It is nothing,' she whispered. 'A dream. I didn't mean to wake you.'

Sayyid rubbed at his eyes, staring groggily toward her. He had brought himself to a sitting position, and he panted from the effort. 'A vision. Nur al-Allah has said—'

'My *brother* needs his sleep, as does his general. Please.'

'Why must you always oppose me, woman?' Sayyid frowned, and Misha knew that he remembered his earlier embarrassment, when in frustration he had battered her, as if he could find release in her pain. 'Tell me,' he insisted. 'I must know if it's something to tell the prophet.'

I am Kahina, she wanted to say. *I'm the one Allah has gifted. Why must you be the one to decide whether to wake Najib? It was not your vision.* But she held back the words, knowing that they led to more pain. 'It was confused,' she told him. 'I saw a man, a Russian by his dress, who handed Nur al-Allah many gifts. Then the Russian was gone, and another man – an American – came with more gifts and laid them at the prophet's feet.' Misha licked dry lips, remembering the panic of the dream. 'Then there was nothing but a feeling of terrible danger. He had gossamer strings knotted to his long fingers, and from each string dangled a person. One of his creatures came forward with a gift. The gift was for me, and yet I feared it, dreading to open the package. I ripped it open, and inside …' She shuddered. 'I … I saw only myself. I know there was more to the dream, but I woke. Yet I know, I know the gift-bearer is coming. He will be here soon.'

'An American?' Sayyid asked.

'Yes.'

'Then I know already. You dream of the plane carrying the Western infidels. The prophet will be ready for them: a month, perhaps more.'

Misha nodded, pretending to be reassured, though the terror of the dream still held her. *He was coming, and he held out his gift for her, smiling.* 'I'll tell Nur al-Allah in the morning,' she said. 'I'm sorry I disturbed your rest.'

'There's more I would talk about,' Sayyid answered.

She knew. 'Please. We're both tired.'

'I'm entirely awake now.'

'Sayyid, I wouldn't want to fail you again …'

She had hoped that would end it, yet had known it would not. Sayyid groaned to his feet. He said nothing; he never did. He lumbered across the room, breathing loudly at the exertion. She could see his huge bulk beside her bed, a darker shade against the night.

He fell more than lowered himself atop her. 'This time,' he breathed. 'This time.'

It was not this time. Misha didn't need to be Kahina to know that it would never be.

FROM *THE JOURNAL*
OF XAVIER DESMOND

December 29, 1986/Buenos Aires:

Don't cry for Jack, Argentina …

Evita's bane has come back to Buenos Aires. When the musical first played Broadway, I wondered what Jack Braun must have thought, listening to Lupone sing of the Four Aces. Now that question has even more poignance. Braun has been very calm, almost stoic, in the face of his reception here, but what must he be feeling inside?

Peron is dead, Evita even deader, even Isabel just a memory, but the Peronistas are still very much a part of the Argentine political scene. They have not forgotten. Everywhere the signs taunt Braun and invite him to go home. He is the ultimate *gringo* (do they use that word in Argentina, I wonder), the ugly but awesomely powerful American who came to the Argentine uninvited and toppled a sovereign government because he disapproved of its politics. The United States has been doing such things for as long as there has been a Latin America, and I have no doubt that these same resentments fester in many other places. The United States and even the dread 'secret aces' of the CIA are abstract concepts, however, faceless and difficult to get a fix on – Golden Boy is flesh and blood, very real and very visible, and *here*.

Someone inside the hotel leaked our room assignments, and when Jack stepped out onto his balcony the first day, he was showered with dung and rotten fruit. He has stayed inside ever since, except for official functions, but even there he is not safe. Last night as we stood in a receiving line at the Casa Rosada, the wife of a union official – a beautiful young woman, her small dark face framed by masses of lustrous black hair – stepped up to him with a sweet smile, looked straight into his eyes, and spit in his face.

It caused quite a stir, and Senators Hartmann and Lyons have filed some sort of protest, I believe. Braun himself was remarkably restrained, almost gallant. Digger was hounding him ruthlessly after the reception; he's cabling a write-up on the incident back to *Aces* and wanted a quote. Braun finally gave him something. 'I've done things I'm not proud of,' he said, 'but getting rid of Juan Peron isn't one of them.'

'Yeah, yeah,' I heard Digger tell him, 'but how did you feel when she spit on you?'

Jack just looked disgusted. 'I don't hit women,' he said. Then he walked off and sat by himself.

Downs turned to me when Braun was gone. 'I don't hit women,' he echoed in a singsong imitation of Golden Boy's voice, then added, 'What a weenie ...'

The world is too ready to read cowardice and betrayal into anything Jack Braun says and does, but the truth, I suspect, is more complex. Given his youthful appearance, it's hard to recall at times how old the Golden Boy really is – his formative years were during the Depression and World War II, and he grew up listening to the NBC Blue Network, not MTV. No wonder some of his values seem quaintly old-fashioned.

In many ways the Judas Ace seems almost an innocent, a bit lost in a world that has grown too complicated for him. I think he is more troubled than he admits by his reception here in Argentina. Braun is the last representative of a lost dream that flourished briefly in the aftermath of World War II and died in Korea and the HUAC hearings and the Cold War. They thought they could reshape the world, Archibald Holmes and his Four Aces. They had no doubts, no more than their country did. Power existed to be used, and they were supremely confident in their ability to tell the good guys from the bad guys. Their own democratic ideals and the shining purity of their intentions were all the justification they needed. For those few early aces it must have been a golden age, and how appropriate that a golden boy be at its center.

Golden ages give way to dark ages, as any student of history knows, and as all of us are currently finding out.

Braun and his colleagues could do things no one else had ever done – they could fly and lift tanks and absorb a man's mind and memories, and so they bought the illusion that they could make a real difference on a global scale, and when that illusion dissolved beneath them, they fell a very long way indeed. Since then no other ace has dared to dream as big.

Even in the face of imprisonment, despair, insanity, disgrace, and death, the Four Aces had triumphs to cling to, and Argentina was perhaps the brightest of those triumphs. What a bitter home-coming this must be for Jack Braun.

As if this was not enough, our mail caught up with us just before we left Brazil, and the pouch included a dozen copies of the new issue of *Aces* with Digger's promised feature story. The cover has Jack Braun and Mordecai Jones in profile, scowling at each other (All cleverly doctored, of course. I don't believe the two had ever met before we all got together at Tomlin) over a blurb that reads, 'The Strongest Man in the World.'

The article itself is a lengthy discussion of the two men and their public careers, enlivened by numerous anecdotes about their feats of strength and much speculation about which of the two is, indeed, the strongest man in the world.

Both of the principals seem embarrassed by the piece, Braun perhaps more acutely. Neither much wants to discuss it, and they certainly don't seem likely to settle the matter anytime soon. I understand that there has been considerable argument and even wagering back in the press compartment since Digger's piece came out (for once, Downs seems to have had an impact on his journal-istic colleagues), but the bets are likely to remain unresolved for a long time to come.

I told Downs that the story was spurious and offensive as soon as I read it. He seemed startled. 'I don't get it,' he said to me. 'What's *your* beef?'

My beef, as I explained to him, was simple. Braun and Jones are scarcely the only people to manifest superhuman strength since the advent of the wild card; in fact, that particular power is a fairly common one, ranking close behind telekinesis and telepathy in Tachyon's incidence-of-occurrence charts. It has something to do with maximizing the contractile strength of the muscles, I believe. My point is, a number of prominent jokers display augmented strength as well – just off the top of my head, I cited Elmo (the dwarf bouncer at the Crystal Palace), Ernie of Ernie's Bar & Grill, the Oddity, Quasiman … and, most notably, Howard Mueller. The Troll's strength does not perhaps equal that of Golden Boy and the Harlem Hammer, but assuredly it approaches it. None of these jokers were so much as mentioned in passing in Digger's story, although the names of a dozen other superstrong aces were dropped here and there. Why was that? I wanted to know.

I can't claim to have made much of an impression unfortunately. When I was through, Downs simply rolled his eyes and said, 'You people are so damned *touchy.*' He tried to be accommodating by telling me that if this story went over big, maybe he'd write up a sequel on the strongest *joker* in the world, and he couldn't comprehend why that 'concession' made me even angrier. And they wonder why we people are touchy …

Howard thought the whole argument was vastly amusing. Sometimes I wonder about him.

Actually my fit of pique was nothing compared to the reaction the magazine drew from Billy Ray, our security chief. Ray was one of the other aces mentioned in passing, his strength dismissed as not being truly 'major league.' Afterward he could be heard the length of the plane, suggesting that maybe Downs would like to step outside with him, seeing as how he was so minor league. Digger declined the offer. From the smile on his face I doubt that Carnifex will be getting any good press in *Aces* anytime soon.

Since then, Ray has been grousing about the story to anyone who will listen. The crux of his argument is that strength isn't everything; he may not be as strong as Braun or Jones, but he's strong enough to take either of them in a fight, and he'd be glad to put his money where his mouth is.

Personally I have gotten a certain perverse satisfaction out of this tempest in a teapot. The irony is, they are arguing about who has the most of what is essentially a minor power. I seem to recall that there was some sort of demonstration in the early seventies, when the battleship *New Jersey* was being refitted at the Bayonne Naval Supply Center over in New Jersey. The Turtle lifted the battleship telekinetically, got it out of the water by several feet, and held it there for almost half a minute. Braun and Jones lift tanks and toss automobiles about, but neither could come remotely close to what the Turtle did that day.

The simple truth is, the contractile strength of the human musculature can be increased only so much. Physical limits apply. Dr. Tachyon says there may also be limits to what the human mind can accomplish, but so far they have not been reached.

If the Turtle is indeed a joker, as many believe, I would find this irony especially satisfying.

I suppose I am, at base, as small a man as any.

THE TINT OF HATRED

PART FOUR

Thursday, January 1, 1987, South Africa:

The evening was cool. Beyond the hotel's wide veranda, the crumpled landscape of the Bushveld Basin seemed pastoral. The last light of the day edged grassy hills with lavender and burnt orange; in the valley the sluggish Olifants's brown waters were touched with gold. Among the stand of acacias lining the river monkeys settled to sleep with occasional hooting calls.

Sara looked at it and felt nausea. It was so damn beautiful, and it hid such a sickness.

There had been enough trouble even keeping the delegation together in the country. The planned New Year's celebration had been wrecked by jet lag and the hassles of getting into South Africa. When Father Squid, Xavier Desmond, and Troll had tried to eat with the others in Pretoria, the head waiter had refused to seat them, pointing to a sign in both English and Afrikaans: WHITES ONLY. 'We don't serve blacks, coloreds, or jokers,' he insisted.

Hartmann, Tachyon, and several of the other high-ranking members of the delegation had immediately protested to the Botha government; a compromise had been reached. The delegation was given the run of a small hotel on the Loskop Game Preserve; isolated, they could intermingle if they wished. The government had let it be known that they also found the idea distasteful.

When they had finally popped the champagne corks, the wine had tasted sour in all their mouths.

The junket had spent the afternoon at a ramshackle kraal, actually little more than a shantytown. There they'd seen firsthand the double-edged sword of prejudice: the new apartheid. Once it had been a two-sided struggle, the Afrikaaners and the English against the blacks, the colored, and the Asians. Now the jokers were the new Uitlanders, and both white and black spat upon them. Tachyon had looked at the filth and squalor of this jokertown, and Sara had seen his noble, sculptured face go white with rage; Gregg had looked ill. The entire delegation had turned on the National Party officials who had accompanied them from Pretoria and begun to rail at the conditions here.

The officials spouted the approved line. This is why we have the Prohibition of Mixed Marriages Act, they said, pointedly ignoring the jokers among the group. Without strict separation of the races we will only produce *more* jokers, *more* colored, and we're sure none of you want that. This is why there's an Immorality Act, a Prohibition of Political Interference Act. Let us do things our way, and we will take care of our own problems. Conditions are bad, yes, but they are getting better. You've been swayed by the African/Jokers National Congress. The AJNC is outlawed, their leader Mandela is nothing more than a fanatic, a troublemaker. The AJNC has steered you to the worst encampment they could find – if the doctor, the senators, and their colleagues had only stayed with *our* itinerary, you would have seen the other side of the coin.

All in all, the year had begun like hell.

Sara put a foot up on the railing, lowered her head until it rested on her hands, and stared at the sunset. *Everywhere. Here you can see the problems so easily, but it's not really different. It's been horrible everywhere whenever you look past the surface.*

She heard footsteps, but didn't turn around. The railing shuddered as someone stood next to her. 'Ironic, isn't it, how lovely this land can be.' Gregg's voice.

'Just what I was thinking,' Sara said. She glanced at him, and he was staring out at the hills. The only other person on the veranda was Billy Ray, reclining against the railing a discreet distance away.

'There are times when I wish the virus were more deadly, that it had simply wiped the planet clean of us and started over,' Gregg said. 'That town today …' He shook his head. 'I read the transcript you phoned in. It brought back everything. I started to get furious all over again. You've a gift for making people respond to what you're feeling, Sara. You'll do more in the long run than I will. Maybe you can do something to stop prejudice; here, and with people like Leo Barnett back home.'

'Thanks.' His hand was very near hers. She touched it softly with her own; his fingers snared hers and didn't let her go. The emotions of the day, of the entire trip, were threatening to overwhelm her; her eyes stung with tears. 'Gregg,' she said very softly, 'I'm not sure I like the way I feel.'

'About today? The jokers?'

She took a breath. The failing sun was warm on her face. 'That, yes.' She paused, wondering if she should say more. 'And about you too,' she added at last.

He didn't say anything. He waited, holding her hand and watching the nightfall. 'It's changed so fast, the way I've seen you,' Sara continued after a time. 'When I thought that you and Andrea …' She paused, her breath trembling. 'You care, you hurt when you see the way people are treated. God, I used to detest you. I saw everything that Senator Hartmann did in that light. I saw you as false and empty of compassion. Now that's gone, and I watch your face when you talk about the jokers and what we have to do to change things, and …'

She pulled him around so that they faced each other. She looked up at him, not caring that he'd see that she'd been crying. 'I'm not used to holding things inside. I like it when everything's out in the open, so forgive me if this isn't something I should say. Where you're concerned, I think I'm very vulnerable, Gregg, and I'm afraid of that.'

'I don't intend to hurt you, Sara.' His hand came up to her face. Softly he brushed moisture from the corner of her eyes.

'Then tell me where we're heading, you and I. I need to know what the rules are.'

'I …' He stopped. Sara, watching his face, saw an inner conflict. His head came down; she felt his warm, sweet breath on her cheek. His hand cupped her chin. She let him lift her face up, her eyes closing.

The kiss was soft and very gentle. Fragile. Sara turned her face away, and he brought her to him, pressing her body to his. 'Ellen …' Sara began.

'She knows,' Gregg whispered. His fingers brushed her hair. 'I've told her. She doesn't mind.'

'I didn't want this to happen.'

'It did. It's okay,' he told her.

She pushed away from him and was glad when he simply let her go. 'So what do we do about it?'

The sun had gone behind the hills; Gregg was only a shadow, his features barely visible to her. 'It's your decision, Sara. Ellen and I always take a double suite; I use the second room as my office. I'm going there now. If you want, Billy will bring you up. You can trust him, no matter what anyone's told you about him. He knows how to be discreet.'

For a moment, his hand stroked her cheek. Then he turned, walking quickly away. Sara watched him speak briefly to Ray, and then he went through the doors into the hotel's lobby. Ray remained outside.

Sara waited until full darkness had settled over the valley and the air had begun to cool from the day's heat, knowing that she'd already made the decision but not certain she wanted to follow it through. She waited, half looking for some sign in the African night. Then she went to Ray. His green eyes, set disturbingly off-line in an oddly mismatched face, seemed to look at her appraisingly.

'I'd like to go upstairs,' she said.

FROM *THE JOURNAL*
OF XAVIER DESMOND

January 16/Addis Ababa, Ethiopia:

A hard day in a stricken land. The local Red Cross representatives took some of us out to see some of their famine relief efforts. Of course we'd all been aware of the drought and the starvation long before we got here, but seeing it on television is one thing, and being here amidst it is quite another.

A day like this makes me acutely aware of my own failures and shortcomings. Since the cancer took hold of me, I've lost a good deal of weight (some unsuspecting friends have even told me how good I look), but moving among these people made me very self-conscious of the small paunch that remains. They were *starving* before my eyes, while our plane waited to take us back to Addis Ababa ... to our hotel, another reception, and no doubt a gourmet Ethiopian meal. The guilt was overwhelming, as was the sense of helplessness.

I believe we all felt it. I cannot conceive of how Hiram Worchester must have felt. To his credit he looked sick as he moved among the victims, and at one point he was trembling so badly he had to sit in the shade for a while by himself. The sweat was just pouring off him. But he got up again afterward, his face white and grim, and used his gravity power to help them unload the relief provisions we had brought with us.

So many people have contributed so much and worked so hard

for the relief effort, but here it seems like nothing. The only realities in the relief camps are the skeletal bodies with their massive swollen bellies, the dead eyes of the children, and the endless heat pouring down from above onto this baked, parched landscape.

Parts of this day will linger in my memory for a long time – or at least as long a time as I have left to me. Father Squid gave the last rites to a dying woman who had a Coptic cross around her neck. Peregrine and her cameraman recorded much of the scene on film for her documentary, but after a short time she had had enough and returned to the plane to wait for us. I've heard that she was so sick she lost her breakfast.

And there was a young mother, no more than seventeen or eighteen surely, so gaunt that you could count every rib, with eyes incredibly ancient. She was holding her baby to a withered, empty breast. The child had been dead long enough to begin to smell, but she would not let them take it from her. Dr. Tachyon took control of her mind and held her still while he gently pried the child's body from her grasp and carried it away. He handed it to one of the relief workers and then sat on the ground and began to weep, his body shaking with each sob.

Mistral ended the day in tears as well. En route to the refugee camp, she had changed into her blue-and-white flying costume. The girl is young, an ace, and a powerful one; no doubt she thought she could help. When she called the winds to her, the huge cape she wears fastened at wrist and ankle ballooned out like a parachute and pulled her up into the sky. Even the strangeness of the jokers walking between them had not awakened much interest in the inward-looking eyes of the refugees, but when Mistral took flight, most of them – not, all, but most – turned to watch, and their gaze followed her upward into that high, hot blueness until finally they sank back into the lethargy of despair. I think Mistral had dreamed that somehow her wind powers could push the clouds around and make the rains come to heal this land. And what a beautiful, vainglorious dream it was …

She flew for almost two hours, sometimes so high and far that she vanished from our sight, but for all her ace powers, all she could raise was a dust devil. When she gave up at last, she was exhausted, her sweet young face grimy with dust and sand, her eyes red and swollen.

Just before we left, an atrocity underscored the depth of the despair here. A tall youth with acne scars on his cheeks attacked a fellow refugee – went berserk, gouged out a woman's eye, and actually *ate* it while the people watched without comprehension. Ironically we'd met the boy briefly when we'd first arrived – he'd spent a year in a Christian school and had a few words of English. He seemed stronger and healthier than most of the others we saw. When Mistral flew, he jumped to his feet and called out after her. 'Jetboy!' he said in a very clear, strong voice. Father Squid and Senator Hartmann tried to talk to him, but his English-language skills were limited to a few nouns, including 'chocolate,' 'television,' and 'Jesus Christ.' Still, the boy was more alive than most – his eyes went wide at Father Squid, and he put out a hand and touched his facial tendrils wonderingly and actually smiled when the senator patted his shoulder and told him that we were here to help, though I don't think he understood a word. We were all shocked when we saw them carrying him away, still screaming, those gaunt brown cheeks smeared with blood.

A hideous day all around. This evening back in Addis Ababa our driver swung us by the docks, where relief shipments stand two stories high in some places. Hartmann was in a cold rage. If anyone can make this criminal government take action and feed its starving people, he is the one. I pray for him, or would, if I believed in a god ... but what kind of god would permit the obscenities we have seen on this trip ...

Africa is as beautiful a land as any on the face of the earth. I should write of all the beauty we have seen this past month. Victoria Falls, the snows of Kilimanjaro, a thousand zebra moving through the tall grass as if the wind had stripes. I've walked among the ruins of proud ancient kingdoms whose very names were unknown to me, held pygmy artifacts in my hand, seen the face of a bushman light up with curiosity instead of horror when he beheld me for the first time. Once during a visit to a game preserve I woke early, and when I looked out of my window at the dawn, I saw that two huge African elephants had come to the very building, and Radha stood between them, naked in the early morning light, while they touched her with their trunks. I turned away then; it seemed somehow a private moment.

Beauty, yes – in the land and in so many of the people, whose faces are full of warmth and compassion.

Still, for all that beauty, Africa has depressed and saddened me considerably, and I will be glad to leave. The camp was only part of it. Before Ethiopia there was Kenya and South Africa. It is the wrong time of year for Thanksgiving, but the scenes we have witnessed these past few weeks have put me more in the mood for giving thanks than I've ever felt during America's smug November celebration of football and gluttony. Even jokers have things to give thanks for. I knew that already, but Africa has brought it home to me forcefully.

South Africa was a grim way to begin this leg of the trip. The same hatreds and prejudices exist at home of course, but whatever our faults we are at least civilized enough to maintain a facade of tolerance, brotherhood, and equality under the law. Once I might have called that mere sophistry, but that was before I tasted the reality of Capetown and Pretoria, where all the ugliness is out in the open, enshrined by law, enforced by an iron fist whose velvet glove has grown thin and worn indeed. It is argued that at least South Africa hates openly, while America hides behind a hypocritical facade. Perhaps, perhaps ... but if so, I will take the hypocrisy and thank you for it.

I suppose that was Africa's first lesson, that there are worse places in the world than Jokertown. The second was that there are worse things than repression, and Kenya taught us that.

Like most of the other nations of Central and East Africa, Kenya was spared the worst of the wild card. Some spores would have reached these lands through airborne diffusion, more through the seaports, arriving via contaminated cargo in holds that had been poorly sterilized or never sterilized at all. CARE packages are looked on with deep suspicion in much of the world, and with good reason, and many captains have become quite adept at concealing the fact that their last port of call was New York City.

When one moves inland, wild card cases become almost non-existent. There are those who say that the late Idi Amin was some kind of insane joker-ace, with strength as great as Troll or the Harlem Hammer, and the ability to transform into some kind of were-creature, a leopard or a lion or a hawk. Amin himself claimed to be able to ferret out his enemies telepathically, and those few enemies who survived say that he was a cannibal who felt human flesh was necessary to maintain his powers. All this is the stuff of rumor and propaganda, however, and whether Amin was a joker, an ace, or a pathetically deluded nat madman, he is assuredly dead, and in this corner of the world, documented cases of the wild card virus are vanishingly hard to locate.

But Kenya and the surrounding nations have their own viral nightmare. If the wild card is a chimera here, AIDS is an epidemic. While the president was hosting Senator Hartmann and most of the tour, a few of us were on an exhausting visit to a half-dozen clinics in rural Kenya, hopping from one village to another by helicopter. They assigned us only one battered chopper, and that at Tachyon's insistence. The government would have much preferred that we spend our time lecturing at the university, meeting with educators and political leaders, touring game preserves and museums.

Most of my fellow delegates were only too glad to comply. The wild card is forty years old, and we have grown used to it – but AIDS, that is a new terror in the world, and one that we have only begun to understand. At home it is thought of as a homosexual affliction, and I confess that I am guilty of thinking of it that way myself, but here in Africa, that belief is given the lie. Already there are more AIDS victims on this continent alone than have ever been infected by the Takisian xenovirus since its release over Manhattan forty years ago.

And AIDS seems a crueler demon somehow. The wild card kills ninety percent of those who draw it, often in ways that are terrible and painful, but the distance between ninety percent and one hundred is not insignificant if you are among the ten who live. It is the distance between life and death, between hope and despair. Some claim that it's better to die than to live as a joker, but you will not find me among their number. If my own life has not always been happy, nonetheless I have memories I cherish and accomplishments I am proud of. I am glad to have lived, and I do not want to die. I've accepted my death, but that does not mean I welcome it. I have too much unfinished business. Like Robert Tomlin, I have not yet seen *The Jolson Story*. None of us have.

In Kenya we saw whole villages that are dying. Alive, smiling, talking, capable of eating and defecating and making love and even babies, alive to all practical purposes – and yet dead. Those who draw the Black Queen may die in the agony of unspeakable transformations, but there are drugs for pain, and at least they die quickly. AIDS is less merciful.

We have much in common, jokers and AIDS victims. Before I left Jokertown, we had been planning for a JADL fund-raising benefit at the Funhouse in late May – a major event with as much big-name entertainment as we could book. After Kenya I cabled instructions back to New York to arrange for the proceeds of the benefit to be split with a suitable AIDS victims' group. We pariahs need to stick together. Perhaps I can still erect a few necessary bridges before my own Black Queen lies face up on the table.

DOWN BY THE NILE

Gail Gerstner-Miller

The torches in the temple burned slowly, steadily, occasionally flickering when someone passed by. Their light illuminated the faces of the people gathered in a small antechamber off the main hall. They were all present, those who looked like ordinary people, and the others who were extraordinary: the cat woman, the jackal-headed man, those with wings, crocodile skin, and bird heads.

Osiris the far-seer spoke. 'The winged one comes.'

'Is she one of us?'

'Will she help us?'

'Not directly,' Osiris answered. 'But within her is that which will have the power to do great things. For now we must wait.'

'We have waited a very long time,' said Anubis the jackal. 'A little longer will not make a difference.'

The others murmured in agreement. The living gods settled back to patiently wait.

The room in Luxor's Winter Palace Hotel was sweltering, and it was still only morning. The ceiling fan stirred the sluggish air tiredly and sweat ran in tickling rivulets over Peregrine's rib cage and breasts as she lay propped up in bed, watching Josh McCoy slip a new film cassette into his camera. He looked at her and smiled.

'We'd better get going,' he said.

She smiled back lazily from the bed, her wings moving gently, bringing more coolness into the room than the slow-moving fan.

'If you say so.' She stood, stretched lithely, and watched McCoy watch her. She walked by him, dancing out of his way as he reached for her. 'Haven't you had enough yet?' she asked teasingly as she took a clean pair of jeans from her suitcase. She wiggled into them, batting her wings to keep her balance. 'The hotel laundry must have washed these in boiling water.' She took a deep breath and pulled on the stubborn zipper. 'There.'

'They look great, though,' McCoy said. He put his arms around her from behind, and Peregrine shivered as he kissed the back of her neck and caressed her breasts, still sensitive from their morning lovemaking.

'I thought you said we had to get going.' She settled back against him.

McCoy sighed and pulled away reluctantly. 'We do. We have to meet the others in' – he checked his wristwatch – 'three minutes.'

'Too bad,' Peregrine said, smiling mischievously. 'I think I could be coaxed into spending all day in bed.'

'Work awaits,' McCoy said, rummaging for his clothes as Peregrine put on a tank top. 'And I'm anxious to see if these self-proclaimed living gods can do all they claim.'

She watched him as he dressed, admiring his lean, muscular body. He was blond and fit, a documentary filmmaker and camera-man, and a wonderful lover.

'Got everything? Don't forget your hat. The sun's fierce, even if it is winter.'

'I've got everything I need,' Peregrine said with a sidelong glance. 'Let's go.'

McCoy turned the DO NOT DISTURB sign hanging on the door handle to the other side, then closed and locked the door. The hotel corridor was quiet and deserted. Tachyon must have heard their muffled footsteps, because he poked his head out as they passed his room.

'Morning, Tachy,' Peregrine said. 'Josh, Father Squid, Hiram, and I are going to catch the afternoon ceremony at the Temple of the Living Gods. Want to come along?'

'Good morning, my dear.' Tachyon, looking resplendent in a white brocade dressing gown, nodded distantly to McCoy. 'No, thank you. I'll see everything I need to see at the meeting tonight. Right now it's much too hot to venture out.' Tachyon looked closely at her. 'Are you feeling all right? You look pale.'

'I think the heat's getting to me too,' Peregrine replied. 'That and the food and water. Or rather the microbes that live in them.'

'We don't need you getting sick,' Tachyon said seriously. 'Come in and let me do a quick examination.' He fanned his face. 'We'll find out what's bothering you, and it will give me something useful to do with my day.'

'We don't have the time right now. The others are waiting for us—'

'Peri,' McCoy interrupted, a concerned look on his face, 'it'll only take a few minutes. I'll go downstairs and tell Hiram and Father Squid you've been delayed.' She hesitated. 'Please,' he added.

'Oh, all right.' She smiled at him. 'I'll see you downstairs.'

McCoy nodded and continued down the hallway as Peregrine followed Tachyon into his ornately appointed suite. The sitting room was spacious, and much cooler than the room she shared with McCoy. Of course, she reflected, they had generated a lot of heat themselves that morning.

'Wow,' she commented, glancing around the luxuriously decorated room. 'I must have gotten the servants' quarters.'

'It's really something, isn't it? I especially like the bed.' Tachyon pointed to a large four-poster draped with white netting that was visible through the bedroom's open door. 'You have to climb steps to get into it.'

'What fun!'

He glanced at her mischievously. 'Want to try it out?'

'No, thanks. I've already had my morning sex.'

'Peri,' Tachyon complained in a teasing tone, 'I don't understand why you're attracted to that man.' He retrieved his red leather medical bag from the closet. 'Sit there,' he said, indicating a plush velvet wingback chair, 'and open your mouth. Say *ahhh*.'

'*Ahh*,' Peregrine repeated obediently after seating herself.

Tachyon peered down her throat. 'Well, that looks nice and healthy.' He swiftly examined her ears and looked into her eyes. 'Seems okay. Tell me about your symptoms.' He removed his stethoscope from his bag. 'Nausea, vomiting, dizziness?'

'Some nausea and vomiting.'

'When? After you eat?'

'No, not really. Anytime.'

'Do you get sick every day?'

'No. Maybe a couple times a week.'

'*Hmmmm*.' He lifted her shirt up and held his stethoscope against her left breast. She jumped at the touch of cold steel against her warm flesh. 'Sorry ... heartbeat is strong and regular. How long has this vomiting been occurring?'

'A couple of months, I guess. Since before the tour started. I thought it was stress related.'

He frowned. 'You've been vomiting for a couple of months, and you didn't see fit to consult me? I am your doctor.'

She squirmed uncomfortably. 'Tachy, you've been so busy. I didn't want to bother you. I think it's all the traveling, the food, different water, different standards of hygiene.'

'Allow *me* to make the diagnosis, if you please, young lady. Are you getting enough sleep, or is your new boyfriend keeping you up all hours?'

'I'm getting to bed early every night,' she assured him.

'I'm certain you are,' he said drily. 'But that wasn't what I asked. Are you getting enough sleep?'

Peregrine blushed. 'Of course I am.'

Tachyon replaced his equipment in his bag. 'How's your menstrual cycle? Any problems?'

'Well, I haven't had a period in a while, but that's not unusual, even though I'm on the pill.'

'Peri, please try to be a little more precise. How long is "a while"?'

She bit her lip and waved her wings gently. 'I don't know, a couple of months, I guess.'

'*Hmmmmm*. Come here.' He led her into his bedroom, and her wings instinctively curled over her body. The air conditioner was going full blast and it felt about twenty degrees cooler. Tachyon gestured at the bed. 'Take off your jeans and lie down.'

'Are you sure this is a medical examination?' she asked him teasingly.

'Do you want me to call a chaperon?'

'Don't be silly. I trust you!'

'You shouldn't,' Tachyon leered. He raised an eyebrow as Peregrine kicked off her Nikes and peeled off her jeans. 'Don't you wear underwear?'

'Never. It gets in the way. Do you want me to take off my shirt too?'

'If you do, you may never leave this room!' Tachyon threatened.

She laughed and kissed his cheek. 'What's the big deal? You've examined me a million times.'

'In the proper surroundings, with you in a medical gown and a nurse in the room,' he retorted. 'Never with you naked, almost naked,' he corrected, 'in my bedroom.' He tossed her a towel. 'Here, cover yourself.'

Tachyon admired her long, tanned legs and shapely buttocks as she arranged herself on his bed, draping the towel discreetly over her hips. The blast of refrigerated air coming from the laboring air conditioner raised goosebumps all over her, but Tachyon ignored them.

'Your hands better be warm,' Peregrine warned as he knelt next to her.

'Just like my heart,' Tachyon said, palpating her stomach. 'Does this hurt?'

'No.'

'Here? Here?'

She shook her head.

'Don't move,' he ordered. 'I need my stethoscope.' This time he warmed the metal head with his hand before placing it on her stomach. 'Have you had much indigestion?'

'Some.'

A strange expression crossed Tachyon's foxy face as he assisted her off the bed. 'Get your jeans on. I'll take a blood sample, and then you can go play tourist with the others.'

He got the syringe ready while she finished tying her track shoes. Peregrine held out her arm, winced as he expertly raised the vein, swabbed the skin above it, inserted the syringe, and withdrew the blood. She watched in fascination and suddenly realized that the sight of blood was making her ill.

'Shit.' She ran into the bedroom, leaving behind a flurry of feathers, and leaned over the toilet vomiting up her room service breakfast and what was left of last night's dinner and champagne.

Tachyon held her shoulders while she was sick, and as she sagged against the tub, exhausted, wiped her face with a warm, wet washcloth.

'Are you all right?'

'I think so.' He helped her to her feet. 'It was the blood. Although the sight of blood has never bothered me before.'

'Peregrine, I don't think that you should go sight-seeing this morning. The place for you is bed, alone, with a cup of hot tea.'

'No,' she protested. 'I'm fine. It's just all this traveling. If I feel sick, Josh will bring me back here.'

'I'll never understand women.' He shook his head sadly. 'To prefer a mere human when you could have me. Come here and I'll bandage that hole I put in your arm.' He busied himself with sterile gauze and tape.

Peregrine smiled gently. 'You're sweet, Doctor, but your heart is buried in the past. I'm getting to the point now that I'm ready for a permanent relationship, and I don't think you would give me that.'

'And he can?'

She shrugged, her wings moving with her shoulders. 'I hope so. We'll see, won't we?'

She picked up her bag and hat from the chair and walked to the door.

'Peri, I wish you would reconsider.'

'What? Sleeping with you or sight-seeing?'

'Sight-seeing, wicked one.'

'I'm fine now. Please stop worrying. Honestly, I've never had so many people worrying about me as on this trip.'

'That's because, my dear, under your New York glamour, you're incredibly vulnerable. You make people want to protect you.' He opened the door for her. 'Be careful with McCoy, Peri. I don't want you to get hurt.'

She kissed him as she left the room. Her wings brushed the doorway and a flurry of fine feathers fell to the floor.

'Damn,' she said, stooping and picking one up. 'I seem to be losing a lot of these lately.'

'Indeed?' Tachyon looked curious. 'No, don't bother with them. The maid will clean them up.'

'Okay. Good-bye. Have fun with your tests.'

Tachyon's eyes were worried as they followed Peregrine's graceful body down the hallway. He closed the door, one of her feathers in his hand.

'This doesn't look good,' he said aloud as he tickled his chin with her feather. 'Not good at all.'

Peregrine spotted McCoy in the lobby talking to a stocky, dark man in a white uniform. Her two other companions were lounging nearby. Hiram Worchester, she reflected, was looking a little haggard. Hiram, one of Peregrine's oldest and dearest friends, was dressed in one of his custom-made tropical-weight suits, but it hung loosely on him, almost as if he had lost some of his three hundred plus pounds. Perhaps he was feeling the strain of constant traveling as much as she was. Father Squid, the kindly pastor of the Church of Jesus Christ, Joker, made Hiram look almost svelte. He was as tall as a normal man and twice as broad. His face was round and gray, his eyes were covered by nictitating membranes, and a cluster of tentacles hung down over his mouth like a constantly twitching mustache. He always reminded her of one of Lovecraft's fictional Deep Ones, but he was actually much nicer.

'Peri,' said McCoy. 'This is Mr. Ahmed. He's with the Tourist Police. Mr. Ahmed, this is Peregrine.'

'This is a pleasure,' said the guide, bending to kiss her hand.

Peregrine responded with a smile and then greeted Hiram and the priest. She turned to Josh, who was watching her closely. 'You okay?' Josh asked. 'You look awful. What did Tachyon do, take a quart of blood?'

'Of course not. I'm fine,' she said, following Ahmed and the others to the waiting limo. And if I keep saying that, she said to herself, maybe I'll even believe it.

'What on earth?' exclaimed Peregrine as they stopped in front of a metal-and-glass guard station. There were two heavily armed men inside the box, which stood next to a high wall that surrounded several acres of desert that was the Temple of the Living Gods. The whitewashed wall was topped with strands of barbed wire and patrolled by men dressed in blue and armed with machine guns. Video cameras tirelessly surveyed the perimeter. The effect of the pure white wall against the shining sand and bright blue Egyptian sky was dazzling.

'Because of the Nur,' explained Ahmed, pointing to the line of tourists waiting to enter the temple grounds, 'everyone has to pass through two detectors, one for metal and the other for nitrates. These fanatics are determined to destroy the temple and the gods. They have already made several attacks against the temple, but so far they've been stopped before doing much damage.'

'Who are the Nur?' Father Squid asked.

'They are the followers of Nur al-Allah, a false prophet determined to unite all Islamic sects under himself,' Ahmed said. 'He has decided that Allah desires the destruction of all those deformed by the wild card virus, and so the Temple of the Living Gods has become one of his sect's targets.'

'Do we have to wait in line with the tourists?' Hiram broke in peevishly. 'After all, we are here by special invitation.'

'Oh, no, Mr. Worchester,' Ahmed hurriedly answered. 'The VIP gate is this way. You will go right through. If you please …'

As they lined up behind Ahmed, McCoy whispered to Peregrine, 'I've never been through a VIP gate, only press gates.'

'Stick with me,' she promised. 'I'll take you lots of places you've never been before.'

'You already have.'

The VIP gate had its own metal and nitrate detectors. They passed through, watched closely by security guards dressed in the blue robes worn by adherents of the living gods, who thoroughly examined Peregrine's bag and McCoy's camera. An elderly man approached as McCoy's equipment was being returned. He was short, deeply tanned and healthy looking, with gray eyes, white hair, and a magnificent white beard that contrasted nicely with his flowing blue robes.

'I am Opet Kemel,' he announced. His voice was deep, mellifluous, and he knew how to use it to demand attention and respect. 'I am the head priest of the Temple of the Living Gods. We are gratifed that you could grace us with your presence.' He looked from Father Squid to Peregrine, Hiram, and McCoy, and then back to Peregrine. 'Yes, my children will be glad that you have come.'

'Do you mind if we film the ceremony?' asked Peregrine.

'Not at all.' He gestured expansively. 'Come this way and I'll show you the best seats in the house.'

'Can you give us some background on the temple?' Peregrine asked.

'Certainly,' Kemel replied as they followed him. 'The Port Said wild card epidemic of 1948 caused many "mutations," I believe they're called, among them of course, the celebrated *Nasr* – Al Haziz, Khôf and other great heroes of past years. Many men of Luxor were working on the Said docks at the time and were also affected by the virus. Some passed it on to their children and grandchildren.

'The true meaning of these mutations struck me over a decade ago when I saw a young boy make clouds drop much-needed rain over his father's fields. I realized that he was an incarnation of Min, the ancient god of crops, and that his presence was a harbinger of the old religion.

'I was an archaeologist then and had just discovered an intact temple complex' – he pointed at their feet – 'beneath the ground right where we stand. I convinced Min of his destiny and found others to join us: Osiris, a man pronounced dead who returned to life with visions of the future; Anubis, Taurt, Thoth … Through the years they have all come to the Temple of the Living Gods to listen to the prayers of their petitioners and perform miracles.'

'Exactly what kind of miracles?' Peregrine asked.

'Many kinds. For example, if a woman with child is having a difficult time, she will pray to Taurt, goddess of pregnancy and childbirth. Taurt will assure that all will be fine. And it will be. Thoth settles disputes, knowing who tells the truth and who lies. Min, as I have said, can make it rain. Osiris sees bits of the future. It's all quite simple.'

'I see.' Kemel's claims seemed reasonable, given the abilities that Peregrine knew the virus could waken in people. 'How many gods are there?'

'Perhaps twenty-five. Some cannot really do anything,' Kemel said in confiding tones. 'They are what you call jokers. However, they look like the old gods – Bast, for example, is covered with fur and has claws – and they give great comfort to the people who come to pray to them. But see for yourselves. The ceremony is almost ready to begin.'

He led them past groups of tourists posing next to statues of the gods, booths that sold everything from Kodak film, key rings, and Coca-Cola to replicas of antique jewelry and little statuettes of the gods themselves. They went past the booths, through a narrow doorway into a sandstone block wall set flush against a cliff face, and then down worn stone steps. Goosebumps rose on Peregrine's skin. It was cool inside the structure, which was lit by electric lights that resembled flickering torches. The stairwell was beautifully decorated with bas-relief carvings of everyday life in ancient Egypt, intricately detailed hieroglyphic inscriptions, and representations of animals, birds, gods, and goddesses.

'What a wonderful job of restoration!' Peregrine exclaimed, enchanted by the beautiful freshness of the reliefs they passed.

'Actually,' Kemel explained, 'everything here is just as it was when I discovered it twenty years ago. We added some modern conveniences, like the electricity, of course.' He smiled.

They entered a large chamber, an amphitheater with a stage faced by banked stone benches. The walls of the chamber were lined with glass cases displaying artifacts that, Kemel said, had been discovered in the temple.

McCoy meticulously recorded them, shooting several minutes of footage of painted wooden statues that looked as fresh as if they had been painted the day before, necklaces, collars, and pectorals of lapis lazuli, emerald, and gold, chalices carved of translucent alabaster, unguent jars of jade intricately carved in the shapes of animals, elaborately inlaid tiny chests, and gaming boards, and chairs ... The exquisite treasures of a dead civilization were displayed before them, a civilization that, Peregrine reflected, Opet Kemel seemed, with his Temple of the Living Gods, to restore.

'Here we are.' Kemel indicated a group of benches at the front of the amphitheater close to the stage, bowed slightly, and departed.

It didn't take long for the amphitheater to fill. The lights dimmed and the theater became silent. A spotlight shone on the stage, strange music that sounded as old and eerie as the temple itself softly played, and the procession of the living gods began. There was Osiris, the god of death and resurrection, and his consort Isis. Behind him came Hapi, carrying a golden standard. Thoth, the ibis-headed judge, followed with his pet baboon. Shu and Tefnut, brother and sister, god and goddess of the air, floated above the floor. Sobek followed them with his dark, cracked crocodile skin and snoutlike mouth. Hathor, the great mother, had the horns of a cow. Bast, the cat-goddess, moved delicately, her face and body covered with tawny fur, claws protruding from her fingers. Min looked like an ordinary man, but a small cloud hovered above him, following him like an obedient puppy wherever he went. Bes, the handsome dwarf, did cartwheels and walked on his hands. Anubis, the god of the underworld, had the head of a jackal. Horus had falconlike wings ...

On and on they came, crossing the stage slowly and then seating themselves on gilded thrones as they were presented to the audience in English, French, and Arabic.

After the introductions the gods began to demonstrate their abilities. Shu and Tefnut were gliding in the air, playing tag with Min's cloud, when the unexpected, deafening sound of gunfire shattered the peaceful scene, evoking screams of terror from the spectators trapped in the amphitheater. Hundreds of tourists leapt up and milled about like terrified cattle. Some bolted for the doors at the back, and the stairways soon became clogged by panicked, shrieking people. McCoy, who had pushed Peregrine to the ground and covered her with his body at the first sound of gunfire, dragged her behind one of the large, elaborately carved stone pillars flanking the stage.

'You okay?' he gasped, peering around the column at the sounds of madness and destruction, his camera whirring.

'Uh-huh. What is it?'

'Three guys with machine guns.' His hands were steady and there was an edge of excitement in his voice. 'They don't seem to be shooting at the people, just the walls.'

A bullet whined off the pillar. The sound of shattering glass filled the air as the terrorists destroyed the cases filled with the priceless artifacts and raked the beautifully carved walls with machine-gun fire.

The living gods had fled when the first shot sounded. Only one remained behind, the man who had been introduced as Min. As Peregrine peeked around the pillar, a cloud appeared from nowhere to hang over the terrorists' heads. It started to rain torrents upon them, and slipping and sliding on the wet stone floor, they scattered, trying to find cover from the blinding cloudburst. Peregrine, digging in her bag for her metal talons, noticed Hiram Worchester standing alone, a look of fierce concentration on his face. One of the attackers gave a distressed shout as his gun slipped from his hands and landed on his foot. He collapsed, screaming, blood spattering from his shattered limb. Hiram turned his gaze to the second terrorist as Peregrine pulled on her guantlets.

'I'm going to try to get above them,' she told McCoy.

'Be careful,' he said, intent on filming the action.

She flexed her fingers, now encased in leather gauntlets tipped with razor-edged titanium claws. Her wings quivered in anticipation as she took a half-dozen running steps, then beat thunderously as she hurled herself forward and launched herself into the air—

– and fell jarringly to the floor.

She caught herself on her hands and knees, skinning her palms on the rough stones and banging her left knee so hard that it went numb after an initial stab of excruciatingly sharp pain.

For a long second Peregrine refused to believe what had happened. She crouched on the floor, bullets whining around her, then sood and beat her wings again, hard. But nothing happened. She couldn't fly. She stood in the middle of the floor, ignoring the gunfire around her, trying to figure out what was happening, what she was doing wrong.

'Peregrine,' McCoy shouted, 'get down!' The third terrorist aimed at her, screaming incoherently. A look of horror suddenly contorted his face and he swooped toward the ceiling. His gun slipped out of his hand and smashed to the floor. Hiram casually let the man drop thirty feet as the other terrorists were clubbed to the floor by temple security guards. Kemel bustled up, a look of incredulous horror on his face.

'Thank the Merciful Ones you weren't injured!' he cried, rushing to Peregrine, who was still dazed and confused at what had hapened to her.

'Yeah,' she said distantly, then her eyes focused on the walls of the chamber. 'But look at all the damage!'

A small wooden statue, gilded and inlaid with faience and precious stones, lay in fragments at Peregrine's feet. She stopped and picked it up gently, but the fragile wood turned to dust at her touch, leaving behind a twisted shell of gold and jewels. 'It survived for so long, only to be destroyed by this madness …' she murmured softly.

'Ah, yes.' Kemel shrugged. 'Well, the walls can be restored, and we have more artifacts to put into display cases.'

'Who were those people?' Father Squid asked, imperturbably brushing dust off of his cassock.

'The Nur,' Kemel said. He spat on the floor. 'Fanatics!'

McCoy rushed up to them, his camera slung over his shoulder. 'I thought I told you to be careful,' he reproached Peregrine. 'Standing in the middle of a room with idiots blazing away with machine guns is not my idea of careful! Thank God that Hiram was watching that guy.'

'I know,' Peregrine said, 'but it shouldn't have happened that way. I was trying to get airborne, but I couldn't. Nothing like this has ever happened to me before. It's strange.' She pushed her long hair out of her eyes, looking troubled. 'I don't know what it is.'

The chamber was still in turmoil. The terrorists could have slaughtered hundreds if they had chosen to shoot people rather than the symbols of the old religion, but as it was, several score of tourists had been hit by stray bullets or injured themselves trying to escape. Temple security guards were trying to help those who were hurt, but there were so many of them lying crumpled on the stone benches, wailing, crying, screaming, bleeding ...

Peregrine turned from McCoy and the others, nauseated to the point of vomiting, but there was nothing in her stomach to throw up. McCoy held her as she was racked by dry heaves. When she stopped shuddering, she leaned against him gratefully.

He took her hand gently. 'We'd better get you to Dr. Tachyon.'

On the way back to the Winter Palace Hotel, McCoy put his arm around her and drew her to him. 'Everything is going to be okay,' he soothed. 'You're probably just tired.'

'What if it isn't that? What if something is really wrong with me? What,' she asked in a horror-stricken whisper, 'if I'll never fly again?' She buried her face against McCoy's shoulder as the others looked on in mute sympathy. Her tears soaked through his shirt as he stroked her long brown hair.

'Everything will be all right, Peri. I promise.'

◆

'Hmmm, I should have expected that,' Tachyon said as Peregrine tearfully told him her story.

'What do you mean?' asked McCoy. 'What's wrong with her?'

Tachyon eyed Josh McCoy coldly. 'It's rather private. Between a woman and her physician. So …'

'Anything that concerns Peri concerns me.'

'It's that way, is it?' Tachyon looked at McCoy hostilely.

'It's all right, Josh,' said Peregrine. She hugged him.

'If that's the way you want it.' McCoy turned to go. 'I'll wait for you in the bar.'

Tachyon closed the door behind him. 'Now, sit down and wipe your eyes. It's nothing serious, really. You're losing your feathers because of hormonal changes. Your mind has recognized your condition and has blocked your power as a means of protection.'

'Condition? Protection? What's wrong with me?'

Peregrine perched on the edge of the sofa. Tachyon sat next to her and took her cold hands in his.

'It's nothing that won't be cleared up in a few months.' His lilac eyes looked straight into her blue ones. 'You're pregnant.'

'What!' Peregrine sank back against the sofa cushions. 'That's impossible! How can I be pregnant? I've been on the pill forever!' She sat up again. 'What will NBC say? I wonder if this is covered in my contract?'

'I suggest you stop taking the pill and all other drugs, including alcohol. After all, you want a happy, healthy baby.'

'Tachy, this is ridiculous! I can't be pregnant! Are you sure?'

'Quite. And judging from your symptoms, I'd say you were about four months along.' He nodded at the door. 'How will your lover feel about being a father?'

'Josh isn't the father. We've only been together for a couple of weeks.' Her mouth dropped open. 'Oh, my God!'

'What is it?' Tachyon asked, concern in his voice and on his face.

She got off the sofa and began walking around the room, her wings fluttering absently. 'Doctor, what would happen to the baby if both parents carried the wild card? Joker mother, ace father, that sort of thing?' She stopped by the marble mantel and fiddled with the dusty knickknacks set on it.

'Why?' Tachyon asked suspiciously. 'If McCoy isn't the father, who is? An ace?'

'Yeah.'

'Who?'

She sighed and put aside the figurine she was playing with. 'I don't think it really matters. I'll never see him again. It was just one night.' She smiled in recollection. 'What a night!'

Tachyon suddenly remembered the dinner at Aces High on Wild Card Day. Peregrine had left the restaurant with – 'Fortunato?' he shouted. 'Fortunato's the father? You went to bed with that, that pimp? Have you no taste? You won't sleep with me, but you'll lay with him!' He stopped shouting and took several deep breaths. He walked to the room's bar and poured himself a brandy. Peregrine looked at him in amazement.

'I cannot believe it,' Tachyon repeated, swallowing most of the glass. 'I have so much more to offer.'

Right, she thought. *Another notch on your bedpost. But then maybe I was just that for Fortunato too.*

'Let's face it, Doctor,' Peregrine said flippantly, angered by his self-centeredness. 'He's the only man I've ever screwed that made me glow. It was absolutely incredible.' She smiled inside at the furious look on Tachyon's face. 'But that's not important now. What about the baby?'

A multitude of thoughts dashed through her mind. *I'll have to redo my apartment*, she thought. *I hope they've fixed the roof. A baby can't live in a house without a roof. Maybe I should move upstate. That would probably be better for a child.* She smiled to herself. *A big house with a large lawn, trees, and a garden. And dogs. I never thought about having a baby. Will I be a good mother? This is a good time to find out. I'm thirty-two and the old biological clock is ticking away.*

But how did it happen? The pill had always worked before. Fortunato's powers, she realized, *are based on his potent sexuality.*

Perhaps they somehow circumvented the contraceptives. Fortunato ... and Josh! How would he react to the news? What would he think?

Tachyon's voice broke into her reverie. 'Have you heard a word I've said?' he demanded.

Peregrine blushed. 'I'm sorry. I was thinking about being a mother.'

He groaned. 'Peri, it's not that simple,' he said gently.

'Why not?'

'Both you and that man have the wild card. Therefore the child will have a ninety percent chance of dying before or at birth. A nine percent chance of being a joker, and one percent, *one percent*,' he emphasized, 'of being an ace.' He drank more brandy. 'The odds are terrible, terrible. The child has no chance. None at all.'

Peregrine began pacing back and forth. 'Is there something you can do, some sort of test, that can tell if the baby is all right now?'

'Well, yes, I can do an ultrasound. It's abysmally primitive, but it'll tell if the child is developing normally or not. If the baby is not, I suggest – no, I urge you, very strongly, to have an abortion. There are already enough jokers in this world,' he said bitterly.

'And if the baby is normal?'

Tachyon sighed. 'The virus often doesn't express itself until birth. If the child survives the birth trauma without the virus manifesting, then you wait. Wait and wonder what will happen, and when it will happen. Peregrine, if you allow the child to be born, you will spend your whole life in agony, worrying and trying to protect it from everything. Consider the stresses of childhood and adolescence, any one of which might trigger the virus. Is that fair to you? To your child? To the man waiting for you downstairs? Providing,' Tachyon added coldly, 'he still wants to be a part of your life when he learns of this.'

'I'll have to take my chances with Josh,' she said swiftly, coming again to the thought that dominated her mind. 'Can you do the ultrasound soon?'

'I'll see if I can make arrangements at the hospital. If we can't do it in Luxor, then you'll have to wait until we get back to Cairo. If the child is abnormal, you must consider an abortion. Actually you should have an abortion, regardless.'

She stared at him. 'Destroy what may be a healthy human being? It might be like me,' she argued. 'Or Fortunato.'

'Peri, you don't know how good the virus was to you. You've parlayed your wings into fame and financial success. You are one of the fortunate few.'

'Of course I am. I mean, I'm pretty, but nothing special. Pretty girls are a dime a dozen. Actually I have you to thank for my success.'

'This is the first time anyone has thanked me for helping to destroy the lives of millions of people,' Tachyon said grimly.

'You tried to stop it,' she said reassuringly. 'It's not your fault Jetboy screwed up.'

'Peri,' Tachyon said grimly, changing the subject as if the failures of the past were too painful to dwell upon, 'if you don't terminate the pregnancy, you'll be showing very shortly. You'd better start thinking about what you're going to tell people.'

'Why, the truth of course. That I'm going to have a baby.'

'What if they ask about the father?'

'That's nobody's business but mine!'

'And, I would submit,' Tachyon said, 'McCoy's.'

'I guess you're right. But the world doesn't have to know about Fortunato. Please don't tell anyone. I'd hate for him to read it in the papers. I'd rather tell him myself.' If I ever see him again, she added silently. 'Please?'

'It is not my place to inform him,' Tachyon said coldly. 'But he must be told. It is his right.' He frowned. 'I don't know what you saw in that man. If it had been me, this would have never happened.'

'You've said that before,' Peregrine said, annoyance showing on her face. 'But it's a little too late for might-have-beens. Eventually everything will be fine.'

'Everything is *not* going to be fine,' said Tachyon firmly. 'The odds are the child will die or be a joker, and I don't think that you're strong enough to deal with either of those possibilities.'

'I'll have to wait and see,' Peregrine said pragmatically. She turned to leave. 'I guess I'd better break the news to Josh. He'll be glad it's nothing serious.'

'And that you're carrying the child of another man?' asked Tachyon. 'If you can maintain your relationship through this, then McCoy is a very unusual man.'

'He is, Doctor,' she assured him, and herself. 'He is.'

Peregrine walked slowly to the bar, remembering the day she and McCoy had met. He had made his interest in her evident from the very first when they were introduced at the NBC offices in November. A talented cameraman and freelance documentary maker, he had jumped at the chance to film the tour, and as he later confessed to Peregrine, the opportunity to meet her up close and personal. Peregrine was almost over her obsession with Fortunato and McCoy's attentions had helped. They had teased and tantalized each other until they finally ended up in bed together in Argentina. They'd shared a room ever since.

But McCoy couldn't arouse in her the sexual passion that Fortunato had. She doubted if any man could. Peregrine had wanted him again after that wild night they'd had together. He was like a drug she craved. Every time the phone had rung or there was a knock at the door, she'd hoped it was Fortunato. But he'd never come back. With Chrysalis's help she had found his mother and learned that the ace had left New York and was somewhere in the Orient, probably Japan.

The realization that he had left her so casually helped her get over him, but now he rushed back into her mind. She wondered how he would feel about her pregnancy, about being a father. Would he ever even know? She sighed.

Josh McCoy, she told herself sternly, *is a wonderful man, and you love him. Don't blow it over a man you'll probably never see again. But if I did see him again, what would it be like?* For the millionth time she relived her hours with Fortunato. Just thinking about it made her want him. Or McCoy.

Josh was drinking a Stella beer. As he saw her, he signaled the waiter and they arrived at his table together.

'I'll have another beer,' McCoy told the waiter. 'Some wine, Peri?'

'Uh, no thanks. Do you have any bottled water?' she asked the waiter.

'Certainly, madam. We have Perrier.'

'That'll be fine.'

'Well?' McCoy asked. 'What did Tachyon have to say? Are you okay?'

I'm not as brave about telling him this as I thought I'd be, Peregrine said to herself. *What if he can't deal with it?* It was best, she decided, to simply tell him the truth.

'There's nothing wrong with me. Nothing that time won't cure.' She took a sip of the drink the waiter placed in front of her and murmured, 'I'm going to have a baby.'

'What?' McCoy almost dropped his beer. 'A baby?'

She nodded, looking at him directly for the first time since she had sat down. *I really love you,* said silently. *Please don't make this any harder on me than it already is.*

'Mine?' he inquired calmly.

This was going to be the hard part. 'No,' she admitted.

Josh downed the rest of his beer and picked up the second bottle. 'If I'm not the father, who is? Bruce Willis?' Peregrine made a face. 'Keith Hernandez? Bob Weir? Senator Hartmann? Who?'

She arched an eyebrow at him. 'Regardless of what the super-market tabloids, and apparently you, think, I do not sleep with every man my name is linked with.' She drank some Perrier. 'In fact, I happen to be rather particular about choosing bedmates.' She grinned mischievously. 'I picked you, after all.'

'Don't try to change the subject,' he warned. 'Who's the father?'

'Do you really want to know?'

Josh nodded curtly.

'Why?'

'Because,' he sighed, 'I happen to love you and I think it's import-ant that I know who is the father of your baby. Does he know yet?'

'How can he? I just found out myself.'

'Do you love him?' McCoy asked, frowning. 'Why did you break off your relationship? Was it him?'

'Josh,' Peregrine explained patiently. 'There was no relationship. It was one night. I met this man, we went to bed. I never saw him again.' *Although not*, she silently added, *for lack of trying*.

McCoy's frown deepened. 'Are you in the habit of going to bed with anybody who catches your fancy?'

Peregrine flushed. 'No. I just told you I'm not.' She laid her hand on his. 'Please understand. I had no idea you were in my future when I met him. You knew you weren't my first the first time we made love, and after all,' she challenged, 'I'm surely not the first woman you've slept with, am I?'

'No, but I was hoping you'd be the last.' McCoy ran his hand through his hair. 'This really puts a cramp into my plans.'

'What do you mean?'

'Well, what about the father? Is he going to just stand quietly by while I marry the mother of his kid?'

'You want to marry me?' For the first time Peregrine felt that everything would work out right.

'Yeah, I do! What's so strange about that? Is this guy going to be a problem? Who is it anyhow?'

'It's an ace,' she said slowly.

'Who?' McCoy insisted.

Oh, hell, she thought. *Josh knows a lot about the New York scene. He's sure to have heard of Fortunato. What if he has the same attitude Tachyon has? Maybe I shouldn't tell him, but maybe he has the right to know.* 'His name's Fortunato—'

'*Fortunato!*' exploded McCoy. 'That guy with all the hookers? Geishas, he calls them! You slept with *him*!' He gulped down more beer.

'I really don't see that it matters now. It happened. And if you must know, he's very charming.'

'Okay, okay.' McCoy glowered.

'If you're going to be jealous of every man I ever slept with, then

I don't give us very much of a chance. And marriage is out of the question.'

'Come on, Peri, give me a break. This is kind of unexpected.'

'Well, it's a shock to me too. This morning I thought I was tired. This afternoon I find out I'm pregnant.'

A shadow fell over their table. It was Tachyon in a lilac silk suit that matched his eyes. 'Do you mind if I join you?' He pulled out a chair without awaiting a reply. 'Brandy,' he snapped to the waiter, who was hovering nearby. They all stared at each other until the waiter made a precise little bow and left. 'I've spoken to the local hospital,' Tachyon said finally. 'We can do the test tomorrow morning.'

'What test?' McCoy asked, looking from Peregrine to Tachyon.

'Did you tell him?' Tachyon asked.

'I didn't have a chance to tell him about the virus,' Peregrine said in a barely audible whisper.

'Virus?'

'Because both Peregrine and For – the father, that is – carry the wild card, the child will have it,' Tachyon said crisply. 'An ultrasound must be performed as soon as possible to determine the status of the fetus. If the child is developing abnormally, Peregrine must have an abortion. If the child is growing normally, I still advise termination, but that will, of course, be her decision.'

McCoy stared at Peregrine. 'You didn't tell me that!'

'I didn't have a chance,' she said defensively.

'There is a one in one hundred chance that the child will be an ace, but a nine in one hundred chance that it will be a joker,' added Tachyon relentlessly.

'A joker! You mean like one of those awful things that lives in Jokertown, something horrible, an atrocity?'

'My dear young man,' began Tachyon angrily, 'not all jokers—'

'Josh,' Peregrine interrupted softly, 'I'm a joker.'

Both men turned to her. 'I am,' she insisted. 'Jokers have physical deformities.' Her wings fluttered. 'Like these. I'm a *joker*.'

'This discussion is getting us nowhere,' said Tachyon after a long silence. 'Peri, I'll see you tonight.' He walked away without touching his brandy.

'Well,' said McCoy. 'Tachyon's little piece of news certainly puts a different light on the subject.'

'What do you mean,' she asked, a chill seizing her.

'I hate jokers,' McCoy burst out. 'They give me the creeps!' His knuckles were white on the beer bottle. 'Look, I can't go on with this. I'll call New York and tell them to send you another cameraman. I'll get my gear out of your room.'

'You're leaving?' Peregrine asked, stunned.

'Yeah. Look, it's been a lot of fun,' he said deliberately, 'and I've really enjoyed you. But I'll be damned if I'm going to spend my life raising some pimp's bastard! Especially,' he added as an afterthought, 'one that's going to develop into some kind of monster!'

Peregrine winced as if she'd been slapped. 'I thought you loved me,' she said, her voice and wings quivering. 'You just asked me to marry you!'

'I guess I was wrong.' He finished his beer and stood up. 'Bye, Peri.'

Peregrine couldn't face him as he left. She stared down at the table, cold and shaken, and didn't notice the intense, lingering look McCoy gave her as he left the bar.

'Ahem.'

Hiram Worchester seated himself across from her in the chair McCoy had just vacated. Peregrine shuddered. *It's true, he's gone*, she thought. *I will never, never*, she told herself fiercely, *get involved with another man. Never!*

'Where's McCoy? Father Squid and I want to know if the two of you will join us for dinner. Of course,' he added when she didn't respond, 'if you have other plans ...'

'No,' she said dully, 'no other plans. It will be just me, I'm afraid. Josh is, ahhh, out filming some local color.' She wondered why she lied to one of her oldest friends.

'Of course.' Hiram beamed. 'Let's get Father Squid and retire to the dining room. Using my power always makes me hungry.' He stood and pulled out her chair.

Dinner was excellent, but she hardly tasted it. Hiram wolfed down huge portions and waxed poetical about the *batarikh* – Egyptian caviar – and lamb shish kebab served with a wine called *rubis d'Égypte*. He loudly urged Tachyon to try some when he joined them, but Tachyon declined with a shake of his head.

'Are you ready for the meeting?' he asked Peregrine. 'Where's McCoy?'

'Out filming,' answered Hiram. 'I suggest we go without him.'

Peregrine murmured her agreement.

'He wasn't invited anyway,' Tachyon sniped.

Dr. Tachyon, Hiram Worchester, Father Squid, and Peregrine met with Opet Kemel in a small antechamber off the amphitheater that had been so severely damaged in the terrorist attack earlier that day.

'There must be Nur spies among us,' Kemel exclaimed, glancing around the room. 'That is the only way those dogs could have gotten through security. Or else they bribed one of my people. We are trying to ferret out the traitor now. The three assassins killed themselves after they were captured,' Kemel said, the hatred in his voice making Peregrine doubt the strict truth of his words. 'They are now *shahid*, martyrs for Allah at the instigation of that madman, Nur al-Allah, may he die a most painful and lingering death.' Kemel turned to Tachyon. 'You see, Doctor, that is why we need your assistance to protect ourselves ...'

His voice dragged on and on. Occasionally Peregrine heard Hiram or Father Squid or Tachyon chime in, but she wasn't really listening. She knew the expression on her face was polite and inquisitive. It was the face she wore when she had boring guests on her show who blathered on and on about nothing. She wondered how Letterman was doing with *Peregrine's Perch*. Probably fine. Her mind refused to stay on unimportant topics and wandered back to Josh McCoy. What could she have done to make him stay? Nothing. Perhaps it was better that he left if that was his real attitude toward those stricken with the wild card. She thought back to Argentina, their first night together. She had summoned up her courage, put on her sexiest dress, and gone to his room with a bottle of champagne. McCoy had been occupied with a woman he'd picked up in the hotel bar. Peregrine, extremely embarrassed, had slunk back to her room and begun drinking the champagne. Fifteen minutes later McCoy had appeared. It had taken so long, he explained, because he had to get rid of the woman.

Peregrine was impressed by his supreme confidence. He was the first man she'd been with since Fortunato, and his touch was wonderful. They'd spent every night since then together, making love at least once a day. Tonight she'd be alone. He hates you, she told herself, because you're a joker. She placed her left hand across her abdomen. *We don't need him*, Peregrine told the baby. *We don't need anyone.*

Tachyon's voice broke through her reverie. 'I'll report this to Senator Hartmann, the Red Cross, and the UN. I'm sure we can assist you somehow.'

'Thank you, thank you!' Kemel reached across the table to take Tachyon's hands in gratitude. 'Now,' he said, smiling at the others, 'perhaps you would like to meet my children? They have expressed a desire to talk to you all, especially you.' He directed his penetrating stare at Peregrine.

'Me?'

Kemel nodded and stood. 'Come this way.'

They passed between the long golden curtains that separated the antechamber from the auditorium, and Kemel led them to another room where the living gods were waiting for them.

Min was there, and bearded Osiris, bird-headed Thoth, and the floating brother and sister, as were Anubis and Isis and a dozen others whose names Peregrine couldn't remember. They immediately surrounded the Americans and Dr. Tachyon, everyone talking at once. Peregrine found herself face-to-face with a large woman who smiled and spoke to her in Arabic.

'I'm sorry,' Peregrine said, smiling back. 'I don't understand.'

The woman gestured to the bird-headed man standing close by, who immediately joined them.

'I am Thoth,' he said in English, his beak giving him a strange clacking accent. 'Taurt has asked me to tell you that the son you bear will be born strong and healthy.'

Peregrine looked from one to the other, incredulity on her face. 'How did you know I'm pregnant?' she demanded.

'Ah, we have known since we heard you were coming to the temple.'

'But this trip was decided upon months ago!'

'Yes. Osiris is cursed by knowing pieces of the future. Your future, your child, was in one of those pieces.'

Taurt said something and Thoth smiled. 'She says not to worry. You will be a very good mother.'

'I will?'

Taurt handed her a small linen pouch with hieroglyphs embroidered on it. Peregrine opened it and found a small amulet made of red stone. She examined it curiously.

'It is an *achet*,' Thoth clacked. 'It represents the sun rising in the east. It will give you the strength and power of Ra the Great. It is for the child. Keep it until the boy is old enough to wear it.'

'Thank you. I will.' She impulsively hugged Taurt, who returned the gesture and then disappeared into the crowded room.

'Come now,' said Thoth, 'the others wish to meet you.'

As Peregrine and Thoth circulated among the gods, she was greeted with great affection by each.

'Why are they acting like this?' she asked after a particularly bone-crushing embrace from Hapi, the bull.

'They are happy for you,' Thoth told her. 'The birth of a child is a wonderous thing. Especially to one with wings.'

'I see,' she said, though she didn't. She had the feeling that Thoth was holding something back, but the bird-headed man slipped back into the crowd before she could question him.

Amid the greetings and extemporaneous speeches she suddenly realized that she was exhausted. Peregrine caught Tachyon's eye where he stood conversing with Anubis. She pointed to her watch and Tachyon beckoned to her. As she joined them, she heard him ask Anubis about the threat of the Nur. Father Squid was close by, discussing theology with Osiris.

'The gods will protect us,' replied Anubis, lifting his eyes upward. 'And from what I understand, security around the temple has been strengthened.'

'Excuse me for interrupting,' Peregrine apologized, addressing Tachyon, 'but don't we have that appointment early tomorrow morning?'

'Burning sky, I'd almost forgotten. What time is it?' He lifted his eyebrows when he saw it was after one. 'We'd best go. It will take us an hour to get back to Luxor, and you, young lady, need your sleep.'

Peregrine entered her room at the Winter Palace Hotel with apprehension. McCoy's things were gone. She sank into a large armchair, and the tears that had been threatening all night came. She cried until she had no more tears left and her head ached with the strain. *Go to bed*, she told herself. *It's been a long day. Someone tries to shoot you, you find out you're pregnant, and the man you love leaves you. Next you'll find out that NBC's canceled* Peregrine's Perch. *At least you know your baby is going to be all right*, she thought as she undressed. She turned off the light and slipped into the lonely double bed.

But her brain wouldn't turn off. *What if Taurt is wrong? What if the ultrasound reveals a deformity? I'll have to have an abortion. I don't want one, but I can't bring another joker into the world. Abortion is against everything I was brought up to believe.*

But do you want to spend the rest of your life taking care of a monster? Can you take the life of a baby, even if it's a joker?

Back and forth she went, until she finally dropped off to sleep. Her last coherent thought was of Fortunato. *What would he want*, she wondered?

She was awakened by Tachyon banging at her door.

'Peregrine,' she foggily heard him call. 'Are you there? It's seven-thirty.'

She rolled out of bed, wrapped herself in the sheet, and opened the locked door. Tachyon stood there, annoyance written all over his face.

He glared at her. 'Do you know what time it is? You were supposed to meet me downstairs a half hour ago.'

'I know, I know. Yell at me while I get dressed.'

She picked up her clothes and headed toward the bathroom. Tachyon closed the door behind him and eyed her sheet-clad body appreciatively.

'What happened here?' he asked. 'Where's your paramour?'

Peregrine poked her head around the bathroom door and spoke around her toothbrush. 'Gone.'

'Do you want to tell me about it?'

'No!' She glanced in the mirror as she quickly brushed her hair and frowned at her exhausted face and swollen, red eyes. *You look like hell*, she told herself. She pulled on her clothes, pushed her feet into a pair of sandals, grabbed her bag, and joined Tachyon, who was waiting by the door.

'I'm sorry I overslept,' she apologized as they hurried through the lobby and to the waiting cab. 'It took me forever to fall asleep.'

Tachyon watched her intently as he helped her into the cab. They rode in silence, her mind full of the baby, McCoy, Fortunato, motherhood, her career. Suddenly she asked, 'If the baby ... if the test ...' She took a deep breath and began again. 'If the test shows that there is some abnormality, will they be able to do the abortion today?'

Tachyon took her cold hands in his. 'Yes.'

Please, she prayed, *please don't let anything be wrong with my baby*. Tachyon's voice broke into her thoughts. 'What?'

'Peri, what happened with McCoy?'

She stared out the window and withdrew her hand from Tachyon's. 'He's gone,' she said dully, twisting her fingers together. 'I guess he went back to New York.' She blinked away tears. 'Everything seemed okay, I mean, about my being pregnant and Fortunato and all. But after he heard that if the baby lived, it would probably be a joker, well ...' Her tears began again. Tachyon handed her his lace-trimmed silk handkerchief. Peregrine took it and wiped her eyes. 'Well,' she said, continuing her story, 'when Josh heard that, he decided he didn't want to have anything to do with me or the baby. So he left.' She rolled Tachyon's handkerchief into a small, damp ball.

'You truly love him, don't you?' Tachyon asked gently.

Peregrine nodded and pushed away more tears.

'If you have an abortion, will he come back?'

'I don't know and I don't care,' she flared. 'If he can't accept me the way I am, then I don't want him.'

Tachyon shook his head. 'Poor Peri,' he said softly. 'McCoy is a jackass.'

It seemed like an eternity before the cab rolled up in front of the hospital. As Tachyon went to consult with the receptionist, Peregrine leaned against the cool, white wall of the waiting room and shut her eyes. She tried to make her mind go blank, but she couldn't stop thinking about McCoy. *If he did come to you, you'd take him back*, she accused herself. *You know you would. He won't, though, not with me carrying Fortunato's child.* She opened her eyes as someone touched her arm.

'Are you sure you're all right?' Tachyon asked.

'Just tired.' She tried to smile.

'Scared?' he asked.

'Yes,' she admitted. 'I'd never really thought about having children, but now that I'm pregnant, I want to have a baby more than anything.' Peregrine sighed and folded her arms protectively over her abdomen. 'But I hope that the baby is all right.'

'They're paging the doctor who'll perform the procedure,' Tachyon said. 'I hope you're thirsty. You have to drink several quarts of water.' He removed a pitcher and a glass from a tray held by the nurse standing beside him. 'You can start now.'

Peregrine began drinking. She'd finished six glasses before a short man in a white coat hurried up to them.

'Dr. Tachyon?' he asked, grasping Tachyon's hand. 'I am Dr. Ali. It is a great pleasure to meet you and welcome you to my hospital.' He turned to Peregrine. 'Is this the patient?'

Tachyon performed the introductions.

Dr. Ali rubbed his hands together. 'Let's get on with it,' he said, and they followed him to the OB-GYN section of the hospital.

'You, young lady, into that room.' He pointed. 'Remove all your clothing and put on the gown you'll find there. Keep drinking water. When you've changed, come back here and we'll perform the sonography.'

When Peregrine rejoined Tachyon, now wearing a white coat over his silken finery, and Dr. Ali, she was told to lie on an examining table. She followed their directions, clutching Taurt's amulet in her hand. A nurse raised the robe up and rubbed a clear gel on Peregrine's stomach.

'Conductive jelly,' Tachyon explained. 'It helps carry the sound waves.'

The nurse began to move a small instrument that looked like a microphone over Peregrine's belly.

'The transducer,' said Tachyon as he and Ali studied the image on the video screen in front of them.

'Well, what do you see?' Peregrine demanded.

'A moment, Peri.'

Tachyon and Ali conferred in low tones.

'Can you print that?' Peregrine heard Tachyon ask. Dr. Ali gave the nurse instructions in Arabic, and very shortly a computer printout of the image appeared.

'You can climb down now,' said Tachyon. 'We've seen everything there is to see.'

'Well?' Peregrine asked anxiously.

'Everything looks fine ... so far,' said Tachyon slowly. 'The child appears to be developing normally.'

'That's wonderful!' She hugged him as he helped her down from the table.

'If you intend to go through with this pregnancy, I insist on an ultrasound every four to five weeks to monitor the baby's growth.'

Peregrine nodded. 'These sound waves won't hurt the baby, will they?'

'No,' said Tachyon. 'The only thing that can injure the child already exists within it.'

Peregrine looked at Tachyon. 'I know you feel you have to keep telling me that, but the baby is going to be just fine, I know it.'

'Peregrine, this is not a fairy tale! You are not going to live happily ever after! This could ruin your life!'

'Growing wings when I was thirteen could have ruined my life, but it didn't. This isn't going to either.'

Tachyon sighed. 'There is no reasoning with you. Go put your clothes on. It's time we got back to Cairo.'

Tachyon was waiting for her outside the dressing room.

'Where's Dr. Ali?' she asked, looking around. 'I wanted to thank him.'

'He had other patients to attend to.' Tachyon steered her down the corridor with his arm around her shoulders. 'Let's get back ...' his voice broke off. Coming down the hallway toward them was Josh McCoy. Peregrine was pleased to see that he looked as awful as she felt. He must not have gotten much sleep either. He stopped in front of them.

'Peri,' he began, 'I've been thinking—'

'Good for you,' Peregrine said crisply. 'Now if you will excuse us—'

McCoy reached out and grabbed her upper arm. 'No. I want to talk to you and I intend to do it now.' He pulled her away from Tachyon.

She had to talk to him, she told herself. Maybe everything could be straightened out. She hoped.

'It's all right,' she said shakily to Tachyon. 'Let's get this over with.'

Tachyon's voice followed them. 'McCoy. You are undoubtedly a fool. And I warn you, if you harm her – in any way – you will regret it for a very long time.'

McCoy ignored him and continued to pull Peregrine down the hall, opening doors until he found an empty room. He dragged her in and slammed the door behind them. He let go of her arm and began pacing back and forth.

Peregrine stood against the wall, rubbing her arm where the marks of his fingers were visible.

McCoy stopped pacing and stared at her. 'I'm sorry if I hurt you.'

'I think it's going to bruise,' she said, inspecting her arm.

'We can't have that,' McCoy said mockingly. 'Bruises on America's sex symbol!'

'That's pretty rotten,' she said, her voice dangerously quiet.

'True, though,' he shot back. 'You are a sex symbol. There's your *Playboy* centerfold, that nude ice sculpture of you at Aces High. And what about that naked poster, "Fallen Angel," that Warhol did?'

'There's nothing wrong with posing nude! I'm not ashamed to show my body or to have other people look at it.'

'No kidding! You strip for anyone who asks you!'

She went white with fury. 'Yes, I do! Including you!' She slapped McCoy's face and turned to the door, her wings quivering. 'I don't have to stand here and take any more abuse from you.'

She reached for the door handle, but McCoy shoved in front of her and held it closed. 'No. I need to talk to you.'

'You're not talking, you're being abusive,' Peregrine retorted, 'and I don't like it one bit.'

'You don't know what abuse is,' he told her, brown eyes glittering angrily. 'Why don't you scream? Tachyon's probably right outside. He'd love to rush in and rescue you. You could fuck him in gratitude.'

'How dare you?' Peregrine shouted. 'I don't need him to protect me! Him or you or anyone! Let me go!' she demanded angrily.

'No.' He pressed her body to the wall. She felt like a butterfly pinned on velvet. She could feel his heavy warmth against her. 'Is this what it's going to be like,' he raged, 'men always wanting to protect you? Men wanting to fuck you just because you're Peregrine? I don't want anyone else touching you. No one but me.

'Peri,' he said more gently. 'Look at me.' When she refused, he forced her chin up until she looked him in the eyes, tears rolling down her cheeks. 'Peri, I'm sorry for everything I said yesterday. And for everything I said just now. I didn't intend to lose my temper, but when I saw that overdressed quiche-eater with his hands on you, I just lost it. The thought of anyone but me touching you makes me furious.' The fingers on her chin tightened. 'Yesterday when you said that Fortunato was the baby's father, all I could see was him in bed with you, holding you, loving you.' He let her go and walked to the window of the small room, staring out unseeing, his hands clenching and unclenching. 'It was then,' he continued, 'that I realized exactly what I was up against. You're famous and beautiful and sexy and everyone wants you. I don't want to be Mr. Peregrine. I don't want to compete with your past. I want your future.

'What I said yesterday about jokers wasn't true. It was the first excuse that I could think of. I wanted to hurt you as bad as I was hurting.' He ran a hand through his blond hair. 'It really hurt me when you told me about the baby, because it's not mine. I don't hate jokers. I like kids and I'll love yours and try to be a good father. If Fortunato shows up, well, I'll deal with it the best I can. Hell, Peri, I love you. Last night without you was terrible. It showed me what the future would be like if I let you go. I love you,' he repeated, 'and I want you to be my life.'

Peregrine put her arms around him and leaned against his back. 'I love you too. Last night was about the worst night of my life. I realized what you meant to me, and also what this baby means. If I can only have one of you, I want my baby. I'm sorry to say that, but I had to tell you. But I want you too.'

McCoy turned and took her hands. He kissed them. 'You sound awfully determined.'

'I am.'

McCoy laughed. 'No matter what happens when the baby is born, we'll do the best we can.' He smiled down at her. 'I have a bunch of nieces and nephews, so I even know how to change diapers.'

'Good. You can teach me.'

'I will,' he promised, his lips touching hers as he pulled her closer.

The door opened. A white-clad figure looked at them disapprovingly. After a moment Doctor Tachyon peered in. 'Are you quite finished?' he asked icily. 'They need this room.'

'We're done with the room, but we're not finished. We're just starting,' Peregrine said, smiling radiantly.

'Well, as long as you're happy,' Tachyon said slowly.

'I am,' she assured him.

They left the hospital with Tachyon. He got into a cab by himself, while McCoy and Peregrine settled into the horse-drawn carriage waiting at the curb behind the taxi.

'We have to get back to the hotel,' Peregrine said.

'Are you propositioning me?'

'Of course not. I have to pack so we can rejoin the tour in Cairo.'

'Today?'

'Yes.'

'Then we'd better hurry.'

'Why?'

'Why?' McCoy trailed kisses over her face and neck. 'We have to make up for last night, of course.'

'Oh.' Peregrine spoke to the driver and the carriage picked up speed. 'We don't want to waste any more time.'

'Enough has already been wasted,' McCoy agreed. 'Are you happy?' he asked softly as she settled in his arms, her head on his chest.

'Happier than I've ever been!' But a little voice in the back of her mind kept reminding her of Fortunato.

His arms tightened around her. 'I love you.'

FROM *THE JOURNAL*
OF XAVIER DESMOND

January 30/Jerusalem:

The open city of Jerusalem, they call it. An international metropolis, jointly governed by commissioners from Israel, Jordan, Palestine, and Great Britain under a United Nations mandate, sacred to three of the world's great religions.

Alas, the apt phrase is not 'open city' but 'open sore.' Jerusalem bleeds as it has for almost four decades. If this city is sacred, I should hate to visit one that was profane.

Senators Hartmann and Lyons and the other political delegates lunched with the city commissioners today, but the rest of us spent the afternoon touring this free international city in closed limousines with bulletproof windshields and special underbody armor to withstand bomb blasts. Jerusalem, it seems, likes to welcome distinguished international visitors by blowing them up. It does not seem to matter who the visitors are, where they come from, what religion they practice, how their politics lean – there are enough factions in this city so that everyone can count on being hated by someone.

Two days ago we were in Beirut. From Beirut to Jerusalem, that is a voyage from day to night. Lebanon is a beautiful country, and Beirut is so lovely and peaceful it seems almost serene. Its various religions appear to have solved the problem of living in comparative harmony, although there are of course incidents – nowhere in the Middle East (or the world, for that matter) is completely safe.

But Jerusalem – the outbreaks of violence have been endemic for thirty years, each worse than the one before. Entire blocks resemble nothing so much as London during the Blitz, and the population that remains has grown so used to the distant sound of machine-gun fire that they scarcely seem to pay it any mind.

We stopped briefly at what remains of the Wailing Wall (largely destroyed in 1967 by Palestinian terrorists in reprisal for the assassination of al-Haziz by Israeli terrorists the year before) and actually dared to get out of our vehicles. Hiram looked around fiercely and made a fist, as if daring anyone to start trouble. He has been in a strange state of late; irritable, quick to anger, moody. The things we witnessed in Africa have affected us all, however. One shard of the wall is still fairly imposing. I touched it and tried to feel the history. Instead I felt the pocks left in the stone by bullets.

Most of our party returned to the hotel afterward, but Father Squid and I took a detour to visit the Jokers' Quarter. I'm told that it is the second-largest joker community in the world, after Jokertown itself ... a distant second, but second nonetheless. It does not surprise me. Islam does not view my people kindly, and so jokers come here from all over the Middle East for whatever meager protection is offered by UN sovereignty and a small, out-manned, out-gunned, and demoralized international peacekeeping force.

The Quarter is unspeakably squalid, and the weight of human misery within its walls is almost palpable. Yet ironically the streets of the Quarter are reputed safer than any other place in Jerusalem. The Quarter has its own walls, built in living memory, originally to spare the feelings of decent people by hiding we living obscenities from their sight, but those same walls have given a measure of security to those who dwell within. Once inside I saw no nats at all, only jokers – jokers of all races and religions, all living in relative peace. Once they might have been Muslims or Jews or Christians, zealots or Zionists or followers of the Nur, but after their hand had been dealt, they were only jokers. The joker is the great equalizer, cutting through all other hatreds and prejudices, uniting all mankind in a new brotherhood of pain. A joker is a joker is a joker, and anything else he is, is unimportant.

Would that it worked the same way with aces.

The sect of Jesus Christ, Joker has a church in Jerusalem, and Father Squid took me there. The building looked more like a mosque than a Christian church, at least on the outside, but inside it was not so terribly different from the church I'd visited in Jokertown, though much older and in greater disrepair. Father Squid lit a candle and said a prayer, and then we went back to the cramped, tumbledown rectory where Father Squid conversed with the pastor in halting Latin while we shared a bottle of sour red wine. As they were talking, I heard the sound of automatic weaponry chattering off in the night somewhere a few blocks away. A typical Jerusalem evening, I suppose.

No one will read this book until after my death, by which time I will be safely immune from prosecution. I've thought long and hard about whether or not I should record what happened tonight, and finally decided that I should. The world needs to remember the lessons of 1976 and be reminded from time to time that the JADL does not speak for all jokers.

An old joker woman pressed a note into my hand as Father Squid and I were leaving the church. I suppose someone recognized me.

When I read the note, I begged off the official reception, pleading illness once again, but this time it was a ruse. I dined in my room with a wanted criminal, a man I can only describe as a notorious international joker terrorist, although he is a hero inside the Jokers' Quarter. I will not give his real name, even in these pages, since I understand that he still visits his family in Tel Aviv from time to time. He wears a black canine mask on his 'missions' and to the press, Interpol, and the sundry factions that police Jerusalem, he is variously known as the Black Dog and the Hound of Hell. Tonight he wore a completely different mask, a butterfly-shaped hood covered with silver glitter, and had no problem crossing the city.

'What you've got to remember,' he told me, 'is that nats are fundamentally stupid. You wear the same mask twice and let your picture get taken with it, and they start thinking it's your face.'

The Hound, as I'll call him, was born in Brooklyn but emigrated to Israel with his family at age nine and became an Israeli citizen. He was twenty when he became a joker. 'I traveled halfway around the world to draw the wild card,' he told me. 'I could have stayed in Brooklyn.'

We spent several hours discussing Jerusalem, the Middle East, and the politics of the wild card. The Hound heads what honesty forces me to call a joker terrorist organization, the Twisted Fists. They are illegal in both Israel and Palestine, no mean trick. He was evasive about how many members they had, but not at all shy about confessing that virtually all of their financial support comes from New York's Jokertown. 'You may not like us, Mr. Mayor,' the Hound told me, 'but your people do.' He even hinted slyly that one of the joker delegates on our tour was among their supporters, although of course he refused to supply a name.

The Hound is convinced that war is coming to the Middle East, and soon. 'It's overdue,' he said. 'Neither Israel or Palestine have ever had defensible borders, and neither one is an economically viable nation. Each is convinced that the other one is guilty of all sorts of terrorist atrocities, and they're both right. Israel wants the Negev and the West Bank, Palestine wants a port on the Mediterranean, and both countries are still full of refugees from the 1948 partition who want their homes back. Everyone wants Jerusalem except the UN, which has it. Shit, they *need* a good war. The Israelis looked like they were winning in '48 until the *Nasr* kicked their asses. I know that Bernadotte won the Nobel Peace Prize for the Treaty of Jerusalem, but just between you and me, it might have been better if they'd fought it out to the bitter end ... any kind of end.'

I asked him about all the people who would have died, but he just shrugged. 'They'd be dead. But maybe if it was over, really *over*, some of the wounds would start to heal. Instead we got two pissed-off half-countries that share the same little desert and won't even recognize each other, we've got four decades of hatred and terrorism and fear, and we're still going to get the war, and soon. It beats me how Bernadotte pulled off the Peace of Jerusalem anyway, though I'm not surprised that he got assassinated for his troubles. The only ones who hate the terms worse than the Israelis are the Palestinians.'

I pointed out that, unpopular as it might be, the Peace of Jerusalem had lasted almost forty years. He dismissed that as 'a forty-year stalemate, not real peace. Mutual fear was what made it work. The Israelis have always had military superiority. But the Arabs had the Port Said aces, and you think the Israelis don't remember? Every time the Arabs put up a memorial to the *Nasr*, anywhere from Baghdad to Marrakesh, the Israelis blow it up. Believe me, they remember. Only now the whole thing's coming unbalanced. I got sources say Israel has been running its own wild card experiments on volunteers from their armed forces, and they've come up with a few aces of their own. Now that's fanaticism for you, to *volunteer* for the wild card. And on the Arab side, you've got Nur al-Allah, who calls Israel a "bastard joker nation" and has vowed to destroy it utterly. The Port Said aces were pussycats compared to his bunch, even old Khôf. No, it's coming, and soon.'

'And when it comes?' I asked him.

He was carrying a gun, some kind of small semiautomatic machine pistol with a long Russian name. He took it out and laid it on the table between us. 'When it comes,' he said, 'they can kill each other all they want, but they damn well better leave the Quarter alone, or they'll have us to deal with. We've already given the Nur a few lessons. Every time they kill a joker, we kill five of them. You'd think they'd get the idea, but the Nur's a slow learner.'

I told him that Senator Hartmann was hoping to set up a meeting with the Nur al-Allah to begin discussions that might lead to a peaceful solution to this area's problems. He laughed. We talked for a long time, about jokers and aces and nats, and violence and non-violence and war and peace, about brotherhood and revenge and turning the other cheek and taking care of your own, and in the end we settled nothing. 'Why did you come?' I finally asked him.

'I thought we should meet. We could use your help. Your

knowledge of Jokertown, your contacts in nat society, the money you could raise.'

'You won't get my help,' I told him. 'I've seen where your road leads. Tom Miller walked that road ten years ago.'

'Gimli?' He shrugged. 'First, Gimli was crazy as a bedbug. I'm not. Gimli wants the world to kiss it and make it all better. I just fight to protect my own. To protect you, Des. Pray that your Jokertown never needs the Twisted Fists, but if you do, we'll be there. I read *Time*'s cover story on Leo Barnett. Could be the Nur isn't the only slow learner. If that's how it is, maybe the Black Dog will go home and find that tree that grows in Brooklyn, right? I haven't been to a Dodger game since I was eight.'

My heart stopped in my throat as I looked at the gun on the table, but I reached out and put my hand on the phone. 'I could call down to our security right now and make certain that won't happen, that you won't kill any more innocent people.'

'But you won't,' the Hound said. 'Because we have so much in common.'

I told him we had nothing in common.

'We're both jokers,' he said. 'What else matters?' Then he holstered his gun, adjusted his mask, and walked calmly from my room.

And God help me, I sat there alone for several endless minutes, until I heard the elevator doors open down the hall – and finally took my hand off the phone.

THE TINT OF HATRED

PART FIVE

Sunday, February 1, 1987, The Syrian Desert:

Najib struck her down with one quick blow, but Misha persisted. 'He's coming,' Misha said. 'Allah's dreams tell me that I must go to Damascus to meet him.'

In the darkness of the mosque Najib glowed like a green beacon from near the *mihrab*, the jeweled prayer niche. It was at night that Nur al-Allah was the most impressive, a fiery vision of a prophet, gleaming with Allah's own fury. He said nothing to Misha's pronouncement, looking first at Sayyid, resting his great bulk against one of the tiled pillars.

'No,' Sayyid grumbled. 'No, Nur al-Allah.' He looked at Misha, kneeling in supplication before her brother, and his eyes were full of a smoldering rage because she would not submit to her brother's will or Sayyid's suggestions. 'You've often said that the abominations are to be killed. You've said that the only way to negotiate with the unbeliever is with the edge of a sword. Let me fulfill those words for you. The entire Ba'th government can do nothing to stop us; al-Assad trembles when Nur al-Allah speaks. I'll take some of the faithful to Damascus. We'll cleanse the abominations and those who bring them with purifying fire.'

Najib's skin flared for a moment, as if Sayyid's advice had excited him. His lips had pulled back in a fierce grimace. Misha shook her head. 'Brother,' she implored. 'Listen also to Kahina. I've had the same dream for three nights. I see the two of us with the Americans. I see the gifts. I see a new, untrodden path.'

'Also tell Nur al-Allah that you woke screaming from the dream, that you felt the gifts were dangerous, that this Hartmann had more than one face in your dreams.'

Misha looked back at her husband. 'A new way is always danger-ous. Gifts always obligate the one who receives them. Will you tell the Nur al-Allah that there's no danger in *your* way, the way of violence? Is Nur al-Allah so strong already that he can defeat the entire West? The Soviets won't help in this; they'll want their hands to be clean.'

'*Jihad* is struggle,' Sayyid grated out.

Najib nodded his head. He raised a brilliant hand before his face, turning it as if marveling at the soft light it radiated. 'Allah smote the unbelievers with His hand,' he agreed. 'Why shouldn't I do the same?'

'Because of Allah's dream,' Misha insisted.

'Allah's dream or *yours*, woman?' Sayyid asked. 'What will the infidels do if Nur al-Allah does as I've asked? The West has done *nothing* about the hostages Islam has taken, they've done nothing about other killings. Will they complain to Damascus and al-Assad? Nur al-Allah rules Syria in all but title; Nur al-Allah has united half of all Islam behind him. They'll complain, they'll bluster. They'll cry and moan, but they won't interfere. What will they do – refuse to trade with us? *Ptah!*' Sayyid spat on the intricate tiles at his feet. 'They will hear Allah's laughter in the wind.'

'These Americans have their own guards,' Misha countered. 'They have the ones they call aces.'

'We have Allah. His strength is all we need. Any of my people would be honored to become *shahid*, a martyr for Allah.'

Misha turned to Najib, still looking at his hand as Sayyid and Misha argued. 'Brother, what Sayyid asks ignores the gifts that Allah has given us. His way ignores the gift of dreams, and it ignores *kuwwa nuriyah*, the power of light.'

'What do you mean?' Najib's hand fell.

'Allah's power is in your voice, your presence. If you meet with these people, they would be swayed the way the faithful are swayed when you speak. *Any* of Allah's people could kill them, but only Nur al-Allah can actually bring the infidels to the faith of Allah. Which of the two is the greater honor to Allah?'

Najib didn't answer. She could see his luminescent face furrowed in a deep frown, and he turned to walk away a few paces. She knew then that she had won. *Praise Allah! Sayyid will beat me again for this, but it's worth it.* Her cheek throbbed where Najib had struck her, but she ignored the pain.

'Sayyid?' Najib asked. He looked from a slitted window to the village. Faint voices hailed the glowing visage.

'It is Nur al-Allah's decision. He knows my counsel,' Sayyid said. 'I'm not a *kahin*. My foresight is limited to war. Nur al-Allah is strong – I think we should demonstrate that strength.'

Najib came back to the *mihrab*. 'Sayyid, will you allow the Kahina to go to Damascus and meet with the Americans?'

'If that's what Nur al-Allah wishes,' Sayyid answered stiffly.

'It is,' Najib said. 'Misha, go back to your husband's house and make yourself ready to travel. You'll meet this delegation, and you'll tell me of them. Then Nur al-Allah will decide how to deal with them.'

Misha bowed, her head to the cool tiles. She kept her eyes down, feeling the heat of Sayyid's gaze as she passed him.

When she had gone, Najib shook his head at Sayyid's sullen posture. 'You think I ignore you for your wife, my friend? Are you insulted?'

'She is your sister, and she is Kahina,' Sayyid replied, his voice neutral.

Najib smiled, and the darkness of his mouth was like a hole in his bright face. 'Let me ask you, Sayyid, are we truly strong enough to do as you suggested?'

'*In sha'Allah*, of course, but I wouldn't have said so if I didn't think it true.'

'And would your plan be easier to execute in Damascus, or here – in our own place, at our own time?'

Comprehension made Sayyid grin. 'Why, *here*, of course, Nur al-Allah. *Here*.'

Tuesday, February 3, 1987, Damascus:
The hotel was near the Suq al-Hamidiyah. Even through the chatter of the air conditioner's ancient compressor, Gregg could hear the market's boisterous energy. The *suq* was swirling with a thousand brightly hued *djellaba*, interspersed with the dull black of the *chador*. The crowds filled the narrow lanes between the stalls' colorful awnings and spilled out into the streets. On the nearest corner a water-seller called his wares: '*Atchen, taa saubi!*' – if you thirst, come to me.

Everywhere there were crowds, from the *suq* to the white minarets of 1200-year-old Umayyad Mosque. 'You'd think the wild card never existed. Or the twentieth century, for that matter,' Gregg commented.

'That's because Nur al-Allah has made sure that no joker dares to walk the streets. They kill jokers here.' Sara, on the bed, laid her orange on the peels littering the copy of *al Ba'th*, the official Syrian newspaper. 'I remember one tale we got from the *Post* stringer here. A joker had the misfortune of being caught stealing food in the *suq*. They buried him in the sand so that only his head showed, then they stoned him to death. The judge – who belonged to the Nur sect, by the way – insisted that only small stones be thrown, so the joker would have sufficient time to contemplate his many sins before he died.'

Gregg laced his fingers in her tousled hair, gently pulled her head back, and kissed her deeply. 'That's why we're here,' he said. 'That's why I hope to meet this Light of Allah.'

'You've been edgy since Egypt.'

'I think this is an important stop.'

'Because the Middle East is going to be one of the main concerns of the next president?'

'You're an impertinent little bitch.'

'I'll take the "little" as a compliment. A "bitch," though, is a female dog, you sexist pig. And I *can* smell a story.' She wrinkled her nose up at him.

'Does that mean I get your vote?'

'It depends.' Sara threw back the sheet, scattering *al-Ba'th*, orange, and peels to the floor, and took Gregg's hand. She kissed his fingers lightly and then moved his hand lower on her body. 'What kind of incentives were you thinking of offering?' she asked.

'I'll do whatever I have to do.' *And that's true.* Puppetman stirred slightly, impatient. *If I make Nur al-Allah a puppet, I influence his action. I can sit down at the table with him and get him to sign whatever I want: Hartmann the Great Negotiator, the world's humanitarian. Nur al-Allah is the key to this region. With him and a few other leaders* ... The thought made him smile. Sara laughed throatily.

'No sacrifice is too great, huh?' She laughed again and pulled him on top of her. 'I like a man with a sense of duty. Well, start earning your vote, Senator. And this time, *you* get the wet spot.'

A few hours later there was a discreet knock on the outer door. Gregg was standing by the window, knotting his tie as he looked out on the city. 'Yes?'

'It's Billy, Senator. Kahina and her group are here. I've told the others. Should I send her on to the conference room?'

'Just a second.'

Sara called quietly from the open door of the bathroom, 'I'll go down to my own room.'

'You might as well stay here for a bit. Billy will make sure no one sees you leave. There'll be a press conference after, so you might want to head down in half an hour.' Gregg went to the door, opened it slightly, and spoke to Billy. Then he stepped quickly to the door leading to the adjoining suite and knocked. 'Ellen? Kahina's on her way.'

Ellen came in as Gregg was putting on his jacket; Sara was brushing her hair. Ellen smiled automatically at Sara, nodding. Gregg could feel a mild annoyance in his wife, a glimmer of jealousy; he let Puppetman smooth that roughness, lathing it with cold blue. He needed very little effort; she had had no delusions about their marriage from the start – they had married because she was a Bonestell, and the New England Bonestells had always been involved in politics in one way or another. She understood how to play the supportive spouse: when to stand beside him; what to say and how to say it. She accepted that 'men had needs' and didn't care as long as Gregg didn't flaunt it in public or stop her from having her own affairs. Ellen was among the most pliable of his puppets.

Deliberately, just for the small pleasure that Ellen's hidden distaste would give him, he hugged Sara. He could feel Sara holding back in Ellen's presence. *I can change that,* Puppetman murmured in his head. *See, there's so much affection in her. Just a twist, and I could ...*

No! The depth of his response surprised Gregg. *We don't force her. We never touched Succubus; we won't touch Sara.*

Ellen watched the embrace blandly, and the smile never left her lips. 'The two of you slept well, I hope.' There was nothing in the tone beyond the mere words. Glacial, distant, her gaze left Sara; she smiled at Gregg. 'Darling, we should go. And I want to talk to you about that reporter Downs – he's been asking me the strangest questions, and he's talking to Chrysalis as well ...'

The meeting wasn't what he'd expected, though John Werthen had briefed him on the necessary protocol. The Arab guards along the wall, armed with a mixture of Uzis and Soviet-made automatic weapons, were unnerving. Billy Ray had carefully beefed up their own security. Gregg, Tachyon, and the other political members of the junket were in attendance. The aces and (especially) jokers were elsewhere in Damascus, as President al-Assad toured the city with them.

Kahina herself was a surprise. She was a small, petite woman. The ebony eyes above the veils were bright, inquisitive, and searching; her dress was plain except for a line of turquoise beads above her forehead. Translators accompanied her. In addition, a trio of burly men in bedouin dress sat nearby, watching.

'Kahina's a woman in a very conservative Islamic society, Senator,' John had said. 'I can't stress that enough. Her even *being* here is a break with tradition, allowed only because she's the prophet-twin of her brother and because they think she has magic, *sihr*. She's married to Sayyid, the general who masterminded Nur al-Allah's military victories. She might be the Kahina, and she's had a liberal education, but she's *not* a Westerner. Be careful. These people are quick to be insulted and very long on holding a grudge. And – Jesus, Senator – tell Tachyon to tone it down.'

Gregg waved to Tachyon, dressed outrageously as usual, but with a new twist. Tachyon had abandoned the satins, too hot for him in this climate. Instead he looked as if he'd raided a bazaar in the *suq*, emerging as a movie-cliché vision of a sheikh: red, baggy silk trousers, a loose linen shirt and jacket with intricate brocade, bead and bangles jingling everywhere. His hair was hidden under an elaborate headdress; the long toes of his slippers turned up and curled back. Gregg decided not to comment. He shook hands with the others and seated Ellen as everyone found chairs. He nodded to Kahina and her entourage, who tore their gazes away from Tachyon.

'Marhala,' Gregg said: greetings.

Her eyes gleamed. She inclined her head. 'I speak only a little English,' she said slowly in a heavily accented, quiet voice. 'It will be easier if my translator, Rashid, speaks for me.'

Headsets had been provided; Gregg put his on. 'We're delighted that Kahina would come to make arrangements for us to meet with Nur al-Allah. This is more honor than we deserve.'

Her translator was speaking softly into his headset. Kahina nodded. She spoke in a stream of rapid Arabic. 'The honor is that you have even gotten this close to meeting him, Senator,' Rashid's husky voice translated. 'The Qur'an says: "For those who disbelieve in Allah and His apostle. We have prepared a blazing fire."'

Gregg glanced toward Tachyon, who raised his eyebrows slightly under the headdress and shrugged. 'We'd like to believe that we share a vision of peace with Nur al-Allah,' Gregg answered slowly.

Kahina seemed almost amused by that. 'Nur al-Allah, for this once, has chosen *my* vision. On his own, he might have stayed in the desert until you were gone ...' Kahina was still speaking, but Rashid's voice had trailed into silence. Kahina glared at the man, saying something that made him grimace. One of the men with Kahina gestured harshly; Rashid cleared his throat and resumed.

'Or ... or perhaps Nur al-Allah might have followed the advice of Sayyid and slain you and the abominations you bring with you.'

Tachyon pressed back in his chair in shock; Lyons, the Republican senator, blustered, leaning over to Gregg to whisper, 'And I thought *Barnett* was sick.'

Inside Gregg, Puppetman stirred hungrily. Even without a direct mindlink, the surging emotions could be felt. Kahina's attendants were frowning, obviously upset by her candor but afraid to interfere with someone who was, after all, part of the twinned prophet. The guards around the wall tensed. The UN and Red Cross representatives consulted in whispers.

Kahina sat calmly in the middle of the turmoil, her hands folded on the tabletop, her regard on Gregg. The intensity of her stare was unnerving; he found himself struggling not to look away.

Tachyon leaned forward, his long fingers interlaced. 'The "abominations" are blameless,' he said bluntly. 'If anything, the responsibility should be laid at *my* feet. Your people would better serve the jokers with kindness than scorn and brutality. They were infected by a blind, horrible, and undiscriminating disease. So were you; you were simply lucky.'

Her attendants muttered at that, darting angry stares at the alien, but Kahina answered calmly, 'Allah is supreme. The virus might be blind, but Allah is not. Those who are worthy, He rewards. Those who are not, He strikes down.'

'And what of the aces we brought with us, who worship another version of God, or perhaps none at all?' Tachyon persisted. 'What of the aces in other countries who worship Buddha or Amaterasu or a Plumed Serpent or no gods at all?'

'The ways of Allah are subtle. I know that what He has spoken in the Qur'an is truth. I know that the visions He grants me contain truth. I know that when Nur al-Allah speaks in His voice, it is truth.

Beyond that, it's folly to claim to understand Allah.' Her voice now held an undertone of irritation, and Gregg knew Tachyon had hit a nerve with her.

Tachyon shook his head. 'And I would claim that the ultimate folly is attempting to understand humans, who have made these gods,' he retorted.

Gregg had listened to the exchange with growing excitement. To have Kahina for a puppet: she might be nearly as useful to him as Nur al-Allah himself. Until now he had dismissed Kahina's influence. He'd thought that a woman within this fundamentalist Islamic movement could wield no real power. Now he saw that his evaluation might have been wrong.

Kahina and Tachyon had locked gazes. Gregg held up his hand, making his voice reasonable, soothing.

'Please. Doctor, let me answer. Kahina, none of us have any intention of insulting your beliefs. We're here only to help your government deal with the problems of the wild card virus. My country has had to cope with the virus for the longest time; we've had the largest affected population. We're also here to learn, to see other techniques and resolutions. We can do that best by meeting with those who have the most influence. Throughout the Middle East we have heard that this person is Nur al-Allah. No one holds more power than he.'

Kahina's gaze now flicked back to Gregg. The resentment had still not left the mahogany pupils. 'You were in Allah's dreams,' she said. 'I saw you. Strings ran from your fingertips. As you tugged, the people held at the other ends moved.'

My God! The shock and panic almost brought Gregg out of his seat. Puppetman snarled like a cornered dog in his head. His pulse pounded against his temples, and he could feel heat on his cheeks. *How could she know …?*

Gregg made himself laugh, forced a smile to his lips. 'That's a common dream of politicians,' he said, as if she'd made a joke. 'I was probably trying to make the voters check the right box on the ballot.' There were chuckles around his side of the table at that. Gregg let his voice drift back to seriousness. 'If I *could* control people, aside from being president already, I'd be pulling those strings that would make your brother meet with us. Could that be the meaning of your dream?'

Unblinking, she looked at him. 'Allah *is* subtle.'

You must take her. No matter that Tachyon is here or that it's dangerous because she's an ace. You must take her because of what she might say. You must take her because you may never meet Nur al-Allah. She is here, now.

The power in Gregg was impatient, eager; he forced it back down. 'What will convince Nur al-Allah, Kahina?'

A burst of Arabic; Rashid's voice spoke in Gregg's ear. 'Allah will convince him.'

'And you. You're his adviser too. What will you tell him?'

'We argued when I said Allah's dreams told me to come to Damascus.' Her escorts were muttering again. One of them touched her shoulder and whispered into her ear fiercely. Kahina shook her head. 'I will tell my brother what Allah's dreams tell me to say. Nothing more. My own words have no weight.'

Tachyon pushed his chair back. 'Senator, I suggest that we waste no further time with this. I want to see the few clinics the Syrian government has bothered to set up. Maybe *there* I can accomplish something.'

Gregg looked around the table; the others were nodding. Kahina's own people looked impatient. Gregg rose. 'Then we'll wait for word from you, Kahina. Please, I beg you, tell your brother that sometimes when you know an enemy, you find that he is no enemy at all. We're here to help. That's all.'

As Kahina stood, taking off her headset, Gregg casually held out his hand to her, ignoring the contempt the gesture elicited from her escorts. When Kahina didn't respond by taking his hand, he kept his hand extended. 'We have a saying that, in Rome, one is supposed to act Roman,' he commented, hoping she would understand the words or that Rashid would translate. 'Still, the first step in understanding someone is to know their customs. One of ours is that peers shake hands to show understanding.'

He thought for a moment that the ploy had failed, that the

opportunity would pass. He was almost glad. Opening the mind and will of an ace who had already terrified him with her unknowing perception, and doing so with Tachyon standing alongside him, watching ...

Then her hand, surprisingly white against the midnight darkness of her robes, brushed against his fingers.

You must ...

Gregg slid along the curving, branching tendrils of the nervous system, watching for blocks and traps, watching especially for any sign of awareness of his presence. Had he felt that, he would have fled as quickly as he'd entered. He'd always been extremely cautious with aces, even with those who he knew had no mental powers. Kahina seemed unaware of his penetration.

He opend her, setting up the entrances he would use later. Puppetman sighed at the swirling maelstrom of emotion he found there. Kahina was rich, complicated. The hues of her mind were saturated and strong. He could sense her attitude toward him: a brilliant gold-green hope, the ocher of suspicion, a vein of marbled pity/disgust for his world. And yet there was glimmering envy underneath as well, and a yearning that seemed tied to her feelings for her brother.

He followed that trail backward and was surprised at the pure, bitter gall he found there. It had been carefully concealed, layered under safer, more benign emotions and sealed with respect for Allah's favoring of Nur al-Allah, but it was there. It throbbed at his touch, alive.

It took only a moment. Her hand had already withdrawn, but the contact was established. He stayed with her for a few more seconds to be sure, and then he came back to himself.

Gregg smiled. It was done, and he was still safe. Kahina hadn't noticed; Tachyon hadn't suspected.

'We're all grateful for your presence,' Gregg said. 'Tell Nur al-Allah that all we wish is understanding. Doesn't the Qur'an itself begin with the exordium "In the name of Allah, the Compassionate, the Merciful"? We've come out of a sense of that same compassion.'

'Is that the gift you bring, Senator?' she asked in English, and Gregg could feel the wistfulness surging from her opened mind.

'I think,' he told her, 'it's the same gift you would give yourself.'

Wednesday, February 4, 1987, Damascus:

The knock on her hotel door woke Sara from sleep. Groggy, she glanced first at her travel clock: 1:35 A.M. local time – it felt much later. *Still jet lagged. Too early for Gregg, though.*

She put a robe on, rubbing her eyes as she went to the door. The security people had been very definite about the risks here in Damascus. She didn't stand directly in front of the door, but leaned over toward the central peephole. Glancing through, she saw the distorted face of an Arabic woman, swathed in the *chador*. The eyes, the fine structure of the face were familiar, as were the sea-blue beads sewn in the *chador*'s headpiece. 'Kahina?' she queried.

'Yes,' came the muffled voice from the hallway. 'Please. I would talk.'

'Just a minute.' Sara ran a hand through her hair. She exchanged the thin, lacy robe she'd put on for a heavier, more concealing one. She unchained the door, opened it a crack.

A heavy hand threw the door entirely open, and Sara stifled a shout. A burly man scowled at her, a handgun gripped in his large fist. He ignored Sara after an initial glance and prowled through her room, opening the closet door, peering into the bathroom. He grunted, then went back to the door. He spoke something in Arabic, and then Kahina entered. Her bodyguard shut the door behind her and stationed himself near it.

'I'm sorry,' Kahina said. Her voice struggled with the English, but her eyes seemed kind. She gestured in the direction of the guard. 'In our society, a woman ...'

'I think I understand,' Sara said. The man was staring rudely at her; Sara tightened the robe's sash and tugged the neckline higher. Involuntarily she yawned. Kahina seemed to smile under her veil.

'Again I am sorry I woke you, but the dream ...' She shrugged. 'May I sit?'

'Please.' Sara waved toward two chairs by the window.

The guard grunted. He spoke in rapid-fire syllables. 'He says not by the window,' Kahina translated. 'Too unsafe.'

Sara dragged the chairs to the center of the room; that seemed to satisfy the guard, who leaned back against the wall. Kahina took one of the chairs, the dark cloth of her robes rustling. Sara seated herself carefully on the other.

'You were at the meeting?' Kahina asked when they were settled.

'At the press conference afterward, you mean? Yes.'

Kahina nodded. 'I saw you there. I knew your face from Allah's dreams. I come here now because of tonight's dream.'

'You say *my* face was in your dreams?'

Kahina nodded. Sara found that the *chador* made it nearly impossible to read the hidden face. There were only Kahina's piercing eyes above the veils. Yet there seemed to be a deep kindness in them, an empathy. Sara felt herself warming to the woman. 'At the ... *conference*' – Kahina stumbled over the word – 'I said that Nur al-Allah waited to hear of my dreams before he would decide to meet with your people. I've just had his dream.'

'Then why come to me instead of your brother?'

'Because in the dream I was told to come to you.'

Sara shook her head. 'I don't understand. We don't know each other; I was just one of a dozen or more reporters there.'

'You're in love with *him*.'

She knew who Kahina meant. She knew, but the protest was automatic. 'Him?'

'The one with a double face. The one with strings. Hartmann.' When Sara didn't answer, Kahina reached out and touched her hand gently. The gesture was sisterly and strangely knowing. 'You love the one you once hated,' Kahina said. Her hand had not left Sara's.

Sara found that she could not lie, not to Kahina's open, vulnerable eyes. 'I suppose so. You're the Seer; can you tell me how it turns out?' Sara said it jokingly, but Kahina either missed the inflection or chose to ignore it.

'You are happy for the moment, even though you are not his wife, even though you sin. I understand that.' Kahina's fingers pressed against Sara's. 'I understand how hate can be a blunted sword, how it can be beat upon until you begin to think it something else.'

'You're confusing me, Kahina.' Sara sat back, wishing she were completely awake, wishing that Gregg were there. Kahina withdrew her hand.

'Let me tell the dream.' Kahina closed her eyes. She folded her hands in her lap. 'I ... I saw Hartmann, with his two faces, one pleasant to see, the other twisted like an abomination of Allah. *You* were beside him, not his wife, and the face that was pleasant smiled. I could see your feelings for him, how your hatred had been turned. My brother and I were there also, and my brother pointed to the abomination within Hartmann. The abomination spat, and the spittle fell upon me. I saw myself, and *my* face was yours. And I saw that I too had another face within my veils, an abomination-face ugly with spite. Hartmann reached out and twisted my head until only the abomination could be seen.

'For a time the images of the dream were confused. I thought I saw a knife, and I saw Sayyid, my husband, struggling with me. Then the images cleared, and I saw a dwarf, and the dwarf spoke. He said: "Tell her that underneath the hate still lives. Tell her to remember that. The hate will protect you." The dwarf laughed, and his laugh was evil. I did not like him.'

Her eyes opened, and there was a distant terror in them.

Sara started to speak, stopped, began again. 'I ... Kahina, I don't know what any of that means. It's just random images, no better than the dreams I have myself. Does it mean something to you?'

'It's Allah's dream,' Kahina insisted, her voice harsh with intensity. 'I could feel His power in it. I understand this: My brother will meet with your people.'

'Gregg – Senator Hartmann – and the others will be glad to know that. Believe me, we mean only to help your people.'

'Then why is the dream so fearful?'

'Maybe because there's always fear in change.'

Kahina blinked. Suddenly the openness was gone. She was isolated, as hidden as her face behind the *veils*. 'I said something very like that to Nur al-Allah once. He did not like the thought any more than I do now.' She rose swiftly to her feet. The guard came to attention by the door. 'I am glad we met,' she said. 'I will see you again in the desert.' She went to the door.

'Kahina—'

She turned, waiting.

'Was that all you wanted to tell me?'

The shadow of her veils hid her eyes. 'I wanted to tell you one thing only,' she said. 'I wore your face in the dream. I think we are very alike; I feel we are … like kin. What this man you love would do to me, he might also do to you.'

She nodded to the guard. They stepped quickly into the hallway and were gone.

Wednesday, February 4, 1987, in the Syrian Desert:

It was the most barren landscape Gregg had ever seen.

The windows were thick with grime kicked up by the 'copter's blades. Below them, the land was desolate. The vegetation was sparse and dry, clinging to life in the volcanic rock of the desert plateau. The land around the coast had been relatively lush, but the date palms and arable farmland had given way to pines as the trio of helicopters left the mountains of Jabal Duriz. Then there were only hawthorns and bristly scrub. The only life they saw was in the occasional settlement, where robed and turbaned men looked up from goat herds with suspicious eyes.

The ride was long, noisy, and distinctly uncomfortable. The air was turbulent, and the faces around Gregg were sour. He glanced back at Sara; she gave him a halfhearted smile and shrug. The choppers began to descend toward a small town that seemed under siege by brightly colored tents, set in the folds of a prehistoric river valley. The sun was setting behind the barren, purpled hills; the lights of campfires dotted the area.

Billy Ray came back as the helicopter threw swirling gales of dust through the canvas. 'Joanne said it's okay to land, Senator,' Billy half-shouted through the clamor of the engines, cupping his mouth. 'I want you to know that I still don't like it.'

'We're safe enough, Billy,' Gregg shouted back. 'The man would have to be crazy to do anything to us.'

Billy gave him a sidelong look. 'Uh-huh. He's a fanatic. The Nur sect has been linked to terrorism everywhere in the Middle East. Going to *his* headquarters, at *his* beck and call, and with the limited resources I have is cutting Security's throat.'

He sounded more excited than worried – Carnifex *enjoyed* fighting – but Gregg could feel a faint, cold undercurrent of fear under Ray's swelling anticipation. He reached into Billy's mind and tweaked that fear, enjoying the sensation as the feeling heightened. Gregg told himself that it wasn't simply for enjoyment, but because paranoia would make Ray even more effective if there was trouble. 'I appreciate your concerns, Billy,' he said. 'But we're here. Let's see what we can do.'

The 'copters landed in a central square near the mosque. They filed out, all but Tachyon shivering in the evening chill. Only a portion of the delegation had taken the flight from Damascus. Nur al-Allah had forbidden any 'loathsome abominations' to come to this place; the list had excluded all obvious jokers such as Father Squid or Chrysalis; Radha and Fantasy had decided on their own to remain in Damascus. Most of the spouses and much of the scientific team had remained behind as well. The haughtiness of Nur al-Allah's 'invitation' had angered many of the contingent; there had been a bitter debate over whether they should go at all. Gregg's insistence had finally won out.

'Look, I find his demands as distasteful as anyone. But the man's a legitimate force here. He rules Syria and a good portion of Jordan and Saudi as well. It doesn't matter who the elected leaders are – Nur al-Allah has united the sects. I don't like his teachings or his methods, but I can't deny his power. If we turn our backs on him, we change *nothing*. His prejudice, his violence, his hatred will continue to spread. If we *do* meet him, well, at least there's a chance we can get him to temper his harshness.'

He'd laughed self-deprecatingly, shaking his head at his own argument. 'I don't think we have a prayer, really. Still ... it's something we're going to face, if not with Nur al-Allah, then back home with fundamentalists such as Leo Barnett. Prejudice isn't going to go away because we ignore it.'

Puppetman, reaching out, had made certain that Hiram, Peregrine, and the others open to him murmured agreement. The rest had reluctantly withdrawn their objections, even if most decided to remain behind in protest.

In the end the aces willing to meet with Nur al-Allah had been Hiram, Peregrine, Braun, and Jones. Senator Lyons had decided to go at the last minute. Tachyon, to Gregg's dismay, insisted on being included. Reporters and security people swelled the ranks further.

Kahina stepped out from the mosque as the *chuff* of the blades slowed and the steps were let down from the doors of the helicopters. She bowed to them as they disembarked. 'Nur al-Allah bids you welcome,' she said. 'Please, follow me.'

Gregg heard Peregrine's sudden intake of breath as Kahina motioned to them. In the same moment he felt a surge of indignation and panic. He glanced over his shoulder to see Peregrine's wings folded protectively around herself, her gaze fixed on the ground near the mosque. He followed her stare.

A fire had flared up between the buildings. In its flickering light they could all see three flyblown bodies crumpled against the wall, rocks scattered around them. The nearest body was unmistakably a joker, the face elongated into a furry snout and the hands horn-like claws. The smell hit them then, ripe and foul; Gregg could feel the swelling of shock and disgust. Lyons was being desperately and loudly sick; Jack Braun muttered a curse. Inside, Puppetman grinned gleefully while Gregg frowned.

'What is this outrage?' Tachyon demanded of Kahina.

Gregg let himself drift into her mind and found shifting hues of confusion. She'd looked back at the bodies herself, and Gregg felt the quick stab of betrayal within her. Yet when Kahina looked back, she'd covered it with the placid emerald of faith, and her voice was a careful monotone, her gaze flat. 'They were ... abominations. Allah placed the mark of their unworthiness on them, and their death is nothing. That is what Nur al-Allah has decreed.'

'Senator, we are *leaving*,' Tachyon declared. 'This is an intolerable insult. Kahina, tell Nur al-Allah that we will protest most strongly to your government.' His aristocratic face was tight with controlled fury, his hands clenched at his sides. But before any of them could move, Nur al-Allah stepped from the arched entrance to the mosque.

Gregg had no doubt that Nur al-Allah had chosen the time to best display himself. In the darkening night he appeared like a medieval painting of Christ, a holy radiance speading out from him. He wore a thin *djellaba* through which his skin gleamed, his beard and hair dark against the glow. 'Nur al-Allah is Allah's prophet,' he said in accented English. 'If Allah would let you go, you may go. If He would bid you stay, you will stay.'

Nur al-Allah's voice was a cello – a glorious, rich instrument. Gregg knew that he should answer, but couldn't. Everyone in the party was silent; Tachyon froze halfway in his turn back to the helicopters. Gregg had to fight to make his mouth work. His mind was filled with cobwebs, and it was only Puppetman's strength that allowed him to break those bonds. When he did reply, his own voice sounded thin and harsh. 'Nur al-Allah allows the murder of innocents.'

'Nur al-Allah allows the murder of innocents. That's not the power of Allah. That's only the failing of a man,' Gregg rasped.

Sara wanted to shout agreement, but her voice wouldn't obey. Everyone stood as if stunned. Alongside Sara, Digger Downs had been scribbling frantically in his notebook; he'd stopped, the pencil forgotten in his hand.

Sarah felt quick fright – for herself, for Gregg, for everyone. *We shouldn't have come. That voice ...* They'd known Nur al-Allah was an accomplished orator; they'd even suspected that some ace power rode in it, but no reports had said that it was this powerful.

'Man fails when he fails Allah,' Nur al-Allah answered placidly. His voice wove a soft spell, a blanketing numbness. When he spoke, his words seemed filled with truth. 'You think me deranged; I'm not. You think me a threat; I threaten only Allah's enemies. You think me harsh and cruel; if that's so, then it's only because Allah is harsh with sinners. Follow me.'

He turned, walking quickly back into the mosque. Peregrine and Hiram were already moving to follow; Jack Braun looked dazed as he strode after the prophet; Downs brushed past Sara. Sara fought the compulsion, but her legs were possessed. She shambled forward with the rest. Of the party, only Tachyon was immune to Nur al-Allah's power. His features strained, he stood stiffly immobile in the middle of the court. As Sara passed him, he looked back at the helicopters; then, with a glare, let himself be drawn with her into the interior of the mosque.

Oil lamps lit shadowed recesses among the pillars. In the front, Nur al-Allah stood on the dais of the *minbar*, the pulpit. Kahina stood at his right hand, and Sara recognized the gargantuan figure of Sayyid at his left. Guards with automatic weapons moved to stations around the room as Sara and the others milled around the *minbar* in confusion.

'Hear the words of Allah,' Nur al-Allah intoned. It was as if some deity were speaking, for his voice thundered and roared. Its fury and scorn made them tremble, wondering that the very stones of the mosque didn't fall as the power throbbed. '"As for the unbelievers, because of their misdeeds, ill fortune shall not cease to afflict them or crouch at their very doorstep." And He also says: "Woe to the lying sinner! He heard the revelations of Allah recited to Him and then, as though he never heard them, persists in scorn. Those that deride Our revelations when they have scarcely heard them shall be put to a shameful punishment. Those that deny the revelations of their Lord shall suffer the torment of a hideous scourge."'

Sara found unbidden tears streaking down her cheeks. The quotations seemed to burn, etching her soul like acid. Though a part of her struggled, she wanted to shout to Nur al-Allah and beg him for forgiveness. She looked for Gregg and saw him near the *minbar*. Tendons corded in his neck; he seemed to be reaching out for Nur al-Allah, and there was no repentance in his face. *Can't you see?* she wanted to say. *Can't you see how wrong we've been?*

And then, though Nur al-Allah's voice was still deep and resonant, the energy was gone from it. Sara wiped away tears angrily as his bright, sardonic face smiled. 'You see? You feel the power of Allah. You came here to know your enemy – then know that he is strong. His strength is God's, and you could no more defeat that than you could crack the spine of the world itself.' He lifted his hand, fisted it before them. 'Allah's power is here. With it I will sweep all unbelievers from this land. Do you think I need guards to hold you?' Nur al-Allah spat. '*Ptah!* My voice alone is your prison; should I want you to die, I'll simply command it of you and you'll place the barrel in your own mouth. I'll raze Israel to the very ground; I will take the ones marked by the Scourge of Allah and make them slaves; those with power that refuse to give themselves to Allah I will kill. That is what I offer to you. No parley, no compromise, only the fist of Allah.'

'And that we cannot allow.' The voice was Tachyon's, from the back of the mosque. Sara allowed herself to feel a desperate hope.

'And that we cannot allow.' Gregg heard the words as his fingers strained toward Nur al-Allah's sandals. Puppetman added his strength, but it was as if Nur al-Allah stood atop a mountain and Gregg were reaching vainly up from the foot. Beads of sweat stood out on his forehead. Sayyid glanced down scornfully, not even deigning to kick Gregg's hand away from his master.

Nur al-Allah laughed at Tachyon's words. 'You'd challenge me, you who do not believe in Allah? I can feel you, Dr. Tachyon. I can feel your power prying at my mind. You believe that my mind can be broken the way you might break the mind of one of your companions. That's not so. Allah protects me, and Allah will punish those who attack him.'

Yet even as he spoke, Gregg saw the strain on Nur al-Allah's face. His radiance seemed to dim, and the barriers holding Gregg loosened. Whatever the prophet's boast, Tachyon's mental attack was getting through. Gregg felt a quick hope.

At that moment, with Nur al-Allah's attention on Tachyon,

Gregg managed to touch the shimmering flesh of the prophet's foot. The emerald radiance burned hot; he ignored it. Puppetman shouted in triumph.

And then quickly recoiled. Nur al-Allah was *there*. He was aware, and Gregg could sense Tachyon's presence as well. *Too dangerous*, Puppetman cried. *He knows, he knows.* From behind, there was a thud and strangled cry, and Gregg looked back over his shoulder at the doctor.

One of the guards had come up behind Tachyon, clubbing the alien on the head with the butt of his Uzi. Tachyon was on his knees, his hands covering his head, moaning. He struggled to rise, but the guard struck him down brutally. Tachyon lay unconcious on the tiled mosaic of the floor, his breathing labored.

Nur al-Allah laughed. He looked down at Gregg, whose hand still reached futilely toward the foot of the prophet. 'There, you see? I am protected: by Allah, by my people. What about *you*, Senator Hartmann, you with Kahina's strings? Do you still want me now? Perhaps I should show you the strings of Allah and make you dance for His pleasure. Kahina said you are a danger, and Sayyid wants you killed. So perhaps you should be the first sacrifice. How would your people react if they saw you confess your crimes and then, begging Allah's forgiveness, kill yourself? Would that be effective, do you think?'

Nur al-Allah pointed a finger at Gregg. 'Yes,' he said. 'I think it would.'

Puppetman yammered in fear.

'Yes, I think it would.'

Misha listened to her brother's words with unease. Everything he had done was a slap in her face: the flaunting of the stoned jokers, the attack on Tachyon, his haughty threats now. Najib betrayed her with every word.

Najib had used her and lied to her, he and Sayyid. He'd let her go to Damascus thinking that she was representing them, that if she brought the Americans, there might be a chance of some agreement. But Najib hadn't cared. He hadn't listened to her warnings that he overreached himself. A slow festering rose inside her, leaching away her faith. *Allah. I believe in Your voice within Najib. But now he shows his own second face. Is it Yours, as well?*

The doubt diluted the magic of Najib's voice, and she dared to speak and interrupt him.

'You move too fast, Najib,' she hissed. 'Don't destroy us with your pride.'

His glowing face contorted, his speech halting in mid-sentence. '*I* am the Prophet,' he snapped. 'Not you.'

'Then at least listen to me, who sees our future. This is a mistake, Najib. This way leads away from Allah.'

'Be *silent!*' he roared, and his fist lashed out. A red-hued dizziness blinded her. In that moment, with Najib's voice dulled by pain, something in her mind gave way, some barrier that had been holding back all the venom. This fury was cold and deadly, poisonous with every insult and abuse Najib had given her over the years, laced with frustration and denial and subjugation. Najib had turned away from her, expecting her obedience. He resumed his tirade, the power of the voice coiling out over the crowd once more.

It could not touch her, not through what spilled from the bitter pool.

She saw the knife in his sash and knew what she had to do. The compulsion was too great for her to resist.

She leapt at Najib, screaming wordlessly.

Sara saw Nur al-Allah point his glowing finger toward Gregg. Yet in following that gesture, her attention was snagged by Kahina. Sara frowned even under the spell of Nur al-Allah's words, for Kahina was trembling – she stared at her brother and there was nothing in her eyes but acid. She shouted something to him in Arabic, and he swung around to her, still pulsing with flaring power. They exchanged words; he struck her.

It was as if that blow had driven her into a divine madness.

Kahina leapt at Nur al-Allah like some predatory cat, screaming as she clawed at him with bare hands. Dark rivulets of blood dimmed the moon of his face. She tugged at the long, curved knife in his sash, pulling it from the bejeweled scabbard. In the same motion she slashed across his throat with the keen edge. Nur al-Allah clutched at his neck, blood pouring between his fingers as a strangled, wet gasping came from him. He toppled backward.

For a moment the horror held everyone in suspension, then the room erupted into shouts. Kahina was standing in shock above Nur al-Allah, the knife dangling from white fingers. Sayyid bellowed in disbelief, swinging a huge arm that sent Kahina tumbling to the floor. Sayyid took a clumsy step forward – Sara realized with a start that the giant was a cripple. Two of the guards seized Kahina, dragging her to her feet as she struggled. Other men crouched beside the stricken Nur al-Allah, trying to stanch the flow of blood.

Sayyid had reached Kahina. He picked up the dagger she'd dropped, staring at the dark stains on it. He wailed, his eyes raised to heaven, and then drew the blade back to stab her.

But he moaned, the blade still raised. He sagged, his knees buckling as if some great weight were pressing down on him from above, crushing him. Sayyid screamed in agony, dropping the weapon. His massive body collapsed in on itself, the skeleton no longer able to support the flesh. Everyone heard the dry, sickening crack of snapping bones. Sara glanced around and saw Hiram sweating, his right fist squeezing into a white-knuckled fist.

Sayyid whimpered, a shapeless mass on the tiles. The guards let go of Kahina in confusion.

Kahina ran. One of the guards brought his Uzi to bear, but he was slammed against the wall by Mordecai Jones. Jack Braun, glowing golden, picked up another of the Nur al-Allah's guards and tossed him bodily across the room. Peregrine, her feathers molting, was unable to take to the air. Still, she slipped on her taloned gloves and slashed at a guard. Billy Ray, with an exultant whoop, spun and kicked the knees of the gunman alongside him.

Kahina ducked through an archway and was gone.

Sara found Gregg in the confusion. He was safe; a wave of relief flooded through her. She began to run toward him, and the relief turned frigid.

There was no more fright on *his* face, no concern at all.

He seemed calm. He almost seemed to smile.

Sara gaped. She felt nothing but a yawning emptiness. 'No,' she whispered to herself.

What he would do to me, he would also do to you.

'No,' she insisted. 'That can't be.'

Nur al-Allah had pointed his accusing finger at Gregg, and Gregg had known that his only hope lay in the bitterness within Kahina. Nur al-Allah was beyond his control, he knew now, but Kahina was his. Gregg's rape of her mind was brutal and ruthless. He'd stripped everything from her but that underlying hate, letting it flood and swell. It had worked beyond his expectations.

But he'd wanted Kahina dead. He'd wanted her silenced. It must have been Hiram that had stopped Sayyid – too chivalrous to give Kahina to Islamic justice and strangely brutal with his power. Gregg berated himself for not having foreseen that; he could have controlled Hiram, long a puppet, even with the strange hues he'd seen in the man lately. Now the moment was gone, the spell broken with the loss of Nur al-Allah's voice. Gregg let himself touch Hiram's mind and saw that faint, odd coloring there again. He had no time to muse on it.

People were shouting. An Uzi chattered, deafening.

In the midst of chaos Gregg felt Sara. He swung about to find her staring at him. Emotions were shifting wildly inside her. Her love was tattered, stretched thin under swelling ocher suspicion. 'Sara,' he called, and her gaze slid sharply away, looking at the press of people around Nur al-Allah.

There was fighting all around him. He thought he saw Billy, glee on his face, dive bodily at a guard.

Let me have Sara or you've lost her. Puppetman sounded oddly sad. *There's nothing you can say to undo the damage. She's all you can salvage from this. Give her to me, or she's gone too.*

No, she can't know. It's not possible that she knows. Gregg protested, but he knew that he was wrong. He could see the damage in her mind. No lie could repair that.

Grieving, he entered her mind and caressed the torn azure fabric of her affection. Gregg watched as – slowly, carefully – Puppetman buried her distrust under bright and soft ribbons of false love.

He hugged her quickly. 'Come on,' he said gruffly. 'We're leaving.'

Out in the room Billy Ray stood over an unconscious guard. His strident voice ordered his security people into position. 'Move! You – get the doctor. Senator Hartmann – now! Let's get out of here!' There was still some resistance on the floor, but Nur al-Allah's people were in shock. Most knelt around Nur al-Allah's prone body. The prophet was still alive: Gregg could sense his fright, his pain. Gregg wanted Nur al-Allah dead, too, but there was no opportunity for that.

Gunfire erupted near Gregg. Braun, glowing intensely now, stepped in front of the hidden gunman; they could hear the whine of the slugs ricocheting from his body. Gregg grunted in shock even as Braun tore the weapon away from the man. A lancing fire slammed into his shoulder, the impact staggering him. 'Gregg!' he heard Sara cry.

On his knees, he groaned. He pulled his hand away from his shoulder and saw his fingers bright with blood. The room spun around him; Puppetman cowered.

'Joanne, get 'em out! The Senator's hit!' Billy Ray moved Sara aside and crouched beside Gregg. He carefully stripped the blood-stained jacket from the senator to examine the wound. Gregg could feel relief flood through the man. 'You'll be okay – a good, long graze, that's all. Let me give you a hand—'

'I can make it,' he grated through clenched teeth, struggling to his feet. Sara took his good arm, helping him up. He gulped air – there was violence all around him, and Puppetman was too dazed to even feed. He forced himself to think, to ignore the throbbing pain. 'Billy, go on. Get the others.' There was little to do. The remainder of Nur al-Allah's people were tending to their prophet;

Peregrine had slipped outside; Jones and Braun were shepherding Lyons and the other dignitaries. Hiram had turned Tachyon nearly weightless and was assisting him outside as the doctor shook his head groggily. No one resisted their retreat.

Sara let Gregg lean against her as they fled. As they tumbled into seats in the helicopter, she hugged him softly.

'I'm glad you're safe,' she whispered. She took his hand as the chopper's blades tore the night air.

It was as if Gregg grasped a doll's wooden hand. It meant nothing. Nothing at all.

FROM *THE JOURNAL OF XAVIER DESMOND*

February 7/Kabul, Afghanistan:

I am in a good deal of pain today. Most of the delegates have gone on a day trip to various historic sights, but I elected to stay at the hotel once again.

Our tour ... what can I say? Syria has made headlines around the world. Our press contingent has doubled in size, all of them eager to get the inside story of what happened out in the desert. For once, I am not unhappy to have been excluded. Peri has told me what it was like ...

Syria has touched all of us, myself included. Not all of my pain is caused by the cancer. There are times when I grow profoundly weary, looking back over my life and wondering whether I have done any good at all, or if all my life's work has been for nothing. I have tried to speak out on behalf of my people, to appeal to reason and decency and the common humanity that unites us all, and I have always been convinced that quiet strength, perseverance, and nonviolence would get us further in the long run. Syria makes me wonder ... how do you reason with a man like the Nur al-Allah, compromise with him, talk to him? How do you appeal to his humanity when he does not consider you human at all? If there is a God, I pray that he forgives me, but I find myself wishing they had killed the Nur.

Hiram has left the tour, albeit temporarily. He promises to rejoin us in India, but by now he is back in New York City, after jetting from Damascus to Rome and then catching a Concorde back to America. He told us that an emergency had arisen at Aces High that demanded his personal attention, but I suspect the truth is that Syria shook him more than he cared to admit. The rumor has swept round the plane that Hiram lost control in the desert, that he hit General Sayyid with far more weight than was necessary to stop him. Billy Ray, of course, doesn't think Hiram went far enough. 'If it'd been me, I would have piled it on till he was just a brown and red stain on the floor,' he told me.

Worchester himself refused to talk about it and insisted that he was taking this brief leave of us simply because he was 'sick unto death of stuffed grape leaves,' but even as he made the joke, I noticed beads of sweat on his broad, bald forehead and a slight tremor in his hand. I hope a short respite restores him; the more we have traveled together, the more I have to come to respect Hiram Worchester.

If clouds do indeed have a silver lining, however, then perhaps one good did come out of the monstrous incident in Syria: Gregg Hartmann's stature seems to have been vastly enhanced by his near brush with death. For a decade now his political fortunes have been haunted by the specter of the Great Jokertown Riot in 1976, when he 'lost his head' in public. To me his reaction was only human – he had just witnessed a woman being torn to pieces by a mob, after all. But presidential candidates are not allowed to weep or grieve or rage like the rest of us, as Muskie proved in '72 and Hartmann confirmed in '76.

Syria may finally have put that tragic incident to rest. Everyone who was there agrees that Hartmann's behavior was exemplary – he was firm, cool-headed, courageous, a pillar of strength in the face of the Nur's barbarous threats. Every paper in America has run the AP photo that was taken as they pulled out: Hiram helping Tachyon into the helicopter in the background, while in the foreground Senator Hartmann waited, his face streaked with dust, yet still grim and strong, his blood soaking through the sleeve of his white shirt.

Gregg still claims that he is not going to be a presidential candidate in 1988, and indeed all the polls show that Gary Hart has an overwhelming lead for the Democratic nomination, but Syria and the photograph will surely do wonders for his name recognition and his standing. I find myself desperately hoping that he will reconsider. I have nothing against Gary Hart, but Gregg Hartmann is something special, and perhaps for those of us touched by the wild card, he is our last best hope.

If Hartmann fails, all my hopes fail with him, and then what choice will we have but to turn to the Black Dog?

I suppose I should write something about Afghanistan, but there is little to record. I don't have the strength to see what sights Kabul has to offer. The Soviets are much in evidence here, but they are being very correct and courteous. The war is being kept at arm's length for the duration of our short stopover. Two Afghan jokers have been produced for our approval, both of whom swear (through Soviet interpreters) that a joker's life is idyllic here. Somehow I am not convinced. If I understand correctly, they are the only two jokers in all of Afghanistan.

The *Stacked Deck* flew directly from Baghdad to Kabul. Iran was out of the question. The Ayatollah shares many of the Nur's views on wild cards, and he rules his nation in name as well as fact, so even the UN could not secure us permission to land. At least the Ayatollah makes no distinctions between aces and jokers – we are all the demon children of the Great Satan, according to him. Obviously he has not forgotten Jimmy Carter's ill-fated attempt to free the hostages, when a half-dozen government aces were sent in on a secret mission that turned into a horrid botch. The rumor is that Carnifex was one of the aces involved, but Billy Ray emphatically denies it. 'If I'd been along, we would have gotten our people out and kicked the old man's ass for good measure,' he says. His colleague from Justice, Lady Black, just pulls her black cloak more tightly about herself and smiles enigmatically. Mistral's father, Cyclone, has often been linked to that doomed mission as well, but it's not something she'll talk about.

Tomorrow morning we'll fly over the Khyber Pass and cross into India, a different world entirely, a whole sprawling subcontinent, with the largest joker population anywhere outside the United States.

February 12/Calcutta:

India is as strange and fabulous a land as any we have seen on this trip … if indeed it is correct to call it a land at all. It seems more like a hundred lands in one. I find it hard to connect the Himalayas and the palaces of the Moguls to the slums of Calcutta and Bengali jungles. The Indians themselves live in a dozen different worlds, from the aging Britishers who try to pretend that the Viceroy still rules in their little enclaves of the Raj, to the maharajas and nawabs who are kings in all but name, to the beggars on the streets of this sprawling filthy city.

There is so *much* of India.

In Calcutta you see jokers on the streets everywhere you go. They are as common as beggars, naked children, and corpses, and too frequently one and the same. In this quasination of Hindu and Moslem and Sikh, the vast majority of jokers seem to be Hindu, but given Islam's attitudes, that can hardly be a surprise. The orthodox Hindu has invented a new caste for the joker, far below even the untouchable, but at least they are allowed to live.

Interestingly enough, we have found no jokertowns in India. This culture is sharply divided along racial and ethnic grounds, and the enmities run very deep, as was clearly shown in the Calcutta wild card riots of 1947, and the wholesale nationwide carnage that accompanied the partition of the subcontinent that same year. Despite that, today you find Hindu and Muslim and Sikh living side by side on the same street, and jokers and nats and even a few pathetic deuces sharing the same hideous slums. It does not seem to have made them love each other any more, alas.

India also boasts a number of native aces, including a few of considerable power. Digger is having a grand time dashing about the country interviewing them all, or as many as will consent to meet with him.

Radha O'Reilly, on the other hand, is obviously very unhappy here. She is Indian royalty herself, it appears, at least on her mother's side ... her father was some sort of Irish adventurer. Her people practice a variety of Hinduism built around Gonesh, the elephant god, and the black mother Kali, and to them her wild card ability makes her the destined bride of Gonesh, or something along those lines. At any rate she seems firmly convinced that she is in imminent danger of being kidnapped and forcibly returned to her homeland, so except for the official receptions in New Delhi and Bombay, she has remained closely closeted in the various hotels, with Carnifex, Lady Black, and the rest of our security close at hand. I believe she will be very happy to leave India once again.

Dr. Tachyon, Peregrine, Mistral, Fantasy, Troll, and the Harlem Hammer have just returned from a tiger hunt in the Bengal. Their host was one of the Indian aces, a maharaja blessed with a form of the midas touch. I understand that the gold he creates is inherently unstable and reverts to its original state within twenty-four hours, although the process of transmutation is still sufficient to kill any living thing he touches. Still, his palace is reputed to be quite a spectacular place. He's solved the traditional mythic dilemma by having his servants feed him.

Tachyon returned from the expedition in as good a spirit as I've seen him since Syria, wearing a golden nehru jacket and matching turban, fastened by a ruby the size of my thumb. The maharaja was lavish with his gifts, it seems. Even the prospect of the jacket and turban reverting to common cloth in a few hours does not seem to have dampened our alien's enthusiasm for the day's activities. The glittering pageant of the hunt, the splendors of the palace, and the maharaja's harem all seem to have reminded Tach of the pleasures and prerogatives he once enjoyed as a prince of the Ilkazam on his home world. He admitted that even on Takis there was no sight to compare to the end of the hunt, when the maneater had been brought to bay and the maharaja calmly approached it, removed one golden glove, and transmuted the huge beast to solid gold with a touch.

While our aces were accepting their presents of fairy gold

and hunting tigers, I spent the day in humbler pursuits, in the unexpected company of Jack Braun, who was invited to the hunt with the others but declined. Instead Braun and I made our way across Calcutta to visit the monument the Indians erected to Earl Sanderson on the site where he saved Mahatma Gandhi from assassination.

The memorial resembles a Hindu temple and the statue inside looks more like some minor Indian deity than an American black who played football for Rutgers, but still ... Sanderson has indeed become some sort of god to these people; various offerings left by worshipers were strewn about the feet of his statue. It was very crowded, and we had to wait for a long time before we were admitted. The Mahatma is still universally revered in India, and some of his popularity seems to have rubbed off on the memory of the American ace who stepped between him and an assassin's bullet.

Braun said very little when we were inside, just stared up at the statue as if somehow willing it to come to life. It was a moving visit, but not entirely a comfortable one. My obvious deformity drew hard looks from some of the higher-caste Hindus in the press of the people. And whenever someone brushed against Braun too tightly – as happened frequently among such a tightly packed mass of people – his biological force field would begin to shimmer, surrounding him with a ghostly golden glow. I'm afraid my nervousness got the better of me, and I interrupted Braun's reveries and got us out of there hastily. Perhaps I overreacted, but if even one person in that crowd had realized who Jack Braun was, it might have triggered a vastly ugly scene. Braun was very moody and quiet on the way back to our hotel.

Gandhi is a personal hero of mine, and for all my mixed feelings about aces I must admit that I am grateful to Earl Sanderson for the intervention that saved Gandhi's life. For the great prophet of nonviolence to die by an assassin's bullet would have been too grotesque, and I think India would have torn itself apart in the wake of such a death, in a fratricidal bloodbath the likes of which the world has never seen.

If Gandhi had not lived to lead the reunification of the

subcontinent after the death of Jinnah in 1948, would that strange two-headed nation called Pakistan actually have endured? Would the All-India Congress have displaced all the petty rulers and absorbed their domains, as it threatened to do? The very shape of this decentralized, endlessly diverse patchwork country is an expression of the Mahatma's dreams. I find it inconceivable to imagine what course Indian history might have taken without him. So in that respect, at least, the Four Aces left a real mark on the world and perhaps demonstrated that one determined man can indeed change the course of history for the better.

I pointed all this out to Jack Braun on our ride home, when he seemed so withdrawn. I'm afraid it did not help much. He listened to me patiently and when I was finished, he said, 'It was Earl who saved him, not me,' and lapsed back into silence.

True to his promise, Hiram Worchester returned to the tour today, via Concorde from London. His brief sojourn in New York seems to have done him a world of good. His old ebullience was back, and he promptly convinced Tachyon, Mordecai Jones, and Fantasy to join him on an expedition to find the hottest vindaloo in Calcutta. He pressed Peregrine to join the foraging party as well, but the thought seemed to make her turn green.

Tomorrow morning Father Squid, Troll, and I will visit the Ganges, where legend has it a joker can bathe in the sacred waters and be cured of his afflictions. Our guides tell us there are hundreds of documented cases, but I am frankly dubious, although Father Squid insists that there have been miraculous joker cures in Lourdes as well. Perhaps I shall succumb and leap into the sacred waters after all. A man dying of cancer can ill afford the luxury of skepticism, I suppose.

Chrysalis was invited to join us, but declined. These days she seems most comfortable in the hotel bars, drinking amaretto and playing endless games of solitaire. She has become quite friendly with two of our reporters, Sara Morgenstern and the ubiquitous

Digger Downs, and I've even heard talk that she and Digger are sleeping together.

Back from the Ganges. I must make my confession. I took off my shoe and sock, rolled up my pants legs, and put my foot in the sacred waters. Afterward, I was still a joker, alas ... a joker with a wet foot.

The sacred waters are filthy, by the way, and while I was fishing for my miracle, someone stole my shoe.

THE TEARDROP OF INDIA

Walton Simons

The people of Colombo had been waiting for the ape since early morning, and the police were having trouble keeping them away from the docks. A few were getting past the wooden barricades, only to be quickly caught and hustled into the bright yellow police vans. Some sat on parked cars; others had children perched on their shoulders. Most were content to stand behind the cordons, craning their necks for a look at what the local press called 'the great American monster.'

Two massive cranes lifted the giant ape slowly off the barge. It hung bound and limp, dark fur poking out from inside the steel mesh. The only indication of life was the slow rising and falling of its fifteen-foot-wide chest. There was a grinding squeal as the cranes pivoted together, swinging the ape sideways until it was over the freshly painted, green railway car. The flatcar groaned as the ape settled onto its broad steel bed. There was scattered cheering and clapping from the crowd.

It was the same as the vision he'd had only a few months ago – the crowd, the calm sea, and clear sky, the sweat on the back of his neck – all the same. The visions never lied. He knew exactly what would happen for the next fifteen minutes or so; after that he could go back to living again.

He adjusted the collar of his nehru shirt and flashed his government ID card to the policeman nearest him. The officer nodded and stepped out of his way. He was a special assistant to the Secretary of the Interior, which gave him a particularly wide range of responsibilities. Sometimes what he did was little more than nurse-maid rich, visiting foreigners. But it was preferable to the twenty-plus years he'd spent in embassies overseas.

There was a group of twenty or thirty Americans around the train. Most wore light gray security uniforms and were busy chaining the beast down to the railway car. They kept an eye on the ape while going about their business but didn't act afraid. A tall man in a Hawaiian print shirt and plaid Bermuda shorts was standing well away, talking to a girl in a light blue cotton sundress. They were both wearing red and black 'King Pongo' visors.

He walked over to the tall man and tapped him on the shoulder.

'Not now.' The man didn't even bother to turn and look at him.

'Mr. Danforth?' He tapped him on the shoulder again, harder. 'Welcome to Sri Lanka. I'm G. C. Jayewardene. You telephoned me last month about your film.' Jayewardene spoke English, Sinhalese, Tamil, and Dutch. His position in the government required it.

The film producer turned, his face blank. 'Jayewardene? Oh, right. The government guy. Nice to meet you.' Danforth grabbed his hand and pumped it a few times. 'We're real busy right now. Guess you can see that.'

'Of course. If it's not too much trouble, I'd like to ride along while you're transporting the ape.' Jayewardene could not help but be impressed with its size. The monster was even taller than the forty-foot Aukana Buddha. 'It seems much larger when you see it up close.'

'No joke. But it'll be worth all the blood, sweat, and tears it took to get it here when the film comes out.' He jerked his thumb toward the monster. 'That baby is great pub.'

Jayewardene put his hand over his mouth, trying to hide his puzzled expression.

'Publicity.' Danforth smiled. 'Have to watch the industry slang, I guess. Sure, G.C., you can ride in the VIP car with us. It's the one in front of our hairy friend.'

'Thank you.'

The giant ape exhaled, stirring the dust and dirt by its open mouth into a small cloud.

'Great pub,' said Jayewardene.

♠

The rhythmic clacking of the train's wheels on the old railway track relaxed him. Jayewardene had ridden the island trains on countless trips in the forty-odd years since he'd boarded one for the first time as a boy. The girl in the blue dress, who'd finally introduced herself as Paula Curtis, was staring out the window at the terraced tea fields. Danforth was working over a map with a red felt-tip pen.

'Okay,' he said, putting the handle end of the pen to his lips. 'We take the train to the end of the line, which is around the headwaters of the Kalu Ganga.' He flattened the map onto his knees and pointed to the spot with his pen. 'That puts us at the edge of the Udu Walawe National Park, and Roger has supposedly scouted out some great locations for us there. Right?'

'Right,' Paula answered. 'If you trust Roger.'

'He's the director, my dear. We have to trust him. Too bad we couldn't afford somebody decent, but the effects are going to take up most of the budget.'

A steward walked over to them, carrying a tray with plates of curried rice and string hoppers, small steamed strands of rice flour dough. Jayewardene took a plate and smiled. '*Es-thu-ti,*' he said, thanking the young steward. The boy had a round face and broad nose, obviously Sinhalese like himself.

Paula turned from the window long enough to take a plate. Danforth waved the boy away.

'I'm not sure I understand.' Jayewardene took a mouthful of the rice, chewed briefly, and swallowed. There was too little cinnamon in the curry for his taste. 'Why spend money on special effects when you have a fifty-foot ape?'

'Like I said earlier, the monster's great pub. But it would be hell trying to get the thing to perform on cue. Not to mention being prohibitively dangerous to everyone around him. Oh, we may use him in a couple of shots, and definitely for sound effects, but most of the stuff will be done with miniatures.' Danforth grabbed a fingerful of rice from Paula's plate and dropped it into his mouth, then shrugged. 'Then, when the movie opens, the critics will say they can't tell the real ape from the model, and people take that as a challenge, see. Figure they can be the one to spot it. It sells tickets.'

'Surely the publicity value is less than the money it took to get the beast from the City of New York and bring it halfway around the world.' Jayewardene dabbed at the corner of his mouth with a cloth napkin.

Danforth looked up, grinning. 'Actually we got the ape for nothing. See, it gets loose every now and then and starts tearing things up. The city is up to its ass in lawsuits every time that happens. If it's not in New York, it can't do any damage. They almost paid us to take the thing off their hands. Of course we have to make sure nothing happens to it, or the zoo would lose one of its main attractions. That's what those boys in gray are for.'

'And if the ape escapes here, your film company will be liable.' Jayewardene took another bite.

'We've got it doped up all the time. And frankly it doesn't seem much interested in anything.'

'Except blond women.' Paula pointed to her short, brown hair. 'Lucky for me.' She looked back out the window. 'What's that mountain?'

'Sri Pada. Adam's Peak. There is a footprint at the top said to be made by the Buddha himself. It is a very holy place.' Jayewardene made the pilgrimage to the top every year. He planned to do so in the near future, as soon as his schedule allowed it. This time with hopes of cleansing himself spiritually so that there were no more visions.

'No kidding.' Paula elbowed Danforth. 'We going to have time to do any sight-seeing?'

'We'll see,' Danforth said, reaching over for more rice.

Jayewardene set his plate down. 'Excuse me.' He got up and walked to the rear of the car, slid the door open, and stepped out onto the platform.

The giant ape's head was only about twelve feet from where

he stood. Its eyes fluttered, then stared up at the rounded top of Adam's Peak. The ape opened its mouth; lips pulled back, revealing the huge yellow-white teeth. There was a rumble, louder than the train engine, from the back of the monster's throat.

'It's waking up,' he yelled at the security men riding at the back of the flatcar.

They walked forward carefully, steadying themselves on the car's side railing, avoiding the ape's manacled hands. One watched the monster, rifle centered on its head. The other changed the plastic bottle hooked up to the IV in the ape's arm.

'Thanks.' One of the guards waved at Jayewardene. 'It'll be okay now. This stuff will put him out for hours.'

The ape twisted its head and looked directly at him, then turned back to Adam's Peak. It sighed and closed its eyes.

There was something in the monster's brown eyes that he couldn't identify. He paused, then went back into the car. The curry aftertaste was sour in the back of his throat.

They reached the camp at dusk. Actually it was more of a hastily thrown together city of tents and portable buildings. There was less activity than Jayewardene had expected. Most of the crew sat around talking or playing cards. Only the zoo security people were busy, carefully unloading the ape onto a broadbed truck. It was still unconscious from the drug.

Danforth told Paula to introduce Jayewardene around. The director, Roger Winters, was busy making changes in the shooting script. He wore a Frank S. Buck outfit, complete with pith helmet to hide his thinning hair. Paula guided Jayewardene away from the director.

'You wouldn't like him,' she said. 'Nobody does. At least nobody I know. But he can bring them in on schedule. Here's somebody you'll be more interested in. You're not married, are you?'

'Widowed.'

'Oh, sorry.' She waved at a blond woman sitting on the bare wooden steps of the camp's main building. The woman wore a black and red 'King Pongo' T-shirt, tight blue jeans, and leather walking boots.

'Hi, Paula,' said the blonde, tossing her hair. 'Who's your friend?'

'Robyn Symmes, meet Mr. G.C. Jayewardene,' Paula said. Robyn extended her hand. Jayewardene lightly shook it.

'Nice to meet you, Miss Symmes.' Jayewardene bowed, embarrassingly aware of the tightness of his shirt across his oversize stomach. He was flattered to be in the company of the only two women he'd seen in the camp. They were both attractive, in a foreign way. He wiped the sweat from his brow and wondered how they would look in saris.

'Look, I have to go settle Danforth in. Why don't you two entertain each other for a while.' Paula was walking away before either of them had time to answer.

'Your name is Jayewardene? Any relation to President Junius Jayewardene?'

'No. It's a common name. How do you like it here?' He sat down next to her. The steps were uncomfortably hot.

'Well, I've only been here a few days, but it's a beautiful place. A bit too hot for my taste, but I'm from North Dakota.'

He nodded. 'We have every kind of beauty imaginable here. Beaches, mountains, jungle, cities. Something for everyone. Except cold weather of course.'

There was a pause. 'So.' Robyn slapped her hands on her thighs. 'What is it you do that your government decided to stick you out here with us?'

'I'm a diplomat of sorts. My job is to make foreign visitors happy here. Or at least to try. We like to maintain a reputation as a friendly country.'

'Well, I sure haven't seen anything to contradict that. The people I've met practically kill you with kindness.' She pointed to the line of trees at the edge of the camp. 'The animals are something again, though. You know what they found this morning?'

He shrugged.

'A cobra. Right over there. *Üffdä*. That's something that you definitely don't get in North Dakota.' She shuddered. 'Most animals I can handle, but snakes …' She made a face.

'Nature is complete and harmonious here.' He smiled. 'But I must be boring you.'

'No. Not really. You're certainly more interesting than Roger, or the gaffers and grips. How long will you be here? I mean, with the film company.'

'Off and on for your entire stay, although I'll be going back to Colombo tomorrow for a few days. Dr. Tachyon, the alien, and a large party from your country will be arriving here then. To study the effect of the virus in my country.' A shiver eased up his spine.

'You are a busy little bee, aren't you?' She looked up. The light was beginning to dim around the swaying treetops. 'I'm going to go get some sleep. You might want to do the same. Paula will show you where. She knows everything. Danforth wouldn't ever finish a film without her.'

Jayewardene watched her walk away, sighing at the memory of pleasure he thought best forgotten, then got up and headed in the direction Paula had gone. He would need sleep to be fresh for the trip back tomorrow. But sleep never came easily to him. And he was afraid to dream. He'd learned to be afraid.

He woke up biting his right hand hard enough to draw blood. His breathing was ragged and his nightshirt was bathed in sweat. The world around him shimmered and then came into focus. Another vision, snatched from the future. They were happening more and more often in spite of his prayers and meditation. It was only a small comfort that this one wasn't about him. Not directly anyway.

He pulled on his pants and shoes, unzipped his tent, and stepped outside. Jayewardene walked quietly toward the truck where the ape was chained. Two men were on guard. One was leaning against the cab; the other was sitting with his back to one of the huge, mud-covered tires. Both had rifles and lit cigarettes. They were speaking softly to each other.

'What's up?' asked the man by the cab as Jayewardene approached. He didn't bother to raise his rifle.

'I wanted to look at the ape again.'

'In the middle of the night? You'll see more tomorrow morning when it's light.'

'I couldn't sleep. And I'll be returning to Colombo tomorrow.' He walked up next to the monster. 'When did the ape first appear?'

'Blackout of '65 in New York City,' said the seated man. 'Showed up in the middle of Manhattan. Nobody knows where it came from, though. Probably had something to do with the wild card. At least that's what people say.'

Jayewardene nodded. 'I'm going to walk around to the other side. To look at his face.'

'Just don't put your head in its mouth.' The guard flicked his cigarette butt onto the ground. Jayewardene crushed it out with his shoe as he walked past.

The ape's breath was hot, organic, but not foul. Jayewardene waited, hoping that the beast would open its eyes again. The vision had told him what was behind them, but he wanted another look. The dreams had never been wrong before, but his reputation would be destroyed if he went to the authorities with this story and it proved wrong. And there would be questions about how he could have known. He would have to answer them without revealing his unusual abilities. Not an easy problem to solve in so little time.

The ape's eyes stayed shut.

The jungle's night sounds were more distant than usual. The animals were staying far away from the camp. Jayewardene hoped it was because they sensed the ape. Sensed the wrongness about it. He glanced at his watch. It would be dawn in a couple of hours. He would speak to Danforth first thing in the morning, then go back to Colombo. Dr. Tachyon had the reputation of being able to work wonders. It would be his task to transform the ape. The vision made that very clear. Perhaps the alien could even help him. If his pilgrimage failed.

He walked back to his tent and spent the next few hours praying to the Buddha for a little less enlightenment.

It was past nine o'clock when Danforth emerged, bleary-eyed, from the main portable building. Jayewardene was on his second cup of tea but was still moving slowly, as if his body were encased in mud.

'Mr. Danforth. I must speak to you before leaving this morning.'

Danforth yawned and nodded. 'Fine. Look, before you get away, I want to take some pictures. You know, the entire crew and the ape. Something to give to the wire services. I'd appreciate it if you'd be in it too.' Danforth yawned again, even wider. 'God, got to get some coffee in me. The boys are supposed to have everything set up by now. I'll be free for a few minutes after that, and we can talk about it then.'

'I think it would be best to discuss it now, privately.' He looked out into the jungle. 'Perhaps take a walk away from the camp.'

'In the jungle? I heard they killed a cobra yesterday. No way.' Danforth backed away. 'I'll talk to you after we get our publicity shots done, not before.'

Jayewardene took another sip of tea and walked over to the truck. He wasn't surprised or disgusted at Danforth's attitude. The man had the weight of a multimillion dollar project on his shoulders. That kind of pressure could skew anyone's values; make him fear the wrong things.

Most of the crew were already assembled in front of the giant ape. Paula was sitting in front, chewing on her fingernails while looking over the production schedule. He knelt down next to her.

'I see his majesty hooked you into doing this just like the rest of us,' Paula said without looking up.

'I'm afraid so. You don't look like you slept very well.'

'It's not that I didn't sleep well. I didn't sleep period. I was up with Roger and Mr. D. all last night. But it comes with the territory.' She leaned her head back and rotated it in a slow, circular motion. 'Well, as soon as Roger, Robyn, and the boss get here, we can get this fun over with.'

Jayewardene downed the rest of his tea. Later in the day a busload of extras, most Sinhalese with a few Tamils and Muslims, was scheduled to arrive. All those selected to be in the film spoke English, which was not uncommon, given the island's history of British involvement.

Danforth showed up with Roger in tow. The producer looked at the group and squinted. 'The ape's facing the wrong way. Somebody get that truck turned around.'

A gray-clad guard waved, jumped up into the cab, and started the truck up.

'Okay. Everybody out of the way so we can get this done quickly.' Danforth motioned them toward him.

Somebody whistled and Jayewardene turned. Robyn was walking toward the group. She was wearing a long, skintight silver dress. She wasn't smiling.

'Why do I have to wear this now? It's going to be bad enough during shooting. I'll probably get heat stroke.' Robyn put her hands on her hips and frowned.

Danforth shrugged. 'Jungle shooting is a pain in the butt. You knew that when you took the part.'

Robyn pressed her lips tightly together and was quiet.

The truck backed into position and Danforth clapped his hands. 'All right. Everybody back where you were before. We'll get this over as quickly as possible.'

One of the guards walked over to Danforth. Jayewardene moved in close enough to hear.

'I think we woke it up when we moved the truck, sir. Want me to dope him up again before you take your pictures?'

'No. It'll look better if there's a little life in the damned thing.' Danforth stroked his chin. 'And feed it when we're done. Then you can knock it out again.'

'Right, sir.'

Jayewardene took his place in front of the truck. The ape's breathing was irregular. He turned. The ape's eyes fluttered and opened. Its pupils were dilated. The eyes moved about slowly, looked at the cameras, and stopped at Robyn. They became bright and purposeful. Jayewardene felt his skin go cold.

The ape took a deep breath and roared, a sound like a hundred lions. Jayewardene started to run but tripped over somebody who'd reacted away from the ape and into him. The ape was rocking back and forth on the truck. One of the tires blew out. The monster continued to roar and pull at the chains. Jayewardene struggled to his feet. He heard the high-pitched squeal of metal straining against metal, then a loud pinging noise as the chains snapped. Steel shrapnel from the broken chains flew in all directions. One piece hit a guard. The man fell, screaming. Jayewardene ran to the man and helped him to his feet. The ground was shaking right behind them. He turned to look back, but the ape was already past them. Jayewardene turned to the injured man.

'Broken rib, I think. Maybe two,' said the guard through gritted teeth. 'I'll be okay.'

A woman screamed. Jayewardene left the man and rushed ahead. He could see most of the ape over the tin tops of the portable buildings. It bent down and picked up something in its right hand. It was Robyn. He heard a gunshot and tried to move faster. His sides ached already.

The ape snatched up a tent and threw it at one of the guards, whose rifle was raised for another shot. The canvas drifted down over the man, spoiling his aim.

'No. No,' Jayewardene yelled. 'You might hit the woman.'

The monster looked over the camp briefly, then waved its free arm disdainfully at the humans and shouldered into the jungle. Robyn Symmes was limp and pale against the huge darkness of its chest.

Danforth sat on the ground, head in hands. 'Oh, shit. What the hell do we do now. This wasn't supposed to happen. Those chains were made of titanium steel. It can't be happening.'

Jayewardene put his hand on the producer's shoulder. 'Mr. Danforth, I'll need your fastest car and your best driver. And it might be better if you came along with us.'

Danforth looked up. 'Where are we going?'

'Back to Colombo. A group of your aces is arriving there in a few hours.' He smiled thinly. 'Long ago our island was called Serendib. The land of fortunate coincidence.'

'Thank god. There's a chance then.' He stood up, the color returning to his face. 'I'll get things moving.'

'Need any help?' Paula dabbed at a cut over her eye with her shirtsleeve.

'Only all I can get,' Danforth said.

The ape roared again. It already seemed impossibly far away.

The car sped along down the road, jolting them at every bump and pothole. They were still a few miles outside Ratnapura. Jayewardene was in the front seat, directing the driver. Paula and Danforth sat silently in the back. As they rounded a corner, he saw several saffron-robed Buddhist priests ahead. 'Stop,' he yelled as the driver braked the car. They went into a skid and off the road, sliding to a stop. The priests, who had been working on the dirt road with shovels, stood to one side and motioned them through.

'Who are they?' asked Paula.

'Priests. Members of an appropriate technologist group,' Jayewardene said as the driver pulled back onto the road. He bowed to the priests as he went past. 'Much of their time is spent doing such work.'

He planned to call ahead from Ratnapura. Let the government know the situation and discourage the military from attacking the creature. That would be difficult, given the amount of damage it could cause. Tachyon and the aces would be the answer. They had to be. His stomach burned. It was dangerous to hinge his plans on people he'd never met, but he had no other choice.

'I wonder what set him off?' Danforth asked, his voice almost too soft to hear.

'Well' – Jayewardene turned to speak to them – 'he looked at the cameras, then at Miss Symmes. It was as if something clicked in his brain, brought him right out of the stupor.'

'If anything happens to her, it'll be my fault.' Danforth looked at the muddy floorboard. 'My fault.'

'Then we'll all have to work hard to make sure nothing does happen to her,' Paula said. 'Okay?'

'Right,' Danforth said weakly.

'Remember,' she said, patting his shoulder. 'It's beauty that kills the beast. Not the other way around.'

'Hopefully we can resolve the situation and keep both beauty and beast alive.' Jayewardene turned to look back at the road. He spotted the buildings of Ratnapura ahead. 'Slow down when you get to town. I'll direct you where we need to go.' He intended to inform the military of the situation and then return to Colombo. Jayewardene sank back into the car seat. He wished he had slept better the night before. Today's work was going to spill into tomorrow and maybe even the next day.

They arrived back in Colombo a little after noon and went directly to Jayewardene's home. It was a large white stucco residence with a red-tiled roof. Even when his wife had been alive, it had been more space than they needed. Now he rattled around in it like a coconut in an empty boxcar. He called his office and found out the American delegation of aces had arrived and was staying at the Galadari Meridien Hotel. After settling Danforth and Paula in, he went to his garden shrine and reaffirmed his pledge of the Five Precepts.

Afterward he hurriedly put on a clean white shirt and pair of pants and ate a few fingerfuls of cold rice.

'Where are you going now?' Paula asked as he opened the door to leave.

'To speak to Dr. Tachyon and the Americans about the ape.' He shook his head as she got up off the couch. 'It would be better for you to rest now. Whatever develops, I'll call you.'

'Okay.'

'Is it all right if we get something to eat?' Danforth already had the refrigerator door open.

'Certainly. Help yourselves.'

Traffic was heavy, even on the Sea Beach Road, which Jayewardene had instructed the driver to take. The car's air conditioner was broken and his clean clothes were soaked with sweat before they were even halfway to the hotel.

The film company driver, his name was Saul, was slowing to stop in front of the Galadari Meridien when the engine died. He turned the key several times, but there was only a clicking sound.

'Look.' Jayewardene pointed toward the hotel entrance. People were scattering around the main doorway as something rose into the air. Jayewardene shaded his eyes as they flew over. One was a full-grown Indian elephant. A common enough sight, but this one was flying. Seated on its back was a well-muscled man. The elephant's ears were extended and appeared to help the creature steer while flying.

'Elephant Girl,' said Saul. Crowds stopped up and down the street, pointing in silence as the aces flew by overhead.

'Do what you can with the car,' he told Saul, who already had the hood up.

Jayewardene walked quickly to the hotel's main entrance. He pushed past the doorman, who was sitting on the sidewalk shaking his head, and into the darkness inside. Hotel employees were busy lighting candles and reassuring the guests in the bar and restaurant.

'Waiter, get those drinks over here.' The male voice came from the bar. He spoke English with an American accent.

Jayewardene let his eyes adjust to the dim lighting, then made his way carefully into the bar. The bartender was setting lamps up next to the mirror behind the bar. Jayewardene pulled out his handkerchief and wiped his sweaty forehead.

They were seated together in a booth. There was a large man with a dark spade-shaped beard, wearing a tailored blue three-piece suit. Across from him was another man. He was middle-aged, but trim, and sat in the booth as if it were a throne. Although he thought he knew the men, the woman sitting between them was instantly recognizable. She was wearing a low-cut, shoulderless black dress, trimmed with sequins. Her skin was transparent. He quickly looked away from her. Her bone and muscles reflected the light in a disturbing manner.

'Pardon me,' he said, walking over to them. 'My name is Jayewardene. I'm with the Department of the Interior.'

'And what do you want?' The large man took a skewered cherry
from his drink and rolled it between his manicured thumb and
forefinger.

The other man stood, smiled, and shook Jayewardene's hand.
The gesture was studied, a political greeting refined by years of
practice. 'I'm Senator Gregg Hartmann. Pleased to meet you.'

'Thank you, Senator. I hope your shoulder is better.' Jayewardene
had read about the incident in the newspapers.

'It wasn't as bad as the press made it sound.' Hartmann looked
at the other end of the booth. 'The man torturing that cherry is
Hiram Worchester. And the lady is—'

'Chrysalis, I believe.' Jayewardene bowed. 'May I join you.'

'Certainly,' Hartmann said. 'Is there something we can do for
you?'

Jayewardene sat down next to Hiram, whose bulk partially obscured Chrysalis. He found her profoundly disturbing to look at.
'Several things perhaps. Where were Elephant Girl and that man
going just now?'

'To catch the ape, of course.' Hiram looked at him as one might
at an embarrassing relative. 'And rescue the girl. We just found
out about it. Catching the beast is something of a tradition.' He
paused. 'For aces.'

'Is that possible? I don't think Elephant Girl and one man can
manage that.' Jayewardene turned to Hartmann.

'The man with her was Jack Braun,' Chrysalis said. Her accent
was more British than American. 'Golden Boy. He can handle
almost anything, up to and including the giant ape. Although he
hasn't been getting his rest lately. His glow's been a little on the
feeble side.' She nudged Hiram. 'Don't you think?'

'Personally I don't really care what happens to Mr. Braun.'
Hiram twirled the small, red plastic sword from his drink. 'And I
think the feeling's mutual.'

Hartmann coughed. 'At the very least they should be able to rescue the actress. That should simplify matters for your government.'

'Yes. One would hope.' Jayewardene folded and unfolded a cloth napkin. 'But such a rescue should be carefully planned out.'

'Yes, they did rather fly off the handle,' Chrysalis said, taking a sip of brandy.

Jayewardene thought he caught a glint of mischief in Hartmann's eyes, but dismissed it as the lighting. 'Could you tell me where to find Dr. Tachyon?'

Hiram and Chrysalis both laughed. Hartmann maintained his poise and gave them a disapproving look. 'He's unavailable right now.'

Chrysalis motioned to the waiter and pointed to her glass. 'Which one of the stewardesses is he trying this time?'

'Upstairs, trapped in the darkness together. If anything will help Tachy get over his problem, this is it. The doctor's not to be disturbed right now.' Hiram held the plastic sword above the table and made a fist with his other hand. The sword fell and stuck in the tabletop. 'Get the point?'

'Could we give him a message for you?' Hartmann asked, ignoring Hiram.

Jayewardene pulled out his snakeskin wallet and handed Hartmann one of his business cards. 'Please have him contact me as soon as possible. I may be busy the rest of the afternoon, but he can reach me at my home. It's the bottom number.'

'I'll do what I can,' Hartmann said, standing to shake hands again. 'I hope we see you again before we leave.'

'Nice meeting you, Mr. Jayewardene,' Chrysalis said. He thought perhaps she was smiling, but couldn't be sure.

Jayewardene turned to leave but stopped short as two people entered the bar. One was a man whom Jayewardene judged to be in his late thirties. He was tall and muscular with blond hair and a camera slung over his shoulder. The woman with him was as stunningly beautiful as any of the photographs Jayewardene had seen of her. Even without the wings she would have attracted attention.

Peregrine was a vision he would willingly linger on. Jayewardene stepped out of their way as they joined the others in the booth.

They were still lighting candles and lamps in the lobby when he left.

♥

It was hard to arrange for a helicopter with the ape on the loose, but the base commander owed him more than one favor. The pilot, headgear under his arm, was waiting for Jayewardene at the chopper. He was dark-skinned, a Tamil, part of the military's new plan to try to integrate the armed forces. The aircraft itself was a large, outdated model, lacking the sleek aerodynamics of the newer attack ships. Olive paint was peeling from the chopper's metal skin and the tires were balding.

Jayewardene nodded to the pilot and spoke to him in Tamil. 'I had requested a bullhorn be put on board.'

'Already done, sir.' The pilot opened the door and crawled up into the cockpit. Jayewardene followed.

The young Tamil was going through a checklist, flipping switches, examining gauges.

'I've never been in a helicopter before,' Jayewardene said, buckling his seat belt. He pulled against the belt, testing it, not exactly happy that it was fraying around the edges.

The pilot shrugged and put on his helmet, then cranked the engine, took the stick, and engaged the rotor. The blades whopped noisily and the helicopter lifted slowly into the sky. 'Where are we going, sir?'

'Let's head down toward Ratnapura and Adam's Peak.' He coughed. 'We'll be looking for a man on a flying elephant. American aces.'

'Do you want to engage them, sir?' The pilot's tone was cool and professional.

'No. No, nothing like that. Just observe them. They're after the ape that escaped.'

The pilot took a deep breath and nodded, then flipped on the radio and picked up the mouthpiece. 'Lion base, this is Shadow One. Can you give us any information on a flying elephant? Over.'

There was a pause and crackle of static before the base

answered. 'Your target reported heading due east from Colombo. Approximate speed one five zero kilometers per hour. Over.'

'Acknowledged. Over and out.' The pilot checked his compass and adjusted his course.

'Hopefully we can find them before they locate the ape. I don't think they have any real idea where to look, but the country isn't that large.' Jayewardene pointed to dark clouds ahead. As he did there was a flash of lightning. 'Are we safe from bad weather?'

'Fairly safe. Do you think these Americans would be stupid enough to fly into a storm?' He pointed the chopper toward a thin spot in the wall of clouds.

'Hard to say. I don't know these people. They've handled the creature before, though.' Jayewardene looked down. The land beneath was rising steadily upward. The jungle was broken here and there with tea and rice fields or water reservoirs. From the air the flooded rice paddies looked like the shards of a broken mirror, the pieces reassembled so that they almost touched each other.

'Something ahead, sir.' The pilot reached under his seat and handed over a pair of binoculars. Jayewardene took them, wiped off the lenses with the tail of his shirt, and looked in the direction the pilot was pointing. There was something. He rotated the adjusting knob and brought it into focus. The man on the elephant was pointing toward the ground.

'It's them,' Jayewardene said, setting the binoculars on his lap. 'Get in close enough for this to be heard.' He raised the bull-horn.

'Yes, sir.'

Jayewardene's mouth and throat were dry. He opened his window as they got closer in. The aces didn't seem to have noticed them yet. He switched on the bullhorn and set the volume control near the top. He saw the ape's shoulders and head above the tree-tops and knew why the Americans were paying no attention to the helicopter.

He stuck the bullhorn out the window as the chopper moved in. 'Elephant Girl. Mr. Braun.' Jayewardene thought Golden Boy was inappropriate for a grown man. 'My name is Jayewardene. I'm an official with the Sri Lankan government. Do you understand what I am saying?' He spoke each word slowly and carefully. The bull-horn vibrated in his sweaty hand.

Jack Braun waved and nodded. The monster had stopped to look up and bare its teeth. It stripped the foliage off the top of a tree and set Robyn in a crook between two bare branches.

'Rescue the woman if you can, but do not harm the ape.' Jaye-wardene's voice sounded almost unintelligible from inside the helicopter, but Braun made a thumbs-up signal to show he understood. 'We'll stand by,' Jayewardene said.

The ape reached down, scooped up a handful of dirt, and crushed the contents down with its palms. The creature roared and threw the dirtball at the aces. The flying elephant dropped out of its path. The missile continued upward. Jayewardene saw it was going to hit the chopper and gripped the seat as tightly as possible. The earth thudded against the side of the aircraft. The helicopter began to spin, but the pilot quickly brought it back under control and pulled up sharply.

'Better keep a safe distance,' the pilot said, making sure the ape stayed in view. 'If the momentum hadn't been spent on that, I don't think we'd still be in the air.'

'Right.' Jayewardene slowly exhaled and wiped his brow. A few scattered raindrops began to dot the windshield.

The Elephant Girl had moved about fifty yards away from the ape and down to treetop level. Braun jumped off her and disappeared into the undergrowth. The elephant gained height again and trumpeted, moving back toward the monster. The ape snarled and beat its chest, the sound like an explosion underground.

The standoff lasted a minute or two, then the ape rocked backward, catching its balance just at the point of falling over. Elephant Girl swooped down quickly toward the woman in the tree. The ape swung his arms at her. The flying elephant banked away, wobbling a bit.

'Did it hit her?' Jayewardene turned to the pilot. 'Should we move in and try to help?'

'I don't think there's much we can do. Possibly distract it. But that could get us knocked down.' The pilot put the stick between his knees and wiped the sweat from his palms.

The ape roared and reached down to pick up something. Jack Braun struggled in the creature's hand, trying to push the giant fingers open. The ape lifted him up to its open mouth.

'No,' Jayewardene said, turning his head away.

The beast roared again and Jayewardene looked back. The monster rubbed its mouth with its free hand. Braun, apparently unhurt, was bracing his back against the ape's fingers and pushing the thumb open. The monster flipped its arm like a baseball pitcher, sending Braun cartwheeling through the air. He came down in heavy jungle several seconds and several hundred yards away.

The Tamil sat with his mouth slightly open, then put the helicopter into a turn toward the spot where Braun had disappeared into the trees. 'It tried to eat him, but he wouldn't go down. I think he broke one of the devil's teeth.'

The Elephant Girl followed behind them. The ape picked Robyn out of the tree and after a final triumphant roar, began wading through the jungle again. Jayewardene bit his lip and looked at the treetops for broken limbs to show where Braun had fallen through.

The rain grew heavier and the pilot switched on the wipers. 'There he is,' the Tamil said, slowing to a hover. Braun was climbing up a large coconut palm tree. His clothes were in tatters, but he didn't appear hurt. Elephant Girl moved in, curled her trunk around his waist, and lifted him onto her back. Braun bent over and held on to her ears.

'Follow us,' Jayewardene said, using the bullhorn again. 'We'll lead you back to the airbase. Are you all right, Mr. Braun?'

The golden ace made a thumbs-up again, this time without looking at them.

Jayewardene said nothing for several minutes. Perhaps his vision had been wrong. The beast appeared so vicious. A normal person would have been crushed to a paste between the monster's teeth. No. The dream had to be true. He couldn't allow any self-doubt, or the ape would have no chance at all.

They outraced the storm back to Colombo.

Jayewardene paused outside Tachyon's door. He'd been sleeping when the alien called. Tachyon had apologized for taking so long to get back to him and began listing the reasons. Jayewardene had interrupted and asked if he could come over immediately. The doctor had said yes with little enthusiasm.

He knocked and waited, then raised his hand again before he heard footfalls from the other side. Tachyon opened the door, wearing a puffy-sleeved white shirt and blue velvet pants sashed with a large red scarf. 'Mr. Jayewardene? Please come in.' Jayewardene bowed and went in.

Tachyon sat down on the bed, underneath an oil painting of Dunhinda Falls. A scarlet-plumed hat and a partially eaten plate of rice were on the bedside table. 'You are the same Mr. Jayewardene from the helicopter? The one Radha told me about.'

'Yes.' Jayewardene lowered himself into the lounger next to the bed. 'I hope Mr. Braun wasn't injured.'

'Only his already battered pride.' Tachyon closed his eyes for a moment, as if trying to gather strength, then reopened them. 'Please tell me how I can help you, Mr. Jayewardene.'

'The military is planning on attacking the ape tomorrow. We must stop them and subdue the creature ourselves.' Jayewardene rubbed his eyes. 'But I'm not starting at the beginning. The military deals with harsh reality. But you, Doctor, work in the context of the extraordinary on a daily basis. I don't know you, but I am in a position of needing to trust you.'

Tachyon placed his dangling feet firmly on the floor and straightened his shoulders. 'I've spent most of my life here trying to live up to the trust of others. I only wish I could believe the trust was warranted. But you say we must stop the military and subdue the ape ourselves. Why? Surely they're better equipped—'

Jayewardene interrupted. 'The virus doesn't affect animals, if I understand correctly.'

'I know the virus doesn't affect animals,' Tachyon replied with a shake of his curly, red hair. 'I helped develop the virus. Every child knows ...' He covered his mouth. 'Ancestors forgive me.' He slid off the bed and walked to the window. 'For twenty years it's been staring me in the face, and I *missed* it. By my own blind stupidity I've sentenced some individual to a living hell. I've failed one of mine again. The trust isn't warranted.' Tachyon pressed his fists against his temples and continued berating himself.

'Your pardon, Doctor,' Jayewardene said. 'I think your energies would be more beneficial if we applied them to the problem at hand.' Tachyon turned, a pained expression on his face. 'I meant no offense, Doctor,' he added, sensing the depth of the alien's guilt.

'No. No, of course not. Mr. Jayewardene, how did you know?'

'Not many of our people have been touched by the virus. I'm one of the very few. I suppose I should be grateful to be alive and whole, but it's in our nature to complain. My ability gives me visions of the future. Always about someone or some place I know, usually myself. And so detailed and vivid.' He shook his head. 'My most recent one showed me the ape's true nature.'

Tachyon sat back down on the bed, tapping his fingertips together. 'What I don't understand is the primitive behavior exhibited by the creature.'

'I'm sure that most of our questions can be answered once he's a man again.'

'Of course. Of course.' Tachyon popped up off the bed again. 'And your ability. Temporal displacement of the cognitive self during dreamstate. This was what my family had in mind when they created the virus. Something that transcends known physical values. Amazing.'

Jayewardene shrugged. 'Yes, amazing. But it's a burden I would gladly give up. I want to view the future from its proper perspective, the here and now. This – power – destroys the natural flow of life. After the ape is restored, I plan to make my pilgrimage to Sri Pada. Perhaps through spiritual purity I may be rid of it.'

'I've had some success reversing the effects at my clinic.' Tachyon twisted his sash. 'Of course the success rate isn't what I'd hoped. And the risk would be yours to take.'

'We must deal with the ape first. After that my path may become more clear.'

'If only we had more time here,' Tachyon complained. 'The tour is supposed to leave for Thailand day after tomorrow. That leaves us little margin for error. And we can't all go chasing out after the creature.'

'I don't think the government would allow it in any case. Not after today. The fewer of your people we involve, the better.'

'Agreed. I can't believe the others went off like that. Sometimes I think we're all suffering from some kind of creeping insanity. Hiram especially.' Tachyon walked to the window and opened the mini-blinds. Lightning flashed on the horizon, briefly silhouetting the wall of towering thunderclouds. 'Obviously I must be included in this little adventure. Radha can give me maneuverability. She's half-Indian. There have been problems between your country and India lately, I believe?'

'Sadly, yes. The Indians support the Tamils, since they have the same cultural heritage. The Sinhalese majority looks at this as support for the Tamil Tigers, a terrorist group.' Jayewardene looked down at the floor. 'It is a conflict with no winners and too many victims.'

'So we must have a cover story. That Radha was hiding out, afraid for her life. She might present the answer to some other problems.' Tachyon closed the blinds. 'What weaponry will be used against the ape?'

'Two waves of helicopters. The first will move in with steel nets. The second, if needed, will be fully armed attack ships.'

'Could you slip us onto their base before the second wave gets off the ground?' Tachyon rubbed his palms together.

'Possibly. Yes, I think I could.'

'Good.' The alien smiled. 'And Mr. Jayewardene, in my own defense, there's been so much in my life, the founding of the clinic, unrest in Jokertown, the Swarm invasion—'

Jayewardene cut him off. 'Doctor, you owe me no explanation.'

'But I will owe him one.'

♠

They'd stopped the car a couple of miles from the gate to put Radha into the trunk. Jayewardene took a sip of tea from his Styrofoam cup. It was thick, coppery, and hot enough to help ward off the predawn chill. Since the road to the air base was bumpy, he had only partially filled his cup. There was a cold ache inside him that even the tea could not reach. Even in his best case scenario he would be forced to resign his post. He was overstepping his authority in an unforgivable manner. But he couldn't worry about what might happen to him; the ape was his first concern. He and Tachyon had stayed up most of the night, trying to cover all the things that might go wrong and what to do if the worst happened.

Jayewardene was in the front seat with Saul. Tachyon was in back between Danforth and Paula. No one spoke. Jayewardene reached for his government ID as they approached the well-lit front gate.

The gate guard was a young Sinhalese. His shoulders were as straight as the creases in his khaki uniform. His eyes were bright and he moved with measured steps to Jayewardene's side of the car.

Jayewardene rolled down his window and handed the guard his ID. 'We wish to speak with General Dissanayake. Dr. Tachyon and two representatives of the American film company are in our party as well as myself.'

The guard looked at the ID, then at the people in the car. 'One moment,' he said, then headed over to the small booth beside the gate and picked up the phone. After speaking for a few moments he walked back and handed the ID back with five laminated visitor badges. 'The general will see you. He's in his office. Do you know the way, sir?'

'Yes, thank you,' Jayewardene said, rolling his window back up and clipping one of the badges onto his shirt pocket.

The guard opened the gate and motioned them past with his red-tipped flashlight. Jayewardene sighed as they drove through and the gate closed behind them. He directed Saul to the officers' complex and patted the driver on the shoulder. 'You know what to do?'

Saul eased the car to a stop between two faded yellow stripes and removed the keys, holding them between his thumb and forefinger. 'As long as the trunk opens, you don't have to worry about my screwing up.'

They got out of the car and walked down the sidewalk toward the building. Jayewardene heard helicopter rotors cutting the air overhead. Once inside, Tachyon stayed at Jayewardene's side as he guided them down the linoleum hallways. The alien was fussing with the cuffs of his coral-pink shirt. Paula and Danforth followed closely behind them, whispering to each other.

The corporal in the general's outer office looked up from his cup of tea and waved them in. The general was sitting behind his desk in a large swivel chair. He was a man of average height and compact build with dark, deep-set eyes and an expression that seldom changed. Some in the military community felt that, at fifty-four, Dissanayake was too young to be a general. But he had been both firm and controlled in his dealing with the Tamil Tigers, a militant separatist group. He had managed to avoid a bloodbath without appearing weak. Jayewardene respected him. The general nodded as they entered, pointing to the group of chairs opposite his cluttered desk.

'Please, sit down,' Dissanayake said, tightening his lips into a half-smile. His English was not as good as Jayewardene's, but was still easily understandable. 'Always a pleasure to see you, Mr. Jayewardene. And of course to welcome our other distinguished visitors.'

'Thank you, General.' Jayewardene waited for the others to seat themselves before continuing. 'We know that you're quite busy now and appreciate your time.'

Dissanayake looked at his gold watch and nodded. 'Yes, I'm supposed to be up at operations right now. The first wave is scheduled to be taking off as we speak. So,' he said, clasping his hands, 'if you could be as brief as possible.'

'We don't think you should attack the ape,' Tachyon said. 'To my knowledge it's never harmed anyone. Are there any reports of casualties so far?'

'None have been reported, Doctor.' Dissanayake leaned back in his chair. 'But the monster is headed for Adam's Peak. If unchecked, there will almost certainly be fatalities.'

'But what about Robyn?' Paula said. 'You go after the ape with attack choppers and she's likely to be killed.'

'And if we do nothing, hundreds could be killed. Possibly thousands if it reaches a city.' Dissanayake bit his lip. 'It is my duty to prevent that from happening. I do understand what it means to have a friend in danger. And be assured, we will do everything possible to rescue Miss Symmes. My men will sacrifice their own lives to save hers, if need be. But to me her safety is no more important than the others who are threatened. Please, try to understand my position.'

'And nothing we can say will persuade you even to postpone the attack?' Tachyon hand-combed his hair back out of his eyes.

'The ape is very near to Adam's Peak. There are many pilgrims at this time of year, and there is no time for a successful evacuation. Delay will almost certainly cost lives.' Dissanayake stood and picked up his cap from the desktop. 'And now I must see to my duties. You're welcome to monitor the operation from here if you like.'

Jayewardene shook his head. 'No, thank you. We do appreciate your taking time to see us.'

The general extended his palms. 'I wish I could have been more helpful. Good luck to us all, even the ape.'

The sky was beginning to brighten when they got back to the car. Saul was leaning against the door, an unlit cigarette in his mouth. Tachyon and Jayewardene walked over to him as Danforth and Paula got into the car.

'Everything proceeding according to plan?' Jayewardene asked.

'She's out and hidden. Nobody seems to have noticed a thing.' Saul pulled out a plastic lighter. 'Now?'

'Now or never,' said Tachyon, sliding into the backseat.

Saul flicked the lighter and stared a moment at the flame before starting up his cigarette. 'Let's get the hell out of Dodge.'

'Five minutes,' said Jayewardene, walking quickly to the other side of the car.

They pulled up next to the front gate. The guard walked slowly over and extended his hand. 'Your badges, please.'

Jayewardene unclipped his and handed it over as the guard collected them.

'Shit,' said Danforth. 'I dropped the damn thing.'

Saul flipped on the car's interior lights. Jayewardene glanced at his watch. They didn't have time for this. Danforth reached into the crack between the edge of the seat and the door, made a face, and pulled out the badge. He handed it quickly to the guard, who took the badges back to his post before swinging the gate open.

The gate creaked closed behind them with less than two minutes left. Saul pushed the accelerator quickly up to fifty, doing his best to avoid the larger potholes.

'I hope Radha can manage this. She's never extended her powers over such a large area before.' Tachyon drummed his fingers on the vinyl car seat. He turned to look back. 'We're far enough away, I think. Stop here.'

Saul pulled over and they all got out and looked back toward the base.

'I don't get it.' Danforth crouched down next to the rear of the car. 'I mean, all she can do is turn into an elephant. I don't see where this gets us.'

'Yes, but the mass has to come from somewhere, Mr. Danforth. And electrical energy is the most easily convertible source.' Tachyon looked at his watch. 'Twenty seconds.'

'You know, if you could make your movies this exciting, Mr D ...' Paula shook her head. 'Come on, Radha.'

The entire base went silently dark. 'Hot damn.' Danforth popped up and bounced on his toes. 'She did it.'

Jayewardene looked at the gray sky above the horizon. A dark shape lifted itself up out of the larger blackness and moved toward them, throwing off occasional blue sparks.

'I think she may be a bit overcharged,' said Tachyon. 'But no gunfire. I'm sure they don't know what hit them.'

'That's fine,' said Danforth. 'Because I'm not really sure what did either.'

'What I understand,' said Saul, leaning into the front seat and starting up the car, 'is that no more choppers are taking off from there for a while. And Miss Elephant Girl owes me a new battery from yesterday.'

Radha flew in and landed next to the car, sparks igniting from each foot as she touched the ground. Jayewardene thought she looked a little bigger than she had the day before. Tachyon walked over and stepped onto her front leg, his hair standing out like a clown's wig as he touched her. Radha lifted him up onto her back.

'We'll see you soon, with luck,' the alien said, waving.

Jayewardene nodded. 'The drive to Adam's Peak should take us about an hour from here. Fly northwest as quickly as you can.'

The elephant rose noiselessly into the air and they were gone before anything else could be said.

The road was narrow. Dense trees grew to its edge and stretched ahead endlessly. They had been alone except for a bus and a few horse-drawn carts. Jayewardene explained to them what the ape really was and how he had come by the knowledge. Discussing his ace ability passed the time during the drive. Saul was pushing as hard as he could on the mud-slicked roads, making better time than Jayewardene had thought possible.

'I don't understand one thing, though,' said Paula, leaning forward from the backseat to put her head next to his. 'If these visions are always true, why are you working so hard to see that things turn out?'

'For myself there is no choice,' Jayewardene said. 'I cannot let the visions dictate how I lead my life, so I try to act as I would have without such knowledge. And a little knowledge of the future is very dangerous. The final outcome is not my only concern. What happens in the interim is equally as important. If anyone was killed by the ape because I knew it would ultimately have its humanity restored, I would be guilty of having caused that death.'

'I think you're being a little hard on yourself.' Paula gave his shoulder a light squeeze. 'There's only so much anyone can do.'

'Those are my beliefs.' Jayewardene turned around and looked into her eyes. She returned the look for an instant, then sank back next to Danforth.

'Something going on up ahead,' Saul said in a level, almost disinterested tone.

They were at the top of a hill. The trees had been cleared away from the roadside for a hundred yards or so on either side, giving them an unobstructed view.

Sri Pada's peak was still shrouded in the early morning mist. Helicopters circled something unseen near the base of the mountain.

'Think it's our boy they're after?' asked Danforth.

'Almost certainly.' Jayewardene wished he had brought along field glasses. One of the circling shapes might be Radha and Tachyon, but from this distance there was no way to tell. The clearing ended, and they were again surrounded by jungle.

'Want me to jack it up a little?' Saul crushed out his cigarette in the ashtray.

'As long as we get there alive,' Paula said, fastening her seat belt.

Saul pushed the accelerator down a little farther, leaving a spray of mud behind them.

They parked behind a pair of abandoned buses that blocked off the road. No one was visible other than the beast and its attackers. The pilgrims had either fled up the mountain or back down the road into the valley. Jayewardene walked as quickly as he could up the stone steps, the others following behind him. The helicopters had kept the ape from making it very far up the mountain.

'Any sign of our elephant?' asked Danforth.

'Can't see them from here.' Jayewardene's sides already hurt from the exertion. He paused to rest a moment and looked up as one of the choppers dropped a steel net. There was an answering roar, but they couldn't tell if the net had found its target.

They worked their way up the steps for several hundred yards, passing through an empty but undamaged rest station. The helicopters were still pressing their attack, although they appeared to be fewer in number now. Jayewardene slipped on one of the wet flagstones and smashed his knee against a step edge. Saul grabbed him by the armpits and lifted him up. 'I'm all right,' he said, painfully straightening his leg. 'Let's keep on.'

An elephant trumpeted in the distance.

'Hurry,' said Paula, taking the stairs in twos.

Jayewardene and the others trotted up after her. After another hundred-yard climb he stopped them. 'We have to cut across the mountain's face here. The footing is very dangerous. Hold on to the trees when you can.' He stepped out onto the moist soil and steadied himself against a coconut palm, then began working slowly toward the direction of the battle.

They were slightly higher than the ape when they got close enough to see what was going on. The monster had a steel net in one hand and a stripped tree in the other. It was holding Radha and the two remaining helicopters at bay like a gladiator with a net and trident. Jayewardene couldn't see Robyn but assumed that the beast had her in the top of a tree again.

'Well, now that we're here, what the hell do we do?' Danforth leaned against a jak tree, breathing hard.

'We go get Robyn.' Paula wiped her muddy hands on her shorts and took a step toward the ape.

'Wait.' Danforth grabbed her hand. 'I can't afford to lose you too. Let's see what Tachyon can do.'

'No,' Paula said, twisting away. 'We have to get her out while the ape's distracted.'

The pair stared hard at each other for a moment, then Jayewardene came between them. 'Let's get a bit closer and see what's possible.'

They half-slid, half-walked down the slope, then hit a ledge that was deep mud. Jayewardene felt it slip uncomfortably into his shoes. Robyn was still nowhere in sight, but the ape hadn't noticed them.

The last helicopter moved into position over the ape and dropped its net. The ape caught it on the end of the tree and deflected it to one side, then tossed the tree at the retreating chopper, which had to bank away sharply to avoid being hit. The ape beat its chest and roared.

Radha and Tachyon moved in from behind at treetop level. The ape reached down, picked up one of the steel nets, and swung it in a blur of motion. There was a pinging thwack as the edge of the net caught Radha on the foreleg. Tachyon slipped off her back and was left dangling from her ear. Radha gained height and pulled Tachyon back up onto her shoulders.

The ape pounded the earth and bared its teeth, then stood there clutching and unclutching its huge, black hands.

'I don't see what they can do,' said Danforth. 'That thing is just too strong.'

'We shall see,' Jayewardene said.

Tachyon leaned in close to one of Radha's immense ears. The elephant dropped down like a stone for a distance, then began circling rapidly around the ape's head. The ape lifted its arms and twisted around, trying to keep its enemy in sight. After a few moments the creature was half a turn behind the elephant. Radha dove directly for the ape's back. Tachyon jumped onto the ape's neck, and the flying elephant moved away quickly to a safe distance. The ape hunched down, then reached back for Tachyon, who was clinging to the thick fur on its shoulder. The beast plucked the alien off easily and held him up for inspection, then roared and brought Tachyon toward its mouth.

'Holy shit,' said Danforth, restraining Paula.

The monster had Tachyon almost into its mouth when it froze, jerked convulsively for a moment, and toppled over backward. The impact jarred water from the trees, streaking the mud on the faces of Jayewardene and his companions. Jayewardene hurried downhill toward the ape, trying to ignore the pain in his knee.

Tachyon was squirming out of the ape's rigid fingers when they arrived at the creature's side. He slid down quickly off the giant body and steadied himself against Jayewardene.

'Burning sky! You were right, Mr. Jayewardene.' He took several deep breaths. 'There is a man inside the beast.'

'How did you stop it?' Danforth asked, staying a few steps farther away than the others. 'And where's Robyn?'

'Headed back to North Dakota,' came a weak voice from a nearby treetop. Robyn waved and began picking her way down.

'I'll see if she's okay,' Paula said, running over.

'To answer your first question, Mr. Danforth,' Tachyon said, counting the missing buttons on his shirt, 'the main portion of the brain is simian and consists mostly of an old black-and-white film. But there is also a human personality, completely subordinate to the ape mentality. I have temporarily given them equal control, thus providing a stasis that has paralyzed it.'

Danforth nodded uncomprehendingly. 'So what do we do now?'

'Dr. Tachyon will now restore the ape to human form.' Jayewardene rubbed his leg. 'The military isn't likely to stay away for long. There isn't much time to do what must be done.' As if to punctuate his remark, one of the helicopters appeared and hovered over them for a moment before turning away.

Tachyon nodded and looked at Jayewardene. 'You saw the transformation in your vision. Was I injured? Just out of curiosity.'

Jayewardene shrugged. 'Would it matter?'

'No. I suppose not.' Tachyon chewed on a fingernail. 'Matter. That's the real problem. When we restore the human mind to dominance, he'll shed all that excess matter as energy. Anyone near, including myself, is likely to be killed.'

Jayewardene pointed to Radha, who was helping Robyn down out of the tree. 'Perhaps if you were held in the air, ungrounded so to speak, the danger would be minimized. And if the energy was channeled into something like a lightning bolt ...' Jayewardene looked up at the overcast sky.

'Yes. That idea has possibilities.' Tachyon nodded and yelled to Radha. 'Don't change back yet.'

A few minutes later everyone was in position. Jayewardene sat next to Paula, who held Robyn's head in her lap. Saul and Danforth stood a few yards away. Radha, some ten feet off the ground, held Tachyon in her trunk a few feet from the ape's head. Saul had torn his shirt into blindfolds for Elephant Girl and Tachyon. They could hear the beast's labored breathing from where they sat.

'You'd better close your eyes or turn away,' said Jayewardene. They did as he suggested.

The vision took over and Jayewardene felt all the air go out of him. He smelled the damp jungle. Heard birds singing and the far-away flap of helicopter rotors. The sun went behind a cloud. An ant crawled up his leg. He shut his eyes. Even through his closed lids the flash was magnesium bright. There was a single deafening boom of thunder. He jumped involuntarily, then waited a moment and opened his eyes.

Through the white streak in his vision caused by the flash, he saw Tachyon kneeling next to a thin, naked, Caucasian man. Radha was stomping out small fires that had broken out in a circle around them.

'How am I going to explain this to the Central Park Zoo?' asked Danforth, his expression dazed.

'Oh, I don't know,' said Jayewardene, moving slowly back down the mountainside toward Tachyon. 'It sounds like great pub to me.'

Tachyon helped the naked man to his feet. He was of average height with plain features. He moved his mouth but made no sound.

'I think he's come through it intact,' said Tachyon, getting his shoulder under the man's armpit. 'Thanks to you.'

Jayewardene shook his head and pulled three identical envelopes out of his pants pocket. 'What happened had to happen. When the military shows up, and they will, I want you to deliver these to them. Say they are from me. One goes to the president, one the Minister of State, the last to the Minister of the Interior. It is my letter of resignation.'

Tachyon took the envelopes and tucked them away. 'I see.'

'As for me, I intend to make the pilgrimage to the top of Sri Pada. Perhaps it will help me achieve my goal. To be rid of these visions.' Jayewardene headed back toward the stone steps.

'Mr. Jayewardene,' Tachyon said. 'If your pilgrimage is not successful, I would be willing to do anything possible to help you.

Perhaps try to put some mental damper to keep you out of touch with your ability. We leave tomorrow. I suspect your government will be glad to see us go. But you'd be more than welcome to come with us.'

Jayewardene bowed and moved over toward Paula and Robyn.

'Mr. Jayewardene,' Robyn said in a rasping voice. Her blond hair was tangled and matted with mud. Her clothes were in shreds. Jayewardene tried not to look. 'Thank you for helping save me.'

'You're most welcome. But you should be gotten to a hospital as soon as possible. Just for observation.' He turned to Paula. 'I plan to make the pilgrimage up the mountain now, if you'd like to come.'

'I don't know,' said Paula, looking down at Robyn.

'Go ahead,' Robyn said. 'I'll be fine.'

Paula smiled and looked back at Jayewardene. 'I'd love to.'

The multicolored neon reflects brokenly from the wet pavement. The Japanese are all around us, mostly men. They stare at Peregrine, who has her beautiful, banded wings folded tight around her. She looks ahead, ignoring them.

We have been walking a long way. My sides burn and my feet ache. She stops at an alleyway and turns to me. I nod. She walks slowly into the darkness. I follow, afraid of making a noise that will attract attention. I feel useless, like a shadow. Peregrine stretches her wings. They almost touch the cold stone on either side of the alleyway. She folds them back.

A door opens and the alley is filled with light. A man steps out. He is thin, tall, with dark skin, almond eyes, and a high forehead. He cranes his head forward to look at us.

'Fortunato?' she asks.

Jayewardene crouched next to the dying embers of the campfire. A few other pilgrims sat wordlessly next to him. The vision had awakened him. Even here there was no escape. Although the pilgrimage was not officially complete until he returned home, he knew that the visions would continue. He was tainted with the wild card virus, perhaps tainted by the years he'd spent in foreign countries. Spiritual purity and completeness was impossible to attain. At least for the present.

Paula came up behind him and put her hands lightly on his shoulders. 'It's beautiful up here, really.'

The others around the campfire looked up at her suspiciously. Jayewardene guided her away. They stood at the edge of the peak, staring out into the dark mist down the mountain.

'Each religion had its own belief about the footprint,' he said. 'We believe it was made by Buddha. The Hindus say it was made by Shiva. Moslems argue that it is where Adam stood for a thousand years, atoning for the loss of paradise.'

'Whoever it was, they had a big foot,' Paula said. 'That print was three feet long.'

The sun came up over the horizon, slowly bringing light to the swirling mists below them. Their shadows grew huge in the grayness. Jayewardene caught his breath. 'The Specter of the Brocken,' he said, closing his eyes in prayer.

'Wow,' said Paula. 'I guess it's my week for things giant.'

Jayewardene opened his eyes and sighed. His fantasies about Paula had been as unrealistic as those about his hope of destroying his power through the pilgrimage. They were like two wheels in a clockwork whose teeth meshed but whose centers forever remained at a distance. 'What you have seen is the rarest of wonders here. One can come here every day for a year and not witness what we have.'

Paula yawned, then smiled weakly. 'Sounds like it's time to go down.'

'Yes. It's time.'

◆

Danforth and Paula met him at the airport. Danforth was shaved and in clean clothes, almost the same cocksure producer he'd met only a few days ago. Paula wore shorts and a tight, white T-shirt.

She seemed ready to get on with her life. Jayewardene envied her.

'How's Miss Symmes?' he asked.

Danforth rolled his eyes. 'Well enough to have called her lawyer three times in the last twelve hours. I'm really in the soup now. I'll be lucky to stay in the business at all.'

'Offer her a five-picture deal and plenty of points,' said Jayewardene, cramming his entire knowledge of film jargon into one sentence.

'Sign this guy up, Mr. D.' Paula grinned and took Jayewardene by the arm. 'He might be able to get you out of some jams even I couldn't.'

Danforth stuck his thumbs through his belt loops and rocked back and forth. 'That's really not a bad idea. Not bad at all.' He took Jayewardene's hand and shook it. 'I really don't know what we would have done without you.'

'Gone right down the drain.' Paula gave Jayewardene a one-shoulder hug. 'I guess this is where we have to say good-bye.'

'Mr. Jayewardene.' A young government courier shouldered his way through the crowd to their side. He was breathing hard, but took time to straighten his uniform before handing Jayewardene an envelope. It bore the presidential seal.

'Thank you,' he said, popping it open with his thumb. He read it silently.

Paula leaned in to look, but the writing was Sinhalese. 'What does it say?'

'That my resignation has not been accepted and I am considered to be on an extended leave of absence. Not exactly the safest thing he could have done, but much appreciated.' He bowed to Danforth and Paula. 'I'll look for the film when it comes out.'

'*King Pongo,*' Danforth said. 'It'll be a monster hit for sure.'

The plane was more crowded than he had expected. People had been wandering around since after takeoff, chatting, complaining, getting drunk. Peregrine was standing in the aisle, talking to the tall, blond man who'd been with her in in the bar. They were keeping their voices low, but Jayewardene could tell from the looks on their faces that it was not a pleasant conversation. Peregrine turned away from the man, took a deep breath, and walked over to Jayewardene.

'May I sit next to you?' she asked. 'I know everyone else on this plane. Some considerably better than I'd like.'

'I'm flattered and delighted,' he said. And it was true. Her features and fragrance were beautiful but intimidating. Even to him.

She smiled, her lips curving in an almost inhumanly attractive manner. 'That man you and Tach saved. He's sitting right over there.' She indicated him with the arch of an eyebrow. 'His name's Jeremiah Strauss. Used to be a minor league ace named the Projectionist. I guess we're all bozos on this bus. Ah, here he comes now.'

Strauss wandered over, his hands clutching the backs of seats as he went. He was pale and afraid. 'Mr. Jayewardene?' He said it as if he'd been practicing the pronunciation for the last ten minutes. 'My name is Strauss. I've been told all that you did for me. And I want you to know that I never forget a favor. If you need a job when we get to New York, U Thant's a friend of the family. We'll work something out.'

'That's very kind of you, Mr. Strauss, but I would have done it in any case.' Jayewardene reached up and shook his hand.

Strauss smiled, straightened his shoulders, and clutched his way back to his seat.

'I'd say he's going to need quite a while to readjust,' Peregrine said in a whisper. 'Twenty-plus years is a lot to lose.'

'I can only wish him a speedy recovery. It's difficult to feel sorry for myself considering his circumstances.'

'Feeling sorry for oneself is an inalienable right.' She yawned. 'I can't believe how much I'm sleeping. Should have time for a nice long nap before we get to Thailand. Do you mind if I use your shoulder?'

'No. Please think of it as your own.' He looked out the window. 'Australia. Then where?'

She rested her head against him and closed her eyes. 'Malaysia,

Vietnam, Indonesia, New Zealand, Hong Kong, China, Japan. Fortunato.' She said the last word almost too quietly for him to hear. 'I doubt we'll be running into him.'

'But you will.' He said it hoping to please her, but she looked at him as if she'd caught him going through her underwear.

'You know this? You've had one of those visions about me?' Someone had obviously told her about his power.

'Yes. I'm sorry. I really have no control over them.' He looked back out the window, feeling ashamed.

She rested her head back onto his shoulder. 'It's not your fault. Don't worry. I'm sure Tach will be able to do something for you.'

'I hope so.'

She'd been asleep for over an hour. He'd eaten one-handed to keep from waking her up. The roast beef he'd had was like a ball of lead in his stomach. He knew he would survive Western food at least until they reached Japan. The air was a low rumble as it rushed by the plane's metal skin. Peregrine breathed softly next to his ear. Jayewardene closed his eyes and prayed for dreamless sleep.

DOWN IN THE DREAMTIME

Edward Bryant

Cordelia Chaisson had dreamed about the murder less frequently during the month past. It surprised her she still thought of it even that much; after all, she had seen far worse. Work consumed her; the job with Global Fun & Games sufficiently exhausted her days; laboring on the AIDS/WCV benefit to be held in May at Xavier Desmond's Jokertown Funhouse took up much of the nights. Most evenings she went to sleep long after the eleven o'clock news. Five in the morning came all too early. There was little time for diversion.

But there were still the occasional bad nights of dreaming:

—Coming up out of the Fourteenth Street station, heels clicking smartly on the dirty concrete, traffic muttering down from above. Hearing the voice a few steps up at street level saying, 'Just give us the purse, bitch!' Hesitating, then going ahead anyway. Fearing, but—

She heard the second voice, the Aussie accent: 'G'day, mates. Some problem here?'

Cordelia emerged from the stairwell into the sweltering night. She saw the instant tableau of two unshaven white punks backing a middle-aged woman into the space between the short row of phone carrels and the plywood butt of a shuttered newsstand. The woman had tight hold of both a yapping black poodle and her handbag.

Sun-burnt and rangy, the man Cordelia assumed was an Aussie

faced down the two youths. He wore a sand-colored outfit that looked like a rougher, more authentic version of a Banana Republic ensemble. There was a bright, well-cared-for knife in one hand.

'A problem, sonny?' he repeated.

'No, no problem, dick-head,' said one of the punks. He pulled out a short-barreled pistol from his jacket and shot the Aussie in the face.

It simply happened too quickly for Cordelia to react. As the man fell to the sidewalk, the assailants ran. The woman with the poodle screamed, momentarily harmonizing with the cries of the dog.

Cordelia ran to the man and knelt beside him. She felt for the pulse in his neck. Almost imperceptible. It was probably too late for CPR. She averted her gaze from the blood pooling beneath the man's head. The hot metallic smell of blood nauseated her. A siren wailed up the scale less than a block away.

'I've still got my purse!' the woman cried.

The man's face twitched. He died. 'Shit,' said Cordelia softly, helplessly. There wasn't a damned thing she could do.

Some kind of trouble now, Cordelia thought, as a dark-suited man she didn't recognize waved her into one of GF&G's executive offices. Deep shit, maybe. The two women standing by the desk examined a stack of printouts. Red-haired and tough, Polly Rettig was marketing chief for the GF&G satellite service. She was Cordelia's immediate boss. The other woman was Luz Alcala, vice president for programming and Rettig's boss. Neither Rettig nor Alcala smiled as they usually did. The man in black stepped back by the door and stood there with his arms folded. Security? Cordelia speculated. 'Good morning, Cordelia,' Rettig said. 'Please have a seat. We'll be with you in just a moment.' She turned her attention back to Alcala and pointed out something on the sheet in her hand.

Luz Alcala slowly nodded. 'Either we buy it first, or we're dead in the water. Maybe hire someone good—'

'Don't even think it,' said Rettig, frowning slightly.

'It might become necessary,' Alcala said. 'He's dangerous.'

Cordelia tried to keep the bewildered look off her face.

'He's also too powerful.' Folding her hands, Rettig turned toward Cordelia. 'Tell me what you know about Australia.'

'I've seen everything Peter Weir ever directed,' Cordelia said, momentarily hesitating. What was going on here?

'You've never been there?'

'New York is the farthest I've ever been from home.' Home was Atelier Parish, Louisiana. Home was a place she'd rather not think about. In most respects it didn't exist.

Rettig was looking at Alcala. 'What do you think?'

'I think yes.' The older woman picked up a thick envelope and handed it across the desk to Cordelia. 'Open it, please.' She found a passport, a sheaf of airline tickets, an American Express card, and a hefty folder of traveler's checks. 'You'll need to sign those.' Alcala indicated the checks and the credit card.

Cordelia looked silently up from the smiling image affixed to the first page of the passport. 'Nice photo,' she said. 'I don't remember applying.'

'There was little time,' said Polly Rettig apologetically. 'We took liberties.'

'The point is,' said Alcala, 'you're leaving this afternoon for the other side of the world.'

Cordelia felt stunned, then recognized the excitement growing. 'All the way to Australia?'

'Commercial flight,' said Alcala. 'Brief stops for fuel in L.A., Honolulu, and Auckland. In Sydney you'll catch an Ansett flight to Melbourne and another plane up to Alice Springs. Then you'll rent a Land-Rover and drive to Madhi Gap. You're going to have a full day,' she added dryly.

A thousand things crowded into Cordelia's mind. 'But what about my job here? And I can't just abandon the benefit – I want to go to New Jersey this weekend to check out Buddy Holly.'

'He can wait till you're back. The whole benefit can wait,' said Rettig firmly. 'PR is fine, but the JADL and the Manhattan AIDS Project don't pay your salary. This is Global Fun & Games business.'

'But—'

'It is important.' Voice smoothly modulated, Alcala made it sound like a pronouncement.

'But what *is* it?' She felt as if she were listening to Auntie Alice on Radio Wonderland. 'What's all this about?'

Alcala seemed to be picking her words carefully. 'You've seen the PR flacking GF&G's plan to inaugurate a worldwide entertainment service via satellite.'

Cordelia nodded. 'I thought that was years down the road.'

'It was. The only thing holding back the plan was the investment capital.'

'We've got the money,' Rettig said. 'We have the help of allied investors. Now we need the satellite time and the ground stations to pipe our programming down to the earth.'

'Unfortunately,' said Alcala, 'we have sudden competition for securing the services of the commercial facility in the telecommunications complex in Madhi Gap. A man named Leo Barnett.'

'The TV evangelist?'

Alcala nodded.

'The ace-baiting, intolerant, psychotic, species-chauvinist son of a bitch,' said Rettig with sudden passion. '*That* TV evangelist. Fire-breather, some call him.'

'And you're sending *me* to Madhi Gap?' said Cordelia excitedly. Incredible, she thought. It was too good to be true. 'Thank you! Thank you very much. I'll do a terrific job.'

Rettig and Alcala glanced at each other. 'Hold on,' said Alcala. 'You're going along to assist, but you're not going to be negotiating.'

It *was* too good to be true. Shit, she thought.

'Meet Mr. Carlucci,' said Alcala.

'Marty,' said a nasal voice from behind Cordelia.

'*Mr.* Carlucci,' Alcala repeated.

Cordelia turned and took another, closer look at the man she had dismissed as some kind of hired help. Medium height, compact build, styled black hair. Carlucci smiled. He looked like a thug. An amiable one, but still a thug. His suit didn't look as if it had come off the rack. Now that she looked more closely, the coat looked expensively tailored to a T.

Carlucci extended his hand. 'It's Marty,' he said. 'We got to spend a day and a night on a plane, we might as well be friendly about it, you know?'

Cordelia sensed disapproval from the two older women. She took Carlucci's hand. She was no jock, but she knew she had a firm grip. Cordelia felt that the man could have squeezed her fingers a *lot* harder had he wished to. Behind his smile, she sensed a glint of something feral. Not a man to cross.

'Mr. Carlucci,' said Alcala, 'represents a large investors' group that has entered into partnership with us in the matter of acquiring a major share in global satellite entertainment. They are providing a portion of the capital with which we expect to set up the initial satellite net.'

'A lot of bucks,' said Carlucci. 'But we'll all make it back and probably ten times as much in about five years. With our resources and your ability to' – he grinned – 'acquire talent, I figure there's no way we can lose. Everybody makes out.'

'But we do wish to saturate the Australian market,' said Alcala, 'and the ground station is already in place. All we need is a signed letter of intent to sell.'

'I can be very persuasive.' Carlucci grinned again. To Cordelia the expression looked like a barracuda showing its teeth. Or maybe a wolf. Something predatory. And definitely persuasive.

'You'd better go pack, dear,' said Alcala. 'Try for one carry-on bag. Enough clothes to last a week. One sophisticated outfit; a more comfortable one for the outback. Anything else you need you can buy there. Alice Springs is isolated, but it is not an uncivilized place.'

'It ain't Brooklyn,' said Carlucci.

'No,' said Alcala. 'No, it isn't.'

'Be at Tomlin,' said Rettig, 'by four.'

Cordelia glanced from Carlucci to Rettig to Alcala. 'I meant it before. Thank you. I'll do a good job.'

'I know you will, dear,' said Alcala, her dark eyes suddenly looking tired.

'I hope so,' Rettig said.

Cordelia knew she was dismissed. She turned and headed for the door.

'See you on the plane,' said Carlucci. 'First class all the way. Hope you don't mind smoking.'

She hesitated only momentarily, then said firmly, 'I do.'

For the first time Carlucci frowned. Polly Rettig grinned. Even Luz Alcala smiled.

♦

Cordelia lived in an apartment with a single roommate in a high rise on Maiden Lane near the Woolworth Building and Jetboy's Tomb. Veronica wasn't home, so Cordelia scrawled a brief note. It took her about ten minutes to pack what she thought she'd need on the trip. Then she called Uncle Jack and asked whether he could meet her before she hopped the Tomlin Express. He could. It was one of his days off.

Jack Robicheaux was waiting for her in the diner when she entered from the avenue. No surprise. He knew the transit system below Manhattan better than anyone else.

Every time Cordelia saw her uncle, she felt as if she were look-ing into a mirror. True, he was male, twenty-five years older, sixty pounds heavier. But the dark hair and eyes were the same. So were the cheekbones. The family resemblance was undeniable. And then there was the less tangible similarity. Both had despaired of any kind of normal growing up in Louisiana; each in young adulthood had fled Cajun country and run away to New York City.

'Hey, Cordie.' Jack rose to his feet when he saw her, gave her a firm hug and a kiss on the cheek.

'I'm going to Australia, Uncle Jack.' She hadn't meant to give away the surprise, but it burst out anyway.

'No kidding.' Jack grinned. 'When?'

'Today.'

'Yeah?' Jack sat down and leaned back in the green Naugahyde seat. 'How come?'

She told him about the meeting.

Jack frowned at the mention of Carlucci. 'You know what I think? Suzanne – Bagabond – has been hanging around Rosemary and the DA's office, feeding me a little spare-time work. I don't hear everything, but I catch enough. I think maybe we're talking about Gambione cash here.'

'GF&G wouldn't go for that,' said Cordelia. 'They're legitimate, even if they do funnel money from the skin mags.'

'Desperation breeds a special blindness. Especially if the money's been laundered through Havana. I know Rosemary's been trying to steer the Gambiones into legitimate enterprise. I guess satellite TV qualifies.'

'That's my job you're talking about,' said Cordelia.

'Better than hooking for the big F.'

Cordelia knew her cheeks were coloring. Jack looked repentant. 'Sorry,' he said. 'I wasn't trying to be bitchy.'

'Listen, this was really a big day for me. I just wanted to share it.'

'I appreciate that.' Jack leaned across the Formica table. 'I know you're gonna do just fine down under. But if you need any help, if you need anything at all, just call.'

'Halfway around the world?'

He nodded. 'Doesn't matter how far. If I can't be there in person, maybe I can suggest something. And if you really need a fourteen-foot 'gator in the flesh' – he grinned – 'give me about eighteen hours. I know you can hold any fort *that* long.'

She knew he meant it. That was why Jack was the only person in the Robicheaux clan who meant anything at all to her. 'I'll be okay. It's going to be terrific.' She got up from the booth.

'No coffee?'

'No time.' She hefted the soft leather carry-on case. 'I need the next train to Tomlin. Please tell C.C. good-bye for me. Bagabond and the cats too.'

Jack nodded. 'Still want the kitten?'

'You better believe it.'

'I'll walk you to the station.' Jack got up and took her case. She resisted only a moment before smiling and allowing him.

'There's something I want you to remember,' said Jack.

'Don't talk to strangers? Take my pill? Eat green vegetables?'

'Shut up,' he said fondly. 'Your power and mine, they may be related, but they're still different.'

'I'm not as likely to get turned into a suitcase,' said Cordelia.

He ignored her. 'You've used the reptile level in your brain to control some pretty violent situations. You killed folks to protect yourself. Don't forget you can use the power for life too.'

Cordelia felt bewildered. 'I don't know how. It scares me. I just would rather ignore it.'

'But you can't. Remember what I'm saying.' Braving cabs, they crossed the avenue to the subway entrance.

'Ever see much Nicolas Roeg?' Cordelia said.

'Everything,' said Jack.

'Maybe this will be my "walkabout."'

'Just make it back in one piece.'

She smiled. 'If I can deal with a bull alligator here, I figure I can handle a bunch of crocodiles in Australia just fine.'

Jack smiled too. It was a warm, friendly expression. But it showed all his teeth. Jack was a shape-shifter and Cordelia wasn't, but the family resemblance was unmistakable.

When she found Marty Carlucci at the United terminal at Tomlin, Cordelia discovered the man was carrying an expensive alligator overnight bag and a similarly appointed attaché case. She was less than pleased, but there wasn't much she could say.

The woman working the computer at the ticketing counter gave them seats one row apart in first class – smoking and nonsmoking. Cordelia suspected it wouldn't make much of a difference to her lungs, but felt she had won a moral decision. Also she suspected she'd feel more comfortable not having to sit with her shoulder rubbing up against his.

A good deal of the excitement of travel had worn off by the time the 747 set down at LAX. Cordelia spent much of the next two hours looking out at the early evening darkness and wondering if she'd ever get to see the La Brea Tar Pits, Watts Towers,

Disneyland, Giant Insect National Monument, the Universal tour. She bought some paperbacks in the gift shop. Finally Carlucci and she were called for the Air New Zealand flight. As with the first leg, they had requested first-class seats on either side of the terminator dividing active smoke from passive.

Carlucci snored much of the way to Honolulu. Cordelia couldn't sleep at all. She divided her time between the new Jim Thompson mystery and staring out the window at the moonlit Pacific thirty-six thousand feet below.

Both Carlucci and she converted some of their traveler's checks into Australian dollars on the concourse in Honolulu. 'The numbers are good.' Carlucci gestured at the conversion chart taped to the window of the change booth. 'I checked the paper before we left the States.'

'We're still in the States.'

He ignored her.

Just to make conversation, she said, 'You know a lot about finance?'

Pride filled his voice. 'Wharton School of Finance and Commerce. Full ride. Family paid for it.'

'You've got rich parents?'

He ignored her.

The Air New Zealand jumbo loaded and took off, and the stewards fed the passengers one last time in preparation for tucking into the long night to Auckland. Cordelia switched on her reading light when the cabin illumination dimmed. Finally she heard Carlucci grumble from the row ahead, 'Get some sleep, kiddo. Jet lag's gonna be bad enough. You got a lotta Pacific to cross yet.'

Cordelia realized the man had a valid point. She waited a few more minutes so that it would look more like it was her own idea, then switched off the light. She pulled the blanket tight around her and scrunched into the seat so she could look out the port. The travel excitement was almost all gone now. She realized she was indeed exhausted.

She saw no clouds. Just the shining ocean. She found it astonishing that anything could be so apparently endless. So enigmatic. It occurred to her that the Pacific could swallow up a 747 without more than the tiniest ripple.

Eer-moonans!

The words meant nothing to her.

Eer-moonans.

The phrase was so soft it could have been a whisper in her mind.

Cordelia's eyes clicked open. Something was very wrong. The reassuring vibration of the jumbo's engines was somehow distorted, blended with the sigh of a rising wind. She tried to throw the suddenly strangling blanket away and clawed her way up the back of the seat ahead, nails biting into the cool leather.

When she looked down the other side, Cordelia sharply drew in her breath. She was staring into the wide, surprised, dead eyes of Marty Carlucci. His body still faced forward. But his head had been screwed around 180 degrees. Viscid blood slowly dripped from his ears, his mouth. It had pooled at the bottom of his eyes and was oozing down over his cheekbones.

The sound of her scream closed in around Cordelia's head. It was like crying out in a barrel. She finally struggled free of the blanket and stared unbelievingly down the aisle.

She still stood in the Air New Zealand 747. And she stood in the desert. One was overlaid on the other. She moved her feet and felt the gritty texture of the sand, heard its rasp. The aisle was dotted with scrubby plants moving as the wind continued to rise.

The jumbo's cabin stretched into a distance her eye couldn't quite follow, diminishing endlessly into perspective as it approached the tail section. Cordelia saw no one moving.

'Uncle Jack!' she cried out. There was, of course, no answer.

Then she heard the howling. It was a hollow ululation rising and falling, gaining in volume. Far down the cabin, in the tunnel that was also the desert, she saw the shapes leaping toward her. The creatures bounded like wolves, first in the aisle, then scrambling across the tops of the seats.

Cordelia smelled a rank, decaying odor. She scrambled into the aisle, recoiling until her spine was flush against the forward bulk-head.

The creatures were indistinct in the half-light. She couldn't even be sure of their numbers. They *were* like wolves, claws clicking and tearing on the seats, but their heads were all wrong. The snouts were blunted off, truncated. Ruffs of shining spines ringed their necks. Their eyes were flat black holes deeper than the surrounding night.

Cordelia stared at the teeth. There were just too many long needle fangs to fit comfortably into those mouths. Teeth that champed and clashed, throwing out a spray of dark saliva.

The teeth reached for her.

Move, goddamnit! The voice was in her head. It was her own voice. Move!

– as teeth and claws sought her throat.

Cordelia hurled herself to the side. The lead wolf-creature smashed into the steel bulkhead, howled in pain, staggered upright confusedly as the second leaping monster rammed into its ribs. Cordelia scrambled past the confusion of horrors into the narrow galleyway.

Focus! Cordelia knew what she had to do. She wasn't Chuck Norris nor did she have an Uzi in her hand. In her instant of respite as the wolf-creatures snarled and spat at one another, she wished again that Jack were here. But he wasn't. Concentrate, she told herself.

One of the blunted muzzles poked around the corner of the galley. Cordelia stared into the pair of deadly matte-black eyes. 'Die, you son of a bitch,' she cried aloud. She sensed the power uncoiling from the reptile level of her brain, felt the force flow into the alien mind of the monster, striking directly for the brain stem. She shut off its heart and respiration. The creature struggled toward her, then collapsed forward on its clawed paws.

The next monster appeared around the corner. How many of them were there? She tried to think. Six, eight, she wasn't sure. Another blunt muzzle protruded. Another set of claws. More gleaming teeth. Die! She felt the power draining from her. This was no feeling she'd known before. It was like trying to jog in quicksand.

The bodies of the wolf-creatures piled up. The surviving monsters scrambled over the barrier, lunging at her. The final one made it all the way into the galley.

Cordelia tried to shut down its brain, felt the power waning as the creature launched itself down the heap of corpses. As the toothy jaws reached for her throat, she swung a double fist and tried to smash them aside. One of the spines from the thing's ruff slid into the back of her left hand. Steaming spittle spattered her face.

She felt the staccato rhythm of the wolf-creature's breathing hesitate and cease as its body slumped onto her feet. But now she felt a chill spreading across her hand and up her arm. Cordelia grasped the spine with her right hand and wrenched it free. The shaft came loose and she hurled it from her, but the coldness didn't abate.

It'll reach my heart, she thought, and that was the last thing that passed through her mind. Cordelia felt herself collapsing, falling across the crazy-quilt arrangement of monstrous bodies. The wind filled up her ears; the darkness took her eyes.

'Hey! You okay, kid? Whattsa matter?' The accent was all New York. It was Marty Carlucci's voice. Cordelia struggled to open her eyes. The man bent over her, breath minty with recent toothpaste. He grasped her shoulders and shook her slightly.

'*Eer-moonans,*' Cordelia said weakly.

'Huh?' Carlucci looked baffled.

'You're ... dead.'

'Damn straight,' he said. 'I don't know how many hours I slept, but I feel like shit. How about you?'

Memories of the night slammed back. 'What's going on?' Cordelia said.

'We're landing. Plane's about half an hour out of Auckland. You wanna use the can, get cleaned up and all, you better do it quick.' He took his fingers away from her shoulders. 'Okay?'

'Okay.' Cordelia sat up shakily. Her head felt as if it were stuffed with sodden cotton. 'Everybody's okay? The plane isn't full of monsters?'

Carlucci stared at her. 'Just tourists. Hey, you have some bad dreams? Want some coffee?'

'Coffee. Thanks.' She grabbed her bag and struggled past him into the aisle. 'Right. Nightmares. Bad ones.'

In the restroom she alternated splashing cold and hot water on her face. Brushing her teeth helped. She slugged down three Midol and unsnarled her hair. Cordelia did her best with makeup. Finally she stared at herself in the mirror and shook her head. 'Shit,' she told herself, 'you look thirty.'

Her left hand itched. She raised it in front of her face and stared at the inflamed puncture wound. Maybe she had caught her hand on something when she'd moved in her sleep, and that had translated into the dream. Perhaps it was stigmata. Either story sounded equally implausible. Maybe this was some weird new menstrual side effect. Cordelia shook her head. Nothing made sense. Weakness flooded over her and she had to sit down on the lid of the toilet. The inside of her skull felt scoured. Maybe she *had* spent much of the night battling monsters.

Cordelia realized someone was knocking on the door of the restroom. Others wanted to get ready for New Zealand. So long as they weren't wolf-creatures ...

The morning was sunny. The North Island of New Zealand was intensely green. The 747 touched down with scarcely a bump and then sat at the end of the runway for twenty minutes until the agriculture people climbed on board. Cordelia hadn't expected that. She watched bemusedly as the smiling young men in their crisp uniforms walked down the aisles, an aerosol jet of pest-killer fogging from the can in each hand. Something about this reminded her perversely of what she'd read of the final moments of Jetboy.

Carlucci must have been thinking something similar. Having promised not to smoke, he'd moved into the seat beside her. 'Sure hope it's pesticide,' he said. 'Be a really nasty joke if it was the wild card virus.'

After the passengers had murmured, griped, wheezed, and coughed, the jumbo taxied to the terminal and everyone debarked. The pilot told them they had two hours before the plane left on the thousand-mile leg to Sydney.

'Just time to stretch our legs, buy some cards, make some phone calls,' said Carlucci. Cordelia welcomed the thought of getting some exercise.

In the main terminal Carlucci went off to place his trans-Pacific calls. The terminal seemed extraordinarily crowded. Cordelia saw camera crews in the distance. She headed for the doors to the outside.

From behind her she heard, 'Cordelia! Ms. Chaisson!' The voice wasn't Carlucci's. Who the hell? She turned and saw a vision of flowing red hair framing a face that looked vaguely like Errol Flynn's in *Captain Blood*. But Flynn had never worn such bright clothing, not even in the colorized *Adventures of Captain Fabian*.

Cordelia stopped and smiled. 'So,' she said. 'Do you like new wave music any better these days?'

'No,' said Dr. Tachyon. 'No, I'm afraid I do not.'

'I fear,' said the tall, winged woman standing beside Tachyon, 'that our good Tacky will never progress much beyond Tony Bennett.' A simply cut, voluminous blue silk dress whispered softly around her. Cordelia blinked. Peregrine was hard to mistake.

'Unfair, my dear.' Tachyon smiled at his companion. 'I have my favorites among contemporary performers. I'm rather fond of Placido Domingo.' He turned back toward Cordelia. 'I'm forgetting my manners. Cordelia, have you formally met Peregrine?'

Cordelia took the proffered hand. 'I've had a call in to your agent for weeks now. Nice to see you.' Shut up, she said to herself. Don't be rude.

Peregrine's dazzling blue eyes regarded her. 'I'm sorry,' she said. 'Is this about the benefit at Dez's club? I'm afraid I've been incredibly busy tidying up other projects in the midst of getting ready for this trip.'

'Peregrine,' said Tachyon, 'this young woman is Cordelia Chaisson. We know each other from the clinic. She's come frequently with friends to visit C.C. Ryder.'

'C.C.'s going to be able to do the Funhouse,' said Cordelia.

'That would be fabulous,' said Peregrine. 'I've admired her work for a long time.'

'Perhaps we could all sit down over a drink,' said Tachyon. He smiled at Cordelia. 'There has been a delay with arranging the senator's ground transport into Auckland. I'm afraid we're stranded at the airport for a bit.' The man glanced back over his shoulder. 'As well, I'm afraid we are trying to avoid the rest of the party. The aircraft does get a bit close.'

Cordelia felt the tempting proximity of fresh air starting to drift away. 'I've got just about two hours,' she said, hesitating. 'Okay, let's have a drink.' As they walked toward the restaurant, Cordelia didn't see Carlucci. He could get along fine by himself. What she did notice was the number of stares following them. No doubt some of the attention was being paid to Tachyon – his hair and wardrobe always ensured that. But mostly people were looking at Peregrine. Probably the New Zealanders weren't all that accustomed to seeing a tall, gorgeous woman with functional wings folded against her back. She *was* spectacular, Cordelia admitted to herself. It would be great to have the looks, the stature, the presence. At once Cordelia felt very young. Almost like a kid. Inadequate. Damn it.

Cordelia ordinarily took her coffee with milk. But if black would help clear her head, then she'd give it a try. She insisted that the three of them wait for a window table. If she wasn't going to breathe the outside air, at least she could sit within inches of it. The colors of the unfamiliar trees reminded her of photos she'd seen of the Monterey Peninsula.

'So,' she said after they'd given orders to the waitress, 'I guess I should say something about a small world. How's the junket? I saw some pictures of the Great Ape on the eleven o'clock news before I left.'

Tachyon rambled on about Senator Hartmann's round-the-world tour. Cordelia remembered reading about it interminably in the *Post* on the subway, but had been so busy with the Funhouse benefit, she hadn't paid much attention. 'Sounds like a back-breaker,' she said when Tachyon finished his gloss.

Peregrine smiled wanly. 'It hasn't exactly been a vacation. I think Guatemala was my favorite. Have your people thought of climaxing the benefit with a human sacrifice?'

Cordelia shook her head. 'I think we're going for a little more festive tone, even considering the occasion.'

'Listen,' Peregrine said. 'I'll do what I can with my agent. In the meantime maybe I can introduce you to a few folks who'll do you some good. Do you know Radha O'Reilly? Elephant Girl?' At Cordelia's head shake she continued, 'When she turns into a flying elephant, it's smoother than anything Doug Henning's dreamed of. You ought to talk to Fantasy too. You could use a dancer like her.'

'That'd be terrific,' Cordelia said. 'Thank you.' She felt the frustration of wanting to do everything herself – *showing* everyone – and yet knowing when to accept the aid that was being graciously extended.

'So,' Tachyon said, breaking in on her thoughts. 'And what are *you* doing here so far from home?' His expression looked expectant; his eyes gleamed with honest curiosity.

Cordelia knew she couldn't get away with claiming she'd won the trip for selling Girl Scout cookies. She opted for honesty. 'I'm going to Australia with a guy from GF&G to try and buy a satellite ground station before it gets scarfed up by a TV preacher.'

'Ah,' said Tachyon. 'Would that evangelist be Leo Barnett, by chance?'

Cordelia nodded.

'I hope you succeed.' Tachyon frowned. 'Our friend Fire-breather's power is growing at a dangerously exponential rate. I, for one, would prefer to see the growth of his media empire retarded.'

'Just yesterday,' said Peregrine, 'I heard from Chrysalis that some of Barnett's youth-group thugs are hanging out in the Village and beating the stuffing out of anybody they think is both a joker and vulnerable.'

'*Die Juden*,' Tachyon murmured. The two women glanced questioningly at him. 'History.' He sighed, then said to Cordelia, 'Whatever help you need in competing with Barnett, let us know. I think you'll find a great deal of support from both aces and jokers.'

'Hey,' said an overly familiar voice from behind Cordelia's scapula. 'What's happening?'

Without looking around Cordelia said, 'Marty Carlucci, meet Dr. Tachyon and Peregrine.' To the latter she said, 'Marty's my chaperon.'

'Hiya.' Carlucci took the fourth chair. 'Yeah, I know you,' he said to Tachyon. He stared at Peregrine, frankly surveying her. All of her. 'You I've seen a lot. I got tapes of every show you've done for years.' His eyes narrowed. 'Say, you pregnant?'

'Thank you,' said Peregrine. 'Yes.' She stared him down.

'Uh, right,' said Carlucci. He turned to Cordelia. 'Kid, come on. We gotta get back on the plane.' More firmly, 'Now!'

Good-byes were said. Tachyon volunteered to pay for the coffee. 'Good luck,' Peregrine said, aimed specifically at Cordelia. Carlucci seemed preoccupied, not noticing.

As the two of them walked toward the boarding gate, he said, 'Dumb fuckin' bitch.'

Cordelia stopped dead still. '*What?*'

'Not you.' Carlucci took her elbow roughly and propelled her toward the security checkpoint. 'That joker who sells info – Chrysalis. I ran into her by the phones. I figured I'd save the price of a call.'

'So?' said Cordelia.

'One of these days she's gonna get her invisible tits caught in the wringer and there's going to be real bright blood all over the laundry room wall. I told New York that too.'

Cordelia waited, but he didn't elaborate. 'So?' she said again.

'What did you tell those two geeks?' said Carlucci. His voice sounded dangerous.

'Nothing,' said Cordelia, listening to the internal warning bells. 'Nothing at all.'

'Good.' Carlucci grimaced. He mumbled, 'She's gonna be fish food, I swear it.'

Cordelia stared at Carlucci. The sheer conviction in his voice kept him from appearing a comic-opera gangster. She thought he meant what he was saying. He reminded her of the wolf-creatures in last night's maybe-dream. All that was missing was the dark spittle.

Carlucci's mood didn't improve on the flight to Australia. In Sydney they cleared customs and transferred to an A-300 Airbus. In Melbourne, Cordelia finally got to stick her head out of doors for a few minutes. The air smelled fresh. She admired the DC-3 suspended from a cable in front of the terminal. Then her companion fussed at her to get to the proper Ansett gate. This time they were seated on a 727. Cordelia was glad she wasn't trusting her bag to checked luggage. Part of Marty Carlucci's gloom involved speculation that *his* checked bag was going to get missent to Fiji or some other improper destination.

'So why didn't you carry everything on?' Cordelia had said.

'There's some stuff you *can't* carry on.'

The 727 droned north, away from the coastal greenery. Cordelia had the window seat. She stared down at the apparently unending desert. She squinted, looking for roads, railroad tracks, any other sign of human intervention. Nothing. The flat brownish-tan wasteland was dotted with cloud shadows.

When word crackled over the cabin speakers that the plane was approaching Alice Springs, Cordelia realized only after she'd performed the actions that she had stowed the tray table, cinched her seat belt, and shoved her bag back under the seat ahead. It had all become utterly automatic.

The airport was busier than she'd expected. Somehow she had anticipated a single dusty runway with a galvanized tin shack beside it. A TAA flight had landed minutes before and the terminal was crowded with people who clearly resembled tourists.

'We rent the Land-Rover now?' she asked Carlucci. The man was leaning impatiently over the luggage belt.

'Uh-uh. We go into town. I've got us reservations at the Stuart Arms. We're both getting a good night's sleep. I don't want to be any nastier than I *have* to be tomorrow at the meeting. It's all set up for three o'clock,' he added as an apparent afterthought. 'The lag's gonna catch up with us real fast. I suggest you get a good supper with me when we get to Alice. Then it's beddy-bye till ten or eleven tomorrow morning. If we pick up the rental and get out of Alice by noon, we should hit the Gap in plenty of time. *There*, you son of a bitch!' He grabbed his alligator case from the conveyor. 'Okay, let's go.'

They took an Ansett coach into Alice. It was half an hour into town and the air-conditioning labored hard against the baking heat outside. Cordelia stared out the window as the bus approached downtown Alice Springs. At first glance it didn't look terribly different from a small, arid American city. Certainly Baton Rouge was more alien than this, Cordelia thought. It didn't look at all as she'd expected from seeing both versions of *A Town Like Alice*.

The air transit terminal turned out to be across the street from the turn-of-the-century architecture of the Stuart Arms, a fact for which Cordelia was grateful. It was getting dark as the passengers climbed down to the pavement and claimed their bags. Cordelia glanced at her watch. The numbers meant absolutely nothing. She needed to reset to local time. *And* change the date as well, she reminded herself. She wasn't even sure what day of the week it was now. Her head had started to throb when she plunged into the heat that lingered even while the dark was falling. She thought longingly of being able to lie straight, stretched out on clean sheets. *After* she'd had a long bath. She checked that. The bath could wait until she'd slept for twenty or thirty hours. At least.

'Okay, kiddo,' said Carlucci. They were standing in front of the antique registration desk. 'Here's your key.' He paused. 'Sure you wouldn't like to shave expenses for GF&G and stay in my room?'

Cordelia didn't have the energy to smile wanly. 'Nope,' she said, taking the key from his hand.

'You wanna know something? You're not on this picnic just because the Fortunato broads think you're such hot shit.'

What was he talking about? She used enough energy to glance at him.

'I've seen you around the GF&G offices. I liked what I saw. I put in the word.'

Cordelia sighed. Aloud.

'Okay,' he said. 'Hey, no offense. I'm bushed too.' Carlucci picked up the alligator bag. 'Let's get the stuff stowed and catch supper.' There was a LIFT OUT OF ORDER sign on the elevator. He turned wearily toward the staircase.

'Second floor,' said Carlucci. 'At least that's a goddamn blessing.' They passed a mimeographed poster in the stairwell advertising a band called Gondwanaland. 'Maybe after we eat, you wanna go dancing?' Even he didn't sound all that enthusiastic.

Cordelia didn't bother to reply.

The landing opened out into a hallway lined with dark wood trim and some unobtrusive glass cases containing aboriginal artifacts. Cordelia glanced at the boomerangs and bull roarers. Doubtless she'd be able to work up a little more interest tomorrow.

Carlucci looked at his key. 'The rooms are next to each other. God, I'm looking forward to bagging it. I really am dead.'

A door slammed open behind them. Cordelia caught a quick flash of two dark figures leaping. They were monsters. Later she decided they must have been wearing masks. *Ugly* masks.

Tired as she was, her reflexes still worked. She'd started to duck to the side when a stiffened forearm caught her across the chest and drove her into one of the glass cases. Glass shattered, shards spraying. Cordelia flailed her arms, trying to keep her equilibrium, as someone or something tried to grapple with her. She thought she heard Marty Carlucci screaming.

Her fingers closed on something hard – the end of a boomerang – as she sensed rather than saw her assailant spin around and spring for her again. She brought the boomerang forward in a whistling arc. Instinct. All instinct. *Shit*, she thought. *I'm going to die.*

The sharp edge of the boomerang sliced into the face of her attacker with the sound of a carving knife slicing into a watermelon. Outstretched fingers slapped her neck and dropped away. A body rolled to the floor.

Carlucci! Cordelia turned and saw a dark figure crouched over her colleague. It straightened, stood, started for her, and she realized it was a man. But now she had a little time. Think! she said to herself. Think think think. Focus. It was as though the power had been blanketed by the smothering layers of fatigue. But it was still there. She concentrated, felt the lowest level of her brain engage and strike out.

Stop, goddamn you!

The figure stopped, staggered, started forward again. And fell. Cordelia knew she'd shut down everything in his autonomic system. The smell as his bowels released made it even worse.

She edged around him and knelt down by Marty Carlucci. He lay on his stomach, looking upward. His head had been screwed around completely, just as it had been in the maybe-dream. Slightly walleyed, his dead eyes stared past her.

Cordelia rocked back on her heels against the wall, putting her fists to her mouth, feeling her incisors bite into the knuckles. She felt the epinephrine still prickling in her arms and legs. Every nerve seemed raw.

Christ! she thought. *What am I gonna* do? She looked both ways along the hall. There were no more attackers, no witnesses. She could call Uncle Jack in New York. Or Alcala or Rettig. She could even try to find Fortunato in Japan. If the number she had was still good. She could attempt to locate Tachyon in Auckland. It came home to her. She was many thousands of miles from anyone she trusted, anyone she even *knew*.

'What am I gonna do?' This time she muttered it aloud.

She scrambled over to Carlucci's alligator case and clicked the catches open. The man had affected an icy calm at customs. She had no doubt there was a reason. Cordelia tore through the clothing, searching for the weapon she knew had to be there. She opened the case marked 'shaver and converter set.' The gun was blued steel and ugly, some kind of snubbed-off, scaled-down automatic weapon. It felt reassuringly heavy in her hand.

Floorboards creaked down in the stairwell. On some level Cordelia caught the scattered words: '... by now he and the bitch should both be dead ...'

She forced herself to get up and step over Marty Carlucci's corpse. Then she ran.

At the end of the hallway farthest from the main staircase, a window overlooked a fire-stairs. Cordelia slid it open, softly cajoling the window when the pane momentarily stuck in the casement. She skinned through, then turned to shut the window after her. She saw shadows writhing at the other end of the hall. Cordelia ducked and scuttled crabwise to the steps down.

She momentarily wished she'd grabbed her overnight bag. At least she had the passport case with the Amex card and traveler's checks in the small handbag slung around her shoulder. Cordelia realized she still had the room key clutched in her left hand. She maneuvered it in her fist so that the key thrust out from between her index and middle fingers.

The steps were metal, but they were old and they creaked. Quick and stealthy, Cordelia discovered, were mutually contradictory here.

She saw she was descending into an alley. The noise from the street, about twenty yards distant, was loud and boisterous. At first she thought it sounded like a party. Then she detected undercurrents of anger and pain. The crowd noise rose. Cordelia heard the flat sounds of what she guessed were fists on flesh.

'Terrific,' she muttered. Then it occurred to her that a riot would provide good cover for her escape. She had already started mulling contingency plans. First, stay alive. Get out of here. Then call Rettig or Alcala and let them know what had happened. They would send someone to replace Carlucci while she stayed out of sight. Wonderful. A brand-new guy in a tailored suit to sign his company's name on a contract. What was so difficult about that? *She* could do it. But not if she was dead.

With both key and gun at the ready Cordelia eased down from the bottom step of the fire-stairs and started toward the mouth of the alley. Then she froze. She *knew* someone was standing directly behind her.

She whirled, driving her left hand forward, aiming the key at a spot she hoped would be right beneath the intruder's chin. Someone was indeed there. Strong fingers clamped around her wrist, easily soaking up all the forward momentum of her thrust.

The figure pulled her forward into what little light spilled down from the Stuart Arms through the stair gratings. Cordelia brought the gun up and stuck the barrel into her assailant's belly. It didn't go far. She pulled the trigger.

Nothing happened.

She caught a glimpse of dark eyes catching hers. The figure reached forward with its free hand and clicked something on the side of the weapon. A male voice said, 'Here, little missy, you left on the safety. Now it will work.'

Cordelia was too astonished to pull the trigger. 'Okay, I get the point. Who are you, and can we get out of here?'

'You can call me Warreen.' Sudden light flooded down from above them, bursting through the gratings, painting quagga stripes of illumination.

Cordelia stared at the bars of light falling across the man's face. She registered the wild, curly black hair, the hooded eyes as dark as hers, the broad flat nose, the high, sharp cheekbones, the strong lips. He was, her mama would have called him, a man of some color. He was, she also realized, the most striking man she had ever seen. Her daddy would have whipped her for that thought alone.

Footsteps clattered down the fire-stairs.

'Now we get out of here,' Warreen said, steering her toward the alley mouth.

Naturally it wasn't as easy as that. 'There are men there,' said Cordelia. She saw an indeterminate number of men holding what seemed to be sticks. They were waiting, silhouetted against the light from the street.

'So there are.' Warreen grinned and Cordelia caught the flash of white teeth. 'Shoot at them, little missy.'

Sounds good to me, Cordelia thought, bringing up the weapon in her right hand. When she pulled the trigger, there was a sound like ripping canvas and bullets screamed off brick. The ragged muzzle flash showed her the men in the alley were now flat in the dirt. She didn't think she had hit any of them.

'Later we worry about marksmanship,' said Warreen. 'Now we go.' He enclosed her left hand in his right, not seeming to notice the key still in place in her fist.

She wondered if they were going to jump from back to back of the prostrate men like Tarzan hopscotching crocodiles in lieu of stepping stones.

◆

They didn't *go* anywhere.

Something akin to heat washed over her. It felt like energy flooding through Warreen's fingers and into her body. The heat seared from the inside out – just like, she thought, a microwave oven.

The world seemed to move sharply two feet to the left and then drop a foot more. The air rotated around her. The night funneled into a blazing speck centered in her chest.

Then it was no longer night.

Warreen and she stood on a reddish-brown plain that joined the distant sky in a far, flat horizon. There were occasional hardy-looking plants and a bit of a breeze. The wind was hot and it eddied the dust.

She realized this was the same plain that had overlaid the cabin of the Air New Zealand jumbo in her nightmare between Honolulu and Auckland.

Cordelia staggered slightly and Warreen caught her arm. 'I've seen this place before,' she said. 'Will the wolf-creatures come?'

'Wolf-creatures?' Warreen looked momentarily puzzled. 'Ah,

little missy, you mean the Eer-moonans, the long-toothed ones from the shadows.'

'I guess so. Lots of teeth? Run in packs? They've got rows of quills around their necks.' Holding the gun loosely, Cordelia massaged the inflamed place on the back of her left hand.

Warreen frowned and examined the wound. 'Pierced by a quill? You're very fortunate. Their venom is usually fatal.'

'Maybe us 'gator types have natural immunity,' Cordelia said, smiling wanly. Warreen looked politely puzzled. 'Never mind. I guess I'm just lucky.'

He nodded. 'Indeed so, little missy.'

'What's this "little missy" crap?' Cordelia said. 'I didn't want to take time to ask back in the alley.'

Warreen looked startled, then grinned widely. 'The European ladies seem to like it. It feeds those delicious colonial impulses, you know? Sometimes I still talk like I'm a guide.'

'I'm not European,' said Cordelia. 'I'm a Cajun, an American.'

'Same thing to us.' Warreen continued to grin. 'Yank's same as a European. No difference. You're all tourists here. So what should I call you?'

'Cordelia.'

His expression became serious as he leaned forward and took the gun from her hand. He examined it closely, gingerly working the action, then clicking the safety back on. 'Scaled down H and K full auto. Pretty expensive hardware, Cordelia. Going shooting dingos?' He gave her back the weapon.

She let it dangle from her hand. 'It belonged to the guy I came to Alice Springs with. He's dead.'

'At the hotel?' said Warreen. 'The minions of the Murga-muggai? Word was out, she was going to ice the agent of the evangelist.'

'Who?'

'The trap-door spider woman. Not a nice lady. She's tried to kill me for years. Since I was a kid.' He said it matter-of-factly. Cordelia thought he still looked like a kid.

'Why?' she said, involuntarily shivering. If she had any phobia, it was spiders. She coughed as the wind kicked red dust up into her face.

'Started as clan vengeance. Now it's something else.' Warreen seemed to reflect, then added, 'She and I both have some powers. I think she feels there is space in the outback for only one such. Very shortsighted.'

'What kind of powers?' said Cordelia.

'You are full of questions. So am I. Perhaps we can trade knowledge on our walk.'

'Walk?' said Cordelia a bit stupidly. Once again events threatened to outstrip her ability to comprehend them. 'Where?'

'Uluru.'

'Where's that?'

'There.' Warreen pointed toward the horizon.

The sun was directly overhead. Cordelia had no idea which compass direction was indicated. 'There's nothing there. Just a lot of countryside that looks like where they shot *Road Warrior*.'

'There will be.' Warreen had started walking. He was already a dozen paces away. His voice drifted back on the wind. 'Shake a pretty leg, little missy.'

Deciding she had little choice, Cordelia followed. 'Agent of the evangelist?' she muttered. That wasn't Marty. Somebody had made a bad mistake.

'Where are we?' said Cordelia. The sky was dotted with small cumulus, but none of the cloud-shadows ever seemed to shade her. She wished mightily that they did.

'The world,' said Warreen.

'It's not my world.'

'The desert, then.'

'I *know* it's the desert,' said Cordelia. 'I can see it's the desert. I can feel it. The heat's a dead giveaway. But what desert is it?'

'It is the land of Baiame,' said Warreen. 'This is the great Nullarbor Plain.'

'Are you sure?' Cordelia scrubbed sweat from her forehead with the strip of fabric she had carefully torn away from the hem of her Banana Republic skirt. 'I looked at the map on the plane all the way up from Melbourne. The distances don't make sense. Shouldn't this be the Simpson Desert?'

'Distances are different in the Dreamtime,' Warreen said simply.

'The Dreamtime?' *What am I in, a Peter Weir movie?* she thought. 'As in the myth?'

'No myth,' said her companion. 'We are now where reality was, is, and will be. We are in the origin of all things.'

'Right.' *I am dreaming*, Cordelia thought. *I'm dreaming – or I'm dead and this is the last thing my brain cells are creating before everything flares and goes black.*

'All things in the shadow world were created here first,' said Warreen. 'Birds, creatures, grass, the ways of doing things, the taboos that must be observed.'

Cordelia looked around her. There was little to see. 'These are the originals?' she said. 'I've only seen the copies before?'

He nodded vigorously.

'I don't see any dune buggies,' she said a bit petulantly, feeling the heat. 'I don't see any airliners or vending machines full of ice-cold Diet Pepsi.'

He answered her seriously. 'Those are only variations. Here is where everything begins.'

I'm dead, she thought glumly. 'I'm hot,' she said. 'I'm tired. How far do we have to walk?'

'A distance.' Warreen kept striding along effortlessly.

Cordelia stopped and set hands to hips. 'Why should I go along?'

'If you don't,' Warreen said back over his shoulder, 'then you shall die.'

'Oh.' Cordelia started walking again, having to run a few steps in order to catch up with the man. The image she couldn't get out of her head was that of cold cans of soda, the moisture beading on the aluminum outsides. She ached to hear the click and hiss as the tabs peeled back. And the bubbles, the taste …

'Keep walking,' said Warreen.

♣

'How long have we been walking?' said Cordelia. She glanced up and shaded her eyes. The sun was measurably closer to the horizon. Shadows stretched in back of Warreen and her.

'Are you tired?' said her companion.

'I'm exhausted.'

'Do you need to rest?'

She thought about that. Her own conclusion surprised her. 'No. No, I don't think I do. Not yet, anyway.' Where was the energy coming from? She *was* exhausted – and yet strength seemed to rise up into her, as though she were a plant taking nourishment from the earth. 'This place is magical.'

Warreen nodded matter-of-factly. 'Yes, it is.'

'However,' she said, 'I *am* hungry.'

'You don't need food, but I'll see to it.'

Cordelia heard a sound apart from the wind and the padding of her own feet on the dusty soil. She turned and saw a brownish-gray kangaroo hopping along, easily pacing them. 'I'm hungry enough to eat one of those,' she said.

The kangaroo stared at her from huge chocolate eyes. 'I should hope not,' it said.

Cordelia closed her mouth with a click. She stared back.

Warreen smiled at the kangaroo and said courteously, 'Good afternoon, Mirram. Will we shortly find shade and water?'

'Yes,' said the kangaroo. 'Sadly, the hospitality is being hoarded by a cousin of the Gurangatch.'

'At least,' said Warreen, 'it is not a bunyip.'

'That is true,' agreed the kangaroo.

'Will I find weapons?'

'Beneath the tree,' said the kangaroo.

'Good,' Warreen said with relief. 'I wouldn't relish wrestling a monster with only my hands and teeth.'

'I wish you well,' said the kangaroo. 'And you,' it said to Cordelia, 'be at peace.' The creature turned at right angles to their path and bounded into the desert where it soon was lost to sight.

'Talking kangaroos?' said Cordelia. 'Bunyips? Gurnagatches?'

'Gurangatch,' Warreen corrected her. 'Something of both lizard and fish. It is, of course, a monster.'

She was mentally fitting pieces together. 'And it's hogging an oasis.'

'Spot on.'

'Couldn't we avoid it?'

'No matter what trail we follow,' Warreen said, 'I think it will encounter us.' He shrugged. 'It's just a monster.'

'Right.' Cordelia was glad she still had tight hold of the H and K mini. The steel was hot and slippery in her hand. 'Just a monster,' she mumbled through dry lips.

Cordelia had no idea how Warreen found the pond and the tree. So far as she could tell, they followed a perfectly straight path. A dot appeared in the sunset distance. It grew as they approached it. Cordelia saw a tough-looking desert oak streaked with charcoal stripes. It seemed to have been struck by lightning more than once and looked as if it had occupied this patch of hardscrabble soil for centuries. A belt of grass surrounded the tree. A gentle slope led down to reeds and then the edge of a pool about thirty feet across.

'Where's the monster?' said Cordelia.

'Hush.' Warreen strode up to the tree and began to strip. His muscles were lean and beautifully defined. His skin shimmered with sweat, glowing almost a dark blue in the dusk. When he skinned out of the jeans, Cordelia at first turned away, then decided this was not an occasion for politeness, whether false or otherwise.

God, she thought. *He's gorgeous.* Depending on gender, her kin would have been either scandalized or triggered to a lynching impulse. Even though she had been reared to abhor such a thought, she wanted to reach and lightly touch him. This, she abruptly realized, was not like her at all. Although she was surrounded in New York by people of other colors, they still made her nervous. Warreen was engendering that reaction, yet it was vastly different in nature and intensity. She *did* want to touch him.

Naked, Warreen neatly folded his clothes and set them in a pile beneath the tree. In turn, he picked up a variety of objects from the grass. He inspected a long club, then set it back down. Finally he straightened with a spear in one hand, a boomerang in the other. He looked fiercely at Cordelia. 'I can be no more ready.'

She felt a chill like ice water run through her. It was a sensation both of fear and of excitement. 'Now what?' She tried to keep her voice low and steady, but it squeaked slightly. God, she hated that.

Warreen didn't have a chance to answer. He gestured toward the dark pool. Ripples had appeared on the far side. The center of those ripples seemed to be moving toward them. A few bubbles burst on the surface.

The water was shrugged aside. What surveyed the couple on the bank was a figure out of a nightmare. *Looks meaner than any joker I've ever seen*, Cordelia thought. As it lifted more of its body from the water, she decided the creature must possess at least the mass of Bruce the Shark. The froglike mouth gaped, revealing a multitude of rust-colored teeth. It regarded the humans with slitted, bulging lizard eyes.

'It is equally sired of fish and lizard,' said Warreen conversationally, as though guiding a European tourist through a wild-game park. He stepped forward and raised his spear. 'Cousin Gurangatch!' he called out. 'We would drink from the spring and rest beneath the tree. We would do this in peace. If we cannot, then I must treat you in the manner employed by Mirragen the Cat-man against your mighty ancestor.'

Gurangatch hissed like a freight train bleeding its brakes. Without hesitation it lunged forward, slamming down on the wet bank with the slap of a ten-ton eel. Warreen lightly leapt back, and the stained teeth clashed together just in front of his face. He poked Gurangatch's snout with the spear. The fish-lizard hissed even louder.

'You are not so lithe as Mirragen,' it said with the voice of a steam hose. Gurangatch jerked away as Warreen pulled loose the spear and stabbed again. This time the pointed end jammed under the shining silver scales surrounding the monster's right eye. The creature twisted, tugging the spear loose from Warreen's fingers.

The monster reared high, gazing at Warreen from ten feet, fifteen, twenty. The man looked up, expectant, the boomerang cocked in his right hand. The hiss was almost a sigh. 'Time to die again, little cousin!' Gurangatch's bull neck flexed, dipped. Jaws gaped.

This time Cordelia remembered to click off the safety. This time she braced herself by holding the H and K with both hands. This time the bullets went exactly where she wished.

She saw the slugs stitch a line down Gurangatch's throat. She released the trigger, raised the gun, fired a quick burst at the monster's face. One of the creature's eyes burst like a balloon full of dye. It cried out in pain, green jelly sloshing down across its snout. The wounds in the neck were oozing crimson. *Christmas colors*, Cordelia thought. *Get a grip, girl. Don't go hysterical.*

As Gurangatch writhed in the water, Warreen swung his arm in a short, tight arc and set the end of the boomerang into the creature's remaining eye. At this, the monster bellowed so loudly, Cordelia winced and recoiled back a step. Then Gurangatch doubled over in the water and dove. Cordelia had a quick impression of a thick, gilalike tail disappearing through the spray. Then the pool was quiet, small wavelets still splashing up on the banks. The ripples flattened and were gone.

'He has dived into the earth,' said Warreen, squatting and peering into the water. 'He will be gone a long time.'

Cordelia put the H and K back on safety.

Hands free of weapons, Warreen turned away from the pool and stood. Cordelia couldn't help herself. She stared. Warreen glanced down, then met her eyes again. With little apparent embarrassment he said, 'It is the excitement of the contest.' Then he smiled and said, 'This wouldn't happen under ordinary circumstances if I were guiding a European lady in the outback.'

It occurred to Cordelia to pick up his folded clothing and hold it out to him.

With dignity Warreen accepted the garments. Before turning away to dress he said, 'If you're ready, it would be a good time for a refreshing drink and some rest. I'm sorry I'm a bit short of tea.'

Cordelia said, 'I'll manage.'

The desert was slow to cool with the sunset. Cordelia continued to feel the heat rise out of the ground beneath her. Warreen and she lay back against the gnarled, semiexposed roots of the tree. The air felt as though it were a quilted comforter pulled up over her face. When she moved, the motion seemed to be at half speed.

'The water was delicious,' she said, 'but I'm still hungry.'

'Your hunger here is an illusion.'

'Then I'll fantasize a pizza.'

'Mmph,' Warreen said. 'Very well.' With a sigh he raised himself to his knees and ran his fingers over the rough bark of the tree. When he found a loose patch, he tugged it away from the trunk. His right hand darted forward, fingers scrambling to catch something Cordelia couldn't see. 'Here.' He displayed his find to her.

Her first impression was of something snakelike and squirming. She saw the pasty color, the segments and the many legs. 'What *is* that?' she said.

'Witchetty grub.' Warreen smiled. 'It's one of our national cuisines.' He thrust his hand forward like a mischievous little boy. 'Does it turn your stomach, little missy?'

'Goddamnit. No,' she said with a flash of anger. 'Don't call me that.' *What are you doing?* she said to herself as she reached for the creature. 'Do I have to eat it live?'

'No. It is not necessary.' He turned and cracked the creature against the desert oak. The witchetty grub convulsed once and ceased struggling.

Forcing herself just to *do* it and not think about the act, she took the witchetty, popped it into her mouth, and started chewing. *God,* she thought, *why do I do these things?*

'How do you find it?' said Warreen with a solemn face.

'Well,' said Cordelia, swallowing, 'it doesn't taste like chicken.'

The stars came out, spangling a belt across the entire sky. Cordelia lay with fingers plaited behind her head. She realized she had lived in Manhattan for close to a year and never looked for the stars at all.

'Nurunderi is up there,' said Warreen, pointing at the sky, 'along with his two young wives, placed there by Nepelle, the ruler of the heavens, after the women ate the forbidden food.'

'Apples?' said Cordelia.

'Fish. Tukkeri – a delicacy given only to the men.' His hand moved, the fingers pointing again. 'There, farther on – you can make out the Seven Sisters. And there is Karambal, their pursuer. You call him Aldebaran.'

Cordelia said, 'I have a lot of questions.'

Warreen paused. 'Not about the stars.'

'Not about the stars.'

'What, then?'

'All of this.' She sat up and spread her arms to the night. 'How am I here?'

'I brought you.'

'I know. But how?'

Warreen hesitated for a long time. Then he said, 'I am of Aranda blood, but was not raised within the tribe. Do you know of the urban aborigines?'

'Like in *The Last Wave*,' Cordelia said. 'I saw *The Fringe Dwellers* too. There aren't really tribal aborigines in the cities, right? Just sort of like individuals?'

Warreen laughed. 'You compare almost everything to the cinema. That is likening everything to the shadow world. Do you know anything of reality?'

'I think so.' In this place she wasn't so sure, but she wasn't about to admit it.

'My parents sought work in Melbourne,' Warreen said. 'I was born in the outback, but cannot recall any of that. I was a boy in the city.' He laughed bitterly. 'My walkabout seemed destined to lead me only among drunken diggers chundering in the gutter.'

Cordelia, listening raptly, said nothing.

'When I was an infant, I nearly died of a fever. Nothing the wirinun – the medicine man – could do helped. My parents, despairing, were ready to take me to the white doctor. Then the fever broke. The wirinun shook his medicine stick over me, looked into my eyes, and told my parents I would live and do great things.' Warreen paused again. 'The other children in the town had taken ill with the same sort of fever. All of them died. My parents told me their bodies shriveled or twisted or turned into unspeakable things. But they all died. Only I survived. The other parents hated me and hated my parents for bearing me. So we left.' He fell silent.

It dawned in Cordelia's mind like a star, rising. 'The wild card virus.'

'I know of it,' said Warreen. 'I think you are right. My childhood was as normal as my parents could make it until I grew the hair of an adult. Then …' His voice trailed off.

'Yes?' Cordelia said eagerly.

'As a man, I found I could enter the Dreamtime at will. I could explore the land of my ancestors. I could even take others with me.'

'Then this truly is the Dreamtime. It isn't some kind of shared illusion.'

He turned on his side and looked at her. Warreen's eyes were only about eighteen inches from hers. His gaze was something she could feel in the pit of her stomach. 'There is nothing more real.'

'The thing that happened to me on the airplane. The Eermoonans?'

'There are others from the shadow world who can enter the Dreamtime. One is Murga-muggai, whose totem is the trap-door spider. But there is something … wrong with her. You would call her psychotic. To me she is an Evil One, even though she claims kinship with the People.'

'Why did she kill Carlucci? Why try to kill me?'

'Murga-muggai hates European holy men, especially the American who comes from the sky. His name is Leo Barnett.'

'Fire-breather,' said Cordelia. 'He is a TV preacher.'

'He would save our souls. In doing so he will destroy us all, as kin and as individuals. No more tribes.'

'Barnett …' Cordelia breathed. 'Marty wasn't one of his people.'

'Europeans look much like one another. It doesn't matter that he didn't work for the man from the sky.' Warreen regarded her sharply. 'Aren't you here for the same purpose?'

Cordelia ignored that. 'But how did I survive the Eer-moonans?'

'I believe Murga-muggai underestimated your own power.' He hesitated. 'And possibly was it your time of the moon? Most monsters will not touch a woman who bleeds.'

Cordelia nodded. She began to be very sorry her period had ended in Auckland. 'I guess I'll have to depend on the H and K.' After a time she said, 'Warreen, how old are you?'

'Nineteen.' He hesitated. 'And you?'

'Going on eighteen.' They both were quiet. A very mature nineteen, Cordelia thought. He wasn't like any of the boys she remembered at home in Louisiana, or in Manhattan either.

Cordelia felt a chill plummeting both in the desert air and inside her mind. She knew the coldness growing within her was because she now had time to think about her situation. Not just thousands of miles from home and among strangers, but also not even in her own world.

'Warreen, do you have a girlfriend?'

'I am alone here.'

'No, you're not.' Her voice didn't squeak. Thank God. 'Will you hold me?'

Time stretched out. Then Warreen moved close and clumsily put his arms around her. She accidentally elbowed him in the eye before they both were comfortable. Cordelia greedily absorbed the warmth of his body, her face tucked against his. Her fingers wound through the surprising softness of his hair.

They kissed. Cordelia knew her parents would kill her if they knew what she was doing with this black man. First, of course, they would have lynched Warreen. She surprised herself. It was no different touching him than it had been touching anyone else she'd liked. There hadn't been many. Warreen felt much better than any of them.

She kissed him many times more. He did the same to her. The night chill deepened and their breathing pulsed faster.

'Warreen ...' she finally said, gasping. 'Do you want to make love?'

He seemed to go away from her, even though he was still there in her arms. 'I shouldn't—'

She guessed at something. 'Uh, are you a virgin?'

'Yes. And you?'

'I'm from Louisiana.' She covered his mouth with hers.

'Warreen is only my boy's name. My true name is Wyungare.'

'What does that mean?'

'He who returns to the stars.'

The moment came when she raised herself to take him and felt Wyungare driving deep within her. Much later she realized she hadn't thought of her mama and what her family would think. Not even once.

The giant first appeared as the smallest nub on the horizon.

'That's where we're going?' said Cordelia. 'Uluru?'

'The place of greatest magic.'

The morning sun rose high as they walked. The heat was no less pressing than it had been the previous day. Cordelia tried to ignore her thirst. Her legs ached, but it was not from trudging. She welcomed the feeling.

Various creatures of the outback sunned themselves by the path and inspected the humans as they passed.

An emu.

A frilled lizard.

A tortoise.

A black snake.

A wombat.

Wyungare acknowledged the presence of each with a courteous greeting. 'Cousin Dinewan' to the emu; 'Mungoongarlie' to the lizard; 'Good morning, Wayambeh' to the tortoise, and so on.

A bat circled them three times, squeaked a greeting, and flew off. Wyungare waved politely. 'Soar in safety, brother Narahdarn.'

His greeting to the wombat was particularly effusive. 'He was my boy-totem,' he explained to Cordelia. 'Warreen.'

They encountered a crocodile sunning itself beside their trail.

'He is your cousin as well,' said Wyungare. He told her what to say.

'Good morning, cousin Kurria,' said Cordelia. The reptile stared back at her, moving not an inch in the baking heat. Then it opened its jaws and hissed. Rows of white teeth flashed in the sun.

'A fortunate sign,' said Wyungare. 'The Kurria is your guardian.'

As Uluru grew in the distance, fewer were the creatures that came to the path to look upon the humans.

Cordelia realized with a start that for an hour or more she had been dwelling within her own thoughts. She glanced aside at Wyungare. 'How was it that you were in the alley at just the right time to help me?'

'I was guided by Baiame, the Great Spirit.'

'Not good enough.'

'It was a sort of a corroboree that night, a get-together with a purpose.'

'Like a rally?'

He nodded. 'My people don't usually engage in such things. Sometimes we have to use European ways.'

'What was it about?' Cordelia shaded her eyes and squinted into the distance. Uluru had grown to the size of a fist.

Wyungare also narrowed his eyes at Uluru. Somehow he seemed to be gazing much farther. 'We are going to drive the Europeans out of our lands. Especially we are not going to allow the men-who-preach to seize further footholds.'

'I don't think that's going to be very easy. Aren't the Aussies pretty well entrenched?'

Wyungare shrugged. 'Have you no faith, little missy? Just because we are outnumbered forty or fifty to one, own no tanks or planes, and know that few care about our cause? Just because we are our own worst enemies when it comes to organizing ourselves?' His voice sounded angry. 'Our way of life has stretched unbroken for sixty thousand years. How long has *your* culture existed?'

Cordelia started to say something placating.

The young man rushed on. 'We find it hard to organize effectively in the manner of the Maori in New Zealand. They are great clans. We are small tribes.' He smiled humorlessly. 'You might say the Maori resemble your aces. We are like the jokers.'

'The jokers can organize. There are people of conscience who help them.'

'We will not need help from Europeans. The winds are rising – all around the world, just as they are here in the outback. Look at the Indian homeland that is being carved with machetes and bayonets from the American jungle. Consider Africa, Asia, every continent where revolution lives.' His voice lifted. 'It's time, Cordelia. Even the white Christ recognizes the turning of the great wheel that will groan and move again in little more than a decade. The fires already burn, even if your people do not yet feel the heat.'

Do I know him? thought Cordelia. She knew she did not. She had suspected none of this. But within her heart she recognized the truth of what he said. And she did not fear him.

'Murga-muggai and I are not the only children of the fever,' said Wyungare. 'There are others. There will be many more, I fear. It will cause a difference here. *We* will make a difference.'

Cordelia nodded slightly.

'The whole world is aflame. All of us are burning. Do your Dr. Tachyon and Senator Hartmann and their entire party of touring Europeans know this?' His black eyes stared directly into hers. 'Do they truly know what is happening outside their limited sight in America?'

Cordelia said nothing. No, she thought. Probably not. 'I expect they don't.'

'Then that is the message you must bear them,' said Wyungare.

'I've seen pictures,' said Cordelia. 'This is Ayers Rock.'

'It is Uluru,' said Wyungare.

They stared up at the gigantic reddish sandstone monolith.

'It's the biggest single rock in the world,' said Cordelia. 'Thirteen hundred feet up to the top and several miles across.'

'It is the place of magic.'

'The markings on the side,' she said. 'They look like the cross section of a brain.'

'Only to you. To me they are the markings on the chest of a warrior.'

Cordelia looked around. 'There should be hundreds of tourists here.'

'In the shadow world there are. Here they would be fodder for Murga-muggai.'

Cordelia was incredulous. 'She eats people?'

'She eats anyone.'

'God, I hate spiders.' She stopped looking up the cliff. Her neck was getting a crick. 'We have to climb this?'

'There is a slightly gentler trail.' He indicated they should walk farther along the base of Uluru.

Cordelia found the sheer mass of the rock astonishing – and something more. She felt an awe that large stones did not ordinarily kindle. *It's gotta be magic*, she thought.

After a twenty-minute hike Wyungare said, 'Here.' He reached down. There was another cache of weapons. He picked up a spear, a club – nullanulla, he called it – a flint knife, a boomerang.

'Handy,' Cordelia said.

'Magic.' With a leather strap Wyungare tied the weapons together. He shouldered the packet and pointed toward the summit of Uluru. 'Next stop.'

To Cordelia the proposed climb looked no easier than it had at the first site. 'You're sure?'

He gestured at her handbag and the H and K. 'You should leave those.'

She shook her head, surveying first his weapons, then hers. 'No way.'

◆

Cordelia lay flat on her belly, peering up the rocky slope. Then she looked down. *I shouldn't have done that*, she thought. It might only have been a few hundred yards, but it was like leaning over an empty elevator shaft. She scrambled for a purchase. The H and K in her left hand didn't help.

'Just let it go,' said Wyungare, reaching back to secure her free hand.

'We might need it.'

'Its power will be slight against the Murga-muggai.'

'I'll risk it. When it comes to making magic, I need all the help I can get.' She was out of breath. 'You're sure this is the easiest ascent?'

'It is the only one. In the shadow world there is a heavy chain fixed to the rock for the first third of this journey. It is an affront to Uluru. Tourists use it to pull themselves up.'

'I'd settle for the affront,' said Cordelia. 'How much farther?'

'Maybe an hour, maybe less. It depends whether Murga-muggai decides to hurl boulders down upon us.'

'Oh.' She considered that. 'Think there's a good chance?'

'She knows we are coming. It depends on her mood.'

'I hope she doesn't have PMS.'

'Monsters don't bleed,' said Wyungare seriously.

They reached the broad, irregular top of Uluru and sat on a flat stone to rest. 'Where is she?' said Cordelia.

'If we don't find her, she'll find us. Are you in a hurry?'

'No.' Cordelia looked around apprehensively. 'What about the Eer-moonans?'

'You killed them all on the shadow plane. There is not an endless supply of such creatures.'

Oh, God, thought Cordelia. *I killed off an endangered species.* She wanted to giggle.

'Got your breath?'

She groaned and got up from the slab.

Wyungare was already up, his face angled at the sky, gauging the temperature and the wind. It was a great deal cooler on top of the rock than it had been on the desert floor. 'It is a good day to die,' he said.

'You've seen too many movies too.'

Wyungare grinned.

They trudged along nearly the entire diameter of the top of Uluru before coming to a wide, flat area about a hundred yards across. A sandstone cliff fell away to the desert only a few yards beyond. 'This looks promising,' said Wyungare. The surface of scoured sandstone was not completely bare. Football-size bits of rock were littered about like grains of sand. 'We are very close.'

The voice seemed to come from everywhere around them. The words grated like two chunks of sandstone rubbing together. 'This is my home.'

'It is not your home,' said Wyungare. 'Uluru is home to us all.'

'You have intruded ...'

Cordelia looked around apprehensively, seeing nothing other than rock and a few sparse bushes.

'... and will die.'

Across the rocky clearing, a sheet of sandstone about ten feet across flipped over, slamming into the surface of Uluru and shattering. Bits of stone sprayed across the area, and Cordelia reflexively stepped back. Wyungare did not move.

Murga-muggai, the trap-door spider woman, heaved herself up out of her hole and scrabbled into the open air.

For Cordelia it was like suddenly leaping into her worst nightmares. There were big spiders at home in the bayous, but nothing of this magnitude. Murga-muggai's body was dark brown and shaggy, the size of a Volkswagen. The bulbous body balanced swaying on eight articulated legs. All her limbs were tufted with spiky brown hair.

Glittering faceted eyes surveyed the human interlopers. A mouth opened wide, papillae moving gently, a clear, viscid liquid dripping down to the sandstone. Mandibles twitched apart.

'Oh, my God,' Cordelia said, wanting to take another step backward. Many more steps. She wished to wake up from this dream.

Murga-muggai moved toward them, legs shimmering as they seemed to slip momentarily in and out of phase with reality. To Cordelia it was like watching well-done stop-motion photography.

'Whatever else she is,' said Wyungare, 'Murga-muggai is a creature of grace and balance. It is her vanity.' He unslung the packet of weapons, unwinding the leather strap.

'Your flesh will make a fine lunch, cousins,' came the abrasive voice.

'You're no relation of mine,' said Cordelia.

Wyungare hefted the boomerang as though considering an experiment, then fluidly hurled it toward Murga-muggai. The honed wooden edge caressed the stiff hairs on top of the spider-creature's abdomen and sighed away into the open sky. The weapon swung around and started to return, but didn't have sufficient altitude to clear the rock. Cordelia heard the boomerang shatter on the stone below Uluru's rim.

'Bad fortune,' said Murga-muggai. She laughed, an oily, sticky sound.

'Why, cousin?' said Wyungare. 'Why do you do any of this?'

'Silly boy,' said Murga-muggai, 'you've lost hold of tradition. It will be the death of you, if not the death of our people. You are so wrong. I must remedy this.'

Apparently in no hurry to eat, she slowly closed the distance between them. Her legs continued to strobe. It was dizzying to watch. 'My appetite for Europeans is growing,' she said. 'I will enjoy today's varied feast.'

'I will have only one chance,' Wyungare said in a low voice. 'If it doesn't work—'

'It will,' said Cordelia. She stepped even with him and touched his arm. *'Laissez les bon temps rouler.'*

Wyungare glanced at her.

'Let the good times roll. My daddy's favorite line.'

Murga-muggai leapt.

The spider-creature descended over them like a wind-torn umbrella with spare, bent struts flexing.

Wyungare jammed the butt of the spear into the unyielding sandstone and lifted the fire-hardened head toward the body of the monster. Murga-muggai cried out in rage and triumph.

The spear-head glanced off one mandible and broke. The supple shaft of the spear at first bent, then cracked into splinters like the shattering of a spine. The spider-creature was so close, Cordelia could see the abdomen pulse. She could smell a dark, acrid odor.

Now we're in trouble, she thought.

Both Wyungare and she scrambled backward, attempting to avoid the seeking legs and clashing mandibles. The nullanulla skittered across the sandstone.

Cordelia scooped up the flint knife. It was suddenly like watching everything in slow motion. One of Murga-muggai's hairy forelegs lashed out toward Wyungare. The tip fell across the man's chest, just below his heart. The force of the blow hurled him backward. Wyungare's body tumbled across the stone clearing like one of the limp rag dolls Cordelia had played with as a girl.

And just as lifeless.

'No!' Cordelia screamed. She ran to Wyungare, knelt beside him, felt for the pulse in his throat. Nothing. He was not breathing. His eyes stared blindly toward the empty sky.

She cradled the man's body for just a moment, realizing that the spider-creature was patiently regarding them from twenty yards away. 'You are next, imperfect cousin,' came the ground-out words. 'You are brave, but I don't think you can help the cause of my people any more than the Wombat.' Murga-muggai started forward.

Cordelia realized she was still clinging to the gun. She aimed the H and K mini at the spider-creature and squeezed the trigger. Nothing happened. She clicked the safety on, then off again. Pulled the trigger. Nothing. Damn. It was finally empty.

Focus, she thought. She stared at Murga-muggai's eyes and willed the creature to die. The power was still there within her. She could feel it. She strained. But nothing happened. She was helpless. Murga-muggai was not even slowed.

Evidently the reptile-level had nothing to say to spiders.

The spider-thing rushed toward her like a graceful, eight-legged express train.

Cordelia knew there was nothing left to do. Except the one thing she dreaded most.

She wondered if the image in her mind would be the last thing she would ever know. It was the memory of an old cartoon showing Fay Wray in the fist of King Kong on the side of the Empire State Building. A man in a biplane was calling out to the woman, 'Trip him, Fay! Trip him!'

Cordelia summoned all the hysterical strength left within her and hurled the empty H and K at Murga-muggai's head. The weapon hit one faceted eye and the monster shied slightly. She leapt forward, wrapping arms and legs around one of the pistoning spider-creature's forelegs.

The monster stumbled, started to recover, but then Cordelia jammed the flint knife into a leg joint. The extremity folded and momentum took over. The spider-thing was a ball of flailing legs rolling along with Cordelia clinging to one hairy limb.

The woman had a chaotic glimpse of the desert floor looming ahead and below her. She let go, hit the stone, rolled, grabbed an outcropping and stopped.

Murga-muggai was propelled out into open space. To Cordelia the monster seemed to hang there for a moment, suspended like the coyote in the Roadrunner cartoons. Then the spider-creature plummeted.

Cordelia watched the flailing, struggling thing diminish. A screech like nails on chalkboard trailed after.

Finally all she could see was what looked like a black stain at the foot of Uluru. She could imagine only too well the shattered remains with the legs splayed out. 'You deserved it!' she said aloud. 'Bitch.'

Wyungare! She turned and limped back to his body.

He was still dead.

For a moment Cordelia allowed herself the luxury of angry tears. Then she realized she had her own magic. 'It's only been a minute,' she said, as if praying. 'Not longer. Not long at all. Only a minute.'

She bent close to Wyungare and concentrated. She felt the power draining out of her mind and floating down around the man, insulating the cold flesh. The thought had been a revelation. In the past she had tried only to shut autonomic nervous systems down. She had never tried to start one up. It had never occurred to her.

Jack's words seemed to echo from eight thousand miles away: 'You can use it for life too.'

The energy flowed.

The slightest heartbeat.

The faintest breath.

Another.

Wyungare began to breathe.

He groaned.

Thank God, thought Cordelia. Or Baiame. She glanced around self-consciously at the top of Uluru.

Wyungare opened his eyes. 'Thank you,' he said faintly but distinctly.

The riot swirled past them. Police clubs swung. Aboriginal heads cracked. 'Bloody hell,' said Wyungare. 'You'd think this was bloody Queensland.' He seemed restrained from joining the fray only by Cordelia's presence.

Cordelia reeled back against the alley wall. 'You've brought me back to Alice?'

Wyungare nodded.

'This is the same night?'

'All the distances *are* different in the Dreamtime,' said Wyungare. 'Time as well as space.'

'I'm grateful.' The noise of angry shouts, screams, sirens, was deafening.

'Now what?' said the young man.

'A night's sleep. In the morning I'll rent a Land-Rover. Then I'll drive to Madhi Gap.' She pondered a question. 'Will you stay with me?'

'Tonight?' Wyungare hesitated as well. 'Yes, I'll stay with you. You're not as bad as the preacher-from-the-sky, but I must find a way to talk you out of what you want to do with the satellite station.'

Cordelia started to relax just a little.

'Of course,' said Wyungare, glancing around, 'you'll have to sneak me into your room.'

Cordelia shook her head. *It's like high school again*, she thought. She put her arm around the man beside her.

There were so many things she needed to tell people. The road south to Madhi Gap stretched ahead. She still hadn't decided whether she was going to call New York first.

'There is one thing,' said Wyungare.

She glanced at him questioningly.

'It has always been the custom,' he said slowly, 'for European men to use their aboriginal mistresses and then abandon them.'

Cordelia looked him in the eye. 'I am not a European man,' she said.

Wyungare smiled.

FROM *THE JOURNAL*
OF XAVIER DESMOND

March 14/Hong Kong:

I have been feeling better of late, I'm pleased to say. Perhaps it was our brief sojourn in Australia and New Zealand. Coming close upon the heels of Singapore and Jakarta, Sydney seemed almost like home, and I was strangely taken with Auckland and the comparative prosperity and cleanliness of its little toy jokertown. Aside from a distressing tendency to call themselves 'uglies,' an even more offensive term than 'joker,' my Kiwi brethren seem to live as decently as any jokers anywhere. I was even able to purchase a week-old copy of the *Jokertown Cry* at my hotel. It did my soul good to read the news of home, even though too many of the headlines seem to be concerned with a gang war being fought in our streets.

Hong Kong has its jokertown too, as relentlessly mercantile as the rest of the city. I understand that mainland China dumps most of its jokers here, in the Crown Colony. In fact a delegation of leading joker merchants have invited Chrysalis and me to lunch with them tomorrow and discuss 'possible commercial ties between jokers in Hong Kong and New York City.' I'm looking forward to it.

Frankly it will be good to get away from my fellow delegates for a few hours. The mood aboard the *Stacked Deck* is testy at best at present, chiefly thanks to Thomas Downs and his rather over-developed journalistic instincts.

Our mail caught up with us in Christchurch, just as we were taking off for Hong Kong, and the packet included advance copies of the latest issue of *Aces*. Digger went up and down the aisles after we were airborne, distributing complimentary copies as is his wont. He ought to have read them first. He and his execrable magazine hit a new low this time out, I'm afraid.

The issue features his cover story of Peregrine's pregnancy. I was amused to note that the magazine obviously feels that Peri's baby is the big news of the trip, since they devoted twice as much space to it as they have to any of Digger's previous stories, even the hideous incident in Syria, though perhaps that was only to justify the glossy four-page footspread of Peregrine past and present, in various costumes and states of undress.

The whispers about her pregnancy started as early as India and were officially confirmed while we were in Thailand, so Digger could hardly be blamed for filing a story. It's just the sort of thing that *Aces* thrives on. Unfortunately for his own health and our sense of camaraderie aboard the *Stacked Deck*, Digger clearly did not agree with Peri that her 'delicate condition' was a private matter. Digger dug too far.

The cover asks, 'Who Fathered Peri's Baby?' Inside, the piece opens with a double-page spread illustrated by an artist's conception of Peregrine holding an infant in her arms, except that the child is a black silhouette with a question mark instead of a face. 'Daddy's an Ace, Tachyon Says,' reads the subhead, leading into a much larger orange banner that claims, 'Friends Beg Her to Abort Monstrous Joker Baby.' Gossip has it that Digger plied Tachyon with brandy while the two of them were inspecting the raunchier side of Singapore's nightlife, managing to elicit a few choice indiscretions. He did not get the name of the father of Peregrine's baby, but once drunk enough, Tachyon displayed no reticence in sounding off about all the reasons why he believes Peregrine ought to abort this child, the foremost of which is the nine percent chance that the baby will be born a joker.

I confess that reading the story filled me with a cold rage and made me doubly glad that Dr. Tachyon is not my personal physician. It is at moments such as this that I find myself wondering how Tachyon can possibly pretend to be my friend, or the friend of any joker. *In vino veritas*, they say; Tachyon's comments make it quite clear that he thinks abortion is the only choice for any woman in Peregrine's position. The Takisians abhor deformity and customarily 'cull' (such a polite word) their own deformed children (very few in number, since they have not yet been blessed with the virus that they so generously decided to share with Earth) shortly after birth. Call me oversensitive if you will, but the clear implication of what Tachyon is saying is that death is preferable to jokerhood, that it is better that this child never live at all than live the life of a joker.

When I set the magazine aside I was so livid that I knew I could not possibly speak to Tachyon himself in any rational manner, so I got up and went back to the press compartment to give Downs a piece of my mind. At the very least I wanted to point out rather forcefully that it was grammatically permissible to omit the adjective 'monstrous' before the phrase 'joker baby,' though clearly the copy editors at *Aces* feel it compulsory.

Digger saw me coming, however, and met me halfway. I've managed to raise his consciousness at least enough so that he knew how upset I'd be, because he started right in with excuses. 'Hey, I just wrote the article,' he began. 'They do the headlines back in New York, that and the art, I've got no control over it. Look, Des, next time I'll talk to them—'

He never had a chance to finish whatever promise he was about to make, because just then Josh McCoy stepped up behind him and tapped him on the shoulder with a rolled-up copy of *Aces*. When Downs turned around, McCoy started swinging. The first punch broke Digger's nose with a sickening noise that made me feel rather faint. McCoy went on to split Digger's lips and loosen a few teeth. I grabbed McCoy with my arms and wrapped my trunk around his neck to try to hold him still, but he was crazy strong with rage and brushed me off easily, I'm afraid. I've never been the physical sort, and in my present condition I fear that I'm pitifully weak. Fortunately Billy Ray came along in time to break them up before McCoy could do serious damage.

Digger spent the rest of the flight back in the rear of the plane, stoked up with painkillers. He managed to offend Billy Ray as well by dripping blood on the front of his white Carnifex costume. Billy is nothing if not obsessive about his appearance, and as he kept telling us, 'those fucking bloodstains don't come out.' McCoy went up front, where he helped Hiram, Mistral, and Mr. Jayewardene console Peri, who was considerably upset by the story. While McCoy was assaulting Digger in the rear of the plane, she was tearing into Dr. Tachyon up front. Their confrontation was less physical but equally dramatic, Howard tells me. Tachyon kept apologizing over and over again, but no amount of apologies seemed to stay Peregrine's fury. Howard says it was a good thing that her talons were packed away safely with the luggage.

Tachyon finished out the flight alone in the first-class lounge with a bottle of Remy Martin and the forlorn look of a puppy dog who has just piddled on the Persian rug. If I had been a crueler man, I might have gone upstairs and explained my own grievances to him, but I found that I did not have the heart. I find that very curious, but there is something about Dr. Tachyon that makes it difficult to stay angry with him for very long, no matter how insensitive and egregious his behavior.

No matter. I am looking forward to this part of the trip. From Hong Kong we travel to the mainland, Canton and Shanghai and Peking and other stops equally exotic. I plan to walk upon the Great Wall and see the Forbidden City. During World War II I'd chosen to serve in the Navy in hopes of seeing the world, and the Far East always had a special glamour for me, but I wound up assigned to a desk in Bayonne, New Jersey. Mary and I were going to make up for that afterward, when the baby was a little older and we had a little more in the way of financial security.

Well, we made our plans, and meanwhile the Takisians made theirs.

Over the years China came to represent all the things I'd never done, all the far places I meant to visit and never did, my own personal Jolson story. And now it looms on my horizon, at last. It's enough to make one believe the end is truly near.

ZERO HOUR

Lewis Shiner

The store had a pyramid of TV sets in the window, all tuned to the same channel. They tracked a 747 landing at Narita Airport, then pulled back to show an announcer in front of a screen. Then the airport scene switched to a graphic featuring a caricature of Tachyon, a cartoon jet, and the English words *Stacked Deck*.

Fortunato stopped in front of the store. It was just getting dark, and all around him the neon ideograms of the Ginza blazed into red and blue and yellow life. He couldn't hear anything through the glass, so he watched helplessly while the screen flashed pictures of Hartmann and Chrysalis and Jack Braun.

He knew they were going to show Peregrine an instant before she flashed on the screen, lips slightly parted, her eyes starting to look away, the wind in her hair. He didn't need wild card powers to have predicted it. Even if he'd still had them. He knew they'd show her because it was the thing he feared. Fortunato watched his reflected image superimposed over hers, faint, ghostlike.

He bought a *Japanese Times*, Tokyo's biggest English-language paper. 'Aces Invade Japan,' the headline said, and there was a special pullout section with color photographs. The crowds surged around him, mostly male, mostly in business suits, mostly on autopilot. The ones that noticed him gave him a shocked glance and looked away again. They saw his height and thinness and foreignness. If they could tell he was half-Japanese, they didn't care; the other half was black American, *kokujin*. In Japan, as in too many other parts of the world, the whiter the skin the better.

The paper said the tour would be staying at the newly remodeled Imperial Hotel, a few blocks from where Fortunato stood. And so, Fortunato thought, the mountain has come to Muhammad. Whether Muhammad wants it or not.

It was time, Fortunato thought, for a bath.

Fortunato crouched by the tap and soaped himself all over, then carefully rinsed it off with his plastic bucket. Getting soap into the *ofuro* was one of two breaches of etiquette the Japanese would not tolerate, the other being the wearing of shoes on tatami mats. Once he was clean, Fortunato walked over to the edge of the pool, his towel hanging to cover his genitals with the casual skill of a native Japanese.

He slipped into the 115-degree water, giving himself over to the agonizing pleasure. A mixture of sweat and condensation immediately broke out across his forehead and ran down his face. His muscles relaxed in spite of himself. Around him the other men in the *ofuro* sat with their eyes shut, ignoring him.

He bathed about this time every day. In the six months he'd spent in Japan he'd become a creature of habit, just like the millions of Japanese around him. He was up by nine in the morning, an hour he'd seen only half a dozen times back in New York City. He spent the mornings in meditation or study, going twice a week to a zen *Shukubo* across the bay in Chiba City.

In the afternoons he was a tourist, seeing everything from the French Impressionists at the Bridgestone to the woodcuts at the Riccar, walking in the Imperial Gardens, shopping in the Ginza, visiting the shrines.

At night there was the *mizu-shōbai*. The water business.

It was what they called the huge underground economy of pleasure, everything from the most conservative of geisha houses to the most blatant of prostitutes, from the mirror-walled nightclubs to the tiny red-light bars where, late at night, after enough saki, the hostess might be talked into dancing naked on the Formica counter. It was an entire world catering to the carnal appetite, unlike anything Fortunato had ever seen. It made his operations back in New York, the string of high-class hookers that he'd naively called geishas, seem puny in comparison. In spite of everything that had happened to him, in spite of the fact that he was still trying to push himself toward leaving the world entirely and shutting himself in a monastery, he couldn't stay away from these women. The *jo-san*, the play-for-play hostesses. If only to look at them and talk to them and then go home alone to masturbate in his tiny cubicle, in case his burned-out wild card ability had started to come back, in case the tantric power was beginning to build inside his Muladhara chakra.

When the water wasn't painful anymore, he got up and soaped and rinsed again and got back into the *ofuro*. It was time, he thought, for a decision. Either to face Peregrine and the others at the hotel, or leave town entirely, maybe stay a week at the *Shukubo* in Chiba City so he wouldn't run into them by accident.

Or, he thought, the third way. Let fate decide. Go on about his business, and if he was meant to find them, he would.

It happened five days later, just before sunset on Tuesday afternoon, and it was not an accident at all. He'd been talking to a waiter he knew in the kitchen of the Chikuyotei, and he'd taken the back door into an alley. When he looked up, she was there.

'Fortunato,' she said. She held her wings straight out behind her. Still, they nearly touched the walls of the alley. She wore a deep blue off-the-shoulder knit dress that clung to her body. She looked to be about six months pregnant. Nothing he'd seen had mentioned it.

There was a man with her, from India or somewhere near it. He was about fifty, thick in the middle, losing his hair.

'Peregrine,' Fortunato said. She looked upset, tired, relieved – all at once. Her arms came up and Fortunato went to her and held her gently. She rested her forehead on his shoulder for a second and then pulled away.

'This … this is G.C. Jayewardene,' Peregrine said. The man put his palms together, elbows out, and ducked his head. 'He helped me find you.'

Fortunato bowed jerkily. Christ, he thought, I'm turning Japanese. Next I'll be stammering nonsense syllables at the beginning of every sentence, not even be able to talk anymore. 'How did you know …' he said.

'The wild card,' Jayewardene said. 'I saw this moment a month ago.' He shrugged. 'The visions come without my asking. I don't know why or what they mean. I'm their prisoner.'

'I know the feeling,' Fortunato said. He looked at Peregrine again. He reached out and put a hand on her stomach. He could feel the baby moving inside her. 'It's mine. Isn't it?'

She bit her lip, nodded. 'But that's not the reason I'm here. I would have left you alone. I know it's what you wanted. But we need your help.'

'What kind of help?'

'It's Hiram,' she said. 'He's disappeared.'

Peregrine needed to sit down. In New York or London or Mexico City there would have been a park within walking distance. In Tokyo the space was too valuable. Fortunato's apartment was a half-hour train ride away, a four-tatami room, six feet by twelve, in a gray-walled complex with narrow halls and communal toilets and no grass or trees. Besides, only a lunatic would try to ride a train at rush hour, when white-gloved railroad employees stood by to shove people into already-packed cars.

Fortunato took them around the corner to a cafeteria-style sushi bar. The decor was red vinyl, white Formica, and chrome. The sushi traveled the length of the room on a conveyor belt that passed all the booths.

'We can talk here,' Fortunato said. 'But I wouldn't try the food. If you want to eat, I'll take you someplace else – but it'd mean waiting in line.'

'No,' Peregrine said. Fortunato could see that the sharp vinegar and fish smells weren't sitting well on her stomach. 'This is fine.'

They'd already asked each other how they'd been, walking over here, and both of them had been pleasant and vague in their answers. Peregrine had told him about the baby. Healthy, she said, normal as far as anyone could tell. Fortunato had asked Jayewardene a few polite questions. There was nothing left but to get down to it.

'He left this letter,' Peregrine said. Fortunato looked it over. The handwriting seemed jagged, unlike Hiram's usual compulsive penmanship. It said he was leaving the tour for 'personal reasons.' He assured everyone he was in good health. He hoped to rejoin them later. If not, he would see them in New York.

'We know where he is,' Peregrine said. 'Tachyon found him, telepathically, and made sure he wasn't hurt or anything. But he refuses to go into Hiram's brain and find out what's wrong. He says he doesn't have the right. He won't let any of us talk to Hiram, either. He says if somebody wants to leave the tour it's not our business. Maybe he's right. I know if I tried to talk to him, it wouldn't do any good.'

'Why not? You two always got along.'

'He's different now. He hasn't been the same since December. It's like some witch doctor put a curse on him while we were in the Caribbean.'

'Did something specific happen to set him off?'

'Something happened, but we don't know what. We were having lunch at the Palace Sunday with Prime Minister Nakasone and all these other officials. Suddenly there's this man in a cheap suit. He just walks in and hands Hiram a piece of paper. Hiram got very pale and wouldn't say anything about it. That afternoon he went back to the hotel by himself. Said he wasn't feeling good. That must have been when he packed and moved out, because Sunday night he was gone.'

'Do you remember anything else about the man in the suit?'

'He had a tattoo. It came out from under his shirt and went down his wrist. God knows how far up his arm it went. It was really vivid, all these greens and reds and blues.'

'It probably covered his whole body,' Fortunato said. He rubbed his temples, where his regular daily headache had set in. 'He was *yakuza*.'

'*Yakuza* ...' Jayewardene said.

Peregrine looked from Fortunato to Jayewardene and back. 'Is that bad?'

'Very bad,' Jayewardene said. 'Even I have heard of them. They're gangsters.'

'Like the Mafia,' Fortunato said. 'Only not as centralized. Each family – they call them clans – is on its own. There's something like twenty-five hundred separate clans in Japan, each with its own *oyabun*. The *oyabun* is like the don. It means "in the role of parent." If Hiram's in trouble with the *yak*, we may not even be able to find out which clan is after him.'

Peregrine took another piece of paper out of her purse. 'This is the address of Hiram's hotel. I ... told Tachyon I wouldn't see him. I told him somebody should have it in case of emergency. Then Mr. Jayewardene told me about his vision ...'

Fortunato put his hand on the paper but didn't look at it. 'I don't have any power left,' he said. 'I used everything I had fighting the Astronomer, and there isn't anything left.'

It had been back in September, Wild Card Day in New York. The fortieth anniversary of Jetboy's big fuckup, when the spores had fallen on the city and thousands had died, Jetboy among them. It was the day a man named the Astronomer chose to get even with the aces who had hounded him and broken his secret society of Egyptian Masons. He and Fortunato had fought it out with blazing fireballs of power over the East River. Fortunato had won, but it had cost him everything.

That had been the night he had made love to Peregrine for the first and last time. The night her child had been conceived.

'It doesn't matter,' Peregrine said. 'Hiram respects you. He'll listen to you.'

In fact, Fortunato thought, he's afraid of me and he blames me for the death of a woman he used to love. A woman Fortunato had used as a pawn against the Astronomer, and lost. A woman Fortunato had loved too. Years ago.

But if he walked away now he wouldn't see Peregrine again. It had been hard enough to stay away from her, knowing that she was so close by. It was a whole other order of difficult to get up and walk away from her when she was right there in front of him, so tall and powerful and overflowing with emotions. The fact that she carried his child made it even harder, made just one more thing he wasn't ready to think about.

'I'll try,' Fortunato said. 'I'll do what I can.'

Hiram's room was in the Akasaka Shanpia, a businessman's hotel near the train station. Except for the narrow hallways and the shoes outside the doors, it could have been any middle-price hotel in the U.S. Fortunato knocked on Hiram's door. There was a hush, as if all noises inside the room had suddenly stopped.

'I know you're in there,' Fortunato said, bluffing. 'It's Fortunato, man. You might as well let me in.' After a couple of seconds the door opened.

Hiram had turned the place into a slum. There were clothes and towels all over the floor, plates of dried-out food and smudged highball glasses, stacks of newspapers and magazines. It smelled faintly of acetone and a mixture of sweat and old booze.

Hiram himself had lost weight. His clothes sagged around him like they were still on hangers. After he let Fortunato in, he walked back to the bed without saying anything. Fortunato shut the door, dumped a dirty shirt off a chair, and sat down.

'So,' Hiram said at last. 'It would seem I've been ferreted out.'

'They're worried. They think you might be in some kind of trouble.'

'It's nothing. There's absolutely nothing for them to be concerned about. Didn't they get my note?'

'Don't bullshit me, Hiram. You've gotten messed up with the *yakuza*. Those are not the kind of people you take chances with. Tell me what happened.'

Hiram stared at him. 'If I don't tell you, you'll just come in and get it, won't you?' Fortunato shrugged, another bluff. 'Yeah. Right.'

'I just want to help,' Fortunato said.

'Well, your help is not required. It's a small matter of money. Nothing else.'

'How much money?'

'A few thousand.'

'Dollars, of course.' A thousand yen were worth a little over five dollars U.S. 'How did it happen? Gambling?'

'Look, this is all rather embarrassing. I'd prefer not to talk about it, all right?'

'You're saying this to a man who was a pimp for thirty years. Do you think I'm going to come down on you? Whatever you did?'

Hiram took a deep breath. 'No. I suppose not.'

'Talk to me.'

'I was out walking Saturday night, kind of late, over on Roppongi Street ...'

'By yourself?'

'Yes.' He was embarrassed again. 'I'd heard a lot about the women here. I just wanted to ... tantalize myself, you know? The mysterious Orient. Women who would fulfill your wildest dreams. I'm a long way from home. I just ... wanted to see.'

It wasn't that different from what Fortunato had been doing the last six months. 'I understand.'

'I saw a sign that said "English-speaking hostesses." I went in and there was a long hallway. I must have missed the place the sign was for. I went back into the building a long way. There was a padded kind of a door at the end, no sign or anything. When I got inside, they took my coat and went away with it somewhere. Nobody spoke English. Then these girls more or less dragged me over to a table and got me buying them drinks. There were three of them. I had one or two drinks myself. More than one or two. It was a sort of a dare. They were using sign language, teaching me some Japanese. God. They were so beautiful. So ... delicate, you know? But with huge dark eyes that would look at you and then skitter away. Half shy and half ... I don't know. Challenging. They said nobody had ever drunk ten jars of saki there before. Like no one had ever been quite man enough. So I did. By then they had me pretty well convinced I would get all three of them for a reward.'

Hiram started to sweat. The drops ran down his face and he wiped them off with the cuff of a stained silk shirt. 'I was ... well, very aroused, shall we say. And drunk. They kept flirting and touching me on the arm, so lightly, like butterflies landing on my skin. I suggested we go somewhere. They kept putting me off. Ordering more drinks. And then I just lost control.'

He looked up at Fortunato. 'I haven't been ... quite myself lately. Something just came over me in that bar. I guess I grabbed one of the girls. Sort of tried to take her dress off. She started screaming and all three of them ran away. Then the bouncer started hustling me toward the door, waving a bill in my face. It was for fifty thousand yen. Even drunk I knew there was something wrong. He pointed at my coat and then at a number. Then the jars of saki and more numbers. Then the girls and more numbers. I think that was what really got to me. Paying so much money just to be flirted with.'

'They were the wrong girls,' Fortunato said. 'Christ, there's a million women for sale in this town. All you have to do is ask a taxi driver.'

'Okay. Okay. I made a mistake. It could happen to anybody. But they went too far.'

'So you walked out.'

'I walked out. They tried to chase me and I glued them to the floor. Somehow I got back to the hotel. It took me forever to find a cab.'

'Okay,' Fortunato said. 'Where exactly was this place? Could you find it again?'

Hiram shook his head. 'I tried. I've spent two days looking for it.'

'What about the sign? Do you remember anything about it? Could you sketch any of the characters?'

'The Japanese, you mean? No way.'

'There must have been something.'

Hiram closed his eyes. 'Okay. Maybe there was a picture of a duck. Side view. Looked like a decoy, back home. Just an outline.'

'Okay. And you've told me everything that happened at the club.'

'Everything.'

'And the next day the *kobun* found you at lunch.'

'*Kobun?*'

'The *yakuza* soldier.'

Hiram blushed again. 'He just walked in. I don't know how he got past the security. He stood right across the table from where I was sitting. He bowed from the waist with his legs spread; his right hand is out like this, palm up. He introduced himself, but I was so scared I couldn't remember the name. Then he handed me a bill. The amount was two hundred and fifty thousand yen. There was a note in English at the bottom. It said the amount would double every day at midnight until I paid it.'

Fortunato worked the figures out in his head. In U.S. money the debt was now close to seven thousand dollars.

Hiram said, 'If it's not paid by Thursday they said ...'

'What?'

'They said I would never even see the man who killed me.'

Fortunato phoned Peregrine from a pay phone, color-coded red for local calls only. He fed it a handful of ten-yen coins to keep it from beeping at him every three minutes.

'I found him,' Fortunato said. 'He wasn't a lot of help.'

'Is he okay?' Peregrine sounded sleepy. It was all too easy for Fortunato to picture her stretched out in bed, covered only by a thin white sheet. He had no powers left. He couldn't stop time or project his astral body or hurl bolts of *prana* or move around inside people's thoughts. But his senses were still acute, sharper than they'd ever been before the virus, and he could remember the smell of her perfume and her hair and her desire as if they were there all around him.

'He's nervous and losing weight. But nothing's happened to him yet.'

'Yet?'

'The *yakuza* want money from him. A few thousand. It's basic-ally a misunderstanding. I tried to get him to back down, but he wouldn't. It's a pride thing. He sure picked the country for it. People die from pride here by the thousands, every year.'

'You think it's going to come to that?'

'Yes. I offered to pay the money *for* him. He refused. I'd do it behind his back, but I can't find out which clan is after him. What scares me is it sounds like they're threatening him with some kind of invisible killer.'

'You mean, like an ace?'

'Maybe. In all the time I've been here I've only heard about one actual confirmed ace, a zen *rōshi* up north on Hokkaido Island. For one thing, I think the spores had pretty much settled out before they could get here. And even if any did, you might never hear about them. We're talking about a culture here that makes self-effacement into a religion. Nobody wants to stand out. So if we're up against some kind of ace, it's possible nobody's even heard of him.'

'Can I do anything?'

He wasn't sure what she was offering and he didn't want to think too hard about it. 'No,' he said. 'Not now.'

'Where are you?'

'A pay phone, in the Roppongi district. The club where Hiram got in trouble is somewhere around here.'

'It's just . . . we never really had a chance to talk. With Jayewardene there and everything.'

'I know.'

'I went looking for you after Wild Card Day. Your mother said you were going to a monastery.'

'I was. Then when I got here I heard about that monk, the one up on Hokkaido.'

'The ace.'

'Yeah. His name is Dogen. He can create mindblocks, a little like the Astronomer could, but not as drastic. He can make people forget things or take away worldly skills that might interfere with their meditation or—'

'Or take away somebody's wild card power. Yours, for instance.'

'For instance.'

'Did you see him?'

'He said he'd take me in. But only if I gave up my power.'

'But you said your power was gone.'

'So far. But I haven't given it a chance to come back. And if I go in the monastery, it could be permanent. Sometimes the block wears off and he has to renew it. Sometimes it doesn't wear off at all.'

'And you don't know if you want to go that far.'

'I want to. But I still feel ... responsible. Like the power isn't entirely *mine*, you know?'

'Kind of. I never wanted to give mine up. Not like you or Jayewardene.'

'Is he serious about it?'

'He sure seems to be.'

'Maybe when this is over,' Fortunato said, 'him and me can go see Dogen together.' Traffic was picking up around him; the day-time buses and delivery vans had given way to expensive sedans and taxis. 'I have to go,' he said.

'Promise me,' Peregrine said. 'Promise me you'll be careful.'

'Yeah,' he said. 'Yeah. I promise.'

The Roppongi district was about three kilometers southwest of the Ginza. It was the one part of Tokyo where the clubs stayed open past midnight. Lately it was overrun with *gaijin* trade, discos and pubs and bars with Western hostesses.

It had taken Fortunato a long time to get used to things closing early. The last trains left the center of the city at midnight, and he'd walked down to Roppongi more than once during his first weeks in Tokyo, still looking for some elusive satisfaction, unwilling to settle for sex or alcohol, not ready to risk the savage Japanese punishment for being caught with drugs. Finally he'd given it up. The sight of so many tourists, the loud, unceasing noise of their languages, the predictable throb of their music, were not worth the few pleasures the clubs had to offer.

He tried three places and no one remembered Hiram or recognized the sign of the duck. Then he went into the north Berni Inn, one of two in the district. It was an English pub, complete with Guinness and kidney pie and red velvet everything. About half the tables were full, either of foreign tourists in twos and threes, or large tables of Japanese businessmen.

Fortunato slowed to watch the dynamics at one of the Japanese tables. Expense accounts kept the water trade alive. Staying out all night with the boys from the office was just part of the job. The youngest and least confident of them talked the loudest and laughed the hardest. Here, with the excuse of alcohol, was the one time the pressure was off, their only chance to fuck up and get away with it. The senior men smiled indulgently. Fortunato knew that even if he could read their thoughts there wouldn't be much there to see. The perfect Japanese businessman could hide his thoughts even from himself, could efface himself so completely that no one would even know he was there.

The bartender was Japanese and probably new on the job. He looked at Fortunato with a mixture of horror and awe. Japanese were raised to think of *gaijin* as a race of giants. Fortunato, over six feet tall, thin, his shoulders hunched forward like a vulture's, was a walking childhood nightmare.

'*Genki desu-ne?*' Fortunato asked politely, with a little bow of the head. 'I'm looking for a nightclub,' he went on in Japanese. 'It has a sign like this.' He drew a duck on one of the red bar napkins and showed it to the bartender. The bartender nodded, backing away, a rigid smile of fear on his face.

Finally one of the foreign waitresses ducked behind the bar and smiled at Fortunato. 'I have a feeling Tosun is not going to do well here,' she said. Her accent was Northern England. Her hair was dark brown and pinned up with chopsticks, and her eyes were green. 'Can I help?'

'I'm looking for a nightclub somewhere around here. It's got a duck on the sign, like this one. Small place, doesn't do a lot of *gaijin* trade.'

The woman looked at the napkin. For a second she had the same look as the bartender. Then she worked her face around into a perfect Japanese smile. It looked horrible on her European features. Fortunato knew she wasn't afraid of him. It had to be the club. 'No,' she said. 'Sorry.'

'Look. I know the *yakuza* are mixed up in this. I'm not a cop, and I'm not looking for any trouble. I'm just trying to pay a debt for somebody. For a friend of mine. Believe me, they *want* to see me.'

'Sorry.'

'What's your name?'

'Megan.' The way she thought before saying it told Fortunato she was lying.

'What part of England are you from?'

'I'm not, actually.' She casually crumpled the napkin and threw it under the bar. 'I'm from Nepal.' She gave him the brittle smile again and walked away.

◆

He'd looked at every bar in the district, most of them twice. At least it seemed that way. Hiram could, of course, have been half a block farther on in the wrong direction, or Fortunato could simply have missed it. By four A.M. he was too tired to look anymore, too tired even to go home.

He saw a love hotel on the other side of the Roppongi Crossing. The hourly rates were on the high, windowless walls by the entrance. After midnight it was actually something of a bargain. Fortunato went in past the darkened garden and slipped his money through a blind slot in the wall. A hand slid him out a key.

The hall was full of size-ten foreign men's shoes paired off with tiny *zōri* or doll-sized spike heels. Fortunato found his room and locked the door behind him. The bed was freshly made with pink satin sheets. There were mirrors and a video camera on the ceiling, feeding a big-screen TV in the corner. By love hotel standards the room was pretty tame. Some featured jungles or desert islands, beds shaped like boats or cars or helicopters, light shows and sound effects.

He turned out the light and undressed. All around him his over-sensitive hearing picked up tiny cries and shrill, stifled laughter. He folded the pillow over his head and lay with his eyes open to the darkness.

He was forty-seven years old. For twenty of those years he'd lived inside a cocoon of power and never noticed himself aging. Then the last six months had begun to teach him what he'd missed. The dreadful fatigue after a long night like this one. Mornings when his joints hurt so badly it was hard to get up. Important memories beginning to fade, trivia haunting him obsessively. Lately there were the headaches, and indigestion and muscle cramps. The constant awareness of being human, being mortal, being weak.

Nothing was as addictive as power. Heroin was a glass of flat beer in comparison. There had been nights, watching an endless throng of beautiful women move down the Ginza or the Shinjuku, virtually all of them for sale, when he'd thought he couldn't go on without feeling that power again. He'd talked to himself like an alcoholic, promising himself he'd wait just one more day. And somehow he'd held out. Partly because the memories of his last night in New York, of his final battle with the Astronomer, were still too fresh, reminding him of the pain the power had cost him. Partly because he was no longer sure the power was there, whether Kundalini, the great serpent, was dead or just asleep.

Tonight he'd watched helplessly as a hundred or more Japanese lied to him, ignored him, even humiliated themselves rather than tell him what they so obviously knew. He'd started to see himself through their eyes: huge, clumsy, sweaty, loud, and uncivilized, a pathetic barbarian giant, a kind of oversized monkey who couldn't even be held accountable for common politeness.

A little tantric magick would change all that.

Tomorrow, he told himself. *If you still feel this way tomorrow then you can go ahead, try to get it back.*

He closed his eyes and finally fell asleep.

♥

He woke up with an erection for the first time in months. It was fate, he told himself. Fate that brought Peregrine to him, that provided the need for him to use his power again.

Was that the truth? Or did he just want an excuse to make love to her again, an outlet for six months of sexual frustration?

He dressed and took a cab to the Imperial Hotel. The tour took up an entire floor of the new thirty-one-story tower, and everything inside was scaled up for Europeans. The halls and the insides of the elevators seemed huge to Fortunato now. By the time he got off on the thirtieth floor his hands were shaking. He leaned against Peregrine's door and knocked quietly. A few seconds later he knocked again, harder.

She answered the door in a loose nightgown that touched the floor. Her feathers were ruffled and she could hardly open her eyes. Then she saw him.

She took the chain off the door and stood aside. He shut the door behind him and took her in his arms. He could feel the tiny creature in her belly moving as he held her. He kissed her. Sparks seemed to be crackling around them, but it could have been just the strength of his desire, breaking out of the chains he'd kept it in for so long.

He pulled the straps of her nightgown down along her arms. It fell to her waist and revealed her breasts, their nipples dark and puffy. He touched one with his tongue and tasted the chalky sweetness of her milk. She put her arms around his head and moaned. Her skin was soft and fragrant as the silk of an antique kimono. She pulled him toward the unmade bed and he broke away from her long enough to take off his clothes.

She lay on her back. The pregnancy was the summit of her body, where all the curves ended. Fortunato knelt next to her and kissed her face and throat and shoulders and breasts. He couldn't seem to get his breath. He turned her on her side, facing away from him, and kissed the small of her back. Then he reached up between her legs and held her there, feeling the warmth and wetness against his palm, moving his fingers slowly through the tangle of her pubic hair. She undulated slowly, clutching a pillow in both hands.

He lay down behind her and went into her from behind. The soft flesh of her buttocks pressed into his stomach and his eyes went out of focus. 'Oh, God,' he said. He began to move slowly inside her, his left arm under her and cupping one breast, his right hand lightly touching the curve of her stomach. She moved with him, both of them in slow motion, her breath coming harder and faster until she cried out and ground her hips against him.

At the last possible moment he reached down and blocked his ejaculation at the perineum. The hot fluid flooded back into his groin and lights seemed to flash around him. He relaxed, ready to feel his astral body come loose from his flesh.

It didn't happen.

He put his arms around Peregrine and held onto her fiercely. He buried his face in her neck, let her long hair cover his head.

Now he knew. The power was gone.

He had a single bright moment of panic, then exhaustion carried him on into sleep.

He slept for an hour or so and woke up tired. Peregrine was on her back, watching him.

'You okay?' she said.

'Yeah. Fine.'

'You're not glowing.'

'No,' he said. He looked at his hands. 'It didn't work. It was wonderful. But the power didn't come back. There's nothing there.'

She turned on her side, facing him. 'Oh, no.' She stroked his cheek. 'I'm sorry.'

'It's okay,' he said. 'Really. I've spent the last six months going back and forth, afraid the power would come back, then afraid it wouldn't. At least now I know.' He kissed her neck. 'Listen. We need to talk about the baby.'

'We can talk. But it's not like I expect anything from you, okay? I mean, there's some things I should probably have told you. There's a guy on the tour name of McCoy. He's the cameraman for this documentary we're doing. It looks like it could get serious with us. He knows about the baby and he doesn't care.'

'Oh,' Fortunato said. 'I didn't know.'

'We had a big fight a couple of days ago. And seeing you again – well, that really was something, that night back in New York. You're quite a guy. But you know there couldn't ever be anything permanent between us.'

'No,' Fortunato said. 'I guess not.' His hand moved reflexively to stroke her swollen stomach, tracing blue veins against the pale skin. 'It's weird. I never wanted kids. But now that it's happened, it's not like I thought it would be. It's like it doesn't really matter what I want. I'm responsible. Even if I never see the kid, I'm still responsible, and I always will be.'

'Don't make this harder than it has to be. Don't make me wish I hadn't come to you with this.'

'No. I just want to know that you're going to be okay. You and the baby both.'

'The baby's fine. Other than the fact that neither one of us has a last name to give it.'

There was a knock at the door. Fortunato tensed, feeling suddenly out of place. 'Peri?' said Tachyon's voice. 'Peri, are you in there?'

'Just a minute,' she said. She put on a robe and handed Fortunato his clothes. He was still buttoning his shirt when she opened the door.

Tachyon looked at Peregrine, at the rumpled bed, at Fortunato. 'You,' he said. He nodded like his worst suspicions had just proved out. 'Peri told me you were … helping.'

Jealous, little man? Fortunato thought. 'That's right,' he said.

'Well, I hope I didn't interrupt.' He looked at Peregrine. 'The bus for the Meiji Shrine is supposed to leave in fifteen minutes. If you're going.'

Fortunato ignored him, went to Peregrine, and kissed her gently. 'I'll call you,' he said, 'when I know something.'

'All right.' She squeezed his hand. 'Be careful.'

He walked past Tachyon and into the hall. A man with an elephant's trunk instead of a nose was waiting there.

'Des,' Fortunato said. 'It's good to see you.' That was not entirely true. Des looked terribly old, his cheeks sunken, the bulk of his body melting away. Fortunato wondered if his own pains were as obvious.

'Fortunato,' Des said. They shook hands. 'It's been a long time.'

'I didn't think you'd ever leave New York.'

'I was due to see a little of the world. Age has a way of catching up with one.'

'Yeah,' Fortunato said. 'No kidding.'

'Well,' Des said. 'I have to make the tour bus.'

'Sure,' Fortunato said. 'I'll walk you.'

There was a time when Des had been one of his best customers. It looked like those times were over.

Tachyon caught up with them at the elevator. 'What do you *want*?' Fortunato said. 'Can't you just leave me alone with this?'

'Peri told me about your powers. I came to tell you I'm sorry. I know you hate me. Though I don't really know why. I suppose the way I dress, the way I behave, is some kind of obscure threat to your masculinity. Or at least you've chosen to see it that way. But it's in your mind, not mine.'

Fortunato shook his head angrily.

'I just want one second.' Tachyon closed his eyes. The elevator chimed and the doors opened.

'Your second's up,' Fortunato said. Still he didn't move. Des got on, giving Fortunato a mournful look, and the elevator closed again. Fortunato heard the cables creaking behind bamboo-patterned doors.

'Your power is still there.'

'Bullshit.'

'You're shutting it inside yourself. Your mind is full of conflicts and contradictions, holding it in.'

'It took everything I had to fight the Astronomer. I hit empty. The bottom of the barrel. Cleaned out. Nothing left to recharge. Like running a car battery dry. It won't even jumpstart. It's over.'

'To take up your metaphor, even a live battery won't start when the ignition key is turned off. And the key,' Tachyon said, pointing at his forehead, 'is inside.' He walked away and Fortunato slammed the elevator button with the flat of his hand.

He called Hiram from the lobby.

'Get over here,' Hiram said. 'I'll meet you out front.'

'What's wrong?'

'Just get over here.'

Fortunato took a cab and found Hiram pacing back and forth in front of the plain gray facade of the Akasaka Shanpia. 'What happened?'

'Come in and see,' Hiram said.

The room had looked bad before, but now it was a disaster. The walls were spattered with shaving cream, the dresser drawers had been thrown into the corner, the mirrors were shattered and the mattress ripped to shreds.

'I didn't even see it happen. I was here the whole time and I didn't see it.'

'What are you talking about? How could you not see it?'

Hiram's eyes were frantic. 'I went to the bathroom about nine this morning and got a glass of water. I know everything was okay then. I came back in here and put the TV on and watched for maybe half an hour. Then I heard something that sounded like the door slamming. I looked up and the room was like you see it. And this note was in my lap.'

The note was in English. 'Zero hour comes tomorrow. You can die this easy. Zero man.'

'Then it is an ace.'

'It won't happen again,' Hiram said. He obviously didn't even believe himself. 'I'll know what to look for. He couldn't fool me twice.'

'We can't risk it. Leave everything. You can buy some new clothes this afternoon. I want you to hit the street and keep moving. Around ten o'clock go into the first hotel you see and get a room. Call Peregrine and tell her where you are.'

'Does she ... does she know what happened?'

'No. She knows it's money trouble. That's all.'

'Okay. Fortunato, I …'

'Forget it,' Fortunato said. 'Just keep moving.'

The shade of the banyan tree had saved a little coolness from the morning. Overhead the milk-colored sky was thick with smog. *Sumoggu*, they called it. It was easy to see what the Japanese thought of the West by the words they borrowed: *rashawa*, rush hour; *sarariman*, salary man, executive; *toire*, toilet.

It helped to be here in the Imperial Gardens, an oasis of calm in the heart of Tokyo. The air was fresher, though the cherry blossoms wouldn't be blooming for another month. When they did, the entire city would turn out with cameras. Unlike New Yorkers, the Japanese could appreciate the beauty that was right in front of them.

Fortunato finished the last piece of boiled shrimp from his *bentō*, the box lunch he'd bought just outside the park, and tossed the box away. He couldn't seem to settle down. What he wanted was to talk to the *rōshi*, Dogen. But Dogen was a day and a half away, and he would have to travel by airplane train, bus, and foot to get there. Peregrine was grounded by her pregnancy, and he doubted Mistral was strong enough for a twelve-hundred-mile round trip. There was no way he could get to Hokkaido and back in time to help Hiram.

A few yards away an old man raked the gravel in a rock garden with a battered bamboo rake. Fortunato thought of Dogen's harsh physical discipline: the 38,000-kilometer walk, equivalent to a trip all the way around the earth, lasting a thousand days, around and around Mt. Tanaka; the constant sitting, perfectly still, on the hard wooden floors of the temple; the endless raking of the master's stone garden.

Fortunato walked up to the old man. *'Sumi-masen,'* he said. He pointed to the rake. 'May I?'

The old man handed Fortunato the rake. He looked like he couldn't decide if he was afraid or amused. There were advantages,

Fortunato thought, to being an outsider among the most polite people on earth. He began to rake the gravel, trying to raise the least amount of dust possible, trying to form the gravel into harmonious lines through the strength of his will alone, channeled only incidentally through the rake. The old man went to sit under the banyan tree.

As he worked, Fortunato pictured Dogen in his mind. He looked young, but then most Japanese looked young to Fortunato. His head was shaved until it glistened, the skull formed from planes and angles, the cheeks dimpling when he spoke. His hands formed *mudras* apparently of their own volition, the index fingers reaching to touch the ends of the thumbs when they had nothing else to do.

Why have you called me? said Dogen's voice inside Fortunato's head.

Master! Fortunato thought.

Not your master yet, said Dogen's voice. *You still live in the world.*

I didn't know you had the power to do this, Fortunato thought.

It is not my power. It is yours. Your mind came to me.

I have no power, Fortunato thought.

You are filled with power. It feels like Chinese peppers inside my head.

Why can't I feel it?

You have hidden yourself from it, the way a fat man tries to hide himself from the yakitori *all around him. This is how it is in the world. The world demands that you have power, and yet the use of it makes you ashamed. This is the way Japan is now. We have become very powerful in the world, and to do it we gave up our spiritual feelings. You have to make the decision. If you want to live in the world you must admit your power. If you want to feed your spirit, you must leave the world. Right now you are pulling yourself into pieces.*

Fortunato knelt in the gravel and bowed low. *Domo arigatō, o sensei. Arigatō* meant 'thank you,' but literally it meant 'it hurts.' Fortunato felt the truth inside the words. If he hadn't believed Dogen, it wouldn't have hurt so much. He looked up and saw the old gardener staring at him in abject fear, but at the same time making a series of short, nervous bows from the waist so as not to seem rude. Fortunato smiled at him and bowed low again. 'Don't worry,' he said in Japanese. He stood up and gave the old man back his rake. 'Just another crazy *gaijin*.'

His stomach hurt again. It wasn't the *bentō*, he knew. It was the stress inside his own mind, eating his body up from within.

He was back on Harumi-Dori, heading toward the Ginza corner. He'd been wandering for hours, while the sun had set and the night had flowered around him. The city seemed like an electronic forest. The long vertical signs crowded each other down the entire length of the street, flashing ideograms and English characters in blazing neon. The streets were crowded with Japanese in jogging outfits or jeans and sport shirts. Packed in with the regular citizens were the *sararimen* in plain gray suits.

Fortunato stopped to lean against one of the graceful f-shaped streetlights. Here it is, he thought, in all its glory. There was no more worldly a place on the planet, no place more obsessed with money, gadgets, drinking, and sex. And a few hours away were wooden temples in pine forests where men sat on their heels and tried to turn their minds into rivers or dust or starlight.

Make up your mind, he told himself. You have to make up your mind.

'*Gaijin-san!* You like girl? Pretty girl?'

Fortunato turned around. It was a tout for a *Pinku Saron*, a unique Japanese institution where the customer paid by the hour for a bottomless saki cup and a topless *jo-san*. She would sit passively in his lap while he fondled her breasts and drank himself into a state where he was prepared to go home to his wife. It was, Fortunato decided, an omen.

He paid three thousand yen for half an hour and walked into a darkened hallway. A soft hand took his and led him downstairs into a completely dark room filled with tables and other couples. Fortunato heard business being discussed all around him. His hostess led him to one end of the room and sat him with his legs pinned under a low table, his back supported by a legless wooden chair. Then she gracefully moved into his lap. He heard her kimono rustle as she opened it to free her breasts.

The woman was tiny and smelled of face powder, sandalwood soap, and, faintly, of sweat. Fortunato reached up with both hands and touched her face, his fingers tracing the lines of her jaw. She paid no attention. 'Saki?' she asked.

'No,' Fortunato said. *'I-ie, domo.'* His fingers followed the muscles of her neck down to her shoulders, out to the edges of her kimono, then down. His fingertips brushed lightly over her small, delicate breasts, the tiny nipples hardening at his touch. The woman giggled nervously, raising one hand to cover her mouth. Fortunato laid his head between her breasts and inhaled the aroma of her skin. It was the smell of the world. It was time either to turn away or surrender, and he had backed himself into a corner, left himself without the strength to resist.

He gently pulled her face down and kissed her. Her lips were tight, nervous. She giggled again. In Japan they called kissing *suppun*, the exotic practice. Only teenagers and foreigners did it. Fortunato kissed her again, feeling himself stiffening, and the electricity went through him and into the woman. She stopped giggling and began to tremble. Fortunato was shaking too. He could feel the serpent, Kundalini, begin to wake up. It moved around in his groin and began to uncoil through his spine. Slowly, as if she didn't understand what she was doing or why, the woman touched him with her little hands, putting them behind his neck. Her tongue touched him lightly on his lips and chin and eyelids. Fortunato untied her kimono and opened it up. He lifted her easily by the waist and sat her on the edge of the table, putting her legs over his shoulders, bending to open her up with his tongue. She tasted spicy, exotic, and in seconds she had come alive under him, hot and wet, her hips moving involuntarily.

She pushed his head away and leaned forward, working at his trousers. Fortunato kissed her shoulders and neck. She moaned softly. There didn't seem to be anyone else in the hot, crowded room, no one else in the world. It was happening, Fortunato thought. Already he could see a little in the darkness, see her plain, square face, the lines beginning to show under her eyes, seeing how her looks had consigned her to the darkness of the *Pinku Saron*, wanting her even more for the desire he could see hidden inside her. He lowered her onto him. She gasped as he went into her, her fingers digging into his shoulders, and his eyes rolled back in his head.

Yes, he thought. Yes, yes, yes. The world. I surrender.

The power rose inside him like molten lava.

It was a little after ten when he walked into the Berni Inn. The waitress, the one who'd told him her name was Megan, was just coming out of the kitchen. She stopped dead when she saw Fortunato. The waitress behind her nearly ran into her with a tray of meat pies.

She stared at his forehead. Fortunato didn't have to see himself to know that his forehead had swollen again, bulging with the power of his *rasa*. He walked across the room to her. 'Go away,' she said. 'I don't want to talk to you.'

'The club,' Fortunato said 'The one with the sign of the duck. You know where it is.'

'No. I never—'

'Tell me where it is,' he ordered.

All expression left her face. 'Across Roppongi. Right at the police box, down two blocks, then left half a block. The bar in front is called Takahashi's.'

'And the place in back? What's it called?'

'It hasn't got a name. It's a *yak* hangout. It's not the Yamaguchi-gumi, none of the big gangs. Just this one little clan.'

'Then why are you so afraid of them?'

'They've got a *ninja*, a shadow-fighter. He's one of those what-you-call-thems. An ace.' She looked at Fortunato's forehead. 'Like you, then, isn't he? They say he's killed hundreds. Nobody's ever seen him. He could be in this room right now. If not now, then he will be later. He'll kill me for having told you this.'

'You don't understand,' Fortunato said. 'They want to see me. I've got just the thing they want.'

It was the way Hiram had described it. The hallway was raw gray plaster and the door at the end of it was padded in turquoise Naugahyde with big brass nailheads. Inside, one of the hostesses came up to take Fortunato's jacket. 'No,' he said in Japanese. 'I want to see the *oyabun*. It's important.'

She was still a little stunned just by the way he looked. His rudeness was more than she could deal with. '*W-w-wakarimasen,*' she stammered.

'Yes, you do. You understand me perfectly well. Go tell your boss I have to speak to him. Now.'

He waited next to the doorway. The room was long and narrow, with a low ceiling and mirrored tiles on the left-hand wall, above a row of booths. There was a bar along the other wall, with chrome stools like an American soda fountain. Most of the men were Koreans, in cheap polyester suits and wide ties. The edges of tattoos showed around their collars and cuffs. Whenever they looked at him, Fortunato stared back and they turned away.

It was eleven o'clock. Even with the power moving through him, Fortunato was a little nervous. He was a foreigner, out of his depth, in the middle of the enemy's stronghold. I'm not here for trouble, he reminded himself. I'm here to pay Hiram's debt and get out.

And then, he thought, everything will be okay. It was not even midnight Wednesday, and Hiram's business was nearly settled. Friday the 747 would be off for Korea and then the Soviet Union, taking Hiram and Peregrine with it. And then he would be on his own, able to think about what came next. Or maybe he should get on the plane himself, go back to New York. Peregrine said they had no future together, but maybe that wasn't true.

He loved Tokyo, but Tokyo would never love him back. It would see to all his needs, give him enormous license in exchange for even the smallest attempt at politeness, dazzle him with its beauty, exhaust him with its exquisite sexual pleasures. But he would always be a *gaijin*, a foreigner, never have a family in a country where family was more important than anything.

The hostess crouched by the last booth, talking to a Japanese with long permed hair and a silk suit. The little finger of his left hand was missing. The *yakuza* used to cut their fingers off to atone for mistakes. The younger kids, Fortunato had heard, didn't hold much with the idea. Fortunato took a breath and walked up to the table.

The *oyabun* sat next to the wall. Fortunato figured him to be about forty. There were two *jo-san* next to him, and another across from him between a pair of heavyset bodyguards. 'Leave us,' Fortunato ordered the hostess. She walked away in the middle of her protest. The first bodyguard got up to throw Fortunato out. 'You too,' Fortunato said, making eye contact with each of them and each of the girls.

The *oyabun* watched it all with a quiet smile. Fortunato bowed to him from the waist. The *oyabun* ducked his head and said, 'My name is Kanagaki. Will you sit down?'

Fortunato sat across from him. 'The *gaijin* Hiram Worchester has sent me here to pay his debt.' Fortunato took out his checkbook. 'The amount, I believe, is two million yen.'

'Ah,' Kanagaki said. 'Another "ace." You have provided us with much amusement. Especially the little red-haired fellow.'

'Tachyon? What does he have to do with this?'

'With this?' He pointed to Fortunato's checkbook. 'Nothing. But many *jo-san* have tried to bring him pleasure these past few days. It seems he is having trouble performing as a man.'

Tachyon? Fortunato thought. Can't get it up? He wanted to laugh. It certainly explained the little man's rotten mood at the hotel. 'This has nothing to do with aces,' Fortunato said. 'This is business.'

'Ah. Business. Very well. We shall settle this in a businesslike way.' He looked at his watch and smiled. 'Yes, the amount is two million yen. In a few minutes it will become four million. A pity. I doubt you will have time to bring the *gaijin* Worchester-*san* here before midnight.'

Fortunato shook his head. 'There is no need for Worchester-*san* to be here in person.'

'But there is. We feel there is some honor at stake here.'

Fortunato held the man's eyes. 'I am asking you to do the needful.' He made the traditional phrase an order. 'I will give you the money. The debt will be canceled.'

Kanagaki's will was very strong. He almost managed to say the words that were trying to get out of his throat. Instead he said in a strangled voice, 'I will honor your face.'

Fortunato wrote the check and handed it to Kanagaki. 'You understand me. The debt is canceled.'

'Yes,' Kanagaki said. 'The debt is canceled.'

'You have a man working for you. An assassin. I think he calls himself Zero Man.'

'Mori Riishi.' He gave the name in Japanese fashion, family name first.

'No harm will come to Worchester-*san*. He is not to be harmed. This Zero Man, Mori, will stay away from him.'

Kanagaki was silent.

'What is it?' Fortunato asked him. 'What is it you're not saying?'

'It's too late. Mori has already left. The *gaijin* Worchester dies at midnight.'

'Christ,' Fortunato said.

'Mori comes to Tokyo with a great reputation, but we have no proof. He was very concerned to make a good impression.'

Fortunato realized he hadn't checked with Peregrine. 'What hotel? What hotel is Worchester-*san* staying in?'

Kanagaki spread his hands. 'Who knows?'

Fortunato started to get up. While he'd been talking to Kanagaki, the bodyguards had come back with reinforcements. They surrounded the table. Fortunato couldn't be bothered with them. He formed a wedge of power around himself and sprinted for the door, pushing them aside as he ran.

Outside, the Roppongi was still crowded. Over at Shinjuku station the late-night drinkers would be trying to push their way onto the last trains of the night. On the Ginza they would be lining up at the cab stands. It was ten minutes to midnight. There wasn't time.

He let his astral body spring loose and rocket through the night toward the Imperial Hotel. The neon and mirrored glass and chrome blurred as he picked up speed. He didn't slow until he was through the wall of the hotel and hovering in Peregrine's room. He let himself become visible, a glowing, golden-rose image of his physical body.

Peregrine, he thought.

She rolled over in bed, opened her eyes. Fortunato saw, with a small, distant sort of pang, that she was not alone.

I need to know where Hiram is.

'Fortunato?' she whispered, then saw him. 'Oh my God.'

Hurry. The name of the hotel.

'Wait a minute. I wrote it down.' She walked naked over to the phone. Fortunato's astral body was free of lust and hunger, but still the sight of her moved him. 'The Ginza Dai-Ichi. Room eight oh one. He says it's a big H-shaped building by the Shimbashi station—'

I know where it is. Meet me there as fast as you can. Bring help.

He couldn't wait for her answer. He snapped back to his physical body and lifted it into the air.

He hated the spectacle of it. Being in Japan had made him even more self-conscious than he ever had been in New York. But there was no choice. He levitated straight up into the sky, high enough that he couldn't make out the faces turned up to stare at him, and arced toward the Dai-Ichi Hotel.

He got to the door of Hiram's room at twelve midnight. The door was locked, but Fortunato wrenched the bolts back with his mind, splintering the wood around them.

Hiram sat up in bed. 'Wha—'

Fortunato stopped time.

It was like a train grinding to a halt. The countless tiny sounds of the hotel slowed to a bass growl, then hung in the silence between beats. Fortunato's own breathing had stopped.

There was nobody in the room but Hiram. It hurt Fortunato to make his head turn; to Hiram it would have seemed like he was moving in a blur of speed. The sliding doors to the bathroom were open. Fortunato couldn't see anyone in there either.

Then he remembered how the Astronomer had been able to hide from him, to make Fortunato not see him. He let time begin to trickle past him again. He brought up his hands, fighting the heavy, clinging air, and framed the room, making an empty square bordered by his thumbs and index fingers. Here was the closet, the doors open. Here was a stretch of bamboo-patterned wall with nothing in it. Here was the foot of the bed, and the edge of a samurai sword moving slowly toward Hiram's head.

Fortunato threw himself forward. His body seemed to take forever to rise into the air and float toward Hiram. He opened his arms and knocked Hiram to the floor, feeling something hard scrape the bottoms of his shoes. He rolled onto his back and saw the sheets and mattress slowly splitting in two.

The sword, he thought. Once he convinced himself it was there, he could see it. Now the arm, he thought, and slowly the entire man took shape in front of him, a young Japanese in a white dress shirt and gray wool pants and bare feet.

He let time start again before the strain wore him out completely. He heard footsteps in the hall. He was afraid to look away, afraid he might loose the killer again. 'Drop the sword,' Fortunato said.

'You can see me,' the man said in English. He turned to look toward the door.

'Put it down,' Fortunato said, making it an order now, but it was too late. He no longer had eye contact and the man resisted him.

Without thinking, Fortunato looked at the doorway. It was Tachyon, in red silk pajamas, Mistral behind him. Tachyon was charging into the room, and Fortunato knew the little alien was about to die.

He looked back for Mori. Mori was gone. Fortunato went cold with panic. The sword, he thought. Find the sword. He looked where the sword would have to be if it were slicing toward Tachyon and slowed time again.

There. The blade, curved and impossibly sharp, the steel dazzling as sunlight. Come to me, Fortunato thought. He pulled at the blade with his mind.

He only meant to take it from Mori's hands. He misjudged his own power. The blade spun completely around, missing Tachyon by inches. It whirled around ten or fifteen times and finally buried itself in the wall behind the bed.

Somewhere in there it had sliced off the top of Mori's head.

Fortunato shielded them with his power until they were on the street. It was the same trick Zero Man had used. No one saw them. They left Mori's corpse in the room, his blood soaking into the carpet.

A taxi pulled up and Peregrine got out. The man who'd been in bed with her got out behind her. He was a bit shorter than Fortunato, with blond hair and a mustache. He stood next to Peregrine and she reached out and took his hand. 'Is everything okay?' she said.

'Yeah,' Hiram said. 'It's okay.'

'Does this mean you're back on the tour?'

Hiram looked around at the others. 'Yeah. I guess I am.'

'That's good,' Peregrine said, suddenly noticing how serious everyone was. 'We were all worried about you.'

Hiram nodded.

Tachyon moved next to Fortunato. 'Thank you,' he said quietly. 'Not only for saving my life. You probably saved the tour as well. Another violent incident – after Haiti and Guatemala and Syria – well, it would have undone everything we were trying to accomplish.'

'Sure,' Fortunato said. 'We probably shouldn't hang around here too long. No point in taking chances.'

'No,' Tachyon said. 'I guess not.'

'Uh, Fortunato,' Peregrine said. 'Josh McCoy.'

Fortunato shook his hand and nodded. McCoy smiled and gave his hand back to Peregrine. 'I've heard a lot about you.'

'There's blood on your shirt,' Peregrine said. 'What happened?'

'It's nothing,' Fortunato said. 'It's all over now.'

'So much blood,' Peregrine said. 'Like with the Astronomer. There's so much violence in you. It's scary sometimes.'

Fortunato didn't say anything.

'So,' McCoy said. 'What happens now?'

'I guess,' Fortunato said, 'me and G.C. Jayewardene will go see a man about a monastery.'

'You kidding?' McCoy said.

'No,' Peregrine said. 'I don't think he is.' She looked at Fortunato for a long time, and then she said, 'Take care of yourself, will you?'

'Sure,' Fortunato said. 'What else?'

'There it is,' Fortunato said. The monastery straggled across the entire hillside, and beyond it were stone gardens and terraced fields. Fortunato wiped the snow from a rock next to the path and sat down. His head was clear and his stomach quiet. Maybe it was just the clean mountain air. Maybe it was something more.

'It's very beautiful,' Jayewardene said, crouching on his heels.

Spring wouldn't get to Hokkaido for another month and a half. The sky was clear, though. Clear enough to see, for instance, a 747 from miles and miles away. But the 747s didn't fly over Hokkaido. Especially not the ones headed for Korea, almost a thousand miles to the southwest.

'What happened Wednesday night?' Jayewardene asked after a few minutes. 'There was all kind of commotion, and when it was over Hiram was back. Do you want to talk about it?'

'Not much to tell,' Fortunato said. 'People fighting over money. A boy died. He'd never actually killed anybody, as it turned out. He was very young, very afraid. He just wanted to do a good job, to live up to the reputation he'd invented for himself.' Fortunato shrugged. 'It's the way of the world. That kind of thing is always going to happen in a place like Tokyo.' He stood up, brushing at the seat of his pants. 'Ready?'

'Yes,' Jayewardene said. 'I've been waiting for this a long time.'

Fortunato nodded. 'Then let's get on with it.'

FROM *THE JOURNAL*
OF XAVIER DESMOND

March 21/en route to Seoul:
A face out of my past confronted me in Tokyo and has preyed on my mind ever since. Two days ago I decided that I would ignore him and the issues raised by his presence, that I would make no mention of him in this journal.

I've made plans to have this volume to be offered for publication after my death. I do not expect a best-seller, but I would think the number of celebrities aboard the *Stacked Deck* and the various newsworthy events we've generated will stir up at least a little interest in the great American public, so my volume may find its own audience. Whatever modest royalties it earns will be welcomed by the JADL, to which I've willed my entire estate.

Yet, even though I will be safely dead and buried before anyone reads these words, and therefore in no position to be harmed by any personal admissions I might make, I find myself reluctant to write of Fortunato. Call it cowardice, if you will. Jokers are notorious cowards, if one listens to the jests, the cruel sort that they do not allow on television. I can easily justify my decision to say nothing of Fortunato. My dealings with him over the years have been private matters, having little to do with politics or world affairs or the issues that I've tried to address in this journal, and nothing at all to do with this tour.

Yet I have felt free, in these pages, to repeat the gossip that has inevitably swirled about the airplane, to report on the various foibles and indiscretions of Dr. Tachyon and Peregrine and Jack Braun and Digger Downs and all the rest. Can I truly pretend that their weaknesses are of public interest and my own are not? Perhaps I could … the public has always been fascinated by aces and repelled by jokers … but I will not. I want this journal to be an honest one, a true one. And I want the readers to understand a little of what it has been like to live forty years a joker. And to do that I must talk of Fortunato, no matter how deeply it may shame me.

Fortunato now lives in Japan. He helped Hiram in some obscure way after Hiram had suddenly and quite mysteriously left the tour in Tokyo. I don't pretend to know the details of that; it was all carefully hushed up. Hiram seemed almost himself when he returned to us in Calcutta, but he has deteriorated rapidly again, and he looks worse every day. He has become volatile and unpleasant, and secretive. But this is not about Hiram, of whose woes I know nothing. The point is, Fortunato was embroiled in the business somehow and came to our hotel, where I spoke to him briefly in the corridor. That was all there was to it … now. But in years past Fortunato and I have had other dealings.

Forgive me. This is hard. I am an old man and a joker, and age and deformity alike have made me sensitive. My dignity is all I have left, and I am about to surrender it.

I was writing about self-loathing.

This is a time for hard truths, and the first of those is that many nats are disgusted by jokers. Some of these are bigots, always ready to hate anything different. In that regard we jokers are no different from any other oppressed minority; we are all hated with the same honest venom by those predisposed to hate.

There are other normals, however, who are more predisposed to tolerance, who try to see beyond the surface to the human being beneath. People of good will, not haters, well-meaning generous people like … well, like Dr. Tachyon and Hiram Worchester to choose two examples close to hand. Both of these gentlemen have proven over the years that they care deeply about jokers in the abstract, Hiram through his anonymous charities, Tachyon through his work at the clinic. And yet both of them, I am convinced, are just as sickened by the simple physical deformity of most jokers as the Nur al-Allah or Leo Barnett. You can see it in their eyes, no matter how nonchalant and cosmopolitan they strive to be. Some of their best friends are jokers, but they wouldn't want their sister to marry one.

This is the first unspeakable truth of jokerhood.

How easy it would be to rail against this, to condemn men like Tach and Hiram for hypocrisy and 'formism' (a hideous word coined by a particularly moronic joker activist and taken up by Tom Miller's Jokers for a Just Society in their heyday). Easy, and wrong. They are decent men, but still only men, and cannot be thought less because they have normal human feelings.

Because, you see, the second unspeakable truth of jokerhood is that no matter how much jokers offend nats, we offend ourselves even more.

Self-loathing is the particular psychological pestilence of Jokertown, a disease that is often fatal. The leading cause of death among jokers under the age of fifty is, and always has been, suicide. This *despite* the fact that virtually every disease known to man is more serious when contracted by a joker, because our body chemistries and very shapes vary so widely and unpredictably that no course of treatment is truly safe.

In Jokertown you'll search long and hard before you'll find a place to buy a mirror, but there are mask shops on every block.

If that was not proof enough, consider the issue of names. Nicknames, they call them. They are more than that. They are spotlights on the true depths of joker self-loathing.

If this journal is to be published, I intend to insist that it be titled *The Journal of Xavier Desmond*, not *A Joker's Journal* or any such variant. I am a man, a particular man, not just a generic joker. Names are important; they are more than just words, they shape and color the things they name. The feminists realized this long ago, but jokers still have not grasped it.

I have made it a point over the years to answer to no name but my own, yet I know a joker dentist who calls himself Fishface, an accomplished ragtime pianist who answers to Catbox, and a brilliant joker mathematician who signs his papers 'Slimer.' Even on this tour I find myself accompanied by three people named Chrysalis, Troll, and Father Squid.

We are, of course, not the first minority to experience this particular form of oppression. Certainly black people have been there; entire generations were raised with the belief that the 'prettiest' black girls were the ones with the lightest skins whose features most closely approximated the Caucasian ideal. Finally some of them saw through that lie and proclaimed that *black* was beautiful.

From time to time various well-meaning but foolish jokers have attempted to do the same thing. Freakers, one of the more debauched institutions of Jokertown, has what it calls a 'Twisted Miss' contest every year on Valentine's Day. However sincere or cynical these efforts are, they are surely misguided. Our friends the Takisians took care of that by putting a clever little twist on the prank they played on us.

The problem is, every joker is unique.

Even before my transformation I was never a handsome man. Even after the change I am by no means hideous. My 'nose' is a trunk, about two feet long, with fingers at its end. My experience has been that most people get used to the way I look if they are around me for a few days. I like to tell myself that after a week or so you scarcely notice that I'm any different, and maybe there's even a grain of truth in that.

If the virus had only been so kind as to give *all* jokers trunks where their noses had been, the adjustment might have been a good deal easier, and a 'Trunks Are Beautiful' campaign might have done some real good.

But to the best of my knowledge I am the only joker with a trunk. I might work very hard to disregard the aesthetics of the nat culture I live in, to convince myself that I am one handsome devil and that the rest of them are the funny-looking ones, but none of that will help the next time I find that pathetic creature they call Snotman sleeping in the dumpster behind the Funhouse. The horrible reality is, my stomach is as thoroughly turned by the more extreme cases of joker deformity as I imagine Dr. Tachyon's must be – but if anything, I am even more guilty about it.

Which brings me, in a roundabout way, back to Fortunato. Fortunato is ... or was at least ... a procurer. He ran a high-priced call girl ring. All of his girls were exquisite; beautiful, sensual, skilled in every erotic art, and by and large pleasant people, as much a delight out of bed as in it. He called them geishas.

For more than two decades I was one of his best customers.

I believe he did a lot of business in Jokertown. I know for a fact that Chrysalis often trades information for sex, upstairs in her Crystal Palace, whenever a man who needs her services happens to strike her fancy. I know a handful of truly wealthy jokers, none of whom are married, but almost all of whom have nat mistresses. The hometown papers we've seen tell us that the Five Families and the Shadow Fists are warring in the streets, and I know why – because in Jokertown prostitution is big business, along with drugs and gambling.

The first thing a joker loses is his sexuality. Some lose it totally, becoming incapable or asexual. But even those whose genitalia and sexual drives remain unaffected by the wild card find themselves bereft of sexual identity. From the instant one stabilizes, one is no longer a man or a woman, only a joker.

A normal sex drive, abnormal self-loathing, and a yearning for the thing that's been lost ... manhood, femininity, beauty, whatever. They are common demons in Jokertown, and I know them well. The onset of my cancer and the chemotherapy have combined to kill all my interest in sex, but my memories and my shame remain intact. It shames me to be reminded of Fortunato. Not because I patronized a prostitute or broke their silly laws – I have contempt for those laws. It shames me because, try as I did over the years, I could never find it in me to desire a joker woman. I knew several who were worthy of love; kind, gentle, caring women, who needed commitment and tenderness and yes, sex, as much as I did. Some of them became my cherished friends. Yet I could never respond to them sexually. They remained as unattractive in my eyes as I must have been in theirs.

So it goes, in Jokertown.

The seat belt light has just come on, and I'm not feeling very well at present, so I will sign off here.

ALWAYS SPRING IN PRAGUE

Carrie Vaughn

April 1987

The delegates were settled in their hotel rooms, the security check of the building and surrounding streets was done, and SCARE agent Joann Jefferson gave herself a moment to pause on the balcony of one of the upper suites to gaze over the vista of Prague and simply enjoy the view. The hotel was on the south bank of the Vltava River, with a good view of the Charles Bridge – a Renaissance construction lined with statues that stood like ghostly pilgrims – and the fortress complex on the hill across the steel-gray water. The city's skyline was unique, identifiably European and medieval, but with exotic, otherworldly touches. Churches with strange, jutting spires; baroque domes; jagged rooflines; and romantic Art Nouveau facades, the gilded remnants of last century's optimism, butting up against neighborhoods with tangled narrow streets. The Communist city seemed tired, but the hints of what it had been – one of the great cultural capitals of Europe – managed to peer through the gray. Afternoon sunlight made the walls and spires of the castle on the hill glow.

Here she was, seeing the world, a dream come true. The irony was that after five months on the road with the WHO tour, Joann was going to need a serious vacation.

Back in the hallway, on the way to the room that was serving as ops for the tour, she ran into Billy Ray, who'd completed his own security sweep. He made a show of being a professional tough guy, with his white fighting suit and broken, oddly-mended face that gave him a constant glowering expression. But he was a conscientious agent. They'd been working together for years, now.

'How's it look?' he asked.

'Fine. Calm. I think everyone's getting worn out.'

'Wouldn't that be nice? Get everyone to stay in their rooms and out of trouble for once?' He crossed his arms and huffed, as if demonstrating how unlikely that was with this bunch.

'That's no way to get your picture in the paper, now, is it?' she said, and Ray chuckled.

He glanced at her sidelong while leaving most of the space of the hallway open between them. Most people who knew her did so. She was used to keeping a good distance between herself and others, but Ray often gave her this look like he was sizing her up – wondering how much of his super-strength and healing could stand up to her life-draining power.

She settled her black and silver cloak more firmly around her, kept her head bowed and hidden under the hood, aware that she presented an image of herself as dangerous and mysterious that she didn't always appreciate. But the cloak helped her control her power, preventing it from lashing out to leech the energy from everything, everyone, around her. She hadn't touched another living soul, except to do damage to them, since she was a child.

He added, 'You might keep your eyes open – a couple of spooks are holed up in the building across the street. Standard spy versus spy shit. They may get pushy.'

'They'd probably learn more about the tour by reading the newspapers than running surveillance.'

'Yeah. I'll take the first shift on call if you want to get some rest.'

'Thanks, I will,' she said, and he waved her off as he marched on to ops.

The security contingent and staff on the tour didn't get the luxury suites that the delegates did. But this was still a five-star hotel, and

Joann was more than happy with her 'plain' room, with its king bed, private bathroom, and claw-foot tub. She was contemplating the extravagance of a hot bath when she got a call on her room's phone.

'Lady Black, this is Representative Cramer. May I have a word with you?'

'Yes, Representative, of course. Is there a problem?' Inwardly, she groaned. If they had a problem, the delegates shouldn't be calling her, they should be calling ops. Unless this was for something unofficial. Unofficial and complicated, of course.

'I would very much like to discuss this in person, if possible.' She worded it as a request, but the tone of command was unmistakable. So much for a bath. Joann took a wistful look back at the expansive bed and bade farewell to an afternoon nap.

Congresswoman Carol Cramer, Republican from Missouri, was one of those accidental women politicians who stepped into the opening left when her husband died – in this case he dropped dead of a heart attack during a re-election campaign. She won the election for his seat three years ago, won re-election for herself, and seemed to be digging in for a long political career. As the most junior political delegate on the tour, she'd kept a very low profile. Her main goal seemed to be to do her duty in representing the Republican Party on the tour while avoiding any kind of scandal that might damage her future political aspirations. Which made calling for a secret conference with a SCARE security agent all the more surprising. Joann reassured herself: how much trouble could a polite southern-midwestern lady like Carol Cramer really get into?

Cramer was watching for her and opened the doorway wide when Joann arrived at her room. Joann declined the offered chair and prepared to listen attentively. Cramer paced. She was in her fifties, very well dressed in a tailored, light blue dress suit, her short ash-colored hair curled and settled. She was the kind of woman who'd never leave her room without checking to make sure her clothing, hair, makeup, everything, were perfect.

'I have … well, a favor to ask. But I'd like it to be kept quiet if at all possible. It's nothing illegal, I'm certain. But it's ... sensitive. Lady Black, I need you to find someone.'

Joann raised an eyebrow and waited for further explanation. 'I have friends – political donors, really, which is why I'd like to keep this quiet. They have a daughter, twenty years old, who dropped out of Smith earlier this year and then all but vanished. The family has considerable resources, of course, and they hired investigators, but they've only made a little progress. They believe she's here in Prague, and they've asked me to confirm that and to talk to her if I can.'

She drew a battered envelope out of the desk drawer. Tipping it open, she slid out a handful of photographs and a typed report. Joann stepped over to look.

The daughter, Katrina Duboss according to the label, was a joker. In place of her left arm a collection of orange, snake-like limbs clustered, Medusa-like. They seemed prehensile, wrapping around the arm of the lawn chair where she sat. The bright, shimmering orange scales from this strange limb continued upward to her neck and partially covered her cheek, giving the impression that she wore a partial mask. The photo was a candid snapshot, taken at some backyard party. In the background, a group of college-age kids were playing Frisbee. Dressed in a tank-top and flowing skirt, she held a can of Coke in her normal hand and rolled her eyes as if the person with the camera had asked her to pose. The young woman seemed shy, but not ashamed. Not trying to hide from the camera, not trying to disguise her deformity. She had lively brown eyes.

'She's a joker,' Joann observed, stating the obvious.

Cramer closed her eyes and sighed, as if it was a tragedy. 'Yes, that happened only a couple of years ago. She became infected and was ill for quite a long time. And – I'm afraid things just haven't been the same for the family since.'

'I imagine not,' Joann said wryly. If she had to judge from the photo, Katrina seemed at ease. Happy, even. She seemed to have adjusted to her transformation. That might not have been true for the rest of the family.

The typed report was a list of known whereabouts over the last year. Katrina Duboss had cashed out a savings account to buy a plane ticket to London. From there, she'd wandered, vanishing for weeks before reappearing in some other European city. She seemed to be doing the itinerant backpacking pilgrimage. Any college student might drop out to travel for a few months, but the Duboss girl seemed to have adopted this as a lifestyle.

'She was studying art in school,' Cramer said. 'Her parents understand her wanting to go to Europe, but like this? They could have helped her, but she hasn't spoken to them in months.'

Joann knew this wasn't the whole story, from watching this scenario play out in dozens of other families. Well-off families suddenly finding a joker in their midst, a puzzle piece that didn't fit into their neat little world, and their first instinct was to bury the problem. That was some people's definition of 'help.' Joann wondered if Katrina's parents had proposed amputation and plastic surgery, thinking that half a body would be better than a deformed one. Nobody could blame Katrina for running away from that. Except maybe someone like Cramer.

She shouldn't be making blanket assumptions about Cramer, the Duboss family, or anything else. But she also shouldn't have to deal with this kind of soap opera when her job was protecting the tour.

'Ma'am, this isn't really in my purview. You should talk to the embassy, they have staff who would be much more helpful—'

'And if I went to them, this would garner publicity that the family really doesn't need. I'm trying to avoid that, and the family would like to avoid any official inquiries.'

Which gave the whole incident a patina of suspicion that Joann didn't at all like. 'Off the record' usually meant 'cover our ass.' What was the family trying to hide? And of course Cramer didn't want to be seen pulling strings for a donor.

'She's over eighteen, the kid can do whatever she wants. We can't force her to go home,' Joann said.

'I know that, but I'd like to talk to her, if I can. For Mark and Barbara's sake.'

The tour would be in Prague for two days. Local security would be taking up part of the burden of babysitting the delegates. Because of that, she was supposed to have a little time off during those two days. Theoretically, she could take a couple of hours to shake some trees and see if the Duboss girl fell out. Most likely she wouldn't, and Joann wouldn't feel too bad about it.

'I'll see what I can do, but I can't promise anything.'

'Thank you,' Representative Cramer said, and held out her hand to shake Joann's. A purely reflexive move, a politician's instinct for graciousness. Joann kept her hands folded underneath her cloak and pressed her lips in apology. She did not shake hands, not even with gloves on. Even that brought her too close to people. Cramer withdrew, wringing her hands awkwardly, and Joann showed herself out.

The next morning, rather than repeating someone else's footwork, Joann tapped sources at the U.S. Embassy. The intelligence people here weren't idiots. They tracked American citizens entering and leaving the country, especially ones who might raise security flags. Katrina Duboss wouldn't necessarily raise any flags, but if Cramer was right, she might be running with a crowd that would. Besides, any joker would stand out in this part of the world. She didn't have to explain herself, her search would stay off the record as Cramer requested. Though Joann was tempted to get the whole thing *on* the record just to see what kind of skeletons turned up. That kind of thing *was* part of her job description. But she'd wait to see what happened before she went that far.

In short order, she got what she needed: a starting point. The embassy clerk was able to give her a list of places where disaffected college students and bohemian artist types gathered. Literally Bohemian, in this part of the world. The original Bohemians. She wondered if they even noticed that, around here.

List in hand, she went for a walk.

If she was going to be searching anyway, she might as well enjoy herself by playing tourist. So she wandered along streets, admiring architecture and stopping at corners to stare at everything from the Art Nouveau splendor of the nineteenth-century opera house to the wicked-looking angled spires of the medieval Týn Church. Wenceslas Square, at one end of a broad-tree lined street that would have been at home in any city in western Europe, with yet another impressive nineteenth-century block of buildings and a grand equestrian statue. And even after World War II and forty years under Communism, the city had a Jewish neighborhood, and an intact medieval synagogue with a distinctive jagged roofline. There, she'd found an eager tour guide who spoke English and insisted that Rabbi Loew's famous golem was stored in the roof. Joann smiled at the story and tipped the guide well.

Turning a corner at the edge of the Old Town, she stumbled across a façade painted with a mural of a gorgeous woman with streaming, curling red hair, a diaphanous gown, surrounded by whorls and lilies. Alphonse Mucha – this was an Alphonse Mucha piece forming a painted arc over a doorway, stuck out here randomly in the middle of the city, obscured by soot but still clearly Mucha. She just stared for a moment. What an odd, incongruous city.

Her dad would love this. Joann took the time to send a postcard to her father, of the Charles Bridge over the river. She'd managed to send him one from almost every city the tour had visited. He should have quite the collection by now, pictures of beaches and monuments, sunsets and Ayers Rock and the pyramids of Giza, the Tokyo skyline, the Casa Rosada in Buenos Aires.

Maybe when she had some time off they could take a trip together. She'd suggest it to him.

The list of gathering places for the city's disaffected youth was about what she expected. Bars, coffee shops, the basement of a used book store, all with a vaguely clandestine air about them. Even behind the Iron Curtain, some things didn't change, and very little could stop young people from gathering to drink and talk about how they were going to change the world. Even if, in a city like this, in a country like this, they might speak very quietly and look over their shoulders while doing so.

People stared at her wherever she went, whether it was because she was black, or because with her height and rippling cloak she always drew the eye. She stood out in New York City, for crying out loud. She was used to it. It also meant that people rarely messed with her. With the dark surface of her cloak facing out, she could contain her energy, make herself almost a shadow. Keep from causing too much of a disturbance when she peeked into coffee houses and scanned for jokers, artists, or anyone who looked like they might know Katrina.

She found the place at dusk. The sixth address on her list, it looked like a normal store front on a back street on the fringes of the Old Town. A short set of stairs led down to a sunken door, a cellar underneath a square stone building. As she hung back and watched, a pair of young women with short hair and worn jeans pushed through the door and left, arm in arm, giggling and conversing softly in Czech.

The door wasn't locked. No secret passwords, no guards. It was hidden in plain sight, the kind of place most people would just walk right by unless they knew it was here. Quickly, she slipped inside.

Wrapped in her cloak, she tried to be unobtrusive, keeping to shadows. When a bleary-eyed kid with an ash-laden cigarette stumbled toward her and to the door, she stepped out of his way, and he never took a second glance. Continuing down the stairs, she emerged into a wide room, and the bustle of a nascent counter-culture. Bare bulbs on sockets strung together with extension cords cast a stark light over the scene. The place was set up like some kind of coffee house cum workshop, small groups gathered at tables that were little more than plywood set on sawhorses. The air smelled of thick-brewed coffee and strong beer. Conversation rumbled. A black-haired, denim-jacketed girl played guitar and sang earnestly, if a little out of tune. Flyers, posters, and even spray paint decorated the walls, advertising British punk bands and anti-communist revolution. Nobody here could have been over twenty-five, and they were all dressed in ripped jeans, T-shirts, army surplus, gypsy skirts and faded tunics, all of it thrift store chic. An anticipatory energy ran through the place, people leaning over their work, exchanging excited words. These kids were like something out of *Hair,* twenty years too late.

And they were in a basement that might have been built six hundred years ago, pale walls and vaulted ceilings, a chill of age and stone pressing close. Those medieval stone walls, now pasted over with slogans and graffiti. She could have wept. But time didn't stand still, did it? This was a city, not a museum.

She spotted the American joker in the back of the hall, leaning over a table and drawing on a wide piece of butcher paper. Joann had actually missed her on her first scan of the room; her left side was turned toward the wall, and from this angle she looked a little like Mucha's nymph, long hair curling down her back, bright eyes and fine features. She was missing the draping clothing, instead wearing a shawl over a green army jacket, paisley dress, stockings and Doc Martens.

Holding back a moment, Joann just watched.

Katrina wasn't the only joker in the room. Joann spotted three others, one with damp and mottled skin like a salamander, another with an extra set of elongated, boneless arms tucked in the pockets of a sleeveless jacket, a third with bright blue hair that might have been dyed, until Joann saw it moving on its own, like seaweed in a current. The jokers didn't cluster together but were scattered throughout the room, working on projects of their own. There weren't enough of them to form their own clique, their own community. Strangely enough, discrimination wasn't as pronounced when the minority became so small as to not cause anxiety. Joann had experienced the phenomenon often enough. Katrina was here because she could be an artist here, not just a joker.

She looked fine. Mostly healthy, smiling. She could stand to eat a little more, maybe.

As Joann watched, patterns in the group's behavior emerged. Different clusters of people appeared to be involved in their own projects and conversations, but on further observation, all the projects had a sameness to them: signs, banners, streamers, noise-makers. All obvious props for some kind of demonstration. Joann's heart sank, thinking how these kids were setting themselves up for a confrontation with the Czech police, maybe even Soviet occupation forces, and that sort of thing never ended well.

A lanky guy with spiked hair and gaunt features that would have been handsomely rugged if he put on a little weight seemed to be the constant, the one who circled the room, checking in on the various clusters of kids, offering direction on their work. He wore a faded T-shirt for an obscure band and ratty jeans, and he moved with authority, talking to people, nodding in approval or shaking his head, and everyone in the little artist colony looked on him with awe. So, this was mostly likely the personality-in-chief around here.

When the guy reached Katrina, he wrapped a possessive arm around her, pulled her close, and kissed her. She laughed. When she tried to pull away to get back to her drawing, he didn't let go. They spoke a few words. The guy spoke English with a German accent.

Joann waited until he finished holding court and departed for another circuit of the room before sidling over to catch the young woman's attention.

'Katrina Duboss?' Joann said gently.

The young woman's eyes went round, stricken with guilt, and she pressed herself to the wall. 'How do you know who I am?'

'I'm Joann Jefferson. Are you familiar with Congresswoman Carol Cramer? She's a friend of your parents?'

'Are you a cop?' she asked. 'Or a PI or something?'

Sort of? How much worse would it be to say she was a Federal agent? 'Not really,' she answered. 'Not here, at least. I'm just doing a favor for Representative Cramer, who's here as a delegate on a U.N. tour and asked me to look in on you. Do you know her? She'd like to talk to you.'

Relaxing, Katrina smirked. 'Yeah. Yeah, I know her. My folks used to drag me to her fundraising dinners. I've never seen a more pretentious group of predators. You can tell her I'm fine. I don't want to talk to her.'

'I understand that,' Joann said. *And I can't say that I blame you.*

'But I think your family's worried about you. Do you have a message, anything you'd like to tell them?'

'They're not really worried about me, you know. It's just that they haven't been able to come up with a good story to tell their friends about what happened to me.' The snakes at her side seemed agitated, twisting and writhing until they curled around her front like a shield. The gesture was very like she'd crossed her arms.

'All right. I'll let Cramer know you're okay.' From across the room, the German punk kid was staring at them. Katrina quickly looked away.

'You'd better get going,' she told Joann. 'You don't really fit in here, you know? You're making people nervous.'

Joann just smiled. 'I get that a lot. So, can you give me a hint about what you're all doing here?

The joker glared. 'What, you think I'm going to spy for you?'

'I'm just curious. I'd hate to see you all get in trouble.'

'You mean more trouble than I'm already in, with my parents' friends sending people like you after me?'

'There's trouble, then there's trouble,' Joann said. 'Just careful, don't get in over your head if you can help it. I don't know exactly when or where you're going to launch the protest you all are obviously putting together, but you might think twice about putting yourself in the middle of that.'

'Thanks for your concern,' Katrina shot back, full of sarcasm and contempt.

She wasn't a kid, Joann reminded herself. She should give the young woman some credit.

Katrina picked up two pieces of charcoal, one with her normal hand and one with a snake limb, which curled around it and wielded it like a sword. She bent over the paper and used both pieces to add marks, swoops and whirls and lines that built into a picture. Katrina's work was beautiful. With just the one color, she'd created a shaded series of images on the paper, a cobbled street turning into a rain of flowers that in turn transformed into a woman's curling hair, and the woman's strong face was upturned, determined. Someone else had been wandering the streets and looking at Mucha's art.

'It's nice,' Joann said, inadequately.

Katrina flashed a smile that managed to express both gratitude and sarcasm.

'Hello, I'm Erik.' The young German man returned, putting his arm protectively around Katrina and glaring at Joann who tried very hard not to smile with amusement. 'And you are?'

'I'm Joann,' she answered calmly. 'You've got quite a community here, Erik. I wish you all the best.'

'And what do you want here?'

'I'm just a tourist, passing through and admiring Katrina's work.' She didn't expect anything different than the look of stark disbelief he gave her. 'I'll let you alone. You all have a good evening.'

After nodding to them both, she slipped out of the basement and back to the street.

Joann was followed most of the way back to the embassy, which didn't surprise her at all. Probably the spooks Ray had spotted staking out the hotel. Tour security had spent enough time warning the delegates that they would likely all be trailed by some kind of foreign intelligence agents if they went into the city, she didn't expect herself to be any different. At night, in the dark, they were easy to spot, mostly because foot traffic had thinned. There were two of them a couple of blocks behind her, one on each side of the street. The one on her side of the street was average height, with close-cropped dark hair atop an angular head. He wore a suit and brown leather jacket and appeared to be looking for an address, checking a card in his hand with street markers posted on building corners and signs above shop fronts. Since he'd been doing this for the past ten blocks, she didn't quite believe his attempts to find a particular address. Not to mention the fact that every five minutes or so, he glanced across the street to his partner. This second man was large, half a head taller than the people he passed on the sidewalk. This was the only clear detail about him. He wore a long overcoat, the collar turned up, hands hidden in the pockets, and walked with his shoulders hunched to his ears. His steps were steady, but slow. He moved like a man walking through a storm, though the sky was clear, the air cool but not uncomfortable. She might have overlooked him as simply an old man lost in thought during an evening walk, except that the smaller man in the leather coat kept looking at him, and the large man would occasionally nod back.

No matter how the medieval streets of the old part of the city twisted and jogged, turning abruptly and merging into squares before breaking off again at an odd angle, they kept on her. This was their city, after all – she pegged them as local, not KGB.

Through the Old Town and along the main tourist drag back to the hotel, few lights illuminated the streets, but those few were enough. Joann pushed her cloak back over her shoulder and raised a hand as if feeling the air for new rainfall. She focused on the lights and breathed in. Two streetlights, one ahead of her and one behind her, sparked and went dark. A faint tracery of light followed her hand, the sign that the electricity was now part of her. She felt it hum along her skin, warming her flesh, and even her in bones. Almost pleasant, if she didn't have to worry so much about what happened after. She was a human capacitor, a burst of lightning contained, wrapped in an insulating cloak to keep it all from roiling out – right until the moment she wanted it to.

She'd left the cobbled medieval streets and now walked along modern asphalt, with a modern steel drain grating on the far corner, between her and the agents who trailed her. This, she targeted, sweeping back her cloak and flicking out her arm, sending a bolt of power arcing to the metal. A crack like thunder echoed, and sparks rained. Joann turned the corner, using the explosion to distract from her exit. Her bolt of lightning shouldn't have done too much damage – scorched the asphalt maybe – but it sure looked exciting.

Let them try to figure that out. They didn't think they could follow her all the way back to the hotel unscathed, did they? A couple of blocks later, she ducked into a doorway to take a look, and sure enough, she seemed to have lost them. She brushed her hands together in a show of satisfaction.

Back at the hotel, Joann had maybe an hour to relax and get

some sleep before going back on duty. Billy Ray caught her in the hotel lobby on her way in; likely, he'd been watching for her.

'Have a nice walk?' Ray asked, raising an eyebrow, leering, or that might have been just the odd shape of his mouth and jaw.

'I did indeed. I had company most of the way, couple of our friends from across the street I'm guessing.'

'They give you any trouble?'

'Nope, not even a little.' He didn't need to know that she might have been a little excessive in her effort to lose them …

'I know, you're perfectly capable of taking care of yourself, don't remind me.'

She pulled off her hood, exposing her head, her close-cropped dark hair, her smile. She felt a static charge a tickling across her cheeks and scalp, the ambient energy in the room calling to her from the wiring, the light bulbs, and even from Ray's beating heart. She'd have to put the hood back up in a minute before the hum turned into an itching, then a burning. She'd suck power in, then launch it back out in a blast that she couldn't control.

'Ray, you're just *itching* to have a go at taking care of me, aren't you?'

He grinned. 'You flirt harder than anyone I know, hon.'

'Is that what this is?'

He took a step toward her – a dangerous step. Energy poured off him, his ace-fueled strength flowing, and all she had to do was reach out and touch that craggy cheek … He knew it, too. For all the grin in his lips, his gaze was clouded. Maybe just a little bit afraid.

'One of these days I'm gonna try it, just to see what happens,' he said, when he was just a hand span away from her. All she'd have to do was lean forward to kiss him.

'You know where to find me,' she said, putting her hood up as she slipped around him and walked away. Behind her, he chuckled.

Joann never remembered a time when her touch did not kill. Her first victim had been her own mother. That time was a blur, thankfully. The accident, the fear, the days of trying to figure out what had happened, and realizing that it was all her fault. Sequestered in the hospital, her father holding her while she cried. He wore a hazmat suit to prevent the least stray contact until the doctors could figure out the exact nature of her murderous ace. Thick rubber, slippery plastic, and hissing gas mask between them. He could hold her, but not touch her; she would never feel a gentle skin-to-skin touch of kindness again. He couldn't kiss her to make it better.

She spent a lot of time thinking about how different her life would have been if her father hadn't stayed with her. If he'd blamed her instead of forgiving her. Rejected her and her freakish powers instead of embracing her – metaphorically, at least. On the days she wanted to wail and break windows and rip off her own flesh, he was there to talk her down. Would she have been able to live with herself, if he hadn't been there to reassure her that this would all be worthwhile, someday?

'This power of yours, of course it's dangerous. It can be destructive, if you aren't careful. But so can electricity, knives, cars – and these are tools we need. Joann, you have to figure out a way to make this thing good. Use it to build things up instead of break things down.'

Because of her father, she'd gone into government service instead of to an institution. Most days, she knew she'd taken the right path. She chose her ace name, Lady Black, herself, and it had many levels of meaning. It was the color of the absorbing side of her cloak, and the color of her skin. It represented the danger of her dark power. The title, the 'Lady,' reminded people to treat her with respect.

The delegates had meetings and tours all the next day. This was another stop where the stated mission of the tour on paper and in reality didn't quite match up. Ostensibly, the delegates were meant to observe with impartial interest an Eastern Block Communist government's innovations in treating the wild card virus, and report on conditions experienced by victims of the virus. In reality, they were treated to another dog-and-pony show of sparkling clean institutions and carefully staged interviews with hand-picked and coached jokers and even a few aces in controlled settings. Czech officials presented a middle-aged man who could telekinetically re-arrange the print in any book to read as *The Communist Manifesto*. Ideologically impressive, no doubt, however questionable the ace's actual usefulness was. The American delegates were polite enough not to ask how many of Czechoslovakia's more powerful aces were working for intelligence agencies or had been recruited by the KGB, and the Czech guides were polite enough not to offer the information.

Joann's excursion in town last night illustrated that at least some of the country's virus victims went unnoticed by the system. The country didn't sequester all its jokers, which made it marginally better than some, she supposed.

In her role as bodyguard and babysitter, Joann accompanied one of the tours, mostly made up of the American politicians and WHO officials rather than the celebrities, who were off with Billy Ray playing the photogenic tourists in the Old Town. After so many weeks of this sort of the thing, the routine was established: Dr. Tachyon grilled the rather stunned local medical professionals, who stammered answers in rough English or sometimes French, or spoke through interpreters. The politicians looked on, feigning interest through glazed expressions. Cramer was here, but Joann hadn't had a chance to speak with her about Katrina. That came after hours, while most of the other delegates were sipping after-noon drinks in the hotel bar, and the congresswoman once again invited Joann to the front room of her suite.

'I found her,' Joann said, and Cramer let out a sigh. 'She's not interested in coming home. Or even talking about it, really.'

'Is she all right? She's not in trouble, is she?' She was sitting at the edge of a straight-back chair with scrolled detail, pulled out from a breakfast table.

That depended on how you define trouble. 'I think she's all right,' Joann said, carefully neutral. 'But like I said, she's an adult. If she doesn't want to talk, we can't make her.' She hoped this would be the end of it.

'Do you think … I would like to talk to her, Lady Black. You know where she is – can you arrange a meeting?'

Not only was this way outside Joann's normal responsibilities, Cramer was bordering on using her position to gain special consideration – a minor abuse of power practiced by politicians from time immemorial, but still an abuse, if Joann chose to call her on it. She didn't want to go hunting down the wayward artist again.

'Ms. Duboss was certain—'

'Her family is worried about her, you must understand that. If I can talk to her myself – at least then I'll be able to give her parents first-hand information about her. That can't be so difficult, can it?'

'I'll see what I can do.' The formal embassy reception was tonight. She really didn't have time. But truth be told, she was curious herself. Another trip to the city center, maybe she'd get a hint about what the kids were up to with their protest plans.

◆

When she arrived at the curved alley with the basement art commune, the place was blocked off with police cars, roof lights flashing. A couple of uniformed cops loitered, looking bored. More cops were passing in and out through the basement doorway, carrying posters torn from the wall, stacks of paper, and even buckets of paint and art supplies. They took their haul to a short moving truck parked at the other end of the alley, tossed everything in, unmindful of how it landed. If she asked, she was certain they'd tell her they were collecting evidence, no matter how haphazard the process looked from the outside. These guys were standard law enforcement, not scary secret service or the like. From her vantage, lingering at the corner to watch the proceedings, eavesdropping on conversations in a language she didn't understand, she couldn't guess what crime they were investigating, if that even mattered. They'd found the artist's base, and they'd shut it down.

In New York, a crowd of onlookers would have gathered at both end of the alleys, elbowing each other and pressing forward for a better look, and half a dozen cops and barriers would be on hand just to keep back the public. Here, no one. Passersby pointedly walked on, heads bowed and gazes averted. Lingering at a scene like this drew unwanted attention. Joann took the hint and left.

She kept an eye out for her friends, the two agents who'd tailed her yesterday. She had a sinking feeling they might have been the ones to put the cops onto the basement hideout – after she'd shown them the way there. They didn't seem to be around for the moment. But then, they didn't need to be.

At the next intersection, a figure reached out, and an orange bundle of tentacles twined around her arm. At the first hint of a touch, Joann leapt backward, getting herself out of reach and wrapping her insulating cloak more firmly around her.

Katrina Duboss, wearing a different sweater, shawl, and bohemian peasant skirt today, stood at the corner, smirking.

'Do I really gross you out that much?' she said.

'My touch kills,' Joann said. 'You could have died, if you'd gotten skin.' The girl paled. And yes, Joann got that reaction a lot. Almost worse than the lack of touch was having to explain it to people – and the look of pity they donned when they understood the implications.

'You're an ace?' Katrina asked. She squinted, peering for a glimpse under Joann's hood. 'Ace, or joker?'

That was a philosophical question for the ages, wasn't it? The way some people recoiled from Joann in fear, she might very well be a joker, no matter what she saw when she looked in the mirror.

'Let's walk, Katrina.' Joann gestured ahead, and she and Katrina continued on, side by side. The joker kept a healthy distance between them.

Joann was about to start the difficult conversation when Katrina asked, 'Is it worth it? Being an ace, if that's the price you have to pay for it?'

Nobody had ever put it to her in such blunt terms, but the question was elegant. Elegant and unanswerable – no one had given her the option of paying a price for her ace. Both the power and the price had landed randomly.

'To tell you the truth, I don't always think of myself as an ace. I'm just doing the best I can with what I have.'

'Yeah. Me too,' she said.

A few more steps, and Joann asked, 'Did everyone get out okay?'

'Oh yeah. We saw them coming. No thanks to you.'

Even if Joann hadn't led the police to their basement, the kids were going to blame her for it. So be it, especially if it kept them from embarking on any potentially dangerous protest plans.

'Representative Cramer wants to meet you in person. You think you can take a few minutes for her? There's a café near the hotel where you two should be able to get together without drawing too much attention.'

'I don't want to talk to her, she's just trying to pander to my parents.'

Couldn't fault the kid for being perceptive. Joann tipped her head in acknowledgement.

Katrina said, 'Why are you even working for Cramer? I looked you up – and the WHO tour. This seems way outside your job description.'

'I was curious. You and your friends are obviously planning something. Or, you were.'

'Still are. This isn't going to stop us. We got out everything we needed, and they can't stop us. We can go tonight, if we want.'

Something about the look in her eye, the way she smiled, made Joann think this wasn't hypothetical. 'What exactly are you planning?' Joann asked.

'You'll have to read it about it in the papers tomorrow.'

'This isn't a game, Katrina. If these guys arrest you for doing something they don't like, you'll be in for a world of hurt. The embassy – your parents – might not be able to bail you out.'

She grimaced. 'Oh, I know. My parents wouldn't lift a finger to help me. The raid was just about intimidation. A scare tactic. It didn't work.' She spoke with the chin-up, fist clenched conviction of youth and righteousness.

'Is that what that Erik guy said? Is he putting you up to this?'

'Because a deluded little thing like me couldn't possibly have my own opinions about it? Or maybe I'm just so grateful that any guy will even *look* at a twisted-up freak like me that I'd do anything for him?' She held up her arm, and the snakes writhed. Glinting light across the orange scales made her look like she held fire. 'I'm not doing this because of Erik, or because I'm crazy, or I'm trying to get back at my parents, or I'm part of a cult, or anything. I'm doing this because I want to, because it's a good thing to do, because I can help. I can use my trust fund money for something good instead of just going on fancy useless shopping sprees or whatever. Because Prague is beautiful, and Mucha and Dvorak and Kafka lived here, and because as stupid as it may look from the outside, protests like this are working. They're going to work. And it doesn't hurt to dream, does it?'

Joann lowered her gaze. Oh, to be young and full of convictions. 'Katrina – be careful. I'll be in Prague for another day. If you get in trouble or need help, contact me.'

'I'll be fine. Tell Cramer I'm *fine*.'

With a flounce of her skirt, Katrina turned and stomped off, her tentacled arm curled protectively around her middle.

Joann didn't get back to the hotel until dusk, and Ray met her at the door.

'You're late,' he said, glaring. 'We're due at the embassy in half an hour.'

'That's right,' she said, shouldering past him. 'Did anything happen while I was gone that you couldn't handle on your own?'

'Well, no.'

'Then I'm back, I'm on duty, and I don't want to hear any more about it.'

'Are you getting into some kind of trouble out there?'

She looked up enough so he could see her expression under her hood and raised a smug brow at him. 'I said I didn't want to hear it. Do you trust me or not?'

He frowned. 'I don't *not* trust you. But you're kind of weird, you know?'

Coming from Billy Ray, that was almost a compliment. 'Agent Ray, I am an ace, which makes me exactly as weird as you are. Now don't you think we should round up the delegates and get a move on?'

He gestured grandly into the lobby. 'Lead on, princess.'

The U.S. Embassy in Prague was an honest-to-God seventeenth century palace, with courtyards, wings, baroque moldings, cavernous ceilings and some hundred rooms. Even Dr. Tachyon seemed impressed, as the group traveled up the garden walk through arched doorways into the formal reception hall. Human beings so rarely lived up to his standards.

Embassy receptions, Joann had learned, all looked pretty much the same. The ambassador and spouse would be gracious hosts, and their staff would be preternaturally adept at smoothing over difficulties, faux-pas, and other mishaps before they became international incidents. The food, drink, and music would be excellent. Some national specialty would be prominently featured – tango in Argentina, sashimi in Japan, and so on. There might or might not be alcohol in an Islamic country, but there'd likely be something to make up for it if it was absent. Amazing coffee, for example. But this was Eastern Europe. There was plenty of alcohol.

It was all like watching a movie, from Joann's perspective. The *same* movie, with this crowd. Dr. Tachyon, downing champagne glassfuls at a time. Hiram Worchester had returned to the tour, at least for the moment, and was holding forth over a tray of hors d'oeuvres. The politicians circulated, shaking hands and conversing. Joann spotted Representative Cramer, in a conservative high-necked gown that seemed more like a dress suit with a long skirt than formal wear. Xavier Desmond, who might insist that he wasn't a politician, was part of the circulating group. Chrysalis, however, was not. Wearing a purple strapless gown that seemed to draw attention to the shifting contours of her visible musculature, she sat on the periphery, watching closely. One change from the start of the tour: Peregrine was no longer modeling svelte, haute couture gowns at every event. She still managed to look gorgeous in shimmering maternity wear that draped artfully around her expanding middle.

All this, taking place in the embassy's finely curtained and carpeted reception hall, made for a strange gathering. Both political, public, sensational, serious. As usual, Joann remained outside it, lurking in her cloak and hood. Observing, and nothing more.

When Cramer detached herself from her conversation and came across the hall toward her, Joann's stomach sank. What now? It couldn't possibly be important enough to interrupt the reception for. For someone who wanted to avoid attention, Cramer was certainly drawing a lot of it to her now. Joann straightened and reminded herself to be professional. No ducking around the corner to escape from this.

'Lady Black. Agent Jefferson. May I speak with you?'

Joann had to keep her sigh to herself. 'Why don't we step outside, Representative Cramer?' The ace led her through a side hall to a secluded corner of the patio, where the light and eavesdroppers didn't reach.

Cramer was impatient when she demanded, 'Were you able to arrange a meeting with Katrina?'

'No, Representative Cramer. Ms. Duboss doesn't seem to want to have anything to do with her family.' *She said you were pandering*, Joann kept to herself.

'She's wise,' Cramer said, and her expression changed, wincing into something like pain. Joann raised a polite eyebrow, inquiring.

The woman started pacing along the edges of the marble patio. 'I spoke on the phone with Katrina's parents this afternoon. I'm afraid … I've been under a bit of a misapprehension. When they asked me to contact her, I believed they wanted her to come home. I assumed – you see, if she were my daughter, I'd want her to come home.'

'What was it they really wanted?' Joann prompted gently.

It had to be bad, the way she took a deep breath before launching in. 'They want evidence that she's broken the terms of her trust so they can disinherit her. If she ever gets arrested, if she's ever convicted of anything more than a parking ticket, she loses her trust fund. And mind you, this isn't because she ran away, this isn't because she's done anything *wrong*, it's simply because of her condition. It's terribly unjust. So you see, Katrina's wise to distance herself. She's their *daughter*, they should be taking care of her.'

The world of trust funds and disinherited children was far outside Joann's experience, but Cramer's consternation was plain. Family was clearly more important than the wild card virus or any other consideration. *That*, Joann understood.

She also understood: Katrina was, right now as they spoke, getting herself into exactly the kind of trouble that would get her disinherited. Cramer would want to know – though it was probably better that she didn't. *Katrina* would want to know ... surely she'd want to stay out of trouble if it meant keeping her trust fund. And pissing off her parents to boot.

Now, if only Joann knew exactly where Katrina was and what she was doing.

Cramer went on. 'I only want to offer her help. She can't go to her family if she gets in trouble, obviously. But I'd like her to have *some* recourse. We get into politics because we think we can fix all the world's problems. That we really can make a difference. I knew it would be hard – but look at this tour, what good are we doing really? But I thought I could at least help this one person.'

Joann was hardly listening, because this wasn't about Cramer anymore. She decided: she had to get out, find Katrina, and keep the police off her back. The rest could wait.

'I'll try to talk to her one more time,' she told the congress-woman.

'I very much appreciate your help, Agent Jefferson.'

That was nice, but at this point Joann was mostly worried about whether Katrina would appreciate it.

She looked around the reception hall and the party that was in full swing. The delegates could not be any more secure than they were here, in the middle of the U.S. Embassy. They could spare her for a couple of hours.

Billy Ray made an impressive show of force all by himself, planted at the arched entrance between the reception hall and the gardens. He wore his white fighting suit and stood, arms crossed and scowling, studying everyone who entered or left. She sidled up to him, swirling her cloak behind her, and spoke over his shoulder.

'Billy, can you cover for me?'

'Why? What's up?'

'This is a personal favor for one of the delegates that has gotten way out of hand, but I'm in it now, so I have to finish it.'

'Hon, you are not making any sense at all. What's wrong?'

Urging him outside, to the shelter of an obliging shrub, she told him the whole story.

'Huh. Great,' he said, lip curling. 'You know you don't owe these people anything, right? Not Cramer, not the rich kid.'

'This isn't about Cramer anymore, that's the whole point,' Joann said, sighing, and looking out over the city as if she expected to see fireworks launching up from their planned protest. The river shone like liquid lead under the city's nighttime lights, and the spires of the Týn Church rose up like a demonic scepter. 'Back in the sixties, a couple of students here set themselves on fire to protest Soviet occupation of the country. *That's* what I'm afraid she's gotten herself into.' Because here was a kid whose life had been turned upside down by the wild card virus, but she was determined to move on, to find meaning, to do something great in the world. Joann understood.

'And if that's what she's determined to do, how are you going to stop her?'

'I just want to find her and talk to her.'

'Then I'll help.'

'Really, that's not necessary, you don't—'

'Seriously. Sounds like more fun than this show.' Indeed, a tipsy Tachyon had just accosted the pianist who'd been providing background music and was imploring him to sing Mozart. Ray leered. 'Besides, you need someone watching your back.'

What harm could he do? Ha.

Together they snuck out of the reception. He touched her shoulder and urged her on, down the sidewalk to the embassy delivery gate. Didn't even think about it; the gesture had been as natural as shading one's eyes from the sun. The fabric of her cloak protected him, and her. So close and yet so far, she thought for the millionth time.

A spring rain shower had fallen that afternoon, giving the streets a slick sheen, giving a fresh chill to the air. The hem of her cloak grew damp as it brushed on the pavement.

When Joann thought about it, their destination was obvious: Wenceslas Square. The broad thoroughfare had been the site of political gatherings and demonstrations for decades. If Katrina and Erik's bunch was planning something – something they wanted to garner a lot of attention – they would go there. She and Ray set off on foot, planning to find a cab once they got off the embassy grounds. But of course, this late and in this part of town, taxis were scarce. The central part of the city wasn't that big, so they kept moving, across the river and into the Old Town.

Where Ray was immediately tackled by an immense figure in a long coat. Her tail from yesterday. The big man had grabbed the ace around the middle at a dead run, and kept going, carrying him off the sidewalk and across the street.

Joann put her back to the wall of the nearest building and looked around for the guy's partner. Spotted him across the street, waiting. The big guy kept going, smashing Ray into the wall, cracking the brick in all directions. Ray slumped, dazed, but kept to his feet and threw a punch that landed on the guy's gut with a dull thud before the guy picked him up and smashed him into the wall again. They must have known about Ray's ace, and that they'd have to do a lot of smashing before they'd drop him. They seemed intent on doing exactly that.

Joann couldn't let that happen. She ran, shifting her cloak over her shoulders, and reaching out for the tough guy. His partner, the smaller man, didn't do anything, which made Joann suspicious. What was he waiting for? Or more likely – what was he hiding?

Keeping an eye on the partner, standing watchfully half a block away, Joann slapped her hand on the large one's back and *pulled*, opening the doors to her power. The feeling was like a vortex in the middle of her gut, a yawning hole that was desperate for power, that would swallow the energy and keep going until her whole being exploded. She had it all planned out – drop him like a rock by sucking him close to dry, then turning and punching a big chunk of his own energy back into him. He'd be off his feet for weeks, if not dead outright.

But nothing happened. She had a firm grip on him, but nothing poured out of him, and she didn't feel so much as a spark. It was like he was dead already – but somehow still upright, still moving. He turned around to stare at her with a stone-like gaze. Then, with surprising deftness, the big guy grabbed her and hoisted her off the ground. Still no effect. She tried the reverse, grabbing his shoulders with both her bare hands to slam a bomb's worth of energy into him. Power bounced off in a cascade of lightning, and he continued holding tight to her. Now, she struggled, kicking and digging fingernails into strangely unyielding flesh. He was solid, his muscles hard, and his expression vaguely bland as he started squeezing.

Here was someone who could touch her – he was touching her, and not falling. Not dying. She could touch this man, he could touch her and not die; the fact thrilled her. Even as he was obviously trying to kill her, she almost leaned in to kiss him. Proposition: for every ace power there existed, somewhere, an equal and opposite power. Every ace had an opposite against whom their power was useless. The idea offered a strangely comforting balance to the universe. If she could drain the lifeforce from anyone, didn't it stand to reason there was an ace, somewhere, whose power meant his lifeforce couldn't be drained?

Of course Murphy's Law intruded – a man who could touch her, and he was trying to kill her.

Her arms were pinned. She kicked at his knees and groin, but he didn't even flinch. All she did was stub her toes on his rock-solid flesh. Joann's big professional secret was that she wasn't at all proficient in martial arts and hand-to-hand combat skills that would usually be required for a Federal agent working security. She could learn movements, but she couldn't realistically spar with anyone without running the risk of killing them with her power. When she could incapacitate anyone with just a wave of her hand, no one ever thought she *needed* proficiency in hand-to-hand combat. Well, so much for that. Caught in the powerful ace's grip, she could do little more than flop, while he squeezed harder. Her ribs creaked, and she choked on a breath when her lungs refused to expand.

Screw this. Wriggling, making herself as slippery as possible, she slid downward in his grip, and right out of her cloak. The guy's hold on her faltered. He grabbed for the cloak's slick fabric, and she stumbled away. More by instinct than thought, she turned and let off a starburst of stored energy, a flash that blasted outward, thunder echoing on stone.

The ace flinched back, sheltering his eyes with an arm as he tossed the cloak away. Her blast didn't kill him, but it seemed to have blinded him.

The other agent still wasn't engaging. Ray was picking himself up off the pavement, rubbing his head – and snarling with rage.

'Ray—' Joann warned.

'Fuck this, I've got it,' he growled. And jumped.

The big man made a fist and swung around to punch Ray, but the white-garbed ace was already out of the way and coming down on top of the giant's head, hooking an arm around his neck, twisting, and landing a punch on the guy's face. Chips of stone flew from his head.

Wait, stone?

The other Czech agent shouted a word of denial and ran for them. Joann held out a hand in a 'stop' gesture. The guy stopped. They both turned back to watch.

The big man blinked in confusion. Ray had done damage – a series of cracks radiated across his face, starting at his cheek and looping around his eye, then across a marking on his forehead, some kind of scar or tattoo. He reached up, scratching at it – and another bit of stone chipped away, and the symbol fell apart.

The man froze, still as a statue. Just like a statue. The cracks in his face widened, the damage increasing, spreading across his entire body until the whole figure fell into rubble, leaving his coat and clothing slumped on top of it.

A weird silence settled over them, confused and watchful. Joann knelt by the remains, the pile of stone and sand, tracing her fingers through it. Blinking in confusion, Ray crouched where he'd fallen when the giant disintegrated. What was going on here?

The remaining Czech agent's expression hardened, grief turning impassive. Finally he said, 'It doesn't matter. I can make another one, and another.'

He was the ace, not his hulking partner. His power: bringing to life stone, making stone men –

Joann's eyes widened. 'You're Jewish. That's where your power comes from. Your ace, it draws on the golem folklore—'

'I'm a good Communist,' he said, straightforward, like he was used to saying it dutifully, over and over again. 'I and my servants are good agents, and I will still find out what you have planned—'

Joann sighed with frustration. 'We don't have anything planned!'

'I know you are conspiring with the foreign demonstrators to provoke civil unrest.'

She couldn't help it; she chuckled. 'You've got it all backwards. I was just—' She shook her head, let it go.

Clenching her fist, she felt a crackle of power. She could drop him where he stood with a touch if she needed to. He was human and had a normal flow of energy through a conventional nervous system. Not like his stone servant. But she didn't, because he wasn't doing anything but standing there. Brushing off her hands, she went to retrieve her cloak. With a practiced twist and sweep, she draped her cloak around herself and drew her power close.

'Joann, you okay?' Ray was back on his feet, bruised, a trickle of blood dripping down his forehead, but otherwise none the worse for wear. She wondered if she should tell him about the blood before it dripped on his suit.

'Yeah, I'm fine,' she said. Her ribs felt bruised, but she'd recover. She regarded the Czech agent. 'I am honestly not here to cause any trouble. We can both walk away and neither of us has to report this.'

'You have all the power here. You can decide what we do.' He lifted his chin, in pride and defiance.

He expected them to kill him. He would have, if the roles were reversed. All she had to do was lift her hand – or say the word and Ray would knock the guy's head off.

'Ray, let's go,' Joann said, settling her cloak more firmly over her shoulders and starting away. 'We've wasted enough time.'

'You're sure?' Ray said.

'Yeah.'

Together they walked to the next intersection. When she looked over her shoulder, the Czech agent was gone.

A mental clock was ticking – had Katrina gotten in trouble yet? How close was she to getting arrested?

This late, traffic was minimal, but they must have passed a dozen police cars along the way. Joann thought for sure they'd get stopped. She had the dark surface of her cloak turned out and could be inconspicuous, but Ray's white suit gleamed like a beacon. The police seemed to be on a mission, driving fast, heading in similar directions. It didn't bode well. Joann hurried, and Ray trailed, keeping a look out.

Joann heard laughter and shouting voices as the broad thoroughfare of the square opened before her. Finally, she spotted them.

A gang of young people, teenagers on up to punks in their mid-twenties, ran across the street several blocks ahead, laughing and carrying on in a tangled mob. She might have spotted Katrina's peasant skirt, sweater, and writhing joker limb, but she wasn't sure. It might have been someone else's scarf. The group certainly looked like the kids from the basement. Joann ran to catch up with them, but they had a head start and no intention of waiting around. Whatever they'd planned, they'd done it, and they'd been successful, and now they were out of here. They pelted down the street, around a distant corner, and out of sight. Not seeing much use in chasing them further, Joann slowed, stopped, and turned to look up the thoroughfare to the heart of Wenceslas Square and the equestrian statue of King Wenceslas that occupied its center.

The statue was covered in flowers. Draped with blankets of them on the horse's flank and neck, garlands around its head, ropes of them around mounted King Wenceslas, spiraling up his spear, hanging off the end of it like a banner. More flowers, spares and strays, lay scattered across the shrubbery around the statue, and a few draped in the trees across the street. The acres of paper flowers were what they'd been making in their basement arts-and-crafts session. They'd transformed the monument into a whimsical garden, springing up in the middle of the city.

Along with the flowers, the kids had posted banners, signs, posters, tying them in the trees, taping them to storefronts, plastering them to the statue's base. Symbols, cartoons, slogans, most of them in Czech, which Joann couldn't read. Some in German, some in English – none in Russian. Pro-democracy, pro-peace slogans. There were drawings of tanks and bombs with red cross-out symbols over them, peace signs, lyrics from songs, and so on. Katrina's beautiful charcoal drawing was among them, destined to be rained on, torn up, and trashed. Joann almost wanted to rescue it, carefully roll it up and save it. But no, it belonged here.

And this was their protest. No marching, no shouting, no disruption. Nothing blown up, no one set on fire. Dawn would come, and the city's residents, police, Soviet occupiers – and photojournalists – would see a bright, colorful work of art, full of energy and hope.

'That's *it?*' Ray declared, coming up to stand next to Joann. 'That's their big protest demonstration whatsit?'

'That's it,' Joann said, chuckling. 'It's pretty, don't you think?'

Ray regarded the scene, expression pursed in confusion, scratching his short hair. 'I guess. Don't know that I'd call it art or anything.'

She looked at him. 'Billy, you wouldn't know art if it smacked you upside the head and bought you dinner.'

'Joann, that almost sounds like you're asking me on a date.'

It was one of those moments when gravity seemed to shift slightly, or maybe the oxygen content of the atmosphere suddenly changed, making her lightheaded. She could say yes, she realized. She could ask the man to dinner. And it wouldn't go anywhere, it wouldn't mean anything, there'd be no point to it. Except … except what if there was a point? She could have said yes, she could have said no, but she didn't say anything. Just stood there looking at him like an idiot, and he was looking back at her with similar bemusement. Then he leaned in.

He was like a kid inching his way to the very edge of a cliff, peering over, seeing how far he could get without tumbling to his death. Maybe convinced that even if he fell, he couldn't possibly get hurt. Well, this *was* Billy Ray, after all. He could be beaten but not broken.

Just this once, she didn't inch away. Didn't put her hood up and turn her shoulder. Didn't protect bystanders, or herself. His finger-tips brushed her chin, trailed up her left cheek. A tingle trailed after his touch, and she humored herself for that fraction of a second that the feeling came from the shock of human contact on her skin, from the surprisingly gentle movement of a seductive hand against her face, inviting her to lean in for more. She could turn her face, brush along his palm, and reach for him. Overcoming a lifetime of instinct to keep her distance would suddenly be very easy.

Ray must have also indulged a moment of wishful thinking, because he grew bolder, pressing his hand to her face instead of just testing, taking another step in like he might actually kiss her. But that pleasant, warm tingle wasn't the thrill of flirting or nascent foreplay; it was energy. Lifeforce sparking between them, power from Ray's hand flowing into her skin, flooding her nerve endings, pouring through her and making her blood feel molten. Ray hissed in pain, shuddered, and his eyes rolled.

He fell back in a dead faint. Instead of lunging forward to catch him as any normal person would have done, Joann wrapped her cloak around her and stepped back. Insulating her power, pulling it close in, forcing her breathing to stay calm even as her heart pounded. She kept control of herself, as she'd practiced doing her whole life.

Ray hit the ground, cracked his head on the pavement, lay there a moment, still. Then, letting out a groan, he put a hand to his head. So, not dead. She was relieved.

'You got a punch like a Mack truck, you know that?' he muttered.

He was one of the tough aces, one of the ones who could take a lot of damage. For just a moment there she'd thought that maybe, just maybe ... But no.

And that was okay. It had to be okay.

'You knew the risks,' she said to Ray, her smile lopsided.

'Nothing ventured,' he muttered back, gasping for breath while pretending not to. 'I'd ask for a hand up ... but no. No offense.' He hauled himself to his feet, creaking like an old man.

'We should get back to the embassy,' she said. 'Make sure the drunk delegates get back to the hotel okay.'

'I think I'd rather have you knock me out cold again.'

Joann was calm enough she could laugh at that.

The WHO tour was scheduled to leave for Krakow the next afternoon, but Joann was able to arrange a meeting between Cramer and Katrina for that morning in a coffee shop halfway between the hotel and the Old Town. They wouldn't draw so much attention, and they would have some privacy.

Cramer was already seated at a table with Joann when Katrina came in, looking bleary-eyed, because of course she did – her group had probably stayed up all night partying after their successful redecoration of Wenceslas Square. The police had cleaned up the square quickly, but not before pictures of it ended up in the papers that morning. The international press had even picked up the story. Maybe Katrina was right, maybe protests like that – enough of them, over time – could work.

Cramer stood, adjusting her sleeves nervously as if she was meeting her own daughter. Katrina saw them, sigh, and walked over.

Cramer held out her hand. 'Katrina dear, I don't know if you remember me—'

'I do, Mrs. Cramer. It's good to see you,' Katrina said and

dutifully shook the woman's hand. The polite daughter of a wealthy family coming to the fore. The façade seemed wrong on her, after getting to know the bright-eyed artist.

They sat, and Katrina put her arm with its tangle of snakes right on the table. Cramer stared a moment, blanching a bit. But to her credit she recovered quickly and turned earnest.

Cramer said, 'I have to confess, I'm very disappointed in your parents—'

'But you'll still take their contributions, I'm sure.'

'And you'll still draw on your trust fund. This isn't about money, not for me. I just want you to know – you have friends. I know that you can't ever go to them for help. But I want you to know you're not alone.'

'I know I'm not, ma'am. Thank you.'

'And when you decide you're ready to come home—'

'I'm sure I'll be able to buy a plane ticket, like everyone else,' Katrina said.

Joann hid a smile behind her hand.

Katrina let the Congresswoman buy her a coffee, and they made awkward small talk for half an hour before Cramer declared she needed to get back to the hotel to rejoin the rest of the delegates for the trip to the airport. Joann managed to get a few minutes alone with Katrina, as she walked the young woman out of the café.

'She's just like my parents,' Katrina explained. 'I mean, not *just* like. She at least seems to have some sense of common decency. But my parents want me to think this is the end of the world, that it'll ruin my life.' She held up her arm, and the snakes writhed, angry and rippling. 'But I can still paint, I can still draw. I can still see the world and find a boyfriend. I still have a life. A good life. Can't they see that?'

'The rest of us see it,' Joann said, because the question didn't seem rhetorical. Katrina needed an answer – validation. But Joann had to pause and turn the question back on herself. She could still have a good life. She'd built herself a good life, dammit. Here she was, traveling the world, which so many people dreamed of and never got to do. She had friends, she had purpose. And maybe, someday, somewhere, she'd meet an ace with the exact power to balance hers. Maybe someone who could produce endless fountains of energy out of nothing. And maybe he'd also be smart, handsome, witty, kind …

Didn't hurt to dream, did it?

'Take care of yourself, Katrina.' Joann said goodbye to the young woman before walking Representative Cramer back to the hotel.

FROM *THE JOURNAL*
OF XAVIER DESMOND

April 10/Stockholm:
Very tired. I fear my doctor was correct – this trip may have been a drastic mistake, insofar as my health is concerned. I feel I held up remarkably well during the first few months, when everything was fresh and new and exciting, but during this last month a cumulative exhaustion has set in, and the day-to-day grind has become almost unbearable. The flights, the dinners, the endless receiving lines, the visits to hospitals and joker ghettos and research institutions, it is all threatening to become one great blur of dignitaries and airports and translators and buses and hotel dining rooms.

I am not keeping my food down well, and I know I have lost weight. The cancer, the strain of travel, my age… who can say? All of these, I suspect.

Fortunately the trip is almost over now. We are scheduled to return to Tomlin on April 29, and only a handful of stops remain. I confess that I am looking forward to my return home, and I do not think I am alone in that. We are all tired.

Still, despite the toll it has taken, I would not have forfeited this trip for anything. I have seen the Pyramids and the Great Wall, walked the streets of Rio and Marrakesh and Moscow, and soon I will add Rome and Paris and London to that list. I have seen and experienced the stuff of dreams and nightmares, and I have learned much, I think. I can only pray that I survive long enough to use some of that knowledge.

Sweden is a bracing change from the Soviet Union and the other Warsaw Pact nations we have visited. I have no strong feelings about socialism one way or the other, but grew very weary of the model joker 'medical hostels' we were constantly being shown and the model jokers who occupied them. Socialist medicine and socialist science would undoubtedly conquer the wild card, and great strides were already being made, we were repeatedly told, but even if one credits these claims, the price is a lifetime of 'treatment' for the handful of jokers the Soviets admit to having.

Billy Ray insists that the Russians actually have thousands of jokers locked away safely out of sight in huge gray 'joker warehouses,' nominally hospitals but actually prisons in all but name, staffed by a lot of guards and precious few doctors and nurses. Ray also says there are a dozen Soviet aces, all of them secretly employed by the government, the military, the police, or the party. If these things exist – the Soviet Union denies all such allegations, of course – we got nowhere close to any of them, with Intourist and the KGB carefully managing every aspect of our visit, despite the government's assurance to the United Nations that this UN-sanctioned tour would receive 'every cooperation.'

To say that Dr. Tachyon did not get along well with his socialist colleagues would be a considerable understatement. His disdain for Soviet medicine is exceeded only by Hiram's disdain for Soviet cooking. Both of them do seem to approve of Soviet vodka, however, and have consumed a great deal of it.

There was an amusing little debate in the Winter Palace, when one of our hosts explained the dialectic of history to Dr. Tachyon, telling him feudalism must inevitably give way to capitalism, and capitalism to socialism, as a civilization matures. Tachyon listened with remarkable politeness and then said, 'My dear man, there are two great star-faring civilizations in this small sector of the galaxy. My own people, by your lights, must be considered feudal, and the Network is a form of capitalism more rapacious and virulent than anything you've ever dreamed of. Neither of us shows any signs of maturing into socialism, thank you.' Then he paused for a moment and added, 'Although, if you think of it in the right light, perhaps the Swarm might be considered communist, though scarcely civilized.'

It was a clever little speech, I must admit, although I think it might have impressed the Soviets more if Tachyon had not been dressed in full cossack regalia when he delivered it. Where does he *get* these outfits?

Of the other Warsaw Bloc nations there is little to report. Yugoslavia was the warmest, Poland the grimmest, Czechoslovakia seemed the most like home. Downs wrote a marvelously engrossing piece for *Aces*, speculating that the widespread peasant accounts of active contemporary vampires in Hungary and Rumania were actually manifestations of the wild card. It was his best work, actually, some really excellent writing, and all the more remarkable when you consider that he based the whole thing on a five-minute conversation with a pastry chef in Budapest. We found a small joker ghetto in Warsaw and a widespread belief in a hidden 'solidarity ace' who will shortly come forth to lead that outlawed trade union to victory. He did not, alas, come forth during our two days in Poland. Senator Hartmann, with greatest difficulty, managed to arrange a meeting with Lech Walesa, and I believe that the AP news photo of their meeting has enhanced his stature back home. Hiram left us briefly in Hungary – another 'emergency' back in New York, he said – and returned just as we arrived in Sweden, in somewhat better spirits.

Stockholm is a most congenial city, after many of the places we have been. Virtually all the Swedes we have met speak excellent English, we are free to come and go as we please (within the confines of our merciless schedule, of course), and the king was most gracious to all of us. Jokers are quite rare here, this far north, but he greeted us with complete equanimity, as if he'd been hosting jokers all of his life.

Still, as enjoyable as our brief visit has been, there is only one incident that is worth recording for posterity. I believe we have un-earthed something that will make the historians around the world sit up and take notice, a hitherto-unknown fact that puts much of recent Middle Eastern history into a new and startling perspective.

It occurred during an otherwise unremarkable afternoon a number of the delegates spent with the Nobel trustees. I believe it was Senator Hartmann they actually wanted to meet. Although it ended in violence, his attempt to meet and negotiate with the Nur al-Allah in Syria is correctly seen here for what it was – a sincere and courageous effort on behalf of peace and understanding, and one that makes him to my mind a legitimate candidate for next year's Nobel Peace Prize.

At any rate, several of the other delegates accompanied Gregg to the meeting, which was cordial but hardly stimulating. One of our hosts, it turned out, had been a secretary to Count Folke Bernadotte when he negotiated the Peace of Jerusalem, and sadly enough had also been with Bernadotte when he was gunned down by Israeli terrorists two years later. He told us several fascinating anecdotes about Bernadotte, for whom he clearly had great admiration, and also showed us some of his personal memorabilia of those difficult negotiations. Among the notes, journals, and interim drafts was a photo book.

I gave the book a cursory glance and then passed it on, as did most of my companions. Dr. Tachyon, who was seated beside me on the couch, seemed bored by the proceedings and leafed through the photographs with rather more care. Bernadotte figured in most of them, of course – standing with his negotiating team, talking with David Ben-Gurion in one photo and King Faisal in the next. The various aides, including our host, were seen in less formal poses, shaking hands with Israeli soldiers, eating with a tentful of bedouin, and so on. The usual sort of thing. By far the single most arresting picture showed Bernadotte surrounded by the *Nasr*, the Port Said aces who so dramatically reversed the tide of battle when they joined with Jordan's crack Arab Legion. Khôf sits beside Bernadotte in the center of the photograph, all in black, looking like death incarnate, surrounded by the younger aces. Ironically enough, of all the faces in that photo, only three are sill alive, the ageless Khôf among them. Even an undeclared war takes it toll.

That was not the photograph that caught Tachyon's attention, however. It was another, a very informal snapshot, showing Bernadotte and various members of his team in some hotel room, the table in front of them littered with papers. In one corner of the photograph was a young man I had not noticed in any of the other pictures – slim, dark-haired, with a certain intense look around the eyes, and a rather ingratiating grin. He was pouring a cup of coffee. All very innocent, but Tachyon stared at the photograph for a long time and then called our host over and said to him privately, 'Forgive me if I tax your memory, but I would be very interested to know if you remember this man.' He pointed him out. 'Was he a member of your team?'

Our Swedish friend leaned over, studied the photograph, and chuckled. 'Oh, him,' he said in excellent English. 'He was ... what is the slang word you use, for a boy who runs errands and does odd jobs? An animal of some sort ...'

'A gofer,' I supplied.

'Yes, he was a *gopher*, as you put it. Actually a young journalism student. Joshua, that was his name. Joshua ... something. He said he wanted to observe the negotiations from within so he could write about them afterward. Bernadotte thought the idea was ridiculous when it was first put to him, rejected it out of hand in fact, but the young man was persistent. He finally managed to corner the Count and put his case to him personally, and somehow he talked him around. So he was not officially a member of the team, but he was with us constantly from that point through the end. He was not a very efficient gopher, as I recall, but he was such a pleasant young man that everyone liked him regardless. I don't believe he ever wrote his article.'

'No,' Tachyon said. 'He wouldn't have. He was a chess player, not a writer.'

Our host lit up with remembrance. 'Why, yes! He played incessantly, now that I recall. He was quite good. Do you know him, Dr. Tachyon? I've often wondered whatever became of him.'

'So have I,' Tachyon replied very simply and very sadly. Then he closed the book and changed the topic.

I have known Dr. Tachyon for more years than I care to contemplate. That evening, spurred by my own curiosity, I managed to seat myself near to Jack Braun and ask him a few innocent questions while we ate. I'm certain that he suspected nothing, but he was willing enough to reminisce about the Four Aces, the things they did and tried to do, the places they went, and more importantly, the places they did *not* go. At least not officially.

Afterward, I found Dr. Tachyon drinking alone in his room. He invited me in, and it was clear that he was feeling quite morose, lost in his damnable memories. He lives as much in the past as any man I have ever known. I asked him who the young man in the photograph had been.

'No one,' Tachyon said. 'Just a boy I used to play chess with.' I'm not sure why he felt he had to lie to me.

'His name was not Joshua,' I told him, and he seemed startled. I wonder, does he think my deformity affects my mind, my memory? 'His name was David, and he was not supposed to be there. The Four Aces were never officially involved in the Mideast, and Jack Braun says that by late 1948 the members of the group had gone their own ways. Braun was making movies.'

'Bad movies,' Tachyon said with a certain venom.

'Meanwhile,' I said, 'the Envoy was making peace.'

'He was gone for two months. He told Blythe and me that he was going on a vacation. I remember. It never occurred to me that he was involved.'

No more has it ever occurred to the rest of the world, though perhaps it should have. David Harstein was not particularly religious, from what little I know of him, but he was Jewish, and when the Port Said aces and the Arab armies threatened the very existence of the new state of Israel, he acted all on his own.

His was a power for peace, not war; not fear or sandstorms or lightning from a clear sky, but pheromones that made people like him and want desperately to please him and agree with him, that made the mere presence of the ace called Envoy a virtual guarantee of a successful negotiation. But those who knew who and what he was showed a distressing tendency to repudiate their agreements once Harstein and his pheromones had left their presence. He must have pondered that, and with the stakes so high, he must have decided to find out what might happen if his role in the process was carefully kept secret. The Peace of Jerusalem was his answer.

I wonder if even Folke Bernadotte knew who his gopher really was. I wonder where Harstein is now, and what he thinks of the peace that he so carefully and secretly wrought. And I find myself reflecting on what the Black Dog said in Jerusalem.

What would it do to the fragile Peace of Jerusalem if its origins were revealed to the world? The more I reflect on that, the more certain I grow that I ought tear these pages from my journal before I offer it for publication. If no one gets Dr. Tachyon drunk, perhaps this secret can even be kept.

Did he ever do it again, I wonder? After HUAC, after prison and disgrace and his celebrated conscription and equally celebrated disappearance, did the Envoy ever sit in on any other negotiations with the world's being none the wiser? I wonder if we'll ever know.

I think it unlikely and wish it were not. From what I have seen on this tour, in Guatemala and South Africa, in Ethiopia and Syria and Jerusalem, in India and Indonesia and Poland, the world today needs the Envoy more than ever.

PUPPETS

Victor W. Milán

MacHeath had a jackknife, so the song went.

Mackie Messer had something better. And it was ever so much easier to keep out of sight.

Mackie blew into the camera store on a breath of cool air and diesel farts from the Kurfürstendamm. He left off whistling his song, let the door hiss to behind him, and stood with his fists rammed down in his jacket pockets to catch a look around.

Light slamdanced on countertops, the curves of cameras, black and glassy-eyed. He felt the humming of the lights down beneath his skin. This place got on his tits. It was so clean and antiseptic it made him think of a doctor's office. He hated doctors. Always had, since the doctors the Hamburg court sent him to see when he was thirteen said he was crazy and penned him up in a *Land* juvie/psych ward, and the orderly there was a pig from the Tirol who was always breathing booze and garlic over him and trying to get him to jerk him off ... and then he'd turned over his ace and walked on out of there, and the thought brought a smile and a rush of confidence.

On a stool by the display counter lay a *Berliner Zeitung* folded to the headline: 'Wild Card Tour to Visit Wall Today.' He smiled, thin.

Yeah. Oh, yeah.

Then Dieter came in from the back and saw him. He stopped dead and put this foolish smile on his face. 'Mackie. Hey. It's a little early, isn't it?'

He had a narrow, pale head with dark hair slicked back in a smear of oil. His suit was blue and ran to too much padding in the shoulders. His tie was thin and iridescent. His lower lip quivered just a little.

Mackie was standing still. His eyes were the eyes of a shark, cold and gray and expressionless as steel marbles.

'I was just, you know, putting in my appearance here,' Dieter said. A hand jittered around at the cameras and the neon tubing and the sprawling shiny posters showing the tanned women with shades and too many teeth. The hand glowed the white of a dead fish's belly in the artificial light. 'Appearances are important, you know. Got to lull the suspicions of the bourgeoisie. Especially today.'

He tried to keep his eyes off Mackie, but they just kept rolling back to him, as if the whole room slanted downward to where he stood. The ace didn't look like much. He was maybe seventeen, looked younger, except for his skin – that had a dryness to it, a touch of parchment age. He wasn't much more than a hundred seventy centimeters tall, even skinnier than Dieter, and his body kind of twisted. He wore a black leather jacket that Dieter knew was scuffed to gray along the canted line of his shoulders, jeans that were tired before he fished them out of a trash can in Dahlem, a pair of Dutch clogs. A brush of straw hair stuck up at random above the drawn-out face of an El Greco martyr, oddly vulnerable. His lips were thin and mobile.

'So you stepped up the timetable, came for me early,' Dieter said lamely.

Mackie flashed forward, wrapped his hand in shiny tie, hauled Dieter toward him. 'Maybe it's too late for you, comrade. Maybe maybe.'

The camera salesman had a curious glossy-pale complexion, like laminated paper. Now his skin turned the color of a sheet of the *Zeitung* after it had spent the night blowing along a Buda-pesterstrasse curb. He'd seen what that hand could do.

'M-mackie,' he stammered, clutching at the reed-thin arm.

He collected himself then, patted Mackie affectionately on a leather sleeve. 'Hey, hey now, brother. What's the matter?'

'You tried to sell us, motherfucker!' Mackie screamed, spraying spittle all over Dieter's after-shave.

Dieter jerked back. His arm twitched with the lust to wipe his cheek. 'What the fuck are you talking about, Mackie? I'd never try—'

'Kelly. That Australian bitch. Wolf thought she was acting funny and leaned on her.' A grin winched its way across Mackie's face. 'She's never going to the fucking *Bundeskriminalamt* now, man. She's *Speck*. Lunchmeat.'

Dieter's tongue flicked bluish lips. 'Listen, you've got it wrong. She was nothing to me. I knew she was just a groupie, all along—'

His eyes informed on him, sliding ever so slightly to the right. His hand suddenly flared up from below the register with a black snub revolver in it.

Mackie's left hand whirred down, vibrating like the blade of a jigsaw. It sheared through the pistol's top strap, through the cylinder and cartridges, and slashed open the trigger guard a piece of a centimeter in front of Dieter's forefinger. The finger clenched spastically, the hammer came back and clicked to, and the rear half of the cylinder, its fresh-cut face glistening like silver, fell forward onto the countertop. Glass cracked.

Mackie grabbed Dieter by the face and hauled him forward. The camera salesman put down his hands to steady himself, shrieked as they went through the countertops. The broken glass raked him like talons, slashing through blue coat sleeve and blue French shirt and fishbelly skin beneath. His blood streamed over Zeiss lenses and Japanese import cameras that were making inroads in the Federal Republic despite chauvinism and high tariffs, ruining their finish.

'We were comrades! Why? *Why?*' Mackie's whole skinny body was shaking in hurt fury. Tears filled his eyes. His hands began to vibrate of their own accord.

Dieter squealed as he felt them rasping at the post-shave stubble he could never get rid of, the only flaw in his neo-sleek grooming. 'I don't know what you're talking about,' he screamed. 'I never meant to do it – I was playing her along—'

'*Liar!*' Mackie yelled. The anger jolted through him like a blast from the third rail, and his hands were buzzing, buzzing, and Dieter was flopping and howling as the flesh began to come off his cheeks, and Mackie gripped him harder, hands on cheekbones, and the rising vibration of his hands was transmitted through bone to the wet mass of Dieter's brain, and the camera salesman's eyes rolled and his tongue came out and the violent agitation flash-boiled the fluids in his skull and his head exploded.

Mackie dropped him, danced back howling like a man on fire, swiping at the clotted stuff that filled his eyes and clung to his cheeks and hair. When he could see, he went around the counter and kicked the quivering body. It slid onto the cuffed linoleum floor. The cash register was flashing orange error-condition warnings, the display case swam with blood, and there were lumps of greasy yellow-gray brains all over everything.

Mackie dabbed at his jacket and screamed again when his hands came away slimy. 'You bastard!' He kicked the headless corpse again. 'You got this shit all over me, you asshole. Asshole, asshole, *asshole!*'

He hunkered down, pulled up the tail of Dieter's suit coat, and wiped the worst lumps off his face and hands and leather jacket. 'Oh, Dieter, Dieter,' he sobbed, 'I wanted to *talk* to you, stupid son of a bitch—' He picked up a cold hand, kissed it, tenderly rested it on a spattered lapel. Then he went back to the john to wash down as best he could.

When he came out, anger and sorrow both had faded, leaving a strange elation. Dieter had tried to fuck with the Faction and he'd paid the price, and what the hell did it matter if Mackie hadn't been able to find out why? It didn't matter, nothing mattered. Mackie was an ace, he was MacHeath made flesh, invulnerable, and in a couple of hours he was going to show the cocksuckers—

The glass doors up front opened and somebody came in.

Laughing to himself, Mackie changed phase and walked through the wall.

Rain jittered briefly on the roof of the Mercedes limo. 'We'll be meeting a number of influential people at this luncheon, Senator,' said the young black man with the long narrow face and earnest expression, riding with his back to the driver. 'It's going to be an excellent opportunity to show your commitment to brotherhood and tolerance, not just for jokers, but for members of oppressed groups of all persuasions. Really excellent.'

'I'm sure it will, Ronnie.' Chin on hand, Hartmann let his eyes slide away from his junior aide and out the condensation-fogged window. Blocks of apartments rolled by, tan and anonymous. This close to the Wall Berlin seemed always to be holding its breath.

'Aide et Amitié has an international reputation for its work to promote tolerance,' Ronnie said. 'The head of the Berlin chapter, Herr Prahler, recently received recognition for his efforts to improve public acceptance of the Turkish "guest workers," though I understand he's a rather, ah, controversial personality—'

'Communist bastard,' grunted Möller from the front seat. He was a strapping blond kid plainclothesman with big hands and prominent ears that made him resemble a hound pup. He spoke English out of deference to the American senator, though between a grandmother from the Old Country and a few college courses, Hartmann knew enough German to get by.

'Herr Prahler's active in *Rote Hilfe*, Red Help,' explained Möller's opposite number, Blum, from the backseat. He was sitting on the other side of Mordecai Jones, who sometimes and with poor grace responded to the nickname Harlem Hammer. Jones was concentrating on *The New York Times* crossword puzzle and acting as if no one else were there. 'He's a lawyer, you know. Been defending radicals since Andy Baader's salad days.'

'Helping damned terrorists get off with a slap on the wrists, you mean.'

Blum laughed and shrugged. He was leaner and darker than

Möller, and he wore his curly black hair shaggy enough to push even the notoriously liberal standards of the Berlin *Schutzpolizei*. But his brown artist's eyes were watchful, and the way he held himself suggested he knew how to use the tiny machine pistol in the shoulder holster that bulked out his gray suit coat in a way not even meticulous German tailoring could altogether conceal.

'Even radicals have a right to representation. This is Berlin, *Mensch*. We take freedom seriously here – if only to set an example for our neighbors, *ja?*' Möller made a skeptical sound low in his throat.

Ronnie fidgeted on the seat and checked his watch. 'Maybe we could go a little faster? We don't want to be late.'

The driver flashed a grin over his shoulder. He resembled a smaller edition of Tom Cruise, though more ferret faced. He couldn't have been as young as he looked. 'The streets are narrow here. We don't want to have an accident. Then we'd be even later.'

Hartmann's aide set his mouth and fussed with papers in the briefcase open on his lap. Hartmann slid another glance toward the bulk of the Hammer, who was still stolidly ignoring everybody. Puppetman was amazingly quiescent, given his gut dread of aces. Maybe he was even feeling a certain thrill at Jones's proximity.

Not that Jones looked like an ace. He appeared to be a normal black man in his mid to late thirties, bearded, balding, solidly built, looking none too well at ease knotted into coat and tie. Nothing out of the ordinary.

As a matter of fact he weighed four hundred and seventy pounds and had to sit in the center of the Merc so it wouldn't list. He might be the strongest man in the world, stronger than Golden Boy perhaps, but he refused to engage in any kind of competition to settle the issue. He disliked being an ace, disliked being a celebrity, disliked politicians, and thought the entire tour was a waste of time. Hartmann had the impression he'd only agreed to come along because his neighbors in Harlem got such a kick out of his being in the spotlight, and he hated to let them down.

Jones was a token. He knew it. He resented it. That was one reason Hartmann had goaded him into coming to the Aide et Amitié luncheon; that and the fact that for all their pious pretensions of brotherhood, most Germans didn't like blacks and were uncomfortable around them; they pretended, but that wasn't the sort of thing you could hide from Puppetman. *He* found the Hammer's pique and the discomfort of their hosts amusing; almost worthwhile to take Jones on as a puppet. But not quite. The Hammer was known primarily as a muscleman ace, but the full scope of his powers was a mystery. Any chance of discovery was too much for Puppetman.

Beyond the minor titillations poking everyone off balance provided, Hartmann was getting fed up with Billy Ray. Carnifex had fumed and blustered when Hartmann ditched him with the rest of the tour back at the Wall – detailed to escort Mrs. Hartmann and the senator's two senior aides back to the hotel – but he couldn't say much without offending their hosts, whose security men were on the job. And anyway, with the Hammer along, what could possibly happen?

'*Scheisse,*' the driver said. He had turned a corner to find a gray and white telephone van parked blocking the street next to an open manhole. He braked to a halt.

'Idiots,' said Möller. 'They're not supposed to do that.' He unlocked the passenger door.

Beside Hartmann, Blum flicked his eyes to the rearview mirror. 'Uh-oh,' he said softly. His right hand went inside his coat.

Hartmann craned his neck. A second van had cranked itself across the street not thirty feet behind them. Its doors were open, spilling people onto pavement wet from the rain spasm. They held weapons. Blum shouted a warning to his partner.

A figure loomed up beside the car. A terrible metal screeching filled the limousine. Hartmann's breath turned solid in his throat as a hand cut through the roof of the car in a shower of sparks.

Möller winced away. He drew his MP5K from its shoulder holster, pressed it to the window, and fired a burst. Glass exploded outward.

The hand snapped back. 'Jesus *Christ,*' Möller shouted, 'the bullets went right through him!'

He threw open the door. A man with a ski mask over his face fired an assault rifle from the rear of the telephone van.

The noise rattled the car's thick windows, on and on. It sounded oddly remote. The windshield starred. The man who'd cut through the roof screamed and went down. Möller danced back three steps, fell against the Mercedes's fender, collapsed to the pavement squirming and screaming. His coat fell open. Scarlet spiders clung to his chest.

The assault rifle ran dry. The sudden silence was thunderous. Puppetman's fingers were clenched on the padded handle of the door as Möller's mindscream jolted into him like speed hitting the main line. He gasped, at the hot mad pleasure of it, at the cold rush of his own fear.

'*Hände hoch!*' shouted a figure beside the van that had boxed them from behind. 'Hands up!'

Mordecai Jones put a big hand on Hartmann's shoulder and pushed him to the floor. He clambered over him, careful not to squash him, put his weight against the door. Metal wailed and it came away with him as Blum, more conventional, pulled the lever on his own door to disengage the latching mechanism, twisted, and shouldered it open. He brought his MP5K up with his left hand clutching the vestigial foregrip, aimed the stubby machine pistol back around the frame as Hartmann yelled, '*Don't shoot!*'

The Hammer was racing toward the telephone van. The terrorist who'd shot Möller pointed his weapon at him, pumped his finger on the empty weapon's trigger in a comic pantomime of panic. Jones backhanded him gently. He sailed backward to rebound off the front of a building and land in a heap on the sidewalk.

The moment hung in air like a suspended chord. Jones squatted, got his hands under the phone van's frame. He strained, straightened. The van came up with him. Its driver screamed in terror. The Hammer shifted his grip and pressed the vehicle over his head as if it were a not-particularly-heavy barbell.

A burst of gunfire stuttered from the second van. Bullets shredded open the back of Jones's coat. He teetered, almost lost it, swung in a ponderous circle with the van still balanced above his head. Then several terrorists fired at once. He grimaced and fell backward.

The van landed right on top of him.

The limo driver had his door open and a little black P7 in his hand. As the Hammer fell, Blum blazed a quick burst at the van behind. A man ducked back as 9mm bullets punched neat holes in thin metal – a joker, Hartmann realized. *What the hell's going on here?*

He ducked his head below window level and grabbed at Blum's coattail. He felt the vehicle shudder on its suspension as bullets struck it. The driver gasped and slumped out of the car. Hartmann heard somebody yelling in English to cease fire. He shouted for Blum to quit shooting.

The policeman turned toward him. 'Yes, sir,' he said. Then a burst punched through his opened door and sugared the glass in the window and threw him against the senator.

Ronnie was plastered against the back of the driver's seat. 'Oh, God,' he moaned. 'Oh, dear God!' He jumped out the door the Hammer had torn from its hinges and ran, with papers scattered from his briefcase swooping around him like seagulls.

The terrorist Mordecai Jones had brushed aside had recovered enough to come to one knee and stuff another magazine into his AKM. He brought it to his shoulder and emptied it at the senator's aide in a juddering burst. A scream and mist of blood sprayed from Ronnie's mouth. He fell and skidded.

Hartmann huddled on the floor in fugue, half-terrified, half-orgasmic. Blum was dying, holding on to Hartmann's arm, the holes in his chest sucking like lamia mouths, his life-force surging into the senator like arrhythmic surf.

'I'm hurt,' the policeman said. 'Oh, mama, mama please—' He died. Hartmann jerked like a harpooned seal as the last of the man's life gushed into him.

Out by the street Hartmann's young aide was dragging himself along with his arms, glasses askew, leaving a snail-trail of blood on the sidewalk. The slightly built terrorist who had shot him ambled up, stuffing a third magazine into his weapon. He positioned himself in front of the wounded man.

Ronnie blinked up at him. Disjointedly Hartmann remembered he was desperately nearsighted, virtually blind without his glasses.

'Please,' Ronnie said, and blood rolled from his mouth. 'Please.'

'Have a *Negerkuss*,' the terrorist said, and fired a single shot into his forehead.

'Dear God,' Hartmann said. A shadow fell across him, heavy as a corpse. He looked up with inhuman eyes at a figure black against the gray-cloud sky beyond. A hand gripped him by the arm, electricity blasted through him, and consciousness exploded in ozone convulsion.

Substantial again, Mackie bounced to his feet and tore off his ski mask. 'You shot at me! You could have killed me,' he shrieked at Anneke. His face was almost black.

She laughed at him.

The world seemed to come on to Mackie in Kodachrome colors. He started for her, hand beginning to buzz, when a commotion behind him brought his head around.

The dwarf had grabbed Ulrich's rifle by the still-hot muzzle brake and spun him round, echoing Mackie's theme, with variations. 'You stupid bastard, you could have killed him!' he screamed. '*You could have offed the fucking senator!*'

Ulrich had fired the final burst that downed the cop in the back of the limousine. Weight lifter though he was, he was only just hanging on to his piece against the dwarf's surprising strength. The two were orbiting each other out there on the street, spitting at one another like cats.

Mackie had to laugh.

Then Mólniya was beside him, touching his shoulder with a gloved hand. 'Let it go. We have to move quickly.'

Mackie arched like a cat to meet the touch. Comrade Mólniya was worried he was still mad at Anneke for shooting at him and then laughing about it.

But that was forgotten. Anneke was laughing too, over the body of the man she'd just finished off, and Mackie had to laugh with her.

'A *Negerkuss*,' he said. 'You said did he want a *Negerkuss*. Huh huh. That was pretty good.' It meant *Negro Kiss*, a small chocolate-covered cake. It was especially funny since they'd told him Negro Kisses were a trademark of the group from back in the old days, back when all of them but Wolf were kids.

It was nervous laughter, relieved laughter. He'd thought he'd lost it when the pig shot at him; he'd just seen the gun come up in time to phase out, and the anger burned black within him, the desire to make his hand vibrate till it was hard as a knife blade and drive it into that fucking cop, to make sure he felt the buzz, to feel the hot rush of blood along his arm and spraying in his face. But the bastard was dead, it was too late now ...

He'd worried again when the black man picked up the van, but then Comrade Ulrich shot him. He was strong, but he wasn't immune to bullets. Mackie liked Comrade Ulrich. He was so self-assured, so handsome and muscular. Women liked him; Anneke could hardly keep her hands off him. Mackie might have envied him, if he hadn't been an ace.

Mackie didn't have a gun himself. He hated them, and anyway he didn't need a weapon – there wasn't any weapon better than his own body.

The American joker called Scrape was fumbling Hartmann's limp body out of the limousine. 'Is he dead?' Mackie called in German, caught up by sudden panic. The dwarf let go of Ulrich's rifle and stared wildly at the car. Ulrich almost fell over.

Scrape looked up at Mackie, face frozen into immobility by its exoskeleton, but his lack of understanding clear from the tilt of his head. Mackie repeated the question in the halting English he'd learned from his mother before the worthless bitch had died and deserted him.

Comrade Mólniya pulled his other glove back on. He wore no mask, and now Mackie noticed he looked a little green at the sight of the blood spilled all over the street. 'He's fine,' he replied for Scrape. 'I just shocked him unconscious. Come now, we must hurry.'

Mackie grinned and bobbed his head. He felt a certain satisfaction at Mólniya's squeamishness, even though he wanted to please the Russian ace almost as much as he did his own cell leader Wolf. He went to help Scrape, though he hated being so close to the joker. He feared he might touch him accidentally; the thought made his flesh crawl.

Comrade Wolf stood by with his own unfired Kalashnikov dangling from one huge hand. 'Get him in the van,' he ordered. 'Him too.' He nodded to Comrade Wilfried, who'd stumbled from the driver's seat of the telephone van and was on his knees pitching breakfast on the wet asphalt.

It started to rain again. Broad pools of blood on the pavement began to fray like banners whipped by the wind. In the distance sirens commenced their hair-raising chant.

They put Hartmann into the second van. Scrape got behind the wheel. Mólniya slid in beside him. The joker backed up onto the sidewalk, turned, and drove away.

Mackie sat on the wheel well, drumming a heavy-metal beat on his thighs. *We did it! We captured him!* He could barely sit still. His penis was stiff inside his jeans.

Out the back window he saw Ulrich spraying letters on a wall in red paint: RAF. He laughed again. That would make the bourgeoisie shit their pants, that was for sure. Ten years ago those initials had been a synonym for terror in the Federal Republic. Now they would be again. It gave Mackie happy chills to think about it.

A joker wrapped head to toe in a shabby cloak stepped up and sprayed three more letters beneath the first with a hand wrapped in bandages: JJS.

The other van heeled way over to the side as its wheels rolled over the supine body of the black American ace, and they were gone.

With her NEC laptop computer tucked under one arm and a a bit of her cheek caught between her small side teeth, Sara strode across the lobby of the Bristol Hotel Kempinski with briskness that an outside observer would probably have taken for confidence. It was a misapprehension that had served her well in the past.

Reflexively she ducked into the bar of Berlin's most luxurious hotel. *The tour proper's long since been mined out, at least of stuff we can print*, she thought, *but what the heck?* She felt heat in her ears at the thought that she was the star of one of the tour's choicer unprintable vignettes.

Inside was dark, of course. All bars are the same song; the polished wood and brass and old pliable leather and elephant ears were grace notes to set apart this particular refrain. She tipped her sunglasses up on top of her nearly white hair, drawn back this afternoon in a severe ponytail, and let her eyes adjust. They always adjusted to dark more quickly than light.

The bar wasn't crowded. A pair of waiters in arm garters and starched highboy collars worked their way among the tables as if by radar. Three Japanese businessmen sat at a table chattering and pointing at a newspaper, discussing either the exchange rates or the local tit bars, depending.

In the corner Hiram was talking shop, in French of course, with the Kempinski's *cordon bleu*, who was shorter than he was but at least as round. The hotel chef had a tendency to flap his short arms rapidly when he spoke, which made him look like a fat baby bird that wasn't getting the hang of flight.

Chrysalis sat at the bar drinking in splendid isolation. There was no joker chic here. In Germany, Chrysalis found herself discreetly avoided rather than lionized.

She caught Sara's eye and winked. In the poor light Sara only knew it because of the way Chrysalis's mascaraed eyelashes tracked across a staring eyeball. She smiled. Professional associates back home, sometime rivals in the bartering of information that was the meta-game of Jokertown, they'd grown to be friends on this trip. Sara had more in common with Debra-Jo than her nominal peers who were along.

At least Chrysalis was dressed. She was showing a different face to Europe than she did the country she pretended wasn't her native one. Sometimes Sara envied her, secretly. People looked at her and saw a joker, an exotic, alluring and grotesque. But they didn't see *her*.

'Looking for me, little lady?'

Sara started, turned. Jack Braun sat at the end of the bar, hardly five feet from her. She hadn't noticed him. She had a tendency to edit him out; the force of him made her uncomfortable.

'I'm going out,' she said. She slapped the computer, a touch harder than necessary, so her fingers stung. 'Down to the main post office to file my latest material by modem. It's the only place you can get a transatlantic connection that won't scramble all your data.'

'I'm surprised you're not off pushing cookies with Senator Gregg,' he said, eyeing her cantwise from beneath bushy eyebrows.

She felt color come to her cheeks. 'Senator *Hartmann* attending a banquet may be a hot item for my colleagues with the celebrity-hunting glossies. But it's not exactly hard news, is it, Mr. Braun?'

It was an open afternoon. There wasn't much hard news here, not the kind to interest readers following the WHO tour. The West German authorities had blandly assured the visitors there was no wild card problem in *their* country, and used the tour as a counter in whatever game they were playing with their Siamese twin to the east – that damp, dreary ceremony this morning, for instance. Of course they were right: even proportionally, the number of German wild card victims was minuscule. The most pathetic or unsightly couple of thousand were kept discreetly tucked away in state housing or clinics. Much as they'd sneered at Americans for their treatment of jokers during the Sixties and Seventies, the Germans were embarrassed by their own.

'Depends on what gets said at the banquet, I guess. What's on your schedule after you file your piece, little lady?' He was grinning that B-movie leading-man grin at her. Golden highlights glimmered on the planes and contour edges of his face. He was flexing his muscles to bring on the glow that gave him his ace name. Irritation tightened the skin at the outskirts of her eyes. He was either coming on to her for real or teasing her. Either way she didn't like it.

'I have work to do. And I could use a little time to catch my breath. Some of us have had a busy time on this tour.'

Is that really the reason you were relieved when Gregg dropped the hint that it might not be discreet to tag along to the banquet with him? she wondered. She frowned, surprised at the thought, and turned crisply away.

Braun's big hand closed on her arm. She gasped and spun back to him, angry and starting to panic. What could she do against a man who could lift a bus? That detached observer inside her, the journalist within, reflected on the irony that Gregg, whom she'd come to hate, yes, obsessively, should be the first man in years whose touch she'd come to welcome—

But Jack Braun was frowning past her, into the lobby of the hotel. It was filling up with purposeful, husky young men in suit coats.

One of them came into the bar, looked hard at Braun, consulted a piece of paper in his hand. 'Herr Braun?'

'That's me. What can I do you for?'

'I am with the Berlin *Landespolizei*. I'm afraid I must ask you not to leave the hotel.'

Braun pushed his jaw forward. 'And why might that be?'

'Senator Hartmann has been kidnapped.'

◆

Ellen Hartmann shut the door with eggshell care and turned away. The flowered vines fading in the carpet seemed to twine about her ankles as she walked back into the suite and sat down on the bed.

Her eyes were dry. They stung, but they were dry. She smiled slightly. It was hard to let her emotions go. She had so much experience controlling her emotions for the cameras. And Gregg—

I know what he is. But what he is is all I have.

She picked up a handkerchief from the bedside table and methodically began to tear it to pieces.

'Welcome to the land of the living, Senator. For the moment at least.'

Slowly Hartmann's mind drained into consciousness. There was a tinny taste in his mouth and a singing in his ears. His right upper arm ached as if from sunburn. Someone hummed a familiar song. A radio muttered.

His eyes opened to darkness. He felt the obligatory twinge of blindness anxiety, but something pressed his eyeballs, and from the small stinging pull at the back of his head he guessed it was taped gauze. His wrists were bound behind the back of a wooden chair.

After the awareness of captivity, what struck hardest was the smells: sweat, grease, mildew, dust, sodden cloth, unfamiliar spices; ancient urine and fresh gun oil, crowding his nostrils clear to his sinuses.

He inventoried all these things before permitting himself to recognize the rasping voice.

'Tom Miller,' he said. 'I wish I could say it's a pleasure.'

'Ah, yes, Senator. But *I* can.' He could feel Gimli's gloating as he could smell his stinking breath – toothpaste and mouthwash belonged to the surface-worshiping nat world. 'I could also say you have no idea how long I've waited for this, but of course you do. You know full well.'

'Since we know each other so well, why don't you undo my eyes, Tom.' As he spoke he probed with his power. It had been ten years since he'd last had physical contact with the dwarf, but he didn't think the link, once created, ever decayed. Puppetman feared loss of control more than anything but discovery; and being discovered itself represented the ultimate loss of power. If he could get his hooks back into Miller's soul, Hartmann could at the very least be sure of holding down the panic that bubbled like magma low in his throat.

'Gimli!' the dwarf shouted. His spittle sprayed Hartmann's lips and cheeks.

Instantly Hartmann dropped the link. Puppetman reeled. For a moment he'd felt Gimli's hatred blazing like an incandescent wire. *He suspects!*

Most of what he'd sensed was the hate. But beneath that, beneath the conscious surface of Gimli's mind lay awareness that there was something out of the ordinary about Gregg Hartmann, something inextricably tied to the bloody shambles of the Jokertown Riots. Gimli wasn't an ace, Hartmann was sure of that. But Gimli's natural paranoia was itself something of a sixth sense.

For the first time in his life Puppetman faced the possibility he had lost a puppet.

He knew he blanched, knew he flinched, but fortunately his reaction passed for squeamishness at being spat on.

'Gimli,' the dwarf repeated, and Hartmann sensed he was turning away. 'That's my name. And the mask stays on, Senator. You know me, but the same doesn't apply to everybody here. And they'd like to keep it that way.'

'That's not going to work too well, Gimli. You think a ski mask is going to disguise a joker with a furry snout? I – that is, if anybody saw you grab me, they'll have little enough trouble identifying you and your gang.'

He was saying too much, he belatedly realized – he didn't want Miller dwelling too much on the fact that Hartmann could make him and some of his accomplices. Whatever had put him out had stirred his brains like omelette batter.

– an electrical shock of some sort, he thought. Back in the Sixties he'd been a freedom rider briefly – it was an up-and-coming New Frontier sort of thing to do, and there was always the hatred, heady as wine, the possibility of lovely violence, crimson and indigo. A peckerwood state trooper had nailed him with a cattle prod during the Selma protests, which was too firsthand for his taste and sent him back north in a hurry. But it had felt like that, back in the limousine.

'Come now, Gimli,' said a gritty baritone voice in accented but clear English. 'Why not have the mask off? The whole world will know us soon enough.'

'Oh, all right,' Gimli said. Puppetman could taste his resentment without having to reach. Tom Miller was having to share stage with someone, and he didn't like it. Little bubbles of interest began to well up through the seethe of Hartmann's incipient panic.

Hartmann heard the scrape of feet on bare floor. Someone fumbled briefly, cursed, and then he caught his breath involuntarily as the tape was unwound, pulling reluctantly away from his hair and skin.

The first thing he saw was Gimli's face. It still looked like a bagful of rotten apples. The look of exultation didn't improve it any. Hartmann pushed his gaze past the dwarf to the rest of the room.

It was a shitty little tenement, like shitty little tenements pretty much everywhere in the world. The wooden floor was stained and the striped wallpaper had patches of damp like a workman's armpits. From the general scatter of crunchy and crinkly trash underfoot, Hartmann guessed the place was derelict. Still, a light-bulb glared in a busted-globe fixture overhead, and he felt a radiator drumming out too much heat the way every radiator in Germany did until it came down June.

For all he knew he could be in the Eastern sector, which was a hell of a cheery thought. On the other hand, he'd been in German homes before. This one smelled *wrong*, somehow.

There were three other overt jokers in the room, one swathed from head to feet in a dusty-looking cowled robe, one covered with yellowish chitin dotted with tiny red pimples, a third the furry one he'd seen next to the van. The three young nats in Hartmann's field of vision looked offensively normal by comparison.

His power felt others behind him. That was strange. He wasn't usually able to taste another's emotions, unless that one was broadcasting strongly, or was a puppet. He sensed a peculiar squirming in the power inside him.

He glanced back. Two more back there, nats to the eye, though the scrawny youth leaning on the stained wall next to the radiator had an odd look to him. A man in his mid-thirties sat next to him in a gaudy plastic chair with his hands in the pockets of an overcoat. Hartmann thought the older man was subconsciously straining away from the younger; when their eyes met he caught a quick impression of sadness.

That's odd, he thought. Maybe tension had heightened his normal perceptions; maybe he was imagining things. But something was coming off that kid as he grinned at Hartmann, something that prickled all around the edges of his awareness. Again he had that evasive feeling from Puppetman.

A shoe crunched debris. He turned, found himself looking up at an enormous nat dressed in suit coat and trousers of an odd tan-green, almost military. The man had no tie; his shirt collar hung unbuttoned around a thick neck, open to a spray of grizzled blond chest hair. Big hands rested on his hips with the coattails swept up behind, like something out of a little theater production of *Inherit the Wind*. His long hair lay combed back from a high forehead.

He smiled. He had one of those rugged ugly faces women fall for and men believe.

'A very great pleasure to meet you, Senator.' It was the rolling sea swell of the voice he'd heard urge Gimli to remove his blindfold.

'You have the advantage.'

'That's true. Oh, but I daresay my name won't be unfamiliar to you. I am Wolfgang Prahler.'

Behind Hartmann someone *tsked* in exasperation. Prahler frowned, then laughed. 'Ah, now, Comrade Mólniya, do I break security? Well, did we not agree that we must come out into the light of day to accomplish a task so important?'

Like many educated Berliners he spoke English with a pronouncedly British cast. From behind, Puppetman felt a flicker of agitation at the name *Mólniya*. It was Russian. It meant *lightning*; the Soviets had a series of communications satellites by that name.

'What exactly is going on here?' Hartmann demanded. His heart lurched at the words. He didn't mean to take that tone with cold-blooded killers who had him altogether at their mercy. But Puppetman, coming suddenly into arrogance, had taken the bit in his teeth. 'Couldn't you wait until the *Aide et Amitié* banquet to make my acquaintance?'

Prahler's laugh resonated up from deep in his chest. 'Very good.

But have you not figured it out? It was never intended you should reach the banquet, Senator. You were, as you Americans say, set up.'

'Drawn to the bait and trapped,' said a slight redheaded woman who wore a black turtleneck and jeans. 'Set cheese for a rat; set a fine banquet to catch a fine lord.'

'Rats and lords,' a voice repeated. 'A fine rat. A fine lord.' It giggled. It was a male voice, cracked and adolescent: the leather boy. Hartmann felt a tickle run along the cord of his scrotum like the fingers of a whore. No doubt about it. He was getting emotion from him like static on a line. A hint of something potent – something terrible. For once Puppetman felt no desire to probe further.

He feared this one. More than the others, Prahler, these casual youths with guns. Even Gimli.

'You went to all this trouble to help Gimli here settle an old, imaginary score?' he made himself say. 'That's generous of you.'

'We're doing this for the revolution,' said a youthful nat with a blond flattop and a heat-lamp tan and the air of having worked hard to memorize the line. His turtleneck and jeans were molded around an athlete's figure. He stood by the wall caressing the muzzle brake of a Soviet assault rifle grounded by his foot.

'You're of no significance, Senator,' the woman said. She flipped her square-cut bangs off her forehead. 'Simply a tool. What your naive egotism tells you notwithstanding.'

'Who the hell are you people?'

'We bear the sacred name of the Red Army Faction,' she told him. She hovered over a stocky youngster who sat cross-legged fiddling with a radio perched on a warped wooden nightstand. He wouldn't meet Hartmann's eyes.

'Comrade Wolf gave it to us,' the blond boy said. 'He used to hang out with Baader and Meinhof and them. They used to be close like this.' He held up a clenched fist.

Hartmann sucked in his lips. Since the terrorist wars had gotten underway for true in the early Seventies, it wasn't uncommon for radical attorneys to come to involve themselves directly in the activities of those they represented in court, especially in Germany and Italy. Apparently, if what the kid said was true, Prahler had been a leader in the Baader-Meinhof group and the RAF all along, without the authorities ever getting wind of the fact.

Hartmann looked at Tom Miller. 'I'll rephrase my question. How did *you* get mixed up in this, Gimli?'

'We just happened to be in the right place at the right time, Senator.'

The dwarf smirked at him. Puppetman felt an urge to crush that smug face, to tear out the dwarf's guts and throttle him with them. The frustration was physical torment.

Sweat crawled down Hartmann's forehead like a centipede. His emotions were oddly distinct from Puppetman's. His other self whipsawed from rage to fear. What he mostly felt now was tired and annoyed.

And sad. *Poor Ronnie. He meant so well. He tried so hard.*

The redhead suddenly slapped the seated man on the shoulder. 'You idiot, Wilfried, there it was! You went past it.' He mumbled apology and dialed back.

'—captured by the Red Army Faction, acting in concert with comrades from the Jokers for a Just Society who have fled persecution in Amerika.' It was Comrade Wolf's voice, pouring like liquid amber from the cheap little radio. 'The terms of his release are these: release of the Palestinian freedom fighter al-Muezzin. An airliner with sufficient fuel to take al-Muezzin to a country in the liberated Third World. Immunity from prosecution for members of this action team. We demand that the Jetboy memorial be torn down and in its place a facility built to provide shelter and medical attention to joker victims of Amerikan intolerance. And finally, just to poke the capitalist swine where it most hurts them, ten million dollars cash, which will be used to aid victims of Amerikan aggression in Central Amerika.

'If these terms are not met by ten o'clock tonight, Berlin time, Senator Gregg Hartmann will be executed.

'We return you now to regularly scheduled programming.'

'We have to do something.' Hiram Worchester tangled his fingers in his beard and gazed out the window at the patchy Berlin sky.

Digger Downs turned over a card. Trey of clubs. He grimaced.

Billy Ray paced the carpet of Hiram's suite like a tyrannosaurus with an itch. 'If I'd been there, this shit would never have happened,' he said, and aimed a green glare at Mordecai Jones.

The Hammer sat on the sofa. It was oak and flowered upholstery, and like many of the hotel's furnishings had survived the war. Fortunately they'd built stout furniture back in the 1890s.

Jones made a dirty-gearbox noise toward the center of him and stared at his big hands, which he was working into tangles between his knees.

The door opened and Peregrine flew into the room. Figuratively, at least, her wings jittering on her back. She wore a loose velour blouse and jeans that muted the advanced state of her pregnancy.

'I just heard on the radio – isn't it terrible?' Then she stopped and stared at the Hammer. 'Mordecai – what on earth are *you* doing here?'

'Just like you, Ms. Peregrine. Won't let me out.'

'But why aren't you in the hospital? The reports said you were terribly injured.'

'Just shot a little.' He slapped his gut. 'Got me a pretty tough hide, kind of like that Kevlar stuff you read about in *Popular Science*.'

Downs turned up a new card. Red eight. 'Shit,' he muttered.

'But a *van* fell on you,' Peregrine said.

'Yeah, but see, I got these funky heavy metals replacing the calcium in my bones, so they're like stronger and more flexible and all, and my innards and whatnot are a lot sturdier than most folks'. And I heal mighty fast – don't even get sick – since I turned up my ace. I'm a pretty durable sort of dude.'

'Then why'd you let them get away?' Bill Ray challenged, almost shouting. 'Goddamn, the senator was your responsibility. You could've kicked some *ass*.'

'To tell you the entire truth, Mr. Ray, it hurt like a sonofabitch. I wasn't good for much for a while there.'

The *Mister* came out differently than *Ms.* had. Billy Ray cocked his head and looked hard at him. Jones ignored him.

'Lay off him, Billy,' said Carnifex's partner, Lady Black, who sat to one side with her long legs crossed at the ankles before her.

Peregrine came and touched Mordecai on the shoulder. 'It must have been awful. I'm surprised they let you out of the hospital.'

'They didn't,' Downs said, splitting open the deck in his left hand to catch a peek inside. 'He released himself. Smashed right through the wall. The public health people are kind of pissed about it.'

Jones looked down at the floor. 'Don't like doctors,' he muttered.

Peregrine looked around. 'Where's Sara? The poor thing. This must be hell for her.'

'They let *her* go over to the crisis control center in City Hall. No other reporter from the tour. Just her.' Downs made a face and went back to his solitaire game.

'Sara took over a statement from Mr. Jones about what he saw and heard during the abduction,' Lady Black said. 'He didn't give one before he left the hospital.' After the accident that triggered his wild card virus, Jones had been held by the Oklahoma Department of Public Health as a lab specimen, a virtual prisoner. The experience had given him an almost pathological fear of medical science and all its appurtenances.

'Funny damn thing,' Jones said, shaking his head. 'I was lying there trying to breathe with this fu – with this van on my chest, and I keep hearing all these people yelling at each other. Like little kids fightin' on a playground.'

Hiram turned from the window. The rings that had been sinking in around his eyes since the tour began were even more pronounced. 'I understand,' he said, bringing his hands up cupped before his chest. They were dainty hands, and fit oddly with his bulk. 'I understand what's happening here. This has been a blow to all of us. Senator Hartmann isn't just the last best hope for jokers to get a fair shake – and maybe aces too, with this crazy Barnett fellow on the loose – he's our *friend*. We're trying to soften the blow by talking around the subject. But it won't do. We have to *do* something.'

'That's what I say.' Billy Ray slammed a fist into his palm. 'Let's kick butts and take names!'

'Whose butt?' Lady Black asked tiredly. 'Whose name?'

'That sawed-off little bastard Gimli for starters. We should have grabbed him when he was dicking around New York last summer—'

'Where are you going to find him?'

He flung out his arm. 'Hell, that's why we ought to be looking for him, instead of sitting here on our duffs wringing our hands and saying how sorry we are the fucking senator's gone.'

'There are ten thousand cops out there combing the streets,' Lady Black said. 'You think we'll find him quicker?'

'But what can we do, Hiram?' Peregrine asked. Her face was pale, and the skin stretched tight over her cheekbones. 'I feel so helpless.' Her wings opened slightly, then folded again.

Hiram's little pink tongue dabbed his lips. 'Peri, I wish I knew. Surely there must be something—'

'They mentioned ransom,' Digger Downs said.

Hiram punched his palm twice in unconscious imitation of Carnifex. 'That's it. That's it! Maybe we can raise enough money to buy him back.'

'Ten million's a lot of bread,' Mordecai said.

'That's just a bargaining position,' Hiram said, sweeping aside objections with his small hands. 'Surely we can work them down.'

'What about their demands this terrorist dude be released? We can't do nothing about that.'

'Money talks,' Downs said. 'Nobody walks.'

'Inelegantly put,' Hiram said, beginning to drift here and there like an ungainly cloud, 'but correct. Surely if we can scrape together sufficient funds, they'll leap at our offer.'

'Now, wait a minute—' Carnifex began.

'I'm a man of not inconsiderable means,' Hiram said, scooping up a handful of mints from a silver salver in passing. 'I can contribute a fair amount—'

'I have money,' Peregrine said excitedly. 'I'll help.'

Mordecai frowned. 'I'm not crazy about politicians, but shoot, I feel I *lost* the man and shit. Count me in, for what it's worth.'

'Hold on, dammit!' Billy Ray said. 'President Reagan has already announced there will be no negotiating with these terrorists.'

'Maybe he'll go for it if we throw in a Bible and a mess of rocket launchers,' Mordecai said.

Hiram elevated his chin. 'We're private citizens, Mr. Ray. We can do as we please.'

'We'll by God see—'

The door opened. Xavier Desmond walked in. 'I couldn't bear to sit alone any longer,' he said. 'I'm so worried – my God, Mordecai, what are you doing here?'

'Never mind that, Des,' Hiram said. 'We've got a plan.'

The man from the Federal Criminal Office tapped his pack of cigarettes on the edge of the desk in the crisis center in City Hall, shook out a cigarette, and put it between his lips. 'What on earth were you thinking of, permitting that to go over the air without consulting me!' He made no move to light the cigarette. He had a young man's face with an old man's wrinkles, and lynx yellow eyes. His ears stuck out.

'Herr Neumann,' the mayor's representative said, trapping the phone receiver between his shoulder and a couple of chins and getting it quite sweaty, 'here in Berlin our reflex is to shy away from censorship. We had enough of that in the bad old days, *na ja?*'

'I don't mean that. How are we to control this situation if we're not even *informed* when steps like this are taken?' He leaned back and stroked a finger down one of the furrows that bracketed his mouth. 'This could turn into Munich all over again.'

Tachyon studied the digital clock built into the high heel of one of the pair of boots he'd bought on the Ku'damm the day before. Aside from the clocks he was in full seventeenth-century regalia. *This tour was a political stunt*, he thought. *But still, we might have accomplished some good. Is this how it's going to end?*

'Who is this al-Muezzin?' he asked.

'Daoud Hassani is his name. He's an ace who can destroy things with his voice, rather like your own late ace Howler,' Neumann said. If he noticed Tachyon's wince he gave no sign. 'He's from Palestine. He's one of Nur al-Allah's people, works out of Syria. He claimed responsibility for the downing of that El Al jetliner at Orly last June.'

'I'm afraid we've heard far from the last of the Light of Allah,' Tachyon said. Neumann nodded grimly. Since the tour had left Syria, there had been three dozen bombings worldwide in retribution for its 'treacherous attack' on the ace prophet.

If only that wretched woman had finished the job, Tach thought. He was careful not to speak it aloud. These Earthers could be sensitive about such things.

Sweat ran down the side of his neck and into the lace collar of his blouse. The radiator hummed and groaned with heat. *I wish they were less sensitive to cold. Why do these Germans insist on making their hot planet so much hotter?*

The door opened. Clamor spilled in from the international press corps crammed into the corridor outside. A political aide slipped inside and whispered to the mayor's man. The mayor's man petulantly slammed down his phone.

'Ms. Morgenstern has come from the Kempinski,' he announced.

'Bring her in at once,' Tachyon said.

The mayor's man jutted his underlip, which gleamed wet in the fluorescents. 'Impossible. She's a member of the press, and we have excluded the press from this room for the duration.'

Tachyon looked at the man down the length of his fine, straight nose. 'I demand that Ms. Morgenstern be admitted at once,' he said in that tone of voice reserved on Takis for grooms who tread on freshly polished boots and serving maids who spill soup on heads of allied Psi Lord houses who are guesting in the manor.

'Let her in,' Neumann said. 'She's brought Herr Jones's tape for us.'

Sara was wearing a white trench coat with a hand-wide belt red as a bloody bandage. Tach shook his head. Like all fashion statements she made, this one jarred.

She came to him. They shared a brief, dry embrace. She turned away, unslinging her heavy handbag.

Tachyon wondered. Had that been a touch of metal in her watercolor eyes, or only tears?

◆

'Did you hear that?' the redhead called Anneke warbled. 'One of the pigs we got today was a Jew.'

Early afternoon. The radio simmered with reports and conjectures about the kidnapping. The terrorists were exalted, strutting and puffing for each other's benefit.

'One more drop of blood to avenge our brothers in Palestine,' said Wolf sonorously.

'What about the nigger ace?' demanded the one who looked like a lifeguard and answered to Ulrich. 'Has he died yet?'

'He's not going to anytime soon,' Anneke said. 'According to the news, he walked out of the hospital within an hour of being admitted.'

'That's bullshit! I hit him with half a magazine. I saw that van fall on him.'

Anneke sidled over from the radio and ran her fingers along the line of Ulrich's jaw. 'Don't you think if he can lift a van all by himself, he might be a little hard to hurt, sweetheart?'

She stood up on the toes of her sneakers and kissed him just behind the lobe of his ear. 'Besides, we killed two—'

'Three,' said Comrade Wilfried, who was still monitoring the airwaves. 'The other, uh, policeman just died.' He swallowed.

Anneke clapped her hands in delight. 'You see?'

'I killed somebody too,' said the boy's voice from behind Hartmann. Just the sound of it filled Puppetman with energy. *Easy, easy,* Hartmann cautioned his other half, wondering, *do I have this one? Is it possible to create a puppet without knowing it? Or is he constantly emoting at such a pitch that I can feel it without having the link?*

The power didn't answer.

The leather boy shuffled forward. Hartmann saw he was hunchbacked. A joker?

'Comrade Dieter,' the teenager said. 'I offed him – *brrr* – like *that*!' He held his hands up in front of him and suddenly they were vibrating like a powersaw blade, a blur of lethality.

An ace! Hartmann's own breath hit him in the chest.

The vibration stopped. The boy showed yellow teeth around at the others. They were very quiet.

Through the pounding in his ears Hartmann heard a scrape of tubular metal on wood as the man in the coat got up from his chair. 'You killed someone, Mackie?' he asked mildly. His German was a touch too perfect to be natural. 'Why?'

Mackie tucked his head down. 'He was an informer, Comrade,' he said sidelong. His eyes jittered between Wolf and the other. 'Comrade Wolf ordered me to take him into custody. But he – he tried to kill me! That was it. He pulled a gun on me and I *buzzed* him off.' He brandished a vibrating hand again.

The man came slowly forward where Hartmann could see him. He was medium height, dressed well but not too well, hair neat and blond. A man just on the handsome side of nondescriptness. Except for his hands, which were encased in what appeared to be thick rubber gloves. Hartmann watched them in sudden fascination.

'Why wasn't I told of this, Wolf?' The voice stayed level, but Puppetman could hear an unspoken shout of anger. There was sadness too – the power was pulling it in, no question now. And a hell of a lot of fear.

Wolf rolled heavy shoulders. 'There was a lot going on this morning, Comrade Mólniya. I learned that Dieter planned to betray us, I sent Mackie after him, things got out of hand. But everything's all right now, everything's going fine.'

Facts dropped into place like tumblers in a lock. *Mólniya – lightning.* Suddenly Hartmann knew what had happened to him in the limousine. The gloved man was an ace, who'd used some kind of electric power to shock him under.

Hartmann's teeth almost splintered from the effort it took to bite back the terror. *An unknown ace! He'll know me, find me out …*

His other self was ice. *He doesn't know anything.*

But how can you know? We don't know his powers.

He's a puppet.

It was a fight to keep his face from matching his emotion. *How the hell can that be?*

I got him when he shocked me. Didn't even have to do anything; his own power fused our nervous systems for a moment. That's all it took.

Mackie squirmed like a puppy caught peeing on the rug. 'Did I do right, Comrade Mólniya?'

Mólniya's lips whitened, but he nodded with visible effort. 'Yes … under the circumstances.'

Mackie preened and strutted. 'Well, there it is. I executed an enemy of the Revolution. You're not the only ones.'

Anneke clucked and brushed fingertips across Mackie's cheek. 'Preoccupied with the search for individual glory, Comrade? You're going to have to learn to watch those bourgeois tendencies if you want to be part of the Red Army Faction.'

Mackie licked his lips and slunk away, flushing. Puppetman felt what was going on inside him, like the roil beneath the surface of the sun.

What about him? Hartmann asked.

Him too. And the blond jock as well. They both handled us after the Russian shocked you. That jolt made me hypersensitive.

Hartmann let his head drop forward to cover a frown. *How could all this happen without my knowledge?*

I'm your subconscious, remember? Always on the job.

Comrade Mólniya sighed and returned to his seat. He felt hairs rise on the back of his hands and neck as his hyperactive neurons fired off. There was nothing he could do about low-level discharges such as this; they happened of their own accord under stress. It was why he wore gloves – and why some of the more lurid tales they told around the Aquarium about his wedding night had damned near come to pass.

He had to smile. *What's there to be tense about?* Even if he were identified for what he was, after the fact, there would be no international repercussions; that was how the game was played, by us and by them. So his superiors assured him.

Right.

Good God, what did I do to deserve being caught up in this lunatic scheme? He wasn't sure who was crazier, this collection of poor twisted men and bloodthirsty political naïfs or his own bosses.

It was the opportunity of the decade, they'd told him. Al-Muezzin was in the vest pocket of the Big K. If we spring him, he'll fall into our hands out of gratitude. Work for us instead. He might even bring the Light of Allah along.

Was it worth the risk? he'd demanded. Was it worth blowing the underground contacts they'd been building in the Federal Republic for ten years? Was it worth risking the Big War, the war neither side was going to win no matter what their fancy paper war plans said? Reagan was president; he was a cowboy, a madman.

But there was only so far you could push, even if you were an ace and a hero, the first man into the Bala Hissar in Kabul on Christmas Day of '79. The gates had closed in his face. He had his orders. He needed no more.

It wasn't that he disagreed with the goals. Their archrivals, the *Komitet Gosudarstvennoi Bezopasnosti* – the State Security Committee – were arrogant, overpraised, and undercompetent. No good GRU man could ever object to taking those assholes down a peg. As a patriot he knew that Military Intelligence could make far better use of an asset as valuable as Daoud Hassani than their better-known counterparts the KGB.

But the method ...

It wasn't for himself he worried. It was for his wife and daughter. And for the rest of the world too; the risk was enormous, should anything go wrong.

He reached into a pocket for cigarettes and a lighter.

'A filthy habit,' Ulrich said in that lumbering way of his.

Mólniya just looked at him.

After a moment Wolf produced a laugh that almost didn't sound forced. 'The kids these days, they have different standards. In the old days – ah, Rikibaby, Comrade Meinhof, she was a smoker. Always had a cigarette going.'

Mólniya said nothing, just kept staring at Ulrich. His eyes bore a trace of epicanthic fold, legacy of the Mongol Yoke. After a moment the blond youth found somewhere else to look.

The Russian lit up, ashamed of his cheap victory. But he had to keep these murderous young animals under control. What an irony it was that he, who had resigned from the *Spetsnaz* commandos and transferred to the Chief Intelligence Directorate of the Soviet General Staff because he could no longer stomach violence, should find himself compelled to work with these creatures for whom the shedding of blood had become addiction.

Oh, Milya, Masha, will I ever see you again?

'*Herr Doktor.*'

Tach scratched the side of his nose. He was getting restive. He'd been cooped up here two hours, unsure of what he might be contributing. Outside ... well, there was nothing to be done. But he might be with his people on the tour, comforting them, reassuring them.

'Herr Neumann,' he acknowledged.

The man from the Federal Criminal Office sat down next to him. He had a cigarette in his fingers, unlit despite the layer of tobacco that hung like a fogbank in the thick air. He kept turning it over and over.

'I wanted to ask your opinion.'

Tachyon raised a magenta eyebrow. He had long since realized the Germans wanted him here solely because he was the tour's leader in Hartmann's absence. Otherwise they would hardly have cared to have a medical doctor, and a foreigner at that, underfoot. As it was, most of the civil and police officials circulating through the crisis center treated him with the deference due his position of authority and otherwise ignored him.

'Ask away,' Tachyon said with a hand wave that was only faintly sardonic. Neumann seemed honestly interested, and he had shown signs of at least nascent intelligence, which in Tach's compass was rare for the breed.

'Were you aware that for the past hour and a half several members of your tour have been trying to raise a sum of money to offer Senator Hartmann's kidnappers as ransom?'

'No.'

Neumann nodded, slowly, as if thinking something through. His yellow eyes were hooded. 'They are experiencing considerable difficulty. It is the position of your government—'

'Not *my* government.'

Neumann inclined his head. '—of the United States government, that there will be no negotiation with the terrorists. Needless to say, American currency restrictions did not permit the members of the tour to take anywhere near a sufficient amount of money from the country, and now the American government has frozen the assets of all tour participants to preclude their concluding a separate deal.'

Tachyon felt his cheeks turn hot. 'That's damned high-handed.'

Neumann shrugged. 'I was curious as to what you thought of the plan.'

'Why me?'

'You're an acknowledged authority on joker affairs – that's the reason you honor our country with your presence, of course.' He tapped the cigarette on the table next to a curling corner of a map of Berlin. 'Also, you come of a culture in which kidnapping is a not uncommon occurrence, if I do not misapprehend.'

Tach looked at him. Though he was a celebrity, most Earthers knew little of his background beyond the fact that he was an alien. 'I can't speak of the RAF, of course—'

'The *Rote Armee Faktion* in its current incarnation consists primarily of middle-class youths – much like its previous incarnations, and for that matter most First World revolutionary groups. Money means little to them; as children of our so-called Economic Miracle, they've been raised always to assume a sufficiency of it.'

'That's certainly not something you can say for the JJS,' Sara Morgenstern said, coming over to join the conversation. An aide moved to intercept her, reaching a hand to shepherd her away from the important masculine conversation. She shied away from him as if a spark had jumped between them and glared.

Neumann said something brisk that not even Tachyon caught. The aide retreated.

'Frau Morgenstern. I am also much interested in what you have to say.'

'Members of the Jokers for a Just Society are authentically poor. I can vouch for that at least.'

'Would money tempt them, then?'

'That's hard to say. They are committed, in a way I suspect the RAF members aren't. Still—' a butterfly flip of the hand – 'they haven't lost any Mideastern aces. On the other hand, when they demand money to benefit jokers, I believe them. Whereas that might mean less to the Red Army people.'

Tach frowned. The demand to knock down Jetboy's Tomb and build a joker hospice rankled him. Like most New Yorkers, he wouldn't miss the memorial – an eyesore erected to honor failure, and one he'd personally prefer to forget. But the demand for a hospice was a slap in his face: *When has a joker been turned away from my clinic? When?*

Neumann was studying him. 'You disagree, *Herr Doktor*?' he asked softly.

'No, no. She's right. But Gimli—' he snapped his fingers and extended a forefinger. 'Tom Miller cares deeply for jokers. But he has also an eye for what Americans call the main chance. You might well be able to tempt him.'

Sara nodded. 'But why do you ask, Herr Neumann? After all, President Reagan refuses to negotiate for the senator's return.' Her voice rang with bitterness. Still, Tach was puzzled. As high-strung as she was, he'd thought that surely worry for Gregg would have broken her down by now.

Instead she seemed to be growing steadier by the hour.

Neumann looked at her for a moment, and Tach wondered if he was in on the ill-kept secret of her affair with the missing senator.

He had the impression those yellow eyes – red-rimmed now from the smoke – missed little.

'Your President has made his decision,' he said softly. 'But it's my responsibility to advise my government on what course to take. This is a German problem too, you know.'

At two-thirty Hiram Worchester came on the air reading a statement in English. Tachyon translated it into German during the pauses.

'Comrade Wolf – Gimli, if you're there,' Hiram said, voice fluting with emotion, 'we want the senator back. We're willing to negotiate as private citizens.

'Please, for the love of God – and for jokers and aces and all the rest of us – please call us.'

Mólniya stared at the door. White enamel was coming away in flakes. Striae of green and pink and brown showed beneath the white, around gouges that looked as if someone had used the door for knife-throwing practice. He was all but oblivious to the others in the room. Even the mad boy's incessant humming; he'd long since learned to tune that out for sanity's sake.

I should never have let them go.

It took him aback when both Gimli and Wolf wanted to make the meet with the tour delegation. It was about the first thing they'd agreed on since this whole comic-opera affair had gotten underway.

He'd wanted to forbid them. He didn't like the smell of this rendezvous ... but that was foolish. Reagan had closed the door on overt negotiation, but didn't the current Irangate hearings with which the Americans were currently amusing themselves prove he was not averse to using private channels to deal with terrorists against whom he'd taken a hard public line?

Besides, he thought, *I've long since learned better than to issue orders I doubt will be obeyed.*

It had been so different in *Spetsnaz*. The men he'd commanded were professionals and more, the elite of the Soviet armed forces, full of esprit and skilled as surgeons. Such a contrast to this muddle of bitter amateurs and murderous dilettantes.

If only he'd at least had someone trained back home, or in a camp in some Soviet client state, Korea or Iraq or Peru. Someone except Gimli, that is – he had the impression years had passed since anything but plastique would open the dwarf's mind enough to accept input from anyone else, nats in particular.

He wished at least he might have gone on the meet. But his place was here, guarding the captive. Without Hartmann they had nothing – except a worldful of trouble.

Does the KGB have this much trouble with its puppets? Rationally he guessed they did. They'd fluffed a few big ones over the years – the mention of Mexico could still make veterans wince – and GRU had evidence of plenty of missteps the Big K thought they'd covered up.

But the Komitet's publicists had done their job well, on both sides of the quaintly named 'Iron Curtain.' Down behind his fore-brain not even Mólniya could shake the image of the KGB as the omniscient puppet master, with its strings wrapping the world like a spider's web.

He tried to envision himself as a master spider. It made him smile.

No. I'm not a spider. Just a small, frightened man whom some-body once called hero.

He thought of Ludmilya, his daughter. He shuddered.

There are strings attached to me, right enough. But I'm not the one who pulls them.

I want him.

Hartmann looked around the squalid little room. Ulrich was pacing, face fixed and sullen at having been left behind. Stocky Wilfried sat cleaning an assault rifle with compulsive care. He always seemed to be doing something with his hands. The two remaining jokers sat by themselves saying nothing. The Russian sat and smoked and stared at the wall.

He studiously didn't look at the boy in the scuffed leather jacket.

Mackie Messer hummed the old song about the shark and its teeth and the man with his jackknife and fancy gloves. Hartmann remembered a mealymouthed version popular when he was a teenager, sung by Bobby Darin or some such teen-idol crooner. He also recalled a different version, one he'd heard for the first time in a dim dope-fogged room on Yale's Old Campus when antiwar activist Hartmann returned to his alma mater to lecture in '68. Dark and sinister, a straighter translation of the original, sung in the whisky baritone of a man who, like old Bertolt Brecht himself, delighted in playing Baal: Thomas Marion Douglas, Destiny's doomed lead singer. Remembering the way the words went down his spine on that distant night, he shuddered.

I want him.

No! his mind shouted. *He's insane. He's dangerous.*

He could be useful, once I get us out of here.

Hartmann's body clenched in rictus terror. *No! Don't do anything! The terrorists are negotiating right now. We'll get out of this.*

He felt Puppetman's disdain. Seldom had his alter ego seemed more discrete, more other. *Fools. What has Hiram Worchester ever been involved in that amounted to anything? It'll fall through.*

Then we just wait. Sooner or later something will be worked out. It's how these things go. He felt slimy vines of sweat twining his body inside his blood-spattered shirt and vest.

How long do you think we have to wait? How long before our jokers and their terrorists friends blow up in each other's faces? I have puppets. They're our only way out.

What can they do? I can't just make someone let me go. I'm not that little mind-twister Tachyon.

He felt a smug vibration within.

Don't forget 1976, he told his power. *You thought you could handle that too.*

The power laughed at him, until he closed his eyes and concentrated and forced it to quiescence.

Has it become a demon, possessing me? he wondered. *Am I just another of Puppetman's puppets?*

No. *I'm the master here. Puppetman's just a fantasy. A personification of my power. A game I play with myself.*

Inside the tangled corridors of his soul, the echo of triumphant laughter.

'It's raining again,' Xavier Desmond said.

Tach made a face and refrained from a rejoinder commending the joker's firm grasp of the obvious. Des was a friend, after all.

He shifted his grip on the umbrella he shared with Desmond and tried to console himself that the squall would soon pass. The Berliners strolling the paths that veined the grassy Tiergarten park and hurrying along the sidewalks of the nearby Bundes Allee clearly thought so, and they should know. Old men in homburgs, young women with prams, intense young men in dark wool sweaters, a sausage vendor with cheeks like ripe peaches; the usual crowd of Germans taking advantage of anything resembling decent weather after the lengthy Prussian winter.

He glanced at Hiram. The big round restaurateur was resplendent in his pin-striped three-piece suit, hat at a jaunty angle, and black beard curled. He had an umbrella in one hand, a gleaming black satchel in the other, and Sara Morgenstern standing primly next to him, not quite making contact.

Rain was dripping off the brim of Tach's plumed hat, which swept beyond the coverage of the cheap plastic umbrella. A rivulet ran down one side of Des's trunk. Tach sighed.

How did I let myself get talked into this? he wondered for the fourth or fifth time. It was idle; when Hiram had called to say a West German industrialist who wished to remain nameless had offered to front them the ransom money, he'd known he was in.

Sara stood stiff. He sensed she was shivering, almost subliminally. Her face was the color of her raincoat. Her eyes were a paleness that somehow contrasted. He wished she hadn't insisted on coming along. But she was the leading journalist on this junket;

they'd have had to lock her up to keep her from covering this meeting with Hartmann's kidnappers at first hand. And there was her personal interest.

Hiram cleared his throat. 'Here they come.' His voice was pitched higher than usual.

Tachyon glanced right without turning his head. No mistake; there weren't enough jokers in West Germany that it was likely to have two just happen along at this moment, even if there could be any doubt about the identity of the small bearded man who walked with the Toulouse-Lautrec roll beside a being who looked like a beige anteater on its hind legs.

'Tom,' Hiram said, voice husky now.

'Gimli,' the dwarf replied. He said it without heat. His eyes glittered at the satchel hanging from Hiram's hand. 'You brought it.'

'Of course … Gimli.' He handed the umbrella to Sara and cracked the satchel. Gimli stood on tiptoe and peered in. His lips pursed in a soundless whistle. 'Two million American dollars. Two more after you hand Senator Hartmann over to us.'

A snaggletoothed grin. 'That's a bargaining figure.'

Hiram colored. 'You agreed on the phone—'

'We agreed to consider your offer once you demonstrated your good faith,' said one of the two nats who accompanied Gimli and his partner. He was a tall man made bulkier by his raincoat. Dark blond hair was slicked back and down from a balding promontory of forehead by the intermittent rain. 'I am Comrade Wolf. Let me remind you, there is the matter of the freedom of our comrade, al-Muezzin.'

'Just what is it that makes German socialists risk their lives and freedom on behalf of a fundamentalist Muslim terrorist?' Tachyon asked.

'We're all comrades in the struggle against Western imperialism. What brings a Takisian to risk his health in our beastly climate on behalf of a senator from a country that once whipped him from its shores like a rabid dog?'

Tach drew his head back in surprise. Then he smiled. 'Touché.' He and Wolf shared a look of perfect understanding.

'But we can only give you money,' Hiram said. 'We can't arrange for Mr. Hassani to be released. We *told* you that.'

'Then it's no sale,' said Wolf's nat companion, a redheaded woman Tach could have found attractive but for a sullen, puffy jut to her lower lip and a bluish cast to her complexion. 'What use is your toilet-paper money to us? We merely demand it to make you pigs sweat.'

'Now, wait a minute,' Gimli said. 'That money can buy a lot for jokers.'

'Are you so obsessed with buying into consumption fascism?' sneered the redhead.

Gimli went purple. 'The money's here. Hassani's in Rikers, and that's a long way away.'

Wolf was frowning at Gimli in a speculative sort of way. Somewhere an engine backfired.

The woman spat like a cat and jumped back, face pale, eyes feral.

Motion tugged at the corner of Tach's eye.

The chubby sausage seller had flipped open the lid of his cart. His hand was coming out with a black Heckler & Koch mini-machine pistol in it.

Ever suspicious, Gimli traced his gaze. 'It's a trap!' he shrieked. He whipped open his coat. He'd been holding one of those compact little Krinkov assault rifles beneath.

Tachyon kicked the foreshortened Kalashnikov from Gimli's hand with the toe of an elegant boot. The nat woman pulled out an AKM from inside her coat and stuttered a burst one-handed. The sound threatened to implode Tach's eardrums.

Sara screamed. Tach threw himself onto her, bore her down to wet, fragrant grass as the female terrorist tracked her weapon from left to right, face a rictus of something like ecstasy.

There was motion all around. Old men in homburgs and young women with prams and intense young men in sweaters were whipping out machine pistols and rushing toward the party clumped around the two umbrellas.

'Wait,' Hiram shouted, 'hold on! It's all a misunderstanding.'

The other terrorists had guns out now, firing in all directions.

Bystanders screamed and scattered. The slick-soled shoes of a man waving a machine pistol with one hand lost traction on the grass and shot out from under him. A man with an MP5K and a business suit tripped over a baby carriage whose operator had frozen on the handle and fell on his face.

Sara lay beneath Tachyon, rigid as a statue. The clenched rump pressed against his crotch was firmer than he would have expected. *This is the only way I'm ever going to get on top of her,* he thought ruefully. It was almost physical pain to realize it was contact with him and not fear of the bullets crackling like static overhead that made her go stiff.

Gregg, you are a lucky man. Should you somehow survive this imbroglio.

Scrambling after his rifle, Gimli ran into a big nat who snatched at him. He picked him up by one leg with that disproportionate strength of his and pitched him into the faces of a trio of his comrades like a Scot tossing the caber.

Des was making love to the grass. *Smart man,* Tachyon thought. His head was full of burned powder and the green and brown aromas of wet turf. Hiram was wandering dazed through a horizontal firestorm, waving his arms and crying, 'Wait, wait – oh, it wasn't supposed to happen like this.'

The terrorists bolted. Gimli ducked between the legs of one nat who flailed his arms at him in a grab, came up and punched a second in the nuts and followed them.

Tach heard a squeal of pain. The snouted joker fell down with black ropy strands of blood unraveling from his belly. Gimli caught him up on the run and slung him over his shoulder like a rolled carpet.

A gaggle of Catholic schoolgirls scattered like blue quail, pigtails flying, as the fugitives stampeded through them. Tachyon saw a man go to one knee, raise his machine pistol for a burst at the terrorists.

He reached out with his mind. The man toppled, asleep.

A van coughed into life and roared from the curb with Gimli thrashing for the handles of the open doors with his stubby arms.

Hiram sat on the wet grass, weeping into his hands. The black satchel wept bundled money beside him.

'The political police,' Neumann said, as if trying to work a shred of spoiled food from inside his mouth. 'They don't call them *Popo* for nothing.'

'Herr Neumann—' the man in mechanic's coveralls began beseechingly.

'Shut up. Doctor Tachyon, you have my personal apology.' Neumann had arrived within five minutes of the terrorists' escape, just in time to keep Tachyon from being arrested for screaming abuse at the police interlopers.

Tachyon sensed Sara beside and behind him like a whiteout shadow. She'd just finished narrating a sketch of what had just happened into the voice-actuated mike clipped to the lapel of her coat. She seemed calm.

He gestured at the ambulances crowded together like whales with spinning blue lights beyond the police cordon, with a hat still bedraggled from being jumped up and down on. 'How many people did your madmen gun down?'

'Three bystanders were injured by gunfire, and one policeman. Another officer will require hospitalization but he, ah, was not shot.'

'What were you *thinking* of?' Tachyon screamed. He thought he'd blasted all his fury out of him, all over the plainclothes officers who'd been stumbling across each other demanding to know how the terrorists could *possibly* have gotten away. But now it was back, filling him up to overflow. 'Tell me, what did you people think you were doing?'

'It wasn't my people,' Neumann said. 'It was the political branch of the Berlin *Land* police. The *Bundeskriminalamt* had nothing to do with it.'

'It was all a setup,' Xavier Desmond said, stroking his trunk with leaden fingers. 'That millionaire philanthropist who lent the ransom—'

'Was fronting for the political police.'

'Herr Neumann.' It was a *Popo* with grass stains on the knees of his once sharply pressed trousers, pointing an accusing finger at Tachyon. 'He let the terrorists go. Pauli had a clear shot at them, and he – he knocked him down with that mind power of his.'

'The officer was aiming his weapon at a crowd of people through whom the terrorists were fleeing,' Tach said tautly. 'He could not have fired without hitting innocent bystanders. Or perhaps I am confused as to who is the terrorist.'

The plainclothesman turned red. 'You interfered with one of my officers! We could have stopped them—'

Neumann reached out and grabbed a pinch of the man's cheek. 'Go elsewhere,' he said softly. 'Really.'

The man swallowed and walked away, sending hostile looks back over his shoulder at Tachyon. Tachyon grinned and shot him the bird.

'Oh, Gregg, my God, what have we done?' sobbed Hiram. 'We'll never get him back.'

Tachyon tugged on his elbow, more trying to encourage him to his feet than help him. He forgot about Hiram's gravity power; the fat man popped right up. 'What do you mean, Hiram, my friend?'

'Are you out of your mind, Doctor? They'll kill him now.'

Sara gasped. When Tach glanced to her she looked quickly away, as if unwilling to show him her eyes.

'Not so, my friend,' Neumann said. 'That's not how the game is played.'

He stuck hands in the pockets of his trousers and gazed off across the misty park at the line of trees that masked the outer fences of the zoo. 'But now the price will go up.'

'The bastards!' Gimli turned, whipping rain from the tail of his raincoat, and beat fists on the mottled walls. 'The cocksuckers. *They set us up!*'

Shroud and Scrape were huddled over the thin, filthy mattress on which Aardvark lay moaning softly. Everybody else seemed to be milling around a room crowded with heavy damp as well as bodies.

Hartmann sat with his head pulled protectively down inside his sweat-limp collar. He agreed with Gimli's character assessment. *Are those fools trying to get me killed?*

A thought went home like a whaler's bomb-lance: *Tachyon! Does that alien demon suspect? Is this a convoluted Takisian plot to get rid of me without a scandal?*

Puppetman laughed at him. "*Never attribute to malice what may adequately be explained by stupidity,*" he said. Hartmann recognized the quote; Lady Black had said it to Carnifex once, during one of his rages.

Mackie Messer stood shaking his head. 'This isn't right,' he said, half-pleading. 'We have the senator. Don't they know that?'

Then he was raging around the room like a cornered wolf, snarling and hacking air with his hands. People jostled to get out of the way of those hands.

'What do they think's going on?' Mackie screamed. 'Who do they think they're fucking with? I'll tell you something. I'll tell you what. Maybe we should send them a few pieces of the Senator here, show them what's what.'

He *buzzed* his hand inches from the tip of the captive's nose.

Hartmann yanked his head back. *Christ, he almost got me!* The intent had been there, for real – Puppetman had felt it, felt it waver at the final millisecond.

'Calm down, Detlev,' Anneke said sweetly. She seemed exalted by the shootout in the park. She'd been fluttering around and laughing at nothing since the group's return, and red spots glowed like greasepaint on her cheeks. 'The capitalists won't be eager to pay all we ask for damaged goods.'

Mackie went white. Puppetman felt fresh anger burst inside him like a bomb. 'Mackie! I'm Mackie Messer, you fucking bitch! Mackie the Knife, just like my song.'

Detlev was slang for *faggot*, Hartmann remembered. He kept his last breath inside.

Anneke smiled at the youthful ace. From the side of his eye

Hartmann saw Wilfried pale, and Ulrich picked up an AKM with an elaborate casualness he wouldn't have thought the blond terrorist could muster.

Wolf put his arm around Mackie's shoulders. 'There, Mackie, there. Anneke didn't mean anything by it.' Her smile made a liar of him. But Mackie pressed against the big man's side and allowed himself to be gentled. Mólniya cleared his throat, and Ulrich set the rifle down.

Hartmann let the breath go. The explosion wasn't coming. Quite yet.

'He's a good boy,' Wolf said, giving Mackie another hug and letting him go. 'He's the son of an American deserter and a Hamburg whore – another victim of your imperialist venture in Southeast Asia, Senator.'

'My father was a general,' Mackie shouted in English.

'Yes, Mackie; anything you say. The boy grew up running the docks and alleys, in and out of institutions. Finally he drifted to Berlin, more helpless flotsam cast up by our own frenetic consumer culture. He saw posters, began to attend study groups at the Free University – he's barely literate, the poor child – and that's where I found him. And recruited him.'

'And he's been *sooo* helpful,' Anneke said, rolling her eyes at Ulrich, who laughed. Mackie glanced at them, then quickly away.

You win, Puppetman said.

What?

You're right. My control isn't perfect. And this one is too unpredictable, too ... terrible.

Hartmann almost laughed aloud. Of all the things he'd come to expect from the power that dwelt within him, humility wasn't one.

Such a waste; he'd be such a perfect puppet. And his emotion, so furious, so lovely – like a drug. But a deadly drug.

So you've given up. Relief flooded him.

No. The boy just has to die.

– But that's all right. I've got it all worked out now.

Shroud squatted over Aardvark like a solicitous mummy, bathing his forehead with a length of his own bandage, which he'd dipped in water from one of the five-liter plastic cans stacked in the bedroom. He shook his head and murmured to himself.

Eyes malice-bright, Anneke danced up to him. 'Thinking of all that lovely money you lost, Comrade?'

'Joker blood's been shed – again,' Shroud said levelly. 'It better not have been for nothing.'

Anneke sauntered over to Ulrich. 'You should have seen them, sweetheart. All ready to hand Senator *Schweinfleisch* over for a suitcase full of dollars.' She pursed her lips. 'I do believe they were so excited they forgot all about the frontline fighter we've sworn to liberate. They would have sold us all.'

'Shut up, you bitch!' Gimli yelled. Spittle exploded from the center of his beard as he lunged for the redhead. With a scratch of chitin on wood Scrape interposed himself, threw his horny arms around his leader as guns came up.

A loud *pop* stopped them like a freeze-frame. Mólniya stood with a bare hand upturned before his face, fingers extended as if to hold a ball. An ephemeral blue flicker limned the nerves of his hand and was gone.

'If we fight among ourselves,' he said calmly, 'we play into our enemies' hands.'

Only Puppetman knew his calm was a lie.

Deliberately Mólniya drew his glove back on. 'We were betrayed. What more can we expect from the capitalist system we oppose?' He smiled. 'Let us strengthen our resolve. If we stand together, we can make them pay for their treachery.'

The potential antagonists fell back away from each other.

Hartmann feared.

Puppetman exulted.

The last of day lay across the Brandenburg plain west of the city like a layer of polluted water. From the next block tinny Near Eastern music skirled from a radio. Inside the little room it was tropical, from the heat billowing out of the radiator that the handy Comrade Wilfried had got going despite the building's derelict status, as well as electricity ; from the humidity of bodies confined under stress.

Ulrich let the cheap curtains drop and turned away from the window. 'Christ, it stinks in here,' he said, doing stretches. 'What do those fucking Turks do? Piss in the corners?'

Lying on the foul mattress next to the wall, Aardvark huddled closer around his injured gut and whimpered.

Gimli moved over beside him, felt his head. His ugly little face was all knotted up with concern. 'He's in a bad way,' the dwarf said.

'Maybe we oughta get him to a hospital,' Scrape said.

Ulrich jutted his square chin and shook his head. 'No way. We decided.'

Shroud knelt down next to his boss, took Aardvark's hand, and felt the low fuzzy forehead. 'He's got some fever.'

'How can you tell?' Wilfried asked, his broad face concerned. 'Maybe he's naturally got a higher temperature than a person, like a dog or something.'

Quick as a teleport Gimli was across the room. He swept Wilfried off his feet with a transverse kick and straddled his chest, pummeling him. Shroud and Scrape hauled him off.

Wifried was holding his hands up before his face. 'Hey, hey, what did I do?' He seemed almost in tears.

'You stupid bastard!' Gimli howled, windmilling his arms. 'You're no better than the rest of the fucking nats! *None of you!*'

'Comrades, please—' Mólniya began.

But Gimli wasn't listening. His face was the color of raw meat. He sent his companions flying with a heave of his shoulders and marched to Aardvark's side.

◆

Puppetman hated to let Gimli off like this, walking away clear. He'd have to kill the evil little fuck someday.

But survival surmounted even vengeance. Puppetman's imperative was to shave the odds against him. This was the quickest way.

Tears streamed over Gimli's lumpy cheeks. 'That's enough,' he sobbed. 'We're taking him for medical attention, and we're taking him *now*.' He bent down and looped a limp furry arm over his neck. Shroud glanced around, eyes alert above the bandage wrap, then joined him.

Comrade Wolf blocked the door. 'Nobody leaves here.'

'What the fuck are you talking about, little man?' Ulrich said pugnaciously. 'He's not hurt that badly.'

'Who says he's not eh?' Shroud said. For the first time Hartmann realized he had a Canadian accent.

Gimli's face twisted like a rag. 'That's shit. He's hurting. He's dying. Dammit, let us go.'

Ulrich and Anneke were sidling for their weapons. 'United we stand, brother,' Wolf intoned. 'Divided we fall. As you *Amis* say.'

A double clack brought their heads around. Scrape stood by the far wall. The assault rifle he'd just cocked was pointed at the buckle of the blond terrorist's army belt. 'Then maybe we just fell, comrades,' he said. 'Because if Gimli says we're going, we're gone.'

Wolf's mouth crumpled in on itself, as if he were old and had forgotten his false teeth. He glanced at Ulrich and Anneke. They had the jokers flanked. If they all moved at once ...

Clinging to one of Aardvark's wrists, Shroud brought up an AKM with his free hand. 'Keep it cool, nat.'

Mackie felt his hands beginning to buzz. Only the touch of Mólniya's hand on his arm kept him from slicing some joker meat. *Ugly monsters! I knew we couldn't trust them.*

'What about the things we're working for?' the Soviet asked.

Gimli wrung Aardvark's hand. '*This* is what *we're* working for. He's a joker. And he needs help.'

Comrade Wolf's face was turning the color of eggplant. Veins stood out like broken fingers on his temples. 'Where do you think you're going?' he forced past grinding teeth.

Gimli laughed. 'Right through the Wall. Where our friends are waiting for us.'

'Then leave. Walk out on us. Walk out on the great things you were going to do for your fellow monsters. We still have the senator; we are going to win. And if we ever catch you—'

Scrape laughed. 'You gonna have trouble catching your breath after this goes down. The pigs'll be crawling all over you, I guarantee. You're such total fuckups I can smell it.'

Ulrich's eyes were rolling belligerently despite the rifle aimed at his midsection. 'No,' Mólniya said. 'Let them go. If we fight everything is lost.'

'Get out,' Wolf said.

'Yeah,' Gimli said. He and Shroud gently carried Aardvark out into the unlit hallway of the abandoned building. Scrape covered them until they were out of sight, then swiftly crossed the room. He paused, gave them as much of a smile as chitin would permit, and closed the door.

Ulrich hurled his Kalashnikov against the door. Fortunately it failed to go off. 'Bastards!'

Anneke shrugged. Clearly she was bored with the psychodrama. 'Americans,' she said.

Mackie sidled over to Mólniya. Everything seemed wrong. But Mólniya would make it right. He knew he would.

The Russian ace was cake.

Ulrick swung around with his big hands tied into fists. 'So what's going to happen? Huh?'

Wolf sat on a stool with his belly on his thighs and hands on his knees. He'd visibly aged as the thrill of high adventure ebbed. Perhaps the exploit he'd hoped to cap his double life with was going sour on his tongue.

'What do you mean, Ulrich?' the lawyer asked wearily.

Ulrich turned him a look of outrage. 'Well, I mean it's our deadline. It's ten o'clock. You heard the radio. They still haven't met our demands.'

He picked up an AKM, jacked a round into the chamber. 'Can't we kill the son of a bitch now?'

Anneke laughed like a ringing bell. 'Your political sophistication never ceases to amaze me, lover.'

Wolf hiked up the sleeve of his coat and checked his wristwatch. 'What happens now is that you, Anneke, and you, Wilfried, will go and telephone the message we agreed upon to the crisis center the authorities have so conveniently established. We've both proved we can play the waiting game; it's time to make things move a little.'

And Comrade Mólniya said, 'No.'

The fear was gathering. Bit by bit it coalesced into a cancer, black and amorphous in the center of his brain. With each minute's passage it seemed Mólniya's heart gained a beat. His ribs felt as if they were vibrating from the speed of his pulse. His throat was dry and raw, his cheeks burned as though he stared into the open maw of a crematorium. His mouth tasted like offal. He had to get out. Everything depended on it.

Everything.

No, a part of him cried. *You've got to stay. That was the plan.*

Behind his eyes he saw his daughter Ludmiyla sitting in a rubbled building with her melted eyes running down blister-bubbled cheeks. *This is at stake, Valentin Mikhailovich*, another, deeper voice replied, *if anything goes wrong. Do you dare entrust this errand to these adolescents?*

'No,' he said. His parched palate would barely produce the word. 'I'll go.'

Wolf frowned. Then the ends of his wide mouth drew up in a smile. Doubtless it occurred to him that would leave him in complete control of the situation. *Fine. Let him think as he will. I've got to get* out of here.

Mackie blocked the door, Mackie Messer with tears thronging the lower lids of his eyes. Mólniya felt fear spike within him, almost ripped off a glove to shock the boy from his path. But he knew the young ace would never harm him, and he knew why.

He mumbled an apology and shouldered past. He heard a sob as the door shut behind him, and then only his footsteps, pursuing him down the darkened hall.

One of my better performances, Puppetman congratulated himself. Cake.

Mackie beat his open palms on the door. Mólniya had abandoned him. He hurt, and he couldn't do anything about the hurt. Not even if he made his hands buzz so they'd cut through steel plate.

Wolf was still here. Wolf would protect him ... but Wolf hadn't. Not really. Wolf had let the others laugh at him – him, Mackie the ace, Mackie the Knife. It had been Mólniya who'd stood up for him the last few weeks. Mólniya who had taken care of him.

Mólniya who was gone. Who wasn't supposed to go. Who was gone.

He turned, weeping, and slid slowly down the door to the floor.

Exhilaration swelled Puppetman. It was all working just as he had planned. His puppets cut the capers he directed and suspected nothing. And here he sat, at breath's distance, drinking their passions like brandy. Danger was no more than added poignance; he was Puppetman, and in control.

And finally the time had come to make an end of Mackie Messer and get himself out of here.

Anneke stood over Mackie, taunting: 'Crybaby. And you call yourself a revolutionary?' He pulled himself upright, whimpering like a lost puppy.

Puppetman reached out for a string, and pulled.

And Comrade Ulrich said, 'Why didn't you just go with the rest of the jokers, you ugly little queer?'

♦

'Kreuzberg,' Neumann said.

Slumped in his chair, Tachyon could barely muster the energy to lift his head and say, 'I beg your pardon?' Ten o'clock was ancient history now. So, he feared, was Senator Gregg Hartmann.

Neumann grinned. 'We have them. It took the Devil's own time, but we traced the van. They're in Kreuzberg. The Turkish ghetto next to the Wall.'

Sara gasped and quickly looked away.

'An antiterrorist team from GSG-9 is standing by,' Neumann said.

'Do they know what they're doing?' Tach asked, remembering the afternoon's fiasco.

'They're the best. They're the ones who sprang the Lufthansa 737 the Nur al-Allah people hijacked to Mogadishu in 1977. Hans-Joachim Richter himself is in charge.' Richter was the head of the Ninth Border Guards Group, GSG-9, especially formed to combat terrorism after the Munich massacre of '72. A popular hero in Germany, he was reputed to be an ace, though nobody knew what his powers might be.

Tach stood. 'Let's go.'

Mackie's left hand cut right down Comrade Ulrich's right side from the base of his neck to the hip. It felt good going through, and the kiss of bone thrilled him like speed.

Ulrich's arm fell off. He stared at Mackie. His lips peeled back away from perfect teeth, which clacked open and closed three times like something in the window of a novelty store.

He looked down at what had been his perfect animal body and shrieked.

Mackie watched in fascination. The scream made his exposed lung work in and out like a vacuum cleaner bag, all grayish purple and moist and veined with blue and red. Then his guts started to spill out the side of him, piling over his fallen rifle, and the blood rushing out of him carried away the strength that kept him standing, and he dropped.

'Holy Mary mother of God,' Wilfried said. Puke slopped from a corner of his mouth as he backed away from the wreckage of his comrade. Then he looked past Mackie and yelled, 'No—'

Anneke aimed her Kalashnikov at the small of the ace's back. Fear knotted her finger sphincter-tight.

Mackie phased out. The burst splashed Wilfried all over the wall.

Mólniya stood with hands on knees and his back against the side of a stripped Volvo, pulling in deep breaths of diesel-flavored Berlin night. It wasn't a part of town in which strangers cared to spend much time alone. That didn't concern him. What he feared was fear.

What came over me? I've never felt like that in my life.

He'd fled the apartment in a bright haze of panic. No sooner had he stepped outside than it evaporated like water spilled on a sun-heated rock in the Khyber. Now he was trying to collect himself, unsure for the moment whether to carry on with his errand or go back and send a couple of Wolf's vicious cubs.

Papertin was right, he told himself. *I've gotten soft. I—*

From above came a familiar heavy stutter. His blood ran like freon through his veins as he raised his head to see fireflashes dancing on chintz curtains two stories up.

It was all over.

If I'm not found here, he thought, *then maybe – conceivably – the Third World War won't happen tonight.*

He turned and walked away down the street, very fast.

Hartmann lay on his side with the floorboards throbbing against the bruise they'd made on his cheekbone. He'd kicked the chair over as soon as things started happening.

What in hell's name went wrong? he wondered desperately. *The bastard wasn't supposed to talk, just shoot.*

It was '76 all over again. Once again Puppetman in his arrogance had overreached himself. And it may just have cost him his ass.

His nostrils buzzed with the stink of hot lubricant and blood and fresh moist shit. Hartmann could hear the two surviving terrorists stumbling around the room shouting at each other. Ulrich was dying in wheezes a few feet away. He could feel the energy running from him like an ebb tide.

'Where is he? Where'd the fucker go?' Wolf was saying.

'He went through the wall,' Anneke said. She was hyperventilating, tearing the words out of the air like pieces of cloth.

'Well, watch for him. Oh, holy Jesus.'

Their terror was stark as crucifixion as they stood trying to cover all three interior walls with their guns. Hartmann shared it. The twisted ace had gone berserk.

Someone shrieked and died.

Mackie stood for a moment with his arm elbow-deep in Anneke's back. He took the buzz off, leaving his hand jutting from the woman's sternum like a blade. Blood oozed greasily around the leather sleeve on Mackie's arm where it vanished into her torso. He enjoyed the look of it, and the intimate way what remained of Anneke's heart kept hugging his arm. The fools hadn't even been looking his way when he slipped back through the wall from the bedroom, not that it would have helped them if they had. Three quick steps and that was it for redheaded little Comrade Anneke.

'Fuck you,' he said, and giggled.

The heart convulsed one last time around Mackie's arm and was still. Putting a slight buzz on, Mackie pulled his arm free. He swung the corpse around as he did so.

Wolf was standing there with his cheeks quivering. He brought up his gun as Mackie turned. Mackie pushed the corpse at him. He fired. Mackie laughed and phased out.

Wolf emptied the magazine in a shivering ejaculation. Plaster dust filled the room. Anneke's corpse collapsed across the senator. Mackie phased back in.

Wolf screamed pleas, in German, in English. Mackie took the Kalashnikov away from him, pinned him against the door, and taking his time about it, sawed his head in two, right down the middle.

Riding in the armored van with the particolored lights of downtown Berlin washing over her and the faces and weapons of the GSG-9 men who sat facing her, Sara Morgenstern thought, *What's come over me?*

She wasn't sure whether she meant now or before – weeks before, when the affair with Gregg began.

How strange, how very strange. How could I have ever have thought I loved … him? I feel nothing for him now.

But that wasn't really true. Where love had left a vacuum an earlier emotion was seeping in. Tainted with a toxic flavor of betrayal.

Andrea, Andrea, what have I done?

She bit her lip. The GSG-9 commando riding across from her saw and grinned, his teeth startling in his blackened face. She was instantly wary, but there was no sex in that smile, only the self-distracting camaraderie of a man facing battle with both pleasure and fear. She made herself smile back and nestled closer against Tachyon, sitting by her side.

He put his arm around her. It wasn't just a brotherly gesture. Even the prospect of danger wasn't enough to drive sex wholly from his mind. Oddly she found she didn't mind the attention. Perhaps it was her acute awareness of how incongruous they were, a pair of small gaudy cockatoos riding among panthers.

And Gregg … did she really care what happened to him?

Or do I hope he never leaves that tenement alive?

The screaming had stopped, and the buzz-saw sounds. Hartmann had feared they might go on forever. He gagged on the reek of friction-burned hair and bone.

He felt like something from a medieval fable as painted by Bosch: a glutton presented with the fullest of feasts, only to have it turn to ashes in his mouth. Puppetman had drawn no nourishment from the terrorists' dying. He'd been nearly as terrified as they.

A humming, coming closer: Morität, *The Ballad of Mackie the Knife*. The mad ace was locked in killing frenzy now, stalking toward him with his terrible hand still dripping brains. Hartmann writhed in his bonds. The woman Mackie had impaled was a dead weight across his legs. He was going to die now. Unless …

Bile surged up his throat at what he was going to do. He choked it back, reached for a string, and pulled. Pulled *hard*.

The humming stopped. The soft tocking of clogs on wood stopped. Hartmann looked up. Mackie leaned over him with glowing eyes.

He pulled Anneke off Hartmann's legs. He was strong for his size. Or maybe inspired. He pulled Hartmann's chair upright. Hartmann winced, dreading contact, fearing death. Fearing the alternative almost as much.

His own breathing nearly deafened him. He could feel the emotion swelling within Mackie. He steeled himself and stroked it, teased it, made it grow.

Mackie went to his knees before the chair. He unfastened the fly of Hartmann's trousers, slipped fingers inside, tugged the senator's cock out into the humid air and fastened his lips around the glans. He began to pump his head up and down, slowly at first, then gaining speed. His tongue went caduceus round and round.

Hartmann moaned. He couldn't let himself enjoy this.

If you don't it's never going to end, Puppetman taunted.

What are you doing to me?

Saving you. And securing the best puppet of all.

But he's so powerful – so … unpredictable. Involuntary pleasure was breaking his thoughts into kaleidiscope fragments.

But I've got him now. Because he wants to be my puppet. He loves you, the way that neurasthenic bitch Sara never could.

God, God, am I still a man?

You're alive. And you're going to smuggle this creature back to

New York. And anyone who stands in our way from now on will die.
– Now relax and enjoy it.

Puppetman took over. As Mackie sucked his cock, he sucked the boy's emotions with his mind. Hot-wet and salty, they gushed into him.

Hartmann's head went back. Involuntarily he cried out.

He came as he had not come since Succubus died.

Senator Gregg Hartmann pushed through a door from which the glass had long since been broken. He leaned against the cold metal frame and stared into a street that was empty except for gutted cars and weeds pushing up through cracks in the pavement.

White light drilled him from the rooftop opposite, fierce as a laser. He raised his head, blinking.

'My God,' a German voice yelled, 'it's the senator.'

The street filled up with cars and whirling lights and noise. It didn't seem to take any time at all. Hartmann saw magenta highlights struck like sparks off Tachyon's hair, and Carnifex in his comic-book outfit, and from doorways and behind the automotive corpses appeared men totally encased in black, trotting warily forward with stubby machine pistols held ready.

Past them all he saw Sara, dressed in a white coat that was the defiant antithesis of camouflage.

'I … got away,' he said, voice creaking like an unused door. 'It's over. They – they killed each other.'

Television spotlights spilled over him, hot and white as milk fresh from the breast. His gaze caught Sara's. He smiled. But her eyes drilled into his like iron rods.

Cold and hard. *She's slipped away!* he thought. With the thought came pain.

But Puppetman wasn't buying pain. Not tonight. He drove himself into her through the eyes.

And she came running for him, arms spread, her mouth a red hole through which love-words poured. And Hartmann felt his puppet wrap her arms around his neck and makeup-streaked tears gush onto his collar, and he hated that part of him that had saved his life.

And down away where light never was, Puppetman smiled.

MIRRORS OF THE SOUL

Melinda M. Snodgrass

April in Paris. The chestnut trees resplendent in their pink and white finery. The blossoms drifting like fragrant snow about the feet of the statues in the Tuileries Garden, and floating like colorful foam atop the muddy waters of the Seine.

April in Paris. The song bubbling incongruously through his head as he stood before a simple gravestone in the Cimetière Montmartre. So hideously inappropriate. He banished it only to have it return with greater intensity.

Irritably Tachyon hunched one shoulder, took a tighter grip on the simple bouquet of violets and lily of the valley. The crisp green florist's paper crackled loudly in the afternoon air. Away to his left he could hear the urgent bleat of horns as the bumper-to-bumper traffic crawled up the Rue Norvins toward Sacré-Coeur. With its gleaming white walls, cupolas, and dome the cathedral floated like an Arabian nights dream over this city of light and dreams.

The last time I saw Paris.

Earl, his face holding all the expression of an ebony statue. Lena, flushed, impassioned. 'You must go!' Looking to Earl for help and comfort. The quiet; 'it would probably be best.' The path of least resistance. So strange from this of all men.

Tachyon knelt, brushed away the petals that littered the stone slab.

Earl Sanderson Jr.
'Noir Aigle'
1919–1974

You lived too long, my friend. Or so it was said. Those busy, noisy activists could have used you better if you'd had the grace to die in 1950. No – even better – while liberating Argentina or freeing Spain or saving Gandhi.

Laid the bouquet on the grave. A sudden breeze set the delicate white bells of the lilies to trembling. Like a young girl's lashes just before she was kissed. Or like Blythe's lashes just before she wept.

The last time I saw Paris.

A cold, bleak December, and a park in Neuilly.

Blythe van Renssaeler, aka Brain Trust, died yesterday …

Gracelessly he surged to his feet, dusted the knees of his pants with a handkerchief. Gave his nose a quick, emphatic blow. That was the trouble with the past. It never stayed buried.

Straddling the slab was a large elaborate wreath. Roses and gladiolas and yards of ribbon. A wreath for a dead hero. A travesty. A small foot came up, sent the wreath tumbling. Contemptuously Tachyon walked over it, grinding the fragile petals beneath his heel.

One cannot propitiate the ancestors, Jack. Their ghosts will follow.

His certainly were.

On the Rue Etex he hailed a cab, fished for the note, read off the name of the Left Bank café in rusty French. Settled back to watch the unlit neon signs flash past. *XXX, Le Filles! 'Les Sexy.'* Strange to think of all this smut at the foot of a hill whose name translated as the Mountain of Martyrs. Saints had died on Montmartre. The Society of Jesus had been founded on the hill in 1534.

They proceeded in noisy and profane lurches. Bursts of heart-stopping speed followed by neck-wrenching stops. A blare of horns, and an exchange of imaginative insults. They shot through the Place Vendome past the Ritz where the delegation was housed. Tachyon hunkered deeper into his seat though it was unlikely he would be spotted. He was so sick of them all. Sara, quiet, sleek, and secretive as a mongoose. She had changed since Syria, but refused to confide. Peregrine flaunting her pregnancy, refusing to accept that she might not beat the odds. Mistral, young and beautiful. She had been tactful and understanding and kept his shameful secret. Fantasy, sly and amused. She had not. Hot blood washed his face. His humiliating condition was now public to be sniggered at and discussed in tones ranging from the sympathetic to the amused. His hand closed tightly on the note. There would be at least one woman he could face without embarrassment. One of his ghosts, but more welcome than the living right now.

She had chosen a café on the Boulevard Saint-Michel in the heart of the Latin Quarter. The area had always despised the bourgeoisie. Tachyon wondered if Danelle still did. Or had the years dampened her revolutionary ardor? One could only hope it had not dampened her other ardors. Then he remembered, and shrunk down once more.

Well, if he could no longer taste passion, he could at least remember it.

She had been nineteen when they'd met in August of 1950. A university student majoring in political philosophy, sex, and revolution. Danelle had been eager to comfort the shattered victim of a capitalist witch-hunt: the new darling of the French intellectual left. She took pride in his sufferings. As if the mystique of his martyrdom could rub off with bodily contact.

She had used him. But by the Ideal he had used her. As a shroud, a buffer against pain and memory. Drowned himself in cunt and wine. Nursing a bottle in Lena Goldoni's Champs-Élysées penthouse listening to the impassioned rhetoric of revolution. Caring far less for the rhetoric than the passion. Red-tipped nails meeting a slash of red for a mouth as Dani puffed inexpertly at larynx-stripping Gauloises. Black hair as smooth as an ebony helmet over her small head. Lush bosoms straining at a too tight sweater, and short skirts that occasionally gave him tantalizing glimpses of pale inner thigh.

God, how they had screwed! Had there ever been any emotion

past mutual using? Yes, perhaps, for she had been one of the last to condemn and reject him. She had even seen him off on that frigid January day. That was when he'd still had luggage and a semblance of dignity. There on the platform of the Montparnasse railway station, she had pressed money and a bottle of cognac onto him. He hadn't refused. The cognac had been too welcome, and the money meant that another bottle would follow.

In 1953 he had called Dani when another fruitless visa battle with the German authorities had sent him careening back into France. Called her hoping for one more bottle of cognac, one more handout, one more round of desperate fornication. But a man had answered, and in the background he had heard a child crying, and when she had finally come to the phone, the message was clear. *Get fucked, Tachyon.* Tittering, he had suggested that was why he'd called. The unpleasant buzz of a disconnected phone.

Later in that cold park in Neuilly he'd read of Blythe's death, and nothing had seemed to matter anymore.

And yet when the delegation arrived in Paris, Dani had reached out. A note in his box at the Ritz. A meeting on the Left Bank as the silver-gray Parisian sky was turning to rose, and the Eiffel Tower became a web of diamond light. So maybe she had cared. And maybe, to his shame, he hadn't.

Dôme was a typical working-class Parisian café. Tiny tables squeezed onto the sidewalk, gay, blue, and white umbrellas, harried, frowning waiters in none-too-clean white smocks. The smell of coffee and *grillade*. Tach surveyed the handful of patrons. It was early yet for Paris. He hoped she hadn't chosen to sit inside. All that smoke. His glance kept flicking across a thickset figure in a rusty black coat. There was a watchful intensity about the raddled face, and—

Dear God, could it ... NO!

'*Bon soir*, Tachyon.'

'Danelle,' he managed faintly, and groped for the back of a chair.

She smiled an enigmatic smile, sucked down some coffee, ground out a cigarette in the dirty ashtray, lit another, leaned back in a horrible parody of her old sexy manner, and eyed him through the rising smoke. 'You haven't changed.'

His mouth worked, and she laughed sadly. 'The platitude a little hard to force out? Of course *I've* changed – it's been thirty-six years.'

Thirty-six years. Blythe would be seventy-five.

Intellectually he had accepted the reality of their pitifully short lifespans. But it had not come home to him before. Blythe had died. Braun remained unchanged. David was lost, so like Blythe remained a memory of youth and charm. And of his new friends, Tommy, Angelface, and Hiram were just entering that uncomfortable stage of middle age. Mark was the merest child. Yet forty-one years ago it had been Mark's father who had impounded Tach's ship. *And Mark hadn't even been born yet!*

Soon (or at least as his people measured time), he would be forced to watch them pass from youth into inevitable decay and thence into death. The chair was a welcome support as his rump hit the cold wrought-iron.

'Danelle,' he said again.

'A kiss, Tachy, for old times' sake?'

Heavy yellowish pouches hung beneath faded eyes. Gray brittle hair thrust into a careless bun, the deep gouges beside her mouth into which the scarlet lipstick had bled like a wound. She leaned in close, hitting him with a wave of foul breath. Strong tobacco, cheap wine, coffee, and rotting teeth combining in a stomach-twisting effluvium.

He recoiled, and this time when the laughter came it seemed forced. As if she hadn't expected this reaction and was covering the hurt. The harsh laugh ended in a long coughing jag that brought him out of his chair and to her side. Irritably she shrugged off his soothing hand.

'Emphysema. And don't you start, *le petit docteur*. I'm too damn old to give up my cigarettes, and too damn poor to get medical attention when the time comes to die. So I smoke faster hoping I'll die faster, and then it won't cost so much at the end.'

'Danelle—'

'*Bon Dieu*, Tachyon! You are dull. No kiss for old times' sake, and apparently no conversation either. Though as I recall, you weren't much of a talker all those years ago.'

'I was finding all the communication I needed in the bottom of a cognac bottle.'

'It doesn't seem to have inconvenienced you any. Behold! A great man.'

She saw the world-renowned figure, a slim figure dressed in brocade and lace, but he, gazing back at the reflections of a thousand memories, saw a cavalcade of lost years. Cheap rooms stinking of sweat, vomit, urine, and despair. Groaning in an alley in Hamburg, beaten almost to death. Accepting a devil's pact with a gently smiling man, and for what? Another bottle. Waking hallucinations in a cell in the Tombs.

'What are you doing, Danelle?'

'I'm a maid at the Hotel Intercontinental.' She seemed to sense his thought. 'Yes, an unglamorous end to all that revolutionary fervor. The revolution never came, Tachy.'

'No.'

'Which doesn't leave you brokenhearted.'

'No. I never accepted your – all of your – versions of utopia.'

'But you stayed with us. Until finally we threw you out.'

'Yes, I needed you, and I used you.'

'My God, such a soul-deep confession? At meetings like these it's supposed to be all "*bonjour*" and "*Comment allez-ous,*" and "My, you haven't changed." But we've already done that, haven't we?' The bitter mocking tone added a razor's edge to the words.

'What do you want, Danelle? Why did you ask to see me?'

'Because I knew it would bother you.' The butt of the Gauloise followed its predecessor into a squashed and ashy death. 'No, that's not true. I saw your little motorcade pull in. All flags and limousines. It made me think of other years and other banners. I suppose I wanted to remember, and alas as one grows older, the memories of youth become fainter, less real.'

'I unfortunately do not share that kindly blurring. My kind do not forget.'

'Poor little prince.' She coughed again, a wet sound.

Tachyon reached into his breast pocket, pulled out his wallet, stripped off bills.

'What's that for?'

'The money you gave me and the cognac and thirty-six years interest.'

She flinched away, eyes bright with unshed tears. 'I didn't call you for charity or pity.'

'No, you called to rip at me, hurt me.'

She looked away. 'No, I called you so I could remember another time.'

'They weren't very good times.'

'For you maybe. I loved them. I was happy. And don't flatter yourself. You weren't the reason.'

'I know. Revolution was your first and final love. I find it hard to accept that you've given it up.'

'Who says I have?'

'But you said ... I thought ...'

'Even the old can pray for change, perhaps even more fervently than the young. By the way' – she drained the last of her coffee with a noisy slurp – 'why wouldn't you help us?'

'I couldn't.'

'Ah, of course. The little prince, the dedicated royalist. You never cared about the people.'

'Not as you use that phrase. You reduce them to slogans. I was bred to lead and to protect and to care for them as individuals. Ours is a better way.'

'You're a parasite!' And in her face he saw a fleeting shadow of the girl she had been.

An almost rueful smile touched his lips. 'No, an aristocrat, which you would probably argue is synonymous.' His long forefinger played among the little pile of francs. 'Despite what you think, it really wasn't my aristocratic sensibilities that kept me from using my power on your behalf. What you were doing was harmless enough – unlike this new breed who think nothing of killing a man merely for being successful.'

She hunched a shoulder. 'Please, get to the point.'

'I'd lost my powers.'

'What? You never told us.'

'I was afraid of losing my mystique if I had.'

'I don't believe you.'

'It's true. Because of Jack's cowardice.' His face darkened. 'The HUAC returned Blythe to the stand. They were demanding the names of all known aces, and because she had my mind, she knew. She was about to betray them, so I used my power to stop her and in so doing broke her mind and left the woman I loved a raving maniac.' He raised trembling fingertips to his damp forehead. The retelling in this of all cities infused it with new power, new pain.

'It took years for me to overcome my guilt, and it was the Turtle who showed me how. I destroyed one woman, but saved another. Does that balance the scales?' He was speaking more to himself than to her.

But she was not interested in his ancient pain; her own memories were too intense. 'Lena was so angry. She called you a disgusting user, taking and taking and giving nothing in return. Everyone wanted you out because you had so spoiled our beautiful plan.'

'Yes, and not *one* person took my side! Not even Earl.' His expression softened, as he looked past the ruin of age, to the beautiful girl he remembered. 'No, that's not true. You defended me.'

'Yes,' she admitted gruffly. 'Little good that it did. It took me years to regain the respect of my comrades.' She stared blindly down at the tabletop.

Tachyon glanced at the watch in his boot heel, rose. 'Dani, I must go. The delegation is due at Versailles by eight, and I must change. It's been ...' He tried again. 'I'm so glad that you contacted me.' The words seemed stilted and insincere even to his own ears.

Her face crumpled, then stiffened into bitter lines. 'That's it? Forty minutes and *au revoir*, you wouldn't even drink with me?'

'I'm sorry, Dani. My schedule—'

'Ah, yes, the great man.' The pile of bills still lay between them on the table. 'Well, I'll take these as an example of your noblesse oblige.'

She lifted up a shapeless bag and fished out a billfold. Scooped up the francs and jammed them into the battered wallet. Then paused and stared at one photo. A cruel little smile played about her wrinkled lips.

'No, better yet. I'll give you value for your money.' Gnarled, arthritic fingers pulled free the picture and tossed it onto the table.

It was a breathtaking still of a young woman. A river of red hair half masking the narrow, shadowed face. A mischievous, knowing look in the uptilted eyes. A delicate forefinger pressed against a full lower lip as if shushing the onlooker.

'Who is she?' Tach asked, but with a breath-stopping certainty that he knew the answer.

'My daughter.' Their eyes locked. Dani's smile broadened. 'And yours.'

'Mine.' The word emerged as a wondering, joyful sigh.

Suddenly all the weariness and anguish of the trip sloughed away. He had witnessed horrors. Jokers stoned to death in the slums of Rio. Genocide in Ethiopia. Oppression in South Africa. Starvation and disease everywhere. It had left him feeling hopeless and defeated. But if *she* walked this planet, then it could be borne. Even the anguish over his impotence faded. With the loss of his virility he had lost a major part of himself. Now it had been returned to him.

'Oh, Dani, Dani!' He reached across and gripped her hand. 'Our daughter. What is her name?'

'Gisele.'

'I must see her. Where is she?'

'Rotting. She's dead.'

The words seemed to shatter in the air, sending ice fragments deep into his soul. A cry of anguish was torn from him, and he wept, tears dropping through his fingers.

Danelle walked away.

Versailles, the greatest tribute to the divine right of kings ever constructed. Tachyon, heels tapping on the parquet floor, paused and surveyed the scene through the distorting crystal of his champagne glass. For an instant he might have been home, and the longing that gripped him was almost physical in its intensity.

There is indeed no beauty to this world. I wish I could leave it forever.

No, not true, he amended as his gaze fell upon the faces of his friends. *There is much here still to love.*

One of Hartmann's polished aides was at his shoulder. Was this the one fortunate enough to have survived the kidnapping in Germany, or had he been flown in specially to serve as cannon fodder for this line-withering tour? Well, perhaps the increased security would keep this young man alive until they could reach home.

'Doctor, Monsieur de Valmy would like to meet you.'

The young man forced a path for Tachyon while the alien studied France's most popular presidential candidate since de Gaulle. Franchot de Valmy, said by many to be the next president of the Republic. A tall, slim figure moving easily through the crowd. His rich chestnut hair was streaked with a single two-inch bar of white. Very striking. More striking, though far less evident, was the fact he was a wild card. An ace. In a country gone mad for aces.

Hartmann and de Valmy were shaking hands. It was an outstanding display of political soft soap. Two eager hunters using one another's power and popularity to catapult them into the highest offices in their lands.

'Sir, Dr. Tachyon.'

De Valmy turned the full force of his compelling green-eyed gaze onto the Takisian. Tachyon, raised in a culture that put a high premium on charm and charisma, found that this man possessed both to an almost Takisian magnitude. He wondered if that was his wild card gift.

'Doctor, I am honored.' He spoke in English.

Tach placed a small hand over his breast and replied in French, 'The honor is entirely mine.'

'I will be interested to hear your comments on our scientists' work on the wild card virus.'

'Well, I have only just arrived.' He fingered his lapel, raised his eyes, and pinned de Valmy with a sharp glance. 'And will I be reporting to *all* the candidates in the race? Will they also wish to hear my comments?'

Senator Hartmann took a small step forward, but de Valmy was laughing. 'You are very astute. Yes, I am – how do you Americans say – counting my chickens.'

'With reason,' said Hartmann with a smile. 'You've been groomed by the President as his heir apparent.'

'Certainly an advantage,' said Tachyon. 'But your status as an ace hasn't hurt.'

'No.'

'I would be curious to know your power.'

De Valmy covered his eyes. 'Oh, Monsieur Tachyon, I'm embarrassed to speak of it. It's such a contemptible little power. Mere parlor tricks.'

'You are very modest, sir.'

Hartmann's aide glared, and Tach stared blandly back, though he regretted the momentary flash of sarcasm. It was ill bred of him to take out his weariness and unhappiness on others.

'I am not above using the advantage granted to me, Doctor, but I hope that it will be my policies and leadership that will give me the presidency.'

Tachyon gave a small laugh and caught Gregg Hartmann's eye. 'It is ironic, is it not, that in this country the wild card bestows a cachet to help a man into high office, while in our country that same information would defeat him.'

The senator pulled a face. 'Leo Barnett.'

'I beg you pardon?' asked de Valmy in some confusion.

'A fundamentalist preacher who's gathering quite a following. He'd restore all the old wild card laws.'

'Oh, worse than that, Senator. I think he would place them in detention camps and force mass sterilizations.'

'Well, this is an unpleasant subject. But on another unpleasant subject I'd like a chance to talk to you, Franchot, about your feelings on the phaseout of medium-range missiles in Europe. Not that I have any standing with the current administration, but my colleagues in the Senate …' He linked arms with de Valmy and they drifted away, their various aides trailing several paces behind like hopeful pilot fish.

Tach gulped down champagne. The chandeliers glittered in the long line of mirrors, multiplying them a hundredfold and throwing back bright light like shards of glass into his aching head. He took another swallow of champagne, though he knew the alcohol was partly to blame for his present discomfort. That and the drilling hum of hundreds of voices, the busy scrape of bows on strings, and outside, the watching presence of an adoring public. Sensitive telepath that he was, it beat on him like an urgent, hungry sea.

As the motorcade had driven up the long chestnut-lined boulevard, they had passed hundreds of waving people all eagerly craning for a glimpse of the *les ases fantastiques*. It was a welcome relief after such hatred and fear in other countries. Still, he was glad that only one country remained, and then he would be home. Not that anything waited for him there but more problems.

In Manhattan, James Spector was on the streets. Death incarnate stalking free. Another monster created by my meddling. Once home I must deal with this. Trace him. Find him. Stop him. I was so stupid to abandon him in favor of pursuing Roulette.

And what of Roulette? Where can she be? Did I do wrong to release her? I am undoubtedly a fool where women are concerned.

'Tachyon.' Peregrine's gay call floated on the strains of Mozart and pulled him from his introspective fog. 'You've got to see this.'

He pinned a smile firmly in place and kept his eyes strictly off the mound of her belly thrust aggressively front and center. Mordecai Jones, the Harlem auto repairman, looking uncomfortable in his tuxedo, nervously eyed a tall gold-and-crystal lamp as if expecting it to attack. The long march of mirrors brought back thoughts of the Funhouse, and Des, the fingers at the end of his elephant's trunk twitching slightly, heightened the memory. *The past*. It seemed to be hanging like a dead weight from his shoulders.

The knot of friends and fellow travelers parted, and a hunched, twisted figure was revealed. The joker lurched around and smiled up at Tach. The face was a handsome one. Noble, a little tired, lines about the eyes and mouth denoting past suffering, a kindly face – *his, in fact*. There was a shout of laughter from the group as Tach gaped down into his own features.

There was a shifting like clay being mashed or a sponge being squeezed, and the joker faced him with his own features in place. A big square head, humorous brown eyes, a mop of gray hair, set atop that tiny, twisted body.

'Forgive me, the opportunity was too enticing to pass up,' chuckled the joker.

'And your expression the best of all, Tachy,' put in Chrysalis.

'You can laugh, you're safe. He can't do you,' harrumphed Des.

'Tach, this is Claude Bonnell, *Le Miroir*. He's got this great act at the Lido.'

'Poking fun at the politicos,' rumbled Mordecai.

'He does this hysterical skit with Ronald and Nancy Reagan,' giggled Peregrine.

Jack Braun, drawn by the laughing group, hovered at its out-skirts. His eyes met Tachyon's, and the alien looked through him. Jack shifted until they were at opposite sides of the circle.

'Claude's been trying to explain to us this alphabet soup that's French politics,' said Digger. 'All about how de Valmy has welded an impressive coalition of the RPR, the CDS, the JJSS, the PCF—'

'No, no, Mr. Downs, you must not include my party among the ranks of those who support Franchot de Valmy. We communists have better taste, and our own candidate.'

'Who won't win,' ejected Braun, frowning down at the tiny joker.

The features blurred, and Earl Sanderson Jr. said softly, 'There were some who supported the goals of world revolution.'

Jack, face gone sickly white, staggered back. There was a sharp *crack* as his glass shattered in his hands, and a flare of gold as his biological force field came to life to protect him. There was an uncomfortable silence after the big ace had left, then Tachyon said coolly, 'Thank you.'

'My pleasure.'

'You are here as a wild card representative?'

'Partly, but I also have an official capacity. I am a member of the party congress.'

'You are a big wheel with the commies,' whistled Digger with his usual lack of tact.

'Yes.'

'How did you pick up Earl? Or have you just made it a point to study those of us on the tour?' asked Chrysalis.

'I have a very low-level telepathy. I can pick up the faces of those who have deeply affected a person.'

Hartmann's aide was once again at his side. 'Doctor, Dr. Corvisart has arrived and wants to meet you.'

Tachyon made a face. 'Duty calls, so pleasure must be forgone. Gentlemen, ladies.' He bowed and walked away.

An hour later Tach was standing by the small chamber orchestra, allowing the soothing strains of Mendelssohn's Trout quintet to work its magic. His feet were beginning to hurt, and he realized that forty years on Earth had robbed him of his ability to stand for hours. Recalling long-past deportment lessons, he tucked in his hips, pulled back his shoulders, and lifted his chin. The relief was immediate, but he decided that another glass would also help.

Flagging down a waiter, he reached for the champagne. Then staggered, and fell heavily against the man as a blinding, directionless mind assault struck his shields.

Mind control!

The source?

Outside ... somewhere.

The focus?

He was dimly aware of crashing glasses as he slumped against his startled support. Forced up lids that seemed infinitely heavy. So distorting was the effect of his own psi search, and the screaming power of the mind control, that reality took on a strange shifting quality. The reception guests in their bright finery faded to gray. He could 'see' the mind probe like a brilliant line of light. Becoming diffuse at its source, impossible to pinpoint. But haloing:

A man.

Uniform.

One of the security captains.

Attaché case.

BOMB!

He reached out with his mind and seized the officer. For a moment the man writhed and danced like a moth in a flame as his controller and Tach fought for supremacy. The strain was too much for his human mind, and consciousness left him like a candle being snuffed. The major went down spraddle-legged on the polished wood floor. Tach found his fingers closing about the edges of the black leather case, though he couldn't remember moving.

Controller knows he's lost focus. Time detonated or command detonated? No time to ponder on it.

The solution, when it came, almost wasn't conscious. He reached out, gripped the mind. Jack Braun stiffened, dropped his drink, and went running for the long windows overlooking the front garden and fountains. People flew like ninepins as the big ace came barreling through them. Tachyon cocked back his arm, prayed to the ancestors for aim and strength, and threw.

Jack, like a hero in a forties football film, leapt, plucked the spinning case from the air, tucked it tight into his chest, and launched himself out the window. Glass haloed his gold-glowing body. A second later, and a tremendous explosion blew out the rest of the windows lining the Hall of Mirrors. Women screamed as razor-edged glass shards bit deep into unprotected skin. Glass and gravel from the yard pattered like hysterical raindrops onto the wood floor.

People rushed to the window to check on Braun.

Tachyon turned his back on the windows and knelt beside the stentoriously breathing major. One should have priorities.

'Let's go over it again.'

Tach eased his aching buttocks on the hard plastic chair, shifted until he could take a surreptitious glance at his watch. *12:10 A.M.* Police were definitely the same the world over. Instead of being grateful for his having averted a tragedy, they were treating him as if he were the criminal. And Jack Braun had been spared all this because the authorities had insisted on carting him off to the hospital. Of course he wasn't hurt, that was why Tachyon had selected him. No doubt by morning the papers would be filled with praise for the brave American ace, thought Tach sourly. *Never noticing my contributions.*

'*Monsieur?*' prodded Jean Baptiste Rochambeau of the French Sûreté.

'To what purpose? I've *told* you. I sensed a powerful, natural mind control at work. Because of the user's lack of training and control, I was unable to pinpoint the source. I could, however, pinpoint its victim. When I fought for control, I read through to the controller's mind, read the presence of the bomb, mind-controlled Braun, tossed him the bomb, he went out the window, the bomb exploded, with him no worse for the wear except perhaps wearing some of the topiary.'

'There is no topiary beyond the windows of the Hall of Mirrors,' sniffed Rochambeau's assistant in his nasal, high-pitched voice.

Tach swung around in the chair. 'It was a little joke,' he explained gently.

'Dr. Tachyon. We are not doubting your story. It's just that it's impossible. No such powerful ... mentat?' – he looked to Tachyon for confirmation – 'exists in France. As Dr. Corvisart has explained, we have every carrier, both latent and expressed, on file.'

'Then one has slipped past you.'

Corvisart, an arrogant gray-haired man with fat cheeks like a chipmunk's and a tiny pursed bud of a mouth, gave a stubborn headshake.

'Every infant is tested and registered at birth. Every immigrant is tested at the border. Every tourist must have the test before they can receive a visa. The only explanation is the one I have suspected for several years. The virus has mutated.'

'That is patent and utter nonsense! With all due respect, Doctor, *I* am the foremost authority on the wild card virus on this or any other world.'

Perhaps something of an exaggeration that, but surely it could be forgiven. He had been enduring fools with such patience for so many hours.

Corvisart was quivering with outrage. 'Our research has been acknowledged as the best in the world.'

'Ah, but *I* don't publish.' Tachyon was on his feet. '*I* don't have to.' A single-step advance. '*I* have a certain advantage.' Another. '*I* helped develop the withering thing!' he bellowed down into the Frenchman's face.

Corvisart held stubbornly firm. 'You are wrong. The mentat exists, he is not on file, ergo the virus has mutated.'

'I want to see your notes, duplicate the research, look over these vaunted files.' This he addressed to Rochambeau. He might have the soul of a policeman, but at least he wasn't an idiot.

The Sûreté officer cocked an eyebrow. 'You have any objections, Dr. Corvisart?'

'I suppose not.'

'You want to start now?'

'Why not? The night's ruined anyway.'

They set him up in Corvisart's office with an impressive computer at his disposal, bulging hardcopy files of research, a foot-high stack of disks, and a cup of strong coffee that Tach liberally laced with brandy from his hip flask.

The research was good, but it was geared toward proving Corvisart's pet premise. The hope of fame in the form of a mutated form – Wild Cardus Corvisartus? – was subtly coloring the Frenchman's interpretations of the data he was collecting. The virus was *not* mutating.

Thank the gods and ancestors, Tach sent up as a heartfelt prayer.

He was scrolling idly through the wild card registry when an anomaly, something not quite right, caught his attention. It was five in the morning, hardly the time to scroll back several years to check if he'd seen what he'd thought he'd seen, but upbringing and his own curious nature could not be denied. After several minutes of fervid key tapping he had the screen divided and both documents called up side by side. He fell back in the chair, rumpling his already tumbled curls with nervous fingers.

'Well, I'll be damned,' he said aloud to the silent room.

The door opened, and the adenoidal sergeant thrust in his head. 'Monsieur? You require something?'

'No, nothing.'

His hand shot out, and he erased the damning documents. What he discovered was for him alone. For it was political dynamite. It would create havoc with an election, cost a man the presidency, and shake the foundations of trust of the electorate should it get out.

Tach pressed his hands into the small of his back, stretched until vertebrae popped, and shook his head like a weary pony. 'Sergeant, I am very much afraid that I have found nothing that is of any help. And I'm too tired to go on. May I please be returned to the hotel?'

♦

But his bed at the Ritz had held no comfort or rest, so here he was leaning over the bridge railing on the Pont de la Concorde watching coal barges slip by, and snuffling eagerly at the smell of baking bread, which seemed to have permeated the city. Every part of his small body seemed to be suffering from some discomfort. His eyes felt like two burned holes in a blanket, his back still ached from that impossible chair, and his stomach was demanding to be fed. But worst of all was what he had dubbed his mental indigestion. He had seen or heard something of significance. And until he hit upon it, his brain was going to continue to seethe like jelly boiling on a stove.

'Sometimes,' he told his mind severely, 'I feel as if you have a mind of your own.'

He began walking through the Place de la Concorde, where Marie Antoinette had lost her head, the spot now marked by a venerable Egyptian obelisk. There were plenty of restaurants to choose from: the Hotel de Crillon, the Hotel Intercontinental, just two blocks from the square, where Dani was no doubt hard at work, and beyond it the Ritz. He hadn't seen any of his companions since the dramatic events of the previous night. His entrance would be met with exclamations, congratulations ... He decided to miss the whole mess.

He was still wearing his reception finery. Pale lavender and rose, and a foam of lace. He frowned when a taxi driver gaped and drove over a curb and almost into one of the central fountains. Embarrassed, Tachyon darted through the richly decorated iron railing and into the Tuileries Gardens. On either side loomed the Jeu de Paume and the Orangerie, ahead the neat rows of chestnut trees, fountains, and a riot of statues.

Tach dropped wearily onto the edge of a basin. The fountain squirted into life and sent a fine spray of mist across his face. For a moment he sat with eyes closed, savoring the cool touch of the water. Retreating to a nearby bench, he pulled out the picture of Gisele and again studied those delicate features. Why was it that whenever he came to Paris, he found only death?

And suddenly the piece fell into place. The puzzle lay complete before him. With a cry of joy he leapt to his feet and broke into a frantic run. The high heels of his formal pumps slipped on the gravel path. Cursing, he hopped along, pulling them off. Then with a shoe in each hand he flew up the stairs and onto the Rue de Rivoli. Horns blared, tires squealed, drivers shrieked. He ran on heedless of it all. Pulled up gasping before the glass and marble entrance to the Hotel Intercontinental. Met the bemused eyes of the doorman, slipped his feet into his shoes, straightened his coat, patted at his tumbled hair, trod casually into the quiet lobby.

'Bonjour.'

The desk clerk's eyes widened in dawning wonder as he recognized the extravagant figure before him. He was a handsome man in his mid-thirties with sleek seal-brown hair and deep blue eyes.

'You have a woman working here. Danelle Moncey. It is vital that I speak with her.'

'Moncey? No, Monsieur Tachyon. There is no one by—'

'Damn! She married. I forgot that. She's a maid, mid-fifties, black eyes, gray hair.' His heart was thundering, setting up an answering pounding in his temples. The young man looked nervously down at Tachyon's hands, which had closed urgently about his lapels, pulling him half over the counter. Releasing the clerk, Tachyon rubbed his fingertips. 'Forgive me. As you can see, this is very important ... very important to me.'

'I'm sorry, but there is no Danelle working here.'

'She's a Communist,' Tach added in desperation.

The man shook his head, but the pert blond behind the exchange counter suddenly said, 'Ah, no, François. You know, Danelle.'

'Then she is here?'

'Oh, *mais oui*. She is on the third floor—'

'Will you get her for me?' Tachyon gave the girl his best come-hither smile.

'Monsieur, she is working,' protested the desk clerk.

'I only require a moment of her time.'

'Monsieur, I cannot have a cleaning woman in the lobby of the Intercontinental.' It was almost a wail.

'Blood's end! Then I'll go to her.'

Danelle was bundling sheets into a hamper. Gasped when she saw him, tried to bull past him using her cleaning cart as a battering ram. He danced aside and caught her by the wrist.

'We must talk.' He was grinning like a fool.

'I'm working.'

'Take the day off.'

'I'll lose my job.'

'You're not going to need this job any longer.'

'Oh, why not?'

A man and his wife stepped out of their room and stared curiously at the couple.

'This won't do.'

She eyed him, checked her cheap wristwatch. 'It's almost my break. I'll meet you at the Café Morens just down from the hotel on the Rue du Juillet. Buy me some cigarettes and my usual.'

'Which is?'

'They'll know. I always take my break there.'

He took her face between his hands and kissed her. Smiled at her confused expression.

'What has happened with you?'

'I'll tell you at the café.'

As he hurried back through the lobby he saw the desk clerk just hanging up the phone in one of the public booths. The young blond woman waved and called, 'Did you find her?'

'Oh, yes. Thank you very much.'

Tachyon fidgeted at one of the tiny tables that had been squeezed out front of the café. The street was so narrow that the parked cars had two wheels cocked up on the sidewalks.

Dani arrived and lit a Gauloise. 'So what is this all about?'

'You lied to me.' He shook a finger coyly under her nose. 'Our daughter is not dead. At Versailles … that was not a wild card, it was my blood kin. I don't blame you for wanting to hurt me, but let me make it up to you. I'll get you both back to America.'

A small car was gunning down the street. As it swept past, the chatter of automatic weapon fire echoed off the gray stone buildings. Danelle jerked in the chair. Tachyon caught her, flung them both down behind one of the parked cars. A white-hot poker burned through his thigh, and his elbow hit the sidewalk with a jarring crack. He lay frozen, cheek pressed to the pavement, something warm running over his hand. His leg had gone numb.

Danelle's breath was rattling in her throat. Tachyon took her mind. Gisele appeared. Reflected a million times over in a million different memories. *Gisele*. A brilliant firefly presence.

Desperately he reached after her, but she was receding, a lost and elusive magic among the darkening pathways of her dying mother's mind.

Danelle died.

Gisele died.

But had left a part of herself. A son. Tach clung to her, violating every rule of advanced mentatics by holding to a dying mind.

Panic seized him, and he fled back from that terrifying boundary.

In the physical world the air was filled with the undulating wail of sirens. *Oh, ancestors, what to do?* Be found here with a murdered hotel maid? Ludicrous. There would be questions to be answered. They would learn of his grandchild. And if wild cards were a national treasure, how much more a treasure was a part-blood Takisian?

The pain was beginning. Tachyon experimentally moved the leg and found that the bullet had missed the bone. The effort had popped sweat and filled the back of his throat with bile. How could he possibly reach the Ritz? He tightened his jaw. Because he was a prince of the house Ilkazam. *It's only two blocks*, he thought encouragingly.

He laid Danelle gently aside, folded her hands on her bosom, kissed her forehead. *Mother of my child*. Later he would mourn her properly. But first came vengeance.

The bullet had passed cleanly through the fleshy part of his thigh. There wasn't much blood. Yet. As he walked it began to pump. Camouflage, something to hide the wound just long enough to get past the desk and up to his room. He checked in parked cars. A folded newspaper. And the window was open. Not perfect, but good enough. Now he just had to find enough control not to limp those few steps from the front door to the elevator.

Piece of cake, as Mark would say. Training was everything. And blood. Blood would always tell.

He had taken a stab at sleeping, but it had been useless. Finally at six Jack Braun kicked aside the entangling bed clothes, stripped off sweat-soaked pajamas, dressed, and went in search of food.

Five months of hunched shoulders and nervous backward glances. Five months in which *he* had *never* spoken. Refused to grant him even eye contact. Had the hope of rehabilitation really been worth this amount of hell?

The Swarm invasion was to blame. It had pulled him back, out of the womb of real estate and California evenings and poolside sex. Here was a real crisis. No ace, no matter how tainted, would be unwelcome. And he'd done good, stomping all over monsters in Kentucky and Texas. And he'd discovered something interesting. Most of the new young aces didn't know who the hell he was. A few, Hiram Worchester, the Turtle, had known and it had mattered. But it was bearable. So maybe there was a way to come back. To be a hero again.

Hartmann had announced the world tour.

Jack had always admired Hartmann. Admired the way he'd led the fight to repeal certain parts of the Exotic Powers Control Act. He'd called the senator and offered to foot part of the bill. Money was always welcome to a politician, even if it wasn't being used to finance a campaign. Jack found himself on the plane.

And most of it hadn't been bad. There'd been plenty of action with women – most notably with Fantasy. They had lain in bed one night in Italy, and she'd told him with vicious wit about Tachyon's impotency. And he'd laughed, too loud and too long. Trying to diminish Tachyon. Trying to make him less of a threat.

Over the years he'd absorbed a bit about Takisian culture from the interviews he'd read. Vengeance was definitely part of the code. So he'd watched his back and waited for Tachyon to act. *And nothing had happened.*

The strain was killing him.

And then had come last night.

He smeared butter on the last roll in the bread basket, washed down the hard crusted bite with a sip of the unbelievably strong French coffee. He sure wished these Frenchies had a concept of a real breakfast. He could order an American breakfast of course, but the cost was as unbelievable as the coffee. This basket of dry bread and coffee was costing him ten dollars. Add in some eggs and bacon, and the cost soared to near thirty dollars. For breakfast!

Suddenly the absurdity of the thought struck him. He was a rich man, not a Depression farm boy from North Dakota. His contribution to this tour had been big enough to buy him a piece of the big 747, or at least the jet fuel to fly it—

Tachyon was entering the hotel, and the hair on the nape of

Jack's neck prickled. The door of the small restaurant gave him only a limited view, and soon the alien was out of sight. Jack felt the muscles in his neck and shoulders relax, and with a sigh he lifted a finger and ordered a full American breakfast.

Tachyon had looked funny. Fork moved mechanically from plate to mouth. *Holding himself real stiff.* Folded newspaper along his thigh like a soldier on dress parade. None of his business what the bastard was getting up to.

But last night was his business.

Anger ate through his belly like a physical pain. Sure the bomb couldn't have hurt him, but *he took my mind.* Casually, like a man tasting a mint. Reducing him in an instant from man to object.

Jack mopped up the last of the yolk while anger and outrage grew. God damn it! It was stupid to be scared of a pint-size fairy in fancy dress.

Not scared, Jack's mind quickly amended. He'd stayed away from the alien out of politeness, an acknowledgment of how much Tachyon hated him. But now Tachyon had changed the rules. He'd taken his mind. That he wasn't going to allow to pass.

They looked like two little red mouths. Bullet in, bullet out. Tach, seated in his undershorts, jabbed in a hypodermic, depressed the plunger, waited for the painkiller to take effect. Just for good measure he'd given himself a tetanus shot and an injection of penicillin. Spent hypos littered the table, a gauze pad lay ready, a roll of cotton. But for the moment he would let it seep. And do some hard thinking.

So Danelle had not lied. She had just not told all. Gisele was dead. The question was, how? Or did that matter? Probably not. What mattered was that she had married and borne a son. *My grandson.* And he had to be found.

And the father? Well, what of him? Assuming he was still alive, he was no fit guardian for the boy. The father – or unknown others – were manipulating this Takisian gift to spread terror.

So where to start? Undoubtedly at Danelle's apartment. Then

to the hall of records to search for the marriage license and birth certificate.

But that attack on Danelle and himself had been no accident. *They*, whoever they were, were watching. So, however distasteful, he was going to have to make an effort to blend in.

Braun spent a few moments dithering in the hall. But outrage won over prudence. He tested the door, found it locked, gave a hard twist, and broke the knob. Stepped over the threshold and froze in astonishment at the sight of Tachyon, scissors at the ready, seated in the midst of a circle of snipped red locks.

The Takisian gaped back, a final hank of that improbable hair clutched in a hand.

'How *dare* you!'

'What in the hell are you doing?'

As their first exchange in almost forty years, it seemed to lack something.

In quick flicks like the shuttering of a camera, the rest of the scene came into focus. Jack's forefinger shot out.

'That's a bullet wound.'

'Nonsense.' The gauze was laid quickly over the white thigh with its peppering of red-gold hairs. 'Now get out of my room.'

'Not until I have some answers out of you. Who the hell has been shooting at you?' He snapped his fingers. 'The bomb at Versailles. You've got a line into the people—'

'NO!' Far too quick and far too strong.

'Have you told the authorities?'

'There is no need. This is not a bullet wound. I know nothing of the terrorists.' The scissors sawed viciously through the last piece of hair. It fluttered to the floor, ironically forming a shape very reminiscent of a question mark.

'Why are you cutting your hair?'

'Because I feel like it! Now get out before I take your mind and make you go.'

'You do, and I'll come back and break your damn neck. You've never forgiven me—'

'You have *that* right!'

'You threw a goddamm bomb at me!'

'Unfortunately I knew it wouldn't hurt you.'

The long slender fingers played about his cropped head, fluttering among the curls until they clustered about his face. It had the effect of making him appear suddenly very young.

Braun stepped in on him, rested his hands on either arm of the chair, effectively trapping Tachyon. 'This tour is important. If you get up to some crazy stunt, it could damage everybody's reputation. *You* I don't give a damn about, but Gregg Hartmann is important.'

The alien looked away and gazed woodenly out the window. Despite being clad only in shirt and shorts he managed to make it seem regal.

'I'll go to Hartmann.'

There was a flicker of alarm deep in the lilac eyes, quickly suppressed. 'Fine, go. Anything to be rid of you.'

Silence stretched between them. Suddenly Braun asked, 'Are you in trouble?' No reply. 'If you are, tell me. Maybe I can help.'

The long lashes lifted, and Tachyon looked him fully in the eyes. There was nothing young about the narrow face now. It looked as cold and old and as implacable as death.

'I've had enough of your help for one lifetime, thank you.'

Jack almost ran from the room.

Tachyon pulled off the soft brown fedora and crumpled it agitatedly in his hands. The tiny two-room flat looked as if it had been struck by a cyclone. Drawers stood open, a cheap picture frame stood forlornly empty on a scarred table. What had it held that was so significant it had to be removed?

The police? he wondered. No, they would have been more careful. So Dani's killers had been here, and the police were yet to come, which meant Tach had to hurry. The newly purchased jeans felt stiff against his skin, and he tugged fretfully at the crotch while he riffled through the paperbacks that littered the front room.

A faint rasp sounded from the bedroom. Tachyon froze, crept cat-footed to the hot plate, and lifted the knife lying next to it. In a quick rush he crossed the room and pressed himself against the wall, ready to stab whatever came through the connecting door.

Careful, quiet footsteps, but enough vibration for Tach to tell that his opponent was big. Two sets of soft breaths from either side of the wall. Tach held his, waited. The man came through the door in a rush; Tachyon lunged in low, ready to drive the blade up beneath the ribs. The blade snapped, and gold light flashed across the dingy apartment walls. Jack Braun, forming his hand into a gun, placed his forefinger firmly between Tachyon's eyes, 'Bang, bang, you're dead.'

'GOD DAMN YOU!' In a blaze of temper he flung the broken knife against the wall. 'What are you doing here?'

'I followed you.'

'I never saw you!'

'I know. I'm pretty good at this.' The implication was clear.

'Why can't you just leave ... me ... alone?'

'Because you're getting in way over your head.'

'I can take care of myself.'

A derisive snort.

'If it hadn't been you, I'd have taken you out,' Tach cried.

'Yeah? And what if there'd been more than one? Or if they'd had guns?'

'I don't have time to discuss this with you. The police may be here any minute,' the alien threw over his shoulder as he stormed into the bedroom and continued his search.

'Police! HOLD IT! What is going on? Why the police?'

'Because the woman who lived in this flat was murdered this morning.'

'Oh, great. And why does this involve you?' Tachyon's mouth tightened mulishly. Braun gathered up the front of the alien's shirt, hefted him off the ground, and held him at eye level, noses almost touching. 'Tachyon.' It was a warning rumble.

'It's a private matter.'

'Not if the police are involved it isn't.'

'I can handle it myself.'

'I don't think so. You couldn't even spot me.' Tachyon sulked. 'Tell me what's going on. I just might help you.'

'Oh, very well,' he snapped pettishly. 'I'm searching for any clue as to the whereabouts of my grandson.'

That took some explaining. Tachyon fired out the tale in quick staccato sentences while they finished pawing through the jumble, turning up absolutely nothing.

'So you see, I have to find him first and get him out of the country before the French authorities realize what they possess,' he concluded, laying his hand on the doorknob. And heard a key rasp in the lock.

'Oh, shit,' whispered Tach.

'Police?' mouthed Jack.

'Undoubtedly,' the Takisian mouthed back.

'Fire escape.' Jack pointed back over his shoulder.

They fled.

'Let's see what we've got.' Braun paused to light a cigarette. Tachyon stopped wolfing down his enormous and very belated lunch and fished the paper from his jeans. Tossed it, only to have it land fluttering in the mustard jar. 'God damn it, be careful,' said Jack, aggrieved, and mopped at the paper with his napkin.

Tachyon continued to shovel it in. With an annoyed grunt the ace pulled out a pair of reading glasses and peered at the Takisian's florid hand:

Gisele Bacourt wed François Andrieux in a civil ceremony on December 5th, 1971.

One child, Blaise Jeannot Andrieux, born May 7, 1975.

Gisele Andrieux killed in a shoot-out with industrialist Simon de Montfort's personal bodyguard, November 28, 1984.

Both husband and wife were members of the French Communist Party.

François Andrieux had been pulled in for questioning, but was released when nothing conclusive could be found.

They had tried the simple expedient of checking the phone book, and – not surprisingly – Andrieux had not been listed. Jack sighed, rocked back in his chair, and returned his glasses to his shirt pocket. The Eiffel Tower cast an elongated shadow across the outdoor café.

'It's getting late, and we've got that dinner at the Tour Eiffel.'

'I'm not going.'

'Oh?'

'No, I'm going to go talk to Claude Bonnell.'

'Who?'

'Bonnell, Bonnell! *Le Miroir*, you know?'

'Why?'

'Because he's a major figure in the Communist Party. He may be able to obtain Andrieux's address for me.'

'And if that fails?' The smoke from the cigarette formed a loop in the air between them.

'I don't want to think about that.'

'Well, you better, if you really want to find this guy.'

'So what's your suggestion?'

'Try tracing the materials used in the bomb. They had to buy the stuff somewhere.'

Tach made a face. 'Sounds slow and tedious.'

'It is.'

'Then I'll pin my hope on Bonnell.'

'Fine, you hope, and I'll pursue my bomb idea. Of course, how we're going to get that information I'm not certain. I suppose you could always go to see Rochambeau and pick his brains …'

Tachyon steepled his fingers before his face and peered speculatively over the top at Jack. 'I have a better idea.'

'What?'

'Don't sound so suspicious. You and Billy Ray could talk to Rochambeau about the bomb. Say that you think it was meant for the senator – it might have been for all we know – suggest that you pool information.'

'Might work.' Jack ground out the cigarette. 'Billy Ray is a Justice Department ace, and Hartmann's bodyguard. 'Course he's bound to ask why I'm involved.'

'Just tell him it's because you're *Golden Boy*.' And the tone was undiluted acid.

◆

Bonnell's dressing room backstage at the Lido was typical. The strong odor of cold cream, greasepaint, and hair spray overlaying the fainter scents of old sweat and stale perfume.

Tachyon straddled a chair, arms resting along the back, and watched the joker put the final touches on his makeup.

'Could you hand me my ruff?'

Bonnell clasped it about his neck, rose, took one final critical look at the black and white harlequin costume, and settled back into the battered wooden chair.

'All right, Doctor. I'm ready. Now tell me what I can do for you.'

'I need a favor.' They spoke in French.

'Which is?'

'Do you have membership lists – addresses – for your members?'

'I assume we're speaking of the Party.'

'Oh, forgive me. Yes.'

'And to answer you, yes, we do.'

Bonnell was not helping him any. Tach plowed awkwardly on. 'Could you obtain an address for me?'

'That would depend on what you want it for.'

'Nothing nefarious, I assure you. A personal matter.'

'*Hmmm.*' Bonnell straightened the already meticulously arranged pots and tubes on his dressing table. 'Doctor, you presume a great deal. We have met only once, yet you come to me asking for private information. And if I were to ask you why?'

'I'd rather not say.'

'I rather thought that would be your answer. So I'm afraid I really must refuse.'

Exhaustion, tension, and the throbbing ache from his leg slammed down like a curling storm wave. Tach laid his head on his arms. Fought tears. Considered just giving up. A gentle but firm hand caught his chin and forced his head up.

'This really means a great deal to you, doesn't it?'

'More than you can know.'

'So tell me so I will know. Can't you trust me? Just a little?'

'I lived in Paris long ago. Have you been a communist for long?' he asked abruptly

'Ever since I was able to comprehend politics.'

'Then I'm surprised I didn't meet you all those long years ago. I knew them all. Thorenz, Lena Goldoni ... Danelle.'

'I wasn't in Paris then. I was still in Marseilles getting the crap beat out of me by my supposedly *normal* neighbors.' His smile was bitter. 'France has not always been so kind to her wild cards.'

'I'm sorry.'

'Why should *you* be?'

'Because it's my fault.'

'That's an exceedingly silly and self-indulgent attitude.'

'Thank you so very much.'

'The past is dead, buried, and gone forever past recall. Only the present and the future matter, Doctor.'

'And I think that's a silly and simplistic attitude. The actions of the past have consequences for the present and the future. Thirty-six years ago I came to this country broken and bitter. I slept with a young girl. Now I return to find that I left a more permanent mark on this place than I had thought. I sired a child who was born, lived, and died without my ever knowing of her existence. I could curse her mother for that, and yet perhaps she was wise. For the first thirteen years of Gisele's life her father was a drunken derelict. What could I have given her?' He paced away and stood rigidly regarding a wall. Then whirled and rested his shoulders against the cool plaster.

'I lost my chance with her, but the Ideal has granted me another. She had a son, my grandchild. And I want him.'

'And the father?'

'Is a member of your party.'

'You say you want him. What? You would steal him from his father?'

Tach rubbed wearily at his eyes. Forty-eight hours without sleep was taking its toll. 'I don't know. I haven't thought that far ahead. All I want is to see him, to hold him, to look into the face of my future.'

Bonnell slapped his hands onto his thighs and pushed up from the chair. '*C'est bien*, Doctor. A man deserves a chance to look upon the intersection of his past, present, and future. I will find you this man.'

'Just give his address, there's no reason for you to be involved.'

'He might take fright. I can reassure him, set up a meeting. His name – ?'

'François Andrieux.'

Bonnell noted it. 'Very good. So, I will speak to this man, and then I will ring you at the Ritz—'

'I'm no longer staying there. You can reach me at the Lys on the Left Bank.'

'I see. Any particular reason?'

'No.'

'I must work on that innocent expression. It is very charming, if not terribly convincing.' Tachyon flushed, and Bonnell laughed. 'There, there, don't take offense. You've told me enough of your secrets tonight. I won't press you for any more.'

The junket was dining at the expensive Tour Eiffel.

Tachyon, leaning on the rail of the observation deck, fidgeted and waited for Braun to emerge. Through the windows of the restaurant he could see that the party had reached the brandy-coffee-cigars-speeches stage. The door opened, and Mistral, giggling, darted out. She was followed by Captain Donatien Racine, one of France's more prominent aces. His sole power was flight, but that coupled with the fact he was career military had ensured that the press dubbed him Tricolor. It was a name he hated.

Gripping the American about her slender waist, Racine carried them over the protective railing. Mistral gave him a quick kiss, pushed free of his encircling arm, and floated away on the gentle breezes that sighed about the tower. Her great blue-and-silver cape spread around her until she resembled an exotic moth drawn by the glittering lights webbing the tower. Watching the couple darting and swooping in an intricate game of tag, Tachyon suddenly felt very weary and very old and very earthbound.

The restaurant doors flew open, and the delegation flowed out like water through a broken dam. After five months of formal dinners and endless speeches, it was no wonder they fled.

Braun, elegant in his white tie and tails, paused to light a cigarette. Tachyon touched him with a thread of telepathy.

Jack.

He stiffened, but gave no other outward sign.

Gregg Hartmann glanced back. 'Jack, are you coming?'

'I'll catch up with you. Think I'll enjoy the air and the view and watch those crazy kids skydive.' He pointed to Mistral and Racine.

A few moments later he joined Tachyon at the rail.

'Bonnell's going to set up a meeting.'

Braun grunted, flicked ash. 'The Sûreté were at the hotel when I got back. They tried to be subtle about questioning the delegation as to your whereabouts, but the news hounds are snuffling. They sense a story.'

The Takisian shrugged it aside with a hunch of the shoulder. 'Will you come with me? To the meeting?'

Ancestors, how it stuck in the throat to ask him for help!

'Sure.'

'I may need help with the father.'

'So you're going to do …'

'Whatever it takes. I want him.'

Montmartre. Where artists, legitimate and otherwise, swarmed like locusts ready to fall upon the unwary tourist. *A portrait of your beautiful wife, monsieur.* The cost politely never mentioned, then when it was completed a charge sufficient to purchase an old master.

Tour buses groaned up the hill and disgorged their eager passengers. The Gypsy children, circling like vultures, moved in. The European travelers, wise to the ways of these innocent-faced thieves, drove them away with loud threats. The Japanese and Americans, lulled by sparkling black eyes in dark faces, allowed them to approach. Later they would rue it when they discovered the loss of wallets, watches, jewelry.

So many people, and one small boy.

Braun, hands on hips, gazed out across the plaza before Sacré-Coeur. It was awash with people. Easels thrust up like masts from a colorful surging sea. He sighed, checked his watch.

'They're late.'

'Patience.'

Braun stared pointedly at his watch again. The Gypsy children attracted by the slim gold band of the Longines crept forward.

'Beat it!' Jack roared. 'Jesus, where do they all come from? Is there a Gypsy factory the same way there's a hooker factory?'

'They're usually sold by their mothers to "talent scouts" from France and Italy. They're then trained to steal and work like slaves for their owners.'

'Jesus, sounds like something out of Dickens.'

Tachyon shaded his eyes with one slim hand and searched for Bonnell.

'You know you were supposed to address a conference of researchers today.'

'Yes.'

'Well, did you call to cancel?'

'No, I forgot. I have more important things on my mind right now than genetic research.'

'I'd say that's exactly what you have on your mind,' came Braun's dry reply.

A taxi pulled up, and Bonnell struggled painfully out. He was followed by a man and a small boy. Tachyon's fingers dug deep into Jack's bicep.

'Look. Dear God!'

'What?'

'That man. He's the clerk from the hotel.'

'Huh?'

'He was at the Intercontinental.'

The trio were walking toward them. Suddenly the father froze, pointed at Jack, gestured emphatically, grabbed the child by the wrist, and hustled for the taxi.

'No, dear God, no.' Tachyon ran forward a few steps. Reached out, his power closing about their minds like a vise. They froze. He walked slowly toward them. Felt his breath go short as he devoured the small, stubborn face beneath its cap of red hair. The boy was fighting with not insignificant power, and only a quarter Takisian. Pride surged through Tach.

Suddenly he was flung to the ground, fists and rocks raining down upon him. He clung desperately to the control while the Gypsy children plucked at him, removing wallet, watch, and all the time continuing the hysterical beating. Jack waded in and began plucking urchins off him.

'No no, catch *them*. Don't worry about me!' screamed Tach. With a leg sweep he brought two to the ground, lurched to one knee, stiffened his fingers, and jabbed them hard into one gangling teenager's throat. The boy fell back, choking.

Jack hesitated, turned toward Andrieux and the boy, broke into a run. Tachyon, distracted, watched his progress. Never even saw the boot come swinging in. Pain exploded in his temple. Distantly he heard someone shouting, then bitter darkness.

Bonnell was wiping his face with a damp handkerchief when he finally came around. Desperately Tachyon levered up onto his elbows, then fell back as the motion sent waves of pain through his head and filled the back of his throat with nausea.

'Did you get them?'

'No.' Jack was holding a bumper like a man displaying a prize catch. 'When you went under they ran for it and made it into the cab. I tried to grab the car, but could only get the bumper. It came off,' he added unnecessarily. Jack eyed the interested crowd that had surrounded them and shooed them away.

'Then we've lost them.'

'What did you expect? You turn up with the Judas Ace,' said Bonnell angrily.

Jack flinched, murmured through stiff lips, 'That was a long time ago.'

'Some of us don't forget. And others of us shouldn't.' He glared at Tachyon. 'I thought I could trust you.'

'Jack, go away.'

'Well, fuck you too.' Long, jerky strides carried him into the crowd and out of sight.

'It's funny, but I feel very badly about that.' He gave himself a shake. 'So what do we do now?'

'First I extract a promise from you that there will be no more stunts like today.'

'All right.'

'I'll reset the meeting for tonight. And this time *come alone*.'

Jack wasn't sure why he did it. After the insult Tachyon had given him, he should have just washed his hands of the whole thing or told the Sûreté everything he knew. Instead he turned up at the Lys with an ice pack and aspirin.

'Thank you, but I do have a medical kit.'

Jack tossed the bottle several times. 'Oh, yeah? Well, then I'll take them. This whole thing is giving me a headache.'

Tach lifted the pack from his eye. 'Why you?'

'Lie down and leave that thing on your eye.' He scratched at his chin. 'Look, let me throw something out to you. Doesn't this whole thing strike you as just a little too convenient?'

'In what way?' But Jack could tell from the little alien's cautious tone that he'd struck a nerve.

'Instead of just giving you Andrieux's address, Bonnell insists on setting up a meeting. They tried to split—'

'Because you were there.'

'Yeah, right. You mind control them, then you just happen to get attacked by a gang of Gypsy children. I've done a little checking around. They *never* do that kind of thing. I think somebody had this arranged ahead of time. To make certain you couldn't use your mind control. And what about Andrieux? You said he was the clerk at the hotel. Then why did he deny any knowledge of Danelle? She was his mother-in-law, for Christ's sake. This thing stinks to high heaven.'

Tachyon flung the ice pack against the wall. 'So what do you suggest I do?'

'Don't work with Bonnell anymore. Don't go to any more meetings. Let me see what I can do with the bomb fragments. Rochambeau has agreed to work with Ray.'

'That could take weeks. We leave in a few days.'

'You are fucking obsessed with this!'

'Yes!'

'Why? Is it because you're impotent? Is that the big deal here?'

'I don't wish to discuss this.'

'I know you don't, but you've got to! You're not thinking this through, Tachyon. What it could do to the tour, to your reputation – to mine for that matter. We're withholding vital evidence pertaining to a murder.'

'You didn't have to become involved.'

'I know that, and sometimes I wish to Christ I hadn't. But I'm into it now, so I'll see it through to the end. So are you going to sit tight and see what I can find?'

'Yes, I'll wait to see what you find out.'

Jack shot him a suspicious glance. 'Well, I guess that'll have to do.'

'Oh, Jack.' The big ace paused, hand on the doorknob, and looked back. 'I apologize for this afternoon. It was wrong of me to send you away.'

It was obvious from the Takisian's expression what this was costing him. 'Okay,' Jack replied gruffly.

♥

It was an old house, a very old house, in the university district. Cracks cut the dingy plaster walls, and the musty odor of mold hung in the air. Bonnell gave Tachyon's arm a hard squeeze.

'Remember not to expect too much. This child doesn't know you.'

Tachyon barely heard him, certainly paid no attention. He was already heading up the stairs.

There were five people in the room, but Tachyon saw only the boy. Perched on a stool, he was swinging one foot, slamming his heel rhythmically into a battered wooden leg. His fine straight hair lacked the metallic copper fire of his grandsire's, but it was none-theless a deep rich red. Tach felt a surge of pride at this evidence of his prepotence. Straight red brows gave Blaise an overly serious expression that set oddly on the narrow child's face. His eyes were a brilliant purple-black.

Standing behind, a hand possessively on his son's shoulder, was Andrieux. Tachyon studied him with the critical eye of a Takisian psi lord evaluating breeding stock. *Not bad, human of course, but not bad.* Definitely handsome, and he appeared intelligent. Still it was hard to tell. If only he could run tests ... He tried to close his mind to the unwelcome suspicion that this man had been instru-mental in Dani's death.

He looked back to Blaise and found the boy studying him with equal interest. There was nothing shy about the gaze. Suddenly Tach's shields repelled a powerful mind assault.

'Trying to pay me back for yesterday?'

'*Mais oui.* You took my mind.'

'You take people's minds.'

'Of course. No one can stop me.'

'I can.' The brows snapped together in a thunderous frown. 'I'm Tachyon. I'm your grandfather.'

'You don't look like a grandfather.'

'My kind live a very long time.'

'Will I?'

'Longer than a human.' The boy seemed pleased with this oblique reference to his alienness.

As they talked, Tach made a preliminary probe of his abilities. An unbelievable mind control aptitude for one so young. And all self-taught, that was the truly amazing thing. With proper instruction he would be a force to be reckoned with. No teke, no precog, and worst of all almost no telepathy. He was virtually mind blind.

That's what comes of unrestricted and unplanned breeding.

'Doctor,' said Claude. 'Won't you sit down?'

'First I would like to give Blaise a hug.' He looked inquiringly at the boy, who made a face.

'I don't like hugs and kisses.'

'Why not?'

'It makes me feel like ants are on me.'

'A common mentat reaction. You will not feel that way with me.'

'Why not?'

'Because I am your kin and kind. I understand you better than anyone else in the world can ever understand you.' François Andrieux shifted angrily.

'Well, I'll try it,' said Blaise decisively, and slid off his stool. Again Tachyon was pleased with his assurance.

As his arms closed about his grandson's small form, tears rushed into his eyes.

'You're crying,' Blaise accused.

'Yes.'

'Why?'

'Because I am so very happy to have found you. To know that you exist in the world.'

Bonnell cleared his throat, a discreet little sound. 'As loath as I am to interrupt this, I'm really afraid I must, Doctor.' Tachyon stiffened warily. 'We have to talk a little business.'

'Business?' The word was dangerously low.

'Yes. I've given you what you want.' He indicated Blaise with a flip of a tiny hand. 'Now you have to give me what I want. François, take him.'

Father and son left. Tachyon speculatively studied the remaining men.

'Please don't consider a mind-assisted escape. There are more of us waiting outside this room. And my companions are armed.'

'I somehow assumed they would be.' Tach settled onto a sagging sofa. It sent up a puff of dust under his weight. 'So, you are a member of this little gang of galloping terrorists.'

'No, sir, I lead it.'

'Umm, and you had Dani killed.'

'No. That was an act of blatant stupidity for which François has been ... *chastised*. I disapprove of subordinates acting on their own initiative. They so often screw up. Don't you agree?'

Tachyon's late cousin Rabdan came instantly to mind, and he found himself nodding. Pulled himself up short. There was something very outré about this chatty little conversation, faced as he was with the man who had attempted to kill hundreds at Versailles.

'Oh, dear, and I had so hoped that Andrieux was bright,' mused Tachyon, then he asked, 'Is this a kidnapping for ransom?'

'Oh, no, Doctor, you're quite beyond price.'

'So I've always thought.'

'No, I need your help. In two days there will be a great debate between all the presidential candidates. We intend to kill as many of them as we can.'

'Even your own candidate?'

'In a revolution sometimes sacrifice is necessary. But for your information, I have little loyalty to the Communist Party. They have betrayed the people, lost the will and the strength to make the difficult decisions. The mandate has passed to us.'

Tach rested his forehead on a hand. 'Oh, please, don't blurt slogans at me. It's one of the most tiresome things about you people.'

'May I outline my plan?'

'I don't see any way I can prevent you.'

'The security will undoubtedly be very tight.'

'Undoubtedly.' Bonnell shot him a sharp glance at the irony. Tachyon gazed innocently back.

'Rather than attempt to run this gauntlet with weapons of our own, we will use those already provided. You and Blaise will mind control as many guards as possible and have them rake the platform with automatic weapons fire. It should have the desired result.'

'Interesting, but what can you possibly gain by this?'

'The destruction of France's ruling elite will throw the country into chaos. When that occurs, I won't need your esoteric powers. Guns and bombs will suffice. Sometimes the simplest things are often the best.'

'What a philosopher you are. Perhaps you should set yourself up as a guide to the young.'

'I already have. I'm Blaise's beloved Uncle Claude.'

'Well, this has of course been instructional, but I very much regret that I must refuse.'

'Not surprising. I had anticipated this. But consider, Doctor, I hold your grandson.'

'You won't harm him, he's too precious to you.'

'True. But my threat is not of death. If you refuse to accommodate me in this, I will be forced to have certain very unpleasant things done to you, being careful to ensure that you live. I will then disappear with Blaise. You might find it somewhat difficult to trace us when you are a bedridden cripple.'

He smiled in satisfaction at the look of horror on Tachyon's face. 'Jean will escort you to your room now. There you can reflect upon my offer and, I'm certain, see your way clear to help me.'

'I doubt it,' gritted Tachyon, regaining command of his voice, but it was hollow bravado, and Bonnell undoubtedly knew it.

The 'room' turned out to be the very cold and dank basement of the house. Hours later Blaise arrived with his dinner.

'I have come to visit with you,' he announced, and Tach sighed, again admiring and regretting Bonnell's cunning. The joker had obviously made a careful study of Tachyon, his attitudes and culture.

He ate while Blaise, chin resting in his cupped hands, gazed thoughtfully at him.

Tach set aside his fork. 'You are very silent. I thought we were going to visit.'

'I don't know what to say to you. It's very strange.'

'What is?'

'Finding out about you. Now I'm not so special anymore, which bothers me, but it's also good to know ...' He considered.

'That you're not alone,' suggested Tach gently.

'Yes, that's it.'

'Why do you help them?'

'Because they are right. The old institutions must fall.'

'But people have died.'

'Yes,' he agreed sunnily.

'Doesn't that bother you?'

'Oh, no. They were bourgeois capitalist pigs and deserved to die. Sometimes killing is the only way.'

'A very Takisian attitude.'

'You will help us, won't you? It will be fun.'

'Fun!'

It's his upbringing, Tach consoled himself. Endow any child with this kind of unsupervised power and they would react the same.

They talked. Tachyon pieced together a picture of unfettered freedom, virtually no formal schooling, the excitement of playing hide-and-seek with the authorities. More chilling was the realization that Blaise did not withdraw from his victims when they died. Rather he rode through the terror and pain of their final moment.

There will be time to correct this, he promised himself.

'So will you help?' Blaise asked, hopping down from the chair. 'Uncle Claude said to be sure and ask you.'

Seconds stretched into minutes as he considered. The noble course would be to tell Bonnell to go to hell. He considered Bonnell's gently worded threats and shuddered. He had been bred and trained to seize the opportunity, to turn defeat into victory. He would trust to that. Surely they could not guard him as closely at the rally.

'Tell Claude that I will help.'

An exuberant hug.

Alone, Tachyon continued to reflect. He did have one other advantage. Jack ... who would surely realize something had gone terribly wrong and alert the Sûreté. But his hope was founded on a man whose weakness was well known to him, and his fears on a man who, despite his civilized exterior, possessed no humanity.

Coming up on twenty-four hours since the little bastard had disappeared. Jack swung at the wall, pulled the punch just in time. Knocking out a wall at the Ritz wasn't going to help.

Was Tachyon in trouble?

Despite his promise, had he gone off with Bonnell? And did that necessarily mean trouble? Was it possible he was merely playing hooky with his grandkid?

If he was out visiting the zoo or whatever and Jack alerted the Sûreté, and they found out about Blaise, Tachyon would never forgive him. It would be another betrayal. Maybe his last one. The Takisian would find a way to get even this time.

But if he's really in trouble?

A knock pulled him from his distracted thoughts. One of Hartmann's interchangeable aides stood in the hall.

'Mr. Braun, the senator would like to invite you to join him at the debate tomorrow.'

'Debate? What debate?'

'All one thousand and eleven' – a condescending little laugh – 'or however many candidates there are in this crazy race, will be taking part in a round-robin debate in the Luxembourg Gardens. The senator would like as many of the tour as possible to be there. To show support for this great European democracy – such as it is. Mr. Braun ... are you all right?'

'Fine, yeah, I'm fine. You tell the senator I'll be there.'

'And Doctor Tachyon? The senator's very concerned by his continued absence.'

'I think I can safely promise the senator that the doctor will be there too.'

Closing the door, Jack quickly crossed to the phone and put in a call for Rochambeau. A probable terrorist attack on the candidates. No need to mention the child. Just an urgent need to call out the troops.

And a long night of praying he had guessed correctly. That he had made the right choice.

◆

He should be sleeping, preparing mind and body for the morrow. His life and the future of his line depended upon his skill and speed and cunning.

And on Jack Braun. Ironic that.

If Jack had drawn the correct conclusion. *If* he had alerted the Sûreté. *If* there were sufficient officers. *If* Tachyon could stretch his talent beyond all limits and hold an unheard of number of minds.

He sat up on the rickety cot and hugged his stomach. Sank back and tried to relax. But it was a night for memories. Faces out of the past. Blythe, David, Earl, Dani.

I'm gambling my life and the life of my grandchild on the man who destroyed Blythe. Lovely.

But the possibility of dying can act as a spur for self-examination. Force a person to strip away the comforting, insulating little lies that buffer one from their most private guilts and regrets.

'*Then give me those names!*'

'*All right ... all right.*'

The power – lancing out – fragmenting her mind ... her mind ... her mind.

But they wouldn't have known but for Jack. And she wouldn't have absorbed their minds but for Holmes, and she wouldn't have been there but for the paranoia of a nation. *And no one would suffer had they not been born*, thought Tach, quoting a favorite adage of his father's. Sometime one must stop excusing, accept responsibility for actions taken.

Tisianne brant Ts'ara, Jack Braun didn't destroy Blythe, you *did*.

He flinched, prepared for it to hurt. Instead he felt better. Lighter, freer, at peace for the first time in so many, many years. He began to laugh, was not surprised when it turned to quiet tears.

They lasted for some time. When the storm ended, he lay back, exhausted but calm. Ready for tomorrow. After which he would return home and *make* a home and raise his child. Calmly and a little regretfully he turned his back on the past.

He was Tisianne brant Ts'ara sek Halima sek Ragnar sek Omian, a prince of the House Ilkazam, and tomorrow his enemies would learn to their pain and regret what it meant to stand against him.

Claude, Blaise, and a driver remained in a car almost a block from the gardens. Tachyon, linked through the barrel of a Beretta with a stone-faced Andrieux, hovered at the out-skirts of an enormous crowd. Parisians were nothing if not enthusiastic about their politics. But spotted throughout this sea of humanity like an insidious infection were the other fifteen members of Bonnell's cell. Waiting. For blood to flow and nurture their violent dreams.

On the stand, the candidates – all seven of them. About half the delegation seated in chairs directly in front of the bunting-hung platform. There was no way they would escape without injury if Tach should fail and the shooting begin. Jack came into view. Hands thrust deep into pants pockets, he paced and frowned out over the throng.

Blaise was a rider in Tachyon's mind. Ready to sense the tiniest use of telepathy. His power might be slight, but he was sensitive enough to detect the shift in focus such mind communication required. His presence suited his grandsire just fine. It would make what was to come all the easier.

Carefully Tachyon constructed a mind-scrim of the scene. A false picture to lull his grandchild. He hedged it around with shields, presented it to Blaise. Then from beneath its protective cover he reached out, touched Jack's mind.

Don't jump, keep frowning.

Where are you?

Near gate, edge of trees.

Got it.

Sûreté?

Everywhere. Terrorists?

Likewise everywhere.

How … !?

They'll come to you.

Wha … ???

Trust.

He withdrew and carefully constructed a trâp. It was similar to the link he enjoyed with Baby when the ship boosted and amplified his own natural powers to allow for transspace communication, but much, much stronger. Its teeth were very deep. What might it do to Blaise? No. There was no time for doubts.

The mind snare snapped down. A mental scream of alarm from the boy. Desperate struggle, panting resignation. The rider had become the ridden.

Tachyon joined Blaise's power to his. It was like a bar of white-hot light. Carefully he split it into strands. Each tendril snapped out like a burning whip. Settled on his captors. They became frozen statues.

He was gasping with effort, sweat bursting from his forehead, running in rivulets into his eyes. He set them marching, a regiment of zombies. As Andrieux stepped from his side, Tachyon forced his hand to move, to close about the Beretta, to pull it from his slave's limp grasp.

Braun was leaping about, gesticulating, summoning help with great arm sweeps.

Hurry! Hurry!

He had to hold them. All of them. If he failed …

Blaise was struggling again. It was like being kicked over and over again in the gut. One thread snapped. To Claude Bonnell. With a cry Tachyon dropped the control, ran for the gate. Behind him there was the vicious snarl of an Uzi. Apparently one of his captives had tried to run and been cut down by the French security forces. Perhaps it had been Andrieux. More gunfire, punctuating screams. A torrent of people swept past, almost knocking him from his feet. He tightened his grip on the Beretta, pumped harder. Slid around the corner just as the dazed driver reached for the key.

A blow from Tachyon's mind, and he collapsed onto the steering wheel, and the blare of the horn was added to the pandemonium.

Bonnell struggled from the car, gripping Blaise by the wrist. He went lurching and stumbling for a narrow, deserted side street.

Tach flew after them, caught Blaise by his free hand, and wrenched him free.

'LET ME GO! LET ME GO!'

Sharp teeth bit deep into his wrist. Tachyon silenced the boy with a crushing imperative. Supported the sleeping child with one arm. He and Bonnell regarded one another over the limp figure.

'Bravo, Doctor. You outfoxed me. But what a media event my trial will be.'

'I'm afraid not.'

'Eh?'

'I require a body. One infected with the wild card. Then the Sûreté will have their mysterious mentat ace and will look no further.'

'You can't be serious! You can't mean to kill me in cold blood.' He read the answer in Tachyon's implacable lilac gaze. Bonnell tottered back, came up short against a wall, moistened his lips. 'I treated you fairly, kindly. You took no hurt from me.'

'But others have not fared so well. You shouldn't have sent Blaise to me. He was quick to tell me of your other *triumphs*. An innocent banker, controlled by Blaise, sent into his bank carrying his own death. That bomb blast killed seventeen. Clearly a triumph.'

Bonnell's face shifted, took on the aspect of Thomas Tudbury, the Great and Powerful Turtle. 'Please, I beg you. At least grant me the opportunity for a trial.'

'No,' The features shifted again – Mark Meadows, Captain Trips blinked confusedly at the gun. 'I think the outcome is fairly predictable.' Danelle, but as she had been all those long years ago. 'I merely hasten your execution.'

A final transformation. Shoulder-length sable hair cascading over the shoulders, long sooty lashes brushing at her cheeks, lifting to reveal eyes of a profound midnight blue. *Blythe*.

'Tachy, please.'

'I'm sorry, but you're dead.'

And Tach shot him.

'Ah, Doctor Tachyon.' Franchot de Valmy rose from his desk, hand outstretched. 'France owes you a great debt of gratitude. How can we ever repay you?'

'By issuing me a passport and visa.'

'I'm afraid I don't understand. You of course—'

'Not for me. For Blaise Jeannot Andrieux.'

De Valmy fiddled with a pen. 'Why not merely apply?'

'Because François Andrieux is currently in custody. Checks will be run, and I can't allow that.'

'Aren't you being a bit forthright with me?'

'Not at all. I know what an expert you are on falsified documents.' The Frenchman froze, then shifted slowly to the back of his chair. 'I know you're not an ace, Monsieur de Valmy. I wonder, how would the French public react to news of such a cheat? It would cost you the election.'

De Valmy forced past stiff lips, 'I am a very capable public servant. I can make a difference for France.'

'Yes, but none of that is half so alluring as a wild card.'

'What you're asking is impossible. What if it's traced to me? What if—' Tachyon reached for the phone. 'What are you doing?'

'Calling the press. I too can arrange press conferences at a moment's notice. One of the privileges of fame.'

'You'll get your documents.'

'Thank you.'

'I'll find out why you're doing this.'

Tachyon paused at the door, glanced back. 'Then we'll each have a secret on the other, won't we?'

The big plane was darkened for the late-night hop to London. The first-class section was deserted save for Tach, Jack, and Blaise, sleeping soundly in his grandfather's arms. There was something about the little tableau that warned everyone to stay well away.

'How long are you gonna keep him under?' The single reading light pulled fire from the twin red heads.

'Until we reach London.'

'Will he ever forgive you?'

'He won't know.'

'About Bonnell maybe, but the rest he'll remember. You betrayed him.'

'Yes.' It was scarcely audible over the rumble of the engines. 'Jack?'

'Yeah?'

'I forgive you.'

Their eyes met.

The human reached down, softly pushed back a lock of silky hair from the child's forehead. 'Then I guess maybe there's hope for you too.'

LEGENDS

Michael Cassutt

I.

The month of April brought little in the way of relief to Muscovites staggered by an unusually cold winter. Following a brief flurry of southern breezes, which sent boys into the newly green football fields and encouraged pretty girls to discard their overcoats, the skies had darkened again, and a dreary, uninspired rain had begun to fall. To Polyakov the scene was autumnal and therefore entirely appropriate. His masters, bending in the new breeze from the Kremlin, had decreed that this would be Polyakov's last Moscow spring. The younger, less-tainted Yurchenko would move up, and Polyakov would retire to a dacha far from Moscow.

Just as well, Polyakov thought, since scientists were saying that weather patterns had changed because of the Siberian airbursts. There might never be a decent Moscow spring again.

Nevertheless, even in its autumn clothes Moscow had the ability to inspire him. From this window he could see the cluster of trees where the Moscow River skirted Gorky Park, and beyond that, looking appropriately medieval in the mist, were the domes of St. Basil's and the Kremlin. In Polyakov's mind age equalled power, but then he was old.

'You wanted to see me?' The voice interrupted his musings. A young major in the uniform of the Chief Intelligence Directorate of the General Staff – uncommonly known as the GRU – had entered. He was perhaps thirty-five, a bit old to still hold the rank of major, Polyakov thought, especially with the Hero of the Soviet Union medal. With his classic White Russian features and sandy hair, the man looked like one of those unlikely officers whose pictures appeared on the cover of *Red Star* every day.

'Mólniya.' Polyakov elected to use the young officer's code name rather than Christian name and patronymic. Initial formality was one of the interrogator's tricks. He held out his hand. The major hesitated, then shook it. Polyakov was pleased to note that Mólniya wore black rubber gloves. So far his information was correct. 'Let's sit down.'

They faced each other across the polished wood of the conference table. Someone had thoughtfully provided water, which Polyakov indicated. 'You have a very pleasant conference room here.'

'I'm sure it hardly compares with those at Dzerzhinsky Square,' Mólniya shot back with just the proper amount of insolence. Dzerzhinsky Square was the location of KGB headquarters.

Polyakov laughed. 'As a matter of fact it's identical, thanks to central planning. Gorbachev is doing away with that, I understand.'

'We've been known to read the Politburo's mail too.'

'Good. Then you know exactly why I'm here and who sent me.'

Mólniya and the GRU had been ordered to cooperate with the KGB, and the orders came from the very highest places. That was the slim advantage Polyakov brought to this meeting … an advantage that, as the saying went, had all the weight of words written on water … since he was an old man and Mólniya was the great Soviet ace.

'Do you know the name Huntington Sheldon?'

Mólniya knew he was being tested and said tiredly, 'He was CIA director from 1966 to 1972.'

'Yes, a thoroughly dangerous man … and last week's issue of *Time* magazine has a picture of him standing right in front of the Lubiyanka – pointing up at the statue of Dzerzhinsky!'

'Maybe there's a lesson in that … cousin.' *Worry about your own security and leave our operations alone!*

'I wouldn't be here if you hadn't had such a spectacular failure.'

'Unlike the KGB's perfect record.' Mólniya didn't try to hide his contempt.

'Oh, we've had our failures, cousin. What's different about our operations is that they've been approved by the Intelligence Council. Now, you're a Party member. You couldn't have graduated from the Kharkov Higher Engineering School without being at least slightly familiar with the principles of collective thought. Successes are shared. So are failures. This operation you and Dolgov cooked up – what were you doing, taking lessons from Oliver North?'

Mólniya flinched at the mention of Dolgov's name, a state secret and, more importantly, a GRU secret. Polyakov continued, 'Are you worried about what we say, Major? Don't be. This is the cleanest room in the Soviet Union.' He smiled. '*My* housekeepers swept it. What we say here is between us.

'So, now, tell me,' Polyakov said, 'what the hell went wrong in Berlin?'

♦

The aftermath of the Hartmann kidnapping had been horrible. Though only a few right-wing German and American newspapers mentioned possible Soviet involvement, the CIA and other Western agencies made the connections. Finding the bodies, even mutilated as they were, of those Red Army Faction punks had allowed the CIA to backtrack through their residences, cover names, bank accounts, and contacts, destroying in a matter of days a network that had been in place for twenty years. Two military attachés, in Vienna and Berlin, had been expelled, and more were to follow.

The involvement of the lawyer Prahler in such a brutal and inept affair would make it impossible for other deep-cover agents of his stature to act ... and make it difficult to recruit new ones.

And who knew what else the American senator was telling.

'You know, Mólniya, for years my service ran moles at the very heart of the British intelligence service ... we even had one who acted as liaison with the CIA.'

'Philby, Burgess, Maclean, and Blount. And old man Churchill, too, if you believe the Western spy novels. Is there a point to this anecdote?'

'I'm just trying to give you some idea of the damage you've done. Those moles paralyzed the British for over twenty years. That's what could happen to us ... to both of us. Your GRU bosses will never admit it; if they do, they certainly won't discuss it with you. But that's the mess I've got to clean up.

'Now ... if you know anything at all about me' – Polyakov was certain that Mólniya knew as much about him as the KGB, which meant that Mólniya did not know one very important thing – 'you know that I'm fair. I'm old, I'm fat, I'm faceless ... but I'm objective. I'm retiring in four months. I have *nothing* to gain from causing a new war between our two services.'

Mólniya merely returned his gaze. Well, Polyakov expected as much. The rivalry between the GRU and KGB had been bloody. At various times in the past each service had managed to have the leaders of its rival shot. There is nothing longer than institutional memory.

'I see.' Polyakov stood up. 'Sorry to have troubled you, Major. Obviously the General Secretary was mistaken ... you have nothing to say to me—'

'Ask your questions!'

Forty minutes later Polyakov sighed and sat back in his chair. Turning slightly, he could see out the window. GRU headquarters was called the Aquarium because of its glass walls. It fit. Polyakov had noticed, as he was driven by another GRU officer past the Institute of Space Biology, which, together with the little-used Frunze Central Airport, surrounded the Aquarium, that this building – perhaps the most inaccessible, indeed even invisible place in the city of Moscow – appeared to be almost transparent. A fifteen-story building with nothing but floor-to-ceiling windows!

To find it inviting was a mistake. Polyakov pitied the theoretical casual visitor. Before even reaching the inner circle, one had to penetrate an outer one consisting of three secret aircraft design bureaus, the even more secret Chelomei spacecraft design bureau, or the Red Banner Air Force Academy.

At the far end of the courtyard below, nestled against the impenetrable concrete wall that surrounded the Aquarium, was a crematorium. The story was that, in the final interview before acceptance into the GRU, every candidate was shown this squat green building and a special film.

The film was of the 1959 execution of GRU Colonel Popov, who had been caught spying for the CIA. Popov was strapped to a stretcher with unbreakable wire and simply fed – alive – into the flames. The process was interrupted so that the coffin of another, substantially more honored GRU employee could be consigned first.

The message was clear: *You leave the GRU only through the crematorium. We are more important than family, than country.* A man such as Mólniya, trained by such an organization, was not vulnerable to any of Polyakov's interrogator's tricks. In almost an hour all Polyakov had pried out of him were operational details ... names, dates, places, events. Material that Polyakov already possessed. There was something more to be learned – a secret of some kind – Polyakov was sure of it. A secret no one else had been able to get out of Mólniya. A secret that, perhaps, no one but Polyakov knew existed. How could he get Mólniya to talk?

What could be more important to this man than that crematorium?

'It must be difficult being a Soviet ace.'

If Mólniya was surprised by Polyakov's sudden statement, he didn't show it. 'My power is just another tool to be used against the imperialists.'

'I'm sure that's what your superiors would like to think. God forbid you should use it for yourself.' Polyakov sat down again. This time he poured himself a glass of water. He held out the bottle to Mólniya, who shook his head. 'You must be tired of the jokes by now. Water and electricity.'

'Yes,' Mólniya said tiredly. 'I have to be careful when it rains. I can't take baths. The only water I like is snow ... Given the number of people who know about me, it's amazing how many jokes I've heard.'

'They have your family, don't they? Don't answer. It's not something I know. It's just ... the only way to control you.'

The wild card virus was relatively dissipated by the time it reached the Soviet Union, but it was still strong enough to create jokers and aces, and to cause the creation of a secret state commission to deal with the problem. In typical Stalinist fashion aces were segregated from the population and 'educated' in special camps. Jokers simply disappeared. In many ways it was worse than the Purge, which Polyakov had seen as a teenager. In the Thirties the knock on the door came for Party members ... those with incorrect ambitions. But *everyone* was at risk during the Wild Card Purge.

Even those in the Kremlin. Even those at the very highest levels.

'I knew someone like you, Mólniya. I used to work for him, not far from here as a matter of fact.'

For the first time Mólniya dropped his guard. He was genuinely curious. 'Is the legend true?'

'Which legend? That Comrade Stalin was a joker and died with a stake driven through his heart? Or that it was Lysenko who had been affected?' Polyakov could tell that Mólniya knew them all. 'I must say I'm shocked to think that such fabrications are circulated by officers of military intelligence!'

'I was thinking of the legend that there was nothing left of Stalin to bury ... that the corpse displayed at the funeral was made up by the same geniuses who maintain Lenin's.'

Very close, Polyakov thought. What *did* Mólniya know? 'You're a war hero, Mólniya. Yet you ran from that building in Berlin like a raw recruit. Why?'

This was another one of the old tricks, the sudden segue back to more immediate business.

As Mólniya replied that he didn't honestly remember running, Polyakov went around the table and, sliding a chair closer, sat down right next to him. They were so close that Polyakov could smell the soap and, under that, the sweat ... and something that might have been ozone. 'Can you tell when someone is an ace?'

Finally Mólniya was getting nervous. 'Not without some demonstration … no.'

Polyakov lowered his voice and jabbed a finger at the Hero's medal on Mólniya's chest. 'What do you think now?'

Mólniya's face flushed and tears formed in his eyes. One gloved hand slapped Polyakov's away. It only lasted an instant.

'I was burning up!'

'Within seconds, yes. Burnt meat.'

'*You're* the one.' There was as much fascination – after all, they had a lot in common – as fear in Mólniya's face. 'That was another one of the legends, that there was a second ace. But you were supposed to be in the Party hierarchy, one of Brezhnev's people.'

Polyakov shrugged. 'The second ace belongs to no one. He's very careful about that. His loyalty is to the Soviet Union. To Soviet ideals and potential, not the pitiful reality.' He remained close to Mólniya. 'And now you know my secret. One ace to another … what do *you* have to tell *me*?'

It was good to leave the Aquarium. Years of institutional hatred had imbued the place with an almost physical barrier – like an electrical charge – that repelled all enemies, especially the KGB.

Polyakov should have been feeling elated: he had gotten some very important information out of Mólniya. Even Mólniya himself did not know how important. No one knew why the Hartmann kidnapping had fallen apart, but what had happened to Mólniya could best be explained by the presence of a secret ace, one with the power to control men's actions. Mólniya could not know, of course, that something much like this had happened in Syria. But Polyakov had seen that report. Polyakov was afraid he knew the answer.

The man who might very well be the next president of the United States was an ace.

II.

'The chairman will see you now.'

To Polyakov's surprise the receptionist was a young woman of striking beauty, a blonde straight out of an American movie. Gone was Seregin, Andropov's old gatekeeper, a man with the physical appearance of a hatchet – appropriately enough – and a personality to match. Seregin was perfectly capable of letting a Politburo member cool his heels for eternity in this outer office, or if necessary, physically ejecting anyone foolish enough to make an unexpected call on the chairman of the Committee for State Security, the chief of the KGB.

Polyakov imagined that this lissome woman was potentially just as lethal as Seregin; nevertheless, the whole idea struck him as ludicrous. An attempt to put a smile on the face of the tiger. Meet your new, caring Kremlin. Today's friendly KGB!

Seregin was gone. But then, so was Andropov. And Polyakov himself was no longer welcome on the top floor ... not without the chairman's invitation.

The chairman rose from his desk to kiss him, interrupting Polyakov's salute. 'Georgy Vladimirovich, how nice to see you.' He was directed to a couch – another new addition, some kind of conversational nook in the formerly Spartan office. 'You're not often seen in these parts.' *By your choice*, Polyakov wanted to say.

'My duties have kept me away.'

'Of course. The rigors of field work.' The chairman, who like most KGB chiefs since Stalin's day was essentially a Party political appointee, had served the KGB as a snitch – a *stukach* – not an operative or analyst. In this he was the perfect leader of an organization consisting of a million *stukachi*. 'Tell me about your visit to the Aquarium.'

Quickly to business. Another sign of the Gorbachev style. Polyakov was thorough to the point of tedium in his replay of the interrogation, with one significant omission. He counted on the chairman's famous impatience and wasn't disappointed.

'These operational details are all well and good, Georgy

Vladimirovich, but wasted on poor bureaucrats, hmm?' A self-deprecating smile. 'Did the GRU give you full and complete cooperation, as directed by the General Secretary.'

'Yes ... alas,' Polyakov said, earning the chairman's equally famous laugh.

'Do you have enough information to salvage our European operations?'

'Yes.'

'"How will you proceed? I understand that the German networks are being rolled up. Every day Aeroflot brings our agents back to us."

'Those not held for trial in the West, yes,' Polyakov said. 'Berlin is a wasteland for us now. Most of Germany is barren and will be for years.'

'Carthage.'

'But we have other assets. Deep-cover assets that have not been utilized in years. I propose to activate one known as the Dancer.'

The chairman drew out pen and made a note to have the Dancer file brought up from the registry. He nodded. 'How much time will this ... recovery take, in your honest estimation?'

'At least two years.'

The chairman's gaze drifted off. 'Which brings me to a question of my own,' Polyakov persisted. 'My retirement.'

'Yes, your retirement.' The chairman sighed. 'I think the only course is to bring Yurchenko in on this as soon as possible, since he'll be the one who has to finish the job.'

'Unless I postpone my retirement.' Polyakov had said the unspeakable. He watched the chairman make an unaccustomed search for an unprogrammed response.

'Well. That would be a problem, wouldn't it? All the papers have been signed. Yurchenko's promotion is already approved. You will be promoted to general and will receive your third Hero's medal. We're prepared to announce it at the plenum next month.' The chairman leaned forward. 'Is it money, Georgy Vladimirovich? I shouldn't mention this, but there is often a pension bonus for extremely ... valuable service.'

It wasn't going to work. The chairman might be a political hack, but he was not without his skills. He had been ordered to clean house at the KGB and clean house he would. Right now he feared Gorbachev more than he feared an old spy.

Polyakov sighed. 'I only want to finish my job. If that is not the … desire of the Party, I will retire as agreed.'

The chairman had been anticipating a fight and was relieved to have won so quickly. 'I understand the difficulty of your situation, Georgy Vladimirovich. We all know your tenacity. We don't have enough like you. But Yurchenko is capable. After all … you trained him.'

'I'll brief him.'

'I tell you what,' the chairman said. 'Your retirement doesn't take effect until the end of August.'

'My sixty-third birthday.'

'I see no reason why we should deprive ourselves of your talents until that date.' The chairman was writing notes to himself again. 'This is highly unusual, as you well know, but why don't you go with Yurchenko? Hmm? Where is this Dancer?'

'France, at the moment, or England.'

The chairman was pleased. 'I'm sure we can think of worse places for a business trip.' He wrote another note with his pen. 'I will authorize you to accompany Yurchenko … to assist in the transition. Charming bureaucratic phrase.'

'Thank you.'

'Nonsense, you've earned it.' The chairman got up and went to the sideboard. That, at least, had not changed. He drew out a bottle of vodka that was almost empty, pouring two glasses full, which finished it. 'A forbidden toast – the end of an era!' They drank.

The chairman sat down again. 'What will happen to Mólniya? No matter how badly he bungled Berlin, he's too valuable to waste in that horrible furnace of theirs.'

'He's teaching tactics now, here in Moscow. In time, if he's good, they may let him return to fieldwork.'

The chairman shuddered visibly. 'What a mess.' His tight smile showed a pair of steel teeth. 'Having a wild card working for you! I wonder, would one ever sleep?'

Polyakov drained his glass. '*I* wouldn't.'

III.

Polyakov loved the English newspapers. *The Sun* … *The Mirror* … *The Globe* … with their screaming three-inch headlines about the latest royal rows and their naked women, they were bread and circus rolled into one. At the moment some MP was on trial, accused of hiring a prostitute for fifty pounds and then, in *The Sun*'s typically restrained words, 'Not getting his money's worth!' ('"It was over so *fast*," tart claims!') Which was the greater sin? Polyakov wondered.

A tiny deck on that same front page mentioned that the Aces Tour had arrived in London.

Perhaps Polyakov's affection for the papers derived from professional appreciation. Whenever he was in the West, his legend or cover was that of a Tass correspondent, which had required him to master enough rudimentary journalistic skills to pass, though most Western reporters he met *assumed* he was a spy. He had never learned to write well – certainly not with the drunken eloquence of his Fleet Street colleagues – but he could hold his liquor and he could find a story.

At that level, at least, journalism and intelligence were not mutually exclusive.

Alas, Polyakov's old haunts were unsuitable for a rendezvous with the Dancer. Recognition of either of them would be disastrous for both. They could not, in fact, use a public house of any kind.

To make matters worse, the Dancer was an uncontrolled agent – a 'cooperative asset' to use Moscow Center's increasingly bland jargon. Polyakov had not even seen him in over twenty years, and that had been an accidental encounter following even more years of separation. There were no prearranged signals, no message drops, no intermediaries, no channels to let the Dancer know that Polyakov had come to collect.

Though the Dancer's notoriety made certain kinds of contacts impossible, it made Polyakov's job easier in one respect: If he wanted to know how to find this particular asset—

—all he had to do was pick up a paper.

◆

His assistant, and future successor, Yurchenko, was busy ingratiating himself with the London *rezident*; both men showed only a passing interest in Polyakov's comings and goings, joking that their soon-to-be-retired friend was spending his time with King's Cross whores – 'Just be sure you don't wind up in the newspapers, Georgy Vladimirovich,' Yurchenko had teased. 'If you do ... at *least* get your money's worth!' – since such behavior by Polyakov was not unprecedented. Well ... he had never married. And years in Germany, particularly in Hamburg, had given him a taste for pretty young mouths at affordable prices. It was also quite true that the KGB did not trust an agent who possessed no notable weakness. One vice was tolerated, so long as it was one of the controllable ones – alcohol, money, or women – rather than, say, religion. A dinosaur such as Polyakov – who had worked for Beria, for God's sake! – having a taste for honey ... well, that was considered rakish, even charming.

From the Tass office near Fleet, Polyakov went alone to the Grosvenor House Hotel, riding in one of the famous English black cabs – this one actually belonged to the Embassy – down Park Lane to Knightsbridge to Kensington Road. It was early on a work day and the cab crawled through a sea of vehicles and humanity. The sun was up, burning off the morning haze. It was going to be a beautiful London spring day.

At Grosvenor House, Polyakov had to talk his way past several very obvious guards while noting the presence of several discreet ones. He was allowed as far as the concierge station, where he found, to his annoyance, another young woman in place of the usual old scout. This one even looked like the chairman's new gatekeeper. 'Will the house telephone put me through to the floors where the Aces Tour is staying?'

The concierge frowned and framed a reply. Clearly the tour's presence here was not common knowledge, but Polyakov preempted her questions, as he had gotten past the guards, by presenting his press credentials. She examined them – they were genuine in any case – then guided him to the telephones. 'They might not be answering at this hour, but these lines are direct.'

'Thank you.' He waited until she had withdrawn, then asked the operator to ring through to the room number one of the Embassy's footmen had already provided.

'Yes?' Polyakov had not expected the voice to change, yet he was surprised that it had not.

'It's been a long time ... Dancer.'

Polyakov was not surprised by the long silence at the other end. 'It's you, isn't it?'

He was pleased. The Dancer retained enough tradecraft to keep the telephone conversations bland. 'Didn't I promise that I would give you a visit someday?'

'What do you want?'

'To meet, what else? To see you.'

'This is hardly the place—'

'There's a cab waiting out front. It'll be easy to spot. It's the only one at the moment.'

'I'll be down in a few minutes.'

Polyakov hung up and hurried out to the cab, not forgetting to nod to the concierge again.

'Any luck?'

'Enough. Thank you.'

He slipped into the cab and closed the door. His heart was pounding. *My God*, he thought, *I'm like a teenager waiting for a girl!*

Before long the door opened. Immediately Polyakov was awash in the Dancer's scent. He extended his hand in the Western fashion. 'Dr. Tachyon, I presume.'

♥

The driver was a young Uzbek from the Embassy whose professional specialty was economic analysis, but whose greatest virtue was his ability to keep his mouth shut. His total lack of interest in Polyakov's activities and the challenge of navigating London's busy streets allowed Polyakov and Tachyon some privacy.

Polyakov's wild card had no face, so he had never been suspected of being an ace or joker. That, and the fact that he had only used his powers twice:

The first time was in the long, brutal winter of 1946–47, the winter following the release of the virus. Polyakov was a senior lieutenant then, having spent the Great Patriotic War as a *zampolit*, or political officer, at the munitions factories in the Urals. When the Nazis surrendered, Moscow Center assigned him to the counterinsurgency forces fighting Ukrainian nationalists – the 'men from the forests' who had fought with the Nazis and had no intentions of giving up. (In fact they continued fighting until 1952.)

Polyakov's boss there was a thug named Suvin, who confessed drunkenly one night that he had been an executioner in the Lubiyanka during the Purge. Suvin had developed a real taste for torture; Polyakov wondered if that was the only possible response to a job that daily required one to shoot a fellow Party member in the back of the neck. One evening Polyakov brought in a Ukrainian teenager, a boy, for questioning. Suvin had been drinking and began to beat a confession out of the kid, which was a waste of time: the boy had already confessed to stealing food. But Suvin wanted to link him to the rebels.

Polyakov remembered, mostly, that he had been tired. Like everyone in the Soviet Union in that year, including those at the very highest levels, he was often hungry. It was the fatigue, he thought shamefully now, not human compassion, that made him leap at Suvin and shove him aside. Suvin turned on him and they fought. From underneath the other man, Polyakov managed to get his hands on his throat. There was no chance he could choke him … yet Suvin suddenly turned red – dangerously red – and literally burst into flames.

The young prisoner was unconscious and knew nothing. Since

fatalities in the war zone were routinely ascribed to enemy action, the bully Suvin was officially reported to have died 'heroically' of 'extreme thoracic trauma' and 'burns,' euphemisms for being fried to a cinder. The incident terrified Polyakov. At first he didn't even realize what had happened; information on the wild card virus was restricted. But eventually he realized that he had a power ... that he was an ace. And he swore never to use the power again.

He had only broken that promise once.

By the autumn of 1955, Georgy Vladimirovich Polyakov, now a captain in the 'organs,' was using the legend of a junior Tass reporter in West Berlin. Aces and jokers were much in the news in those days. The Tass men monitored the Washington hearings with horror – it reminded some of them of the Purge – and delight. The mighty American aces were being neutralized by their own countrymen!

It was known that some aces and their Takisian puppet master (as *Pravda* described him) had fled the U.S. following the first HUAC hearings. They became high-priority targets for the Eighth Directorate, the KGB department responsible for Western Europe. Tachyon in particular was a personal target for Polyakov. Perhaps the Takisian held some clue to the secret of the wild card virus ... something to explain it ... something to make it go away. When he heard that the Takisian was on the skids in Hamburg, he was off.

Since Polyakov had made prior 'research' trips to Hamburg's red-light district, he knew which brothels were likely to cater to an unusual client such as Tachyon. He found the alien in the third establishment he tried. It was near dawn; the Takisian was drunk, passed out, and out of money. Tachyon should have been grateful: the Germans as a race had little liking for drunken indigents; masters of Hamburg whorehouses had even less. Tachyon would have been lucky to have been dumped in the canal ... alive.

Polyakov had him taken to a safe house in East Berlin, where, after a prolonged argument among the *rezidenti*, he was supplied with controlled amounts of alcohol and women while he slowly regained his health ... and while Polyakov and at least a dozen others questioned him. Even Shelepin himself took time out from his plotting back in Moscow to visit.

Within three weeks it was clear that Tachyon had nothing left to give. More likely, Polyakov suspected, the Takisian had regained sufficient strength to withstand any further interrogation. Nevertheless, he had supplied them with so much data on the American aces, on Takisian history and science, and on the wild card virus itself, that Polyakov half-expected his superiors to give the alien a medal and a pension.

They did almost as much. Like the German rocket engineers captured after the war, Tachyon's ultimate fate was to be quietly repatriated … in this case to West Berlin. They transferred Polyakov to the illegals residence there at the same time, hoping for residual contacts, and allowing both men a simultaneous introduction to the city. Because of East Berlin, they would never be friends. Because of their time in the western sector, they could never be total enemies.

'In forty years on this world I've learned to alter my expectations every day,' Tachyon told him. 'I honestly thought you were dead.'

'Soon enough I will be,' Polyakov said. 'But you look better now that you did in Berlin. The years truly pass slowly for your kind.'

'Too slowly at times.' They rode in silence for a while, each pretending to enjoy the scenery while each ordered his memories of the other.

'Why are you here?' Tachyon asked.

'To collect on a debt.'

Tachyon nodded slightly, a gesture that showed how thoroughly assimilated he had become. 'That's what I thought.'

'You knew it would happen one day.'

'Of course! Please don't misunderstand! My people honor their commitments. You saved my life. You have a right to anything I can give you.' Then he smiled tightly. 'This one time.'

'How close are you to Senator Gregg Hartmann?'

'He's a senior member of this tour, so I've had some contact with him. Obviously not much lately, following that terrible business in Berlin.'

'What do you think of him ... as a man?'

'I don't know him well enough to judge. He's a politician, and as a rule I despise politicians. In that sense he strikes me as the best of a bad lot. He seems to be genuine in his support for jokers, for example. This is probably not an issue in your country, but it's a very emotional one in America, comparable to abortion rights.' He paused. 'I doubt very much he would be susceptible to any kind of ... arrangement, if that's what you're asking.'

'I see you've taken up reading spy novels,' Polyakov said. 'I'm more interested in ... let's call it a political analysis. Is it possible that he will become president of the United States?'

'Very possible. Reagan has been crippled by his current crisis and is not, in my judgment, a well man. He has no obvious successor, and the American economy is likely to worsen before the election.'

The first piece of the puzzle: There is one American politician who has left in his wake a series of mysterious deaths worthy of Beria or Stalin ... The second: The same politician is kidnapped – twice. And escapes under mysterious circumstances – twice.

'The Democrats have several candidates, none without major weaknesses. Hart is sure to eliminate himself. Biden, Dukakis, any of the others could disappear tomorrow. If Hartmann can put together a strong organization, and if the right opening occurs, he could win.'

A recent Moscow Center briefing had predicted that Dole would be the next U.S. president. Strategists at the American Institute were already creating an expert psychological model of the senator from Kansas. But these were the same analysts who predicted Ford over Carter and Carter over Reagan. On the principle that events never turn out the way experts say, Polyakov was inclined to believe Tachyon.

Even the theoretical possibility of a Hartmann presidency was important ... if he was an ace! He needed to be watched, stopped if necessary, but Moscow Center would never authorize such a move, especially if it contradicted its expensive little studies.

The driver, by prearrangement, headed back toward Grosvenor

House. The rest of the trip was spent in reminiscence of the two Berlins, even of Hamburg. 'You aren't satisfied, are you?' Tachyon said finally. 'You want more from me than a superficial political analysis, surely.'

'You know the answer to that.'

'I have no secret documents to give you. I'm hardly inconspicuous enough to work as a spy.'

'You have your *powers*, Tachyon—'

'*And* my limitations! You know what I will and will not do.'

'I'm not your enemy, Tachyon! I'm the only one who even remembers your debt, and in August I'll be retired. At this point I'm just an old man trying to put together the pieces of a puzzle.'

'Then tell me about your puzzle—'

'You know better than that.'

'Then how can I possibly help you?' Polyakov didn't answer. 'You're afraid that by even asking me a direct question, I'll learn too much. Russians!'

For a moment Polyakov wished for a wild card power that would let him read minds. Tachyon had many human characteristics, but he was Takisian … all of Polyakov's years of training did not help him decide whether or not he was lying. Must he depend on Takisian honor?

The cab pulled up to the curb and the driver opened the door. But Tachyon didn't get out. 'What's going to happen to you?'

What, indeed? Polyakov thought. 'I'm going to become an honored pensioner, like Khrushchev, able to go to the front of a queue, spending my days reading and reliving my exploits over a bottle of vodka for men who will not believe them.'

Tachyon hesitated. 'For years I hated you … not for exploiting my weakness, but for saving my life. I was in Hamburg because I wanted to die. But now, finally, I have something to live for … it's only been very recent. So I *am* grateful, you know.'

Then he got out of the cab and slammed the door. 'I'll see you again,' he said, hoping for a denial.

'Yes,' Polyakov said, 'you will.' The driver pulled away. In the rearview mirror Polyakov saw that the Takisian watched them drive off before going into his hotel.

No doubt he wondered where and when Polyakov would turn up again. Polyakov wondered too. He was all alone now ... mocked by his colleagues, discarded by the Party, loyal to some ideal that he only barely remembered. Like poor Mólniya in a way, sent out on some misguided mission and then abandoned.

The fate of a Soviet ace is to be betrayed.

He was scheduled to remain in London for several weeks yet, but if he could no longer extract useful information from a relatively cooperative source such as the Dancer, there was no point in staying. That night he packed for the return to Moscow and his retirement. After a dinner in which he was joined only by a bottle of Stolichnaya, Polyakov left the hotel and took a walk, down Sloane, past the fashionable boutiques. What did they call the young women who shopped here? Yes, Sloane Rangers. The Rangers, to judge from the stray samples still hurrying home at this hour, or from the bizarre mannequins in the windows, were thin, wraithlike creatures. Too fragile for Polyakov.

In any case, his ultimate destination ... his farewell to London and the West ... was King's Cross, where the women were more substantial.

On reaching Pont Street, however, he noticed an off-duty black cab following him. In moments he considered possible assailants, ranging from renegade American agents to Light of Allah terrorists to English hoodlums ... until he read, in the reflection from a shop window, the license number of a vehicle belonging to the Soviet Embassy. Further examination revealed that the driver was Yurchenko.

Polyakov dropped his evasions and simply met the car. In the back was a man he didn't know. 'Georgy Vladimirovich,' Yurchenko shouted. 'Get in!'

'There's no need to yell,' Polyakov said. 'You'll draw attention.' Yurchenko was one of those polished young men for whom tradecraft came so easily that, unless reminded, he often neglected to use it.

As soon as Polyakov was aboard in the front seat, the car jumped into traffic. They were quite obviously going for a ride.

'We thought we were losing you,' Yurchenko said pleasantly.

'What's this all about?' Polyakov said. He indicated the silent man in the backseat. 'Who's your friend?'

'This is Dolgov of the GRU. He's presented me with some very disturbing news.'

For the first time in years Polyakov felt real fear. Was *this* to be his retirement? An 'accidental' death in a foreign country?

'Don't keep me in suspense, Yurchenko. The last time I checked, I was still your boss.'

Yurchenko couldn't look at him. 'The Takisian is a double agent. He's working for the Americans and has for thirty years.'

Polyakov turned toward the GRU man. 'So now the GRU is *sharing* its precious intelligence. What a great day for the Soviet Union. I suppose I'm suspected of being an agent.'

The GRU man spoke for the first time. 'What did the Takisian give you?'

'I'm not talking to you. What my agents give me is KGB business—'

'The GRU will share with you, then. Tachyon has a grandson named Blaise, whom he found in Paris last month. Blaise is a new kind of ace ... potentially the most powerful and dangerous in the world. And he was snatched right out of our hands to be taken to America.'

The car was crossing Lambeth Bridge, heading toward a gray and depressing industrial district, a perfect location for a safe house ... the perfect setting for an execution.

Tachyon had a grandson with powers! Suppose this child came into contact with Hartmann – the potential was horrifying. Life in a world threatened by nuclear destruction was safe compared to one dominated by a wild card Ronald Reagan. How could he have been so stupid?

'I didn't know,' he said finally. 'Dancer was not an active agent. There was no reason to place him under surveillance.'

'But there was,' Dolgov persisted. 'He's a goddamned alien, for one thing! And if his presence on the tour itself wasn't enough, there was the situation in Paris!'

It was easy for the GRU to spy on someone in Paris: the embassy there was full of its operatives. Of course the sister service hadn't bothered to pass its vital information along to the KGB. Polyakov would have acted differently with Mólniya had he known about Blaise!

Now he needed time to think. He realized he had been holding his breath. A bad habit. 'This is serious. We should obviously be working together. I'm ready to do whatever I can—'

'Then why are you packed?' Yurchenko interrupted, sounding genuinely anguished.

'You've been watching me?' He looked from Yurchenko to Dolgov. My God, they *actually* thought he was going to defect!

Polyakov turned slightly, his hand brushing Yurchenko, who recoiled as if slapped. But Polyakov didn't let go. The cab sideswiped a parked car and skidded back into traffic just as Polyakov saw Yurchenko's eyes roll up ... the heat had already boiled his brain.

Dolgov threw himself into the front seat, grabbing for the wheel, and managed to steer right into another parked car, where they stopped. Polyakov had braced for the impact, which threw Yurchenko's smoking body off him ... freeing him to reach out for Dolgov, who made the mistake of grabbing back.

For an instant Dolgov's face was the face of the Great Leader ... the Benevolent Father of the Soviet People ... himself turned into a murderous joker. Polyakov was just a young courier who carried messages between the Kremlin and Stalin's dacha – sufficiently trusted that he was allowed to know the secret of Great Stalin's curse – not an assassin. He had never intended to be an assassin. But Stalin had already ordered the execution of *all* wild cards ...

If it was his destiny to carry this power, it must also be his destiny to use it. As he had eliminated Stalin, so he eliminated Dolgov.

He didn't allow the man to say a word, not even the final gesture of defiance, as he burned the life out of him.

The impact had jammed the two front doors, so Polyakov would have to crawl out the back. Before he did, he removed the silencer and the heavy service revolver Dolgov carried ... the weapon he was to have pressed to the back of Polyakov's neck. Polyakov fired a round into the air, then put the revolver back where Dolgov carried it. Scotland Yard and the GRU could think what they liked ... another unsolved murder with the murderers themselves the victims of an unlucky accident.

The fire from the two bodies reached the tiny trickle of gasoline spilled in the crash ... The crematorium would not get Dolgov.

The explosion and flames would attract attention. Polyakov knew he should go ... yet there was something attractive in the flames. As if an aged, dutiful KGB colonel were dying, too, to be reborn as a superhero, the one true Soviet ace ...

This would be a legend of his *own* creation.

IV.

There were many signs in Russian at the British Airways terminal at Robert Tomlin International Airport, placed there by members of Jewish Relief, headquartered in nearby Brighton Beach. For Jews who managed to emigrate from the Eastern bloc, even those who dreamed of eventually settling in Palestine, this was their Ellis Island.

Among those debarking this day in May was a stocky man in his early sixties, dressed like a typical middle-class émigré, in brown shirt buttoned to the neck and well-worn gray jacket. A woman from Relief stepped forward to help him. 'Strasvitye s Soyuzom Statom,' she said in Russian, 'Welcome to the United States.'

'Thank you,' the man replied in English.

The woman was pleased. 'If you already speak the language, you will find things very easy here. May I help you?'

'No, I know what I'm doing.'

Out there, in the city, waited Dr. Tachyon, living in fear of their next encounter, wondering what it would mean to his very special grandson. To the south, Washington, and Senator Hartmann, a formidable target. But Polyakov would not work alone. No sooner had he gone underground in England than he had managed to contact the shattered remains of Mólniya's network. Next week Gimli would be joining him in America ...

As he waited for customs to clear his meager luggage, Polyakov could see through the windows that it was a beautiful American summer day.

FROM *THE JOURNAL*
OF XAVIER DESMOND

April 27/somewhere over the Atlantic:

The interior lights were turned out several hours ago, and most of my fellow travelers are long asleep, but the pain has kept me awake. I've taken some pills, and they are helping, but still I cannot sleep. Nonetheless, I feel curiously elated ... almost serene. The end of my journey is near, in both the larger and smaller senses. I've come a long way, yes, and for once I feel good about it.

We still have one more stop – a brief sojourn in Canada, whirl-wind visits to Montreal and Toronto, a government reception in Ottawa. And then home. Tomlin International, Manhattan, Jokertown. It will be good to see the Funhouse again.

I wish I could say that the tour had accomplished everything we set out to do, but that's scarcely the case. We began well, per-haps, but the violence in Syria, West Germany, and France undid our unspoken dream of making the public forget the carnage of Wild Card Day. I can only hope that the majority will realize that terrorism is a bleak and ugly part of the world we live in, that it would exist with or without the wild card. The bloodbath in Berlin was instigated by a group that included jokers, aces, and nats, and we would do well to remember that and remind the world of it forcefully. To lay that carnage at the door of Gimli and his pathetic followers, or the two fugitive aces still being sought by the German police, is to play into the hands of men like Leo Barnett and the

Nur al-Allah. Even if the Takisians had never brought their curse to us, the world would have no shortage of desperate, insane, and evil men.

For me, there is a grim irony in the fact that it was Gregg's courage and compassion that put his life at risk, and hatred that saved him, by turning his captors against each other in that fratricidal holocaust.

Truly, this is a strange world.

I pray that we have seen the last of Gimli, but meanwhile I can rejoice. After Syria it seems unlikely that anyone could still doubt Gregg Hartmann's coolness under fire, but if that was indeed the case, surely all such fears have now been firmly laid to rest by Berlin. After Sara Morgenstern's exclusive interview was published in the *Post*, I understand Hartmann shot up ten points in the polls. He's almost neck and neck with Hart now. The feeling aboard the plane is that Gregg is definitely going to run.

I said as much to Digger back in Dublin, over a Guinness and some fine Irish soda bread in our hotel, and he agreed. In fact, he went further and predicted that Hartmann would get the nomination. I wasn't quite so certain and reminded him that Gary Hart still seems a formidable obstacle, but Downs grinned in that maddeningly cryptic way of his beneath his broken nose and said, 'Yeah, well, I got this hunch that Gary is going to fuck up and do something really stupid, don't ask me why.'

If my health permits, I will do everything I can to rally Jokertown behind a Hartmann candidacy. I don't think I'm alone in my commitment either. After the things we have seen, both at home and abroad, a growing number of prominent aces and jokers are likely to throw their weight behind the senator. Hiram Worchester, Peregrine, Mistral, Father Squid, Jack Braun ... perhaps even Dr. Tachyon, despite his notorious distaste for politics and politicians.

Terrorism and bloodshed notwithstanding, I do believe we accomplished some good on this journey. Our report will open some official eyes, I can only hope, and the press spotlight that has shone on us everywhere has greatly increased public awareness of the plight of jokers in the Third World.

On a more personal level, Jack Braun did much to redeem himself and even buried his thirty-year emnity with Tachyon; Peri seems positively radiant in her pregnancy; and we did manage, however belatedly, to free poor Jeremiah Strauss from twenty years of simian bondage. I remember Strauss from the old days, when Angela owned the Funhouse and I was only the maître d', and I offered him a booking if and when he resumes his theatrical career as the Projectionist. He was appreciative, but noncommittal. I don't envy him his period of adjustment. For all practical purposes, he is a time traveler.

And Dr. Tachyon ... well, his new punk haircut is ugly in the extreme, he still favors his wounded leg, and by now the entire plane knows of his sexual dysfunction, but none of this seems to bother him since young Blaise came aboard in France. Tachyon has been evasive about the boy in his public statements, but of course everyone knows the truth. The years he spent in Paris are scarcely a state secret, and if the boy's hair was not a sufficient clue, his mind control power makes his lineage abundantly clear.

Blaise is a strange child. He seemed a little awed by the jokers when he first joined us, particularly Chrysalis, whose transparent skin clearly fascinated him. On the other hand, he has all of the natural cruelty of an unschooled child (and believe me, any joker knows how cruel a child can be). One day in London, Tachyon got a phone call and had to leave for a few hours. While he was gone, Blaise grew bored, and to amuse himself he seized control of Mordecai Jones and made him climb onto a table and recite 'I'm a Little Teapot,' which Blaise had just learned as part of an English lesson. The table collapsed under the Hammer's weight, and I don't think Jones is likely to forget the humiliation. He didn't much like Dr. Tachyon to begin with.

Of course not everyone will look back on this tour fondly. The trip was very hard on a number of us, there's no gainsaying that. Sara Morgenstern has filed several major stories and done some of the best writing of her career, but nonetheless the woman is edgier and more neurotic with every passing day. As for her colleagues in the back of the plane, Josh McCoy seems alternately madly in love with Peregrine and absolutely furious with her, and it cannot be easy for him with the whole world knowing that he is not the father of her child. Meanwhile, Digger's profile will never be the same.

Downs is, at least, as irrepressible as he is irresponsible. Just the other day he was telling Tachyon that if he got an exclusive on Blaise, maybe he would be able to keep Tach's impotence off-the-record. This gambit was not well received. Digger has also been thick as thieves with Chrysalis of late. I overheard them having a very curious conversation in the bar one night in London. 'I know he is,' Digger was saying. Chrysalis told him that knowing it and proving it were two different things. Digger said something about how they *smelled* different to him, how he'd known ever since they met, and Chrysalis just laughed and said that was fine, but smells that no one else could detect weren't much good as proof, and even if they were, he'd have to blow his own cover to go public. They were still going at it when I left the bar.

I think even Chrysalis will be delighted to return to Jokertown. Clearly she loved England, but given her Anglophile tendencies, that was hardly a surprise. There was one tense moment when she was introduced to Churchill during a reception, and he gruffly inquired as to exactly what she was trying to prove with her affected British accent. It is quite difficult to read expressions on her unique features, but for a moment I was sure she was going to kill the old man right there in front of the Queen, Prime Minister, and a dozen British aces. Thankfully she gritted her teeth and put it down to Lord Winston's advanced age. Even when he was younger, he was never precisely reticent about expressing his thoughts.

Hiram Worchester has perhaps suffered more on this trip than any of us. Whatever reserves of strength were left to him burned out in Germany, and since then he has seemed exhausted. He shattered his special custom seat as we were leaving Paris – some sort of miscalculation with his gravity control, I believe, but it delayed us nearly three hours while repairs were made. His temper has been fraying too. During the business with the seat, Billy Ray made one too many fat jokes, and Hiram finally snapped and turned on him in a white rage, calling him (among other things) an 'incompetent little guttermouth.' That was all it took. Carnifex just grinned that ugly little grin of his, said, 'For that you get your ass kicked, fat man,' and started to get out of his seat. 'I didn't say you could get up,' Hiram replied; he made a fist and trebled Billy's weight, slamming him right back into the seat cushion. Billy was still straining to get up and Hiram was making him heavier and heavier, and I don't know where it might have ended if Dr. Tachyon hadn't broken it up by putting both of them to sleep with his mind control.

I don't know whether to be disgusted or amused when I see these world-famous aces squabbling like petty children, but Hiram at least has the excuse of ill health. He looks terrible these days: white-faced, puffy, perspiring, short of breath. He has a huge, hideous scab on his neck, just below the collar line, that he picks at when he thinks no one is watching. I would strongly advise him to seek out medical attention, but he is so surly of late that I doubt my counsel would be welcomed. His short visits to New York during the tour always seemed to do him a world of good, however, so we can only hope that homecoming restores his health and spirits.

◆

And lastly, me.

Observing and commenting on my fellow travelers and what they've gained or lost, that's the easy part. Summing up my own experience is harder. I'm older and, I hope, wiser than when we left Tomlin International, and undeniably I am five months closer to death.

Whether this journal is published or not after my passing, Mr. Ackroyd assures me that he will personally deliver copies to my grandchildren and do everything in his power to make sure that they are read. So perhaps it is to them that I write these last, concluding words ... to them, and all the others like them ...

Robert, Cassie ... we never met, you and I, and the blame for that falls as much on me as on your mother and your grandmother. If you wonder why, remember what I wrote about self-loathing and please understand that I was not exempt. Don't think too harshly of me ... or of your mother or grandmother. Joanna was far too young to understand what was happening when her daddy changed, and as for Mary ... we loved each other once, and I cannot go to my grave hating her. The truth is, had our roles been reversed, I might well have done the same thing. We're all only human, and we do the best we can with the hand that fate has dealt us.

Your grandfather was a joker, yes. But I hope as you read this book you'll realize that he was something else as well – that he accomplished a few things, spoke up for his people, did some good. The JADL is perhaps as good a legacy as most men leave behind them, a better monument to my mind than the Pyramids, the Taj Mahal, or Jetboy's Tomb. All in all, I haven't done so badly. I'll leave behind some friends who loved me, many treasured memories, much unfinished business. I've wet my foot in the Ganges, heard Big Ben sound the hour, and walked on the Great Wall of China. I've seen my daughter born and held her in my arms, and I've dined with aces and TV stars, with presidents and kings.

Most important, I think I leave the world a slightly better place for my having been in it. And that's really all that can be asked of any of us.

Remember me to your children, if you will.

My name was Xavier Desmond, and I was a man.

FROM *THE NEW YORK TIMES*

July 17, 1987

Xavier Desmond, the founder and president emeritus of the Jokers' Anti-Defamation League (JADL) and a community leader among the victims of the wild card virus for more than two decades, died yesterday at the Blythe van Rensselaer Memorial Clinic, after a long illness.

Desmond, who was popularly known as the 'Mayor of Jokertown,' was the owner of the Funhouse, a well-known Bowery night spot. He began his political activities in 1964, when he founded the JADL to combat prejudice against wild card victims and promote community education about the virus and its effects. In time, the JADL became the nation's largest and most influential joker rights organization, and Desmond the most widely-respected joker spokesman. He sat on several mayors' advisory committees, served as a delegate on the recent global tour sponsored by the World Health Organization. Although he stepped down as president of the JADL in 1984, citing age and ill health, he continued to influence the organization's policies until his death.

He is survived by his former wife, Mary Radford Desmond, his daughter, Mrs. Joanna Horton, and his grandchildren, Robert Van Ness and Cassandra Horton.

SHUFFLING THE DECK

or, Book Four and the World Tour

by George R.R. Martin

Here there be spoilers! You do *not* want to read what follows until after you've finished *Aces Abroad* and the three books before it

Wild Cards began with a three-book contract, but the series was always intended to be open-ended. So when the first three volumes were published to excellent reviews and very strong sales and Bantam asked me for more, my writers and I were pleased to oblige. We loved this world and the characters who peopled it, and knew we had many more stories to tell about them.

The question was, where should we go from here?

Jokers Wild had brought the first triad to a climactic close. The Astronomer was dead, his Egyptian Freemasons smashed and dispersed, and out in the dark of space the Swarm had been tamed and turned away from Earth ... but our characters remained, and damned few of them had been left to live happily ever after. Yeoman was still on the streets with his bow, fighting his one-man war against the Shadow Fist. Croyd Crenson still woke transformed every time he surrendered to sleep. James Spector remained on the loose, his eyes brimming with death. The Great and Powerful Turtle had been killed in *Jokers Wild* ... or had he? Was the Turtle sighting that evening authentic? Just what had happened to Tom Tudbury after the Astronomer's minions had sent his shell crashing into the Hudson?

And we had larger issues to deal with as well. We'd had some fun pitting our aces against the menace of the Swarm and the evil of the Astronomer, but we were ploughing ground that had been ploughed a thousand times before. Aliens and supervillains had been staples of the funny books since the first one came rolling off the press. Our versions had been grittier and more visceral, perhaps, but there was nothing really new in those types of adventures.

The most widely acclaimed story in the first three books had been Walter Jon Williams' Nebula finalist, 'Witness,' a powerful tale of human frailty where the villain was neither the Swarm nor the Astronomer, but rather the House of Un-American Activities Committee (a few of our readers seemed to think that Walter made up HUAC, but never mind). There was a lesson there, if we wanted *Wild Cards* to be all that it could be. Plenty of comic books featured superheroes fighting supervillains and alien invasions, but very few seriously explored the deeper issues that would arise if a handful of superhumans had 'powers and abilities far beyond those of mortal men.' The responsibilities and temptation sof great power, randomly bestowed. The ways society would deal with those who were more than human, and with the new underclass, the jokers. Aces as objects of hero worship and aces as objects of fear. The cult of the celebrity. All this should be grist for our mill, and the thematic heart and soul of *Wild Cards*.

We also wanted to broaden our canvas. The first triad had been very tightly focused on New York City. Oh, we got some glimpses of what was happening in the rest of the world during the Swarm War, and earlier as well, when the Four Aces were chasing Peron from Argentina and losing China to the Communists ... but that was all they were, glimpses. For the most part our eyes remained fixed on the towers of Manhattan and the mean streets of Jokertown. It was time we showed what the Takisian virus had done to the rest of the world.

In my Afterword to the ibooks edition of *Jokers Wild*, I talked about my belief that the most effective shared worlds were those that maximized the sharing. That was a lesson that carried over into the second triad. We wanted a series where the whole was always greater than the sum of its parts. I had been fortunate enough to assemble the most gifted group of writers ever to work together on a collaborative project of this nature, and in the first three books they had given us a richly textured world with its own history, full of fascinating characters and conflicts ... but to build on that foundation we needed to start working together more closely than we had previously. I wanted to draw our plot threads together, and make the second *Wild Cards* triad much more tightly woven than the first.

In later years, much of the planning for the *Wild Cards* books would be done on line, in a private category on the Genie BBS service, but back then the series and the Internet were both still in their infancy. Instead the New Mexico *Wild Cards* contingent assembled in the living room of Melinda Snodgrass's old house on 2nd Street, where we argued over coffee, and from time to time phoned up some of our out-of-town contributors to draw them into the dialogue as well.

As with the earlier triad, we decided that the first two volumes would feature a series of individual stories linked by an interstitial narrative, while the third and concluding volume would bring everything together in a full mosaic novel along the lines of *Jokers Wild*. The Astronomer and his Masonic cult had been the major overarching threat in the first three books. In this new triad, that role would be filled by Senator Gregg Hartmann, a wonderfully complex character who showed a noble, idealistic face to the world as he led the fight for joker rights, while concealing the sadistic ace Puppetman within. Hartmann's 1976 bid for the presidency had failed in book one, but there was no reason he should not try again.

The Hartmann story would be the major unifying thread of these next three books – the overplot, we called it – but there would be other conflicts going on as well. Both John Miller and Leanne Harper had given us a glimpse into New York's criminal underworld, and it seemed inevitable that John's Asian mob and Leanne's old line Mafia family would come into conflict. So that became a second major plot thread, the focus of the middle book of this triad, volume five in the overall series, which would eventually be titled *Down & Dirty*.

The fourth book, the one you've just finished, would be built around a global junket led by Senator Hartmann, its stated purpose to investigate the impact of the wild card virus on other parts of the world. That would serve to reintroduce Hartmann and Puppetman and get the overplot rolling, while simultaneously allowing us to tell some stories we would never have been able to tell had the series remained tightly based in New York City.

Of course, it wasn't that simple. With *Wild Cards*, nothing ever was. I have sometimes likened *Wild Cards* to a big band or symphony, but writers are not accustomed to following a conductor. In *this* band, sometimes two people would leap in to play the same solo, determined to drown each other out. At other times, while most of the band was attempting Beethoven's Fifth, there would be one oboe off in the corner stubbornly playing Mozart instead, and another guy on the harmonica doing the theme song to 'My Mother, the Car.' As editor, sometimes I felt as if I were herding cats. Big cats, and me with neither a chair nor a whip … though I did have a checkbook, which works better than a whip on writers.

The triad which began with *Aces Abroad* was indeed much more tightly plotted than the first … though not nearly as tightly as some of the later triads would be. *Wild Cards* was more interwoven than any shared world series that preceded it (or that followed it, for that matter), but that meant we were exploring virgin territory, so none of us really knew the way. No, not even Your Humble Editor, though editors are usually infallible, as is well known. Looking back on *Aces Abroad* all these years later, I think that perhaps I should have cracked my checkbook-whip a little more often at several points in the proceedings. Having Hartmann kidnapped *twice* during the same tour was a bit much, really, and I should have insisted that my writers juggle with the balls they *already* had up in the air before allowing them to toss up so many new ones. It is all very well when the plot thickens, but if it gets too bloody thick you're likely to throw your wrist out stirring.

Still, it all worked out in the end, more or less. And if perhaps there were too many new characters being introduced, well, many of them would go on to greatly enrich the series in later books. It was here we first met the Living Gods and Ti Malice, here that

Mackie Messer first cut a bloody path into our hearts, here that the Hero Twins and the Black Dog and Dr. Tachyon's darling grandson Blaise made their debuts, and Kahina and the Nur al-Allah as well. Polyakov came on stage for the first time, as did Ed Bryant's aboriginal shaman Wyungare ... though the new character destined to play the largest role down the line was not actually new at all.

That was Jerry Strauss, introduced in the first book as the Projectionist, before becoming a Great Ape for a decade and a half. It was only *after* he was restored to humanity in *Aces Abroad* that our readers, like Dr. Tachyon, found themselves slapping their heads and remembering that the wild card *never* affects animals. As the Projectionist and the Great Ape, Jerry was just a bit player, but later as Nobody he would become somebody. So to speak.

Aces Abroad was a book for goodbyes as well. Lew Shiner's heroic pimp Fortunato had been a *Wild Cards* mainstay since the first volume. In those early days he was one of our two most popular characters, judging from the mail we got, and what our readers told us at conventions. (Dr. Tachyon was the only character to equal Fortunato's popularity, but the readers who loved Tach inevitably hated Fortunato, and vice versa. 'The wimp and the pimp' dichotomy, we called it.) Lew had sent Fortunato off to Japan after his climactic battle with the Astronomer in *Joker's Wild*, to give the character some closure. But Gail Gerstner Miller threw him a curve ball when she had Peregrine turn up pregnant by Fortunato ... and then we brought the tour *to* Japan, right to his doorstep. That managed to coax one last Fortunato story out of Lew ... after which the pimp shuffled permanently offstage, leaving the wimp to reign in solitary splendor for a time.

Aces Abroad also marked the end for my own Xavier Desmond, the 'Mayor of Jokertown,' whose voice I used for the interstitial narrative. Writing the interstitial segments was always one of the most challenging assignments in doing a *Wild Cards* book. Not only did you need to tell a good story of your own, you also had to tie together all the *other* stories, bridge any gaps your fellow writers might have left, and patch up holes in the overplot. Later in the series, I would farm out the interstitials to various other brave souls, but in the beginning I did them all myself. 'The Journal of Xavier Desmond' was the best of my interstitials, I think, and one of the most powerful things I ever wrote for *Wild Cards*.

All in all, the second *Wild Cards* triad got off to a flying start when our aces and jokers boarded the *Stacked Deck* for their trip around the world, little realizing what storms lay ahead for the characters, writers, and editor alike – the madness that was *Down & Dirty* and the monstrous runaway growth of book six.

But those are tales for another day.

George R.R. Martin
January 2, 2002

Copyright Acknowledgements

EYEWITNESS TRAVEL

AUSTRALIA

DK

LONDON, NEW YORK,
MELBOURNE, MUNICH AND DELHI
www.dk.com

Produced by Duncan Baird Publishers
London, England

MANAGING EDITOR Zoë Ross
MANAGING ART EDITORS Vanessa Marsh
(with Clare Sullivan and Virginia Walters)
EDITOR Rebecca Miles
COMMISSIONING DESIGNER Jill Mumford
DESIGNERS DAWN DAVIS-COOK, Lucy Parissi

CONSULTANT Helen Duffy
MAIN CONTRIBUTORS Jan Bowen, Helen Duffy,
Paul Kloeden, Jacinta le Plaistrier, Sue Neales,
Ingrid Ohlssen, Tamara Thiessen.

PHOTOGRAPHERS
Max Alexander, Alan Keohane, Dave King,
Rob Reichenfeld, Peter Wilson.

ILLUSTRATORS
Richard Bonson, Jo Cameron, Stephen Conlin, Eugene Fleury,
Chris Forsey, Steve Gyapay, Toni Hargreaves, Chris Orr, Robbie
Polley, Kevin Robinson, Peter Ross, John Woodcock.

Reproduced by Colourscan (Singapore)
Printed and bound by South China Printing Co. Ltd., China

First published in Great Britain in 1998
by Dorling Kindersley Limited
80 Strand, London WC2R 0RL

**Reprinted with revisions
1999, 2000, 2001, 2002, 2003, 2005, 2006**
Copyright 1998, 2006 © Dorling Kindersley Limited, London
A Penguin Company

ISBN 13: 978 1 40531 498 5
ISBN 10: 1 40531 498 2

Front cover main image: Great Barrier Reef, Queensland

CONTENTS

HOW TO USE
THIS GUIDE **6**

INTRODUCING AUSTRALIA

DISCOVERING
AUSTRALIA **10**

PUTTING AUSTRALIA
ON THE MAP **14**

A PORTRAIT OF
AUSTRALIA **16**

AUSTRALIA THROUGH
THE YEAR **40**

Giraffe in Sydney's Taronga Zoo

THE HISTORY OF
AUSTRALIA **46**

SYDNEY

INTRODUCING
SYDNEY **62**

THE ROCKS AND
CIRCULAR QUAY **74**

CITY CENTRE AND
DARLING
HARBOUR **86**

BOTANIC GARDENS
AND THE DOMAIN **104**

KINGS CROSS,
DARLINGHURST AND
PADDINGTON **116**

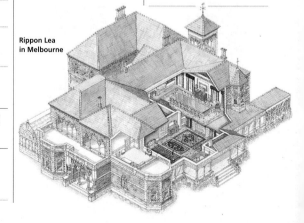

Ben Boyd National Park on the south coast of New South Wales

PRACTICAL
INFORMATION **128**

SYDNEY STREET
FINDER **148**

NEW SOUTH
WALES AND ACT

INTRODUCING NEW
SOUTH WALES
AND ACT **158**

THE BLUE MOUNTAINS
AND BEYOND **164**

THE SOUTH COAST
AND SNOWY
MOUNTAINS **182**

CANBERRA AND
ACT **190**

QUEENSLAND

INTRODUCING
QUEENSLAND **210**

BRISBANE **218**

SOUTH OF
TOWNSVILLE **234**

NORTHERN
QUEENSLAND **248**

THE NORTHERN
TERRITORY

INTRODUCING THE
NORTHERN
TERRITORY **260**

DARWIN AND THE
TOP END **266**

THE RED CENTRE **278**

WESTERN
AUSTRALIA

INTRODUCING WESTERN
AUSTRALIA **292**

PERTH AND THE
SOUTHWEST **298**

NORTH OF PERTH **320**

SOUTH AUSTRALIA

INTRODUCING SOUTH
AUSTRALIA **334**

ADELAIDE AND THE
SOUTHEAST **340**

THE YORKE AND EYRE
PENINSULAS **358**

VICTORIA

INTRODUCING
VICTORIA **372**

MELBOURNE **380**

WESTERN VICTORIA **422**

EASTERN VICTORIA **438**

TASMANIA

INTRODUCING
TASMANIA **454**

TASMANIA **456**

TRAVELLERS'
NEEDS

WHERE TO STAY **474**

WHERE TO EAT **518**

SHOPPING **564**

SPECIALIST HOLIDAYS
AND ACTIVITIES **566**

SURVIVAL GUIDE

PRACTICAL
INFORMATION **572**

TRAVEL
INFORMATION
582

Rippon Lea
in Melbourne

HOW TO USE THIS GUIDE

This guide helps you to get the most from your visit to Australia. *Introducing Australia* maps the whole country and sets it in its historical and cultural context. The 17 regional chapters, including *Sydney*, describe important sights with maps, pictures and illustrations, as well as introductory features on subjects of regional interest. Suggestions on restaurants, accommodation, shopping and entertainment are in *Travellers' Needs*. The *Survival Guide* has tips on getting around the country. The cities of Sydney, Melbourne and Brisbane also have their own *Practical Information* sections.

SYDNEY

The centre of Sydney has been divided into four sightseeing areas. Each area has its own chapter which opens with a list of the sights described. All the sights are numbered and plotted on an *Area Map*. Information on each sight is easy to locate within the chapter as it follows the numerical order on the map.

Sights at a Glance lists the chapter's sights by category: Historic Streets and Buildings, Museums and Galleries, Parks and Gardens etc.

All pages relating to Sydney have orange thumb tabs.

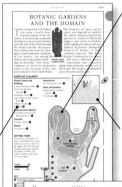

1 Area Map
Sights are numbered on a map. Sights in the city centre are also shown on the Sydney Street Finder (see pp148–55). *Melbourne also has its own* Street Finder (see pp414–21).

A locator map shows where you are in relation to other areas of the city centre.

2 Street-by-Street Map
This gives a bird's-eye view of the heart of each sightseeing area.

A suggested route for a walk covers the more interesting streets in the area.

Stars indicate sights that no visitor should miss.

3 Detailed Information on Each Sight
All the sights in Sydney are described individually. Useful addresses, telephone numbers, opening hours and other practical information are provided for each entry. The key to all the symbols used in the information block is shown on the back flap.

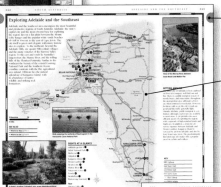

ADELAIDE AND THE SOUTHEAST

1 Introduction
The landscape, history and character of each region is described here, showing how the area has developed over the centuries and what it offers to the visitor today.

AUSTRALIA AREA BY AREA

Apart from Sydney, Australia has been divided into 16 regions, each of which has a separate chapter. The most interesting towns and places to visit are numbered on an *Regional Map* at the beginning of each chapter.

Each area of Australia can be identified quickly by its own colour coding, which is shown on the inside front cover.

2 Regional Map
This shows the main road network and gives an illustrated overview of the whole area. All interesting places to visit are numbered and there are also useful tips on getting around the region.

3 Detailed Information
All the important towns and other places to visit are described individually. They are listed in order, following the numbering on the Regional Map. *Within each town or city, there is detailed information on important buildings and other sights.*

For all the top sights, a visitors' checklist provides the practical information needed to plan your visit.

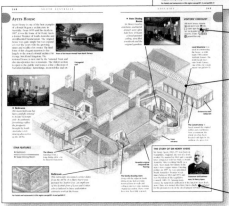

4 Australia's Top Sights
Historic buildings are dissected to reveal their interiors; museums and galleries have colour-coded floorplans; the national parks have maps showing facilities and trails. Major towns have maps, with sights picked out and described.

Story boxes explore specific subjects further.

INTRODUCING
AUSTRALIA

DISCOVERING AUSTRALIA 10–13

PUTTING AUSTRALIA ON THE MAP 14–15

A PORTRAIT OF AUSTRALIA 16–39

AUSTRALIA THROUGH THE YEAR 40–45

THE HISTORY OF AUSTRALIA 46–59

DISCOVERING AUSTRALIA

Australia offers unequalled experiences and a wealth of diversity. Its 18,000-km (11,180-mile) coastline boasts everything from the world's best coral reefs, to endless white sandy bays, stunning tropical islands and buzzing surf beaches. The massive interior includes vast red deserts, ancient Aboriginal sites, snow-topped

Aboriginal necklace

mountains and lush green vineyards. You will be spoilt for choice whether you want to experience thrilling outdoor adventure, enjoy the laid-back beach culture, or sample the best in international cuisine and wine. These pages detail regional highlights that will whet your appetite and help you to plan and make the most of your trip.

SYDNEY

- Stunning Sydney Harbour
- Sydney Opera House
- The historic Rocks
- Relaxed beach culture

Australia's largest city offers a magnificent array of cultural and architectural delights. The city's crowning glory is **Sydney Harbour** *(see pp70-73)* – a stunning natural asset that other cities can only dream about. **Sydney Opera House** *(see pp84-5)* is a world-class venue and an architectural icon that enjoys the most spectacular setting of any cultural institution. Nearby is the pretty historic quarter, **The Rocks** *(see pp76-7)*, where the first British fleet settled in 1788. A string of gorgeous ocean beaches line the east coast, such as famous **Bondi** *(see p126-7)*, where surfers gather at dawn and the beach cafés are perfect for people-watching.

Sydney Opera House, one of the world's most striking buildings

THE BLUE MOUNTAINS AND BEYOND

- Outdoor activities
- Hunter Valley wine tasting
- Prehistoric Mungo World Heritage Area

Escape from Sydney to the cool refuge of the **Blue Mountains** *(see pp170-73)*. The striking Three Sisters rocks at Echo Point frame a breathtaking panorama, and act as a backdrop for adventure activities, such as bushwalking and rock climbing. **Hunter Valley** *(see pp174-75)* is world-famous for its superb wines, which can be sampled in local cellars. North of Newcastle, secluded towns dot the coast all the way to Queensland. Some are sleepy hideaways, but for those seeking a party, Byron Bay *(see pp178-79)* is the place to go. Out west, the **Mungo World Heritage**

Lush vineyards in the fertile Hunter Valley, New South Wales

Area *(see p181)* reminds visitors of the Aborigine's 40,000-year occupation of this ancient land.

THE SOUTH COAST AND SNOWY MOUNTAINS

- Glorious hiking and cycling
- Browsing in antique shops
- World-class skiing

Perfect for those who love the great outdoors, this region boasts the **Royal National Park** *(see p186)* on Sydney's southeastern fringe – a fantastic playground for cyclists, bushwalkers and hang-gliders. Further south are the lush, idyllic villages of the **Southern Highlands** *(see pp186-7)*. Known as a retreat for Sydneysiders in summer, they are ideal in winter for browsing antique shops. The **South Coast**'s *(see pp188–9)* fishing villages are a hit with anglers and families, while the **Snowy Mountains** *(see p187)* offer world-class ski resorts, trout fishing and horse-riding in summer.

CANBERRA AND ACT

- **Impressive city architecture**
- **World-class art and artefacts**
- **A breathtaking wilderness**

Australia's capital sprang to life under the harmonious designs of its architect, Walter Burley Griffin. Impressive colonial and indigenous art and artefacts are displayed at the world-class **National Museum of Australia** *(see p205)* and the **National Gallery of Australia** *(see pp202-03)*. To the south, the wild **Namadgi National Park** *(see p207)* offers great hiking amid snowy mountains, glistening river valleys and ancient Aboriginal rock art.

The Great Barrier Reef, one of the natural wonders of the world

Cuddly Koala at the Lone Pine Koala Sanctuary, Brisbane

BRISBANE

- **Arts and culture**
- **Exotic botanic gardens**
- **Bustling Southbank**

Cosmopolitan Brisbane has as its creative hub the **Queensland Cultural Centre** *(see pp228–9)*. This thriving institution houses the state's Museum, Art Gallery, Library and Performing Arts Centre. The **Botanic Gardens** *(see p230)* feature exotic herbs, delicate mangrove and walking trails. Across the river, **Southbank Parklands** *(see p227)* abounds with buskers, markets and cafés. Admire adorable koalas at the **Lone Pine Koala Sanctuary** *(see p230)*.

SOUTH OF TOWNSVILLE

- **The magnificent Great Barrier Reef**
- **Sunshine and beaches**
- **Fraser Island's giant dunes**

With astonishing natural wonders, this region is one of Australia's highlights, and its undisputed gem is the **Great Barrier Reef** *(see pp212-17)*. The world's largest coral reef is a must-see for anyone who has ever dreamt of coming face to face with tropical fish. The **Sunshine Coast** *(see p240)* lives up to its name, with a sunny climate and superb resorts. **Fraser Island** *(see p242)* is the world's biggest sand island, with interior rainforests and endless beaches.

NORTHERN QUEENSLAND AND THE OUTBACK

- **Partying in Cairns**
- **Coastal rainforest**
- **The vast Gulf Savannah**

Cairns *(see p254)* is famed for its party atmosphere. The city also makes a good base for exploring the Great Barrier Reef and **Daintree National Park** *(see p253)*, where the rainforest meets the sea. The **Gulf Savannah** *(see p256)* is an empty wilderness of salt pans and flatlands, a breeding ground for birds in spring and a birdwatchers' paradise. Drive into the Outback and discover the harsh realities of life as an Aussie farmer in the town of **Longreach** (see p257).

DARWIN AND THE TOP END

- **Spectacular landscapes at Kakadu National Park**
- **Ancient Aboriginal rock art**
- **Bathurst Island culture**

Darwin's *(see p270)* remote location and history of migration have given it a multicultural, wild-west character. The world's best Aboriginal art collection is displayed at Darwin's **Museum and Art Gallery of the Northern Territory** *(see p277)*. Rock art is also a highlight of one of Australia's most extraordinary places, **Kakadu National Park** *(see p276)*, with its dramatic escarpments and spectacular lightning storms in the build-up to the wet season. Day trips from Darwin to **Bathurst Island** *(see p274)* offer a unique glimpse of Aboriginal, Indonesian and Tiwi islanders' traditional way of life.

Aboriginal cave art, Kakadu National Park, Darwin

THE RED CENTRE

• **Awe-inspiring Uluru**
• **Desert wildflowers in spring**
• **Adventure camel treks**

At the heart of this vast red landscape is a site of enormous spiritual significance for the Aboriginal community: **Uluru** *(see pp286-9)*. The chance to admire the immense presence and ever-changing colours of this monolith is one of the highlights of a trip to Australia. Spring is a magical time to visit as, after the rains, the desert erupts into a carpet of wildflowers. Lively **Alice Springs** *(see pp282–3)* is the Red Centre's only city, and from here you can arrange outdoor adventure activities, such as **camel treks** *(see p567)* in the desert.

Uluru, the emblem of Australia and a sacred Aboriginal site

Surfing off the coast of Perth, Western Australia

PERTH AND THE SOUTHWEST

• **The isolated city of Perth**
• **Bike rides on Rottnest Island**
• **Surfing at Margaret River**

Perth *(see pp302–7)*, the world's most remote city, is a modern metropolis with superb beaches and great surf. On lovely **Rottnest Island** *(see pp308–9)* you can hire bikes to explore its idyllic coves and encounter its unique furry inhabitants: the quokkas. Within easy access of Perth, the historic port of **Fremantle** *(see pp310–11)* is the ideal spot for a laid-back café crawl. To the southwest lies one of the region's prettiest coastal towns, **Margaret River** *(see p314)*, which has become synonymous with gourmet food, fine wine and international surf competitions.

NORTH OF PERTH AND THE KIMBERLEY

• **The extraordinary Pinnacles**
• **Dazzling Ningaloo Reef**
• **The dramatic Kimberley**

Remote Western Australia contains hidden treasures. Strange limestone Pinnacles stand to attention amid the dunes at **Nambung National Park** *(see p324)*, while the magnificent **Ningaloo Reef** *(see p328)* is a snorkeller's dream. Swim from exquisite turquoise bays to observe its sea turtles, whale sharks and reef fish. Spring is the best time to explore the **Kimberley** *(see p330)*, with its vast deserts and deep-river canyon.

Coastal dunes on the Eyre Peninsula, South Australia

ADELAIDE AND THE SOUTHEAST

• **Charming Adelaide**
• **Barossa Valley vineyards**
• **Unspoilt Kangaroo Island**

Adelaide *(see pp344–7)*, the graceful "City of Churches", is a cosmopolitan city with a vibrant restaurant scene. Don't miss a tour of one of the world-class wineries set amid the rolling hills of the **Barossa Valley** *(see pp356–7)*. To the southwest of Adelaide, **Kangaroo Island** *(see p354)* is a haven for wildlife, while the beautiful lagoons of **Coorong National Park** *(see p351)* are protected from the Southern Ocean by sand dunes.

THE YORKE AND EYRE PENINSULAS AND THE FAR NORTH

• **Coffin Bay Oysters**
• **Walk the Flinders Ranges**
• **Going underground at Coober Pedy**

Some of Australia's best oysters are to be had at **Coffin Bay National Park** *(see p366)* on the Eyre Peninsula *(see p360)*, which is also home to wonderful spring wildflowers and birdlife. To the west, clifftops are prime vantage points for whale watching. Inland, the arid **Flinders Ranges** *(see p369)* are popular with bushwalkers, while in **Coober Pedy** *(see p368)*, residents live in subterranean dwellings to escape the extreme temperatures.

MELBOURNE

- A botanical paradise
- European café culture
- International cuisine
- Great sporting venues

Melbourne *(see pp380–405)* prides itself on its green spaces, multicultural lifestyle and strong sporting tradition. Take a stroll though the tranquil 19th-century **Royal Botanic Gardens and Kings Domain** *(see pp398–9)* and enjoy one of the finest botanic collections in the world. Melbourne is also home to several great sporting venues, notably Australia's world-famous cricketing temple, the **Melbourne Cricket Ground** *(see p397)*, and the international tennis mecca at **Melbourne Park** *(see p397)*. European, Middle-Eastern and Asian immigrants have given the city a variety of world-class restaurants and a lively, usually alfresco, café culture *(see pp552–6)*.

Outdoor café in the centre of Federation Square, Melbourne *(see p402)*

National Park *(see p427)*. Paddlesteamers cruise the lazy **Murray River** *(see p430)* passing pioneer river towns such as **Swan Hill** *(see p431)*. Down south, the highlight is scenic drive down the **Great Ocean Road** *(see pp428–9)*, a winding coast road that hugs the rugged clifftops overlooking the mighty Twelve Apostles, giant eroded monoliths.

Fairy penguin, Phillip Island

WESTERN VICTORIA

- Gold fever in Ballarat
- Awesome climbing
- Drive the mighty Great Ocean Road

The 19th-century gold-rush went wild in **Ballarat** *(see pp434–5)*, **Bendigo** and **Maldon** *(see p432)*, where the extravagant buildings are evidence of former wealth. Westwards, climbers and bushwalkers have a field day in the rugged **Grampians**

EASTERN VICTORIA

- Majestic Yarra Valley
- Alpine National Park Skiing
- Penguins of Phillip Island

Fertile Eastern Victoria boasts intense natural beauty. The **Yarra Valley** *(see p443)* is home to some of Australia's finest vineyards, and the **Healesville Sanctuary** *(see p443)*, is a fascinating wildlife park that features indigenous species, such as the elusive platypus. Victoria's **Alpine National Park** *(see p448)* offers world-class cross-country and downhill ski

resorts. Tranquil **Phillip Island** *(see p442)* is famous for the thousands of Fairy penguins waddle out of the ocean at dusk. **Wilsons Promontory** *(see p444)* is a stunning coastal park with shady gullies, secluded beaches and windswept heathlands that are made for nature-lovers. The calm waters of **90 Mile Beach** *(see p444)*, an unbroken stretch of beaches and sand dunes, and the beautiful **Gippsland Lakes** *(see p445)*, Australia's largest inland lake system, offer fantastic sailing, fishing, camping and diving.

TASMANIA

- Historic Hobart
- Port Arthur gaol
- White-water rafting at Franklin-Gordon Wild Rivers

Steeped in maritime history, pretty **Hobart** *(see pp460–61)*, is Australia's second oldest city. Its beautiful waterfront bustles with markets, cafés, restaurants, entertainment and nightlife. The city's dark past as a penal colony has been preserved at isolated **Port Arthur** prison *(see pp470–71)*. **Cradle Mountain Lake Saint Clair National Park** *(see p467)* is loved by bushwalkers, many of whom make the pilgrimage to its pristine alpine lake. **The Franklin-Gordon Wild Rivers National Park** *(see p468)* is a wild region of cool-climate rainforests, fern gullies and white-water rafting.

Tasmania, an island of stunning natural beauty

Putting Australia on the Map

Australia lies in the southern hemisphere and covers 7,772,535 sq km (3,842,675 sq miles) of land. A continent, it is bordered by the Pacific Ocean to the east and the Indian Ocean to the west. More than 70 per cent of its 20 million people reside along the coastline with its more hospitable climate. The capital, Canberra, is in the Australian Capital Territory, but the most populous city is Sydney. Tasmania, an island state, lies 240 km (150 miles) off the south tip of the country, across the Bass Strait.

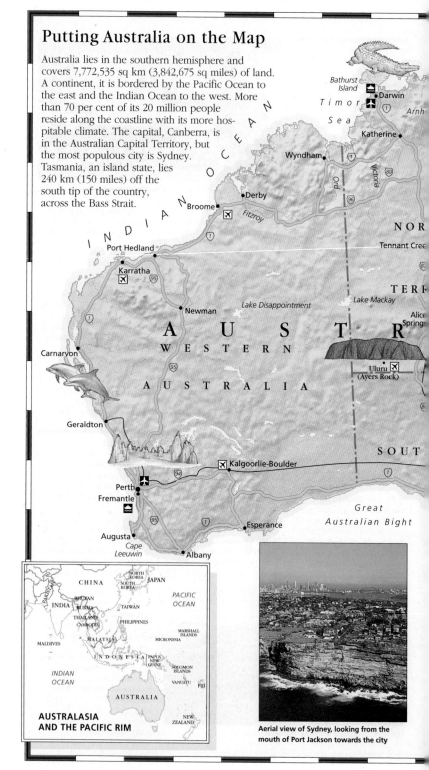

Bathurst Island

Darwin

Timor Sea

Katherine

Arnh

Wyndham

Ord

Victoria

Derby

Broome

Fitzroy

N O R

Port Hedland

Tennant Cree

Karratha

Lake Disappointment

Lake Mackay

T E R I

Newman

Alice
Springs

A U S T R

W E S T E R N

Uluru
(Ayers Rock)

A U S T R A L I A

Carnarvon

Geraldton

S O U T

Kalgoorlie-Boulder

Perth

Fremantle

*Great
Australian Bight*

Augusta
*Cape
Leeuwin*

Esperance

Albany

I N D I A N   O C E A N

**AUSTRALASIA
AND THE PACIFIC RIM**

CHINA

NORTH KOREA

SOUTH KOREA

JAPAN

*PACIFIC
OCEAN*

INDIA

BHUTAN

BURMA

TAIWAN

THAILAND

PHILIPPINES

CAMBODIA

MARSHALL
ISLANDS

MALAYSIA

MICRONESIA

MALDIVES

I N D O N E S I A

PAPUA
NEW
GUINEA

SOLOMON
ISLANDS

*INDIAN
OCEAN*

VANUATU

FIJI

AUSTRALIA

NEW
ZEALAND

**Aerial view of Sydney, looking from the
mouth of Port Jackson towards the city**

For additional map symbols *see back flap*

Aerial view of Melbourne, along the
Yarra River looking towards the casino

rafura Sea

Torres *Strait*

Cape York

Gulf

*Groote
Eylandt*

of

Carpentaria

*Mornington
Island*

Cooktown

Cairns

ERN

Flinders

Townsville

Great Barrier Reef

Mount Isa

ORY

Mackay

QUEENSLAND

Longreach

Rockhampton

Diamantina

Blackall

*Fraser
Island*

Charleville

Maroochydore

Brisbane

Toowoomba

Coolangatta

*Lake
Eyre*

Moree

Lake Torrens

*Lake
Gairdner*

Bourke

Coffs Harbour

USTRALIA

Darling

NEW
SOUTH
WALES

Whyalla

Broken Hill

Dubbo

Maitland

Newcastle

Port
Lincoln

Murray

Mildura

SYDNEY

Adelaide

Wagga Wagga

Wollongong

CANBERRA

AUSTRALIAN
CAPITAL
TERRITORY

*Kangaroo
Island*

VICTORIA

Melbourne

Geelong

KEY

Tasman Sea

International airport

*King
Island*

Bass Strait

*Flinders
Island*

Domestic airport

Passenger ship terminal

Freeway or motorway

Launceston

Railway

TASMANIA

State boundary

Hobart

0 kilometres   500

0 miles   250

PACIFIC OCEAN

A PORTRAIT OF AUSTRALIA

Australia is the world's oldest continent, inhabited for more than 60,000 years by Aborigines. It was settled by the British just over 200 years ago, in 1788, and since then has transformed from a colonial outpost into a nation with a population of about 20 million people. For visitors, its ancient, worn landscape contrasts with the vitality and youthful energy of its inhabitants.

Covering an area as large as the United States of America or the entire European continent, Australia's landscape is highly diverse, encompassing the dry Outback, the high plateaus of the Great Dividing Range, the lush woods of Tasmania, the rainforests and coral reefs of the tropical north and almost 18,000 km (11,000 miles) of coastline. The Great Dividing Range forms a spine down eastern Australia, from Queensland to Victoria, separating the fertile coastal strip from the dry and dusty interior.

Dominating the vegetation is the eucalypt, known as the "gum tree", of which there are some 500 varieties.

Aboriginal image of Namerredje

Australian trees shed their bark rather than their leaves, the native flowers have no smell and, with the exception of the wattle, bloom only briefly.

Australia has a unique collection of fauna. Most are marsupials, such as the emblematic kangaroo and koala. The platypus and echidna are among the few living representatives in the world of mammals that both lay eggs and suckle their young. The dingo, brought to Australia by the Aborigines, is considered the country's native dog.

Australia's antiquity is nowhere more evident than in the vast inland area known as the Outback.

Sydney Opera House, jutting into Sydney Harbour

◁ Typical red soil and spinifex grass of Australia's Outback

Ancient, eroded landscape of the Olgas, part of Uluru-Kata Tjuta National Park in the Northern Territory

Once a huge inland sea, its later aridity preserved the remains of the creatures that once inhabited the area. Some fossils found in Western Australia are 350 million years old – the oldest forms of life known on earth.

THE ABORIGINES

The indigenous inhabitants of Australia, the Aborigines, today constitute almost 1.6 per cent of the national population. Their rights and social status are gradually being improved.

Aboriginal Australian

The early days of European colonialism proved disastrous for the Aborigines. Thousands were killed in hostilities or by unfamiliar diseases. During the 1850s, many Aborigines were confined to purpose-built reserves in a misguided attempt to overcome widespread poverty.

Since the 1950s there have been serious efforts to redress this lack of understanding. Conditions are improving, but even today, in almost every aspect of life, including health care, education and housing, Aborigines are worse off than other Australians. In 1992, a milestone occurred when the High Court overturned the doctrine of *terra nullius* – that Australia belonged to no one at the time of British settlement. The Native Title Act followed, which, in essence, states that where Aborigines could establish unbroken occupancy of an area, they could then claim that land as their own.

Almost all Australians support this reconciliation and are increasingly aware of the rich heritage of the Aborigines. The Aboriginal belief in the Dreamtime *(see pp30–31)* may never be completely assimilated into

The kangaroo, a famous icon of Australia

the Australian consciousness, but an understanding of ancestral beings is an invaluable guide to traditional lifestyles. Aboriginal painting is now respected as one of the world's most ancient art forms and modern Aboriginal art began to be taken seriously in the 1970s. Aboriginal writers have also come to the forefront of Australian literature. Younger Aborigines are beginning to capitalize on this new awareness to promote equal rights and, with Aboriginal cultural centres being set up throughout the country, it is unlikely that Australia will dismiss its native heritage again.

SOCIETY

Given Australia's size and the fact that early settlements were far apart, Australian society is remarkably homogeneous. Its citizens are fundamentally prosperous and the way of life in the major cities and towns is much the same however many miles divide them. It takes a keen ear to identify regional accents.

However, there is some difference in lifestyle between city dwellers and the country people. Almost 90 per cent of the population lives in the fast-paced cities along the coast and has little more than a passing familiarity with the Outback. The major cities preserve pockets of colonial heritage, but the

A fortified wine maker takes a sample from a barrel of port in the Barossa Valley, South Australia

overall impression is modern, with new buildings reflecting the country's youth. In contrast, the rural communities tend to be slow-moving and conservative. For many years, Australia was said to have "ridden on the sheep's back", a reference to wool being the country's main money-earner. However, the wool industry is no longer dominant. Much of Australia's relatively sound economy is now achieved from coal, iron ore and wheat, and as the largest diamond producer in the world. Newer industries such as tourism and wine making are also increasingly important. Australians are generally friendly and relaxed, with a self-deprecating sense of humour. On the whole, Australia has a society without hierarchies, an attitude generally held to stem from its convict beginnings.

Isolated Outback church in Silverton, New South Wales

Yet, contrary to widespread belief, very few Australians have true convict origins. Within only one generation of the arrival of the First Fleet in 1788, Australia had become a nation of immigrants. Originally hailing almost entirely from the British Isles, today one in three Australians comes from elsewhere. Australia's liberal postwar immigration policies led to an influx of survivors from war-torn Europe, most notably Greeks, Italians, Poles and Germans.

Indonesian satay stall at Parap Market in Darwin in the Northern Territory

The emphasis has shifted in recent years and today the majority of new immigrants hail from Southeast Asia. Although some racism does exist, this blend of nations has, on the whole, been a successful experiment and Australia is justifiably proud to have one of the most harmonious multicultural communities in the world.

POLITICS

Since 1901, Australia has been a federation, with its central government based in the purpose-built national capital, Canberra. Each state also has its own government. The nation inherited the central parliamentary system from England, and there is a two-party system consisting of the left (Labor) and the right (a coalition of Liberal and National Parties). The prime minister is the head of federal government, while the heads of states are premiers. Australia is a self-governing member of the British Commonwealth and retains the English monarch as its titular head of state. At present, the national representative of the monarch is the governor general, but the nation is involved in an ongoing debate about its future as a republic. There is opposition from those who argue that the system currently in place has led to one of the most stable societies in the world, while others believe that swearing allegiance to an English monarch has little meaning for the current population, many of whom are immigrants. A referendum in November 1999 saw the monarchy retained with some 55 per cent of the votes. The debate continues.

The nation's character has always been shaped by its sparsely populated island location, far distant from its European roots and geographically closer to Southeast Asia. Today

View of the Parliamentary area and Lake Burley Griffin in Canberra

there is a growing realization that the country must look to the Pacific region for its future. Closer ties with Asia, such as business transactions with Indonesia and Japan, are being developed.

ART AND CULTURE

Blessed with a sunny climate and surrounded by the sea, outdoor leisure is high on the list of priorities for Australians – going to the beach is almost a national pastime. Australians are also mad about sport: football, cricket, rugby, tennis and golf are high on the national agenda.

Yet despite this reputation, Australians actually devote more

Australian Rules football match in Melbourne

of their time and money to artistic pursuits than they do to sporting ones, and as a result the national cultural scene is very vibrant. It is no accident that the Sydney Opera House is one of the country's most recognizable symbols. The nation is probably best known for its opera singers, among whom have been two of the all-time greats, Dame Nellie Melba and Dame Joan Sutherland. Opera Australia and the Australian Ballet, both in Sydney, are acknowledged for their high standards. Every state also has its own thriving theatre company and symphony orchestra. Major art galleries abound throughout the country, from the many excellent state galleries exhibiting international works to a multitude of small

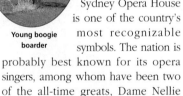

Young boogie boarder

private galleries exhibiting local and contemporary Australian and Aboriginal art.

The Australian film industry has also come into its own since the 1970s. The best-known Australian film is possibly *Crocodile Dundee* (1985), but lower budget productions such as *Shine* (1996) and *Muriel's Wedding* (1994) have an attractive, understated quality which regularly wins them international film awards.

This is not to say that Australia's cultural pursuits are entirely highbrow. Low-budget television soap operas such as *Neighbours* have become high-earning exports. Rock bands such as AC/DC also have an international following.

In almost all aspects, it seems, Australia lives up to its nickname of "the lucky country" and it is hard to meet an Australian who is not thoroughly convinced that this young and vast nation is now the best country on earth.

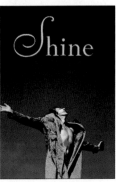

Film poster of the Academy-Award winning *Shine*

Australia's Landscape

Geological stability has been largely responsible for creating the landscape of the earth's oldest, flattest and driest inhabited continent. Eighty million years ago, Australia's last major bout of geological activity pushed up the Great Dividing Range, but since then the continent has slept. Mountains have been eroded down, making it difficult for rain clouds to develop. Deserts have formed in once lush areas and today more than 70 per cent of the continent is arid. However, with some of the oldest rocks on earth, its landscapes are anything but uniform, and include rainforests, tropical beaches, glacial landforms, striking coastlines and flood plains.

Australia's drift *towards the equator has brought a northern monsoon climate, as in Kakadu National Park (see pp276–7).*

Cradle Mountain (see p467) *in southwest Tasmania was created by geological upheaval, glaciation and erosion. Here jagged mountain ranges, ravines and glacial lakes have formed a landscape that is quite unique in Australia.*

KATA TJUTA (THE OLGAS)
Geological remnants of an immense bed of sedimentary rock now almost covered by sand from erosion, Kata Tjuta's weathered domes may once have been a single dome many times the size of Uluru *(see pp286–9).*

Western
Plateau

Central
Lowlands

Great
Dividing
Range

There are three *main geological regions in Australia: the coastal plain including the Great Dividing Range; the Central Lowlands; and the Western Plateau. The Great Dividing Range is a relatively new feature in geological terms. It contains Australia's highest mountains, deep rivers, spectacular gorges and volcanic landforms. The Central Lowlands subsided when the continental margins on either side rose up – a result of rifting caused by continental drift. The Western Plateau contains many of Australia's large deserts and is composed of some of the most ancient rocks in the world.*

The area to the east *of Queensland was flooded at the end of the last Ice Age, creating ideal conditions for a coral reef. The Great Barrier Reef* (see pp212–17) *now forms one of the world's most stunning sights.*

The Nullarbor Plain (see p367) *was created by the upthrust of an ancient sea floor. Today, sheer cliffs drop away from this desert landscape dotted with sinkholes and plunge into the sea below, creating one of Australia's most startling coastlines.*

THE AUSTRALIAN CONTINENT

The Australian continent finally broke away from its last adjoining landmass, Antarctica, 40 million years ago and embarked on a long period of geographical isolation. During this time Australia's unique flora and fauna evolved and flourished *(see pp24–5)*. Aboriginal people lived undisturbed on this continent for at least 40,000 years, developing the land to their own needs, until the arrival of Europeans in 1770 *(see pp46–51)*.

Two hundred million years ago, the area of land that is now continental Australia was attached to the lower half of the earth's single landmass, Pangaea.

Between 200 and 65 million years ago, Pangaea separated to form two supercontinents, Gondwanaland in the south and Laurasia in the north.

Fifty million years ago, Gondwanaland had broken up into the various southern continents with only Antarctica and Australia still attached.

Today, the drifting of the continents continues and Australia is moving northwards towards the equator at the rate of 8 cm (3 ins) a year.

Flora and Fauna

Forty million years of isolation from other major land masses have given Australia a collection of flora and fauna that is unique in the world. Low rainfall and poor soil has meant meagre food sources, and animals and plants have evolved some curious adaptations to help them cope. Surprisingly, these adverse conditions have also produced incredible biodiversity. Australia has more than 25,000 species of plants, and its rainforests are among the richest in the world in the number of species they support. Even its desert centre has 2,000 plant species and the world's greatest concentration of reptile species.

The platypus *lives in an aquatic environment like a fish, suckles its young like a mammal, lays eggs and has the bill of a duck!*

The lush rainforest is a haven for many endemic species of flora and fauna.

Epiphytes, ferns and vines abound around this rainforest creek.

At least 30 species of spinifex cover many of Australia's desert plains.

RAINFORESTS

The east coast rainforests are among the most ancient ecosystems on earth. At least 18,000 plant species exist here. Some trees are more than 2,500 years old, and many are direct descendants of species from Gondwana *(see p23)*.

ARID REGIONS

The vast reaches of Australia's arid and semi-arid regions teem with life. Desert plants and animals have developed unique and specific behavioural and physical features to maximize their survival chances in such harsh conditions.

The golden bowerbird *of the rainforest builds spectacular bowers out of sticks as a platform for its mating displays. Some bowers reach well over 2 m (6.5 ft) in height.*

The boab (baobab) tree *sheds its leaves in the dry season to survive.*

Spinifex grass, *found across the desert, stores water and needs frequent exposure to fire to thrive.*

The Wollemi pine *was discovered in 1994 and caused a sensation. It belongs to a genus thought to have become extinct between 65 and 200 million years ago.*

The thorny devil *feeds only on ants and can consume more than 3,000 in one meal.*

MAMMALS

Australian mammals are distinctive because the population is dominated by two groups that are rare or non-existent elsewhere. Monotremes, such as the platypus, are found only in Australia and New Guinea, and marsupials, represented by 180 species here, are scarce in other parts of the world. In contrast, placental mammals, highly successful on other continents, have been represented in Australia only by bats and rodents, and more recently by dingos. Mass extinctions of larger placentals occurred 20,000 years ago.

Red kangaroos *are the most common of many species of this marsupial found in Australia.*

The dingo *was introduced into Australia by migrating humans c. 5,000 years ago.*

Eucalypt trees provide food for possums and koalas.

Moist fern groundcover shelters a variety of small mammals and insects.

This coral garden is home to many molluscs, crustaceans and brightly coloured fish.

OPEN WOODLAND

The woodlands of the eastern seaboard, the southeast and southwest are known as the Australian bush. Eucalypt trees predominate in the hardy vegetation that has developed to survive fire, drought and poor-quality soil.

SEALIFE

Australia's oceans are poor in nutrients but rich in the diversity of life they support. Complex ecosystems create beautiful underwater scenery, while the shores and islands are home to nesting seabirds and giant sea mammals.

Koalas *feed only on nutrient-poor eucalypt leaves, and have evolved low-energy lives to cope, such as sleeping for 20 hours a day.*

Seagrass beds *have high-saline conditions which attract many sea creatures. Shark Bay shelters the highest number of sea mammals in the world* (see pp326–7).

Kookaburras *are very efficient breeders: one of the young birds is kept on in the nest to look after the next batch of hatchlings, leaving both parents free to gather food.*

The Australian sealion *is one of two seal species unique to Australia. Its extended breeding cycle helps it contend with a poor food supply.*

World Heritage Areas of Australia

The World Heritage Convention was adopted by UNESCO in 1972 in order to protect areas of universal cultural and natural significance. Eleven sites in Australia are inscribed on the World Heritage List and include unusual landforms, ancient forests and areas of staggering biodiversity. Four of the locations (Kakadu National Park, Willandra Lakes, the Tasmanian wilderness and Uluṟu-Kata Tjuṯa National Park) are also listed for their Aboriginal cultural heritage.

Fossil sites *in Riversleigh (see p257)* and Naracoorte *chart Australia's important evolutionary stages.*

Kakadu National Park *is a landscape of wetlands and tropical splendour. Art sites document the interaction between Aborigines and the land* (see pp276–7).

NORTHERN TERRITORY

WESTERN AUSTRALIA

SOUTH AUSTRALIA

Australian Fossil Mammal Site at Naracoorte *(see p355)*

Shark Bay *is home to a vast colony of sea mammals. The bay's stromatolites (algae-covered rocks) are the oldest form of life known on earth (see pp326–7).*

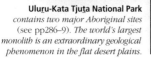

Uluṟu-Kata Tjuṯa National Park *contains two major Aboriginal sites (see pp286–9). The world's largest monolith is an extraordinary geological phenomenon in the flat desert plains.*

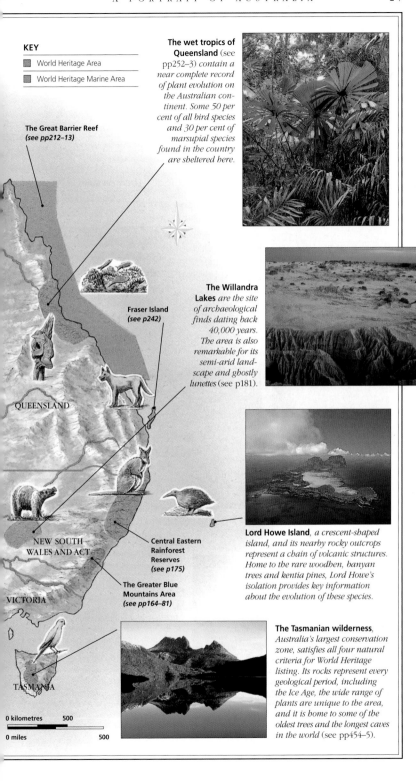

KEY

- World Heritage Area
- World Heritage Marine Area

The wet tropics of Queensland (see pp252–3) *contain a near complete record of plant evolution on the Australian continent. Some 50 per cent of all bird species and 30 per cent of marsupial species found in the country are sheltered here.*

The Great Barrier Reef *(see pp212–13)*

Fraser Island *(see p242)*

The Willandra Lakes *are the site of archaeological finds dating back 40,000 years. The area is also remarkable for its semi-arid landscape and ghostly lunettes (see p181).*

QUEENSLAND

NEW SOUTH WALES AND ACT

Central Eastern Rainforest Reserves *(see p175)*

The Greater Blue Mountains Area *(see pp164–81)*

VICTORIA

Lord Howe Island, *a crescent-shaped island, and its nearby rocky outcrops represent a chain of volcanic structures. Home to the rare woodhen, banyan trees and kentia pines, Lord Howe's isolation provides key information about the evolution of these species.*

The Tasmanian wilderness, *Australia's largest conservation zone, satisfies all four natural criteria for World Heritage listing. Its rocks represent every geological period, including the Ice Age, the wide range of plants are unique to the area, and it is home to some of the oldest trees and the longest caves in the world (see pp454–5).*

TASMANIA

0 kilometres   500

0 miles   500

The Australian Outback

Perenite goanna in the Outback

The Outback is the heart of Australia and one of the most ancient landscapes in the world. It is extremely dry – rain may not fall for several years. Dramatic red rocks, ochre plains and purple mountains are framed by brilliant blue skies. Development is sparse: "towns" are often no more than a few buildings and facilities are basic. There may be hundreds of miles between one petrol station and another. The Outback isn't easy to explore, but it can be a rewarding experience. Make sure you are well equipped (*see p590*), or take an organized tour.

LOCATOR MAP

    The Australian Outback

Camels *were brought to Australia in the 1870s from the Middle East, as a means of desert transport. The Outback is now home to the only wild camels in the world. Camel safaris for tourists are available in many places.*

Saltbush, which gets its name from its ability to withstand saline conditions, is a typical form of vegetation.

Camping *in the bush is one of the highlights of any trip into Australia's Outback, whether independently or with an organized tour. You will need a camping permit, a swag (canvas-covered bed roll), a mosquito net and a good camping stove to eat and sleep in relative comfort under the stars.*

OUTBACK LIFE

The enduring image of Australia's Outback is red dust, solitary one-storey shacks and desert views as far as the eye can see. Although small areas of the Outback have seen towns spring up over the past 100 years, and many interstate roads are now suitable for most vehicles, this image remains true to life across vast stretches of the interior landscape. Most of the Outback remains pioneering country far removed from the modern nation.

The film industry *has long been a fan of the Outback's vast open spaces and dramatic colours. Films such as the 1994 comedy* The Adventures of Priscilla, Queen of the Desert *made spectacular use of the Red Centre's sparse and dusty landscape.*

Australian "hotels" in Outback areas often operate only as public houses, re-named hotels to counteract Australia's once strict licensing laws.

PIONEERS AND EXPLORERS

Many European explorers, such as Edward Eyre and John Stuart, ventured into the Outback during the 19th century. The most infamous expedition was Robert O'Hara Burke's from Victoria to the Gulf of Carpentaria *(see p53)*. Ironically, it was the rescue missions due to his inexperience which brought about the pioneers' most significant investigations of Australia's interior.

Robert O'Hara Burke 1820–61

A solitary building set against vast areas of open desert landscape can be an evocative landmark in the Outback.

The Birdsville Races *in Queensland are the biggest and best of the many horse races held in the Outback, where locals gather to bet and socialize.*

Opal mining *in towns such as Coober Pedy (see p368) is one source of the Outback's wealth. Tourists need a miner's permit, available from state tourist offices, to hunt for gems.*

Aboriginal Culture

Far from being one homogeneous race, at the time of European settlement in the 18th century, the estimated 750,000 Aborigines in Australia had at least 300 different languages and a wide variety of lifestyles, depending on where they lived. The tribes of northern coastal areas, such as the Tiwis, had most contact with outsiders, especially from Indonesia, and their culture was quite different from the more isolated Pitjantjatjaras of Central Australia's deserts or the Koories from the southeast. However, there were features common to Aboriginal life and these have passed down the centuries to present-day traditions.

Ancient stone axe

Men's Dreaming by Clifford Possum Tjapaltjarri

Aboriginal artifacts and tools, decorated in traditional ornate patterns

TRADITIONAL ABORIGINAL LIFESTYLES

For thousands of years, the Aborigines were a race of hunters leading a nomadic existence. They made lightweight, versatile tools such as the boomerang, and built temporary mud dwellings. The extent of their wanderings differed from region to region – people who lived in areas with a plentiful supply of food and water were relatively more static than those in areas where such essentials were scarce.

Through living in small groups in a vast land, Aboriginal society came to be broken up into numerous clans separated by different languages and customs. Even people with a common language would live apart in "core" family groups, consisting of a husband, wife, children and perhaps some close friends to share the responsibilities of daily life. Groups would come together from time to time to conduct religious ceremonies, arrange marriages and settle inter-clan disputes. Trade was an important part of social life. Shell, ochre and wood were some of the goods exchanged along trade routes that criss-crossed the entire country.

The nomadic way of life largely ended when English settlers claimed vast tracts of land, but other aspects of traditional life have survived. In Aboriginal communities, senior members are still held in great respect, and are responsible for maintaining laws and meting out punishments to those who break them or divulge secrets of ancient rituals. Such rituals are part of the Aboriginal belief system called "Dreamtime".

THE DREAMTIME

The dreamtime (or Dreaming) is the English term for the Aboriginal system of laws and beliefs. Its basis is a rich mythology about the earth's creation. "Creation ancestors" such as giant serpents are believed to have risen up from the earth's core and roamed the world, creating valleys, rivers and mountains. Other progenitors caused the rain and sun, and created the people and wildlife. Sites where ancestral beings are thought to have emerged from the earth are sacred and are still used as the locations for ceremonies and rituals today.

The belief in the Dreamtime is, in essence, a religious ideology for all Aborigines, whatever their tribe, and forms the basis of Aboriginal life. Every Aborgine is

THE BOOMERANG

Contrary to popular belief, not all boomerangs will return to the thrower. Originally, "boomerang" simply meant "throwing stick". They were used for hunting, fighting, making fire, stoking the coals when cooking and in traditional games. A hunter did not normally require a throwing stick to return since its purpose was to injure its target sufficiently to enable capture. Over time, intricate shapes were developed that allowed sticks to swirl in a large arc and return to the thrower. The returning boomerang is limited to games, killing birds and directing animals into traps. Light and thin, with a deep curvature, its ends are twisted in opposite directions. The lower surface is flat and the upper surface convex.

Aboriginal boomerang

believed to have two souls – one mortal and one immortal, linked with their ancestral spirit (or totem). Each family clan is descended from the same ancestral being. These spirits provide protection: any misfortune is due to disgruntled forebears. As a consequence, some clan members have a responsibility for maintaining sacred sites. Anyone failing in these duties is severely punished.

Each Dreamtime story relates to a particular landscape; as one landscape connects with another, these stories form a "track". These "tracks" are called Songlines and criss-cross the Australian continent. Aborigines are able to connect with other tribes along these lines.

ABORIGINAL SONG AND DANCE

Aboriginal songs tell stories of Dreamtime ancestors and are intrinsically linked to the worship of spirits – the words of songs are often incomprehensible due to the secrecy of many ancestral stories. Simple instruments accompany the songs, including the didgeridoo, a 1-m (3-ft) long wind instrument with a deep sound.

Aborigines also use dance as a means of communicating with their ancestors. Aboriginal dance is experiencing a cultural renaissance, with new companies performing both traditional and new works.

Aborigines being painted with white paint to ward off evil spirits

ABORIGINAL ISSUES

Although few Aborigines now maintain a traditional nomadic lifestyle, the ceremonies, creation stories and art that make up their culture remain strong.

The right to own land has long been an issue for present-day Aborigines; they believe that they are responsible for caring for the land entrusted to them at birth. The Land Rights Act of 1976 has done much to improve these rights. The Act established Aboriginal Land Councils which negotiate between the government and Aborigines to claim land for its traditional owners *(see pp58–9)*. Where Aboriginal rights have been established, that land cannot be altered in any way.

Decorating bark with natural ochre stains

In areas of large Aboriginal inhabitance, the government has also agreed that white law can exist alongside black law, which allows for justice against Aboriginal offenders to be meted out according to tribal law. In many cases, this law is harsh and savage, but it allows for Aborigines to live by their own belief system.

The revival of Aboriginal art was at the forefront of seeing Aboriginal culture in a more positive light by Australians. Aboriginal artists such as Emily Kame Kngwarreye combine traditional materials such as bark and ochre with acrylics and canvas, while telling Dreaming stories in a modern idiom.

Many Aborigines have now moved away from their traditional lifestyle and live within the major cities, but they remain distinctly Aboriginal and generally choose to live within Aboriginal communities. Within designated Aboriginal lands *(see pp262–3)*, many still follow bush medical practices and perform traditional rituals.

It cannot be denied that Aborigines are still disadvantaged in comparison with the rest of Australia, particularly in terms of housing, health and education. But the growing awareness of their culture and traditions is gradually leading to a more harmonious coexistence.

Aborigines performing a traditional dance at sunset

Aboriginal Art

Aboriginal rock art sign

As a nomadic people with little interest in decorating their temporary dwellings, Aborigines have long let loose their creativity on landscape features such as rocks and caves *(see pp47–8)*. Many art sites are thousands of years old, although they have often been re-painted over time to preserve the image. Rock art reflects daily Aboriginal life as well as religious beliefs. Some ancient sites contain representations of now extinct animals; others depict human figures with blue eyes, strange weapons and horses – evidently the arrival of Europeans. Aboriginal art is also seen in everyday objects – utensils and accessories such as belts and headbands.

Bark painting, *such as this image of a fish, has disappeared from southern areas, but still flourishes in Arnhem Land and on Melville and Bathurst islands.*

Cave rock was a popular "canvas" for traditional Aboriginal art, particularly when tribes took cover during the rainy season.

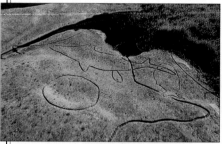

The outline style *of rock engraving was developed most fully in the Sydney-Hawkesbury area, due to vast areas of soft Hawkesbury sandstone. More than 4,000 figures have been recorded, often gigantic in size – one whale engraving is more than 20 m (65 ft) long. Groups of engravings can cover more than 1 ha (2.5 acres).*

Figures showing the human anatomy are often depicted in basic but exaggerated, stylized forms.

Darwin

Brisbane •

Perth •

Sydney

Adelaide •

Melbourne •

Hobart

MAJOR ABORIGINAL ART SITES

- Arnhem Land, Northern Territory
- Central Desert
- Uluru-Kata Tjuta National Park
- Laura, Queensland
- Melville and Bathurst islands
- Sydney-Hawkesbury area

Quinkans *are stick-like figures found in far north Queensland's Laura region. They represent spirits that are thought to emerge suddenly from rock crevices and startle people, to remind them that misbehaviour will bring swift retribution.*

Burial poles *are an example of how important decoration is to Aborigines, even to commemmorate death. These brightly coloured Pukumani burial poles belong to the Tiwi people of Melville and Bathurst islands (see p274).*

The crocodile image personifies the force of nature, as well as symbolizing the relationship between humans and the natural environment. Both are common themes within Aboriginal art.

Bush Plum Dreaming *(1991) by Clifford Possum Tjapaltjarri is a modern example of ancient Aboriginal techniques used by the Papunya tribe.*

"X-ray art", *such as this figure at Nourlangie Rock in Kakadu National Park (see pp276–7), shows the internal and external anatomy of living subjects, including a range of animals.*

ARNHEM LAND ROCK ART
Arnhem Land is the 80,285-km (49,890-mile) Aboriginal territory which stretches from east of Darwin to the Gulf of Carpentaria *(see pp262–3)*. Magnificent rock art "galleries" in this region date from 16,000 BC *(see p47)* – some of the oldest Aboriginal art in the country.

Totemic art *at Uluru (see pp286–9) is thought to portray the beings in Aboriginal culture who are believed to have created the rock.*

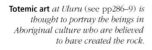

Australian Artists and Writers

The first Europeans to paint Australia were those who arrived in the *Endeavour (see pp50–51)*, but it was not until the prosperity generated by the 1850s gold rushes that art gained any public recognition. There had been colonial artists, of whom Conrad Martens (1801–78) was the best known, but in a country where survival was the most immediate problem, art was not a high priority. The first writings were also journals of early settlers; it was 100 years before Australia could claim the beginnings of a literary tradition, when Rolf Boldrewood (1826–1915) wrote *Robbery Under Arms* (1888), a heroic tale of the bush.

Frederick McCubbin

Sir Russell Drysdale

ARTISTS

The so-called "Heidelberg School", named after an area around Melbourne, was the first distinctive Australian school of painting at the end of the 19th century. Its mainstays included Tom Roberts (1856–1931), Charles Conder (1868–1909), Frederick McCubbin (1855–1917) and Arthur Streeton (1867–1943). The group drew strongly on the *plein air* methods of the French Impressionists to capture the distinctive light and openness of the Australian landscape. Then, in the early 1900s, Hans Heysen captured the national imagination with his delicately coloured gum trees and his view of the Australian landscape. Sir Sidney Nolan (1917–92),

best known for his "Ned Kelly" series of the 1940s based on the country's most notorious bushranger *(see p394)*, also produced landscape paintings which propelled Australian art on to the international scene for the first time.

The best known of the talented Boyd family, Arthur Boyd (1920–99), is another great on the Australian art scene; his "Half-Caste Bride" series catapulted him into the art world in 1960.

Probably the greatest interpreter of Australia's Outback is Sir Russell Drysdale (1912–81), whose paintings depict the harshness of this landscape. Brett Whiteley (1939–92) is a more recent talent whose sensual work reflects his view of the world.

Winner of the Archibald Prize for portraiture, William Dobell (1899–1970) is often regarded as the figurehead of the Sydney Modernist movement. He achieved some level of notoriety when, in 1944, two fellow artists mounted a legal challenge to the granting of the Archibald for his portrait of Joshua Smith, claiming it was "not a portrait but a caricature". The action was unsuccessful, but all Dobell's further work generated publicity for the wrong reasons.

Possibly the most popularly recognized Australian artist is Ken Done. Often dismissed for blatant commercialism, his brilliantly coloured work has achieved sales of which most artists only dream.

The most significant collection of Australian art can be seen at Canberra's National Gallery *(see pp202–3)*.

Toberua (1994) by Ken Done

THE ANTIPODEANS

Formed in Melbourne in 1959, the Antipodeans consisted of seven of Australia's best-known modern artists, all born in the 1920s: Charles Blackman, Arthur Boyd, David Boyd, John Brack, Robert Dickerson, John Perceval and Clifton Pugh. The aim of the group was to support figurative painting rather than abstraction. The group denied that they were creating a national style and the name Antipodeans was adopted to avoid too narrow a focus on Australia, as the group aimed for international recognition at exhibitions in London. Ironically, it later came to apply to Australian art in general.

Kelly in Spring (1956), one of Sir Sidney Nolan's "Ned Kelly" series

Portrait of Miles Franklin by Marie McNiven

WRITERS

Much of Australian fiction is concerned with the difficulties Europeans experienced in a harsh land, or the relationship between white settlers and Aborigines. The themes can be traced back to an early Australian novelist, Henry Handel Richardson, the pseudonym of Ethel Robertson (1870–1946). Her trilogy, *The Fortunes of Richard Mahoney* (1929), was published to great acclaim, including a nomination for the Nobel Prize for Literature. Contemporary novelist David Malouf (born in 1934) continues to explore these issues in *Remembering Babylon* (1993), winner of the Prix Baudelaire, and *Conversations at Curlow Creek* (1996).

Film poster of *Schindler's List*, based on *Schindler's Ark*

Australia's most celebrated novelist is undoubtedly Patrick White (1912–90), who won the Nobel Prize in 1973 with *The Eye of the Storm*. White had made his mark in 1957 with *Voss*, the story of the explorer Ludwig Leichhardt, while his later novels include *A Fringe of Leaves* (1976) and *The Twyborn Affair* (1979).

Campaigner for women's suffrage, Louisa Lawson (1848–1920), is credited with Australia's first feminist journal, *Dawn*, written between 1888 and 1905. At the same time, another feminist, Miles Franklin (1879–1954), defied traditional women's roles of the time by pursuing an independent life in Australia, England and the USA. Her life was documented in several autobiographies, beginning with *My Brilliant Career* (1901).

For descriptions of pre- and postwar Sydney life in the slums, the novels of Ruth Park (born in 1922), such as *Harp in the South* (1948) and *Fence around the Cuckoo* (1992), are unbeatable. Novelist Thomas Keneally (born in 1935) won the 1982 Booker Prize with *Schindler's Ark*, later made by Steven Spielberg into the acclaimed film *Schindler's List*.

Aboriginal writer Sally Morgan (born in 1951) has put indigenous Australian writing on the map with her 1988 autobiography *My Place*.

POETS

Australia's early poets were mostly bush balladeers, articulating life in the bush and the tradition of the Australian struggle. "The Man from Snowy River" and "Clancy of the Overflow" by AB "Banjo" Paterson (1864–1941) are 19th-century classics still committed to

memory by every Australian schoolchild. Writing from the late 1800s until his death in 1922, Henry Lawson similarly wrote some enduring bush verse, but his poetry also had a more political edge. His first published poem in the *Bulletin* literary magazine in 1887 was the rallying "Song of the Republic".

Poets such as Judith Wright (born in 1945) and, in particular, Oodgeroo Noonuccal (1920–93), have sensitively and powerfully expressed the anguish of Aboriginal people in verse.

Henry Lawson

PLAYWRIGHTS

Australia's most prolific contemporary playwright is David Williamson, born in 1942. A satirist exploring middle-class life and values, Williamson has been an international success and several of his plays, such as *Dead White Males* (1995), have been performed both in London and New York.

Ray Lawler gained renown in 1955 with *Summer of the Seventeenth Doll*, which challenged the deep-rooted Australian concept of male friendship. The play has been adapted as an opera, with music by Australian composer Richard Meale.

Other notable contemporary playwrights are Nick Enright, Stephen Sewell and Louis Nowra.

The Wines of Australia

Penfold's Grange

Grapes and wine have been produced in Australia virtually since European settlement in 1788 *(see pp50–51)*. The first vineyards were planted in Sydney in 1791 and over the next 40 years vines were planted in the Hunter Valley (1827), the Barossa Valley at Jacobs Creek (1847), the Yarra Valley (1930), and Adelaide (1937). John and Elizabeth Macarthur became Australia's first commercial wine producers with a small vintage in 1827 from their Sydney farm *(see p127)*. In the 1960s, with the introduction of international grape varieties, such as Chardonnay, small oak-barrel maturation and modern wine-making technology, the wine industry really developed. Since the 1990s Australia has earned an excellent reputation for high-quality wines and there are about 1,465 wineries operating today.

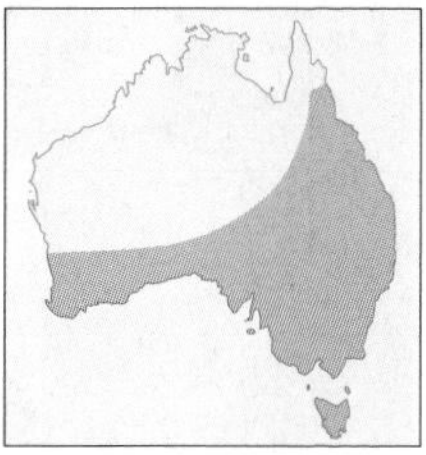

LOCATOR MAP

Major wine-producing regions of Australia

0 kilometres 500

0 miles 500

Leeuwin Estate winery *in Margaret River, Western Australia* (see pp314–15) *is one of the nation's largest producers of top-quality table wines, including Chardonnay and Cabernet Sauvignon.*

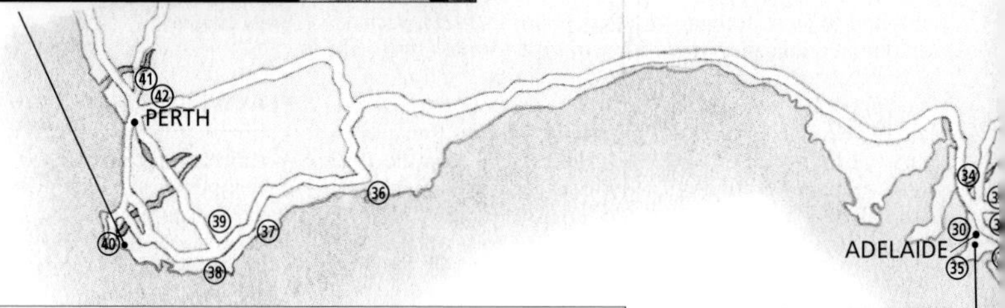

THE FATHER OF AUSTRALIAN WINE

James Busby

James Busby is often regarded as the father of the Australian wine industry. Scottish-born, he arrived in Sydney in 1824. During the voyage to Australia he wrote the country's first wine book, detailing his experiences of French vineyards. He established a property at Kirkton in the Hunter Valley, New South Wales, and returned to Europe in 1831, collecting 570 vine cuttings from France and Spain. These were cultivated at Kirkton and at the Sydney and Adelaide Botanic Gardens. In 1833, having founded Australia's first wine-producing region, he emigrated to New Zealand.

Mount Hurtle winery *produces distinctive white table wines. It is located in one of South Australia's main wine regions, McLaren Vale* (see pp338–9).

WINE REGIONS OF AUSTRALIA

Since signing a trade agreement with the European Union, Australia has had to implement a new classification system for its wine producing regions. The whole of Australia has 28 wine zones, which can be whole state (Tasmania) or parts of states (Western Victoria). Within these zones are 61 wine regions, such as Barossa Valley *(see p356–7)*, with the main ones listed below. Some of the up-and-coming areas in Australia are Mudgee and Orange (NSW), and Geelong (VIC).

- 1 **South Burnett**
- 2 **Granite Belt**
- 3 **Hastings River**
- 4 **Hunter Valley**
- 5 **Mudgee**
- 6 **Orange**
- 7 **Cowra**
- 8 **Lachlan Valley**
- 9 **Canberra**
- 10 **Gundagai**
- 11 **Hilltops**
- 12 **Sydney**
- 13 **Shoalhaven**
- 14 **Riverina**
- 15 **Murray Darling**
- 16 **Swan Hill**
- 17 **Rutherglen**
  Glenrowan
  King Valley
- 18 **Yarra Valley**
- 19 **Mornington Peninsula**
- 20 **Geelong**
- 21 **Tasmania**
- 22 **Sunbury**
- 23 **Macedon**
- 24 **Pyrenees**
- 25 **Grampians**
- 26 **Coonawarra**
- 27 **Mount Benson**
- 28 **Padthaway**
- 29 **Langhorne Creek**
- 30 **McLaren Vale**
- 31 **Adelaide Hills**
- 32 **Eden Valley**
- 33 **Barossa Valley**
- 34 **Clare Valley**
- 35 **Kangaroo Island**
- 36 **Esperance**
- 37 **Great Southern**
- 38 **Pemberton**
- 39 **Manjimup**
- 40 **Margaret River**
- 41 **Swan District**
- 42 **Perth Hills**

Balmoral House *is part of the Rosemount Estate in the Upper Hunter Valley* (see pp162–3). *The house gives its name to the winery's excellent Balmoral Shiraz.*

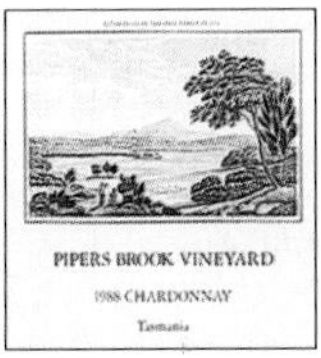

Pipers Brook *in Tasmania was established in 1973 and produces fine Chardonnays.*

VISITING A WINERY

Wine tourism is increasingly popular in Australia and information and maps are readily available at information bureaux. Most wineries are open daily (but you should ring ahead to avoid disappointment) and if they charge for tastings it will be refunded against a purchase. Winery restaurants are also popular and some have barbeques and entertainment for children while others have a wine-food paired menu. With strict drink-drive laws it may be better to take a guided tour – these can be by bus or tailor-made by limousine.

Surfing and Beach Culture

Lifeguard and her surfboard

Australia is the quintessential home of beach culture, with the nation's beaches ranging from sweeping crescents with rolling waves to tiny, secluded coves. Almost all Australians live within a two-hour drive of the coast, and during the hot summers it is almost second nature to make for the water to cool off. The clichéd image of the sun-bronzed Australian is no longer the reality it once was, but popular beaches are still packed with tanned bodies basking on golden sands or frolicking in deep blue waves. Fines levied for inappropriate behaviour mean that the atmosphere is calm and safe at all times. Surfing has always been a national sport, with regular carnivals and competitions held on the coastline. There are also opportunities for beginners to try their hand at this daring sport.

Baked-brown bodies *and sun-bleached hair were once the epitome of beach culture.*

Surf carnivals *attract thousands of spectators, who thrill to races, "iron man" competitions, dummy rescues and spectacular lifeboat displays.*

SURFER IN ACTION

Riding the waves is a serious business. Wetsuit-clad "surfies" study the surfing reports in the media and think nothing of travelling vast distances to reach a beach where the best waves are running.

Crouching down into the wave's crest increases stability on the board.

WHERE TO SURF

The best surfing to be found in Australia is on the New South Wales coast *(see pp178–9)*, the southern Queensland coast, especially the aptly named Surfer's Paradise and the Sunshine Coast *(pp238–9)* and the southern coastline of Western Australia *(pp312–13)*. Tasmania also has some fine surfing beaches on its northwestern tip *(pp466–7)*. Despite superb north Queensland beaches, the Great Barrier Reef stops the waves well before they reach the mainland. In summer, deadly marine stingers (jellyfish) here make surf swimming impossible in many areas, unless there is a stinger-proof enclosure.

Surf lifesaving *is an integral part of the Australian beach scene. Trained volunteer life-savers, easily recognized by their red and yellow swimming caps, ensure that swimmers stay within flag-defined safe areas and are ready to spring into action if someone is in trouble.*

BEACH ACTIVITIES

Australian beaches are not only the preserve of surfers. Winter temperatures are mild in most coastal areas, so many beach activities are enjoyed all year. Weekends see thousands of pleasure boats, from small runabouts to luxury yachts, competing in races or just out for a picnic in some sheltered cove. The sails of windsurfers create swirls of colour on gusty days. Kite-flying has become an art form, with the Festival of the Winds a September highlight at Sydney's Bondi Beach *(see p40)*. Beach volleyball, once a knockabout game, is now an Olympic sport.

Festival of the Winds

Takeaway snack food *at the beach is an Australian tradition, since many sunlovers spend entire days by the ocean. Fish and chips, kebabs and burgers are on sale at beach cafés.*

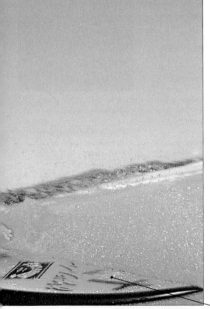

Surfboards, once made out of wood, are now built of light fibreglass, often in bright colours, improving speed and visibility.

The Australian crawl *revolutionized swimming throughout the world in the 1880s. For most Australians, swimming is an everyday sport, learned at a very early age.*

SAFETY

Beaches are safe provided you follow a few guidelines:
- *Always swim "between the flags".*
- *Don't swim alone.*
- *Note signs warning of strong currents, blue bottles or stingers.*
- *If you get into difficulty, do not wave but signal for help by raising one arm straight in the air.*
- *Use Factor 30+ sunscreen and wear a shirt and hat.*

AUSTRALIA
THROUGH THE YEAR

The seasons in Australia are the exact opposite of those in the northern hemisphere. In the southern half of the country spring comes in September, summer is from December to February, autumn runs from March to May, while winter begins in June. In contrast, the tropical climate of the north

Reveller enjoying the Melbourne Festival

coast is more clearly divided into wet and dry seasons, the former between November and April. Australia's vast interior has a virtually unchanging desert climate – baking hot days and cool nights. The weather throughout Australia is reliable enough year-round to make outdoor events popular all over the country.

SPRING

With the warm weather, the profusion of spring flowers brings gardens and national parks to life. Food, art and music festivals abound in cities. Footballers finish their seasons, cricketers warm up for summer matches and the horse-racing fraternity gets ready to place its bets.

Australian Football League Grand Final in September

SEPTEMBER

Open Garden Scheme *(Sep–May)*. The country's most magnificent private gardens open to the public *(see p374)*.
Mudgee Wine Festival *(date varies)*. Includes bush dances as well as wine *(see p177)*.
Festival of the Winds *(Sun, date varies)*, Bondi Beach *(see p39)*. Multicultural kite-flying festival; music, dance.

Royal Melbourne Show *(last two weeks)*. Agricultural exhibitions, rides and displays.
Australian Football League Grand Final *(last Sat in Sep)*, Melbourne *(see p397)*.
Australian Rugby League Grand Final *(last weekend)*, Sydney. National event.
Tulip Festival *(last week Sep–first week Oct)*, Bowral. The Corbett Gardens are carpeted with flowers *(see p186)*.
Carnival of Flowers *(date varies)*, Toowoomba. Popular floral festival including spectacular garden and flower displays *(see p240)*.

OCTOBER

Melbourne Fringe Festival *(late Sep–early Oct, dates vary)*. The arts festival showcases hundreds of events, such as live performances, films, visual arts, multi-media exhibits and comedy shows.

Floriade, the October spring flower festival in Canberra

Melbourne International Arts Festival *(most of Oct)*, Dance, theatre, music and visual arts events.
Henley-on-Todd Regatta *(third Sat)*, Alice Springs. Races in bottomless boats along the dry Todd River.
Melbourne Marathon *(date varies)*. Fun-run through the centre of the city.
Lygon Street Festa *(last weekend)*, Melbourne. Street carnival through the city's Italian district *(see p395)*.

Henley-on-Todd Regatta at Alice Springs

Floriade *(first three weeks)*, Canberra. Magnificent flower festival in Commonwealth Park *(see p195)*.

Leura Garden Festival *(second to third weekends)*, Blue Mountains. Village fair and garden shows *(see p172)*.

Rose and Rodeo Festival *(last weekend)*, Warwick. Australia's oldest rodeo attracts riders from all over the world *(see p240)*.

Jacaranda Festival *(last week)*, Grafton. Australia's oldest flower festival features a Grand Float procession through the town *(see p178)*.

Maldon Folk Festival *(last weekend)*. Folk music concerts in this country town.

Santa Claus celebrating Christmas on Bondi Beach, Sydney

Race-goers dressed up for the Melbourne Cup in November

NOVEMBER

Sculpture by the Sea *(first week)*, Sydney. Great outdoor sculptures can be seen at Bondi beach.

Great Mountain Race of Victoria *(first Sat)*, Mansfield. Bush riders compete cross-country *(see p447)*.

Melbourne Cup *(first Tue)*. Australia's most popular horse race virtually brings the nation to a halt.

SUMMER

The beginning of the school holidays for Christmas marks the start of the summer in Australia and the festivities continue until

Australia Day on 26 January. Summer, too, brings a feast for sport lovers, with tennis, surfing events and a host of cricket matches. Arts and music lovers make the most of organized festivals.

DECEMBER

Carols by Candlelight *(24 Dec)*, Melbourne. Top musicians unite with locals to celebrate Christmas.

Christmas at Bondi Beach *(25 Dec)*. Holiday-makers hold parties on the famous beach *(see p126)*.

Sydney to Hobart Yacht Race *(26 Dec)*. Sydney Harbour teems with yachts setting off for Hobart *(see p458)*.

Boxing Day Test Match *(26 Dec)*, Melbourne.

New Year's Eve *(31 Dec)*, Sydney Harbour. Street parties and firework displays.

JANUARY

Hanging Rock Picnic Races *(1 Jan & 26 Jan)*. Premier country horse racing event *(see p437)*.

Festival of Sydney *(first week –end Jan)*. City comes alive during this cultural festival.

Australian Open *(last two weeks)*, Melbourne. Australia's popular Grand Slam tennis tournament.

Country Music Festival *(last two weeks)*, Tamworth. Australia's main country music festival, culminating in the Golden Guitar Awards *(see p177)*.

Midsumma Festival *(mid-Jan–first week Feb)*,

Melbourne. Melbourne's annual Gay and Lesbian festival includes street parades.

Tunarama Festival *(last weekend)*, Port Lincoln. Tuna tossing competitions and fireworks *(see p366)*.

Australia Day Concert *(26 Jan)*, Sydney. Free concert commemorating the birth of the nation *(see p56)*.

Chinese New Year *(late Jan or early Feb)*, Sydney.

Cricket Test Match, Sydney.

Fireworks in Sydney for the Australia Day celebrations

FEBRUARY

Gay and Lesbian Mardi Gras Festival *(whole month)*, Sydney. Flamboyant street parades and events.

Festival of Perth *(Feb–Mar)*. Australia's oldest arts festival.

Leeuwin Estate Winery Music Concert *(mid-Feb–Mar)*, Margaret River. Concert attracting stars *(see p314)*.

Adelaide Fringe *(mid-Feb–mid-Mar)*. Second-largest fringe festival in the world.

Australian Grand Prix, held in Melbourne in March

AUTUMN

After the humidity of the summer, autumn brings fresh mornings and cooler days that are tailor-made for outdoor pursuits such as bushwalking, cycling and fishing, as well as outdoor festivals. There are numerous sporting and cultural events to tempt the visitor. Many of the country's wineries open their doors during the harvest season and hold gourmet food and wine events. Anzac Day (25 April) – the day in 1915 when Australian and New Zealand forces landed at Gallipoli – has been observed annually since 1916 and is a national holiday on which Australians commemorate their war dead.

Yarra Valley wine

MARCH

Australian Formula One Grand Prix *(first weekend)*, Melbourne. Top Formula One drivers compete, while the city celebrates with street parties *(see p403)*.

Yarra Valley Grape Grazing *(early Mar)*. Grape pressing, barrel races, good food and wine.

Begonia Festival *(first two weeks)*, Ballarat. Begonia displays in the Botanical Gardens *(see p435)*.

Moomba Festival *(second week)*, Melbourne. International aquatic events on the Yarra River *(see pp400–1)*, as well as cultural events throughout the city.

St Patrick's Day Parade *(17 Mar or Sun before)*, Sydney. Pubs serve green beer and a flamboyant parade travels from Hyde Park.

APRIL

Melbourne International Comedy Festival *(end Mar–early Apr)*. Comedy acts from around the world perform in theatres, pubs and outdoors.

Royal Easter Show *(week preceding Good Fri)* Sydney. Agricultural shows, funfair rides, local arts and crafts displays and team games.

Rip Curl Pro Surfing Competition *(Easter weekend)*, Bells Beach. Pros and amateurs from all over the world take part in this premier competition *(see p428)*.

Easter Fair *(Easter weekend)*, Maldon. An Easter parade and a colourful street carnival takes over this quaint country town *(see p432)*.

International Flower and Garden Show *(early Apr)*, Melbourne. Spectacular floral event held in the beautiful Exhibition Gardens *(see p395)*.

Bright Autumn Festival *(last week Apr–mid-May)*, Bright. Winery tours, art exhibitions and street parades *(see p447)*.

Anzac Day *(25 Apr)*. Australia's war dead and war veterans are honoured in remembrance services throughout the country.

MAY

Australian Celtic Festival *(first weekend)*, Glen Innes. Traditional Celtic events celebrate the town's British heritage *(see p176)*.

Kernewek Lowender Cornish Festival *(mid-May)*, Little Cornwall. A biennial celebration of the area's Cornish heritage which began with the copper discoveries of the 1860s *(see p363)*.

Torres Strait Cultural Festival *(even-numbered years)*, Thursday Island. Spiritual traditions of the Torres Strait Islanders celebrated through dance, song and art.

Anzac Day ceremony along Canberra's Anzac Parade

Racing in Alice Springs' Camel Cup

WINTER

Winter in the east can be cool enough to require warm jackets, and it is often icy in Victoria and Tasmania. Many festivals highlight the change of climate in celebration of freezing temperatures. Other events, such as film festivals, are arts-based and indoors. The warm rather than sweltering climate of the Outback in winter offers the opportunity for pleasurable outdoor events.

JUNE

Three-day Equestrian event *(first weekend)*, Gawler. Spectacular riding skills are displayed at Australia's oldest equestrian event.
Sydney Film Festival *(two weeks mid-Jun)*. The latest blockbusters film releases are combined with retrospectives and showcases.
Laura Dance & Cultural Festival *(odd-numbered years)*, Cape York. Celebration of Aboriginal culture.

Darling Harbour Jazz Festival *(mid-Jun)*, Sydney. Hugely popular festival featuring jazz bands.

JULY

Yulefest *(throughout Jun, Jul, Aug)*, Blue Mountains. Hotels, guesthouses and some restaurants celebrate a mid-winter "traditional Christmas" with log fires and all the usual yuletide trimmings.
Brass Monkey Festival, *(throughout Jul)*, Stanthorpe. Inland Queensland turns the freezing winter temperatures into an opportunity for celebration *(see p240)*.
Alice Springs Show *(first weekend)*. Agricultural and historical displays combined with arts, crafts and cookery demonstrations.
Cairns Show *(mid-Jul)*. A cultural celebration of historical and contemporary life in the Australian tropics *(see p254)*.
Melbourne International Film Festival *(last week Jul–mid-Aug)*. The largest and most popular film festival.

Camel Cup *(mid-Jul)*, Alice Springs. Camel racing on the dry Todd River.

Mount Isa Rodeo in August

AUGUST

Almond Blossom Festival *(first week)*, Mount Lofty. Includes almond cracking.
City to Surf Race *(second Sun)*, Sydney. A 14-km (9-mile) fun run to Bondi.
Shinju Matsuri Festival *(last weekend–first week Sep)*, Broome. Pearl festival.
Melbourne Contemporary Art Fair *(mid-Aug)*. Biennial modern art fair.
Mount Isa Rodeo *(mid-Aug)*. Largest rodeo *(see p257)*.

Dragon Boat race, part of the Shinju Matsuri in Broome

The Climate of Australia

This vast country experiences a variable climate. Three-quarters of its land is desert or scrub and has low, unreliable rainfall. The huge, dry interior is hot year-round during the day but can be very cold at night. The southern half of Australia, including Tasmania, has warm summers and mild winters. Further north, seasonal variations lessen and the northern coast has just two seasons: the dry, and the wet, with its monsoon rains and occasional tropical cyclones.

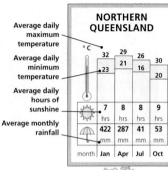

NORTHERN QUEENSLAND

- Average daily maximum temperature
- Average daily minimum temperature
- Average daily hours of sunshine
- Average monthly rainfall

°C	Jan	Apr	Jul	Oct
max	32	29	26	30
min	23	21	16	20
sunshine	7 hrs	8 hrs	8 hrs	9 hrs
rainfall	422 mm	287 mm	41 mm	53 mm

NORTH OF PERTH

°C	Jan	Apr	Jul	Oct
max	33	34	28	33
min	26	22	14	22
sunshine	8 hrs	9 hrs	7 hrs	9 hrs
rainfall	160 mm	30 mm	5 mm	1 mm

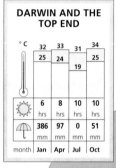

DARWIN AND THE TOP END

°C	Jan	Apr	Jul	Oct
max	32	33	31	34
min	25	24	19	25
sunshine	6 hrs	8 hrs	10 hrs	10 hrs
rainfall	386 mm	97 mm	0 mm	51 mm

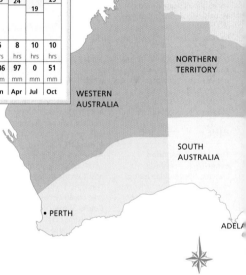

DARWIN

NORTHERN TERRITORY

WESTERN AUSTRALIA

SOUTH AUSTRALIA

PERTH

ADELAIDE

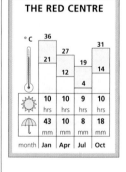

THE RED CENTRE

°C	Jan	Apr	Jul	Oct
max	36	27	19	31
min	21	12	4	14
sunshine	10 hrs	10 hrs	9 hrs	10 hrs
rainfall	43 mm	10 mm	8 mm	18 mm

PERTH AND THE SOUTHWEST

°C	Jan	Apr	Jul	Oct
max	29	24	17	21
min	17	14	9	12
sunshine	10 hrs	7 hrs	5 hrs	8 hrs
rainfall	8 mm	43 mm	170 mm	56 mm

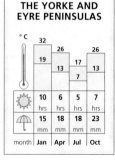

THE YORKE AND EYRE PENINSULAS

°C	Jan	Apr	Jul	Oct
max	32	26	17	26
min	19	13	7	13
sunshine	10 hrs	6 hrs	5 hrs	7 hrs
rainfall	15 mm	18 mm	18 mm	23 mm

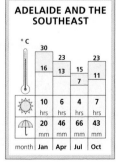

ADELAIDE AND THE SOUTHEAST

°C	Jan	Apr	Jul	Oct
max	30	23	15	23
min	16	13	7	11
sunshine	10 hrs	6 hrs	4 hrs	7 hrs
rainfall	20 mm	46 mm	66 mm	43 mm

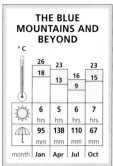

THE BLUE MOUNTAINS AND BEYOND

°C

°C			
26	23		23
18	13	16	15
		9	

	Jan	Apr	Jul	Oct
☀	6 hrs	5 hrs	6 hrs	7 hrs
☂	95 mm	138 mm	110 mm	67 mm
month	Jan	Apr	Jul	Oct

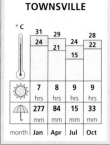

SOUTH OF TOWNSVILLE

°C

°C			
31	29		28
24	21	24	22
		15	

	Jan	Apr	Jul	Oct
☀	7 hrs	8 hrs	9 hrs	9 hrs
☂	277 mm	84 mm	15 mm	33 mm
month	Jan	Apr	Jul	Oct

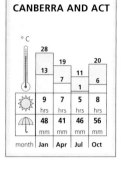

CANBERRA AND ACT

°C

°C			
28		19	20
	13	7	11	
		1	6

	Jan	Apr	Jul	Oct
☀	9 hrs	7 hrs	5 hrs	8 hrs
☂	48 mm	41 mm	46 mm	56 mm
month	Jan	Apr	Jul	Oct

BRISBANE

°C

°C			
29	26		27
21	16	20	16
		9	

	Jan	Apr	Jul	Oct
☀	8 hrs	7 hrs	7 hrs	8 hrs
☂	163 mm	94 mm	56 mm	64 mm
month	Jan	Apr	Jul	Oct

SYDNEY

°C

°C			
26	22		22
18	14	16	13
		8	

	Jan	Apr	Jul	Oct
☀	7 hrs	6 hrs	6 hrs	7 hrs
☂	89 mm	135 mm	117 mm	71 mm
month	Jan	Apr	Jul	Oct

QUEENSLAND

BRISBANE ●

NEW SOUTH WALES AND ACT

● SYDNEY
● CANBERRA

VICTORIA
●
MELBOURNE

TASMANIA
● HOBART

THE SOUTH COAST AND SNOWY MOUNTAINS

°C

°C			
24	21		22
19	15	14	15
		8	

	Jan	Apr	Jul	Oct
☀	7 hrs	5 hrs	6 hrs	6 hrs
☂	85 mm	140 mm	122 mm	75 mm
month	Jan	Apr	Jul	Oct

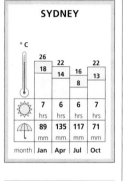

EASTERN VICTORIA

°C

°C			
27		19	21
	12	10	12	8
		4	

	Jan	Apr	Jul	Oct
☀	8 hrs	6 hrs	4 hrs	7 hrs
☂	40 mm	52 mm	45 mm	59 mm
month	Jan	Apr	Jul	Oct

WESTERN VICTORIA

°C

°C			
	25		17
11	18	10	9
	9	3	

	Jan	Apr	Jul	Oct
☀	7 hrs	5 hrs	5 hrs	6 hrs
☂	38 mm	50 mm	77 mm	70 mm
month	Jan	Apr	Jul	Oct

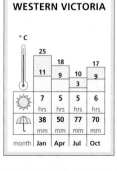

MELBOURNE

°C

°C			
	26		19
14	20	13	9
	11	6	

	Jan	Apr	Jul	Oct
☀	8 hrs	5 hrs	4 hrs	6 hrs
☂	48 mm	58 mm	48 mm	66 mm
month	Jan	Apr	Jul	Oct

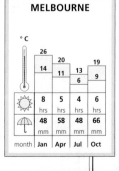

TASMANIA

°C

°C			
22	17		17
12	9	11	8
		4	

	Jan	Apr	Jul	Oct
☀	8 hrs	5 hrs	4 hrs	6 hrs
☂	48 mm	48 mm	53 mm	58 mm
month	Jan	Apr	Jul	Oct

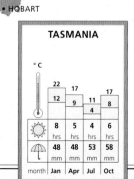
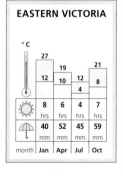

THE HISTORY OF AUSTRALIA

*A*ustralia is a young nation in an ancient land. It is a nation of immigrants, past and present, forced and free. The first European settlers occupied a harsh country; they explored it, exploited its mineral wealth and farmed it. In so doing, they suffered at the hands of nature, as well as enduring depressions and wars. Out of all this, however, has emerged a modern and cosmopolitan society.

The first rocks of the Australian landscape began to form some four-and-a-half billion years ago. Over time many older rocks were covered by more recent rocks, but in places such as the Pilbara region of Western Australia erosion has exposed a landscape 3,500 million years old *(see pp330–31)*. About 500 million years ago Australia, together with South America, South Africa, India and the Antarctic, formed a supercontinent known as Gondwanaland. This landmass moved through a series of different climatic zones; today's desert interior was once a shallow sea *(see pp22–3)*.

Australian coat of arms

THE FIRST IMMIGRANTS

Australia was first settled by Aboriginal people who arrived by sea from Asia more than 60,000 years ago. On landing, they quickly adapted to the climatic and geographical conditions. Nomadic hunters and gatherers, the Aborigines moved with the seasons and spread across the continent, reaching Tasmania 35,000 years ago. They had few material possessions beyond the tools and weapons required for hunting and obtaining food. The early tools, known today as core tools, were very simple chopping implements, roughly formed by grinding stone. By 8,000 BC Aborigines had developed the sophisticated returning boomerang *(see p30)* and possibly the world's first barbed spear. So-called flaked tools of varying styles were in use 5,000 years later, finely made out of grained stones such as flint to create sharp cutting edges.

Beneath the apparently simple way of life, Aboriginal society was complex. It was based on a network of mainly nomadic bands, comprising between 50 and 100 people, bound by kin relationships, who lived according to strictly applied laws and customs. These laws and beliefs, including the spiritual significance of the land, were upheld through a tradition of song, dance and art *(see pp30–33)*. With no centralized or formal system of government, individual groups were led by prominent, generally older men, who were held in great respect. Across the continent there were more

TIMELINE

60,000 BC	50,000 BC	40,000 BC	30,000 BC	20,000 BC	10,000 BC

43,000–38,000 BC Tools found in a grave pit beside Nepean River are among the oldest firmly dated signs of human occupation in Australia

35,000 BC Aborigines reach Tasmania

Diprotodon 20,000 BC

13,000 End of Ice Age

170–60,000 BC Aborigines thought to have reached Australia

42,000 BC Aboriginal engravings at Olary, South Australia

25,000 BC Woman is cremated at Lake Mungo – the world's oldest known cremation

20,000 BC Humans live in the Blue Mountains despite Ice Age. Remains of the largest marsupial, Diprotodon, date back to this period

◁ *Desmond, A New South Wales Chief* **(about 1825) by Augustus Earle**

than 200 languages spoken and approximately 800 dialects. In many respects, Aboriginal life was also very advanced: excavations at Lake Mungo provide fascinating evidence of ancient burial rituals,

Woodcut of an "antipodean man" (1493)

including what is believed to be the world's oldest cremation 25,000 years ago *(see p181)*.

THEORIES OF A SOUTHERN LAND

In Europe, the existence of a southern land was the subject of debate for centuries. As early as the 5th century BC, with the European discovery of Australia some 2,000 years away, the mathematician Pythagoras speculated on the presence of southern lands necessary to counterbalance those in the northern hemisphere. In about AD 150, the ancient geographer Ptolemy of Alexandria continued this speculation by drawing a map showing a landmass enclosing the Atlantic and Indian oceans. Some scholars went so far as to suggest that it was inhabited by

"antipodes", a race of men whose feet faced backwards. Religious scholar St Augustine (AD 354–430) declared categorically that the southern hemisphere contained no land; the contrary view was heretical. But not all men of religion agreed: the 1086 *Osma Beatus,* a series of maps illustrating the works of the monk Beatus, showed the hypothetical land as a populated region.

It was not until the 15th century, when Europe entered a golden age of exploration, that these theories were tested. Under the patronage of Prince Henry of Portugal (1394–1460), known as Henry the Navigator, Portuguese sailors crossed the equator for the first time in 1470. In 1488 they sailed around the southern tip of Africa, and by 1502 they claimed to have located a southern land while on a voyage to explore South America. The Italian navigator, Amerigo Vespucci, described it as Paradise, full of trees and colourful birds. The location of this land is not clear but it was definitely not Australia.

In 1519 another Portuguese expedition set off, under the command of Ferdinand Magellan, and was the first to circumnavigate the world. No drawings of the lands explored survive, but subsequent maps show Tierra del Fuego as the tip of a landmass south of the Americas. Between 1577 and 1580 the Englishman Sir Francis Drake also circumnavigated the world, but his maps indicate no such land. Meanwhile, maps prepared in Dieppe in France between 1540 and 1566 show a southern continent, Java la Grande, lying southeast of Indonesia.

First known map of Australia known as the *Dauphin Chart*, 1530–36

TIMELINE

5,000 BC Dingo is the first domesticated animal to reach Australia from Southeast Asia	**500 BC** Pythagoras speculates on existence of southern lands	**AD 150** Ptolemy believes the southern land encloses the Atlantic and Indian oceans	**450** Macrobius, in his *Dream of Scorpio,* envisages uninhabited southern land

5,000 BC	1,000 BC	AD 1	1000

400 St Augustine declares south to be all ocean and rejects idea of antipodeans

1086 Beatus, on his *Mappa mundi,* shows a southern land inhabited by a monster with one large foot

Copperplate print of a dingo

Abel Tasman's Dutch discovery ships

THE DUTCH DISCOVERY

By the 17th century Portugal's power in Southeast Asia was beginning to wane, and Holland, with its control of the Dutch East Indies (Indonesia), was the new power and responsible for the European discovery of Australia.

Willem Jansz, captain of the ship *Duyfken*, was in search of New Guinea, a land thought to be rich in gold, when he sailed along the Cape York Peninsula in 1606. He found the coast inhospitable. In 1616 Dirk Hartog, commanding the *Eendracht*, was blown off course on his way to the East Indies. He landed on an island off Western Australia and nailed a pewter plate to a pole *(see p326)*.

Dutch navigator Abel Tasman charted large parts of Australia and New Zealand between 1642 and 1644, including Tasmania which he originally named Van Diemen's Land in honour of the Governor-General of the East Indies. It became Tasmania in 1855.

The Dutch continued to explore the country for 150 years, but although their discoveries were of geographic interest they did not result in any economic benefit.

THE FORGOTTEN SPANIARD

In 1606, the same year that Willem Jansz first set foot on Australian soil, Luis Vaez de Torres, a Spanish Admiral, led an expedition in search of "Terra Australia". He sailed through the strait which now bears his name between Australia and New Guinea *(see p252)*.

Bronze relief of Luis Vaez de Torres

His discovery, however, was inexplicably ignored for 150 years. He sent news of his exploration to King Felipe III of Spain from the Philippines but died shortly after. Perhaps his early death meant that the news was not disseminated and the significance of his maps not realized.

THE FIRST ENGLISHMAN

The first Englishman to land on Australian soil was the privateer William Dampier in 1688. He published a book of his journey, *New Voyage Round the World*, in 1697. Britain gave him command of the *Roebuck*, in which he explored the northwest Australian coast in great detail. His ship sank on the return voyage. The crew survived but Dampier was court martialled for the mistreatment of his subordinates.

Portrait of William Dampier

Sir Francis Drake

1577–80 Sir Francis Drake circumnavigates the world but indicates no austral region beneath South America

Dampier's compass

1688 William Dampier lands on Australian soil

1200	1400	1600

1300 Marco Polo describes a southern land which is later added to the imaginary Terra Australis on Renaissance maps

Hartog's plate

1616 Dirk Hartog sails from Amsterdam and lands on the western shore of Australia, nailing a pewter plate to a pole

1756 Final Dutch voyage of the *Buis* to Australia

The Colonization of Australia

Hat made from cabbage palm

By the mid-18th century England had taken over as the world's main maritime power. In 1768 Captain James Cook set off to find Australia in the *Endeavour* and in 1770 King George III formally claimed possession of the east coast, named New South Wales. Overcrowding of jails and the loss of American colonies in the War of Independence led the English to establish a penal colony in the new land. The First Fleet, consisting of two men-of-war and nine transport ships, arrived in Sydney Cove in 1788. The initial settlement consisted of 750 convicts, approximately 210 marines and 40 women and children. Faced with great hardship, they survived in tents, eating local wildlife and rations from England.

Captain James Cook *(c.1800)*
The English navigator charted eastern Australia for the first time between 1770 and 1771.

Boat building at the Government dockyard

England Takes Possession
In 1770 the Union Jack was raised on the east coast of Australia, and England finally claimed possession of this new-found land.

Aborigines depicted observing the new white settlement.

Sir Joseph Banks
Aboard the Endeavour *with Captain Cook, botanist Joseph Banks was responsible for the proposal of Botany Bay as the first penal settlement.*

A VIEW OF SYDNEY COVE

This idyllic image, drawn by Edward Dayes and engraved by F Jukes in 1804, shows the Aboriginal peoples living peacefully within the infant colony alongside the flourishing maritime and agricultural industries. In reality, by the end of the 18th century they had been entirely ostracized from the life and prosperity of their native land. The first settlement was founded at Port Jackson, renamed Sydney Cove.

First Fleet Ship
This painting by Francis Holman (c.1787) shows three views of the Borrowdale, *one of the fleet's three commercial store ships.*

Scrimshaw
Engraving bone or shell was a skilful way to pass time during long months spent at sea.

Buildings looked impressive but were poorly built.

Convict housing

Governor Phillip's House, Sydney
This grand colonial mansion, flanked by landscaped gardens, was home to Australia's first government.

Barracks housing NSW Rum Corps

Prison Hulks
Old ships, unfit for naval service, were used as floating prisons to house convicts until the mid-19th century.

TIMELINE

1768 Captain James Cook sets out from England for Tahiti on his ship, the *Endeavour*

1775 English overcrowding of jails and prison hulks

Aborigine Bennelong

1788 Aborigine Bennelong is captured and held for five months, then taken to England to meet King George III

1770	1780	1790

1770 Cook discovers the east coast of Australia and takes possession for England

1779 Botanist Joseph Banks recommends Botany Bay for penal settlement

Merino sheep

1797 John Macarthur introduces merino sheep from the Cape of Good Hope *(see p127)*

EXPLORING THE COASTLINE

Once the survival of the first settlement was assured, both the government and the free settlers began to look beyond its confines. Faced with a vast, unknown continent and fuelled by desires for knowledge and wealth, they set out to explore the land. The 19th century was a period of exploration, discovery and settlement.

Between 1798 and 1799 the English midshipman Matthew Flinders and surgeon George Bass charted much of the Australian coastline south of Sydney. They also circumnavigated Tasmania, known at that time as Van Diemen's Land (*see p49*). In 1801 Flinders was given command of the sloop *Investigator* and explored the entire Australian coastline, becoming the first man to successfully circumnavigate the whole continent.

John Batman and local Aboriginal chiefs

EXPLORING THE INTERIOR

Inland New South Wales was opened up for settlement in 1813, when George Blaxland, William Wentworth and William Lawson forged a success-ful route across the Blue Mountains (*see pp170–71*). In 1824 explorers Hamilton Hume and William Hovell opened up the continent further when they travelled overland from New South Wales to Port Phillip Bay, the present site of Melbourne.

Between 1828 and 1830 Charles Sturt, a former secretary to the New South Wales Governor, led two expeditions along Australia's inland river systems. On his first journey he discovered the Darling River. His second expedition began in Sydney and followed the Murray River to the sea in South Australia. This arduous task left Sturt, like many such explorers before and after him, suffering from ill health for the rest of his life.

NEW COLONIES

Individual colonies began to emerge across the continent throughout the 19th century. First settled in 1804, Tasmania became a separate colony in 1825; in 1829 Western Australia became a colony with the establishment of Perth. Originally a colony of free settlers, a labour shortage led to the westward transportation of convicts.

In 1835 a farmer, John Batman, signed a contract with local Aborigines to acquire 250,000 ha (600,000 acres) of land where Melbourne now stands (*see p381*). His action resulted in a rush for land in the area. The settlement was recognized in 1837, and the separate colony of Victoria was proclaimed in 1851, at the start of its gold rush (*see pp54–5*). Queensland became a separate colony in 1859.

Sturt's party shown being attacked by Aborigines
on their journey to the Murray River

E J Eyre

1798–9 Matthew Flinders and George Bass circumnavigate Tasmania	1808 Major Johnston leads an insurrection against rum being abolished as currency	1825 Van Diemen's Land (later Tasmania) becomes a separate colony	1840–41 Sheep farmer Edward John Eyre is the first European to cross the Nullarbor Plain
1800	**1810**	**1820**	**1830**	**1840**

| 1801–3 Flinders circumnavigates Australia | 1804 Hobart Town is established

1813 The first currency, the "holey dollar" and "dump", is introduced | *Holey dollar and dump, made from Spanish coins* | 1833 Port Arthur opens as a penal establishment. It remains in use until 1877

1829 Western Australia is annexed, using convicts for cheap labour |

A typical colonial house in Hobart Town (now Hobart), Tasmania, during its early days in 1856

South Australia was established in 1836 as Australia's only convict-free colony. Based on a theory formulated by a group of English reformers, the colony was funded by land sales which paid for public works and the transportation of free labourers. It became a haven for religious dissenters, a tradition that still continues today.

CROSSING THE CONTINENT

Edward John Eyre, a sheep farmer who arrived from England in 1833, was the first European to cross the Nullarbor Plain from Adelaide to Western Australia in 1840.

In 1859 the South Australian government, anxious to build an overland telegraph from Adelaide to the north coast, offered a reward to the first person to cross the continent from south to north. An expedition of 20 to 40 men and camels left Melbourne in 1860 under the command of police officer Robert O'Hara Burke and surveyor William Wills. Burke, Wills and two other men travelled from their base camp at Cooper Creek to the tidal mangroves of the Flinders River which they mistook

THE RUM REBELLION

In 1808, the military, under the command of Major George Johnston and John Macarthur *(see p127)*, staged an insurrection known as the Rum Rebellion. At stake was the military's control of the profitable rum trade. Governor William Bligh (1754–1817), target of a mutiny when captain of the *Bounty*, was arrested after he tried to stop rum being used as currency. The military held power for 23 months until government was restored by Governor Lachlan Macquarie.

William Bligh

for the ocean, before heading back south. They returned to the base camp only hours after the main party, who now believed them dead, had left. Burke and Wills died at the base camp from starvation and fatigue.

The crossing from south to north was finally completed by John McDouall Stuart in 1862. He returned to Adelaide sick with scurvy and almost blind.

The return of Burke and Wills to Cooper Creek in 1860

1851 Gold discovered near Bathurst, New South Wales, and at Ballarat and Bendigo, Victoria *(see pp54–5)*

1862 John Stuart is the first explorer to cross from south to north Australia

1872 Overland telegraph from Adelaide to Darwin, via Alice Springs

1873 Uluṟu (Ayers Rock) first sighted by Europeans

1899 Australians fight in the Boer War

| 1850 | 1860 | 1870 | 1880 | 1890 |

1854 Eureka Stockade *(see p54)*

1853 Last convicts transported to Tasmania

1868 Last transportation of convicts to Australia arrive in Western Australia

1876 Last full-blooded Tasmanian Aborigine, Truganini, dies *(see p469)*

1880 Ned Kelly hanged *(see p451)*

Death mask of Ned Kelly

The 1850s Gold Rush

19th-century gold decoration

Gold was discovered near Bathurst in New South Wales and at Ballarat and Bendigo in Victoria in 1851. Established towns were almost deserted as men from all over the country, together with immigrants from Europe and China, rushed to the gold fields. Some became extremely wealthy, while others returned empty-handed. By the 1880s, Australia was a prosperous country and cities were lined with ornate architecture, some of which was constructed by the last waves of convict labour. Despite gold found in Western Australia in the 1890s, however, the final decade of the 19th century was a period of depression, when wool prices fell, Victoria's land boom collapsed and the nation suffered a severe drought.

Edward Hargraves
In 1851 Hargraves made his name by discovering gold in Bathurst, New South Wales.

Lamp

Panning dish

Pick axe

Gold Mining Utensils
Mining for gold was initially an un-skilled and laborious process that required only a few basic utensils. A panning dish to swill water, a pick axe to loosen rock and a miner's lamp were all that were needed to commence the search.

Eureka Stockade
In 1854 an insurrection took place just outside the town of Ballarat when miners rebelled against costly licences and burned them at a stockade (see p434).

DIGGING FOR GOLD
Edwin Stocqueler's painting *Australian Gold Diggings* (1855) shows the varying methods of gold mining and the hard work put in by thousands of diggers in their quest for wealth. As men and their families came from all over the world to make their fortune, regions rich in gold, in particular Victoria, thrived. Previous wastelands were turned into tent settlements and gradually grew into impressive new cities.

Might versus Right *(c.1861)*
ST Gill's painting depicts the riots on the Lambing Flag gold fields in New South Wales in 1861. Chinese immigrants, who came to Australia in search of gold, were met with violent racism by European settlers who felt their wealth and position were in jeopardy.

Tent villages covered the Victoria landscape in the 1850s.

Gold panning was the most popular extraction method.

Prosperity in Bendigo
The buildings of Williamson Street in Bendigo (see p432) display the prosperity that resulted from gold finds in Victoria.

Chinese Miners' Medal
Racism against the Chinese eventually subsided. This medal was given by the Chinese to the district of Braidwood, Victoria, in 1881.

Miners wore hats and heavyweight trousers to protect them from the sun.

The sluice was a trough which trapped gold in its bars as water was flushed through.

Gold Prospecting Camel Team
Just as the gold finds dried up in Victoria, gold was discovered in Western Australia in the 1890s. Prospectors crossed the continent to continue their search.

Souvenir handkerchief of the Australian Federation

FEDERAL BEGINNINGS

Following the economic depression at the end of the 19th century, Australia entered the 20th century on an optimistic note: the federation of its six colonies formed the Australian nation on 1 January 1901. Within the federation, there was one matter on which almost everyone agreed: Australia would remain "European" with strong ties to Britain. One of the first acts of the new parliament was to legislate the White Australia Policy. The Immigration Restriction Act required anyone wishing to emigrate to Australia to pass a dictation test in a European language. Unwanted immigrants were tested in obscure languages such as Gaelic. Between 1901 and 1910 there were nine different governments led by five different prime ministers. None of the three major political groups, the Protectionists, the Free Traders and the Labor Party, had sufficient support to govern in its own right. By 1910, however, voters were offered a clear choice between two parties, Labor and Liberal. The Labor Party won a landslide victory and since then the Australian government has come solely from one of these two parties.

WORLD WAR I

When Britain entered World War I in 1914, Australia followed to defend the "mother land". Most Australians supported the war, but they would not accept conscription or compulsory national service.

Enlisting poster

Australia paid a very high price for its allegiance, with 64 per cent of the 331,781 troops killed or wounded. Memorials to those who fought and died are found throughout the country, ranging from the simple to the impressive such as the Australian War Memorial in Canberra *(see pp200–1)*. World War I was a defining moment in Australia's history. Anzac Day, rather than Australia Day, is felt by many to be the true national day. It commemorates the landing of the Australian and New Zealand Army Corps at Gallipoli in Turkey on the 25th April 1915, for their unsuccessful attempt to cross the Dardanelles and

Labor government publicity poster

TIMELINE

1901 The Commonwealth of Australia comes into being. The White Australia Policy becomes law with the passage of the Immigration Restriction Bill	*Australia's national flag*	**1919** Postwar immigration includes the Big Brother movement, which welcomes adolescents		**1921** Edith Cowan becomes the first woman MP in the country
1900	**1905**	**1910**	**1915**	**1920**
	1902 Women's suffrage is granted in Australia	**1912** Walter Burley Griffin is chosen to design Canberra *(see p191)*		**1920** Qantas is formed as a local airline
		1914–18 Australia takes part in World War I	**QANTAS** *Qantas logo*	

link up with the Russians. This was the first battle in which Australian soldiers fought as a national force and, although a failure, they gained a reputation for bravery and endurance. It is an event which many believe determined the Australian character and saw the real birth of the Australian nation.

BETWEEN THE WARS

During the 1920s, Australia, boosted by the arrival of some 300,000 immigrants, entered a period of major development. In 1920 Qantas (Queensland and Northern Territory Aerial Service Ltd) was formed, which was to become the national airline, and made its first international flight in 1934. Building of the Sydney Harbour Bridge began in 1923 *(see pp80–81)*. Australia's population reached 6 million in 1925, but this new optimism was not to last.

In 1929 Australia, along with much of the world, went into economic decline. Wool and wheat prices, the country's major export earners, fell dramatically. By 1931, a third of the

Celebrating the opening of Sydney Harbour Bridge

country was unemployed. People slept in tents in city parks; swagmen (workers with their possessions on their backs) appeared as men left cities in search of work in the country.

Prices began to increase again by 1933 and manufacturing revived. From 1934 to 1937 the economy improved and unemployment fell. The following year, however, Australia again faced the prospect of war.

WORLD WAR II

Though World War II was initially a European war, Australians again fought in defence of freedom and the "mother land". However, when Japan entered the war, Australians felt for the first time that their national security was at risk. In 1942 Darwin, Broome and Townsville were bombed by the Japanese, the first act of war on Australian soil. The same year two Japanese midget submarines entered Sydney Harbour.

Britain asked for more Australian troops but for the first time they were refused: the men were needed in the

Swagmen during the Great Depression

1923
Vegemite first produced

Jar of Vegemite

1932 Sydney Harbour Bridge opens

1933 Western Australia produces a referendum in favour of secession from Britain, but parliament rejects it

1939–45 Australia takes part in World War II

1941 Australian War Memorial opens in Canberra

| 1925 | 1930 | 1935 | 1940 | 1945 |

1927 First federal parliament held in Canberra in temporary Parliament House

1929 The Great Depression hits Australia, bringing great hardship

1928 Royal Flying Doctor service starts

First Australian car

1948 Holden is the first car produced that is entirely made in Australia

Pacific. This was a major shift in Australian foreign policy away from Britain and towards the USA. Australians fought alongside the Americans in the Pacific and nearly 250,000 US troops spent time in Australia during the war. This led, in 1951, to the signing of Australia's first defence treaty with a foreign country: the ANZUS treaty between Australia, New Zealand and the United States.

Again, war affected most Australian communities and towns. Nearly one million of Australia's seven million population went to fight: 34,000 were killed and 180,000 wounded.

Poster promoting travel and tourism in 1950s Australia

immigrants arrived in Australia in the 20 years following World War II, 800,000 of whom were not British. In 1956, the status of "permanent resident" allowed non-Europeans to claim citizenship. In 1958, the dictation entry test was abolished. Yet until 1966 non-Europeans had to have 15 years' residence before gaining citizenship, as opposed to five years for Europeans.

THE MENZIES ERA
From 1949 until 1966, Prime Minister Robert Menzies "reigned", winning eight consecutive elections. The increasing population and international demand for Australian raw materials during this time provided a high standard of living.

POSTWAR IMMIGRATION
The proximity of the fighting in World War II left Australia feeling vulnerable. The future defence of the country was seen to be dependent upon a strong economy and a larger population.

The postwar immigration programme welcomed not only British immigrants but also Europeans. Almost two million

British migrants arriving in Sydney in 1967 as part of the postwar wave of immigration

MABO AND BEYOND

In 1982, Edward Koiki (Eddie) Mabo, a Torres Strait Islander, took action against the Queensland government claiming that his people had ancestral land rights. After a ten-year battle, the High Court ruled that Aborigines and

Edward Koiki Mabo

Torres Strait Islanders may hold native title to land where there has been no loss of traditional connection. This ended the concept of *terra nullius* – that Australia belonged to no one when Europeans arrived there – and acknowledged that Aborigines held valid title to their land. Subsequent legislation has provided a framework for assessing such claims.

TIMELINE

1955 Australian troops sent to Malaya	**1966–72** Demonstrations against the Vietnam War	**1967** Referendum on Aborigines ends legal discrimination	**1973** Sydney Opera House opens (see pp84–5)
	1958 Immigration dictation test abolished		

Sydney Opera House

1955	1960	1965	1970	1975	1980

1956 Melbourne hosts the Olympic Games	**1965** Australian troops sent to Vietnam as part of their National Service	**1971** Neville Bonner becomes Australia's first Aboriginal MP	**1976** "Advance Australia Fair" becomes national anthem	**1979** Severe droughts in the country last three years	**1981** Preferenc given to immig with family me already in Aus Increase in As immigration

Neville Bonner

Anti-Vietnam demonstrations as US President Johnson arrives in Australia

In 1972, the Labor Party, under Edward Gough Whitlam, was elected on a platform of social reform. It abolished conscription, introduced free university education, lowered the voting age from 21 to 18 and gave some land rights to Aborigines. In 1974, an immigration policy without any racial discrimination was adopted. At the same time, however, inflation was increasing and there was talk of economic mismanagement.

Menzies understood his people's desire for peace and prosperity, and gave Australians conservatism and stability. He did, however, also involve them in three more wars, in Korea (1950), Malaya (1955) and Vietnam (1965). Vietnam was the first time Australia fought in a war in which Britain was not also engaged.

SOCIAL UNREST AND CHANGE

Opposition to conscription and the Vietnam War increased in the late 1960s and led to major demonstrations in the capital cities. At the same time there was concern for issues such as Aboriginal land rights and free education. In 1967, a constitutional referendum was passed by 90.8 per cent of the voters, ending the ban on Aboriginal inclusion in the national census. It also gave power to the federal government to legislate for Aborigines in all states, ending state discriminations.

RETURN TO CONSERVATISM

In 1975, the Liberal leader Malcolm Fraser won the election. Subsequent governments, both Liberal under Fraser (1975–83) and Labor under Bob Hawke and Paul Keating (1983–96), were concerned with economic rather than social agendas. The boom of the 1980s was followed by recession in the 1990s. During this period Australia shifted its focus from Europe towards Asia and, by 1986, all legislative ties with Great Britain were broken.

Following 9/11, Australia has been at the forefront in the fight against terrorism. It has also experienced increased racial tensions and even riots.

Australia continues to take centre stage at international sporting events, hosting both the Commonwealth and Olympic Games.

Prime Minister Whitlam hands over Aboriginal land rights in 1975

1983 Bob Hawke elected as prime minister

1986 Proclamation of Australia Act breaks legal ties with Britain

1991 Paul Keating elected as Prime minister

1996 John Howard is elected as prime minister

2006 Commonwealth Games held in Melbourne

1985	1990	1995	2000	2005	2010

1983 America's Cup victory

americas cup

1988 Bicentenary new federal Parliament House opened in Canberra

1992–3 High Court rules that Aborigines held valid claims to land

2000 Sydney hosts Olympic Games

2005 Race riots in Sydney between White and Lebanese-Muslim youths

SYDNEY

INTRODUCING SYDNEY 62–73

THE ROCKS AND CIRCULAR QUAY 74–85

CITY CENTRE AND DARLING HARBOUR 86–103

BOTANIC GARDENS AND THE DOMAIN 104–115

KINGS CROSS, DARLINGHURST AND
PADDINGTON 116–125

FURTHER AFIELD 126–127

PRACTICAL INFORMATION 128–147

SYDNEY STREET FINDER 148–155

Central Sydney

This guide divides the centre of Sydney into four distinct areas, and the majority of the city's main sights are contained in these districts. The Rocks and Circular Quay are the oldest part of inner Sydney. The City Centre is the central business district, and to its west lies Darling Harbour, which includes Sydney's well-known Chinatown. The Botanic Gardens and The Domain form a green oasis almost in the heart of the city. To the east are Kings Cross and Darlinghurst, hub of the café culture, and Paddington, an area that still retains its charming 19th-century character.

The Lord Nelson Hotel *is a traditional pub in The Rocks (see p480) which first opened its doors in 1834. Its own specially brewed beers are available on tap.*

KEY

▨	Major sight
▨	Other building
🚆	CityRail station
🅿	Monorail station
🚆	Sydney Light Rail station (SLR)
🚌	Bus station
🚌	Coach station
⛴	Ferry boarding point
🚢	JetCat/RiverCat boarding point
🚓	Police station
🅿	Car park
🛈	Tourist information
✚	Hospital with casualty unit
✝	Church
✡	Synagogue

Queen Victoria Building *is a Romanesque former produce market, built in the 1890s. It forms part of a fine group of Victorian buildings in the City Centre (see p90). Now a shopping mall, it retains many of its original features, including its ornate roof statues.*

◁ **Sydneysiders enjoying the sunshine in front of the distinctive Sydney Opera House**

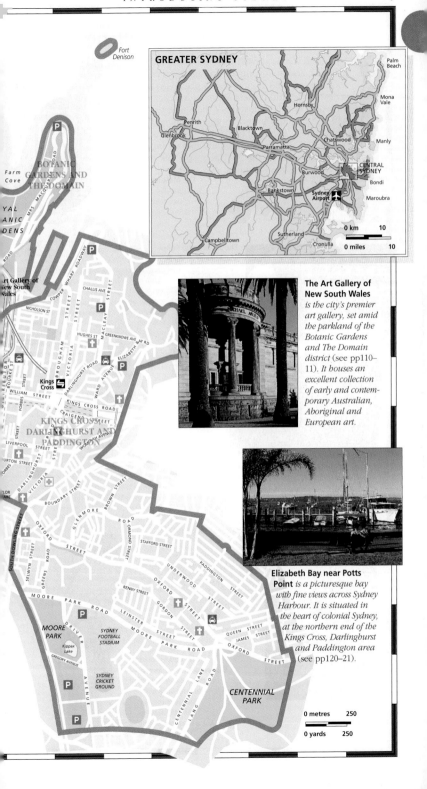

GREATER SYDNEY

Palm Beach

Mona Vale

Hornsby

Manly

Penrith

Blacktown

Chatswood

Glenbrook

Parramatta

CENTRAL SYDNEY

Burwood

Bondi

Bankstown

Sydney Airport

Maroubra

Campbelltown

Sutherland

Cronulla

0 km 10

0 miles 10

Fort Denison

Farm Cove

BOTANIC GARDENS AND THE DOMAIN

ROYAL BOTANIC GARDENS

Art Gallery of New South Wales

The Art Gallery of New South Wales *is the city's premier art gallery, set amid the parkland of the Botanic Gardens and The Domain district (see pp110–11). It houses an excellent collection of early and contemporary Australian, Aboriginal and European art.*

KINGS CROSS, DARLINGHURST AND PADDINGTON

Kings Cross

Elizabeth Bay near Potts Point *is a picturesque bay with fine views across Sydney Harbour. It is situated in the heart of colonial Sydney, at the northern end of the Kings Cross, Darlinghurst and Paddington area (see pp120–21).*

MOORE PARK

SYDNEY FOOTBALL STADIUM

Kippax Lake

SYDNEY CRICKET GROUND

CENTENNIAL PARK

0 metres 250

0 yards 250

Sydney's Best: Museums and Galleries

Sydney is well endowed with museums and galleries, and, following the current appreciation of social history, much emphasis is placed on the life-styles of past and present Sydneysiders. Small museums are also a feature of the Sydney scene, with a number of historic houses recalling the colonial days. Most of the major collections are housed in architecturally significant buildings – the Classical façade of the Art Gallery of NSW makes it a city landmark, while the MCA or Museum of Contemporary Art has given new life to a 1950s Art Deco-style building at Circular Quay.

Bima figure, Powerhouse Museum

The Museum of Sydney *includes* The Edge of the Trees, *an interactive installation (see p92).*

THE ROCKS AND CIRCULAR QUAY

The Justice and Police Museum *illustrates Sydney's early legal and criminal history. It includes some macabre relics of notorious crimes (see p83).*

CITY CENTRE AND DARLING HARBOUR

The Museum of Contemporary Art *has an excellent Aboriginal art section, with works such as* Mud Crabs *by Tony Dhanyula Nyoka, a Ramingining artist (see p78).*

The National Maritime Museum *is the home port for HMB* Endeavour, *a replica of the vessel that charted Australia's east coast in 1770, with Captain Cook in command (see pp100–1).*

The Powerhouse Museum, *set in a former power station, uses both traditional and interactive displays to explore Australian innovations in science and technology (see pp102–3).*

| 0 metres | 500 |
| 0 yards | 500 |

The Art Gallery of New South Wales *includes colonial watercolours in its Australian collection, which, to avoid deterioration, are only shown for a few weeks each year. Charles Meere's Australian Beach Pattern (1940) is a recent work (see pp110–13).*

Elizabeth Bay House is *elegantly furnished to the 1840s period, when the Colonial Secretary Alexander Macleay briefly lived in the house that ultimately caused his bankruptcy (see p120).*

BOTANIC GARDENS AND THE DOMAIN

KINGS CROSS, DARLINGHURST AND PADDINGTON

The Hyde Park Barracks were *originally built by convicts for their own incarceration. They were later home to poor female immigrants. Exhibits recall the daily life of these occupants (see p114).*

The Sydney Jewish Museum *documents the history of the city's Jewish community. Exhibits include reconstructed scenes, such as George Street in 1848, a Jewish business area (see p121).*

The Australian Museum *is Australia's largest natural history museum. Dinosaurs such as this large mammal or "megafauna" Diprotodon skeleton are a major attraction (see pp94–5).*

Sydney's Best: Architecture

For such a young city, Sydney possesses a great
diversity of architectural styles. They range from the
simplicity of Francis Greenway's Georgian buildings
(see p169) to Jørn Utzon's Expressionist Sydney Opera
House *(see pp84–5)*. Practical colonial structures gave
way to elaborate Victorian edifices such as Sydney
Town Hall. The same passion for detail is seen in
Paddington's terraces. Later, Federation warehouses and
bungalows introduced a uniquely Australian style.

Colonial convict *structures were
simple with shingled roofs, based
on the English homes of the first
settlers. Cadman's Cottage
is an example of this style
(see p78).*

Contemporary
*architecture abounds in
Sydney, including
Governor Phillip Tower.
The Museum of Sydney is
at its base (see p92).*

Colonial Georgian *buildings
include St James Church (see
p115). Francis Greenway's
design was adapted to suit
the purposes of a church.*

**American
Revivalism** *took up
the 1890s vogue of
arcades connecting
many different
streets. The Queen
Victoria Building is
a fine example
(see p90).*

THE ROCKS
AND
CIRCULAR
QUAY

Victorian
*architecture
abounds in the city.
Sydney Town Hall
includes a metal
ceiling, installed for
fear that the organ
would vibrate a plaster
one loose (see p93).*

CITY
CENTRE &
DARLING
HARBOUR

Contemporary Expressionism's *main
emphasis is roof design and the silhouette.
Innovations were made in sports stadiums
and museums, such as the National
Maritime Museum (see p100–1).*

Interwar Architecture
*encapsulates the spirit of Art Deco,
as seen in the Anzac Memorial in
Hyde Park (see p93).*

| 0 metres | 500 |
| 0 yards | 500 |

Modern Expressionism
*includes one of the world's greatest
examples of 20th-century architecture.
The construction of Jørn Utzon's Sydney
Opera House began in 1959. Despite the
architect's resignation in 1966, it was
opened in 1973 (see pp84–5).*

Australian Regency *was popular
during the 1830s. The best-designed
villas were the work of John Verge. The
beautiful Elizabeth Bay House is considered his masterpiece (see p120).*

Early Colonial's
*first buildings, such as
Hyde Park Barracks
(see p114), were mainly
built for the government.*

BOTANIC
GARDENS AND
THE DOMAIN

KINGS CROSS,
DARLINGHURST &
PADDINGTON

Colonial military *buildings were both
functional and ornate. Victoria Barracks,
designed by engineers, is a fine example of a
Georgian military compound (see p124).*

Colonial Grecian *and
Greek Revival were the
most popular styles for
public buildings
designed during the
1820–50 period. The
Darlinghurst Court
House is a particularly
fine example (see p121).*

Victorian iron lace
*incorporated filigree
of cast-iron in prefab-
ricated patterns.
Paddington's verandas
are fine examples of
this 1880s style
(see pp122–3).*

Sydney's Best: Parks and Reserves

Flannel flower

Sydney is almost completely surrounded by national parks and intact bushland. There are also a number of national parks and reserves within Greater Sydney itself. Here, the visitor can gain some idea of how the landscape looked before the arrival of European settlers. The city parks, too, are filled with plant and animal life. The more formal plantings of both native and exotic species are countered by the indigenous birds and animals that have adapted and made the urban environment their home. One of the highlights of a trip to Sydney is the huge variety of birds to be seen, from large birds of prey such as sea eagles and kites, to the shyer species such as wrens and tiny finches.

Garigal National Park
is made up of rainforest and moist gullies, which provide shelter for superb lyrebirds and sugar gliders.

North Arm Walk
is covered in spring with grevilleas and flannel flowers blooming profusely.

Lane Cove National Park *is an open eucalypt forest dotted with grass trees, as well as fine stands of blue gums and apple gums. The rosella, a type of parrot, is common in the area.*

Bicentennial Park *is situated at Homebush Bay (see p147). The park features a mangrove habitat and attracts many water birds, including pelicans.*

Hyde Park *is situated on the edge of the city centre (see p93). The park provides a peaceful respite from the hectic streets. The native iris is just one of the plants found in the lush gardens. The sacred ibis, a water bird, is often seen.*

Middle Head and Obelisk Bay *are dotted with gun emplacements, tunnels and bunkers built in the 1870s to protect Sydney from invasion. The superb fairy wren lives here, and water dragons can at times be seen basking on rocks.*

North Head *is covered with coastal heathland, with banksias, tea trees and casuarinas dominating the cliff tops. On the leeward side, moist forest surrounds tiny, secluded harbour beaches.*

Grotto Point's paths, winding through the bush to the lighthouse, are lined with bottlebrushes, grevilleas and flannel flowers.

Bradleys Head *is a nesting place for the ringtail possum. Noisy flocks of rainbow lorikeets are also often in residence. The views across the harbour to Sydney are spectacular.*

South Head contains unique plant species such as the sundew.

Nielsen Park is inhabited by the kookaburra, easily identified by its call, which sounds like laughter.

The Domain *features palms and Moreton Bay figs. The Australian magpie, with its black and white plumage, is a frequent visitor (see p109).*

Moore Park is filled with huge Moreton Bay figs which provide an urban habitat for the flying fox.

Centennial Park *contains open expanses and groves of paper-bark and eucalypt trees, bringing sulphur-crested cockatoos en masse. The brushtail possum is a shy creature that comes out at night (see p125).*

| 0 kilometres | 4 |
| 0 miles | 2 |

Garden Island to Farm Cove

Waterlily in the Royal Botanic Gardens

Sydney's vast harbour, also named Port Jackson after a Secretary in the British Admiralty who promptly changed his name, is a drowned river valley which was transformed over millions of years. Its intricate coastal geography of headlands and secluded bays can sometimes confound even lifelong residents. This waterway was the lifeblood of the early colony, with the maritime industry a vital source of wealth and supply. The legacies of recessions and booms can be viewed along the shoreline: a representation of a nation where an estimated 70 per cent of the population cling to the coastal cities, especially in the east.

The city skyline *is a result of random development. The 1960s' destruction of architectural history was halted, and towers now stand amid Victorian buildings.*

Two harbour beacons,
known as "wedding cakes" because of their three tiers, are solar powered and equipped with a fail-safe back-up service. There are around 350 buoys and beacons now in operation.

The barracks for the naval garrison date from 1888.

Garden Island marks a 1940s construction project with 12 ha (30 acres) reclaimed from the harbour.

Sailing on the harbour *is a pastime not exclusively reserved for the rich elite. Of the several hundred thousand pleasure boats registered, some are available for hire while others take out groups of inexperienced sailors.*

Mrs Macquaries Chair *is a carved rock seat by Mrs Macquaries Road (see p108). In the early days of the colony this was the site of a fruit and vegetable garden which was farmed until 1805.*

0 metres	250
0 yards	250

The Andrew (Boy) Charlton Pool *is a favourite bathing spot for inner-city residents, and is named after the 16-year old who won an Olympic gold medal in 1924. It was erected in 1963 on the Domain Baths' site, which had a grandstand for 1,700.*

Woolloomooloo Finger Wharf was a disembarkation point when most travellers arrived by sea.

LOCATOR MAP
See Street Finder, *map 2*

THE ROCKS
AND CIRCULAR
QUAY

BOTANIC
GARDENS AND
THE DOMAIN

CITY CENTRE
AND
DARLING
HARBOUR

KINGS CROSS,
DARLINGHURST
AND PADDINGTON

Harry's Café de Wheels, *a snack van, has been a Sydney culinary institution for more than 50 years. Photographs of celebrity customers are pinned to the van, attesting to its fame.*

The Royal Botanic Gardens *display both flowering and non-flowering plants. Here the first trees were planted by the new European colonists; some of these trees survive today (see pp106–107).*

Farm Cove *has long been a mooring place for visiting naval vessels. The land opposite, now the Botanic Gardens, has been continuously cultivated for over 200 years.*

Sydney Cove to Walsh Bay

It is estimated that over 70 km (43 miles) of harbour foreshore have been lost as a result of the massive land reclamation projects carried out since the 1840s. That the 13 islands existing when the First Fleet arrived in 1788 have now been reduced to just eight is a startling indication of rapid and profound geographical transformation. Redevelopments around the Circular Quay and Walsh Bay area from the 1980s have opened up the waterfront for public use and enjoyment, acknowledging it as the city's greatest natural asset. Sydney's environmental and architectural aspirations recognize the need to integrate city and harbour.

Detail from railing at Circular Quay

Conservatorium of Music

1857 Man O'War Steps

The Sydney Opera House *was designed to take advantage of its spectacular setting. The roofs shine during the day and seem to glow at night. The building appears as a visionary landscape to the onlooker (see pp84–5).*

Government House, a Gothic Revival building, was home to the state's governors until 1996.

Harbour cruises *regularly depart from Circular Quay, taking visitors out and about both during the day and in the evening. They are an incomparable way to see the city and its waterways.*

The Sydney Harbour Bridge *was also known as the "Iron Lung" at the time of its construction. During the Great Depression it provided on-site work for approximately 1,400, while others worked in specialist workshops (see pp80–81).*

0 metres   250
0 yards   250

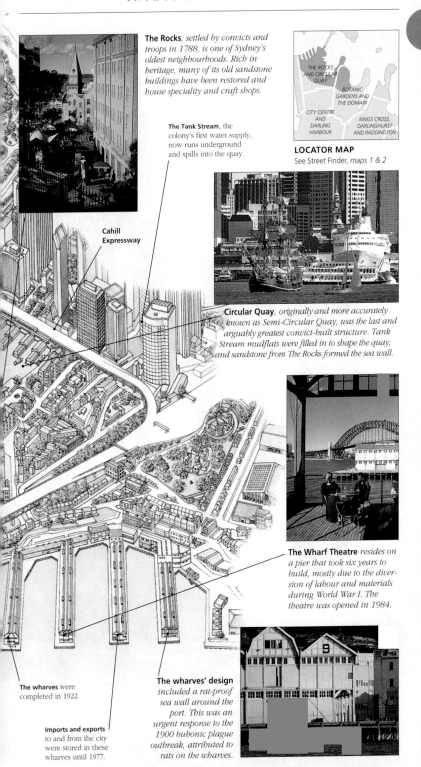

The Rocks, *settled by convicts and troops in 1788, is one of Sydney's oldest neighbourhoods. Rich in heritage, many of its old sandstone buildings have been restored and house speciality and craft shops.*

The Tank Stream, the colony's first water supply, now runs underground and spills into the quay.

LOCATOR MAP
See Street Finder, maps 1 & 2

THE ROCKS AND CIRCULAR QUAY

BOTANIC GARDENS AND THE DOMAIN

CITY CENTRE AND DARLING HARBOUR

KINGS CROSS, DARLINGHURST AND PADDINGTON

Cahill Expressway

Circular Quay, *originally and more accurately known as Semi-Circular Quay, was the last and arguably greatest convict-built structure. Tank Stream mudflats were filled in to shape the quay, and sandstone from The Rocks formed the sea wall.*

The Wharf Theatre *resides on a pier that took six years to build, mostly due to the diversion of labour and materials during World War I. The theatre was opened in 1984.*

The wharves were completed in 1922.

The wharves' design *included a rat-proof sea wall around the port. This was an urgent response to the 1900 bubonic plague outbreak, attributed to rats on the wharves.*

Imports and exports to and from the city were stored in these wharves until 1977.

THE ROCKS AND CIRCULAR QUAY

Circular Quay, once known as Semi-Circular Quay, is often referred to as the "birth-place of Australia". It was here, in January 1788, that the First Fleet landed its human freight of convicts, soldiers and officials, and the new British colony of New South Wales was declared. Sydney Cove became a rallying point whenever a ship arrived bringing much-needed supplies from "home". Crowds still gather here whenever there is a national or civic celebration. The Quay and The Rocks

Sculpture on the AMP Building, Circular Quay

are focal points for New Year's Eve festivities. Circular Quay was the setting for huge crowds when, in 1994, Sydney was awarded the year 2000 Olympic Games. The Rocks area offers visitors a taste of Sydney's past, but it is a far cry from the time, less than 100 years ago, when most inhabitants lived in rat-infested slums, and gangs ruled its streets. Now scrubbed and polished, The Rocks forms part of the colourful promenade from the Sydney Harbour Bridge to the spectacular Sydney Opera House.

SIGHTS AT A GLANCE

Museums and Galleries
Justice and Police Museum **15**
Museum of
   Contemporary Art **2**
National Trust Centre **11**
The Rocks
   Discovery Museum **5**
Sailors' Home **4**
Susannah Place **1**

Theatres and Concert Halls
*Sydney Opera House
   pp84–5* **17**

Historic Streets and Buildings
Cadman's Cottage **3**
Campbell's Storehouses **6**
Customs House **14**
Hero of Waterloo **8**
Macquarie Place **13**
*Sydney Harbour Bridge
   pp80–81* **7**

Sydney Observatory **10**
Writers' Walk **16**

Churches
Garrison Church **9**
St Philip's Church **12**

GETTING THERE
Circular Quay is the best stop for ferries and trains. Sydney Explorer and bus routes 431, 432, 433 and 434 run regularly to The Rocks, while most buses through the city go to the Quay.

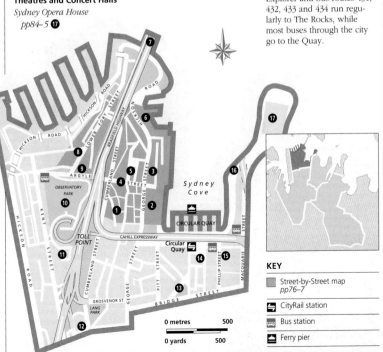

KEY

	Street-by-Street map *pp76–7*
	CityRail station
	Bus station
	Ferry pier

◁ The brilliant white walls of the Sailors' Home, parts of which date back to 1864

Street-by-Street: The Rocks

THE·HERO·OF WATERLOO

Named for the rugged cliffs that were once its dominant feature, this area has played a vital role in Sydney's development. In 1788, the First Fleeters under Governor Phillip's command erected makeshift buildings here, with the convicts' hard labour used to establish more permanent structures in the form of rough-hewn streets. The Argyle Cut, a road carved through solid rock using just hammer and chisel, took 18 years to build, beginning in 1843. By 1900, The Rocks was overrun with disease; the street now known as Suez Canal was once Sewer's Canal. Today, the area is still rich in colonial history and colour.

Governor Arthur Phillip

Hero of Waterloo
Lying beneath this historic pub is a tunnel originally used for smuggling **8**

★ Sydney Observatory
The first European structure on this prominent site was a windmill. The present museum holds some of the earliest astronomical instruments brought to Australia **10**

Garrison Church
Columns in this church are decorated with the insignia of British troops stationed here until 1870. Australia's first prime minister was educated next door **9**

Argyle Cut

Suez Canal

★ Museum of Contemporary Art
The stripped Classical façade belies the avant-garde nature of the Australian and international art displayed in an ever-changing programme **2**

Walkway along Circular Quay West foreshore

For hotels and restaurants in this region see pp478–81 and pp524–8

The Rocks Discovery Museum
Key episodes in The Rocks' history are illustrated by this museum's collection of maritime images and other artefacts **5**

LOCATOR MAP
See Street Finder, map 1

The Rocks Market
is a hive of activity every weekend, offering an eclectic range of craft items and jewellery utilizing Australian icons from gum leaves to koalas *(see p133)*.

★ Cadman's Cottage
John Cadman, government coxswain, resided in what was known as the Coxswain's Barracks with his family. His wife Elizabeth was also a significant figure, believed to be the first woman to vote in New South Wales, a right she insisted on **3**

0 metres	100
0 yards	100

KEY

– – – Suggested route

STAR SIGHTS

★ Cadman's Cottage

★ Museum of Contemporary Art

★ Sydney Observatory

The Overseas Passenger Terminal is where some of the world's luxury cruise liners, including the *QEII*, berth during their stay in Sydney.

Old-fashioned Australian goods at the corner shop, Susannah Place

Susannah Place ●

58–64 Gloucester St, The Rocks.
Map 1 B2. **Tel** (02) 9241 1893.
Sydney Explorer, 431, 432, 433, 434.
Circular Quay, Wynyard.
10am–5pm Sat & Sun, Tue–Thu.
Good Fri, 25 Dec.
www.hht.net.au

This terrace of four brick and
sandstone houses dating back
to 1844 has a rare history of
continuous domestic
occupancy from the 1840s
through to 1990. It is now a
museum examining the living
conditions of its former inhabitants. Rather than re-creating
a single period, the museum
retains the renovations carried out by different tenants.

Built for Edward and Mary
Riley, who arrived from Ireland
with their niece Susannah in
1838, these houses have basement kitchens and backyard
outhouses. Piped water and
sewerage were probably
added by the mid-1850s.

The terrace escaped the
wholesale demolitions that
occurred after the outbreak of
bubonic plague in 1900, as
well as later clearings of land
to make way for the Sydney
Harbour Bridge (see pp80–81)
and the Cahill Expressway. In
the 1970s it was saved once
again when the Builders
Labourers' Federation imposed
a "green ban" on The Rocks,
temporarily halting all redevelopment work which was destructive to cultural heritage.

Museum of Contemporary Art ●

Circular Quay West, The Rocks. **Map**
1 B2. **Tel** (02) 9245 2400. 431, 432,
433, 434, Sydney Explorer. 10am–
5pm daily. 25 Dec. book in
advance. **www**.mca.com.au

When Sydney art collector
John Power died in 1943, he
left his entire collection and a
financial bequest to the
University of Sydney. In 1991
the collection, which by then
included works by Hockney,
Warhol, Lichtenstein and
Christo was transferred to this
1950s Art Deco-style building
at Circular Quay West. As well
as showing its permanent
collection, the museum hosts
exhibitions by local and
overseas artists. The MCA
Store sells distinctive gifts by
Australian designers.

Cadman's Cottage ●

110 George St, The Rocks. **Map** 1 B2.
Tel (02) 9247 5033. 431, 432,
433, 434. 9:30am–4:30pm
Mon–Fri, 10am–4:30pm Sat–Sun.
Good Fri, 25 Dec.

Built in 1816 as barracks for
the crews of the governor's
boats, this sandstone cottage
is Sydney's oldest surviving
dwelling and now serves as
the information centre for the
Sydney Harbour National Park.

The cottage is named after
John Cadman, a convict who
was transported in 1798 for
horse-stealing. By 1813, he was
coxswain of a timber boat and
later, coxswain of government
craft. He was granted a full
pardon and in 1827 he was
made boat superintendent and
moved to the four-room cottage that now bears his name.

Cadman married Elizabeth
Mortimer in 1830, another ex-
convict who was sentenced to
seven years' transportation for
the theft of one hairbrush.
They lived in the cottage until
1845. Cadman's Cottage was
built on the foreshore of
Sydney Harbour. Now, as
a result of successive land
reclamations, it is set well
back from the water's edge.

Art Deco-style façade of the Museum of Contemporary Art

Sailors' Home **4**

106 George St, The Rocks. **Map** 1 B2. 🚌 *Sydney Explorer, 339, 340, 431, 432, 433, 434.*

Built in 1864 as lodgings for visiting sailors. The first and second floors were dormitories, but these were later divided into 56 cubicles or "cabins" which were arranged around open galleries and lit by four enormous skylights. At the time it was built, the Sailors' Home was a welcome alternative to the many seedy inns and brothels in the area, saving sailors from the perils of "crimping". "Crimps" would tempt newly arrived men into bars providing much sought-after entertainment. While drunk, the sailors would be sold on to departing ships, waking miles out at sea and returning home in debt.

Sailors used the home until 1980. In 1994, it opened as a tourist information centre, which has now moved to The Rocks Centre.

The Rocks Discovery Museum **5**

Kendall Lane, The Rocks. **Tel** *1800 067 676.* 🚌 *Sydney Explorer, 431, 432, 433, 434.* 🚢 *Circular Quay.* ☐ *10am–5pm daily.* ● *Good Fri, 25 Dec.* ♿

This Museum, in a restored 1850s coach house, is home to a unique collection of archaeological artefacts and images that detail the story of The Rocks from the pre-European days to the present. There are four exhibitions which are highly interactive, making use of touch screens and audio and visual technology to bring the history alive. Some of the artefacts were found at the archaeological site on Cumberland Street The musuem has been developed in close consultation with local Aboriginal groups, so that their story of the area is properly told.

Opened in late 2005, entry to the museum is free.

Terrace restaurants at Campbell's Storehouses on the waterfront

Campbell's Storehouses **6**

7–27 Circular Quay West, The Rocks. **Map** 1 B2. 🚌 *Sydney Explorer, 431, 432, 433, 434.* ♿

Robert Campbell, a prominent Scottish merchant in the early days of Sydney, purchased this land on Sydney Cove in 1799. In 1802 he began constructing a private wharf and storehouses in which to house the tea, sugar, spirits and cloth he imported from India. Campbell was the only merchant operating in Australia who managed to infiltrate the monopoly held by the British East India Company. The first five sandstone bays were built between 1839 and 1844. A further seven bays were built between 1854 and 1861. The full row of storehouses were finally completed in 1890, including a brick upper storey. Part of the old sea wall and 11 of the original stores are still standing. The pulleys that were used to raise cargo from the wharf can be seen near the top of the preserved buildings.

The area fell into disrepair during the first half of the 20th century. However, in the 1970s the Sydney Cove Redevelopment Authority finalized plans and began renovating the site. Today the bond stores contain a range of fine restaurants catering to all tastes, from contemporary Australian to Chinese and Italian. Their virtually unimpeded views across Circular Quay towards the Sydney Opera House *(see pp84–5)* and Sydney Harbour Bridge *(see pp80–81)* make

these outdoor eating venues very popular with local business people and tourists alike.

Sydney Harbour Bridge **7**

See pp80–81.

The Hero of Waterloo Inn

Hero of Waterloo **8**

81 Lower Fort St, The Rocks. **Map** 1 A2. **Tel** *(02) 9252 4553.* 🚌 *431, 432, 433, 434.* ☐ *10am–11pm Mon–Wed, 10am–11:30pm Thu–Sat, 10am–10pm Sun.* ● *Good Fri, 25 Dec.* ♿ *limited.*

This picturesque old inn is especially welcoming in the winter with its log fires.

Built in 1844, this was a favourite drinking place for the nearby garrison's soldiers. Some sea captains were said to use the hotel to recruit. Patrons who drank too much were pushed into the cellars via a trapdoor. Tunnels then led to the wharves and on to waiting ships.

Sydney Harbour Bridge ❼

Completed in 1932, the construction of the Sydney Harbour Bridge was an economic feat, given the depressed times, as well as an engineering triumph. Prior to this, the only links between the city centre on the south side of the harbour and the residential north side were by ferry or a circuitous 20-km (12-mile) road route which involved five bridge crossings. The single-span arch bridge, colloquially known as the "Coathanger", took eight years to build, including the railway line. The bridge was manufactured in sections on the latter-day Luna Park site. Loans for the total cost of approximately 6.25 million old Australian pounds were eventually paid off in 1988.

Ceremonial scissors

The 1932 Opening
The ceremony was disrupted when zealous royalist Francis de Groot rode forward and cut the ribbon, in honour, he claimed, of King and Empire.

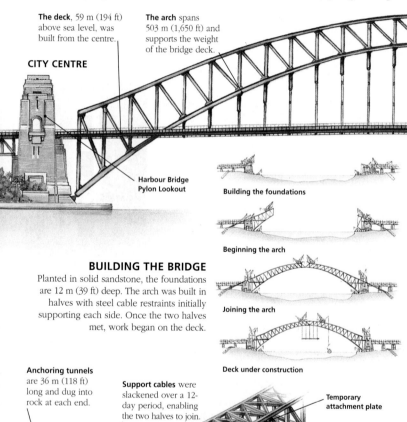

The deck, 59 m (194 ft) above sea level, was built from the centre.

CITY CENTRE

The arch spans 503 m (1,650 ft) and supports the weight of the bridge deck.

Harbour Bridge Pylon Lookout

Building the foundations

Beginning the arch

BUILDING THE BRIDGE

Planted in solid sandstone, the foundations are 12 m (39 ft) deep. The arch was built in halves with steel cable restraints initially supporting each side. Once the two halves met, work began on the deck.

Joining the arch

Deck under construction

Anchoring tunnels are 36 m (118 ft) long and dug into rock at each end.

Support cables were slackened over a 12-day period, enabling the two halves to join.

Temporary attachment plate

The Bridge Design
The steel arch of the bridge supports the deck, with hinges at either end bearing the bridge's full weight and spreading the load to the foundations. The hinges allow the structure to move as the steel expands and contracts in response to wind and extreme temperatures.

BridgeClimb
Thousands of people have enjoyed the spectacular bridge-top views after a 3.5-hour guided tour up ladders, catwalks and finally the upper arch of the bridge.

Over 150,000 vehicles cross the bridge each day, about 15 times as many as in 1932.

Bridge Workers
The bridge was built by 1,400 workers, 16 of whom were killed in accidents during construction.

NORTH SHORE

Maintenance
Painting the bridge has become a metaphor for an endless task. Approximately 30,000 litres (6,593 gal) of paint are required for each coat, enough to cover an area equivalent to 60 soccer pitches.

The vertical hangers support the slanting crossbeams which, in turn, carry the deck.

Paying the Toll
The initial toll of sixpence helped pay off the construction loan. The toll is now used for maintenance and to pay for the 1992 Sydney Harbour Tunnel.

FATHER OF THE BRIDGE

Chief engineer Dr John Bradfield shakes the hand of the driver of the first train to cross the bridge. Over a 20-year period, Bradfield supervised all aspects of the bridge's design and construction. At the opening ceremony, the highway linking the harbour's south side and northern suburbs was named in his honour.

A FLAGPOLE ON THE MUDFLATS

The modest flagpole on Loftus Street, near Customs House, flies a flag, the Union Jack, on the spot where Australia's first ceremonial flag-raising took place. On 26 January 1788, Captain Arthur Phillip hoisted the flag to declare the foundation of the colony. A toast to the king was drunk and a musket volley fired. On this date each year, the country marks Australia Day with a national holiday *(see p43)*. In 1788, the flagpole was on the edge of mudflats on Sydney Cove. Today, due to land reclamations, it is set back from the water's edge.

The Founding of Australia by Algernon Talmage

Garrison Church **9**

Cnr Argyle & Lower Fort sts, Millers Point. **Map** 1 A2. **Tel** (02) 9247 1268. 431, 433. 9am–6pm daily.

Officially named the Holy Trinity Church, this was dubbed the Garrison Church because it was the colony's first military church.

Henry Ginn designed the church and, in 1840, the foundation stone was laid. In 1855, it was enlarged to hold up to 600 people. Regimental plaques hanging along interior walls recall the church's military associations. A museum contains Australian military and historical items.

Other features to look out for are the brilliantly coloured east window and the carved red cedar pulpit.

East window, Garrison Church

Sydney Observatory **10**

Watson Rd, Observatory Hill, The Rocks. **Map** 1 A2. **Tel** (02) 9241 3767. Sydney Explorer, 343, 431, stop 22. 10am–5pm daily. **Night viewings** call to book. 25 Dec. www.sydneyobservatory.com.au

In 1982 this domed building, which had been a centre for astronomical observation and research for almost 125 years, became the city's astronomy museum. It has interactive displays and games, along with night sky viewings; it is essential to book for these.

The building began life in the 1850s as a time-ball tower. At 1pm daily, the ball on top of the tower dropped to signal the correct time. At the same time, a cannon was fired at Fort Denison. This custom continues today *(see p108)*.

During the 1880s Sydney Observatory became known around the world when some of the first astronomical photographs of the southern sky were taken here. From 1890 to 1962 the observatory mapped some 750,000 stars as part of an international project that resulted in an atlas of the entire night sky.

National Trust Centre **11**

Observatory Hill, Watson Rd, The Rocks. **Map** 1 A3. **Tel** (02) 9258 0123. Sydney Explorer, 343, 431, 432, 433, 434. 9am–5pm Tue–Fri. **Gallery** 11am–5pm Tue–Sun. Public hols. www.nsw.nationaltrust.org.au

The buildings that form the headquarters of the National Trust of Australia, date from 1815, when Governor Macquarie chose the site for a military hospital. Today they house a café, a National Trust shop and the SH Ervin Gallery, containing works by 19th- and 20th-century Australian artists such as Margaret Preston and Conrad Martens *(see p34)*.

St Philip's Church **12**

3 York St (enter from Jamison St). **Map** 1 A3. **Tel** (02) 9247 1071. George St routes. 9am–5pm Tue–Fri. 26 Jan. Phone first. 1pm Wed, 8am, 10am, 6:15pm Sun, 4pm 1st & 3rd Sun of month. www.stphilips-sydney.org.au

This Victorian Gothic church may seem overshadowed in its modern setting, yet when it was first built, the square tower was a local landmark.

Begun in 1848, St Philip's is by Edmund Blacket. In 1851 work was disrupted when its stonemasons left for the gold fields, but by 1856 the building was finally completed.

A peal of bells was donated in 1888 to mark Sydney's centenary and they still announce the services each Sunday.

Interior and pipe organ of St Philip's Church

Macquarie Place ⑬

Map 1 B3. 🚌 *Circular Quay routes.*

Governor Macquarie created this park in 1810 on what was once the vegetable garden of the first Government House. The sandstone obelisk, designed by Francis Greenway *(see p169)*, was erected in 1818 to mark the starting point for all roads in the colony. The gas lamps recall the fact that this was also the site of the city's first street lamp in 1826.

Also in this area are the remains of the bow anchor and cannon from HMS *Sirius*, flagship of the First Fleet. The statue of Thomas Mort, a successful 19th-century industrialist, is today a marshalling place for the city's somewhat kamikaze bicycle couriers.

Customs House ⑭

31 Alfred St, Circular Quay. **Map** 1 B3. **Tel** (02) 9242 8595. 🚌 *Circular Quay routes.* ⏰ 8am–7pm Mon–Fri, 10am–4pm Sat, 12pm–4pm Sun. 📷 ♿ 🖥 🍴 **www.** sydneycustomshouse.com.au

Colonial architect James Barnet designed this 1885 sandstone Classical Revival building on the same site as a previous Customs House. Its recalls the bygone days when trading ships berthed at Circular Quay. The building stands near the mouth of Tank Stream, the fledgling colony's freshwater supply. Among its many fine features are tall veranda columns made out of polished granite, a finely sculpted coat of arms and an elaborate clock face, added in 1897, which features a pair of tridents and dolphins.

A complete refurbishment was completed in 2005. Facilities include a City Library with a reading room and exhibition space, and an open lounge area with an international newspaper and magazine salon, internet access and bar. On the roof, Café Sydney offers great views.

Detail from Customs House

Montage of criminal "mug shots", Justice and Police Museum

Justice and Police Museum ⑮

Cnr Albert & Phillip sts. **Map** 1 C3. **Tel** (02) 9252 1144. 🚌 *Circular Quay routes.* ⏰ 10am–5pm Sat & Sun (open daily in Jan). 🚫 *Good Fri, 25 Dec.* 📷 📹 🎦 ♿ *limited.* **www.**hht.net.au

The buildings housing this museum originally comprised the Water Police Court, designed by Edmund Blacket in 1856, the Water Police Station, designed by Alexander Dawson in 1858, and the Police Court, designed by James Barnet in 1885. Here the rough-and-tumble underworld of quayside crime, from the petty to the violent, was dealt swift and, at times, harsh justice. The museum exhibits illustrate that turbulent period, as they re-create legal and criminal history.

Formalities of the late-Victorian legal proceedings can be easily imagined in the fully restored courtroom. Menacing implements from knuckledusters to bludgeons are displayed as the macabre relics of notorious crimes. Other interesting aspects of policing, criminality and the legal system are highlighted in special changing exhibitions. The museum powerfully evokes the realities of Australian policing and justice.

Writers' Walk ⑯

Circular Quay. **Map** 1 C2. 🚌 *Circular Quay routes.*

This series of plaques is set in the pavement at regular intervals between East and West Circular Quay. It gives the visitor the chance to ponder the observations of famous Australian writers, both past and present, on their home country, as well as the musings of some noted literary visitors.

Each plaque is dedicated to a particular writer, consisting of a personal quotation and a brief biographical note. Australian writers in the series include the novelists Miles Franklin and Peter Carey, poets Oodgeroo Noonuccal and Judith Wright *(see pp34–5)*, humorists Barry Humphries and Clive James, and the influential feminist writer Germaine Greer. Among the international writers included who visited Sydney are Mark Twain, Charles Darwin and Joseph Conrad.

Strolling along a section of the Writers' Walk at Circular Quay

Sydney Opera House ⑰

Advertising poster

No other building on earth looks like the Sydney Opera House. Popularly known as the "Opera House" long before the building was complete, it is, in fact, a complex of theatres and halls linked beneath its famous shells. Its birth was long and complicated. Many of the construction problems had not been faced before, resulting in an architectural adventure which lasted 14 years. An appeal fund was set up, eventually raising A$900,000, while the Opera House Lottery raised the balance of the A$102 million final cost. Today it is the city's most popular tourist attraction, as well as one of the world's busiest performing arts centres.

★ Opera Theatre
Mainly used for opera and ballet, this 1,507-seat theatre is big enough to stage grand operas such as Verdi's Aïda.

The Opera Theatre's ceiling and walls are painted black to focus attention on the stage.

Detail of The Possum Dreaming *(1988)*
The mural in the Opera Theatre foyer is by Michael Tjakamarra Nelson, an artist from the central Australian desert.

Opera House Walkway
Extensive public walkways around the building offer the visitor views from many different vantage points.

STAR FEATURES

★ Concert Hall

★ Opera Theatre

★ The Roofs

Northern Foyers
The Utzon Room and the large northern foyers of the Opera Theatre and Concert Hall have spectacular views over the harbour and can be hired for conferences, lunches, parties and weddings.

★ **Concert Hall**
This is the largest hall, with seating for 2,690. It is used for symphony, choral, jazz, folk and pop concerts, chamber music, opera, dance and everything from body building to fashion parades.

VISITORS' CHECKLIST

Bennelong Point. **Map** 1 C2. **Tel**
(02) 9250 7111. **Box office** *(02)
9250 7777.* 🚌 *Sydney Explorer,
111, 311, 380, 389, 392, 394, 396,
397, 399, 890.* 🚆 🚢 *Circular
Quay.* ⭕ *tours and performances.*
⬤ *Good Fri, 25 Dec.* ♿ *limited
(02) 9250 7777.* 📞 *9–5, call
(02) 9250 7209. TTY for hearing
impaired 9250 7347.* 🍴 ♿ 🚻
www.sydneyoperahouse.com

The Monumental Steps and forecourt are used for outdoor performances.

Guillaume at Bennelong
This is one of the finest restaurants in Sydney (see p528).

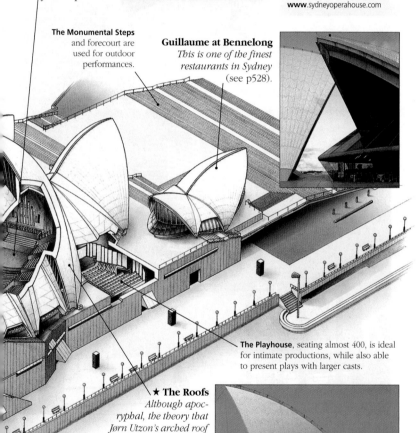

The Playhouse, seating almost 400, is ideal for intimate productions, while also able to present plays with larger casts.

★ **The Roofs**
Although apocryphal, the theory that Jørn Utzon's arched roof design came to him while peeling an orange is enchanting. The highest point is 67 m (221 ft) above sea level.

Detail of Utzon's Tapestry *(2004)*
Jørn Utzon's original design for this Gobelin-style tapestry, which hangs floor to ceiling in the refurbished Utzon Room, was inspired by the music of Carl Philipp Emanuel Bach.

View from Harbourside Shopping Centre looking east towards the city

SIGHTS AT A GLANCE

Museums and Galleries
Australian Museum
  pp94–5 ❿
Australian National Maritime
  Museum pp100–1 ⓯
Museum of Sydney ❼
Powerhouse Museum pp102–3 ⓲

Parks and Gardens
Chinese Garden ⓱
Hyde Park ❾

Cathedrals and Synagogues
Great Synagogue ⓫
St Andrew's Cathedral ⓭
St Mary's Cathedral ❽

**Historic Streets and
Buildings**
Chinatown ⓴
Lands Department Building ❻
Martin Place ❹
Queen Victoria Building ❶

Strand Arcade ❸
Sydney Tower p91 ❺
Sydney Town Hall ⓬

Entertainment
King Street Wharf ⓰
State Theatre ❷
Sydney Aquarium ⓮

Markets
Paddy's Markets ⓳

CITY CENTRE
AND DARLING HARBOUR

George Street, Australia's first thoroughfare, was originally lined with mud and wattle huts, but following the gold rush shops and banks came to dominate the area. The city's first skyscraper, Culwulla Chambers, was completed in 1913. Hyde Park, on the edge of the city centre, was once a racecourse, attracting gambling taverns to Elizabeth Street. Today it provides a peaceful oasis,

Mosaic floor detail, St Mary's Cathedral

while the city's commercial centre is an area of department stores and arcades. The country's industrial age began in Darling Harbour in 1815 with the opening of a steam mill, but later the area became rundown. In the 1980s, it was the site of the largest urban redevelopment project ever carried out in Australia. Today, Darling Harbour contains many fine museums.

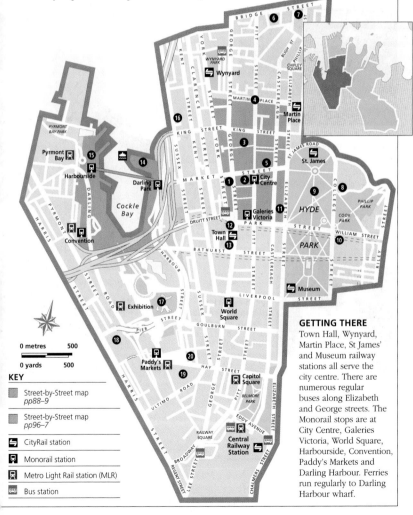

KEY

	Street-by-Street map pp88–9
	Street-by-Street map pp96–7
🚆	CityRail station
🚇	Monorail station
🚋	Metro Light Rail station (MLR)
🚌	Bus station

0 metres 500
0 yards 500

GETTING THERE

Town Hall, Wynyard, Martin Place, St James' and Museum railway stations all serve the city centre. There are numerous regular buses along Elizabeth and George streets. The Monorail stops are at City Centre, Galeries Victoria, World Square, Harbourside, Convention, Paddy's Markets and Darling Harbour. Ferries run regularly to Darling Harbour wharf.

Street-by-Street: City Centre

Sculpture outside the MLC Centre

Although closely rivalled by Melbourne, Sydney is the business and commercial capital of Australia. Vibrant by day, at night the streets are far less busy when office workers and shoppers have gone home. The comparatively small city centre of this sprawling metropolis seems to be almost jammed into a few city blocks.

Because Sydney grew in such a haphazard fashion, with many of today's streets following tracks from the harbour originally made by bullocks, there was no allowance for the expansion of the city into what has become a major international centre. A colourful night scene of cafés, restaurants and theatres is emerging, however, as more people return to the city centre to live.

★ **Queen Victoria Building**
Taking up an entire city block, this 1898 former produce market has been lovingly restored and is now a shopping mall ❶

State Theatre
A gem from the era when the movies reigned, this glittering and richly decorated 1929 cinema was once hailed as "the Empire's greatest theatre" ❷

To Sydney Town Hall

The Queen Victoria Statue was found after a worldwide search in 1983 ended in a small Irish village. It had lain forgotten and neglected since being removed from the front of the Irish Parliament in 1947.

STAR SIGHTS

★ AMP Tower

★ Martin Place

★ Queen Victoria Building

0 metres	100
0 yards	100

KEY

– – – Suggested route

Marble Bar was once a landmark bar in the 1893 Tattersalls hotel. It was carefully dismantled and re-erected in the Sydney Hilton in 1973.

Strand Arcade

A reminder of the late 19th century Victorian era when Sydney was famed as a city of elegant shopping arcades, this faithfully restored example is said to have been the finest of them all **3**

LOCATOR MAP
See Street Finder, maps 1 & 4

GEORGE STREET

KING STREET

PITT STREET

MARTIN PLACE

CASTLEREAGH STREET

ELIZABETH STREET

MLC Centre

★ **Martin Place**
Martin Place's 1929 Art Deco Cenotaph is the site of annual Anzac Day war remembrance services **4**

Theatre Royal

Skygarden is one of the city's many arcades. It features elegant shops with designer labels and a popular food court on the top level.

Hyde Park's northern end

★ **Sydney Tower**
The tower tops the city skyline, giving a bird's eye view of the whole of Sydney. It rises 305 m (1,000 ft) above the ground and can be seen from as far away as the Blue Mountains **5**

Queen Victoria Building ❶

455 George St. **Map** 1 B5. *Tel* (02)
9264 9209. ▦ George St routes.
◯ 9am–6pm Mon–Wed, 9am–9pm
Thu, 9am–6pm Fri & Sat, 11am–5pm
Sun; 11am–5pm public hols. ♿ ✦
See **Shopping** pp132–7.
www.qvb.com.au

French designer Pierre Cardin
called the Queen Victoria
Building "the most beautiful
shopping centre in the
world". Yet this ornate
Romanesque building, better
known as the QVB, began
life as the Sydney produce
market. Completed to the
design of City Architect
George McRae in 1898, the
dominant features are the
central copper dome
and the glass roof
which lets in a
flood of natural
light.

The market
closed at the end
of World War I.
By the 1950s, the
building was
threatened with demolition.

Refurbished at a cost of over
A$75 million, the QVB re-
opened in 1986 as a shopping
gallery with more than 190
shops. A wishing well incorporates a stone from Blarney
Castle, a sculpture of Islay,
Queen Victoria's dog and a
statue of the queen herself.

Inside the QVB, suspended
from the ceiling, is the Royal
Clock. Designed in 1982 by
Neil Glasser, it features part
of Balmoral Castle above a
copy of the four dials of Big
Ben. Every hour, a fanfare is
played with a parade depicting various English monarchs.

**Roof detail,
Queen Victoria Building**

Ornately decorated Gothic foyer of the State Theatre

State Theatre ❷

49 Market St. **Map** 1 B5. *Tel* (02)
9373 6852. ▦ George St routes.
Box office ◯ 9am–5:30pm
Mon–Fri. ◉ Good Friday, 25 Dec.
♿ ✦ (bookings necessary).
www.statetheatre.com.au

When it opened in 1929, this
cinema was hailed as the
finest that local craftsmanship
could achieve. The State
Theatre is one of the best

examples of ornate period
cinemas in Australia.

Its Baroque style is evident
in the foyer, with its high
ceiling, mosaic floor,
marble columns and
statues. The audito-
rium is lit by a
20,000-piece
chandelier. The
beautiful Wurlitzer
organ (under
repair) rises from
below stage before
performances. The
theatre is now one of the
city's special events venues.

Strand Arcade ❸

412–414 George St. **Map** 1 B5. *Tel*
(02) 9232 4199. ▦ George St routes.
◯ 9am–5:30pm Mon–Wed & Fri,
9am–9pm Thu, 9am–4pm Sat, 11am–
4pm Sun. ◉ 25, 26 Dec, some public
hols. ♿ See **Shopping** pp132–7.
www.strandarcade.com.au

Victorian Sydney was a city of
grand shopping arcades. The
Strand, joining George and

Pitt Street entrance to the
majestic Strand Arcade

Pitt streets and designed by
English architect John
Spencer, was the finest of all.
Opened in April 1892, it was
lit by natural light pouring
through the glass roof and the
chandeliers, each carrying 50
jets of gas as well as 50 lamps.

After a fire in 1976, the
building was restored to its
original splendour. Shopping,
followed by a visit to one of
the beautiful coffee shops.

Martin Place ❹

Map 1 B4. ▦ George St & Elizabeth
St routes. ▣ Martin Place.

This plaza was opened in
1891 and made a traffic-free
precinct in 1971. It is busiest
at lunchtime as city workers
enjoy their sandwiches while
watching free entertainment
in the amphitheatre near
Castlereagh Street.

Every Anzac Day (see p42)
the focus moves to the Cenotaph at the George Street end.
Past and present service
personnel attend a dawn
service and wreath-laying
ceremony, followed by a
march past. The shrine, by
Bertram MacKennal, was
unveiled in 1929.

On the southern side of the
Cenotaph is the façade of the
Renaissance-style General Post
Office, considered to be the
finest building by James Bar-
net, colonial architect in 1866.

A stainless steel sculpture
of upended cubes, the Dobell
Memorial Sculpture, is a tribute
to Australian artist William
Dobell, created by Bert
Flugelman in 1979.

For hotels and restaurants in this region see pp478–81 and pp524–8

Sydney Tower ❺

The highest observation deck in the southern hemisphere, the Sydney Tower was conceived as part of the 1970s Centrepoint shopping centre, but was not completed until 1981. About one million people per year admire the stunning views. On the podium level, visitors can enjoy a multimedia journey around Australia on a virtual adventure ride called Oz Trek, and as from 2005, they will be able to venture outside the tower on a Skywalk tour.

VISITORS' CHECKLIST

100 Market St. **Map** 1 B5.
Tel (02) 9333 9222. Sydney
Explorer, all city routes.
Darling Harbour. St James,
Town Hall. City Centre.
9am–10:30pm Mon–Fri & Sun,
9:30am–11:30pm Sat. **Last entry:**
45 mins before closing. 25
Dec.
www.sydneyskytour.com.au

Observation Level
Views from Level 4 stretch north to Pittwater, Botany Bay to the south, west to the Blue Mountains, and along the harbour out to the open sea.

The **30-m (98-ft) spire** completes the total 305 m (1,000 ft) of the tower's height.

The **water tank** holds 162,000 l (35,000 gal) and acts as an enormous stabilizer on very windy days.

Skywalk

Level 4: Observation

Level 3: Coffee shop

Level 2: Buffet restaurant

Level 1: A la carte restaurant

The turret's nine levels, with room to hold almost 1,000 people at a time, include two revolving restaurants, a coffee shop and the Observation Level.

The windows comprise three layers. The outer has a gold dust coating. The frame design prevents panes falling outwards.

The 56 cables weigh seven tonnes each. If laid end to end, they would reach from New Zealand to Sydney.

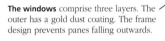

The shaft is designed to withstand wind speeds expected only once in 500 years, as well as unprecedented earthquakes.

The stairs are two separate, fireproofed emergency escape routes. Each year in April or May Sydney's fittest race up the 1,504 stairs.

Construction of Turret
The nine turret levels were erected on the roof of the base building, then hoisted up the shaft using hydraulic jacks.

Double-decker lifts can carry up to 2,000 people per hour. At full speed, a lift takes only 40 seconds to ascend the 76 floors to the Observation Level.

New Year's Eve
Every year, fireworks are set off on top of the Tower as part of the official public fireworks displays to mark the New Year.

Lands Department Building ❻

23 Bridge St. **Map** 1 B3. 🚌 *325, George St routes.* ⬜ *only 2 weeks in the year.* ♿

Designed by the colonial architect James Barnet, this three-storey Classical Revival sandstone edifice was built between 1877 and 1890. Pyrmont sandstone was used for the exterior, as it was for the GPO building.

All the decisions about the subdivision of much of rural eastern Australia were made in the offices within. Statues of explorers and legislators who "promoted settlement" fill 23 of the façade's 48 niches; the remainder are still empty. The luminaries include the explorers Hovell and Hume, Sir Thomas Mitchell, Blaxland, Lawson and Wentworth, Ludwig Leichhardt, Bass, Matthew Flinders and botanist Sir Joseph Banks.

The Lookout on Level 3 of the Museum of Sydney

Museum of Sydney ❼

Cnr Phillip & Bridge sts. **Map** 1 B3. **Tel** *(02) 9251 5988.* 🚌 *Circular Quay routes.* ⬜ *9:30am–5pm daily.* ⬜ *Good Fri, 25 Dec.* 🚫 🎫 📷 ♿ 🍴 🛍

Situated at the base of Governor Phillip Tower, the Museum of Sydney is a modern museum built on a historic site and details the history of Sydney from 1788 to the present. Its many attractions include the archaeological remains of the

Terrazzo mosaic floor in the crypt of St Mary's Cathedral

colony's first Government House, as well as exhibits that explore the evolution of Sydney over two centuries and honour the original Cadigal people.

Indigenous Peoples

A new gallery explores the culture, history, continuity and place of Sydney's original inhabitants. The collectors' chests hold items of daily use such as flint and ochre. In the square outside the complex, the *Edge of the Trees* sculptural installation symbolizes the first contact between the Aborigines and Europeans. Inscribed in the wood are signatures of First Fleeters and names of botanical species in native languages and Latin.

History of Sydney

Outside the museum, a paving pattern outlines the site of the first Government House. The original foundations, below street level, can be seen through a window. A segment of wall has now been reconstructed using the original sandstone.

The Colony display on Level 2 focuses on Sydney

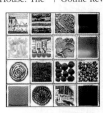

Display from Trade Exhibition on Level 2

during the critical decade of the 1840s: convict transportation ended, the town officially became a city and then suffered economic depression. On Level 3, 20th century Sydney is explored against a panorama of images.

St Mary's Cathedral ❽

St Marys Rd. **Map** 1 C5. **Tel** *(02) 9220 0400.* 🚌 *Elizabeth St routes.* ⬜ *6:30am–6pm Mon–Fri, 6:30am–7pm Sat–Sun.* ♿ *with advance notice.* 📷 *noon Sun.* **www**.sydney.catholic.org.au

Although Catholics arrived with the First Fleet, the celebration of Mass was at first prohibited as it was feared priests would provoke civil strife among the colony's Irish Catholic population. It was not until 1820 that the first Catholic priests were officially appointed and services were permitted. In 1821, Governor Macquarie laid the foundation stone for St Mary's Chapel on the first land granted to the Catholic Church in Australia.

The initial section of this Gothic Revival-style cathedral was opened in 1882 and completed in 1928, but without the twin southern spires originally proposed by the architect William Wardell. By the entrance are statues of Australia's first cardinal, Moran, and Archbishop Kelly, who laid the stone for the final stage in 1913. They were sculpted by Bertram MacKennal, also responsible for the Martin Place Cenotaph *(see p89)*. The crypt's terrazzo mosaic floor took 15 years to complete.

Hyde Park ❾

Map 1 B5. 🚌 *Elizabeth St routes.*

Hyde Park was named after its London equivalent by Governor Macquarie in 1810. The fence around the park marked the outskirts of the township. Once an exercise field for garrison troops, it later incorporated a racecourse and a cricket pitch. Though much smaller today than the original park, it is still a quiet haven in the middle of the bustling city centre, with many notable features.

The 30-m (98-ft) high Art Deco Anzac Memorial commemorates Australians who have died for their country. Opened in 1934 it now includes a military exhibition downstairs.

Sandringham Garden, filled with mauve wisteria, is a memorial to kings George V and George VI, opened by Queen Elizabeth II in 1954.

The bronze and granite Archibald Fountain commemorates the French and Australian World War I alliance. It was completed by François Sicard in 1932 and donated by JF Archibald, one of the founders of the popular *Bulletin* literary magazine.

The *Emden* Gun, on the corner of College and Liverpool Streets, commemorates a World War I naval action. HMAS *Sydney* destroyed the German raider *Emden* off the Cocos Islands on 9 November 1914, and 180 crew members were taken prisoner.

Australian Museum ❿

See pp94–5.

Great Synagogue ⓫

187 Elizabeth St, entrance at 166 Castlereagh St. **Map** 1 B5. **Tel** *(02) 9267 2477.* 🚌 *394, 396, 380, 382.* ⭕ *for services and tours only.* ♿ *by arrangement.* 🔵 *public and Jewish hols.* 📷 📹 *noon Tue & Thu.* **www**.greatsynagogue.org.au

Candelabra in the Great Synagogue

The longest established Jewish Orthodox congregation in Australia assembles in this synagogue (consecrated in 1878). Although Jews had arrived with the First Fleet, worship did not commence until the 1820s. With its carved porch columns and wrought-iron gates, the synagogue is perhaps the finest work of Thomas Rowe, architect of Sydney Hospital *(see p113)*. The interior features a stunning panelled ceiling.

Sydney Town Hall ⓬

483 George St. **Map** 4 E2. **Tel** *(02) 9265 9333.* 🚌 *George St routes.* ⭕ *8am–6pm Mon–Fri.* 🔵 *public hols.* ♿ **www**.cityofsydneyvenues.com.au

The steps of Sydney Town Hall have been a favourite meeting place since it opened in 1869. Walled burial grounds originally covered the site.

Grand organ in Centennial Hall

It is a fine example of High Victorian architecture, even though the plans of the original architect, JH Wilson, were beyond the builders' capabilities. A succession of designers was then brought in. The vestibule, an elegant salon with stained glass and a crystal chandelier, is the work of Albert Bond. The clock tower was completed by the Bradbridge brothers in 1884. From 1888–9, other architects designed Centennial Hall, with its imposing 19th-century Grand Organ with over 8,500 pipes.

Some people believe this became Sydney's finest building by accident, as each architect strove to outdo the other. Today, it makes a good venue for concerts, dances and balls.

St Andrew's Cathedral ⓭

Sydney Square, cnr George & Bathurst sts. **Map** 4 E3. **Tel** *(02) 9265 1661.* 🚌 *George St routes* ⭕ *contact the cathedral for opening times.* ♿ 📷 **www**.cathedral.sydney.anglican.asn.au

While the foundation stone for the country's oldest cathedral was laid in 1819, the building was not consecrated until 1868. The Gothic Revival design, by Edmund Blacket, was inspired by York Minster in England. Inside are memorials to Sydney pioneers, a 1539 Bible and beads made from olive seeds collected in the Holy Land.

The southern wall includes stones from London's St Paul's Cathedral, Westminster Abbey and the House of Lords.

Game in progress on the giant chessboard in Hyde Park

Australian Museum ⑩

Model head of
Tyrannosaurus rex

The Australian Museum, the nation's leading natural science museum, founded in 1827, was the first museum established and remains the premier showcase of Australian natural history. The main building, an impressive sandstone structure with a marble staircase, faces Hyde Park. Architect Mortimer Lewis was forced to resign his position when building costs began to far exceed the budget. Construction was completed in the 1860s by James Barnet. The collection provides a journey across Australia and the near Pacific, covering prehistory, biology, botany, environment and cultural heritage. Australian Aboriginal traditions are celebrated in a community access space also used for dance and other performances.

Museum Entrance
The façade features massive Corinthian square pillars or piers.

Chapman Mineral Collection

Planet of Minerals
This section features a walk-through re-creation of an underground mine with a display of gems and minerals.

Rhodochrosite   **Cuprite**

Mesolite with green apophyllite

Education Centre

Indigenous Australians
From the Dreaming to the struggle for self-determination and land rights, this exhibit tells the stories of Australia's first peoples.

Ground floor

Main entrance

MUSEUM GUIDE
Indigenous Australians and skeleton galleries are on the ground floor. Mineral and rock exhibits are in two galleries on Level 1. Birds and Insects are found on Level 2, along with Kids' Island, Biodiversity: Life Supporting Life and Search & Discover.

STAR EXHIBITS

★ Biodiversity: Life Supporting Life

★ Kids' Island

★ Search & Discover

The Skeletons Gallery, on the ground floor, provides a different perspective on natural history.

★ Search & Discover
Sydneysiders bring bugs, rocks and bones to this area for identification. The public can also access CD-Roms for research.

Level 2

Level 1

★ Kids' Island
Displays designed especially for children aged five and under are heartily enjoyed both by kids and their families. An imaginative place for play and learning.

Birds and Insects
Australia's most poisonous spider, the male of the funnel-web species, dwells exclusively in the Greater Sydney region.

★ Biodiversity: Life Supporting life
The displays of live animals, such as this Gidgee Skink, are the most popular attractions in this exhibition, which also features freshwater crocodiles and a rock pool ecosystem. The aim of the exhibition is to highlight the importance of maintaining biodiversity in nature.

KEY TO FLOORPLAN

- Plants and Minerals
- Kids' Island
- Birds and Insects Gallery
- Indigenous Australians
- The Skeletons Gallery
- Search and Discover
- Biodiversity: Life Supporting Life
- Temporary exhibition space
- Non-exhibition space

"WELCOME STRANGER" GOLD NUGGET

In 1869, the largest gold nugget ever found in Australia was discovered in Victoria. It weighed 71.06 kg (156 lb). The museum holds a cast of the original in a display examining the impact of the gold rush, when the Australian population doubled in ten years.

←— 67.5 cm (26½ in) wide —→

Street-by-Street: Darling Harbour

**Carpentaria lightship,
National Maritime Museum**

Darling Harbour was New South Wales' bicentennial gift to itself. This imaginative urban redevelopment, close to the heart of Sydney, covers a 54-ha (133-acre) site that was once a busy industrial centre and international shipping terminal catering for the developing local wool, grain, timber and coal trades. In 1984 the Darling Harbour Authority was formed to examine the area's commercial options. The resulting complex opened in 1988, complete with the Australian National Maritime Museum and Sydney Aquarium, two of the city's tourist highlights. Free outdoor entertainment, appealing to children in particular, is a regular feature, and there are many shops, waterside cafés and restaurants, as well as several major hotels overlooking the bay (www.darlingharbour.com.au).

Harbourside Complex offers restaurants and cafés with superb views over the water to the city skyline. There is also a wide range of speciality shops, selling unusual gifts and other items.

The Sydney Convention and Exhibition Centre complex presents an alternating range of international and local trade shows displaying everything from home decorating suggestions to bridal wear.

DARLING DRIVE

WESTERN DISTRIBUTOR

WESTERN DISTRIBUTOR

The Tidal Cascades sunken fountain was designed by Robert Woodward, also responsible for the El Alamein Fountain *(see p120)*. The double spiral of water and paths replicates the circular shape of the Convention Centre.

IMAX large-screen cinema

Chinese Garden of Friendship

The Chinese Garden of Friendship is a haven of peace and tranquillity in the heart of Sydney. Its landscaping, with winding pathways, waterfalls, lakes and pavilions, offers an insight into the rich culture of China.

STAR SIGHTS

★ Sydney Aquarium

★ Australian National Maritime Museum

For hotels and restaurants in this region see pp478–81 and pp524–8

Pyrmont Bridge
opened in 1902 to service the busy harbour. It is the world's oldest swingspan bridge and opens for vessels up to 14 m (46 ft) tall. The monorail track above the walkway also opens up for even taller boats.

LOCATOR MAP
See Street Finder, maps 3 & 4

Swingspan supports
for Pyrmont Bridge are sunk 10 m (33 ft) below the harbour floor.

Star City Casino

★ **Australian National Maritime Museum**
Compelling exhibits detail the nation's seafaring history before and after European settlement **15**

The *Vampire*
destroyer (1959) is the largest in the vessel fleet moored outside the museum.

King Street Wharf →

Wharf for harbour cruise departures

★ **Sydney Aquarium**
The aquatic life of Sydney Harbour, the open ocean and the Great Barrier Reef is displayed in massive tanks which can be seen from underwater walkways **14**

Cockle Bay Wharf is vibrant and colourful, and is an exciting food and entertainment precinct.

0 metres	100
0 yards	100

KEY

– – – Suggested route

Sydney Aquarium ⑭

Aquarium Pier, Darling Harbour.
Map 4 D2. **Tel** (02) 8251 7800.
🚌 Sydney Explorer. 🚢 Darling
Harbour. 🚊 Town Hall. 🚉 Darling
Park. 🕘 9am–10pm daily (last adm
9pm). ♿ 🅿 📷 🛒
www.sydneyaquarium.com.au

Sydney Aquarium contains
the country's most com-
prehensive collection of Australian aquatic species. More
than 11,500 animals from
approximately 650 species are
held in a series of re-created
marine environments.

For many visitors, the highlight is a walk "on the ocean
floor", passing through two
floating oceanaria with 145 m
(480 ft) of acrylic underwater
tunnels. These allow close
observation of sharks, stingrays and schools of many
types of fish. Fur and harbour
seals may be viewed above
and below water in a special
seal sanctuary. Other
exhibits
include a
Great Barrier
Reef display,
which docu-
ments the world's
largest coral reef
(see pp212–17), and a Touch
Pool, where visitors may touch
marine invertebrates such as
sea urchins and tubeworms.

**A tang fish in the Great
Barrier Reef display**

The Oceanarium display
enables visitors to be
surrounded by one of the
world's most extensive
collections of sharks.

Australian National Maritime Museum ⑮

See pp100–1.

King Street Wharf ⑯

Lime St, between King and Erskine
sts. **Map** 4 D1. 🚉 Darling Park. 🚢
Darling Harbour. 🏧 🍴 📷 🛒 ♿
www.ksw.com.au

Journalists from nearby
newspaper offices and city
workers flock to this
harbourside venue, which
combines an aggressively
modern glass and steel shrine
to café society with a working
wharf. Passengers arrive and
depart in style on harbour
cruises, ferries, water
taxis and rivercats.
The complex is
flush with bars
that vie for the
best views, and
restaurants includ-
ing Thai, Japanese,
Italian and Modern Australian.
Midway along the wharf is
a boutique brewery that
caters for those who revere

**Night lights at King Street Wharf,
Darling Harbour**

the best kind of cleansing
ales. This is not just a party
circuit, there are residents
here as well in low-rise
apartments set back from the
water on the city side.

Chinese Garden ⑰

Darling Harbour. **Map** 4 D3. **Tel** (02)
9281 6863. 🚌 Sydney Explorer.
🚉 Haymarket. 🚢 Darling Harbour.
🕘 9:30am–5pm daily. 🔴 25 Dec.
📷 ♿ about 60 percent.
www.chinesegarden.com.au

Known as the Garden of
Friendship, the Chinese
Garden was built in 1984. It is
a tranquil refuge from the city
streets. The garden's design
was a gift to Sydney from its
Chinese sister city of Guangdong. The Dragon Wall is in
the lower section beside the
lake. It has glazed carvings
of two dragons, one representing Guangdong province
and the other the state of
New South Wales. In the

Structuralist design of the Sydney Aquarium and Pier

For hotels and restaurants in this region see pp478–81 and pp524–8

Twin Pavilion in the Chinese Garden, decorated with carved flowers

centre of the wall, a carved pearl, symbolizing prosperity, is lifted by the waves. The lake is covered with lotus and water lilies for much of the year and a rock monster guards against evil. On the other side of the lake is the Twin Pavilion. Waratahs (New South Wales' floral symbol) and flowering apricots are carved into its woodwork in Chinese style, and are also planted at its base.

A tea house at the top of the stairs in the Tea House Courtyard serves Chinese and Western light refreshments .

Powerhouse Museum ⑱

See pp102–3.

Paddy's Markets ⑲

Cnr Thomas & Hay sts, Haymarket. **Map** 4 D4. **Tel** 1300 361 589. *Sydney Explorer.* Paddy's Market. 9am–5pm Thu–Sun & public hols. 25 Apr, 25 Dec. See also **Shopping** pp128–31. **www**.paddysmarkets.com.au

The Haymarket district, near Chinatown, is home to Paddy's Markets, Sydney's

oldest and best-known market. It has been in this area, on a number of sites, since 1869 (with only one five-year absence). The origin of the name is uncertain, but is believed to have come from either the Chinese who originally supplied much of its produce, or the Irish who were among their main customers.

Once the shopping centre for the inner-city poor, Paddy's Markets is now an integral part of the Market City Shopping Centre, which includes cut-price fashion outlet stores, an Asian food court and a cinema complex. Yet despite this transformation, the familiar clamour, smells and chaotic bargain-hunting atmosphere of the original marketplace remain. Every weekend the market is filled with up to 800 stalls selling everything from fresh produce to electrical products, homewares, leather goods, and pets, including rabbits, puppies and chickens.

Chinese food products in Chinatown

Chinatown ⑳

Dixon St Plaza, Sydney. **Map** 4 D4. Haymarket.

Originally concentrated around Dixon and Hay streets, Chinatown is now expanding to fill Sydney's Haymarket area, stretching as far west as Harris Street, south to Broadway and east to Castlereagh Street. It is close to the Sydney Entertainment Centre, where some of the world's best-known rock and pop stars perform in concert and many indoor sporting events are held *(see p142)*.

For years, Chinatown was little more than a run-down district at the edge of the city's produce markets, where many Chinese immigrants worked at traditional businesses. Today, Dixon Street, its main thoroughfare, has been spruced up to equal many of the other popular Chinatowns around the world. There are authentic-looking street lanterns and archways, and a new wave of Asian immigrants fills the now upmarket restaurants.

Chinatown is a distinctive area and now home to a new wave of Sydney's Asian population. There are excellent greengrocers, traditional herbalists and butchers' shops with wind-dried ducks hanging in their windows. Asian jewellers, clothes shops and confectioners fill the arcades. There are also two Chinese-language cinema complexes, screening the increasingly popular new Chinese films.

Traditional archway entrance to Chinatown in Dixon Street

Australian National Maritime Museum ⑮

1602 Willem Blaeu Celestial Globe

Bounded as it is by the sea, Australia's history is inextricably linked to maritime traditions. The museum displays material in a broad range of permanent and temporary thematic exhibits, many with interactive elements. As well as artifacts relating to the enduring Aboriginal maritime cultures, the exhibits survey the history of European exploratory voyages in the Pacific, the arrival of convict ships, successive waves of migration, water sports and recreation, and naval life. Historic vessels on show at the wharf include a flimsy Vietnamese refugee boat, sailing, fishing and pearling boats, a navy patrol boat and a World War II commando raider.

Museum Façade
The billowing steel roof design by Philip Cox suggests both the surging sea and the sails of a ship.

Passengers
The model of the Orcades *reflects the grace of 1950s liners. This display also charts harrowing sea voyages made by migrants and refugees.*

Merana Eora Nora – First People traces the seafaring traditions of Aboriginal peoples and Torres Strait Islanders.

The Tasman Light was used in a Tasmanian lighthouse.

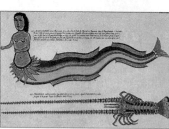

★ Navigators
This 1754 engraving of an East Indian sea creature is a European vision of the uncharted, exotic "great south".

The *Sirius* anchor is from a 1790 wreck off Norfolk Island.

Main entrance (sea level)

The Navy exhibit examines naval life in war and peace, as well as the history of colonial navies.

Linked by the Sea honours enduring links between the US and Australia. American traders stopped off in Australia on their way to China.

STAR EXHIBITS

★ Navigators and Merana Eora Nora

★ Watermarks

★ Vampire

KEY TO FLOORPLAN

- ☐ Navigators and Merana Eora Nora
- ☐ Passengers
- ☐ Commerce
- ☐ Watermarks
- ☐ Navy
- ☐ Linked by the Sea: USA Gallery
- ☐ Temporary exhibitions
- ☐ Non-exhibition space

Commerce
This 1903 Painters' and Dockers' Union banner was carried by waterfront workers in marches. It shows the Niagara *entering the dry dock at Cockatoo Island.*

VISITORS' CHECKLIST

Darling Harbour. **Map** 3 C2. *Tel* 9298 3777. 443, Sydney Explorer. Town Hall. Harbourside. Pyrmont Bay Wharf. 9:30am–5pm daily. 25 Dec. (special exhibitions, submarine and destroyer only). www.anmm.gov.au

★ Watermarks
This 1960s poster for Bondi beach is part of the museum's Watermarks – adventure, sport and play *exhibition. The displays, including fully-rigged boats and profiles of world champion scullers and swimmers, celebrate Australia's love affair with the water.*

A replica of Captain Cook's *Endeavour* moors at this wharf when in Sydney.

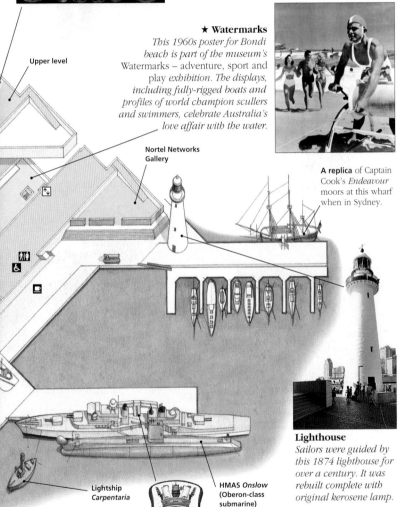

Upper level

Nortel Networks Gallery

Lighthouse
Sailors were guided by this 1874 lighthouse for over a century. It was rebuilt complete with original kerosene lamp.

Lightship *Carpentaria*

HMAS *Onslow* (Oberon-class submarine)

★ Vampire
The museum's largest vessel is the 1959 Royal Australian Navy destroyer, whose insignia is shown here. Tours of "The Bat" are accompanied by simulated battle action sounds.

MUSEUM GUIDE
The Leisure, Navy and Linked by the Sea: USA Gallery exhibits are located on the main entrance level (sea level). The First Australians, Discovery, Passengers and Commerce sections are found on the first level. There is access to the fleet from both levels.

Powerhouse Museum ⑱

This former power station, completed in 1902 to provide power for Sydney's tramway system, was redesigned to cater for the needs of a modern, hands-on museum. Revamped, the Powerhouse opened in 1988. The early collection was held in the Garden Palace hosting the 1879 international exhibition of invention and industry from around the world. Few exhibits survived the devastating 1882 fire, and today's huge and ever-expanding holdings were gathered after this disaster. The buildings' monumental scale provides an ideal context for the epic sweep of ideas encompassed within: everything from the realm of space and technology to the decorative and domestic arts. The museum emphasizes Australian innovations and achievements celebrating both the extraordinary and the everyday.

Silver cricket trophy

Cyberworlds: Computers and Connections
This display explores the past, present and future of computers. Pictured here is a Japanese tin toy robot.

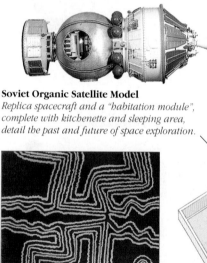

Soviet Organic Satellite Model
Replica spacecraft and a "habitation module", complete with kitchenette and sleeping area, detail the past and future of space exploration.

Bayagul: Contemporary Indigenous Australian Communication
This handtufted rug, designed by Jimmy Pike, is displayed in an exhibit showcasing Aboriginal and Torres Strait Island cultures.

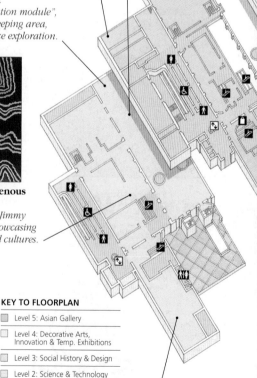

Level 3

Level 2

MUSEUM GUIDE

The museum is two buildings: the former powerhouse and the Neville Wran building. There are over 20 exhibitions on four levels, descending from Level 5. The shop, entrance and main exhibits are on Level 4. Level 3 has thematic exhibits and a Design Gallery. Level 2 has displays on space, transport and computers.

KEY TO FLOORPLAN

☐	Level 5: Asian Gallery
☐	Level 4: Decorative Arts, Innovation & Temp. Exhibitions
☐	Level 3: Social History & Design
☐	Level 2: Science & Technology
☐	Non-exhibition space

For hotels and restaurants in this region see pp478–81 and pp524–8

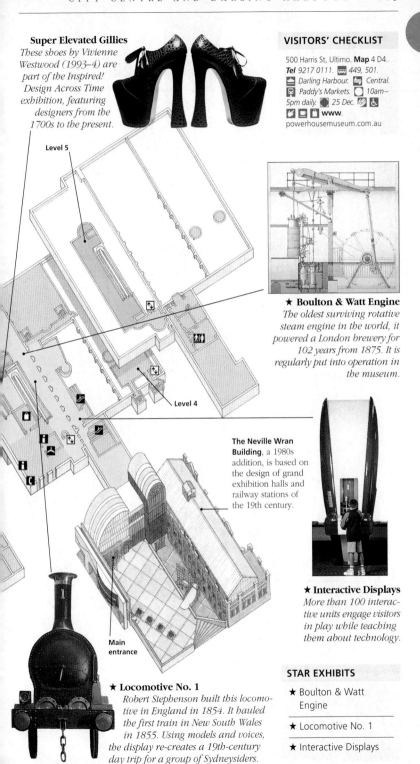

Super Elevated Gillies
These shoes by Vivienne Westwood (1993–4) are part of the Inspired! Design Across Time exhibition, featuring designers from the 1700s to the present.

Level 5

Level 4

★ Boulton & Watt Engine
The oldest surviving rotative steam engine in the world, it powered a London brewery for 102 years from 1875. It is regularly put into operation in the museum.

The Neville Wran Building, a 1980s addition, is based on the design of grand exhibition halls and railway stations of the 19th century.

★ Interactive Displays
More than 100 interactive units engage visitors in play while teaching them about technology.

Main entrance

★ Locomotive No. 1
Robert Stephenson built this locomotive in England in 1854. It hauled the first train in New South Wales in 1855. Using models and voices, the display re-creates a 19th-century day trip for a group of Sydneysiders.

STAR EXHIBITS

★ Boulton & Watt Engine

★ Locomotive No. 1

★ Interactive Displays

BOTANIC GARDENS AND THE DOMAIN

This tranquil part of Sydney can seem a world away from the bustle of the city centre. It is rich in the remnants of Sydney's convict and colonial past: the site of the first farm and the boulevard-like Macquarie Street where the barracks, hospital, church and mint – bastions of civic power – are among the oldest surviving public buildings in Australia. This street continues to assert its dominance today as the location of the state government of New South Wales.

The Domain, an open, grassy space, was originally set aside by the colony's first governor for his private use. Today it is filled with joggers and touch footballers sidestepping picnickers and sunbathers. In January, during the Festival of Sydney, it hosts outdoor concerts. The Royal Botanic Gardens has for almost 200 years collected, grown, researched and conserved plants from Australia and the rest of the world. The result is a parkland of great diversity and beauty.

Wooden angel, St James Church

SIGHTS AT A GLANCE

Historic Streets and Buildings
Conservatorium of Music **2**
Hyde Park Barracks Museum **11**
The Mint **10**
Parliament House **8**
State Library of New South Wales **7**
Sydney Hospital **9**

Museums and Galleries
Art Gallery of New South Wales pp110–13 **5**

Churches
St James Church **12**

Islands
Fort Denison **4**

Monuments
Mrs Macquaries Chair **3**

Parks and Gardens
The Domain **6**
Royal Botanic Gardens pp106–7 **1**

GETTING THERE
Visit on foot, if possible. St James' and Martin Place train stations are close to most of the sights. The 311 bus from Circular Quay runs near the Art Gallery of NSW. The Sydney Explorer also stops at several sights.

| 0 metres | 500 |
| 0 yards | 500 |

KEY

Royal Botanic Gardens pp106–7

CityRail station

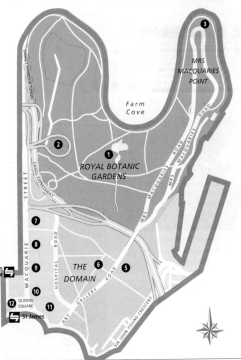

◁ Succulents and cacti from the Succulent Garden in the Royal Botanic Gardens

Royal Botanic Gardens ❶

Statue in the Botanic Gardens

The Royal Botanic Gardens, a 30-ha (75-acre) oasis in the heart of the city, occupy a superb position, wrapped around Farm Cove at the harbour's edge. Established in 1816 as a series of pathways through shrubbery, they are the oldest scientific institution in the country and house an outstanding collection of plants from Australia and overseas. A living museum, the gardens are also the site of the first farm in the fledgling colony. Fountains, statues and monuments are today scattered throughout. The diversity is amazing, there are thousands of trees, stands of bamboo, a cactus garden, a rainforest walk, one of the world's finest collections of palms, a herb garden and a garden containing rare and threatened plant species.

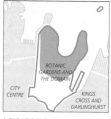

LOCATOR MAP
See Street Finder, maps 1 & 2

Government House (1897)

★ **Palm Grove**
Begun in 1862, this cool summer haven is one of the world's finest outdoor collections of palms. There are about 180 species in the grove.

Conservatorium of Music *(see p108)*

★ **Herb Garden**
Herbs from around the world used for a wide variety of purposes – culinary, medicinal and aromatic – are on display here. A sensory fountain and a sundial modelled on the celestial sphere are also features.

★ **Sydney Tropical Centre**
Two glasshouses contain tropical ecosystems in miniature. Native vegetation is displayed in the Pyramid, while the Arc holds plants not found locally, commonly known as exotics.

| 0 metres | | 200 |
| 0 yards | | 200 |

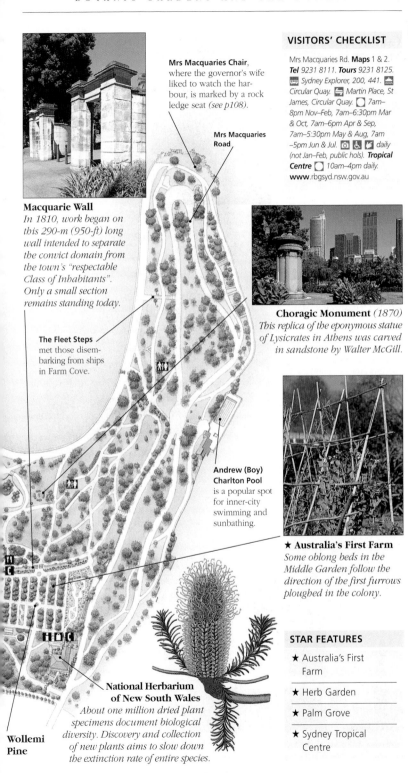

VISITORS' CHECKLIST

Mrs Macquaries Rd. **Maps** 1 & 2.
Tel 9231 8111. **Tours** 9231 8125.
Sydney Explorer, 200, 441.
Circular Quay. Martin Place, St
James, Circular Quay. 7am–
8pm Nov–Feb, 7am–6:30pm Mar
& Oct, 7am–6pm Apr & Sep,
7am–5:30pm May & Aug, 7am
–5pm Jun & Jul. daily
(not Jan–Feb, public hols). **Tropical
Centre** 10am–4pm daily.
www.rbgsyd.nsw.gov.au

Mrs Macquaries Chair,
where the governor's wife
liked to watch the har-
bour, is marked by a rock
ledge seat *(see p108)*.

**Mrs Macquaries
Road**

Macquarie Wall
*In 1810, work began on
this 290-m (950-ft) long
wall intended to separate
the convict domain from
the town's "respectable
Class of Inhabitants".
Only a small section
remains standing today.*

The Fleet Steps
met those disem-
barking from ships
in Farm Cove.

Choragic Monument (1870)
*This replica of the eponymous statue
of Lysicrates in Athens was carved
in sandstone by Walter McGill.*

**Andrew (Boy)
Charlton Pool**
is a popular spot
for inner-city
swimming and
sunbathing.

★ Australia's First Farm
*Some oblong beds in the
Middle Garden follow the
direction of the first furrows
ploughed in the colony.*

**National Herbarium
of New South Wales**
*About one million dried plant
specimens document biological
diversity. Discovery and collection
of new plants aims to slow down
the extinction rate of entire species.*

**Wollemi
Pine**

STAR FEATURES

★ Australia's First
Farm

★ Herb Garden

★ Palm Grove

★ Sydney Tropical
Centre

Conservatorium of Music ❷

Macquarie St. **Map** 1 C3. **Tel** (02) 935
1 1222. 🚌 Sydney Explorer, Circular
Quay routes. ⏰ 9am–5pm Mon–Fri,
9am–4pm Sat, public areas only.
Phone for details of concerts. 🚹 ⬤
public holidays, Easter Sat, 24 Dec–2
Jan. 🎫 phone 9351-1296 for details.

When it was finished in 1821,
this striking castellated
Colonial Gothic building was
meant to be the stables and
servants' quarters for
Government House, but
construction of the latter was
delayed for almost 25 years.
That stables should be built
in so grand a style, and at
such great cost, brought forth
cries of outrage and led to
bitter arguments between the
architect, Francis Greenway
(see p169), and Governor
Macquarie – and a decree
that all future building plans
be submitted to London.

Between 1908 and 1915
"Greenway's folly" underwent
a dramatic transformation. A
concert hall, roofed in grey
slate, was built on the central
courtyard and the building in
its entirety was converted for
the use of the new Sydney
Conservatorium of Music.

Recently added facilities
include a café, which holds
lunchtime concerts during the
school term and an upper level
with great harbour views. "The
Con" continues to be a training ground for future musicians
and a great place to visit.

**Resting on the carved stone seat of
Mrs Macquaries Chair**

Mrs Macquaries Chair ❸

Mrs Macquaries Rd. **Map** 2 E2.
🚌 Sydney Explorer, 111. 🚹 🎫

The Scenic Mrs Macquaries
Road winds alongside much
of what is now the city's
Royal Botanic Gardens,
stretching from
Farm Cove to
Woolloomooloo
Bay and back
again. The road
was built in
1816 at the
instigation of
Elizabeth
Macquarie, wife
of the Governor. In the same
year, a stone bench, inscribed
with details of the new road
and its commissioner, was
carved into the rock at the
point where Mrs Macquarie
would often stop to rest and

admire the view on her daily
stroll. Although today the
outlook is much changed, it is
just as arresting, taking in the
broad sweep of the harbour
with all its landmarks.

Rounding the cove to the
west leads to Mrs Macquaries
Point. These lawns are a popular picnic spot with Sydneysiders, particularly at sunset.

Fort Denison ❹

Sydney Harbour. **Map** 2 E1. **Tel** (02)
9247 5033. ⛴ Circular Quay.
⏰ Daily tours: for prices and times
contact 9247 5033 or email
cadman.cottage@environment.nsw.
gov.au. ⬤ 25 Dec. 🎫 🎫

First named Rock Island, this
prominent, rocky outcrop in
Sydney Harbour was also
dubbed "Pinchgut". This was
probably because of the meagre rations given to convicts
who were confined there as
punishment. It had a grim
history of incar-
ceration in the
early years of
the colony.

In 1796, the
convicted mur-
derer Francis
Morgan was
hanged on the
island in chains.

Fort Denison in 1907

His body was left to rot on the
gallows for three years as a
warning to the other convicts.

Between 1855 and 1857, the
Martello tower (the only one
in Australia), gun battery and
barracks that now occupy the
island were built as part of
Sydney's defences. The site
was renamed after the governor of the time. The gun, still
fired at 1pm each day, helped
mariners to set their ships'
chronometers accurately.

Today the island is the
perfect setting for watching
the many harbour activities,
such as the New Year
fireworks displays (see p41).
To explore Fort Denison,
book one of the tours from
Cadman's Cottage.

Art Gallery of New South Wales ❺

See pp110–11.

Conservatorium of Music at the edge of the Royal Botanic Gardens

The Domain

Art Gallery Rd. **Map** 1 C4.
Sydney Explorer, 111, 411.

The many people who swarm
to the January concerts and
other Festival of Sydney
events in The Domain are
part of a long-standing tradition. They come equipped
with picnic baskets and
blankets to enjoy the ongoing
entertainment.

Once the governor's private
park, this extensive space is
now public and has long been
a rallying point for crowds of
Sydneysiders whenever emo-
tive issues of public importance have arisen. These have
included the attempt in 1916
to introduce military conscription and the sudden dismissal
of the elected federal government by the then governor-
general in 1975.

From the 1890s, part of The
Domain was also used as the
Sydney version of "Speakers'
Corner". Today, you are more
likely to see joggers or office
workers playing touch football in their lunch hours, or
simply enjoying the shade.

Harbour view from The Domain

State Library of New South Wales

Macquarie St. **Map** 4 F1. **Tel** (02)
9273 1414. *Sydney Explorer,
Elizabeth St routes.* 9am–9pm
Mon–Fri, 11am–5pm Sat & Sun.
*most public hols, Mitchell Library
closed Sun.*
www.sl.nsw.gov.au

The state library is housed in
two separate buildings
connected by a passageway
and a glass bridge. The older
building, the Mitchell Library

Mosaic replica of the Tasman Map, State Library of New South Wales

wing (1906), is a majestic
sandstone edifice facing the
Royal Botanic Gardens *(see
pp106–7)*. Huge stone
columns supporting a vaulted
ceiling frame the impressive
vestibule. On the vestibule
floor is a mosaic replica of an
old map illustrating the two
voyages made to Australia by
Dutch navigator Abel Tasman
in the 1640s *(see p49)*. The
two ships of the first voyage
are shown off the south coast,
the two from the second
voyage are seen to the northwest. The original Tasman
Map is held in the Mitchell
Library as part of its collection of historic Australian
paintings, books, documents
and pictorial records.

The Mitchell wing's vast
reading room, with its huge
skylight and oak panelling,
is just beyond the main vestibule. The newest section is
an attractive contemporary
structure that faces Macquarie
Street *(see pp114–15)*. This
area now houses the
State Reference Library.
Beyond the Mitchell
wing is the Dixson
Gallery, housing
cultural and histor-
ical exhibitions which
change regularly.

Outside the library,
facing Macquarie
Street, is a statue of
the explorer Matthew
Flinders, who first
ventured into central
Australia *(see pp52–3)*. On the
windowsill behind him
is a statue of his travelling
companion, his cat, Trim.

**Malby's
celestial globe,
Parliament House**

Parliament House

Macquarie St. **Map** 4 F1. **Tel** (02) 9230
2111. *Sydney Explorer, Elizabeth St
routes.* *Martin Place.*
9:30am–4:30pm Mon–Fri. *public
hols.* (02) 9230 3444 *to book.*
www.parliament.nsw.gov.au

The central section of this
building, which houses the
State Parliament, is part of the
original Sydney Hospital built
from 1811–16 *(see p113)*. It
has been a seat of government since 1829 when the
newly appointed Legislative
Council first held meetings
here. The building was
extended twice during the
19th century and again during
the 1970s and 1980s. The
current building contains the
chambers for both houses of
state parliament, as well as
parliamentary offices.

Parliamentary memorabilia
is on view in the Jubilee
Room, as are displays
showing Parliament
House's development
and the legislative
history of the state.

The corrugated
iron building with
a cast-iron façade
tacked on at the
southern end was
a prefabricated kit
from England. In
1856, this dismantled
kit became the cham-
ber for the new Legislative
Council. Its packing cases were
used to line the chamber; the
rough timber can still be seen.

Art Gallery of New South Wales ❺

Established in 1874, the art gallery has occupied its present imposing building since 1897. Designed by the Colonial Architect WL Vernon, the gallery doubled in size following 1988 building extensions. Two equestrian bronzes – *The Offerings of Peace* and *The Offerings of War* – greet the visitor on entry. The gallery itself houses some of the finest works of art in Australia. It has sections devoted to Australian, Asian, European, photographic and contemporary and photographic works, along with a strong collection of prints and drawings. The Yiribana Gallery, the largest in the world to exclusively exhibit Aboriginal and Torres Strait Islander art and culture, was opened in 1994.

Lower Level 3

Cycladic figure (c.2,500 BC)

Sofala *(1947)*
Russell Drysdale's visions of Australia show "ghost" towns laid waste by devastating natural forces such as drought.

Sunbaker *(1937)*
Max Dupain's iconic, almost abstract, Australian photograph of hedonism and sun worship uses clean lines, strong light, and geometric form. The image's power lies in its simplicity.

Madonna and Child with Infant St John the Baptist
This oil on wood (c.1541) is the work of Siena Mannerist artist Domenico Beccafumi.

STAR EXHIBITS

★ The Golden Fleece – Shearing at Newstead by Tom Roberts

★ Pukumani Grave Posts

GALLERY GUIDE

There are five levels. The Upper Level has the Rudy Komon Gallery for temporary exhibitions, which are also held on Lower Level 1. The Ground Level has European and Australian works, 20th-century European prints are on Lower Level 2 and the Yiribana Aboriginal Gallery is on Lower Level 3.

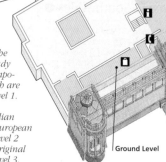

Ground Level

For hotels and restaurants in this region see pp478–81 and pp524–8

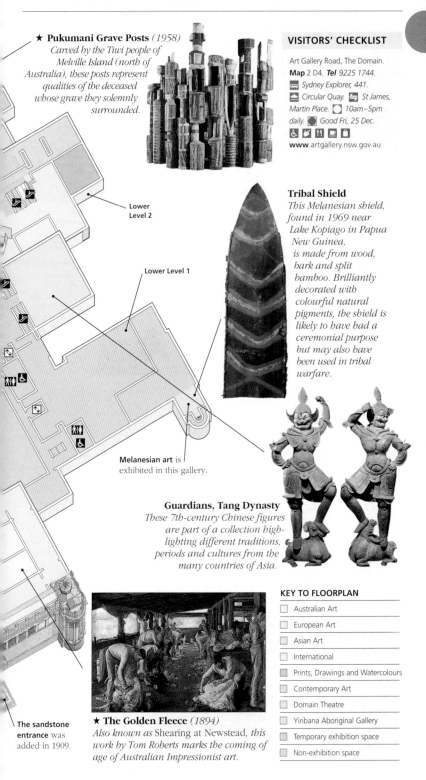

★ **Pukumani Grave Posts** *(1958)*
*Carved by the Tiwi people of
Melville Island (north of
Australia), these posts represent
qualities of the deceased
whose grave they solemnly
surrounded.*

VISITORS' CHECKLIST

Art Gallery Road, The Domain.
Map 2 D4. **Tel** 9225 1744.
Sydney Explorer, 441.
Circular Quay. St James,
Martin Place. 10am–5pm
daily. Good Fri, 25 Dec.
www.artgallery.nsw.gov.au

Lower
Level 2

Lower Level 1

Tribal Shield
*This Melanesian shield,
found in 1969 near
Lake Kopiago in Papua
New Guinea,
is made from wood,
bark and split
bamboo. Brilliantly
decorated with
colourful natural
pigments, the shield is
likely to have had a
ceremonial purpose
but may also have
been used in tribal
warfare.*

Melanesian art is
exhibited in this gallery.

Guardians, Tang Dynasty
*These 7th-century Chinese figures
are part of a collection highlighting different traditions,
periods and cultures from the
many countries of Asia.*

**The sandstone
entrance** was
added in 1909.

★ **The Golden Fleece** *(1894)*
Also known as Shearing at Newstead, *this
work by Tom Roberts marks the coming of
age of Australian Impressionist art.*

KEY TO FLOORPLAN

☐ Australian Art
☐ European Art
☐ Asian Art
☐ International
☐ Prints, Drawings and Watercolours
☐ Contemporary Art
☐ Domain Theatre
☐ Yiribana Aboriginal Gallery
☐ Temporary exhibition space
☐ Non-exhibition space

Exploring the Art Gallery's Collection

Although local works had been collected since 1875, the gallery did not seriously begin seeking Australian and non-British art until the 1920s, and not until the 1940s did it begin acquiring Aboriginal and Torres Strait Islander paintings. These contrasting collections are now its greatest strength. The gallery also stages major temporary exhibitions regularly, with the annual Archibald, Wynne and Sulman prizes being among the most controversial and highly entertaining.

Study for Self Portrait, a Francis Bacon painting from 1976

Grace Cossington Smith's 1955 *Interior with Wardrobe Mirror*

AUSTRALIAN ART

Among the most important colonial works is John Glover's *Natives on the Ouse River, Van Diemen's Land* (1838), an image of doomed Tasmanian Aborigines. The old wing also holds paintings from the Heidelberg school of Australian Impressionism *(see p34)*. Tom Roberts' *The Golden Fleece – Shearing at Newstead* (1894) hangs alongside fine works by Charles Conder, Frederick McCubbin and Arthur Streeton.

Australia was slow to take up Modernism. *Western Australian Gum Blossom* (1928)

is Margaret Preston at her most assertive during the 1920s. Sidney Nolan's works range from *Boy in Township* (1943) to *Burke* (c.1962), exploiting myths of early Australian history. There are also fine holdings of William Dobell, Russell Drysdale, Arthur Boyd, Grace Cossington Smith and Brett Whiteley *(see p34)*.

The Yiribana Aboriginal Gallery exhibits works by Aboriginal and Torres Strait Islanders. These contemporary artists apply traditional styles to new media forms while retaining "Aboriginality".

Significant early purchases were natural pigment paintings on bark and card, often containing a figurative motif of everyday life. The bark painting *Three Mimis Dancing* (1964) by Samuel Wagbara examines themes of ancestral spirits and the creation cycles. *Pukumani Grave Posts Melville Island* (1958) is a ceremonial work dealing with death. Emily Kame Kngwarreye honours the land from which she comes with very intricate dot paintings, created using new tools and technology.

Henry Moore's *Reclining* *Figure: Angles* (1980)

EUROPEAN ART

The European collection ranges from medieval to modern. British art from the 19th and 20th centuries forms a large component, including artists such as Francis Bacon. Among the Old Masters are significant Italian works. Neo-Classical works are also held. *Chaucer at the Court of Edward III* (1845–51) by Ford Madox Brown is a fine Pre-Raphaelite work.

The Impressionists and Post-Impressionists are represented by Pissarro and Monet. *Nude in a Rocking Chair* (1956) by Picasso, was bought in 1981. Among the sculptures is Henry Moore's *Reclining Figure: Angles* (1980).

PHOTOGRAPHY

Australian photography from 1975 to the present day is represented in all its various forms. Recently, however, the emphasis has been on building up a body of 19th-century Australian work. Nearly 3,000 prints constitute this collection with pieces by Charles Kerry, Charles Bayliss and Harold Cazneaux, a major figure of early 20th-century Pictorialism.

Such international photographers as Muybridge, Robert Mapplethorpe and Man Ray are also represented here.

Brett Whiteley's vivid *The Balcony (2)* from 1975

ASIAN ART

This collection is one of the finest in Australia. Chinese art is represented from the pre-Shang dynasty (c.1600 –1027 BC) to the 20th century. The Ming porcelains, earthenware funerary pieces (*mingqi*) and the sculptures deserve close attention.

The Japanese collection has fine examples by major artists of the Edo period (1615–1867). The Southeast Asian and Indian art consists of lacquer, ceramics and sculptures.

PRINTS AND DRAWINGS

This collection represents the European tradition from the High Renaissance to the 19th and 20th centuries, with work by Rembrandt, Constable, William Blake, Edvard Munch and Egon Schiele. A strong bias towards Sydney artists of the past 100 years has resulted in an exceptional gathering of work by Thea Proctor, Norman and Lionel Lindsay and Lloyd Rees.

Egon Schiele's *Poster for the Vienna Secession* (1918)

CONTEMPORARY ART

The Contemporary Art collection highlights the themes that have been central to art practice since the 1970s. Works by Australian artists such as Imants Tillers, Ken Unsworth and Susan Norrie are on display alongside pieces by international artists such as Cindy Sherman, Yves Klein and Philip Guston.

Il Porcellino, **the bronze boar in front of Sydney Hospital**

Sydney Hospital ⑨

Macquarie St. **Map** 1 C4. *Tel* (02) 9382 7111. 🚌 *Sydney Explorer, Elizabeth St routes.* ◯ *daily.* 🎫 *for tours.* ♿ 🎥 *book in advance.*

This imposing collection of Victorian sandstone buildings stands on the site of what was once the central section of the original convict-built Sydney Hospital. It was known locally as the Rum Hospital because the builders were paid by being allowed to import rum for resale. Both the north and south wings of the Rum Hospital survive as Parliament House (*see p109*) and the Sydney Mint. The central wing was demolished in 1879 and the new hospital, which is still operational, was completed in 1894.

The Classical Revival building boasts a Baroque staircase and elegant stained-glass windows in its central hall. Florence Nightingale approved the design of the 1867 nurses' wing. In the inner courtyard, there is a brightly coloured Art Deco fountain (1907), somewhat out of place among the surrounding heavy stonework.

At the front of the hospital sits a bronze boar called *Il Porcellino*. It is a replica of a 17th-century fountain in Florence's Mercato Nuovo. Donated in 1968 by an Italian woman whose relatives had worked at the hospital, the statue is an enduring symbol of the friendship between Italy and Australia. Like his Florentine counterpart, *Il Porcellino* is supposed to bring good luck to all those who rub his snout. Coins tossed in the pool at his feet for luck and fortune are collected for the hospital.

Stained glass at Sydney Hospital

The Mint ⑩

10 Macquarie St. **Map** 1 C5. *Tel* (02) 8239 2288. 🚌 *Sydney Explorer, Elizabeth St routes.* ◯ *9am–5pm Mon–Fri.* ● *Good Fri, 25 Dec.* 📷 ♿ *ground floor only.* 💻 **www**.hht.net.au

The gold rushes of the mid-19th century transformed colonial Australia (*see pp54–5*). The Sydney Mint opened in 1854 in the south wing of the Rum Hospital in order to turn recently discovered gold into bullion and currency. This was the first branch of the Royal Mint to be established outside London, but it was closed in 1927 as it was no longer competitive with the mints in Melbourne (*see p387*) and Perth (*see p305*). The Georgian building then went into decline after it was converted into government offices. The Mint's artefacts are now in the Powerhouse Museum (*see pp102–3*). The head office of the Historic Houses Trust of NSW is now located here and you can look through the front part of the building.

Hyde Park Barracks Museum  ⑪

Queens Square, Macquarie St. **Map** 1 C5. **Tel** (02) 8239 2311. 🚉 St James, Martin Place. ⬜ 9:30am–5pm daily. 🔴 Good Fri, 25 Dec. 🈺 ♿ ground floor only. 🎫 on request. 📷 www.hht.net.au

Described by Governor Macquarie as "spacious" and "well-aired", the beautifully proportioned barracks are the work of Francis Greenway and are considered his masterpiece *(see p169)*. They were completed in 1819 by convict labour and designed to house 600 convicts. Until that time convicts had been forced to find their own lodgings after their day's work. Subsequently, the building

Replica convict hammocks on the third floor of Hyde Park Barracks

then housed, in turn, young Irish orphans and single female immigrants, before it later became courts and legal offices. Refurbished in 1990,

the barracks reopened as a museum on the history of the site and its occupants. The displays include a room reconstructed as convict quarters of the 1820s, as well as pictures, models and artifacts. Many of the objects recovered during archaeological digs at the site and now on display survived because they had been dragged away by rats to their nests; today the rodents are acknowledged as valuable agents of preservation.

The Greenway Gallery on the first floor holds varied exhibitions on history and culture. Elsewhere, the Barracks Café, which incorporates the original cell area, offers views of the courtyard, today cool and attractive but in the past the scene of brutal convict floggings.

MACQUARIE STREET

Described in the 1860s as one of the gloomiest streets in Sydney, this could now claim to be the most elegant. Open to the harbour breezes and the greenery of The Domain, a stroll down this tree-lined street is a pleasant way to view the architectural heritage of Sydney.

This wing *of the library was built in 1988 and connected to the old section by a glass walkway.*

The Mitchell Library wing's portico (1906) has Ionic columns.

Parliament House was once the convict-built Rum Hospital's northern wing.

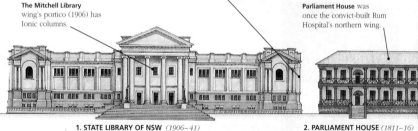

1. STATE LIBRARY OF NSW *(1906–41)*

2. PARLIAMENT HOUSE *(1811–16)*

The roof *of The Mint has now been completely restored to replicate the original wooden shingles in casuarina (she-oak).*

The Mint, *like its twin, Parliament House, has an unusual double-colonnaded, two-storeyed veranda.*

Hyde Park Barracks Café

4. THE MINT *(1816)*

St James Church ⑫

179 King St. **Map** 1 B5. **Tel** (02) 9232 3022. 🚇 St James, Martin Place. ⏰ 8am–5pm Mon–Fri, 8am–4pm Sat, 7:30am–4pm Sun. ♿ **Concerts** 1:15pm Wed (free).

This fine Georgian building, constructed by convict labour, was originally designed as a courthouse in 1819. The architect, Francis Greenway, had to build a church instead when plans to construct a cathedral on George Street were abandoned. Greenway designed a simple yet elegant church. Consecrated in 1824, it is the city's oldest church. Many additions were carried out, including designs by John Verge in which the pulpit faced the high-rent pews, while convicts and the military sat directly behind the preacher where the service was inaudible. A Children's Chapel was created in 1929. Prominent members of early 19th-century society, many of whom died violently, are honoured with marble tablets. These tell the stories of luckless explorers, the governor's wife dashed to her death from her carriage, and shipwreck victims.

Detail from the Children's Chapel mural in the St James Church crypt

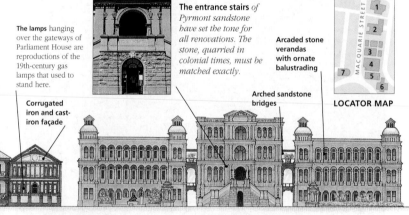

The lamps hanging over the gateways of Parliament House are reproductions of the 19th-century gas lamps that used to stand here.

Corrugated iron and cast-iron façade

The entrance stairs of Pyrmont sandstone have set the tone for all renovations. The stone, quarried in colonial times, must be matched exactly.

Arched sandstone bridges

Arcaded stone verandas with ornate balustrading

LOCATOR MAP

3. SYDNEY HOSPITAL (1868–94)

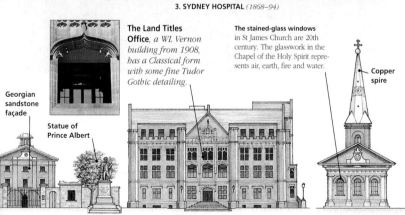

The Land Titles Office, a WL Vernon building from 1908, has a Classical form with some fine Tudor Gothic detailing.

The stained-glass windows in St James Church are 20th century. The glasswork in the Chapel of the Holy Spirit represents air, earth, fire and water.

Copper spire

Georgian sandstone façade

Statue of Prince Albert

HYDE PARK BARRACKS MUSEUM (1817–19)   **6. LAND TITLES OFFICE** (1908–13)   **7. ST JAMES** (1820)

The front entrance to a lovingly restored Victorian terrace house in Paddington

SIGHTS AT A GLANCE

Historic Streets and Buildings
Darlinghurst Court House **7**
Elizabeth Bay House **3**
Five Ways **8**
Fox Studios Entertainment Quarter **16**
Juniper Hall **10**
Old Gaol, Darlinghurst **6**
Paddington Street **14**

Paddington Town Hall **11**
Paddington Village **9**
Victoria Barracks **12**
Victoria Street **2**

Parks and Gardens
Beare Park **4**
Centennial Park **15**

Museums and Galleries
Sydney Jewish Museum **5**

Monuments
El Alamein Fountain **1**

Markets
Paddington Markets **13**

KINGS CROSS, DARLINGHURST AND PADDINGTON

Sydney's Kings Cross and Darlinghurst districts are still remembered for their 1920s gangland associations. However, both areas are now cosmopolitan and densely populated parts of the city. Kings Cross has a thriving café society, in spite of the nearby red light district. Darlinghurst comes into its own every March, during the

Façade detail, Del Rio (see p119)

flamboyant Gay and Lesbian Mardi Gras parade. The Victorian terraces of Paddington are still admired for their wrought-iron "lace" verandas. Paddington is also famed for its fine restaurants, galleries and antiques shops. On Saturdays, people flock to Paddington Markets, spilling out into the pubs and cafés of the surrounding area.

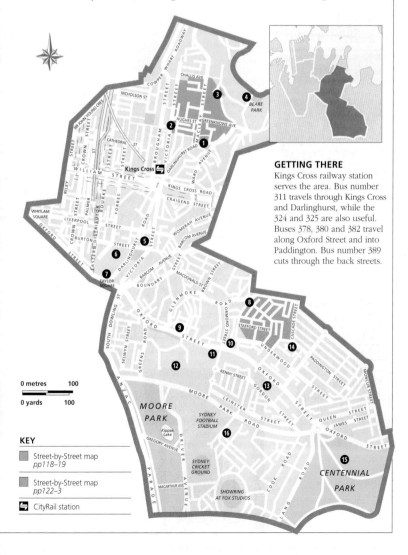

GETTING THERE

Kings Cross railway station serves the area. Bus number 311 travels through Kings Cross and Darlinghurst, while the 324 and 325 are also useful. Buses 378, 380 and 382 travel along Oxford Street and into Paddington. Bus number 389 cuts through the back streets.

KEY

Street-by-Street map pp118–19

Street-by-Street map pp122–3

CityRail station

0 metres 100
0 yards 100

Street-by-Street: Potts Point

Beare Park fountain detail

The substantial Victorian houses filling the streets of this old suburb are excel-lent examples of the 19th-century concern with architectural harmony. New building projects were designed to enhance rather than contradict the surrounding buildings and general streetscape. Monumental structures and fine details of moulded stuccoed parapets, cornices and friezes, even the spandrels in herringbone pattern, are all integral parts of a grand suburban plan. (This plan included an 1831 order that all houses cost at least £1,000.) Cool, dark verandas extend the street's green canopy of shade, leaving an impression of cold drinks enjoyed on summer days in fine Victorian style.

The McElhone Stairs were preceded by a wooden ladder that linked Woolloomooloo Hill, as Kings Cross was known, to the estate far below.

Horderns Stairs

These villas, from the Georgian and Victorian eras, can be broadly labelled as Classical Revival and are fronted by leafy gardens.

★ Victoria Street
From 1972–4, residents of this historic street fought a sometimes violent battle against developers wanting to build high-rise towers, motels and blocks of flats ❷

Kings Cross Station

Werrington, a mostly serious and streamlined building, also has flamboyant Art Deco detailing which is now hidden under brown paint.

Tusculum Villa was just one of a number of 1830s houses subject to "villa conditions". All had to face Government House, be of a high monetary value and be built within three years.

STAR SIGHTS

★ Elizabeth Bay House

★ Victoria Street

LOCATOR MAP
See Street Finder, map 2

Challis Avenue is a fine and shady complement to nearby Victoria Street. This Romanesque group of terrace houses has an unusual façade, with arches fronting deep verandas and a grand ground floor colonnade.

Rockwall, a symmetrical and compact Regency villa, was built to the designs of the architect John Verge in 1830–37.

Landmark Hotel

Del Rio is a finely detailed high-rise apartment block. It clearly exhibits the Spanish Mission influence that filtered through from California in the first quarter of the 20th century.

CHALLIS AVENUE

STREET

MACLEAY

ONSLOW PLACE

BILLYARD AVENUE

ICK AVENUE

ONSLOW AVENUE

AVENUE

ROAD

The Arthur McElhone Reserve

★ Elizabeth Bay House
A contemporary exclaimed over the beauty of the 1830s garden: "Trees from Rio, the West Indies, the East Indies, China . . . the bulbs from the Cape are splendid." ❸

Art Deco Birtley Towers

0 metres   50

0 yards   50

KEY

– – – Suggested route

Elizabeth Bay was part of the original land grant to Alexander Macleay. He created a botanist's paradise with ornamental ponds, quaint grottoes and promenades winding all the way down to the harbour.

El Alamein Fountain, commemorating the World War II battle

El Alamein Fountain ❶

Fitzroy Gardens, Macleay St, Potts Point. **Map** 2 E5. 🚌 *222, 311.*

This dandelion of a fountain in the heart of the Kings Cross district has a reputation for working so spasmodically that passers-by often murmur facetiously, "He loves me, he loves me not." Built in 1961, it commemorates the Australian army's role in the siege of Tobruk, Libya, and the battle of El Alamein in Egypt during World War II. At night, when it is brilliantly lit, the fountain looks surprisingly ethereal.

Victoria Street ❷

Potts Point. **Map** 5 B2. 🚌 *311, 324, 325, 389.*

At the Potts Point end, this street of 19th-century terrace houses, interspersed with a few incongruous-looking high-rise blocks, is, by inner-city standards, almost a boulevard. The gracious street you see today was once at the centre of a bitterly fought conservation struggle, one which almost certainly cost the life of a prominent heritage campaigner.

In the early 1970s, many residents, backed by the "green bans" put in place by the Builders' Labourers Federation of New South Wales, fought to prevent demolition of old buildings for high-rise

Juanita Nielsen

development. Juanita Nielsen, heiress and publisher of a local newspaper, vigorously took up the conservation battle. On 4 July 1975, she disappeared without trace. An inquest into her disappearance returned an open verdict.

As a result of the actions of the union and residents, most of Victoria Street's superb old buildings still stand. Ironically, they are now occupied not by the low-income residents who fought to save them, but by the well-off professionals who eventually displaced them.

Elizabeth Bay House ❸

7 Onslow Ave, Elizabeth Bay. **Map** 2 F5. **Tel** *(02) 9356 3022.* 🚌 *Sydney Explorer, 311.* 🕙 *10am–4:30pm Tue–Sun.* 🔴 *Good Fri, 25 Dec.* 📷 🎫 groundfloor. **www**.hht.net.au

Elizabeth Bay House contains the finest colonial interior on display in Australia. It is a potent expression of how the depression of the 1840s cut short the 1830s' prosperous optimism. Designed in Greek Revival style by John Verge, it was built for Colonial Secretary Alexander Macleay, from 1835–39. The oval saloon with its dome and cantilevered staircase is recognized as Verge's masterpiece. The exterior is less satisfactory, as the intended colonnade and portico were not finished owing to a crisis in Macleay's financial affairs.

The present portico dates from 1893. The interior is furnished to reflect Macleay's occupancy from 1839–45, and is based on inventories drawn up in 1845 for the transfer of the house and contents to his son, William Sharp. He took the house in return for paying off his father's debts, leading to a rift that was never resolved.

Macleay's original 22-ha (55-acre) land grant was subdivided for flats and villas from the 1880s to 1927. In the 1940s, the house itself was divided into 15 flats. In 1942, the artist Donald Friend saw the ferry *Kuttabul* hit by a torpedo from a Japanese midget submarine from his flat's balcony.

The house was restored and opened as a museum in 1977. It is a property of the Historic Houses Trust of NSW.

The sweeping staircase under the oval dome, Elizabeth Bay House

Beare Park ❹

Ithaca Rd, Elizabeth Bay. **Map** 2 F5. 🚌 *311, 350.*

Originally a part of the Macleay Estate, Beare Park is now encircled by a jumble of apartment blocks. A refuge from hectic Kings Cross, it is one of only a few parks serving a populated area. Shaped like a natural amphitheatre, the park has glorious views of Elizabeth Bay.

The family home of JC Williamson, a famous theatrical entrepreneur who came to Australia from America in the 1870s, formerly stood at the eastern extremity of the park.

Star of David in the lobby of the Sydney Jewish Museum

Sydney Jewish Museum ❺

148 Darlinghurst Rd, Darlinghurst.
Map 5 B2. *Tel* (02) 9360 7999.
▣ *Sydney, Bondi & Bay Explorer,
311, 389.* ◯ *10am–4pm Sun–
Thu, 10am–2pm Fri.* ◉ *Sat,
Jewish hols.* ▨ ◐ ◪
www.sydneyjewishmuseum.com.au

Sixteen Jewish convicts were on the First Fleet, and many more were to be transported before the end of the convict era. As with other convicts, most would endure and some would thrive, seizing all the opportunities the colony had to offer.

The Sydney Jewish Museum relates stories of Australian Jewry within the context of the Holocaust. The ground floor display explores present-day Jewish traditions and culture within Australia. Ascending the stairs to the mezzanine levels 1–6, the visitor passes through chrono-logical and thematic exhibi-tions which unravel the tragic history of the Holocaust.

From Hitler's rise to power and *Kristallnacht,* through the evacuation of the ghettos and the Final Solution, to the ulti-mate liberation of the infamous death camps and Nuremberg Trials, the harrowing events are graphically documented. This horrific period is recalled using photographs and relics, some exhumed from mass graves, as well as audiovisual exhibits and oral testimonies.

Holocaust survivors act as guides and their presence, bearing witness to the recorded events, lends considerable power and moving authenticity to the exhibits in the museum.

Old Gaol, Darlinghurst ❻

Cnr Burton & Forbes sts, Darlinghurst.
Map 5 A2. *Tel* (02) 9339 8744. ▣
378, 380, 382, 389. ◯ *9am–5pm
Mon–Fri.* ◉ *public hols.* ◪

Originally known as the Woolloomooloo Stockade and later as Darlinghurst Gaol, this complex is now the National Art School. It was constructed over a 20-year period from 1822.

Surrounded by walls almost 7 m (23 ft) high, the cell blocks radiate from a central round-house. The jail is built of stone quarried on the site by convicts which was then chiselled by them into blocks.

No fewer than 67 people were executed here between 1841 and 1908. Perhaps the most notorious hangman was Alexander "The Strangler" Green, after whom Green Park, outside the jail, is thought to have been named. Green lived near the park until public hostility forced him to live in relative safety inside the jail.

Some of Australia's most noted artists, including Frank Hodgkinson, Jon Molvig and William Dobell, trained or taught at the art school which was established here in 1921.

The former Governor's house, Old Gaol, Darlinghurst

Darlinghurst Court House ❼

Forbes St, Darlinghurst. **Map** 5 A2.
Tel (02) 9368 2947. ▣ *378, 380,
382.* ◯ *Feb–Dec: 10am–4pm
Mon–Fri.* ◉ *Jan, mid-Dec, public
hols.* ◪ ◪ *groups only.*

Abutting the grim old gaol, to which it is connected by undergronahiund passages, and facing tawdry Taylors Square, this unlikely gem of Greek Revival architecture was begun in 1835 by colonial architect Mortimer Lewis. He was only responsible for the central block of the main building with its six-columned Doric portico with Greek embel-lishments. The side wings were not added until the 1880s.

The Court House is still used by the state's Supreme Court, mainly for criminal cases, and these are open to the public.

Beare Park, a quiet inner-city park with harbour views

Street-by-Street: Paddington

Paddington began to flourish in the 1840s, when the decision was made to build the Victoria Barracks. At the time much of it was "the most wild looking place... barren sandhills with patches of scrub, hills and hollows galore."

The area began to fill rapidly, as owner builders bought into the area and built rows of terrace houses, many very narrow because

Victorian finial in Union Street

of the lack of building regulations. After the Depression, most of the district was threatened with demolition, but was saved and restored by the large influx of postwar migrants.

★ **Five Ways**
This shopping hub was established in the late 19th century on the busy Glenmore roadway trodden out by bullocks ❽

Duxford Street's terrace houses in toning pale shades constitute an ideal of town planning: the Victorians preferred houses in a row to have a pleasingly uniform aspect.

"Gingerbread" houses can be seen in Broughton and Union streets. With their steeply pitched gables and fretwork bargeboards, they are typical of the rustic Gothic Picturesque architectural style.

The London Tavern opened for business in 1875, making it the suburb's oldest pub. Like many of the pubs and delicatessens in this well-serviced suburb, it stands at the end of a row of terraces.

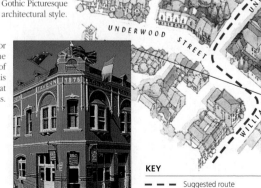

STAR SIGHTS

★ Five Ways

★ Paddington Street

KEY

- - - Suggested route

The Sherman Gallery is housed in a strikingly modern building. It is designed to hold Australian and international contemporary sculpture and paintings. Suitable access gates and a special in-house crane enable the movement of large-scale artworks, including textiles.

LOCATOR MAP
See Street Finder, maps 5 & 6

Paddington's streets are a treasure trove of galleries, bars and restaurants. A wander through the area should prove an enjoyable experience.

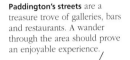

Warwick, built in the 1860s, is a minor castle lying at the end of a row of humble terraces. Its turrets, battlements and assorted decorations, in a style somewhat fancifully described as "King Arthur", even adorn the garages at the rear.

Windsor Street's terrace houses are, in some cases, a mere 4.5 m (15 ft) wide.

Street-making in Paddington's early days was often an expensive and complicated business. A cascade of water was dammed to build Cascade Street.

★ Paddington Street
Under the established plane trees, some of Paddington's finest Victorian terraces exemplify the building boom of 1860–90. Over 30 years, 3,800 houses were built in the suburb ⑭

0 metres 50

0 yards 50

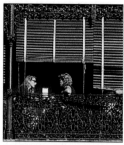

Pretty cast-iron balcony, the typical architecture of Paddington

Five Ways ⑧

Cnr Glenmore Rd & Heeley St. **Map** 5 C3. 🚌 389.

At this picturesque intersection, where three streets cross on Glenmore Road, a shopping hub developed by the tramline that ran from the city to Bondi Beach *(see p126)*. On the five corners stand 19th- and early 20th-century shops, one now a restaurant.

Much of the architecture in Paddington features decorative cast-iron "lacework" balconies, using mixed Victorian and Classical Revival styles. Streets lined with pretty houses make this one of Sydney's most desirable areas.

Paddington Village ⑨

Cnr Gipps & Shadforth sts. **Map** 5 C3. 🚌 378, 380, 382.

Paddington began its life as a working-class suburb of Sydney. The community mainly consisted of the carpenters, quarrymen and stonemasons who supervised the convict gangs that built the Victoria Barracks in the 1840s.

The 19th-century artisans and their families occupied a tight huddle of spartan houses crowded into the area's narrow streets. A few of these houses still remain. Like the barracks, these dwellings and surrounding shops and hotels were built of locally quarried stone.

The terraces of Paddington Village are now a popular address with young, up-and-coming Sydneysiders.

Juniper Hall ⑩

250 Oxford St. **Map** 5 C3. 🚌 378, 380, 382. ⬤ *closed to the public.*

The emancipist gin distiller Robert Cooper built this superb example of colonial Georgian architecture for his third wife, Sarah. He named it after the main ingredient of the gin that made his fortune.

Completed in 1824, the two-storey home is the oldest dwelling still standing in Paddington. It is probably also the largest and most extravagant house ever built in the suburb. It had to be: Cooper already had 14 children when he declared that Sarah would have the finest house in Sydney. Once resident in the new house, he subsequently fathered 14 more.

Juniper Hall was saved from demolition in the mid-1980s and has been restored. Now under the auspices of the National Trust, the building is used as private offices.

Paddington Town Hall ⑪

Cnr Oxford St & Oatley Rd. **Map** 5 C3. 🚌 378, 380, 382. ◯ 10am–4pm Mon–Fri. ⬤ public hols.

Paddington Town Hall was completed in 1891. A design competition was won by local architect JE Kemp. The Classical Revival building still dominates the area.

No longer a centre of local government, the building now houses a cinema, library and a large ballroom.

Paddington Town Hall

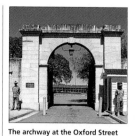

The archway at the Oxford Street entrance to Victoria Barracks

Victoria Barracks ⑫

Oxford St. **Map** 5 B3. **Tel** (02) 9339 3330. 🚌 378, 380, 382. **Museum** ◯ 10am–12:30pm Thu; 10am–3:45pm Sun. ⬤ Sun. ⬤ 25 Dec. ♿ 🎫 **Parade & tour:** 10am Thu *(phone 9339 3170 to book).*

Victoria Barracks are the largest and best-preserved group of late Georgian architecture in Australia, covering almost 12 ha (30 acres). They are widely considered to be one of the best examples of a military barracks in the world.

Designed by the colonial engineer Lieutenant Colonel George Barney, the barracks were built between 1841 and 1848 using local sandstone that were quarried by convict labour. The barracks were originally intended to house 800 men, and they have been in continuous use ever since and still operate as a centre of military administration.

The main block is 225 m (740 ft) long and has symmetrical two-storey wings with cast-iron verandas flanking a central archway. The perimeter walls have foundations 10 m (40 ft) deep in places. A former gaol block now houses a museum tracing New South Wales' military heritage.

Paddington Markets ⑬

395 Oxford St. **Map** 6 D4. **Tel** (02) 9331 2923. 🚌 378, 380, 382. ◯ 10am–4pm Sat. ⬤ 25 Dec. ♿ See **Shopping** p133. **www**.paddingtonmarket.com.au

This market, which began in 1973 as Paddington Bazaar, takes place every Saturday, come rain or shine, in the grounds of Paddington Village Uniting Church. It is probably the most colourful in Sydney – a place to meet and be seen as much as to shop. Stallholders come from all over the world and young designers, hoping to launch their careers, display their wares. Other offerings are jewellery, pottery and other arts and crafts, as well as new and second-hand clothing. Whatever you are looking for you are more than likely to find it here.

Paddington Street terrace house

Paddington Street ⓮

Map 6 D3. 🚌 *378, 380, 382.*

With its huge plane trees shading the road and fine terrace houses on each side, Paddington Street is one of the oldest and loveliest of the suburb's streets.

Paddington grew rapidly as a commuter suburb in the late 19th century and most of the terraces were built for renting to Sydney's artisans. They were decorated with iron lace, Grecian-style friezes, worked parapets and cornices, pilasters and scrolls.

By the 1900s, the terraces became unfashionable and people moved out to newly emerging "garden suburbs". In the 1960s, however, their architectural appeal came to be appreciated again and the area was reborn.

Paddington Street now has a chic atmosphere where small art galleries operate out of quaint and grand shopfronts.

Centennial Park ⓯

Map 6 E5. **Tel** *(02) 9339 6699.*
🚌 *Clovelly, Coogee, Maroubra, Bronte, Randwick, City, Bondi Beach & Bondi Junction routes.* ⭕
Mar–Apr & Sep–Oct: 6am–6pm daily; May–Aug: 6:30am–5:30pm daily; Nov–Feb: 5:45am–8pm daily. ♿ 🍴
🅿 📷 *upon request.*
www.cp.nsw.go.au

Entering this 220-ha (544-acre) park through one of its sandstone and wrought-iron gates, the visitor may wonder how such an extensive and idyllic place has survived so close to the centre of the city. Formerly a common, Centennial Park was dedicated "to the enjoyment of the people of New South Wales forever" on 26 January 1888, the centenary of the foundation of the colony. On 1 January 1901, 100,000 people gathered here to witness the Commonwealth of Australia come into being, when the first Australian federal ministry was sworn in by the first governor-general (*see p56*).

The park boasts landscaped lawns and rose gardens as well as ornamental ponds, an Avenue of Palms with 400 trees, and a playing field. Once the source of the city's water supply, the swamps are home to many species of waterbirds. Picnickers, painters, runners as well as those on horseback, bikes and in-line skates (all of which can be hired nearby) make enthusiastic and regular use of this vast recreation area, which is located so close to the city's centre. There is also a café serving gourmet meals.

Fox Studios Entertainment Quarter ⓰

Lang Rd, Moore Park. **Tel** *9383 4000.* **Map** 5 C5. 🚌 *339, 355.* ⭕ *Many retail shops open 10am–10pm.*
www.foxstudios.com.au

There is a vibrant atmosphere at Fox Studios, which is located next door to the working studios that produced some very famous movies, such as *The Matrix* and *Moulin Rouge*.

There are 16 cinema screens where you can watch the latest movies, and at the La Premiere cinema you can enjoy your movie with wine and cheese, sitting on comfortable sofas. There are four live-entertainment venues which regularly feature the latest local and international acts. You can also enjoy a game of miniature golf, bungy trampolining, bowling or seasonal ice-skating, and children love the play areas. There are many restaurants, cafés and bars offering a range of snacks, meals and drinks.

Every Wednesday you can sample fresh produce at the Farmers Market – many of the stalls offer free tastings.

The weekend market is a merchandise market and there are many handmade items as well as food. There is also an International Food Market on Friday evenings until 9pm. Shops are open until late every day, and there is a good selection of products. There is plenty of undercover parking and the Studios are a pleasant stroll from the Paddington end of Oxford Street.

The lush green expanse of Centennial Park

Further Afield

Beyond Sydney's inner city, numerous places vie for the visitor's attention. Around the harbour shores are picturesque suburbs, secluded beaches and historic sights. To the north is the beautiful landscape of Ku-ring-gai Chase National Park. Manly is the city's northern playground, while Bondi is its eastern counterpart. Further west at Parramatta there are sites that recall and evoke the first days of European settlement.

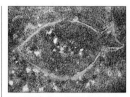

Aboriginal rock art in Ku-ring-gai Chase National Park

SIGHTS AT A GLANCE

Bondi Beach ❸
Ku-ring-gai Chase
   National Park ❶
Manly ❷
Parramatta ❺
Sydney Olympic Park ❹

KEY

▦	Central Sydney
▢	Greater Sydney
③	Metroad (city) route
▬	Highway
▬	Major road

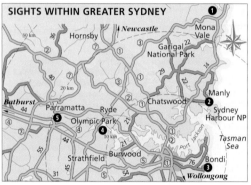

SIGHTS WITHIN GREATER SYDNEY

10 km = 6 miles

Ku-ring-gai Chase National Park ❶

McCarrs Creek Rd, Church Point. ▯
Kalkari Discovery Centre (02) 9472 9300. ⬭ *10am–4pm Mon–Fri, 10am–5pm Sat–Sun.* ⬤ *25 Dec.*

Ku-ring-gai Chase National Park lies on Sydney's northernmost outskirts, 30 km (19 miles) from the city, and covers 15,000 ha (37,000 acres). It is bounded to the north by Broken Bay, at the mouth of the Hawkesbury River, with its eroded valleys formed during the last Ice Age. Sparkling waterways and golden beaches are set against the backdrop of the national park. Picnicking, bushwalking, surfing, boating and windsurfing are popular with visitors.

The Hawkesbury River curls around an ancient sandstone landscape rich in Aboriginal rock art. The national park has literally hundreds of Aboriginal art sites, the most common being rock engravings thought to be 2,000 years old. They include whales up to 8 m (26 ft) long, sharks, wallabies and echidnas, as well as ancestral spirits.

Manly ❷

⬛ *Manly. Oceanworld Manly West Esplanade.* **Tel** *(02) 8251 7877.* ⬭ *10am–5:30pm daily.* ⬤ *25 Dec.* ▨ ⬛ *www.*oceanworld.com.au

If asked to suggest a single excursion outside the city, most Sydneysiders would nominate the 11-km (7-mile) ferry ride from Circular Quay to Manly. This narrow stretch of land lying between the harbour and the ocean was named by Governor Phillip, even before the township of

Brass band playing on The Corso, Manly's esplanade

Sydney got its name, for the impressive bearing of the Aboriginal men.

To the right of the rejuvenated Manly wharf are shops, restaurants and bars on the adjacent pier and, on the left, the tranquil harbourside beach known as Manly Cove. **Oceanworld Manly** is at the far end of Manly Cove, where visitors can see sharks, giant stingrays and other species in an underwater viewing tunnel. You can also dive with the sharks.

The Corso is a lively pedestrian thoroughfare of souvenir shops and fast food outlets. It leads to Manly's ocean beach, popular with sunbathers, with its promenade lined by towering Norfolk pines.

Bondi Beach ❸

⬛ *380, 382, 381.*

This long crescent of golden sand (it is approximately a kilometre long) has long been a mecca for the sun and surf set *(see pp144–5).* The word *bondi* is Aboriginal for "water breaking over rocks". Surfers visit from far and wide

For hotels and restaurants in this region see pp478–81 and pp524–8

Crescent-shaped Bondi Beach, Sydney's most famous beach, looking towards North Bondi

in search of the perfect wave, and inline skaters hone their skills on the promenade.

People also seek out Bondi for its trendy seafront cafés and cosmopolitan milieu as much as for the world-famous beach. The pavilion, built in 1928 as changing rooms, is now a busy venue for festivals, plays, films and arts and crafts displays.

Sydney Olympic Park ❹

Sydney Olympic Park. **Tel** 9714 7888. 🚉 Olympic Park. **Visitors Centre** 1 Showground Rd. 🕐 9am–5pm daily. 🔴 Good Fri, 25 Dec, 26 Dec, 1 Jan. 🎫 👤 📺 🎶 **www.** sydneyolympicpark.nsw.gov.au

Once host to the 27th Summer Olympic Games and Paralympic Games, Sydney Olympic Park is situated at Homebush Bay. Visitors can buy a ticket for a guided tour of the park or the main Olympic Stadium. Bicycles can also be hired. There is a tour of the wetlands of Bicentennial Park as well as Breakfast with the Birds – breakfast after a morning of birdwatching. All tickets for tours can be bought at the Visitor's Centre.

Other facilities include the Aquatic Centre with a water-park, and a Tennis Centre. There is also a market on the fourth Sunday of every month.

Parramatta ❺

📮 Parramatta. 🚉 Parramatta.
🛈 346a Church St (02) 8839 3311.

The fertile soil of this Sydney suburb resulted in its foundation as Australia's first rural settlement, celebrating its first wheat crop in 1789. The area is now an excellent place to visit to gain an insight into the city's early European history.

Elizabeth Farm, dating from 1793, is the oldest surviving home in Australia. Once the home of John Macarthur, the farm played a major role in breeding merino sheep, so vital to the country's economy *(see p51)*. The house is now an innovative hands-on museum, detailing the lives of its first inhabitants from 1793–1850.

Old Government House in Parramatta Park is the oldest intact public building in Australia, built in 1799. The Doric porch, added in 1816, has been attributed to Francis Greenway *(see p169)*. A collection of early 19th-century furniture is housed inside the National Trust building.

Sydney's early history can also be witnessed at **St John's Cemetery**, where many of the settlers who arrived on the First Fleet *(see p50)* are buried.

🏛 **Elizabeth Farm**
70 Alice St, Rosehill. **Tel** (02) 9635 9488. 🕐 10am–5pm daily. 🔴 Good Fri, 25 Dec. 📷 👤 🎶 🛒 📺

🏛 **Old Government House**
Parramatta Park (entry by Macquarie St). **Tel** (02) 9635 8149. 🕐 daily. 🔴 Good Fri, 25 Dec. 👤 🎶

🏛 **St John's Cemetery**
O'Connell St. **Tel** (02) 9635 5904. 👤

Drawing room in Old Government House in Parramatta

GETTING AROUND SYDNEY

Sydney taxi company sign

In general, the best way to see Sydney's many sights and attractions is on foot, coupled with use of the public transport system. Buses and trains will take visitors to within easy walking distance of anywhere in the inner city. They also serve the suburbs and outlying areas. Passenger ferries provide a fast and scenic means of travel between the city and the many harbourside suburbs. Of the many composite and multi-ride tickets available, most visitors will find it best to invest in one that includes all three modes of public transport.

DRIVING IN SYDNEY

Driving is not the ideal way to get around Sydney: the city road network is confusing, traffic is congested and parking can be expensive. If using a car, it is best to avoid the peak hours (about 7:30–9:30am and 5–7:30pm).

Overseas visitors can use their usual driving licences to drive in Sydney, but must have proof that they are simply visiting and keep the licence with them when driving.

Parking in Sydney is strictly regulated, with fines for any infringements. Vehicles can be towed away if parked illegally. Contact the **Transport Management Centre** if this happens. There are many car parks in and around the city. Also look for blue and white "P" signs or metered parking zones, many of which apply seven days a week, but it varies from council to council.

TAXIS

Taxis are plentiful in the city: there are many taxi ranks and taxis are often found outside the large city hotels.

Meters indicate the fare plus any extras, such as booking fees and waiting time. It is customary to round the fare up to the next dollar.

Sydney has a fleet of taxis that cater to disabled passengers, including those in wheelchairs. Book these with any major taxi company.

Cycling in Centennial Park

SYDNEY BY BICYCLE

While cycling is permitted on all city and suburban roads, visitors are advised to stay within designated cycling tracks or areas with light motor traffic. Centennial Park is a popular cycling spot. Helmets are compulsory by law. Those who wish to take advantage of Sydney's undulating terrain can seek advice from **Bicycle New South Wales**. Bicycles are permitted on CityRail trains (*see p130*) but you may have to pay an extra fare.

TRAMS

In 1997, Sydney reintroduced trams to its transport system, after an absence of 36 years. A fleet of seven trams journey around the downtown area, from Central Station (*see p130*) to Lilyfield via Pyrmont, taking in a large proportion of the area's sights (*see pp76–7*). Tickets can be purchased at Central Station.

COMPOSITE TICKETS

Sydney's transport is good value, particularly with one of the composite tickets available from **Sydney Buses Transit Shop** or railway stations.

TravelTen tickets, as the name suggests, entitle you to make ten bus journeys. TravelPasses allow unlimited seven-day travel on Sydney's buses, trains and ferries within stipulated zones. The SydneyPass allows three, five or seven days' travel in any eight-day period on buses and ferries.

A BusTripper allows one day's unlimited travel on regular buses. DayTripper allows one day's unlimited travel on both buses and ferries.

USEFUL INFORMATION

Bicycle New South Wales
Lvl 5, 822 George St.
Map 4 E5.
Tel (02) 9281 4099.

Transport Management Centre
Tel 13 17 00. (24-hour service.)

Sydney Buses Transit Shop Circular Quay
Cnr Loftus and Alfred sts.
Map 1 B3.
Tel (02) 9244 1990.

Transport Infoline
Tel 13 15 00.

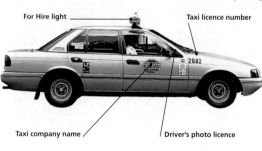

For Hire light — — — — — — — — — — — — Taxi licence number

2882

Taxi company name — — — — — — Driver's photo licence

Travelling by Bus

Sydney buses provide a punctual service that links up conveniently with the city's rail and ferry systems. As well as covering city and suburban areas, there are two excellent sightseeing buses – the Sydney Explorer and the Bondi Explorer. The **Transport Infoline** can advise you on routes, fares and journey times for all Sydney buses. Armed with the map printed on the inside back cover of this book and a composite ticket, you can enjoy travelling about the city without the difficulties and expense of city parking.

Automatic stamping machine for validating composite tickets

USING SYDNEY BUSES

Route numbers and journey destinations are displayed on the front, back and left side of all Sydney buses. An "X" in front of the number means that it is an express bus. Day-Tripper and single-journey tickets can be purchased on board regular buses. Single fares are bought from the driver. Try to have coins ready as drivers are not always able to change large notes. You will be given a ticket valid for that journey only – if you change buses you must pay again.

If using a TravelTen ticket or TravelPass, you must insert it in the automatic stamping machine as you board. Make sure that the arrow is facing towards you and pointing downwards. If sharing a TravelTen ticket, insert it into the machine once for each person travelling.

Front seats must be given up to elderly or disabled passengers. Eating, drinking, smoking and playing music are prohibited on buses. To signal that you wish to alight, press one of the stop buttons – they are mounted on the vertical handrails on each seat – well before the bus reaches your stop. The doors are electronic and can only be opened by the bus drivers.

BUS STOPS

Bus stops are indicated by yellow and black signs displaying a profile of a bus. Below this symbol, the numbers of all buses along the route are clearly listed.

Timetables are usually found at main bus stops. Public holidays follow the Sunday timetable. While bus stop timetables are kept as up-to-date as possible, it is best to carry a current timetable with you. They are available from Sydney Buses Transit Shops, as well as some tourist information facilities.

Express bus

SIGHTSEEING BY BUS

Two Sydney bus services, the red Sydney Explorer and the blue Bondi Explorer, offer flexible sightseeing with commentaries. The Sydney Explorer covers a 32-km (20-mile) circuit and stops at 26 of the city's most popular attractions. The Bondi Explorer travels through a number of Sydney's eastern suburbs, taking in much of the area's coastal scenery.

The red Sydney Explorer buses run daily every 20 minutes, the blue every 30 minutes. The great advantage of these services is that you can explore at will, getting on and off the buses as often as you wish in the course of a day. The best way to make the most of your journey is to choose the sights you most want to see and plan a basic itinerary. Be sure to note the various opening times of museums, art galleries and shops; the bus drivers can often advise you about these. Explorer bus stops are clearly marked by the colours of the bus (red or blue).

Tickets for both Explorer buses can be bought when boarding and are also available from Sydney Buses Transit Shops.

A typical Sydney bus used for standard services

The Bondi Explorer bus

The Sydney Explorer bus

Travelling by Train and Monorail

CityRail logo

As well as the key link between the city and suburbs, Sydney's railway network also serves a large part of the central business district and reaches out to Newcastle to the north, Lithgow to the west, Nowra to the south and Goulburn to the southeast. CityRail's double-decker trains operate on 15 major lines. The City Circle loop stops as Central, Town Hall, Wynyard, Circular Quay, St James and Museum stations. Most suburban lines pass through Central and Town Hall.

Pedestrian concourse outside Central Railway Station

FINDING YOUR WAY AROUND CITYRAIL

Part of state rail, Sydney's CityRail system is mainly used by commuters. It is the most efficient and economical way to travel to and from the suburbs such as Parramatta. The system is easy to follow and **CityRail Information** will offer all details of services and timetables.

Trains run from 4:15am until after 1:30am. When using trains at night: stand in the "Nightsafe" areas and only use carriages near the train guard, marked by a blue light.

USING THE CITYRAIL ROUTE MAP

The 15 cityrail lines are colour-coded and route maps are displayed at all CityRail stations and inside train carriages. Simply trace the line from where you are to your destination, noting if and where you need to change and make connections.

Note that the distances shown on the CityRail map are not to the correct scale.

COUNTRY AND INTER-URBAN TRAINS

State rail has **Countrylink Travel Centres** throughout the city, which provide information about rail and coach services and also take ticket bookings (see their website).

Inter-urban trains run to a variety of areas, including the Blue Mountains *(see pp170–73)*, Wollongong *(see p186)* and Newcastle *(see p169)*.

SIGHTSEEING BY MONORAIL

More novel than practical, Sydney's Monorail runs along a scenic loop through

Monorail leaving the city centre, backed by Sydney Tower

central Sydney, Chinatown and Darling Harbour. Although it only covers a short distance, the Monorail can be a convenient way to travel from the city centre to Darling Harbour.

It runs from 7am–10pm Monday to Thursday, 7am to midnight on Friday and Saturday, and 8am to 10pm on Sunday. Trains run every 5 minutes and the full circuit takes about 12 minutes. Ticket machines are found at each station. They accept most Australian notes and coins and give change.

A Monorail Day Pass allows unlimited rides for an entire day. It can be bought from any of the Monorail information booths.

USEFUL ADDRESSES

CityRail Information
Central Railway Station
Map 4 E5.
Tel (02) 131500.
Circular Quay Railway Station
Map 1 B3.
Tel (02) 9224 3553.
www.cityrail.info

Countrylink Travel Centres
Central Railway Station
Sydney Terminal.
Map 4 E5.
Tel (02) 132232.
www.countrylink.info

Metro Light Rail & Monorail
Tel (02) 9285 5600.
www.metrolightrail.com.au

THE METRO LIGHT RAIL

The MLR is Sydney's most recent transport development and is designed to link Central Railway Station with Glebe and Lilyfield, via Darling Harbour. These efficient and environmentally friendly trains offer a quicker and quieter means of travelling around parts of the city. Tickets are available on board from the conductor.

Travelling by Ferry and Water Taxi

For more than a century, Sydney ferries have been a picturesque, as well as a practical, feature of the Sydney scene. Today, they are as popular as ever. Travelling by ferry is both a pleasure and an efficient way to journey between Sydney's various harbour suburbs. Sightseeing cruises are operated by various private companies as well as by Sydney Ferries Corporation *(see p128)*. Water taxis can be a convenient and fast alternative, although they are more expensive.

A water taxi on Sydney Harbour

WATER TAXIS

Small, fast taxi boats are available for hire to carry passengers around the harbour. You can flag them down like normal road cabs if you spot one cruising for a fare. Try King Street Wharf or Circular Quay, near the Overseas Passenger Terminal.

Water taxis will pick up and drop off passengers at any navigable pier. However, this novel way of getting around the harbour is certainly not cheap. Rates vary, with some drivers charging for the boat (about $40) and a fee per person (about $10).

Sydney ferries coming and going at Circular Quay Ferry Terminal

USING SYDNEY'S FERRIES

There is a steady procession of State Transit Sydney Ferries traversing the harbour between 6am and 10pm daily. They service most of Sydney Harbour, Manly and also several stops along the Parramatta River.

Staff at the **Sydney Ferries Information Office**, open 7am–6pm daily, will answer passenger queries and provide ferry timetables.

All ferry journeys start at the Circular Quay Ferry Terminal. Electronic destination boards at the entrance to each wharf indicate the wharf from which your ferry will leave, and also give departure times and all stops made en route. Tickets and TravelPasses can be bought from the ticket booths that are located on each wharf. On some ferries, tickets can be purchased on board.

Manly's ferry terminal is serviced both by ferries and the speedy JetCats. Tickets and information can be obtained from the ticket windows in the centre of the terminal. No food or drink is permitted on JetCat or Supercat ferries.

SIGHTSEEING BY FERRY

Sydney Ferries has a variety of well-priced cruises which take in the history and sights of Sydney Harbour. They are a cheap alternative to the commercial harbour cruises. There are morning, afternoon and evening tours, all with a commentary throughout. The day cruises show aspects of the city that are rarely seen, while the evening cruises offer spectacular views of the sun setting over the city's landmarks at sunset. Food and drink are available on board, but passengers may bring their own.

The **Australian Travel Specialists** has information on all river and harbour cruises from Circular Quay and Darling Harbour.

USEFUL INFORMATION

Australian Travel Specialists
Wharf 6, Circular Quay; Harbourside Shopping Centre, Darling Harbour. **Map** 1 B3, 3 C2. *Tel* (02) 9211 3192. www.atstravel.com.au

Sydney Ferries Lost Property
Wharf 3, Circular Quay. **Map** 1 B3. *Tel* (02) 9207 3101; 131 500 *(timetable information)*. www.sydneyferries.info

Water Taxi Companies
Harbour Taxi Boats
Tel (02) 9955 1155.
Sydney Harbour Water Taxis
Tel (02) 9299 0199.
Water Taxis Combined
Tel (02) 9555 8888.
www.watertaxis.com.au

Electronic destination board for all ferries leaving Circular Quay

SHOPPING IN SYDNEY

For most travellers, shopping can be as much of a voyage of discovery as sightseeing. The variety of shops in Sydney is wide and the quality of goods is high. The city has many elegant arcades, shopping galleries

Gowings menswear store logo

and popular weekly and monthly markets. The range of merchandise available is vast and local talent is promoted. Nor does the most interesting shopping stop at the city centre; there are several "satellite" alternatives.

A jumble of bric-a-brac in a typical Sydney junk shop

SHOPPING HOURS

Most shops are open from 9am to 5:30pm Monday to Saturday, though some may close early on Saturdays. High-end boutiques open from 10am to 6pm. On Thursdays, most shops stay open until 9pm. Most shops in Chinatown are open late every evening and on Sundays.

HOW TO PAY

Major credit cards are accepted almost everywhere. You will need identification, such as a passport or driver's licence, when using traveller's

cheques. Department stores will exchange goods or refund your money if you are not satisfied, provided you have kept your receipt. Other stores will only refund if an item is faulty. There is also a Goods and Services Tax (GST) which is almost always included in the marked price.

SALES

Many shops conduct sales all year round. The big department stores of **David Jones** and **Myer** have two gigantic and chaotic clearance sales every year. The post-Christmas sales start on 26 December and last into January. The other major sale time is during July, after the end of the financial year

TAX-FREE SALES

Duty-free shops are found in the centre of the city as well as at Kingsford Smith Airport *(see p582)*. You can save around 30 per cent on goods such as perfume, jewellery, watches and alcohol at duty-free shops but you must show your passport and onward ticket. Some stores will also deliver your

goods to the airport to be picked up on departure. Duty-free items must be kept in their sealed bags until you leave the city.

You can claim back the GST paid on most goods, purchased for (or in a single transaction of) A$150 or more, at the airport.

Chifley Tower, with the Chifley Plaza shopping arcade at its base

ARCADES AND MALLS

Arcades and shopping malls in Sydney range from the ornately Victorian to modern marble and glass. The Queen Victoria Building *(see p90)* is Sydney's most palatial shopping space. Four levels contain more than 200 shops.

The elegant Strand Arcade *(see p90)* was originally built in 1892. Jewellery, lingerie, high fashion, antiques and fine cafés are its stock in trade.

Pitt Street Mall has several shopping centres including **Sydney Central Plaza**, which features upmarket stores.

Next door to the Hilton, the **Galeries Victoria** house the fantastic Kinokuniya bookstore, which sells Australian and American imprints, as well as Chinese and Japanese language books. The **Mid City**

Gleebooks, popular with students and Glebe locals *(see pp134–5)*

Centre is home to the HMV music store and shops selling clothes, accessories and gifts.

Both the MLC Centre and nearby Chifley Plaza cater to the prestige shopper. Gucci, Cartier and Tiffany & Co are just some of the shops found in these arcades.

Harbourside Shopping Centre has dozens of shops selling articles of fine art, jewellery and Australiana, along with a range of waterfront restaurants.

BEST OF THE DEPARTMENT STORES

The spring floral displays at David Jones are legendary, as is the luxurious perfumery and cosmetics hall on the ground floor. The store spreads out in two buildings, across the road from each other on Market and Elizabeth streets. The food hall is famous for its gourmet fare and fine wines. Myer has a ground floor packed with makeup and accessories, including a large MAC counter. Both stores sell women's clothing, lingerie, menswear, baby goods, children's clothes, toys, stationery, kitchenware, furniture, china crystal and silver.

Gowings, a Sydney institution, has been operating since 1868. This unpretentious menswear store also sells such things as sunglasses, wat ches, Swiss Army knives, fishing gear, miners' lamps and genuine Australiana such as kangaroo leather wallets and plaited leather belts.

Part of the spring floral display in David Jones department store

Canopy over the harbourside Rocks Market

MARKETS

Scouring markets for the cheap, the cheerful and the unusual has become a popular pastime in Sydney.

Balmain Market, held each Saturday, includes a food hall selling Japanese, Thai and Indian dishes. The Bondi Beach Market on Sundays is known for its trendy second-hand clothing. The Glebe Market is a treasure-trove for the junk shop enthusiast and canny scavenger. The market is bright and popular with the inner-city grunge set.

The Rocks Market, held all weekend under a canopy, has around 140 stalls. Posters, lace, stained glass and leather are among the goods. You can watch a sculptor making art out of stone or have your portrait sketched in charcoal.

Sydney Fish Market is the place to go for fresh seafood. You can choose from more than 100 species, both live and prepared. Above the market, the Sydney Seafood School offers lessons in preparing and serving seafood. The Good Living Growers' Market sells everything you need for a gourmet feast, and is where you will find native Australian bushfoods, such as lemon myrtle linguini, dried bush tomatoes, nutty wattleseed and pepperberries.

The Sydney Opera House Market on Sundays displays an eclectic mix of arts and crafts in a spectacular setting next to the Opera House.

Other good markets are Paddy's Markets (see p99), Fox Studio Markets (see p125) and Paddington Markets (see p125).

(see p99), (see p125) and (see p125)

DIRECTORY

ARCADES AND MALLS

Chifley Plaza
2 Chifley Square. Map 1 B4.
Tel (02) 9221 6111.
www.chifleyplaza.com.au

Galeries Victoria
2 Park St. Map 4 E2.
Tel (02) 9261 0456.

Harbourside Shopping Centre
Darling Harbour. Map 3 C2.
Tel (02) 9281 3999.
www.harbourside.com.au

Mid City Centre
197 Pitt Street Mall. Map 1 B5.
Tel (02) 9221 2422.

MLC Centre
19–29 Martin Place. Map 1 B4.
Tel (02) 9224 8333.
www.mlccentre.com.au

Sydney Central Plaza
100 Market St. Map 4 E2.
Tel (02) 8224 2000.

DEPARTMENT STORES

David Jones
Cnr Elizabeth & Castlereagh sts.
Map 1 B5. *Tel (02) 9266 5544.*

Gowings
319 George St. Map 1 B5.
Tel (02) 9287 6394.

Myer
436 George St. Map 1 B5.
Tel (02) 9238 9111.

MARKETS

Balmain Market
Cnr Darling St & Curtis Rd, Balmain.

Bondi Beach Market
Bondi Beach Public School,
Campbell Parade, North Bondi.

Glebe Market
Glebe Public School, Glebe Point Rd, Glebe. Map 3 B5.

Sydney Fish Market
Cnr Pyrmont Bridge Rd & Bank St,
Blackwattle Bay. Map 3 B2.

Sydney Opera House Market
Western Boardwalk, Sydney Opera House. Map 1 C2.

The Good Living Growers' Market
Pyrmont Bay Park. Map 3 C1

The Rocks Market
George St, The Rocks. Map 1 B2.

Specialist Shopping in Sydney

Sydney offers an extensive range of gift and souvenir ideas, from unset opals and jewellery to Aboriginal art and hand-crafted souvenirs. Museum shops, such as at the Museum of Sydney *(see p92)* and the Art Gallery of NSW *(see pp110–13)*, often have specially commissioned items that make great presents or reminders of your visit.

ONE-OFFS

Specialist shops abound in Sydney – some practical, some eccentric, others simply indulgent. **Ausfurs** sells everything from luxurious sheepskin coats and jackets to pure wool handknits and mohair rugs.

Wheels & Doll Baby designs clothes that are the perfect mix of 1950s chic, rock'n'roll and Hollywood glamour. **The Hour Glass** stocks traditional- style watches, while designer sunglasses such as Armani and Jean Paul Gaultier can be found at **The Looking Glass**.

For a touch of celebrity glamour, **Napoleon Perdis Cosmetics** sells a huge array of make-up and bears the name of Australia's leading make-up artist to the "stars". Or, for some eclectic fashion and homewares, try a branch of **Orson & Blake**, the one in Surry Hills has a good café.

AUSTRALIANA

Australiana has become more than just a souvenir genre; it is now an art form in itself.

Done Art and Design has distinctive prints by Ken and Judy Done on a wide range of clothes, swimwear and accessories, while at **Weiss Art** you will find tasteful, mainly black and white, minimalist designs on clothes, umbrellas, baseball caps and cups. **Makers Mark** is a showcase for exquisite work by artisans in wood, glass and silver. The Queen Victoria Building *(see p90)* is dominated by shops selling Australiana: souvenirs, silver, antiques, art and crafts.

The Australian Museum *(see pp94–5)* has a small shop on the ground floor. It sells slightly unusual gift items such as native flower presses, bark paintings and Australian animal puppets, puzzles and games.

BOOKS

The larger chains such as **Dymocks** and **Angus & Robertson's Bookworld** have a good range of guide books and maps on Sydney. For more eclectic browsing, try **Abbey's Bookshop, Ariel** and **Gleebooks**, while **Berkelouw Books** has three floors of new, second-hand and rare books. **The Bookshop Darlinghurst** specializes in gay and lesbian fiction and non-fiction. The State Library of NSW *(see p109)* bookshop has a good choice of Australian books, particularly on history.

MUSIC

Several specialist music shops of international repute can be found in Sydney. **Red Eye Records** is for the streetwise, with its collectables, rarities, alternative music and concert tickets. **Central Station Records and Tapes** has mainstream grooves, plus rap, hip hop and cutting edge dance music. **Birdland** has a good stock of blues, jazz, soul and avant-garde. **Anthem Records** is Australia's oldest record and CD import store, selling funk, soul and R&B for over 30 years. **Folkways** specializes in world music, **Waterfront** in world and left-of-centre and **Utopia Records** in hard rock and heavy metal. **Michael's Music Room** sells classical music only, specializing in historical and contemporary opera recordings.

ABORIGINAL ART

Traditional paintings, fabric, jewellery, boomerangs, carvings and cards can be bought at the **Aboriginal and Pacific Art.** You can find tribal artifacts from Aboriginal Australia at several shops in the Harbourside Shopping Centre, Darling Harbour. The **Coo-ee Aboriginal Art Gallery** boasts a large selection of limited edition prints, hand-printed fabrics, books and Aboriginal music. The long-established **Hogarth Galleries Aboriginal Art Centre** has a fine reputation and usually holds work by Papunya Tula and Balgo artists and respected painters such as Clifford Possum Tjapaltjarri *(see p30)*. Works by urban indigenous artists can be found at the **Boomalli Aboriginal Artists' Cooperative**.

OPALS

Sydney offers a variety of opals in myriad settings. **Flame Opals** is a family run store, selling stones from all the major Australian opal fields. At **Opal Fields** you can view a museum collection of opalized fossils, before buying from the wide range of gems. **Giulian's** has unset opals, including blacks from Lightning Ridge, whites from Coober Pedy and boulder opals from Quilpie.

JEWELLERY

Long-established Sydney jewellers with 24-carat reputations include **Fairfax & Roberts, Hardy Brothers** and **Percy Marks**. World-class pearls are found in the waters off the northwestern coast of Australia. Rare and beautiful examples can be found at **Paspaley Pearls**.

Victoria Spring Designs evokes costume jewellery's glory days, with filigree and glass beading worked into its sumptuous pendants, rings, earrings and Gothic crosses. **Dinosaur Designs** made its name with colourful, chunky resin jewellery, while at **Love & Hatred**, jewelled wrist cuffs, rings and crosses recall lush medieval treasures. **Jan Logan** is an iconic Australian jewellery designer, with stores in Melbourne, Hong Kong, and London. Choose from beautiful and unusual contemporary pieces, otherwise the shop also carries antiques.

DIRECTORY

ONE-OFFS

Ausfurs
136 Victoria Rd,
Marrickville.
Tel 9557 4040.

The Hour Glass
142 King St.
Map 1 B5.
Tel 9221 2288.

The Looking Glass
Queen Victoria Building.
Map 1 B5.
Tel 9261 4997.

Napoleon Perdis Cosmetics
74 Oxford St,
Paddington.
Map 5 A2.
www.napoleoncosmetics.com

Orson & Blake
78 and 83–85 Queen St,
Woollahra. **Map** 6 E4.
Tel 9326 1155.
Also at:
483 Riley St, Surry Hills.
Map 4 F5.
Tel 8399 2525.
www.orsanandblake.com.au

Wheels & Doll Baby
259 Crown St,
Darlinghurst.
Map 5 A2.
Tel 9361 3286.

AUSTRALIANA

Done Art and Design
123 George St, The Rocks.
Map 1 B2.
Tel 9251 6099.
One of several branches.

Makers Mark
72 Castlereagh St.
Map 1 B5.
Tel 9231 6800.

Weiss Art
85 George St, The Rocks.
Map 1 B2.
Tel 9241 3819.
Also at: Harbourside
Shopping Centre, Darling
Harbour. **Map** 3 C2.
Tel 9281 4614.

BOOKS

Abbey's Bookshop
131 York St. **Map** 1 A5.
Tel 9264 3111.

Angus & Robertson's Bookworld
Pitt St Mall, Pitt St. **Map** 1 B5. *Tel* 9235 1188.
One of many branches.

Ariel
42 Oxford St, Paddington.
Map 5 B3.
Tel 9332 4581.

Berkelouw Books
19 Oxford St, Paddington
Map 5 B3.
Tel 9360 3200.
Also at:
70 Norton St, Leichhardt.
Tel 9560 3200.
www.berkelouw.com.au

The Bookshop Darlinghurst
207 Oxford St,
Darlinghurst. **Map** 5 A2.
Tel 9331 1103.

Dymocks
424 George St.
Map 1 B5.
Tel 9235 0155.
One of many branches.

Gleebooks
49 Glebe Point Rd, Glebe.
Map 3 B5.
Tel 9660 2333.

MUSIC

Anthem Records
9 Albion Place. **Map** 4 E3.
Tel 9267 7931.

Birdland
231 Pitt St. **Map** 1 B5.
Tel 9267 6811.

Central Station Records and Tapes
46 Oxford St, Darlinghurst.
Map 4 F4.
Tel 9361 5222.

Folkways
282 Oxford St,
Paddington. **Map** 5 C3.
Tel 9361 3980

Michael's Music Room
Shop 17, Town Hall
Square. **Map** 4 E3.
Tel 9267 1351.

Red Eye Records
66 King St, Sydney.
Map 1 B5.
Tel 9299 4233.

Utopia Records
Hoyts Cinema Complex,
505 George St. **Map** 4 E3.
Tel 9283 2423.

Waterfront
89 York St. **Map** 1 A5.
Tel 9283 2423.

ABORIGINAL ART

Aboriginal and Pacific Art
2 Danks St, Waterloo.
Tel 9699 2111.

Boomalli Aboriginal Artists' Cooperative
191 Parramatta Rd,
Annandale. **Map** 3 A5.
Tel 9560 2541.

Coo-ee Aboriginal Art Gallery
31 Lamrock Ave, Bondi
Beach.
Tel 9300 9233.

Hogarth Galleries Aboriginal Art Centre
7 Walker Lane, off Brown
St, Paddington.
Map 5 C3.
Tel 9360 6839.
One of two branches.

OPALS

Flame Opals
119 George Street,
The Rocks. **Map** 1 B2.
Tel 9247 3446.

Giulian's
2 Bridge St. **Map** 1 B3.
Tel 9252 2051.

Opal Fields
190 George St,
The Rocks.
Map 1 B2.
Tel 9247 6800.
One of three branches.

JEWELLERY

Dinosaur Designs
Strand Arcade.
Map 1 B5.
Tel 9223 2953.
One of several branches.

Fairfax & Roberts
44 Martin Place.
Map 1 B4.
Tel 9232 8511.

Hardy Brothers
77 Castlereagh St.
Map 1 B5.
Tel 9232 2422.

Jan Logan
36 Cross St, Double Bay.
Tel 9363 2529.

Love & Hatred
Strand Arcade.
Map 1 B5.
Tel 9233 3441.

Paspaley Pearls
142 King St.
Map 1 A4.
Tel 9232 7633.

Percy Marks
60–70 Elizabeth St.
Map 1 B4.
Tel 9233 1355.

Victoria Spring Designs
110 Oxford St,
Paddington.
Map 5 D3.
Tel 9331 7862.

Clothes and Accessories

Australian style was once an oxymoron. Sydney now offers a plethora of chic shops as long as you know where to look. Top boutiques sell both men's and women's clothing, as well as accessories. The city's "smart casual" ethos, particularly in summer, means there are plenty of luxe but informal clothes available.

AUSTRALIAN FASHION

A number of Sydney's fashion designers have attained a global profile, including **Collette Dinnigan** and **Akira Isogawa**. Dinnigan's is filled with lacy evening gowns whereas Japanese-born Isogawa makes artistic clothing for women and men.

Young jeans labels such as **Tsubi** (for men and women) and **Sass & Bide** (women only) have also shot to fame, with celebrities wearing their denims. Nearby is **Scanlan & Theodore**, a stalwart of the Australian fashion scene.

Other shops are **Dragstar**, with its selection of retro women's and children's clothing, such as bright sundresses and minis. The quirky **Capital L** and **Fat** boutiques house the hottest names in Aussie fashion, while **Zimmermann** offers women's and girls' clothes and is famous for its swimwear. **Lisa Ho** is the place to go for a frock, with designs ranging from pretty sundresses to glam gowns. Head to **Farage Man & Farage Women** for quality suits and shirts.

High-street clothing can be found in and around Pitt Street Mall and Bondi Junction. Here you will find both international and homegrown fashion outlets. **Sportsgirl** sells funky clothes that appeal to both teens and adult women. The **Witchery** stores are a favourite among women for their stylish designs. **Just Jeans** doesn't just sell jeans; it stocks the latest trends for men and women.

General Pants has funky street labels such as One Tea-spooon and Just Ask Amanda. Surry Hills is the place for discount and vintage clothing; check out **Zoo Emporium**. New designers try out their wares in Bondi, Glebe and Paddington markets *(see p133)*.

INTERNATIONAL LABELS

Many Sydney stores sell designer imports. For the best ranges, visit **Belinda** – a women's and men's boutique – as well as others in Double Bay, including the **Belinda Shoe Salon**. In **Robby Ingham Stores** you will find women's and men's ranges including Chloé, Paul Smith and Comme des Garçons. **Cosmopolitan Shoes** stocks labels such as Dolce & Gabbana, Sonia Rykiel, Dior and Jimmy Choo. **Hype DC** also offers all the latest ranges. New Zealand designers **Zambesi** offer their own designs for women and men as well as a range of Martin Margiela pieces.

LUXURY BRANDS

Many visitors like to shop for international labels such as **Gucci** and **Louis Vuitton**. You will find both in Castlereagh Street, along with **Chanel** and **Versace**. The Queen Victoria Building *(see p90)* is home to **Bally**, and Martin Place has resident designer A-listers such as **Prada** and **Armani**. **Diesel** is further afield on Oxford Street.

SURF SHOPS

For the latest surf gear, look no further than Bondi where the streets are lined with shops selling clothing, swimwear as well as boards of all sizes to buy and hire. Serious surfers and novices should check out **Mambo Friendship Store** and **Bondi Surf Co.** Besides stocking its own beachwear label, **Rip Curl** also sells Australian brands such as Tigerlily and Billabong. **Labyrinth** and **The Big Swim** are hugely popular swimwear shops packed with bikinis by designers including Jet and Seafolly.

CLOTHES FOR CHILDREN

Department stores, **David Jones** and **Myer** *(see p133)*, are one-stop shops for children's clothes, from newborn to teenage. Look out for good quality

SIZE CHART

Women's clothes

Australian	6	8	10	12	14	16	18	20
American	4	6	8	10	12	14	16	18
British	6	8	10	12	14	16	18	20
Continental	38	40	42	44	46	48	50	52

Women's shoes

Australian	6–6½	7	7½–8	8½	9–9½	10	10½–11
American	5	6	7	8	9	10	11
British	3	4	5	6	7	8	9
Continental	36	37	38	39	40	41	42

Men's suits

Australian	44	46	48	50	52	54	56	58
American	34	36	38	40	42	44	46	48
British	34	36	38	40	42	44	46	48
Continental	44	46	48	50	52	54	56	58

Men's shirts

Australian	36	38	39	41	42	43	44	45
American	14	15	15½	16	16½	17	17½	18
British	14	15	15½	16	16½	17	17½	18
Continental	36	38	39	41	42	43	44	45

Men's shoes

Australian	7	7½	8	8½	9	10	11	12
American	7	7½	8	8½	9½	10½	11	11½
British	6	7	7½	8	9	10	11	12
Continental	39	40	41	42	43	44	45	46

Australian labels such as Fred Bare and Gumboots. Mambo, Dragstar and Zimmermann also sell fun and unusual kidswear.

ACCESSORIES

The team behind **Dinosaur Designs** are some of Australia's most celebrated designers. They craft chunky bangles, necklaces and rings, and also bowls, plates and vases, from jewel-coloured resin. **Collect**, the retail outlet of Object Gallery, is another place to look for handcrafted jewellery, scarfs, textiles, objects, ceramics and glass by leading and emerging Australian designers. At **Makers Mark** *(see pp134)* the jewels feature unique South Sea pearls, classic sapphires and diamonds or unusual materials, such as wood. In her plush store, **Jan Logan** sells exquisite jewellery, using all kinds of precious and semi-precious stones.

Australian hat designer, **Helen Kaminski**, uses fabrics, raffia, straw, felt and leather to make hats and bags. In a different style altogether, **Crumpler** use high-tech fabrics to make bags that will last a century. And in a street of designer names, **Andrew McDonald**'s little studio shop doesn't cry for attention, but he does sell handcrafted shoes for men and women.

DIRECTORY

AUSTRALIAN FASHION

Akira Isogawa
12A Queen St, Woollahra.
Map 6 E4. **Tel** 9361 5221.

Capital L
333 S Dowling St,
Darlinghurst. **Map** 5 A3.
Tel 9361 0111.

Collette Dinnigan
33 William St,
Paddington. **Map** 6 D3.
Tel 9360 6691.

Dragstar
96 Glenayr Ave, Bondi.
Tel 9365 2244.

Farage Man & Farage Women
Shops 54 & 79, Level 1
Strand Arcade. **Map** 1 B5.
Tel 9231 3479,

Fat
18 Oxford St, Woollahra.
Map 6 D4.
Tel 9380 6455.

General Pants
Queen Victoria Building.
Map 4 E2. **Tel** 9264 2842.

Just Jeans
Mid City Centre, Pitt St.
Map 4 E2. **Tel** 9223 8349.

Lisa Ho
2a–6a Queen St,
Woollahra. **Map** 6 D4.
Tel 9360 2345.

Sass & Bide
132 Oxford St,
Paddington. **Map** 5 B3.
Tel 9360 3900.

Scanlan & Theodore
122 Oxford St,
Paddington. **Map** 5 B3.
Tel 9380 9388.

Sportsgirl
Skygarden, 77 Castlereagh
St. **Map** 1 B5.
Tel 9223 8255.

Tsubi
16 Glenmore Rd,
Paddington. **Map** 5 B3.
Tel 9361 6291.

Witchery
Sydney Central Plaza,
Pitt St. **Map** 4 E2.
Tel 9231 1245.

Zimmermann
1/387 Oxford St,
Paddington. **Map** 6 D4.
Tel 9357 4700.

Zoo Emporium
332 Crown St, Surry Hills.
Tel 9380 5990.

INTERNATIONAL LABELS

Belinda
39 & 29 William St,
Paddington. **Map** 6 D3.
Tel 9380 8728.

Belinda Shoe Salon
14 Transvaal Ave,
Double Bay.
Tel 9328 6288.

Cosmopolitan Shoes
Cosmopolitan Centre,
Knox St, Double Bay.
Tel 9362 0510.

Hype DC
Cnr Market St &
Pitt St Mall. **Map** 1 B5.
Tel 9221 5688.

Robby Ingham Stores
424–428 Oxford St,
Paddington. **Map** 6 D4.
Tel 9332 2124.

Zambesi
8 Cross St, Double Bay.
Tel 9363 1466.

LUXURY BRANDS

Armani
4 Martin Place.
Map 1 B4. **Tel** 8233 5888.

Bally
Ground floor, Queen
Victoria Building.
Map 1 B5. **Tel** 9267 3887.

Chanel
70 Castlereagh St.
Map 1 B5. **Tel** 9233 4800.

Diesel
408–410 Oxford St,
Paddington. **Map** 6 D4.
Tel 9331 5255.

Gucci
MLC Centre, 15–25
Martin Place. **Map** 1 B4.
Tel 9232 7565.

Louis Vuitton
63 Castlereagh St.
Map 1 B5. **Tel** 9236 9624.

Prada
44 Martin Place.
Map 1 B4. **Tel** 9231 3929.

Versace
128 Castlereagh St.
Map 1 B5. **Tel** 9267 3232.

SURF SHOPS

The Big Swim
74 Campbell Parade, Bondi
Beach. **Tel** 9365 4457.

Bondi Surf Co.
72–76 Campbell Parade,
Bondi Beach.
Tel 9365 0870.

Labyrinth
30 Campbell Parade, Bondi
Beach. **Tel** 9130 5092.

Mambo Friendship Store
17 Oxford St, Paddington.
Map 5 B3. **Tel** 9331 8034.

Rip Curl
82 Campbell Parade,
Bondi Beach.
Tel 9130 2660.

CLOTHES FOR CHILDREN

David Jones
Cnr Elizabeth &
Castlereagh sts.
Map 1 B5. **Tel** 9266 5544.

Myer
436 George St.
Map 1 B5.
Tel 9238 9111.

ACCESSORIES

Andrew McDonald
58 William St, Paddington.
Map 6 D3.
Tel 9358 6793.

Collect
88 George St, The Rocks.
Map 1 B2. **Tel** 9247 7984.

Crumpler
30 Oxford St, Paddington.
Map 5 B3.
Tel 9331 4660.

Dinosaur Designs
See pp134–5.

Helen Kaminski
Shop 3, Four Seasons
Hotel, 199 George St.
Map 1 B3. **Tel** 9251 9850.

Jan Logan
36 Cross St, Double Bay.
Tel 9363 2529.

Makers Mark
72 Castlereagh St.
Map 1 B5. **Tel** 9231 6800.

ENTERTAINMENT IN SYDNEY

A Wharf Theatre production poster

Sydney has the standard of entertainment and nightlife you would expect from a cosmopolitan city. Everything from opera and ballet at Sydney Opera House to Shakespeare by the Sea at the Balmoral Beach amphitheatre is on offer. Venues such as the Capitol, Her Majesty's Theatre and the Theatre Royal play host to the latest musicals, while Sydney's many smaller theatres are home to interesting fringe theatre, modern dance and rock and pop concerts. Pub rock thrives in the inner city and beyond; and there are many nightspots for jazz, dance and alternative music. Movie buffs are well catered for with film festivals, art-house films and foreign titles, as well as the latest Hollywood blockbusters. One of the features of harbourside living is the free outdoor entertainment, which is very popular with children.

Recently built Sydney Theatre (see p140) on Hickson Road, Walsh Bay

INFORMATION

For details of events in the city, you should check the daily newspapers first. They carry cinema, and often arts and theatre, advertisements daily. The most comprehensive listings appear in the *Sydney Morning Herald's* "Metro" guide every Friday. The *Daily Telegraph* has a daily gig guide, with opportunities to win free tickets to special events. The *Australian's* main arts pages appear on Fridays, and all the papers review new films in weekend editions.

Tourism NSW information kiosks have free guides and the quarterly *What's on in Darling Harbour*. Kiosks are found at Town Hall, Circular Quay and Martin Place. *Where Magazine* is available at the airport and the **Sydney Visitor Centre** at The Rocks. Hotels also offer free guides, or try **www.sydney.citysearch.com.au**.

Music fans are well served by the free weekly guides *Drum Media*, *3-D World* and *Brag*, found at video and music shops, pubs and clubs.

Many venues have leaflets about forthcoming attractions, while the major venues have information telephone lines and websites.

BUYING TICKETS

Some of the most popular operas, shows, plays and ballets in Sydney are sold out months in advance. While it is better to book ahead, many theatres do set aside tickets to be sold at the door on the night.

You can buy tickets from the box office or by telephone. Some orchestral performances do not admit children under seven, so check with the box office before buying. If you make a phone booking using a credit card, the tickets can be mailed to you.

Alternatively, tickets can be collected from the box office half an hour before the show. The major agencies will take overseas bookings.

Buying tickets from touts is not advisable, if you are caught with a "sold on" ticket you will be denied access to the event. If all else fails, hotel concierges have a reputation for being able to secure hard-to-get seats.

CHOOSING SEATS

If booking in person at either the venue or the agency, you will be able to look at a seating plan. Be aware that in the State Theatre's stalls, row A is the back row. In Sydney, there is not as much difference in price between stalls and dress circle as in other cities.

If booking by phone with one of the agencies, you will only be able to get a rough idea of where your seats are. The computer will select the "best" tickets.

The annual Gay and Lesbian Mardi Gras Festival's dog show (see p41)

BOOKING AGENCIES

Sydney has two main ticket agencies: **Ticketek** and **Ticketmaster**. Between them, they represent all the major entertainment and sporting events. Ticketek has more than 60 outlets throughout NSW and the ACT, open from 9am to 5pm weekdays, and Saturdays from 9am to 4pm. Opening hours vary between agencies and call centres, so check with Ticketek to confirm. Phone bookings: 8:30am–10pm, Monday to Saturday, and 8:30am–5pm Sunday. For internet bookings, visit their website.

Ticketmaster outlets are open 9am–5pm Monday to Friday. Phone bookings: 9am–9pm Monday to Saturday and 10am–5pm Sunday. Agencies accept traveller's cheques, bank cheques, cash, Visa, MasterCard (Access) and Amex. Some agencies do not accept Diners Club. A booking fee applies, plus a postage and handling charge if tickets are mailed out. There are generally no refunds (unless a show is cancelled) or exchanges. If one agency has sold out its allocation for a show, it is worth checking with another.

The Spanish firedancers *Els Comediants* at the Sydney Festival

A busker at Circular Quay

DISCOUNT TICKETS AND FREE ENTERTAINMENT

Tuesday is budget-price day at most cinemas. Some independent cinemas have special prices throughout the week. The Sydney Symphony Orchestra and Opera Australia *(see p140)* offer a special Student Rush price to full-time students under 28 but only if surplus tickets are available. These can be bought on the day of the performance, from the box office at the venue.

Outdoor events are especially popular in Sydney, and many are free *(see pp40–3)*. Sydney Harbour is a splendid setting for the fabulous New Year's Eve fireworks, with a display at 9pm for families as well as the midnight display.

The Sydney Festival in January is a huge extravaganza of performance and visual art. Various outdoor venues in the Rocks, Darling Harbour and in front of the **Sydney Opera House** *(see pp84-5)* feature events to suit every taste, including musical productions, drama, dance, exhibitions and circuses. The most popular free events are the symphony and jazz concerts held in the Domain. Also popular are the Darling Harbour Circus and Street Theatre Festival at Easter, and the food and wine festival held in June at Manly Beach.

DISABLED VISITORS

Many older venues were not designed with the disabled visitor in mind, but this has been redressed in most newer buildings. It is best to phone the box office beforehand to request special seating and

Publicity shot of the Australian Chamber Orchestra *(see p140)*

other requirements or call **Ideas Incorporated**, who have a list of Sydney's most wheel-chair-friendly venues. The Sydney Opera House has disabled parking, wheelchair access and a loop system in the Concert Hall for the hearing impaired. A brochure, *Services for the Disabled*, is also available.

DIRECTORY

USEFUL NUMBERS

Ideas Incorporated

Tel 1800 029 904.

Sydney Opera House

Information Desk

Tel (02) 9250 7111.

Disabled Information

Tel (02) 9250 7185.

Sydney Visitor Centre

Tel 1800 067 676 or

(02) 9240 8788.

www.sydneyvisitorcentre.

com.au

Tourism NSW

Tel 132 077.

www.visitnsw.com.au

TICKET AGENCIES

Ticketek

Tel 13 28 49.

www.ticketek.com.au

Ticketmaster

Tel 136 100.

www.ticketmaster7.com

Performing Arts and Cinema

Sydney has a wealth of orchestral, choral, chamber and contemporary music from which to choose, and of course every visitor should enjoy a performance of some kind at the Sydney Opera House. There is also a stimulating range of musicals, classic plays and Shakespeare by the Sea, as well as contemporary, fringe, experimental theatre and comedy. Prominent playwrights include David Williamson, Debra Oswald, Brendan Cowell, Stephen Sewell and Louis Nowra. Australian film-making has also earned an excellent international reputation. A rich variety of both local and foreign films are screened throughout the year.

CLASSICAL MUSIC

Much of Sydney's orchestral music and recitals are the work of the famous **Sydney Symphony Orchestra (SSO)**. Numerous concerts are given, mostly in the Sydney Opera House Concert Hall *(see pp84–5)*, the **City Recital Hall** and the **Sydney Town Hall**.

The **Australian Chamber Orchestra** also performs at the Opera House and City Recital Hall, and has won high acclaim for its creativity. The **Australia Ensemble** is the resident chamber music group at the University of New South Wales.

Many choral groups and ensembles, such as the **Macquarie Trio** of violin, piano and cello, book St James Church *(see pp115)* because of its atmosphere and acoustics.

Formed in 1973, the respected **Sydney Youth Orchestra** stages performances in major concert venues. The **Australian Youth Choir** is booked for many private functions, but if you are lucky, you may catch one of their major annual performances.

Comprising the 120-strong Sydney Philharmonia Symphonic Choir and the 40-member Sydney Philharmonia Motet Choir, the **Sydney Philharmonia Choirs** are the city's finest.

One of Sydney's most impressive vocal groups is the **Café of the Gate of Salvation**, which has been described as an "Aussie blend of *a capella* and gospel".

Originally specialized in chamber music, **Musica Viva** now presents string quartets, jazz, piano groups, percussionists, soloists and international avant-garde artists as well.

Synergy is one of Australia's foremost percussion quartets, commissioning works from all over the world.

COMEDY

Sydney's most established comedy venue, the **Comedy Store** is known for its themed nights. Tuesday is open-mic night; Wednesday, new comics; Thursday, cutting edge; Friday and Saturday are reserved for the best of the best. Monday is comedy night at **The Old Manly Boatshed**, where both local and visiting comics perform. Monday is also comedy night at the **Bridge Hotel**, where live entertainment is offered most nights of the week.

DANCE

The **Australian Ballet** has two seven-week Sydney seasons at the Opera House: one in March/April, the other in November/December. **Sydney Dance Company** is the city's leading modern dance group. Productions are mostly staged at the Sydney Opera House.

Bangarra Dance Theatre uses traditional Aboriginal and Torres Strait Islander dance and music as its inspiration. The startling and original **Legs on the Wall** are a physical theatre group, brilliantly combining circus and aerial techniques with dance and narrative, often performed while suspended from skyscrapers.

OPERA

In 1956, the Australian Opera (now called **Opera Australia**) was formed. It presented four Mozart productions in its first year. But it was the opening of the Sydney Opera House in 1973 that heralded new public interest. Opera Australia's summer season is held from early January to early March; the winter season from June to the end of October. Every year at the popular Opera in The Domain, members of Opera Australia perform excerpts from famous pieces.

THEATRE

Sydney's larger, mainstream musicals are staged at the **Theatre Royal**, the opulent **State Theatre** *(see p90)* and the **Capitol Theatre**. The **Star City** entertainment and casino complex boasts two theatres, the Showroom, and the first-rate Lyric Theatre.

Smaller venues also offer a range of interesting plays and performances. These include the **Seymour Theatre Centre**, the **Belvoir Street Theatre** and the **Ensemble Theatre**. The **Stables Theatre** specializes in works by new Australian playwrights, while the new **Parade Theatre** at the National Institute of Dramatic Arts (NIDA) showcases work by NIDA's students. The well-respected **Sydney Theatre Company (STC)** has just introduced an ensemble of actors, employed full time, who will perform a minimum of two plays each season. Most STC productions are performed at **The Wharf**.

The **Bell Shakespeare Company** productions are ideal for the young or the more wary theatre-goers. **Shakespeare by the Sea**, at lovely Balmoral Beach *(see p144)*, puts on outdoor productions in the summer and has no need for painted backdrops.

The **Sydney Festival** provides an enjoyable celebration of original, often quirky, Australian theatre, dance, music and visual arts.

FILM

The city's main commercial cinema, the **Greater Union Hoyts Village Complex**, is on George Street to the south of the Town Hall. A similar multiplex is in the Fox Studios Entertainment Quarter *(see p125)*. The **IMAX Theatre** in Darling Harbour has a giant, 8-storey screen showing 2D and 3D films.

Cinephiles flock to **Palace Cinemas** on Oxford Street and **Dendy Cinema** at Circular Quay. **Cinema Paris** shows arthouse and indie films, as well as many Bollywood productions. The **Reading Cinema** regularly shows new Chinese films.

Most foreign films are screened in the original language with English subtitles. The latest screenings are usually at 9:30pm, although most major cinemas run later shows. Commercial cinema houses offer half-price tickets on Tuesday, while Palace does so on Monday.

The Sydney Film Festival is one of the highlights of the city's calendar *(see p43)*. The main venue is the State Theatre. The **Flickerfest International Short Film Festival** is held at the Bondi Pavilion Amphitheatre at Bondi Beach in early January. It screens shorts and animated films. In February, **Tropfest** shows local short films.

Run by Queer Screen, the **New Mardi Gras Film Festival**, starts mid-February and continues for 15 days.

DIRECTORY

CLASSICAL MUSIC

Australia Ensemble
Tel 9385 4874.
www.ae.unsw.edu.au

Australian Chamber Orchestra
www.aco.com.au

Australian Youth Choir
www.niypaa.com.au

Café of the Gate of Salvation
www.cafeofthegateof
salvation.com.au

City Recital Hall
Angel Place.
Map 1 B4.
Tel 8256 2222.
www.cityrecitalhall.com

Macquarie Trio
Tel 9850 6355. www.
macquarietrio.com.au

Musica Viva
www.mva.org.au

Sydney Philharmonia Choirs
Tel 9251 3115.
www.sydneyphilharmonia.
com.au

Sydney Symphony Orchestra
Tel 9334 4600.
www. symphony.org.au

Sydney Town Hall
483 George Street.
Map 4 E2.
Tel 9265 9333.

Sydney Youth Orchestra
Tel 9251 2422.
www.syo.com.au

Synergy
www.synergypercussion.
com

COMEDY

Bridge Hotel
135 Victoria Rd, Rozelle.
Tel 9810 1260. www.
bridgehotel.com.au

Comedy Store
Entertainment Quarter,
Driver Ave, Moore Park.
Map 5 C5. *Tel* 9357 1419.
www.comedystore.com.au

The Old Manly Boatshed
40 The Corso, Manly.
Tel 9977 4443.

DANCE

Australian Ballet
Tel 9252 5500. www.
australianballet.com.au

Bangarra Dance Theatre
www.bangarra.com.au

Legs on the Wall
Tel 9560 9479. www.
legsonthewall.com.au

Sydney Dance Company
www.sydneydance.com.au

OPERA

Opera Australia
Tel 9319 1088. www.
opera-australia.org.au

THEATRE

Bell Shakespeare Company
Tel 9241 2722. www.
bellshakespeare.com.au

Belvoir St Theatre
25 Belvoir St, Surry Hills.
Tel 9699 3444.
www.belvoir.com.au

Capitol Theatre
13 Campbell St, Haymarket.
Map 4 E4. *Tel* 136 100.
www.capitoltheatre.com.au

Ensemble Theatre
78 McDougall St, Kirribilli.
Box office tel 9929 0644.
www.ensemble.com.au

Parade Theatre
215 Anzac Parade,
Kensington. **Map** 5 B4
Tel 9697 7613.

Seymour Theatre Centre
Cnr Cleveland St & City Rd,
Chippendale.
Tel 9351 7940.

Shakespeare by the Sea
Band Rotunda, Balmoral
Beach. *Tel* 9590 8305.
www.shakespeare-by-
the-sea.com

Stables Theatre
10 Nimrod St, Kings Cross.
Map 5 B1. *Tel* 9250 7799.

Star City
80 Pyrmont St, Pyrmont.
Map 3 B1. *Tel* 9777 9000.

State Theatre
49 Market St. **Map** 1 B5.
Box office tel 136 100.
www.statetheatre.com.au

Sydney Festival
Tel 8248 6500. www.
sydneyfestival.org.au

Sydney Theatre Co.
Tel 9250 1777. www.
sydneytheatre.com.au

Theatre Royal
MLC Centre, King St. **Map**
1 B5. *Tel* 9224 8444.

The Wharf
Pier 4, Hickson Rd, Walsh
Bay. **Map** 1 A1. *Tel* 9250
1777.

FILM

Cinema Paris
Entertainment Quarter,
Driver Ave, Moore Park.
Map 5 C5. *Tel* 9332 1633.

Dendy Cinema
Shop 9/2, East Circular
Quay. **Map** 1 C2.
Tel 9247 3800.

Flickerfest
www.flickerfest.com.au

Greater Union Hoyts Village Complex
505–525 George St.
Map 4 E3. *Tel* 9267 8666.
www.greaterunion.com.au

IMAX Theatre
Southern Promenade,
Darling Harbour. **Map** 4
D3. *Tel* 9281 3300.
www.imax.com.au

New Mardi Gras Festival
www.queerscreen.com.au

Palace Cinemas
Academy Twin 3a Oxford
St, Paddington. *Tel* 9361
4453. **Verona** 17 Oxford
St, Paddington. *Tel* 9360
6099. **Map** 5 B3.

Reading Cinema
Level 3, Market City, 9 Hay
St, Haymarket. **Map** 4 E4.
Tel 9280 1202. www.
readingcinemas.com.au

Tropfest
www.tropfest.com

Music Venues and Nightclubs

Sydney attracts some of the biggest names in modern music all year round. Venues range from the cavernous Sydney Entertainment Centre to small and noisy back rooms in pubs. Visiting international DJs frequently play sets at Sydney clubs. Some venues cater for a variety of music tastes – rock and pop one night, jazz, blues or folk the next. There are several free weekly gig guides available, including *Drum Media*, *3-D World* and *Brag (see p138)*, which tell you what is on.

GETTING IN

Tickets for major shows are available through booking agencies such as Ticketek and Ticketmaster *(see p138)*. Prices vary considerably, depending on the shows that are going to take place. You may pay from A$30 to A$70 for a gig at the Metro, but over A$150 for seats for a Rolling Stones concert. **Moshtix** also sells tickets for smaller venues across Sydney and their website gives a good idea of the various venues and what is on. Buying online also prevents you from having to queue early for tickets from the door.

You can also pay at the door on the night at most places, unless the show is sold out. Nightclubs often have a cover charge, but some venues will admit you free before a certain time in the evening or on weeknights.

Most venues serve alcohol, so shows are restricted to those at least 18 years of age. This is the usual case unless a gig is specified "all ages". It is advisable that people under 30 years old carry photo identification, such as a passport or driver's licence, because entry to some establishments is very strict. You are also not allowed to carry any kind of bottle into most nightclubs or other venues. Similarly, any cameras and recording devices are usually prohibited.

Dress codes vary, but generally shorts (on men) and flip flops are not welcome. Wear thin layers, which you can remove when you get hot, instead of a coat, and avoid carrying a big bag, because many venues do not have a cloakroom.

ROCK, POP AND HIP HOP

Pop's big names and famous rock groups perform at the **Sydney Entertainment Centre**, **Hordern Pavilion** and sports grounds such as the Aussie Stadium at **Sydney Olympic Park** *(see p127)* in Homebush Bay. More intimate locations include the **State Theatre** *(see p90)*, **Enmore Theatre** and Sydney's best venue, **The Metro Theatre**. Hip Hop acts usually play in rock venues rather than in nightclubs. You are almost as likely to find a crew rapping or as a band strumming and drumming at the Metro Theatre, the **Gaelic Club**, **@Newtown** or the **Hopetoun Hotel**. It is not unusual to catch a punk, garage or electro-folk band at **Spectrum** or the **Annandale Hotel** on Parramatta Road.

Pub rock is a constantly changing scene in Sydney. Weekly listings appear on Fridays in the "Metro" section of the *Sydney Morning Herald* and in the street press *(see p138)*. Music stores are also full of flyers for gigs at the Metro Theatre and Gaelic Club, where international and Australian acts perform every week. These shows usually sell out very quickly.

JAZZ, FOLK AND BLUES

For many years, the first port of call for any jazz, funk, groove or folk enthusiast has been **The Basement**. Visiting luminaries play some nights, talented but struggling local musicians others, and the line-ups now also include increasingly popular world music and hip-hop bands. **Soup Plus**, Margaret Street, plays jazz while serving reasonably priced food, including soup. Experimental jazz is offered on Fridays and Saturdays at the **Seymour Theatre Centre** *(see p141)*. **The Vanguard**, a newer venue, also offers dinner and show deals, as well as show-only tickets, and has been drawing an excellent roster of jazz, blues and roots talent. Annandale's **Empire Hotel** is Sydney's official home of the blues, and the **Cat & Fiddle Hotel** in Balmain of acoustic music and folk. **Wine Banq**, a plush bar and restaurant in the central business district, dishes up smooth jazz most nights of the week.

HOUSE, BREAKBEATS AND TECHNO

Sydney's only super club, **Home Sydney** in Cockle Bay features three levels and a gargantuan sound system. Friday night is the time to go, as the DJs present a pulsating mix of house, trance, drum and bass and breakbeats. A mainstream crowd flocks to the nearby **Bungalow 8** on King Street Wharf. Once the sun has set, house DJs turn the place into a club. At the swank **Tank** on Bridge Lane, the emphasis is on pure house music and the decor is a throwback to Studio 54 in New York. **Cave**, at Star City, is another mainstream house club.

For something a little more hip, try **Candy's Apartment** on Bayswater Road, or the fashionable tech-electro **Mars Lounge** on Wentworth Avenue, with its red lacquered interior. Enter **Goodbar** on Oxford Street in Paddington by a barely marked door, descend a flight of stairs, and you will find yourself in one of Sydney's longest established nightclubs. There is hip hop some nights, house others. Down the road, **Q Bar** on Oxford Street, Darlinghurst, has arcade games for when you need a breather. Or try the low-ceilinged **Chinese Laundry** on Sussex Street, tucked under the gentrified pub, Slip Inn.

GAY AND LESBIAN PUBS AND CLUBS

Sunday night is the big night for many of Sydney's gay community, although there is plenty of action throughout the week. A number of venues have a gay or lesbian night on one night of the week and attract a mainstream crowd on the other nights. Wednesday is lesbian night at the **Bank Hotel** in Newtown and some Sundays are queer nights at Home Sydney and Mars Lounge. **Club Kooky**, on William Street, offers an alternative to the mainstream gay clubs with a mixed crowd, excellent DJs and live electronic music and an anything-goes vibe on Sunday nights.

ARQ on Flinders Street is the largest of the gay clubs, with pounding commercial house music. The main dance floor is overlooked by a mezzanine for watching the writhing mass of bodies below. **Midnight Shift** on Oxford Street is for men only, and **Stonewall** plays camp anthems and is patronized mostly by men and their straight female friends. Drag shows are performed every night at **The Venus Room** cabaret club on Roslyn Street.

The **Colombian** is the best of the Oxford Street bars, with a mock Central American jungle and large windows that open out to the street. The **Oxford Hotel** and its upper-level cocktail bars are popular too. Both the **Newtown Hotel** and **Imperial Hotel** have drag shows on most nights of the week.

DIRECTORY

ROCK, POP AND HIP HOP

Annandale Hotel
17–19 Parramatta Rd, Annandale.
Tel 9550 1078.
www.
annandalehotel.com

Enmore Theatre
130 Enmore Rd, Newtown.
Tel 9550 3666.
www.
enmoretheatre.com.au

Gaelic Club
64 Devonshire St, Surry Hills. *Tel 9211 1687.*
www.thegaelicclub.com

Hopetoun Hotel
416 Bourke St, Surry Hills.
Tel 9361 5257.

Hordern Pavilion
Driver Ave, Moore Park.
Map 5 C5.
Tel 9921 5333.
www.playbillvenues.com

The Metro Theatre
624 George St.
Map 4 E3. *Tel 9264 2666.*
www.
metrotheatre.com.au

Moshtix
Tel 9209 4614.
www.moshtix.com.au

@Newtown
52 Enmore Rd, Newtown.
Tel 9557 5044.
www.atnewtown.com.au

Spectrum
34 Oxford St,
Darlinghurst. **Map** 4 F4.
www.pashpresents.com

State Theatre
49 Market St. **Map** 1 B5.
Tel 9373 6655.
Box office tel 136 00.
www.statetheatre.com.au

Sydney Entertainment Centre
Harbour St, Haymarket.
Map 4 D4.
Tel 9320 4200.

Sydney Olympic Park
Homebush Bay.
Tel 9714 7958.
www.sydneyolympicpark.
nsw.gov.au

JAZZ, FOLK AND BLUES

The Basement
29 Reiby Place.
Map 1 B3.
Tel 9251 2797. **www.**
thebasement.com.au

Cat & Fiddle Hotel
456 Darling St, Balmain.
Tel 9810 7931.
www.thecatandfiddle.net

Empire Hotel
Cnr Johnston St & Paramatta Rd, Annandale.
Tel 9557 1701.
www.sydneyblues.com

Seymour Theatre Centre
Cnr Cleveland St & City Rd, Chippendale.
Tel 9351 7940.

Soup Plus
1 Margaret St (cnr Clarence St). **Map** 4 E1.
Tel 9299 7728.
www.soupplus.com.au

The Vanguard
42 King St, Newtown.
Tel 9557 7992. **www.**
thevanguard.com.au

Wine Banq
53 Martin Pl. **Map** 1 B4.
Tel 9222 1919.
www.winebanq.com.au

HOUSE, BREAKBEATS AND TECHNO

Bungalow 8
The Promenade,
King St Wharf.
Tel 9299 4660.

Candy's Apartment
22 Bayswater Rd,
Kings Cross. **Map** 5 B1.
Tel 9380 5600.

Cave
Star City, Pirrama Rd,
Pyrmont. **Map** 3 C1.
Tel 9566 4755.

Chinese Laundry
Slip Inn 111 Sussex St.
Map 1 A3. *Tel 8295 9999.*

Goodbar
11a Oxford St,
Paddington. **Map** 5 B3.
Tel 9360 6759.

Home Sydney
Wheat Rd, Cockle Bay,
Darling Harbour.
Map 4 D2.
Tel 9266 0600.
www.homesydney.com

Mars Lounge
16 Wentworth Avenue,
Darlinghurst. **Map** 4 F4
Tel 9267 6440.

Q Bar
Level 2, 44 Oxford St,
Darlinghurst.
Map 4 F4.
Tel 9360 1375.

Tank
3 Bridge Lane.
Tel 9240 3094.

GAY AND LESBIAN CLUBS AND PUBS

ARQ
16 Flinders St, Taylor
Square. **Map** 5 A2.
Tel 9380 8700.

Bank Hotel
324 King St. Newtown.
Tel 9565 1730.

Club Kooky
77 William St, East Sydney.
Map 5 A1.
Tel 9361 4981.

Colombian
Cnr Oxford and Crown
Sts, Surry Hills. **Map** 5 A2.
Tel 9360 2151.

Imperial Hotel
35 Erskineville Rd,
Erskineville.
Tel 9519 9899.

Midnight Shift
85 Oxford St, Darlinghurst.
Map 5 A2.
Tel 9360 4319.

Newtown Hotel
174 King St, Newtown.
Tel 9557 1329.

Oxford Hotel
134 Oxford St,
Darlinghurst. **Map** 5 A2.
Tel 9331 3467.

Stonewall
175 Oxford St,
Darlinghurst. **Map** 5 A2.
Tel 9360 1963.

The Venus Room
2 Roslyn St, Kings Cross.
Map 5 C1.
Tel 8354 0888.

Sydney's Beaches

Being a city built around the water, it is no wonder that many of Sydney's recreational activities involve the sand, sea and sun. There are many harbour and surf beaches in Sydney, most of them accessible by bus *(see p129)*. Even if you're not a swimmer, the beaches offer a chance to get away from it all for a day or weekend and enjoy the fresh air and relaxed way of life.

SWIMMING

You can swim at either harbour or ocean beaches. Harbour beaches are generally smaller and sheltered. Popular ones are Camp Cove, Shark Bay and Balmoral Beach.

At the ocean beaches, surf lifesavers in their red and yellow or blue caps are on duty. Swimming rules are strongly enforced. Surf life-saving carnivals are held throughout the summer. Call **Surf Life Saving NSW** for a calendar. Well-patrolled, safer surf beaches include Bondi, Manly and Coogee.

The beaches can become polluted, especially after heavy rainfall. The **Beach Watch Info Line** provides updated information.

SURFING

Surfing is more a way of life than a leisure activity for some Sydneysiders. If you're a beginner, try Bondi, Bronte, Palm Beach or Collaroy.

Two of the best surf beaches are Maroubra and Narrabeen. Bear in mind that local surfers know one another well and do not take kindly to "intruders" who drop in on their

waves. To hire a surfboard, try Bondi Surf Co on Campbell Parade, Bondi Beach, or Aloha Surf on Pittwater Road, Manly. If you would like to learn, there are two schools: **Manly Surf School** and **Lets Go Surfing** at Bondi Beach. They also hire out boards and wetsuits.

WINDSURFING AND SAILING

There are locations around Sydney suitable for every level of windsurfer. Boards can be hired from **Balmoral Windsurfing, Sailing & Kayaking School & Hire**.

Good spots include Palm Beach, Narrabeen Lakes, La Perouse, Brighton-Le-Sands and Kurnell Point (for beginner and intermediate boarders) and Long Reef Beach, Palm Beach and Collaroy (for more experienced boarders).

One of the best ways to see the harbour is while sailing. A sailing boat, including a skipper, can be hired for the afternoon from the **East Sail** sailing club. If you'd like to learn how to sail, the sailing club has two-day courses and also hires out sailing boats and motor cruisers to experienced sailors.

Scuba diving at Gordons Bay

SCUBA DIVING-

The great barrier reef it may not be, but there are some excellent dive spots around Sydney, especially in winter when the water is clear, if a little cold. Favoured spots are Shelly Beach, Gordons Bay and Camp Cove.

Pro Dive Coogee offers a complete range of courses, escorted dives, introductory dives for beginners, and hire equipment. **Dive Centre Manly** also runs courses, hires equipment and conducts boat dives seven days a week.

DIRECTORY

Balmoral Windsurfing and Kitesurfing School
Balmoral Sailing Club, Balmoral Beach. *Tel 9960 5344.*
www.sailboard.net.au

Beach Watch Info Line
Tel 1800 036 677.

Dive Centre Manly
10 Belgrave St, Manly. *Tel 9977 4355.* **www**.divesydney.com
Also at Bondi.

East Sail
d'Albora Marinas, New Beach Rd, Rushcutters Bay. *Tel 9327 1166.*
www.eastsail.com.au

Lets Go Surfing
128 Ramsgate Ave North Bondi.
Tel 9365 1800.
www.letsgosurfing.com.au

Manly Surf School
North Steyne Rd, Manly.
Tel 9977 6977.
www.manlysurfschool.com

Pro Dive Coogee
27 Alfreda St, Coogee.
Tel 9665 6333.

Surf Life Saving NSW
Tel 9984 7188.
www.surflifesaving.com.au

Rock baths and surf lifesaving club at Coogee Beach

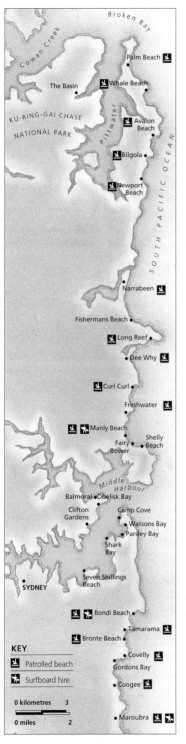

TOP 30 BEACHES

These beaches have been selected for their safe swimming, water sports, facilities available or their picturesque setting.

	SWIMMING POOL	SURFING	WINDSURFING	FISHING	SCUBA DIVING	PICNIC/BARBECUE	RESTAURANT/CAFE
AVALON	☆	☆	☆	☆		☆	
BALMORAL	☆		☆	☆	☆	☆	☆
THE BASIN	☆					☆	
BILGOLA							
BONDI BEACH	☆	☆		☆	☆	☆	☆
BRONTE	☆	☆		☆	☆	☆	☆
CAMP COVE					☆		
CLIFTON GARDENS	☆		☆	☆	☆	☆	
CLOVELLY				☆	☆	☆	
COOGEE	☆		☆	☆	☆	☆	☆
CURL CURL	☆	☆		☆			
DEE WHY	☆	☆		☆	☆	☆	☆
FAIRY BOWER					☆		
FISHERMANS BEACH		☆	☆	☆	☆		
FRESHWATER	☆	☆		☆	☆	☆	
GORDONS BAY				☆	☆		
LONG REEF		☆	☆	☆	☆		
MANLY BEACH	☆	☆			☆	☆	☆
MAROUBRA		☆	☆	☆	☆	☆	
NARRABEEN	☆	☆		☆		☆	
NEWPORT BEACH	☆	☆	☆	☆		☆	
OBELISK BAY							
PALM BEACH	☆	☆	☆	☆		☆	☆
PARSLEY BAY						☆	
SEVEN SHILLINGS BEACH	☆					☆	
SHARK BAY	☆					☆	☆
SHELLY BEACH					☆	☆	☆
TAMARAMA		☆	☆	☆	☆	☆	☆
WATSONS BAY	☆				☆		☆
WHALE BEACH	☆	☆	☆	☆		☆	☆

FISHING IN SYDNEY

Surprisingly for a thriving city port, there is a wide variety of fish to be caught. From the rocks and headlands of the northern beaches, such as Palm Beach and Bilgola, tuna, whiting and blenny abound. The Narrabeen Lakes offer estuary fishing, with a population of flathead and bream. The sheltered Middle Harbour has many angling spots. A NSW Recreational Fishing Fee must be paid by everyone.

Triplefin blenny

SPORTING SYDNEY

Throughout Australia sport is a way of life and Sydney is no exception. On any day you'll see locals on golf courses at dawn, running on the streets keeping fit, or having a quick set of tennis after work. At weekends, during summer and winter, there is no end to the variety of sports you can watch. Thousands gather at the Aussie Stadium (Sydney Football Stadium) and Sydney Cricket Ground every weekend while, for those who cannot make it, sport reigns supreme on weekend television.

CRICKET

During the summer months Test cricket and one-day internationals are played at the Sydney Cricket Ground (SCG). Tickets for weekday sessions of the Tests can often be bought at the gate, although it is advisable to book well in advance (through **Ticketek**) for weekend sessions of Test matches and for all the one-day international matches.

RUGBY LEAGUE AND RUGBY UNION

The popularity of rugby league knows no bounds in Sydney. This is what people are referring to when they talk about "the footie". There are three major competition levels: local, State of Origin – which matches Queensland against New South Wales – and Tests. The "local" competition fields teams from all over Sydney as well as Newcastle, Canberra, Brisbane, Perth, the Gold Coast and Far North Queensland.

These matches are held all over Sydney, although the Aussie Stadium is by far the biggest venue. Tickets for State of Origin and Test

Australia versus the All Blacks

matches often sell out as soon as they go on sale. Call Ticketek to check availability.

Rugby union is the second most popular football code. Again, matches at Test level sell out very quickly. For some premium trans-Tasman rivalry, catch a Test match between Australia's "Wallabies" and the New Zealand "All Blacks" at the Aussie Stadium. Phone Ticketek for details.

GOLF AND TENNIS

Golf enthusiasts need not do without their round of golf. There are many courses throughout Sydney where visitors are welcome at all times. These include **Moore Park**,

St Michael's and Warringah golf courses. It is sensible to phone beforehand for a booking, especially at weekends.

Tennis is another favoured sport. Courts available for hire can be found all over Sydney. Many centres also have floodlit courts available for night time. Try **Cooper Park** or **Parkland Sports** Centre.

Playing golf at Moore Park, one of Sydney's public courses

AUSTRALIAN RULES FOOTBALL

Although not as popular as in Melbourne, "Aussie Rules" has a strong following in Sydney. The local team, the Sydney Swans, plays its home games at the Sydney Cricket Ground during the season. Check a local paper for details. Rivalry between the Sydney supporters and their Melbourne counterparts is always strong. Busloads of diehard fans from the south arrive to cheer on their teams. Tickets can usually be bought at the ground on the day of the game.

BASKETBALL

Basketball has grown in popularity as both a spectator and recreational sport in recent years. Sydney has male and female teams competing in the National Basketball League. The games, held at the Sydney Entertainment

One-day cricket match between Australia and the West Indies, SCG

Aerial view of the Aussie Stadium at Moore Park

Centre, Haymarket, have much of the pizzazz, colour and excitement of American basketball. Tickets can be purchased by phone or on the internet from Ticketek.

CYCLING AND INLINE SKATING

Sydney boasts excellent, safe locations for the whole fam-ily to go cycling. One of the most frequented is Centennial Park *(see p128)*. You can hire bicycles and safety helmets from **Centennial Park Cycles**.

Another popular pastime in summer is inline skating. **Total Skate**, located opposite Centennial Park, hires inline skates and protective gear, and also offers lessons. **Rollerblading.com** runs tours starting at Milsons Point to all parts of Sydney. If you are a little unsteady on your feet, they offer private and group lessons. Or keep both feet firmly on the ground and watch skateboarders and inline skaters practising their moves at the ramps at Bondi Beach *(see p145)*.

Inline skaters enjoying a summer evening on the city's streets

HORSE RIDING

For a leisurely ride, head to Centennial Park or contact the **Centennial Parklands Equestrian Centre**. They will give you details of the four rid-ing schools that operate in the park. **Samarai Park Riding School** conducts trail rides through Ku-ring-gai Chase National Park *(see p126)*.

Further afield, you can enjoy the magnificent scenery of the Blue Mountains *(see pp170–71)* on horseback. The **Megalong Australian Heritage Centre** has trail rides from one hour to an overnight ride. All levels of experience are catered for.

Horse riding in one of the parks surrounding the city centre

ADVENTURE SPORTS

Sydney offers a wide range of adventure sports for those seeking a more active and thrill-filled time. You can participate in guided bush-walking, mountain biking, canyoning, rock climbing and abseiling expeditions in the nearby Blue Mountains National Park. The **Blue Mountains Adventure Company** runs one-day or multi-day courses and trips for all standards of adventurer.

DIRECTORY

Blue Mountains Adventure Company
84a Bathurst Rd, Katoomba.
Tel 4782 1271.
www.bmac.com.au

Centennial Park Cycles
50 Clovelly Rd, Randwick.
Tel 9398 5027.
www.cyclehire.com.au

Centennial Parklands Equestrian Centre
Cnr Lang & Cook Rds, Moore Park. **Map** 5 D5.
Tel 9332 2809.

Cooper Park Tennis Courts
Off Suttie Rd, Double Bay.
Tel 9389 9259.

Megalong Australian Heritage Centre
Megalong Valley Rd, Megalong Valley. *Tel 4787 8188.*

Moore Park Golf Club
Cnr Cleveland St & Anzac Parade, Moore Park. **Map** 5 B5.
Tel 9663 1064.

Parkland Sports
Lang Rd, Moore Park.
Tel 9662 7033.

Rollerblading.com
Tel 0411 872 022.
www.rollerblading.com.au/
rollerbladingsydney

St Michael's Golf Club
Jennifer St, Little Bay.
Tel 9311 0621.
www.stmichaelsgolf.com.au

Samarai Park Riding School
90 Booralie Rd, Terrey Hills.
Tel 9450 1745.

Ticketek
Tel 13 28 49.
www.ticketek.com.au

Total Skate
36 Oxford St, Woollahra.
Map 6 D4. *Tel 9380 6356.*
www.totalskate.com.au

Warringah Golf Club
397 Condamine St, North Manly.
Tel 9905 4028. www.
warringah.golfagent.com.au

SYDNEY STREET FINDER

The page grid superimposed on the *Area by Area* map below shows which parts of Sydney are covered in this *Street Finder*. Map references given for all sights, hotels, restaurants, shopping and entertainment venues described in this guide refer to the maps in this section. All the major sights are clearly marked so they are easy to locate. The key, set out below, indicates the scale of the maps and shows what other features are marked on them, including railway stations, bus terminals, ferry boarding points, emergency services, post offices and tourist information centres. Map references are also given for hotels *(see pp478–517)* and restaurants *(see pp524–63)*.

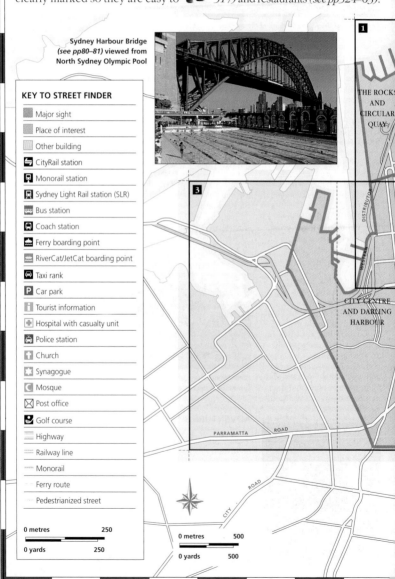

Sydney Harbour Bridge *(see pp80–81)* viewed from North Sydney Olympic Pool

THE ROCKS AND CIRCULAR QUAY

CITY CENTRE AND DARLING HARBOUR

PARRAMATTA ROAD

CITY ROAD

KEY TO STREET FINDER

- Major sight
- Place of interest
- Other building
- CityRail station
- Monorail station
- Sydney Light Rail station (SLR)
- Bus station
- Coach station
- Ferry boarding point
- RiverCat/JetCat boarding point
- Taxi rank
- P Car park
- Tourist information
- Hospital with casualty unit
- Police station
- Church
- Synagogue
- Mosque
- Post office
- Golf course
- Highway
- Railway line
- Monorail
- Ferry route
- Pedestrianized street

0 metres   250
0 yards   250

0 metres   500
0 yards   500

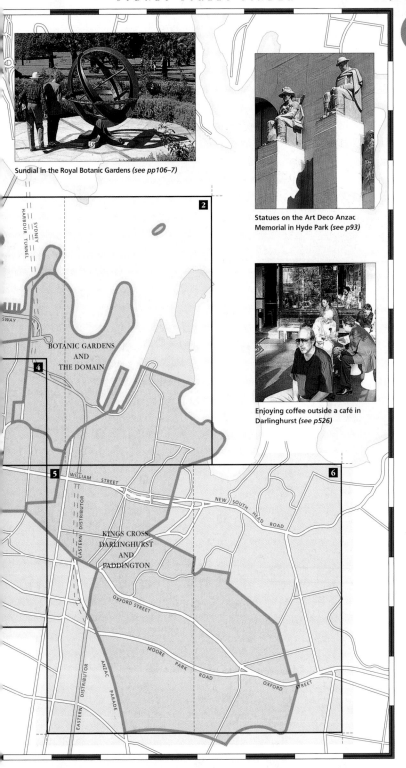

Sundial in the Royal Botanic Gardens *(see pp106–7)*

Statues on the Art Deco Anzac Memorial in Hyde Park *(see p93)*

Enjoying coffee outside a café in Darlinghurst *(see p526)*

HARBOUR TUNNEL

SYDNEY

2

SWAY

BOTANIC GARDENS
AND
THE DOMAIN

4

5 WILLIAM STREET

EASTERN DISTRIBUTOR

NEW SOUTH HEAD ROAD

KINGS CROSS
DARLINGHURST
AND
PADDINGTON

6

OXFORD STREET

MOORE PARK ROAD

OXFORD STREET

EASTERN DISTRIBUTOR

ANZAC PARADE

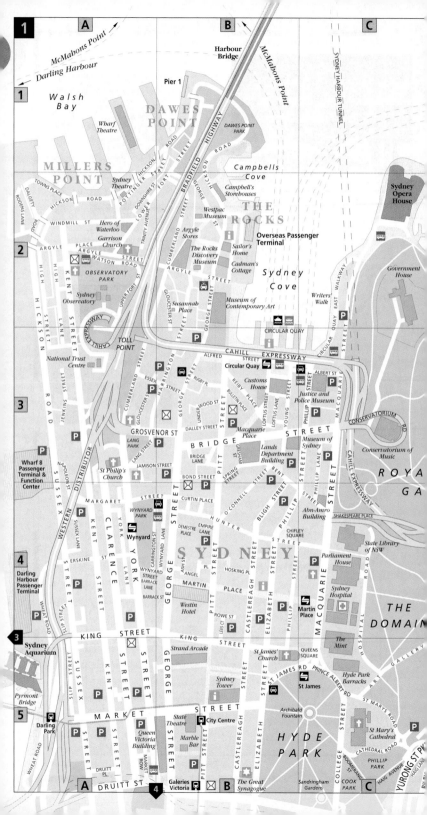

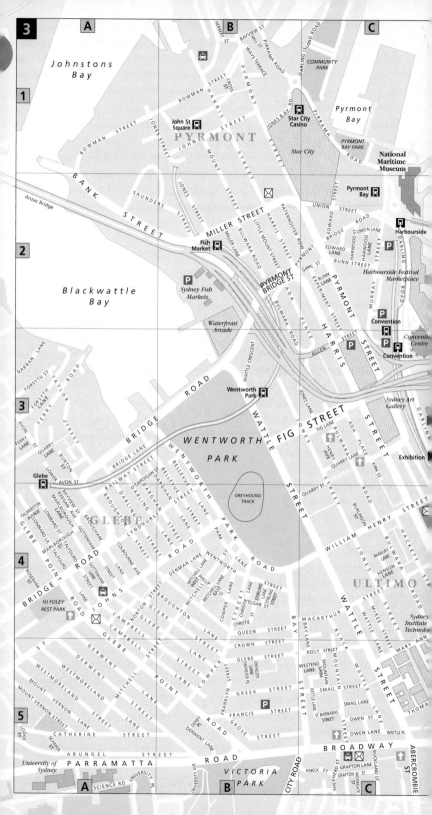

3

A   B   C

1

Johnstons Bay

HERBERT ST

BAYVIEW ST

MILL ST

PIRRAMA ROAD

WAYS TERRACE

DARLING ISLAND ROAD

COMMUNITY PARK

BOWMAN STREET

HARRIS STREET

CROSS STREET

PYRMONT STREET

JONES BAY RD

Pyrmont Bay

PYRMONT

John St Square

JOHN STREET

MOUNT STREET

PIRRAMA ROAD

Star City Casino

Star City

PYRMONT BAY PARK

National Maritime Museum

2

Anzac Bridge

BANK STREET

SAUNDERS STREET

JONES STREET

MILLER STREET

MILLER LANE

LITTLE MOUNT STREET

HARRIS STREET

PATERNOSTER ROW

BULWARA ROAD

UNION STREET

EDWARD STREET

HARWOOD ROAD

UNION LANE

BRIDGE ROAD

Pyrmont Bay

Harbourside

Blackwattle Bay

Fish Market

PYRMONT BRIDGE ST

Sydney Fish Markets

Waterfront Arcade

GIPPS ST

ADA

BULWARA ROAD

BUNN STREET

EXPERIMENT STREET

BUNN LANE

EDWARD LANE

MURRAY

Harbourside Festival Marketplace

Convention

HARRIS STREET

Convention

3

GARRAN LANE

FORSYTH ST

TAYLOR ROAD

FORSYTH LANE

FERRY STREET

AVON LANE

QUARRY LANE

AVON ST

BRIDGE ROAD

BRIDGE LANE

WATTLE CRESCENT

Wentworth Park

WATTLE STREET

JONES LANE

ALLEN ST

PLACE

FIG STREET

FIG LANE

HENRY AVE

ADA PLACE

QUARRY LANE

BULWARA ROAD

KIRK ST

Sydney Art Gallery

Exhibition

Glebe

WENTWORTH PARK

GREYHOUND TRACK

FIG STREET

QUARRY STREET

KENT

ROAD

BURLINSON

4

PALMERSTON AVENUE

BAYVIEW ST

KEGAN AVE

MARLBOROUGH LANE

LOMBARD ST

LOMBARD LA

TALFOURD

BROUGHAM ST

GLEBE POINT ROAD

RAILWAY STREET

DARLING STREET

CARDIGAN LANE

BELLEVUE STREET

DARGHAN STREET

BELLEVUE LANE

LYNDHURST STREET

COLBOURNE AVE

WENTWORTH PARK ROAD

DENMAN LANE

MITCHELL LANE WEST

MITCHELL LANE

WELL PHILLIP

COWPER LANE

MITCHELL LANE EAST

CHRISTIE STREET

ELGAR ST

STIRLING LANE

STIRLING STREET

BAY STREET

WILLIAM HENRY STREET

JONES STREET

PARBURY LANE

BULWARA ROAD

HENSON LANE

HACKETT STREET

ULTIMO

WATTLE STREET

Sydney Institute Technolo...

ROSEBANK ST

BRIDGE ROAD

GLEBE POINT ROAD

JOHNS LANE

NORTON LANE

BROUGHTON LANE

CAMPBELL STREET

CHRISTIE LANE

QUEEN STREET

CROWN STREET

GLEBE STREET

HJ FOLEY REST PARK

GLEBE

DERWENT ST

WESTMORELAND ST

WESTMORELAND LANE

MOUNT VERNON ST

MOUNT VERNON LANE

LODGE ST

SEAMER ST

CATHERINE STREET

ARUNDEL STREET

MITCHELL STREET

DERWENT LANE

GLEBE POINT ROAD LANE

COWPER LANE

FRANKLYN STREET

EBENEZER LANE

EBENEZER PL

GREEK STREET

FRANCIS STREET

GROSE STREET

DERBY PL

GLEBE STREET

CROWN STREET

EBENEZER STREET

KELLY STREET

WESTEND LANE

MOUNTAIN LANE

SMAIL STREET

ST BARNABAS STREET

BLACK MOUNTAIN STREET

KETTLE LANE

SMAIL LANE

MCKEE STREET

WATTLE LANE

WATTLE STREET

OWEN STREET

OWEN LANE

WATTLE PL

MARY ANN

THOMAS

MACARTHUR STREET

5

University of Sydney

PARRAMATTA STREET

SCIENCE RD

UNIVERSITY PL

UNIVERSITY AVE

CITY ROAD

VICTORIA PARK

ROAD

BROADWAY

GRAFTON LANE

SHEPHERD ST

GRAFTON STREET

KNOX ST

BUCKLAND STREET

MOORGATE ST

ABERCROMBIE ST

A   B   C

NEW SOUTH WALES AND ACT

INTRODUCING NEW SOUTH WALES
AND ACT 158–163

THE BLUE MOUNTAINS AND BEYOND 164–181

THE SOUTH COAST AND
SNOWY MOUNTAINS 182–189

CANBERRA AND ACT 190–207

New South Wales and ACT at a Glance

This southeastern corner of the continent, around
Sydney Cove, was the site of the first European
settlement in the 18th century and today it is the
most densely populated and varied region in Australia,
and home to its largest city, Sydney *(see pp60–155)*, as
well as Canberra, the nation's capital. It also contains
the country's highest mountain, Mount Kosciuszko. In
the east there are farmlands and vineyards, the Blue
Mountains and the ski resorts of the Snowy Mountains.
To the west is a desert landscape. The coastline is
tropically warm in the north, cooler in the south.

Broken Hill *is one of the few 19th-
century mining towns in Australia
that continues to survive on its
mineral resources* (see p181). *It is
also the location of the Royal Flying
Doctor Service headquarters, and
tours detailing the history of the
service are popular with visitors.*

**THE BLUE
MOUNTAINS AND
BEYOND**
(see pp164–81)

Bourke's *major
attraction is its
remote location.
Irrigated by the Darling
River, the town is also a
successful agricultural centre*
(see p181). *A lift-up span
bridge crosses the river.*

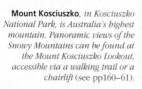

Mount Kosciuszko, *in Kosciuszko
National Park, is Australia's highest
mountain. Panoramic views of the
Snowy Mountains can be found at
the Mount Kosciuszko Lookout,
accessible via a walking trail or a
chairlift* (see pp160–61).

◁ The Breadknife rock formation in the Warrumbungle National Park north of Dubbo, New South Wales

Tenterfield's School of Arts *building has a proud history as the site of Sir Henry Parkes' Federation speech in 1889, which was followed, 12 years later, by the founding of the Commonwealth of Australia (see p56). A museum in the town details the event.*

Tamworth *is the heart of Australian country music. The Golden Guitar Hall, fronted by a model guitar, holds concerts (see p177).*

The Three Sisters *rock formation is the most famous sight within the Blue Mountains National Park. At night it is floodlit for a spectacular view (see pp170–71).*

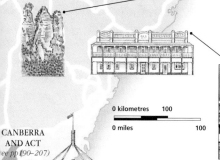

CANBERRA
AND ACT
(see pp190–207)

THE SOUTH
COAST AND
SNOWY
MOUNTAINS
(see pp182–9)

0 kilometres   100

0 miles   100

Windsor *is one of the best preserved 19th-century towns in the state. The Macquarie Arms Hotel is considered to be the oldest operational hotel in Australia (see p168).*

Canberra *was designed as the new national capital in 1912 by architect Walter Burley Griffin. Anzac Parade offers fine views of New Parliament House, atop Capital Hill (see pp194–5).*

The Snowy Mountains

The Snowy Mountains stretch 500 km (310 miles) from Canberra to Victoria. Formed more than 250 million years ago, they include Australia's highest mountain, Mount Kosciuszko, and the country's only glacial lakes. In summer, wildflowers carpet the meadows; in winter, snow gums bend beneath the cold winds. The Snowy Mountains are preserved within the Kosciuszko National Park and are also home to two of Australia's largest ski resorts, Thredbo and Perisher. The Snowy Mountains Scheme dammed four rivers to supply power to much of inland eastern Australia (see p183).

The Snowy Mountains *are home to the Kosciuszko National Park which was declared a World Biosphere Reserve by UNESCO in 199*

The Snowy River *rises below Mount Kosciuszko and is now damned and diverted to provide hydroelectricity for Melbourne and Sydney as part of the Snowy Mountains Scheme.*

Blue Lake is a spectacular glacial lake, one of only a few in the country, which lies in an ice-carved basin 28 m (90 ft) deep.

Seaman's Hut, built in honour of a skier who perished here in 1928, has saved many lives during fierce blizzards.

The Alpine Way offers a spectacular drive through the mountains, best taken in spring or summer, via the Thredbo River Valley.

Geehi River

Snowy River

Perisher Valley •

MOUNT KOSCIUSZKO
▲
2,228 m (7,310 ft)

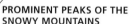
Alpine Way

Thredbo

Dead Horse Gap is a striking pass named after a group of "brumbies" (wild horses) that perished in a snow drift here during the 19th century.

PROMINENT PEAKS OF THE SNOWY MOUNTAINS

Mount Kosciuszko is Australia's highest mountain, and may be approached by gentle walks across alpine meadows from Thredbo or from Charlottes Pass. Mount Townsend is only slightly lower but, with a more pronounced summit, is often mistaken for its higher and more famous neighbour.

Charlottes Pass *marks the start of the summit walk to Mount Kosciuszko. It was named after Charlotte Adams, who, in 1881, was the first European woman to climb the peak.*

```
0 kilometres   5
0 miles        5
```

KEY

▬	Major road
═	Minor road
▪▪▪	Walking trail
⚡	Ski trail
△	Camp site
ℹ	Tourist information
✲	Viewpoint

Downhill and cross-country skiing *and snow-boarding are popular in the Snowy Mountains between June and September.*

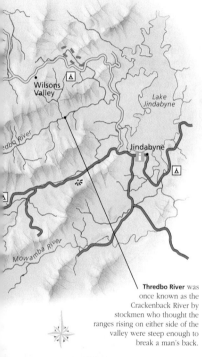

• Wilsons Valley

Lake Jindabyne

Jindabyne

Thredbo River was once known as the Crackenback River by stockmen who thought the ranges rising on either side of the valley were steep enough to break a man's back.

The Yarrangobilly Caves, *about 130 km (80 miles) north of Thredbo, are a system of 70 limestone caves formed 750,000 years ago. They contain magnificent white columns, cascading frozen waterfalls and delicate underground pools.*

VISITORS' CHECKLIST

Kosciusko Road, Jindabyne (02) 6450 5600. **www**.snowy mountains.com.au **Perisher Valley** www.*perisherblue. com.au* **Charlotte Pass www.** charlottepass.com.au **Yarrango-billy** 9–5 daily.

FLORA AND FAUNA

The Snowy Mountains are often harsh, windswept and barren, yet myriad flowers, trees and wildlife have evolved to survive all seasons. Almost all species here are unique to the alpine regions of Australia.

Silver snow daisies, *with their white petals and yellow centres, are the most spectacular of all the alpine flowers en masse.*

Mountain plum pine *is a natural bonsai tree, which grows slowly and at an angle. The pygmy possum feeds on its berries.*

Sphagnum moss *surrounds the springs, bogs and creeks in the highest regions, and helps to protect primitive alpine plants.*

Corroboree frogs *live only in the fragile sphagnum moss bogs of the region.*

Mountain pygmy possums *live under the snow, high up in the mountains.*

Brown and rainbow trout, *both introduced species, thrive in the cool mountain streams.*

Wines of New South Wales and ACT

New South Wales and ACT were the cradle of Australian wines. A small consignment of vines was on board the First Fleet when it landed at Sydney Cove in January 1788 (see pp50–51), and this early hope was fulfilled in the steady development of a successful wine industry. New South Wales is now the home of many fine wineries with an international reputation. The state is currently in the vanguard of wine industry expansion, planting new vineyards and developing established districts to meet steadily rising domestic and export demand.

Rosemount Chardonnay

LOCATOR MAP

New South Wales wine regions

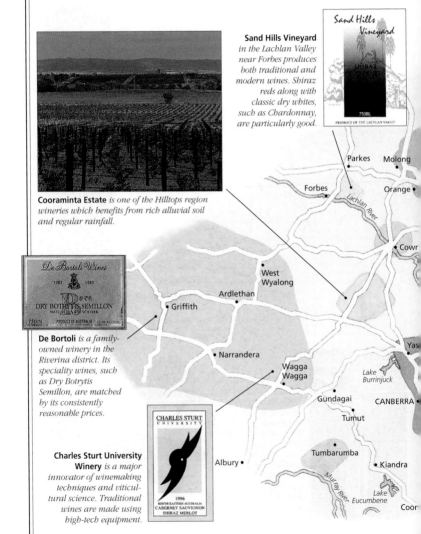

Sand Hills Vineyard *in the Lachlan Valley near Forbes produces both traditional and modern wines. Shiraz reds along with classic dry whites, such as Chardonnay, are particularly good.*

Cooraminta Estate *is one of the Hilltops region wineries which benefits from rich alluvial soil and regular rainfall.*

De Bortoli *is a family-owned winery in the Riverina district. Its speciality wines, such as Dry Botrytis Semillon, are matched by its consistently reasonable prices.*

Charles Sturt University Winery *is a major innovator of winemaking techniques and viticultural science. Traditional wines are made using high-tech equipment.*

Parkes · Molong
Forbes · Orange ·
· Cowr
West Wyalong
Ardlethan ·
· Griffith
· Narrandera · Yas
Wagga Wagga · Lake Burrinjuck
Gundagai · CANBERRA ·
Tumut
Tumbarumba
Albury · · Kiandra
Lake Eucumbene
Coor

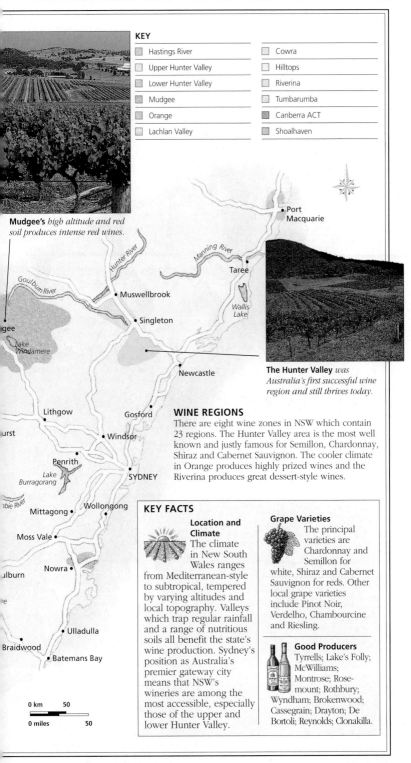

KEY

- Hastings River
- Upper Hunter Valley
- Lower Hunter Valley
- Mudgee
- Orange
- Lachlan Valley
- Cowra
- Hilltops
- Riverina
- Tumbarumba
- Canberra ACT
- Shoalhaven

Mudgee's *high altitude and red soil produces intense red wines.*

The Hunter Valley *was Australia's first successful wine region and still thrives today.*

WINE REGIONS

There are eight wine zones in NSW which contain 23 regions. The Hunter Valley area is the most well known and justly famous for Semillon, Chardonnay, Shiraz and Cabernet Sauvignon. The cooler climate in Orange produces highly prized wines and the Riverina produces great dessert-style wines.

KEY FACTS

Location and Climate

The climate in New South Wales ranges from Mediterranean-style to subtropical, tempered by varying altitudes and local topography. Valleys which trap regular rainfall and a range of nutritious soils all benefit the state's wine production. Sydney's position as Australia's premier gateway city means that NSW's wineries are among the most accessible, especially those of the upper and lower Hunter Valley.

Grape Varieties

The principal varieties are Chardonnay and Semillon for white, Shiraz and Cabernet Sauvignon for reds. Other local grape varieties include Pinot Noir, Verdelho, Chambourcine and Riesling.

Good Producers

Tyrrells; Lake's Folly; McWilliams; Montrose; Rosemount; Rothbury; Wyndham; Brokenwood; Cassegrain; Drayton; De Bortoli; Reynolds; Clonakilla.

0 km 50

0 miles 50

THE BLUE MOUNTAINS AND BEYOND

Think of northern New South Wales and vibrant colours spring to mind. There are the dark blues of the Blue Mountains; the blue-green seas of the north coast; the verdant green of the rainforests near the Queensland border; and the gold of the wheat fields. Finally, there are the reds and yellows of the desert in the far west.

Ever since English explorer Captain James Cook claimed the eastern half of Australia as British territory in 1770 and named it New South Wales, Sydney and its surroundings have been at the forefront of Australian life.

On the outskirts of Sydney, at Windsor and Richmond, early convict settlements flourished into prosperous farming regions along the fertile Hawkesbury River. The barrier of the Blue Mountains was finally penetrated in 1812, marking the first spread of sheep and cattle squatters north, west and south onto the rich plains beyond. In the middle of the 19th century came the gold rush around Bathurst and Mudgee and up into the New England Tablelands, which led to the spread of roads and railways.

Following improved communications in the late 19th and early 20th centuries, northern New South Wales now contains more towns, a denser rural population and a more settled coastline than anywhere else in the country. Fortunately, all this development has not robbed the region of its natural beauty or assets. From the grand and daunting wilderness of the Blue Mountains to the blue waters and surf of Byron Bay, the easternmost point in Australia, the region remains easy to explore and a delight to the senses. It is most easily divided into three parts: the coastline and mild hinterland, including the famous Hunter Valley vineyards; the hills, plateaus and flats of the New England Tablelands and Western Plains with their rivers, national parks and thriving farming areas; and the remote, dusty Outback, west of the vast Great Dividing Range.

The combination of urban civilization, with all the amenities and attractions it offers, and the beautiful surrounding landscape, make this region a favourite holiday location with locals and tourists all year round.

Cape Byron lighthouse on Australia's most easterly point

◁ **The Three Sisters rock formation in the Blue Mountains National Park, seen from Echo Point**

Exploring the Blue Mountains and Beyond

Distances can be long in northern New South Wales so the extent of any exploration will depend on the time available. Within easy reach of Sydney are historic gold rush towns such as Windsor and those between Bathurst and Mudgee, the cool retreats of the Blue Mountains, and the gentle, green hills of the Hunter Valley and its vineyards. The north coast and its hinterland are best explored as part of a touring holiday between Sydney and the Queensland capital, Brisbane, or as a short break to the beaches and fishing areas around Port Macquarie, Taree and Coffs Harbour.

KEY

The Blue Mountains and Beyond

West of the Divide pp180–81

Impressive Three Sisters rocks in the Blue Mountains National Park

SIGHTS AT A GLANCE

Armidale ❼
Barrington Tops WHA ❻
Blue Mountains National Park pp170–73 ❶
Gibraltar Range National Park ❽
Gosford ❸
Inverell ❿
Mudgee ⓬
Newcastle ❹
Tamworth ⓫
Tenterfield ❾
Windsor ❷

Tour
Hunter Valley ❺

West of the Divide
See pp180–81
Bourke ⓯
Broken Hill ⓰
Dubbo ⓭
Lightning Ridge ⓮
Wagga Wagga ⓲
Willandra National Park ⓱

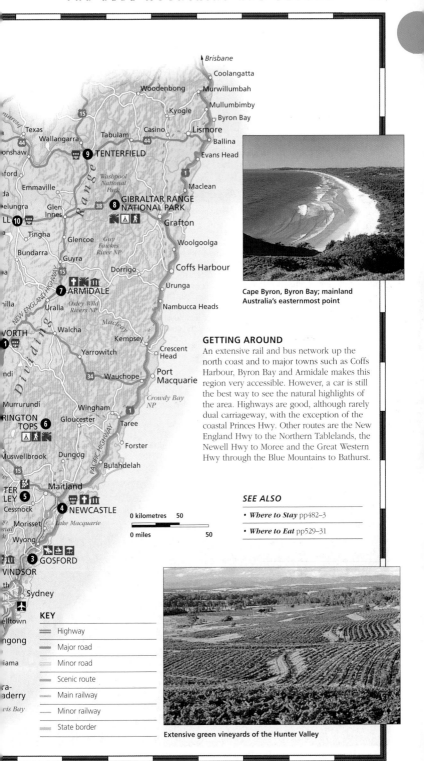

Brisbane
Coolangatta
Woodenbong   Murwillumbah
Mullumbimby
Kyogle
Byron Bay
Texas   Tabulam   Casino   Lismore
Wallangarra   Ballina
onshaw
9 TENTERFIELD   Evans Head
nford
Emmaville   Maclean
da   Washpool
elungra   National
Glen   Park
LL **10**   Innes   GIBRALTAR RANGE **8**
NATIONAL PARK
Tingha   Grafton
Glencoe   Guy
Bundarra   Fawkes   Woolgoolga
Guyra   River NP
Dorrigo   Coffs Harbour
Urunga
7 ARMIDALE
nilla   Nambucca Heads
Uralla   Oxley Wild
Rivers NP
/ORTH   Walcha
1   Kempsey   Crescent
Yarrowitch   Head
ndi   Wauchope   Port
34   Macquarie
Crowdy Bay
Murrurundi   Wingham   NP
RINGTON   Gloucester   Taree
TOPS **6**
Forster
Muswellbrook   Dungog
Bulahdelah
Maitland
TER
LEY **5**
Cessnock   Lake Macquarie
Morisset   **4** NEWCASTLE
Wyong
3 GOSFORD
VINDSOR
Sydney

Cape Byron, Byron Bay; mainland
Australia's easternmost point

GETTING AROUND

An extensive rail and bus network up the
north coast and to major towns such as Coffs
Harbour, Byron Bay and Armidale makes this
region very accessible. However, a car is still
the best way to see the natural highlights of
the area. Highways are good, although rarely
dual carriageway, with the exception of the
coastal Princes Hwy. Other routes are the New
England Hwy to the Northern Tablelands, the
Newell Hwy to Moree and the Great Western
Hwy through the Blue Mountains to Bathurst.

SEE ALSO

• *Where to Stay* pp482–3

• *Where to Eat* pp529–31

0 kilometres   50

0 miles   50

KEY

═══ Highway

── Major road

── Minor road

── Scenic route

═══ Main railway

── Minor railway

── State border

Extensive green vineyards of the Hunter Valley

Blue Mountains National Park ❶

See pp170–3.

Windsor ❷

🏯 *1,850.* 🚉 🚌 🚏 ℹ *Windsor St, Clarington (02) 4578 0233.* **www**.hawkesbury.com.au

Windsor was named by Governor Macquarie and this well-preserved colonial settlement is one of the five "Macquarie towns". Established on the banks of the Hawkesbury River in 1794, the town provided farmers with both fertile land and the convenience of river transport.

In the centre of town, St Matthew's Church, designed by Francis Greenway, is a fine example of Georgian colonial architecture and is considered to be his most successful work. Other buildings of interest include the Macquarie Arms, which claims to be Australia's oldest hotel, and the **Hawkesbury Museum**, set in a Georgian residence. The museum chronicles Windsor's early colonial history.

🏛 **Hawkesbury Museum**
7 Thompson Square. **Tel** (02) 4577 2310. 🕐 *call first to check hours.* ⬤ *Good Fri, 25 Dec.* 🖼

St Matthew's Church in Windsor, designed by Francis Greenway

Environs
One of the other five "Macquarie towns" is Richmond, which lies 6 km (3.5 miles) west of Windsor. This attractive settlement was established five years earlier, in 1789. The farmstead of Mountainview, built in 1804, is one of the oldest surviving homes in the country.

Gosford ❸

🏯 *154,654.* 🚉 🚌 🚏 ⛴ ℹ *Rotary Park, Terrigal Dr, Terrigal, (02) 4385 4430.* **www**.visitcentralcoast.com.au

Gosford is the principal town of the popular holiday region known as the Central Coast, and provides a good base for touring the surrounding area. The rural settlements that once dotted this coastline have now evolved into one continuous beachside suburb, stretching as far south as Ku-ring-gai Chase National Park *(see p126)*. Gosford itself sits on the calm northern shore of Brisbane Waters, an excellent spot for sailing and other recreational activities. The nearby coastal beaches are renowned for their great surf, clear lagoons and long stretches of sand. The beaches here are so numerous that it is still possible to find a deserted spot in any season except high summer. The **Australian Rainforest Sanctuary** is located in a valley of subtropical and

Preserved 18th-century Custom House at Old Sydney Town near Gosford

temperate rainforest. There are picnic areas, play areas, a kiosk and barbeque facilities in addition to beautiful rainforest walks.

The **Australian Reptile Park** is home to many types of reptiles, including crocodiles, massive goannas, snakes and other species.

Australian Rainforest Sanctuary
Ourimbah Creek Rd, Ourimbah. *Tel* (02) 4362 1855. ☐ 10am–5pm Wed– Sun, daily in school hols. Good Fri, 25 Dec, 1 Jan, 25 Apr. 🅿 limited.
www.australianrainforest.com.au

Australian Reptile Park
Pacific Hwy, Somersby. *Tel* (02) 4340 1022. ☐ 9am–5pm daily. 25 Dec. 🅿 **ww**.reptilepark.com.au

Environs
There are several national parks within a short distance of Gosford. Worth a visit is the Bulgandry Aboriginal site in Brisbane Waters National Park, which has rock engravings of human and animal figures dating back thousands of years.

Newcastle ❹

140,000. ✈ 🚗 🚌 🚢
361 Hunter St (02) 4974 2999.
www.visitnewcastle.com.au

One visitor to Newcastle, Australia's second-oldest city, remarked in the 1880s: "To my mind the whole town appeared to have woke up in fright at our arrival and to have no definite ideas of a rendezvous whereat to rally." The chaos to which he referred was largely the result of the city's reliance on coal mining and vast steel works. Building progressed only as profits rose with no planning.

Today this chaos only adds to Newcastle's charm. The city curls loosely around a splendid harbour and its main streets rise randomly up the surrounding hills. Industry is still the mainstay, but this does not detract from the city's quaint beauty. The main thoroughfare of Hunter Street has many buildings of diverse architectural styles. The Court-house follows a style known as Late Free Classical; the

Italianate post office in Newcastle

Court Chambers are High Victorian; the post office was modelled on Palladio's Basilica in Venice and the town's cathedral, Christ Church, is an elaborate and impressive example of Victorian Gothic.

The modern **Newcastle Region Art Gallery** houses works by some of the country's most prominent 19th- and 20th-century artists, including the Newcastle-born William Dobell, Arthur Boyd and Brett Whiteley (*see pp34–5*).

Queens Wharf is the main attraction of the harbour foreshore. It was redeveloped during the 1980s as part of a bicentennial project. There are splendid views from its promenade areas and outdoor

cafés (*see p530*). On the southern side of the harbour, Nobbys Lighthouse sits at the end of a long causeway; the vista back over old Newcastle makes the brief walk worthwhile.

Further on lies **Fort Stratchley**, built originally to repel the coal-seeking Russians in the 1880s. Despite constant surveillance, the fort did not open fire until the 1940s, when the Japanese shelled Newcastle during World War II. Good surfing beaches lie on either side of the harbour's entrance.

🏛 Newcastle Region Art Gallery
Cnr Darby & Laman sts. *Tel* (02) 4974 5100. ☐ 10am–5pm Tue–Sun. 25 Dec, Good Fri. ♿

⛫ Fort Scratchley
Nobbys Rd. *Tel* (02) 4929 3066.
Museum ☐ 10:30am–4pm Tue–Fri. **Fort & Tunnels** ☐ noon–4pm Sat & Sun. Good Fri, 25 Dec. 🅿 ♿

Environs
Four times the size of Sydney Harbour (*see pp74–103*), Lake Macquarie lies 20 km (12 miles) south of Newcastle. The lake's vast size facilitates nearly every kind of water sport imaginable. On the western shore, at Wangi Wangi, is Dobell House, once home to the renowned local artist, William Dobell.

FRANCIS GREENWAY, CONVICT ARCHITECT

Until recently, Australian $10 notes bore the portrait of the early colonial architect Francis Greenway. This was the only currency in the world to pay tribute to a convicted forger. Greenway was transported from England to Sydney in 1814 to serve a 14-year sentence for his crime. Under the patronage of Governor Lachlan Macquarie, who appointed him Civil Architect in 1816, Greenway designed more than 40 buildings, of which 11 still survive today. He received a full King's Pardon in 1819, but soon fell out of favour because he charged exorbitant fees for his architectural designs while still on a government salary. Greenway eventually died in poverty in 1837.

Francis Greenway (1777–1837)

Blue Mountains National Park ❶

Kookaburra

The landscape of the Blue Mountains was more than 250 million years in the making as sediments built up then were eroded, revealing sheer cliff faces and canyons. Home to Aboriginal communities for an estimated 14,000 years, the rugged terrain proved, at first, a formidable barrier to white settlers *(see p172)*, but since the 1870s it has been a popular holiday resort. The mountains get their name from the release of oil from the eucalyptus trees which causes a blue haze. Excellent drives and walking trails allow for easy exploration of the region.

The Cathedral of Ferns an area of green foliage set amid streams, resembling tropical rainforest

Mount Wilson
A basalt cap, the result of a now extinct volcano, provides the rich soil for the gar-dens of this attractive summer retreat.

The Zig Zag Railway is a steam train line between Sydney and Lithgow.

FLORA AND FAUNA IN THE BLUE MOUNTAINS

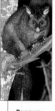

Possum

Many flora and fauna species which are unique to Australia can be easily seen in the Blue Mountains. For example, the superb lyrebird is a fan-tailed bird found in the forests, distinguishable by its high-pitched cry. The sassafras (*Doryphora sassafras*) tree is one of the species of the warm temperate rainforest and produces tiny white flowers. The shy brushtail possum seeks shelter in the woodlands by day and forages at night.

MUDGEE

Lithgow

Bells Line of Road

Bell

Hartley

Mount Victoria

Blackheath

Jenolan Caves Road

Hampton

JENOLAN STATE FOREST

Jenolan Caves
Nine spectacular limestone caves are open to the public; stalactites and stalagmites can be seen in beautiful and striking formations.

Katoomba is the largest town in the vicinity of the national park and has a full range of accommodation for tourists.

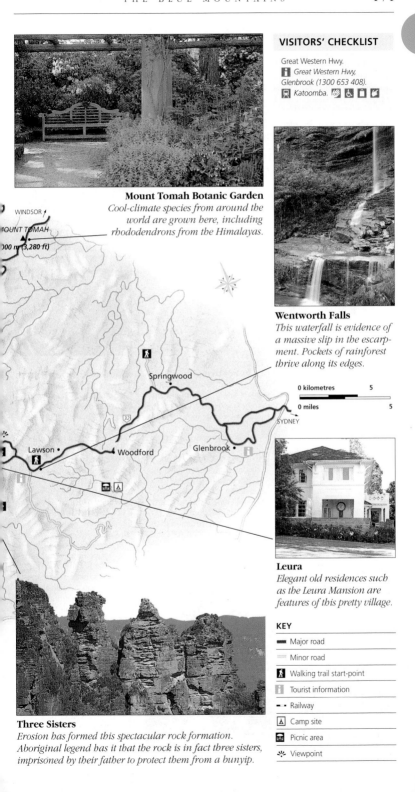

Mount Tomah Botanic Garden
Cool-climate species from around the world are grown here, including rhododendrons from the Himalayas.

VISITORS' CHECKLIST

Great Western Hwy.
🛈 *Great Western Hwy, Glenbrook (1300 653 408).*
🚉 *Katoomba.* ♻ ♿ 🚻 🛒

Wentworth Falls
This waterfall is evidence of a massive slip in the escarpment. Pockets of rainforest thrive along its edges.

0 kilometres 5

0 miles 5

Leura
Elegant old residences such as the Leura Mansion are features of this pretty village.

KEY

▬	Major road
▭	Minor road
🚶	Walking trail start-point
🛈	Tourist information
--	Railway
⛺	Camp site
⛽	Picnic area
🔭	Viewpoint

Three Sisters
Erosion has formed this spectacular rock formation. Aboriginal legend has it that the rock is in fact three sisters, imprisoned by their father to protect them from a bunyip.

Exploring the Blue Mountains

The Blue Mountains, reaching 1,100 m (3,600 ft) above sea level at their highest point, at first made the early colonists virtual prisoners of the Sydney Cove area. Many settlers were convinced that plains suitable for grazing and crops would be found beyond the mountains, but attempts to reach the imagined pastures repeatedly failed. In 1813, however, three farmers, Gregory Blaxland, William Lawson and William Charles Wentworth, set out on a well-planned mission, following the ridge between the Grose and Cox rivers, and emerged successfully on the western side of the mountains. The construction of roads and a railway made the mountains an increasingly attractive destination, and resorts and country homes were soon established. In 1959, the Blue Mountains National Park was gazetted, ensuring the preservation of the large tracts of remaining wilderness.

🏛 Norman Lindsay Gallery and Museum

14 Norman Lindsay Crescent, Faulconbridge. *Tel* (02) 4751 1067. ◯ 10am–4pm daily. ◯ 25 Dec.

Norman Lindsay, one of Australia's most recognized artists, inspired considerable controversy during his lifetime with his sumptuous nudes and risqué novels. Born in 1879, he bought his mountain retreat in 1913 and set about producing an enormous body of work, much of which reflects his rejection of the moral and sexual restraints of his era.

His beautifully preserved home is now a gallery for his many paintings, cartoons, mythological garden sculptures and children's books. There is a whole room devoted to *The Magic Pudding*, a perennial favourite with children and adults alike. There is also a re-creation of the interior of his original studio, and a peaceful garden set amid the mountain bushland.

Leura

ℹ Echo Point, Katoomba. *Tel* 1300 653 408. 📅 first Sunday of the month.

This small town on the Great Western Highway, with its European gardens and Art Deco architecture, recalls the elegance of life in the 1920s. Its secluded, tree-lined main street is a magnet for fine art galleries, cafés, shops and up-market restaurants.

Six km (3.5 miles) from Leura, Everglades House is an Art Deco fantasy of curves, balconies and rose-pink walls. The Everglades gardens are considered classic examples of cool-climate design from the 1930s. They include a shaded alpine garden, a grotto pool, rhododendron stands, an arboretum and peacocks roaming around the grounds.

Some other gardens in the area are opened to the public during the Leura Garden Festival each October *(see p41)*.

Visitors can get an overview of the surrounding landscape by taking the Cliff Drive to Katoomba. The lookout at Sublime Point, at the end of Sublime Point Road, also provides startling views across the Jamison Valley.

Scenic Skyway ride over the Blue Mountains from Katoomba

Katoomba

ℹ Echo Point, Katoomba. *Tel* 1300 653 408. www.bluemountainstourism.org.au

Katoomba is the bustling tourism centre of the Blue Mountains and a good base from which to explore the mountains. However, it still manages to retain a veneer of its gracious former self, when it first attracted wealthy Sydneysiders in need of mountain air during the 1870s. The Paragon Café, with its dark-wood panelling and mirrored walls, is a reminder of these glory days, as are the imposing guesthouses with their fresh air and beautiful views across the Jamison Valley.

Within a few minutes' drive of the town are the region's most popular attractions. Echo Point is home to a large information centre and lookout, with views across to the imposing bulk of Mount Solitary and the most famous of icons, the Three Sisters *(see pp170–71)*. A short walk leads down to this striking rock formation, while further on the Giant Staircase – steps hewn out of the rock face –

Picturesque tree-lined Main Street in Leura

curls around its eastern side. Beyond the Staircase is the Leura Forest, which is a warm temperate rainforest.

On the western side of town the world's first glass-floor Skyway, 270 m (885 ft) above the valley floor, departs regularly. The Scenic Skyway traverses 205 m (670 ft) above the mountains, while the Scenic Railway offers a nerve-wracking plummet down a mountain gorge. Reputed to be the steepest rail track in the world, it was originally built in the 1880s to transport miners down to the valley's rich coal deposits.

Blackheath

⚐ 4,100. ⓘ Govetts Leap Rd. **Tel** (02) 4787 8877.

Blackheath is a small village that offers a quieter prospect than many of the busy mountain towns further east. The excellent standard of restaurants and accommodation available in the town often induces visitors to stay one or two nights here, rather than make the return to Sydney the same day. But the real draw of this area is the chance to explore the mist-enshrouded rifts and ravines of the beautiful Grose Valley.

The best place to start is the Heritage Centre, 3 km (2 miles) from Blackheath along Govetts Leap Road. Displays document the geological, Aboriginal and European histories of the region and local flora and fauna, while park officers are available to offer advice on the best walks in the area. Govetts Leap, with its heady views across Grose Valley, provides a point of orientation and is the starting place for a number of tracks. A clifftop track leads off in a southerly direction past Bridal Falls, the highest waterfalls in the Blue Mountains, and through stretches of exposed mountain heathland.

A steep and arduous 8-hour return trek into the valley leads to Blue Gum Forest, so called because of the smoky blue trunks of the eucalypt species that dominate this pretty woodland. The Grand Canyon is a destination only for the fit – this 5-hour walk,

Eroded gorge in Grose Valley, near the town of Blackheath

through deep gorges and sandstone canyons, sheds some light on the geological mysteries of the mountains.

🏛 Jenolan Caves

Jenolan Caves Rd. **Tel** (02) 6359 3911. ⏱ 9am–5pm daily. 🎫 ♿ to small section of Orient and Chifley caves.

The Jenolan Caves lie southwest of the mountain range. The Great Western Highway passes the grand old hotels of Mount Victoria before a south turn is taken at Hartley, the centre of the first grazing region established by Blaxland, Lawson and Wentworth from 1815 onwards. The southern stretch of the road, cutting across the escarpment of Kanimbla Valley, is one of the most scenic in the mountains.

Limestone formations in the Jenolan Caves

The Jenolan Caves were first discovered in 1838 and are remarkable for their complexity and accessibility. More than 300 subterranean chambers were formed in a limestone belt that was deposited more than 300 million years ago. The nine caves that are open to the public are replete with a variety of delicately wrought limestone formations, pools and rivers, including the ominously named Styx River.

🌿 Mount Tomah Botanic Gardens

Bells Line of Road. **Tel** (02) 4567 2154. ⏱ 10am–5pm daily. ⬤ 25 Dec. 🎫 ♿

Mount Tomah lies along the Bells Line of Road, a quiet but increasingly popular route with tourists to the area.

Tomah takes its name from an indigenous word for "fern". The Botanic Gardens were set up as an annex to Sydney's Royal Botanic Gardens (see pp106–7) in order to house species that would not survive the coastal conditions. Of special interest are the southern hemisphere plants which developed in isolation once Australia broke away from Gondwanaland (see p23).

The overall layout of the gardens is a feat of engineering and imagination, and the views north and south across Grose Valley are breathtaking.

A Tour of the Hunter Valley ❺

The first commercial vineyards in Australia were established on the fertile flats of the Hunter River in the 1830s. Originally a specialist area for fortified wines, Tyrell's helped shift the focus towards new, high-quality modern wines. February and March are busy months with the Harvest Festival taking place from March to May and the Jazz in the Vines festival in October. With beautiful scenery and 74 wineries, mostly open daily, the Hunter Valley is one of the top tourist destinations in New South Wales.

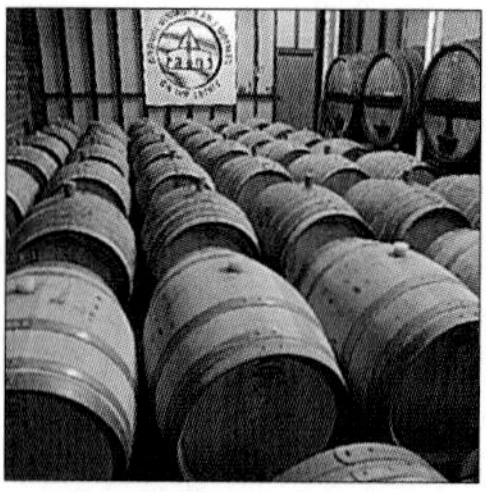

Lake's Folly ③
Max Lake started this vineyard in the 1960s, successfully growing Cabernet Sauvignon grapes in the Hunter Valley for the first time since the 1900s.

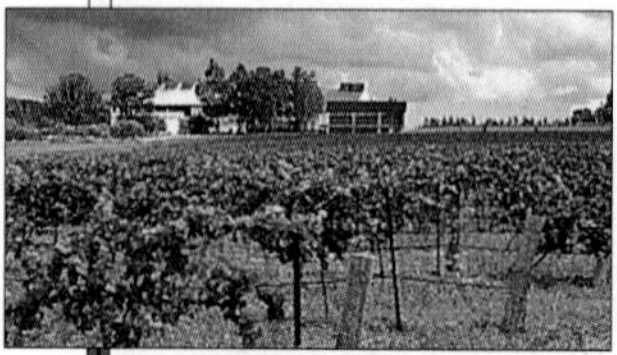

Rothbury Estate ④
Cask Hall was the vision of wine writer Len Evans. The vineyard's wines are now world famous, as are its music concerts.

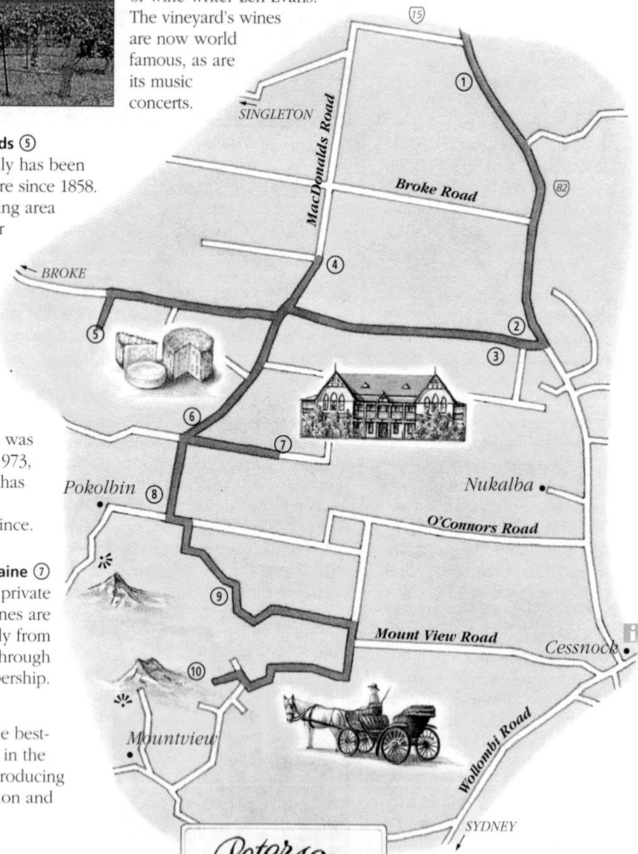

Tyrrells' Vineyards ⑤
The Tyrrell family has been making wine here since 1858. An outdoor tasting area gives views over the vineyards.

Brokenwood ⑥
The first vintage was picked here in 1973, and this winery has attracted a loyal following ever since.

Tamburlaine ⑦
A small private producer – wines are available only from the winery or through winery membership.

Lindemans ⑧
This is one of the best-known wineries in the Hunter Valley, producing legendary Semillon and Shiraz wines.

McWilliams Mount Pleasant Winery ⑨
Phil Ryan, the legendary winemaker, ran this winery for many years. It is home to the Mount Pleasant Elizabeth Semillon, one of Australia's best quality white wines.

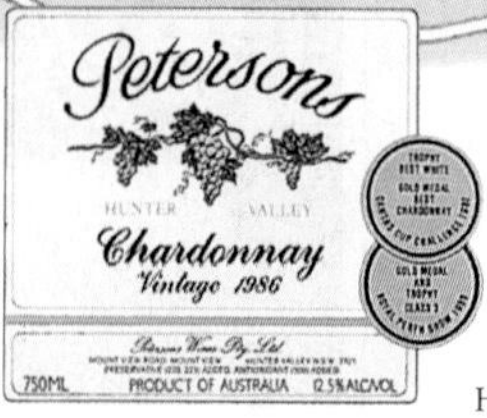

Petersons Winery ⑩
This small family winery is known for its unique experimentation with champagne-style wine production in the Hunter Valley.

Rothbury ①
An early morning champagne breakfast and hot-air balloon flight over the Hunter Valley from this town are a luxurious way to start a day touring the wineries.

The Hunter Valley Wine Society ②
This group organizes wine tastings from many local vineyards and offers excellent advice for the novice. Shiraz and Semillon are the two most recognizable Hunter Valley styles.

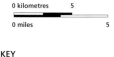

| 0 kilometres | 5 |
| 0 miles | 5 |

KEY

▬▬ Tour route

── Other road

❖ Viewpoint

TIPS FOR DRIVERS

Tour length: 60 km (37 miles). While there are no limits on the numbers of wineries that can be visited, three or four in one day will give time to taste and discuss the wines leisurely. Don't forget Australia's strict drink-driving laws (see p589).

Starting point: Cessnock is the gateway to the Hunter Valley and is home to its major visitors' centre.

Stopping-off points: Apart from the picnic areas and restaurants at the wineries, Pokolbin has plenty of cafés, a general store and a bush picnic area. The Mount Bright lookout gives a panoramic view over the region.

Panoramic mountain view from Barrington Tops

Barrington Tops World Heritage Area ❻

🏞 Gloucester. ℹ 27 Denison St, Gloucester (02) 6558 1408. ⬜ daily. www.gloucester.org.au

Flanking the north of the Hunter Valley is the mountain range known as the Barringtons. One of the highest points in Australia, its high country, the "Barrington Tops", reaches 1,550 m (5,080 ft), and light snow is common in winter. The rugged mountains, cool-climate rainforest, gorges, cliffs and waterfalls make Barrington Tops a paradise for hikers, campers, birdwatchers and climbers. Its 280,000 ha (690,000 acres) of forest, with 1,000-year-old trees, are protected by the Barrington Tops National Park. The rainforest was declared a World Heritage Area in 1986 and a Wilderness Area in 1996 as part of the Central Eastern Rainforest Reserves *(see pp26–7)*.

Spinning wheel from the Armidale Folk Museum

Barrington Tops has been a favourite weekend escape for Sydneysiders for more than 100 years. Tourist operators organize environmentally friendly 4WD trips into the heart of the wild forests, with camping along the Allyn River, hiking trails at Telegherry and Jerusalem Creek and swimming in the rock pool at Lady's Well.

Barrington Tops is best reached through Dungog or from Gloucester.

Armidale ❼

🏫 22,000. ✈ 🚉 🏢 🚌 ℹ 82 Marsh St 1800 627 736. ⬜ daily. www.armidaletourism.com.au

Lying in the heart of the New England Tablelands, Armidale is a sophisticated university city surrounded by some of the state's most magnificent national parks, while concerts, plays, films and lectures fill its many theatres, pubs and university halls.

Some 35 buildings in Armidale are classified by the National Trust, testament to the land booms of the 19th century, including the town hall, courthouse and St Peter's Anglican Cathedral. The **New England Regional Art Museum** holds the A$20 million Howard Hinton and Chandler Coventry collections, with many works by Australian artists, including Tom Roberts and Norman Lindsay *(see p34)*. To the east of Armidale is the 90-ha (220-acre) **Oxley Wild Rivers National Park**, containing the 220-m (720-ft) high Wollomombi Gorge, one of the highest waterfalls in Australia.

🏛 **New England Regional Art Museum**
Kentucky St. **Tel** (02) 6772 5255.
⬜ 10am–5pm Tue–Sun.
● 1 Jan, Good Fri, 25 Dec. 🖼 ♿

♣ **Oxley Wild Rivers National Park**
Waterfall Way. **Tel** (02) 6776 0000.
⬜ daily. ♿ limited.

Northern New South Wales Coastline

The northern New South Wales coastline is known for its mix of natural beauty, mild climate and good resorts. Australia's most easterly mainland point, Byron Bay, is an attractive, up-market resort which is enhanced by its unspoiled landscape and outstanding beaches. Elsewhere, clean and isolated beaches directly abut rainforest, with some national parks and reserves holding World Heritage status *(see pp26–7)*. Sugar cane and bananas are commonly grown in the region.

Coffs Harbour *is one of the most popular tourist destinations in New South Wales. Surrounded by excellent beaches, there is also an attractive man-made harbour and a range of top-quality tourist facilities.*

Red Cliff Beach ④

🌊 🏄 🛟 🚻 ⛺

Adjacent to the beautiful Yuraygir National Park, Red Cliff is one of several sandy, isolated beaches in the immediate vicinity.

Moonee Beach ⑤

🌊 🏄 🛟 🚻 ⛺

A creek meandering through bush country to the ocean offers perfect opportunities for safe swimming, picnics and camping.

Urunga ⑥

🌊 🏄 🏖 🛟 🚻

Two rivers, the Bellingen and the Kalang, reach the ocean in this picturesque beach resort. Its safe waters make it a particularly popular holiday site for families.

Arakoon ⑨

🌊 🏄 🛟

This picturesque headland is part of a state recreation area. Nearby is Trial Bay Gaol, a progressive 19th-century prison that re-opened during World War I to house prisoners of war from various countries.

Third Headland Beach ⑦

🌊 🛟 🚻 ⛺

Like its neighbour Hungry Head Beach, 5 km (3 miles) north, Third Headland is a popular surfing beach with strong waves hitting the headland cliffs.

Grafton *is a quaint 19th-century rural town, with elegant streets and riverside walks. The town is best known for its abundance of jacaranda trees, whose striking purple blooms are celebrated in a festival each October* (see p41).

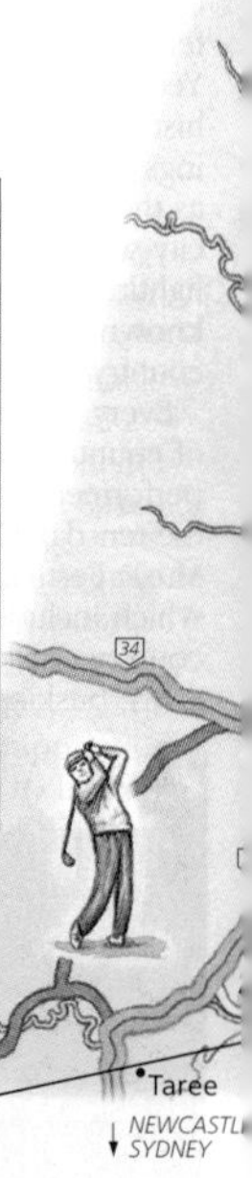
34
Taree
NEWCASTL
SYDNEY

★ Crowdy Bay ⑫

🌊 🏄 🏖 🛟 🚻

Part of a national park, Crowdy Bay's lagoons, forests and swamps are abundant with native wildlife here. Coarse-fishing is a popular activity from the sea's edge.

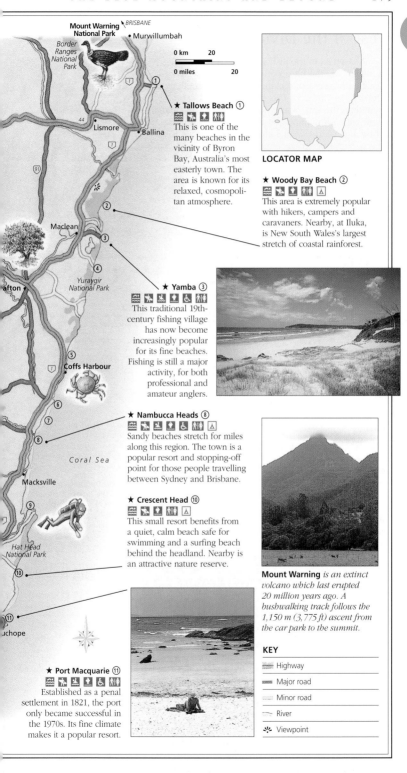

Mount Warning National Park
BRISBANE
Murwillumbah

Border Ranges National Park

0 km   20
0 miles   20

Lismore
Ballina

★ Tallows Beach ①

This is one of the many beaches in the vicinity of Byron Bay, Australia's most easterly town. The area is known for its relaxed, cosmopolitan atmosphere.

LOCATOR MAP

★ Woody Bay Beach ②

This area is extremely popular with hikers, campers and caravaners. Nearby, at Iluka, is New South Wales's largest stretch of coastal rainforest.

Maclean

Yuraygir National Park

Grafton

★ Yamba ③

This traditional 19th-century fishing village has now become increasingly popular for its fine beaches. Fishing is still a major activity, for both professional and amateur anglers.

Coffs Harbour

★ Nambucca Heads ⑧

Sandy beaches stretch for miles along this region. The town is a popular resort and stopping-off point for those people travelling between Sydney and Brisbane.

Coral Sea

Macksville

★ Crescent Head ⑩

This small resort benefits from a quiet, calm beach safe for swimming and a surfing beach behind the headland. Nearby is an attractive nature reserve.

Hat Head National Park

Mount Warning *is an extinct volcano which last erupted 20 million years ago. A bushwalking track follows the 1,150 m (3,775 ft) ascent from the car park to the summit.*

KEY

Wauchope

★ Port Macquarie ⑪

Established as a penal settlement in 1821, the port only became successful in the 1970s. Its fine climate makes it a popular resort.

▓▓	Highway
▬	Major road
⋯	Minor road
⤳	River
☆	Viewpoint

West of the Divide

In stark contrast to the lush green of the Blue
Mountains and the blue waters of the New South Wales
coastline, the western region of the state is archetypal
of Australia's Outback. This dusty, dry landscape,
parched by the sun, is an understandably remote area,
dotted with a few mining towns and national parks.
Dubbo and Wagga Wagga are the main frontier towns,
but anything beyond is commonly referred to as "Back
o' Bourke" and ventured into by only the most determined of tourists. Even the most adventurous
should avoid the area in high summer.

LOCATOR MAP

- West of the Divide
- The Blue Mountains
  pp164–79

SIGHTS AT A GLANCE

Bourke ⑮
Broken Hill ⑯
Dubbo ⑬
Lightning Ridge ⑭
Wagga Wagga ⑱
Willandra National Park ⑰

KEY

═══ Major road

──── Minor road

── ── Track

▬▬▬ Main railway

▨▨▨▨ Regional border

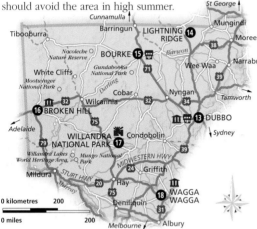

Dubbo ⑬

🚶 38,000. ✈ 🚉 🚌 🚍 🛈 cnr
Newell Hwy & Macquarie St (02)
6884 1422.
www.dubbotourism.com.au

Dubbo is located at the
geographical heart of
the state and is the regional
capital of western New South
Wales. The area was first noted
for its rich agricultural potential in 1817 by explorer John
Oxley, sited as it is on the
banks of the Macquarie River.
The city has since grown into
a rural centre producing $45
million worth of food and
agricultural goods annually.

Dubbo also has a strong
colonial history and period
architecture. Among the more
interesting buildings are the
1876 Dubbo Museum, with its
ornate ceilings and cedar staircase, the 1890 Italianate courthouse and the 1884 Macquarie
Chambers, with their Tuscan
columns and terracotta tiles.

At the **Old Dubbo Gaol**,
visitors can hear the tragic

story of Jacky Underwood, an
Aborigine hung for his part in
the Breelong massacre of
1900, when eleven white
settlers were killed. Dubbo
magistrate Rolf Boldrewood
drew on the characters of the
gaol's inmates to write the
classic novel *Robbery Under
Arms (see p34)*.

The most popular sight in
Dubbo is the **Western Plains**

Rhinoceros in Western Plains Zoo

Zoo, 5 km (3 miles) from the
town. The zoo's emphasis is
on breeding endangered species. Visitors can see over
1,000 animals living freely.

🏛 **Old Dubbo Gaol**
Macquarie St. **Tel** (02) 6801 4460.
⬤ 9am–4:30pm daily. ⬤ Good
Fri, Dec 25.

🦘 **Western Plains Zoo**
Obley Rd. **Tel** (02) 6882 5888.
⬤ 9am–5pm daily. 🈂 🈳 ⬤

Lightning Ridge ⑭

🚶 5,000. ✈ 🚉 🛈 Morilla St
(02) 6829 1670.

Lightning Ridge is a small
mining village and home of
the treasured black opal – a
rare dark opal shot with red,
blue and green. Gem enthusiasts from around the world
come to try their luck on the
opal fields. The town is also
famous for its hearty welcome
to visitors, unusual within
mining communities, and its
mine tours, plethora of opal
shops and hot bore spas.

For hotels and restaurants in this region see pp482–3 and pp529–31

Bourke ⓯

🏃 *3,000.* ✈ 🚗 🚌
ℹ *24 Anson St (02) 6872 1222.*
www.visitbourke.com

Situated on the Darling River, part of Australia's longest river system, Bourke is a colourful town that was once the centre of the world's wool industry. It still produces 25,000 bales per year.

Bourke's heyday is evident in the colonial buildings and the old weir, wharf, lock and lift-up span bridge which recall the days of the paddle-steamer trade to Victoria *(see p431)*. The town's cemetery tells something of Bourke's history: Afghan camel drivers who brought the animal to Australia from the Middle East in the 19th century are buried here.

Broken Hill ⓰

🏃 *21,000.* ✈ 🚗 🚗 🚌 ℹ *cnr Blende and Bromide sts (08) 8088 9700.* **www**.visitbrokenhill.com.au

The unofficial centre of Outback New South Wales, Broken Hill is a mining city perched on the edge of the deserts of inland Australia. The town was established in 1883, when vast deposits of zinc, lead and silver were discovered in a 7-km (4-mile) long "Line of Lode" by the then-fledgling company, Broken Hill Pty Ltd. Broken Hill has since grown into a major town and BHP has become Australia's biggest corporation.

Broken Hill's now declining mining industry is still evident; slag heaps are piled up, there

MUNGO WORLD HERITAGE AREA

Lake Mungo is an area of great archaeological significance. For 40,000 years, it was a 15-m (50-ft) deep lake, around which Aborigines lived. The lake then dried up, leaving its eastern rim as a wind-blown sand ridge known as the Walls of China. Its age was determined in the 1960s when winds uncovered an Aboriginal skeleton known as Mungo Man. Lake Mungo has been protected as part of the Willandra Lakes World Heritage Area since 1981 *(see pp26–7)*.

Walls of China sand ridges

are more pubs per head than any other city in the state and streets are named after metals.

Surprisingly, Broken Hill also has more than 20 art galleries featuring desert artists. The city is also the base of the Royal Flying Doctor Service *(see p257)* and School of the Air.

To the northwest of Broken Hill is **Silverton**, once a thriving silver mining community and now a ghost town. It is popular as a location for films, such as *Mad Max* and *Priscilla, Queen of the Desert*.

Willandra National Park ⓱

ℹ *Hilston Mossgiel Rd (02) 6967 8159.* ⭕ *daily.* ⬤ *in wet weather.* ♿ 🏠 *to homestead.*
www.nationalparks.nsw.gov.au

Less than 20,000 years ago, Willandra Creek was a major river system and tributary of the Lachlan River, providing wetlands of at least 1,000 sq

km (400 sq miles). Now the Willandra Lakes are dry and Willandra Creek is little more than a small stream.

A glimpse of the area's past is found in Willandra National Park. Wetlands emerge each year after the spring rain, providing sanctuary for waterbirds.

Wagga Wagga ⓲

🏃 *57,000.* ✈ 🚗 🚗
ℹ *Tarcutta St (02) 6926 9621.*
www.tourismwaggawagga.com.au

Named by its original inhabitants, the Widadjuri people, as "a place of many crows", Wagga Wagga has grown into a large, modern city serving the surrounding farming community. It has won many accolades for its wines and the abundance of gardens has earned it the title of "Garden City of the South".

The large Botanic Gardens and the Wagga Historical Museum are well worth a visit. The Widadjuri track is a popular walk along the Murrumbidgee River banks.

Environs

The gentle town of **Gundagai**, nestling beneath Mount Parnassus on the banks of the Murrumbidgee River, has been immortalized in the bush ballad "Along the Road to Gundagai". More tragic is Gundagai's place in history as the site of Australia's greatest natural disaster when floods swept away the town in 1852.

Historic pub in the ghost town of Silverton, near Broken Hill

THE SOUTH COAST AND SNOWY MOUNTAINS

lthough the busiest highway in Australia runs through southern New South Wales, the area remains one of the most beautiful in the country. Its landscape includes the Snowy Mountains, the surf beaches of the far south, the historic Southern Highland villages and the farming towns of the Murray and Murrumbidgee plains.

Ever since European settlers crossed the Blue Mountains in 1812 *(see p172)*, the southern plains of New South Wales around Goulburn, Yass and Albury have been prime agricultural land. Yet the wilderness of the Snowy Mountains to the east and the steep escarpment which runs the length of the beautiful South and Sapphire coasts, from Wollongong to the Victoria border, has never been completely tamed. Today, the splendour of southern New South Wales is protected by a number of large national parks.

The great Snowy Mountains offer alpine scenery at its best. In summer, the wildflower-scattered meadows, deep gorges and cascading mountain creeks seem to stretch endlessly into the distance; in winter, the jagged snow-capped peaks and twisted snow gums turn this summer walking paradise into a playground for keen downhill and cross-country skiers.

The area also has a long and colourful cultural heritage: Aboriginal tribes, gold diggers and mountain cattlemen have all left their mark here. During the 1950s and 1960s, the region became the birthplace of multicultural Australia, as thousands of European immigrants came to work on the Snowy Mountains Scheme, an engineering feat which diverted the flow of several rivers to provide hydroelectricity and irrigation for southeastern Australia.

But southern New South Wales is more than just landscapes; civilization is never far away. There are excellent restaurants and hotels along the coast, Wollongong is an industrial city and the gracious towns of the Southern Highlands offer historic attractions.

Snowy Mountains landscape in autumn

◁ Red rocks and blue waters of the Sapphire Coast at Merimbula Wharf

Exploring the South Coast and Snowy Mountains

The Great Dividing Range, which runs from the Blue Mountains *(see pp170–73)* down to the Snowy Mountains and into Victoria, divides the region into three areas. There is the coastal strip, a zone of beautiful beaches, which starts at Wollongong and runs south for 500 km (310 miles) to Eden, hemmed in by the rising mountain range to its west. On the range lie the Southern Highlands, Mount Kosciuszko and the Snowy Mountains. West of the range are the farming plains of the Murrumbidgee River.

Waterfall in the beautiful Morton National Park

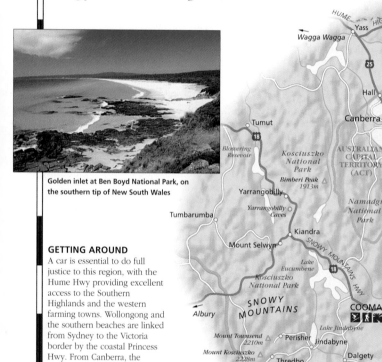

Golden inlet at Ben Boyd National Park, on the southern tip of New South Wales

GETTING AROUND

A car is essential to do full justice to this region, with the Hume Hwy providing excellent access to the Southern Highlands and the western farming towns. Wollongong and the southern beaches are linked from Sydney to the Victoria border by the coastal Princess Hwy. From Canberra, the Monaro Hwy is the best route to the Snowy Mountains. From Bega to the east or Gundagai and Tumut in the west, take the Snowy Mountains Hwy. A train service between Sydney and Canberra stops at the Southern Highlands and Hume Hwy towns, while the coastal resorts are serviced by buses from both Sydney and Melbourne.

SEE ALSO

- *Where to Stay* pp484–5
- *Where to Eat* pp531–3

0 kilometres   25

0 miles   25

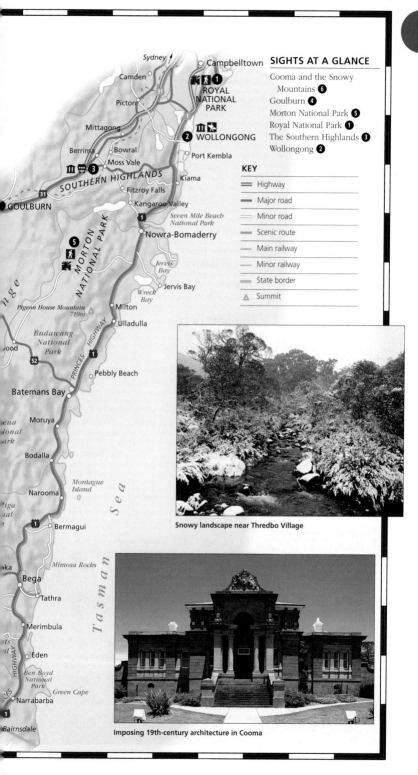

Sydney

Campbelltown

Camden

ROYAL NATIONAL PARK ❶

Picton

Mittagong

WOLLONGONG ❷

Berrima Bowral
Moss Vale
SOUTHERN HIGHLANDS ❸

Port Kembla

31
GOULBURN

Kiama

Fitzroy Falls

Kangaroo Valley

Seven Mile Beach National Park

Nowra-Bomaderry

❺
MORTON NATIONAL PARK

Jervis Bay

Jervis Bay

Wreck Bay

Pigeon House Mountain 719m

Milton

Budawang National Park

Ulladulla

Jood

52

PRINCES HIGHWAY

1

Pebbly Beach

Batemans Bay

Moruya

eua ional ark

Bodalla

Montague Island

Narooma

iga al

1

Bermagui

ka

Minnosa Rocks

Bega

Tathra

Merimbula

sts al

Eden

HIGHWAY

Ben Boyd National Park

Green Cape

Narrabarba

1

Bairnsdale

n
g
e

T a s m a n   S e a

SIGHTS AT A GLANCE

Cooma and the Snowy
  Mountains ❻
Goulburn ❹
Morton National Park ❺
Royal National Park ❶
The Southern Highlands ❸
Wollongong ❷

KEY

═══ Highway

▬▬▬ Major road

──── Minor road

──── Scenic route

──── Main railway

──── Minor railway

▬▬▬ State border

△ Summit

Snowy landscape near Thredbo Village

Imposing 19th-century architecture in Cooma

Royal National Park ❶

📖 *Loftus, then tram to Audley (Sun public hols only).* 🚌 *Bundeena from Cronulla.* ℹ️ *Sir Bertram Stevens Drive, Audley (02) 9542 0648.* 🖥️ **www**.nationalparks.nsw.gov.au

Designated a national park in 1879, the "Royal" is the oldest national park in Australia and the oldest in the world after Yellowstone in the USA. It covers 16,500 ha (37,000 acres) of spectacular landscape.

To the east, waves from the Pacific Ocean have undercut the sandstone and produced coastal cliffs, interspersed by creeks, waterfalls, lagoons and beaches. Sea eagles and terns nest in caves at the Curracurrang Rocks. Heath vegetation on the plateau merges with woodlands on the upper slopes and rainforest in the gorges. The park is ideal for bushwalking, swimming and bird-watching.

Wollongong ❷

🏙️ *280,000.* 📖 ✈️ 🚌 ℹ️ *93 Crown St (02) 4227 5545.* **www**.tourismwollongong.com

The third largest city in the state, Wollongong is situated on a coastline of beautiful surf beaches. Mount Kembla and Mount Keira provide a backdrop to the city. Originally a coal and steel industrial city – the BHP steel mill at Port Kembla is still a major employer – Wollongong is fast building a reputation as a leisure centre. Northbeach is the most famous of its 17 surf beaches. Flagstaff Point, with its lighthouse, boat harbour, beach views and seafood restaurants, is popular with visitors. Fresh seafood is also on offer at the fish market in Wollongong harbour. The city boasts Australia's largest regional art gallery, and the Nan Tien Temple, the largest Buddhist temple in the southern hemisphere, built for Sydney's Chinese community.

Figure in Nan Tien Temple

The Southern Highlands ❸

🚌 📖 *Bowral, Moss Vale, Mittagong, Bundanoon.* ℹ️ *62–70 Main St, Mittagong (02) 4871 2888.* **www**.southern-highlands.com.au

Quaint villages, country guesthouses, homesteads and beautiful gardens are scattered across the lush landscape of the Southern Highlands. The region has been a summer retreat for Sydneysiders for almost 100 years. Villages such as Bowral, Moss Vale, Berrima and Bundanoon are also ideal places in the winter for pottering around antiques shops, dining on hearty soups, sitting by open fires and taking bush walks and country drives. The region's gardens are renowned for their blaze of colours in the spring and autumn. The Corbett Gardens at Bowral are a showpiece during its Tulip Festival *(see p40).* Bowral is also home to the **Bradman Museum**, where a fascinating collection of photos and cricketing memorabilia commemorates the town's famous son, cricketer Sir Donald Bradman. Bradman is said to have first showed signs of greatness as a child, hitting a golf ball against a water tank stand with a wicket-wide strip of wood.

Visiting the village of Berrima is like stepping back in time. The settlement, now home to an abundance of antiques and craft shops, is one of the most unspoilt examples of a small Australian town of the 1830s.

Popular walks in the area include Mount Gibraltar, Carrington Falls, the magnificent Fitzroy Falls at the northern tip of Morton-Budawang National Park and the majestic Kangaroo Valley. The five Wombeyan Caves, west of the

Fishing boats moored along Wollongong Harbour

For hotels and restaurants in this region see pp484–5 and pp531–3

Impressive peak of Pigeon House in Morton-Budawang National Park

town of Mittagong, form an imposing underground lime-stone cathedral.

🏛 **Bradman Museum**
St Jude St, Bowral. *Tel* (02) 4862 1247. ⭕ 10am–5pm daily. 🚫 25 Dec. 🖼 🚻 🔲

Sandstone house in Goulburn

Goulburn ❹

🏃 24,500. 🚋 ✈ 🚌 🛈 201 Sloane St (02) 4823 4492.

Goulburn is at the heart of the Southern Tablelands, with its rich pastoral heritage. Proclaimed in 1863, the town's 19th-century buildings, such as the courthouse, post office and railway station, are testament to the continuing prosperity of the district.

The Big Merino, a giant, hollow concrete sheep, marks Goulburn as the "fine wool capital of the world".

Environs
The town of **Yass** is known for its fine wool and cool-climate wines. Worth a visit is the historic Cooma Cottage, now owned by the National Trust. It was once the home of Australian explorer Hamilton Hume, between 1839 and 1873.

Morton National Park ❺

📷 Bundanoon. 🚌 Fitzroy Falls. 🛈 Fitzroy Falls (02) 4422 2346.

Morton National Park stretches for 200 km (125 miles) from Batemans Bay to Nowra. Fitzroy Falls are at the northern end of the park. At Bundanoon, magnificent sand-stone country can be explored along walking tracks.

To the south, views of the coastline and Budawang wild-erness can be found at Little Forest Plateau and the top of Pigeon House Mountain.

Cooma and the Snowy Mountains ❻

🏃 8,000. ✈ 🚋 🚌 🛈 119 Sharp St (02) 6450 1742.
www.visitcooma.com.au

Colourful Cooma has a rich history as a cattle, engi-neering and ski town. During the construction of the Snowy Mountains Scheme *(see p183)*, Cooma was also the weekend base for the thousands of immigrants working up in the mountains during the week. Stories surviving from this era include tales of frontier-like shootouts in the main street, interracial romances and bush mountain feats. However, Cooma is now a sleepy rural town that acts as the gateway to the Snowy Mountains and the southern ski slopes.

The modern resort town of Jindabyne on Lake Jindabyne is home to the Kosciuszko National Park information centre, a myriad of ski shops and lodges, and plenty of nightlife. The two major ski resorts are Thredbo Village along the Alpine Way and the twin resort of Perisher Blue, linked by the ski tube train to Lake Crackenback and the Blue Cow ski fields. Take the chairlift from Thredbo in sum-mer to walk to the summit of Australia's highest mountain, Mount Kosciuszko *(see p160)*, or simply to stroll among the wildflowers and snow gums in the alpine meadows. Another recommended walk is to Blue Lake and the Cas-cades from Dead Horse Gap. Lake Eucumbene and the Thredbo and Eucumbene rivers offer excellent fly-fishing.

Environs
The ghost settlement of **Kiandra** has a marked historic walking trail detailing the gold rush era in the town *(see pp54–5)*. Nearby is the gentle ski resort of Mount Selwyn and the spectacular Yarrangobilly Caves with their underground walks set among limestone stalactites and stalagmites.

Resort town of Jindabyne in the Snowy Mountains

The South Coast

From Nowra to the border with Victoria, the south coast of New South Wales is a magical mix of white sand beaches, rocky coves and coastal bush covered with spotted gums and wattles, and alive with a variety of birds. The coastline is rich in Aboriginal sites, fishing villages and unspoilt beach settlements. The 400 km (250 miles) of coast are divided into three distinct areas – the Shoalhaven Coast to the north, the Eurobodalla ("Land of Many Waters") Coast in the centre and the Sapphire Coast in the far south.

Whale Museum harpoon gun

Ulladulla *is a small fishing village flanked by the dovecote-shaped peak of Pigeon House Mountain in the Morton-Budawang National Park. A bushwalk offers breathtaking coastal views.*

Central Tilba *is a delightful historic farming village, backed by the 800-m (2,600-ft) Mount Dromedary. The town itself is famous for its weatherboard cottages and shops, now housing some of the region's finest cafés and arts and crafts shops, and its cheese and wine. The cheese factory and wineries are all open to visitors.*

★ **Horseshoe Bay Beach, Bermagui** ⑦

Writer Zane Grey brought fame to this tiny game fishing town with his tales of marlin fishing.

★ **Merimbula Beach** ⑩

The tourist centre of the Sapphire Coast is famous for its oysters, deep-sea fishing and surrounding white sandy beach.

★ **Eden** ⑪

Set on the deep Twofold Bay, this was once a whaling station. It is now the centre of whale-watching on the south coast during spring. It is also a major tuna fishing town and centre for the local timber industry.

Nowra *is the town centre of the beautiful Shoalhaven Coast, near the mouth of the Shoalhaven River. The name means "black cockatoo" in the local Aboriginal language. Nearby are the resorts of Culburra and Shoalhaven Heads, adjacent to Seven Mile Beach National Park.*

0 kilometres 25

0 miles 25

ORBOST ↓

De Natic Pa

Moruy

Bodal

Cent Tilba

Bega

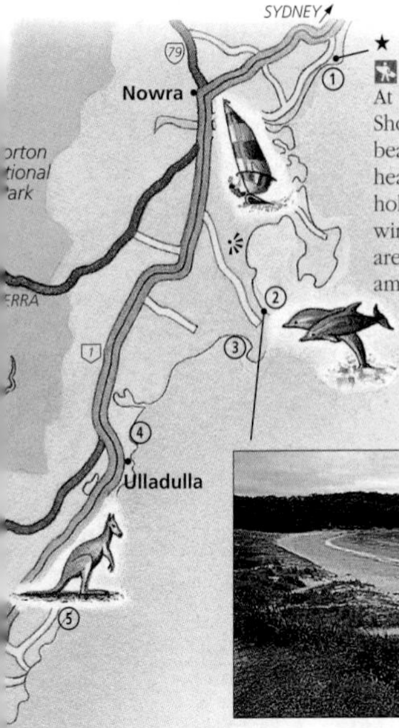

★ Shoalhaven Heads ①

🚶 🌊 🏖 🚻 ⛺

At the mouth of the Shoalhaven River, this beach resort is at the heart of a popular holiday area. Sailing and windsurfing on the river are popular activities among the locals.

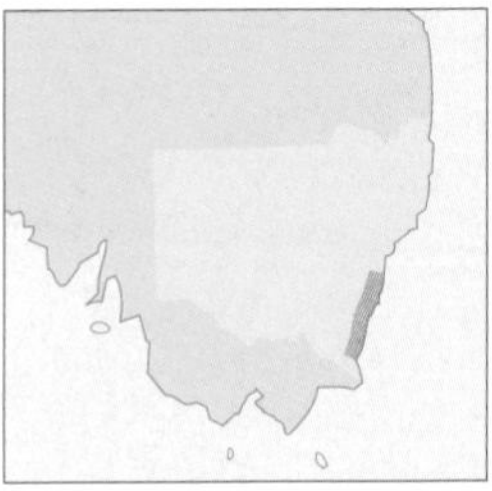

LOCATOR MAP

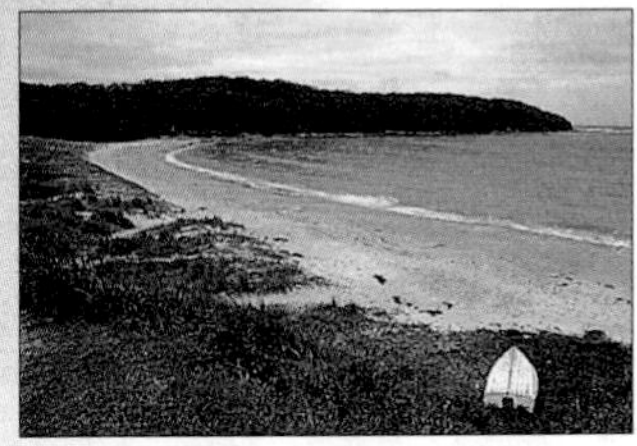

★ Jervis Bay ②

🌊 🏖 🚻 ⛺

This is one of the most beautiful natural harbours in Australia, famous for its naval bases, national park, tiny settlements of Husskinson and Vincentia, and some of the whitest beaches and crystal clear waters in the world.

Wreck Bay ③

🌊 🏖

This area, within Jervis Bay National Park, abounds with Aboriginal history. The cultural centre offers walkabout tours of local bushlife and archaeology. Nearby Cave Beach is one of the region's most popular for its secluded location.

Lake Conjola ④

🌊 🚻 ⛺

This lake, 10 km (6 miles) north of Ulladulla, is one of many lakes in the region popular with canoeists. Camp sites are also available.

Batemans Bay ⑥

🚶 🌊 🏖 🚻 ⛺

The Clyde River enters the sea here, marking the start of the Eurobodalla coastline with its rivers, lakes and chain of heavenly quiet beaches popular with Canberrans.

Mimosa Rocks ⑧

🏖 ⛺

This coastal park, just off the south coast road, offers exceptional bushwalking opportunities and idyllic beaches. Secluded camp sites, with minimum facilities, are popular with families and anglers.

Tathra Beach ⑨

🚶 🌊 🏖 🚻 ⛺

This tiny fishing village and holiday haven includes a maritime museum, housed in a 150-year-old wharf building.

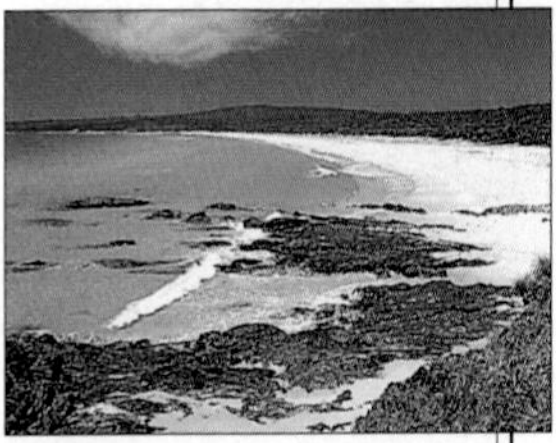

Ben Boyd National Park ⑫

🌊 🏖 ⛺

Camping, bushwalks and fine beaches are all features of this park. Temperate rainforests begin to take over the landscape in the surrounding region. The ascent to Mount Imlay offers panoramic views of the coast.

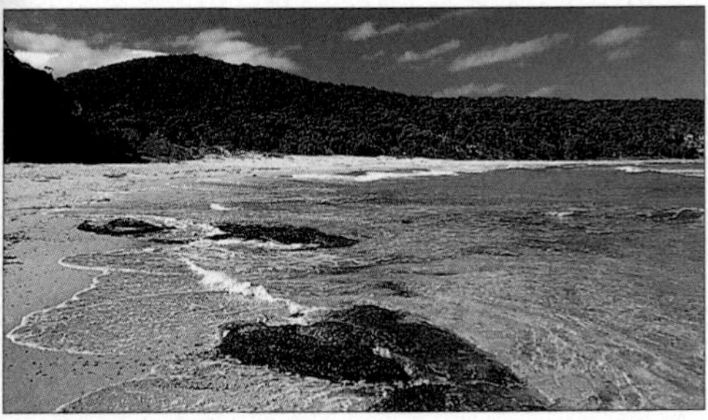

★ Pebbly Beach ⑤

🚶 🌊 🏖

Set within Murramarang National Park, this beach is famous for its tame kangaroos which sometimes venture into the water at dusk and dawn, and have been seen to "body surf".

KEY

- Highway
- Major road
- Minor road
- River
- Viewpoint

CANBERRA AND AUSTRALIAN CAPITAL TERRITORY

*L*ocated within New South Wales, some 300 km (185 miles) southwest of Sydney, Canberra is Australia's capital and its political heart-land. The city was planned in 1908 as the new seat of federal parliament to end rivalry between Sydney and Melbourne. The surrounding Australian Capital Territory features bush and mountain terrain.

Canberra was once little more than a sheep station on the edge of the Molonglo River. American architect Walter Burley Griffin won an international competition to design the city. He envisaged a spacious, low-level, modern city, with its major buildings centred on the focal point of Lake Burley Griffin. Canberra (its name is based on an Aboriginal word meaning "meeting place") is a city of contradictions. It consists of more than just politics, diplomacy and monuments. Lacking the traffic and skyscrapers of Australia's other main cities, it has a serenity and country charm suited to strolling around the lake, bush driving and picnicking.

Canberra is the national capital and the centre of political and administrative power in Australia, yet it is also a rural city, ringed by gum trees, with the occasional kangaroo seen hopping down its suburban streets. The city holds the majority of the nation's political, literary and artistic treasures, and contains important national institutions such as the High Court of Australia, the Australian National University and the Australian War Memorial, but it has a population of fewer than 500,000. These contradictions are the essence of the city's attraction. Canberra's hidden delights include Manuka's elegant cafés *(see pp533–4)*, excellent local wines and sophisticated restaurants. Special events include the annual spring flower festival, Floriade, which turns the north shore of the lake into a blaze of colour, and the spectacular hot-air ballooning festival in April.

Outside the city lie the region's natural attractions. Tidbinbilla Nature Reserve is home to wild kangaroos, wallabies, emus, koalas and platypuses. The Murrumbidgee River is excellent for canoeing, and the wild Namadgi National Park has bush camping, Aboriginal art sites, alpine snow gums and mountain creeks for trout fishing.

Hot-air ballooning festival over Lake Burley Griffin, near the National Library of Australia

◁ **The imposing flag-topped Parliament House in Canberra**

Exploring Canberra and ACT

Central Canberra lies around Lake Burley Griffin,
framed by the city's four hills – Black Mountain and
Mount Ainslie to the north and Capital Hill and Red
Hill to the south. Most of Canberra's main sights
are accessible from the lake. Scattered throughout the
northern suburbs are other places of interest such as
the Australian Institute of Sport. To the south lies the
wilderness and wildlife of Namadgi National Park.

View of Canberra from Mount Ainslie

SIGHTS AT A GLANCE

Historic Streets and Buildings
*Australian War Memorial
    pp200–1* **8**
Civic Square **7**
Government House **3**
Mount Stromlo Observatory **14**
Royal Australian Mint **2**
Telstra Tower **10**
Yarralumla **5**

Parks and Gardens
Australian National Botanic
    Gardens **9**
Namadgi National Park p207 **18**
Red Hill **1**

Modern Architecture
Parliament House pp198–9 **4**

Museums and Galleries
Australian Institute of Sport **12**
Canberra Space Centre **16**
National Gallery pp202–3 **6**
National Museum of Australia **13**

**Aquariums and Nature
Reserves**
National Zoo and Aquarium **11**
Tidbinbilla Nature Reserve **17**

Rivers
Murrumbidgee River **15**

0 kilometres   1

0 miles   1

SEE ALSO

- *Where to Stay* pp486–7

- *Where to Eat* pp533–4

GETTING AROUND

Many of the sights around Lake Burley Griffin are within walking distance of each other. The Canberra Explorer red bus also travels between attractions. The city centre's layout can make driving difficult, but to explore the bush suburbs a car is essential as there is no suburban train system. Most of the sights in ACT are within half an hour's drive of the city.

NEW SOUTH WALES
Sydney
CANBERRA AND ACT
VICTORIA
Melbourne

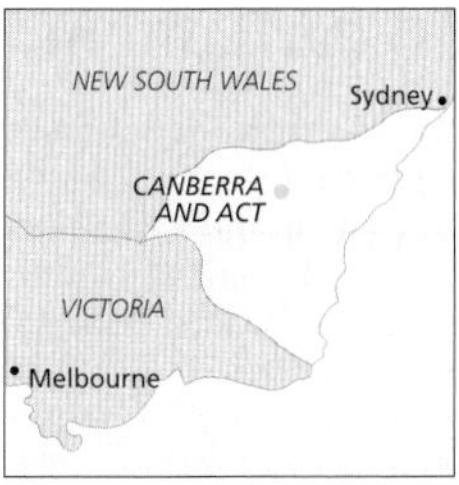

LOCATOR MAP

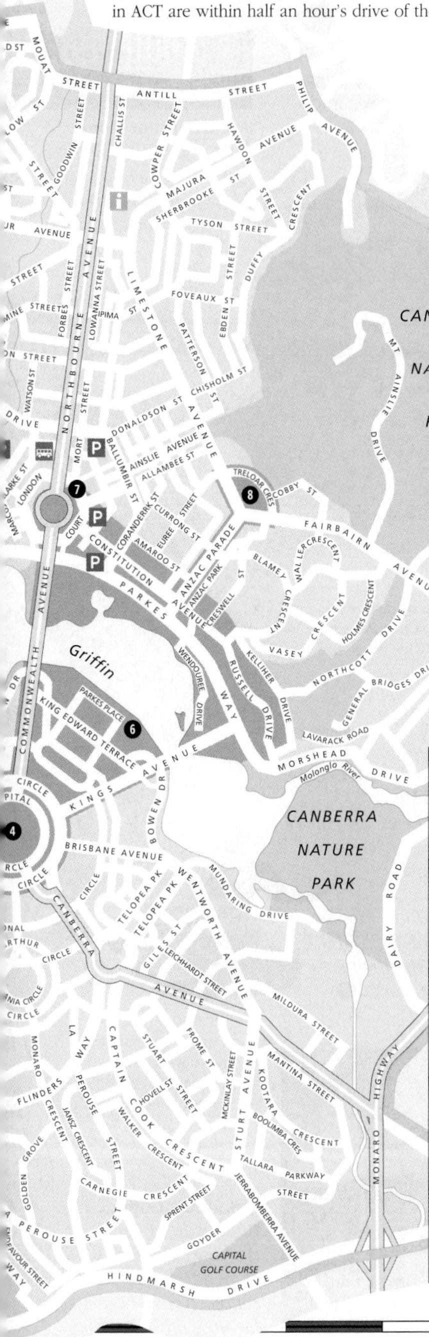

CANBERRA NATURE PARK
MT AINSLIE DRIVE
FAIRBAIRN AVENUE
NORTHBOURNE AVENUE
COMMONWEALTH AVENUE
CONSTITUTION AVENUE
PARKES WAY
ANZAC PARADE
LIMESTONE AVENUE
Griffin
KING EDWARD TERRACE
PARKES PLACE
KINGS AVENUE
BRISBANE AVENUE
MORSHEAD DRIVE
Molonglo River
GOLF COURSE
CANBERRA NATURE PARK
DAIRY ROAD
WENTWORTH AVENUE
CANBERRA AVENUE
MONARO HIGHWAY
CAPITAL GOLF COURSE
HINDMARSH DRIVE

KEY

- Street-by-Street area *pp194–5*
- Bus station
- Car Park
- Tourist information
- Metroad (city) route
- Highway
- Major road
- Minor road
- Territory boundary

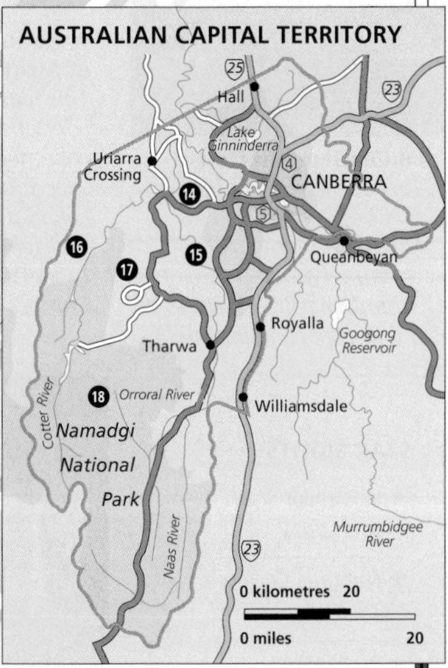

AUSTRALIAN CAPITAL TERRITORY
Hall
Lake Ginninderra
Uriarra Crossing
CANBERRA
Queanbeyan
Royalla
Googong Reservoir
Tharwa
Orroral River
Williamsdale
Cotter River
Namadgi National Park
Naas River
Murrumbidgee River
0 kilometres 20
0 miles 20

The Parliamentary Triangle

Canberra's major monuments, national buildings and key attractions are all situated around Lake Burley Griffin within the Parliamentary Triangle. Designed to be the focal point of Canberra's national activities by the architect Walter Burley Griffin *(see p197)*, the Parliamentary Triangle has Capital Hill at its apex, topped by Parliament House. Commonwealth Avenue and Kings Avenue fan out from Capital Hill, cross the lake and end at Parkes Way. Running at a right angle from the base of the triangle is Anzac Parade, which leads to the Australian War Memorial *(see pp200–1)* and completes the basic symmetry of Burley Griffin's plan.

★ Parliament House
Completed in 1988, this is one of the world's most impressive parliamentary buildings ❹

Capital Hill

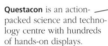

Questacon is an action-packed science and technology centre with hundreds of hands-on displays.

Kings Avenue

Old Parliament House
This was the first parliamentary building in the new capital. Built in 1927, it remained as the centre of Australian politics until 1988. It is now open to the public.

★ National Gallery of Australia
This impressive art gallery contains an excellent collection of Australian colonial and Aboriginal art, as well as many significant European works ❻

The High Court of Australia is the highest court of justice in the country.

STAR SIGHTS

- ★ Australian War Memorial
- ★ National Gallery of Australia
- ★ Parliament House

Blundell's Cottage
Built in 1858, this is a fine example of an early colonial cottage typical of remote farming life of the time.

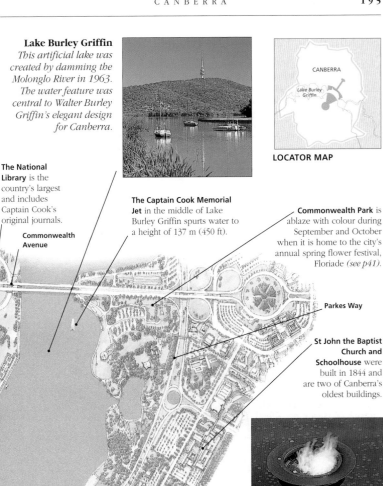

Lake Burley Griffin
This artificial lake was created by damming the Molonglo River in 1963. The water feature was central to Walter Burley Griffin's elegant design for Canberra.

LOCATOR MAP

CANBERRA

Lake Burley Griffin

The National Library is the country's largest and includes Captain Cook's original journals.

Commonwealth Avenue

The Captain Cook Memorial Jet in the middle of Lake Burley Griffin spurts water to a height of 137 m (450 ft).

Commonwealth Park is ablaze with colour during September and October when it is home to the city's annual spring flower festival, Floriade *(see p41)*.

Parkes Way

St John the Baptist Church and Schoolhouse were built in 1844 and are two of Canberra's oldest buildings.

★ **Australian War Memorial**
The nation's tribute to its 102,000 war dead is also a remarkable museum **8**

The Australian-American Memorial was given to Australia by the United States as a thank you for the Pacific alliance during World War II *(see pp57–8)*.

Anzac Parade
Nine memorials line the boulevard, commemorating Australia's war efforts in the 20th century.

0 metres	500
0 yards	500

Exploring the Parliamentary Triangle

Canberra, with its still lake and impressive national monuments and institutions, can at first glance appear cold and somewhat forbidding to visitors. But venture inside the various buildings dotted around Lake Burley Griffin within the Parliamentary Triangle, and a treasure trove of architecture, art, history and politics will be revealed. The lake itself, surrounded by gardens, cycle paths and outdoor sculptures and memorials, is a picturesque location for relaxing picnics and leisurely strolls. Exploring the entire Parliamentary Triangle can take one or two days. It is, however, more easily tackled by dividing it into two parts, taking in first the north and then the south of the lake.

🏛 Old Parliament House
King George Terrace, Parkes.
Tel *(02) 6270 8222.* ☐ *9am–5pm daily.* ● *25 Dec.* 🖾 ♿ 🖋 🖵
www.oph.gov.au
Built in 1927 as the first parliamentary building in the new national capital, Old Parliament House was the centre of Australian politics for more than 60 years. It was replaced by the new Parliament House in 1988 *(see pp198–9).*

This building has witnessed many historic moments: Australia's declaration of war in 1939; news of the bombing of Australia's northern shores by the Japanese in 1942; the disappearance and presumed drowning of Prime Minister Harold Holt in 1967 and the dismissal of the Whitlam government by Sir John Kerr in 1975 *(see pp58–9).*

Kings Hall, the old House of Representatives and Senate chambers can all be explored. Visitors can also examine the hidden peephole in the wall of the prime minister's office, discovered during renovations in 1990. Several historical exhibitions about Australia are housed here. The National Portrait Gallery's main collection is held here – they also have an annexe in Commonwealth Place.

Blundell's Cottage

🏛 Blundell's Cottage
Wendouree Drive, Parkes. ***Tel*** *(02) 6273 2667.* ☐ *11am–4pm Mon–Sun.* ● *25 Dec.* 🖾
This small sandstone farmhouse was built in 1858 by the Campbell family, owners of a large farming property at Duntroon Station, for their head ploughman. It was later occupied by bullock driver George Blundell, his wife, Flora, and their eight children.

This excellent example of a colonial cottage also conveys all the remoteness of early farming life. Blundell's Cottage once looked out over sheep paddocks, but these were flooded by Lake Burley Griffin *(see pp194–5).*

🏛 National Capital Exhibition
Commonwealth Park.
Tel *(02) 6257 1068.* ☐ *9am–5pm daily.* ● *25 Dec.* ♿ 🖵 🖵
The rotunda housing the National Capital Exhibition, north of Lake Burley Griffin at Regatta Point, is recommended as a starting point for any tour of Canberra. Inside are models, videos and old photographs showing the history and growth of Canberra as the federal capital of Australia. These provide an excellent orientation of the city.

From the windows of the rotunda is a clear view of Lake Burley Griffin, the Parliamentary Triangle and the Captain Cook Memorial Jet, National Carillion and Globe. The jet fountain and bronze, copper and enamel globe on the edge of the lake were added to the city's special features in 1970, as a bicentennial commemoration of the claiming of the east coast of Australia by British navy officer Captain James

Neo-Classical façade of Old Parliament House and its impressive forecourt

Cook in 1770 *(see p46)*. The elegant fountain lifts a column of water 147 m (480 ft) out of the lake from 11am until 2pm, provided the weather is not too windy. The National Carillion has 55 bronze bells and there are regular recitals.

🏛 National Library of Australia

Parkes Place, Parkes. *Tel* (02) 6262 1111. ☐ 9am–9pm Mon–Thu, 9am–5pm Fri, 9am–5pm Sat, 1:30–5pm Sun. ⬤ Good Fri, 25 Dec. ⬤ 📷 💻 **www**.nla.gov.au

This five-storey library, considered to be an icon of 1960s architecture, is the repository of Australia's literary and documentary heritage. Containing more than 7 million books, as well as copies of most newspapers and magazines published in Australia, thousands of tapes, manuscripts, prints, maps and old photographs, it is the nation's largest library and leading research and reference centre. There are also historic items in a rotating display such as Captain Cook's original journal from his *Endeavour* voyages.

The building, designed by Sydney architect Walter Bunning and completed in 1968, includes some notable works of art. Foremost are the modern stained-glass windows by Australian architect and artist Leonard French, made of Belgian chunk glass and depicting the planets. There are also the Australian life tapestries by French artist Mathieu Mategot.

Leonard French stained glass

🏛 Questacon – The National Science and Technology Centre

Cnr King Edward Terrace & Parkes Place, Parkes. *Tel* (02) 6270 2800. ☐ 9am–5pm daily. ⬤ 25 Dec. 📷 ⬤ **www**.questacon.edu.au

With 200 hands-on exhibits in six different galleries arranged around the 27-m (90-ft) high cylindrical centre of the building, science need never be dull again. A must for anyone visiting Canberra, Questa-

con clearly demonstrates that science can be fascinating, intriguing, fun and an everyday part of life.

Visitors can freeze their shadow to a wall, play a harp with no strings, experience an earthquake and feel bolts of lightning. You can also enjoy giant slides and a roller coaster simulator, and there are also regular science demonstrations and special lectures.

🏛 High Court of Australia

Parkes Place, Parkes. *Tel* (02) 6270 6811. ☐ 9:45am–4:30pm Mon–Fri. ⬤ Sat–Sun, public hols. ⬤ 💻

British and Australian legal traditions are embodied in this imposing lakeside structure, opened in 1980 by Queen Elizabeth II. The High Court is centred on a glass public hall, designed to instil respect for the justice system. Two six-panel murals by artist Jan Sensbergs look at the Australian constitution, the role of the Federation and the significance of the High Court. There are three courtrooms, and chambers for the Chief Justice and six High Court judges. Sittings are open to the public.

On one side of the ramp at the entrance is a sculpture of a waterfall constructed out of speckled granite. This feature is intended to convey how the decisions of this legal institution trickle down to all Australian citizens.

Jan Sensbergs mural in the High Court

🔒 St John the Baptist Church and Schoolhouse Museum

Constitution Ave, Reid. *Tel* (02) 6249 6839. ☐ 10am–noon Wed, 2–4pm Sat, Sun. ⬤ Good Fri, 25 Dec. 📷 ⬤

Built in 1844 of local bluestone and sandstone, the Anglican church of St John the Baptist and its adjoining schoolhouse are Canberra's oldest surviving buildings. They served the pioneer farming families of the region. Memorials on the walls of the church commemorate many early settlers, including statesmen, scientists and scholars.

Within the schoolhouse is a museum containing various 19th-century memorabilia.

WALTER BURLEY GRIFFIN

In 1911, the Australian government, then located in Melbourne, decided on Canberra as the best site for a new national capital. An international competition for a city plan was launched, and the first prize was awarded to a 35-year-old American landscape architect, Walter Burley Griffin. Influenced by the design of Versailles, his plan was for a garden city, with lakes, avenues and terraces rising to the focal point of Parliament House atop Capital Hill. On 12 March 1913, a foundation stone was laid by Prime Minister Andrew Fisher, but bureaucratic arguments and then World War I intervened. By 1921, little of Canberra had begun to be constructed, and Burley Griffin was dismissed from his design post. He stayed in Australia until 1935, when, reduced to municipal designs, he left for India. He died there in 1937, although his original vision lives on in the ever-expanding city of Canberra.

Walter Burley Griffin

Red Hill ❶

Via Mugga Way, Red Hill.

One of the highlights of a visit to Canberra is a drive to the top of Red Hill, which offers excellent views over Lake Burley Griffin,

Panoramic view of Canberra from Red Hill

Parliament House, Manuka and the embassy suburb of Yarralumla (see p200). Behind Red Hill stretch the southern suburbs of Canberra, with the beautiful green of the Brinda-bella Ranges to the west.

An alternative view of Canberra, offering a better understanding of Walter Burley Griffin's carefully planned city design, can be seen from the top of Mount Ainslie, on the north side of the lake behind the Australian War Memorial (see pp200–1).

Royal Australian Mint ❷

Denison St, Deakin. **Tel** (02) 6202 6999. 🚌 30, 31. ⭘ 9am–4pm Mon–Fri; 10am–4pm Sat–Sun, public hols. ⭘ Good Fri, 25 Dec. ♿

The Royal Australian Mint is the sole producer of Australia's circulating coin currency as well as being the country's national mint. It has produced over 11 billion circulating coins and today has the capacity to mint over two million coins per day, or over 600 million per year. The Mint is dedicated to commemorating Australia's culture and history through its

Parliament House ❹

Parliament House is the meeting place of Australia's Parliament and the focal point of Australia's democracy. Opened in 1988, the building on Capital Hill is the third home of the Federal Parliament since 1901. The building is set on a 32-hectare (80-acre) site and is the focal point of Canberra. Its architecture reflects Australia's commitment to open government.

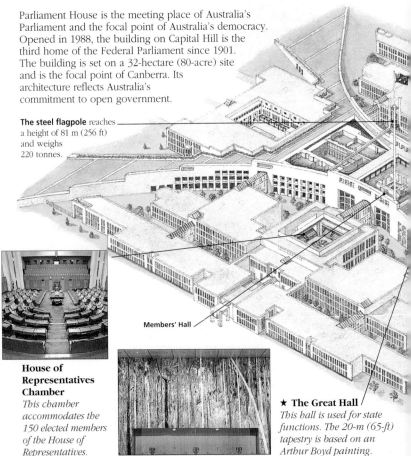

The steel flagpole reaches a height of 81 m (256 ft) and weighs 220 tonnes.

Members' Hall

House of Representatives Chamber
This chamber accommodates the 150 elected members of the House of Representatives.

★ **The Great Hall**
This hall is used for state functions. The 20-m (65-ft) tapestry is based on an Arthur Boyd painting.

numismatic programme. When touring the Mint you can see the history of Australian currency as well as how coins are made. You can even view the production process as the coins come off the presses.

Government House ❸

Dunrossil Drive, Yarralumla. **Tel** (02) 6283 3533. ⬤ various dates – phone ahead to check. 🖼 📷 obligatory.

Elegant façade and front grounds of Government House

Government House has been the official residence of the Governor General, the representative of the monarch in Australia, since 1927. The house was once part of a large sheep station called Yarralumla, which was settled in 1828, and is now where heads of state and the Royal Family stay when visiting Australia.

The house is closed to the public, except on special open days; however, a lookout point on Lady Denman Drive offers good views of the residence and the large gardens.

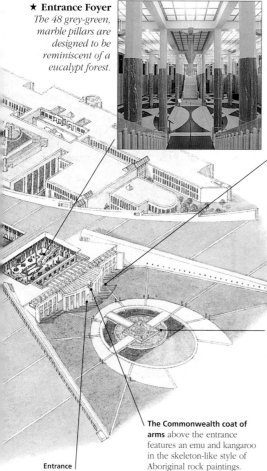

★ **Entrance Foyer**
The 48 grey-green, marble pillars are designed to be reminiscent of a eucalypt forest.

The Commonwealth coat of arms above the entrance features an emu and kangaroo in the skeleton-like style of Aboriginal rock paintings.

Entrance

VISITORS' CHECKLIST

Capital Hill. **Tel** (02) 6277 7111. 🚌 31, 34, 39. ⬤ 9am–5pm daily. ⬤ 25 Dec. 🕐 every 30 mins until 4pm. 📷 ♿ 🛍 🖥

The Great Veranda is clad with white Italian marble cut from a single cliff face. Its grand design marks both the ceremonial and the public entrance for Parliament House.

Forecourt
The Aboriginal mosaic, red gravel and pool represent Australia's landscape and native inhabitants.

STAR FEATURES

★ Entrance Foyer
─────────────
★ The Great Hall

Yarralumla ❺

Yarralumla. 📞 (02) 6205 0044.
🚌 901, 31. 🌐 for embassy open
days. ♿ variable. 📷

The suburb of Yarralumla, on
the edge of Capital Hill, is
home to more than 80 of
Australia's foreign embassies
and diplomatic residences. A
drive through the tree-lined
streets gives a fascinating view

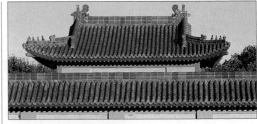

The traditional style of the Chinese Embassy in Yarralumla

of the architecture and cultures of each country represented, as embodied in their
embassies and grand ambassadorial residences.

Distinctive buildings include
the vast Chinese Embassy at
No. 15 Coronation Drive, with
its red columns, dragon statues and pagoda-shaped roofs.

On Moonah Place, the Indian
Embassy has pools, a shallow
moat and a white temple
building in the Mogul architectural style, with a gold spire on

Australian War Memorial ❽

The Australian War Memorial was built
to commemorate all Australians who
have died while serving their country. The
Roll of Honour and the symbolic Tomb
000of the Unknown Australian Soldier
serve as a reminder of the horror and
sadness of war. Other galleries in the
memorial document the history of all the
wars in which Australia has participated.

Façade of the Australian War Memorial

STAR FEATURES

★ Roll of Honour

★ Tomb of the Unknown
   Soldier

First World War Gallery

Orientation
Gallery

★ Roll of Honour
Names of all the 102,600
Australians killed in
action are written
on bronze panels
in the cloisters.

The Pool of
Reflection is a peaceful
place where families can
mourn their loved ones.
Rosemary planted by
the pool symbolizes
remembrance.

Eternal flame

Entrance

top. The High Commission of Papua New Guinea on Forster Crescent is built as a Spirit House, with carved totem poles outside; the Mexican Embassy on Perth Avenue boasts a massive replica of the Aztec Sun Stone.

Just across Adelaide Avenue is The Lodge, the official residence of the Australian prime minister and his family.

National Gallery of Australia ❻

See pp202–3.

Civic Square ❼

Civic Centre. 🚌 *many routes.*

The commercial heart of Canberra is the Civic Centre, on the north side of Lake Burley Griffin close to the northwest corner of the Parliamentary Triangle *(see pp194–5)*. It is the centre of many administrative, legal and local government functions in Canberra, as well as having the highest concentration of offices and private

Ethos Statue, Civic Square

sector businesses. It is also the city's main shopping area.

The central Civic Square, as envisaged by Walter Burley Griffin in his original city plan, is a common meeting place and relaxing area. It is dominated by the graceful bronze statue of Ethos, by Australian sculptor Tom Bass, located at the entrance of the ACT Legislative Assembly. In the adjacent Petrie Plaza is a traditional carousel, a much-loved landmark among the citizens of Canberra.

Hall of Memory
Adorning the golden dome is one of the world's largest mosaics, built in part by war widows.

Aircraft Hall

Second World War Gallery

Stained-Glass Windows
The figures on these windows represent the personal, social and fighting skills of all Australians during wartime.

★ Tomb of the Unknown Soldier
Beneath this red marble slab is buried an unknown Australian soldier who died during World War I. He symbolizes all Australians who have been killed while serving their country.

National Gallery of Australia ⑥

Australian society is diverse, multicultural and vibrant, and the 100,000 works of art owned by the National Gallery of Australia reflect the spirit of the country. The National Gallery opened in 1982, and the core of its collection consists of Australian art, from European settlement to present day, by some of its most famous artists, such as Tom Roberts, Arthur Boyd, Sidney Nolan and Margaret Preston *(see p34)*. The oldest art in Australia is that of its indigenous inhabitants *(see pp32–3)*, and the Aboriginal art collection offers fine examples of both ancient and contemporary works. The gallery's Asian and international collections are also growing. Modern sculptures are on display in the gardens.

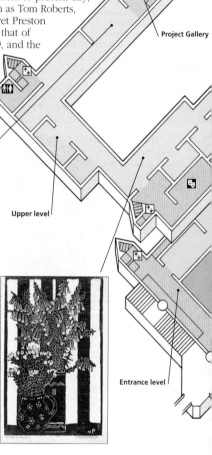

Project Gallery

Upper level

Entrance level

★ In a Corner on the MacIntyre *(1895)*
Tom Roberts' depiction of this country's bushland is painted in the fractured light style of the Australian School of Impressionists.

Native Fuchsia *(1925)*
This painting is typical of the hand-coloured wood-block techniques of artist Margaret Preston, best known for depicting Australian flowers.

SCULPTURE GARDEN

The National Gallery makes the most of its picturesque, lakeside gardens as the site for an impressive collection of sculptures, from classical, such as Aristide Maillol's *The Mountain*, to modern. Two of the best known and loved contemporary sculptures in the garden are *Cones* by Bert Flugelman and *The Pears* by George Baldessin.

The Mountain by Aristide Maillol

GALLERY GUIDE

The National Gallery is easily visited within two hours, although an excellent one-hour tour of the highlights is offered twice daily. On the entrance level is the Aboriginal art collection, which is not to be missed, and the international collections. Also highly recommended, on the upper level, is the extensive Australian art collection. Touring "blockbuster" art shows are hung in rooms in what is actually a later addition to the original building.

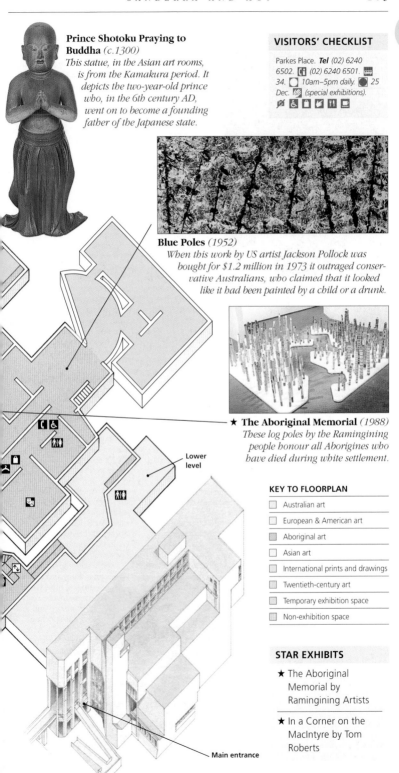

Prince Shotoku Praying to Buddha *(c.1300)*
This statue, in the Asian art rooms, is from the Kamakura period. It depicts the two-year-old prince who, in the 6th century AD, went on to become a founding father of the Japanese state.

VISITORS' CHECKLIST

Parkes Place. **Tel** *(02) 6240 6502.* ☐ *(02) 6240 6501.* ☐ *34.* ☐ *10am–5pm daily.* ☐ *25 Dec.* ☐ *(special exhibitions).*
🚫 ♿ ☐ 📷 🍴 🛍

Blue Poles *(1952)*
When this work by US artist Jackson Pollock was bought for $1.2 million in 1973 it outraged conservative Australians, who claimed that it looked like it had been painted by a child or a drunk.

★ **The Aboriginal Memorial** *(1988)*
These log poles by the Ramingining people honour all Aborigines who have died during white settlement.

Lower level

Main entrance

KEY TO FLOORPLAN

☐ Australian art
☐ European & American art
☐ Aboriginal art
☐ Asian art
☐ International prints and drawings
☐ Twentieth-century art
☐ Temporary exhibition space
☐ Non-exhibition space

STAR EXHIBITS

★ The Aboriginal Memorial by Ramingining Artists

★ In a Corner on the MacIntyre by Tom Roberts

Rock Garden section of the Australian National Botanic Gardens

Australian National Botanic Gardens ❾

Clunies Ross St, Acton. **Tel** (02) 6250 9540. ◯ Feb–Dec: 8:30am–5pm daily, Jan: 8:30am–6pm daily. ◉ 25 Dec. ♿ 📷 🅿

On the slopes of Black Mountain, the Australian National Botanic Gardens hold the finest scientific collection of native plants in the country. Approximately 90,000 plants of more than 5,000 species are featured in its displays.

The Rainforest Gully, one of the most popular attractions, features the plants from the rainforests of eastern Australia. One fifth of the nation's eucalypt species are found on the Eucalypt Lawn, which is also ideal for picnics. The Aboriginal Trail is a self-guided walk that details how Aborigines have utilized plants over thousands of years.

Telstra Tower ❿

Black Mountain Drive, Acton. **Tel** (02) 6219 6111. ◯ 9am–10pm daily. 📷 ♿

Known affectionately by locals as "the giant syringe", the Telstra Tower soars 195 m (640 ft) above the summit of

Black Mountain. The tower houses state-of-the-art communications equipment, such as television transmitters, radio pagers and cellular phone bases. The tower also features an exhibition on the history of telecommunications in Australia, from its first telegraph wire in Victoria in 1854 and on into the 21st century.

There are three viewing platforms at different levels of the tower offering spectacular 360° views of Canberra and the surrounding countryside both by day and by night. There is also a revolving restaurant. In 1989, Telstra Tower was made a member of the World Federation of Great Towers, which includes such buildings as the Empire State Building in New York.

National Zoo and Aquarium ⓫

Lady Denman Drive, Scrivener Dam. **Tel** (02) 6287 8400. ◯ 9am–5pm daily. ◉ 25 Dec. ♿ 📷 by arrangement. **www**.zooquarium.com.au

A wonderful collection of Australia's fish, from native freshwater river fish to brilliantly coloured cold sea, tropical and coral species are on display in the National Zoo and Aquarium. This is Australia's only combined zoo and aquarium. There are about 20 aquariums on show, including a number of smaller tanks containing freshwater and marine animals. They have some eight different species of shark on display.

The 9-ha (22-acre) landscaped grounds of the adjacent **Zoo** have excellent displays of numerous native

animals including koalas, wombats, dingoes, fairy penguins, Tasmanian devils, emus and kangaroos. As well as the native residents of the zoo there are many favourites from all over the world, including several big cats (the zoo has the largest collection of big cats in the country), primates, two giraffes and African antelopes.

The zoo also organizes "Meet a Cheetah" encounters. Under the supervision of a keeper, you will enter the cheetah enclosure and actually be able to touch and pat the animals. For even more close encounters, there is the two-hour ZooVenture tour, which would appeal to those animal lovers who want to enjoy a more hands-on behind-the-scenes kind of experience. Both this tour and "Meet a Cheetah" have age and height restrictions, and must be booked well in advance of your visit.

Australian Institute of Sport ⓬

Leverrier Crescent, Bruce. **Tel** (02) 6214 1010. 🚍 80. ◯ **Tours** 10am, 11:30am, 1pm, 2:30pm daily. ◉ 25 Dec. 📷 ♿ 📷 obligatory. **www**.ais.org.au

Australian Olympic medallists are often on hand to show visitors around the world-class Australian Institute of Sport (AIS). This is the national centre of Australia's sports efforts. Here you can see where the athletes sleep, train and eat. You can see how your fitness levels compare and test your sporting skills. There is also an exhibition of interactive sports displays, the Sportex exhibition, which includes themes such as "Heroes and Legends" and "How do you measure up?" Athletes also take visitors on guided tours around the amazing facilities. A shop and a café are also open to visitors.

Turtle in the National Aquarium

The *Harvest of Endurance* scroll, depicting the 1861 Lambing Flat Riots, in the National Museum of Australia

National Museum of Australia 🚱

Acton Peninsula. *Tel* (02) 6208 5000. 🚌 34. ⬭ 9am-5pm daily. ⬤ 25 Dec. 🗒 by arrangement. 📷 (special exhibitions). **www**.nma.gov.au

Established by an Act of Parliament in 1980, the National Museum of Australia moved to its permanent home on the Acton Peninsula in early 2001. It shares its location with the Australian Institute of Aboriginal and Torres Strait Islander Studies. The innovative, purpose-built facility quickly became an architectural landmark. Its unique design was inspired by the idea of a jigsaw puzzle.

Before beginning a tour of the museum, visitors can experience an audiovisual introduction to the museum in the Circa, a novel rotating cinema. A huge, three-dimensional map of Australia is visible from three floors. Using digital animation and interactive media stations, it helps to place the displays in their geographical context.

The permanent exhibitions explore the people, events and issues that have shaped and influenced the country. The museum's aim is to be a focus for sharing stories and promoting debate, and interactive displays involve visitors by inviting their contributions. Many rare objects from the museum's collection are also on display.

The **First Australians** gallery is the largest permanent exhibition and relates the stories and experiences of Aboriginal and Torres Strait Islander people. It not only illuminates their history but also deals frankly with contemporary social issues. Displays include Central Australian desert art, stone tools and Aboriginal jewellery made from Tasmanian seashells and a Torres Island outrigger canoe.

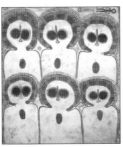

Untitled by Charlie Alyungurra, in the First Australians gallery

Nation: Symbols of Australia uses more than 700 props and artifacts to look at the way symbols help to define a sense of national identity. Exhibits include the kangaroo, as well as official symbols, such as the flag and Anzac Day. The **Horizons** gallery reviews the ways in which immigration has shaped the country. Since 1788 more than 10 million people have arrived in Australia as immigrants, and this gallery uses individual stories, as well as objects from the museum's collection, to look at the remarkable diversity of the Australian experience.

One of the more moving exhibitions is **Eternity**, in which the personal stories of 50 Australians are brought to life. The intention of this unique display is to explore history through emotion. "Your Story", an interactive exhibit, allows visitors to record their own stories, which then become part of the collection.

The museum also acknowledges the significance of the land in Australia's identity. In **Tangled Destinies**, the relationship between people and the environment is examined.

The landscaping of the museum is also notable and includes the striking Garden of Australian Dreams, which incorporates many symbols of Australian culture. The Backyard Café spills out into the innovative garden.

In addition, the museum hosts a range of temporary exhibitions. There are also children's galleries and performance spaces, as well as a television broadcast studio.

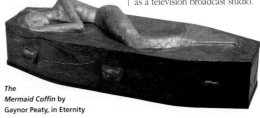

The Mermaid Coffin by Gaynor Peaty, in Eternity

Further Afield in the ACT

More than 70 per cent of the Australian Capital Territory is bushland. A one-day tour along Tourist Drive 5 provides an opportunity to see native animals in the wild, swim in the majestic Murrumbidgee River, visit a deep-space tracking station, and relax in the lovely gardens of the historic Lanyon Homestead.

Distinctive silver dome of Mount Stromlo Observatory

Mount Stromlo Observatory ⑭

Via Cotter Rd. *Tel (02) 6125 0232.* ☐ 10am–5pm Wed–Sun. ◑ 25 Dec. ♿ ▣

Mount Stromlo Observatory has been a central part of Canberra's astronomical world since 1942. However, the science centre only opened up its fascinating exhibits to the general public in 1997.

Set in the Mount Stromlo pine forest just outside the city, this elevated area has clear views of the night skies. Self-guided tours are available of the high-powered telescope, astronomers talk about their work and interactive displays explain the stellar formations of the southern hemisphere.

Murrumbidgee River ⑮

ℹ️ ACT Parks and Conservation Service (02) 6207 2425.

The Murrumbidgee River meets the Cotter River at Casuarina Sands, a beautiful place to fish and canoe. Nearby is Cotter Dam, good for picnics, swimming and camping.

Situated on the bank of the Murrumbidgee River south of Canberra is **Lanyon Homestead**, a restored 1850s home

attached to a sheep station. The house is complemented by peaceful gardens.

On the same property is the Sidney Nolan Gallery, which features the Ned Kelly series of paintings *(see p34)*. Nolan considered Lanyon a good place for his paintings to rest.

▥ Lanyon Homestead
Tharwa Drive, Tharwa. *Tel (02) 6235 5677.* ☐ 10am–4pm Tue–Sun. ◑ Good Fri, 24 & 25 Dec. 🎫 ♿

Canberra Space Centre ⑯

Via Paddys River Rd (Tourist Drive 5). *Tel (02) 6201 7880.* ☐ 9am–5pm daily. ♿ 🎫 by arrangement.

Canberra Space Centre at the Canberra Deep Space Communication Complex is managed by the Common-wealth Scientific and Industrial Research Organization (CSIRO)

Tracking dish at Canberra Space Centre, known as an "antenna"

and the American NASA organization. It is one of only three such deep-space tracking centres in the world linked to the NASA control centre in California.The centre has six satellite dishes, the largest of which measures 70 m (230 ft) in diameter and weighs a hefty 3,000 tonnes.

Visitors to the Space Centre can see a piece of moon rock 3.8 billion years old, examine a real astronaut's space suit, learn about the role of the complex during the Apollo moon landings and see recent photographs sent back from Mars, Saturn and Jupiter.

Emu at Tidbinbilla Nature Reserve

Tidbinbilla Nature Reserve ⑰

Via Paddys River Rd (Tourist Drive 5). *Tel (02) 6205 1233.* ☐ 9am–6pm daily. ◑ 25 Dec. 🎫 ♿ limited. 🎫

The tranquil Tidbinbilla Nature Reserve, with its 5,450 ha (13,450 acres) of forests, grasslands, streams and mountains, is a paradise for wildlife lovers. Kangaroos and their joeys bask in the sun, emus strut on the grassy flats, platypuses swim in the creeks, koalas thrive on the eucalypt branches and bower birds and superb lyrebirds can be seen in the tall forests.

The reserve is set at the end of a quiet valley. Visitors hike up to Gibraltar Rock or take a night stroll with a ranger to see sugar gliders and possums. The Birrigai Time Trail is a 3-km (2-mile) walk through different periods of history. The visitors' centre features Aboriginal artifacts and pioneer relics.

Namadgi National Park ⑱

Namadgi National Park covers almost half of the Australian Capital Territory. It is a beautiful, harsh landscape of snow, mountains, river valleys and Aboriginal rock art. Only 35 km (22 miles) south of Canberra, Namadgi is remote and solitary. Many days could be spent exploring the park, but even a day's walking will reward you with breathtaking views of the country.

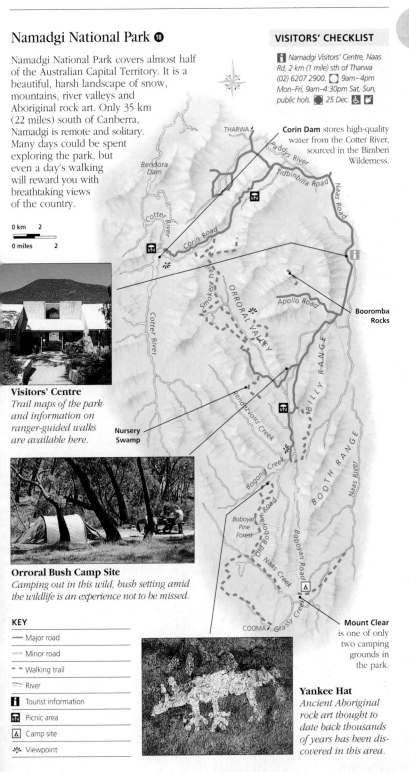

Corin Dam stores high-quality water from the Cotter River, sourced in the Bimberi Wilderness.

0 km 2
0 miles 2

Visitors' Centre
Trail maps of the park and information on ranger-guided walks are available here.

Nursery Swamp

Booromba Rocks

Orroral Bush Camp Site
Camping out in this wild, bush setting amid the wildlife is an experience not to be missed.

Mount Clear
is one of only two camping grounds in the park.

Yankee Hat
Ancient Aboriginal rock art thought to date back thousands of years has been discovered in this area.

KEY

— Major road
— Minor road
- - Walking trail
〜 River
ℹ Tourist information
⛫ Picnic area
△ Camp site
⁂ Viewpoint

QUEENSLAND

INTRODUCING QUEENSLAND 210–217

BRISBANE 218–233

SOUTH OF TOWNSVILLE 234–247

NORTHERN AND OUTBACK
QUEENSLAND 248–257

Queensland at a Glance

Australia's second-largest state encompasses some 1,727,000 sq km (667,000 sq miles) and is the country's most popular tourist destination, after Sydney, due to its tropical climate. Brisbane, the state capital, is a modern city, with skyscrapers looking out over the Brisbane River. The southern coastline is a haven for surfers and is the region that most typifies the nation's beach culture. Further north is the Great Barrier Reef, one of the natural wonders of the world. Inland, cattle stations and copper mines generate Queensland's wealth. The Far North remains remote and unspoiled, with rainforests and savannah land abundant with native wildlife.

Cairns *is Queensland's most northerly city and is a popular boarding point for touring the Great Barrier Reef. The city's hub is its esplanade, lined with cafés (see p254).*

NORTHERN AND OUTBACK QUEENSLAND *(see pp248– 57)*

Mount Isa *is Australia's largest inland city and revolves almost entirely around its copper, zinc and lead mining industries (see p257).*

0 kilometres   150

0 miles   150

Longreach *is in the heart of Queensland's Outback, and its most popular sight is the Stockman's Hall of Fame, documenting Australia's Outback history. Longreach is also the site of Qantas' original hangar (see p257).*

◁ **Fairy basslets among the coral in the Great Barrier Reef**

The Great Barrier Reef *is the largest coral reef in the world. Hundreds of islands scatter the coastline, but only a few are developed for tourists, who come here to dive among the coral and tropical fish (see pp212–17).*

Maryborough *is known for its Queenslander houses, their wide verandas shading residents from the tropical sun (see p241).*

Brisbane, *the state capital, is a highly modern yet relaxing city. Skyscrapers blend with older edifices, such as the impressive City Hall (see pp218–33).*

SOUTH OF TOWNSVILLE
(see pp234–47)

Surfers Paradise *is the main city of the Gold Coast region and more than lives up to its name. Chic hotels, pulsating nightclubs, high fashion stores and beach poseurs can all be found here (see p239).*

The Great Barrier Reef

Coral reefs are among the oldest and most primitive forms of life, dating back at least 500 million years. Today, the Great Barrier Reef is the largest reef system in the world, covering 2,000 km (1,250 miles) from Bundaberg to the tip of Cape York and an area of approximately 350,000 sq km (135,000 sq miles). Between the outer edges of the reef and the mainland, there are more than 2,000 islands and almost 3,000 separate reefs, of differing types. On islands with a fringing reef, coral can be viewed at close hand, although the best coral is on the outer reef, about 50 km (30 miles) from the mainland.

Saddled butterfly fish

LOCATOR MAP

The channel of water between the inner reef and Queensland's mainland is often as deep as 60 m (200 ft) and can vary in width between 30 km (20 miles) and 60 km (40 miles).

Coral is formed by tiny marine animals called polyps. These organisms have an external "skeleton" of limestone. Polyps reproduce by dividing their cells and so becoming polyp colonies.

Fringing reefs *surround islands or develop off the mainland coast as it slopes away into the sea.*

TYPICAL SECTION OF THE REEF

In this typical section of the Great Barrier Reef, a deep channel of water runs close to the mainland. In shallower water further out are a variety of reef features including coral cays, platform reefs and lagoons. Further out still, where the edge of the continental shelf drops off steeply, is a system of ribbon reefs.

Platform reef

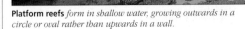

Platform reefs *form in shallow water, growing outwards in a circle or oval rather than upwards in a wall.*

Coral cays are sand islands, formed when reef skeletons and other debris such as shells are exposed to the air and gradually ground down by wave movement into fine sand.

Queensland's tropical rainforest *is moist and dense, thriving on the region's heavy, monsoon-like rains and rich soil.*

HOW THE REEF WAS FORMED

The growth of coral reefs is dependent on sea level, as coral cannot grow above the water line or below 30 m (100 ft). As sea level rises, old coral turns to limestone, on top of which new coral can build, eventually forming barrier reefs. The Great Barrier Reef consists of thousands of separate reefs and is comparatively young, most of it having formed since the sea level rose after the end of the last Ice Age. An outer reef system corresponds with Queensland's continental shelf. Reef systems nearer the mainland correspond with submerged hills.

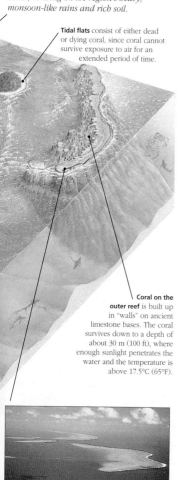

Tidal flats consist of either dead or dying coral, since coral cannot survive exposure to air for an extended period of time.

Coral on the outer reef is built up in "walls" on ancient limestone bases. The coral survives down to a depth of about 30 m (100 ft), where enough sunlight penetrates the water and the temperature is above 17.5°C (65°F).

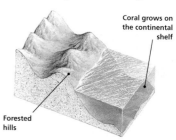

Coral grows on the continental shelf

Forested hills

1 Approximately 18,000 years ago, during the last Ice Age, waters were low, exposing a range of forested hills. Coral grew in the shallow waters of the continental shelf.

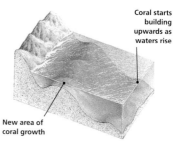

Coral starts building upwards as waters rise

New area of coral growth

2 Approximately 9,000 years ago, following the last Ice Age, the water level rose to submerge the hills. Coral began to grow in new places.

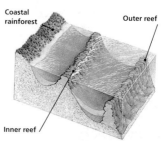

Coastal rainforest

Outer reef

Inner reef

3 Over succeeding millennia, coral formed "walls" on the continental shelf (the outer reef), while an array of fringing and platform reefs, coral cays and lagoons formed around the former hills (the inner reef).

Ribbon reefs *are narrow strips that occur only in the north along the edge of the continental shelf. Exactly why they form here remains a mystery to marine biologists.*

Life on the Great Barrier Reef

Blue-faced angelfish

More than 2,000 species of fish and innumerable species of hard and soft coral are found in the waters of the Great Barrier Reef. The diversity of life forms is extraordinary, such as echinoderms (including sea urchins), crustaceans and sponges. There is also an array of invertebrates, such as the graceful sea slug, some 12 species of sea grasses and 500 types of algae. The reef islands and coral cays support a wonderfully colourful variety of tropical birdlife. This environment is protected by the Great Barrier Reef Marine Park Authority, established by an Act of Parliament in 1975.

Diving amid the dazzling colours and formations of soft coral.

Hard coral is formed from the outer skeleton of polyps (*see p204*). The most common species is staghorn coral.

Soft coral has no outer skeleton and resembles the fronds of a plant, rippling in the waves.

Wobbegongs *are members of the shark family. They sleep during the day under rocks and caves, camouflaged by their skin tones.*

Manta rays are huge fish, measuring up to 6 m (20 ft) across. Despite their size, they are gentle creatures that are happy to be touched by divers.

Potato cod are known for their friendly demeanour and are often happy to swim alongside divers.

Great white sharks are occasional visitors to the reef, although they usually live in the open ocean and swim in schools.

Giant clams, which are large bivalves, are sadly a gourmet delicacy. Australian clams are now protected by law to save them from extinction.

The sea bed of the Barrier Reef is 60 m (195 ft) deep at its lowest point.

Coral groupers *inhabit the reef waters and grow up to 15 kg (33 lbs). They are recognizable by their deep red skin.*

THE FRAGILE REEF

Ecotourism is the only tourism that is encouraged on the Great Barrier Reef. The important thing to remember when on the reef is to look but not touch. Coral is easily broken; avoid standing on it and be aware that the taking of coral is strictly forbidden and carefully monitored. Camping on the reef's islands requires a permit from the Great Barrier Reef Marine Park Authority.

Beaked coralfish *are abundant and some of the most attractive fish of the Barrier Reef. They often swim in pairs, in shallow waters and around coral heads.*

Gobies feed on sand, ingesting the organic matter. They are found near the shoreline.

Blenny

Butterfly fish

THE REEF AS A MARINE HABITAT

Hard corals are the building blocks of the reef. Together with soft corals, they form the "forest" within which the fish and other sea creatures dwell.

Schultz pipefish

Goatfish

Clown anemonefish have an immunity to the stinging tentacles of sea anemones, among which they reside.

Batfish *swim in large groups and colonize areas of the reef for long periods before moving on elsewhere. They mainly feed on algae and sea jellies.*

Moray eels grow to 2 m (6 ft) in length, but are gentle enough to be hand-fed by divers.

The crown of thorns starfish *feeds mainly on staghorn coral. In the 1960s, a sudden growth in the numbers of this starfish led to worries that it would soon destroy the whole reef. However, many now believe that such a population explosion is a natural and common phenomenon. It contributes to reef life by destroying old coral and allowing new coral to generate.*

BIRDS OF THE GREAT BARRIER REEF

Gulls, gannets, frigate birds, shearwaters and terns all make use of the rich environment of the islands of the Great Barrier Reef to breed and rear their young, largely safe from mainland predators such as cats and foxes. The number of sea birds nesting on some of the coral cays (*see p204*) is astounding – for example, on the tiny area of Michaelmas Cay, 42 km (26 miles) northeast of Cairns, there are more than 30,000 birds, including herons and boobies.   **Red-footed booby**

Activities on the Great Barrier Reef

Ornate butterfly fish

Fewer than 20 of the Great Barrier Reef's 2,000 islands cater for tourists (see map and table below). Accommodation on the islands ranges from luxury resorts to basic camp sites. To make the most of the coral, take a tourist boat trip to the outer reef; most operators provide glass-bottomed boats or semi-submersibles to view the coral. The best way of seeing the reef, however, is by diving or snorkelling. There are numerous day trips from the mainland to the reef and between the islands.

Reef walking *involves walking over dead stretches of the reef at low tide. Wear strong shoes and be very careful to avoid standing on living coral under the water.*

Snorkelling *is one of the most popular activities in the Great Barrier Reef, offering the chance to see beautiful tropical fish at close range.*

THE MAIN ISLANDS

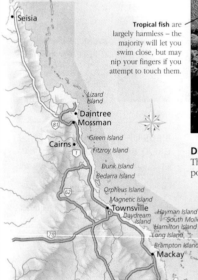

• Seisia

Tropical fish are largely harmless – the majority will let you swim close, but may nip your fingers if you attempt to touch them.

Lizard Island

• **Daintree**
• **Mossman**

Green Island

Cairns •
Fitzroy Island

Dunk Island
Bedarra Island

Orpheus Island
Magnetic Island
• **Townsville**
Daydream Island   *Hayman Island*
  South Molle Island
  Hamilton Island
  Long Island
  Brampton Island
• **Mackay**

Great Keppel Island

Heron Island
Rockhampton • **Gladstone**

Lady Elliot Island

Bundaberg •

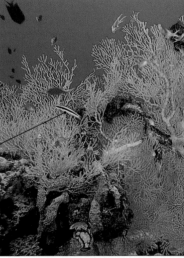

DIVING ON THE GREAT BARRIER REEF

The Great Barrier Reef is one of the most popular, as well as one of the more reasonably priced, places to learn to dive in the world. The best places to find dive schools are Townsville or Cairns, although many schools exist along the coast. Some boat trips also offer hand-held dives for complete beginners; some offer night dives.

KEY

▭▭	Highway
▭▭	Unsealed road

0 km 150

0 miles 150

Heron Island *is one of the few coral cay resorts and is known for its excellent diving. From October to March, turtle-spotting is a popular activity as they make their way up the beach to lay their eggs. Bird-watching is also popular as the island's pisonia trees are home to thousands of birds, including Noddy terns. Guided nature walks around the cay are available.*

Gorgonian fan coral grows in thickets in the deep waters of the Barrier Reef and is recognizable by its orange-yellow colour.

Scuba is an acronym for Self-contained Underwater Breathing Apparatus.

GETTING TO THE TOURIST ISLANDS

Bedarra Island 🚤 *from Dunk Island.* **Brampton Island** ✈ 🚤 *from Mackay.* **Daydream Island** 🚤 *from Shute Harbour.* **Dunk Island** ✈ *from Cairns.* 🚤 *from Mission Beach.* **Fitzroy Island** 🚤 *from Cairns.* **Great Keppell Island** 🚤 *from Rockhampton.* **Green Island** 🚤 *from Cairns.* **Hamilton Island** ✈ *from state capitals & Cairns.* 🚤 *from Shute Harbour.* **Hayman Island** 🚤 *from Shute Harbour.* **Heron Island** ✈ 🚤 *from Gladstone.* **Lady Elliot Island** ✈ *from Bundaberg, Hervey Bay.* **Lizard Island** ✈ *from Cairns.* **Long Island** 🚤 *from Shute Harbour.* **Magnetic Island** ✈ 🚤 *from Townsville.* **Orpheus Island** ✈ *from Cairns & Townsville.* **S. Molle Island** 🚤 *from Shute Harbour.*

Hamilton Island *is a popular resort island featuring a wide range of activities, including para-sailing, skydiving, golf, tennis and children's entertainments.*

ACTIVITIES ON THE TOURIST ISLANDS

These islands are easily accessible and offer a range of activities.

	DIVING	SNORKELLING	FISHING	DAY TRIPS	BUSHWALKING	WATERSPORTS	FOR CHILDREN
Bedarra Island	●	■	●	■	●	■	
Brampton Island		■	●	■	●	■	
Daydream Island	●	■	●	■	●	■	●
Dunk Island *(see p255)*	●	■	●	■	●	■	●
Fitzroy Island	●	■	●	■	●	■	
Gt Keppell Island		■	●	■	●	■	
Green Island *(see p253)*	●	■	●	■	●	■	
Hamilton Island	●	■	●	■	●	■	
Hayman Island	●	■	●	■	●	■	●
Heron Island	●	■	●	■		■	●
Lady Elliot Island	●	■		■			●
Lizard Island	●	■	●	■	●	■	
Long Island	●	■	●	■	●	■	
Magnetic Island *(see p247)*	●	■	●	■	●	■	
Orpheus Island	●	■	●	■	●	■	
South Molle Island	●	■	●	■	●	■	

The Low Isles, *25 km (15 miles) offshore from Port Douglas, are a perfect example of the reef's day-trip opportunities. This glass-bottomed boat offers sunbathing areas, snorkelling, views of reef life and lunch, before returning to the mainland.*

BRISBANE

Brisbane is the capital of Queensland and, with a population of over 1.6 million, ranks third in size in Australia after Sydney and Melbourne. Situated on the Brisbane River and surrounded by misty blue hills, the city is known for its scenic beauty, balmy climate and friendly atmosphere. Its tropical vegetation is a great attraction, particularly the bougainvillea, poinciana and fragrant frangipani.

In 1823, the Governor of New South Wales, Sir Thomas Brisbane, decided that some of the more intractable convicts in the Sydney penal settlement needed more secure incarceration. The explorer John Oxley was dispatched to investigate Moreton Bay, noted by Captain Cook on his journey up the east coast 50 years earlier. Oxley landed at Redcliffe and thought he had stumbled across a tropical paradise. He was soon disappointed and it was decided to move the colony inland up the Brisbane River. This was mainly due to Brisbane's more reliable water supply and the fact that the river had a bend in it, which made escape more difficult for the convicts.

Free settlers began arriving in 1837, although they were not permitted to move closer than 80 km (50 miles) to the famously harsh penal settlement. This set a pattern of decentralization which is still evident today: Brisbane consists of several distinct communities as well as the central area. The city's growth was rapid and, in 1859, when Queensland became a self-governing colony, Brisbane was duly named as the state capital.

As Queensland's natural resources, including coal, silver, lead and zinc, were developed, so its major city flourished. Brisbane's status as a truly modern city, however, is relatively recent, beginning with a mining boom in the 1960s. Hosting the Commonwealth Games in 1982 and the 1988 Expo were also milestones, bringing thousands of visitors to the city. Today, Brisbane is a cosmopolitan place boasting some superb restaurants, streetside cafés and a lively arts scene. Yet amid all the high-rises and modernity, pockets of traditional wooden cottages with verandas can still be found, and the relaxed manner of the locals tempers the urban bustle.

Sheep in the Australian Woolshed animal park in Brisbane

◁ An old paddlesteamer on the Brisbane River, set against the city's modern skyline

Exploring Central Brisbane

Brisbane's city centre fits neatly in a U-shaped loop of the Brisbane River, so one of the best ways to get acquainted with the city is by ferry. The city centre can also be easily explored on foot. The streets follow a grid and are named after British royalty: queens and princesses run north–south, kings and princes run east–west. Brisbane's suburbs also have their own distinct feel: to the east is chic Kangaroo Point; just west of the centre is trendy Paddington; while to the northwest Fortitude Valley has a diverse and multicultural population.

Cenotaph in Anzac Square

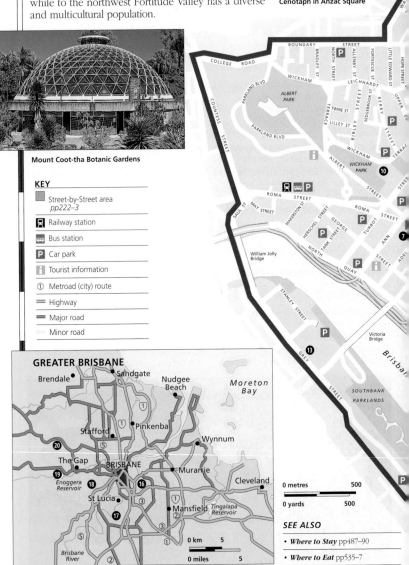

Mount Coot-tha Botanic Gardens

KEY

	Street-by-Street area *pp222–3*
🚈	Railway station
🚌	Bus station
🅿	Car park
ℹ	Tourist information
①	Metroad (city) route
	Highway
	Major road
	Minor road

GREATER BRISBANE

Brendale •   • Sandgate
    Nudgee
    Beach
Moreton Bay

Stafford •   Pinkenba
Wynnum •

The Gap •
BRISBANE
• Murarrie
Cleveland •

Enoggera Reservoir
St Lucia •
Mansfield •
Tingalapa Reservoir

Brisbane River

0 km	5
0 miles	5

0 metres	500
0 yards	500

SEE ALSO

- *Where to Stay* pp487–90
- *Where to Eat* pp535–7

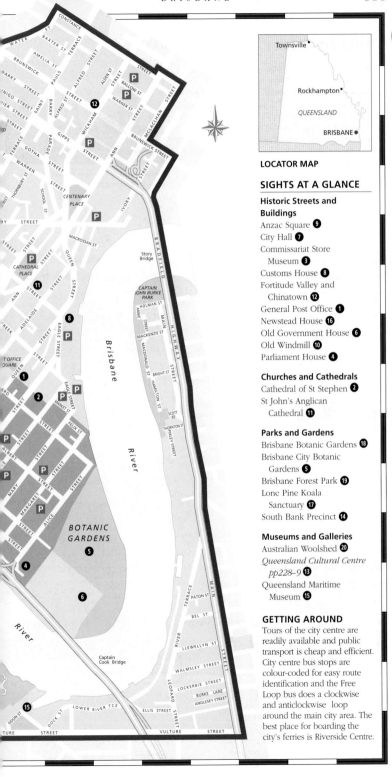

LOCATOR MAP

SIGHTS AT A GLANCE

Historic Streets and Buildings

Anzac Square **9**

City Hall **7**

Commissariat Store Museum **3**

Customs House **8**

Fortitude Valley and Chinatown **12**

General Post Office **1**

Newstead House **16**

Old Government House **6**

Old Windmill **10**

Parliament House **4**

Churches and Cathedrals

Cathedral of St Stephen **2**

St John's Anglican Cathedral **11**

Parks and Gardens

Brisbane Botanic Gardens **18**

Brisbane City Botanic Gardens **5**

Brisbane Forest Park **19**

Lone Pine Koala Sanctuary **17**

South Bank Precinct **14**

Museums and Galleries

Australian Woolshed **20**

Queensland Cultural Centre pp228–9 **13**

Queensland Maritime Museum **15**

GETTING AROUND

Tours of the city centre are readily available and public transport is cheap and efficient. City centre bus stops are colour-coded for easy route identification and the Free Loop bus does a clockwise and anticlockwise loop around the main city area. The best place for boarding the city's ferries is Riverside Centre.

Street-by-Street: Central Brisbane

Central Brisbane is a blend of glass and
steel high-rises co-existing with graceful
19th-century constructions. The latter fortunately managed to survive the frenzy of demol-
ishing old buildings that took place throughout
the country during the 1970s. Queen Street,
now a pedestrian mall, is the hub of the city.
Reflecting the city's beginnings as a port, most
of the historic buildings are found near the
river. Near the city's first Botanical Gardens, which border Alice Street, many
old pubs have been renovated to cater
for a largely business-lunch clientele.

Central Brisbane's modern skyline, looming
over the Brisbane River

Cathedral of St Stephen
*One of the landmarks of
Brisbane's city centre is
this Gothic-style cathedral.
Particularly notable are
its white twin spires* **2**

Elizabeth Arcade
is filled with New
Age, alternative
and bohemian-
style bookstores
and retail shops.

★ Commissariat Store Museum
*The original façade of these former 19th-
century granary stores has been preserved,
although the interior is now a museum
detailing Queensland's history* **3**

0 metres   100

0 yards   100

The former Coal Board building was erected in the mid-1880s and is an example of the elaborate warehouses that once dominated the city.

Smellie & Co. was a 19th-century hardware merchant housed in this attractive building. Note the Baroque doorway on the eastern side.

Queensland Club
This charming old building has housed the private, men-only Queensland Club since 1884. Panelled wood walls and elegant columns were intended to emulate British gentlemen's clubs.

LOCATOR MAP

KEY

--- Suggested route

STAR SIGHTS

★ Commissariat Store Museum

★ Parliament House

The Mansions
The Mansions are a row of 1890s three-storey, red brick terrace houses. The arches of lighter coloured sandstone create a distinctive design. Stone cats sit atop the parapets at each end of the building.

★ Parliament House
This stained-glass window depicting Queen Victoria is one of the many beautiful features of this late 19th-century building. Unlike many early parliamentary buildings in Australia, it is still used for its original purpose ❹

STREET

STREET

ALICE STREET

South façade of the restored colonial Commissariat Store Museum

General Post Office ❶

261 Queen St. *Tel* 13 13 18.
🚆 Brisbane Central. 🚌 Free Loop.
⛴ Eagle St Pier. ⏰ 7am–6pm
Mon–Fri. ♿

Built between 1871 and 1879, this attractive Neo-Classical building was erected to house the city's first official postal service. It replaced the barracks for female convicts which had previously occupied the site. The building continues to operate as central Brisbane's main post office.

Post Office Square, opposite the General Post Office, is a pleasant place to relax, while looking out over the landscaped greenery and fountains of Anzac Square.

Cathedral of St Stephen ❷

249 Elizabeth St. *Tel* (07) 3336 9111.
🚆 Brisbane Central. 🚌 Free Loop.
⛴ Eagle St Pier. ⏰ 8am–6pm
Mon–Fri, 7am–6pm Sat–Sun. ♿ 🚻

Early settlers provided the funds for this lovely English Gothic-style Catholic cathedral, designed by noted colonial architect Benjamin Backhouse and completed in 1874. The main façade features restored twin spires on each side of the elaborate stained-glass windows.

Next door is St Stephen's Chapel, the original cathedral. It was designed by AW Pugin, an English architect who also worked on London's Houses of Parliament.

Commissariat Store Museum ❸

115 William St. *Tel* (07) 3221 4198.
🚆 South Brisbane. 🚌 Free Loop.
⛴ North Quay. ⏰ 10am–4pm
Tue–Fri & most Sun. 🏛 Good Fri,
Easter Sun, 25 Dec, 26 Dec. 🚻 ♿

The Commissariat Stores, constructed by convict labour in 1829, is the only surviving building from Brisbane's penal colony days open to the public. Having been restored in 2000, it is now open to visitors and houses the Royal Historical Society of Queensland.

Parliament House ❹

Cnr George and Alice sts. *Tel* (07)
3406 7562. 🚆 Brisbane Central. 🚌
1a, 1b, 5, 5b, 5c, 7, 7a, Free Loop. ⛴
Gardens Point. ⏰ 9:30am–4:15pm
Mon–Fri, 10am–2pm Sat–Sun. 🏛
public hols. ♿ 📷 obligatory.

Queensland's Parliament House was designed in French Renaissance style by architect Charles Tiffin, who won an architectural competition. Begun in 1865, it was completed in 1868. Tiffin added features more suited to Queensland's tropical climate, such as shady colonnades, shutters and an arched roof which is made from Mount Isa copper *(see p257).* Other notable features are the cedar staircases and the intricate gold leaf detailing on the Council Chamber ceilings.

The building is still used for its original purpose and the public is permitted into the chambers when parliament is not in progress. Unlike other state parliaments, consisting of an Upper and Lower House, Queensland has only one parliamentary body.

Parliament House is also notable as being the first legislative building in the British Empire to be lit by electricity.

Interior of the Assembly Chamber in Parliament House

Brisbane City Botanic Gardens ❺

Alice St. *Tel* (07) 3403 8888.
🚆 Brisbane Central. 🚌 Free Loop.
⛴ Edward St. ⏰ 24 hours. ♿

Brisbane's first Botanic Gardens on the Brisbane River are the second oldest botanic gardens in Australia. Their peaceful location is a

Mangrove boardwalk in the Botanic Gardens

For hotels and restaurants in this region see pp487–90 and pp535–7

Arcade and arches of the north façade of Old Government House

welcome haven from the city's high-rise buildings.

In its earliest incarnation, the area was used as a vegetable garden by convicts. It was laid out in its present form in 1855 by the colonial botanist Walter Hill, who was also the first director of the gardens. An avenue of bunya pines dates back to the 1850s, while an avenue of weeping figs was planted in the 1870s.

Hundreds of water birds, such as herons and plovers, are attracted to the lakes dotted throughout the gardens' 18 ha (44 acres). Brisbane River's renowned mangroves are now a protected species and can be admired from a specially built boardwalk.

Old Government House ❻

Queensland University of Technology Campus, Gardens Point, George St. *Tel* (07) 3864 8005. 🚆 Brisbane Central. 🚌 Free Loop. 🚢 Gardens Point. ⏱ 10am–4pm Mon–Fri. public hols. 🚻 ground floor only. 📷

Home to the National Trust of Queensland since 1973, the state's first Government House was designed by colonial architect Charles Tiffin and completed in 1862. The graceful sandstone building served not only as the state governor's residence, but also as the administrative base and social centre of the state of Queensland until 1910. Following its vice-regal term

of office, the building was occupied by the fledgling University of Queensland (now situated in the suburb of St Lucia). Of particular architectural note are the Norman-style arches and arcades on the ground floor.

City Hall ❼

King George Square. *Tel* (07) 3403 4048. 🚆 Brisbane Central. 🚌 Free Loop. 🚢 Eagle St Pier. ⏱ 8am–5pm Mon–Fri; 10am–5pm Sat–Sun. public hols. 🚻 📷 **Clocktower** ⏱ 10am–3pm Mon–Fri, 10am–2.30pm Sat. public hols. **Museum of Brisbane** ⏱ 10am–5pm daily. www.brisbane.qld.gov.au

Completed in 1930, the Neo-Classical City Hall is home to Brisbane City Council, the largest council in Australia.

Brisbane's early settlement is depicted by a beautiful sculpted tympanum above the main entrance. In the King George Square foyer, are some fine examples of traditional crafts-manship are

evident in the floor mosaics, ornate ceilings and woodwork carved from Queensland timbers. City Hall's 92-m (300-ft) Italian Renaissance-style tower gives a panoramic view of the city from a platform at its top. A display of contemporary art and Aboriginal art and ceramics is housed in the Museum of Brisbane.

The attractive King George Square, facing City Hall, continues to resist the encroachment of high-rise office blocks and has several interesting statues, including *Form del Mito* by Arnaldo Pomodoro. The work's geometric forms and polished surfaces, for which this Italian sculptor is noted, reflect the changing face of the city from morning through to night. The bronze *Petrie Tableau*, by Tasmanian sculptor Stephen Walker, was designed for Australia's bicentenary. It commemorates the pioneer families of Brisbane and depicts one of Queensland's earliest explorers, Andrew Petrie, being bid farewell by his family as he departs on an inland expedition.

Façade of City Hall, with its Italian Renaissance clocktower

Customs House ❽

399 Queen St. *Tel (07) 3365 8999.*
🚋 *Brisbane Central.* 🚌 *Free Loop.*
⛴ *Riverside.* ◯ *9am–5pm Mon,
9am–10pm Tue–Sat, 9am–4pm Sun.*
◉ *public hols.* ♿ 📷 *Sun.* 🍴

Restored by the University
of Queensland in 1994,
Customs House, with its
landmark copper dome and
stately Corinthian columns, is
now open to the public.
Commissioned in 1886, this is
one of Brisbane's oldest
buildings, predating both City
Hall *(see p225)* and the
Treasury. Early renovations
removed the hall and
staircase, but these have now
been carefully reconstructed
from the original plans.
Today, the building is used
for numerous civic functions
and there is also a restaurant.

Anzac Square ❾

Ann & Adelaide sts. 🚋 *Brisbane
Central.* 🚌 *Free Loop.* ⛴
Waterfront Place, Eagle St Pier.

All Australian cities commemorate those who have
given their life for their
country. Brisbane's war
memorial is centred on Anzac
Square, an attractive park
planted with, among other
flora, rare boab (baobab) trees.
The Eternal Flame burns in a
Greek Revival cenotaph at the
Ann Street entrance to the
park. Beneath the cenotaph
is the Shrine of Memories,
containing various tributes
and wall plaques to those
who gave their lives in war.

Distinctive view of Old Windmill

Old Windmill ❿

Wickham Terrace. 🚋 *Brisbane
Central.* 🚌 *City Sights.* ◉ *to public.*

Built in 1828, the Old Windmill is one of two buildings
still standing in Brisbane
from convict days, the old
Commissariat Stores being the
other survivor *(see p224).*
Originally the colony's first
industrial building, it proved
unworkable without the availability of trained operators,
so it was equipped with
treadmills to punish recalcitrant
convicts. It later served as a
time signal, with a gun fired
and a ball dropped each day
at exactly 1pm.

The picturesque mill was
also chosen as the first television image in Australia in the
1920s. The windmill is not
open to the public, but it
makes a striking photograph.

St John's Anglican Cathedral ⓫

373 Ann St. *Tel (07) 3835 2231.* 🚋
Brisbane Central. 🚌 *Free Loop.* ⛴
Riverside Centre. ◯ *9:30am–
4:30pm daily.* ♿ 📷

Designed along French
Gothic lines in 1888, with the
foundation stone laid in 1901,
St John's Anglican Cathedral is
regarded as one of the most
splendid churches in the
southern hemisphere. The
interior is of Helidon sandstone.
On display are numerous
examples of local needlework,
wood, glass and stone craft.
Over 400 cushions depicting
Queensland's flora and fauna
attract a lot of interest.

It was at the adjacent
Deanery in 1859 that
Queensland was made a
separate colony (it had been
part of NSW). The Deanery
was the temporary residence of
Queensland's first governor.

**Nave and altar of St John's Anglican
Cathedral**

Fortitude Valley and Chinatown ⓬

Brunswick & Ann sts, Fortitude Valley.
🚋 *Brunswick St.* 🚌 *City Sights.*

The ship *Fortitude* sailed
from England and up the
Brisbane River in 1859 with
250 settlers on board, and
the name stuck to the valley
where they disembarked.
For a time the area was the
trading centre of the city and
some impressive buildings
were erected during the 1880s

Greek cenotaph in Anzac Square

For hotels and restaurants in this region see pp487–90 and pp535–7

Entrance to the Pedestrian Hall in Chinatown, Fortitude Valley

and 1890s. It then degenerated into one of Brisbane's seedier areas.

In the 1980s, the city council began to revive the district. It is now the bohemian centre of Brisbane, with some of the city's best restaurants (*see pp535–7*). McWhirter's Emporium, an Art Deco landmark, was originally a department store. Shops now occupy the lower levels with apartments above. On weekends, there is also a busy outdoor market in Brunswick Street.

Also within the valley is Brisbane's Chinatown, a bustling area of Asian restaurants, supermarkets, cinemas and martial arts centres. The lions at the entrance to the area were turned around when a *feng shui* expert considered their original position to be bad for business.

Queensland Cultural Centre **⑬**

See pp228–9.

South Bank Precinct **⑭**

Brisbane River foreshore, South Bank.
![] South Bank. ![] 12, Adelaide St & George St routes. ![] South Bank 1, 2, 3. ![] **Visitors' Centre** *Tel* (07) 3867 2051. ![] 9am–5pm daily.
www.south-bank.net.au

The South Bank of the Brisbane River was the site of Expo '88 and has now been redeveloped into a 17 ha (42 acres) centre of culture, entertainment and recreation. The area known as the parklands includes the Queensland Performing Arts Centre, the State Library, the Queensland Museum, Queensland Art Gallery, the Conservatorium, Opera Queensland, two colleges and an exhibition centre. The South Bank area abounds with restaurants, cafés, weekend market stalls and street entertainers. Classical music and pop concerts are also regularly held here. There is even a man-made lagoon with

Butterfly at South Bank Parklands

a "real" sandy beach, complete with suntanned lifesavers. South Bank Cinema screens the latest-release movies.

One of the most recent additions includes a 450-m (1,500-ft) pedestrian and cycle bridge, linking the southern end of the area with the city's Botanic Gardens.

Queensland Maritime Museum **⑮**

End of Goodwill Bridge, South Bank. *Tel* (07) 3844 5361. ![] South Bank. ![] 174, 175, 203, 204. ![] River Plaza, South Bank 3. ![] 9:30am–4:30pm daily. ![] Good Fri, 25 Apr (am), 25 Dec, 26 Dec. ![] ![] ![]
www.maritimemuseum.com.au

Queensland Maritime Museum lists among its exhibits shipbuilders' models, reconstructed cabins from early coastal steamers and relics from early shipwrecks in the area. In the dry dock, as part of the National Estate, sits HMAS *Diamantina*, a frigate that served during World War II.

A coal-fired tug, *Forceful*, is maintained in running order and cruises with passengers to Moreton Bay two seasons a year. Also on display is the pearling lugger *Penguin* and the bow of a Japanese pleasure boat, a *yakatabume*, donated to Brisbane by Japan after Expo '88.

HMAS *Diamantina* at the Queensland Maritime Museum

Queensland Cultural Centre ⑬

The Queensland Cultural Centre is the hub of
Brisbane's arts scene. It incorporates the
Queensland Art Gallery, a museum, performing arts
centre and library. The Gallery is the most
renowned of these, first established in 1895 and
part of the cultural centre since 1982. It has a fine
collection of Australian art, including works by
Sidney Nolan and Margaret Preston, together with
Aboriginal art. The international collection includes
15th-century European art and Asian art from the
12th century. Also noteworthy is the collection of
indigenous art and contemporary Asian art.

★ **Under the Jacaranda**
*R. Godfrey Rivers'
work is part of a
collection of
Australian art.*

Level 4

Level 3

Bushfire *(1944)*
*Russell Drysdale is known for his depiction
of harsh Outback life, such as this farmhouse destroyed by a natural disaster.*

★ **La Belle Hollandaise** *(1905)*
*One of Picasso's transitional
works between his blue and
rose periods, this was
painted during a visit to
the Netherlands. The
gallery paid a then
world record price of
£55,000 in 1959 for the
work of a living artist.*

Bathers *(1906)*
*One of Australia's
most highly regarded
artists, Rupert
Bunny achieved
international fame
with his paintings of
Victorian life. Here
the luxurious bathing
scene is matched by
the sumptuous scale
and composition.*

Level 2

STAR PAINTINGS

★ Under the Jacaranda

★ La Belle Hollandaise

For hotels and restaurants in this region see pp487–90 and pp535–7

KEY

- Contemporary, indigenous and Asian art
- Australian art, pre-1970s
- European art
- Decorative art
- Works on paper
- Non-exhibition space
- Water mall
- Sculpture courtyard

☐ Queensland Museum

Tel (07) 3840 7555. 9:30am–5pm daily. Good Fri, 25 Apr (until 1:30pm), 25 Dec.

This imaginative natural history museum is filled with full-scale models, both prehistoric and current. A large-scale model of Queensland's unique dinosaur, the *Muttaburrasaurus*, stands in the foyer. There are also displays on local megafauna and endangered species.

QUEENSLAND ART GALLERY GUIDE

The collection is housed over three levels. Contemporary, indigenous and Asian art are found on Levels 2 and 4. Decorative art is displayed on Level 2. European art also begins on this level and moves up to Level 3. Level 3 also contains Australian art after 1970.

The Sculpture Courtyard and surrounding fountains are a pleasant place to relax or enjoy a picnic.

Indoor lake

Restaurant

Art library

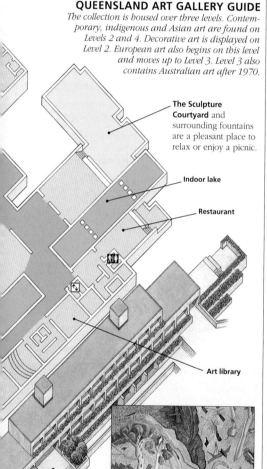

Performers of the acclaimed Queensland Ballet company

☐ Queensland Performing Arts Centre

Tel 13 62 46. performances only. advise when booking.
Queensland's Performing Arts Centre (QPAC) comprises a main concert hall and three theatres. Internationally acclaimed opera, classical music and a wide range of theatrical productions are staged at the centre. The highly respected Queensland Ballet is also based here.

☐ State Library of Queensland

Tel (07) 3840 7666. daily. Good Fri, 25–26 Dec.
The State Library houses collections from around the world. Its extensive resources cover all interests and most of its services are free. There are innovative displays and exhibitions, multimedia facilities, Indigenous Knowledge Centre, reading rooms, an auditorium and free films every Sunday.

Main entrance

Level 1

William and Shirley, Flora and Fauna *(1985)*
William Robinson's Queensland landscape is part of a fine collection by this contemporary artist.

Newstead House 🅰

Newstead Park, Breakfast Creek Rd,
Newstead. **Tel** (07) 3216 1846.
🚇 Bowen Hills. 🚌 300, 306, 322.
🕐 10am–4pm Mon–Fri, 2–5pm
Sun. ⬤ Good Fri, 25 Apr, 25–26
Dec. 📷 🎫 by arrangement.

Built in 1846 for Patrick
Leslie, one of the first
European settlers in the Darling Downs region, Newstead
House is the oldest surviving
home in Brisbane. Overlooking the river, this charming
building was sold in 1847 to
government resident and magistrate, Captain John Wickham.
The centre of the new
colony's social life, Newstead
House was the scene of lavish
parties. A huge fig tree, under
which elegant carriages once
waited, still graces the drive.
In 1939, it became the first
Australian house to be
preserved by its very own
act of parliament. Restored
by the Newstead House
Trust from 1976, the house
has been refurnished with
Victorian antiques.

Music box in Newstead House

Lone Pine Koala Sanctuary 🅱

Jesmond Rd, Fig Tree Pocket. **Tel**
(07) 3378 1366. 🚌 430, 445. ⛴
North Quay. 🕐 8:30am–5pm daily;
8:30am–4pm on 25 Dec. ⬤ until
1:30pm 25 April. 📷 ♿

The oldest Koala Sanctuary
in Australia, opened in 1927,
is now one of Brisbane's most
popular tourist attractions. Lone
Pine has more than 100
koalas, as well as kangaroos,
emus, possums, dingoes,

wombats, reptiles and many
Australian birds, including
various species of parrot.
Lone Pine insists that it is more
than just a zoo, a claim that is
supported by its nationally
respected koala breeding
programme. For a small fee,
visitors can have their photograph taken holding a koala.
A pleasant and scenic way
to get to Lone Pine Sanctuary
is by ferry. There are daily
departures at 10am from
Victoria Bridge.

Brisbane Botanic Gardens 🅲

Mt Coot-tha Rd, Toowong.
Tel (07) 3403 2535. 🚌 333.
🕐 daily.

Brisbane Botanic Gardens, in
the foothills of Mount Coot-
tha Forest Park 8 km (5 miles)
from the city centre, were
founded in 1976 and feature
more than 20,000 specimens,
representing 5,000 species, of
exotic herbs, shrubs and trees
laid out in themed beds.
Highlights include eucalypt
groves, a Japanese Garden, a
Tropical Display Dome,
which includes lotus lilies and
vanilla orchids, a Lagoon and
Bamboo Grove, Fern House,
National Freedom Wall
(celebrating 50 years of
peace) and a large collection
of Australian native plants.
Many arid and tropical plants,
usually seen in greenhouses,
thrive in the outdoor setting.
Also in the Gardens complex,
the Sir Thomas Brisbane

Planetarium is the largest of
Australia's planetariums.
Mount Coot-tha Forest Park
offers both spectacular views
and attractive picnic areas.
The Aboriginal name means
"place of wild honey", a
reference to the tiny bees
found in the area. On a
clear day, from the summit
lookout you can see
Brisbane, snugly encircled
by the river, Moreton and
Stradbroke islands, the
Glasshouse Mountains (so
named by Captain Cook
because they reminded him
of the glass furnaces in his
native Yorkshire) and the
Lamington Plateau backing
onto the Gold Coast (see
pp238–9). The park also
contains some excellent,
easygoing walking trails
through the woodland,
including Aboriginal trails
which detail traditional uses
of native plants.

Brisbane Forest Park 🅳

🚌 385. ℹ The Gap (07) 3300
4855. 🕐 9am–4:30pm daily.
⬤ 25 Dec.

Brisbane Forest Park, within
the D'Aguilar Mountain
Range, stretches for more
than 50 km (30 miles) northwest of Brisbane city centre.
Covering more than 28,500
ha (70,250 acres) of natural
bushland and eucalypt
forests, the park offers
driving routes with breathtaking views over the sur-

Koala at Lone Pine Koala Sanctuary

Lush landscape of the Brisbane Botanic Gardens backed by one of the city's modern skyscrapers

rounding countryside. The most scenic driving route is along Mount Nebo Road, which winds its way through the lush mountains.

Another scenic drive extends from Samford up to the charming mountain village of Mount Glorious and down the other side. It is worth stopping from time to time to hear the distinctive calls of bellbirds and whipbirds.

Six km (3.5 miles) past Mount Glorious is the Wivenhoe Outlook, with spectacular views down to Lake Wivenhoe, an artificial lake created to prevent the Brisbane River from flooding the city. One km (0.6 miles) north of Mount Glorious is the entrance to Maiala Recreation Area, where there are picnic areas, some wheelchair accessible, and several walking trails of varying lengths, from short walks to longer, 8-km (5-mile) treks. These pass through the rainforest, which abounds with animal life. Other excellent walks are at Manorina and at Jolly's Lookout, the oldest formal lookout in the park, which has a good picnic area. Also in the park is the Westridge Outlook, a boardwalk with sweeping views.

The engrossing **Walkabout Creek Wildlife Centre** at the park's headquarters is a re-created large freshwater environment. Water dragons, pythons, water rats, catfish and tiny rainbow fish flourish within these natural surroundings. Visitors also have the chance to see the extraordinary lungfish, a unique species which is equipped with both gills and lungs. The on-site restaurant looks out over the beautiful bush landscape.

About 4 km (2 miles) from the park headquarters is Bellbird Grove, which includes an outdoor Aboriginal collection of bark huts. It has a picnic area and also grassed picnic areas at Ironbark Gully and Lomandra.

Walkabout Creek Wildife Centre
60 Mt Nebo Rd, The Gap.
Tel (07) 3300 4855.
9am–4:30pm daily.
25 Dec. limited.

Australian Woolshed 20

148 Samford Rd, Ferny Hills.
Tel (07) 3872 1100. Ferny Grove.
8:30am–4pm daily. 25 Dec.
ram show: 9:30am, 11am, 1pm, 2:30pm.

The Australian Woolshed offers an instant insight into Australian country life. Ram shows are held daily, with trained rams of various breeds going through their paces, along with commentary explaining the way different breeds are used in Australian farming. In a recreated outback, working sheep dogs gather sheep for demonstrations of shearing and, later, wool-spinning.

Koalas, kangaroos and other native animals roam free in the grounds. Visitors have the opportunity to hand-feed kangaroos and wallabies, or have a digital picture taken while holding a koala.

The Woolshed Restaurant is a good place to stop for lunch and, on selected dates throughout the year, visitors can participate in bush dinner dances. There are also water slides, bungee trampoline and an animal farm with young animals.

Traditional sheep shearing at the Australian Woolshed

BRISBANE PRACTICAL INFORMATION

Time Off listings guide

Brisbane, built around a serpentine river, takes full advantage of its idyllic subtropical weather. Trendy riverside cafés, heritage trails, miles of boardwalk and a floating walkway, ferries and fast catamaran-style CityCats make Brisbane a relaxed holiday destination. The city offers centrally located five-star hotels, budget inns and historic guesthouses (see pp487–90). There are dining choices in all price ranges, such as silver service at luxury hotels, riverfront cafés, ethnic cuisine and alfresco restaurants, most offering menus based on superb local produce and fresh seafood (see pp535–7). Public transport is reasonably priced and easily accessed. Taxi stands are well signposted, and tourist information centres, identified by the international "I" symbol, are situated throughout the city.

SHOPPING

Brisbane is a shopping heaven, with its hidden arcades, small boutiques, quaint tea shops, lively galleries, pedestrian malls and multi-storied shopping centres. Finding what you are looking for is not difficult as the city is divided into small precincts each offering a unique shopping experience. The pedestrianized **Queen Street Mall** has over 1,200 boutiques, three department stores and five shopping centres. **Brisbane Arcade**, one of Brisbane's most elegant shopping areas runs off the Mall. With classic marbled interior and polished wood balustrades, it was opened in 1923 and offers quality jewellers and stylish

Restored interior of the 19th-century Brisbane Arcade

The lively art and crafts market on the Southbank, held every weekend

fashion. Using the river to move from one precinct to another is a convenient and relaxing option. The **Fireworks Gallery** exhibits aboriginal art and local artists, and is just another river stop away at Stratton Street, in Newstead. The **James Street Precinct** in Fortitude Valley has developed around an urban inner-city lifestyle. It is a great place for coffee, small delicatessens, trendy fashion shops, designer boutiques and galleries. Brisbane's weather encourages outdoor markets. The **Riverside Markets** with over 250 stalls are open every Sunday, displaying a huge variety of local arts, crafts, clothes and jewellery. The **Southbank Markets** are held every weekend. With its parklands, man-made beach, cafés and restaurants, this is a great place for shopping.

ENTERTAINMENT

Brisbane has entertainment options for everyone. The **Queensland Performing Arts Centre** has an exciting calendar of events, including opera, classical and contemporary dance, and live stage shows. The **La Boite Theatre** in Spring Hill is a 200-seat theatre in the round, and home to one of the oldest production companies in Australia. Brisbane hosts a myriad of music festivals throughout the year, including the Brisbane River Festival. For live music there are night-clubs in the Fortitude Valley and Caxton Street areas. **Conrad Treasury Brisbane** casino is open 24 hours. Entertainment listings can be found in free magazines such as *This Week in Brisbane* and *Time Off*, which offers a

CityCat ferry service on the Brisbane River

great Gig Guide. Tickets for most events can be obtained from **Ticketek**.

GETTING AROUND

Brisbane is a compact city which can be explored on foot. Maps are available from most hotels and information centres. There are excellent self-guided heritage trails and riverside pathways on both sides of the river.

Public transport in Brisbane includes buses, commuter trains and ferries. The TransLink system allows to use of one ticket for all forms of transport. The river has become one of the main ways of moving about the city. CityCat ferries service some of the most popular locations including South Bank, Eagle Street, Riverside, Dockside, New Farm and Kangaroo Point. The two main points of departure are in Eagle Street. Tour boats supply a commentary and lunch or dinner.

The most economical way to travel on all Brisbane's

CityCat ferry sign

public transport if you are making several journeys is with a Daily ticket, available from any public transport service. This can offer unlimited travel for a day, or at off-peak times within nominated zones.

Another flexible and economical way to see the city is on a **City Sights Bus Tour**. There is a standard fare and you can get on and off whenever you choose. To get back on a Bus, simply hail one from one of the City Sights' stops and show your ticket.

Brisbane's Free Loop service travels around the centre of the city, with a bus every ten minutes. The Cityxpress buses service the suburbs. All buses stop at the Queen Street Bus Station near the Myer Centre.

Commercially operated bus companies also offer tours of the city's highlights, as well as to the surrounding areas, including Stradbroke Island, Moreton Bay and Surfers Paradise (*see pp238–9*) and

the mountainous hinterland (*see pp240–41*).

All types of public transport run until midnight, and taxis are plentiful in the city centre at night. As with any modern city, driving is increasingly difficult. There are numerous, well-maintained bike tracks around the city.

DIRECTORY

SHOPPING

Brisbane Arcade
160 Queen Street Mall
Tel (07) 3221 5977.

Fireworks Gallery
11 Stratton Street, New Stead.
Tel (07) 3216 1250.

James Street Precinct
James Street, Fortitude Valley.
Tel (07) 3403 8888.

Queen Street Mall
Queen Street.
Tel (07) 3006 6290.

Riverside Markets
Markets Cnr Eagle & Charlotte
Streets. *Tel (07) 3870 2807.*

Southbank Markets
Stanley Street, South Bank.
Tel (07) 3867 2051.

ENTERTAINMENT

Conrad Treasury
21 Queen St. *Tel (07) 3306 8888.*

La Boite Theatre
21 Queen St. *Tel (07) 3007 8600.*
info@laboite.com.au

Queensland Performing Arts Centre
Cnr Grey & Melbourne sts, South
Bank. *Tel 13 67 46.*

Ticketek
Tel 13 28 49.

PUBLIC TRANSPORT

Administration Centre
George Street.
Tel (07) 3403 8888. (24 hrs)

City Sights Bus Tour
Tel 13 12 30.

Transinfo
(for public transport information)
Tel 13 12 30.

TOURIST INFORMATION CENTRES

Brisbane Marketing
Tel (07) 3006 6200.

City Sights Bus Tour, an easy way to see central Brisbane

SOUTH OF TOWNSVILLE

S outhern Queensland is renowned for two distinct features: its fine coastal surfing beaches and, inland, some of the richest farming land in Australia. The area is the centre of the country's beef and sugar industries, and the Burdekin River Delta supports a fertile "salad basin" yielding tomatoes, beans and other small crops. Ports such as Mackay and Gladstone service some rich inland mines.

Recognizing the land's potential, pastoralists followed hard on the heels of the explorers who opened up this region in the 1840s. Sugar production had begun by 1869 in the Bundaberg area and by the 1880s it was a flourishing industry, leading to a shameful period in the country's history. As Europeans were considered inherently unsuited to work in the tropics, growers seized on South Sea Islanders for cheap labour. Called Kanakas, the labourers were paid a pittance, housed in substandard accommodation and given the most physically demanding jobs. Some Kanakas were kidnapped from their homeland (a practice called "blackbirding"), but this was outlawed in 1868 and government inspectors were placed on all Kanakas ships to check that their emigration was voluntary. It was not until Federation in 1901 that the use of island labour stopped but by then some 60,000 Kanakas had been brought to Queensland.

In tandem with this agricultural boom, southern Queensland thrived in the latter half of the 19th century when gold was found in the region. Towns such as Charters Towers have preserved much of their 19th-century architecture as reminders of the glory days of the gold rush. Although much of the gold has been extracted, the region is still rich in coal and has the world's largest sapphire fields. Amid this mineral landscape, there are also some beautiful national parks.

Today, the area is perhaps best known for its coastal features. Surfers from all over the world flock to the aptly named resort of Surfers Paradise, and the white sand beaches of the Gold Coast are crowded throughout the summer months. The region is also the gateway to the southern tip of the Great Barrier Reef and the Whitsunday Islands, and is popular with both locals and visitors.

Beach fishing as dawn breaks in Surfers Paradise

◁ Sandstone Bluff near the entrance of Violet Gorge in the ruggedly beautiful Carnarvon National Park

Exploring South of Townsville

With easy access from Brisbane *(see pp218–33)*, the southern coastline of Queensland is one of the most popular holiday locations in Australia, with its sunny climate, sandy beaches and good surf. Fraser Island is one of the region's undisputed highlights with its vast beaches, cool blue lakes and interior rainforests. Behind the fertile coastal plains are many of the 1850s gold rush "boom towns", while the Capricorn Hinterland, inland from Rockhampton, has the fascinating sapphire gem fields near Emerald and the dramatic sandstone escarpments of the Carnarvon and Blackdown Tableland national parks. To the north of the region is the busy city of Townsville, a major gateway to the Whitsundsays and the islands of the Great Barrier Reef *(see pp212–17)*.

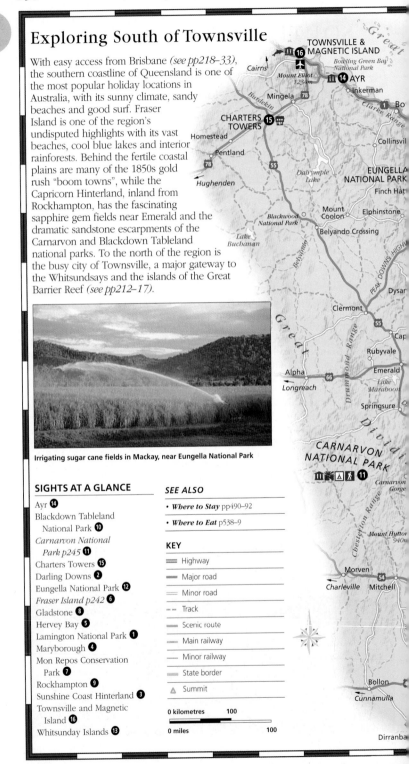

Irrigating sugar cane fields in Mackay, near Eungella National Park

TOWNSVILLE & MAGNETIC ISLAND 16
Great
Bowling Green Bay National Park
Cairns
Mount Elliot 1234m
14 AYR
Inkerman
Mingela
78
Burdekin
Clarke Range
Bo
CHARTERS TOWERS 15
Homestead
Collinsvil
Pentland
78
55
Hughenden
Dalrymple Lake
EUNGELLA NATIONAL PARK
Finch Hat
Mount Coolon
Elphinstone
Blackwood National Park
Belyando Crossing
Lake Buchanan
Belyando
PEAK DOWNS HIGHW
Dysar
Clermont
55
Great
Cap
Drummond Range
Rubyvale
Alpha
66
Emerald
Longreach
Lake Maraboon
Springsure
Divid
CARNARVON NATIONAL PARK
11
Carnarvon Gorge
Chesterton Range
Mount Hutton 940m
Morven
54
Charleville
Mitchell
Bollon
Cunnamulla
Dirranba

SIGHTS AT A GLANCE

Ayr 14
Blackdown Tableland National Park 10
Carnarvon National Park p245 11
Charters Towers 15
Darling Downs 2
Eungella National Park 12
Fraser Island p242 6
Gladstone 8
Hervey Bay 5
Lamington National Park 1
Maryborough 4
Mon Repos Conservation Park 7
Rockhampton 9
Sunshine Coast Hinterland 3
Townsville and Magnetic Island 16
Whitsunday Islands 13

SEE ALSO

- ***Where to Stay*** pp490–92
- ***Where to Eat*** p538–9

KEY

- Highway
- Major road
- Minor road
- Track
- Scenic route
- Main railway
- Minor railway
- State border
- Summit

0 kilometres 100
0 miles 100

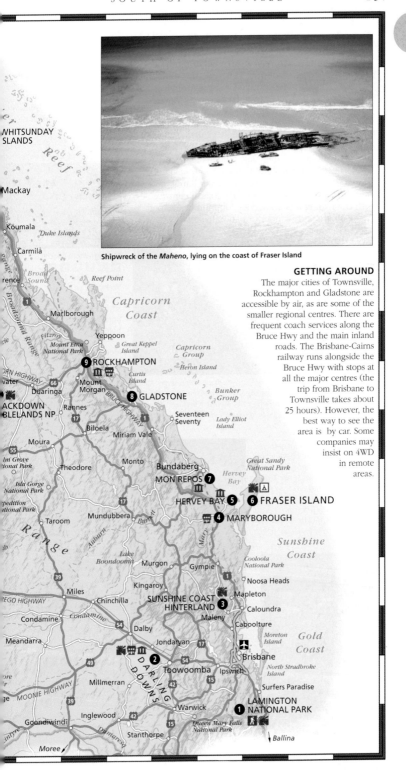

Shipwreck of the *Maheno*, lying on the coast of Fraser Island

GETTING AROUND

The major cities of Townsville, Rockhampton and Gladstone are accessible by air, as are some of the smaller regional centres. There are frequent coach services along the Bruce Hwy and the main inland roads. The Brisbane-Cairns railway runs alongside the Bruce Hwy with stops at all the major centres (the trip from Brisbane to Townsville takes about 25 hours). However, the best way to see the area is by car. Some companies may insist on 4WD in remote areas.

Southern Queensland Coastline

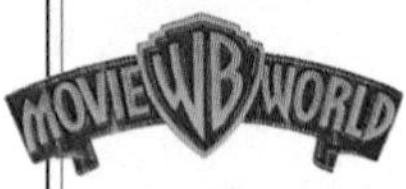

Movie World entrance sign on the Gold Coast

An hour's drive either north or south of Brisbane, the southern Queensland coast is Australia's most popular beach playground. The famous Gold Coast extends 75 km (45 miles) south of Brisbane and is a flashy strip of holiday apartments, luxury hotels, shopping malls, nightclubs, a casino and, above all, 42 km (25 miles) of golden sandy beaches. To the north, the Sunshine Coast is more restrained and elegant. Inland, the Great Dividing Range provides a cool alternative to the hot coastal climate, with flourishing arts and crafts communities, superb bushwalking and wonderful panoramas.

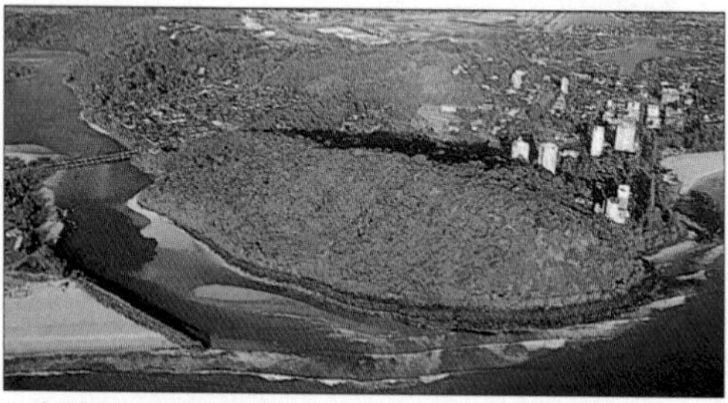

Burleigh Heads National Park *is a tiny park which preserves the dense eucalypt forests that once covered the entire region. The nutritious volcanic soil stemming from Mount Warning, 30 km (20 miles) southwest of the park, allows the rainforest to thrive.*

The Gold Coast *has three theme parks. Sea World has dolphin, sea lion and penguin displays; Warner Bros. Movie World features stunt shows and tours of replica film sets; Dreamworld is a family fairground park with wildlife attractions that include Bengal tigers.*

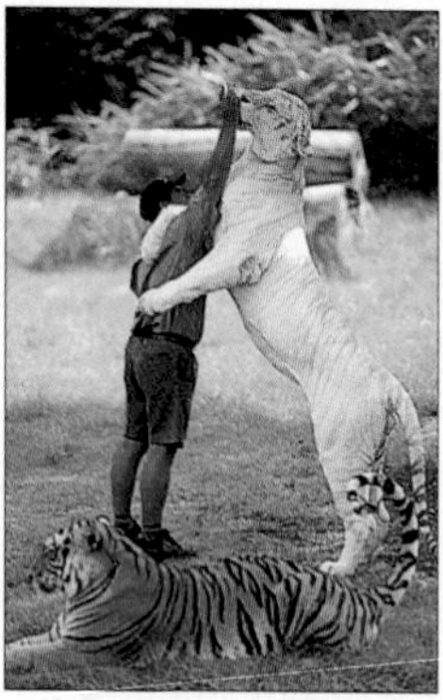

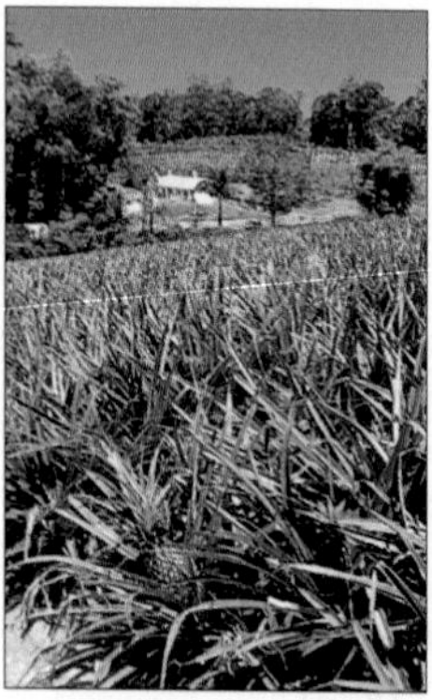

The Big Pineapple *is a vast pineapple plantation. Pineapples are one of Queensland's major crops. Trips around the plantation are available on a cane train. The entrance is marked by a giant fibreglass model of a pineapple.*

Tewantin ②
⛑
This well-known town is in the heart of the Sunshine Coast area, with spectacular sunsets and beautiful beaches. It is also the ferry access point to Cooloola National Park.

MARYBOROUG

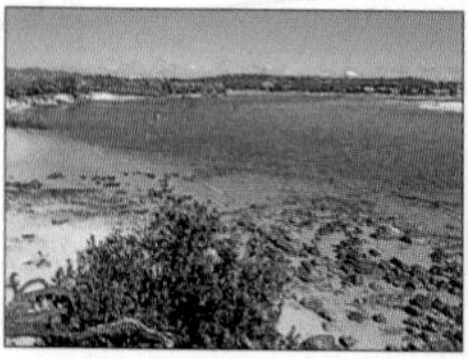

Maroochydore Beach ⑤
🏄 🌊 🏊 ⛑ ♿ 🚻
An ocean beach and the Maroochy river front make the main commercial centre of the Sunshine Coast a popular holiday destination, with good hotels and restaurants.

Mooloolaba Wharf ⑥
🏄 🌊 🏊 ⛑ ♿
The wharf at Mooloolaba is a popular tourist development. Underwater World, said to be the largest oceanarium in the southern hemisphere, contains crocodiles and barramundi.

Bulcock Beach, Caloundra ⑦
🌊 🏊 ⛑ ♿ 🚻
The central location of sandy Bulcock Beach means it is often crowded with tourists and families. Nearby Golden Beach and Shelly Beach are also beautiful, but quieter.

Moreton Bay ⑧
🌊 🏊 ⛑ ♿ 🚻
This is the access point to some 370 offshore islands, the most popular being Moreton, Bribie and South Stradbroke. Fishing, bird-watching and boating are the main activities.

Coolangatta ⑫
🏄 🌊 🏊 ⛑ ♿ 🚻
On the Queensland–New South Wales border, Coolangatta has some of the best surfing waters in the area, but relatively uncrowded beaches. Surfing tuition and boards for hire are available here.

Key to Symbols *see back flap*

★ **Cooloola National Park** ①

Attractive lakes and sclerophyll woodland abound in this area. A 60-km (35-mile) 4WD to Rainbow Beach passes the Teewah Coloured Sands, produced by natural chemicals.

LOCATOR MAP

★ **Noosa Heads, Main Beach** ③

Extraordinary natural beauty, a north-facing beach and an extensive river system have combined to make Noosa a fashionable holiday resort.

★ **Noosa National Park** ④

Consisting of 380 ha (940 acres) of headland surrounded by coastline containing secluded coves, this national park is inhabited with koalas.

★ **Sanctuary Cove** ⑨

Situated on Hope Island, the glamorous resort of Sanctuary Cove is aimed particularly at golfers and includes two luxury golf courses.

★ **South Stradbroke Island Beach** ⑩

This unspoiled sand island offers peaceful but relatively basic accommodation. Catching crabs and bird-watching are popular activities.

0 kilometres 20

0 miles 20

★ **Surfers Paradise Beach** ⑪

This is the focal point of the Gold Coast with block after block of high-rise developments and a range of entertainment options for visitors.

Big Pineapple ②

• Caloundra

• Caboolture

• Redcliffe

BRISBANE

Moreton Island

North Stradbroke Island

Coomera

Burleigh Heads National Park •

BYRON BAY ↓

KEY

▬▬ Highway

▬ Major road

▬ Minor road

～ River

☀ Viewpoint

Lamington National Park ❶

🚌 *Canungra.* 🛈 *Park Ranger Office (07) 5544 0634.* ⬜ *Mon–Fri.*

Lamington National Park, set within the McPherson Mountain Range, is one of Queensland's most popular parks. Declared in 1915, it contains 200 sq km (78 sq miles) of thick wooded country, with more than 160 km (100 miles) of walking tracks through subtropical rainforests of hoop pine, black booyongs and strangler figs. The highest ridges in the park reach more than 1,000 m (3,280 ft) and are lined with Antarctic beech trees – the most northerly in Australia. Some 150 species of birds, such as the Albert's lyrebird, make bird-watching a popular pastime. The global importance of the area was recognized in 1994, when Lamington was declared a World Heritage Area.

Nearby Macrozamia National Park has macrozamia palms (cycads) – one of the oldest forms of vegetation still growing in the world.

Darling Downs ❷

🚌 *Toowoomba.* 🚍 *Toowoomba.* 🛈 *Toowoomba (07) 4639 3797.*

Only 90 minutes' drive from Brisbane, stretching west of the Great Dividing Range, is the fertile country of the Darling Downs. The first area to be settled after Brisbane, the region encompasses some of the most productive agricultural land in Australia, as well as one of the most historic areas in Queensland.

Toowoomba is the main centre of the Downs and is also one of Queensland's biggest cities. Early settlers transformed this one-time swamp into the present "Garden City", famous for its jacarandas and Carnival of Flowers *(see p40)*.

About 45 km (28 miles) northwest of Toowoomba along the Warrego Hwy is the

Jondaryan Woolshed. Built in 1859 to handle 200,000 sheep in one season, it has now been restored as a working memorial to the early pioneers of the district.

South of Toowoomba is Warwick, the oldest town in Queensland after Brisbane and known for its roses and its 19th-century sandstone buildings. It also claims one of the oldest rodeos in Australia, dating from 1857 when £50 (a year's pay) was wagered on the outcome of the riding contest. Today the rodeo follows the Rose and Rodeo Festival in October and offers prize money of more than A$70,000 *(see p41)*.

About 60 km (40 miles) south of Warwick and 915 m (3,000 ft) above sea level, Stanthorpe actively celebrates its freezing winter temperatures with the Brass Monkey Season *(see p43)*.

Stunning king parrot

The town is at the heart of the Granite Belt, one of Queensland's few wine regions *(see p37)*.

Near Warwick, Queen Mary Falls National Park is a 78-ha (193-acre) rainforest park with picnic areas and a 40-m (130-ft) waterfall.

🏛 **Jondaryan Woolshed**
Evanslea Rd, Jondaryan. *Tel* (07) 4692 2229. ⬜ *9am–4pm daily.* ● *Good Fri, 25 Dec.* 🎟 ♿

Sunshine Coast Hinterland ❸

🚍 *Bus link at Landsborough station.* 🛈 *Cnr 6th Ave & Melrose Pde, Maroochydore (07) 5479 1566; 1800 882 032.*

To the west of the Sunshine Coast is the Blackall Range. The area has become a centre for artists and artisans, with numerous guesthouses and some fine restaurants. The

Waterfall in Queen Mary Falls National Park, Darling Downs

The Glasshouse Mountains, a Queensland landmark on the hinterland of the Sunshine Coast

most attractive centres are Montville and Maleny. The drive from Maleny to Mapleton is one of the most scenic in the region, with views across to Moreton Island, encompassing pineapple and sugar cane fields.

Consisting of ten volcanic cones, the Glasshouse Mountains were formed 20 million years ago. They were named by Captain Cook in 1770 because they reminded him of the glass furnaces in his native Yorkshire.

Maryborough ❹

🏠 *25,500.* ✈ 🚃 🚌
ℹ *Travel Stop (07) 4121 4111; City Hall, Kent St (07) 4190 5742.*

Situated on the banks of the Mary River, Maryborough has a strong link with Australia's early history. Founded in 1843, the town provided housing for Kanakas' labour *(see p235)* and was the only port apart from Sydney where free settlers could enter. This resulted in a thriving town – the buildings reflecting the wealth of its citizens.

Many of these buildings survive, earning Maryborough the title of "Heritage City". A great many of the town's private residences also date from the 19th century, ranging from simple workers' cottages to beautiful old "Queenslanders". These houses are distinctive to the state, set high off the ground to catch the cool air currents and with graceful verandas on all sides.

Hervey Bay ❺

🏠 *52,000.* ✈ 🚃 🚢 ℹ *401 The Esplanade, Scarness, Hervey Bay (07) 4124 4050.*

As recently as the 1970s Hervey Bay was simply a string of five fishing villages. However, the safe beaches and mild climate have quickly turned it into a metropolis of 30,000 people and one of the fastest growing holiday centres in Australia.

Hervey Bay is also the best place for whale-watching. Humpback whales migrate more than 11,000 km (7,000 miles) every year from the Antarctic to northern Australian waters to mate and calve. On their return, between August and October, they rest at Hervey Bay to give the calves time to develop a protective layer of blubber before they begin their final run to Antarctica.

Bundaberg rum

Since whaling was stopped in the 1960s, numbers have quadrupled from 300 to approximately 5,000.

Environs
The sugar city of central Queensland, Bundaberg is 62 km (38 miles) north of Hervey Bay. It is the home of Bundaberg ("Bundy") rum, the biggest selling spirit label in Australia.

Bundaberg is an attractive town with many 19th-century buildings. The city's favourite son, Bert Hinkler (1892–1933), was the first man to fly solo from England to Australia in 1928. His original "Ibis" aircraft is displayed in the **Bundaberg and District Historical Museum**.

🏛 **Bundaberg and District Historical Museum**
Young St, Botanic Gardens. **Tel** (07) 4152 0101. ⏰ *10am–4pm daily.* 🌐 *Good Fri, 25 Apr, 25 Dec.* ♿ 🖼

Classic Queenslander-style house in Maryborough

Fraser Island ❻

Situated off the Queensland coast near Maryborough *(see p241)*, Fraser Island World Heritage area is the largest sand island in the world. Measuring 123 km (76 miles) in length and 25 km (16 miles) across, the island is a mix of hills and valleys, rainforest and clear lakes. Ferries to the island operate from Urangan, River Heads and Inskip Point. There is a range of resorts and numerous camp sites on the island. Vehicle (4WD only) and camping permits are required.

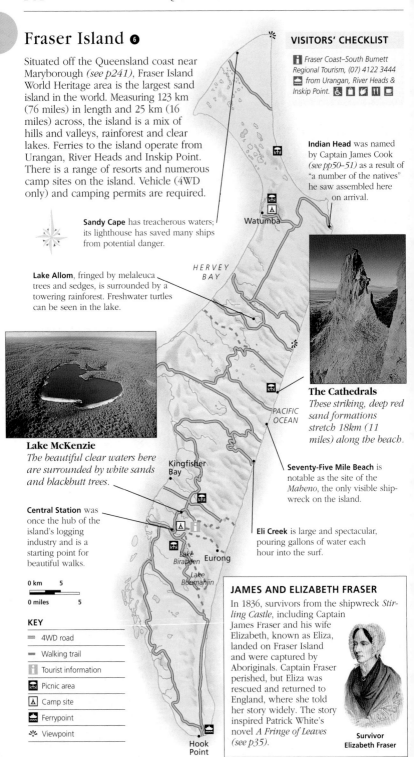

VISITORS' CHECKLIST

ℹ️ Fraser Coast–South Burnett Regional Tourism, (07) 4122 3444
⛴ from Urangan, River Heads & Inskip Point. ♿ 🚻 🅿️ 🍴 🛍️

Indian Head was named by Captain James Cook *(see pp50–51)* as a result of "a number of the natives" he saw assembled here on arrival.

Sandy Cape has treacherous waters; its lighthouse has saved many ships from potential danger.

Lake Allom, fringed by melaleuca trees and sedges, is surrounded by a towering rainforest. Freshwater turtles can be seen in the lake.

HERVEY BAY

Watumba

PACIFIC OCEAN

The Cathedrals
These striking, deep red sand formations stretch 18km (11 miles) along the beach.

Lake McKenzie
The beautiful clear waters here are surrounded by white sands and blackbutt trees.

Kingfisher Bay

Seventy-Five Mile Beach is notable as the site of the *Maheno*, the only visible shipwreck on the island.

Central Station was once the hub of the island's logging industry and is a starting point for beautiful walks.

Lake Birabeen
Eurong
Lake Boomanjin

Eli Creek is large and spectacular, pouring gallons of water each hour into the surf.

0 km	5
0 miles	5

KEY

═══ 4WD road
─── Walking trail
ℹ️ Tourist information
🏞️ Picnic area
⛺ Camp site
⛴ Ferrypoint
☼ Viewpoint

JAMES AND ELIZABETH FRASER

In 1836, survivors from the shipwreck *Stirling Castle*, including Captain James Fraser and his wife Elizabeth, known as Eliza, landed on Fraser Island and were captured by Aboriginals. Captain Fraser perished, but Eliza was rescued and returned to England, where she told her story widely. The story inspired Patrick White's novel *A Fringe of Leaves* *(see p35)*.

Survivor Elizabeth Fraser

Hook Point

Loggerhead turtle laying eggs on Mon Repos Beach

Mon Repos Conservation Park ❼

Tel (07) 4159 1652, tour bookings (07) 4153 8888. ☐ daily. 🐢 Turtle tours. ♿ ☑ obligatory Nov–Mar.

Mon Repos Beach, 15 km (9 miles) from Bundaberg (*see p241*), is one of the most significant and accessible turtle rookeries on the Australian mainland. Egg-laying of loggerhead and other turtles takes place from November to February. By January, the first young turtles begin to hatch and make their way down the sandy beach to the ocean.

There is an information centre within the environmental park which has videos and other information about these fascinating reptiles. Supervised public viewing ensures that the turtles are not unduly disturbed by curious tourists.

Just behind Mon Repos Beach is an old stone wall built by Kanakas and now preserved as a memorial to these South Sea Island inhabitants (*see p235*).

Gladstone ❽

🏃 28,000. ✈ 🚌 🚉 🚌
ℹ️ Gladstone Marina, Bryan Jordan Drive (07) 4972 9000.

Gladstone is a town dominated by industry. However, industry is in harmony with tourism and the environment. Tours of the area are popular with visitors. The world's largest alumina refinery is located here, processing bauxite mined in Weipa on the west coast of Cape York Peninsula. Five per cent of the nation's wealth and 20 per cent of Queensland's wealth is generated by Gladstone's industries. Gladstone's port, handling more than 35 million tonnes of cargo a year, is one of the busiest in Australia.

There are, however, more attractive sights in and around the town. The town's main street has an eclectic variety of buildings, including the Grand Hotel, rebuilt to its 1897 form after fire destroyed the original in 1993. Gladstone's Botanic Gardens were first opened in 1988 as a bicentennial project and consist entirely of native Australian plants. South of Gladstone are the tiny coastal villages of Agnes Waters and the quaintly named "1770" in honour of Captain Cook's brief landing here during his journey up the coast (*see p50*). About 20 km (12 miles) out of town lies the popular holiday location of Boyne Island.

Gladstone is also the access point for Heron Island, considered by many to be one of the most desirable of all the Great Barrier Reef islands, with its wonderful coral and diving opportunities. Other islands in the southern half of the reef can also be accessed from Gladstone by boat or helicopter (*see pp216–17*).

Pretty coastal village of Agnes Waters, near Gladstone

Rockhampton ❾

👥 66,000. 🚉 🚌 🚆 ℹ️ Capricorn Info. Centre, Gladstone (07) 4927 2055.

Rockhampton is situated 40 km (25 miles) inland, on the banks of the Fitzroy River. Often referred to as the "beef capital" of Australia, the town is also the administrative and commercial heart of central Queensland. A spire marks the fact that, geographically, the Tropic of Capricorn runs through the town.

Rockhampton was founded in 1854 and contains many restored 19th-century buildings. Quay Street flanks the tree-lined river and has been classified in its entirety by the National Trust. Particularly outstanding is the sandstone Customs House, with its semi-circular portico. The beautiful **Botanic Gardens** were established in 1869, and have a fine collection of tropical plants. There is also on-site accommodation.

Built on an ancient tribal meeting ground, the **Aboriginal Dreamtime Cultural Centre** is owned and operated by local Aboriginals. Imaginative displays give an insight into their life and culture.

Plaque at base of the Tropic of Capricorn spire

🌸 **Botanic Gardens**
Spencer St. *Tel* (07) 4922 1654.
⭕ 6am–6pm daily. ♿

🏛 **Aboriginal Dreamtime Cultural Centre**
Bruce Hwy. *Tel* (07) 4936 1655.
⭕ 10am–3:30pm Mon–Fri.
⭕ public hols. 🅿️ 📷

Sandstone cliff looking out over Blackdown Tableland National Park

Environs

The heritage township of Mount Morgan is 38 km (25 miles) southwest of Rockhampton. A 2 sq km (0.5 sq mile) open-cut mine of first gold, then copper, operated here for 100 years and was an important part of the state's economy until the minerals ran out in 1981.

Some 25 km (15 miles) north of Rockhampton is Mount Etna National Park, containing spectacular limestone caves, discovered in the 1880s. These are open to the public via Olsen's Capricorn Caverns and Camoo Caves. A major feature of the caves is "cave coral" – stone-encrusted tree roots that have forced their way through the rock. The endangered ghost bat, Australia's only carnivorous bat, nests in these caves.

The stunning sandy beaches of Yeppoon and Emu Park are only 40 km (25 miles) northeast of the city. Rockhampton is also the access point for Great Keppel Island (*see pp216–17*).

Blackdown Tableland National Park ❿

Off Capricorn Hwy, via Dingo. **Park Ranger** *Tel* (07) 4986 1964.

Between Rockhampton and Emerald, along a 20-km (12-mile) untarmacked detour off the Capricorn Highway, is Blackdown Tableland National Park. A dramatic sandstone plateau which rises 600 m (2,000 ft) above the flat surrounding countryside, the Tableland offers spectacular views, escarpments, open forest and tumbling waterfalls. Wildlife includes gliders, brushtail possums, rock wallabies and the occasional dingo.

Emerald is a coal mining centre and the hub of the central highland region, 75 km (45 miles) west of the park; the town provides a railhead for the surrounding agricultural areas. Its ornate 1900 railway station is one of the few survivors of a series of fires that occurred between 1936 and 1969 that destroyed much of the town's heritage. About 60 km (37 miles) southwest of Emerald is Cullin-la-ringo, where there are headstones marking the mass grave of 19 European settlers killed in 1861 by local Aboriginals. At Comet is a tree carved with the initials of explorer Ludwig Leichhardt during his 1844 expedition to Port Essington (*see p249*).

More in tune with its name, Emerald is also the access point for the largest sapphire fields in the world. The lifestyle of the gem diggers is fascinating, making it a popular tourist area.

Façade of Customs House on Quay Street, Rockhampton

For hotels and restaurants in this region see pp490–92 and pp538–9

Carnarvon National Park ⓫

The main access to Carnarvon National Park lies 250 km (155 miles) south of Emerald, while the park itself covers some 298,000 ha (730,000 acres). There are several sections of the park, but the stunning Carnarvon Gorge is the most accessible area to visitors. A 32-km (20-mile) canyon carved by the waters of Carnarvon Creek, the gorge consists of white cliffs, crags and pillars of stone harbouring plants and animals which have survived through centuries of evolution. The area is also rich in Aboriginal culture, and three cultural sites are open to the public. Comfortable cabin accommodation is available or there are various camp sites, provided you have an advance booking and a camping permit *(see p477)*.

VISITORS' CHECKLIST

🛈 *Visitors' Centre, Carnarvon Gorge, via Rolleston (07) 4984 4505.* ⭘ *8am–5pm daily.* ♿ 🚻

KEY

═══ Major road

- - - Walking trail

═══ River

🛈 Tourist information

Ⓐ Camp site

☀ Viewpoint

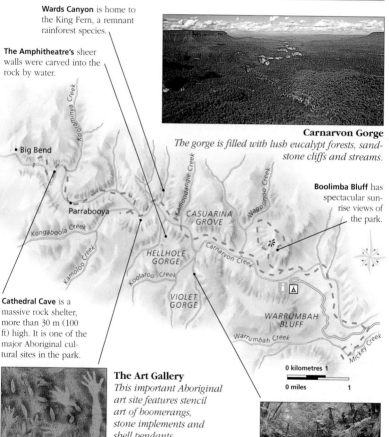

Wards Canyon is home to the King Fern, a remnant rainforest species.

The Amphitheatre's sheer walls were carved into the rock by water.

• Big Bend

Parrabooya

Kooramindie Creek

Kamoodangie Creek

Kongaboola Creek

Kamoroo Creek

CASUARINA GROVE

Wagoonoo Creek

HELLHOLE GORGE

Koolaroo Creek

Carnarvon Creek

VIOLET GORGE

WARRUMBAH BLUFF

Warrumbah Creek

Mickey Creek

Cathedral Cave is a massive rock shelter, more than 30 m (100 ft) high. It is one of the major Aboriginal cultural sites in the park.

Carnarvon Gorge
The gorge is filled with lush eucalypt forests, sandstone cliffs and streams.

Boolimba Bluff has spectacular sunrise views of the park.

0 kilometres 1

0 miles 1

The Art Gallery
This important Aboriginal art site features stencil art of boomerangs, stone implements and shell pendants.

Moss Garden
This lush greenery of ferns, creepers, hornworts and liverworts is sustained by seepage from the spring waters down the rock walls.

Stunning estuary at Whitehaven Beach, the highlight of the Whitsundays

Eungella National Park ⑫

🏨 Mackay. 🚌 Mackay. 🛈 Mackay (07) 4944 5888. **Park Ranger Tel** (07) 4958 4552.

Eungella National Park is the main wilderness area on the central Queensland coast and encompasses some 50,000 ha (125,000 acres) of the rugged Clarke Ranges. Volcanic rock covered with rainforest and subtropical flora is cut by steep gorges, crystal clear pools and impressive waterfalls tumbling down the mountainside.

Finch Hatton Gorge is the main destination for tourists, where indigenous wildlife includes gliders, ring-tailed possums, bandicoots and pademelons (a kind of wallaby). Broken River is one of the few places in Australia where platypuses can be spotted at dusk and dawn.

The main access point for Eungella is the prosperous sugar town of **Mackay**. Somewhat low-key from a tourist point of view, Mackay boasts a balmy climate by way of the surrounding mountains trapping the warm coastal air even in winter. Thirty beautiful white sand beaches are lined with casuarinas. All around the town sugar cane can be seen blowing in the wind in the many sugar cane fields.

The town centre of Mackay also has a number of historic buildings worth visiting, including the Commonwealth Bank and Customs House, both classified by the National Trust. The second-largest coal-loader in the world is at Hay Point, where trains more than 2 km (1 mile) long haul coal from the western mines for shipping overseas.

Whitsunday Islands ⑬

🏨 Proserpine. 🚌 Airlie Beach. ✈ Hamilton Island; Proserpine. ⛴ Shute Harbour. **www**.whitsundaytourism.com

The Whitsunday Islands are an archipelago of 74 islands, situated within the Great Barrier Reef Marine Park, approximately 1,140 km (700 miles) north of Brisbane and 640 km (400 miles) south of Cairns. These beautiful islands and sandy atolls are among the most stunning holiday destinations in Australia. Whitehaven Beach on Whitsunday Island is recognized as one of the world's best beaches, with 9 km (5.6 miles) of pure white silica sand and turquoise sea.

Only a few of the islands offer accommodation, including Hamilton, Daydream, Hayman, South Molle and Lindeman, while some 66 islands remain uninhabited. A wide range of accommodation is available including luxury hotels, hostels, guesthouses and self-catering apartments.

There are many activities on offer include scuba diving, whale watching, seaplane flights and charter sailing. Many companies at Airlie Beach on the mainland offer sailing packages, which include diving or snorkelling and a night or two moored on the Great Barrier Reef.

Ayr ⑭

🏨 8,600. 🚌 🚉 🛈 Plantation Park, Bruce Hwy (07) 4783 5988.
The busy town of Ayr, at the heart of the Burdekin River Delta, is the major sugar cane-growing area in Australia.

Within the town itself is the modern Burdekin Cultural Complex, which includes a 530-seat theatre, a library and an art gallery. Among its art collection are the renowned

"Living Lagoon" sculpture at the Burdekin Complex, Ayr

"Living Lagoon" sculptures crafted by the contemporary Australian sculptor Stephen Walker. The Ayr Nature Display consists of an impressive rock wall made from 2,600 pieces of North Queens-land rock, intricate pictures made from preserved insects and a display of Australian reptiles, shells, fossils and Aboriginal artifacts. In Plantation Park is the Juru walking trail and Gubulla Munda, a giant snake sculpture 15 m (50 ft) long.

Environs
Approximately 55 km (35 miles) north of Ayr is Alligator Creek, which is the access point for Bowling Green Bay National Park. Here you will find geckos and chirping cicadas living alongside each other in this lush landscape. Within the park are rock pools, perfect for swimming, and plunging waterfalls.

For hotels and restaurants in this region see pp490–92 and pp538–9

Ornate 19th-century façade of City Hall in Charters Towers

Charters Towers ⑮

🏃 10,000. 🚉 🚌 🚆 ℹ️ 74
Mosman St (07) 4752 0314.

Charters Towers was once the second-largest town in Queensland with a population of 27,000, following the 1871 discovery of gold in the area by a 10-year-old Aboriginal boy. Gold is still mined in the area, as well as copper, lead and zinc.

The old Charters Towers Stock Exchange is a historic gem set amid a group of other splendid 19th-century buildings in the city centre. This international centre of finance was the only such exchange in Australia outside a capital city and was built during the gold-mining days.

Charters Towers fell into decline when the gold ran out in the 1920s. Its economy now depends on the beef industry and its status as the educational centre for Queensland's Outback and Papua New Guinea – school students make up one-fifth of the population.

Townsville and Magnetic Island ⑯

🏃 155,000. ✈️ 🚉 🚌 🚆 ⛴️
ℹ️ 303 Flinders Mall (07) 4721 3660.

Townsville is the second-largest city in Queensland and a major port for the beef, sugar and mining industries. Boasting, on average, 300 sunny days a year, the beachfront is a source of local pride.

The city was founded in the 1860s by Robert Towns, who began the practice of "blackbirding" – kidnapping Kanakas from their homeland and bringing them to Australia as cheap labour (see p235).

Among the city's tourist attractions is **Reef HQ**, a "living coral reef aquarium" and the **Museum of Tropical Queensland**, which displays artifacts from the *Pandora*. Townsville is also an access point for the Barrier Reef and a major diving centre, largely because of the nearby wreck of the steamship *Yongala*, which sank in 1911.

Situated 8 km (5 miles) offshore and officially a suburb of Townsville, Magnetic Island has 2,500 inhabitants and is the only reef island with a significant permanent population. It was named by Captain Cook, who erroneously believed that magnetic fields generated by the huge granite boulders he could see were causing problems with his compass. Today, almost half of the island is a national park.

🐠 Reef HQ
Flinders St East. **Tel** (07) 4750 0800.
⭕ daily. ● 25 Dec. 📷 ♿
🏛 Musuem of Tropical Qld
Flinders St East. **Tel** (07) 4726 0606
⭕ daily. ● 25 Dec, 25 Apr (am),
Good Fri. 📷

Idyllic blue waters of Rocky Bay on Magnetic Island

NORTHERN AND OUTBACK QUEENSLAND

*E*uropean explorers who made epic journeys into the previously impenetrable area of Northern and Outback Queensland in the 1800s found a land rich in minerals and agricultural potential. They also discovered places of extreme natural beauty, such as the Great Barrier Reef and other unique regions now preserved as national parks.

Northern Queensland was first visited by Europeans when Captain Cook was forced to berth his damaged ship, the *Endeavour*, on the coast. The area remained a mystery for almost another 100 years, however, until other intrepid Europeans ventured north. These expeditions were perilous and explorers were faced with harsh conditions and hostile Aboriginal tribes. In 1844, Ludwig Leichhardt and his group set out from Brisbane to Port Essington, but most of the men were wounded or killed by Aboriginals. In 1848, Edmund Kennedy led an expedition from Cairns to the top of Cape York. All but two of this party perished, including Kennedy, who was killed by Aboriginals.

In the late 19th century, Northern Queensland found sudden prosperity when gold was discovered in the region. The population rose and towns grew up to service the mines, but by the beginning of the 20th century much of the gold had dried up. These once thriving "cities" are now little more than one-street towns, lined with 19th-century architecture as a reminder of their glory days. Today, much of the area's wealth stems from its booming tourist trade. Luxury resorts line the stunning coastline, and tourists flock to experience the spectacular natural wonders of the Great Barrier Reef.

Queensland's Outback region has a strong link with Australia's national heritage. The Tree of Knowledge at Barcaldine marks the meeting place of the first Australian Labor Party during the great shearer's strike of 1891. The town of Winton is where "Banjo" Paterson *(see p35)* wrote Australia's national song "Waltzing Matilda" in 1895. Today, the vast Outback area is known for agriculture and a wide range of mining operations.

A rodeo rider and clown perform in Laura near Lakefield National Park in Northern Queensland

◁ The beautiful coral cay of Green Island on the Great Barrier Reef

Exploring Northern Queensland

The area north of Townsville leading up to Cairns is Australia's sugar-producing country, the cane fields backed by the Great Dividing Range. Northern Queensland is sparsely populated: Cairns is the only city, while Port Douglas and Mossman are small towns. The only other villages of note in the region are Daintree and Cooktown. Cape York Peninsula is one of the last untouched wildernesses in the world, covering 200,000 sq km (77,220 sq miles) – roughly the same size as Great Britain. The landscape varies according to the time of year: in the green season (November–March) the rivers are swollen and the country is green; during the dry winter the riverbeds are waterless and the countryside is bare and arid.

Lush rainforest in Daintree National Park, near Cairns

Pier Marketplace and Marlin Marina in Cairns

GETTING AROUND

Cairns is well served by public transport, with regular air, train and coach connections from southern Queensland and other states. It also benefits from an international airport. North of Cape Tribulation to Cooktown and the Outback requires approved hire cars unless you take an organized tour. The 326-km (202-mile) coast road from Cairns to Cooktown requires a 4WD vehicle after Cape Tribulation, although most car rental companies will insist on a 4WD all the way. During the wet season, Cape York is generally impassable.

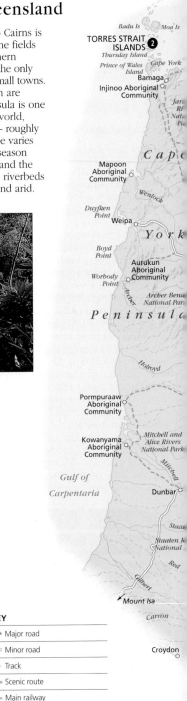

KEY

▬	Major road
═	Minor road
‑ ‑	Track
▬	Scenic route
▬	Main railway
▬	Minor railway

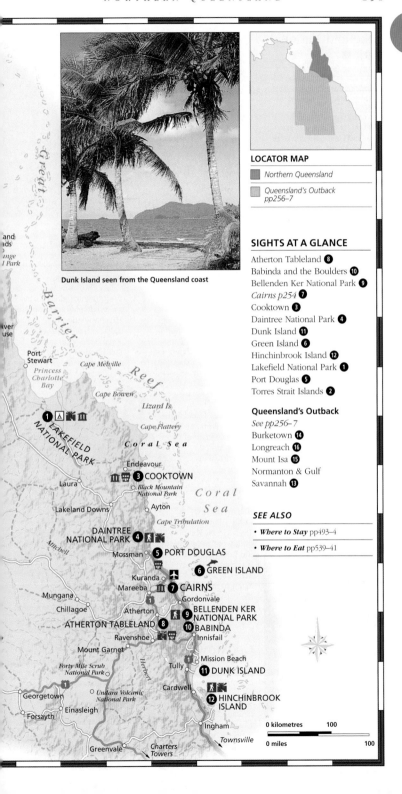

Dunk Island seen from the Queensland coast

LOCATOR MAP

☐ *Northern Queensland*

☐ *Queensland's Outback pp256–7*

SIGHTS AT A GLANCE

Atherton Tableland **8**
Babinda and the Boulders **10**
Bellenden Ker National Park **9**
Cairns p254 **7**
Cooktown **3**
Daintree National Park **4**
Dunk Island **11**
Green Island **6**
Hinchinbrook Island **12**
Lakefield National Park **1**
Port Douglas **5**
Torres Strait Islands **2**

Queensland's Outback

See pp256–7
Burketown **14**
Longreach **16**
Mount Isa **15**
Normanton & Gulf
Savannah **13**

SEE ALSO

• *Where to Stay* pp493–4

• *Where to Eat* pp539–41

0 kilometres   100

0 miles   100

Lakefield National Park ❶

🚗 Cooktown. 🏠 Cooktown (07)
4069 5446. **Park Office** Lakefield
(07) 4069 5777. ◻ Mon–Fri.

Covering approximately
540,000 ha (1,300,000 acres),
Lakefield National Park is the
second-largest national park
in Queensland. It encom-
passes a wide variety of landscapes, including river forests,
plains and coastal flats. The
centre of the park abounds
with birds. Camping is the
only accommodation option
and a permit must be obtained
at the self-registration stations
throughout the park. The
park is largely inaccessible
during the wet season between
December and April when
the rivers flood the plains.

The nearby town of **Laura**,
at the base of the Cape York
Peninsula, is a typical Australian Outback town, with a
newly sealed road flanked by
a pub, a general store and a
few houses. During the late
19th century, Laura was the
rail terminus for the Palmer
River gold fields and some
20,000 people passed through
here each year. Today, it is
almost forgotten, but the
discovery in 1959 of Aboriginal art sites of great antiquity is reviving interest in the
area. One of the most notable
sites is the "giant horse
gallery", which contains huge
horse paintings thought to
record the first sightings of
European explorers.

**River forest in Lakefield
National Park**

Thursday Island, in the Torres Strait island group

Torres Strait Islands ❷

✈ from Cairns. ⛴ from Cairns.
🏠 Cairns (07) 4051 3588.

The Torres Strait divides
the northern coastline
of Australia from Papua New
Guinea and is dotted with
numerous islands. Approximately 19 of these islands are
inhabited and have been
governed by Queensland
since 1879.

Thursday Island is the
"capital" island and was
once the centre of the
local pearling
industry. Many
Japanese
pearlers who
lost their lives
in this occupa-
tion are buried
in the island's cemetery. In
1891, Green Hill Fort was
built to prevent invasion by
the Russians. Murray Island
was the birthplace of Eddie
Mabo, who, in 1992, won his
claim to traditional land in
the Australian High Court and
changed Aboriginal–European
relations (see p58).

Cooktown ❸

🏛 2,000. ✈ 🚗 ⛴ 🚢 🏠
Charlotte St (07) 4069 5446.

When the *Endeavour* was
damaged by a coral reef in
1770, Captain Cook and his
crew spent six weeks in this
area while repairs to the ship
were made (see pp50–51).

**Chinese gravestone
in Cooktown**

Cooktown's proud boast,
therefore, is that it was the
site of the first white settlement in Australia.

Like most towns in the area,
Cooktown originally serviced
the gold fields and its present-
day population of less than
2,000 is half the 4,000
inhabitants who once
sustained its 50 pubs.
However, many of its historic
buildings survive, including
the Westpac Bank,
originally the Old
National Bank, with
its stone columns
supporting an iron-lace
veranda. The **James
Cook Museum**,
which houses the
old anchor from
the *Endeavour*,
started life in
the 1880s as a
convent. In the
cemetery of the town, a
memorial and numerous
gravestones are testimony
to the difficulties faced by
the many Chinese who came
to the gold fields in the
1870s (see p55).

Between Cooktown and
Bloomfield, Black Mountain
National Park is named after
the geological formation of
huge black granite boulders.
The boulders were formed
around 260 million years ago
below the earth's surface and
were gradually exposed as
surrounding land surfaces
eroded away.

🏛 **James Cook Museum**
Cnr Helen & Furneaux sts.
Tel (07) 4069 5386. ◻ 9:30am–
4pm daily. 🈲 ♿

Daintree National Park ❹

🚌 from Port Douglas. ℹ️ Port Douglas (07) 4099 5599. **Park Office** Mossman (07) 4098 2188. ⏰ daily. **www**.epa.qld.gov.au

Daintree National Park, north of Port Douglas, covers more than 76,000 ha (188,000 acres). The Cape Tribulation section of the park is a place of great beauty, and one of the few places where the rainforest meets the sea. Captain Cook named Cape Tribulation in rueful acknowledgment of the difficulties he was experiencing navigating the Great Barrier Reef. Today, it is a popular spot with backpackers.

The largest section of the park lies inland from Cape Tribulation. It is a mostly inaccessible, mountainous area, but 5 km (3 miles) from Mossman lies the Mossman Gorge, known for its easy and accessible 2.7-km (1-mile) track through the rainforest.

Port Douglas ❺

🏘️ 3,500. 🚌 🚏 ℹ️ 23 Macrossan St (07) 4099 5599.

Situated 75 km (47 miles) from Cairns, Port Douglas was once a tiny fishing village. Today it is a tourist centre, but it has managed to preserve some of its village atmosphere.

Macrossan Street is typical of Australian country thoroughfares, and at the end of the

Tropical Myall Beach in Daintree National Park

street is the beautiful Four-Mile Beach, which is a very popular walking spot. Many 19th-century buildings still line the street, such as the Courthouse Hotel, and the modern shopping centres have been designed to blend with the town's original architecture.

The original port was set up during the gold rush of the 1850s, but it was superseded by Cairns as the main port of the area. A disastrous cyclone in 1911 also forced people to move elsewhere, leaving the population at less than 500. The construction of the luxurious Sheraton Mirage Resort in the early 1980s heralded the beginning of a new boom, and now a range of accommodation and restaurants is on offer (see p494 and p541).

Port Douglas is also the main departure point for Quicksilver, a major Great Barrier Reef tour operator.

Green Island ❻

⛴️ from Cairns. ℹ️ (07) 4051 3588.

Green Island is one of the few inhabited coral cays of the Great Barrier Reef (see pp216–17). Despite its small size (a brisk walk around the entire island will take no more than 15 minutes), it is home to an exclusive, luxurious five-star resort which opened in 1994.

Green Island's proximity to the mainland tourist areas and the consequent marine traffic and pollution means that the coral is not as spectacular as around islands further afield. But its accessibility by ferry from Cairns makes the island very popular.

Also on Green Island is the Marineland Melanesia complex, where there are crocodile enclosures and an aquarium of sea creatures.

Green Island, a coral cay at the heart of the Great Barrier Reef

Cairs ⑦

Boomerang from Kuranda craft market

Cairns is the main centre of Northern Queensland. Despite its beachfront esplanade, it has a city atmosphere and instead of sandy beaches there are mud-flats, abundant with native birdlife. Its main attraction is as a base for exploring the Great Barrier Reef *(see pp212–17)*, the Daintree Rainforest *(p253)* and the Atherton Tableland *(p255)*. However, Cairns itself does have several places of interest to visit.

VISITORS' CHECKLIST

🏙 130,000. ✈ 6 km (3.5 miles) N of the city. 🚉 Cairns railway station, Bunda St. 🚌 Lake St Terminus, Lake St; (interstate); Trinity Wharf, Wharf St. ⛴ Reef trips, Pier Point Rd. 🛈 51 The Esplanade (07) 4051 3588. 🎭 The Reef Festival (Oct); Cairns Show (Jul).

🌴 Flecker Botanic Gardens
Collins Ave, Edge Hill. **Tel** (07) 4044 3398. ⬜ daily. ♿ 🖼
Dating from 1886, the Flecker Botanic Gardens are known for their collection of more than 100 species of palm trees. They also house many other tropical plants. The gardens include an area of Queensland rainforest, complete with native birdlife. The gardens' Centenary Lakes were created in 1976 to commemorate the city's first 100 years.

🏛 Cairns Museum
City Place, cnr Lake & Shield sts. **Tel** (07) 4051 5582. ⬜ 10am–4pm Mon–Sat. 🚫 Good Fri, 25 Apr, 25 Dec. 🖼
Housed in the 1907 School of Arts building, this museum is a fine

Tropical orchid in the Flecker Botanic Gardens

example of the city's early architecture. Among the exhibits are the contents of an old Chinese joss house.

⛴ Reef Fleet Terminal
Pier Point Rd
This is the departure point for most cruises to the Great Barrier Reef. Some

19th-century façades nearby offer a glimpse of the city's early life.

Cairns is the game-fishing centre of Australia and, from August to December, tourists crowd Marlin Jetty to see the anglers return with their catch.

Adjacent Pier Marketplace has boutiques, restaurants, markets and accommodation.

Environs
On the eastern edge of the Atherton Tablelands is the tiny village of **Kuranda**. A hippie hang-out in the 1960s, it has since developed into an arts and crafts centre with markets held here four times a week. Nearby, at Smithfield, is the Tjapukai Cultural Centre, home to the renowned Aboriginal Tjapukai Dance Theatre.

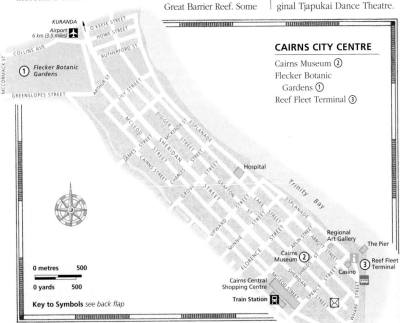

CAIRNS CITY CENTRE

Cairns Museum ②
Flecker Botanic Gardens ①
Reef Fleet Terminal ③

0 metres   500
0 yards   500

Key to Symbols see back flap

Mount Hypipamee Crater's green lake, Atherton Tableland

Atherton Tableland **8**

🛈 Cnr Silo & Main St, Atherton (07) 4091 4222. ⬜ 9am–5pm daily. ▣ 1 Jan, Good Fri, Easter Sun, 25 Dec, 26 Dec.

Rising sharply from the coastal plains of Cairns, the northern landscape levels out into the lush Atherton Tableland. At their highest point, the tablelands are 900 m (3,000 ft) above sea level. The cool temperature, heavy rainfall and rich volcanic soil make this one of the richest farming areas in Queensland. For many decades, tobacco was the main crop, but, with the worldwide decline in smoking, farmers have diversified into peanuts, macadamia nuts, sugar cane, bananas and avocados.

The town of **Yungaburra**, with its many historic buildings, is listed by the National Trust. Nearby is the famed "curtain fig tree". Strangler figs attach themselves to a host tree and eventually kill the original tree. In this case, the aerial roots, growing down from the tree tops, form a 15-m (50-ft) screen. Southwest of Yungaburra is the eerie, green crater lake at Mt Hypipamee. Stretching 60 m (200 ft) in diameter.

Millaa Millaa contains the most spectacular waterfalls of the region. A 15-km (9-mile) sealed circuit drive takes in the Zillie and Ellinjaa falls, while not far away are the picturesque Mungalli Falls.

Atherton is the main town of the region, named after its first European settlers, John and Kate Atherton, who established a cattle station here in the mid-19th century. The wealthy agricultural centre of Mareeba now stands on the site of this former ranch.

Bellenden Ker National Park **9**

🚂 Innisfail. 🚌 Innisfail. 🛈 1 Edith St, Innisfail (07) 4063 2655.

Bellenden Ker National Park contains the state's two highest mountains. Bartle Frere, reaching 1,611 m (5,285 ft) and Bellenden Ker, rising to 1,591 m (5,220 ft), are often swathed in cloud. Cassowaries (large flightless birds, under threat of extinction) can often be spotted on the mountains.

Much of the park is wilderness, although tracks do exist. A popular area to visit is Josephine Falls to the south of the park, about 8 km (5 miles) from the Bruce Highway.

Babinda and the Boulders **10**

🏯 1,300. 🛈 Cnr Munro St & Bruce Hwy, Babinda (07) 4067 1008.

The rural town of Babinda is a quaint survivor of old-world Queensland, lined with veranda-fronted houses and a wooden pub.

The Babinda Boulders, 7 km (4 miles) inland, are water-worn rock shapes and a popular photographic subject.

Dunk Island **11**

🚂 Tully. 🚌 Mission Beach. ⛴ Mission Beach. 🛈 Mission Beach (07) 4068 7099.

Dunk Island is one of the best known of the Great Barrier Reef islands (see p217). The rugged terrain is covered with a variety of vegetation. Day trips from the mainland are popular, offering snorkelling, diving and windsurfing.

Dunk Island is perhaps best known as the setting for EJ Banfield's 1906 book, Confessions of a Beachcomber. Today it is also known for its resident artists' colony and as a convenient stepping stone to exclusive Bedarra Island, 30 minutes away by launch.

Hinchinbrook Island **12**

🚂 Ingham. 🚌 Cardwell. ⛴ Lucinda, Cardwell. 🛈 Ingham (07) 4776 5211.

Hinchinbrook is the largest island national park in Australia, covering 635 sq km (245 sq miles). Dense rainforest, much of which remains unexplored, makes the island popular with bushwalkers. Hinchinbrook's highest point, Mount Bowen, rises 1,121 m (3,678 ft) above sea level and is often capped with cloud. The native wildlife includes wallabies, dugongs and the magnificent blue Ulysses butterfly. The island is separated from the mainland town of Cardwell by a narrow, mangrove-fringed channel.

Water-worn boulders near the town of Babinda

Queensland's Outback

In stark contrast to the lush green of the eastern rainforests, the northwest of Queensland is made up of dry plains, mining areas and Aboriginal settlements. The vast distances and high temperatures often dissuade tourists from venturing into this harsh landscape; yet those willing to make the effort will be rewarded with unique wildlife and an insight into Australia's harsh Outback life.

LOCATOR MAP

Queensland's Outback

Northern Queensland
pp248–55

SIGHTS AT A GLANCE

Burketown ⑭
Longreach ⑯
Mount Isa ⑮
Normanton and
Gulf Savannah ⑬

KEY

── Major road

══ Minor road

-- Track

── Minor railway

══ State border

Normanton and Gulf Savannah ⑬

🚂 Normanton. 🛈 Normanton (07) 4745 1065.

Normanton, situated 70 km (45 miles) inland on the Norman River, is the largest town in the region. It began life as a port, handling copper from Cloncurry and then gold from Croydon. The famous Gulflander train still commutes once a week between Normanton and Croydon.

En route from Normanton to the Gulf of Carpentaria, savannah grasses give way to glistening salt pans, barren of all vegetation. Once the rains come in November, however, this area becomes a wetland and a breeding ground for millions of birds, including jabirus, brolgas, herons and cranes, as well as crocodiles,

prawns and barramundi. Karumba, at the mouth of the Norman River, is the access point for the Gulf of Carpentaria and the headquarters of a multi-million-dollar prawn and fishing industry. It remains something of an untamed frontier town, especially when the prawn trawlers are in.

Covering approximately 350,000 sq km (135,000 sq miles), the most northwesterly region of Queensland is the Gulf Savannah. Largely

flat and covered in savannah grasses, abundant with bird and animal life, this is the remotest landscape in Australia. The economic base of the area is fishing and cattle. Prawn trawlers go out to the Gulf of Carpentaria for months at a time and cattle stations cover areas of more than 1,000 sq km (400 sq miles). Given the distances, local pastoralists are more likely to travel via light aircraft than on horseback.

Gum trees and termite mounds on the grassland of Gulf Savannah

For hotels and restaurants in this region see pp493–4 and pp539–41

QUEENSLAND'S OUTBACK **257**

Mount Isa, dominated by Australia's largest mine

Burketown ⑭

🏃 160. ✈ ℹ 19 Musgrave St (07) 4745 5177, 65 Musgrave St (07) 4745 5100.

In the late 1950s, Burketown found fleeting fame as the setting for Neville Shute's famous novel about life in a small Outback town, *A Town Like Alice*. Situated 30 km (18 miles) from the Gulf of Carpentaria, on the Albert River, Burketown was once a major port servicing the hinterland. The spectacular propagating roll cloud known as a Morning Glory appears here in the early mornings from September to November. Burketown is rich in history and Aboriginal culture. It is also famous for the World Barramundi Fishing Championship.

About 150 km (90 miles) west of Burketown is Hell's Gate, an area so named at the beginning of the 20th century because it was the last outpost where the state's police guaranteed protection.

Mount Isa ⑮

🏃 23,000. ✈ 🚆 🚌
ℹ 19 Marian St (07) 4749 1555.

Mount Isa is the only major city in far western Queensland. Its existence is entirely based around the world's largest silver and lead mine, which dominates the town's industry and landscape. Ore was first discovered at Mount Isa in 1923 by a prospector called John Campbell Miles and the

first mine was set up in the 1930s. In those early days, "the Isa" was a shanty town, and Tent House, now owned by the National Trust, is an example of the half-house-half-tents that were home to most early settlers. Also in town is **Outback at Isa**, which incorporates mine tours, the Riversleigh Fossil Centre and Isa Experience Gallery *(see pp26–7)*.

One of the most popular events in town is the Mount Isa Rodeo in August *(see p43)*. With prize money totalling more than A$100,000, riders come from all over the world to perform spectacular displays of horsemanship.

🏛 **Outback at Isa**
19 Marian St. **Tel** *(07) 4749 1555*.
◯ daily. ⬤ Good Fri, 25 Dec.
🚫 ♿

Environs
Cloncurry, 120 km (75 miles) east of Mount Isa, was the departure point for the Queensland and Northern Territory Aerial Service's (QANTAS) first flight in 1921. Now Australia's national airline, Qantas is also the oldest airline in the English-speaking world.

Longreach ⑯

🏃 4,500. ✈ 🚆 🚌 ℹ Qantas Park, Eagle St (07) 4658 3555.

Situated in the centre of Queensland, Longreach is the main town of the central west of the state.

From 1922 to 1934, Longreach was the operating base of Qantas and there is a Founders Museum at Longreach Airport. Opened in 1988, the **Australian Stockman's Hall of Fame** is a fascinating tribute to Outback men and women. Aboriginal artifacts, as well as documented tales of the early European explorers are included in the impressive displays.

There are daily flights or a 17-hour coach ride from Brisbane to Longreach. Other access points are Rockhampton and Townsville.

🏛 **Australian Stockman's Hall of Fame**
Landsborough Hwy. **Tel** *(07) 4658 2166*. ◯ daily. ⬤ 25 Dec. 🚫 ♿
🅿 🛈

THE ROYAL FLYING DOCTOR SERVICE

The Royal Flying Doctor Service was founded by John Flynn, a Presbyterian pastor who was sent as a missionary to the Australian Outback in 1912. The young cleric was disturbed to see that many of his flock died due to the lack of basic medical care and he founded the Australian Inland Mission together with Hudson Fysh (the founder of Qantas),

A Royal Flying Doctor plane flying over Australia's Outback

self-made millionaire Hugh Victor McKay, Alfred Traeger (the inventor of the pedal wireless) and Dr Kenyon St Vincent Welch. Today, the Royal Flying Doctor Service deals with some 130,000 patients a year, and most Outback properties have an airstrip on which the Flying Doctor can land. Emergency medical help is rarely more than two hours away and advice is available over a special radio channel.

THE NORTHERN TERRITORY

INTRODUCING THE
NORTHERN TERRITORY 260–265

DARWIN AND THE TOP END 266–277

THE RED CENTRE 278–289

The Northern Territory at a Glance

That most famous of Australian icons, the red monolith of Uluru (Ayers Rock) lies within the Northern Territory, but it is just one of the area's stunning natural features, which also include the tropical splendour of Kakadu National Park. The main centres are Darwin in the lush north and Alice Springs in the arid Red Centre. Much of the Outback land is Aboriginal-owned, enabling their ancient culture to flourish. The Northern Territory has yet to achieve full statehood owing to its low population and relatively small economy, but it has been self-governing since 1978.

Melville and Bathurst Islands (see p274) *lie 80 km (50 miles) off the north coast. The islands are inhabited by Tiwi Aboriginals, who have preserved a culture distinct from the mainland which includes unique characteristics such as these burial poles.*

0 kilometres 150

0 miles 150

Darwin (see pp270–73) *is the Northern Territory's capital city with an immigrant population of more than 50 nationalities (see pp264–5). The colonial Government House is one of the few 19th-century survivors in what is now a very modern city.*

THE RED CENTRE
(see pp278–289)

Kakadu National Park (see pp276–7) *is an ancient landscape of tropi-cal rain-forest and majestic rock formations. Covering 1.7 million ha (4.3 million acres), it is the largest national park in Australia. The Jim Jim Falls are the most impressive in the park, and the Aboriginal rock art sites are among the most important in the country.*

Uluru-Kata Tjuta National Park (see pp286–9) *is dominated by the huge sandstone rock rising up out of the flat, arid desert and the nearby Olgas, a series of 36 mysterious rock domes.*

◁ Desert oaks (*Allocasuarina*) in the heart of the Northern Territory

DARWIN AND THE
TOP END
(see pp266–277)

Elsey Homestead Replica, *110 km (70 miles) southeast of Katherine* (see pp274–5), *was the setting for Jeannie Gunn's novel* We of the Never Never, *depicting 19th-century Outback life.*

Devil's Marbles (see p285) *are a remarkable collection of granite boulders in the heart of the flat, sandy desert. Caused by millions of years of erosion, they are traditionally believed to be the eggs of the Rainbow Serpent.*

Alice Springs (see pp282–3) *lies at the heart of Australia. Its Old Telegraph Station Historical Reserve was the site of the area's first settlement in 1871.*

Chambers Pillar Historical Reserve (see p284) *is a strange, 50-m (165-ft) sandstone column which served as a landmark for explorers of the area in the 19th century.*

For additional map symbols *see back flap*

Aboriginal Lands

**ABORIGINAL
FREEHOLD LAND
NO ENTRY
PENALTY $1000**

Sign for
Aboriginal site

Aboriginal people are thought to have lived in the Northern Territory for between 20,000 and 50,000 years. The comparatively short 200 years of European settlement have damaged their ancient culture immensely, but in the Northern Territory more traditional Aboriginal communities have survived intact than in other states – mainly due to their greater numbers and determination to preserve their identity. Nearly one-third of the Northern Territory's people are Aboriginal and they own almost 50 per cent of the land via arrangements with the federal government (*see p59*). For Aboriginals, the concept of land ownership is tied to a belief system that instructs them to care for their ancestral land.

This X-ray image (*see p33*) *of the dreaming spirit Namarrgon at Nourlangie Rock is centuries old, but was continually repainted until the 1900s.*

Nourlangie Rock *in Kakadu National Park is significant to Aborigines as home of the Lightning Dreaming (see pp276–7).*

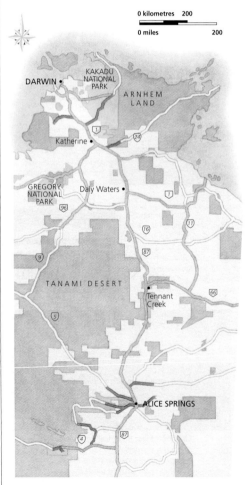

0 kilometres 200

0 miles 200

DARWIN •

KAKADU NATIONAL PARK

ARNHEM LAND

Katherine •

GREGORY NATIONAL PARK

Daly Waters •

TANAMI DESERT

Tennant Creek

ALICE SPRINGS

KEY

	Aboriginal land
	National park
	Highway
	Major road
	Unsurfaced road

ACCESS AND PERMITS

Northern Land Council
Tel (08) 8920 5100.
For access to all Aboriginal land in the Top End, including Arnhem Land.

Northern Territory Parks and Wildlife Commission
Tel (08) 8999 4555. *For permits to Gurig National Park. (08) 8999 4814.*

Tiwi Land Council
Tel (08) 8981 4898.
For access to Melville and Bathurst islands.

Central Land Council
Tel (08) 8951 6320.
For access to all Central Australian Aboriginal lands.

ABORIGINAL TOURISM

Most visitors who come to the Northern Territory are keen to learn more about the region's unique Aboriginal culture. There are now many Aboriginal organizations which take tourists into Aboriginal areas that would otherwise be inaccessible, and explain the Aboriginal view of the land. Excursions available include boat trips in Kakadu National Park *(see pp276–7)* with a Guluyambi guide; bush camping with the Manyallaluk community near Katherine; or a safari camp in Arnhem Land with Umorrduk Safaris. Also well worth visiting are the information and cultural centres, such as those in Kakadu and Uluṟu-Kata Tjuṯa national parks, where native owners share their creation stories and culture, adding another layer to visitors' appreciation of these special places.

Ubirr *in Kakadu National Park is one of the finest Aboriginal rock art sites in the Northern Territory. Many paintings in Ubirr's gallery depict the area's wildlife in an x-ray style (see p33), such as this barramundi. They date from 20,000 years ago to the present day.*

Visitors climbing to the lookout at Ubirr

Uluṟu (see pp286–9) *has many sites sacred to the Anangu people around its base. Almost all of these are closed to the public, but it is possible to walk around the area and learn the associated stories.*

Bush Tucker Dreaming, *painted in 1991 by Gladys Napanangka of the Papunya community of the Central Western Desert, records the Dreaming or creation stories passed down to the artist through hundreds of generations (see pp30–31).*

ABORIGINAL CULTURE AND LAW

Every Aboriginal tribe lives according to a set of laws linking the people with their land and their ancestors. These laws have been handed down through generations and are embedded in Aboriginal creation stories. The stories, which tell how the first spirits and ancestors shaped and named the land, also form a belief system which directs all aspects of Aboriginal life. All Aboriginals are born into two groups: their family clan and a "Dreaming" totem group such as the crocodile – determined by place and time of birth. These decide their links with the land and place in the community and the creation stories they inherit.

Aboriginals in body make-up for a traditional tribal dance

Multicultural Northern Territory

Thai dish

The Northern Territory, with its proximity to Indonesia and the Pacific Islands, has long served as Australia's "front door" to immigrants. Around 500 years ago, Portuguese and Dutch ships charted the waters of the northern coast and from the 1700s traders from the Indonesian archipelago visited the northern shores. From 1874, when Chinese gold prospectors arrived in Darwin, the tropical north has appealed to Southeast Asians and, being closer to Indonesia than to Sydney or Melbourne, the city markets itself as Australia's gateway to Asia. There are now more than 50 ethnic groups living in Darwin, including Greeks and Italians who arrived in the early 20th century, and East Timorese, Indonesians, Thais and Filipinos, together with the town's original mix of Aboriginals and those of Anglo-Celtic stock.

Harry Chan, *elected in 1966, was the first Mayor of Darwin of Chinese descent.*

Mindil Beach market *is one of several Asian-style food markets in the Darwin area. More than 60 food stalls serve Thai, Indonesian, Indian, Chinese, Sri Lankan, Malaysian and Greek cuisine (see p272).*

The Indonesian language Bahasa is taught in many of Darwin's schools due to Indonesia's proximity to the city.

THE CHINESE IN THE TOP END

In 1879, a small carved figure dating from the Ming dynasty (1368–1644) was found in the roots of a tree on a Darwin beach, causing much speculation that a Chinese fleet may have visited this coast in the 15th century. If so, it was the start of an association between China and the Top End which endures today. Chinese came here in search of gold in the 1870s. By 1885, there were 3,500 Chinese in the Top End, and 40 years later Darwin had become a Chinese-run shanty town

Chinese man using buffalo to haul wood in early 19th-century Darwin

with Chinese families managing its market gardens and general stores. Today, many of the area's leading families are of Chinese origin; Darwin has had two Lord Mayors of Chinese descent, and fifth-generation Chinese are spread throughout the city's businesses.

Aboriginal people are believed to have arrived in the Northern Territory 20,000 to 50,000 years ago, overland from Asia when the sea level was much lower. Here, young male initiates from an Arnhem Land tribe are carried to a ceremony to be "made men".

With a quarter of its present population born overseas and another quarter Aboriginal, Darwin's racial mix is best seen in the faces of its children.

THE CHILDREN OF DARWIN

The faces of Darwin's children show an incredible ethnic diversity, something many believe will be typical of all Australia in 50 years time. The Northern Territory, and especially Darwin, is renowned for a relaxed, multicultural society and a racial tolerance and identity rarely found in other Australian cities.

Darwin's children, whatever their ethnic origin, are united by their casual Australian clothes and relaxed attitude.

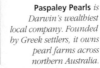

The Filipino community *in Darwin preserves its traditions, as seen by these two girls in national costume at the Festival of Darwin.*

Paspaley Pearls *is Darwin's wealthiest local company. Founded by Greek settlers, it owns pearl farms across northern Australia.*

The East Timorese *community of Darwin performs traditional dancing at a city arts festival. Most of the East Timorese have arrived in the city since 1975, in the wake of Indonesia's invasion of East Timor.*

DARWIN AND THE TOP END

The tropical tip of the Northern Territory is a lush, ancient landscape. For thousands of years it has been home to large numbers of Aboriginals and contains the greatest and oldest collection of rock art in the world. Its capital, Darwin, is small and colourful. The World Heritage-listed Kakadu National Park has a raw beauty combined with the fascinating creation stories of its Aboriginal tribes.

The Port of Darwin was first named in 1839, when British captain John Lort Stokes, commander of HMS *Beagle*, sailed into an azure harbour fringed by palm trees, sandy beaches and mangroves, and named it after his friend Charles Darwin. Although the biologist would not publish his theory of evolution in the *Origin of the Species* for another 20 years, it proved to be a wonderfully apt name for this tropical region, teeming with unique and ancient species of birds, plants, reptiles and mammals. The Aboriginal tribes that have lived for many thousands of years in the northern area known as the Top End are recognized by anthropologists as one of world's oldest races.

Darwin itself is a city that has fought hard to survive. From 1869, when the first settlement was established at Port Darwin, it has endured isolation, bombing attacks by the Japanese in World War II *(see p270)* and devastation by the force of Cyclone Tracy in 1974 *(see p272)*. Despite having been twice rebuilt, it has grown into a multicultural modern city, with a relaxed atmosphere, great beauty and a distinctly Asian feel.

Beyond Darwin is a region of Aboriginal communities and ancient art sites, wide rivers and crocodiles, lotus-lily wetlands and deep gorges. For visitors, Kakadu National Park superbly blends sights of great scenic beauty with a cultural and spiritual insight into the complex Aboriginal culture. Also to be enjoyed are the plunging waterfalls and giant termite mounds of Litchfield National Park, the deep red-rock gorge of Nitmiluk (Katherine Gorge) National Park, and expeditions into the closed Aboriginal communities of Arnhem Land and Melville and Bathurst Islands.

An Aboriginal child gathering water lilies in the lush and tropical Top End

◁ Katherine Gorge cutting an awesome scar across the landscape

Exploring Darwin and the Top End

The top end is a seductive, tropical region on the remote tip of the massive Northern Territory. On the turquoise coast there are palm trees; inland are winding rivers, grassy wetlands, gorge pools and ochre escarpments. The Territory's capital, Darwin, has many attractions and is a good base for day trips to areas such as Berry Springs and Melville and Bathurst Islands. The climate is hot, but the dry season has low humidity, making it the best time to visit. The wet season, however, compensates for its humidity and tropical downpours with the spectacle of thundering rivers and waterfalls, and lush vegetation.

Pearl lugger-turned-cruise boat in Darwin Harbour

GETTING AROUND

The Top End's reputation as an isolated region is long gone. Darwin is linked by the Stuart Highway to Alice Springs, Adelaide and Melbourne in the south, and along interstate hwys to Mount Isa, Cairns and Brisbane in the east. The centre of Darwin can be explored on foot or using the open trolley Tour Tub which stops at all the main attractions in an hourly circuit. The Top End's major attractions, such as Kakadu National Park and Katherine Gorge, can be visited without driving on a dirt road. Bus connections to the main towns are regular, but a car is vital to make the most of the scenery. Distances are not great for Australia; Kakadu is 210 km (130 miles) from Darwin and Katherine 300 km (186 miles) away on the Stuart Hwy.

Spectacular Jim Jim Falls in Kakadu National Park

For additional map symbols *see back flap*

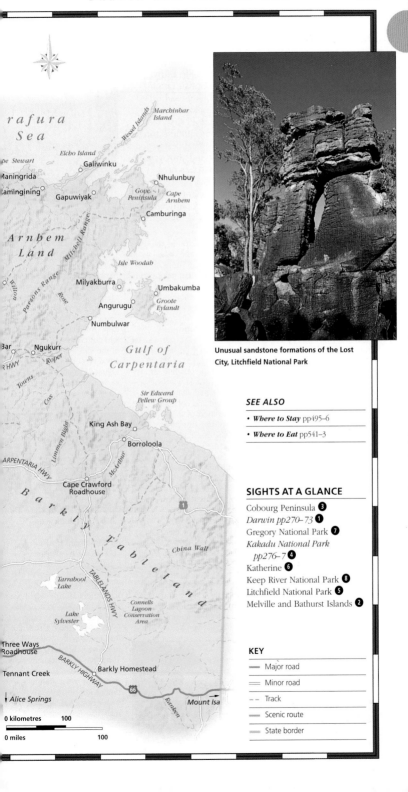

*rafura
Sea*

pe Stewart

Maningrida

Lamingining

Elcho Island

Galiwinku

Gapuwiyak

Wessel Islands

*Marchinbar
Island*

Nhulunbuy

*Gove
Peninsula*

*Cape
Arnhem*

Camburinga

*Arnhem
Land*

Parsons Range

Mitchell Range

Wilton

Rose

Isle Woodah

Milyakburra

Angurugu

Numbulwar

Umbakumba

*Groote
Eylandt*

Bar

Ngukurr

HWY

Roper

Towns

Cox

Limmen Bight

McArthur

*Gulf of
Carpentaria*

*Sir Edward
Pellew Group*

ARPENTARIA HWY

Cape Crawford
Roadhouse

Barkly

King Ash Bay

Borroloola

China Wall

Tableland

Tarrabool
Lake

TABLELANDS HWY

Lake
Sylvester

*Connells
Lagoon
Conservation
Area*

Three Ways
Roadhouse

Tennant Creek

↓ Alice Springs

BARKLY HIGHWAY

Barkly Homestead

66

Ranken

Mount Isa

| 0 kilometres | 100 |
| 0 miles | 100 |

Unusual sandstone formations of the Lost
City, Litchfield National Park

SEE ALSO

• *Where to Stay* pp495–6

• *Where to Eat* pp541–3

SIGHTS AT A GLANCE

Cobourg Peninsula **3**
Darwin pp270–73 **1**
Gregory National Park **7**
*Kakadu National Park
   pp276–7* **4**
Katherine **6**
Keep River National Park **8**
Litchfield National Park **5**
Melville and Bathurst Islands **2**

KEY

───	Major road
═══	Minor road
--	Track
───	Scenic route
───	State border

Darwin ❶

Following European settlement in 1864, for the first century of its life Darwin was an outpost of the British Empire, with vast cattle farms being established around it. In its short, colourful history it has experienced the gold rush of the 1890s, life as an Allied frontline during World War II and almost total destruction in 1974 by the fearful winds of Cyclone Tracy *(see p272)*. Darwin has now emerged as a modern but relaxed town where more than 50 ethnic groups of Asian-born Australians mingle with Aboriginals, Europeans, particularly Greeks, and Chinese from earlier periods of immigration.

Old pearl diver's helmet

Shady palm trees in Bicentennial Park, seen from The Esplanade

Old Town Hall
Smith St.
The limestone ruin of the Old Darwin Town Hall lies at the bottom of Smith Street. The original council chambers, built in 1883, became a naval workshop and store in World War II. Subsequently it was a bank and then a museum, before being destroyed by Cyclone Tracy in 1974. Curved brick paving built against the remaining wall symbolizes the fury of the cyclone's winds.

Brown's Mart
12 Smith St. *Tel* (08) 8981 5522.
Directly opposite the town hall ruins is Brown's Mart, built in 1885 during the gold boom. It was once a mining exchange and is now home to an intimate theatre.

Old Police Station and Courthouse
Cnr Smith St & The Esplanade. *Tel* (08) 8999 7103.
The 1884 limestone Old Police Station and Courthouse have both been restored after being damaged by Cyclone Tracy and are now administration offices.
Across the road is Survivors' Lookout, which overlooks the harbour. Here photographs

and written accounts tell of Darwin's wartime ordeal as an Allied frontline. Thousands of US and Australian troops were based in the Top End, which endured 65 bombing raids by Japanese forces *(see p57)*.

Lyons Cottage
Cnr Knuckey St & The Esplanade. *Tel* (08) 8981 1750. ☐ 10am–4:30pm daily. ● *Easter, 25 Dec.*
The old stone building known as Lyons Cottage was built in 1925. It is maintained in a 1920s style and contains an exhibition of photographs detailing life in the Top End during that era.

Smith Street Mall
Bennett & Knuckey sts.
The heart of Darwin's shopping area is Smith Street Mall, with its glass air-conditioned plazas shaded by tall tropical trees. Always full of buskers, tour operators offering trips, locals and visitors, the mall is a favourite meeting place. Noteworthy buildings include the 1890 Victoria Hotel, a popular landmark and one of the few old structures in the town to survive Cyclone Tracy.

Bicentennial Park
The Esplanade.
This lush, green park, with its pleasant shady walks and panoramic lookouts, is home to many World War II memorials. One commemorates the attack by Japanese bombers which flew over Darwin Harbour on 19 February 1942, sinking 21 of the 46 US and Australian naval vessels in port and killing 243 people. It was the closest Australia came to war on its own soil.

Front entrance of Parliament House

Parliament House
State Square. *Tel* (08) 8946 1434. ☐ *daily.*
Dominating the edge of Darwin's sea cliffs is the new Parliament House, which was opened in 1994. With architecture that appears to borrow from both Middle Eastern and Russian styles, this imposing building is home to the Territory's 25 parliamentarians, who administer just 200,000 people. It has a granite and timber interior which is filled with Aboriginal art. Visitors may also get a glimpse of the parliamentarian chambers and use the library – the largest in the territory, with an excellent local reference section.

Darwin's Old Police Station and Courthouse

For hotels and restaurants in this region see pp495–6 and pp541–3

♿ Government House

The Esplanade. *Tel (08) 8999 7103.* ♿

On a small plateau above the harbour, Government House is Darwin's oldest surviving building, built in 1879. It has withstood the ravages of three cyclones and bombing attacks. It is now home to the Administrator of the Northern Territory, the representative of the Queen and Commonwealth of Australia in the territory.

♿ Old Admiralty House

Cnr Knuckey St & The Esplanade.

Across the road from Lyons Cottage is Old Admiralty House, once the headquarters of the Australian navy and one of the oldest surviving buildings in Darwin. It was built in the 1930s by the territory's principal architect, Beni Carr Glynn Burnett, in an elevated tropical style using louvres, open eaves and three-quarter-high walls to aid ventilation.

♿ Stokes Hill Wharf

McMinn St. ♿ ▢

The long, wooden Stokes Hill Wharf, stretching out into Darwin Harbour, was once the town's main port area. Now a centre for tourist and local life, it has restaurants and shops. Boats leave on tours from the wharf.

At the wharf entrance is the excellent Indo-Pacific Marine exhibit, which has re-created local coral reef ecosystems, with bright tropical fish in its tanks. In the same building, the Australian Pearling Exhibition describes the history and science of local pearl farming.

Restaurant at the end of Stokes Hill Wharf overlooking the harbour

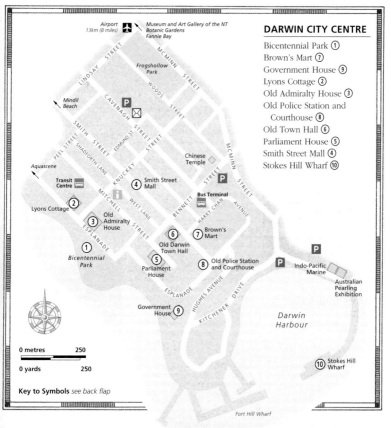

DARWIN CITY CENTRE

Bicentennial Park ①
Brown's Mart ⑦
Government House ⑨
Lyons Cottage ②
Old Admiralty House ③
Old Police Station and Courthouse ⑧
Old Town Hall ⑥
Parliament House ⑤
Smith Street Mall ④
Stokes Hill Wharf ⑩

Airport 13km (8 miles)

Museum and Art Gallery of the NT
Botanic Gardens
Fannie Bay

Frogshollow Park

Mindil Beach

Aquascene

Transit Centre

Lyons Cottage ②

Old Admiralty House ③

Bicentennial Park ①

Chinese Temple

Smith Street Mall ④

Bus Terminal

Old Darwin Town Hall ⑥

Brown's Mart ⑦

Parliament House ⑤

Old Police Station and Courthouse ⑧

Indo-Pacific Marine

Australian Pearling Exhibition

Government House ⑨

Darwin Harbour

Stokes Hill Wharf ⑩

0 metres   250
0 yards   250

Key to Symbols *see back flap*

Fort Hill Wharf

Greater Darwin

Many of Darwin's best attractions are not in the city centre but located a short drive away. The Tour Tub, an open-sided trolley bus that picks up from major hotels, does an hourly circuit of tourist attractions, allowing visitors to hop on and off at will for a daily charge. Outside Darwin, alongside the mango farms and cattle stations, there are some fine bush and wetland areas which provide excellent opportunities for swimming, fishing and exploring.

Decorated emu egg

Feeding the friendly fish at Aquascene in Doctor's Gully

➤ Aquascene

Doctor's Gully, cnr of Daly St & The Esplanade. *Tel* (08) 8981 7837. ☐ *daily, with the tide.* ● *25 Dec.* ♿

Ever since the 1950s, the fish of Darwin Harbour have been coming in on the tides for a feed of stale bread in Doctor's Gully. At Aquascene, visitors can feed and play with hundreds of scats, catfish, mullet and milkfish. Feeding times vary from day to day.

Ethnic food stall at Mindil Beach Sunset Markets

🎪 Mindil Beach Sunset Markets

Mindil Beach. *Tel* (08) 8981 3454. ☐ *May–Oct: Thu, Sun.* ♿

Thursday and Sunday nights during the dry season are when Darwinians flock to Mindil Beach at dusk to enjoy some 60 outdoor food stalls, street theatre, live music and over 200 craft stalls.

♣ George Brown Darwin Botanic Gardens

Gardens Rd, Stuart Park. *Tel* (08) 8981 1958. ☐ *daily.* ♿ *limited.*

Just north of town, the 42-ha (100-acre) Botanic Gardens, established in the 1870s, boast over 1,500 tropical species, including 400 palm varieties and wetland mangroves.

🏯 East Point Military Museum and Fannie Bay Gaol

Alec Fong Lim Drive, East Point. *Tel* (08) 8981 9702. ☐ *9:30am–5pm daily.* ♿

An attraction for all the family this attractive harbourside reserve contains an artificial lake, ideal for swimming, and the East Point Military Museum. Nearby Fannie Bay Gaol is now an interesting museum.

🏛 Australian Aviation Heritage Centre

557 Stuart Hwy, Winnellie. *Tel* (08) 8947 2145. 🚌 *5, 8.* ☐ *9am–5pm daily.* ● *Good Fri, 25 Dec.* ♿ ♿

Along the Stuart Highway at Winnellie, 6 km (4 miles) from the city centre, Darwin's Aviation Centre displays a variety of historic and wartime aircraft. Its exhibits are dominated by a B-52 bomber, one of only two in the world on display outside the US.

🦎 Territory Wildlife Park

Cox Peninsula Rd, Berry Springs. *Tel* (08) 8988 7200. ☐ *8:30am–6pm daily.* ● *25 Dec.* ♿ ♿ ▯

Only 60 km (37 miles) from Darwin is the town of Berry Springs and the Territory Wildlife Park with its hundreds of unique indigenous species, in natural surroundings. Nearby, Berry Springs Nature Reserve has a series of deep pools, fringed with vegetation, that make for great swimming.

🦃 Howard Springs Nature Park

Howard Springs Rd. *Tel* (08) 8983 1001. ☐ *daily.* ♿ *limited.*

This nature park, 35 km (22 miles) from Darwin, has clear, freshwater spring-fed pools, filled with barramundi and turtles. After a good wet season these are an ideal place for a cool swim and a barbecue after a hot day exploring.

CYCLONE TRACY

Late Christmas Eve, 1974, a weather warning was issued that Cyclone Tracy, gathering force off the coast, had turned landward and was heading for Darwin. Torrential rain pelted down and winds reached a record 280 km/h (175 mph) before the measuring machine broke. On Christmas morning, 66 people were dead, thousands injured and 95 per cent of the buildings flattened. More than 30,000 residents were airlifted south in the biggest evacuation in Australia's history. The city ruins were bulldozed and Darwin has been rebuilt, stronger and safer than before.

Cyclone Tracy's devastation

For hotels and restaurants in this region see pp494–6 and pp541–3

Museum and Art Gallery of the Northern Territory

The Museum and Art Gallery of the Northern Territory has exhibitions on regional Aboriginal art and culture, maritime history, visual arts and natural history.

The museum's collection of Aboriginal art is considered to be the best in the world and has some particularly fine carvings and bark paintings, along with explanations of Aboriginal culture. Other displays include a chilling exhibition on Cyclone Tracy and displays that explain the evolution of some of the Top End's unique and curious wildlife, including the popular stuffed crocodile named "Sweetheart".

VISITORS' CHECKLIST

Conacher St. **Tel** (08) 8999 8201.
4, 5. 9am–5pm Mon–Fri,
10am–5pm Sat & Sun. some
public hols.

KEY

- ☐ Aboriginal Art Gallery
- ☐ Natural Sciences Gallery
- ☐ Cyclone Tracy Gallery
- ☐ Visual Art Gallery
- ☐ Amphitheatre
- ☐ Maritime Galleries
- ☐ Temporary exhibitions
- ☐ Non-exhibition space
- ☐ Monsoon Forest Pathway
- ☐ Fish Pond

★ **Aboriginal Art Gallery**
In this gallery, exhibits describe both the anthropology and creation stories of local Aboriginal groups as an introduction to the artworks on display that portray their lives and culture.

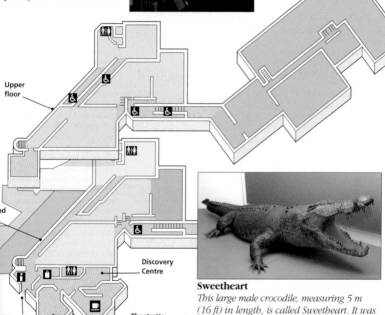

Upper floor

Discovery Centre

Entrance

Theatrette

Sweetheart
This large male crocodile, measuring 5 m (16 ft) in length, is called Sweetheart. It was caught in 1979 in the Finnis River, which is between Darwin and Kakadu.

Façade of the Museum and Art Gallery
Located 4 km (2.5 miles) north of Darwin's centre, the museum's stylish low-level building is in a tropical beachside setting overlooking Fannie Bay.

STAR FEATURES

★ Aboriginal Art Gallery

Tiwi islander making handicrafts from local fibres, Bathurst Island

Melville and Bathurst Islands ❷

✕ ℹ *Tiwi Tours (08) 8924 1115.*

Just 80 km (50 miles) north of Darwin lie the Tiwi Islands, the collective name given to the small island of Bathurst and its larger neighbour, Melville. The latter is the second-largest island off the Australian coast after Tasmania and is rich in history and Aboriginal culture. The islands' inhabitants, the Tiwi people, had little contact with mainland Aboriginals until the 20th century.

With beautiful waters, sandy beaches and lush forest, the islands are a tropical paradise, but, because of their ownership by the Tiwi, only Bathurst Island is visited on tours from Darwin. Running May to October, day trips offer a glimpse of the unique blend of Aboriginal, Indonesian and Tiwi traditions. Tourists can visit Aboriginal art centres, Tiwi batik printworks and a *pukumani* burial site with painted wood burial poles.

Cobourg Peninsula ❸

ℹ *Venture North Australia, Darwin (08) 8927 5500.*
www.northernaustralia.com

The Cobourg Peninsula is one of the most remote parts of Australia. It is only accessible by vehicle during the dry season and with an access permit *(see p262)*, travelling through the closed Aboriginal Arnhem Land to the wild coastal beaches of Gurig National Park. The number of vehicles allowed to enter the region each week is restricted and there are permit fees, too, so going on a tour is sometimes a convenient option.

Gurig is a large park, with sandy beaches and the calm waters of Port Essington. Two attempts by the British to settle this area in the early 19th century were abandoned, due to inhospitable Aborigines and malaria epidemics. The ruins of Victoria Settlement can be reached by boat from Smith Point. Luxury accommodation is available at Seven Spirit Bay Wilderness Lodge, reached by plane from Darwin.

Kakadu National Park ❹

See pp276–7.

Litchfield National Park ❺

ℹ *National Parks and Wildlife Commission for Northern Territory (08) 8976 0282.*

The spectacular Litchfield National Park, only 129 km (80 miles) south of Darwin, is very popular with Darwinians. There are waterfalls, gorges and deep, crocodile-free pools for swimming at Florence Falls, Wangi, in the wet season, and

Giant magnetic termite mound in Litchfield National Park

Buley Rockhole. The park has some amazing giant magnetic termite mounds. They are so-called because they point north in an effort by the termites to control temperature by having only the mound's thinnest part exposed to the sun. Also popular are the sandstone block formations further south, known as the "Lost City" due to their resemblance to ruins.

Katherine ❻

🚹 *11,000.* ✕ 🚌 🚍 ℹ *Cnr Stuart Hwy & Lindsay St (08) 8972 2650.*

The town of Katherine, situated on the banks of the Katherine River, 320 km (200 miles) south of Darwin, is both a thriving regional centre and a major Top End tourist destination. Home for thousands of years to the Jawoyn Aboriginals, Katherine River has long been a rich source of food for the Aboriginal people. The river was first crossed by white explorers in 1844, and the area was not settled by Europeans until 1872, with the completion of the Overland Telegraph Line. Springvale Homestead was built on the Katherine River in 1879. It is now the oldest building in the Territory and is open to the public.

Only 30 km (20 miles) from town lies the famous **Nitmiluk (Katherine Gorge) National Park**. Its string of 13 separate gorges along 50 km (30 miles) of the Katherine River has been carved out by torrential summer rains cutting through cliffs of red sandstone which are 1,650 million years old. The result is a place of deep pools, silence and grandeur.

The best way to explore the park is by boat or canoe. Canoe trips are self-guided, with nine navigable gorges and overnight camping possible. There are also boat trips operated by the Jawoyn people, who own the park and run it in conjunction with the Northern Territory's Parks and Wildlife Commission. Each gorge can be explored in a separate boat, interspersed with swimming holes and short walks. There are also

Upper waterfall and pools of Edith Falls, Nitmiluk (Katherine Gorge) National Park near Katherine

100 km (60 miles) of marked trails in the park, ranging from the spectacular but easy look-out walk to the five-day 72-km (45-mile) hike to Edith Falls, which can also be reached by car from the Stuart Highway.

Environs

Just 27 km (17 miles) south of Katherine are the Cutta Cutta caves, limestone rock formations 15 m (50 ft) under the earth's surface and formed five million years ago. They are home to both the rare orange horseshoe bat and the brown tree snake.

Further southeast, 110 km (70 miles) from Katherine, lies the small town of Mataranka. This is "Never Never" country, celebrated by female pioneer Jeannie Gunn in her 1908 novel, *We of the Never Never*, about life at nearby Elsey Station at the turn of the century. The area is called Never Never country because those who live here find they never, never want to leave it. About

8 km (5 miles) east of Mataranka is Elsey National Park. Visitors can swim in the hot waters of the Mataranka Thermal Pool which flow from Rainbow Springs to this idyllic spot surrounded by rainforest. Built in 1916 **Mataranka Homestead** is now back-packer accommodation and part of the Mataranka Homestead resort, which includes a motel, cabins and camping.

Mataranka Homestead
Tel (08) 8975 4544. ◻ *daily.*
▦ ▐▌ ◻

Gregory National Park ❼

ℹ Timber Creek (08) 8975 0888, Katherine (08) 8973 8888.
◻ 7am–4pm Mon–Fri.

This massive national park is in cattle country, 280 km (174 miles) by road southwest of Katherine. Broken into two sections, its eastern part contains a 50-km (31-mile) section of the Victoria River gorge, mostly inaccessible. In the north of the larger western section of the park are some crocodile-infested areas of the Victoria River. Here boat trips combine close-up views of

Walking trail by a sandstone escarp-ment, Keep River National Park

the crocodiles. In the west of the park, the stunning Limestone Gorge has dolomite blocks, huge cliffs and good fishing opportunities.

Keep River National Park ❽

ℹ Victoria Hwy (08) 9167 8827.
◻ Apr–Sep: daily; Oct–Mar: Mon–Fri. Closed when inaccessible.

Located only 3 km (2 miles) from the Western Australian border, Keep River National Park includes the dramatic Keep River gorge and some of Australia's most ancient rock art sites. The park, once the location of an ancient Aboriginal settlement, today has some superb walking trails for all levels of trekkers.

Limestone Gorge, Gregory National Park

Kakadu National Park ❹

Aboriginal calendar at the
Bowali Visitors' Centre

The vast 19,757 sq km (7,628 sq miles) of Kakadu National Park, with its stunning diversity of stony plateaux, red escarpment cliffs, waterfalls, billabongs, long twisting rivers, flood plains and coastal flats, is one of Australia's most extraordinary places. A UNESCO World Heritage Area *(see pp26–7)*, Kakadu encompasses both scenic wonders and huge galleries of Aboriginal rock art. The park is Aboriginal land leased back to the government *(see p59)* and is managed jointly. The entire catchment area of the South Alligator River lies within the park, and is home to thousands of plant and animal species. Some areas in Kakadu are not accessible during the wet season.

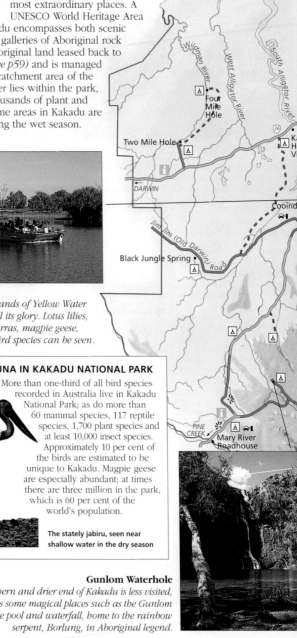

Yellow Water
A cruise on the wetlands of Yellow Water shows Kakadu in all its glory. Lotus lilies, crocodiles, kookaburras, magpie geese, jabirus and other bird species can be seen.

FLORA AND FAUNA IN KAKADU NATIONAL PARK

More than one-third of all bird species recorded in Australia live in Kakadu National Park; as do more than 60 mammal species, 117 reptile species, 1,700 plant species and at least 10,000 insect species. Approximately 10 per cent of the birds are estimated to be unique to Kakadu. Magpie geese are especially abundant; at times there are three million in the park, which is 60 per cent of the world's population.

The stately jabiru, seen near shallow water in the dry season

Gunlom Waterhole
The southern and drier end of Kakadu is less visited, but holds some magical places such as the Gunlom plunge pool and waterfall, home to the rainbow serpent, Borlung, in Aboriginal legend.

Guluyambi Cultural Cruises take visitors up the East Alligator River with Aboriginal guides who explain local Aboriginal traditions and culture.

VISITORS' CHECKLIST

Hwy 36. ℹ️ *Visitors' Centre, Kakadu Hwy, 2.5 km (1.5 miles) south of Jabiru (08) 8938 1120.*

Ubirr
This rock has many Aboriginal rock art galleries, some with paintings more than 20,000 years old (see p33).

Oenpelli is a small Aboriginal town in Arnhem Land outside Kakadu. Some day tours take visitors to this restricted area.

Jabiru is a small town that provides accommodation for visitors to the park.

Ranger Uranium Mine
This mine is rigorously monitored to ensure that the natural and cultural values of the park are not endangered.

Bowali Visitors' Centre
This award-winning centre features excellent displays describing the animals, Aboriginal culture and geology of Kakadu.

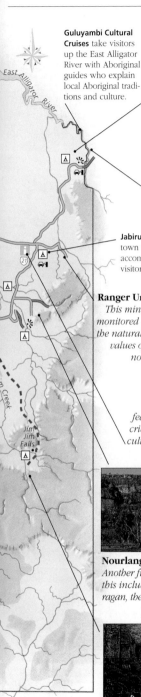

Nourlangie Rock
Another fine Aboriginal rock art site, this includes paintings of Namaragan, the Lightning Man (see p262).

KEY

▬	Highway
▬	Major road
▪ ▪	4WD only
—	National park boundary
🚗⛽	Petrol station
⛺	Camp site
ℹ️	Tourist information
✲	View Point

Twin Falls
This waterfall (accessible by 4WD and boat transfer) flows in the dry season but is dramatic in the wet, when it thunders over a high plateau into deep rock pools.

0 kilometres   20

0 miles   20

THE RED CENTRE

The Red Centre stretches roughly from Tennant Creek to the South Australian border, and is made up almost entirely of huge desert areas. The region occupies the centre of the Australian continent, with its main town, Alice Springs, at the country's geographical heart. Its signature colour is red: red sand, soil, rocks and mountains are all pitched against a typically blue sky.

The Red Centre contains some of the finest natural scenery in the world, much of it dating back about 800 million years. At that time, central Australia was covered by an inland sea; here sediments were laid down which form the basis of some of the region's best-known topographical features today. These include the huge monolith Uluṟu (formerly Ayers Rock), the domes of Kata Tjuṯa (also known as the Olgas), the giant boulders of the Devil's Marbles and the majestic MacDonnell Ranges. Between these sights are vast open spaces where remnants of tropical plant species grow beside desert-hardy stock. Verdant plants fed by occasional rains flourish next to animal skeletons.

Aboriginal people have lived in the region for more than 30,000 years, and their ancient tradition of rock painting is one of many tribal rituals still practised. By comparison, the history of white settlement here is recent. Explorers first arrived in the area during the 1860s. Alice Springs, founded in 1888, was a tiny settlement until improved communications after World War II led to the town's growth. It is now a modern, bustling town with much to offer. Tennant Creek, the only other sizeable settlement in the area, lies on the main Stuart Highway that bisects the Red Centre.

Much of the Territory has now been returned to its Aboriginal owners (*see pp262–3*), and today many Aborigines are actively involved in tourism. Access to Aboriginal lands is restricted but visiting them is a rewarding encounter to add to the unforgettable experience of the Red Centre.

Trekking through the desert landscape on a camel safari near Alice Springs

◁ **The monolith Uluṟu, sacred to the Aborigines, set against a brilliant blue sky**

Exploring the Red Centre

The Red Centre's biggest draw is its stunning array of natural features. Alice Springs is the main city, with other towns at Yulara (Ayers Rock Resort) and Tennant Creek. The best time to travel is from April to October, thus avoiding the intense summer heat. The MacDonnell Ranges run like a huge spine on either side of Alice Springs; elsewhere the land is largely flat, formed by millions of years of erosion, and covered by spinifex grasslands. The region's gorges have been carved out by rivers, many of which flow only once or twice a year, soaking the surrounding desert plains.

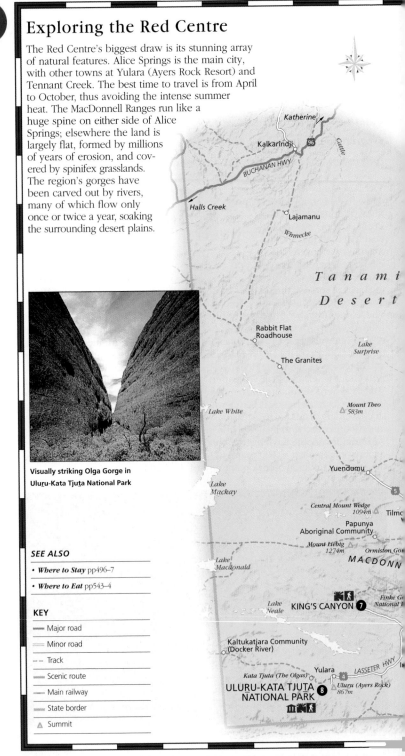

Visually striking Olga Gorge in Uluṟu-Kata Tjuṯa National Park

SEE ALSO

- **Where to Stay** pp496–7

- **Where to Eat** pp543–4

KEY

▬▬	Major road
═══	Minor road
- - -	Track
▬▬	Scenic route
▬▬	Main railway
▬▬▬	State border
△	Summit

Katherine
Kalkarindji 96
Cattle
BUCHANAN HWY
Halls Creek
Lajamanu
Winnecke

Tanami Desert

Rabbit Flat Roadhouse
Lake Surprise
The Granites
Mount Theo △ 583m
Lake White
Yuendumu
Lake Mackay
Central Mount Wedge 1094m △ Tilm
Papunya Aboriginal Community
Mount Liebig 1274m Ormiston Gor
MACDONN
Lake Macdonald
Lake Neale KING'S CANYON ⑦ Finke Ge National F
Kaltukatjara Community (Docker River)
Kata Tjuta (The Olgas) Yulara LASSETER HWY
ULURU-KATA TJUTA NATIONAL PARK ⑧ Uluru (Ayers Rock) 867m

SIGHTS AT A GLANCE

Alice Springs pp282–3 **1**
Chambers Pillar Historical
    Reserve **2**
Devil's Marbles
    Conservation Reserve **5**
Henbury Meteorites
    Conservation Reserve **3**
Kings Canyon **7**
MacDonnell Ranges **4**
Tennant Creek **6**
*Uluṟu-Kata Tjuṯa National
    Park pp286–9* **8**

Colourful mural painted on a shopping centre in Alice Springs

GETTING AROUND

There is a wide range of transport options available in central
Australia. Domestic airports serve Alice Springs and Yulara.
Overland, coaches connect the region with all the state capital
cities, and the famous Ghan railway *(see p283)* operates
between Alice Springs and Adelaide. The most popular
way to explore the region, however, is by car, and
there are many car rental companies in the area.
Standard vehicles are adequate for most
journeys, but 4WD is advisable for off-
road travel. Alternatively, many guided
tours are also available. The Stuart
Hwy is the main road running
through the area, linking
Port Augusta in South
Australia with Darwin
in the north. Alice
Springs itself has
taxis, bike hire and a
town bus service, but
the relatively short
distances within
the city also make
walking popular.

0 kilometres   100

0 miles   100

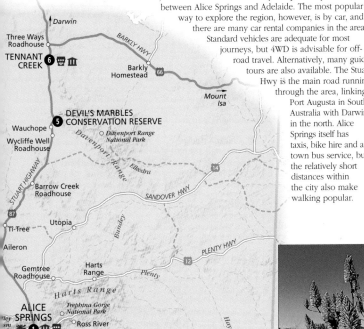

Darwin

Three Ways
Roadhouse
TENNANT 6 🖼 🏛
CREEK

BARKLY HWY

Barkly
Homestead 66

Mount
Isa

**DEVIL'S MARBLES
CONSERVATION RESERVE**
Wauchope **5**   Davenport Range
                    National Park
Wycliffe Well
Roadhouse   *Davenport Range*

                        Elkedra   14

Barrow Creek
Roadhouse   SANDOVER HWY

STUART HIGHWAY

87
Ti-Tree

Utopia   *Bundey*

Aileron

Gemtree   PLENTY HWY
Roadhouse   Harts
               Range   *Plenty*   12

Harts Range

ALICE   Trephina Gorge
SPRINGS   National Park
         1 🏛 🖼 Ross River

RANGES
🏛   *Hay*

es   Ranges   *Hale*

**HENBURY METEORITES
CONSERVATION RESERVE**

**2 CHAMBERS PILLAR
HISTORICAL RESERVE**

rldunda   S i m p s o n

         Finke   D e s e r t
Kulgera
Roadhouse

Coober Pedy

Desert wildflowers in Simpsons
Gap, near Alice Springs

Alice Springs ❶

Alice Springs is named after the Alice Spring permanent waterhole, near which a staging post for the overland telegraph line was built in the 1870s. The waterhole was named after Alice Todd, wife of the line's construction manager. The town developed nearby in the 1880s, but with no rail link until 1929 and no surfaced road link until the 1940s, it grew slowly. The huge increase in tourism since the 1970s, however, has brought rapid growth and Alice Springs is now a lively city with around 400,000 visitors a year, many of whom use it as a base from which to tour the surrounding spectacular natural sights.

Exploring Alice Springs
Although many of its sights are spread around the city, Alice Springs is small enough to tour on foot. Its compact centre, just five streets across running from Wills Terrace in the north to Stuart Terrace in the south, contains many of the town's hotels and restaurants, as well as the pedestrianized Todd Mall. The city's eastern side is bordered by Todd River, dry and sandy most of the time and scene of the celebrated Henley-on-Todd Regatta *(see p40)*.

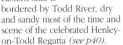

Meteorite fragment in the Museum of Central Australia

🎿 Anzac Hill
West Terrace. 👓
At the northern end of Alice Springs, Anzac Hill overlooks the city and affords fine views of the MacDonnell Ranges *(see p284)*. Named after the 1934 Anzac memorial at the site, the hill is a perfect vantage point for visitors to familiarize themselves with the city's layout, as well as for viewing the area at sunrise or sunset, when it is bathed in a beautiful light.

View over central Alice Springs from the top of Anzac Hill

🏛 Museum of Central Australia
Alice Springs Cultural Precinct, Larapinta Dr. *Tel (08) 8951 1121.* ◯ daily. ● Good Fri, 25 Dec. 🖼 👓
This museum, situated in the Cultural Precinct, concentrates on local natural history with displays of fossils, flora and fauna, meteorite pieces and minerals. It also has a fine collection of Aboriginal art and artefacts.

🏚 Adelaide House
Todd Mall. *Tel (08) 89521856.* ◯ Mon–Fri. ● Good Fri. 🖼 👓
Adelaide House, Alice Springs' first hospital, opened in 1926. It was designed by John Flynn, founder of the Royal Flying Doctor Service *(see p257)*, and is preserved as a museum dedicated to his memory.

🏚 Old Courthouse
Cnr Parsons & Hartley sts. *Tel (08) 8952 9006.* ◯ 10am–5pm daily. ● mid-Dec–1 Feb. 🖼 👓
Built in 1928 by Emil Martin, who was also responsible for The Residency, the Old Courthouse was in use until 1980, when new law courts were opened nearby. The building has recently been restored and now features exhibitions devoted to the achievements of Australia's pioneer women.

Stuart Town Gaol

🏚 Stuart Town Gaol
8 Parsons St. *Tel (08) 8952 4516.* ◯ Mon–Sat. ● mid Dec–1 Feb, public hols. 🖼 👓
The oldest surviving building in central Alice Springs is the Stuart Town Gaol, which operated as a jail between 1909 and 1938 when a new prison was built on Stuart Terrace. The gaol is now open to the public.

🏚 The Residency
29 Parsons St. *Tel (08) 8953 6073.* ◯ 10am–5pm Mon–Fri. ● Dec–Mar, Good Fri, 25 Dec. 🖼 **Donation.**
The Residency, built in 1927 for the regional administrator of Central Australia, was the home of Alice Springs' senior public servant until 1973. After restoration, it was opened to the public in 1996 and now houses a local history display.

🏛 Panorama Guth
65 Hartley St. *Tel (08) 8952 2013.* ◯ Feb–mid Dec: daily. ● mid Dec–1 Feb. 🖼
Panorama Guth is a fantastic 360-degree painting of the Red Centre's main attractions, by Dutch-born artist Hendrik Guth who has lived in the town for more than 30 years. Also on display is an interesting exhibition of Aboriginal artefacts.

🏚 Alice Springs Telegraph Station Historical Precinct
Off Stuart Hwy. *Tel (08) 8952 3993.* ◯ 8am–5pm daily. ● 25 Dec. 🖼 👓
This, the site of the first settlement in Alice Springs, features the original buildings and

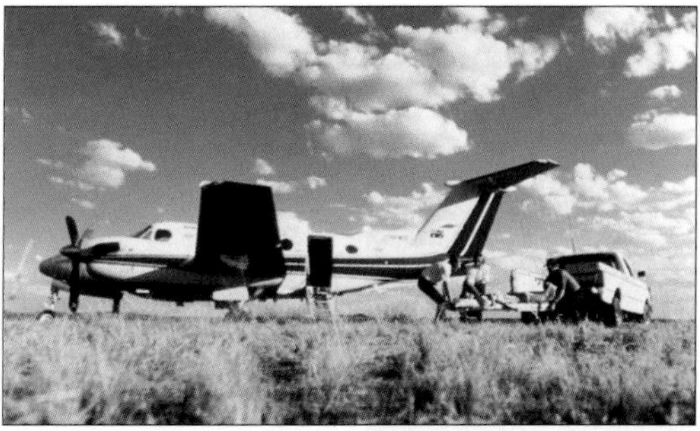

Plane used for the Royal Flying Doctor Service

equipment of the telegraph station built in 1871. A small museum describes the amazing task of setting up the station and operating the overland telegraph.

Alice Springs Desert Park

Larapinta Drive. ***Tel*** *(08) 8951 8788.* 🕐 *7:30am–6pm daily.* ⛔ *25 Dec.* 📷 ♿

An excellent introduction to Central Australia, this park lies on the western edge of the town and features three habitat types: desert river, sand country and woodlands. Visitors may see many of the birds and animals of Central Australia here at close range.

🏛 Old Ghan Train Museum

MacDonnell Siding, Norris Bell Ave. ***Tel*** *(08) 8955 5047.* 🕐 *daily.* ⛔ *Good Fri, 25 Dec.* 📷 🍴 🛍 ♿

South of the city centre, this museum has an extensive collection of Ghan memorabilia. The Ghan train first ran from Adelaide to Alice Springs in 1929. It was named after the Afghans who once ran camel trains along the same route.

VISITORS' CHECKLIST

👥 *27,000.* ✈ *14 km (8.5 miles) S of town.* 🚌 *George Crescent.* ℹ *Gregory Terrace (08) 8952 5800.* 🎉 *Henley-on-Todd Regatta (Oct); Camel Cup (Jul).* **www**.travelnt.com

🏛 Royal Flying Doctor Service Visitor Centre

8–10 Stuart Terrace. ***Tel*** *(08) 8952 1129.* 🕐 *9am–4pm Mon–Sat, 1–4pm Sun.* ⛔ *25 Dec, 1 Jan.* 📷 👤 *obligatory.* 🛍 🍴 ♿ **www**.flyingdoctor.net

The centre can only be seen with a guide, and visitors are taken on a 45-minute tour of the base that includes the Radio Communications centre, where staff recount the history of the Service and explain the day to day operations. There is also a museum, containing old medical equipment, model aircraft and an original Traeger Pedal Radio. The Visitor Centre opened in the late 1970s but was recently redevoloped and extended to include a café and Bush Kitchen.

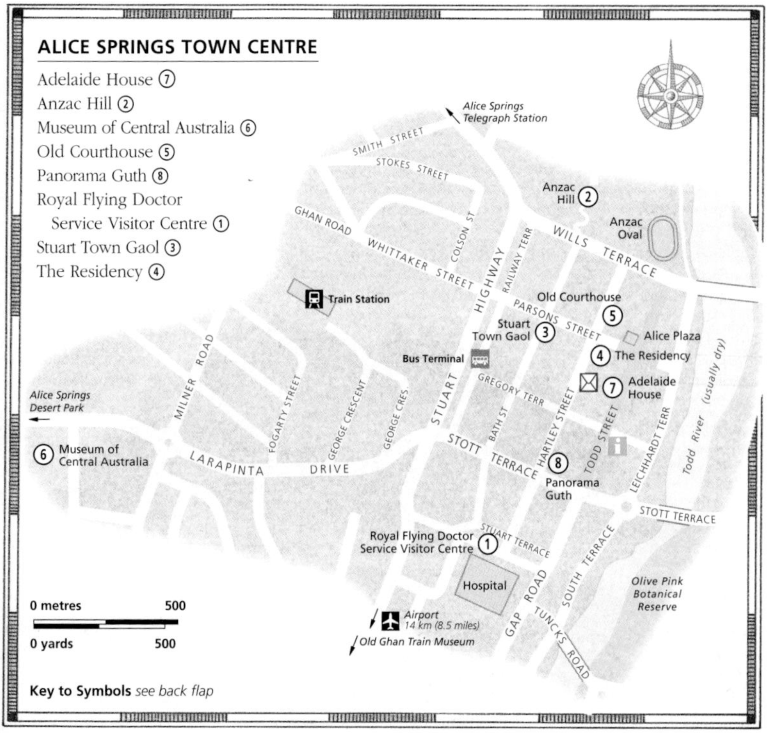
ALICE SPRINGS TOWN CENTRE
Adelaide House ⑦
Anzac Hill ②
Museum of Central Australia ⑥
Old Courthouse ⑤
Panorama Guth ⑧
Royal Flying Doctor Service Visitor Centre ①
Stuart Town Gaol ③
The Residency ④
Alice Springs Telegraph Station
Smith Street
Stokes Street
Ghan Road
Whittaker Street
Colson St
Highway
Railway Terr
Wills Terrace
Anzac Hill ②
Anzac Oval
Train Station
Old Courthouse ⑤
Parsons Street
Stuart Town Gaol ③
Alice Plaza
④ The Residency
Bus Terminal
Gregory Terr
⑦ Adelaide House
Todd River (usually dry)
Alice Springs Desert Park
Milner Road
Fogarty Street
George Crescent
George Cres.
Stuart
Bath St
Hartley Street
Todd Street
Leichhardt Terr
⑥ Museum of Central Australia
Larapinta Drive
Stott Terrace
⑧ Panorama Guth
Stott Terrace
Royal Flying Doctor Service Visitor Centre ①
Stuart Terrace
Hospital
South Terrace
Gap Road
Tuncks Road
Olive Pink Botanical Reserve
Airport 14 km (8.5 miles)
Old Ghan Train Museum
0 metres 500
0 yards 500
Key to Symbols see back flap

Chambers Pillar Historical Reserve ❷

Tel (08) 8951 8250. 🚗 *Alice Springs.* 🚗 *Alice Springs.* 📷
www.nt.gov.au/ipe/pwcnt

Chambers Pillar, a 50-m (165-ft) high sandstone obelisk, was used by explorers as an important navigational landmark during early colonial exploration. The pillar is made of mixed red and yellow sandstone deposited more than 350 million years ago. Many of the explorers, such as John Ross who visited the area in 1870, carved their names and inscriptions into the rock.

Located 160 km (110 miles) south of Alice Springs, with the final section of the journey accessible only by 4WD vehicles, the pillar is also a sacred Aboriginal site.

Henbury Meteorites Conservation Reserve ❸

Tel (08) 8951 8250. 🚗 *Alice Springs.* 🚗 *Alice Springs.* 📷

This cluster of 12 craters, located 145 km (89 miles) southwest of Alice Springs, was formed by a meteorite which crashed to earth several thousand years ago. It is believed that local Aborigines witnessed the event, as one of the Aboriginal names for the area suggests a fiery rock falling to earth. The largest crater in the group is 180 m (590 ft) across and is 15 m (50 ft) deep. Signs on a trail mark significant features.

Lush Palm Valley in Finke Gorge National Park, MacDonnell Ranges

MacDonnell Ranges ❹

🚗 *Alice Springs.* 🚗 *Alice Springs.* 🛈 *Alice Springs (08) 8952 5800.* **Simpsons Gap** ◯ *daily.* ♿ **Standley Chasm** ◯ *daily.* 🈲 ♿ www.nt.gov.au/ipe/pwcnt

The Macdonnell Ranges are the eroded remnants of an ancient mountain chain which was once as monumental as the Himalayas. Still impressive and filled with striking scenery, the East and West MacDonnells contain gorges, waterholes and walking tracks. Running east and west of Alice Springs and easily accessible, they are popular with day-trippers. Visitors will notice the ranges' thrust-up layers of rock, evidence of geological movements more than 300 million years ago. Culturally, they contain many areas sacred to the Aranda people.

In the West MacDonnells, 7 km (4 miles) from Alice Springs, is John Flynn's Memorial Grave, which honours Presbyterian minister, Rev John Flynn, who founded the Royal Flying Doctor Service *(see p257)*.

A further 10 km (6 miles) from town, **Simpsons Gap** is the first of a series of attractive gorges in the MacDonnells. A pretty spot, it is home to some rare local plant species. Nearby is **Standley Chasm**, a narrow, deep gorge whose sheer rock-faces glow a glorious red, particularly under the midday sun.

The large 18-m (60-ft) deep permanent waterhole within Ellery Gorge at Ellery Creek Big Hole is a good swimming spot. Serpentine Gorge, 20 km (12 miles) further west, is another narrow gorge created by an ancient river. A walking track leading to a lookout gives a fine view of its winding path.

Pushed up out of Ormiston Creek, the 300-m (985-ft) high walls of Ormiston Gorge are an awesome sight. The gorge consists of two layers of quartzite, literally doubled over each other, thus making it twice the height of others in the region.

Along Larapinta Drive is the small Aboriginal settlement of Hermannsburg, site of an 1870s Lutheran Mission which predates Alice Springs. Famous as the home of the popular Aboriginal painter Albert Namatjira (1902–59), most of the town is contained within the **Hermannsburg Historic Precinct**, which includes a museum devoted to the mission and an art gallery.

Twenty km (12 miles) south of here lies the popular **Finke Gorge National Park**, home to Palm Valley,

Sacred site of Corroboree Rock in the East MacDonnell Ranges near Alice Springs

an unusual tropical oasis in the dry heart of the country with a host of rare and ancient palm species.

On the other side of Alice Springs, the East MacDonnell Ranges boast some beautiful sites accessible via the Ross Highway. Close to town is Emily Gap, one of the most significant Aranda sites in Australia. Further east, Corroboree Rock, a strangely shaped outcrop, has a crevice once used to store sacred Aranda objects. Trephina Gorge is the most spectacular of the East MacDonnell sights, with quartzite cliffs and red river gums.

🏛 Hermannsburg Historic Precinct
Larapinta Drive. *Tel* (08) 8956 7402. ⬤ daily. ⬤ 25 Dec. 🎑 ♿

🌿 Finke Gorge National Park
🚌 Alice Springs. 🚌 Alice Springs. ℹ Alice Springs (08) 8952 5800.

Spherical boulders of the Devil's Marbles

Devil's Marbles Conservation Reserve ➎

Tel 1800 500 879. 🚌 Tennant Creek. 🚌 from Tennant Creek Tourist Information. ♿ 🎑

Approximately 104 km (65 miles) south of Tennant Creek, the Devil's Marbles Conservation Reserve comprises a collection of huge, spherical, red granite boulders, scattered across a shallow valley in the Davenport Ranges. The result of geological activity occurring 1,700 million years ago, the boulders were created when molten lava was compressed to create huge domes just below the earth's surface. Subsequent erosion of the overlying rock exposed the marbles. They are particularly beautiful at sunset.

Mining building at Battery Hill, Tennant Creek

Tennant Creek ➏

🏘 3,500. ✈ 🚌 ℹ Battery Hill Regional Centre, Peko Rd 1800 500 879.

Tennant Creek was chosen as the site of a telegraph station on the Overland Telegraph Line in the late 1800s. The town grew after gold was discovered in the area in 1932. The **Battery Hill Mining Centre** is now a working museum, crushing ore to extract the gold.

Tennant Creek today is the second-largest town in the Red Centre. Nearly 500 km (310 miles) north of Alice Springs, it is also a major stopover along the Stuart Highway, between Darwin and South Australia. Other local attractions include the recreational Mary Ann Dam, 5 km (3 miles) out of town and ideal for boating and swimming. The remote **Telegraph Station**, 12 km (8 miles) north of the town, built in 1874, is now a museum.

🏛 Battery Hill Mining Centre
Battery Hill Regional Centre, Peko Rd. *Tel* 1800 500 879. ⬤ daily. ⬤ Good Fri, 25 Dec. 🎑 ♿ 🎑

🏛 Telegraph Station
ℹ Battery Hill Regional Centre, Peko Rd 1800 500 879. ♿

Kings Canyon ➐

🚌 Alice Springs. 🚌 Alice Springs, Yulara. ℹ Alice Springs (08) 8952 5800.

The spectacular sandstone gorge of Kings Canyon, set within Watarrka National Park, has walls more than 100 m (330 ft) high that have been formed by millions of years of erosion. They contain the fossilized tracks of ancient marine creatures, and even ripplemarks of an ancient sea are visible. Several walking tracks take visitors around the rim of the gorge where there are some stunning views of the valley below. Watarrka National Park has many waterholes and areas of lush vegetation that contain more than 600 plant species. The park also provides a habitat for more than 100 bird species and 60 species of reptiles.

Rich vegetation deep in the sandstone gorge of Kings Canyon

Uluru-Kata Tjuta National Park **8**

Thorny devil

The most instantly recognizable of all Australian symbols is the huge, red monolith of Uluru (Ayers Rock). Rising high above the flat desert landscape, Uluru is one of the world's natural wonders, along with the 36 rock domes of Kata Tjuta (The Olgas) and their deep valleys and gorges. Both sights are in Uluru-Kata Tjuta National Park, 463 km (288 miles) southwest of Alice Springs, which was established in 1958 and was named as a World Heritage site in 1987 *(see pp26–7).* The whole area is sacred to Aboriginal people and, in 1985, the park was handed back to its indigenous owners and its sights reassumed their traditional names. As Aboriginal land, it is leased back to the Australian government and jointly managed with the local Anangu people. Within the park is an excellent cultural centre which details the Aboriginal lives and traditions of the area. Yulara, 12 km (7 miles) from Uluru, is the park's growing tourist resort *(see p289).*

The Maruku Gallery
This Aboriginal-owned gallery sells traditional and modern Aboriginal crafts.

Kata Tjuta's domes rise in the distance behind Uluru.

Kata Tjuta (The Olgas)
This magnificent view of Kata Tjuta's domes is from the sunset viewing area. The site has drinking water and interpretive panels giving information on local flora and fauna.

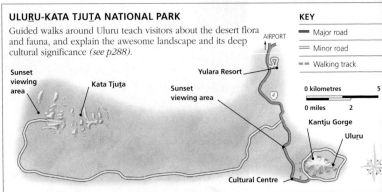

ULURU-KATA TJUTA NATIONAL PARK

Guided walks around Uluru teach visitors about the desert flora and fauna, and explain the awesome landscape and its deep cultural significance *(see p288).*

AIRPORT

Sunset viewing area

Kata Tjuta

Yulara Resort

Sunset viewing area

Kantju Gorge

Uluru

Cultural Centre

KEY

― Major road

═ Minor road

‐‐ Walking track

0 kilometres   5

0 miles   2

Olga Gorge
This scenic gorge runs between two of Kata Tjuta's huge domes. A walking track leads to a cliff face at the end where there is a rock pool and a trickling stream.

VISITORS' CHECKLIST

Hwy 4. ☒ Connellan Airport, 5 km (3 miles) N of Yulara/Ayers Rock Resort. ⓘ Cultural Centre (08) 8956 1128. ◯ daily. ◷ Ø in Cultural Centre. ♿ 🚻 🏠 🛍 www.deh.gov.au/parks/uluru

Uluru is famous for its colour changes, which range from deep red at sunrise and sunset to shiny black after rain.

Hare Wallaby
This mammal is significant to the Anangu people, who call it Mala. According to tradition, Mala people lived at Uluru and created many of the rock formations that are seen today.

DEHYDRATION IN THE DESERT

Uluru-Kata Tjuta National Park is in the heart of Australia's vast desert region. It can experience summer daytime temperatures of more than 45°C (113°F). To avoid dehydration and heat exhaustion all visitors are advised to wear hats, long-sleeved shirts with collars and sunscreen, and to avoid any strenuous activity between 10am and 4pm. Most importantly, each person should drink one litre of water per hour while walking in hot weather.

Vegetation is sparse on this desert plain except for a few areas of greenery found in sheltered spots where rainwater collects.

Mala Walk
This free, ranger-guided walk leads visitors to places created and used by the ancestral Mala people. It ends at Kantju Gorge, sacred to the Anangu, which contains a waterhole beneath a waterfall.

Exploring Uluṟu-Kata Tjuṯa National Park

Welcome to Aboriginal Land

Pukul ngaḻyanama Anangukudwards ngurakutu

Pukulpa pitjama Anangku ngurakutu

Entrance sign to Uluṟu-Kata Tjuṯa National Park

It is impossible to arrive at Uluṟu-Kata Tjuṯa National Park and not be filled with awe. The sheer size of the world's largest monolith, Uluṟu, rising from the flat desert plain, is a moving and impressive sight. Just as magical are the rounded humps of Kata Tjuṯa not far distant. All the rocks change colour from oranges and reds to purple during the day. Getting around the park, understanding some of its deep Aboriginal significance and learning about its geology, flora and fauna should not be rushed. There is much more to this fascinating area than can be seen or experienced in one day, and a two- or three-day stay is recommended.

Blue-tongued lizard basking in the sun

Tourists enjoying the Mala walk around part of the base of Uluṟu

🏞 Uluṟu (Ayers Rock)

Uluṟu, 3.6 km (2.25 miles) long and 2.4 km (1.5 miles) wide, stands 348 m (1,142 ft) above the plains. It is made from a single piece of sandstone which extends 5 km (3 miles) beneath the desert surface. Besides its immense Aboriginal cultural significance, Uluṟu is an outstanding natural phenomenon, best observed by watching its changing colours at dusk and taking a guided walk at the rock's base.

There are a number of walking trails around Uluṟu. The three-hour, 9.5-km (6-mile) tour around the base gives the greatest sense of its size and majesty. Sacred sights en route are fenced off, and entering is an offence. The Mala (hare wallaby) walk takes in several caves, some with rock art. The Liru (snake) walk starts at the cultural centre, with Aboriginal tour guides explaining how they use bush materials in their daily lives. The Kuniya (python) walk visits the Mutijulu waterhole on the southern side of Uluṟu where local Aṉangu people tell creation stories and display art describing various

legends. Details of all walks can be found at the Uluṟu-Kata Tjuṯa Cultural Centre.

🏞 Kata Tjuṯa (The Olgas)

Kata Tjuṯa, meaning "many heads", is a collection of massive rounded rock domes, 42 km (25 miles) to the west of Uluṟu. Beyond lies a vast, remote desert; permits from the Central Land Council *(see*

p262), 4WDs and full travel survival kits are needed in this inhospitable land.

Kata Tjuṯa is not one large rock; it is a system of gorges and valleys that you can walk around, making it a haunting quiet and spiritual place. To the Aṉangu people, it is of equal significance to Uluṟu, but fewer stories about it can be told as they are restricted to initiated tribal men. The tallest rock, Mount Olga, is 546 m (1,790 ft) high, nearly 200 m (660 ft) higher than Uluṟu. There are two recommended walking trails. The Valley of the Winds walk takes about three hours and wanders through several deep gorges. This walk is partially closed when the temperature exceeds 36°C (97°F).

CLIMBING ULURU

The climbing of Uluṟu by the chain-rope path that has been in place since the 1960s is a contentious issue. Physically, it is a steep, 1.6-km (1-mile) climb in harsh conditions, and several tourists die each year from heart attacks or falls. Culturally, the route to the top follows the sacred path taken by the ancestral Mala (hare wallaby) men for important ceremonies. The Aṉangu ask that visitors respect their wishes and do not climb the rock. Despite increasing numbers of visitors to Uluṟu, fewer people climb each year.

If you do decide to climb, the ascent takes about two hours. Climbing the rock is banned for the remainder of the day if the temperature at any point of the climb reaches 36°C (97°F). A dawn climb is most popular.

Sign warning tourists of the dangers of climbing Uluṟu

THE ANANGU OF ULURU

Archaeological evidence suggests that Aboriginal people have lived at Uluru for at least 22,000 years and that both Uluru and Kata Tjuta have long been places of enormous ceremonial and cultural significance to a number of Aboriginal tribes.

The traditional owners of Uluru and Kata Tjuta are the Anangu people. They believe that both sites were formed during the creation period by ancestral spirits who also gave them the laws and rules of society that they live by today. The Anangu believe they are direct descendants of these ancestral beings and that, as such, they are responsible for the protection and management of these lands.

The Anangu Aborigines performing a traditional dance

The Olga Gorge (Walpa Gorge) walk leads up the pretty Olga Gorge to its dead-end cliff face and a rock pool. Walkers here may spot the small brown spinifex bird or the thorny devil spiked lizard.

🏛 Uluru-Kata Tjuta Cultural Centre

Tel (08) 8956 1128.
☐ daily. 📷 ♿

Near to the base of Uluru is an award-winning cultural centre, with multilingual displays, videos and exhibitions. It is an excellent introduction to the park and well worth visiting before exploring the rock and its surrounding area. The Nintiringkupai display focuses on the history and management of Uluru-Kata Tjuta National Park and includes up-to-date brochures and information on walking trails, sights and tours. The Tjukurpa display, with its art, sounds and videos, is a good introduction to the complex system of Anangu beliefs and laws. Attached to the cultural centre is the Aboriginal-owned Maruku Arts and Craft shop, where artists are at work and dancers and musicians give performances for the tourists. The traditional art, on bark and canvas, tells the story of Uluru Tjukurpa legends.

Ayers Rock Resort

Yulara Drive. 📞 *(08) 8957 7377.*
www.ayersrockresort.com.au
Yulara is an environmentally friendly, modern tourist village well equipped to cater for the 500,000 annual visitors. Nestling between the desert dunes 20 km (12 miles) north of Uluru and just outside the national park boundary, it serves as a comfortable, green and relaxing base for exploring Uluru and Kata Tjuta. The resort offers all standards of accommodation, from five-star luxury to backpacker accommodation and camping grounds, and is the only option for those who want to stay in the immediate vicinity (see pp497).

The visitors' centre at Yulara has information about the park and its geology, flora and fauna. It also sells souvenirs and helps to arrange tours with the licensed operators in the park. Every day at 7:30am there is a free, early morning guided walk through the wonderful native garden of the Sails in the Desert Hotel (see p497). Each evening at the Amphitheatre there is an hour-long concert of Aboriginal music featuring a variety of indigenous instruments, including the didgeridoo. A Night Sky Show is also available, and this describes both the Anangu and ancient Greek stories of the stars.

Yulara also has a shopping centre, which includes a post office, bank and supermarket, and many different restaurants and outdoor eating options (see p544). Other facilities include a childcare centre for children up to the age of eight.

Aerial view of Yulara Resort, with Uluru in the distance

WESTERN
AUSTRALIA

INTRODUCING WESTERN AUSTRALIA 292–297

PERTH AND THE SOUTHWEST 298–319

NORTH OF PERTH AND
THE KIMBERLEY 320–331

Western Australia at a Glance

The huge state of Western Australia encompasses a land mass of more than 2,500,000 sq km (1,000,000 sq miles). In recent years, the state's popularity as a tourist destination has increased, with large numbers of visitors drawn to its many areas of extreme natural beauty. The landscape ranges from giant karri forests, imposing mountains and meadows of wildflowers to vast expanses of untamed wilderness with ancient gorges and rock formations. The coastline has an abundance of beaches, ideal for surfing, and some stunning offshore reefs. In the east, great deserts stretch to the state border. The capital, Perth, is home to 80 per cent of the state's population, but there are many historic towns scattered around the southwest, such as the gold field settlements of Kalgoorlie and Coolgardie.

Shark Bay World Heritage and Marine Park *is Australia's westernmost point. Visitors flock to this protected area to watch the dolphins swim in the waters close to the shore* (see pp326–7).

Perth *is Australia's most isolated yet most modern state capital. Gleaming skyscrapers, an easy-going atmosphere and its coastal setting make it a popular destination* (see pp302–7).

Fremantle's *heyday as a major port was at the end of the 19th century. Many of its historic buildings remain. Today the town is renowned for its crafts markets* (see pp310–11).

◁ **Perth city skyline at night**

Karijini National Park *is in the Pilbara region and is a spectacular landscape of gorges, pools and waterfalls. The area is particularly popular with experienced hikers; guided tours are also available for more novice bushwalkers (see p329).*

Purnululu (Bungle Bungle) National Park *is one of Australia's most famous natural sights, with its multi-coloured rock domes. Access is limited, but helicopter flights offer views of the area (see p331).*

NORTH OF PERTH AND
THE KIMBERLEY
(see pp320–31)

Wave Rock *is 15 m (50 ft) high, 110 m (360 ft) long and is so named because its formation resembles a breaking wave. The illusion is further enhanced by years' worth of water stains running down its face (see p318).*

PERTH AND THE
SOUTHWEST
(see pp298–319)

Kalgoorlie *made its name in the 1890s when gold was discovered in the region. Much of its 19th-century architecture has been preserved (see p318).*

0 km   100

0 miles   100

Wildflowers of Western Australia

Western Australia is truly the nation's wildflower state. In the spring, from August to November, more than 11,000 species of flowers burst into brilliantly coloured blooms, carpeting deserts, plains, farmland and forests with blazing reds, yellows, pinks and blues.

A staggering 75 per cent of these flowers are unique to the state, giving it one of the world's richest floras. It is home to such remarkable plants as the kangaroo paw, the cowslip orchid and the carnivorous Albany pitcher plant, as well as giant jarrah and karri forests.

The elegant kangaroo paw *looks exactly like its name suggests. The state's floral emblem, it has many different species and mostly grows in coastal heath and dry woodland areas.*

WHEN AND WHERE TO SEE THE WILDFLOWERS

Bushwalking or driving among the flower carpets of Western Australia is an experience not to be missed. Most of the wildflowers bloom in spring, but exactly when depends on their location in this vast state. The wildflower season begins in the northern Pilbara in July and culminates in the magnificent flowering around the Stirling Ranges and the south coast in late October and November.

The Albany pitcher plant *grows near coastal estuaries around Albany in the southwest. One of the world's largest carnivorous plants, it traps and devours insects in its sticky hairs.*

The magnificent royale hakea *is one of many hakea species in Western Australia. It is found on the coast near Esperance and in Fitzgerald River National Park.*

Red flowering gum *trees in the Stirling Ranges burst into bright red flowers every November, attracting honey bees.*

The cowslip orchid *is a bright yellow orchid with red streaks and five main petals. It can usually be found in October, in the dramatic Stirling Ranges region.*

Much of Western Australia is arid, dusty outback country where the only vegetation is dry bush shrubs and, after rainfall, wildflowers.

Many wild flowers possess an incredible ability to withstand even the driest, hottest ground.

Leschenaultia biloba *is a brilliant blue, bell-shaped flower found in jarrah forests near Collie, or in drier bush and plain country where it flowers in carpets of blue.*

The boab (baobab) tree *is a specimen related to the African baobab. Growing in the rocky plains of the Kimberley (see pp330–31), it holds a great deal of water in its swollen trunk and can grow many metres in circumference.*

The bright daisy flowers of the everlastings come in a host of creams, pinks, yellows, oranges and reds.

GIANTS OF THE WESTERN AUSTRALIAN FOREST

It is not only the native flowers that are special to Western Australia. So, too, are the trees – especially the towering jarrah and karri eucalypts of the southern forests. A major hardwood timber industry, harvesting the jarrah and karri, remains in the state's southwest near Manjimup and Pemberton *(see p315)*. Today, however, thousands of trees are preserved in national parks such as Shannon and Walpole-Nornalup, which has a walkway high in the trees for visitors.

Giant karri trees *grow to a height of 85 m (280 ft). They live for up to 300 years, reaching their maximum height after 100 years.*

EVERLASTING FLOWERS

Native to Australia, everlastings carpet vast areas in many parts of Western Australia. Especially prolific in the southeast, they can also be seen from the roadside in the north, stretching as far as the eye can see.

Everlastings are so called because the petals stay attached to the flower even after it has died.

The scarlet banksia (see p454), *is one of 41 banksia species found in Western Australia. It is named after Sir Joseph Banks, the botanist who first noted this unusual tree and its flower in 1770.*

Sturt's desert pea *is actually South Australia's floral emblem, but is also prolific in the dry inland areas of Western Australia. Its bright flowers spring up after rain in the deserts, sometimes after lying dormant for years.*

The Kimberley

Dingo cave painting

One of the last truly remote regions in Australia, the Kimberley in north-western Australia covers 421,000 sq km (165,000 sq miles), yet has a population of less than 25,000. Geologically it is one of the oldest regions on earth. Its rocks formed up to 2,000 million years ago, with little landscape disturbance since. Aboriginal people have lived here for thousands of years, but this unique land has been a tourist attraction only since the 1980s.

KEY

━━ Highway

━━ Major road

══ Unsealed road

── National park boundary

THE BUNGLE BUNGLES

The tiger-striped beehive mountains that comprise the Bungle Bungle range were only discovered by tourists in the 1980s. These great geological and scenic wonders are now protected in Purnululu National Park *(see p331)*. The large, weathered sandstone domes are most easily viewed by air from Kununurra or Halls Creek, but visitors who make the effort to explore this 4WD-only park will also encounter some stunning narrow gorges and clear pools.

The black and orange moulded domes of the Bungle Bungles

Windjana Gorge National Park is one of the three stunning Devonian Reef national parks *(see p331)*.

The Great Northern Highway is a sealed road that runs from the Northern Territory border to Broome and Perth beyond.

Cape Leveque

Charnley River

Isdell River

King Sound

Derby

Windjana Gorge National Park

Meda River

Gibb River Road

Tunnel Creek National Park

Geikie Gorge National Park

0 kilometres 100

0 miles 100

Broome

GREAT SANDY DESERT

Fitzroy River

Fitzroy Crossing

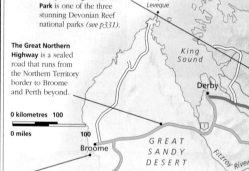

Cable Beach *at Broome attracts many visitors with its vast white beaches and gentle surf. Tourism in the Kimberley is still in its infancy, but some 50,000 tourists now enjoy Broome's tropical atmosphere each year.*

The Cockburn Ranges *have deep, inaccessible caves and sandstone cliffs separating the summit from the surrounding plains. The ranges tower above the crocodile-infested Pentecost River on the Gibb River Road. As with many sites in the region, they hold great Aboriginal significance.*

THE ABORIGINES OF THE KIMBERLEY

Legend suggests that the first Aborigines arrived on the continent, near Broome, 200,000 years ago *(see p47)*. While this view has yet to be validated by scientific evidence, the fact that many of the "songlines" *(see p31)* marked by landmarks and ceremonial sites all end or start around the Kimberley certainly suggests that the area has seen a very long period of human habitation.

Two-thirds of the region's population remains Aboriginal, and Aboriginal culture here is one of the most traditional in Australia. Local Aboriginal communities equip their children with a strong identity to help them cope with the demands of living in a mixed-race society.

Aboriginal art in the Kimberley differs from most other parts of Australia. Dot art does not predominate; instead there are the outstanding Wandjina figures of the central Kimberley, and the object paintings of the Purnululu community based near the Bungle Bungles.

The mysterious *Wandjina figures can be seen throughout the Kimberley region.*

Aboriginal rock art *in the Kimberley has now been dated back 125,000 years, 80,000 years earlier than previously thought.*

Gibb River Road is a rough highway which is used by locals and adventurous travellers.

Emma Gorge *is one of hundreds of deep, cool waterholes hidden across the Kimberley. Located near El Questro Station, it was made by waterfalls cascading off the red sandstone plateau into gorges and valleys below.*

PERTH AND THE SOUTHWEST

Western Australia's pretty capital, Perth, is the most isolated city in the world, closer to Southeast Asia than it is to any other Australian city. The state's stunning southern region takes in magnificent forests and diverse coastal scenery. To the east, the vast Nullarbor Plain covers more than 250,000 sq km (100,000 sq miles), and rolling wheat fields lead to the arid interior and the gold fields.

Aborigines have lived in the southern region of Western Australia for at least 30,000 years. However, within 20 years of the settlement of the state's first European colony, in 1829, most Aboriginal groups had been either forcibly ejected from the region, imprisoned or stricken by European diseases.

Europeans visited the southern part of the state as early as 1696, but it was not until 1826 that British colonist Captain James Stirling arrived in the Swan River area, declaring the Swan River Colony, later Perth, in 1829. Convicts arrived in 1850 and helped to build public buildings and the colony's infrastructure, until transportation to Western Australia ceased in 1868.

In the 1890s, gold strikes in Coolgardie and Kalgoorlie led to a wave of prosperity in the region. Many ornate late Victorian-style buildings were erected, many of which are still standing.

The beginning of the 20th century saw huge changes: a telegraph cable was laid connecting Perth with South Africa and London, and, in 1917, the railway arrived to join Kalgoorlie with the eastern states. In the 1920s, immigrants and returning World War I servicemen were drafted to the area to clear and develop land under the Group Settlement Scheme. Much of the land, however, was intractable and many people abandoned it.

Today, Perth and the Southwest are fast becoming popular international tourist destinations. Blessed with superb beaches and a glorious climate, the region has everything to offer visitors from climbing the tallest fire-lookout tree in the country to whale-watching along the coast. World-class wineries abound in the Margaret River region and, in springtime, vast tracts of the south are covered with wildflowers.

Dramatic beauty of the Stirling Ranges rising from the plains in the southwest of the state

◁ **The glittering night skyline of Western Australia's vibrant state capital, Perth**

Exploring Perth and the Southwest

The city of Perth lies on the Swan River, just 10 km (6 miles) from where it flows into the Indian Ocean. The coastal plain on which it stands is bordered to the north and west by the Darling Range, beyond which lie the region's wheat fields. To the south is a diverse landscape: forests with some of the tallest trees on earth, mountains that dramatically change colour during the course of each day and a spectacular coastline. Inland are the gold fields that kept the colony alive in the 1890s; beyond lies the Nullarbor Plain, bordering the raging Southern Ocean.

GETTING AROUND

Perth's public transport is fast and reliable, and travel within the city centre is free. Westrail, Greyhound and Skywest (the state's airline) offer rail, coach and air services to many of the region's towns. Distances are not overwhelming, so travelling by car allows visits to the many national parks in the area. The arterial routes are fast roads often used by gigantic road trains. However, there are many tourist routes which lead to places of interest and great natural beauty. Some national parks have unsealed roads, and a few are accessible only by 4WD.

SIGHTS AT A GLANCE

Albany 11
Bridgetown 7
Bunbury 4
Busselton 5
Denmark 10
Fremantle pp310–11 3
Manjimup 8
Margaret River 6
Northam 14
Pemberton 9
Perth pp302–7 1
Rottnest Island pp308–9 2
Stirling Range National Park 12
York 13

The Goldfields and Nullarbor Plain *See pp318–19*
Esperance 18
Kalgoorlie-Boulder 16
Norseman 17
Nullarbor Plain 19
Wave Rock 15

SEE ALSO

- ***Where to Stay*** pp497–500
- ***Where to Eat*** pp544–6

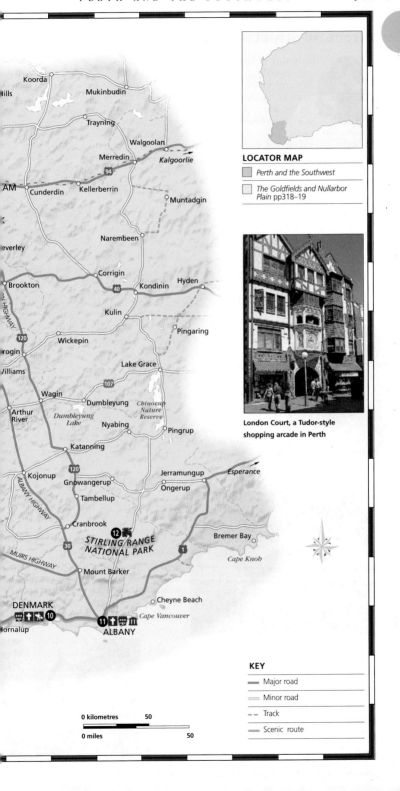

Koorda
Mukinbudin
Hills
Trayning
Walgoolan
Merredin *Kalgoorlie*
94
AM Cunderdin Kellerberrin
Muntadgin
everley
Narembeen
Brookton Corrigin Kondinin Hyden
40
Kulin
Pingaring
rogin Wickepin
120
Williams Lake Grace
107
Wagin Dumbleyung *Chinocup Nature Reserve*
Arthur River *Dumbleyung Lake* Nyabing
Katanning Pingrup
Kojonup *Esperance*
120 Gnowangerup Jerramungup
Tambellup Ongerup
Cranbrook
12 Bremer Bay
30 STIRLING RANGE NATIONAL PARK *Cape Knob*
1
Mount Barker
DENMARK Cheyne Beach
10 *Cape Vancouver*
ornalup **11** ALBANY

LOCATOR MAP

▢ *Perth and the Southwest*

▢ *The Goldfields and Nullarbor Plain pp318–19*

London Court, a Tudor-style shopping arcade in Perth

KEY

— Major road

— Minor road

-- Track

— Scenic route

0 kilometres 50

0 miles 50

Street-by-Street: Perth ❶

Fire Brigade badge

The history of Perth has been one of building and rebuilding. The makeshift houses of the first settlers were soon replaced with more permanent buildings, many erected by convicts in the latter half of the 19th century. The gold rush of the 1890s and the mining boom of the 1960s and 1970s brought waves of prosperity, encouraging the citizens to replace their older buildings with more prestigious symbols of the state's wealth. As a result, much of the early city has gone, but a few traces remain, hidden between skyscrapers or in the city's public parks.

Swan Bells

Barrack Square

Supreme Court Gardens

★ St George's Anglican Cathedral
This Victorian Gothic Revival-style cathedral, built in the late 19th century, has a fine rose window (see p304).

Government House
Hidden behind walls and trees, the original residence of the state governor was built by convicts between 1859 and 1864. The building's patterned brickwork is typical of the period.

The Deanery
Built in 1859, the Deanery was originally the residence of the Dean of St George's. It now houses the Cathedral administration.

STAR SIGHTS

★ Perth Mint

★ St George's Anglican Cathedral

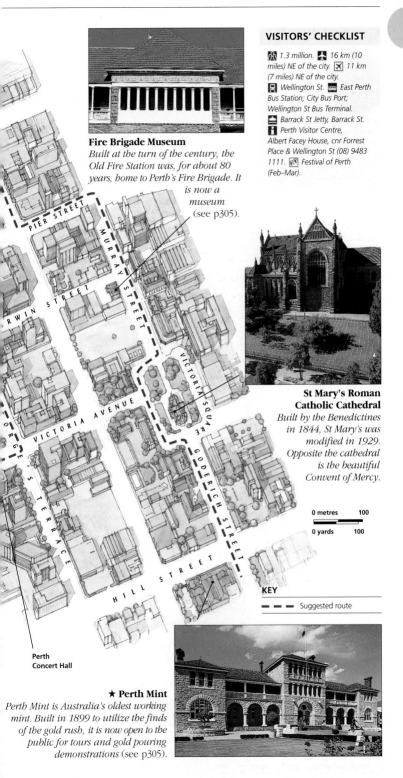

Fire Brigade Museum
Built at the turn of the century, the Old Fire Station was, for about 80 years, home to Perth's Fire Brigade. It is now a museum (see p305).

VISITORS' CHECKLIST

1.3 million. 16 km (10 miles) NE of the city. 11 km (7 miles) NE of the city. Wellington St. East Perth Bus Station; City Bus Port; Wellington St Bus Terminal. Barrack St Jetty, Barrack St. Perth Visitor Centre, Albert Facey House, cnr Forrest Place & Wellington St (08) 9483 1111. Festival of Perth (Feb–Mar).

St Mary's Roman Catholic Cathedral
Built by the Benedictines in 1844, St Mary's was modified in 1929. Opposite the cathedral is the beautiful Convent of Mercy.

0 metres 100

0 yards 100

KEY

– – – Suggested route

Perth Concert Hall

★ Perth Mint
Perth Mint is Australia's oldest working mint. Built in 1899 to utilize the finds of the gold rush, it is now open to the public for tours and gold pouring demonstrations (see p305).

Central Perth

Bronze plaque in St George's Cathedral

Perth is a relatively small and quiet city compared with those on the east coast. Its main commercial and shopping areas can be easily explored on foot. The city's atmosphere is brisk but not hurried, and traffic is by no means congested. Redevelopment projects in the 1970s brought skyscrapers and more roads, but they also made space for city parks and courtyards lined with cafés and shady trees. The city centre is bordered to the south and east by a wide stretch of the Swan River known as Perth Water, and to the north lies Northbridge, Perth's restaurant and entertainment centre.

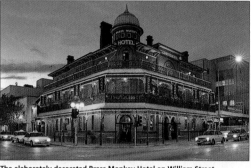

The elaborately decorated Brass Monkey Hotel on William Street

Exploring Central Perth

St Georges Terrace is Perth's main commercial street. At its western end stands Parliament House, and in front of this is Barracks Archway. Further east, the Cloisters, built in 1850 as a school, boast some fine decorative brickwork. Nearby is the Old Perth Boys' School, a tiny one-storey building that was Perth's first school for boys.

Perth's shopping centre lies between William and Barrack streets. It is a maze of arcades, plazas and elevated walkways. The main areas are Hay Street Mall and Murray Street Mall. On the corner of William Street and St Georges Terrace lies the Town Hall (1870), close to the site where Perth was founded.

Beyond the railway tracks is Northbridge, the focus of much of Perth's nightlife. James Street is lined with many restaurants, cafés and food halls offering a variety of ethnic cuisines. The ornate façade of the former Brass Monkey Hotel (now a pub), is a perfect example of colonial gold rush architecture.

🐎 Barracks Archway

Cnr St Georges Terrace & Elder St.
Barracks Archway is all that remains of the 1863 barracks that once housed the soldiers who were brought in to police the convict population.

🏛 Perth Cultural Centre

James St. **Tel** (08) 9224 7300.
◻ 10am–5pm daily. ● 25 Dec, 1pm–5pm 26 Dec , Good Fri, 1pm–5pm 25 Apr. ♿
The Perth Cultural Centre is a pedestrianized complex on

Perth Cultural Centre plaza

several levels, with garden areas. The centre is home to the Art Gallery of Western Australia, which contains a collection of modern Aboriginal and Australian art, and some European and Asian pieces. The Perth Institute of Contemporary Art (PICA) and the State Library are also here.

🏛 Western Australian Museum

Francis St. **Tel** (08) 9427 2700. ◻ 9:30am–5pm daily. ● 1pm–5pm 25 Apr, Good Fri, 25 Dec, 1pm–5pm 26 Dec, 1 Jan. ♿ limited.
In the same area as the Perth Cultural Centre stands the Western Australian Museum complex. Among its buildings are the Old Perth Gaol (1856), with exhibitions on life in the original Swan River colony, and Roe Street Cottage (1863), one of the colony's first homes. The museum's jewel is its exhibition entitled "Patterns of Life in a Vast Land", which covers the history, lifestyle and culture of Western Australian Aborigines and the work of archaeologists in the state.

⛪ St George's Anglican Cathedral

Cnr Pier St & St Georges Terrace (enter from Cathedral Ave).
Tel (08) 9325 5766. ◻ daily. ♿
St George's Cathedral, consecrated in 1888, was only the second permanent Anglican place of worship in Perth. Between 1841 and 1845 Perth's first Anglican church was built, in Classical Revival style, on the site of the existing cathedral, but in 1875 a more prestigious place of worship was required and the old church was demolished after St George's was built, but some artifacts remain, including some of the jarrah pews and the carved eagle lectern. This Gothic Revival building has some notable features including the intricate English alabaster *reredos* at the base of the east window, the modernistic medallions cast for the Stations of the Cross and some original 19th-century Russian icons.

Western façade of St George's Cathedral showing rose window

🏛 Perth Mint

310 Hay St. **Tel** *(08) 9421 7277.*
🕙 *9am–4pm Mon–Fri, 9am–1pm Sat–Sun.* ⬤ *Good Fri, 25 April, 25 Dec, 1 Jan.* 📷 ♿

Perth Mint was opened in 1899, under British control, to refine gold from Western Australia's gold fields to make British sovereigns and half-sovereigns. Although it no longer produces coins for circulation, the mint produces proof coins and specialist pure precious-metal coins, making it Australia's oldest operating mint. The mint contains a museum with coins, precious metal exhibits and displays on gold mining and refining. Every hour a "Gold Pour" takes place in the Melting House that has been in operation over a century.

🏛 Fire Brigade Museum

Cnr Murray & Irwin sts.
Tel *(08) 9323 9468.*
🕙 *10am–3pm Mon–Fri.*
⬤ *public hols.* ♿

Perth City Fire Brigade moved from this, its original home, to a much larger site in 1979. The old fire station is now a fascinating museum charting the history of the fire service in Perth and Western Australia, and a fire safety centre. Educational exhibits here include some well-preserved old fire appliances and reconstructions showing the original use of various rooms in the station.

🏛 Swan Bells Tower

Barrack St Jetty. **Tel** *(08) 9218 8183.*
🕙 *10am–4:30pm daily.*
⬤ *Good Fri, 25 Dec.* 📷 ♿
www.swanbells.com.au

Opened in 2001, and one of Perth's main attractions, the Swan Bells Tower contains 12 bells from St Martin-in-the-Fields, in England. There are displays and exhibitions inside the tower and an observation deck. The bells ring daily, except Wednesday and Friday, when there is a bell handling demonstration instead.

Perth Fire Station's original fire bell

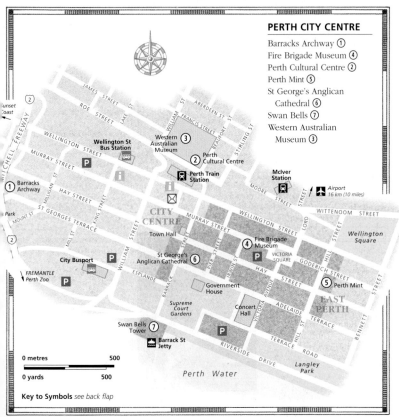

PERTH CITY CENTRE

Barracks Archway ①
Fire Brigade Museum ④
Perth Cultural Centre ②
Perth Mint ⑤
St George's Anglican Cathedral ⑥
Swan Bells ⑦
Western Australian Museum ③

0 metres 500
0 yards 500

Key to Symbols *see back flap*

Exploring Greater Perth

Kings Park memorial

Beyond the city centre, Greater Perth covers the Darling Range in the northeast to the Indian Ocean in the west. It has several large parks, including Kings Park, overlooking the river. On the coast, beaches stretch from Hillarys Boat Harbour in the north to Fremantle in the south *(see pp310–11)*. Perth's suburbs are accessible by train, local bus or car.

SIGHTS AT A GLANCE

AQWA **6**
Hills Forest **3**
Kings Park **1**
Museum of Childhood **7**
Perth Zoo **5**
Sunset Coast **2**
Whiteman Park **4**

KEY

▢	Central Perth
▢	Greater Perth
═	Highway
▬	Major road
═	Minor road

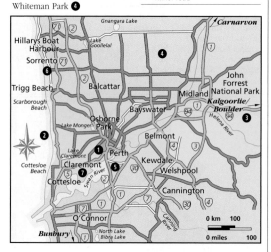

Dolphin performing for crowds at AQWA, north of Perth

➤ AQWA, Aquarium of Western Australia

Hillarys Boat Harbour, Southside Drive, Sorrento. **Tel** *(08) 9447 7500.* ⏲ *10am–5pm daily.* ● *25 Dec.* 🅿 & **www**.aqwa.com.au

At Hillarys Boat Harbour, to the north of Perth's Sunset Coast, this is a magnificent aquarium complex. A transparent submerged tunnel allows visitors to observe native sea creatures, including sharks and stingrays. There is a Touch Pool, where rays and sharks can be stroked. The denizens of the outside seal pool never fail to delight visitors of all ages.

🏛 Museum of Childhood

Edith Cowan University, Claremont Campus, Bay Rd, Claremont. **Tel** *(08) 9442 1373.* ⏲ *10am–4pm Mon–Fri.* ● *public hols.* 🅿 &

In the suburb of Claremont, this engaging museum is dedicated to the history of childhood in Australia. Its comprehensive collection exhibits toys and games, and details schooling and home life.

📷 Sunset Coast

Via West Coast Hwy.

Perth's Sunset Coast is lined with 30 km (20 miles) of white sandy beaches, many of them virtually deserted during the week. There are beaches to suit all tastes. Cottesloe Beach, at the southern end, is fringed with grassland and trees, and offers safe swimming and good services, making it popular with families, as is Sorrento Beach in the north.

🌿 Kings Park

Fraser Ave, West Perth.
Tel *(08) 9480 3600.* ⏲ *daily.* &
www.kpbg.wa.gov.au

Established at the end of the 19th century, Kings Park is 400 ha (1,000 acres) of both wild and cultivated parkland. Situated on Mount Eliza, it offers fine views of the city and the Swan River. Most of the park is bushland, which can be seen from the top of the DNA Lookout Tower, the park's highest point. There are many trails.

A landscaped area on the eastern side includes the Botanic Gardens and a series of artificial ponds and waterfalls. The War Memorial on Anzac Bluff is dedicated to the Western Australians who died in the two world wars.

The Minmara Gun Gun and Pioneer Women's Memorial are monuments to the women who helped build the Swan River Colony and, later, the state.

Bronze statue of a mother and child in Kings Park Botanic Gardens

Scarborough Beach is very popular with surfers, but it is for experienced swimmers only as strong currents can make it dangerous on windy days. Trigg Beach just above Scarborough is also a good surfing spot. Just north of Cottesloe, Swanbourne Beach is a naturist beach.

Many of the city's beaches have no shade whatsoever and Perth residents are constantly advised that the sun's rays, unshielded due to the hole in the ozone layer, can burn within minutes. Beachgoers are strongly advised to take sunscreen, a hat, T-shirt and sun umbrella.

Students admiring a magnificent tiger in Perth Zoo

Surfing on Cottesloe Beach

✂ Perth Zoo
20 Labouchere Rd. **Tel** (08) 9474 0444. ◯ 9am–5pm daily. 🈂 🅰
www.perthzoo.wa.gov.au
In South Perth, a ferry-ride away from the city centre, lies Perth Zoo. Dedicated to conservation, it has all the features of an international-standard zoo, here delightfully set amid pretty gardens. Attractions include a very interesting Nocturnal House, a wildlife park and an African savannah exhibit.

🍂 Hills Forest
Via Great Western Hwy.
Only 30 minutes' drive from Central Perth, Hills Forest lies in the Darling Range and offers a wide range of bush-related activities. Conserved since 1919 as the catchment area for the Mundaring Reservoir, which provided water for the southern gold fields in the 19th century *(see p55)*, Hills Forest is now managed as a conservation and recreation area. It is well served with barbecue and picnic areas and camp sites. At Mundaring Weir landscaped gardens are a lovely backdrop for picnics. On the northern edge of the forest is John Forrest National Park, Western Australia's first national park. It consists of woodland and heathland with trails leading to beautiful pools and waterfalls, including Hovea Falls.

🍂 Whiteman Park
Lord St, Whiteman. **Tel** (08) 9249 2446. ◯ 8:30am–6pm daily. 🅿 🅰
Northeast of the city centre lies popular Whiteman Park. Visitors can tour the park on a 1920s tram or by train. A craft village displays local craftsmanship and there is also a motor museum with a collection of vehicles from the last 100 years. As well as an emu and kangaroo enclosure, there is also a museum displaying farm machinery and a café offering refreshments.

A horse-drawn wagon taking visitors on a tour of Whiteman Park

Rottnest Island ❷

Less than 20 km (12 miles) west of Fremantle lies the idyllic island of Rottnest. Settled by Europeans in 1831, it was used as an Aboriginal prison between 1838 and 1902. In 1917, in recognition of its scenic beauty and rich bird life, the island became a protected area and today it is a popular tourist destination. Rottnest's oldest settlement, Thomson Bay, dates from the 1840s. The island's other settlements, all built in the 20th century, are found at Longreach Bay, Geordie Bay and Kingstown. Rottnest's rugged coastline comprises beaches, coves and reefs – ideal for many water-based activities – salt lakes and several visible shipwrecks. Private cars are not allowed on the island, so the only way to get around is by bicycle or bus, or on foot.

Aerial View of Rottnest
Rottnest is 12 km (7.5 miles) long, 4.5 km (3 miles) wide, and is governed by strict conservation regulations.

City of York Bay was named after Rottnest's most tragic shipwreck. In 1899, a sea captain mistook a lighthouse flare for a pilot's signal and headed towards the rocks.

Rottnest Lighthouse
The lighthouse on Wadjemup Hill was built in 1895. Wadjemup is the Aboriginal name for the island.

Rocky Bay
Overlooked by the sandy Lady Edeline beach, this popular, picturesque bay also contains the wreck of the barque Mira Flores *which sank in 1886.*

Strickland Bay
was named after Sir Gerald Strickland, governor of Rottnest from 1909 to 1912, and is a prime surfing spot.

0 metres		1000
0 yards		1000

Cape Vlamingh Lookout
Named after Dutch explorer Willem de Vlamingh, Rottnest's most famous early European visitor, this lookout stands at the furthest tip of the island, 10.5 km (6.5 miles) from Thomson Bay. The view is spectacular.

KEY

═══	Minor road
– –	Paths and trails
🏕	Camp site
🏕	Picnic area
✈	Aerodrome
⛴	Ferry
ℹ	Tourist information
⚹	Viewpoint

The Rottnest Hotel
*With its turrets and
crenellations, this
was built in 1864 as
the state governor's
summer residence.
Known locally as
the Quokka Arms,
it is now a hotel.*

VISITORS' CHECKLIST

ℹ️ *Visitors' Centre, Main Jetty (08)
9372 9752.* 🚢 *from Perth,
Fremantle, Hillarys Boat Harbour.*
♿ 🏕 📷 🍴 🛏 🖥
www.rottnest.wa.gov.au

The Basin is the most
popular beach on Rottnest
Island, particularly with families
camping with children, as it is
easily accessible on foot from
Thomson Bay.

The Rottnest Museum is
housed in the old granary,
which dates from 1857.
Exhibits cover the island's
geology, its many ship-
wrecks, flora and fauna,
and memorabilia of the
early settlers and convicts.

Little Parakeet Bay is
popular with snorkellers.
The bay is also an excellent
spot to see the rock parrots
after which it is named.

Thomson
Bay
Settlement

Geordie/
Longreach
Settlement

Lake Baghdad

*Herschell
Lake*

PERTH

*Serpentine
Lake*

*Government
House Lake*

● Kingstown

Henrietta Rocks are
a hazardous place for
shipping. No less than
three ships have been
wrecked in the waters
off this point.

Mabel Cove

Oliver Hill
*At this lookout stand two 9.2-inch
(23.5-cm) guns, brought here for
coastal defence purposes in 1937,
but obsolete since the end of World
War II. A railway to the hill has been
renovated recently by volunteers.*

THE QUOKKA

When de Vlamingh first visited Rottnest in 1696,
he noted animals somewhat bigger than a cat, with
dark fur. Thinking they were a species of rat, he
called the island the "rats' nest". In fact the animals
were a type of wallaby, called
quokkas by the Aborigines.
Although there is a small
mainland population in
Western Australia, this is the
best place to see these timid
creatures in areas of
undergrowth. On Rottnest
such habitat is scarce, and
they are often visible at
dusk. Quokkas are wild
and should not be fed.

Fremantle ❸

Fremantle is one of Western Australia's most historic cities. A wealth of 19th-century buildings remains, including superb examples from the gold rush period. Founded on the Indian Ocean in 1829, at the mouth of the Swan River, Fremantle was intended to be a port for the new colony, but was only used as such when an artificial harbour was dredged at the end of the 19th century. The town still has thriving harbours and, in 1987, it hosted the America's Cup. Many sites were renovated for the event, and street cafés and restaurants sprang up.

Anchor from the Maritime Museum

Busy fruit and vegetable stall in the Fremantle Markets

Twelve-sided Round House

⛫ The Round House
10 Arthur Head Rd. *Tel* (08) 9336 6897. ⏲ 10:30am–3:30pm daily. ♿
Built in 1830, the Round House is Fremantle's oldest building. It was the town's first gaol and, in 1844, site of the colony's first hanging. Its cells overlook a small courtyard. Beneath the gaol is a tunnel, dug in 1837, which allowed whalers to transfer their cargo easily from the jetty to the High Street.

To the left of the site, where the port's first courthouse once stood, there are clear views across Bathers Bay to Rottnest Island *(see pp308–9)*.

🏛 Western Australian Maritime Museum
Cnr Cliff St & Marine Terrace. *Tel* (08) 9431 8444. ⏲ 9:30am–5pm daily. ● Good Fri, 25 Dec. **Donation.** ♿ www.musuem.wa.gov.au
This museum's most prized possession is a reconstruction of part of the hull of the Dutch East Indiaman *Batavia* from timbers discovered at the site of its wreck off the Abrolhos Islands in 1628 *(see p324)*. The exhibit tells the story of the shipwreck and mutiny of the vessel and gives an insight into life on board. The museum has also reconstructed a stone arch from blocks found in the coral near the wreck, apparently cut in Holland and meant to be erected in Jakarta, Indonesia, the ship's original destination.

The museum's curators research, locate and explore the many shipwrecks in this part of the Indian Ocean. On display are beautiful and sometimes valuable salvaged items.

Another popular exhibit is the submarine HMAS *Ovens*, which can be toured every half hour throughout the day.

🛒 Fremantle Markets
Cnr South Terrace & Henderson St. *Tel* (08) 9335 2515. ⏲ Fri–Sun, public hols. ● Good Fri, 25 Dec. ♿
In 1897, a competition was announced to design a suitable building to act as Fremantle's market hall. The winning design was built in 1892 and still stands today. It underwent renovation in 1975, and has been used as a market ever since. There are more than 170 stalls offering a variety of wares, from fresh vegetables to opals. The market stays open to 10pm on Fridays.

⛪ St John the Evangelist Anglican Church
Cnr Adelaide & Queen sts. *Tel* (08) 93 35 2213. ⏲ daily. ♿
This charming church, completed in 1882, replaced a smaller church on the same site. Its Pioneer Window tells the story of a pioneer family across seven generations, from its departure from England in the 18th century, to a new life in a Western Australian farming community. The window next to it came from the old church. St John's ceiling and altars are made out of local jarrah wood.

THE AMERICA'S CUP BONANZA
The America's Cup yachting race has been run every four years since 1851. Not until 1983, however, did a country other than the United States win this coveted trophy. This was the year that *Australia II* carried it home. In 1987, the Americans were the challengers, and the races were run in *Australia II*'s home waters, off Fremantle. Investment poured into the town, refurbishing the docks, cafés, bars and hotels for the occasion.

The Americans regained the trophy, but Fremantle remains forever changed by being, for once, under the world's gaze.

The 1983 winner, *Australia II*

🏛 Fremantle Museum and Arts Centre

Cnr Ord & Finnerty sts. ***Tel*** *(08) 9430 9555.* ◯ *10am–5pm daily.* ● *Good Fri, 25 Dec, 26 Dec, 1 Jan.* **Donation.** ♿ *limited.*

Surprisingly, this beautiful Gothic Revival mansion with its shady gardens was first conceived as an asylum for the insane. The main wing was built between 1861 and 1865, and now houses the Fremantle Museum. It was extended between 1880 and 1902, and the newer section contains the Fremantle Arts Centre.

The building, used variously as an asylum, the wartime headquarters for US forces, and the home of the Western Australian Maritime Museum, was slated for demolition in 1967. But, principally through the efforts of Fremantle's mayor, it was rescued and renovated.

The Fremantle Museum is dedicated to the study of the daily lives of the people who came to Western Australia in the 19th century in search of a new life. Its exhibits describe how they lived the obstacles they overcame and the lives and families they left behind.

The Fremantle Arts Centre showcases local contemporary artists and many of the works are for sale. It also stages open-air concerts and sponsors various events in the grounds.

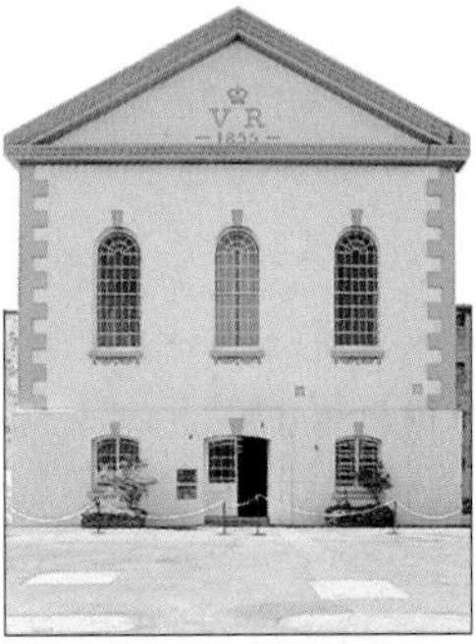

Fremantle Prison's striking façade

VISITORS' CHECKLIST

👥 *25,000.* 🚆 *Elder Place.* 🚌 *Elder Place.* ℹ *Town Hall, Kings Square (08) 9431 7878.* 🎉 *Festival Fremantle (Nov).*

🏛 Fremantle Prison

The Terrace, off Hampton Rd. ***Tel*** *(08) 9336 9200.* ◯ *10am–5pm daily.* ● *Good Fri, 25 Dec.* 📷 ✋ ♿ *limited.*

In the 1850s, when the first group of convicts arrived in the Swan River Colony, the need arose for a large-scale prison. Fremantle Prison, an imposing building with a sturdy gatehouse and cold, forbidding limestone cell blocks, was built by those first convicts in 1855. It was not closed until 1991. Today, visitors tour the complex, visiting cells (some have murals painted by inmates), punishment cells, the chapel and the chilling gallows room, last used in 1964. Candlelight tours are available.

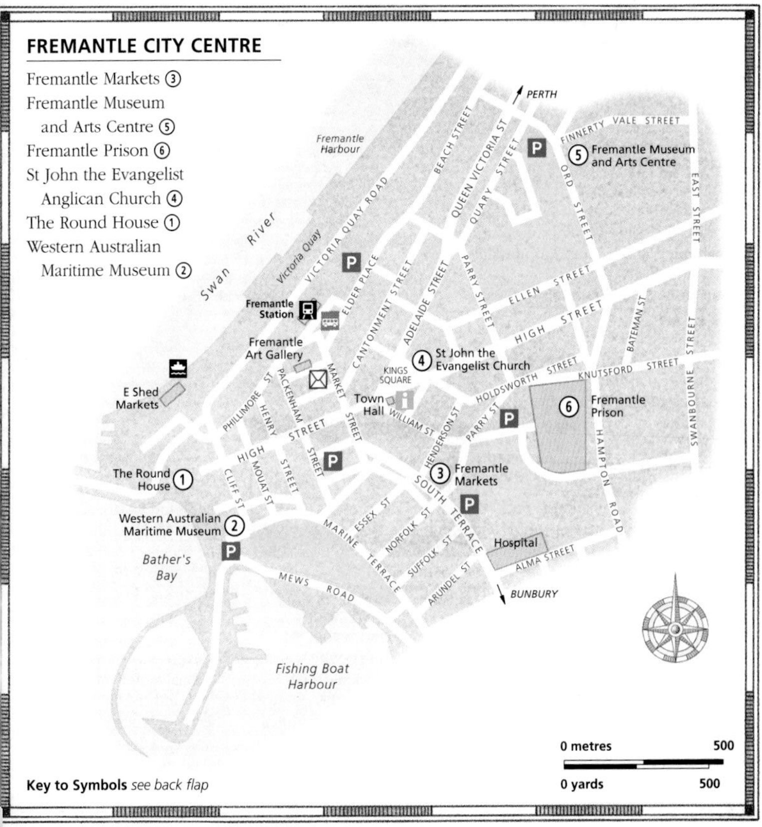
FREMANTLE CITY CENTRE
Fremantle Markets ③
Fremantle Museum and Arts Centre ⑤
Fremantle Prison ⑥
St John the Evangelist Anglican Church ④
The Round House ①
Western Australian Maritime Museum ②
PERTH
Fremantle Harbour
Swan River
Victoria Quay
VICTORIA QUAY ROAD
BEACH STREET
QUEEN VICTORIA ST
QUARY STREET
FINNERTY VALE STREET
Fremantle Museum and Arts Centre
ORD STREET
EAST STREET
ELDER PLACE
CANTONMENT STREET
ADELAIDE STREET
PARRY STREET
ELLEN STREET
HIGH STREET
BATEMAN ST
SWANBOURNE STREET
Fremantle Station
Fremantle Art Gallery
St John the Evangelist Church
KINGS SQUARE
HOLDSWORTH STREET
KNUTSFORD STREET
E Shed Markets
PHILLIMORE ST
PACKENHAM
HENRY
MARKET STREET
Town Hall
WILLIAM ST
HENDERSON ST
PARRY ST
Fremantle Prison
HAMPTON ROAD
HIGH STREET
MOUAT ST
The Round House
CLIFF ST
SOUTH TERRACE
Fremantle Markets
Western Australian Maritime Museum
ESSEX ST
NORFOLK ST
SUFFOLK ST
ARUNDEL ST
MARINE TERRACE
Hospital
ALMA STREET
Bather's Bay
MEWS ROAD
BUNBURY
Fishing Boat Harbour
0 metres 500
0 yards 500
Key to Symbols see back flap

The Southern Coastline

Western Australia's southwest corner has diverse coastal scenery. Two oceans meet here, the Indian and the Southern, resulting in discernible climate changes: the southern coastline is often windy and cooler than the western coast, and the oceans are much less gentle. Lined by national parks, the coast incorporates limestone, reefs, granite formations, beautiful sand dunes and crags topped by low vegetation. There are also world-class surfing spots in the region.

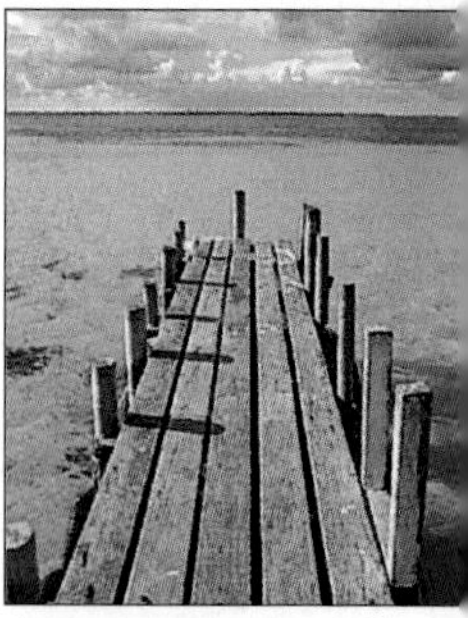

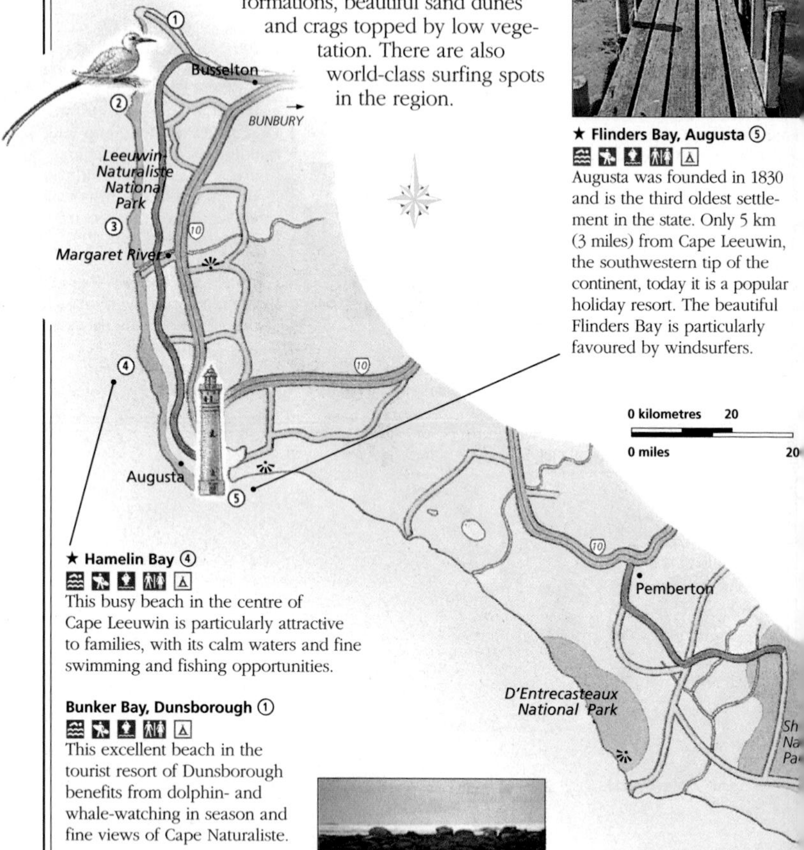

Busselton
BUNBURY
Leeuwin-Naturaliste National Park
Margaret River
10
Augusta
Pemberton
D'Entrecasteaux National Park
0 kilometres 20
0 miles 20

★ Flinders Bay, Augusta ⑤

🌊 🏄 🛟 🚻 ⛺

Augusta was founded in 1830 and is the third oldest settlement in the state. Only 5 km (3 miles) from Cape Leeuwin, the southwestern tip of the continent, today it is a popular holiday resort. The beautiful Flinders Bay is particularly favoured by windsurfers.

★ Hamelin Bay ④

🌊 🏄 🛟 🚻 ⛺

This busy beach in the centre of Cape Leeuwin is particularly attractive to families, with its calm waters and fine swimming and fishing opportunities.

Bunker Bay, Dunsborough ①

🌊 🏄 🛟 🚻 ⛺

This excellent beach in the tourist resort of Dunsborough benefits from dolphin- and whale-watching in season and fine views of Cape Naturaliste.

Smiths Beach, Yallingup ②

🌊 🏄 🛟 🚻 ⛺

This popular honeymoon spot (Yallingup is indigenous word for "place of lovers") is also a haven for surfers. Nearby is the spectacular Yallingup Cave.

Boodjidup Beach, Margaret River ③

🌊 🏄 🛟 🚻 ⛺

The coastline in this holiday town consists of long beaches, sheltered bays and cliff faces looking out on to the surf.

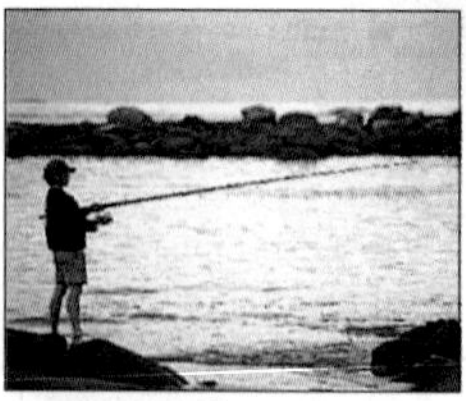

Peaceful Bay ⑦

🌊 🏄 🛟 🚻 ⛺

Keen anglers and sailors can often be spotted within this aptly named inlet, which is also a popular picnic spot. Nearby Walpole is the gateway to Walpole-Nornalup National Park, with its impressive karri and eucalypt trees.

Middleton Beach, Albany ⑩

🌊 🏄 🛟 🚻 ⛺

The waters of Middleton Beach are regularly filled with windsurfers and boogeyboarders (surfing the waves on a short body board). A short drive around the point is Torndirrup National Park, with a multitude of natural coastal formations, including offshore islands and some excellent locations for whale-watching in season.

Lake Cave, *near Margaret River, is just one of an estimated 200 underground caves along the Leeuwin-Naturaliste Ridge that runs from Busselton to Augusta. It is one of the few caves open to the public and is a fairyland of limestone formations, reflected in dark underground waters.*

LOCATOR MAP

D'Entrecasteaux National Park, *40 km (25 miles) southwest of Pemberton, is a wild and rugged park with spectacular coastal cliffs, pristine beaches and excellent coastal fishing. Much of the park, including some isolated beach camp sites, is only accessible by 4WD. Inland, heathland is home to a range of animal and plant habitats.*

Leeuwin-Naturaliste National Park *is a 15,500-ha (40,000-acre) protected area of scenic coastline, caves, heathlands and woodlands. Its rugged limestone coast with long beaches and sheltered bays faces the Indian Ocean. It has long been popular as a holiday destination and has excellent opportunities for swimming, surfing and fishing.*

★ **Ocean Beach, Denmark** ⑧

Denmark is a well-known and popular haunt for surfers from many countries. Ocean Beach, in particular, is the setting for international surfing competitions *(see pp34–5).*

★ **Wilson Inlet** ⑨

From Denmark's main street it is a relatively short walk through well-kept woodland to Wilson Inlet where there are some spectacular and varied coastal views.

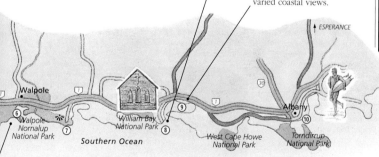

★ **Conspicuous Beach** ⑥

Impressive cliffs face on to the beautiful white sands of Conspicuous Beach. It is also the access point for the Valley of the Giants, with its massive red tingle trees.

KEY

▦▦	Highway
▬	Major road
▭	Minor road
⌒	River
☆	Viewpoint

Wide first-floor veranda and ornate ironwork of the Rose Hotel, Bunbury

Bunbury ❹

🏛 28,000. 🚆 🏢 🚌 🚢
ℹ️ Old Railway Station, Carmody Place (08) 9721 7922.
www.bunburybreaks.com.au

The city of Bunbury lies about 180 km (110 miles) south of Perth at the southern end of the Leschenhault Inlet. The state's second-largest city, it is the capital of the south-west region. Since the 19th century it has grown into a thriving port and a centre for local industry. It is also a popular holiday destination, with many water sports available.

Historic buildings in Bunbury include the Rose Hotel, built in 1865, with its first-floor veranda and intricate ironwork detail. The Roman Catholic St Patrick's Cathedral contains the beautiful Pat Usher Memorial Window, in memory of Bunbury's mayor from 1972 to 1983. St Boniface (Anglican) Cathedral also contains some pretty stained glass. Nearby are the Bunbury Art Galleries, housed in the former Sisters of Mercy convent built in the 1880s. Today they are the centre for community arts events.

On the beachfront stands the **Dolphin Discovery Centre**, which has fascinating audio-visual exhibits. Wild dolphins regularly appear off the coast here, and visitors come to see them and swim with them.

The **King Cottage Museum**, is run by the Bunbury Historical Society. It exhibits local artifacts dating from the 1880s to the 1920s and a wealth of photographs.

🐬 **Dolphin Discovery Centre**
Koombana Drive. **Tel** (08) 9791 3088. ⬜ daily. ⬤ 25 Dec. 🎦 ♿

🏛 **King Cottage Museum**
77 Forrest Ave. **Tel** (08) 9721 7546.
⬜ phone for opening times. 🎦 ♿

Busselton ❺

🏛 14,200. ✈️ 🏢 ℹ️ 38 Peel Terrace (08) 9752 1288.
www.downsouth.com.au

Standing on the shores of Geographe Bay, Busselton boasts more than 30 km (19 miles) of beaches and a vast array of water-based activities, including scuba-diving, fishing and whale-watching. Busselton Jetty, 2 km (1 mile) long and once the longest in Australia, is a reminder of the town's beginnings as a timber port.

Some of Busselton's oldest surviving buildings are located

Entrance to Busselton's original courthouse building

at the Old Courthouse site, now used as an arts complex. Here, the jail cells, police offices, courthouse and bond store all date from 1856. Local crafts are sold in the old jail cells, and other outbuildings act as studio space for artists.

The 1871 *Ballarat*, the first steam locomotive used in the state, stands in Victoria Park.

Environs

About 10 km (6 miles) north of Busselton is **Wonnerup House**, a lovingly restored house built by pioneer George Layman in 1859 and now owned by the National Trust. Three other buildings share the site, the earliest being the first house Layman erected in the 1830s. Both buildings stand in pretty grounds within farmland and are furnished with Layman family memorabilia and artifacts. In 1874, Layman's son built a school and in, 1885, a teacher's house close by.

About 20 km (12 miles) north of Busselton is the beautiful Ludlow Tuart Forest National Park, probably the largest area of tuart trees left in the world.

🏚 **Wonnerup House**
Layman Rd. **Tel** (08) 9752 2039. ⬜ daily. ⬤ Good Fri, 25 Dec. 🎦 ♿

Margaret River ❻

🏛 6,000. ✈️ 🏢 🚌
ℹ️ Bussell Hwy (08) 9757 2911.
www.margaretriver.com

The attractive town of Margaret River, close to the Indian Ocean, was first settled by Europeans in the 1850s. The town became the centre of an agricultural and timber region, but in the past few decades has gained fame for its wineries *(see pp36–7)*, and for its splendid surfing beaches.

Within the town is the **Margaret River Museum**, a privately owned outdoor museum detailing the lives of those who worked on the Group Settlement Scheme in the 1920s *(see p57)*. The museum buildings include a group house, a blacksmith's shop and a schoolhouse. Set in 12 ha (30 acres) of bush on the outskirts of town, the **Eagles**

Heritage Raptor Wildlife Centre has a huge collection of birds of prey and gives eagle-flying displays.

🏛 **Margaret River Museum**
Bussell Hwy at Rotary Bridge.
Tel (08) 9757 9335. ⬜ *daily*
● 24–26 Dec. 🎫 🖻

🦅 **Eagles Heritage Raptor Wildlife Centre**
Lot 303 Boodjidup Rd. *Tel* (08) 9757 2960. ⬜ *daily.* ● 25 Dec. 🎫 ♿

Environs
Eight km (5 miles) north of Margaret River stands the region's first homestead, Ellensbrook, built by pioneer Alfred Bussell in the 1850s. The stone cottage is close to a forest trail which leads to the pretty Meekadarribee Falls.

Visiting Margaret River's outlying wineries is very popular. Many, from Vasse-Felix, the oldest, to the large Leeuwin Estates Winery, offer tastings.

Ellensbrook Pioneer Homestead, near the town of Margaret River

Bridgetown ❼

🏘 *3,000.* 🚌 🛈 *154 Hampton St* (08) 9761 1740.
www.bridgetownvisitors.com.au

Nestled amid rolling hills on the banks of Blackwood River, Bridgetown began as a single one-room homestead in the 1850s. It was built by settler John Blechynden and can still be seen standing next to the second home he built, Bridgedale House. Both are National Trust properties.

The town's tourist centre is home to its municipal history museum and the unusual Brierly Jigsaw Gallery, which has hundreds of puzzles.

Hilltop view of picturesque Bridgetown

Sutton's Lookout, off Philips Street, offers panoramic views of the town and surrounding countryside. The Blackwood River and local jarrah and marri forests afford opportunities for walks and drives, and several river-based activities, including canoeing and marron fishing.

Manjimup ❽

🏘 *5,000.* 🚌 🛈 *Giblett St (08) 9771 1831.*

If you are travelling south from Perth, Manjimup acts as the gateway to the great karri forests for which the southwest is so famous. The town was settled in the late 1850s, and has been associated with the timber industry ever since. The tourist office is within the **Manjimup Timber Park**, with its Timber Museum, Historical Hamlet and Bunnings Age of Steam Museum. A sculpture of a woodsman at the entrance commemorates the region's timber industry pioneers.

🏛 **Manjimup Timber & Heritage Park**
Cnr Rose & Edwards sts. *Tel* (08) 9771 1831 ⬜ *daily.* ● 25 Dec. ♿

Environs
About 25 km (16 miles) west of Manjimup on Graphite Road lies Glenoran Pool, a pretty swimming hole on the Donnelly River. The adjacent One-

Tree Bridge is the site where early settlers felled a huge karri and used it to carry a bridge across the river. Nearby are the Four Aces, four giant karri trees in a straight line, thought to be up to 300 years old.

Pemberton ❾

🏘 *1,200.* 🚌 🛈 *Brockman St* (08) 9776 1133.
www.pembertontourist.com.au

At the heart of karri country, Pemberton has the look and feel of an old timber town. The Pemberton Tramway, originally built to bring the trees to mills in town, now takes visitors through the forests. The **Karri Forest Discovery Centre** provides information on the ecology of the karri forest.

🏛 **Karri Forest Discovery Centre**
Brockman St. *Tel* (08) 9776 1133. ⬜ *daily.* ● 25 Dec. **Donations.** ♿

Environs
Southeast of the town lies Gloucester National Park, home to the famous giant karri, the Gloucester Tree. At 61 m (200 ft), it is one of the highest fire lookout trees in the world. Southwest of Pemberton is Warren National Park with its beautiful cascades, swimming holes and fishing spots. Attractive Beedelup National Park is northwest of Pemberton.

Sculpture of a woodsman at Manjimup Timber Park

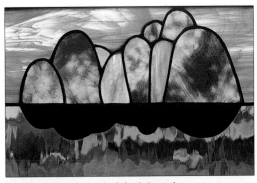

Example of Andy Ducker's stained glass in Denmark

Denmark ⑩

🏃 3,500. 🚆 ℹ️ 60 Strickland St
(08) 9848 2055.
www.denmarkvisitorcentre.com.au

Lying on Western Australia's southern coastline, Denmark was founded as a timber company settlement in 1895, but by the 1920s it was a fully fledged town. The town now attracts a host of visitors, many of whom come seeking the good surf of the Southern Ocean. There is also a large population of artists and artisans, and the atmosphere is distinctly bohemian.

Denmark's oldest building is St Leonard's Anglican Church, built by volunteers in 1899. Its Scandinavian-style pitched roof and interior detail are reminders of the Norwegian timber workers in the town at that time.

Nearby is Mandala Studio, one of Denmark's many craft galleries, where visitors can admire and buy stained-glass items made by local artist Andy Ducker.

Berridge Park is often the scene for open-air concerts.

Environs
Denmark has many beautiful beaches. A popular surfing spot is Ocean Beach; more sheltered locations for swimmers include Cosy Corner and Peaceful Bay. The coastline and Wilsons Inlet are popular with boaters and anglers.

Albany ⑪

🏃 29,000. ✈️ 🚌 🚆 ℹ️ Old Railway Station, Proudlove Parade (08) 9841 1088. **www**.albanytourist.com.au

Albany was first visited by Captain Vancouver in 1791, but it was not until 1826 that the British settled here. Until Fremantle harbour was constructed *(see pp310–11)*, Albany acted as the colony's main port and the harbour is still the commercial heart of the city. Whale migrations bring them close to the city's shores, which made it a base for whalers in the last century.

The town includes many old buildings. **St John the Evangelist Anglican Church**, built in 1848, was the first Anglican church consecrated in Western Australia and is the epitome of an English country church. Inside, the Lady Chapel contains a piece of an arch from St Paul's Cathedral in London.

Much of the stained glass was brought from England at the beginning of the 19th century.

Ship's wheel in
Jaycee's Whaleworld

A number of old buildings stand near the western end of Stirling Terrace. The Residency Museum, originally part of the convict hiring depot built in the 1850s, details the history of the town and its surrounding area. The convict hiring depot itself and the Old Gaol now house the collection of the Albany Historical Society.

In Duke Street is Patrick Taylor Cottage, built before 1836 of wattle and daub, and the oldest building in Albany.

On Albany's foreshore is an impressive, fully-fitted replica of the brig *Amity*, which brought the first settlers here from Sydney in 1826.

🔒 **St John the Evangelist Anglican Church**
York St. **Tel** (08) 9841 5015.
⬜ daily. ♿

Environs
The world's largest whaling museum is **Whale World** Tour guides take visitors around the remains of the Cheyne Beach whaling station and explain the process of extracting whale oil. From July to October, incredible breaching displays of migrating whales can sometimes be seen offshore.

🏛 **Whale World**
Frenchman Bay Rd. **Tel** (08) 9844 4021. ⬜ daily. ⬤ 25 Dec. 📷💻♿

Replica of the brig *Amity*

Stirling Range National Park ⑫

🚗 Albany. ℹ️ Albany (08) 9841 1088. **Park Ranger & information Tel** (08) 9827 9230.

Overlooking the rolling farmland to the north of Albany is the Stirling Range National Park. The mountain peaks, noted for their colour changes from purple to red to blue, rise to more than 1,000 m (3,300 ft) above sea level and stretch for more than 65 km (40 miles). The highest peak is Bluff Knoll, which reaches 1,073 m (3,520 ft). Because of its sudden rise from the

View of Stirling Range National Park from Chester Pass Road

surrounding plains, the park has an unpredictable climate which encourages a wide range of unique flora and fauna, including ten species of mountain bell. No less than 60 species of flowering plants are endemic to the park. They are best seen from October to December, when they are likely to be in flower. The park offers visitors a number of graded and signposted walks in the mountains (all are steep) and there are several picturesque barbecue and picnic areas.

York ⑬

🏘 3,000. 🚌 ⓘ 81 Avon Terrace (08) 9641 1301. 🎪 Festival of Motoring (Jul). **www**.yorkwa.org

The town of York was founded in 1831, in the new colony's drive to establish its self-sufficiency via agriculture. Now registered as a historic town, it retains many mid–19th-century buildings, the majority of which are on Avon Terrace, the main street. The cells of York's Old Gaol, in use from 1865 until 1981, provide a chilling insight into the treatment of 19th-century offenders. Other historic buildings include Settler's House (1860s), now a hotel and restaurant (see p500), and Castle Hotel, built in stages between 1850 and 1932, with its unusual timber verandas.

Nearby stands the **York Motor Museum**, with one of the largest collections of veteran cars and vehicles in Australia. These include the 1886 Benz (the world's first car), the very rare 1946 Holden Sedan Prototype and the extraordinary Bisiluro II Italcorsa racing car.

Also of note is the York Residency Museum, housed in the former home of York magistrate Walkinshaw Cowan, father-in-law to Edith Cowan, the state's first female Member of Parliament (see p56). This extensive collection of artifacts and photographs is justly said to be the finest small museum in the state.

York's 1892 flour mill has now been converted into the Jah-Roc Mill Gallery, which exhibits and sells furniture made from jarra wood and other arts and crafts.

🏛 York Motor Museum
116 Avon Terrace. **Tel** (08) 9641 1288. ◯ daily. ⬤ 25 Dec. 📷 ♿

Original 1925 Rolls Royce in the York Motor Museum

Northam ⑭

🏘 7,000. 🚌 🚃 ⓘ Fitzgerald St (08) 9622 2100. **www**.northamwa.com.au

At the heart of the Avon Valley and the state's wheat belt, Northam is Western Australia's largest inland town. Settled as an agricultural centre early in the colony's history, the town became a gateway to the gold fields of Kalgoorlie-Boulder for prospectors in the 1890s (see p310). It retains a number of historic buildings, including the Old Girls' School (1877), now the town's Art Centre, and the beautiful St John's Church (1890). The town's jewel is Morby Cottage, built in 1836 and a fine example of the architectural style adopted by the early colonists.

Spanning the Avon River is the longest pedestrian suspension bridge in the country, offering views of the river.

The Gold Fields and Nullarbor Plain

Western Australia's southeast is a sparsely populated, flat region of extreme aridity and little fresh water. Vast stretches of its red, dusty landscape are inhabited by small Aboriginal communities and mining companies. The gold rush around Kalgoorlie in the 1890s ensured the state's success, but many places waned and ghost towns now litter the plains. Traversing the Nullarbor Plain, the Eyre Highway runs from Norseman to South Australia, 730 km (455 miles) away, and beyond. To the south is the windswept coast of the Great Australian Bight.

LOCATION MAP

⬜ The Gold Fields and Nullarbor Plain

⬜ Perth and the Southwest pp298–317

SIGHTS AT A GLANCE

Esperance ⑱
Kalgoorlie-Boulder ⑯
Norseman ⑰
Nullarbor Plain ⑲
Wave Rock ⑮

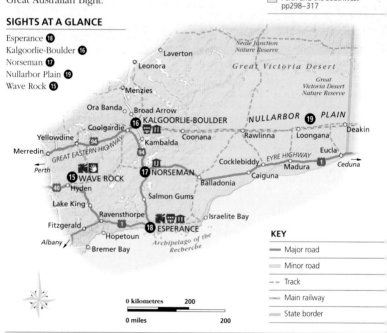

KEY

▬▬ Major road

═══ Minor road

-- Track

▬▬ Main railway

▦▦ State border

0 kilometres 200

0 miles 200

**Wave Rock, in the shape of a
perfect wave about to break**

Wave Rock ⑮

🚻 Hyden. **Visitors' Centre Tel** (08) 9880 5200. ⬜ 9am–6pm daily. 🅿️ ♿ 🚻 by arrangement.

In Western Australia's wheat belt, 5 km (3 miles) east of the small settlement of Hyden, stands one of the state's most surprising rock formations. A great granite wave has been created from a huge outcrop by thousands of years of chemical erosion, and reaction with rainwater has given it red and grey stripes. Other rock formations nearby include the Breakers and Hippo's Yawn. Facing Wave Rock, Lace Place is the unusual location for the largest collection of lacework in the southern hemisphere.

About 20 km (12 miles) northeast of Hyden lies Mulka's Cave, where several Aboriginal rock paintings can be seen.

Kalgoorlie-Boulder ⑯

🚻 30,000. ✈ 🚉 🚌 🚐 ℹ️ 250 Hannan St (08) 9021 1966. **www**.kalgoorlie.com

Kalgoorlie and the nearby town of Boulder, with which it was amalgamated in 1989, constantly remind visitors of their gold-fever past. Gold was first discovered here by Irishman Paddy Hannan in 1893, and, within weeks, the area was besieged with prospectors. Gold fields in other areas soon dwindled, but this field has yielded rich pickings to this day, bolstered by nickel finds in the 1960s. Today, gold is mined in the world's largest open-cut mine and more than 150,000 visitors a year come to see historic Kalgoorlie.

A variety of heritage trails and tours are available, and details are at the tourist office. The **WA Museum Kalgoorlie–Boulder** has an impressive collection of gold nuggets and jewellery, as well as natural history displays and a history of the gold rush. At the Mining Hall of Fame, visitors can go down a shaft and see gold pours and panning demonstrations.

The ornate buildings hastily erected during the boom years are best seen on Hannan Street, in the York and Exchange hotels, classic examples of gold rush architecture, and Kalgoorlie Town Hall.

Around Kalgoorlie-Boulder are ghost towns, such as Ora Banda and Broad Arrow, deserted by prospectors in search of new mines.

Bronze statue of Paddy Hannan

🏛 **WA Museum Kalgoorlie–Boulder**
17 Hannan St. **Tel** (08) 9021 8533. ◔ 10am–4:30pm daily. ● Good Fri, 25 Dec. **Donation.** ♿

Baxters Cliff, east of Esperance, on the shores of the Southern Ocean

Norseman ⓱

🏚 11,000. 🚌 🛈 68 Roberts St (08) 9039 1071.

At the start of the Eyre Highway, Norseman is the gateway to the Nullarbor Plain and the eastern states beyond. Like Kalgoorlie-Boulder, the town stands on a gold field, discovered when a horse pawed the ground, uncovering gold deposits. In gratitude, miners named the town after the horse, and its statue was erected in the main street. Many visitors try fossicking, or learn more about the history of gold mining in the area at the **Norseman Historical and Geological Museum** housed in the old School of Mines. Nearby, Beacon Hill offers a panoramic view of the town and surrounding countryside.

🏛 **Norseman Historical and Geological Museum**
Battery Rd. **Tel** (08) 9039 1593. ◔ Mon–Sat. ● Good Fri, Easter Mon, 25 Apr, 25 Dec. 📷

Esperance ⓲

🏚 10,000. ✈ 🚌 🛈 Museum Village, Demster St (08) 9071 2330.

Although this area was visited by Europeans as far back as 1627, it was not until 1863 that British colonists arrived here to establish a settlement. Fronting the Southern Ocean, this part of the coast is said to have some of the most beautiful beaches in Australia. Offshore is the Recherche Archipelago, with its 100 islands, one of which, Woody Island, is a wildlife sanctuary and can be visited.

In Esperance itself, Museum Village includes the town's art gallery and several historic buildings, and Esperance Municipal Museum contains a fine array of local artifacts.

Nullarbor Plain ⓳

🚌 Kalgoorlie. 🚌 Norseman. 🛈 Norseman (08) 9039 1071.

The Nullarbor Plain stretches across the southeast of the state and into South Australia (see p367). "Nullarbor" derives from the Latin meaning "no trees", and this is indeed a vast treeless plain. Only one road, the Eyre Highway, leads across the plain – one of the great Australian road journeys.

A few tiny settlements consisting only of roadhouses lie along the Eyre Hwy. Cocklebiddy, lying 438 km (270 miles) east of Norseman, has one of the world's longest caves and, at Eucla, 10 km (6 miles) from the state border, a telegraph station's remains can be seen. Nearby Eucla National Park has some fine views of the coastal cliffs.

York Hotel in Hannan Street, Kalgoorlie (see p498)

NORTH OF PERTH AND THE KIMBERLEY

Western Australia covers one-third of Australia, and visitors to the area north of Perth start to get a feel for just how big the state really is. The region has many treasures: Ningaloo Reef and the Pinnacles rock formations; the Kimberley gorges; and a host of national parks, including the amazing Bungle Bungles.

The first people to set foot on the Australian land mass, the Aborigines, did so some 60,000 years ago in the north of Western Australia. This area is rich in Aboriginal petroglyphs, and some are thought to be more than 20,000 years old. The north of Western Australia was also the site of the first European landing in 1616 *(see p49)*. In 1688, English explorer William Dampier charted the area around the Dampier Peninsula and, on a later voyage, discovered Shark Bay and the area around Broome.

In the 1840s, the Benedictines set up a mission in New Norcia and, by the 1860s, settlements had sprung up along the coast, most significantly at Cossack, where a pearling industry attracted immigrants from Japan, China and Indonesia. In the 1880s, pastoralists set up cattle and sheep stations in a swathe from Derby to Wyndham. Gold was struck in 1885 at Halls Creek, and the northern part of the state was finally on the map. In the 1960s, mining came to prominence again with the discovery of such minerals as iron ore, nickel and oil, particularly in the Pilbara region.

Today, the region is fast becoming a popular tourist destination, particularly with those visitors interested in ecotourism *(see p568)*. Its climate varies from Mediterranean-style just north of Perth to the tropical wet and dry pattern of the far north. Wildlife includes endangered species such as the dugongs of Shark Bay. Even isolated spots, such as the Kimberley and the resorts of Coral Bay and Broome, are receiving more visitors every year.

Visitors enjoying close contact with the dolphins of Monkey Mia in Shark Bay World Heritage and Marine Park

◁ The strange silica- and lichen-covered domes of the Bungle Bungles in Purnululu National Park

Exploring North of Perth

The north of Western Australia is a vast area of diverse landscapes and stunning scenery. North of Perth lies Nambung National Park, home to the bizarre Pinnacles Desert. Kalbarri National Park is a region of scenic gorges on the Murchison River. The Indian Ocean coastline offers uninhabited islands, coral reefs, breathtaking cliffs and sandy beaches, none more spectacular than in Shark Bay World Heritage and Marine Park. At the tip of the region is the Pilbara, the state's mining area and home to the fascinating national parks of Karijini and Millstream-Chichester.

St Francis Xavier Cathedral, Geraldton

The Pinnacles in Nambung National Park at dusk

SIGHTS AT A GLANCE

Carnarvon **7**
Cossack Historical Town **12**
Dampier **10**
Exmouth **9**
Geraldton **3**
Houtman Abrolhos **4**
Kalbarri National Park **5**
Karijini National Park **14**
Nambung National Park **2**
New Norcia **1**
Ningaloo Reef Marine Park **8**
Point Samson **13**

Roebourne **11**
Shark Bay World Heritage and Marine Park pp326–7 **6**

The Kimberley and the Deserts *See pp330–31*
Broome **15**
Derby **16**
Halls Creek **17**
Purnululu (Bungle Bungle) National Park **18**
Wyndham **19**

Monte Bello
Islands

Barrow
Island

Thevenard
Island

Muiron
Islands   Onslow

North West Cape

9 EXMOUTH

Cape Range
National Park   Learmouth

Nanutarra
Roadhouse

**NINGALOO
REEF MARINE
PARK** **8**

Coral Bay

Giralia Range

NORTH WEST COASTAL HIGHWAY

Cape Farquhar

Minilya

Minilya
Roadhouse

Red Bluff

Quobba   Lake
Macleod

Kennedy Range

Blowholes

CARNARVON 7

Gascoyne

Dorre
Island   Shark
Bay

Gascoyne
Junction

François Peron
National Park

Dirk Hartog
Island   Monkey
Mia

Denham   Wooramel
Roadhouse

Useless
Loop

6 **SHARK
BAY**

Overlander
Roadhouse

Wannoo
Billabong
Roadhou

1

Zuytdorp Cliffs

**KALBARRI
NATIONAL PARK 5**

Kalbarri

Northampton   Mul

GERALD

4   **3**

*HOUTMAN
ABROLHOS*

Minge

Dongara

Beekeepers
Nature Reserve

Eneabl

Leeman

Cervantes

**NAMBUNG
NATIONAL PARK**

Lan

0 kilometres   100

0 miles   100

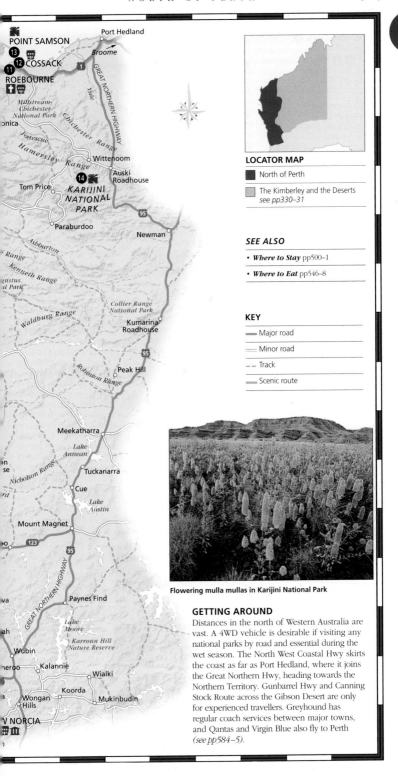

POINT SAMSON
Port Hedland
Broome
COSSACK
ROEBOURNE
GREAT NORTHERN HIGHWAY
Millstream-
Chichester
National Park
Yule
onica
Fortescue
Chichester Range
Hamersley
Range
Wittenoom
Auski
Roadhouse
Tom Price
KARIJINI
NATIONAL
PARK
Paraburdoo
95
Newman
Asburton
Range
Kenneth Range
ustus
al Park
Collier Range
National Park
Waldburg Range
Kumarina
Roadhouse
95
Robinson Range
Peak Hill
Meekatharra
Lake
Annean
Tuckanarra
Nicholson Range
Cue
Lake
Austin
Mount Magnet
123
95
Paynes Find
GREAT NORTHERN HIGHWAY
va
Lake
Moore
ah
Karroun Hill
Nature Reserve
Wubin
neroo
Kalannie
Wialki
Wongan
Hills
Koorda
Mukinbudin
V NORCIA

LOCATOR MAP

■ North of Perth

▨ The Kimberley and the Deserts
see pp330–31

SEE ALSO

• **Where to Stay** pp500–1

• **Where to Eat** pp546–8

KEY

— Major road

═ Minor road

-- Track

▬ Scenic route

Flowering mulla mullas in Karijini National Park

GETTING AROUND

Distances in the north of Western Australia are
vast. A 4WD vehicle is desirable if visiting any
national parks by road and essential during the
wet season. The North West Coastal Hwy skirts
the coast as far as Port Hedland, where it joins
the Great Northern Hwy, heading towards the
Northern Territory. Gunbarrel Hwy and Canning
Stock Route across the Gibson Desert are only
for experienced travellers. Greyhound has
regular coach services between major towns,
and Qantas and Virgin Blue also fly to Perth
(see pp584–5).

New Norcia ❶

🚶 70. 🅿 ℹ️ *New Norcia Museum and Art Gallery, Great Northern Highway (08) 9654 8056.*

One of Western Australia's most important heritage sites is New Norcia, 130 km (80 miles) northeast of Perth. A mission was established here by Spanish Benedictine monks in 1846, and it is still home to a small monastic community who own and run the historic buildings. There are daily tours of the monastery and visitors can stay at a guesthouse.

The town, known for its Spanish colonial architecture, has a pretty cathedral, built in 1860, at its centre. Also of note are two elegant colleges built early in the 20th century: St Gertrude's Residence for Girls and St Ildephonsus' Residence for Boys. The **New Norcia Museum and Art Gallery** has some fine art treasures and artifacts tracing the town's history.

🏛 **New Norcia Museum and Art Gallery**
Great Northern Hwy. *Tel (08) 9654 8056.* 🕐 *daily.* ● *25 Dec.* 📷 ♿ *ground floor only.*

Minarets adorning St Ildephonsus' Residence for Boys, New Norcia

Nambung National Park ❷

ℹ️ *CALM office at Cervantes (08) 9652 7043.* 🕐 *Mon–Fri.*

This unusual national park is composed of beach and sand dunes, with the dunes extending inland from the coast. It is best seen in spring when wildflowers bloom and the heat is not too oppressive. The park is famous for The Pinnacles, a region of curious

The extraordinary Pinnacles, Nambung National Park

limestone pillars, the tallest of which stand 4 m (13 ft) high. Visitors can take either a 3-km (2-mile) driving trail or a shorter walking trail which leads to lookouts with stunning views of the Pinnacles and the coastline.

Most of the park animals are nocturnal, but some, including kangaroos, emus and many reptiles, may be seen in the cool of dawn or dusk.

Geraldton ❸

🚶 26,000. ✈️ 🅿 🚌 ℹ️ *cnr Chapman Rd & Bayly St (08) 9921 3999.* **www**.geraldtontourist.com.au

The city of Geraldton lies on Champion Bay, about 425 km (265 miles) north of Perth. It is known as "Sun City" because of its average eight hours of sunshine per day. The pleasant climate brings hordes of sun-seekers from all over Australia who take advantage of fine swimming and surfing beaches. It can also be very windy at times, a further enticement to windsurfers, for whom Geraldton (particularly Mahomets Beach) is a world centre.

The history of European settlement in the area extends back to the mutiny of the Dutch ship *Batavia*, after it was wrecked on the nearby Houtman Abrolhos in 1628. Two crew members were marooned here

as a punishment. In 1721, the Dutch ship *Zuytdorp* was wrecked, and it is thought that survivors settled here for a brief period. Champion Bay was first mapped in 1849 and a lead mine was established shortly afterwards. Geraldton grew up as a lead shipping point, and today is a port city with a large rock-lobster fleet.

The city retains many of its early historic buildings. The **WA Museum**, **Geraldton** includes Geraldton Maritime Museum, which contains relics of the area's early shipwrecks. The Old Railway Building has exhibits on local history, wildlife and geology. Geraldton has two fine cathedrals: the modern Cathedral of the Holy Cross, with its beautiful stained glass, and St Francis Xavier Cathedral, built from 1916 to 1938, in Byzantine style.

Point Moore Lighthouse, with its distinctive red and white stripes, was shipped here from Britain and has been in continuous operation since 1878. The 1870 **Lighthouse Keeper's Cottage**, the town's first lighthouse, now houses Geraldton's Historical Society. Also in town, the **Geraldton Art Gallery** is one of the best galleries in the state, exhibiting the work of local artists and pieces from private and public collections.

A number of lookouts such as Separation Point Lookout and Mount Tarcoola Lookout give panoramic views of the city and ocean.

Geraldton's Point Moore Lighthouse

🏛 **WA Museum, Geraldton**
1 Museum Place, Batavia Coast
Marina. **Tel** (08) 9921 5080. ◯
10am–4pm daily. ⬤ Good Fri, 25
& 26 Dec. **Donation.** ♿

🏚 **Lighthouse Keeper's
Cottage**
355 Chapman Rd. **Tel** (08) 9921
8505. ◯ 10am–12pm Tue,
2pm–4pm Sat. ⬤ 25 Dec.

🏛 **Geraldton Art Gallery**
24 Chapman Rd. **Tel** (08) 9964
7170. ◯ daily. ⬤ Good Fri, 25
Dec–1 Jan. ♿

Houtman Abrolhos ❹

🚉 Geraldton. 🛥 from Geraldton.
🛈 Geraldton (08) 9921 3999.

About 60 km (37 miles) off
Geraldton lie more than 100
coral islands called the
Houtman Abrolhos. The
world's southernmost coral
island formation. While it is
not possible to stay on the
islands, tours enable visitors
to fly over them or to fish and
dive among the coral.

Kalbarri National Park ❺

🚉 Kalbarri. 🛈 Kalbarri (08) 9937
1104. ◯ sunrise–sunset daily.

The magnificent landscape
of Kalbarri National Park
includes stunning coastal
scenery and beautiful inland
gorges lining the Murchison
River. The park
has a number of
coastal and river
walking trails
which lead to
breathtaking
views and
fascinating rock
formations. The
trails vary in
length, from brief
two-hour strolls to
four-day hikes. Highlights of
the park include Hawks Head,
a picnic area with views of the
gorge; Nature's Window,
where a rock formation frames
a view of the river; and Ross
Graham Lookout, where
visitors can bathe in the river
pools. By the ocean, Pot Alley
provides awesome views of
the rugged coastal cliffs and
Rainbow Valley is made up of
layers of multi-coloured rocks.

The access town for the
park, Kalbarri, is situated on
the coast and provides good
tourist facilities. The park's
roads are accessible to most
vehicles, but are unsuitable for
caravans or trailers. The best
time to visit is from July to
October, when the weather is
dry and the temperatures are
not prohibitive. In summer,
they can soar to 40°C (104°F).

Shark Bay World Heritage and Marine Park ❻

See pp 326–7.

Fine arts and crafts centre in Carnarvon

Carnarvon ❼

🏘 7,000. ✈ 🚌 🚃 🛈 Civic Centre,
11 Robinson St (08) 9941 1146.

The town of Carnarvon,
standing at the mouth of the
Gascoyne River, acts as the
commercial and administrative
centre for the surrounding
Gascoyne region, the gateway
to Western Australia's north.
Tropical fruit plantations line
the river for 16 km (10 miles),
some offering tours and
selling produce.

In Carnarvon itself, One
Mile Jetty on Babbage Island
is a popular place for fishing,
and Jubilee Hall, built in 1887,
houses a fine arts and crafts
centre. Carnarvon is also
home to a busy prawn and
scallop processing industry.

Environs

About 70 km (43 miles) north
of Carnarvon lie the
Blowholes, a spectacular
coastal rock formation where
air and spray is forced through
holes in the rocks in violent
spurts up to 20 m (66 ft) high.

Stunning gorge views from Hawks Head Lookout, Kalbarri National Park

Shark Bay World Heritage and Marine Park ⑥

Historical jetty sign, Monkey Mia

Shark Bay Marine Park was designated a World Heritage Area in 1991 *(see pp26–7)*. The park is home to many endangered species of both plants and animals, and various unusual natural processes have, over the millennia, given rise to some astounding natural features and spectacular coastal scenery. Because this is a World Heritage Area, visitors are asked to abide by conservation rules, particularly when fishing. The only way to travel around the park is by car, and large areas are only accessible by 4WD.

BERNIER ISLAND

DORRE ISLAND

François Peron National Park

At the tip of Peron Peninsula, this national park, now accessible by 4WD, was a vast sheep station until 1990.

Cape Inscription is the place where Dutchman Dirk Hartog became the first known European to set foot in Australia in 1616 *(see p49).*

DIRK HARTOG ISLAND

Denham Sound   *FRANÇOIS PERON NATIONAL PARK*

Peron Homestead

Originally the centre of the Peron sheep station, the homestead offers an insight into pastoral life. The station also has two artesian bores which carry hot water (44°C, 111°F) to tubs at the surface in which visitors may bathe.

Denham was originally settled as a pearling community, but is now mainly a fishing and tourist centre.

Useless Loop

Steep Point faces the Indian Ocean and is the westernmost point of mainland Australia. From here it is possible to see the Zuytdorp Cliffs.

Useless Loop Road

Eagle Bluff

The top of this bluff offers fine panoramic views across Freycinet Reach, with a chance of seeing the eagles that nest on the offshore islands and marine creatures in the clear ocean waters.

The Zuytdorp Cliffs are named after the Dutch ship *Zuytdorp*, wrecked in these waters in 1721.

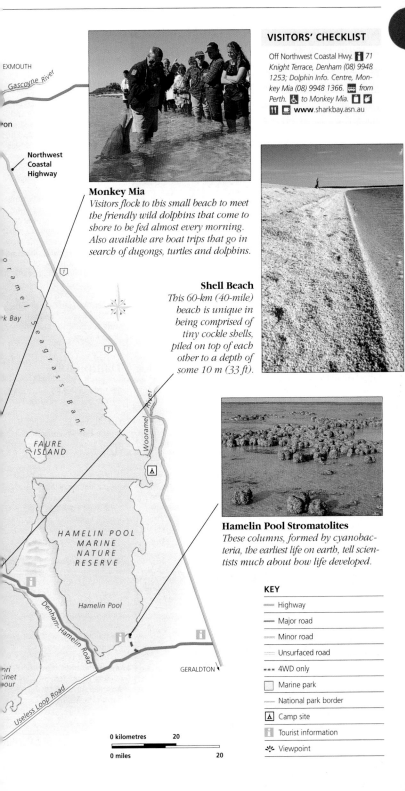

VISITORS' CHECKLIST

Off Northwest Coastal Hwy. **71**
Knight Terrace, Denham (08) 9948
1253; Dolphin Info. Centre, Monkey Mia (08) 9948 1366. from
Perth. to Monkey Mia.
www.sharkbay.asn.au

Monkey Mia
*Visitors flock to this small beach to meet
the friendly wild dolphins that come to
shore to be fed almost every morning.
Also available are boat trips that go in
search of dugongs, turtles and dolphins.*

Shell Beach
*This 60-km (40-mile)
beach is unique in
being comprised of
tiny cockle shells,
piled on top of each
other to a depth of
some 10 m (33 ft).*

Hamelin Pool Stromatolites
*These columns, formed by cyanobac-
teria, the earliest life on earth, tell scientists much about how life developed.*

KEY

	Highway
	Major road
	Minor road
	Unsurfaced road
- - -	4WD only
	Marine park
	National park border
⛺	Camp site
ℹ	Tourist information
☀	Viewpoint

0 kilometres   20

0 miles   20

Ningaloo Reef Marine Park ⑧

🔲 Exmouth. 🔳 Milyering Visitors' Centre, Yardie Creek Rd, Cape Range National Park (08) 9949 2808. ⬜ daily. ⬛ Good Fri, 25 Dec.

This marine park runs for 260 km (162 miles) along the west coast of Exmouth Peninsula and around the tip into Exmouth Gulf. The Ningaloo Reef is the largest fringing barrier reef in the state and offers many of the attractions of the east coast's Great Barrier Reef *(see pp212–17)*. In many places, it lies very close to the shore, and its turquoise waters are popular with snorkellers. Apart from numerous types of coral and brightly coloured fish, the marine park also protects a number of species. Several beaches at the northern end of the park are used by sea turtles as mating and breeding areas. Further offshore, it is possible to see the gentle whale shark from late March to May. Capable of growing to up to 18 m (60 ft), this is the largest fish in the world.

The best areas for snorkelling are Turquoise Bay or the still waters of Coral Bay. A number of companies offer organized scuba diving outings. Visitors can camp on the park's coastline at several sites managed by the Department of Conservation and Land Management (CALM). Fishing is another popular pursuit here, but catches are very strictly controlled.

Yardie Creek Gorge in Cape Range National Park, near Exmouth

Exmouth ⑨

🏙 3,100. ✈ 🚌 🔳 Murat Rd (08) 9949 1176.

Situated on the eastern side of the Exmouth Peninsula, this small town was originally built in 1967 to service the local airforce base. A military presence is still very much in evidence, but today the town is more important as a tourist destination, used as a base for exploring the Ningaloo Reef Marine Park and the Cape Range National Park. Giant turtles and whale sharks can frequently be seen from the nearby coastline.

Slightly outside of town, at Vlaming Head, lies the wreck of the SS *Mildura*, a cattle transporter which sank in 1907 and is still visible from the shore. Nearby stands the Vlaming Lighthouse, on a high bluff offering striking, panoramic views across the entire peninsula.

Environs

Cape Range National Park contains a low mountain range with spectacular gorges and rocky outcrops. This area was originally under water and it is possible to discern the fossils of ancient coral in the limestone. Local wildlife includes kangaroos, emus and large lizards. There are two main wilderness walks, but visitors should not attempt these in summer as temperatures can reach as high as 50°C (120°F).

Yardie Creek is on the western side of the park, only 1 km (0.5 miles) from the ocean. A short walk along gorge cliffs leads visitors into the spectacular canyon, where it is possible to catch sight of rock wallabies on the far canyon wall. A cruise through the gorges is also available.

Dampier ⑩

🏙 1,100. ✈ 🚌 🔳 4548 Karratha Rd, Karratha (08) 9144 4600.

Dampier stands on King Bay on the Burrup Peninsula, facing the 40 or so islands of the Dampier Archipelago. It was established and still acts as a service centre and port for mining areas inland; natural gas from the nearby Northwest Shelf Project is processed here for domestic and export markets. The town also has the largest desalination plant in Australia. This can be viewed from the Dampier Solar Evaporated Salt Mine Lookout. Dampier is also a popular base for offshore and beach anglers. Every August, game-fishing enthusiasts converge on the town for the Dampier Classic and Game Fishing Classic.

The Burrup Peninsula is one of the most renowned ancient Aboriginal art sites in Australia, created by the Yapurrara Aborigines.

Environs

The Dampier Archipelago, within 45 km (28 miles) of the town, offers a range of activities

White sands of Turquoise Bay in Ningaloo Reef Marine Park

Honeymoon Cove, one of the most popular beaches in Point Samson

from game fishing to whale-watching. Sport fishing here is particularly good, with reef and game species such as tuna, trevally and queenfish on offer.

Almost half of the islands are nature reserves and are home to rare species, including the Pilbara olive python and the king brown snake. Access to the islands is by boat only.

Simple façade of the Holy Trinity Church in Roebourne

Roebourne ⑪

🏠 1,400. 🚐 ℹ️ Queen St (08) 9182 1060.

About 14 km (9 miles) inland, Roebourne, established in 1866, is the oldest town in the Pilbara. The town retains several late 19th-century stone buildings, including the Old Gaol which now houses the tourist office and a craft gallery and the Holy Trinity Church (1894). Roebourne also marks the start of the 52-km (32-mile) Emma Withnell Heritage Trail, which takes a scenic route from here to Cossack and Point Samson. Trail guides are available at the tourist office.

Environs:
Some 150 km (93 miles) inland lies the 200,000-ha (500,000-acre) Millstream-Chichester National Park with its lush freshwater pools.

Cossack Historical Town ⑫

🚐 ℹ️ Queen St, Roebourne (08) 9182 1060.

In 1863, the town of Tien Tsin Harbour was established and quickly became the home of a burgeoning pearling industry that attracted people from as far away as Japan and China. The settlement was renamed Cossack in 1872 after a visit by Governor Weld aboard HMS Cossack. However, the town's moment soon passed. The pearling industry moved on to Broome (see p330) and by 1910 Cossack's harbour had silted up. In the late 1970s, restoration work of this ghost town began and today, under the management of the Shire of Roebourne, it has become a curiosity that continues to fascinate many visitors.

Old courthouse in Cossack Historical Town

Point Samson ⑬

🏠 200. ℹ️ Queen St, Roebourne (08) 9182 1060.

This small settlement was founded in 1910 to take on the port duties formerly performed by Cossack. Today, there is a modest fishing industry and two harbours. The town's best beaches are found at Honeymoon Cove and Samson Reef, where visitors can snorkel among the coral or search for rock oysters at low tide.

Karijini National Park ⑭

ℹ️ Tom Price (08) 9188 1112.
🕐 daily (weather permitting).

Set in the Hamersley Range, in the heart of the Pilbara region, Karijini National Park covers some 600,000 ha (1,500,000 acres). It is the second-largest national park in the state after Purnululu National Park (see p331).

The park has three types of landscape: rolling hills and ridges covered in eucalypt forests; arid, low-lying shrubland; and, in the north, spectacular gorges. The best times to visit the park are in winter, when the days are temperate, and in spring, when carpets of wildflowers are in spectacular bloom.

The Kimberley and the Deserts

Pearler's diving helmet, Broome

Australia's last frontier, the Kimberley is a vast, remote upland region of dry, red landscape. Deep rivers cut through mountain ranges, and parts of the coastline have the highest tidal range in the southern hemisphere. Seasonal climatic extremes add to the area's sense of isolation as the harsh heat of the dry season and the torrential rains of the wet hamper access to the hostile terrain. April to September is the best time to visit, offering views of the country's best natural sights such as the Wolfe Creek Meteorite Crater and the Bungle Bungles. To the south lie the huge, inhospitable Great Sandy and Gibson deserts.

LOCATOR MAP

■ The Kimberley and the Deserts

☐ North of Perth pp320–29

SIGHTS AT A GLANCE

Broome ⑮
Derby ⑯
Halls Creek ⑰
Purnululu (Bungle Bungle)
  National Park ⑱
Wyndham ⑲

KEY

━━ Major road

═══ Minor road

– – Track

▬▬ State border

For hotels and restaurants in this region see pp500–1 and pp546–8

Broome ⑮

🏚 13,000. ✈ 🚃 🚌 🛈 cnr Bagot Rd & Broome Hwy (08) 9192 2222. **www**.broomevisitorcentre.com.au

Broome, first settled by Europeans in the 1860s, soon became Western Australia's most profitable pearling region. Pearl divers from Asia swelled the town in the 1880s and helped give it the multicultural flavour that remains today. The tourist industry has now superseded pearling, but the town's past can still be seen in several original stores, as well as the Chinese and Japanese cemeteries that contain the graves of hundreds of pearl divers.

Just outside town is the popular Cable Beach. On Cable Beach Road, **Broome Crocodile Park** has more than 1,000 of these animals.

✗ Broome Crocodile Park
Cable Beach Rd. **Tel** (08) 9192 1489. ☐ daily. 🗺 ♿

Camel trekking along the famous Cable Beach near Broome

A freshwater crocodile basking in the sun, Windjana Gorge, near Derby

Derby ⑯

🏃 *5,000.* ✈ 🚌 ℹ️ *2 Clarendon St (08) 9191 1426.*

Derby is the gateway to a region of stunning gorges. Points of interest in the town include the 1920s Wharfingers House, Old Derby Gaol, and the Botanical Gardens.

South of town is the 1,000-year old Prison Boab (baobab) tree, 14 m (45 ft) in circumference. At the end of the 19th century, it was used to house prisoners overnight before their final journey to Derby Gaol.

Environs

Derby stands at the western end of the Gibb River Road, which leads towards the three national parks collectively known as the **Devonian Reef National Parks**. The parks of Windjana Gorge, Tunnel Creek and Geikie Gorge contain spectacular gorge scenery.

🌿 **Devonian Reef National Parks**
🚌 *to Derby.* ℹ️ *Derby (08) 9191 1426.* ◯ *Mon–Sat.* ⬤ *public hols.*

Halls Creek ⑰

🏃 *1,400.* 🚌 ℹ️ *Community Resource Centre, Great Northern Hwy (08) 9168 6262.*

Halls Creek was the site of Western Australia's first gold rush in 1885, and today is a centre for mineral mining. Close to the original town site is a vertical wall of quartz rock, known as China Wall. About

130 km (80 miles) to the south is the world's second-largest meteorite crater, in **Wolfe Creek Crater National Park**.

🌿 **Wolfe Creek Crater National Park**
🚌 *Halls Creek.* ℹ️ *Halls Creek (08) 9168 6262.* ◯ *Apr–Sep: daily.* ⬤ *wet weather (roads impassable).*

Purnululu (Bungle Bungle) National Park ⑱

🚌 *Kununurra, Halls Creek.*
ℹ️ *Kununurra (08) 9168 1177.*
◯ *Apr–Nov: daily.* 🅿️ ✓

Covering some 320,000 ha (790,000 acres) of the most isolated landscape in Western Australia, Purnululu National Park was declared in 1987. It is home to the local Kija and

The intriguing domes of the Bungle Bungles, Purnululu National Park

Jaru people, who co-operate with national park authorities to develop cultural tourism.

The most famous part of the park is the Bungle Bungle Range, consisting of unique beehive-shaped domes of rock encased in a skin of silica and cyanobacterium.

Wyndham ⑲

🏃 *900.* ✈ 🚌 ℹ️ *Kimberley Motors, 6 Great Northern Hwy (08) 9161 1281.*

The port of Wyndham lies at the northern tip of the Great Northern Highway, on Cambridge Gulf. The town was established in 1888, partly to service the Halls Creek gold rush and partly as a centre for the local pastoral industry. It also provided supplies, which were carried by Afghan camel-trains, for cattle stations in the northern Kimberley. The town's Afghan cemetery is a reminder of those hardy traders who were essential to the survival of pioneer home-steads in the interior.

The part of the town known as Old Wyndham Port was the original town site and still contains a number of 19th-century buildings, including the old post office, the old courthouse and Anthon's Landing, where the first jetty was erected. The Port Museum displays a vivid photographic history of the port.

The area around Wyndham has a large crocodile popula-tion. Freshwater and saltwater crocodiles can be seen at **Wyndham Crocodile Park** or occasionally in the wild at Blood Drain Crocodile Lookout and Crocodile Hole. To complete the picture, a 4-m (13-ft) high concrete saltwater crocodile greets visitors at the entrance to the town. Saltwater crocodiles have a taste for people, so exercise caution.

About 25 km (15 miles) from Wyndham, Aboriginal petro-glyphs can be seen at the pic-nic spot of Moochalabra Dam.

🐊 **Wyndham Crocodile Farm**
Barylettes Rd. **Tel** *(08) 9161 1124.* ◯ *daily.* ⬤ *25 Dec.* 🅿️ ♿

SOUTH AUSTRALIA

INTRODUCING SOUTH AUSTRALIA 334–339

ADELAIDE AND THE SOUTHEAST 340–357

THE YORKE AND EYRE PENINSULAS
AND THE FAR NORTH 358–369

South Australia at a Glance

South Australia contains a wide range of landscapes. A striking coastline of sandy beaches and steep cliffs gives way to lush valleys, mountains and rolling plains of wheat and barley. Further inland, the terrain changes starkly as the climate becomes hotter and drier. The Far North encompasses huge areas and includes the Flinders Ranges and Coober Pedy, the opal-mining town with "dugout" homes. Most of the state's population lives in the capital, Adelaide, and the wine-making towns of the Clare and Barossa valleys.

THE YORKE AND EYRE PENINSULAS AND THE FAR NORTH
(see pp358–69)

Coober Pedy's *golf course is one of the few features above ground in this strange Outback mining town. Many of the town's houses are built underground to escape the area's harsh, dusty climate (see p368).*

Port Augusta (see p365) *is a major road and rail hub that also serves as the gateway to the Far North of the state. It retains several early homesteads among its modern buildings.*

Kangaroo Island (see p354) *is an unspoilt haven for abundant native wildlife. At Kirkpatrick Point in the southwest lie the Remarkable Rocks, sculpted by the wind, rain and sea.*

0 kilometres   100

0 miles   10

◁ **Profile of the rich red soil in a Coonawarra winery in South Australia**

Quorn (see p369) *was an important railway town at the end of the 19th century and has many reminders of its pioneerng days. Today it marks the start of the Pichi Richi Railway, a restored track running vintage trains and locomotives for tourists.*

The Flinders Ranges (see p369) *stretch from north of St Vincent's Gulf far into the Outback. They include some of South Australia's most rugged scenery and offer fine bushwalking.*

The Barossa wine region *encompasses the Barossa Valley and Eden Valley. Both are lush areas of rolling hills and home to dozens of famous wineries dating from the 19th century (see pp356–7).*

Adelaide (see pp344–59) *is an elegant state capital with many well-preserved colonial buildings. Its cosmopolitan atmosphere is enhanced by a lively restaurant, arts and entertainment scene.*

ADELAIDE
AND THE
SOUTHEAST
(see pp340–57)

Mount Gambier (see p354) *lies on the slopes of an extinct volcano of the same name. One of the volcano's crater lakes, Blue Lake, shows its intense hue in the summer months.*

Birds of South Australia

The vast, varied habitats of South Australia are home to some 380 bird species. Gulls, sea eagles and penguins live along the coast, while waders, ducks and cormorants are found in the internal wetlands. Rosellas and other parrots are common in Adelaide's parkland. The mallee scrub, which once covered much of the state, is home to the mallee fowl

South Australian budgerigar

and an array of honeyeaters. The Flinders Ranges and the Far North are the domain of birds of prey such as the peregrine falcon and the wedge-tailed eagle. Although much land has been cleared for farming, many habitats are protected within the state's national parks.

Little penguins *are the smallest penguins found in Australia. The only species to breed on the mainland, they feed on fish and squid skilfully caught underwater.*

THE FLINDERS RANGES AND OUTBACK HABITAT

The rugged mountains and deep gorges of the Flinders Ranges support a wide variety of bird species. Most spectacular are the birds of prey. Wedge-tailed eagles' nests can be found in large gum trees or on rock ledges, and the eagles are commonly seen feeding on dead animals in the arid Outback regions.

MALLEE SCRUB HABITAT

Much of this low-level scrubland has been cleared for agriculture. Remaining areas such as Billiat National Park near Loxton provide an important habitat for several elusive species. Golden whistlers, red and brush wattlebirds and white-eared honeyeaters can be seen here by patient bird-watchers. The best seasons to visit are late winter, spring and early summer.

Wedge-tailed eagles, *with their huge wingspan of up to 2.3 m (7 ft 6 in), typically perch on dead trees and telephone poles.*

Mallee fowls, *a wary species, stand 60 cm (24 in) tall and move quietly. They lay their eggs in a ground nest made of decomposing leaves and twigs.*

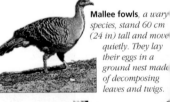

Peregrine falcons *do not build nests, but lay their eggs on bare ledges or in tree hollows. Magnificent in flight, they descend on their prey at great speed with wings half or fully closed.*

Western whipbirds *are scarce and extremely secretive, keeping to the undergrowth. They run and fly swiftly, and are usually first noted by their harsh, grating call.*

THE EMU

Emus are huge flightless birds unique to Australia. Second only to the ostrich in height, they stand 1.5–1.9 m (5–6 ft 3 in) tall. They have long powerful legs and can run at speeds of up to 50 km/h (30 mph) over short distances. The females have a distinctive voice like a thudding drum. They lay their eggs on the ground on a thin layer of grass and leaves. The male incubates them for seven weeks, then broods and accompanies the young for up to 18 months. Common all over Australia, emus are found mainly in open, pastoral areas. Moving alone or in flocks, they are highly mobile and have a large home range.

Alert gaze of the Australian emu

Soft, grey-black plumage of the emu

WETLAND HABITAT

Wetlands such as Coorong National Park (*see p351*) are vital feeding and breeding grounds for a wide range of water birds. They provide essential refuge in times of drought for many endangered birds. Migratory birds, such as sharp-tailed sandpipers from Siberia, use these areas to feed and rest before continuing on their annual journeys.

Brolgas *stand up to 1.3 m (4 ft 3 in) tall, with a wingspan of up to 2.3 m (7 ft 6 in). They are renowned for their impressive dancing displays, leaping, bowing and flapping.*

Freckled ducks *are similar to primitive waterfowl, with swan-like characteristics. Dark, with no obvious markings, they are hard to spot. This is one of the world's rarest ducks.*

WOODLAND HABITAT

Habitats in woodland areas such as the Belair National Park near Adelaide support many species such as honeyeaters, rosellas and kookaburras. There is usually an abundance of food in such places and good opportunities to nest and roost. Despite increased human settlement in these areas, the birdlife is still rich. Dawn and dusk are the best times for seeing birds.

Adelaide rosellas *are commonly found in the Mount Lofty Ranges and the parklands of Adelaide. Their plumage is in brilliant shades of red, orange and blue.*

Laughing kookaburras *are the world's largest kingfishers. They are renowned for their loud, manic laughing call, often begun by one bird and quickly taken up by others.*

Wines of South Australia

South Australia produces almost half of Australia's wines, including many of its finest. From its numerous vineyards comes a dazzling diversity of wines – several are made from some of the oldest vines in the world. The state has a long history of wine-making and is home to some very famous producers, such as Hardys, Penfolds, Jacob's Creek and Banrock Station. Virtually all wineries welcome tourists for tastings.

Sevenhill Cellars *is in the heart of the Clare Valley, one of South Australia's prime wine-producing regions.*

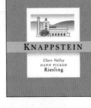

Tim Knappstein, *an award-winning Clare Valley winery, produces Riesling that is European in style.*

Bridgewater Mill *winery is renowned in the area for its excellent restaurant. Daily tastings of its own labels and Petaluma wines are offered at the cellar door.*

WINE REGIONS

South Australia has eight designated wine zones and within these zones are many well-known regions. These include the Barossa Valley *(see pp356–7)*, which has been producing wine for 150 years; the Clare Valley, which is noted for its Rieslings, Cabernet Sauvignon and Shiraz; and Coonawarra, which is Australia's best red wine region, due to its soil. McLaren Vale, the Murray Valley, the Adelaide Plains, the Riverland, the Limestone Coast, and the Adelaide Hills are the other major districts.

Kadina   Clare •

Gawler •
ADELAIDE

Cape Jervis

Alexan

Cabernet Sauvignon *grapes are very successful in the state, with a ripe, fruity flavour.*

The Adelaide Hills *are known for their excellent Pinot Noir, Chardonnay and Riesling grapes.*

Wolf Blass *' Barossa Black Label has a rich, oaky flavour, and is just one of this world-renowned vintner's individual wines. Blass has earned more than 2,000 international medals for his wine.*

KEY		KEY	
☐	Clare Valley	☐	Riverland
☐	Barossa Valley	☐	Langhorne Creek
☐	Eden Valley	☐	Padthaway
☐	Adelaide Hills	☐	Wrattonbully
☐	McLaren Vale	☐	Coonawarra

KEY FACTS

Location and Climate

The climate of Australia's central state ranges from Mediterranean-style in the Murray Valley to the cool Adelaide Hills and districts in the southeast. Vintage begins in high summer, when grapes are often picked and crushed at night to preserve the maximum flavour.

Grape Varieties

The diverse climate ensures that a wide range of grape varieties is planted. These include the whites of Riesling, Semillon, Sauvignon Blanc, Chardonnay; and the reds of Shiraz, Grenache, Pinot Noir, Cabernet Sauvignon, Merlot.

Good Producers

Penfolds, Bethany, Grant Burge, St Hallett, Henschke, Seppelt, Charles Melton, Turkey Flat, Mountadam, Hardys, Orlando, Wolf Blass, Yalumba, Rockford, Willows, Petaluma, Grosset, Wendoree, Pauletts, Pikes, Wynns, Bowen, Chapel Hill, d'Arenberg, Peter Lehmann, Noons, Bridgewater Mill, Hollicks. (This list represents only a sampling of the state's quality producers.)

Barrel maturation *at the Berri Renmano winery in the Murray Valley is one of the traditional techniques still used in the production of top-quality table wines.*

Wynns Winery *at Coonawarra is known for fine Cabernet Sauvignon and other reds. The winery itself is equally distinctive – an image of its triple gable architecture appears on the wine labels.*

Yalumba 'Menzies' Vineyard, *founded in 1849, is one of the oldest in the Coonawarra region. The grapes are grown here, but the wine is made at the winery in the Barossa Valley (see page 357). The climate in the Coonawarra area is similar to that of Bordeaux in France.*

ADELAIDE AND THE SOUTHEAST

The Southeast is a region rich with pine forests, wineries and a spectacular coastline. The state capital, Adelaide, is a vibrant city, whose surrounding hills abound with vineyards from the Barossa Valley to McLaren Vale. To the east, the great Murray River meanders from the Victoria border down to the Southern Ocean. Just off the Fleurieu Peninsula lies Kangaroo Island, a haven for wildlife.

Home to Aborigines for more than 10,000 years, this region was settled by Europeans in 1836 when Governor John Hindmarsh proclaimed the area a British colony. William Light, the Surveyor General, chose the site of the city of Adelaide.

The settlement was based on a theory of free colonization funded solely by land sales, and no convicts were transported here. Elegant Adelaide was carefully planned by Colonel Light: its ordered grid pattern, centred on pretty squares and gardens, is surrounded by parkland. Wealth from agriculture and mining paid for many of Adelaide's fine Victorian buildings. In the mid-20th century, the city established a significant manufacturing industry, in particular of motor vehicles and household appliances. Adelaide still has a focus on high technology.

South Australia has always had a tradition of tolerance. Many of the first settlers were non-conformists from Great Britain seeking a more open society. Other early migrants included Lutherans escaping persecution in Germany. They settled in Hahndorf and the Barossa Valley, where they established a wine industry.

With high rainfall and irrigated by the Murray River, the region is the most fertile in the state. The coastline includes the Fleurieu Peninsula and the beautiful Coorong National Park. Offshore, Kangaroo Island has stunning scenery and bountiful native wildlife.

Port and sherry casks at a winery in the Barossa Valley

◁ The tall twin spires of the neo-Gothic St Peter's Cathedral in Adelaide

Exploring Adelaide and the Southeast

Adelaide and the Southeast area encompass the most bountiful and productive regions of South Australia. Adelaide, the state's capital city and the most obvious base for exploring the region, lies on a flat plain between the Mount Lofty Ranges and the popular white sandy beaches of Gulf St Vincent, to the east of Cape Jervis. The city itself is green and elegant, with many historic sites to explore. To the northeast, beyond the Adelaide Hills, are quaint 19th-century villages and the many wineries of the Barossa Valley region. To the east and south lie Australia's largest river, the Murray River, and the rolling hills of the Fleurieu Peninsula. Further to the southeast the beauty of the coastal Coorong National Park and the Southern Ocean coastline contrasts with the flat, agricultural area inland. Offshore lies the natural splendour of Kangaroo Island, with its abundance of native wildlife and striking rock formations.

0 kilometres   50

0 miles   50

SEE ALSO

- **Where to Stay** pp501–4
- **Where to Eat** pp548–51

Birds enjoying the wetlands of Bool Lagoon in the Naracoorte Caves National Park

St Peter's Anglican Cathedral, seen across Adelaide parkland

SIGHTS AT A GLANCE

Adelaide pp344–9 ❶
Belair National Park ❷
Birdwood ❼
Hahndorf ❹
Kangaroo Island ❽
Mount Gambier ❾
Mount Lofty ❻
Murray River ⓬
Naracoorte Caves ⓫
Penola ❿
Strathalbyn ❺
Warrawong Sanctuary ❸

Tour

Barossa Valley ⓭

View of the Murray River, between Swan Reach and Walker Flat

GETTING AROUND

The inner city of Adelaide is best explored on foot; it is compact, well laid out and flat. There is a public transport system of mostly buses, and some trains, throughout the metropolitan area, although services are often restricted at weekends. However, for those with a car, the city's roads are good and the traffic generally light. Outside Adelaide, public transport is very limited, although coach tours are available to most areas. A car provides the most efficient means of exploring the region, with a network of high-standard roads and highways. In addition, a domestic air service operates between Adelaide and Mount Gambier. Kangaroo Island is serviced by air from Adelaide and also by ferry from Cape Jervis. The predominantly flat landscape also makes this a popular area for cyclists and walkers.

KEY

▬▬	Highway
▬▬	Major road
──	Minor road
▬▬	Scenic route
▬▬▬	Main railway
────	Minor railway
▬▬▬	State border

Street-by-Street: Adelaide **❶**

Adelaide's cultural centre lies between the grand, tree-lined North Terrace and the River Torrens. Along North Terrace is a succession of imposing 19th-century public buildings, including the state library, museum and art gallery and two university campuses. To the west, on the bank of the river, is the Festival Centre. This multipurpose complex of theatres, including an outdoor amphitheatre, is home to the renowned biennial Adelaide Festival of Arts *(see p41)*. To the east, also by the river, lie the botanic and zoological gardens.

Museum figure

River Torrens
Visitors can hire paddleboats to travel along this gentle river and see Adelaide from water level.

The Migration and Settlement Museum tells the stories of the thousands of people from more than 100 nations who left everything behind to start a new life in South Australia.

Festival Centre
Completed in 1977, this arts complex enjoys a picturesque riverside setting and is a popular place for a picnic.

VICTORI

KINTORE AVENUE

KING WILLIAM ROAD

Parliament House
Ten marble Corinthian columns grace the façade of Parliament House, which was completed in 1939, more than 50 years after construction first began.

★ **Botanic Gardens**
Begun in 1855, these peaceful gardens cover an area of 20 ha (50 acres). They include artificial lakes and the beautiful Bicentennial Conservatory in which a tropical rainforest environment has been re-created.

VISITORS' CHECKLIST

1.1 million. West Beach, 10 km (6 miles) W of city. North Terrace (suburban); Richmond Rd, Keswick (interstate). Central Bus Station, Franklin St. Glenelg Jetty, Glenelg Beach. 18 King William St (08) 8303 2033. Adelaide Festival of Arts; Womadelaide (both Feb, alternate years).

Art Gallery of South Australia
Contemporary works, such as Christopher Healey's Drinking Fountains, *feature here alongside period painting and sculpture.*

| 0 metres | 100 |
| 0 yards | 100 |

KEY

— — — Suggested route

STAR SIGHTS

★ Botanic Gardens

★ South Australian Museum

★ **South Australian Museum**
Chiefly a natural history museum, the South Australian Museum has an excellent reputation for its fine Aboriginal collection, including this painting on bark, Assembling the Totem, *by a Melville Island artist (see p274).*

Exploring Adelaide

South Australian Museum boomerangs

Adelaide, a city of great charm with an unhurried way of life, is easily explored on foot. Well planned on a grid pattern, it is bordered by wide terraces and parkland. Within the city are a number of garden squares and gracious stone buildings. However, while Adelaide values its past, it is very much a modern city. The balmy climate and excellent local food and wine have given rise to an abundance of streetside restaurants and cafés. With its acclaimed arts-based Adelaide Festival *(see p41)*, the city also prides itself on being the artistic capital of Australia.

Detail of the ornate front parapet of Edmund Wright House

🏛 Victoria Square
Flinders & Angas sts.

Victoria Square lies at the geographic heart of the city. In its centre stands a fountain designed by sculptor John Dowie in 1968. Its theme is the three rivers from which Adelaide draws its water: the Torrens, the Murray and the Onkaparinga. Government buildings were erected around much of the square during colonial days and many of these buildings still stand as reminders of a bygone age.

On the north side of Victoria Square stands the General Post Office, an impressive building with an ornate main hall and a clock tower. Opened in 1872, it was hailed by English novelist Anthony Trollope as the "grandest edifice in the town".

On the corner of Wakefield Street, to the east of Victoria Square, stands St Francis Xavier Catholic Cathedral. The original cathedral, dedicated in 1858, was a simpler building and plans for expansion were hampered by the lack of rich Catholics in the state. The

cathedral was only completed in 1996, when the spire was finally added.

To the south of the square is Adelaide's legal centre and the Magistrates Court. The Supreme Court, built in the 1860s, has a Palladian façade.

🏛 Adelaide Town Hall
128 King William St. **Tel** *(08) 8203 7203.* ⬜ *Mon–Fri.* ⬛ *public hols.* ♿ **www**.adelaidetownhall.com.au

When Adelaide Town Hall, designed in Italianate style by Edmund Wright, was built in 1866, it became the most significant structure on King William Street. It was not long before it took over as the city's premier venue for concerts and civic receptions and is still used as such today. Notable features include its grand staircase and decorative ceiling.

🏛 Edmund Wright House
59 King William St. ♿

Edmund Wright House, originally built for the Bank of South Australia in 1878, was set to be demolished in 1971. However, a general outcry led to its public

purchase and restoration. The building was renamed after its main architect, Edmund Wright. The skill and workmanship displayed in the finely proportioned and detailed façade is also evident in the beautiful interior. Today the building is the Migrant Resource Centre with limited access to the public.

Further along King William Street, at the corner of North Terrace, stands one of Adelaide's finest statues, the South African War Memorial. It shows a "spirited horse and his stalwart rider" and stands in memory of those who lost their lives in the Boer War.

Apples on display in Adelaide's Central Market

🏛 Central Market
Gouger St. **Tel** *(08) 8203 7494.* ⬜ *Tue, Thu–Sat.* ⬛ *public hols.* ♿

Just west of Victoria Square, between Gouger and Grote streets, Adelaide Central Market has provided a profusion of tastes and aromas in the city for more than 125 years. The changing ethnic pattern of Adelaide society is reflected in the diversity of produce available. Asian shops now sit beside older European-style butchers and delicatessens, and part of the area has become Adelaide's own little Chinatown. Around the market are dozens of restaurants and cafés where local food is adapted to various international cuisines.

View overlooking Victoria Square in the centre of Adelaide

For hotels and restaurants in this region see pp501–4 and pp548–51

🏛 Tandanya

253 Grenfell St. ***Tel*** *(08) 8224 3200.* 🕒 *10am–5pm daily.* ⛔ *Good Fri, 25 Dec, 1 Jan.* 📷 ☕ 🛍 ♿ **www**.tandanya.com.au

Tandanya, the Kaurna Aboriginal people's name for the Adelaide area (it means "Place of the red kangaroo"), is an excellent cultural institute celebrating the Aboriginal and Torres Strait Islander art and cultures. It was established in 1989 and is the first Aboriginal-owned and run arts centre in Australia. The institute features indigenous art galleries, educational workshops and performance areas. It is also possible for visitors to meet indigenous people. Tandanya also has a café (offering bush tucker) and a great gift shop.

🏛 Migration Museum

82 Kintore Ave. ***Tel*** *(08) 8207 7580.* 🕒 *daily.* ⛔ *Good Fri, 25 Dec.* ♿ **www**.history.sa.gov.au

The Migration Museum is located behind the State Library in what was once Adelaide's Destitute Asylum. It reflects the cultural diversity of South Australian society by telling the stories of people from many parts of the world who came here to start a new life. Exhibits, including re-creations of early settlers' houses, explain the immigrants' reasons for leaving their homeland and their hopes for a new life. The site is also home to two other institutes, the Maritime and Motor museums.

🏛 South Australian Museum

North Terrace. ***Tel*** *(08) 8207 7500.* 🕒 *10am–5pm daily.* ⛔ *Good Fri, 25 Dec.* ♿ **www**.samusuem.sa.gov.au

This museum, whose entrance is framed by huge whale skeletons, has a number of interesting collections including an Egyptian room and natural history exhibits. Its most important collection is its internationally acclaimed collection of Aboriginal artifacts which boasts more than 37,000 individual items and 50,000 photographs, as well as many sound and video recordings.

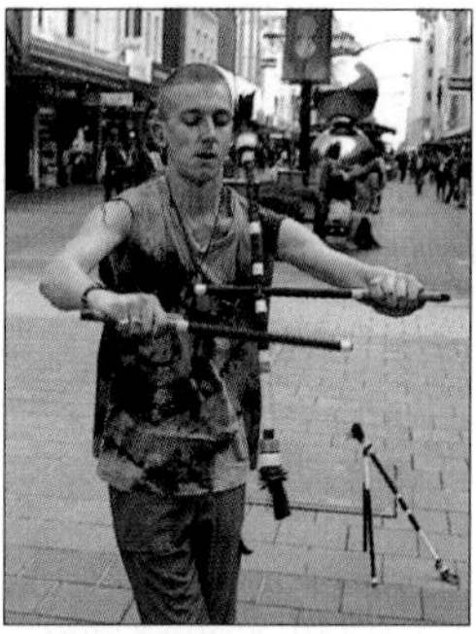

A street performer in Rundle Mall, Adelaide's main shopping precinct

🛍 Rundle Mall

Adelaide Arcade. ***Tel*** *(08) 8223 5522.* 🕒 *daily.* ⛔ *public hols.*

Adelaide's main shopping area is centred on Rundle Mall, with its mixture of department stores, boutiques and small shops. Several arcades run off the mall, including Adelaide Arcade. Built in the 1880s, it has Italianate elevations at both ends and a central dome. The interior was modernized in the 1960s, but has since been fully restored to its former glory.

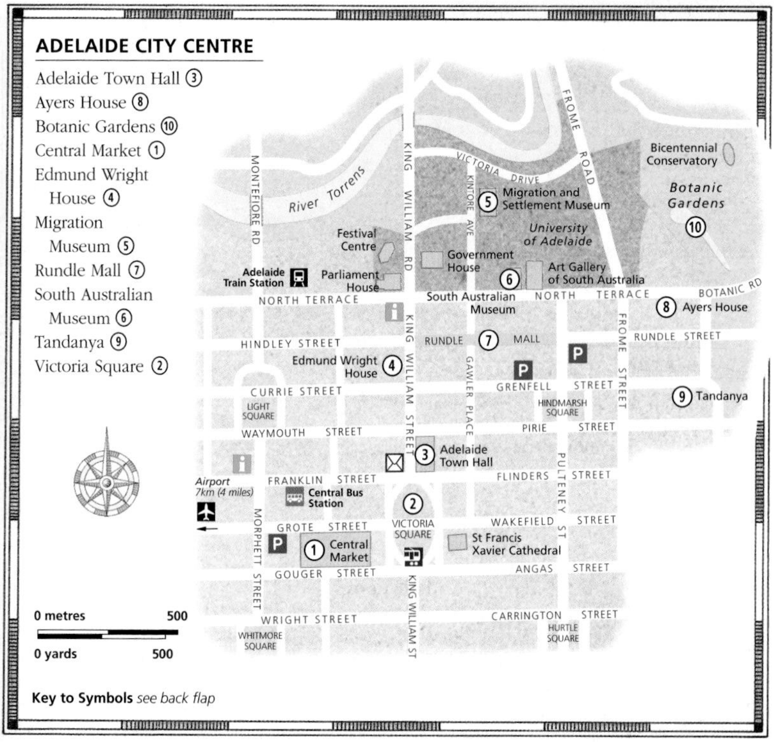
ADELAIDE CITY CENTRE
Adelaide Town Hall 3
Ayers House 8
Botanic Gardens 10
Central Market 1
Edmund Wright House 4
Migration Museum 5
Rundle Mall 7
South Australian Museum 6
Tandanya 9
Victoria Square 2
River Torrens
Festival Centre
Adelaide Train Station
Parliament House
Government House
Migration and Settlement Museum
University of Adelaide
Art Gallery of South Australia
Bicentennial Conservatory
Botanic Gardens
South Australian Museum
Ayers House
Tandanya
Edmund Wright House
Adelaide Town Hall
Central Bus Station
Central Market
St Francis Xavier Cathedral
Airport 7km (4 miles)
NORTH TERRACE
HINDLEY STREET
RUNDLE MALL
RUNDLE STREET
CURRIE STREET
GRENFELL STREET
WAYMOUTH STREET
PIRIE STREET
FRANKLIN STREET
FLINDERS STREET
WAKEFIELD STREET
GROTE STREET
GOUGER STREET
ANGAS STREET
WRIGHT STREET
CARRINGTON STREET
VICTORIA DRIVE
FROME ROAD
FROME STREET
BOTANIC RD
KING WILLIAM RD
KING WILLIAM STREET
KING WILLIAM ST
KINTORE AVE
GAWLER PLACE
PULTENEY ST
MONTEFIORE RD
MORPHETT STREET
LIGHT SQUARE
HINDMARSH SQUARE
VICTORIA SQUARE
WHITMORE SQUARE
HURTLE SQUARE
0 metres 500
0 yards 500
Key to Symbols see back flap

Ayers House

Ayers House is one of the best examples of colonial Regency architecture in Australia. From 1855 until his death in 1897, it was the home of Sir Henry Ayers, a former Premier of South Australia and an influential businessman. The original house was quite simple but was expanded over the years with the growing status and wealth of its owner. The final form of this elegant mansion is due largely to the noted colonial architect Sir George Strickland Kingston. The restored house is now run by the National Trust and also incorporates two restaurants. The oldest section is open to the public and houses a fine collection of Victorian furniture, furnishings, memorabilia and art.

Front of the house viewed from North Terrace

Corrugated roof

★ **Bedroom**
The main bedroom has been carefully restored to its late-Victorian style. Its authentic furnishings reflect the prosperity brought by South Australia's rich mining discoveries in the 1870s.

STAR FEATURES

★ Bedroom

★ State Dining Room

The Library, furnished with a long dining table, can be hired for functions.

Ballroom
This intricately decorated cornice dates from the 1870s. It is likely that it was painted by Charles Gow, an employee of the Scottish firm of Lyon and Cottier, who is believed to have undertaken extensive work at the house.

★ **State Dining
Room**
*Sir Henry loved to
entertain, and lavish
dinners were often
held here. It boasts
a hand-painted
ceiling, stencilled
woodwork and the
original gasoliers.*

VISITORS' CHECKLIST

288 North Terrace, Adelaide.
Tel (08) 8223 1234. 🚉 99c.
🕐 10am–4pm Tue–Fri; 1–4pm
Sat, Sun & public hols. ⬤ Mon,
Good Fri, 25 Dec. 📷 📁 📷
♿ ground floor only.

Local bluestone was
used in constructing
the house, as with
many 19th-century
Adelaide houses. The
north façade faces
onto North Terrace,
one of the city's main
streets *(see pp344–5)*.

**Entrance to main
restaurant**

The Conservatory is
based around the original
stables and coachhouse.
Now a restaurant, the
whole area has been
flooded with light by the
addition of a glass roof.

**Front
entrance**

**Veranda's original
chequered tile
flooring**

The family drawing room,
along with the adjacent family
dining room, had test strips
removed from its walls and
ceiling to uncover some stunning
original decoration. These rooms
have now been fully restored.

THE STORY OF SIR HENRY AYERS

Sir Henry Ayers (1821–97) was born in
Hampshire, England, the son of a dock
worker. He married in 1840 and, a month
later, emigrated with his bride to South
Australia. After working briefly as a
clerk, Ayers made his fortune in the
state's new copper mines. Entering
politics in 1857, he was appointed
South Australia's Premier seven
times between 1863 and 1873, and
was President of the Legislative
Council, 1881–93. Among many
causes, he supported exploration of the interior (Ayers Rock,
now Uluru, was named after him), but is chiefly remembered
for his prominent role in the development of South Australia.

**Statesman and business-
man, Sir Henry Ayers**

The Southeast Coastline

The coastline south of Adelaide is rich and varied with beautiful beaches, magnificent coastal scenery and abundant birdlife. The southern coastline of the Fleurieu Peninsula is largely exposed to the mighty Southern Ocean. Here there are good surfing beaches, long expanses of sand, sheltered bays and harbours and stark, weathered cliffs. The western side of the peninsula is more sheltered. There are very few commercial developments on the southeast's coastline and it is easy to find quiet, secluded beaches for swimming, surfing, fishing or walking. Just off South Australia's mainland, Kangaroo Island boasts both pristine swimming beaches and ruggedly beautiful windswept cliffs.

★ Cape Jervis ②

Visitors to the tiny hamlet of Cape Jervis can see Kangaroo Island (see p354), 16 km (10 miles) away across Backstairs Passage. The cape has good boating and fishing and is a hang-gliding centre.

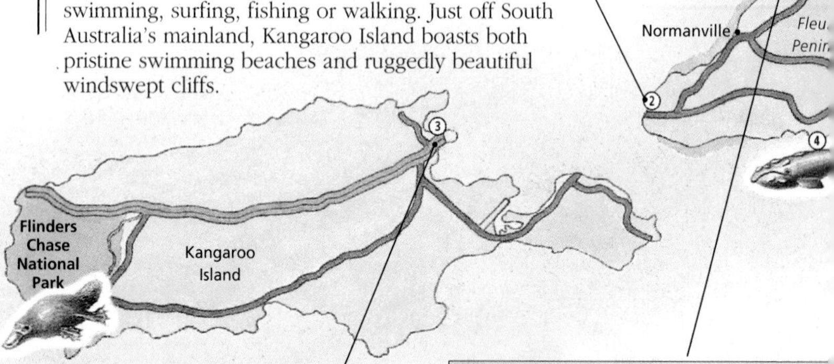

Normanville · Fleu. Penir

Flinders Chase National Park

Kangaroo Island

★ Kingscote, Kangaroo Island ③

Kingscote, the island's largest town has a small sandy beach with a tidal pool. There is rich birdlife in swampland south of the town.

★ Port Noarlunga ①

Port Noarlunga boasts a fantastic beach and a protected reef with marine ecosystems that can be explored by snorkellers and scuba divers on a fully marked 800-m (2,600-ft) underwater trail.

Flinders Chase National Park *covers the western end of Kangaroo Island with undisturbed eucalypt forests and grassland, and seal-inhabited windswept beaches.*

Waitpinga Beach ④

Waitpinga Beach, on the southern coast of the Fleurieu Peninsula, is a spectacular surfing beach with waves rolling in off the Southern Ocean. Strong, unpredictable currents make the beach unsafe for swimming and suitable for experienced surfers only. The long stretch of clean white sand is a favourite for beach walkers.

Victor Harbor ⑤

Holiday homes have been built in Victor Harbor since the 19th century. It later became a whaling station, but today southern right whales can be seen from June to October frolicking offshore.

Port Elliot ⑥

Port Elliot, together with nearby Victor Harbor, has long been a favourite place to escape the summer heat of Adelaide. Established in 1854 as a port for the Murray River trade, the town has a safe swimming beach and a fine cliff-top walk.

Hindmarsh Island ⑦

The quiet escapist destination of Hindmarsh Island can be reached by a free ferry from the town of Goolwa 24 hours a day. On the island there are several good vantage points from which visitors can see the mouth of the Murray River.

Key to Symbols *see back flap*

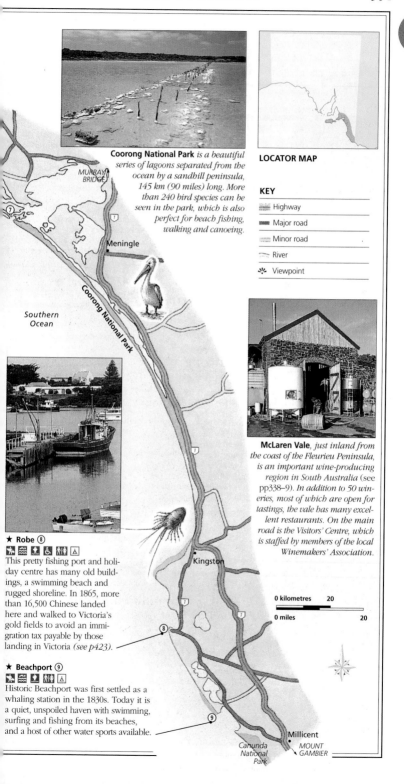

Coorong National Park *is a beautiful series of lagoons separated from the ocean by a sandhill peninsula, 145 km (90 miles) long. More than 240 bird species can be seen in the park, which is also perfect for beach fishing, walking and canoeing.*

LOCATOR MAP

KEY

≈≈≈ Highway

▬▬▬ Major road

═══ Minor road

〜 River

✺ Viewpoint

Southern Ocean

Meningle

MURRAY BRIDGE

Coorong National Park

McLaren Vale, *just inland from the coast of the Fleurieu Peninsula, is an important wine-producing region in South Australia (see pp338–9). In addition to 50 wineries, most of which are open for tastings, the vale has many excellent restaurants. On the main road is the Visitors' Centre, which is staffed by members of the local Winemakers' Association.*

Kingston

0 kilometres   20

0 miles   20

★ **Robe** ⑧

This pretty fishing port and holiday centre has many old buildings, a swimming beach and rugged shoreline. In 1865, more than 16,500 Chinese landed here and walked to Victoria's gold fields to avoid an immigration tax payable by those landing in Victoria *(see p423)*.

★ **Beachport** ⑨

Historic Beachport was first settled as a whaling station in the 1830s. Today it is a quiet, unspoiled haven with swimming, surfing and fishing from its beaches, and a host of other water sports available.

Millicent

Canunda National Park

MOUNT GAMBIER

Old Government House in Belair National Park

Belair National Park ❷

Tel *(08) 8278 5477.* 🚌 *from Adelaide.* ⏰ *8am–4:30pm.* ⬤ *25 Dec.* 🅿️ *for cars only.* ♿ *limited.*

Established in 1891, Belair is the eighth-oldest national park in the world. Only 9 km (5 miles) from Adelaide, it is one of the most popular parks in South Australia. Tennis courts and pavilions are available for hire and there are picnic facilities throughout the park. Visitors can meander through the tall eucalypt forests and cool valleys, and see kangaroos, emus, echidnas and other native wildlife.

In spring, many native plants bloom. The park is closed occasionally in summer on days of extreme fire danger.

Within the park lies **Old Government House**. Built in 1859 as the governor's summer residence, it offers a glimpse of the lifestyle enjoyed by the colonial gentry.

🏛️ **Old Government House**
Belair National Park. *Tel* *(08) 8278 5477.* ⏰ *Sun, public hols.* ⬤ *Good Fri, 25 Dec.* 🅿️

Warrawong Sanctuary ❸

Tel *(08) 8370 9197.* 🚌 *Aldgate.* ⬤ *Closed to the public for restructuring work.*

Warrawong Sanctuary attempts to reverse the disastrous trends of recent years which have seen the extinction of 32 mammal species from South Australia.

Only 20 km (13 miles) from Adelaide, via the town of Stirling, the 32 ha (80 acres) of privately owned native bushland is surrounded by a vermin-proof fence. Into this environment Warrawong's owners have introduced some 15 mammal species, many of which are endangered. These include bettongs, potoroos and quolls (see p455). Warrawong Sanctuary is also the location of Australia's only successful platypus breeding programme.

The sanctuary is currently, and for the forseeable future, closed as it undergoes an extensive programme of changes and improvements.

Hahndorf ❹

🏘️ *1,750.* 🚌 *from Adelaide.* ℹ️ *41 Main St (08) 8388 1185.*

Hahndorf is the oldest surviving German settlement in Australia. The first settlers arrived in 1838 aboard the *Zebra* under the command of Captain Dirk Hahn. Escaping religious persecution in their homeland, they settled in the Adelaide Hills and established Hahndorf (Hahn's Village), a German-style town.

The tree-lined main street has many examples of classic German architecture, such as houses with *fachwerk* timber framing filled in with wattle

Kangaroo roaming through Warrawong Sanctuary in the Adelaide Hills

For hotels and restaurants in this region see pp501–4 and pp548–51

Nineteenth-century mill in the historic town of Hahndorf

and daub, or brick. Visitors can take a stroll around the town and enjoy its historic atmosphere.

Just outside Hahndorf is **The Cedars**, the former home of South Australia's best-known landscape artist, the late Sir Hans Heysen *(see p34)*. Both his home and his studio are open to the public. South of the town is Nixon's Mill, a stone mill built in 1842.

🏛 The Cedars
Heysen Rd. ***Tel*** *(08) 8388 7277.*
🕒 *10am–4pm Sun–Fri.*
⛔ *25 Dec.* 💳 ♿

Strathalbyn ❺

👥 *2,700.* 🚆 🚌 ℹ *Railway Station, South Terrace (08) 8536 3212.*

The designated heritage town of Strathalbyn was originally settled by Scottish immigrants in 1839. Links with its Scottish ancestry can still be seen today in much of the town's architecture, which is reminiscent of small highland towns in Scotland.

Situated on the banks of the Angas River, Strathalbyn is dominated by St Andrew's Church with its sturdy tower. A number of original buildings have been preserved. The police station, built in 1858, and the 1865 courthouse together house the National Trust Museum. The prominent two-storey London House, built as a general store in 1867, has, like a number of buildings in or near the High Street, found a new use as an antiques store. As in many country towns in Australia, the hotels and banks are also architectural reminders of the past.

About 16 km (10 miles) southeast of Strathalbyn, on the banks of the Bremer River, is Langhorne Creek, renowned as one of the earliest wine-growing regions in Australia.

St Andrew's Church, Strathalbyn

Mount Lofty ❻

🚌 *Mount Lofty Summit Rd.* ℹ *Mount Lofty Summit Information Centre (08) 8370 1054.* 🛍 ☕ 🍴

The hills of the Mount Lofty Ranges form the backdrop to Adelaide. The highest point, Mount Lofty, reaches 727 m (2,385 ft) and offers a fine view of the city from the modern lookout at the summit, where there is also an interpretive centre. The hills are dotted with grand summer houses to which Adelaide citizens retreat during the summer heat.

Just below the summit is the **Cleland Wildlife Park** where visitors can stroll among the resident kangaroos and emus, have a photograph taken with a koala or walk through the aviary to observe native birds at close quarters.

About 1.5 km (1 mile) south of here, Mount Lofty Botanic Gardens feature temperate-climate plants such as rhododendrons and magnolias.

🦘 Cleland Wildlife Park
Mount Lofty Summit Rd. ***Tel*** *(08) 8339 2444.* 🕒 *9am–5pm daily.*
⛔ *25 Dec.* 💳 ♿ 🛍 ☕

Birdwood ❼

👥 *600.* ℹ *National Motor Museum, Shannon St (08) 8568 5577.*

Nestled in the Adelaide Hills is the quiet little town of Birdwood. In the 1850s, wheat was milled in the town and the old wheat mill now houses Birdwood's most famous asset: the country's largest collection of vintage, veteran and classic motor cars, trucks and motorbikes. The **National Motor Museum** has more than 300 on display and is considered to be one of the best collections of its kind in the world.

🏛 National Motor Museum
Shannon St. ***Tel*** *(08) 8568 5006.* 🕒
9am–5pm daily. ⛔ *25 Dec.* 💳 ♿

Hand-feeding kangaroos at Cleland Wildlife Park, Mount Lofty

Kangaroo Island 8

🚢 Sea Link ferry connection from Cape Jervis. 🛈 The Gateway Information Centre, Howard Drive, Penneshaw (08) 8553 1185. ♿ 🅿

Kangaroo Island, Australia's third-largest island, is 155 km (96 miles) long and 55 km (34 miles) wide. Located 16 km (10 miles) off the Fleurieu Peninsula, the island was the site of South Australia's first official colonial settlement, established at Reeves Point in 1836. The settlement was short-lived, however, and within just four years had been virtually abandoned. The island was then settled by degrees during the remainder of the 19th century as communications improved with the new mainland settlements.

There is no public transport on Kangaroo Island and visitors must travel on a tour or by car. Though the roads to the main sights are good, many roads are unsealed and extra care should be taken.

Remarkable Rocks at Kirkpatrick Point, Kangaroo Island

Sparsely populated and geographically isolated, the island has few introduced predators and is a haven for a wide variety of animals and birds, many protected in its 19 conservation and national parks.

At Kingscote and Penneshaw fairy penguins can often be seen in the evenings, and the south coast windswept beach of Seal Bay is home to a large colony of Australian sea lions. In Flinders Chase National Park, kangaroos will sometimes approach visitors, but feeding them is discouraged.

The interior is dry, but does support tracts of mallee scrub and eucalypts. The coastline, however, is varied. The north coast has sheltered beaches ideal for swimming. The south coast, battered by the Southern Ocean, has more than 40 shipwrecks. At Kirkpatrick Point to the southwest stands a group of large rocks. Aptly named Remarkable Rocks, they have been eroded into weird formations by the winds and sea.

Mount Gambier 9

🏙 23,000. ✈ 🚌 🚆 🛈 Jubilee Hwy East (08) 8724 9750.

Mount Gambier is a major regional city midway between Adelaide and Melbourne, named after the extinct volcano on the slopes of which the city lies. Established in 1854, it is now surrounded by farming country and large pine plantations. The volcano has four crater lakes which are attractive recreation spots, with walking trails, picnic facilities and a wildlife park. The Blue Lake, up to 85 m (280 ft) deep, is a major draw between November and March when its water mysteriously turns an intense blue. From April to October, it remains a dull grey.

There are also a number of caves to explore within the city. Engelbrecht Cave is popular with cave divers, and the exposed Umpherston Sinkhole has fine terraced gardens.

Strange and vividly coloured water of Mount Gambier's Blue Lake

For hotels and restaurants in this region see pp501–4 and pp548–51

Sharam's Cottage, the first house built in Penola

Penola ❿

🚶 3,400. 🚌 ℹ️ *27 Arthur St*
(08) 8737 2855.

One of the oldest towns in the Southeast, Penola is the commercial centre of the Coonawarra wine region *(see pp338–9)*. The region's first winery was built in 1893. There are now some 20 wineries, most of which are open for sales and tastings.

Penola itself is a quiet town which takes great pride in its history. A heritage walk takes visitors past most of its early buildings, including the restored Sharam's Cottage, which was built in 1850 as the first dwelling in Penola.

Environs

Situated 27 km (17 miles) north of Penola, Bool Lagoon (designated a wetland of international significance by UNESCO), is an important refuge for an assortment of native wildlife including more than 150 species of birds. The park provides an opportunity to observe at close quarters many of these local and migratory birds *(see p337)*.

Naracoorte Caves Conservation Park ⓫

Tel *(08) 8762 2340.* 🚌 *from Adelaide.* ⏰ *9am–5pm daily (last tour 3:30pm).* ⛔ *25 Dec.* 🎦 📷 ♿

Located 12 km (7 miles) south of Naracoorte is the Naracoorte Caves Conservation Park. Within this 600-ha (1,500-acre) park, there are 60 known caves, most notably Victoria

Cave, which has been placed on the World Heritage List as a result of the remarkable fossil deposits discovered here in 1969 *(see pp26–7)*. Guided tours of this and three other caves are available.

From November to February thousands of bent wing bats come to breed in the Maternity Cave. They can be seen leaving the cave en masse at dusk to feed. Entrance to this cave is forbidden, but visitors can view the inside via infra-red cameras in the park.

Ancient stalactites inside one of the Naracoorte caves

Murray River ⓬

🚌 *from Adelaide.* ℹ️ *Renmark (08) 8586 6704.*

Australia's largest river is a vital source of water in this, the driest state in Australia. As well as supplying water for Adelaide it supports a vigorous local agricultural industry

which produces 40 per cent of all Australian wine *(see pp338–9)*. It is also a popular destination for houseboating, water-skiing and fishing.

The town of Renmark, close to the Victoria border, lies at the heart of the Murray River irrigation area and is home to the Riverlands' first winery. At the town's wharf is the restored paddlesteamer *Industry*, now a floating museum and a reminder of days gone by.

Just south of Renmark, Berri is the area's commercial centre and site of the largest combined distillery and winery in the southern hemisphere. The Murray River meanders through Berri and on to the small town of Loxton before winding up towards the citrus centre of Waikerie. Surrounded by more than 5,000 ha (12,000 acres) of orchards, Waikerie is a favourite gliding centre and has hosted the world gliding championships.

Another 40 km (25 miles) downstream, the Murray River reaches the town of Morgan, its northernmost point in South Australia, before it turns south towards the ocean. The **Port of Morgan Museum**, located in the old railway station, aims to recapture the river-trading days, telling the story of what was once the second-busiest port in the state. The *Mayflower*, the oldest surviving paddlesteamer in the state, is moored next to the museum.

🏛️ **Port of Morgan Museum**
Morgan Railway Station. **Tel** *(08) 8540 2130.* ⏰ *2–4pm Tue, Sat, Sun.* ⛔ *25 Dec.* ♿

An old paddlesteamer cruising along the Murray River

Barossa Valley Tour ⑬

The Barossa, which is comprised of the Barossa and Eden valleys, is one of Australia's most famous wine regions and has an international reputation. First settled in 1842 by German Lutheran immigrants, villages were established at Bethany, Langmeil (now Tanunda), Lyndoch and Light's Pass. Signs of German traditions can be seen in the 19th-century buildings, churches and in the region's food, music and festivals. The Barossa Festival takes place in April in every even-numbered year and there is a Music Festival every October.

Riesling grapes

Orlando ①
Established in 1847, this is one of the largest wineries in Australia. Famous for its popular Jacob's Creek range, it is the country's top wine exporter and includes labels such as Wyndham Estate, Poet's Corner and Richmond Grove.

Seppelt ⑤
Between Tanunda and Greenoch this winery was established in 1851 by the pioneering German family Seppelt. A historic complex of splendid stone buildings, it is reached via an avenue of palm trees planted in the 1920s.

Mararnanga
⑤ Seppeltsfield Road
④
Tanunda
Gomersal Road
Turkey Flat
St Hallet
② Barossa Valley Way · Krondorf Road ③
Charles Melton
①
Rowland Flat
ADELAIDE

Peter Lehmann ④
A significant producer of quality Barossa wines, this winery was established by Peter Lehmann, a well-known character in the valley. The winery was awarded International Winemaker of the Year in 2004.

Grant Burge ②
Grant and Helen Burge founded this historic winery in 1988 and undertook restoration work on the buildings. The beautifully restored tasting room has custom-made chandeliers and ornamental glass. The winery produces traditional style Barossa wines – the Meshach Shiraz is one of the region's finest.

KEY
▰▰ Tour route
═══ Other road
🏰 Vineyard

0 km 2
0 miles 2

Rockford ③
This winery uses 100-year-old equipment to make its famous traditional hand-crafted wines. In the summer months visitors can see the old equipment working. The winery itself is also more than a century old.

For additional map symbols *see back flap*

Penfolds ⑥

Established in 1844, Penfolds moved to this site on the outskirts of Nuriootpa in 1974. This major winery (home of the famous *Grange*) matures its range of red and white table wines and ports in barrels made on the premises. Many wines are available for tasting and buying at the cellar door.

Wolf Blass ⑦

One of the younger wineries in the Barossa, established in 1973, Wolf Blass boasts elaborate tasting rooms and a wine heritage museum. It specializes in premium red and white table wines, and sparkling and fortified wines.

Saltram ⑧

Established in 1859, this historic winery is set in beautiful gardens on a Barossa hillside outside Angaston. Popular with red and fortified wine enthusiasts, Saltram also has an excellent restaurant, which is open for lunch daily and dinner Thursday to Saturday.

SALTRAM

Collingrove Homestead, Angaston ⑨

Now owned by the National Trust, Collingrove was built in 1856 as a home for a member of the influential pioneering Angas family. It has original furnishings and is set in an English-style garden. Accommodation is available.

Henschke ⑩

This winery is one of the world's greatest producers. Their wines are made from single vineyards, some with 100-year-old vines. After visiting the cellar be sure to walk through the vineyards – with some of the oldest vines in the world.

TIPS FOR DRIVERS

Although a tour of the Barossa Valley can be made in a day from Adelaide, the region is best seen and enjoyed by taking advantage of the excellent local accommodation and restaurants. The roads are generally good, although drivers should take special care on those that are unsealed. Visitors planning to visit a number of wineries and sample the produce may prefer to take one of the many tours or hire a chauffeur-driven vehicle.

THE YORKE AND EYRE PENINSULAS AND THE FAR NORTH

F*rom the lush Clare Valley and the dunes of the Simpson Desert, to the saltbush of the Nullarbor Plain, the land to the north and west of Adelaide is an area of vast distances and dramatic changes of scenery. With activities ranging from surfing on the coast to bushwalking in the Flinders Ranges, one is never far from awesome natural beauty.*

South Australia was first settled by Europeans in 1836, but suffered early financial problems partly due to economic mismanagement. These were largely remedied by the discovery of copper at Kapunda, north of Adelaide, in 1842, and at Burra, near Clare, in 1845. As these resources were depleted fresh discoveries were made in the north of the Yorke Peninsula, in the area known as Little Cornwall, at the town of Wallaroo in 1859 and at Moonta in 1861. By the 1870s, South Australia was the British Empire's leading copper producer, and copper, silver and uranium mining still boosts the state's economy today.

The Yorke and Eyre peninsulas are major arable areas, producing more than 10 per cent of Australia's wheat and much of its barley. They also have several important fishing ports, most notably Port Lincoln, the tuna-fishing capital of the country. Both peninsulas have stunning coastal scenery. The Yorke Peninsula, only two hours'

drive from Adelaide, is a popular holiday destination with excellent fishing, reef diving and surfing opportunities. The much larger Eyre Peninsula is also renowned for fishing and has many superb beaches. Despite extensive arable use, it still retains about half of its land area as parks, reserves and native bushland.

To the west, the vast Nullarbor Plain stretches far into Western Australia *(see p319)*, with the Great Victoria Desert extending above it. Much of this region is protected Aboriginal land and the Woomera prohibited military area.

North of the Yorke Peninsula lies the rugged majesty of the Flinders Ranges. Rich with sights of deep Aboriginal spiritual and cultural significance, the ranges are also home to abundant flora and fauna, and make for superb bushwalking. Further north, the immense, inhospitable but starkly beautiful desert regions of the South Australian Outback provide a challenging but rewarding destination for adventurous travellers.

Oyster beds in Coffin Bay at the southern tip of the Eyre Peninsula

◁ Rock climbing at Moonarie in the spectacular Flinders Ranges National Park

Exploring the Yorke and Eyre Peninsulas

Just north of Adelaide *(see pp344–9)* lie the green hills of the Clare Valley; then, further inland, as the rainfall diminishes, the countryside changes dramatically. First comes the grandeur of the Flinders Ranges with rugged mountains and tranquil gorges. West of Adelaide are two peninsulas, at the head of which is the industrial triangle of Port Pirie, Port Augusta and Whyalla. The Yorke Peninsula is Australia's richest barley growing district. Eyre Peninsula is also a wheat and barley producing area. From here the barren Nullarbor Plain runs beyond the Western Australian border.

Fishing boats moored in the harbour of Port Lincoln

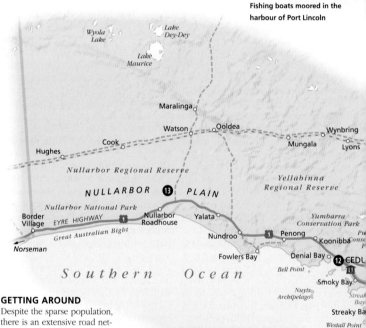

GETTING AROUND

Despite the sparse population, there is an extensive road network throughout the region. The Stuart Hwy runs up from Adelaide to Coober Pedy and beyond into the Northern Territory, and the Eyre Hwy wends its way from Adelaide along the tops of the Yorke and Eyre peninsulas, across the Nullarbor Plain and into Western Australia. There is no state railway, but interstate trains running from Sydney to Perth, and Adelaide to Alice Springs and Melbourne, stop at major towns in the region. Scheduled buses serve most towns, and there are air services from Adelaide to regional airports in Port Lincoln, Ceduna, Coober Pedy, Whyalla, Port Augusta and Renmark.

Raging waters of the Great Australian Bight

SIGHTS AT A GLANCE

Ceduna 12
Clare Valley 6
Coffin Bay National Park 11
Little Cornwall 5
Maitland 4
Minlaton 2
Nullarbor Plain 13
Port Augusta 8
Port Lincoln 10
Port Pirie 7
Port Victoria 3
Whyalla 9
Yorketown 1

The Far North

See pp368–9

Coober Pedy 14
Flinders Ranges 18
Lake Eyre National Park 17
Simpson Desert Conservation Park 16
Witjira National Park 15

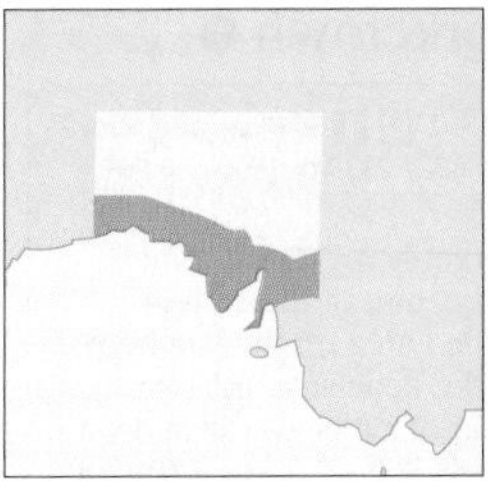

LOCATOR MAP

The Yorke and Eyre Peninsulas

The Far North pp368–9

Saltbush landscape of the Eyre Peninsula

KEY

Major road
Minor road
Track
Scenic route
Main railway
Minor railway
State border
Summit

SEE ALSO

• ***Where to Stay*** pp504–5
• ***Where to Eat*** pp551–2

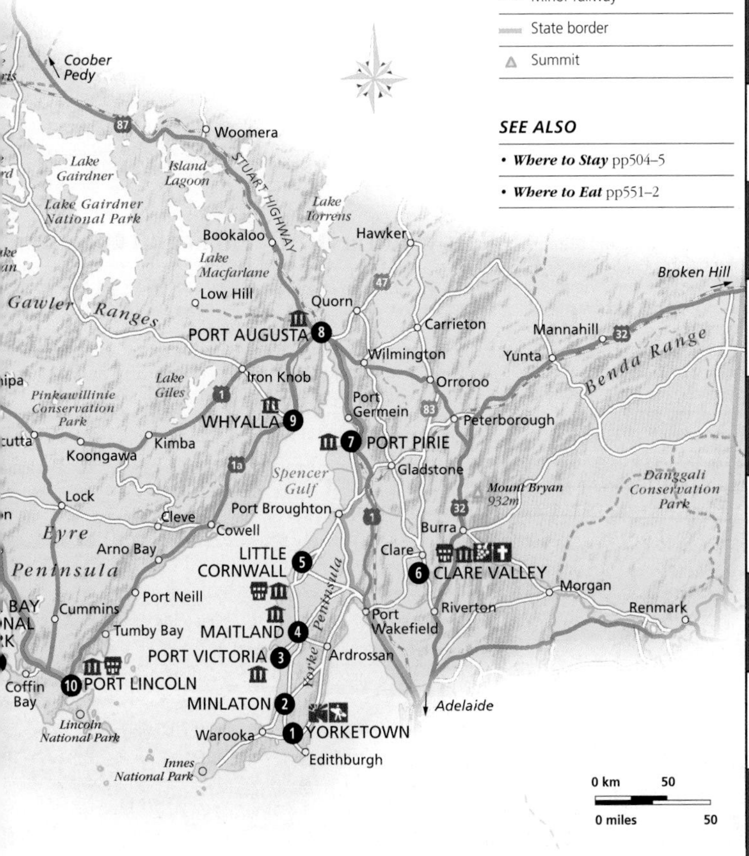
Coober Pedy
Woomera
Lake Gairdner
Island Lagoon
Lake Gairdner National Park
STUART HIGHWAY
Lake Torrens
Bookaloo
Hawker
Lake Macfarlane
Low Hill
Quorn
Broken Hill
Gawler Ranges
PORT AUGUSTA 8
Carrieton
Mannahill
Wilmington
Yunta
Benda Range
Iron Knob
Orroroo
Lake Giles
Pinkawillinie Conservation Park
Port Germein
WHYALLA 9
Peterborough
Kimba
7 PORT PIRIE
Koongawa
Gladstone
Spencer Gulf
Mount Bryan 932m
Danggali Conservation Park
Lock
Port Broughton
Cleve
Cowell
Burra
Eyre Peninsula
Arno Bay
LITTLE CORNWALL 5
Clare
6 CLARE VALLEY
Morgan
Port Neill
Cummins
Port Wakefield
Riverton
Renmark
Tumby Bay
MAITLAND 4
Yorke Peninsula
PORT VICTORIA 3
Ardrossan
Coffin Bay
10 PORT LINCOLN
MINLATON 2
Adelaide
Lincoln National Park
Warooka
1 YORKETOWN
Edithburgh
Innes National Park
0 km 50
0 miles 50

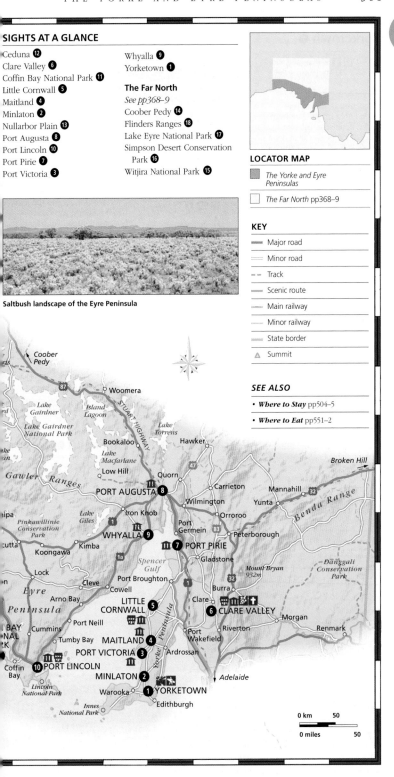

Yorketown ❶

🏠 750. 🚉 🛈 50 Moonta Rd, Kadina (08) 8821 2333 or 1800 654 991.

Yorketown is the commercial centre of the earliest settled area on the southern Yorke Peninsula. It lies at the heart of a region scattered with nearly 300 salt lakes, many of which mysteriously turn pink at various times of the year, depending on climatic conditions. From the late 1890s until the 1930s, salt harvesting was a major industry in this part of South Australia.

Approximately 70 km (40 miles) southwest of Yorketown, at the tip of the Yorke Peninsula, is the spectacular Innes National Park. The park's geography changes from salt lakes and low mallee scrub inland to sandy beaches and steep, rugged cliffs along the coast. Kangaroos and emus have become accustomed to the presence of humans and are commonly seen, but other native inhabitants, such as the large mallee fowl, are more difficult to spot.

There is good surfing, reef diving and fishing in the park, especially at Browns Beach, the wild Pondalowie Bay, Chinamans Creek and Salmon Hole. Other beaches are considered unsafe for swimming. Also in the park are the rusting remains of the shipwrecked barque *Ethel*, which ran aground in 1904 and now lies with part of its hull protruding through the sand below the limestone cliffs of Ethel Beach.

"Red Devil" fighter plane in Minlaton

Minlaton ❷

🏠 800. 🚉 🚌 🛈 59 Main St (08) 8853 2600.

Centrally located, Minlaton is a service town to the surrounding farming community. Minlaton's claim to fame, however, is as the destination of the very first air mail flight across water in the southern hemisphere. Pilot Captain Harry Butler, a World War I fighter ace, set off on this record-breaking mission in August 1919 from Adelaide. Minlaton's Butler Memorial houses his 1916 Bristol fighter plane, "Red Devil", believed to be the only one left in the world, as well as displays detailing Butler's life.

Port Victoria ❸

🏠 350. 🛈 50 Moonta Rd, Kadina (08) 8821 2333.

Lying on the west coast of the Yorke Peninsula, Port Victoria is today a sleepy holiday destination, popular with anglers, swimmers and divers.

In the early part of the 20th century however, it was a busy sea port with large clippers and windjammers loading grain bound for the northern hemisphere. The last time a square rigger used the port was in 1949. The story of these ships and their epic voyages is told in the **Maritime Museum**, located adjacent to the jetty in a timber goods shed.

About 10 km (6 miles) off the coast lies Wardang Island around which are eight known shipwrecks dating from 1871. Divers can follow the Wardang Island Maritime Heritage Trail to view the wrecks, each of which has an underwater plaque. Boats to the island can be chartered, but permission to land must be obtained from the Community Council in Point Pearce, the nearby Aboriginal settlement which administers the island.

🏛 **Maritime Museum**
Main St, Foreshore. **Tel** (08) 8834 2057. ⬜ Sun. 🈺 ♿

Maitland ❹

🏠 1,100. 🚉 🚌 🛈 50 Moonta Rd, Kadina (08) 8821 2333.

Surrounded by some of the most productive farmland in Australia, Maitland lies in the centre of the Yorke Peninsula, on a ridge

Vast expanse of the salt lakes in the Yorketown region

For hotels and restaurants in this region see pp504–5 and pp551–2

overlooking the Yorke Valley and Spencer Gulf. Originally proclaimed in 1872, it is now the service centre for the surrounding community.

The pretty town, laid out on a classic grid pattern, retains many fine examples of colonial architecture, including the Maitland Hotel, built in 1874, and the 1875 St Bartholomew's Catholic Church.

The **Maitland Museum** has an agricultural and folk collection housed in three buildings and focuses on the region's history and development.

🏛 **Maitland Museum**
Cnr Gardiner & Kilkerran terraces.
Tel (08) 8832 2220. ☐ Sun, school hols. ⬤ Good Fri, 25 Dec. 🔄 ♿

Miners' cottages in Little Cornwall

Little Cornwall ❺

🚗 Kadina. 🚌 Kadina. 🛈 50 Moonta Rd, Kadina (08) 8821 2333.

The three towns of Moonta, Kadina and Wallaroo were established after copper discoveries on Yorke Peninsula in 1859 and 1861. Collectively the towns are known as "The Copper Coast" or "Australia's Little Cornwall". Many miners from Cornwall, England, came here in the 19th century seeking their fortunes. The biennial festival "Kernewek Lowender" (see p42) celebrates this Cornish heritage. The wealth created by the mines has left the towns with fine architecture.

Wallaroo, the site of the first copper ore smelting works, was also a shipping port for ore. When mining finished,

Former timber shed now home to the Maritime Museum, Port Victoria

the port was important for agricultural exports. The **Wallaroo Heritage and Nautical Museum** is in the old post office.

Moonta, once home to Australia's richest copper mine, contains a group of sites and buildings in the **Moonta Mines State Heritage Area**. The 1870 Miner's Cottage is a restored wattle and daub cottage. The history museum is in the old Moonta Mines Model School. Also of interest is the Moonta Mines Railway, a restored light-gauge locomotive.

Kadina, where copper was originally found, is the Yorke Peninsula's largest town. The

Farmshed Museum and Tourism Centre has interesting displays on mining and folk history of the area.

🏛 **Wallaroo Heritage and Nautical Museum**
Jetty Rd. *Tel* (08) 8823 3015.
☐ Tue–Thu, Sat–Sun, daily in school hols. ⬤ 25 Dec. 🔄 ♿

🚂 **Moonta Mines State Heritage Area**
Moonta Rd. *Tel* (08) 8825 1891.
☐ Call for opening hours.
⬤ Good Fri, 25 Dec. 🔄 ♿

🏛 **Farmshed Museum and Tourism Centre**
50 Moonta Rd. *Tel* (08) 8821 2333.
☐ daily. ⬤ 25 Dec. 🔄 ♿

FISHING AND DIVING ON THE YORKE PENINSULA

There are fantastic opportunities for on- and offshore fishing and diving in the waters off the Yorke Peninsula. Many of the coastal towns have jetties used by keen amateur fishermen, and around Edithburgh anglers may catch tommy ruff, garfish and snook. Divers can enjoy the southern coast's stunning underwater scenery with brightly coloured corals and fish.

Offshore, the wreck of the *Clan Ranald* near Edithburgh is a popular dive, and off Wardang Island, eight wrecks can be explored on a unique diving trail. Angling from boats can be equally fruitful and local charter boats are available for hire.

A large blue grouper close to a diver in waters off the Yorke Peninsula

Restored 19th-century buildings at Burra Mine near the Clare Valley

Clare Valley ⑥

🚉 Clare. 🛈 Town Hall, 229 Main North Rd, Clare (08) 8842 2131.

Framed by the rolling hills of the northern Mount Lofty Ranges, the Clare Valley is a picturesque and premium wine-producing region. At the head of the valley lies the town of Clare. This pretty, regional centre has many historic buildings, including the National Trust Museum, housed in the old Police Station, and Wolta Wolta, an early pastoralist's home, built in 1864, which has a fine collection of antiques.

Sevenhill Cellars, 7 km (4 miles) south of Clare, is the oldest vineyard in the valley. It was established by Austrian Jesuits in 1851, originally to produce altar wine for the colony. The adjacent St Aloysius Church was completed in 1875. The winery is still run by Jesuits and now produces both altar and table wines.

East of Sevenhill lies the pleasant heritage town of Mintaro, with many buildings making extensive use of the slate quarried in the area for more than 150 years. Also worth visiting is **Martindale Hall**, an elegant 1879 mansion situated just southeast of town.

Twelve km (7 miles) north of Clare lies **Bungaree Station**. This self-contained Merino sheep-farming complex was established in 1841 and is now maintained as a working 19th-century model. From the historic exhibits visitors can learn about life and work at the station.

About 35 km (22 miles) northeast of Clare is the charming town of Burra. Five years after copper was discovered here in 1845, Burra was home to the largest mine in Australia. As such it was the economic saviour of the fledgling state, rescuing it from impending bankruptcy. Once five separate townships, Burra is now a State Heritage Area.

The **Burra Mine** site, with its ruins and restored buildings around the huge open cut, is one of the most exciting industrial archaeological sites in Australia. An interpretive centre at the Bon Accord Mine allows visitors access to the original mine shaft. The miners' dugouts, still seen on the banks of Burra Creek, were once home to more than 1,500 mainly Cornish miners. Paxton Square Cottages, built between 1849 and 1852, are unique in Australian mining history as the first decent accommodation provided for miners and their families. Many old buildings, including the police lockup and stables, the Redruth Gaol and the Unicorn Brewery Cellars, have been carefully restored, as have a number of the 19th-century shops and houses. A museum with various displays chronicling the local history is located in Burra market square.

🏰 **Sevenhill Cellars**
College Rd, Sevenhill. **Tel** (08) 8843 4222. ⬜ daily. ⬤ 25 Dec, 1 Jan, Good Fri. ♿

🏛 **Martindale Hall**
Manoora Rd, Mintaro. **Tel** (08) 8843 9088. ⬜ daily. 📷

🏛 **Bungaree Station**
Port Augusta Rd, Clare. **Tel** (08) 8842 2677. ⬜ tours only. 📷 ♿

🏛 **Burra Mine**
Market St, Burra. **Tel** (08) 8892 2154 ⬜ daily. ⬤ 25 Dec. 📷 ♿ limited.

Port Pirie ⑦

🚶 15,000. 🚉 🚌 🛈 Mary Elie St (08) 8633 8700.

Port Pirie was the state's first provincial city. An industrial hub, it is the site of the largest lead smelter in the southern hemisphere.

In the town centre, the **National Trust Museum** comprises three well-preserved buildings: the pavilion-style railway station built in 1902, the former Customs House and the Old Police Building. The Regional Tourism and Arts Centre, located in the former 1967 railway station, features artworks on lead, zinc and copper panels interpreting the city's historic wealth.

Every October, Port Pirie hosts the South Australian Festival of Country Music.

🏛 **National Trust Museum**
Ellen St. **Tel** (08) 8632 2272. ⬜ daily. ⬤ 25 Dec. ♿ limited.

Victorian grandeur of Port Pirie's old railway station

Harbour view of Port Augusta, backed by its power stations

Port Augusta ❽

🏃 14,000. ✈ 🚗 🚌 🚆 ℹ 41
Flinders Terrace (08) 8641 0793.

Situated at the head of Spencer Gulf, Port Augusta is at the crossroads of Australia; here lies the intersection of the Sydney–Perth and Adelaide–Alice Springs railway lines, as well as the major Sydney–Perth and Adelaide–Darwin highways. Once an important port, its power stations now produce 40 per cent of the state's electricity. The coal-fired Northern Power Station, which dominates the city's skyline, offers free conducted tours.

Port Augusta is also the beginning of South Australia's Outback region. The School of the Air and the Royal Flying Doctor Service offices, both of which provide essential services to inhabitants of remote stations, are open to the public (see p257). The **Wadlata Outback Centre** imaginatively tells the story of the Far North from 15 million years ago when rainforests covered the area, through Aboriginal and European history, up to the present day and into the future.

Australia's first **Arid Lands Botanic Garden** was opened nearby in 1996. This 200-ha (500-acre) site is an important research and education facility, as well as a recreational area. It also commands fine panoramic views of the Flinders Ranges to the east (see p369).

🏛 **Wadlata Outback Centre**
Flinders Terrace. **Tel** (08) 8642 4511. 🕐 daily. ● 25 Dec. 📷 ♿

🌿 **Arid Lands Botanic Garden**
Stuart Hwy. **Tel** (08) 8641 1049. 🕐 daily. ● 25 Dec. ♿ limited.

Whyalla ❾

🏃 26,000. ✈ 🚗 ℹ Port Augusta Rd, Lincoln Hwy, 1800 088 589.

At the gateway to the Eyre Peninsula, Whyalla is the state's largest provincial city. Originally a shipping port for iron ore mined at nearby Iron Knob, the city was transformed in 1939 when a blast furnace was established, a harbour created and a shipyard constructed. The shipyard closed in 1978; however, the first ship built there, the HMAS *Whyalla* (1941), is now a major display of the **Whyalla Maritime Museum**.

Although an industrial centre, Whyalla has a number of fine beaches and good fishing. The **Whyalla Wildlife and Reptile Sanctuary** has a collection of native and exotic animals, including koalas, monkeys and a black leopard.

🏛 **Whyalla Maritime Museum**
Lincoln Hwy. **Tel** (08) 8645 8900. 🕐 daily. ● Good Fri, 25 Dec. 📷 ♿ museum only.

🐾 **Whyalla Wildlife and Reptile Sanctuary**
Lincoln Hwy. **Tel** (08) 8645 7044. 🕐 daily. ● 25 Dec. 📷 ♿

HMAS *Whyalla*, docked beside the Whyalla Maritime Museum

Stunning coastline of Whalers Way at the southern end of the Eyre Peninsula near Port Lincoln

Port Lincoln ⑩

🏘 *13,000.* ✈ 🚌 ℹ *3 Adelaide Pl, 1800 629 911 or (08) 8683 3544.*

At the southern end of the Eyre Peninsula, Port Lincoln sits on the shore of Boston Bay, one of the world's largest natural harbours. A fishing and seafood processing centre, it is home to Australia's largest tuna fleet.

Locals celebrate the start of the tuna season every January with the Tunarama Festival *(see p41)*. This raucous event includes processions, concerts and a tuna-tossing competition.

Fishing and sailing are popular activities. Visitors can take a boat trip to Dangerous Reef, 31 km (20 miles) offshore, to view great white sharks from the relative safety of the boat or submerged cage. In the middle of the bay lies Boston

Island, a working sheep station including an 1842 slab cottage.

The Port Lincoln area has several buildings of note. South of Port Lincoln, **Mikkira Station**, established in 1842, is one of the country's oldest sheep stations. Today it is ideal for picnics or camping, with a restored pioneer cottage and a koala colony. The **Koppio Smithy Museum**, located in the Koppio Hills 40 km (25 miles) north of Port Lincoln, is an agricultural museum with a furnished 1890 log cottage and a 1903 smithy that gives a glimpse into the lives of the pioneers.

Just 20 km (12 km) south of Port Lincoln is Lincoln National Park with its rocky hills, sheltered coves, sandy beaches and high cliffs. The park is also rich in birdlife. Emus and parrots are common and ospreys and sea eagles frequent the coast. Just west of the park, Whalers

Way has some of Australia's most dramatic coastal scenery. This land is private and entry is via a permit available from the visitors' centre.

🏕 **Mikkira Station**
Fishery Bay Rd. **Tel** *(08) 8685 6020.* 🈶

🏛 **Koppio Smithy Museum**
Via White Flat Rd. **Tel** *(08) 8684 4243.* ⌚ *10am–5pm Tue–Sun.* ⬤ *25 Dec.* 🈶 ♿

The prime surfing spot of Almonta Beach in Coffin Bay National Park

Coffin Bay National Park ⑪

🚌 *Port Lincoln.* ℹ *(08) 8688 3111.* ⌚ *daily.* ⬤ *25 Dec.* 🈶 *per vehicle.* ♿ *limited.*

To the west of the southern tip of the Eyre Peninsula is Coffin Bay Peninsula, which is part of the Coffin Bay National Park. This unspoilt area of

---

Wedge-tailed eagle

WILDLIFE OF THE EYRE PENINSULA

An enormous variety of wildlife inhabits the Eyre Peninsula. Emus and kangaroos are common, and the hairy-nosed wombat is found in large numbers on the west coast. Wedge-tailed eagles soar over the Gawler Ranges, while sea eagles, ospreys, albatrosses and petrels are all seen over the coast. In the water, dolphins, sea lions and occasional great white sharks feast on an abundance of marine life. The most spectacular sight, however, are the southern right whales which breed at the head of the Great Australian Bight every June to October. They can be seen from the cliffs at the Head of Bight, just east of the Nullarbor National Park.

---

coastal wilderness has exposed cliffs, sheltered sandy beaches, rich birdlife and fantastic fishing. Wildflowers in the park can be quite spectacular from early spring to early summer.

There are several scenic drives through the park, but some roads are accessible to 4WD vehicles only. A favourite route for conventional vehicles is the Yangie Trail from the small town of Coffin Bay to Yangie and Avoid bays. To the east of Point Avoid is one of Australia's best surfing beaches, Almonta Beach.

Coffin Bay town has long been a popular centre for windsurfing, swimming, sailing and fishing. It now also produces high-quality oysters. The Oyster Walk is a pleasant walking trail along the foreshore through native bushland.

Ceduna ⑫

🏘 3,600. ✈ 🚌 ℹ 58 Poynton St (08) 8625 2780.

At the top of the west side of the Eyre Peninsula, sitting on the shores of Murat Bay, Ceduna is the most westerly significant town in South Australia before the start of the Nullarbor Plain. The town's name comes from the Aboriginal word *cheedoona*, meaning "a place to rest".

Today, Ceduna is the commercial centre of the far west. Within the town is the **Old Schoolhouse National Trust Museum** with its collections of restored farm equipment

An Indian-Pacific train crossing the vast Nullarbor Plain

from early pioneer days. It also has an interesting display on the British atomic weapons tests held at nearby Maralinga in the 1950s, and a small selection of Aboriginal artifacts.

In the 1850s, there was a whaling station on St Peter Island, just off the coast of Ceduna, but now the town is a base for whale-watchers. Southern right whales can be seen close to the shore from June to October from the head of the Bight, 300 km (185 miles) from Ceduna.

The oyster farming industry has established itself west and east of Ceduna at Denial and Smoky bays. Between Ceduna and Penong, a tiny hamlet 73 km (45 miles) to the west, there are detours to surfing beaches including the legendary Cactus Beach. Keen surfers are found here all year round trying to catch some of the best waves in Australia, rolling in from the great Southern Ocean.

🏛 Old Schoolhouse National Trust Museum
Park Terrace. **Tel** (08) 8625 2780.
⬜ Mon–Sat. ⬛ 25 Dec. 🎫 ♿

Nullarbor Plain ⑬

🚉 Port Augusta. 🚌 Ceduna.
ℹ Ceduna (08) 8625 2780.
⬜ 9am–5:30pm Mon–Fri, 10am–4pm Sat–Sun. ⬛ Good Fri, 25 Dec.

The huge expanse of the Nullarbor Plain stretches from Nundroo, about 150 km (95 miles) west of Ceduna, towards the distant Western Australia border 330 km (200 miles) away, and beyond into Western Australia (see p319).

This dry, dusty plain can be crossed by rail on the Trans-Australian Railway or by road on the Eyre Highway. The train travels further inland than the road, its route giving little relief from the flat landscape. The highway lies nearer the coast, passing a few isolated sights of interest on its way west.

Just south of the small town of Nundroo lies Fowlers Bay. Good for fishing, it is popular with anglers seeking solitude. West of here, the road passes through the Yalata Aboriginal Lands and travellers can stop by the roadside to buy souvenirs from the local people. Bordering Yalata to the west is Nullarbor National Park. This runs from the Nullarbor Roadhouse hamlet, 130 km (80 miles) west of Nundroo, to the border with Western Australia 200 km (125 miles) away. The Eyre Highway passes through the park, close to the coastal cliffs. This stretch of the plain has some spectacular views over the Great Australian Bight.

The world's longest cave system runs beneath the plain, and the border area has many underground caves and caverns. These should only be explored by experienced cavers, however, as many are flooded and dangerous.

Watching southern right whales from Head of Bight, near Ceduna

The Far North

South Australia's outback is an enormous area of harsh but often breathtaking scenery. Much of the region is untamed desert, broken in places by steep, ancient mountain ranges, huge salt lakes, gorges and occasional hot springs. Although very hot and dry for most of the year, many places burst into life after heavy winter rains and hundreds of species of wildflowers, animals and birds can be seen. The area's recent history is one of fabled stock routes, now Outback tracks for adventurous travellers. Isolated former mining and railway towns now cater for Outback tourists. Vast areas in the west form extensive Aboriginal lands, accessible by permit only.

LOCATOR MAP

  The Far North

  The Yorke and Eyre Peninsulas see pp358–67

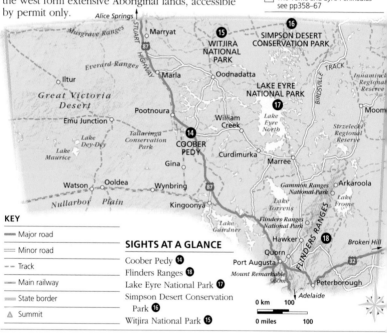

KEY

━━━ Major road

═══ Minor road

- - - Track

━━━ Main railway

━━━ State border

△ Summit

SIGHTS AT A GLANCE

Coober Pedy ⑭

Flinders Ranges ⑱

Lake Eyre National Park ⑰

Simpson Desert Conservation Park ⑯

Witjira National Park ⑮

Coober Pedy ⑭

🏚 3,500. ✈ 🚉 ℹ 773 Hutchison St, 1800 637 078 or (08) 8672 5298.

One of Australia's most famous Outback towns, Coober Pedy, 850 km (530 miles) northwest of Adelaide, is an unusual settlement in the heart of an extremely hostile landscape. Frequent duststorms and a colourless desert landscape littered with abandoned mines contribute to the town's desolate appearance, yet the small population has a cultural mix of over 42 nationalities.

Opal was discovered here in 1915, and today Coober Pedy

produces 70 per cent of the world's supply. Mining claims, limited to one per person, can measure no more than 100 m by 50 m (320 ft by 160 ft). For this reason opal mining is the preserve of individuals, not large companies, and this adds to the town's "frontier" quality.

Underground "dugout" home in Coober Pedy

Coober Pedy's name comes from the Aboriginal *kupa piti*, meaning white man in a hole, and it is apt indeed. Not only the mines, but also houses, hotels and churches are built underground. This way, the residents escape the extreme temperatures of up to 50°C (122°F) during the day and 0°C (32°F) at night. Several such homes are open to the public.

The **Underground Art Gallery** displays Aboriginal art. It also has displays relating to opal mining, and visitors can dig for their own opals.

🏛 **Underground Art Gallery** Main St. **Tel** (08) 8672 5985. ◻ daily. ⬤ 25 Dec. ♿ ⬤

For hotels and restaurants in this region see pp504–5 and pp551–2

Witjira National Park ⓯

📍 *Pink Roadhouse, Oodnadatta (08) 8670 7822.* 🔲 *daily.* **Park Office** *1800 816 078.* 🔲 *24 hours. Desert Parks pass required.*

About 200 km (125 miles) north of Coober Pedy lies the small town of Oodnadatta, where drivers can check the road and weather conditions before heading further north to Witjira National Park.

Witjira has dunes, saltpans, boulder plains and coolibah woodlands, but it is most famous for its hot artesian springs. Dalhousie Springs has more than 60 active springs with warm water rising from the Great Artesian Basin. These springs supply essential water for Aborigines, pastoralists and wildlife, including water snails, unique to the area.

Simpson Desert Conservation Park ⓰

📍 *Pink Roadhouse, Oodnadatta (08) 8670 7822.* 🔲 *daily. Desert Parks pass required.* **Park Office** *1800 816 078.* 🔲 *24 hours.*

The Simpson Desert Conservation Park is at the very top of South Australia, adjoining both Queensland and the Northern Territory. It is an almost endless series of sand dunes, lakes, spinifex grassland and gidgee woodland.

The landscape is home to some 180 bird, 92 reptile and 44 native mammal species, some of which have developed nocturnal habits as a response to the aridity of the region.

Dunes stretching to the horizon in Simpson Desert Conservation Park

Lake Eyre National Park ⓱

📍 *Coober Pedy, (08) 8672 5298.* 🔲 *Mon–Fri.* ⚫ *public hols.* **Park Office** *1800 816 078.* 🔲 *24 hours.*

Lake Eyre National Park encompasses all of Lake Eyre North and extends eastwards into the Tirari Desert. Lake Eyre is Australia's largest salt lake, 15 m (49 ft) below sea level at its lowest point, with a salt crust said to weigh 400 million tonnes. Vegetation is low, comprising mostly blue bush, samphire and saltbush. On the rare occasions when the lake floods, it alters dramatically: flowers bloom and birds such as pelicans and gulls appear, turning the lake into a breeding ground.

Flinders Ranges ⓲

🚉 *Hawker, Wilpena.* 📍 *Wilpena (08) 8648 0048.* 🔲 *daily.* **Park Office** *(08) 8648 0049.*

The Flinders Ranges extend for 400 km (250 miles) from Crystal Brook, just north of the Clare Valley, far into South Australia's Outback. A favourite with bushwalkers, the ranges encompass a great diversity of stunning scenery and wildlife, much of it protected in several national parks.

In the southern part of the Flinders Ranges is Mount Remarkable National Park, renowned for its fine landscape, abundant wildflowers and excellent walking trails.

About 50 km (30 miles) north of here is the town of Quorn, start of the restored Pichi Richi Railway. North of Quorn lie the dramatic Warren, Yarrah Vale and Buckaring gorges.

Much of the central Flinders Ranges are contained within the Flinders Ranges National Park. This beautiful park's best-known feature is Wilpena Pound, an elevated natural basin covering some 90 sq km (35 sq miles) with sheer outer walls 500 m (1,600 ft) high.

To the north is Gammon Ranges National Park, with mountain bushwalking for the experienced only. Just outside the park is **Arkaroola**, a tourist village with a wildlife sanctuary and a state-of-the-art observatory.

✈ **Arkaroola**
Via Wilpena or Leigh Creek. **Tel** *1800 676 042.* 🔲 *daily.* 📷 *for tours.*

Shimmering expanse of Lake Eyre, the largest salt lake in Australia

VICTORIA

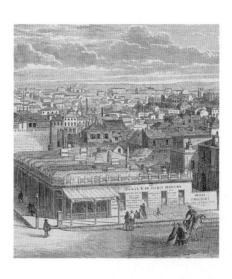

INTRODUCING VICTORIA 372–379

MELBOURNE 380–421

WESTERN VICTORIA 422–437

EASTERN VICTORIA 438–451

Victoria at a Glance

The state of Victoria can be easily
divided into two distinct geographical
halves, east and west. Western Victoria is
known for its unusual landforms, including
the Grampians and the Twelve Apostles.
It was also the site of Australia's wealthiest
gold rush during the 19th century, the
legacy of which can be seen in the ornate
buildings in the many surviving gold rush
towns *(see pp54–5)*. Eastern Victoria's
cooler climate benefits the vineyards that
produce world-class wines, while the
Alps are Victoria's winter playground.
The rugged coastline is known for its
lakes, forests and wildlife. Melbourne,
the state's capital, is the second most
populous city in Australia.

WESTERN VICTORIA
(see pp422–37)

Halls Gap *is the main entrance to the
Grampians National Park (see p427). This
beautiful area is filled with dramatic rock
formations, spectacular ridges and wildflowers
unique to the region.*

**The Twelve
Apostles** *is the
evocative name
given to these
eroded limestone
rock formations
in Port Campbell
National Park,
seen from the
Great Ocean Road
(see pp428–9).
Sunset is the best
time to fully appre-
ciate the view.*

Ballarat's *Arch of Victory on the
Avenue of Honour commemorates
the soldiers of World War I. It is also
the western entrance to this provincial city, which grew up during the
1850s gold rush (see pp434–5).*

◁ **The Cathedral in Mount Buffalo National Park**

Tahbilk Wines *is one of the best known of all the northeastern Victorian vineyards, not only for its excellent wines but also for the pagoda-style architecture of its winery. Eastern Victoria's cool climate has led to a range of successful wineries (see pp450–51).*

The Victorian Alps *come into their own during the winter months as a premier ski area (see p446).*

EASTERN VICTORIA
(see pp438–51)

MELBOURNE
(see inset)

0 kilometres   100

0 miles   100

MELBOURNE
(see pp380–421)

Parliament House
in Melbourne, begun in 1856, is one of the city's finest surviving public buildings (see pp392–3).

Flinders Street Station
is the main rail terminus, set in a fine 19th-century edifice *(see p402).*

Rippon Lea's *ornamental garden is an impressive feature of this 19th-century home (see pp404–5).*

0 km   2

0 miles   2

Melbourne's Best: Parks and Gardens

Visitors to Melbourne should not miss the city's magnificent public and private gardens. A large proportion of the city's parks and gardens were created in the 19th century and have a gracious quality which has earned Victoria the nickname of Australia's "Garden State". Central Melbourne is ringed by public gardens, including the outstanding Royal Botanic Gardens, visited by more than one million people each year. Melbourne also has a network of public parks which offer a mix of native flora and fauna with recreational activities. The annual Open Garden Scheme *(see p40)* allows visitors into some of the best private gardens in Victoria and Australia.

LANDSCAPE GARDENS

Melbourne abounds with carefully planned and formal 19th-century gardens, designed by prominent landscape gardeners.

A variety of trees from all over the world lines the formal avenues of **Carlton Gardens**, designed in 1857 by Edward La Trobe Bateman. The aim of the design was for every path and flowerbed to focus attention on the Exhibition Building, constructed in 1880 *(see p395)*. The main entrance path leads from Victoria Street to the Hochgurtel Fountain, in front of the Exhibition Building, decorated on its upper tier

Statue of Simpson and his donkey in Kings Domain

with stone birds and flowers which are indigenous to the state of Victoria.

The attractive **Fitzroy Gardens** in the heart of the city were also first designed by Bateman in 1848. His original plans were later revised by a Scotsman, James Sinclair, to make them more sympathetic to the area's uneven landscape. The avenues of elms that lead in to the centre of the gardens from the surrounding streets create the shape of the Union Jack flag and are one of the most distinctive features of the gardens *(see pp392–3)*. Fitzroy Gardens' Conservatory is renowned for its five popular annual plant shows.

Statue of Queen Victoria in her eponymous gardens

The **Queen Victoria Gardens** are considered one of the city's most attractive gardens. They were created as a setting for a new statue of the queen, four years after her death, in 1905. Roses now surround the statue. A floral clock near St Kilda Road was given to Melbourne by Swiss watchmakers in 1966. It is embedded with some 7,000 flowering plants.

Kings Domain *(see p398)* was the dream of a German botanist, Baron von Mueller, who designed this impressive garden in 1854. The garden is dominated by elegant statues, including one of Simpson, a stretcher bearer during World War I, with his faithful donkey. There are also fountains, silver birch and the imposing Shrine of Remembrance.

BOTANIC GARDENS

Begun in 1846, the **Royal Botanic Gardens** now cover 36 ha (90 acres). Botanist Baron von Mueller became the director of the gardens in 1857 and began to plant both indigenous and exotic shrubs on the site, intending the gardens to be a scientific aid to fellow biologists. Von Mueller's successor, William Guilfoyle made his own mark on the

Conservatory of flowers in Fitzroy Gardens

Ornamental lake in the Royal Botanic Gardens

WHERE TO FIND THE PARKS AND GARDENS

Alexandra Gardens **Map** 3 A2.
Carlton Gardens **Map** 2 D1.
Fawkner Park **Map** 3 C5.
Fitzroy Gardens *pp384–5*.
Flagstaff Gardens **Map** 1 A2.
Kings Domain *p390*.
Princes Park, Royal Parade, Carlton.
Queen Victoria Gardens **Map** 2 D4.
Royal Botanic Gardens *p399*.
Treasury Gardens *p392*.
Yarra Park **Map** 2 F3.

design, by adding wide paths across the gardens and an ornamental lake.

Today, the gardens are home to more than 10,000 plant species *(see pp398–9)*.

RECREATIONAL GARDENS AND PARKS

Melburnians are avid sports participants as well as spectators, and many of the city's gardens offer a range of sporting facilities in attractive surroundings.

Flagstaff Gardens take their name from the site's role as a signalling station from 1840, warning of ships arriving in the Port of Melbourne. In the 1860s, with advances in communication, this role was no longer required and gardens were laid out on the land instead. Today the gardens are used for their recreational facilities, which include tennis courts, a children's playground and a barbecue area.

The **Alexandra Gardens** were designed in 1904 as a riverside walk along the Yarra River. Today, as well as the major thoroughfare of Alexandra Avenue, there is an equestrian path, a cycle path, boat sheds and barbecue facilities.

The **Treasury Gardens** were designed in 1867 and are lined along its avenues with Moreton Bay Figs, which offer very welcome shade in the summer heat. The location in the centre of the city makes these gardens very popular with office workers during their lunch breaks. The gardens also host regular evening concerts and other entertainment gatherings.

Established in 1856, **Yarra Park** is today home to the city's most well-known sports grounds, Melbourne Park, home of the Australian Open, and the Melbourne Cricket Ground *(see p397)*. The wood and bark of the indigenous river red gums in the park were once used for canoes and shields by local Aborigines and many still bear the scars.

Fawkner Park, named after Melbourne's co-founder, John Fawkner *(see pp52–3)*, was laid out in 1862 and became a large sports ground in the 1890s. Despite a temporary role as a camp site for the Armed Services during World War II, the 40 ha (100 acres) of the park are still used for cricket, football, hockey and softball games.

Another popular sporting area with Melburnians is **Princes Park**. Two sports pavilions were constructed in 1938, as were two playing fields. The park now contains a football oval and the unique "Fun and Fitness Centre", a jogging track lined with exercise equipment at stages along its 3-km (1.8-mile) route. A gravel running track was also added in 1991.

Cricket match in progress in Fawkner Park

Melbourne's Best: Architecture

In 1835, Melbourne was a village of tents and imper-
manent dwellings. Fed by the wealth of the 1850s'
gold rush and the economic boom of the 1880s, it
rapidly acquired many graceful buildings. Today, the
city's architecture is very eclectic, with a strong Victorian element. The range of architectural styles is
impressive, from beautiful restorations to outstanding
contemporary novelties. The city's tallest building is
the Eureka Tower, which is 300 m (985 ft) high.

Early colonial Cook's Cottage

EARLY COLONIAL

In colonial days, it was
quite common for small
edifices, such as La Trobe's
Cottage, to be shipped
from England as skilled
builders were in short
supply. Other imported
structures included timber
cottages and corrugated
iron dwellings.

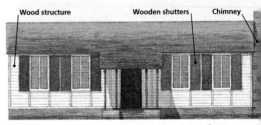
Wood structure   Wooden shutters   Chimney

La Trobe's Cottage *is a prefabricated wooden cottage of 1839.*

HIGH VICTORIAN

During the 19th century, Melbourne erected several grand state
buildings equal to those in the USA and Europe. State Parliament
House, begun in 1856, included a central dome in its original
design which was omitted due to lack of funds *(see p392)*. South
of the city is the 1934 Shrine of Remembrance, which demonstrates the 20th century's yearning for classical roots *(p398)*.

Detail of Parliament House

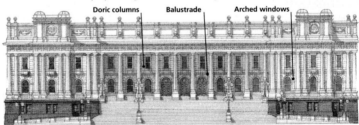
Doric columns   Balustrade   Arched windows

State Parliament House *has an impressive entrance with its grand Doric columns.*

Cast-iron lacework at Tasma Terrace

TERRACE HOUSING

Terrace houses with cast-iron lace balconies
were popular during the Victorian era. Tasma
Terrace (1868–86) was designed by Charles
Webb and is unusual for its three-storey
houses, double-storey being more typical.

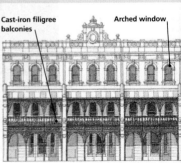
Cast-iron filigree
balconies   Arched window

Tasma Terrace *is now home to the National Trust.*

MODERNISM AND POST-MODERNISM

The latter half of the 20th century has seen a range of post-modern buildings erected in Melbourne. The National Gallery of Victoria was designed by Sir Roy Grounds *(see p402)* and completed in 1968 (further modified in 2003 by Mario Bellini). It was the first time bluestone, widely used in the 19th century, was used in a modern structure. The stained-glass ceiling of the Great Hall was designed by Leonard French.

Melbourne's unique bluestone used in the walls of the National Gallery of Victoria

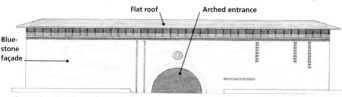

Flat roof   Arched entrance

Bluestone façade

The National Gallery of Victoria *has a monumental façade, impressive for its smooth simplicity and lack of ornamental details.*

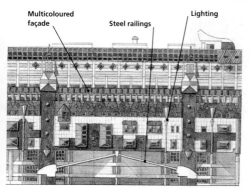

Multicoloured façade   Steel railings   Lighting

Royal Melbourne Institute of Technology's *Building 8 façade is a complex blend of bright colours and diverse shapes.*

CONTEMPORARY

Melbourne is known for its vibrant, experimental architecture scene. Some of the most radical Australian buildings of the 1990s can be found here. The Royal Melbourne Institute of Technology's Building 8 was designed by Peter Corrigan in 1994. The building's interior and façade is both gaudy and Gaudían, with its bold use of primary colours. Whatever your judgment, it cannot help but attract the attention of every visitor to the northern end of the city.

SPORTS ARCHITECTURE

Melbourne's modern architecture clearly reflects the importance of sport to its citizens. Melbourne Park, built in 1988, has a retractable roof, a world first, and seats more than 15,000 people at its centre court.

Aerial view of the glass roof and stadium at Melbourne Park

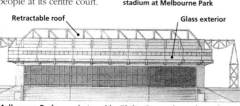

Retractable roof   Glass exterior

Melbourne Park *was designed by Philip Cox and now hosts the annual Australian Open tennis championships.*

WHERE TO FIND THE BUILDINGS

La Trobe's Cottage
  p399.
National Gallery of Victoria
  p402.
Melbourne Park
  Map 2 F4.
Royal Melbourne Institute of
  Technology's Building 8,
  Swanston Street.
  Map 1 C2.
Shrine of Remembrance
  p398.
State Parliament House
  p392.
Tasma Terrace,
  Parliament Place.
  Map 2 E2.

Wines of Victoria

Victoria has approximately 320 wineries located in 19 distinct wine regions, some easily reached in less than an hour by car from the state capital, Melbourne. The northeast is famous for its unique fortified Muscats and Tokays (often described as liquid toffee), while from the cooler south come silky Chardonnays and subtle Pinot Noirs. There is no better way to enjoy Victorian wine than in one of the many restaurants and bistros in cosmopolitan Melbourne *(see pp552–6)*.

Wentworth

MILDURA

Ouyen

Sea L

Horsham

Glaneig River

Hamilton

BA

Co

Best's is one of the oldest family-owned wineries in Australia. This producer makes excellent Shiraz, Merlot, Dolcetto and Riesling wines. Tours of its 100-year-old wooden cellar are available on request.

Cellar stacked with wine at Seppelt's Great Western

KEY FACTS

Location and Climate
Warm in the north, cool in the south, Victoria's climate spectrum yields a diversity of wines. Many small, high-quality producers have been in the vanguard of the Australian wine revolution, which began in the 1970s.

Grape Varieties
Victoria's varied climate and soil means it is possible to grow a full range of grape varieties.

Reds include Shiraz, Merlot, Cabernet Sauvignon and Pinot Noir. Whites include Semillon, Gewürztraminer, Riesling, Chardonnay, Marsanne, Frontignac and Pinot Gris. Victoria also produces excellent sparkling wine.

Good Producers
Morris, Campbells, Brown Bros, de Bortoli, Trentham Estate, Seppelts, Bests, Mount Langi Ghiran, Jaspers Hill, Yarra Yering, Coldstream Hills, Tahbilk Wines, Mitchelton.

2002

four sisters

SOUTH EASTERN AUSTRALIA
sauvignon blanc
semillon
750ML 12.5%VOL

Four Sisters/*Mount Langi Ghiran has established itself as a pioneer by winemaker Trevor Mast.*

Mick Morris sampling his famous Muscat from barrels

HOW VICTORIA'S FAMOUS MUSCATS AND TOKAYS ARE MADE

Brown Muscat and Muscadelle grapes are picked late, when they are at their sweetest, to produce fine Muscats and Tokays respectively. Once the grapes have been crushed, the resulting juice is often fermented in traditional open concrete tanks which have been in use for generations. The wine is then fortified with top-quality grape spirit, which will give it an ultimate alcohol strength of around 18.5 per cent. The solera system, in which young vintages are blended with older ones, gives more depth to the wines and also ensures that they retain a consistent quality. Some wineries, such as Morris, use a base wine combined with vintages going back more than a century. The flavour of wine in the oldest barrel is so intense that one teaspoon can add a new dimension to 200 l (45 gal) of base wine.

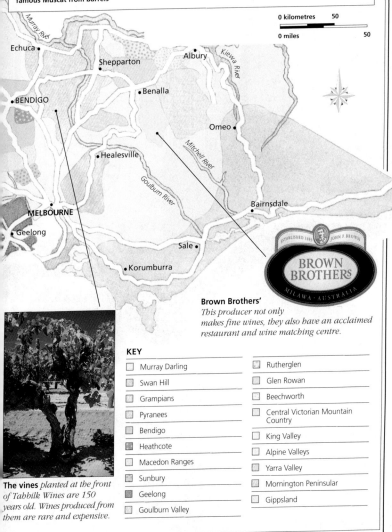

0 kilometres   50

0 miles   50

Murray River

Echuca

Shepparton

Albury

Kiewa River

BENDIGO

Benalla

Omeo

Healesville

Mitchell River

Goulburn River

Bairnsdale

MELBOURNE

Geelong

Sale

Korumburra

Brown Brothers'
This producer not only makes fine wines, they also have an acclaimed restaurant and wine matching centre.

ESTABLISHED 1889   JOHN F. BROWN
BROWN BROTHERS
MILAWA · AUSTRALIA

The vines *planted at the front of Tabbilk Wines are 150 years old. Wines produced from them are rare and expensive.*

KEY

☐ Murray Darling	☐ Rutherglen
☐ Swan Hill	☐ Glen Rowan
☐ Grampians	☐ Beechworth
☐ Pyranees	☐ Central Victorian Mountain Country
☐ Bendigo	☐ King Valley
☐ Heathcote	☐ Alpine Valleys
☐ Macedon Ranges	☐ Yarra Valley
☐ Sunbury	☐ Mornington Peninsular
☐ Geelong	☐ Gippsland
☐ Goulburn Valley	

MELBOURNE

*J*ohn Batman, the son of a Sydney convict, arrived in what is now known as the Port Phillip district in 1835 and met with Aboriginal tribes of the Kulin, from whom he "purchased" the land. In just over two decades Melbourne grew from a small tent encampment to a sprawling metropolis. Today it is thriving as the second-largest city in Australia.

Melbourne's rapid growth was precipitated in the 1850s by the huge influx of immigrants seeking their fortunes on the rich gold fields of Victoria. This caused a population explosion of unprecedented proportions as prospectors decided to stay in the city. The enormous wealth generated by the gold rush led to the construction of grand public buildings. This development continued throughout the land boom of the 1880s, earning the city the nickname "Marvellous Melbourne". By the end of the 19th century, the city was the industrial and financial capital of Australia. It was also the home of the national parliament until 1927, when it was moved to purpose-built Canberra *(see p191)*.

Fortunate enough to escape much damage in World War II, Melbourne hosted the summer Olympics in 1956. Dubbed the "Friendly Games", the event generated great changes in the city's consciousness. The postwar period also witnessed a new wave of immigrants who sought better lives here. Driven by the will to succeed, they introduced Melburnians to a range of cultures, transforming the British traditions of the city. This transformation continues today with the arrival of immigrants from all parts of Asia.

Melbourne holds many surprises: it has the most elaborate Victorian architecture of all Australian cities; it has a celebrated range of restaurant cuisines and its calendar revolves around hugely popular spectator sports and arts events *(see pp40–41)*. While the climate is renowned for its unpredictability, Melburnians still enjoy an outdoor lifestyle, and the city possesses a unique charm that quietly bewitches many visitors.

Melbourne's café society relaxing along Brunswick Street

◁ Flinders Street Station and St Paul's Cathedral, seen from Queens Bridge

Exploring Melbourne

Melbourne is organized informally into precincts. Collins Street is a business centre and the site of the city's smartest stores. To the east is the parliamentary precinct. Swanston Street contains some fine Victorian architecture. The south bank of the river is arts-orientated and includes the Victorian Arts Centre. The city also devotes much land to parks and gardens.

Shrine of Remembrance near the Royal Botanic Gardens

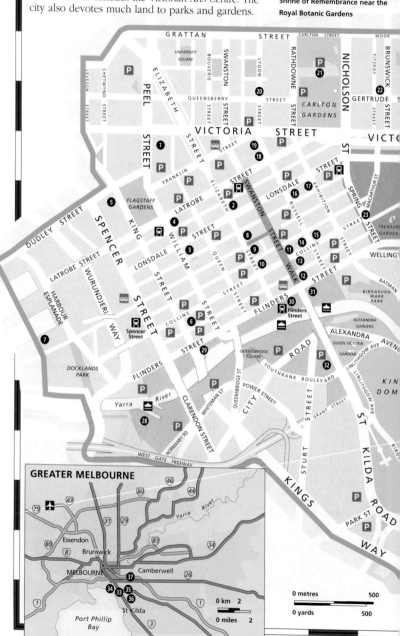

GREATER MELBOURNE

| 0 km | 2 |
| 0 miles | 2 |

| 0 metres | 500 |
| 0 yards | 500 |

For additional map symbols *see back flap*

GETTING AROUND

Despite the comprehensive Metlink transport system of trams, trains and buses, many Melburnians use cars for commuting *(see pp412–13)*. This has resulted in a network of major roads and highways that lead in all directions from Melbourne's central grid through inner and outer suburbs. CityLink is a tollway linking several of the city's major access routes; drivers must purchase a pass in advance of travelling on CityLink roads. The city's flat landscape is also well suited to bicycles.

LOCATOR MAP

SIGHTS AT A GLANCE

Historic Streets and Buildings
Brunswick Street & Fitzroy **22**
Chapel Street **35**
Chinatown **16**
Como Historic House and Garden **37**
Docklands **7**
Federation Square **31**
Fitzroy & Acland streets **33**
Flinders Street Station **30**
General Post Office **8**
Lygon Street **20**
Melbourne Town Hall **11**
No. 120 Collins Street **15**
Old Magistrate's Court **18**
Old Melbourne Gaol **19**
Regent Theatre **13**
Rippon Lea pp404–5 **36**
Royal Exhibition Building **21**
Royal Mint **4**
Supreme Court **3**

Shops and Markets
Block Arcade **10**
Queen Victoria Market **1**
Royal Arcade **9**

Churches and Cathedrals
St Francis' Church **2**
St James' Old Cathedral **5**
St Paul's Cathedral **12**
Scots' Church **14**

Museums and Galleries
Australian Gallery of Sport and Olympic Museum **24**
City Museum **23**
Melbourne Aquarium **29**
Melbourne Maritime Museum **28**
Melbourne Museum **21**
Museum of Chinese Australian History **17**
National Gallery of Victoria **32**

Parks and Gardens
Royal Botanic Gardens and Kings Domain pp398–9 **27**

Modern Architecture
Rialto Towers **6**

Sports Ground
Albert Park **34**
Melbourne Cricket Ground **25**
Melbourne Park **26**

SEE ALSO

- *Street Finder* pp416–21
- *Where to Stay* pp505–9
- *Where to Eat* pp552–6

KEY

Swanston Street Precinct *see pp384–5*

Street-by-Street map *see pp392–3*

The Yarra River *see pp400–1*

Bus station

Train station

Car park

River boat stop

Gothic turrets of the Old Magistrate's Court

Swanston Street Precinct

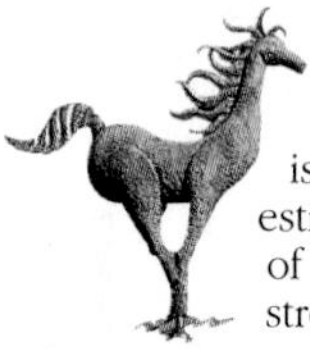

Swanston Street sculpture

Swanston Street, home to Melbourne's town hall and other major civic buildings, has always been a hub of the city. It is also exemplary of one of the most interesting relics of Melbourne: an ordered grid of broad, evenly measured and rectilinear streets, lanes and arcades. The street is also an eclectic illustration of the city's Victorian and 20th-century public architecture. In 1992, the area between Flinders Street and La Trobe Street was converted into a pedestrian precinct until 7pm at night.

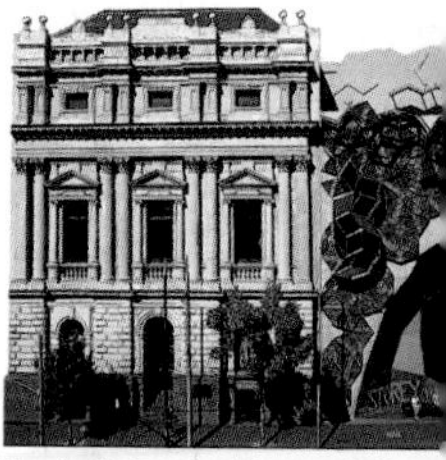

Classically inspired Storey Hall, neighbour of the RMIT Building

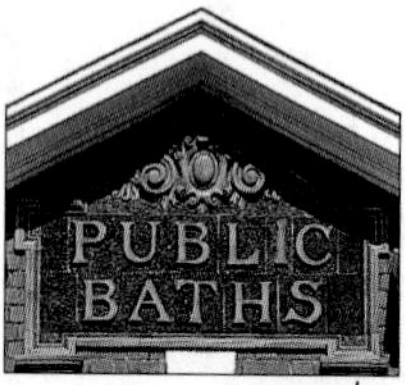

The City Baths are set in a beautiful Edwardian building with twin cupolas as a distinctive feature. They have been carefully restored to their original 1903 condition.

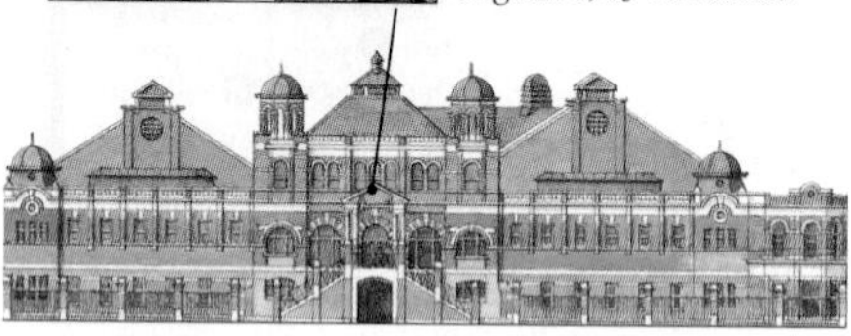

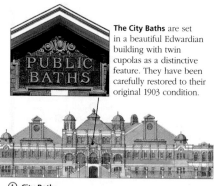

① City Baths

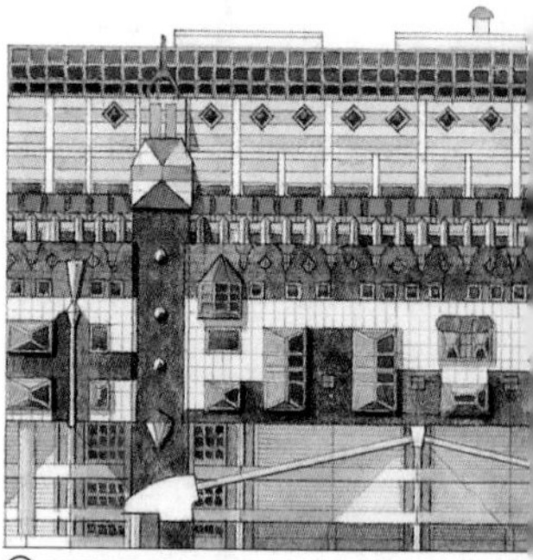

② RMIT Building 8

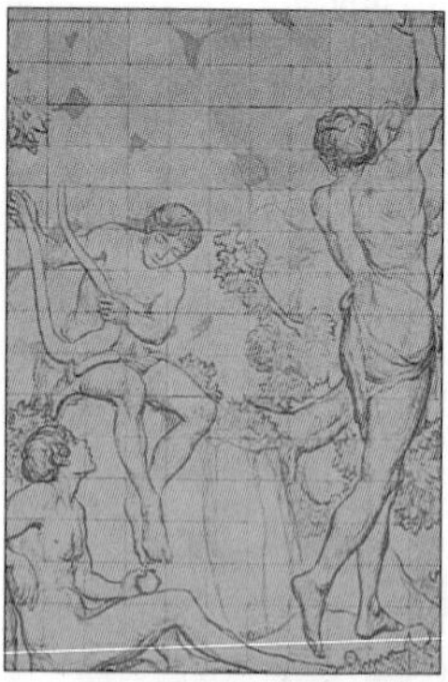

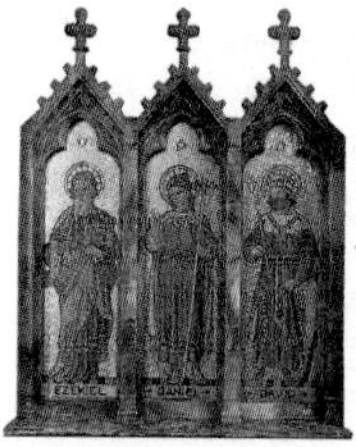

St Paul's Cathedral
Architect William Butterfield designed St Paul's in a Gothic Revival style in the 1880s ⓬

Melbourne Town Hall
The city's town hall was built in 1867, funded by proceeds of the gold rush (see pp54–5) ⓫

Neo-Classical columns

Sandstone façade

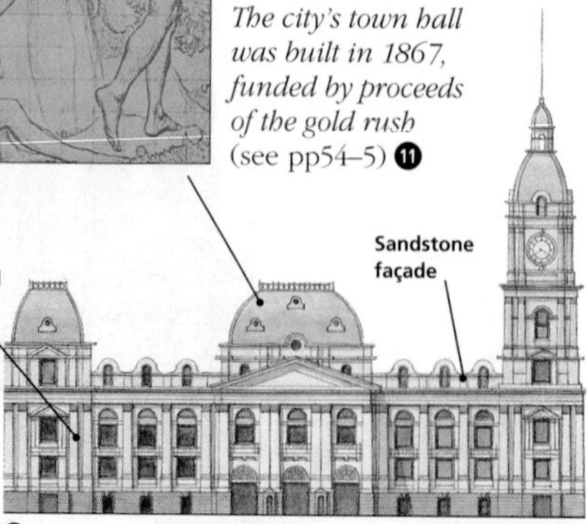

④ Melbourne Town Hall

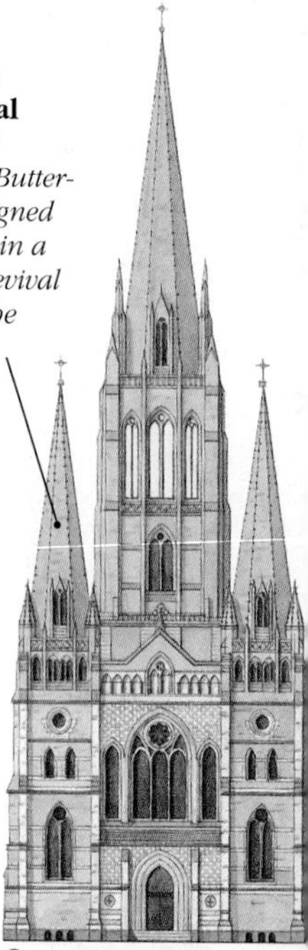

⑤ St Paul's Cathedral

Building 8, RMIT (Royal Melbourne Institute of Technology), is a gaudy, contemporary blend of bold, primary colours utilized within horizontal and vertical lines. It was met with very mixed reviews by Melburnians when it was completed.

LOCATOR MAP
See Melbourne Street Finder, Map 1

The State Library was the first design by noted architect Joseph Reed in 1854. Inside is an attractive octagonal reading room, covered by the central dome which was added in 1913.

Neo-Classical Corinthian columns line the façade.

③ **State Library of Victoria**

Flinders Street Station
Melbourne's busiest rail terminus is one of the most recognizable sights in the city ㉚

Young and Jackson's, a 19th-century hotel known for its nude portrait *Chloe*, is protected by the National Trust.

The Atrium in Federation Square is a remarkable building made of glass, steel and zinc. The Square itself has become the cultural centre of the city, with its restaurants, various attractions and outdoor events.

Station clock

⑥ **Flinders Street Station**   ⑦ **Young and Jackson's**   ⑧ **Federation Square**

Fruit stall in Queen Victoria Market

Queen Victoria Market ❶

Elizabeth, Therry, Peel & Victoria sts.
Map 1 A2. **Tel** (03) 9320 5822.
🚉 Flagstaff & Melbourne Central
(Elizabeth St exit). 🚋 Elizabeth St
routes. ⏱ 6am–2pm Tue & Thu;
6am–6pm Fri; 6am–3pm Sat;
9am–4pm Sun. ⬤ Mon, Wed,
Good Fri, 25 Apr, 25 Dec. ♿ ⬤

Melbourne's main fresh
produce and general goods
market has a strange history,
occupying the site of the
original Melbourne General
Cemetery, which was first
used in 1837. In 1877, the idea
of converting part of the original cemetery into a marketplace for fruit and vegetables
was considered a practical
one. At the time, it involved
the relocation of only three
graves. However, the choice
created controversy which did
not settle down for some time,
as the market's popularity
made it necessary to acquire
further portions of the cemetery. In 1917, an act of Parliament granted the removal of
10,000 remains and the cemetery was razed.

The market began with the
construction of the Wholesale
Meat Market. In 1884, the
Meat Market and Elizabeth
Street shop façades were built.
Further extensions continued
to be built until 1936. Today
the complex, occupying 7 ha
(17 acres), attracts 130,000
visitors per week. Its decorative high-vaulted ceilings and
open sides add to its ornate
atmosphere. About 1,000 stalls
sell fresh fruit and vegetables,
fish, meat, cheese and organic
food. Every Wednesday from
November to February there
is a Gaslight Night Market,
which also has musical and
theatrical performances.

St Francis' Church ❷

326 Lonsdale St. **Map** 1 C2. **Tel** (03)
9663 2495. 🚉 Melbourne Central.
🚋 Elizabeth St routes. ⏱ 7am–
6:30pm daily. ♿ ⬤ by arrangement.

St Francis' Church today is
Australia's busiest Roman
Catholic church, with 10,000
visitors each week. Built
between 1841 and 1845 on
the site of an earlier church,
it is also Victoria's oldest.

Renowned for its beauty,
the church began as a simple
Neo-Gothic building and has
undergone many alterations.
It was the target of a $2.8
million restoration appeal,
and major renovations were
completed in the early 1990s.

During the ceiling restoration,
treasures from the 1860s,
such as a painting of angels,
stars and a coat of arms, were
discovered and beautifully
restored. Vandalized statues
have since been replaced by
faithful copies.

The church holds regular
services, and has one of
Australia's most celebrated
resident choirs.

Roof detail of St Francis' Church

Supreme Court ❸

210 William St. **Map** 1 B3. **Tel** (03)
9603 6111. 🚉 Flagstaff. 🚋 City
Circle & Bourke St routes.
⏱ 8am–5pm Mon–Fri; courts sit
10am–4:15pm. ♿

When the Port Phillip district
was still part of the New
South Wales colony, criminal
and important civil cases
were heard in Sydney. To
ease the inconvenience,
Melbourne's first resident
judge arrived in 1841 to set

Domed library in the Supreme Court

up a Supreme Court in the city. Following the Separation Act of 1850, which established the Colony of Victoria, the city set up its own Supreme Court in 1852. The court moved to the present building, with a design inspired by the Four Courts of Dublin in Ireland, in 1884.

The Supreme Court is an imposing building, with street façades on Lonsdale, William and Little Bourke streets. Its style is Classical, with a projecting portico and a double arcade with Doric and Ionic columns. Internally, a labyrinthine plan is centred on a beautiful domed library. The large bronze figure of Justice, defying tradition, is not blindfolded: rumour has it that an early Melbourne judge persuaded the authorities that Justice should be "wide-eyed if not innocently credulous". The Supreme Court is now classified by the National Trust.

Royal Mint ❹

280 William St. **Map** 1 B3. **Tel** (03) 9670 1219. 🚇 Flagstaff. 🚋 23, 24, 30, 34. 🚌 Lonsdale & Queen sts routes. 🚫 to the public.

This former Mint, built between 1871 and 1872, contains two courts which were until recently used to cope with the overflow from the Supreme Court.

The building replaced Melbourne's first Exhibition Building, erected in 1854 and subsequently destroyed by fire. When the mint opened in 1872 it processed finds from the Victoria gold fields and was a branch of the Royal Mint of London. The actual coining processes took place in an area now occupied by the car park. After the Commonwealth of Australia was founded in 1901 *(see p56)*, new silver coinage was designed, which the mint produced from 1916 to the mid-1960s. The Melbourne site ceased production in 1967 when the Royal Mint

St James' Old Cathedral tower

was relocated to Canberra. Although the Royal Mint building is now closed to the general public, visitors can still take in its imposing structure from the outside.

St James' Old Cathedral ❺

Cnr King & Batman sts. **Map** 1 A2. **Tel** (03) 9329 0903. 🚇 Flagstaff. 🚋 23, 24, 30, 34, 48, 75. 🚌 220, 232. 🕙 10am– 3:30pm Mon– Wed & Fri; 10am service Sun. ● public hols. ♿ 📷 by appointment.

St James' was the first Anglican cathedral in the city, used until St Paul's opened in 1891 *(see p389)*. It was first built near the corner of Little Collins and William streets to replace a wooden hut, known as the "Pioneers' Church". It was relocated to its present site between 1913 and 1914. The stones were numbered to ensure that the original design was replicated. However, a few changes were made, such as a lower ceiling, a shortening of the sanctuary and a reshaping of the bell tower.

Royal Mint crest

St James' was designed in a colonial Georgian style. The foundations are made of bluestone and the main walls were constructed with local sandstone. The cathedral was opened for worship on 2 October 1842, but was not consecrated until 1853. Charles Perry, the city's first bishop,

was enthroned here in 1848. The cathedral is still used for regular services. A small museum contains photographs, historic documents and cathedral mementos.

Rialto Towers ❻

525 Collins St (between King and William sts). **Map** 1 B4. **Tel** (03) 9629 8222. 🚇 Spencer St. 🚋 Collins St routes. 🕙 10am–10pm Sun–Thu; 10am–11pm Fri & Sat. 💰 ♿

Rialto Towers is a member of the World Federation of Great Towers. It has 58 floors above street level and 8 below. From street level up, it measures 253 m (830 ft).

The structure was built in 1986 by Australian developer Bruno Grollo, who was also responsible for the city's new casino on the Yarra River *(see p401)*. An observation deck was opened on the 55th floor in 1994 and now draws 1,500 visitors a day to see panoramic views of the city. There is also a half-hourly screening of a 20-minute film introducing visitors to the sights of Melbourne.

The lift travels from the ground floor to the 55th floor in 38 seconds and is one of the fastest in the world.

The mighty Rialto Towers

General Post Office's magnificent and architecturally eclectic interior

Docklands ❼

Map 1 A4 **Tel** 1300 66 3008.
Spencer Street. City Circle
11, 31, 42, 48, 86. 236.
Yarra River Shuttle
www.docklands.com

The spectacular redevelopment of Melbourne Docklands has created a vibrant, dynamic urban environment, which is worth visiting for the modern architecture alone. The total area to be redeveloped covers some 200 hectares (490 acres) and has 3 km (2 miles) of Yarra River frontage. The project is being undertaken in stages, with the final stage to be completed in 2020.

Docklands is an exciting place to live, work and visit. It has a beautiful harbour and marina (Melbourne's Blue Park @ Docklands), magnificent public spaces, such as Harbour Esplanade, Grand Plaza and Docklands Park, historic wharves, a great variety of urban art (by Australian artists such as Bruce Armstrong), numerous shops and many restaurants, bars and cafés. It hosts many events, such as the Summer Boat Show held every February, and is home to the huge Telstra Dome (www.telstradome.com.au).

General Post Office ❽

Cnr Little Bourke St Mall & Elizabeth St. **Map** 1 C3. **Tel** (03) 9663 0066.
Flinders St & Melbourne Central.
Bourke & Elizabeth sts routes.
10am–6pm Mon–Thu & Sat,
10am–9pm Fri, 11am–6pm Sun.
Good Fri, 25 Dec, 1 Jan.
via Little Bourke St.
www.gpomelbourne.com.au

Melbourne's first postal service was operated from a site near the corner of Kings Street and Flinders Lane. Frequent floods, for which the area became renowned, forced a move to the current site, where the post office opened in 1841.

The present structure was begun in 1859 and completed in 1907. The first and second floors were built between 1859 and 1867, with the third floor and clocktower added between 1885 and 1890. These various stages have resulted in an unusual combination of styles, with Doric columns on the ground floor, Ionic on the second and Corinthian on the topmost level.

The building underwent a number of changes to adapt its 19th-century design to the requirements of a major postal system. This included a post-World War I redesign of its main hall under the direction of architect Walter Burley Griffin (see p197). It closed as a post office in 1993 and after many setbacks, including a fire in 2001, it opened as a beautiful shopping complex in 2004.

Royal Arcade entrance

Royal Arcade ❾

Elizabeth, Bourke & Little Collins sts.
Map 1 C3. **Tel** (03) 9670 7777.
Flinders St. Bourke, Elizabeth
& Collins sts routes. 9am–6pm
Mon–Thu, 9am–9pm Fri,
9am–5:30pm Sat, 10am–5pm Sun.

Royal Arcade is Melbourne's oldest surviving arcade. It is part of a network of lanes and arcades which sprang up to divide the big blocks of the city grid into smaller segments. The network was designed in 1837 by the government surveyor, Robert Hoddle.

The original arcade, built in 1869 and designed by Charles Webb, runs between Bourke Street Mall and Little Collins Street. An annexe, with an entrance on Elizabeth Street, was added in 1908. A statue of Father Time, originally on

Docklands with the Telstra Dome and the city's CBD in the background

For hotels and restaurants in this region see pp505–9 and pp552–6

the Bourke Street façade, is now located inside the arcade at the northern end.

The arcade's most famous inhabitants are statues of Gog and Magog, mythical representations of the conflict between the ancient Britons and the Trojans. They are modelled on identical figures in the Guildhall in the City of London. Between them is Gaunt's Clock, crafted by an original tenant of the arcade, Thomas Gaunt.

Chapel of Ascension in St Paul's Cathedral

Block Arcade ⑩

282 Collins St. **Map** 1 C3. **Tel** (03) 9654 5244. 🚉 Flinders St. 🚋 Swanston & Collins sts routes. 🕐 9am–5pm Mon–Wed, 9am–6pm Thu–Fri, 9am–5pm Sat, 11am–5pm Sun (not all shops). 🌑 Good Fri, 25 Dec. 🚻 📷

Built between 1891 and 1893, with period details including a mosaic floor and a central dome, Melbourne's most opulent arcade was named after the promenade taken by fashionable society in the 1890s. Known as "doing the block", the walk involved strolling down Collins Street between Elizabeth and Swanston streets.

The arcade was restored in 1988. It still includes the Hopetoun Tea-rooms, which have been in place since the structure was opened. Guided tours of the arcade are available.

Block Arcade façade

Melbourne Town Hall ⑪

Swanston St. **Map**1 C3. **Tel** (03) 9658 9658. 🚉 Flinders St. 🚋 Swanston & Collins sts routes. 🕐 9am–6pm Mon–Fri, 9am–5pm Sat–Sun (ground level foyer only). 🌑 public hols. 🚻 📷 obligatory for areas other than ground level foyer.

Melbourne Town Hall was completed in 1870, designed by Joseph Reed's company, Reed & Barnes. The portico was added in 1887. From here there are views of Swanston Street (see pp 384–5) and the Shrine of Remembrance in the Botanic Gardens (see p398).

An adjacent administration block and the council's second chamber were added in 1908. This chamber combines a Renaissance-style interior with uniquely Australian motifs, such as a ceiling plasterwork of gum nuts.

A fire in 1925 destroyed much of the building's interior, including the main hall which had to be rebuilt. The entrance to the building shows four motifs on the young city's coat of arms: a whale, a ship, a bull and a sheep, signifying the main colonial industries. In 1942, the College of Arms ordered an inversion of the motifs according to heraldic convention. This explains the discrepancy between earlier and later coats of arms.

Stained glass in Melbourne Town Hall

St Paul's Cathedral ⑫

Cnr Swanston & Flinders sts. **Map** 2 D3. **Tel** (03) 9650 3791. 🚉 Flinders St. 🚋 Swanston, Flinders & Collins sts routes. 🕐 8:30am–6pm daily. 🚻 📷

St Paul's Cathedral was built in 1866 to replace a far smaller church of the same name on the site.

Construction, however, was plagued by difficulties, with dissension between the English architect, William Butterfield, and the Cathedral Erection Board. Butterfield was contemptuous of the board's wish to have the cathedral face Princes Bridge and their choice of stones for the construction, such as Barrabool and Hawkesbury sandstone. Building began in 1880, but Butterfield tendered his resignation in 1884. The final stages of construction were supervised by the architect Joseph Reed, who also designed many of the fittings. The cathedral was eventually consecrated in 1891.

There are many outstanding internal features, including the reredos (altar screen) made in Italy from marble and alabaster inset with glass mosaics. The organ, made by TC Lewis & Co. of London, is the best surviving work of this great organ-builder. The cathedral also has a peal of 13 bells – a rarity outside the British Isles.

Regent Theatre

191 Collins St. **Map** 2 D3. **Tel** (03) 9299 7500. 🚉 Flinders St. 🚋 Swanston & Collins sts routes. ♿ 🎫 outside performance times.

When the Regent Theatre's auditorium was destroyed by fire in April 1945, the Lord Mayor of Melbourne promised the public that it would be rebuilt, despite the scarcity of building materials due to World War II. Such was the popularity and local importance of the theatre.

Known as "Melbourne's Palace of Dreams", it was first constructed and opened by the Hoyts Theatre Company in 1929. Its lavish interiors emulated both the glamour of Hollywood and New York's impressive Capitol Theater.

The building had two main venues. The auditorium upstairs, for live stage and musical entertainment, was known as the Regent Theatre. Downstairs, the Plaza Theatre was originally a ballroom, but, following the success of the "talkies", it was converted into a cinema.

Fortunately, the magnificent decor of the Plaza Theatre was not damaged in the fire of 1945. The renovated auditorium opened to the public again in 1947.

Assembly hall adjacent to Scots' Church

The advent of television soon resulted in dwindling cinema audiences, and the Regent Theatre closed for almost three decades. The complex has now been restored again and was re-opened in 1996.

Scots' Church

99 Russell St (cnr Collins St). **Map** 2 D3. **Tel** (03) 9650 9903. 🚉 Flinders St & Parliament. 🚋 Swanston & Collins sts routes. ◯ Mon–Wed (call to check times). ✝ 1pm, Wed; 11am & 7pm, Sun. ♿ 🎫 on request.

Scots' Church, completed in 1874, was intended at the time to be "the most beautiful building in Australia". It was designed by Joseph Reed in an "early English" style, with

bluestone used in the foundations and local Barrabool stone making up the superstructure.

The site also includes an assembly hall which was completed in 1913.

No. 120 Collins Street

120 Collins St. **Map** 2 D3. **Tel** (03) 9654 4944. 🚉 Flinders St & Parliament. 🚋 Collins St routes. ◯ 9am–5pm Mon–Fri. ♿

Built in 1991, No. 120 Collins Street was designed by Daryl Jackson and Group Hassell. This office block is now a city landmark. Its communications tower is the highest point in the city,

Grandiose foyer of the Regent Theatre, restored to its original glory

For hotels and restaurants in this region see pp505–9 and pp552–6

standing 262 m (860 ft) tall. Original 1908 Federation-style professional chambers, which were built on the grounds of the 1867 St Michael's Uniting Church, are incorporated into the building.

The major tenant of this 52-storey building is the Australian company BHP Petroleum.

Chambers at No. 120 Collins Street

Chinatown ⑯

Little Bourke St. **Map** 2 D2.
🚆 *Parliament.* 🚎 *Swanston & Bourke sts routes.*

When Chinese immigrants began arriving in Melbourne to seek gold during the 1850s, many European residents were decidedly hostile. Only recent arrivals in the area themselves, they were still insecure about how strongly their own society had been established. This led to racial tension and violence.

The very first Chinese immigrants landed in Australia as early as 1818, but it was during the late 1840s that larger contingents arrived. These newcomers replaced the pool of cheap labour which had dried up with the winding down of convict settlements in the new colonies. This wave of immigration was harmonious until the vast influx of Chinese visitors who came not for labour, but to seek their fortune in the Victorian gold fields in the 1850s. The large numbers of

immigrants and a decline in gold finds made the Chinese targets of vicious and organized riots.

This attitude was sanctioned by government policy. The Chinese were charged a poll tax in most states of £10 each – a huge sum, particularly as many were peasants. Even harsher was a restriction on the number of passengers that boat-owners could carry. This acted as a disincentive for them to bring Chinese immigrants to Australia. What resulted were "Chinese marathons", as new arrivals dodged the tax by landing in "free" South Australia and walking to the gold fields, covering distances of up to 800 km (500 miles) *(see pp54–5)*.

As an immigrant society in Melbourne, the Chinese were highly organized and self-sufficient. A city base was established during the 1850s, utilizing the cheap rental district of the city centre. As with other Chinatowns around the world, traders could live and work in the same premises and act as a support network for other Chinese immigrants. The community largely avoided prejudice by starting up traditional Asian businesses which included market gardening, green grocers and furniture-making (but work had to be stamped "Made by Chinese labour").

Stone lion in the Museum of Chinese Australian History

Traditional gateway in Little Bourke Street, Chinatown

Today, Chinatown is known for its restaurants and Chinese produce shops, with the community's calendar culminating in its New Year celebrations in February *(see p41)*. Ironically, in view of the early prejudices, this community is now one of Australia's oldest and most successful.

Museum of Chinese Australian History ⑰

22 Cohen Place (off Little Bourke St). **Map** 2 D2. **Tel** (03) 9662 2888.
🚆 *Parliament.* 🚎 *Swanston & Bourke sts routes.* 🕐 *10am–5pm daily.* ⬤ *Good Fri, 25 Dec, 1 Jan.*
📷♿🎫

Opened in 1985 to preserve the heritage of Australians of Chinese descent, this museum is in the heart of Chinatown. The subjects of its displays range from the influx of Chinese gold-seekers in the 1850s to exhibitions of contemporary Chinese art, thus offering a comprehensive history of the Chinese in Victoria and their cultural background. The second floor holds regular touring exhibitions from China and displays of Chinese art. On the third floor is a permanent exhibition covering many aspects of Chinese-Australian history, including elaborate costumes, furniture and temple regalia.

In the basement, another permanent exhibition traces the experiences of Chinese gold miners – visitors step into a booth which creaks and moves like a transport ship, then view dioramas of gold field life, a Chinese temple and a tent theatre used by Chinese performers to entertain miners. A guided heritage walk through Chinatown is also available.

The museum also houses the beautiful Melbourne Chinese dragon, the head of which is the largest of its kind anywhere in the world.

Street-by-Street: Parliament Area

St Patrick's Cathedral icon

The Parliament precinct on Eastern Hill is a gracious area of great historic interest. Early founders of the city noted the favourable aspect of the hill and set it aside for Melbourne's official and ecclesiastical buildings. The streets still retain the elegance of the Victorian era; the buildings, constructed with revenue from the gold rush *(see pp54–5)*, are among the most impressive in the city. The Fitzroy Gardens, on the lower slopes of the hill, date back to the 1850s *(see pp374–5)* and provide a peaceful retreat complete with woodlands, glades, seasonal plantings and magnificent elm tree avenues.

The Windsor Hotel, with its long and ornate façade, was built in 1884 and is the grandest surviving hotel of its era in Australia *(see p508).*

Stanford Fountain
The beautiful centrepiece of the elegant Gordon Reserve was sculpted by the prisoner William Stanford while he was serving his sentence.

★ Treasury Building
This Renaissance Revival style building was designed by draughtsman John James Clark in 1857. Built as government offices, with vaults to house the treasury's gold, it is now the City Museum.

Cook's Cottage
This cottage was the English home of the parents of Captain James Cook (see p50). It was shipped to Australia in 1933 piece by piece and now houses displays about Cook and 18th-century life.

For hotels and restaurants in this region see pp505–9 and pp552–6

★ Parliament House
The Legislative Council in this 1850s building sits in a lavish, Corinthian chamber. The crimson colour scheme is copied from the UK's House of Lords.

LOCATOR MAP
See Melbourne Street Finder, map 2

Tasma Terrace is a superb example of Melbourne's distinctive terrace houses with ornate cast-iron decoration *(see pp376–7)*. It is now the headquarters of the National Trust.

St Patrick's Cathedral
This is one of the best examples of Gothic Revival church architecture in the world. It was constructed between 1858 and 1897, with its impressive spires completed in 1937.

CATHEDRAL PLACE

ALBERT STREET

★ Fitzroy Gardens
Landscape gardener James Sinclair was responsible for the superb features of these formal gardens, including winding paths, a fern gully, flowerbeds and avenues of blue gums, planes and elms.

STAR SIGHTS

★ Fitzroy Gardens

★ Parliament House

★ Treasury Building

| 0 metres | 100 |
| 0 yards | 100 |

KEY

- - - Suggested route

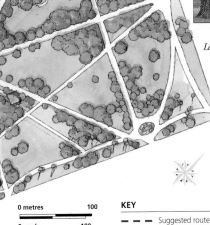

Old Magistrate's Court ⑱

Cnr La Trobe & Russell sts. **Map** 1 C2. 🖼 *Museum.* 🚊 *La Trobe & Swanston sts routes.* 🚭 *to public.*

The Melbourne Magistrate's Court, also called City Court, occupied this building until 1995. The area was formerly known as the police precinct – this is because the court lies opposite the former police headquarters, a very striking Art Deco skyscraper completed in the early 1940s, and next door to the Old Melbourne Gaol.

Built in 1911, the court's façades are made of native Moorabool sandstone. The building's intricate, Romanesque design features gables, turrets and arches. It originally contained three courtrooms and offices, with a two-storey octagonal main vestibule at the centre of its labyrinth of rooms.

The future use of the Old Court is still being decided.

Corridor of cells in Old Melbourne Gaol

Ornate Romanesque tower of the Old Magistrate's Court

Old Melbourne Gaol ⑲

Russell St. **Map** 1 C2. **Tel** (03) 9663 7228. 🖼 *Melbourne Central.* 🚊 *La Trobe & Swanston sts routes.* ◯ *9:30am–5pm daily.* ⬤ *Good Fri, 25 Dec.* 📷 ⬛ 🚭 *limited.* **www**.nattrust.com.au

Visiting the Old Melbourne Gaol, Victoria's first extensive gaol complex, is a chilling experience, especially on a night tour. Between 1845 and 1929, it was the site of 135 executions. Today's National Trust penal museum is housed in the Second Cell Block. Behind this was the Female Ward for women prisoners, now demolished. Still in existence, though not part of the museum, is the prison chapel.

Ghosts are often reported at the gaol, which is hardly surprising given the tragic and grisly accounts of prisoners' lives and deaths. Conditions, based on London's Pentonville Model Prison, were grim: regulated, silent and anonymous. When first incarcerated, prisoners were held in solitary confinement and were not permitted to mix with other prisoners until a later date, set according to their sentence. Exhibits showing these conditions include prisoners' chains and a frame used for flogging. But perhaps the most compelling exhibits are the many accounts of prisoners who were condemned to die at the gaol, accompanied by their death masks. Ned Kelly's death mask is the most famous of those on display.

Many inmates were badly treated. Basilio Bondietto, an Italian immigrant, was convicted of murder in 1876 on circumstantial evidence. He spoke no English, had no interpreter at his trial and apparently did not understand that he was condemned to death until hours before his execution. Another case is that of Frances Knorr, hanged in 1894 amid much public controversy after being convicted of murdering three babies in her care. Knorr had been left pregnant and penniless when her husband was

NED KELLY

The most well-known execution at the Melbourne Gaol was that of Ned Kelly, Australia's most famous bushranger, on 11 November 1880. Edward "Ned" Kelly was the son of Ellen and ex-convict "Red" Kelly. At the time of Ned's final imprisonment and execution, Ellen was serving a sentence in the gaol's Female Ward after hitting a policeman over the head when he visited her house. She was therefore able to visit her son, who

Ned Kelly's death mask

had been captured at Glenrowan on 28 June 1880 *(see p451)*. A crowd of 4,000 waited outside the gaol when Kelly was executed, most of them to lend their support to a man perceived to be rightfully rebelling against the English-based law and police authorities. In one instance, the Kelly Gang burned a bank's records of outstanding loans so they no longer had to be repaid. The controversy over whether Kelly was hero or villain continues to this day.

jailed for selling furniture bought on hire purchase. Her appointed hangman committed suicide days before her execution, after his own wife threatened to leave him if he was the one to execute Knorr.

Italian restaurant in Lygon Street

Lygon Street ⑳

Lygon St, Carlton. **Map** 1 C1.
🚋 *1, 22.* 🚌 *200, 201, 207.*

This Italian-influenced street is one of the main café, restaurant and delicatessen areas in central Melbourne *(see pp552–6).*

The strong Italian tradition of Lygon Street began at the time of mass post-World War II immigration. With a general exodus to the suburbs in the 1940s, Carlton became unfashionable and new immigrants were able to buy its 19th-century houses and shops cheaply. More importantly, the immigrants were central in protecting these Victorian and Edwardian houses, which were built with post-gold rush wealth, from government plans to fill the area with low-income Housing Commission homes.

A distinctive architectural trait of Lygon Street's two-storey shops is their street verandas, built to protect both customers and merchandise from the sun. In the mid-1960s, the area became fashionable with university students, many of whom moved in to take advantage of its cheap accommodation, then stayed on after graduating to become the base of the suburb's contemporary middle-class and professional community. The

Coffee grinder in a Lygon Street coffee house

street is only one block from the main University of Melbourne campus and can be reached from the city centre by foot, bus or tram. Its wide street resembles a French boulevard and is well suited to the Lygon Street Festa held here every year *(see p40).*

Melbourne Museum ㉑

Carlton Gardens, Melbourne. **Map** 2 D1. **Tel** *(03) 8341 7777.* 🚋 *86, 96.* ⏰ *10am–5pm daily.* ⊘ *25 Dec, Good Fri.* 📷 🚻 🏪 ♿ **www. melbourne.museum.vic.gov.au**

Having opened in 2001, this museum is one of the newest in the city. Housed in an ultra-modern facility in verdant Carlton Gardens, it has exhibits over six levels, half of which are below ground level. Diverse displays offer insights into science, technology, the environment, the human mind and body, Australian society and indigenous cultures.

One of the highlights is Bunjilaka, the Aboriginal Centre. It combines exhibition galleries with a performance space and meeting rooms. *Wurreka,* the 50-m- (150 feet) long zinc wall etching at the entrance is by Aboriginal artist Judy Watson. The Two Laws gallery deals with the Indigenous Australians' systems of knowledge, law and property.

The Forest Gallery is a living, breathing exhibit, featuring 8,000 plants from

120 different species. It is also home to around 20 different vertebrate species, including snakes, birds, fish and hundreds of insects. This gallery explores the complex ecosystem of Australia's temperate forests, using plants and animals, art and multimedia installations, soundscapes and other activities.

A dedicated children's museum is in a gallery that resembles a tilted, blue cube. The Blue Box houses multi-sensory displays exploring the theme of growth. There are also Children's Pathways throughout the rest of the museum, providing activities for children in other galleries.

One of the most popular exhibits is in the Australia Gallery. This treats the life of Phar Lap, the champion Australian racehorse of the early 1930s. Exhibits include race memorabilia of the period. Phar Lap himself is seen in an Art-Deco inspired showcase. Other curiosities on show in the museum include the skeleton of a blue whale, a car from Melbourne's first tram, a windmill and the Hertel, the first car to be imported.

Adjacent to the Melbourne Museum is the **Royal Exhibition Building**, offering an interesting 19th-century counterpoint to the Museum's modern architecture. The Exhibition Building was built for the 1880 International Exhibition and is one of the few remaining structures from the 19th-century world fairs. It was designed by Joseph Reed, whose work can be found throughout Melbourne.

Elegant Royal Exhibition Building, near the Melbourne Museum

Leisurely café society in Brunswick Street

Brunswick Street and Fitzroy ㉒

Brunswick St. **Map** 2 E1. 🚋 *11.*

Next to the university suburb of Carlton, Fitzroy was the natural choice for a post-1960s populace of students and other bohemian characters, who took advantage of the area's cheap postwar Housing Commission properties, unwanted by wealthier Melburnians. Despite some recent gentrification, Fitzroy's main strip, Brunswick Street, maintains an alternative air and a cosmopolitan street life.

Today, Brunswick Street is a mix of cafés, restaurants and trendy shops. The Brunswick Street parade, held for the opening of the city's Fringe Festival each September, is very popular. Nearby Johnston Street is home to Melbourne's Spanish quarter. Both streets are most lively on Saturday nights.

City Museum ㉓

Old Treasury Building, Spring Street (top of Collins Street). **Map** 2 D2. **Tel** (03) 9651 2233. 🚋 *109.* 🕐 *9am–5pm Mon–Fri, 10am–4pm Sat, Sun & Public Hols.* 🔴 *Good Fri, 25 & 26 Dec.* 🎦 📷 *11am & 3pm.* ♿ 🏛 **www.**citymuseummelbourne.org

The City Museum is housed within Melbourne's beautiful, 19th-century Old Treasury Building *(see p392)*. Designed in 1857 by John James Clark, a nineteen year old architectural prodigy, it provided secure storage for gold that flooded into Melbourne from the wealthy Victorian gold fields. It also served as office accommodation for the Governor of Victoria (a role it still fulfils to this day).

As well as an opportunity to see the building itself, a visit to the museum includes a look at the gold vaults that lie beneath the building. The vaults contain a dynamic multi-media exhibition *Built on Gold*, which tells the story of how Melbourne developed into a city of enormous wealth in a remarkably short period of ten years. In this time it went from a small colonial outpost to a vibrant city with magnificent buildings and grand boulevards, a dynamic theatre culture, a passion for sport and political activism.

Making Melbourne, a permanent exhibition on the ground floor, explores Melbourne's history from the gold rushes of 1852 up until the present day. This more traditional exhibition, which includes a number of famous paintings of Melbourne from the National Gallery of Victoria, provides visitors with an opportunity to explore the economic, cultural and recreational aspects of the city's contemporary life.

Drawn from galleries and musuems from all over Australia, the temporary exhibition gallery hosts a new exhibition every six weeks. On display are a range of visual arts including sculpture, textiles, photography and architecture.

Australian Gallery of Sport and Olympic Museum ㉔

Melbourne Cricket Ground, Yarra Park, Jolimont. **Map** 2 F3. **Tel** (03) 9657 8879. 🚉 *Richmond.* 🚋 *70.* 🕐 *9:30am–4:30pm daily.* 🔴 *Good Fri, 25 Dec.* 🎦 ♿ 📷

Located at the Melbourne Cricket Ground (MCG), this museum is currently closed due to redevelopment at the MCG in preparation for the Commonwealth Games in 2006. It is due to reopen by November in that year, but in the meantime, you can still take a tour which includes the Arena, the Great Southern Stand, the Ponsford Stand, the football and cricket change rooms, heritage artworks and the corporate suites. Tours leave from Light Tower No.4 every half hour between 10am and 3pm, but only on non-event days.

When it reopens, the Olympic Museum will have displays of the history of all summer Olympic meets, reincarnated in Athens in 1896. Australia, Greece and the United Kingdom are the only three countries to have competed at all of the modern summer games.

The Australian Cricket Hall of Fame, which opened with ten Australian players as initial members, includes Sir Donald Bradman. Each player is presented through a comprehensive historical display.

Olympic Cauldron on display in the Olympic Museum

For hotels and restaurants in this region see pp505–9 and pp552–6

World-famous Melbourne Cricket Ground backed by the city skyline

Melbourne Cricket Ground ㉕

Yarra Park, Jolimont. **Map** 2 F3. **Tel** *(03) 9657 8879.* 🚆 *Jolimont.* 🚋 *48, 75 (special trams run on sports event days).* ⬤ *for tours or sports events only.* 🖼 ♿ 🎥 *obligatory.*

Melbourne Cricket Ground (MCG) is Australia's premier sports stadium and a cultural icon. The land was granted in 1853 to the Melbourne Cricket Club (MCC), itself conceived in 1838.

The MCG predominantly hosts cricket and Australian Rules football, being the site for test matches and the first one-day international match and for the Australian Football League Grand Final, held on the last Saturday of September *(see p40).* Non-sporting events, such as pop concerts, are also held at the venue.

There have been numerous stands and pavilions over the years, each superseded at different times by reconstructions of the ground. An 1876 stand, now demolished, was reversible, with spectators able to watch cricket on the ground and football in the park in winter. The most recent development was the Great Southern Stand, completed in 1992; the MCG can now seat crowds of more than 100,000. The Olympic and Members stands are also under reconstruction. Guided tours usually take visitors to the members' pavilion, which includes the Cricket Museum. However, the museum is closed due to the currrent redevelopment of the stands, and is due to reopen late 2006.

Melbourne Park ㉖

Batman Ave. **Map** 2 F4. **Tel** *(03) 9286 1234.* 🚆 *Flinders St & Richmond.* 🚋 *70.* ⬤ *8:30am–5:30pm Mon–Fri, or during events.* ♿

Melbourne Park (formerly known as the National Tennis Centre) on the northern bank of the Yarra River, is Melbourne's sports and large-scale concerts venue. Events include the Australian Open *(see p41),* one of the four Grand Slam competitions of tennis, played under Melbourne Park's unique retractable roof *(see p377).* There are also 23 outdoor and five indoor tennis courts for public use.

Next to Melbourne Park is the Vodafone Arena, which is home to the popular Victorian Titans basketball team. It also hosts a stadium for tennis, basketball, cycling and concerts, all covering an area of 2.4 ha (6 acres). Opposite the park is the Sports and Entertainment Centre, which was originally built for the 1956 Olympics but is now being redeveloped.

Nearby Olympic Park is the location for international and national athletics meets, as well as regular soccer and rugby competitions.

Australian Open tennis championship in Melbourne Park

Royal Botanic Gardens and Kings Domain ㉗

Shrine of Remembrance crypt plaque

These adjoining gardens, established in 1852, form the green heart of Melbourne on what was originally a swamp on the edge of the city. The Botanic Gardens house one of the finest collections of botanic species in the world, as well as being highly regarded for their landscape design. William Guilfoyle, curator of the Gardens between 1873 and 1909, used his knowledge of English garden design to create a horticultural paradise. Kings Domain, once an inner-city wilderness, became instead a gracious parkland. Its civic function grew over the years, with the establishment of its monuments, statues, cultural venues and the hilltop residence of the Governor of Victoria.

Sidney Myer Music Bowl is an architecturally acclaimed music "shell" which can accommodate up to 15,000 people for open-air concerts and ballets. In winter the stage becomes an ice rink.

Pioneer Women's Garden
This sunken, formal garden was built in 1934 to honour the memory of Victoria's founding women. A still, central pool is adorned by a bronze, female statue.

Observatory Gate Precinct

★ **Shrine of Remembrance**
Based on the description of the Mausoleum of Halicarnassus in Asia Minor, now Turkey, this imposing monument honours Australian soldiers who gave their lives in war.

0 metres   200

0 yards   200

★ Government House
This elaborate Italianate building is a landmark of the gardens. Tours of the state rooms are held each week.

VISITORS' CHECKLIST

St Kilda Rd. **Map** 2 F5. 🛈 *Birdwood Ave (03) 9252 2300.* 🚃 3, 5, 6, 8, 15, 16, 64, 67, 72. 🕐 7:30am daily. 🔵 vary seasonally. ♿ 📷 11am & 2pm Sun–Fri. 🚻 🖥 www.nattrust.com.au

The Perennial Border, based on designer Gertrude Jekyll's traditional colour scheme, is planted with pastels, contrasting with grey and silver foliage.

The Temple of the Winds

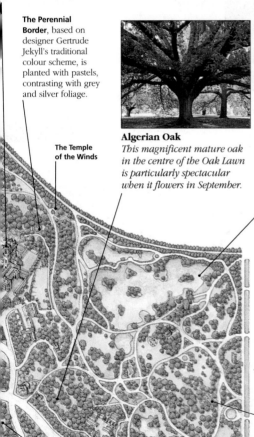

Algerian Oak
This magnificent mature oak in the centre of the Oak Lawn is particularly spectacular when it flowers in September.

★ Ornamental Lake
William Guilfoyle's lake forms the centrepiece of the Gardens. It reflects his adherence to 18th-century English garden design, which used water as a feature.

Arid Garden
Desert region plants from Australia and around the world thrive in this special garden, watered by a small stream which acts as a natural oasis.

Children's Garden

La Trobe's Cottage was shipped from England in 1839 and was home to Victoria's first governor, Charles La Trobe. The building is now preserved by the National Trust.

STAR FEATURES

★ Government House

★ Ornamental Lake

★ Shrine of Remembrance

The Yarra River

The Yarra River winds for 240 km (150 miles) from its source in Baw Baw National Park to the coast. The river has always been vital to the city, not just as its major natural feature, but also in early settlement days as its gateway to the rest of the world. Today, the Yarra is a symbol of the boundary between north and south Melbourne and many citizens live their whole lives on one side or the other. Since the 1980s, the rejuvenation of the central section of the river has given the south bank an important focus. The river is also used for sport: rowers in training are a daily sight and cycle trails run along much of the river.

LOCATOR MAP
See Melbourne Street Finder, maps 1, 2

★ **National Gallery of Victoria**
Recently redeveloped, the Gallery houses one of the largest collections of international works of art in Australia 32

The Victorian Arts Centre is home to the Australian Ballet and the Melbourne Theatre Company. The 115-m (375-ft) spire is now a Melbourne landmark.

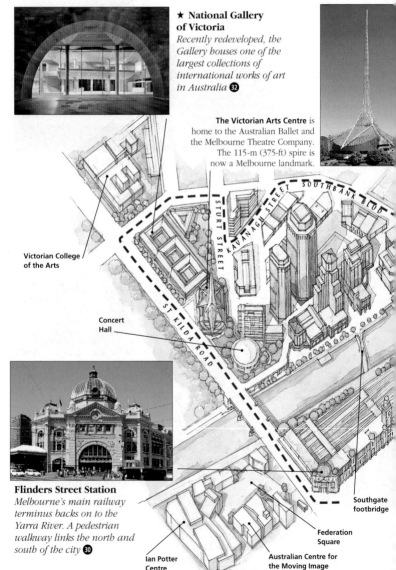

Victorian College of the Arts

Concert Hall

Flinders Street Station
Melbourne's main railway terminus backs on to the Yarra River. A pedestrian walkway links the north and south of the city 30

Ian Potter Centre

Australian Centre for the Moving Image

Federation Square

Southgate footbridge

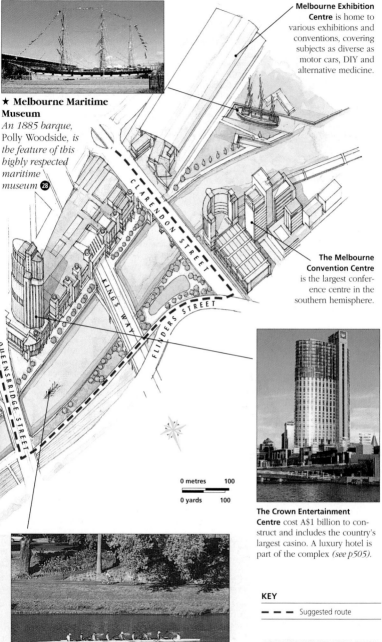

Melbourne Exhibition Centre is home to various exhibitions and conventions, covering subjects as diverse as motor cars, DIY and alternative medicine.

★ **Melbourne Maritime Museum**
An 1885 barque, Polly Woodside, is the feature of this highly respected maritime museum ㉘

The Melbourne Convention Centre is the largest conference centre in the southern hemisphere.

The Crown Entertainment Centre cost A\$1 billion to construct and includes the country's largest casino. A luxury hotel is part of the complex *(see p505).*

0 metres   100
0 yards   100

KEY

– – – Suggested route

STAR SIGHTS

★ National Gallery of Victoria

★ Polly Woodside Maritime Museum

Yarra River Rowers
Professional and amateur rowing teams are a regular sight on the Yarra River, and regattas are a regular event. Rowing boats can be hired at various points along the riverbanks.

For hotels and restaurants in this region see pp505–9 and pp552–6

Polly Woodside barque moored on the Yarra River

Melbourne Maritime Museum ②⑧

Lorimer St East, Southbank. **Map** 1 A5. **Tel** (03) 9699 9760. 🚉 *Spencer St.* 🚍 *12, 96, 109.* 🚢 *Grimes Street Bridge.* 🕐 *10am–4pm daily.* ⬤ *Good Fri, 25 Dec.* 📷 🚻 *except for ship.* 📖 *book in advance.* **www**.nattrust.com.au

The Maritime Museum is also known as the "Home of *Polly Woodside*", an 1885 barque built in Belfast. When she was retired from service in the 1960s, she was the only deep-water commercial ship still afloat in Australia. Even in 1885, she was rare, as only one in four ships were then built with sails. The last 40 years of her working life were spent as a coal hulk. Donated to the National Trust in 1968, she has now been restored and visitors can see how her crews lived on board and study old boat-building skills and various nautical models, displays and memorabilia.

Maritime museum exhibit

Melbourne Aquarium ②⑨

Cnr Flinders & King sts. **Map** 1 B4. **Tel** (03) 9620 0999. 🚉 *Spencer St, Flinders St.* 🕐 *9:30am–6pm daily (to 9pm in Jan).* 📷 🚻 💻 🎁

Featuring species from the southern oceans, the Melbourne Aquarium puts humans close to some of the exotic inhabitants of the deep. Among the exhibits is the 2.2m-litre Oceanarium, housing sharks and rays as well as vibrantly coloured fish, which is approached through a viewing cylinder that places visitors in the middle of the swarming ocean life. Also worth a view is the coral atoll.

Flinders Street Station ③⓪

Cnr Flinders & Swanston sts. **Map** 1 C4. **Tel** 13 16 38. 🚍 *Swanston St and Flinders St. routes.* 🚻

Flinders Street Station is the central metropolitan train terminus of Melbourne and one of the city's favourite meeting places. Generations of Melburnians have met each other on the corner steps of the station "under the Clocks". Although the original clocks are now operated by computer rather than by hand, they remain in working order. The Flinders Street site has been part of the public transport network since the city's early days. The first steam train in Australia left Flinders Street Station, then a small wooden building at the end of Elizabeth Street, in 1854. The present station building, completed in 1910, was designed by Fawcett & Ashworth. The bronze domed building with its bright yellow brickwork was fully restored and refurbished in 1981.

Federation Square ③①

Cnr Flinders & Swanston sts. **Map** 1 C4. **Tel** (03) 9655 1900. 🚍 *Swanston St and Flinders St routes.* 🚻 **www**.federationsquare.com.au **The Ian Potter Centre – NGV Tel** (03) 8662 1555. **ACMI Tel** (03) 8663 2200. **Champions Tel** (03) 1300 139 407. **National Design Centre Tel** (03) 9654 6335.

Melbourne's newest public space, Federation Square commemorates the centenary of the federation of the Australian states and was opened in October 2002. The square hosts up to 2,000 events each year. Its architectural highlight is the geometric design of the Atrium building, a covered public space. There are many outstanding attractions. **The Ian Potter Centre – NGV: Australia**, an offshoot of the National Gallery of Victoria *(see p403)*, is the world's first major gallery dedicated exclusively to the display of Australian art. Nearby, the **Australian Centre for the Moving Image (ACMI)** celebrates images on multimedia and film. Across four floors of the Alfred Deakin Building, the ACMI has two multi-format cinemas and the world's largest screen gallery. Also worth a visit are **Champions – Australian Racing Museum and Hall of Fame** and the **National Design Centre**. The square has two information points: the Melbourne Visitor Centre and the Melbourne Mobility Centre.

Modern architecture of the Atrium building at Federation Square

View of Albert Park Lake and its wetlands

National Gallery of Victoria ❷

180 St Kilda Rd and Federation Square. **Map** 2 D4. **Tel** (03) 8620 2222. ☐ 10am–5pm daily. ⊗ Good Fri, 25 Apr, 25 Dec. **NGV Australia** Mon; **NGV International** Tue. ⬚ ▧ ▨ ▣

The first public art gallery in Australia, the National Gallery of Victoria opened in 1861 and housed the original State Museum *(see p389)*. The gallery moved to St Kilda Rd in 1968 and contains the largest and widest ranging art collection in the country. Its most significant bequest, from Melbourne entrepreneur Alfred Felton in 1904, included works by many great artists, and it is considered to have one of the finest collections of Old Masters in the world. Its collection of contemporary Australian art is also oustanding.

Following major renovations, the international collection can be seen at 180 St Kilda Road *(see p400)* while the Australian collection is housed at Federation Square *(see p402)*.

Fitzroy and Acland Streets ❸

St Kilda. **Map** 5 B5. ▦ 96. ▦ 246, 600, 623, 606. ⬚ St Kilda Pier.

Situated 6 km (4 miles) south of the city centre, St Kilda has long been the most popular seaside suburb of Melbourne. Given the built-up, suburban nature of many of the bay's beaches, it is the closest Melbourne comes to possessing a beach resort.

During the boom-time era of the 1880s *(see pp54–5)*, the suburb was inhabited by many wealthy families before it became more fashionable to live in the suburb of Toorak or on the peninsulas. Other well-off Victorians would holiday in St Kilda during the summer. St Kilda Pier, still a magnet for visitors, was erected in 1857.

Today St Kilda is densely populated, with many Art Deco apartment blocks. The neighbourhood's main streets are Fitzroy and Acland. The latter, renowned as a district of Jewish delicatessens and cake shops, is packed with visitors on Sundays. Fitzroy Street is filled with up-market restaurants and shops. Rejuvenated in the 1980s, the beachside esplanade attracts crowds to its busy arts and crafts market each Sunday.

Another popular outing is a ferry trip across the bay, including a visit to the World Trade Centre on the Yarra River *(see pp400–1)* and destinations further afield.

Melbourne tram running along the City Circle route

Albert Park ❸

Canterbury Rd, Albert St & Lakeside Drive. **Map** 5 B3. ▦ 96.

Encompassing the remains of a former natural swampland, Albert Park Lake is the attractive centrepiece of a 225-ha (555-acre) parkland which includes sporting fields, a public golf course and many other recreational facilities. However, it is now predominantly known as the site of the annual Australian Formula One Grand Prix, which covers a 5,260-m (5,754-yd) circuit around the lake *(see p42)*. Apart from the Grand Prix, the park is used for a variety of purposes. There is a new, popular aquatic and indoor sports centre. Wetlands have also been developed to promote a diverse wildlife. One of the most popular activities at the park is sailing, whether by small yacht, rowing boat or model boat.

A large, ancient river red gum tree standing in the centre of the park is also reputed to have been the site of many Aboriginal *corroborees* (festive night dances).

Chapel Street ❸

South Yarra, Prahran and Windsor. **Map** 6 E3. ▦ South Yarra, Prahan. ▦ 6, 8, 72.

Chapel Street, Melbourne's most fashionable street, with price-tags to match, is lined with shops selling local and international fashion designs. A youthful clientele swarms the street at weekends. Up-market restaurants and cafés abound and the nearby Prahran Market sells the best in fresh, delicatessen produce.

Crossing Chapel Street is Toorak Road, whose "village" is patronized by Melbourne's wealthiest community. More akin to the bohemian area of Brunswick Street *(see p396)* is Greville Street to the west, with its cafés, bars and chic second-hand shops.

A food and fashion festival is sometimes held on the last Sunday before the Melbourne Cup *(see p41)* .

Rippon Lea 36

Rippon Lea Mansion, designed by Joseph
Reed and built in 1868, is now part of a
National Trust estate. The house is a
much loved fixture of the city's heritage.
The first family of Rippon Lea were the
Sargoods, who were renowned party
hosts during the 1880s and 1890s. The
next owner, Premier Sir Thomas Bent,
sold off parts of the estate in the early
1900s. The Nathans bought Rippon Lea
in 1910 and restored its reputation as a
family home. Benjamin Nathan's daughter
Louisa added a ballroom and swimming
pool to the house, which were the
venue for parties in the 1930s and 1940s.
The formal gardens are a main highlight.

Façade of the elegant mansion, Rippon Lea

Arched windows are
a recurring decorative
theme throughout the
house, bordered by
polychrome bricks.

Victorian Bathroom
*The decor of the bathroom has been
restored to its original Victorian style
as installed by the Sargoods. The
earth closets were ingeniously
processed into liquid man-
ure and recycled for use
in the garden.*

The conservatory
housed ferns and orchids,
beloved flowers of both
Frederick Sargood and
Benjamin Nathan. Horticultural
experts were regularly invited
to Rippon Lea.

Main entrance

STAR FEATURES

★ Dining Room

★ Sitting Room

The main staircase is oak and mahogany like much
of the rest of the house. Mirrors, another recurring
theme in the house, are fitted into an archway at the
foot of the stairs, courtesy of Louisa Jones.

★ Dining Room
American walnut blends with an Italian Renaissance style for the dining furniture of Louisa Jones.

The Tower was an unusual feature in the design of a domestic house. In this case, it may have been inspired by Sargood, who wanted his home to have the ornateness of a church.

The brickwork was inspired by a trip by Joseph Reed to Lombardy in Italy, where he came across this polychrome design.

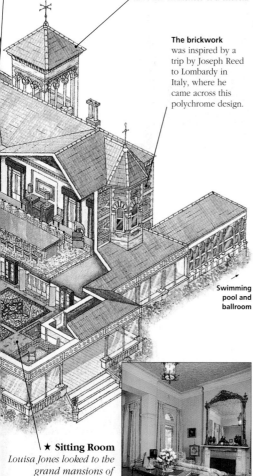

Swimming pool and ballroom

★ Sitting Room
Louisa Jones looked to the grand mansions of Hollywood film stars in the 1930s for much of her interior design, including the plush sitting room.

Como House and its driveway

Como Historic House and Garden ③⑦

Cnr Williams Rd & Lechlade Ave, South Yarra. **Map** 4 F4. **Tel** (03) 9827 2500. 🚉 South Yarra. 🚌 8. ⬤ 10am–5pm daily. ⬤ Good Fri, 25 Dec. 🎟 ♿ ground floor and grounds only. 🎫 obligatory.

Begun in 1847 by Edward Eyre Williams, Como House was occupied by the Armytage family for almost a century (1865–1959).

One of Como's highlights is its vast collection of original furnishings. These include pieces collected by the Armytage matriarch, Caroline, whilst on a Grand Tour of Europe during the 1870s, and include marble and bronze statues. The tour was undertaken as an educational experience for her nine children after the death of her husband, Charles Henry. It was important to this prominent Melbourne family to be seen as well educated. On their return, they held a series of sophisticated parties here.

Set in the picturesque remnants of its once extensive gardens, the house overlooks Como Park and the Yarra River. The original facets of the magnificent grounds, designed by William Sangster (who also had an input at Rippon Lea), remain: the fountain terrace, croquet lawn and hard standing area at the front of the house.

Como was managed by the Armytage women from 1876 until it was purchased by the National Trust in 1959. The house has undergone major restoration work over the years since then; the most recent efforts were in 2001.

SHOPPING IN MELBOURNE

The Central Business District (CBD) is a magnet for the city's shoppers. Major department stores are supplemented by a network of boutiques and specialist shops, many of which are tucked away in arcades and lanes. There is also a network of inner-city and suburban shopping streets: fashionable clothing and retail stores abound in urban areas, while large one-stop shopping towns are a feature

Dinosaur Designs, South Yarra

of Greater Melbourne. There are areas known for particular products, such as High Street, which runs through Armadale and Malvern, with its antiques stores. The city's multicultural society is also reflected in its shopping districts: Victoria Street, Richmond, has a stretch of Vietnamese stores; Sydney Road, Brunswick, is renowned for its shops selling Middle Eastern goods; and Carlisle Street, St Kilda, has many Jewish delicatessens.

Ornate and elegant Royal Arcade, which was built in 1869

SHOPPING HOURS

In Victoria, most traders are open every day. Some small businesses close on Sundays but, increasingly, many stay open, competing with the long hours of chain stores and supermarkets (some of which are open 24 hours a day). Standard hours are 9am to 5:30pm (10am to 6pm in the CBD), although some retailers have extended hours on Thursdays or Fridays. Hours can vary at weekends. Most shops close on Christmas Day and Good Friday.

DEPARTMENT STORES

There are two major department stores in central Melbourne: **Myer Melbourne** and **David Jones**, both are open for business seven days a week.

Australia's largest department store, Myer Melbourne, encompasses a full two blocks of the city centre, with seven floors in Lonsdale

Street and six in Bourke Street. Its main entrance is in Bourke Street Mall. Myer have nine other stores throughout Melbourne. David Jones, known to locals as DJs, has more up-market stock and high-quality service. The store has three sites within the city, with a main entrance adjacent to Myer in Bourke Street Mall; opposite is its menswear department. A third section is accessed in Little Bourke Street, again adjacent to Myer.

Two other popular stores are **Target** and K-mart. Both offer discounted prices on a range of goods. There are many branches of K-mart but they are located outside the CBD.

ARCADES, MALLS AND SHOPPING CENTRES

Melbourne's best arcades and malls are located in the heart of the CBD. Chief among these are Bourke Street Mall, with shopfronts for the Myer and David Jones department stores. Occupied mostly by

speciality stores and boutiques, other arcades and malls include the **Galleria Shopping Plaza**, with an emphasis on Australiana and Australian-owned stores. The ABC Shop sells merchandise associated with the national television and radio network, such as books, videos and DVDs. Australian Geographic is an excellent shop for information on Australian landscape and geology.

Located on Collins Street, renowned for its up-market shops, clothing and shoes, are **Australia on Collins**, Block Arcade (see p389) and 234 Collins Street. Australia on Collins comprises 60 shops on five levels, with fashion, homeware and other retail stores. The Sportsgirl Centre is known for its designer fashion shops, which are located on three levels. Both complexes have food halls. Block Arcade, itself of historic interest, sells more classic clothing amid a beautifully

Upmarket window display in Melbourne Central shopping centre

Locally grown fruit on sale at Queen Victoria Market

restored 1890s interior; there is an entrance on Elizabeth Street. Also on Elizabeth Street is the GPO *(see p388)*, which has been recently transformed into a beautiful shopping complex.

Further up on Collins Street, past Russell Street, there are stores located in Collins Place, and in the Royal Arcade *(see p388)* nearby, which is also of historic and architectural interest. Running between Bourke Street Mall and Little Collins Street, further east, you will find **The Walk Arcade**, containing a small selection of smart and exclusive boutiques.

Little Bourke Street, above Elizabeth Street, and the intersecting Hardware Lane, are well known for a range of stores specializing in travel and adventure products. **Melbourne Central** and **QV** are two outstanding shopping centres located on Lonsdale and Swanston streets. Between them, there are literally hundreds of shops to visit. Away from the city centre, the **Southgate Complex**, with its 40 shops on three levels, should not be missed by the avid shopper. Products include up-market fashion and shoes, music, furniture, jewellery and ethnic products.

MARKETS

Melbourne has a number of fresh food markets. The most notable is the Queen Victoria Market *(see p386)*.

Other kinds of market are also popular. There is a huge range of second-hand goods for sale each Sunday at the **Camberwell Market**. For arts and crafts, **St Kilda Market** is held on Sundays on Upper Esplanade. Other Sunday markets include the food market in **Prahran** and the arts and crafts market at the Victorian Arts Centre *(see p411)*. One of the oldest markets is the **South Melbourne Market**, which has has been in continuous operation since 1867. It is open every Friday to Sunday, and also Wednesday.

Brunswick Street has vintage clothing stores and retro boutiques

SHOPPING STRIPS

Village-style shopping centres abound in the many suburbs of Melbourne. Popular spots include High Street in Armadale; Sydney Road in Brunswick; Brunswick Street in Fitzroy; Bridge Road in Richmond; Chapel Street in South Yarra; and Mailing Road in Canterbury.

Another major shopping centre in South Yarra is the **Como Centre**, which has stores selling furniture, homewares and fashion.

DIRECTORY

DEPARTMENT STORES

David Jones
310 Bourke St Mall. **Map** 1 C3.
Tel (03) 9643 2222.
www.davidjones.com.au

Myer Melbourne
314 Bourke St Mall. **Map** 1 C3.
Tel (03) 9661 1111.
www.myer.com.au

Target
236 Bourke St. **Map** 1 C3. **Tel** (03) 9653 4000. **www**.target.com.au

ARCADES, MALLS AND SHOPPING CENTRES

Australia on Collins
260 Collins St. **Map** 1 C3.
Tel (03) 9650 4355.
www.AustraliaonCollins.com.au

Como Centre
650 Chapel St, South Yarra.
Map 4 E5. **Tel** (03) 9645 9400.

Galleria Shopping Plaza
Cnr Bourke & Elizabeth sts.
Map 1 C3. **Tel** (03) 9604 5800.

Melbourne Central
300 Lonsdale St. **Map** 1 C2.
Tel (03) 9922 1100.
www.melbournecentral.com.au

QV
Cnr Swanston and Lonsdale sts.
Map 1 C2. **Tel** (03) 9658 0100.
www.qv.com.au

Southgate Complex
3 Southgate Ave, Southbank.
Map 2 D4. **Tel** (03) 9686 1000.

The Walk Arcade
309-325 Bourke St Mall.
Map 1 C3. **Tel** (03) 9654 6744.

MARKETS

Camberwell Market
Station St, Camberwell.
Tel 1300 367 712.
www.sundaymarket.com.au

Prahran Market
Commercial Rd (near Chapel St).
Map 6 D1. **Tel** (03) 8290 8220.
www.prahranmarket.com.au

St Kilda Market
Upper Esplanade.
Tel (03) 9209 6777.

South Melbourne Market
Cnr Cecil and Coventry sts.
Tel (03) 9209 6295.

Specialist Shops and Souvenirs

Melbourne is Australia's most fashion-conscious capital and hosts major fashion weeks. The Melbourne Fashion Festival in March sees young designers launch their autumn/winter collections, while established labels showcase their spring/summer collections during Spring Fashion Week in September. New boutiques have opened in the Flinders Lane and Little Collins Streets precincts, either side of Swanston Street, and in the Central Business District's (CBD) revitalized arcades and laneways. This area rivals Fitzroy's Brunswick Street for funky shopping. Melbourne is also a great place to buy outdoor gear, with several retailers located around Hardware Lane and Little Bourke Street. The city has a reputation for excellent bookshops and record stores, most of which are found in the city centre and inner suburbs of Carlton, Fitzroy, St Kilda and South Yarra.

MEN'S CLOTHING

The **Marcs** range is characterised by lightweight and colourful sweaters, shirts, t-shirts and trousers. Myer Melbourne *(see pp406–07)* stocks a limited range of Marcs items, often on sale. For sharp designer suits, head for **Calibre**, who also stock imported designer accessories. Little Collins Street east of Swanston Street has a selection of menswear stores, including **Déclic**, which specialises in business shirts and designer ties with names such as Duchamp, Vivienne Westwood and Zegna. Down the hill, **Ben Sherman** in the beautiful shopping complex at the General Post Office or GPO *(see p388)* has a good range of smart casual gear. **Out of the Closet**, opposite Flinders Street Station, stocks groovy vintage wear. They also have a store in Brunswick Street, Fitzroy. Nearby, **Route 66** stocks worn-in 501s, cowboy boots, bowling shirts and vintage western gear. Brunswick Street is a good place to browse for vintage clothing, and Chapel Street, South Yarra is great for jeanswear.

WOMEN'S CLOTHING

The CBD is the centre for haute couture in Melbourne. The appointment-only **Le Louvre**, at the "Paris End" of Collins Street, has been Melbourne society's couturier for decades. **Alannah Hill**'s and **Bettina Liano**'s fashions are feminine and sophisticated, the latter with a glam edge. **Scanlon & Theodore** have made a name for themselves with elegant outfits, earthy tones and breezy designs. **Issey Miyake** is one of several international design houses represented in Melbourne. Young design outfit **Fat** has shops in Fitzroy, Prahran and at the GPO shopping complex. **Genki** has a range of funky tops and t-shirts designed for women that are also very popular with the kids, while **Kinki Gerlinki** stocks a appealing range of retro clothing. Ben Sherman and Marcs stock a good range of casual gear for women. **Sabi** is a Melbourne design team that prides itself on comfortable sleepwear and lingerie, while **Smitten Kitten** offers imported lingerie, jewellery and exotic accessories. Bridge Road, Richmond has numerous discount fashion outlets.

CHILDREN'S CLOTHING

Brunswick Street, Fitzroy is a good starting point for hunting down kids' clothes. Check out Kinki Gerlinki's offspring, **Gerlinki Junior**, for smart but tough kids' gear. **World Wide Wear**, which started life in Fitzroy, has relocated to an outer-suburban shopping centre, but it is worth the trip to lay your hands on groovy kids' t-shirts, jackets, jeans and outdoor gear. **Genki** sells a cute range of t-shirts for babies and young children.

JEWELLERY

Kozminsky's on Bourke Street has been a Melbourne institution for decades. It specialises in fine art and antique jewellery. Collins Street has a profusion of jewellery stores and international fashion labels, including **Bulgari**. **Maker's Mark** showcases exquisite designer jewellery and glassware. Their flagship store is opposite the Rialto Building and their original boutique is at the Paris End of Collins Street. **Dinosaur Designs** fashion distinctive and contemporary jewellery, and homewares from lustrous resins. They have several stores, including one in Chapel Street.

SHOES AND BAGS

The Grand Hyatt building in Collins Street is home to **Miss Louise**, a favourite with Melbourne's well-healed women. The GPO has several retailers selling groovy casual shoes for men and women, stylish boots and classy bags. Melbourne's **Catherine Manuell** designs colourful handbags, daypacks, kids' bags and travel gear. **Crumpler** bags are the brainchild of a former bicycle courier who saw a market for comfortable, durable and funky shoulder bags. They come in a variety of styles and types to suit everything from laptops, to videos to homework: a Melbourne design icon.

OUTDOOR GEAR

To stock up on ski equipment and apparel, rock-climbing gear, tents, sleeping bags, maps and designer outdoor clothing, head for the Hardware Lane and Little Bourke Street precinct. There are numerous shops with good quality gear. Both **Paddy Pallin**, an established name in outdoor equipment, and **Snowgum**, which has shops across Melbourne, are recommended outlets. Smith Street, Collingwood has several factory shops for outdoor retailers selling discount clothing.

BOOKS AND MUSIC

The US chain **Borders** is well represented in Melbourne with five outlets, including one store at Melbourne Central. **Readings** is a homegrown favourite, which regularly hosts literary events. Its flagship store is in Carlton, although it recently opened a new shop in Acland Street, St Kilda. The **Brunswick Street Bookstore** is a quiet and relaxed venue for browsing quality books and magazines. **Discurio**, in a quiet corner of the CBD, is the place for Coltrane, Bach and alternative grooves. **Gaslight Records** stocks a good range of alternative music.

DIRECTORY

MEN'S CLOTHING

Ben Sherman
Shop G10, GPO, Melbourne 3000.
Map 1 C3.
Tel (03) 9663 7911.
www.bensherman.com.au

Calibre
483 Chapel St, Sth Yarra 3141. **Map** 6 E1.
Tel (03) 9826 4394.
www.calibreclothing
.com.au

Déclic
186 Little Collins St, Melbourne 3000. **Map** 1 C3. *Tel (03) 9650 2202.*
www.declic.com.au

Marcs
576-584 Chapel St, Sth Yarra 3141. **Map** 6 E1.
Tel (03) 9826 4906.
www.marcs.com.au

Out of the Closet
238B Flinders St, Melbourne 3000.
Map 1 C3.
Tel (03) 9639 0980.

Route 66
Shop 7, Cathedral Arcade, 37 Swanston St, Melbourne 3000.
Map 1 C3.
Tel (03) 9639 5669
www.route66.com.au

WOMEN'S CLOTHING

Alannah Hill
533 Chapel St, Sth Yarra 3141. **Map** 4 E5.
Tel (03) 9826 2755.
www.alannahhill.com.au

Bettina Liano
269 Little Collins St, Melbourne 3000. **Map** 1 C3. *Tel (03) 9654 1912.*
www.bettinaliano.com

Fat
272 Chapel St, Sth Yarra 3141. **Map** 6 E2.
Tel (03) 9510 2311.
www.fat4.com

Genki
Shop 5, Cathedral Arcade, 37 Swanston St, Melbourne 3000. **Map** 1 C3.
Tel (03) 9650 6366.
www.genki.com.au

Issey Miyake
Shop 2, 177 Toorak Rd, Sth Yarra 3141. **Map** 4 E5.
Tel (03) 9826 4900.
www.isseymiyake.com

Kinki Gerlinki
22 Centre Place, Melbourne 3000. **Map** 1 C3.
Tel (03) 9650 0465.

Le Louvre
74 Collins St, Melbourne 3000. **Map** 2 D3.
Tel (03) 9650 1300.

Sabi
265 Little Collins St, Melbourne 3000.
Map 1C3 .
Tel (03) 9654 4111.
www.sabi.com.au

Scanlon & Theodore
566 Chapel St, Sth Yarra 3141. **Map** 4 E5.
Tel (03) 9824 1800.
www.scanlonandtheodore
.com.au

Smitten Kitten
20 Presgrave Place, Melbourne 3000.
Map 1 C3.
Tel (03) 9654 2073.
www.smittenkitten.com.au

CHILDREN'S CLOTHING

Gerlinki Junior
217 Brunswick St, Fitzroy 3065. *Tel (03) 9419 9169*

World Wide Wear
Shop B10-B11, Chadstone Shopping Centre, 1341 Dandenong Rd, 3148. *Tel (03) 9530 9864.*
www.worldwidewear.
com.au

JEWELLERY

Bulgari
199 Collins St, Melbourne 3000. **Map** 2 D3
Tel (03) 9663 8100
www.bvlgari.com.au

Dinosaur Designs
562 Chapel St, Sth Yarra 3141. **Map** 4 E5.
Tel (03) 9827 2600.
www.dinosaurdesigns.
com.au

Kozminsky
421 Bourke St, Melbourne 3000. **Map** 1 C3.
Tel (03) 9670 1277.
www.kozminsky.com.au

Maker's Mark
88 and 464 Collins St, Melbourne 3000.
Map 2 D3 and **Map** 1 B4.
Tel (03) 9654 8488.
www.makersmark.com.au

SHOES AND BAGS

Catherine Manuell
277 Little Lonsdale St, Melbourne 3000. **Map** 1 C2. *Tel (03) 9671 4545*
www.catherinemanuellde
sign.com

Crumpler
355 Little Bourke St, Melbourne 3000. **Map** 1 C3. *Tel (03) 9600 3799.*
www.crumpler.com.au

Miss Louise
Grand Hyatt, Shop 601, 123 Collins St, Melbourne 3000. **Map** 2 D3.
Tel (03) 9654 7730.

OUTDOOR GEAR

Paddy Pallin
360 Little Bourke St, Melbourne 3000. **Map** 1 C3 *Tel (03) 9670 4845.*
www.paddypallin.com.au

Snowgum
370 Little Bourke St, Melbourne 3000.
Map 1 C3
Tel (03) 9600 0099.
www.snowgum.com.au

BOOKS AND MUSIC

Borders
Shop 106, Melbourne Central, Melbourne 3000.
Map 1 C2.
Tel (03) 9663 8909.
www.bordersstores.com

Brunswick Street Bookstore
305 Brunswick Street, Fitzroy 3065.
Tel (03) 9416 1030.
www.brunswickstreetboo
kstore.com

Discurio
113 Hardware St, Melbourne 3000.
Map 1 B3.
Tel (03) 9600 1488.
www.discurio.com.au

Gaslight Records
85 Bourke St, Melbourne 3000. **Map** 2 D2
Tel (03) 9650 9009
www.gaslight.com.au

Readings
309 Lygon St, Carlton 3053. *Tel (03) 9347 6633.*
112 Acland St, St. Kilda, 3182. *Tel (03) 9525 3852.*
www.readings.com.au

ENTERTAINMENT IN MELBOURNE

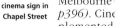

Art Deco cinema sign in Chapel Street

Melbourne could be defined as Australia's city of the arts. All year round there is a wealth of cultural events and entertainment on offer. The city's major festivals include the Melbourne Festival and Moomba *(see pp41–2)*. There are also fringe festivals and many other independent events. The Victorian Arts Centre, which includes the Melbourne Concert Hall *(see p400)*, is home to the state's theatrical companies and hosts both national and international groups. Large concerts are held at Melbourne Park Entertainment Centre or the Melbourne Cricket Ground *(see p396)*. Cinema chains are supplemented by smaller venues devoted to arthouse and revival films.

Evening concert at the Sidney Myer Music Bowl *(see p398)*

INFORMATION

The best guide to the range of events in Melbourne is the entertainment guide in the *Age*, published each Friday. This has comprehensive listings, along with more information on all the up-coming highlights. The tabloid newspaper *Herald Sun* and both newspapers' Sunday editions are also good sources of information and reviews. There is an array of free publications covering arts, entertainment and the nightclub scene. Visitors can obtain these from retailers and cafés in main inner-city precincts such as Fitzroy *(see p403)* and St Kilda. The

Melbourne Visitor Information Centre has a range of publications listing events.

There are also a number of websites that provide good events coverage, as well as other information helpful to visitors: www.melbourne. citysearch.com.au, www. visitvictoria.com and www. thatsmelbourne.com.au are worth a look. The **Victorian Arts Centre** *(see p400)* has a bi-monthly diary which it mails out free of charge worldwide, covering all up-to-date events at the complex. Most ticket agencies and some venues also provide information of events taking place in the city.

TICKET BOOKING AGENCIES

Buying tickets in Melbourne is reasonably straightforward. There are two major ticket booking agencies in Victoria, **Ticketmaster** (with more than 50 outlets) and **Ticketek** (with more than 30 outlets). One other agency, **Save Time Services**, charges a slightly higher rate for tickets, but customers can make advance

Grand 1930s foyer of the Regent Theatre *(see p390)*

bookings (before tickets are officially released) and are always provided with the best seats available. There are some venues which handle their own bookings independently, but these are rare and tickets for most major events are more easily purchased at these agencies.

Bookings can either be made in person at the various outlets, or with a credit card by phone, fax or post. The agencies also accept bookings from overseas. If not bought directly over the counter, tickets can be mailed out to customers for a small handling fee. If the event is impending, tickets can usually be picked up at the venue half-an-hour before the booked performance starts.

The hours for outlets vary according to their location, but almost all are open Monday through to Saturday, and some are open on Sundays. Neither Ticketmaster nor Ticketek offer refunds or exchanges, unless a show is

Façade of the Princess Theatre, by the Parliamentary Precinct *(see p392)*

Street entertainers, a regular sight throughout Melbourne

cancelled. Remember that a nominal booking fee will be added to all ticket prices bought via a ticket agency.

TICKET DEALS

Some major companies, particularly those playing at the Victorian Arts Centre, offer special "rush hour" ticket deals. These are available for tickets purchased in person after 6pm. The **Half Tix** booth at the Melbourne Town Hall on Swanston Street offers half-price deals for many events. Tickets must be bought in person and paid for in cash. They are also generally available only on the day of performance. Shows with tickets available are displayed at the booth.

Half Tix ticket booth sign on Swanston Street

SECURING THE BEST SEATS

If booking in person, you can usually consult a floor-plan showing the location of available seats. Over the telephone, both Ticketmaster and Ticketek have a "best available" system, with remaining seats arranged in a best-to-last order by

individual venues. It is also possible to request particular seats and the booking agency will check their availability. Some seats are retained for sale at the venue itself and this can be a way of getting good seats at the last minute.

DISABLED VISITORS

The vast majority of venues have access and facilities for disabled visitors. Booking agencies will take this into account. You should also enquire at individual venues and the Mobility Centre, Federation Square (www.melbourne.vic.gov.au).

OUTDOOR AND STREET ENTERTAINMENT

Despite its changeable climate, Melbourne has a strong tradition of outdoor and street entertainment. Every summer there is a broad programme of theatre and music for adults and children in most major parks and gardens. Many performances in summer are held in the evenings at sunset.

Street buskers, many travelling on an international circuit, also frequent a number of areas, the most popular being Fitzroy *(see p403)* and St Kilda, and appear at festivals. The main spot in the city centre for regular street performances is the Bourke Street Mall, outside Myer and David Jones department stores and at the Southgate Complex *(see p406)*. The Victorian Arts Centre also has regular programmes featuring free weekend street entertainment.

MELBOURNE PRACTICAL INFORMATION

Melbourne is well served by public transport and is easy to negotiate, given the grid structure of the city centre and the flat layout of its suburbs. The state government has upgraded many public facilities in recent years, aimed at attracting both business

Road sign

and tourists. Driving in the city is also easy and taxis are plentiful. Bureaux de change and automatic cash dispensers are located throughout the city. Melbourne is safe compared with many major cities, but common sense will also keep you out of trouble.

DRIVING AND CYCLING IN MELBOURNE

Driving in Melbourne is straightforward. Cars queue on the left to turn right at some intersections, marked by Safety Zone signs, to accommodate trams. Cars left in No Parking zones will be towed away. The city has a long tollway system known as CityLink, which uses electronic tolling: drivers must purchase a pass before travelling.

Melbourne's flat landscape is well suited to cyclists and there are many cycle tracks. Helmets are compulsory. Information on bicycle hire and good cycle routes can be found at **Bicycle Victoria**.

TRAVELLING BY PUBLIC TRANSPORT

Melbourne has a comprehensive system of trains, buses and trams, known as Metlink. This system also provides access to country and interstate travel, operated by the **CountryLink** network.

The main railway station for suburban services is Flinders Street Station (see p402). The refurbished Southern Cross Station is the main terminus for country and interstate trains.

The free City Circle Tram circuits the city every 15 minutes while the City Explorer is a hop-on hop-off tourist bus, departing at half-hour intervals.

TRAM ROUTES

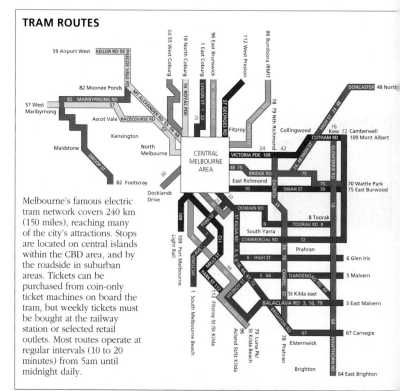

Melbourne's famous electric tram network covers 240 km (150 miles), reaching many of the city's attractions. Stops are located on central islands within the CBD area, and by the roadside in suburban areas. Tickets can be purchased from coin-only ticket machines on board the tram, but weekly tickets must be bought at the railway station or selected retail outlets. Most routes operate at regular intervals (10 to 20 minutes) from 5am until midnight daily.

Flinders Street Station, the city's main suburban rail terminus

Details are available from the **Melbourne Visitor Information Centre**.

Another way to get around the city is via water taxis and cruises along the Yarra River.

TICKETS

Metropolitan tickets can be bought from railway stations, on board trams or from newsagencies. Tourists can buy a CitySaver metcard allowing travel around the centre and admission to some attractions. The SmartVisit

Central Melbourne area

KEY

■	Swanston Street
□	Elizabeth Street
■	William Street
■	Latrobe Street
■	Bourke Street
■	Collins Street
■	Flinders Street
■	Batman Street
■	City Circle
■	Suburban trams

card allows entry to more than 50 attractions and is available for 2, 3 or 7 days.

TOURIST INFORMATION

The main Tourist Information stop is the Melbourne Visitor Information Centre, which has free maps and guides to all attractions and activities. They also provide information on accommodation and arrange bookings.

There is a range of free travel publications available from information centres, covering attractions in Melbourne and Victoria.

DISABLED TRAVELLERS

The useful "CBD Mobility Map" is available from the Melbourne Visitor Information Centre and Mobility Centre (see p411), showing access and facilities available in the city. The majority of public facilities in the city have disabled access and toilets. Parking zones are allocated in the city and suburbs for disabled drivers; disabled driver permits are available from Melbourne Town Hall (see p389).

River cruise boats providing a leisurely way to see the city

DIRECTORY

DRIVING AND CYCLING

Bicycle Victoria
Tel (03) 9328 3000.

CityLink
Tel 13 26 29.

Royal Automobile Club of Victoria
Tel 13 11 11.

Transport Information Line
Tel 13 16 38.

PUBLIC TRANSPORT

CountryLink
Spencer Street Station.
Tel 13 22 32.

Coach Terminus and Booking Centre
Travel Coach Australia
58 Franklin St.
Tel (03) 9663 3299.

Metlink
www.metlink.com.au

Skybus Information Service
Tel (03) 9335 3066.

RIVER CRUISES

Melbourne Water Taxis
Southgate.
Tel (03) 9686 0914.

Williamstown Bay and River Cruises
Southgate, No 7
Exhibition Centre, St Kilda Pier.
Tel (03) 9397 2255
www.williamstownferries.com.au

TOURIST INFORMATION

Melbourne Visitor Information Centre
Federation Square
Cnr Swanston & Flinders sts.
Tel (03) 9658 9658.

Victorian Tourism Information Service
Tel 13 28 42.
www.visitvictoria.com

MELBOURNE STREET FINDER

The key map below shows the areas of Melbourne covered in the *Street Finder*. All places of interest in these areas are marked on the maps in addition to useful information, such as railway stations, bus termini and emergency services. The map references given for sights described in the Melbourne chapter refer to the

Bourke Street sculpture

maps on the following pages. Map references are also given for the city's shops and markets *(see pp406–9)*, entertainment venues *(see pp410–11)*, as well as hotels *(see pp505–9)* and restaurants *(see pp552–6)*. The different symbols used for catalogue sights and other major features on the *Street Finder* maps are listed in the key below.

KEY TO STREET FINDER

	Major sight
	Place of interest
	Other building
Ⓡ	CityRail station
	Bus station
Ⓒ	Coach station
	Ferry boarding point
	Taxi rank
P	Car Park
i	Tourist information
+	Hospital with casualty unit
	Police station
+	Church
✡	Synagogue
C	Mosque
✕	Post office
	Golf course
	Highway
	Railway line
	Pedestrian street

| 0 metres | 250 |
| 0 yards | 250 |

| 0 kilometres | 1 |
| 0 miles | 1 |

VICTORIA   STREE

SPENCER STREET

FLINDERS STREET

Deborah Halpern sculpture at the city's Southgate complex *(see pp400–1)*

ed brick façade of the City Baths on Swanston Street *(see pp384–5)*

Ornamental lake at Rippon Lea *(see pp404–5)*

View of the Collins Street area from Princes Bridge on the Yarra River

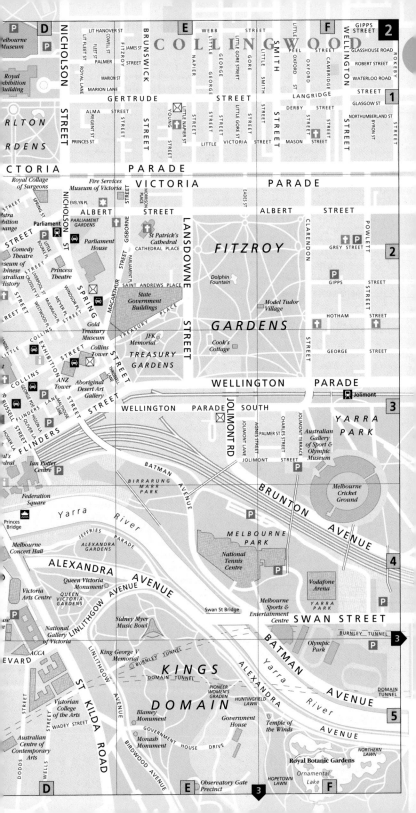

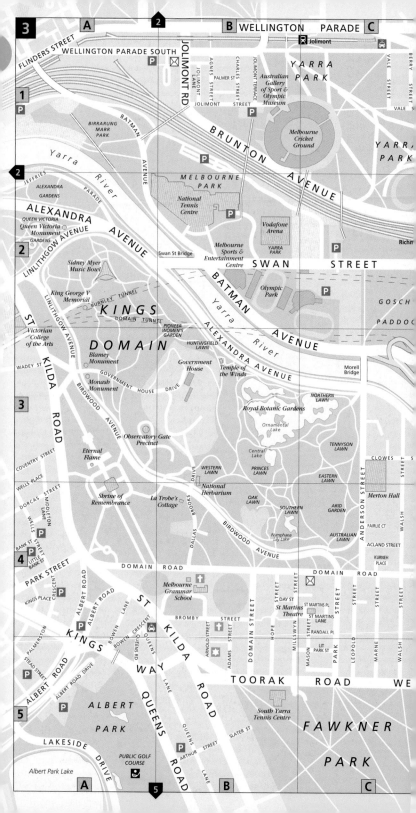

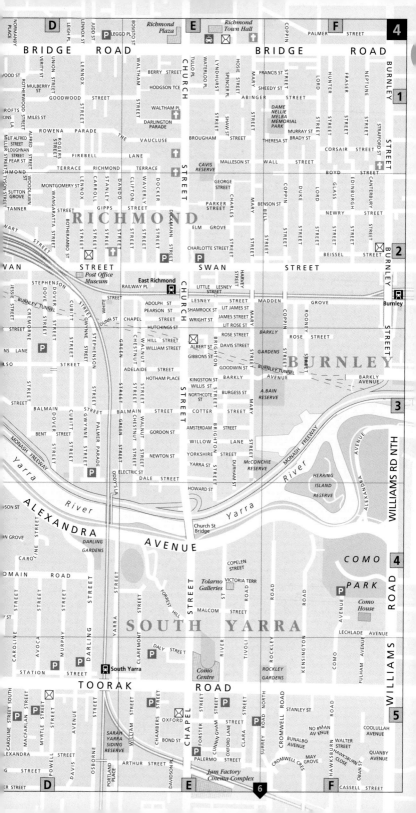

WESTERN VICTORIA

The theme of Western Victoria is diversity. For nature lovers, there is the bare beauty of the mallee deserts of the north or the forested hills and coastal scenery of the south. For a sense of the region's history, 19th-century gold-mining towns lie in the centre, surrounded by beautiful spa towns which have attracted visitors for more than a century. The area's sights are all within easy reach of one another.

Just as the Aboriginal tribes of Western Victoria had their lives and culture shaped by the region's diverse landscape, so the lives of the early European settlers were inevitably determined by the region's geographical features and immense natural resources.

The discovery of gold was the single most important event in Victoria's economic history, drawing prospectors from all over the world and providing the state with unprecedented wealth. Part of the legacy of this period is seen in the grand 19th-century buildings still standing in a number of central western towns. Also of interest are the spa towns clustered nearby, which draw their therapeutic waters from the same mineral-rich earth.

To the northwest, Victoria's major agricultural region, the Murray River, supports several large townships. The area is blessed with a Mediterranean-type climate, resulting in wineries and fruit-growing areas. In the south, the spectacular Grampian mountain ranges have long been of significance to the Aborigines. Fortunately, the steep cliffs and heavily forested slopes offered little prospect for development by early settlers and this beautiful area is today preserved as a wilderness. Wheat and sheep farmers have settled in parts of the mallee region in the north of Western Victoria but, as in the Grampians, other settlers have been discouraged by its semi-arid conditions, and large areas of this stunning desert vegetation and its native wildlife have been left intact.

The southwestern coast was the site of the first settlement in Victoria. Its towns were developed as ports for the rich farmland beyond and as whaling stations for the now outlawed industry. Besides its history, this coastline is known for its extraordinary natural scenery of sandstone monoliths, sweeping beaches, forests and rugged cliffs.

Pioneer Settlement Museum, a re-created 19th-century port town on the Murray River at Swan Hill

◁ The spectacular coastal rock formations of the Twelve Apostles in Port Campbell National Park

Exploring Western Victoria

Western Victoria abounds with holiday possibilities. The spa towns close to Melbourne make perfect weekend retreats, with excellent facilities set amid gentle rural scenery. By contrast, the large number of historic sites and architectural splendours of the gold fields region requires an investigative spirit and sightseeing stamina. The Grampians National Park contains trekking opportunities and rugged views, while the mallee region offers wide open spaces and undulating sandhills. The Murray River towns have their fair share of historic sites, as well as many recreational facilities, restaurants and accommodation. The Great Ocean Road is a popular touring destination – set aside several days to explore the historic towns and scenic beauty of the coastline.

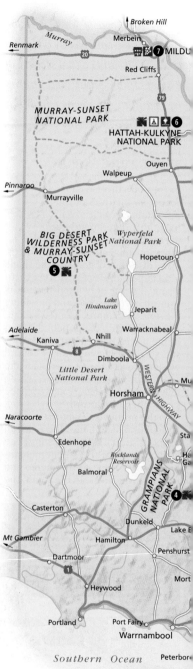

Rupertswood mansion in the Macedon Ranges

GETTING AROUND

The roads in Western Victoria are well signed and offer good roadside facilities. The Western Hwy is the route to Ballarat, the Grampians and the mallee region. The Calder Hwy leads to the spa country and beyond to Bendigo, where it connects with highways to Mildura, Swan Hill and Echuca. Take the Princes Hwy to reach Geelong and the Great Ocean Road. All these places can also be reached by rail or a combination of rail and connecting coaches. However, in remoter areas, public transport may be a problem. A good solution is to take one of the many tours offered by Melbourne's private bus companies *(see p413)*.

For additional map symbols *see back flap*

SEE ALSO

- ***Where to Stay*** pp510–12
- ***Where to Eat*** pp557–9

0 kilometres 50

0 miles 50

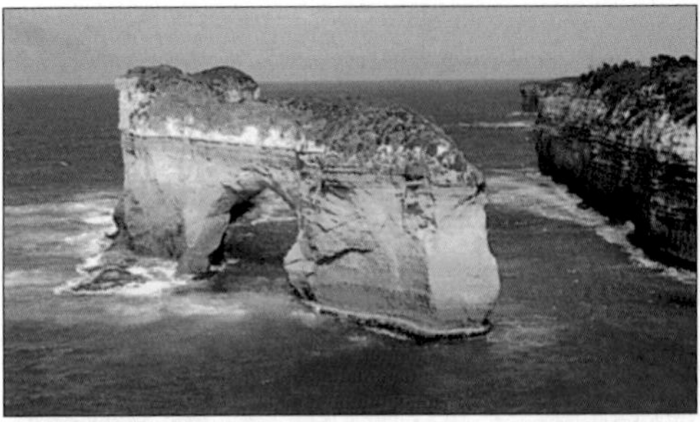

Sandstone arch at Loch Ard Gorge along the Great Ocean Road

SIGHTS AT A GLANCE

Ballarat pp434–5 13
Bellarine Peninsula 2
Bendigo 10
Big Desert Wilderness Park & Murray-Sunset Country 5
Castlemaine 12
Echuca 9
Geelong 3
Grampians National Park 4
Hattah-Kulkyne National Park 6
Maldon 11
Mildura 7
Sovereign Hill 14
Swan Hill 8
Werribee Park 1

Tour

Macedon Ranges and Spa Country 15

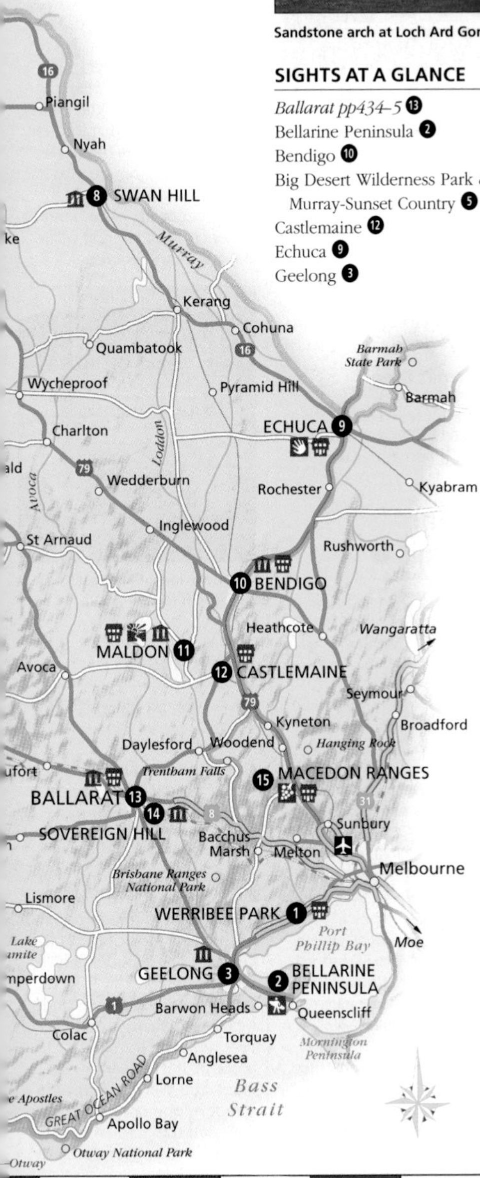

16
Piangil
Nyah
8 SWAN HILL
Murray
Kerang
Cohuna
Quambatook
16
Barmah State Park
Barmah
Wycheproof
Pyramid Hill
ECHUCA 9
Charlton
Loddon
79
Wedderburn
Avoca
Rochester
Kyabram
Inglewood
St Arnaud
Rushworth
10 BENDIGO
Heathcote
Wangaratta
MALDON 11
12 CASTLEMAINE
Avoca
Seymour
79
Kyneton
Broadford
Daylesford
Woodend
Hanging Rock
Trentham Falls
15 MACEDON RANGES
BALLARAT 13
14
SOVEREIGN HILL
8
31
Sunbury
Bacchus Marsh
Melton
Melbourne
Brisbane Ranges National Park
Lismore
WERRIBEE PARK 1
Port Phillip Bay
Moe
GEELONG 3
2 BELLARINE PENINSULA
1
Barwon Heads
Queenscliff
Colac
Torquay
Anglesea
Mornington Peninsula
Lorne
GREAT OCEAN ROAD
Bass Strait
Apollo Bay
Otway National Park

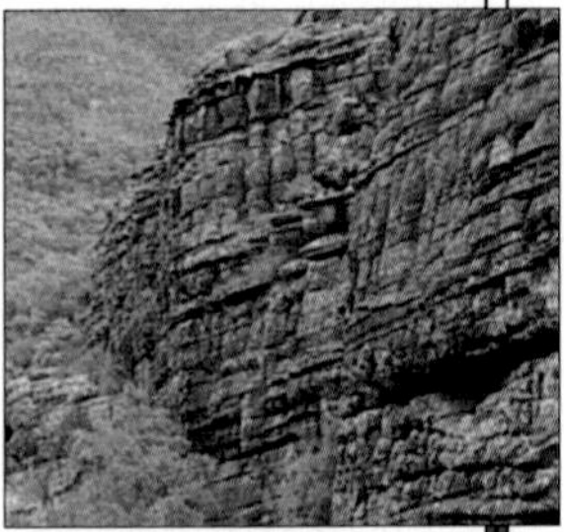

Striking rock formations of Grampians National Park

KEY

- Highway
- Major road
- Minor road
- Track
- Scenic route
- Major railway
- Minor railway
- State border

Flamboyant Italianate façade of Werribee Park Mansion

Werribee Park ❶

Werribee. **Tel** *(03) 9741 2444.*
🚉 *Werribee.* ⏲ *daily.* ⬤ *25 Dec.*
♿ *ground floor only.* 📷

From 1860 until 1890, the
wool boom made millionaires
of Australia's sheep farmers,
with the Chirnside family of
Werribee Park and later of
Victoria's Western District
among the richest and most
powerful. Their former
mansion is a striking Italianate house, built between 1873
and 1878. It has now been
restored to reflect the lifestyle
of wealthy pastoral families.
Visitors can stroll through the
sandstone mansion and see
the room where renowned
opera singer Dame Nellie
Melba once slept. A wing
added in the 1930s has been
converted into a luxury hotel.

Next to Werribee Park Mansion and its formal gardens
with popular picnic areas is
the Victoria State Rose Garden,
laid out in a symbolic Tudor
Rose-shaped design. It contains more than 4,500 beautiful rose bushes of different
varieties and colours that
are in flower from
November to
April. Also
attached to
Werribee Park
is **Victoria's
Open Range Zoo**,
containing a range

**Chaise longue in
Werribee Park**

of exotic animals, including
giraffes and hippopotami. The
State Equestrian Centre is also
part of the estate. This is
home to some of Australia's
premier show-jumping and
polo events. For bird-watchers,

the nearby Werribee sewage
farm and Point Cook Coastal
Park provide magnificent views
of some rare species from
specially designated hides.
Migratory birds such as the
eastern curlew and tiny red-
necked stint spend the whole
summer in these protected
wetlands before flying north
to Japan and Siberia.

🦒 **Victoria's Open
Range Zoo**
Werribee Park Mansion. **Tel** *(03)
9731 9600.* ⏲ *9am–5pm daily.*
📷 ♿ 🚐 *preferred.*

Bellarine
Peninsula ❷

🚉 *Geelong.* 🚌 *Ocean Grove,
Point Lonsdale, Portarlington,
Queenscliff.* ⛴ *Queenscliff.*
ℹ *Queenscliff (03) 5258 4843.*

The Bellarine Peninsula, at
the western entrance to Port
Phillip *(see p430)*, is
one of Melbourne's many
summer resorts. The white
sand beaches of Barwon
Heads, Point
Lonsdale
and Ocean
Grove mark
the start of the
Great Ocean
Road and its
famous surf
beaches *(see
pp428–9)*.

The little village of **Point
Lonsdale** lies at the entrance
to the treacherous Heads –
the most dangerous entry to
any bay in the world due to
its churning seas and whirl-
pools. It is only 3 km (2 miles)

from Point Lonsdale, across
the swirling water (known as
the Rip) with its hidden rocks,
to Point Nepean on the Mornington Peninsula in Eastern
Victoria *(see p442)*.

The graceful old town of
Queenscliff faces Port
Phillip Bay so its beaches are
calm. Its fort was the largest
British defence post in the
southern hemisphere during
the 1880s, when a Russian
invasion was feared. At the
time Queenscliff was also a
fashionable resort for
Melburnians – its elegant
hotels, such as the Vue Grand,
are reminders of that opulent
era *(see p512)*. St Leonards
and Portarlington are also
popular holiday villages.

The peninsula has around 20
wineries, most offering cellar
door sales and tastings.

**Graceful wrought-iron detail on a
Queenscliff façade**

Geelong ❸

🚏 *180,000.* ✈ 🚉 🚌 🚐 ℹ
26–32 Moorabool St (03) 5222 2900.

Geelong is the second largest
city in the state and has
a rural and industrial past.
Positioned on the north-facing
and sheltered Corio Bay, the
city has started to look once
again on its port as a recreational front door, so popular
in the first years of the 20th
century. The wooden 1930s
bathing complex at Eastern
Beach, with its lawns, sandy
beach and shady trees, was
restored to its former Art Deco
glory in 1994. Steampacket
Place and Pier are part of
a redevelopment project that
has seen the gradual renovation of the old warehouses
into a thriving waterfront

quarter filled with excellent seafood restaurants, cafés, shops and hotels.

Opposite Steampacket Place are the historic wool stores. Wool was auctioned, sold and stored here prior to its being shipped around the globe from the 1880s until the 1970s. This generated Geelong's wealth. Now these buildings are being transformed; the largest houses the award-winning **National Wool Museum**, tracing Australia's wool heritage from the shearing shed to the fashion catwalks.

A short drive from Geelong is the Brisbane Ranges National Park, near Anakie, which has lovely walks and native wildflowers, with grevilleas, wattles and wild orchids, in bloom between August and November. Nearby is Steiglitz, a ghost town from the 1850s gold rush. Only a few buildings remain of this once thriving town, among them the elegant 1870s courthouse.

🏛 National Wool Museum

26–32 Moorabool St. *Tel* (03) 5227 0701. 🕘 9:30am–5pm daily. 🔒 Good Fri, 25 Dec. 📷 ♿

Grampians National Park ❹

🚉 Stawell. 🚌 Halls Gap.
🛈 Stawell (03) 5358 2314; Brambuk National Park and Cultural Centre (03) 5356 4381 or 5356 4452. 🕘 daily.

The mountains, cliffs and sheer rock faces of the Grampians rise like a series of

---

FLORA AND FAUNA OF THE GRAMPIANS

The Grampians are a haven for a wide range of birds, animals, native wildflowers and plants. The park is home to almost one-third of all Victorian plant species, with many, such as the Grampians guinea flower and boronia, found only within its rocky walls. Koalas grunt at night around Halls Gap and the kangaroos at Zumsteins are unusually tame and friendly. The air, trees and scrub teem with beautiful blue wrens, rainbow lorikeets, gang gang cockatoos, scarlet robins and emus. In spring, various wildflowers, orchids and pink heath burst from every crevasse and valley floor, and the creeks and rivers are full of rare brown-tree frogs. Just south of the Grampians in the town of Hamilton, a surviving eastern barred bandicoot, once thought to be extinct, was recently discovered on the town rubbish tip. It was quickly rescued and has now become part of an active breeding and protection programme.

Rainbow lorikeet

---

waves above the flat western plains. Within this awesome national park, the third largest in Victoria, is a diversity of natural features and wildlife.

There are craggy slopes, cascading waterfalls and sandstone mountain tops, all formed 400 million years ago by an upthrust of the earth's crust. It has been known as *gariwerd* for thousands of years to local Aboriginal tribes, for whom it is a sacred place, and 80 percent of Victoria's indigenous rock art is here. The Brambuk National Park and Cultural Centre is partly run by local Aboriginal communities who conduct tours to the many sites.

The Grampians offer many different experiences for tourists. Day trips take in the spectacular MacKenzie Falls and the Balconies rock formation. Longer stays offer bush camping, wildflower studies, exploration of the Victoria Valley over the mountains from Halls Gap and overnight hiking trips in the south of the park. Experienced rock climbers come from around the world to tackle the challenging rock forms in the park and also at the nearby Mount Arapiles.

Excellent maps of the area and guides to the best walks are all available from the park's visitors' centre.

Panoramic view from the rugged crags of the Grampians

The Great Ocean Road Coastline

The Great Ocean Road is one of the world's great scenic drives. Close to Melbourne, pretty holiday towns are linked by curving roads with striking views at every turn. Inland, the road cuts through the Otways, a forested landscape, ecologically rich and visually splendid. Between Port Campbell and Port Fairy is a landscape of rugged cliffs and swirling seas. The giant eroded monoliths, the Twelve Apostles, in Port Campbell National Park, are an awesome spectacle. To the far west, old whaling ports provide an insight into one of Australia's early industries; at Warrnambool, southern right whales can still be seen.

Portland, *a deep-water port at the end of the Princes Highway, was the site of the first European settlement in Victoria in 1834. Stunning scenery of craggy cliffs, blowholes and rough waters can be found near the town at Cape Bridgewater.*

MOUNT GAMBIER Portland

Tower Hill Game Reserve

CAMPERDOWN

Lady Julia Percy Island

Southern Ocean

★ **Warrnambool** ②

This coastal town is best known for the southern right whales that can often be spotted off Logans Beach between May and October. The town itself has many fine art galleries, museums and old churches.

★ **Port Fairy** ①

The tiny cottages of Port Fairy are reminders of the days when the town thrived as a centre for whaling in the 1830s and 1840s. Although the whaling industry has come to an end, the town is now a popular tourist destination.

0 kilometres   25

0 miles   25

KEY

Highway
Major road
Minor road
River
Viewpoint

Tower Hill Game Reserve, *13 km (8 miles) west of Warrnambool, is set in an extinct volcano crater. Dusk is the best time to visit and spot emus, koalas and kangaroos roaming the forests.*

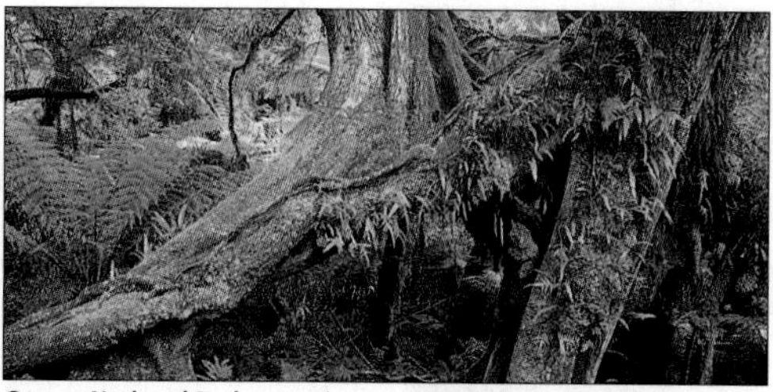

Otway National Park *provides an introduction to some of the species of the southern temperate rainforest, including a famed 400-year-old myrtle beech tree.*

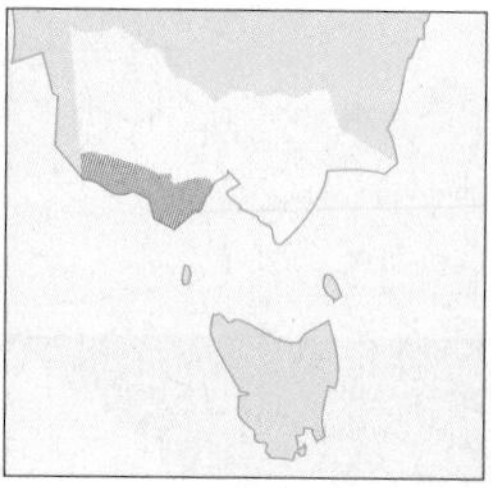

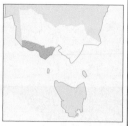

LOCATOR MAP

★ Loch Ard Gorge [5]

♿

This treacherous area claimed the clipper *Loch Ard* in 1878. Local walks focus on the shipwreck, geology and Aboriginal history of the site.

★ Johanna Beach [7]

🏄 🌊 🛟 🚻 ⛺

Another of Victoria's renowned surf beaches is backed by rolling green hills. The area is quite remote, but popular with campers in summer.

★ Lorne [9]

🏄 🌊 🚣 🛟 ♿ 🚻 ⛺

Very crowded in summer, this charming seaside village boasts excellent cafés, restaurants and accommodation. Nearby forests provide a paradise for walkers.

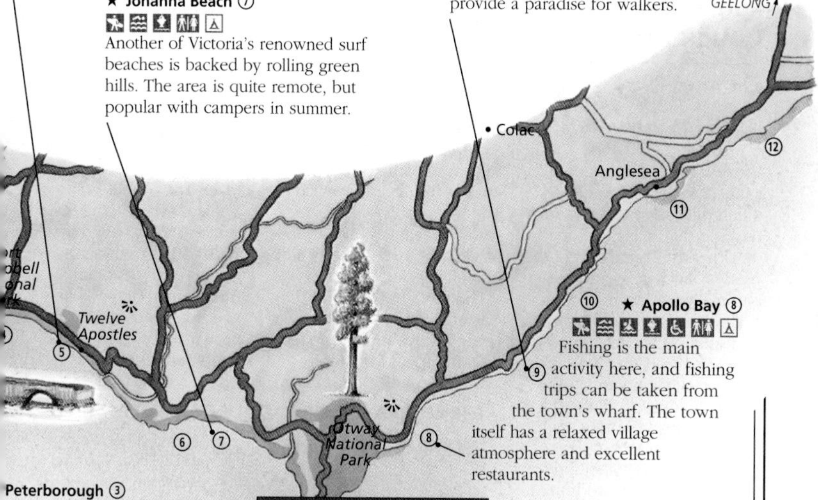
GEELONG
Colac
Anglesea
Twelve Apostles
Otway National Park
[5]
[6]
[7]
[8]
[9]
[10]
[11]
[12]

★ Apollo Bay [8]

🏄 🌊 🚣 🛟 ♿ 🚻 ⛺

Fishing is the main activity here, and fishing trips can be taken from the town's wharf. The town itself has a relaxed village atmosphere and excellent restaurants.

Peterborough [3]

🏄 🌊 🛟 🚻 ⛺

Victoria's dairy industry is based on this stretch of coastline. A popular rock pool beneath the cliff is known as the Grotto.

Port Campbell [4]

🏄 🌊 🛟 ♿ 🚻 ⛺

Port Campbell beach is a sandy bay, safe for swimming. The town, set on a hill, has great views of the ocean.

Moonlight Head [6]

🛟

Massive cliffs give way to rock platforms here in the heart of Otway National Park. Embedded anchors are reminders of the many ships lost along this perilous coastline.

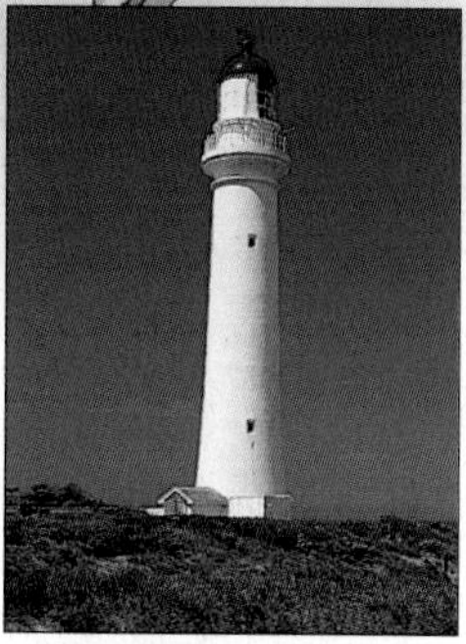

Aireys Inlet [10]

🏄 🌊 🚣 🛟 ♿ 🚻 ⛺

The red and white lighthouse is a landmark of this tiny coastal town with its beautiful ocean views.

Point Addis [11]

🏄 🛟

The Great Ocean Road leads right to the headland with spectacular views from the car park of waves beating the rocks. There are also steps leading down the cliff for a more exhilarating experience of the rolling surf.

Bells Beach [12]

🏄 🛟 🚻

An underwater rock platform is one of the natural features which contribute to the excellent surfing conditions at Bells. An international surfing competition is held here at Easter, bringing thousands of tourists to the area *(see p42)*.

Murrayville track in the Big Desert Wilderness Park

Big Desert Wilderness Park and Murray-Sunset Country ❺

Hopetoun. Hopetoun. 75 Lascelles St, Hopetoun (03) 5083 3001; Parks Victoria Information Line 131963.

Victoria is so often seen as the state of mountains, green hills, river valleys and beaches that many visitors don't realize a large part of the west of the state is arid desert and mallee scrubland.

These are areas of beauty and solitude, with sand hills, dwarf she-oaks, lizards, snakes and dry creek systems. Big Desert Wilderness Park and Murray-Sunset Country are true deserts, with hot days and freezing nights. Murray-Sunset Country is also home to Australia's rarest bird, the black-eared minor.

To the south, Wyperfeld and Little Desert national parks are not true deserts, as they contain lake systems that support diverse flora and fauna.

Hattah-Kulkyne National Park ❻

Mildura. Mildura. Mildura (03) 5021 4424; Parks Victoria Information Line 13 19 63.

Unlike its drier mallee region counterparts, Hattah-Kulkyne National Park is a haven of creeks and lakes that are linked to the mighty Murray River through a complex billabong (natural waterhole) overflow system.

Its perimeters are typical dry mallee country of low scrub, mallee trees and native pine woodland, but the large lakes, including Lake Hattah, Mournpoul and Lockie, are alive with bird and animal life. Ringed by massive red gums, the surrounding habitat is home to an abundance of emus, goanna lizards and kangaroos. The freshwater lakes teem with fish, while pelicans, ibis, black swans and other water birds flock on the surface.

The lakes are ideal for canoeing, and the twisting wetlands and billabongs along the Murray and in Murray-Kulkyne Park make for fine fishing, picnics, camping and bird-watching. The region is also home to Victoria's largest flower, the Murray lily.

Mildura ❼

25,000. 180–190 Deakin Ave (03) 5021 4424.

In 1887, Mildura was little more than a village on the banks of the Murray River, situated in the middle of a red sandy desert. That year, two Canadian brothers, William and George Chaffey, came to town direct from their successful irrigation project in California and began Australia's first large-scale irrigation scheme. Since then, the red soil, fed by the Murray and Darling rivers, has become a vast plain of farms stretching for nearly 100 km (60 miles).

Today, Mildura is a modern city with a thriving tourist trade. The former home of William Chaffey, the magnificent **Rio Vista**, is worth a visit. Built in 1890, it has now been restored with its original furnishings. Grapes, olives, avocados and citrus fruit are grown successfully in the region and the area is rapidly

---

THE MURRAY RIVER PADDLESTEAMERS

Old paddlesteamer on the Murray River

Between the 1860s and 1880s, Australia's economy "rode on the sheep's back" – from the Western District of Victoria to the Diamantina Plains in central Queensland, wool was king. But the only way to transport it from the remote sheep stations to coastal ports and then on to its thriving English market was by river. There were no roads other than a few dirt tracks, so the paddlesteamers that plied the Murray, Murrumbidgee and Darling river systems were the long-distance lorries of the day. Towing barges loaded with wool, they reached the Port of Echuca after sailing for days from inland Australia. Then, stocked up with supplies for the sheep stations and distant river settlements, they returned upriver. However, by the 1890s railway lines had crept into the interior and the era of the paddlesteamer was gone. Now the Port of Echuca is once again home to beautifully restored, working paddlesteamers, such as the PS *Emmylou*, PS *Pride of the Murray* and PS *Adelaide*.

Rio Vista, the elaborate home of irrigation expert William Chaffey, in Mildura

expanding its vineyards and wineries (see pp378–9).

The stark desert of Mungo National Park is only 100 km (60 miles) to the east of town.

🚊 Rio Vista
199 Cureton Ave. **Tel** (03) 5021 4424. ◯ 10am–5pm daily. ● Good Fri, 25 Dec. 📷 🔊 ground floor only.

Swan Hill ⑧

🏨 10,000. 🚗 🚇 🚌 🅸 306 Campbell St (03) 5032 3033.

Black Swans are noisy birds, as the early explorer Major Thomas Mitchell discovered in 1836 when his sleep was disturbed by their early morning calls on the banks of the Murray River. That's how the vibrant river town of Swan Hill got its name, and the black swans are still a prominent feature.

One of the most popular attractions of Swan Hill is the **Pioneer Settlement Museum**, a 3-ha (7-acre) living and working re-creation of a river town in the Murray-Mallee area during the period from 1830 to 1930. The settlement buzzes with the sound of printing presses, the black-smith's hammer, the smell of the bakery and general daily life. "Residents" dress in period clothes and produce old-fashioned goods to sell

to tourists. Some of the log buildings are made of Murray pine, a hardwood tree impenetrable to termites. The sound and light show at night is particularly evocative, providing a 45-minute journey through the town with accompanying sound effects, such as pounding hooves and a thundering steam locomotive.

🚊 Pioneer Settlement Museum
Horseshoe Bend, Swan Hill. **Tel** (03) 5036 2410. ◯ 8:30am–5pm Tue–Sun. ● Mon (except school hols), 25 Dec. 📷 🖥 🔊 www.pioneersettlement.com.au

Echuca ⑨

🏨 11,000. 🚗 🚇 🚌 🅸 2 Heygarth St (03) 5480 7555.

Ex-convict and entrepreneur Henry Hopwood travelled to the Murray River region in 1853, at the end of his prison sentence. He seized upon the need for a river punt at the Echuca crossing by setting up a ferry service, as well as the Bridge Hotel. However, Echuca really came into its own in 1864 when the railway from Melbourne reached the port. Suddenly the town, with its paddle-steamers on the Murray River, became the largest inland port in Australia.

Today the port area features horse-drawn carriages, working steam engines and old-fashioned timber mills. Tours of the area are available, along with regular river trips on a paddlesteamer. Visit the Star Hotel and discover the secret tunnel that let patrons leave after hours. There is also a paddlesteamer display opposite the hotel.

Approximately 30 km (19 miles) upstream from Echuca is Barmah Forest, the largest red gum forest in the world. A drive in the forest, with its 300-year-old river red gums and important Aboriginal sites, is highly recommended, as is the wetlands ecocruise that operates out of Barmah.

Gum trees on the road to Barmah Forest, outside Echuca

Bendigo ⓿

🏃 85,000. ✈ 🚉 🚌 🚊
ℹ 51–67 Pall Mall (03) 5444 4445.

Bendigo celebrated the gold rush like no other city, and with good reason – the finds here were legendary.
In 1851, the first year of gold mining, 23 kg (50 lbs) of gold were extracted from only one bucketful of dirt. When the surface gold began to disappear, the discovery of a gold-rich quartz reef in the 1870s reignited the boom.

Reflecting the city's wealth, Bendigo's buildings are vast and extravagant, often combining several architectural styles within one construction. Government architect GW Watson completed two buildings, the Law Courts and Post Office, in the French and Italian Renaissance styles. The tree-lined boulevard Pall Mall is reminiscent of a French provincial city. The elegant Shamrock Hotel opened to great fanfare in 1897 and is still in operation *(see p510)*. The European-style building is given a distinctly Australian feel with its front veranda. Self-guided heritage walk brochures are available from Bendigo's information centre, and the Vintage Talking Tram provides an excellent commentary on the town's history.

A major part of Bendigo's gold rush history was made by its Chinese population. The **Joss House**, dating from the 1860s, is a restored Chinese temple. It is a reminder of the

Entrance to the Chinese Joss House in Bendigo

Typical 19th-century building in Maldon

important role played by the Chinese in the history of Bendigo and continues to be used as a place of worship.
The **Golden Dragon Museum** also has displays that chart the history of the Chinese in the city. A ceremonial archway links the museum with the **Garden of Joy**, built in 1996. Based on a traditional Asian design, the garden resembles the Chinese landscape in miniature, with valleys, mountains, trees and streams.

The **Bendigo Art Gallery** has a splendid collection of Australian painting, including works depicting life on the gold fields. Nearby are shops selling pieces from Australia's oldest working pottery, established in 1858.

The **Central Deborah Goldmine** takes visitors down 86 m (260 ft) into the last deep reef mine in town.

Bendigo's local pottery

🏛 **Joss House**
Finn St, North Bendigo. **Tel** (03) 5442 1685. 🕐 Thu–Mon. ● Tue–Wed, 25 Dec. 🖼

🏛 **Golden Dragon Museum and Garden of Joy**
5–11 Bridge St. **Tel** (03) 5441 5044. 🕐 9am–5pm daily. ● 25 Dec. 🖼 🅰

🏛 **Bendigo Art Gallery**
42 View St. **Tel** (03) 5443 4991. 🕐 10am–5pm daily. ● 25 Dec. 🖼 🅰 by arrangement.

🏛 **Central Deborah Goldmine**
76 Violet St. **Tel** (03) 5443 8322. 🕐 daily. ● 25 Dec. 🖼 🅰

Maldon ⓫

🏃 1,200. 🚉 🚌 ℹ High St (03) 5475 2569.

The perfectly preserved town of Maldon offers an outstanding experience of an early gold-mining settlement. This tiny town is set within one of the loveliest landscapes of the region. The hills, forests and exotic trees are an attractive setting for the narrow streets and 19th-century buildings. Maldon was declared Australia's "First Notable Town" by the National Trust in 1966. Cafés, galleries and museums cater to the town's stream of tourists.

Other attractions include Carmen's Tunnel, an old gold mine, and a 70-minute round-trip ride aboard a steam train to Muckleford. Visit at Easter to see the glorious golden leaves of the plane, oak and elm trees. There is also an Easter Fair, including an Easter parade and a street carnival (see p42).

Castlemaine ⓬

🏃 7,000. 🚉 🚌 🚊 ℹ Market Building, Mostyn St (03) 5470 6200.

Castlemaine's elegance reflects the fact that gold finds here were brief but extremely prosperous. The finest attraction is the Market Hall, built in 1862. Architect William Benyon Downe designed this building in the Palladian style, with a portico and a large arched entrance leading into the building's restrained interior. The building is now the Visitors' Information Centre. **Buda Historic Home and Garden** was occupied from 1863 to 1981 by Hungarian silversmith, Ernest Leviny, and his family. The house displays an extensive collection of arts and crafts works. The property is also noted for its largely intact 19th-century garden, a unique survivor of its period.

Castlemaine is also home to many writers and artists from Melbourne and has a lively collection of museums, cafés and restaurants.

🏠 Buda Historic Home and Garden
42 Hunter St. **Tel** (03) 5472 1032. ☐ *Wed–Sun.* ☐ *Good Fri, 25 Dec.* 🈳 🅱 *teahouse and upper garden area.*

Ballarat ⑬

Sovereign Hill ⑭

Bradshaw St, Ballarat. **Tel** (03) 5337 1100. ☐ *daily.* ☐ *25 Dec.* 🈳 🅱 www.sovereignhill.com.au

Sovereign Hill is the gold fields' living museum. Located on the outskirts of Ballarat *(see pp434–5)*, it

THE CHINESE ON THE GOLD FIELDS

The first Chinese gold-seekers landed in Melbourne in 1853. Their numbers peaked at around 40,000 in 1859. They worked hard in large groups to recover the tiniest particles of gold, but the Europeans became hostile, claiming that the new arrivals were draining the colony's wealth. In 1857, several Chinese were murdered. The state government tried to quell hostility by introducing an entry tax on Chinese who arrived by boat – the Chinese then landed in neighbouring states and walked overland to Victoria. At the end of the gold rush many stayed on to work as gardeners, cooks and factory hands. There is still a large Chinese community in the state.

Chinese working on the gold fields

offers visitors the chance to explore a unique period of Australia's history. Blacksmiths, hoteliers, bakers and grocers in full period dress ply their trades on the main streets, amid the diggers' huts, tents, old meeting places and the Chinese Village. Among the most absorbing displays are those that reproduce gold mining methods. The town's fields produced an estimated 640,000 kg (630 tonnes) of gold before being exhausted in the 1920s.

The nearby Gold Museum is part of the Sovereign Hill complex. Its changing exhibits focus on the uses of gold throughout history.

Sovereign Hill opens in the evenings for an impressive sound and light show, which re-enacts the events of the Eureka Stockade *(see p434)*.

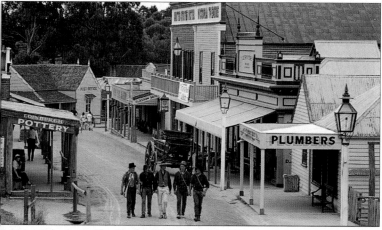

Actors in period costume walking along the main street in Sovereign Hill

Ballarat ⑬

Ballarat gold nugget

In 1851, the cry of "Gold!" shattered the tranquillity of this pleasant, pastoral district. Within months, tent cities covered the hills and thousands of people were pouring in from around the world, eager to make their fortune. While there were spectacular finds, the sustainable prosperity was accrued to traders, farmers and other modest industries, and Ballarat grew in proportion to their growing wealth. The gold rush petered out in the late 1870s. However, the two decades of wealth can still be seen in the lavish buildings, broad streets, ornate statuary and grand gardens. Today, Ballarat is Victoria's largest inland city.

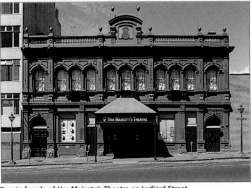

Ornate façade of Her Majesty's Theatre on Lydiard Street

🏛 Lydiard Street

The wealth of the gold fields attracted a range of people, among them the educated and well travelled. Lydiard Street reflects their influence as a well-proportioned streetscape, boasting buildings of exemplary quality and design.

At the northern end lies the railway station. Built in 1862, it features an arched train entrance and Tuscan pilasters. A neat row of four banks was designed by prominent architect Leonard Terry, whose concern for a balanced streetscape is clearly expressed in their elegant façades. Her Majesty's Theatre is an elaborate 19th-century structure and Australia's oldest surviving purpose-built theatre.

Opposite the theatre is Craig's Royal Hotel, begun in 1852. The hotel was extensively renovated in 1867 for a visit by Prince Alfred, Duke of Edinburgh, including the construction of a special Prince's Room and a further

22 bedrooms. In 1881, royal lanterns were constructed outside to honour a visit by the Duke of Clarence and the Duke of York (later King George V). This historic hotel is still in operation *(see p510)*.

🏛 Ballarat Fine Art Galley

40 Lydiard St North. *Tel (03) 5320 5858.* ☐ *daily.* ● *Good Fri, 25 Dec.* 🖼 ♿

Ballarat has always enjoyed the spirit of benefaction. Huge fortunes were made overnight and much of these found their way into the town's institutions. Ballarat Fine Art Gallery has been a major recipient of such goodwill, enabling it to establish an impressive reputation as Australia's largest and arguably best provincial art institution.

More than 6,000 works chart the course of Australian art from colonial to contemporary times. Gold field artists include Eugene von Guerard, whose work *Old Ballarat as it was in the summer of 1853–54* is an extraordinary evocation of the town's early tent cities. The gallery's star exhibit is the original Eureka Flag, which has since come to symbolize the basic democratic ideals which are so much a part of modern Australian society.

🏛 Eureka Centre

Cnr Eureka and Rodier streets. *Tel (03) 5333 1854.* ☐ *9am–4:30pm daily (last entry 4pm).* ● *25 Dec.* 🖼 ♿

The Eureka Centre is located in East Ballarat at what was the site of the Eureka Stockade. The $4 million centre, opened in 1998, commemorates the sacrifices of those who took part in a rebellion that came

---

THE EUREKA STOCKADE

An insurrection at Eureka in 1854, which arose as a result of gold diggers' dissatisfaction with high licensing fees on the gold fields, heralded the move towards egalitarianism in Australia. When hotel-owner Peter Bentley was acquitted of murdering a young digger, James Scobie, after a row about his entry into the Eureka Hotel, it incited anger among the miners. Led by the charismatic Peter Lalor, the diggers built a stockade, burned their licences and raised the blue flag of the Southern Cross, which became known as the Eureka Flag. On Sunday, 3 December 1854, 282 soldiers and police made a surprise attack on the stockade, killing around 30 diggers. After a public outcry over the brutality, however, the diggers were acquitted of treason and the licence system was abolished.

Rebel leader Peter Lalor

For hotels and restaurants in this region see pp510–12 and pp557–9

Lily pond in Ballarat's beautiful Botanical Gardens

VISITORS' CHECKLIST

86,000. ✈ 12 km (7.5 miles) from city centre. 🚊 Lydiard St. 🚌 Ballarat Coachlines, Ballarat Railway Station. 🛈 39 Sturt St 1800 446633. 🎭 Organs of the Ballarat Goldfields (Jan); Begonia Festival (Mar); Eureka Week (Dec).

to signify "a fair go for all" and even, some would argue, the birthplace of Australian democracy. The five exhibition galleries bring the story of the Eureka Stockade to life using clever background sounds, back projection and life-sized displays. After visiting the centre, take a stroll in the centre's gardens, which are a place for contemplation and reflection.

🌼 Botanical Gardens

Wendouree Drive. **Tel** (03) 5320 7444. ☐ daily. ● 25 Dec. 🚻 🚹

The Botanical Gardens, in the northwest of the city, are a telling symbol of Ballarat's desire for Victorian gentility. The rough and ready atmosphere of the gold fields could be easily overlooked here among the statues, lush green lawns and exotic plants.

The focus of the gardens has always been aesthetic rather than botanical, although four different displays are exhibited each year in the Robert Clark Conservatory. The most famous of these is the lovely begonia display, part of the Begonia Festival held here each March (see p42).

There is a Statuary Pavilion featuring female biblical figures in provocative poses, as well as a splendid centrepiece, *Flight from Pompeii*. The Avenue of Prime Ministers is a double row of staggered busts of every Australian prime minister to date, stretching off into the distance. The gardens run along the shores of the expansive Lake Wendouree.

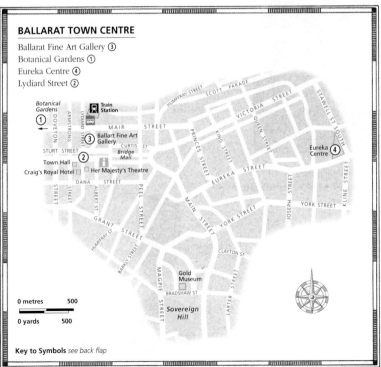

BALLARAT TOWN CENTRE

Ballarat Fine Art Gallery ③
Botanical Gardens ①
Eureka Centre ④
Lydiard Street ②

Botanical Gardens ①

Train Station

Ballarat Fine Art Gallery ③

Town Hall

Craig's Royal Hotel

Her Majesty's Theatre

Eureka Centre ④

Gold Museum

Sovereign Hill

| 0 metres | 500 |
| 0 yards | 500 |

Key to Symbols see back flap

Tour of the Macedon Ranges and Spa Country 🟡

Victoria's Macedon Ranges and Spa Country lie to the northwest of Melbourne. The landscape is dotted with vineyards, small townships, craft markets and bed-and-breakfasts *(see pp510–12)*. The tour follows the Calder Highway, once taken by gold prospectors to the alluvial fields of Castlemaine and Bendigo *(see pp432–3)* before heading west into the spa country around Daylesford. The region's wealthy past is reflected in the 19th-century bluestone buildings, including wool stores and stately homes.

Malmsbury ⑧
During the gold rush, this peaceful hamlet was a busy stop for prospectors on their way to the gold fields.

Hepburn Springs ⑨
The Mineral Reserve is a large area of native bushland. It is an idyllic place for walkers and those who want to "take the waters" from the old-fashioned pumps.

Trentham Falls ⑩
Victoria's largest single-drop falls, 33 m (108 ft) high, are a few minutes' walk from Falls Road.

RUPERTSWOOD AND THE ASHES

During the Christmas of 1882, eight members of the touring English cricket team were house guests of Sir William John Clarke at Rupertswood. The English won a social game between them and their hosts. Lady Clarke burnt a bail, placed the ashes in an urn and presented them to the English captain, Ivo Bligh. The urn was later presented to Marylebone Cricket Club by Bligh's widow, and thus the cricketing tradition of contesting for The Ashes began.

The original 1882 Ashes urn

0 kilometres 5
0 miles 5

KEY

■ Tour route
═ Other roads
※ Viewpoint

Kyneton ⑦
Historic Kyneton was once a supply town for diggers during the gold rush. It still has part of its 19th-century streetscape intact. The town is hidden from the road by trees.

Woodend ⑥
Named for its location at the edge of the Black Forest, Woodend has long been a haven for travellers. It has many restaurants, hotels and speciality shops.

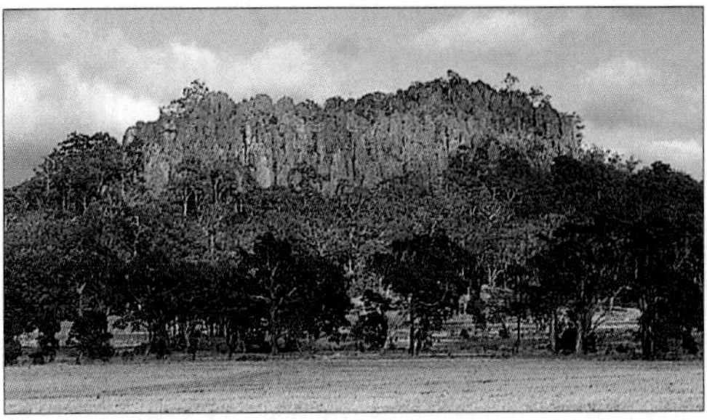

Hanging Rock ⑤
This rock was formed 6 million years ago when lava rose up from the earth's surface and solidified. Erosion has caused the fissures through which you can now walk. Scene of the film *Picnic at Hanging Rock*, the area is steeped in Aboriginal history.

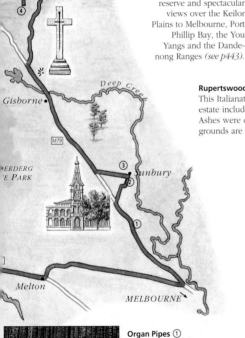

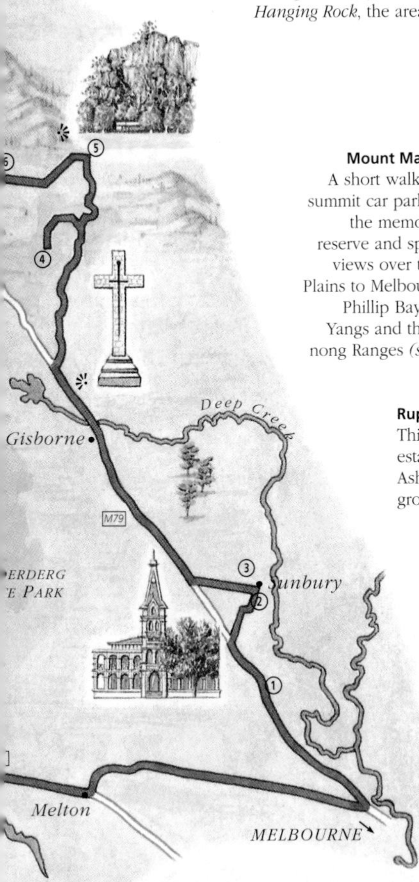
Deep Creek
Gisborne
M79
Sunbury
Melton
MELBOURNE

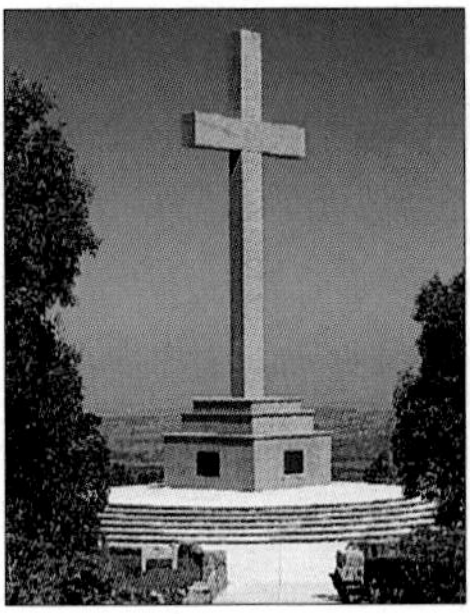

Mount Macedon ④
A short walk from the summit car park leads to the memorial cross reserve and spectacular views over the Keilor Plains to Melbourne, Port Phillip Bay, the You Yangs and the Dandenong Ranges *(see p443)*.

Rupertswood ③
This Italianate mansion was built in 1874. The estate includes the cricket field on which The Ashes were created. The once magnificent grounds are now used by a boys' school.

Goona Warra ②
The original vineyards of this 1863 bluestone winery were replanted during the 1980s. They now produce highly respected cool-climate wines, available for tasting and sales daily from the cellar door *(see pp378–9)*.

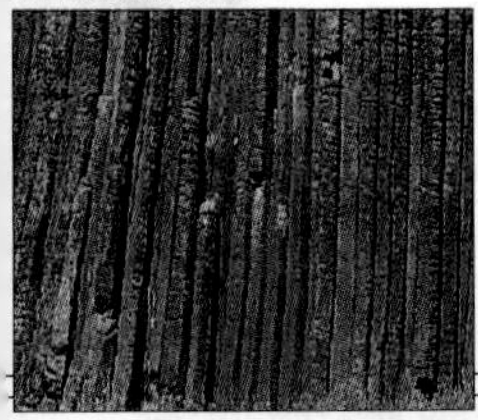

Organ Pipes ①
These 20-m (65-ft) basalt columns were formed by lava flows a million years ago. The Pipes can be seen from a viewing area near the car park or via a trail down to the creek bed.

TIPS FOR DRIVERS

Tour length: *215 km (133 miles).*
Stopping off points: *There are numerous places to stay and eat along the route, particularly at Woodend and Daylesford. Daylesford is also ideal for a romantic dinner or weekend lunch* (see p558).

EASTERN VICTORIA

*E*astern Victoria is a region of immense natural beauty with snow-topped mountains, eucalyptus forests, fertile inland valleys, wild national parks and long sandy beaches. Some of the state's finest wine-growing areas are here, set around historic towns of golden sandstone. Fast rivers popular with rafters flow through the region and ski resorts resembling Swiss villages are found in the Victoria Alps.

Eastern Victoria has a range of attractions for the visitor. The fertile plains of the north-east, crossed by the Goul-burn, Ovens, King and Murray rivers, offer a feast for the tastebuds: Ruther-glen red wines; Milawa mus-tards; local cheeses; and luscious peaches, pears and apricots from Shepparton. Historic 19th-century towns such as Beechworth and Chil-tern are beautifully preserved from their gold-mining days. Glenrowan is the site where Australia's most famous bushranger, Ned Kelly, was captured. An old-fashioned paddlesteamer rides regularly on the broad Murray River near Wodonga.

But towards the Victoria Alps and the towns of Bright and Mansfield another landscape emerges. This one is wild and very beautiful. In winter, there is exciting downhill skiing among the snow gums and peaks at village resorts such as Mount Buller and Falls Creek *(see pp 448–9)*. In summer, walk among the wildflow-ers in Alpine National Park, hike to the summit of Mount Feathertop, or try a rafting expedition down rivers such as the mighty Snowy.

To the east of Melbourne are the mag-nificent beaches of the Gippsland region. Favourite attractions here include Phillip Island with its fairy penguins, and Wilsons Promontory National Park with its wildlife, granite coves and pristine waters. Near the regional centres of Sale and Bairnsdale lie the Gippsland Lakes, Australia's largest inland waterway and an angler's paradise. Beyond, stretching to the New South Wales border, is Croajingo-long National Park and 200 km (125 miles) of deserted coastline.

Canoeing down the Kiewa River near Beechworth in Eastern Victoria

◁ **Mount Buller Alpine Village ski resort high in the Victorian Alps**

Exploring Eastern Victoria

Excellent highways give access to the most popular tourist attractions and towns of Eastern Victoria. The Dandenong Ranges, Yarra Valley and Phillip Island are within an easy day trip from Melbourne; the region's coastline, which includes Gippsland Lakes, around Lakes Entrance, Wilsons Promontory and Croajingolong National Park, is further to the south and east. The mountains, ski resorts and inland farm valleys are better accessed from the northeast of the state. While most of the major sights can be reached by road, some areas of the Gippsland forests and the Victorian Alps must be explored in 4WD vehicles.

0 kilometres 25

0 miles 25

The 19th-century post office in Beechworth

KEY

━━ Highway

━━ Major road

━━ Minor road

-- Track

━━ Scenic route

━━ Main railway

━━ Minor railway

━━ State border

△ Summit

SEE ALSO

• **Where to Stay** pp512–15

• **Where to Eat** pp559–61

For additional map symbols see back flap

SIGHTS AT A GLANCE

Beechworth **12**
Benalla **16**
Bright **11**
Chiltern **13**
Dandenong Ranges **4**
Glenrowan **15**
Lake Eildon **8**
Licola **7**

Mansfield **9**
Marysville **6**
Mornington Peninsula **2**
Mount Beauty **10**
Northeastern Wineries **14**
Phillip Island **1**
Royal Botanical Gardens, Cranbourne **3**
Shepparton **17**
Yarra Valley **5**

Upper Murray Valley in the heart of northeastern Victoria

GETTING AROUND

There are regular train services to the Dandenongs and the Gippsland Lakes. Bus tours can be arranged to Phillip Island and the Yarra Valley, while regular buses run in winter to the ski resorts. However, the best way of exploring is by car. The Hume Hwy provides access to the northeast, the Princes Hwy to the Gippsland Lakes and the South Gippsland Hwy to Phillip Island and Wilsons Promontory.

Lake Eildon at the gateway to the Victorian Alps

Phillip Island ❶

🏠 Cowes. 🚌 Cowes. ℹ️ *Newhaven (03) 5956 7447.* ⏰ *9am– 5pm daily; summer hols: 9am–6pm daily.*

The penguin parade on Phillip Island is an extraordinary natural spectacle and one of Eastern Victoria's most popular tourist attractions. Every evening at sunset at all times of the year, hundreds of little penguins come ashore at Summerland Beach and waddle across the sand to their burrows in the spinifex tussocks (spiky clumps of grass), just as their ancestors have been doing for generations. Once ashore, the small penguins spend their time in the dunes preening themselves and, in summer, feeding their hungry chicks, seemingly oblivious to visitors watching from raised boardwalks.

At Seal Rocks, off the rugged cliffs at the western end of the island, is Australia's largest colony of fur seals. There is estimated to be approximately 7,000 of these seals, which can be seen playing in the surf, resting in the sun or feeding their pups on the rocks. Tourists can watch them from the cliff top or on an organized boat trip. There is also a large koala colony on Phillip Island.

Cape Woolamai, with its red cliffs and wild ocean seas, has good walking trails, excellent bird-watching opportunities and some great surfing. The peaceful town of Cowes is ideal for swimming, relaxing and dining out on the island's fine seafood *(see p522).*

Fairy penguins making their way up the sand dunes of Phillip Island

Rock pools at Sorrento on the Mornington Peninsula

Mornington Peninsula ❷

🏠 *Frankston.* 🚌 *to most peninsula towns.* 🚢 *Stony Point, Sorrento.* ℹ️ *Dromana (03) 5987 3078.*

Only an hour's drive from Melbourne, on the east side of Port Phillip Bay, the Mornington Peninsula is the city's summer and weekend getaway. From Frankston down to Portsea near its tip, the area is ideal for relaxing beach holidays. The sandy beaches facing the bay are sheltered and calm, perfect for windsurfing, sailing or paddling, while the rugged coast fronting the Bass Strait has rocky reefs, rock pools and surf beaches.

Arthur's Seat, a high, bush ridge, has a spectacular chairlift ride offering views of the peninsula. The surrounding Red Hill wineries are fast gaining a reputation for their fine Chardonnays and Pinot Noirs. Sip a glass of one of these wines in the historic village of Sorrento or take a ferry trip across the narrow and treacherous Rip to the beautiful 19th-century town of Queenscliff *(see p416).*

Running the length of the peninsula, the Mornington Peninsula National Park has lovely walking tracks. Point Nepean, formerly a quarantine station and defence post, is now part of the national park. The beach at the tip of The Heads and Cheviot Beach, where Prime Minister Harold Holt disappeared while surfing in 1967, are both beautiful spots.

Environs

The village of Flinders is a peaceful, chic seaside resort, while Portsea is the summer playground of Melbourne's rich and famous. The atmosphere at the remote French Island, a short ferry trip from Crib Point, is unique, with no electricity or telephones. The island also teems with wildlife, including rare potoroo.

Royal Botanic Gardens, Cranbourne ❸

Off South Gippsland Hwy, 1000 Ballarto Rd. **Tel** *(03) 5990 2200.* 🏠 *Cranbourne.* 🚌 *Cranbourne.* ⏰ *9am–5pm daily.* ⊘ *Good Fri, 25 Dec, days of total fire ban.* ♿

The Royal Botanic Gardens in Melbourne are the city's pride and joy *(see pp398–9),* but they have not concentrated exclusively on native flora. The Cranbourne Botanic Gardens fill that niche. Amid the lakes, hills and dunes of this bushland park, banksias, wattles, grevilleas, casuarinas, eucalypts and pink heath bloom, while wrens, honeyeaters, galahs, rosellas, cockatoos and parrots nestle among the gardens' trees.

Dandenong Ranges ❹

🚉 Ferntree Gully & Belgrave. 🚌 to most towns. 🛈 Upper Ferntree Gully (03) 9758 7522. ⏰ 9am–5pm daily.

Since the mid-19th century, the Dandenong Ranges, to the east of Melbourne, have been a popular weekend retreat for city residents. The cool of the mountain ash forests, lush fern gullies and bubbling creeks provide a welcome relief from the bayside heat. The area abounds with plant nurseries, bed-and-breakfasts and tearooms, reached via twisting mountain roads that offer striking views over Melbourne and the bay.

The great gardens of the Dandenongs, many of which once belonged to the mansions of wealthy families, are magnificent for walks and picnics. Particularly popular is the Alfred Nicholas Memorial Garden at Sherbrooke with its oaks, elms, silver birches and Japanese maples around a boating lake. Flowers are the obvious attraction of the National Rhododendron Gardens at Olinda and Tesselaar's Tulip Farm at Silvan. A steam train, Puffing Billy, runs several times daily from Belgrave through 24 km (15 miles) of gullies and forests to Emerald Lake and on to Gembrook.

The superb lyrebird makes its home in the Dandenongs, particularly in Sherbrooke Forest. The 7-km (4-mile)

Domaine Chandon vineyard in the Yarra Valley

Eastern Sherbrooke Lyrebird Circuit Walk through mountain ash offers a chance to glimpse these beautiful but shy birds. Another tranquil walk is the 11-km (6-mile) path from Sassafras to Emerald.

Healesville Sanctuary, with its 30 ha (75 acres) of natural bushland, remains the best place to see indigenous Australian animals in relatively relaxed captivity. Highlights of any visit are the sightings of rare species such as platypuses, marsupials and birds of prey. This is a popular place to bring children who want to learn about Australian wildlife.

Sparkling wine of the Yarra Valley

🦘 **Healesville Sanctuary**
Badger Creek Rd, Healesville. **Tel** (03) 5957 2800. ⏰ 9am–5pm daily. 📷 ♿ www.zoo.org.au

Yarra Valley ❺

🚉 Lilydale. 🚌 Healesville service. 🛈 Healesville (03) 5962 2600.

The beautiful Yarra Valley, at the foot of the Dandenong Ranges, is home to some of Australia's best cool-climate wineries (see pp378–9). They are known for their *Méthode Champenoise* sparkling wines, Chardonnays and Pinot Noirs. Most of the wineries are open daily for wine tastings. Several also have restaurants, serving food to accompany their fine wines.

Just past the bush town of Yarra Glen with its old hotel, the Yarra Glen Grand (see p490), is the historic Gulf Station. Owned by the National Trust, it provides an authentic glimpse of farming life at the end of the 19th century.

Famous Puffing Billy steam train, making its way through the Dandenong Ranges

Eastern Victoria's Coastline

The beautiful coastline of Gippsland is equal to any natural wonder of the world. Approximately 400 km (250 miles) of deserted beaches, inlets and coves are largely protected by national park status. There is the largest inland lake system in Australia, Gippsland Lakes, the pristine sands of Ninety Mile Beach and rare natural features such as the Mitchell River silt jetties. Birds, fish, seals and penguins abound in the area. With little commercial development, the coastline is a popular location with anglers, sailors, divers, swimmers and campers.

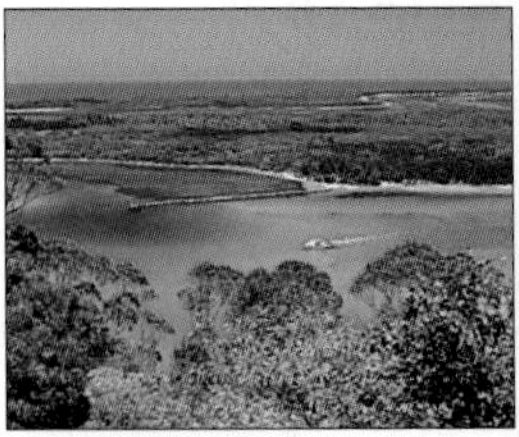

★ Lakes Entrance ⑨

🏄 🌊 🚣 ⛑ ♿ 🚻

Lakes Entrance is the only entrance from the Gippsland Lakes to the sea, through the treacherous Bar. This major fishing port is also well equipped with motels, museums and theme parks for children.

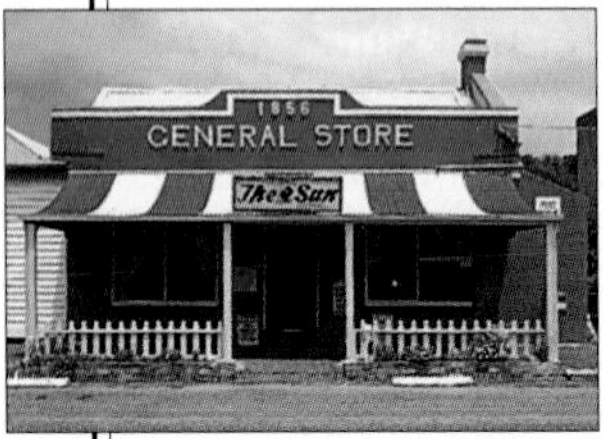
1856
GENERAL STORE
The Sun

Port Albert, *the oldest port in Gippsland, was used by thousands of gold diggers heading for the Omeo and Walhalla gold fields in the 1850s. Quaint buildings with shady verandas line its streets, and it is home to the oldest pub in the state.*

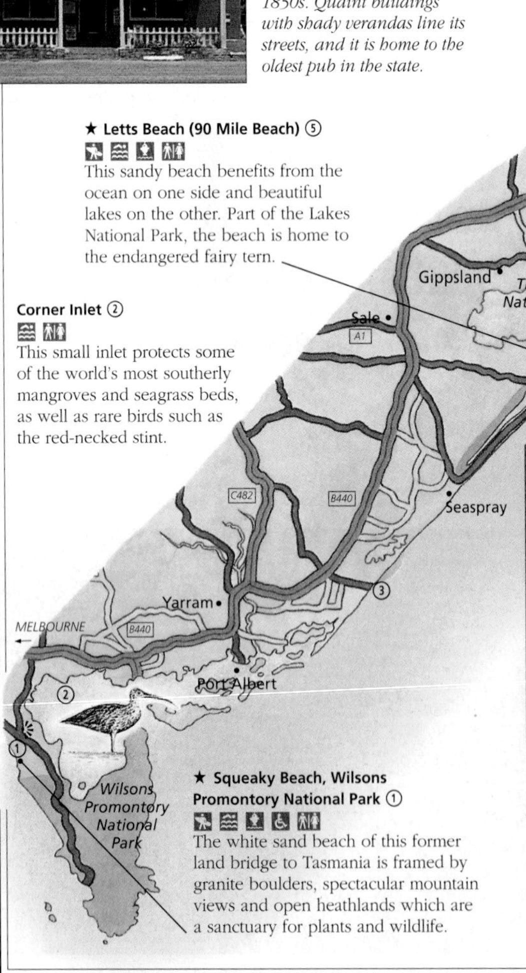
B500
Bairnsdale
Paynesville
Gippsland
The Lakes National Park
Sale
A1
Bass Strait
Seaspray
C482
B440
Yarram
MELBOURNE
B440
Port Albert
Wilsons Promontory National Park

★ Letts Beach (90 Mile Beach) ⑤

🏄 🌊 ⛑ 🚻

This sandy beach benefits from the ocean on one side and beautiful lakes on the other. Part of the Lakes National Park, the beach is home to the endangered fairy tern.

Corner Inlet ②

🌊 🚻

This small inlet protects some of the world's most southerly mangroves and seagrass beds, as well as rare birds such as the red-necked stint.

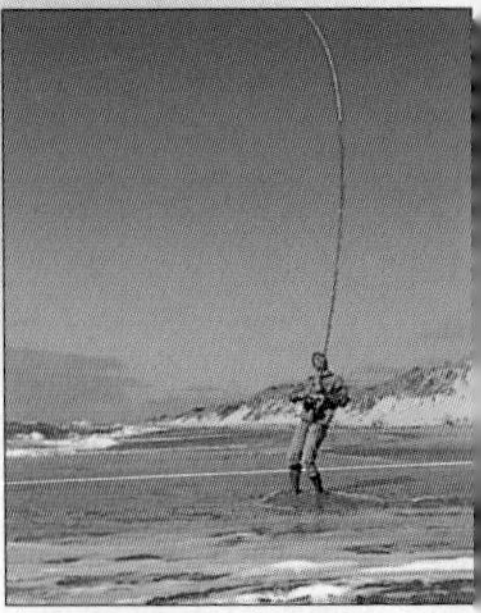

★ Golden Beach (90 Mile Beach) ④

🏄 🌊 ⛑ 🚻

The calm waters of this stretch of ocean make it a popular destination for water sports enthusiasts. Fishing and sailing are two of the regular activities available in the area.

★ Squeaky Beach, Wilsons Promontory National Park ①

🏄 🌊 ⛑ ♿ 🚻

The white sand beach of this former land bridge to Tasmania is framed by granite boulders, spectacular mountain views and open heathlands which are a sanctuary for plants and wildlife.

Key to Symbols *see back flap*

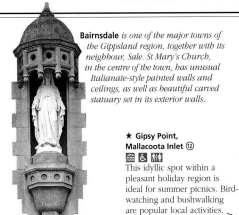

Bairnsdale *is one of the major towns of the Gippsland region, together with its neighbour, Sale. St Mary's Church, in the centre of the town, has unusual Italianate-style painted walls and ceilings, as well as beautiful carved statuary set in its exterior walls.*

★ **Gipsy Point, Mallacoota Inlet** ⑫
This idyllic spot within a pleasant holiday region is ideal for summer picnics. Bird-watching and bushwalking are popular local activities.

LOCATOR MAP

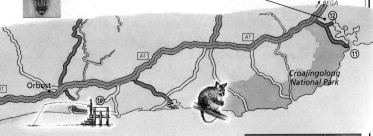

BEGA
⑫
A1
A1
A1
⑪
Orbost
⑩
Croajingolong National Park

Woodside Beach ③
This easily accessible white sandy beach is popular with families, sunbathers and surfers. The area behind the beach benefits from many well-signposted bushwalks.

Gippsland Lakes ⑥
The lagoons, backwaters, islands and lakes of this region make up Australia's biggest inland waterway. Lakeside settlements are home to large sailing and fishing fleets.

Eagle Point ⑦
Silt banks from the Mitchell River stretch 8 km (5 miles) out into Lake King from Eagle Point. The silt banks are second only in length to those of the Mississippi River.

Metung ⑧
This pretty boating and holiday region, popular with campers, benefits from hot mineral pools.

Marlo ⑩
Located at the mouth of the great Snowy River, Marlo is a popular holiday destination, particularly with avid local anglers. Nearby is the large town of Orbost, the centre of East Gippsland's extensive timber industry.

Mallacoota ⑪
This remote fishing village is extremely popular with both Victorian and overseas tourists. It is set on an inland estuary of the Bass Strait, ideal for canoeing, fishing and sailing.

Croajingolong National Park *is a magnificent stretch of rugged and coastal wilderness, classified as a World Biosphere Reserve. Captain Cook caught his first sight of Australia in 1770 at Point Hicks.*

```
0 kilometres        25

0 miles             25
```

KEY

▨	Freeway
▨	Major road
▨	Minor road
⌇	River
☆	Viewpoint

Steavenson Falls, near Marysville, have five cascades and a total descent of 122 m (400 ft)

Marysville ⑥

🏛 670. 🚉 ℹ️ *Marysville Visitors' Information Centre, Murchison St (03) 5963 4567.*

Within a two-hour drive of Melbourne, through the tall trees of the Black Spur and the Dom Dom Saddle in the Upper Yarra Ranges, is the 19th-century resort town of Marysville. Gracious old guesthouses provide a picturesque base from which to follow Lady Talbot Drive along the snow-fed Taggerty River or take walks in the "Beeches" temperate rainforest, home to the rare Leadbeater's possum.

Just outside town are the Steavenson Falls, which are floodlit at night. Nearby are the mountains of the Cathedral Ranges and the snow fields and trails of Lake Mountain (*see pp448–9*).

Licola ⑦

🏛 20. 🚉 *Heyfield.* ℹ️ *Maffra Visitor Information Centre, 8 Johnson St (03) 5141 1811.*

Licola is a tiny village perched on the edge of Victoria's mountain wilderness. North of Heyfield and Glenmaggie, follow the Macalister River Valley north to Licola. The 147-km (90-mile) journey from Licola

to Jamieson, along unsealed roads, takes in the magnificent scenery of Victoria's highest peaks. Only 20 km (12 miles) from Licola is Mount Tamboritha and the start of the popular Lake Tarli Karng bushwalk in the Alpine National Park. It is a popular starting point or base for the more adventurous tourists who are keen to explore the surrounding country. Head for the village general store for information.

Licola is entirely owned by the Lions Club of Victoria (the only privately owned village in the state). The club has developed the Lions Wilderness Village, which provides camp sites and a whole range of activities for young people.

Lake Eildon ⑧

🚉 *Eildon.* ℹ️ *Eildon Visitors' Information Centre, Main St, Eildon (03) 5774 2909.* **www**.lakeeildon.com

Lake Eildon, the catchment for five major rivers, including the Goulburn River, is a vast irrigation reserve that turns into a recreational haven in summer. Surrounded by the Great Dividing Range and Fraser and Eildon national parks, the lake is a good location for water-skiing, houseboat holidays, horse-riding, fishing and hiking. Kangaroos,

koalas and rosellas abound around the lake, and trout and Murray cod are common in the Upper Goulburn River and in the lake. Canoeing on the Goulburn River is also a popular activity.

A variety of accommodation is available, from rustic cabins and camp sites in Fraser National Park to luxurious five-star lodges and guesthouses (*see pp512–15*).

Farmland near the tiny mountain village of Licola

Mansfield ⑨

🏛 2,500. 🚉 ℹ️ *Visitors' Information Centre, Historic Mansfield Railway Station (03) 5775 1464.*

Mansfield, a country town surrounded by mountains, is the southwest entry point to Victoria's alpine country. A memorial in the main street of Mansfield, just near to the 1920s cinema, commemorates the death of three troopers shot by the infamous Ned Kelly and his gang at nearby Stringybark Creek in 1878 – the crime for which he was

Blue waters of Lake Eildon, backed by the Howqua Mountain Ranges

Classic 19th-century architecture in the rural town of Mansfield

hung in Melbourne in 1880 (see p394).

The scenery of Mansfield became well known as the location for the 1981 film *The Man from Snowy River*, which was based on the poet "Banjo" Paterson's legendary ballad of the same name (see p35). Many local horsemen rode in the film and they still contest Crack's Cup each November (see p41). Riders traverse a mountainous track through tall mountain ash, cross rivers and descend steep hills, demonstrating traditional bush skills of both horse and rider.

Environs

The excellent downhill slopes of the Mount Buller ski resort (see pp448-9) is less than one hour's drive from Mansfield. Mount Stirling (see pp448-9) offers year-round activities, such as mountain bike riding (see p567).

Mount Beauty ⓾

⚐ 2,300. ⊟ ℹ *Kiewa Valley Hwy (03) 5754 1962.*

The town of Mount Beauty was first built to house workers on the Kiewa hydro-electricity scheme in the 1940s. It has since developed into a good base for exploring the beauty of the Kiewa Valley, with its tumbling river and dairy farms. Also nearby is the wilderness of the Bogong High Plains and the Alpine National Park (see pp448-9), with their walks, wildflowers and snow gums.

Within the national park, Mount Bogong, Victoria's highest mountain, rises an impressive 1,986 m (6,516 ft)

above the town. The sealed mountain road to Falls Creek (see pp448-9) is one of the main access routes to the region's ski slopes in winter. In summer, Rocky Valley Dam near Falls Creek is a popular rowing and high-altitude athletics training camp. There are beautiful bush walks, and at the top of the High Plains, there are opportunities for fishing, mountain biking, horse-riding and hang-gliding.

Bright ⓫

⚐ 2,500. ⊟ ℹ *119 Gavan St (03) 5755 2275.*

Bright is a picturesque mountain town near the head of the Ovens River Valley, with the towering rocky cliffs of Mount Buffalo (see pp448-9) to the west and the peak of

the state's second highest mountain, Mount Feathertop, to its south. The trees along Bright's main street flame into spectacular colours of red, gold, copper and brown for its Autumn Festival in April and May (see p42). In winter, the town turns into a gateway to the snow fields, with the resorts of Mount Hotham and Falls Creek in the Victorian Alps close by (see pp448-9). In summer, swimming and fly-fishing for trout in the Ovens River are popular activities.

The spectacular **Mount Buffalo National Park** is also popular all year round; visitors can camp amid the snow gums by Lake Catani and walk its flower-flecked mountain pastures and peaks, fish for trout, hang-glide off the granite tors over the Ovens Valley or rock-climb the imposing sheer cliffs. The gracious Mount Buffalo Chalet, built by the state government in 1910, retains its old-world charm and regularly hosts summer musical events, such as Opera in the Alps (see p37). In winter, its cosy fires and grand dining room make it a popular hotel for skiers avoiding the jetset life of other resorts (see p514).

🌿 **Mount Buffalo National Park**
Mount Buffalo Rd. *Tel* 13 19 63.
📷 ♿ some areas.

Buffalo River meandering through Mount Buffalo National Park

Skiing in the Victorian Alps

Child skiing

Australia offers fantastic skiing opportunities that rival the best in the world. Most of the resorts fall within Alpine National Park *(see pp440–41)*, and are open for business from June to late September. Given that the season is so short, conditions can be variable. Mount Buller, Falls Creek and Mount Hotham are the main resort villages, and the whole region is very fashionable. There are chic lounge bars, top-end lodges and fine dining prepared by some of Melbourne's best chefs. Pistes are not as long as those in Europe and the USA, but the views of the High Plains are an unmissable experience.

Mount Buffalo
These less-crowded slopes are popular with beginners intermediates and cross-country skiers.

Mount Stirling Entry to Mount Buller includes free cross-country skiing on Mount Stirling's groomed trails.

Mount Buller
This is the most accessible of the major resorts, and hence the busiest and trendiest. Slopes suit beginners through to advanced skiers, with 80 km (48 miles) of groomed trails and a 405-m (1,300 ft) vertical drop. The entrance car park at Mirimbah is 16 km (10 miles) from the village.

Lake Mountain This resort is ideal for cross-country skiing and snowball fights with the kids. Most runs are for beginners to intermediates. There is no on-mountain accommodation. Nearby Mount Donna Buang is fine for snowmen and toboggan runs.

Mount Buffalo
(5558ft/1695m)

Lake Buffalo

MT BU
NATIC
PA

Mount Stirling
Alpine Resort

Mansfield

Mount Buller
Alpine Village

Lake Eildon

Mount Buller
(5922 ft/1805m)

ALPINE
NATIONAL
PARK

Eildon   Jamieson

Lake Mountain

Licola

YARRA RANGES
NATIONAL
PARK

Mount St Gwinear
(4915ft/1509m)

Mount Baw Baw
(513ft/1565m)

Thomson
Reservoir

Mount
Baw Baw
Alpine Village

Walhalla

Mount Baw Baw
The closest downhill ski resort to Melbourne is an excellent option for beginners, families and skiers on a budget. Nearby Mount St Gwinear offers superb cross-country skiing but no on-mountain accommodation.

Australian Alps Walking Track
The 655-km (393-mile) Australian Alps Walking Track runs from historic Walhalla north-east to the Brindabella Ranges outside Canberra.

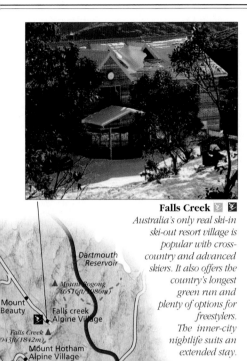

Falls Creek

Australia's only real ski-in ski-out resort village is popular with cross-country and advanced skiers. It also offers the country's longest green run and plenty of options for freestylers. The inner-city nightlife suits an extended stay.

ADVICE FOR SKIERS

Costs
Entry fees range from A$25 to A$30 per car per day. Lifts cost A$57 to A$85 per day per adult.

Transport and Equipment Hire
Roads are sealed to all resorts except Dinner Plain, Mount Baw Baw and Mount Stirling. By law, vehicles must carry chains. Equipment can be hired from the resorts listed here. Coaches run from Melbourne to every resort except Mount Baw Baw. Aircraft and helicopters from Melbourne and Sydney fly to Mount Hotham and Mount Buller. A helicopter shuttle flies between Mount Hotham and Falls Creek.

Ski Resorts
Dinner Plain
www.dinnerplain.com
Tel (03) 5159 6426.

Falls Creek
www.fallscreek.com.au
Tel (03) 5758 3224.

Lake Mountain
www.lakemountainresort.com.au
Tel (03) 59 577 222.

Mount Baw Baw
www.mountbawbaw.com.au
Tel (03) 5165 1136.

Mount Buffalo
www.mtbuffaloresort.com.au
Tel 1800 037 038.

Mount Buller
www.mtbuller.com.au
Tel (03) 5777 6077.

Mount Hotham
www.mthotham.com.au
Tel (03) 5759 4444.

Mount Stirling
www.mtstirling.com.au
Tel (03) 5777 6441.

For hotels in the area, see pp512–15.

KEY

▲ Peak

Resorts

Major road

Minor road

-- Walking track

Beginner

Intermediate

Advanced

Mount Hotham

Featuring mostly challenging terrain, this area best suits intermediate to more advanced skiers. The resort has definitely gone more up-market in recent years. There is an airstrip 20 km (12 miles) from the village. Nearby Dinner Plain is popular with cross-country skiers.

Typical 19th-century honey granite building in Beechworth

Beechworth ⓬

🏃 3,500. 🚉 ℹ️ Shire Hall, Ford St (03) 5728 3233.

Beautifully sited in the foothills of the Victorian Alps, Beechworth was the centre of the great Ovens gold fields during the 1850s and 1860s (see pp54–5). At the height of its boom, the town had a population of 42,000 and 61 hotels.

Today, visiting Beechworth is like stepping back in time. One of the state's best-preserved gold rush towns, it contains more than 30 19th-century buildings now classified by the National Trust. Its tree-lined streets feature granite banks and a courthouse, hotels with wide verandas and dignified brick buildings on either side. The majority of these are still in daily use, modern life continuing within edifices of a bygone era.

A large majority of the old buildings are now restaurants, and bed-and-breakfasts. Dine in the stately old bank which is now the Bank Restaurant (see p560), stand in the dock of the courthouse where Ned Kelly was finally committed for his trial in Melbourne (see p394) and marvel at the old channel blasted through the granite to create a flow of water in which miners panned for gold.

The evocative Chinese cemetery is also worth a visit as a poignant reminder of the hundreds of Chinese who worked and died on the gold fields (see pp54–5).

Chiltern ⓭

🏃 1,500. 🚉 ℹ️ 30 Main St (03) 5726 1611.

This sleepy village was once a booming gold mining town with 14 suburbs. Only 1 km (0.6 miles) off the Hume Highway, halfway between the major towns of Wangaratta and Wodonga, today its colonial architecture and quiet atmosphere, as yet unspoiled by large numbers of tourists, make a visit to this pleasant town a worthwhile experience.

Chiltern has three National Trust properties: Dow's Pharmacy; the Federal Standard newspaper office; and Lakeview House. The last is the former home of Henry Handel Richardson, the pen name of Ethel Robertson, who wrote The Getting of Wisdom (see p35). Chiltern was her childhood home. The house, on Lake Alexander, has been restored with period furniture, and gives an insight into the life of the wealthy at the turn of the 20th century.

An unusual sight is the **Famous Grapevine Attraction** museum. This shows the oldest and largest grapevine in the southern hemisphere – it once covered Chiltern's Star Hotel in its entirety.

For opening hours and other information on these attractions, check with the tourist information office in the town.

Lakeview House in Chiltern

Northeastern Wineries ⓮

🚉 Wangaratta & Rutherglen. 🚌 Wangaratta & Rutherglen. ℹ️ Rutherglen (02) 6032 9428; Wangaratta (03) 5721 5711. **Campbells Winery Tel** (02) 6032 9458. ⏰ 9am–5pm Mon–Sat; 10am–5pm Sun. 🔴 Good Fri, 25 Dec. **Chambers Winery Tel** (02) 6032 8641. ⏰ 9am–5pm Mon–Sat, 10am–5pm Sun & public hols. 🔴 Good Fri, 25 Dec. **Brown Bros Tel** (03) 5720 5500. ⏰ 9am–5pm daily. 🔴 Good Fri, 25 Dec. **www**.northeastvalleys.info

The Northeastern area of Victoria is famous throughout the world for its vineyards and wineries (see pp378–9). In a region that now spreads south to encompass the King and Ovens valleys around Glenrowan, Milawa, Everton, Rutherglen and Whitfield, the wines produced can vary in style enormously, depending on the elevation and microclimate of each vineyard.

Rutherglen is best known for its full-bodied "Rutherglen Reds", such as Cabernet

Rows of grapevines in one of northeastern Victoria's many vineyards

For hotels and restaurants in this region see pp512–15 and pp559–61

Elegant Benalla Art Gallery on the shores of Lake Benalla

Sauvignons from 100-year-old wineries including Campbells and Chambers. The Muscats, Tokays and ports from both Rutherglen and Glenrowan are even more internationally renowned, with Bullers, Morris and Bailey's among the best. Rutherglen itself is a graceful town lined with antiques shops, and a selection of hotels and restaurants.

The grapes grown in the cool-climate region around Whitfield and Milawa make for crisp whites and lighter, softer reds. One of the more popular wineries in Northeastern Victoria is Brown Brothers at Milawa. The winery is open daily for both wine tasting and sales at the cellar door, and its excellent restaurant specializes in local delicacies from the region, including particularly good trout, cheese, honey and lamb. While at Milawa, visits to the Milawa Cheese Factory and Milawa Mustards are recommended.

Iron effigy of Ned Kelly

Glenrowan **⑮**

🏠 *1,000.* 🚍 🚆 *Wangaratta*
ℹ️ *Kate's Cottage, Gladstone St (03) 5766 2448.*

Glenrowan was the site of the last stand by Australia's most notorious bushranger, Ned Kelly, and his gang *(see p394).* In a shoot-out with police in 1880, on Siege Street near the town's railway station, Kelly was finally captured after more than two years on the run. During this time he had earned almost hero status among Victoria's bush poor, particularly its many Irish Catholic farming families, as a Robin Hood-type character. Kelly knew the country around Glenrowan, especially the lovely Warby Ranges, in great detail and often used Mount Glenrowan, west of town, as a lookout. He was later hanged at Melbourne Gaol.

Today Glenrowan thrives on its Kelly history as a tourist attraction. A giant iron effigy of the bushranger greets visitors at the entrance to the town and there are various displays, museums and re-enactments depicting the full Kelly story, including his last defeat.

Benalla **⑯**

🏠 *8,500.* ✈️ 🚍 🚆 ℹ️ *The Creators' Gallery, 14 Mair St (03) 5762 1749.*

The rural town of Benalla is where Ned Kelly grew up and first appeared in court at the age of 15. Today it is most famous for its art gallery, built over Lake Benalla, which contains a fine collection of contemporary and Australian art. A Rose Festival is held in its magnificent rose gardens each November *(see p41).*

The town is also known as the Australian "capital" of gliding, with excellent air thermals rising from both the hot plains and nearby mountains.

Shepparton **⑰**

🏠 *30,000.* ✈️ 🚍 🚆 🚌 ℹ️ *534 Wyndham St (03) 5831 4400, 1800 808 839.*

The modern city of Shepparton, at the heart of the fertile Goulburn River Valley, is often called the "fruit bowl of Australia". The vast irrigation plains around the town support Victoria's most productive pear, peach, apricot, apple, plum, cherry and kiwi fruit farms. A summer visit of the town's biggest fruit cannery, SPC, when fruit is being harvested, reveals a hive of activity.

The area's sunny climate is also ideal for grapes. The two well-known wineries of Mitchelton and Tahbilk Wines, 50 km (30 miles) south of town, are both open for tours and tastings *(see pp378–9).*

Harvesting fruit in Shepparton's orchards

TASMANIA

INTRODUCING TASMANIA 454–455

TASMANIA 456–471

Tasmania's Wildlife and Wilderness

Tasmanian blue gum

Tasmania's landscape varies dramatically within its small area. Parts of Tasmania are often compared to the green pastures of England; however, the west of the state is wild and untamed. Inland there are glacial mountains and wild rivers, the habitat of flora and fauna unique to the island. More than 20 per cent of the island is now designated as a World Heritage Area *(see pp26–7)*.

Russell Falls at Mount Field National Park

MOUNTAIN WILDERNESS

Inland southwest Tasmania is dominated by its glacial mountain landscape, including the beautiful Cradle Mountain – the natural symbol of the state. To the east of Cradle Mountain is the Walls of Jerusalem National Park, an isolated area of five rocky mountains. To the south is Mount Field National Park, a beautiful alpine area of glacial tarns and eucalypt forests, popular with skiers in the winter months.

Deciduous beech (Nothofagus gunnii) *is the only such native beech in Australia. The spectacular golden colours of its leaves fill the mountain areas during the autumn.*

Cradle Mountain, looking down over a glacial lake

The Bennett's wallaby (Macropus rufogriseus) *is native to Tasmania's mountain regions. A shy animal, it is most likely to be spotted at either dawn or dusk.*

COASTAL WILDERNESS

Tasmania's eastern coastline is often balmy in climate and sustains a strong fishing industry. The western coast, however, bears the full brunt of the Roaring Forties winds, whipped up across the vast expanses of ocean between the island state and the nearest land in South America. As a result, the landscape is lined with rocky beaches and raging waters, the scene of many shipwrecks during Tasmania's history.

The Tasmanian devil (Sarcophilus harrisii) *is noisy, potentially vicious and one of only three marsupial carnivores that inhabit the island.*

Banksia *comes in many varieties in Tasmania, including* Banksia serrata *and* Banksia marginata. *It is distinctive for its seed pods.*

Rugged coastline of the Tasman Peninsula

◁ **Autumn in Pine Valley, Cradle Mountain Lake St Clair National Park**

Calm area of Franklin Lower Gordon Wild River

RIVER WILDERNESS

The southwest of Tasmania is well known for its wild rivers, particularly among avid whitewater rafters. The greatest wild river is the 120-km (75-mile) Franklin River, protected within Franklin-Gordon Wild Rivers National Park by its World Heritage status. This is the only undammed wild river left in Australia, and despite its sometimes calm moments it often rages fiercely through gorges, rainforests and heathland.

Huon pine (Lagarostrobus franklinii) *is found in the southwest and in the south along the Franklin-Gordon River. It is prized for its ability to withstand rot. Some examples are more than 2,000 years old.*

Brown trout (Salmo trutta), *an introduced species, is abundant in the wild rivers and lakes of Tasmania, and a popular catch with fly-fishers.*

The eastern quoll (Dasyurus viverrinus) *thrives in Tasmania, where there are no predatory foxes and forests are in abundance.*

PRESERVING TASMANIA'S WILDERNESS

An inhospitable climate, rugged landforms and the impenetrable scrub are among the factors that have preserved such a large proportion of Tasmania as wilderness. Although there is a long history of human habitation in what is now the World Heritage Area (Aboriginal sites date back 35,000 years), the population has always been small. The first real human threat occurred in the late 1960s when the Tasmanian government's hydro-electricity programme drowned Lake Pedder despite conservationists' protests. A proposal two decades later to dam a section of the Franklin River was defeated when the federal government intervened. The latest threat to the landscape is tourism. While many places of beauty are able to withstand visitors, others are not and people are discouraged from visiting these areas.

Protest badges

Dam protests *were common occurrences in Tasmania during the 1980s, when conservationists protested against the damming of the Franklin River. The No Dams sticker became a national symbol of protest.*

TASMANIA

uman habitation of Tasmania dates back 35,000 years, when Aborigines first reached the area. At this time it was linked to continental Australia, but waters rose to form the Bass Strait at the end of the Ice Age, 12,000 years ago. Dutch explorer Abel Tasman set foot on the island in 1642 and inspired its modern name. He originally called it Van Diemen's Land, after the governor of the Dutch East Indies.

Belying its small size, Tasmania has a remarkably diverse landscape that contains glacial mountains, dense forests and rolling green hills. Its wilderness is one of only three large temperate forests in the southern hemisphere; it is also home to many plants and animals unique to the island, including a ferocious marsupial, the Tasmanian devil. Tasmanians are fiercely proud of their landscape and the island saw the rise of the world's first Green political party, the "Tasmanian Greens". One-fifth of Tasmania is protected as a World Heritage Area *(see pp26–7)*.

The Tasmanian Aboriginal population was almost wiped out with the arrival of Europeans in the 19th century, however more than 4,000 people claim Aboriginality in Tasmania today. Evidence of their link with the landscape has survived in numerous cave paintings. Many Aboriginal sites remain sacred and closed to visitors, but a few, such as the cliffs around Woolnorth, display this indigenous art for all to see.

The island's early European history has also been well preserved in its many 19th-century buildings. The first real settlement was at the waterfront site of Hobart in 1804, now Tasmania's capital and Australia's second-oldest city. From here, European settlement spread throughout the state, with the development of farms and villages, built and worked by convict labour.

Today, Tasmania is a haven for wildlife lovers, hikers and fly-fishermen, who come to experience the island's many national parks and forests. The towns scattered throughout the state, such as Richmond and Launceston, with their rich colonial histories, are well worth a visit, and make excellent bases from which to explore the surrounding wilderness.

The historic port area of Battery Point in Hobart

◁ Breathtaking natural scenery in the Walls of Jerusalem National Park

Exploring Tasmania

Part, and yet not a part, of Australia, Tasmania's distinctive landscape, climate and culture are largely due to its 300-km (185-mile) distance from the mainland. The isolation has left a legacy of unique flora and fauna, fresh air, an abundance of water and a relaxed lifestyle. More than 27 per cent of Tasmania's land surface is given over to agriculture, with the emphasis on wine and fine foods. The state also benefits from vast expanses of open space, since approximately 40 per cent of Tasmanians live in the capital, Hobart. Tasmania, therefore, offers the perfect opportunity for a relaxing holiday in tranquil surroundings.

Nelson Falls in Franklin-Gordon Wild Rivers National Park

Yachts in Constitution Dock, Hobart

KING ISLAND

0 km 15
0 miles 15

KING ISLAND

TASMANIA

Cape Wickham
Egg Lagoon
Yambacoona
16 KING ISLAND
Naracoopa
Currie
Grassy
Stokes Point

Three Hummock Island
Hunter Island

17 WOOLNORTH
15 STANLEY
Smithton
Marrawah   Trowutta   Wynyard
Arthur   BURNIE **14**   Pengu
Temma   DEVONPO
                        Gunns Plains
Sandy Cape
Savage River   Waratah   Sheff
Corinna   Cradle Valley
Pieman River
State Reserve   Roseberry   **18**
Zeehan   CRADLE
                        MOUNTAIN
Southern   LAKE ST CLAIR
Ocean   Queenstown   NATIONAL
                        PARK
Strahan   Lake St Clair
                    Derwent Bridge
MACQUARIE **19**
HARBOUR   **20**
                    FRANKLIN-
                    GORDON
                    WILD RIVERS
                    NATIONAL PAR

Strathgordon

Lake Pedder
South
Nati
Pa

0 km 25
0 miles 25

KEY

━━ Major road
═══ Minor road
━━ Scenic route

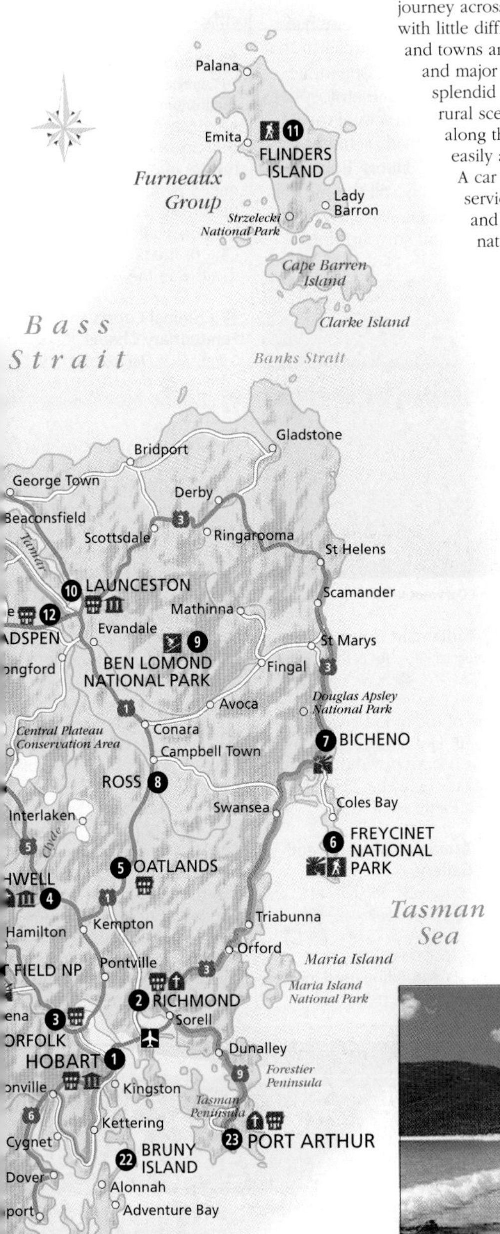
Palana
Emita
FLINDERS ISLAND
[11]
Furneaux Group
Lady Barron
Strzelecki National Park
Cape Barren Island
Clarke Island
Bass Strait
Banks Strait
Gladstone
Bridport
George Town
Derby
Beaconsfield
Scottsdale
Ringarooma
St Helens
Tamar
LAUNCESTON
[10]
Scamander
Mathinna
[12]
Evandale
[9]
St Marys
BEN LOMOND NATIONAL PARK
Fingal
Avoca
Douglas Apsley National Park
Central Plateau Conservation Area
Conara
[7]
BICHENO
Campbell Town
ROSS
[8]
Swansea
Coles Bay
Interlaken
[6]
FREYCINET NATIONAL PARK
Clyde
[5]
OATLANDS
[4]
Hamilton
Kempton
Triabunna
Tasman Sea
Orford
Maria Island
Pontville
Maria Island National Park
[2]
RICHMOND
[3]
Sorell
Dunalley
HOBART
[1]
Forestier Peninsula
Kingston
Tasman Peninsula
Kettering
Cygnet
[23]
PORT ARTHUR
[22]
BRUNY ISLAND
Dover
Alonnah
Adventure Bay

GETTING AROUND

Within this small, compact island, traffic is rarely a problem, and any visitor can journey across the diverse landscape with little difficulty. While all major cities and towns are linked by fast highways and major roads, some of the most splendid mountain, lake, coastal and rural scenery lies off the key routes, along the many alternative and easily accessible country roads.

A car is recommended, but coach services run between most towns and to some of the state's natural attractions.

SIGHTS AT A GLANCE

Ben Lomond National Park [9]
Bicheno [7]
Bothwell [4]
Bruny Island [22]
Burnie [14]
Cradle Mountain Lake St Clair National Park [18]
Devonport [13]
Flinders Island [11]
Franklin-Gordon Wild Rivers National Park [20]
Freycinet National Park [6]
Hadspen [12]
Hobart pp460–61 [1]
King Island [16]
Launceston [10]
Macquarie Harbour [19]
Mount Field National Park [21]
New Norfolk [3]
Oatlands [5]
Port Arthur pp470–71 [23]
Richmond [2]
Ross [8]
Stanley [15]
Woolnorth [17]

SEE ALSO

- ***Where to Stay*** pp515–17
- ***Where to Eat*** pp561–3

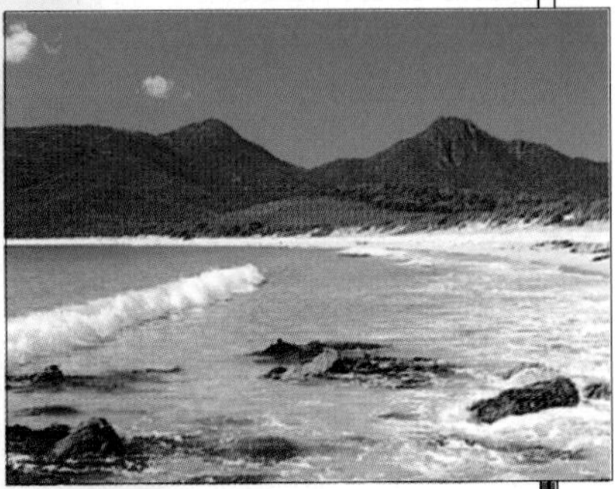

Wineglass Bay in Freycinet National Park

Hobart ❶

Drunken Admiral

Spread over seven hills between the banks of the Derwent River and the summit of Mount Wellington, Australia's second oldest city has an incredible waterfront location, similar to that of her "big sister", Sydney. Hobart began life on the waterfront and the maritime atmosphere is still an important aspect of the city. From Old Wharf, where the first arrivals settled, round to the fishing village of Battery Point, the area known as Sullivans Cove is still the hub of this cosmopolitan city. Like the rest of the state, the capital city makes the most of its natural surroundings.

General view of Hobart and its docks on the Derwent River

🏛 Constitution Dock
Davey St.
The main anchorage for fishing boats and yachts also serves as the finish line of the annual Sydney to Hobart Yacht Race. This famous race attracts an international field of competitors *(see p41)*.

Constitution Dock borders the city and the old slum district of Wapping, which has now been redeveloped. Many of the old warehouses have been restored to include restaurants and cafés. One houses the idiosyncratic restaurant, the Drunken Admiral.

🏛 Hunter Street
Once joined to Hobart Town by a sandbar and known as Hunter Island, this historic harbour-side locale is Hobart's newest art and culture precinct. It is lined with colonial warehouses and was formerly the site of the Jones & Co. IXL jam factory. The heart of this redevelopment is the award-winning Henry Jones Art Hotel *(see p516)*. Hunter Street is just around the corner from the Federation Concert Hall.

🏛 Parliament House
Salamanca Place. **Tel** *(03) 6233 2200.*
⬜ *Mon–Fri.* ⬤ *public hols.* ♿ 🅿
10am & 2pm non-sitting days.
One of the oldest civic buildings in Hobart, designed by John Lee Archer and built by convicts between 1835 and 1841. Partly open to the public.

🏛 Tasmanian Museum and Art Gallery
40 Macquarie St. **Tel** *(03) 6211 4177.* ⬜ *10am–5pm daily.* ⬤ *Good Fri, 25 April, 25 Dec.* ♿ 🅿
www.tmag.tas.gov.au
This 1863 building, designed by the city's best-known colonial architect, Henry Hunter, is now home to a fine collection of prints and paintings of Tasmania, Aboriginal artfacts, and botanical displays.

🏛 Theatre Royal
29 Campbell St. **Tel** *(03) 6233 2299.*
Auditorium ⬜ *Mon–Sat.* ⬤
public hols. 🅿 *for shows only.* ♿
Built in 1837, this is the oldest theatre in Australia. Almost gutted by fire in the 1960s, the ornate decor has since been meticulously restored. One of the most charming theatres in the world.

🏛 Criminal Courts and Penitentiary Chapel
6 Brisbane St. **Tel** *(03) 6231 0911.*
⬜ *daily.* ⬤ *Good Fri, 25 Dec.* 🅿
🎟 *obligatory, 10am, 11:30am,*
1pm, 2:30pm.
In colonial days, courts and prison chapels were often next to each other, making the dispensing of swift judgment convenient. The complex also exhibits solitary confinement cells and an execution yard.

🏛 Salamanca Place
Once the site of early colonial industries, from jam-making to metal foundry and flour milling, this graceful row of sandstone warehouses at Salamanca Place is now the heart of Hobart's lively atmosphere and creative spirit.

Mount Wellington towers above the buildings lining the waterfront, which have been converted into art and craft galleries, antique furniture stores and antiquarian book shops. The Salamanca Arts Centre includes contemporary artists' studios, theatres and exhibition galleries. The

Bustling Saturday market in Salamanca Place

area also has some of the city's best pubs, cafés and restaurants *(see pp562)*. The quarter's pulse reaches a peak every Saturday morning, with the Salamanca Market.

Battery Point

☎ *(03) 6230 8233 to book.*

This maritime village grew up on the hilly promontory adjacent to the early settlement and wharves. The strategic site, with its views down to the Derwent River, was originally home to a gun battery, positioned to ward off potential enemy invasions. The old guardhouse, built in 1818, now lies within a leafy park, just a few minutes' walk from Hampden Road with its range of antiques shops, art galleries, tea-rooms and restaurants.

Battery Point retains a strong sense of history, with its narrow gas-lit streets lined with tiny fishermen's and workers' houses, cottage gardens and colonial mansions and pubs, such as the Shipwright's Arms. The informative Hobart Historic Walks depart daily at 10am from the Visitors Centre on Davey and Elizabeth streets.

Maritime Museum

Cnr Davey & Argyle sts. ***Tel*** *(03) 6234 1427.* 🕘 *9am–5pm daily.* ● *Good Fri, 25 Dec.* 🎫 ♿

Steeped in seafaring history, the Maritime Museum is housed in the Carnegie Building, the former Hobart Public Library It contains a fascinating collection of old relics, manuscripts and voyage documents, as well as an important photographic collection which records Tasmania's maritime history.

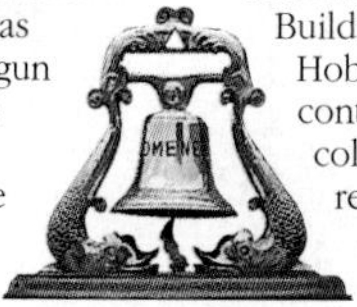

Maritime Museum bell

Castray Esplanade

Castray Esplanade was originally planned in the 19th century as a riverside walking track and it still provides the most pleasurable short stroll within the city.

VISITORS' CHECKLIST

Hobart. 👥 *195,000.* ✈ *20 km (12 miles) NE of the city.* 🚌 *Red Line Coaches, Transit Centre, 199 Collins St.* ℹ *20 Davey St (03) 6230 8233.* 🎉 *Sydney–Hobart Yacht Race (26–29 Dec).*
www.discovertasmania.com.au

En route are the old colonial Commissariat Stores. These have now been beautifully renovated for inner-city living, architects' offices and art galleries, focussing on Tasmanian arts and crafts.

Narryna Heritage Museum

103 Hampden Rd, Battery Point. ***Tel*** *(03) 6234 2791.* 🕘 *10:30am–5pm Tue-Fri, 2–5pm Sat & Sun.* ● *July, 25 Dec, Good Fri, 25 Apr.*

Located in an elegant 1836 Georgian house called Narryna, in Battery Point, this is the oldest folk museum in Australia. Beautiful grounds make a fine backdrop for an impressive collection of early Tasmanian pioneering relics.

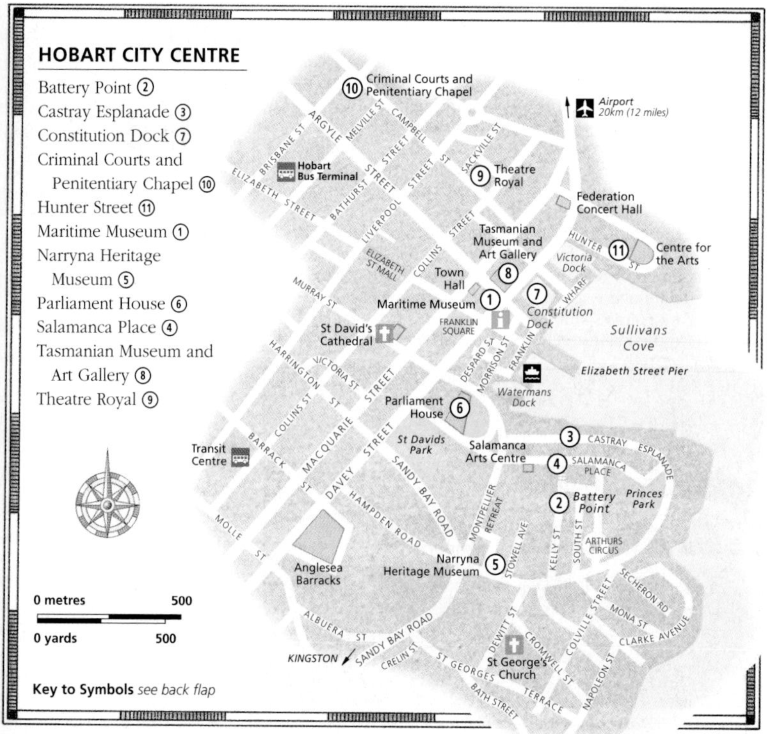
HOBART CITY CENTRE
Battery Point 2
Castray Esplanade 3
Constitution Dock 7
Criminal Courts and Penitentiary Chapel 10
Hunter Street 11
Maritime Museum 1
Narryna Heritage Museum 5
Parliament House 6
Salamanca Place 4
Tasmanian Museum and Art Gallery 8
Theatre Royal 9
Criminal Courts and Penitentiary Chapel
Airport 20km (12 miles)
Hobart Bus Terminal
Theatre Royal
Federation Concert Hall
Tasmanian Museum and Art Gallery
Centre for the Arts
Victoria Dock
Town Hall
Maritime Museum
Constitution Dock
St David's Cathedral
Franklin Square
Sullivans Cove
Elizabeth Street Pier
Watermans Dock
Parliament House
St Davids Park
Salamanca Arts Centre
Transit Centre
Battery Point
Princes Park
Arthurs Circus
Anglesea Barracks
Narryna Heritage Museum
St George's Church
Kingston
0 metres 500
0 yards 500
Key to Symbols see back flap

Hop farm on the Derwent River in New Norfolk

Richmond ❷

🏛 800. 🚌 ℹ️ *Old Hobart Town, Bridge St (03) 6260 2502.*

In the heart of the country-side, 26 km (16 miles) from Hobart, lies the quaint village of Richmond. This was the first area granted to free settlers from England for farming, and at its centre they established a township reminiscent of their homeland. Richmond now includes some of Australia's oldest colonial architecture. Most of the buildings were constructed by convicts, including the sandstone bridge built in 1823, the gaol of 1825 and the Roman Catholic Church of 1834.

Today, Richmond is a lively centre for rural artists and artisans. On the main street, between the old general store and post office, they occupy many of the historic homes and cottages.

New Norfolk ❸

🏛 5,900. 🚌 ℹ️ *Circle St (03) 6261 3700.*

From Hobart, the Derwent River heads north, then veers west through the Derwent River Valley. The hop farms and oast houses along the willow-lined river are testimony to the area's history of brewing.

At the centre of the valley, 38 km (24 miles) from Hobart, is the town of New Norfolk. Many of the first settlers in the region abandoned the colonial settlement of Norfolk Island to come here, hence the name. One of Tasmania's classified historic towns, it contains many interesting buildings, such as the Bush Inn of 1815, which claims to be one of Australia's oldest licensed pubs.

Typical 19th-century building in Bothwell

Bothwell ❹

🏛 400. 🚌 ℹ️ *Australasian Golf Museum, Market Place (03) 6259 4033.*

Nestled in the Clyde River Valley, Bothwell's wide streets are set along a river of the same name, formerly known as the "Fat Doe" river after a town in Scotland. The area's names were assigned by early Scottish settlers, who arrived from Hobart Town in 1817 with their families and 18-l (5-gal) kegs of rum loaded on bullock wagons.

The town's heritage is now preserved with some 50 National Trust buildings dating

Richmond Bridge, constructed with local sandstone

For hotels and restaurants in this region see pp515–17 and pp561–3

from the 1820s, including the Castle Hotel, the Masonic Hall (now an art gallery), Bothwell Grange Guest House and the Old Schoolhouse, now home to the Australasian Golf Museum. The stone heads above the door of the Presbyterian St Luke's Church depict a Celtic god and goddess. Even the town's golf course has a claim on history as the oldest in Australia, as it was laid out in the 1820s.

The town lies at the centre of the historic sheep-farming district of Bothwell, stretching along Lakes Hwy from the southern midlands to the famous trout fishing area of the Great Lakes. It is also the gateway to the ruggedly beautiful Central Plateau Conservation Area – a tableland which rises abruptly from the surrounding flat countryside to an average height of 600 m (nearly 2,000 ft).

Coles Bay, backed by the Hazards Mountains, Freycinet Peninsula

Oatlands ❺

🏛 *550.* 🚌 ℹ *Central Tasmanian Tourism Centre, 77 High St.* *(03) 6254 1212.*

Oatlands was one of a string of military stations established in 1813 during the construction of the old Midlands Hwy by convict chain gangs. Colonial Governor Lachlan Macquarie ordered the building of the road in 1811, to connect the southern settlement of Hobart *(see pp460–61)* with the northern settlement of Launceston *(see p464)*. During a later trip, he chose locations for the townships en route, naming them after places in the British Isles. The road ran through the area of Tasmania corresponding in name and geography to that of the British Midlands region, giving it its original name, but since the 1990s it has been dubbed the Heritage Hwy.

Oatlands soon became one of the colonial coaching stops for early travellers. Today, it has the richest endowment of Georgian buildings in the country, mostly made of local sandstone, including the 1829 courthouse and St Peter's Church (1838). As a result,

the township is classified by the National Trust. Its most distinctive building, the Oatlands Flour Mill, was in operation until 1890.

Distinctive façade of the Oatlands Flour Mill

Freycinet National Park ❻

📷 *from Bicheno.* **Visitors' Centre** *Tel (03) 6256 7000.* ⏰ *8am–5pm daily.* 🚫 *25 Dec.* **www**.parks.tas.gov.au

The Freycinet Peninsula on the east coast of Tasmania is a long, narrow neck of land jutting south, dominated by the granite peaks of the Hazards Mountain Range. Named after an early French maritime explorer, the peninsula consists of ocean beaches on its eastern rim and secluded coves and inlets to the west. The fishing village of Coles Bay lies in the largest cove, backed by the Hazards.

Freycinet National Park on the tip of the peninsula is criss-crossed with walking tracks along beaches, over mountains, around headlands

and across lagoons. The most popular walk is Wineglass Bay – a short, steep trip up and over the saddle of the mountains. The blue waters of the bay are cupped against a crescent of golden sand, which inspired the name.

The drive up the east coast is a highlight of Tasmania. There are ocean views, cliffs, sandy coves and marshlands inhabited by black swans. There are many small towns en route such as Orford and Swansea for overnight stays.

Bicheno ❼

🏛 *750.* 🚌 ℹ *69 Burgess St (03) 6375 1500.*

Together with Coles Bay, Bicheno is the holiday centre of Tasmania's east coast. In summer, the bay is very popular due to its sheltered location, which means temperatures are always a few degrees warmer than elsewhere in the state.

The area also includes Tasmania's smallest national park, the 16,080 ha (39,700 acre) Douglas Apsley National Park. It contains the state's largest dry sclerophyll forest, patches of rainforest, river gorges, waterfalls and spectacular views along the coast. This varied landscape can be taken in along a three-day north to south walking track through the park. The north of the park is only accessible by 4WD. Other attractions in the area include the Apsley Gorge Winery and a 3-km long penguin breeding colony.

Man-O-Ross Hotel at the Four Corners of Ross crossroads

Ross ❽

🏛 300. 🅿 ℹ Tasmanian Wool Centre, Church St (03) 6381 5466.

Set on the banks of the Macquarie River, Ross, like Oatlands (see p463), was once a military station and coaching stop along the Midlands Hwy. It lies at the heart of the richest sheep farming district in Tasmania, internationally recognized for its fine merino wool. Some of the large rural homesteads in the area have remained within the same families since the 1820s when the village was settled.

The town's most famous sight is Ross Bridge, built by convict labour and opened in 1836. It features 186 unique carvings by convict sculptor Daniel Herbert, who was given a Queen's Pardon for his intricate work. The town centres on its historic crossroads, the Four Corners of Ross: "Temptation, Damnation, Salvation and Recreation". These are represented respectively on each corner by the Man-O-Ross Hotel, the jail, the church and the town hall.

Man O'Ross hotel sign

Ben Lomond National Park ❾

📷 when ski slopes are open. ℹ National Parks & Wildlife Service, 167 Westbury Rd Prospect, Launceston (03) 6336 5312.

In the hinterlands between the Midlands and the east coast, 50 km (30 miles) south-east of Launceston, Ben Lomond is the highest mountain in northern Tasmania and home to one of the state's two main ski slopes. The 16,000-ha (40,000-acre) national park surrounding the mountain covers an alpine plateau of barren and dramatic scenery, with views stretching over the northeast of the state. The vegetation includes alpine daisies and carnivorous sundew plants. The park is also home to wallabies, wombats and possums. From Conara Junction on the Heritage Hwy, take the Esk Main Road east before turning off towards Ben Lomond National Park.

The mountain's foothills have been devastated by decades of mining and forestry, and many of the townships, such as Rossarden and Avoca, have since suffered an economic decline. The road through the South Esk Valley along the Esk River loops back to the valley's main centre of Fingal. From here, you can continue through the small township of St Marys before joining the Tasman Hwy and travelling up the east coast.

Launceston ❿

🏛 67,000. ✈ 🚌 Georgetown to Devonport, then bus (summer only). ℹ Travel & Information Centre (inside Cornwall Square Transit Centre), cnr St John & Cimitiere sts (03) 6336 3133.

In colonial days, the coach ride between Tasmania's capital, Hobart, and the township of Launceston took a full day, but today the 200-km (125-mile) route is flat and direct. Nestling in the Tamar River Valley, Launceston was settled in 1804 and is Australia's third-oldest city. It has a charming ambience of old buildings, parks, gardens, riverside walks, craft galleries

Alpine plateau in Ben Lomond National Park, backed by Ben Lomond Mountain

For hotels and restaurants in this region see pp515–17 and pp561–3

Riverside view of Penny Royal World in Launceston

and hilly streets lined with weatherboard houses. The **Queen Victoria Museum and Art Gallery** has the country's largest provincial display of colonial art, along with an impressive modern collection. It also shows Aboriginal and convict relics, and has displays on minerals, flora and fauna of the region.

Penny Royal World in Paterson Street is a complex of historic windmills, corn mills and gunpowder mills, which were carefully dismantled and moved from their original locations stone by stone. The working replica of a 19th-century gunpowder mill has 14 barges that take visitors underground so that they can observe the production process.

Cataract Gorge Reserve is alive with birds, wallabies, pademelons, potoroos and bandicoots, only a 15-minute walk from the city centre. A chairlift, believed to have the longest central span in the world, provides a striking aerial overview.

🏛 **Penny Royal World**
147 Paterson St, Launceston.
Tel (03) 6331 6699. ☐ Sep–May:
9am–4:30pm daily. 🎫 🔥 limited.

🏛 **Queen Victoria Museum and Art Gallery**
Museum 2 Wellington St, Royal Pk, Launceston; **Gallery** 2 Invermay Rd, Inveresk. **Tel** (03) 6323 3777. ☐ 10am–5pm daily. ● Good Fri, 25 Dec. 🔥 www.qvmag.tas.gov.au

Environs:
In the 1830s, the Norfolk Plains was a farmland district owned mainly by wealthy settlers who had been enticed to the area by land grants. The small town of **Longford**, with its historic inns and churches, is still the centre of a rich agricultural district. It also has the greatest concentration of colonial mansions in the state. Many, such as Woolmers and Brickendon, are open for public tours.

Cape Barren geese in the Patriarch Sanctuary on Cape Barren Island

Flinders Island ⓫

✈ from Launceston, Melbourne. 🚢 from Bridport. 🛈 Travel & Information Centre (inside Cornwall Square Transit Centre), cnr St John & Cimitiere sts, Launceston (03) 6336 3133.

On the northeastern tip of Tasmania, in the waters of the Bass Strait, Flinders Island is the largest within the Furneaux Island Group. These 50 or so dots in the ocean are all that remains of the land bridge which once spanned the strait to the continental mainland (see pp22–3).

Flinders Island was also the destination for the last surviving 133 Tasmanian Aborigines. With the consent of the British administration, the Reverend George Augustus Robinson brought all 133 of them here in the 1830s. His aim was to "save" them from extinction by civilizing them according to European traditions and converting them to Christianity. In 1847, however, greatly diminished by disease and despair, the 47 survivors were transferred to Oyster Cove, a sacred Aboriginal site south of Hobart, and the plan was deemed a failure. Within a few years, all full-blooded Tasmanian Aborigines had died.

Much of Flinders is now preserved as a natural reserve, including Strzelecki National Park, which is particularly popular with hikers. Off the island's south coast is Cape Barren Island, home to the Patriarch Sanctuary, a protected geese reserve.

Flinders Island is reached by air from Launceston and Melbourne. There is also a leisurely ferry trip aboard the *Matthew Flinders* from Launceston and the small coastal town of Bridport.

Entally House in Hadspen

Hadspen ⑫

🚶 1,700. 🚌 ℹ️ *Travel & Information Centre, cnr St John & Cimitiere sts, Launceston (03) 6336 3133.*

Heading west along the Bass Highway, a string of historic towns pepper the countryside from Longford through to Deloraine, surrounded by the Great Western Tiers Mountains. The tiny town of Hadspen is a picturesque strip of Georgian cottages and buildings which include an old 1845 coaching house.

The town is also home to one of Tasmania's most famous historic homes open to the public. Built in 1819 on the bank of the South Esk River, the beautiful **Entally House**, with its gracious veranda, has its own chapel, stables, horse-drawn carriages and lavish 19th-century furnishings.

Period furniture in Entally House

🏛️ Entally House
Meander Valley Rd, via Hadspen.
Tel (03) 6393 6201. ⏰ 10am–4pm daily. 🚫 Good Fri, 25 Dec. 📷 ♿

Devonport ⑬

🚶 23,000. ✈️ 🚌 🚆 ⛴️
ℹ️ *Devonport Visitor Centre, 92 Formby Rd (03) 6424 4466.*

Named after the county of Devon in England, the state's third-largest city is strategically sited as a river and sea port. It lies at the junction of the Mersey River and the Bass Strait, on the north coast. The dramatic rocky headland of Mersey Bluff is 1 km (0.6 miles) from the city centre, linked by a coastal reserve and parklands. Here Aboriginal rock paintings mark the entrance of **Tiagarra**, the Tasmanian Aboriginal art and culture centre, with its collection of more than 2,000 ancient artifacts.

From Devonport, the overnight car and passenger ferry *Spirit of Tasmania* sails to the Port of Melbourne on the mainland several times each week. With a local airport, Devonport is also an excellent starting point for touring northern Tasmania. Heading northwest, the old coast road offers unsurpassed views of the Bass Strait.

🏛️ Tiagarra
Mersey Bluff, Devonport. **Tel** (03) 6424 8250. ⏰ 9am–5pm daily. 🚫 Good Fri, 25 Dec, Jun. 📷 ♿

Burnie ⑭

🚶 16,000. ✈️ 🚌 🚆 ℹ️ *Civic Square Precinct (03) 6434 6111.*

Further along the northern coast from Devonport is Tasmania's fourth-largest city, founded in 1829. Along its main streets are many attractive 19th-century buildings decorated with wrought ironwork. Until recently, Burnie's prosperity centred on a thriving wood-pulping industry. One of the state's main enterprises, Associated Pulp and Paper Mills, established in 1938, was sited here. The city in recent times has shed its industrial character, although some industry survives, notably the Lactos company, which has won many awards for its French- and Swiss-style cheeses. The sampling room has tastings and a café. Burnie also has a number of gardens, including Fern Glade, where platypuses are often seen feeding at dusk and dawn. Situated on Emu Bay, the area's natural attractions include forest reserves, fossil cliffs, waterfalls and canyons and panoramic ocean views from nearby Round Hill.

"The Nut" chairlift in Stanley

Stanley ⑮

🚶 470. 🚌 ℹ️ *Stanley Visitors Centre, 45 Main Rd (03) 6458 1330.*

The rocky promontory of Circular Head, known locally as "the Nut", rises 152 m (500 ft) above sea level and looms over the fishing village of Stanley. A chairlift up the rock face offers striking views of the area.

Stanley's quiet main street runs towards the wharf, lined with fishermen's cottages and many bluestone buildings dating from the 1840s. Stanley also contains numerous top-quality bed-and-breakfasts and cafés serving fresh, local seafood *(see p517)*.

Nearby, **Highfield House** was the original headquarters of the Van Diemen's Land

Company, a London-based agricultural holding set up in 1825. The home and grounds of its colonial overseer are now open for public tours.

🏠 **Highfield House**
Green Hills Rd, via Stanley. **Tel** (03) 6458 1100. ⬜ Sep–May: 10am–4pm daily. ⬤ Jun–Aug: weekends. 🖼

King Island ⑯

✉ 🏢 Tasmanian Travel and Information Centre, cnr Davey & Elizabeth sts, Hobart (03) 6230 8233.

Lying off the northwestern coast of Tasmania in the Bass Strait, King Island is a popular location for wildlife lovers. Muttonbirds and elephant seals are among the unusual attractions.

Divers also frequent the island, fascinated by the shipwrecks that lie nearby. The island is also noted for its cheese, beef and seafood.

Woolnorth ⑰

Via Smithton. 🏢 Woolnorth Rd (03) 6452 1493. 📷 obligatory.

The huge sheep, cattle and dairy farming property on the outskirts of Smithton is the only remaining land holding of the Van Diemen's Land Company. The last four Tasmanian tigers held in captivity were caught in the bush backing on to Wool-

Elephant seal bull on King Island – males can weigh up to 3 tonnes

north in 1908. Day-long tours of the property, booked in advance, include a lunch of local beef fillet and a trip to Cape Grim, known for the cleanest air in the world.

Cradle Mountain Lake St Clair National Park ⑱

🚗 Cradle Mountain, Lake St Clair. 🏢 Cradle Mountain (03) 6492 1110 (shuttle from gate is every 20mins in summer, infrequent at other times). Lake St Clair (03) 6289 1172. 🖼 ♿

The distinctive jagged peaks of Cradle Mountain are now recognized as an international symbol of the state's natural environment. The second-highest mountain in Tasmania reaches 1,560 m (5,100 ft) at the northern end of the 161,000-ha (400,000-acre) this national park. The park then

stretches 80 km (50 miles) south to the shores of Lake St Clair, the deepest freshwater lake in Australia.

In 1922, the area became a national park, founded by Austrian nature enthusiast Gustav Weindorfer. His memory lives on in his forest home Waldheim Chalet, now a heritage lodge in Weindorfer's Forest. Nearby at Ronny Creek is the registration point for the celebrated Overland Track, which traverses the park through scenery ranging from rainforest, alpine moors, buttongrass plains and waterfall valleys. Walking the track takes an average of six days, stopping overnight in tents or huts. At the halfway mark is Mount Ossa, the state's highest peak at 1,617 m (5,300 ft). In May, the park is ablaze with the autumn colours of Tasmania's deciduous beech *Nothofagus gunnii*, commonly known as "Fagus" (*see p454*).

Lake St Clair backed by the jagged peaks of Cradle Mountain

Boats sailing on the deceptively calm waters of Macquarie Harbour

Macquarie Harbour ⑲

🚌 Strahan. 🛈 The Esplanade, Strahan (03) 6471 7622.

Off the wild, western coast of Tasmania there is nothing but vast stretches of ocean until the southern tip of Argentina, on the other side of the globe. The region bears the full brunt of the "Roaring Forties" – the name given to the tremendous winds that whip southwesterly off the Southern Ocean.

In this hostile environment, Tasmania's Aborigines survived for thousands of years before European convicts were sent here in the 1820s and took over the land. Their harsh and isolated settlement was a penal station on Sarah Island, situated in the middle of Macquarie Harbour.

The name of the harbour's mouth, "Hell's Gates", reflects conditions endured by both seamen and convicts – shipwrecks, drownings, suicides and murders all occurred here. Abandoned in 1833 for the "model prison" of Port Arthur (see pp458–9), Sarah Island and its penal settlement ruins can be viewed on a guided boat tour available from the fishing port of Strahan.

Strahan grew up around an early timber industry supported by convict labour. It became well-known in the early 1980s when protesters from across Australia came to Strahan to fight government plans to flood the wild and beautiful Franklin River for a hydroelectric scheme. A fascinating exhibition at the visitor centre in Strahan charts the drama of Australia's most famous environmental protest.

Strahan today is one of Tasmania's loveliest towns, with its old timber buildings, scenic port and natural backdrop of fretted mountains and dense bushland. The town's newest attraction is a restored 1896 railway, which travels 35 km (22 miles) across rivers and mountains to the old mining settlement at Queenstown.

Franklin-Gordon Wild Rivers National Park ⑳

🚌 Strahan. 🛈 The Esplanade, Strahan (03) 6471 7622.

One of Australia's great wild river systems flows through southwest Tasmania. This spectacular region consists of high ranges and deep gorges. The Franklin- Gordon Wild Rivers National Park extends southeast from Macquarie Harbour and is one of four national parks in the western part of Tasmania that make up the Tasmanian Wilderness World Heritage Area (see pp26–7). The park takes its name from the Franklin and Gordon rivers, both of which were saved by conservationists in 1983.

Within the park's 442,000 ha (1,090,000 acres) are vast tracts of cool temperate rainforest, as well as waterfalls and dolerite- and quartzite-capped mountains. The flora within the park is as varied as the landscape, with impenetrable horizontal scrub, lichen-coated trees, pandani plants and the endemic conifers, King William, celery top and Huon pines. The easiest way into this largely trackless wilderness is via a boat cruise from Strahan. Visitors can disembark and take a short walk to see a 2,000-year-old Huon pine. The park also contains the rugged peak of

Imposing Frenchmans Cap looming over the Franklin-Gordon Wild Rivers National Park

Idyllic, deserted beach on the rugged Bruny Island

Frenchmans Cap, accessible to experienced bushwalkers. The Franklin River is also renowned for its rapids, which challenge whitewater rafters.

The Wild Way, linking Hobart with the west coast, runs through the park. Sections of the river and forest can be reached from the main road along short tracks. Longer walks into the heart of the park require a higher level of survival skills and equipment.

Russell Falls in Mount Field National Park

Mount Field National Park ㉑

🛈 *Lake Dobson Rd, at entrance to the Park, (03) 6288 1149.*

Little more than 70 km (45 miles) from Hobart along the Maydena Road, Mount Field National Park's proximity and beauty make it a popular location with nature-loving tourists. As a day trip from

Hobart, it offers easy access to a diversity of Tasmanian vegetation and wildlife along well-maintained walking tracks.

The most popular walk is also the shortest: the 10-minute trail to Russell Falls starts out from just within the park's entrance through a temperate rainforest environment. Lake Dobson car park is 15 km (9.5 miles) from the park's entrance up a steep gravel path. This is the beginning of several other short walks and some more strenuous day walks.

The 10-km (6-mile) walk to Tarn Shelf is a bushwalker's paradise, especially in autumn, when the glacial lakes, mountains and valleys are spectacularly highlighted by the red-orange hues of the deciduous beech trees. Longer trails lead up to the higher peaks of Mount Field West and Mount Mawson, southern Tasmania's premier ski slope.

Bruny Island ㉒

Travel by car only – no public transport or taxis on Bruny Island. 🛈 *Bruny D'Entrecasteaux Visitors' Centre, ferry terminal, Kettering (03) 6267 4494.*

On Hobart's back doorstep, yet a world away in landscape and atmosphere, the Huon Valley and D'Entrecasteaux Channel can be

enjoyed over several hours or days. In total, the trip south from Hobart, through the town of Huonville, the Hartz Mountains and Southport, the southernmost town in the country, is only 100 km (60 miles). On the other side of the channel are the orchards, craft outlets and vineyards around Cygnet. The attractive marina of Kettering, just 40 minutes' drive from Hobart, is the departure point for a regular ferry service to Bruny Island.

Truganini, the Bruny Island Aborigine

The name Bruny Island actually applies to two islands joined by a narrow neck. The south island townships of Adventure Bay and Alonnah are only a half-hour drive from the ferry terminal in the north. Once home to a thriving colonial whaling industry, Bruny Island is now a haven for bird-watchers, boaters, swimmers and camel riders along its sheltered bays, beaches and lagoons.

Unfortunately, Bruny Island also has a sadder side to its history. Truganini, of the Wuenonne people of Bruny Island, is said to have been one of Tasmania's last full-blooded Aborigines. It was also from the aptly named Missionary Bay on the island that Reverend Robinson began his ill-fated campaign to round up the indigenous inhabitants of Tasmania for incarceration (*see p465*).

Port Arthur ❷

Handcuffs from Port Arthur museum

Port Arthur was established in 1830 as a timber station and a prison settlement for repeat offenders. While transportation to the island colony from the mainland ceased in 1853, the prison remained in operation until 1877, by which time some 12,000 men had passed through what was commonly regarded as the harshest institution of its kind in the British Empire. Punishments included incarceration in the Model Prison, a separate building from the main penitentiary, where inmates were subjected to sensory deprivation and extreme isolation in the belief that such methods promoted "moral reform". Between 1979 and 1986, a conservation project was undertaken to restore the prison ruins. The 40-ha (100-acre) site is now Tasmania's most popular tourist attraction.

Commandant's House
One of the first houses at Port Arthur, this cottage has now been restored and furnished in early 19th-century style.

The Semaphore was a series of flat, mounted planks that could be arranged in different configurations, in order to send messages to Hobart and across the peninsula.

MASON COVE

The Guard Tower was constructed in 1835 in order to prevent escapes from the prison and pilfering from the Commissariat Store, which the tower overlooked.

To Isle of the Dead cemetery

JETTY ROAD

0 metres 50

0 yards 50

★ Penitentiary
This building was thought to be the largest in Australia at the time of its construction in 1844. Originally a flour mill, it was converted into a penitentiary in the 1850s and housed almost 500 prisoners in dormitories and cells.

STAR FEATURES

★ Separate Prison

★ Penitentiary

For hotels and restaurants in this region see pp515–17 and pp561–3

Hospital
This sandstone building was completed in 1842 with four wards of 18 beds each. The basement housed the kitchen with its own oven, and a morgue, known as the "dead room".

Asylum
By 1872, Port Arthur's asylum housed more than 100 mentally ill or senile convicts. When the settlement closed, it became the town hall, but now serves as a museum and café.

The Paupers' Mess was the dining area for poor prisoners.

Museum and café

The Separate Prison was influenced by Pentonville Prison in London. Completed in 1849, the prison was thought to provide "humane" punishment. Convicts lived in 50 separate cells in silence and anonymity, referred to by number not by name.

Trentham Cottage was owned by the Trentham family who lived in Port Arthur after the site closed. The refurbished interior is decorated with early 19th-century furnishings.

Government Cottage was built in 1853 and was used by visiting dignitaries and government officials.

Church
Built in 1836, Port Arthur's church was never consecrated because it was used by all denominations. The building was gutted by fire in 1884, but the ruins are now fully preserved.

TRAVELLERS'
NEEDS

WHERE TO STAY 474–517

WHERE TO EAT 518–563

SHOPPING IN AUSTRALIA 564–565

SPECIALIST HOLIDAYS AND
OUTDOOR ACTIVITIES 566–569

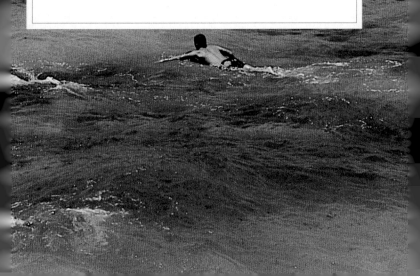

WHERE TO STAY

The wide range of places to stay in Australia is a reflection of the country's size, diversity and emergence as a major tourist destination. There are tropical island resorts, luxury and "boutique" city hotels, ski lodges, converted shearers' quarters on vast sheep stations, colonial cottage bed-and-breakfasts, self-catering apartments,

Sydney hotel doorman

youth hostels, houseboats and, of course, all the usual international chain hotels. Whether you simply want a bed for the night or an all-inclusive holiday resort, the appropriate accommodation can always be found. The listings on pages 478–517 give full descriptions of places to stay to suit all budgets throughout the country.

Art Deco façade of the Criterion Hotel in Perth (see p499)

GRADINGS AND FACILITIES

Australia has no formal national grading system. Terms such as four- and five-star are often used, but have no official imprimatur. State motoring organizations and some state and regional tourism bodies do, however, produce their own rankings and they are a useful indicator of standards and facilities.

In hotels and motels, air-conditioning in summer and heating in winter are almost always provided. Other standard features generally include coffee- and tea-making facilities, televisions, radios and refrigerators. En suite bathrooms are the norm, but specify if you want a bathtub: shower cubicles are more common. For double rooms, you will need to stipulate whether you require a double bed or twin beds. Luxury accommodation often features on-site swimming pools, exercise facilities and a hotel bar or restaurant.

PRICES

Prices for accommodation vary according to location and the facilities on offer. At the top end of the scale, the presidential, or similar, suite in a luxury hotel may have a four-figure daily rate, while a bed in a backpacker hotel will generally cost less than A$20. Budget motels and the majority of bed-and-breakfasts operate within the A$50–A$100 range. Prices may be increased slightly during peak seasons, but equally many hotels offer discount rates during the low season.

BOOKINGS

Pressure on room availability is increasing, especially in the capital cities and the Queensland coastal destinations. This becomes particularly acute during any major cultural and sporting events (see pp40–41). It is therefore advisable to book as far in advance as possible and also to specify if any special needs or requests are required.

State tourist offices can help with or make bookings. Major airlines serving Australia also often have discounted packages on offer to cater to all price ranges (see pp582–5).

CHILDREN

Travelling with children is relatively easy throughout Australia. Almost all accommodation will provide a small bed or cot in family rooms, often at no extra charge – enquire about any special rates in advance. Many major

Hyatt Hotel near the Parliamentary Triangle in Canberra (see p487)

◁ **Surfers waiting for the next big wave at Bronte Beach, Sydney**

Ornate Victorian architecture of the Vue Grand Hotel in Queenscliff *(see p512)*

hotels also offer baby-sitting services, while smaller establishments will be happy to check on a sleeping child while the parents are dining.

However, some of the country house hotels are strictly child-free zones.

Conrad Treasury luxury hotel in Brisbane *(see p488)*

DISABLED TRAVELLERS

Australian building codes now stipulate that any new buildings or renovations must provide facilities for the disabled. It is always advisable, however, to check on the facilities in advance.

LUXURY HOTELS AND RESORTS

The capital cities of each state are well endowed with luxury hotels. Well-known, international names such as **Hyatt, Hilton, Regent, Sheraton, Inter-Continental, Westin** and **Four Seasons** stand side by side with such local institutions as The Windsor in Melbourne *(see p508)*.

Major tourist destinations abound with both luxury and budget beach resorts.

CHAIN HOTELS

There are various chain hotels and motels throughout Australia, which offer reliable and comfortable, if occasionally bland and indistinctive, accommodation. They vary in style and price, but the more reasonable end of the market includes reliable and well-known chains such as **Choice Hotels**, and motels such as **Metro Inns, Best Western, Country Comfort** and **Travelodge**. These hotels are popular with business travellers and often have facilities such as fax and internet connection available.

Stained glass at Simpsons in Sydney *(see p480)*

COUNTRY HOUSE HOTELS

Country house hotels, ranging from elegant mansions to simple bed-and-breakfast cottages, now exist throughout Australia. These offer personalized accommodation and an insight into the Australian way of life, in contrast to chain hotels. Many of these hotels have only one or two rooms so that stays are extremely peaceful, with many of the comforts of home.

Among the best country houses are those found in the wine regions *(see pp36–7)*, around the old gold fields *(see pp54–5)* and in Tasmania *(see pp452–71)*. The **Australian Tourist Commission** and state tourist offices will be able to supply full, up-to-date listings of bed-and-breakfast accommodation available in each area of the country.

Indoor pool at the Observatory Hotel in Sydney *(see p481)*

"The Grand" ballroom in the Windsor Hotel, Melbourne *(see p508)*

BOUTIQUE HOTELS

Many of the "boutique" hotels in Australia offer high-quality accommodation, often with luxury facilities, within an intimate atmosphere and few rooms.

Most boutique hotels do not advertise in glossy brochures, but operate through recommendations. However, tourist offices can provide information and many can be found on the internet. Some of the best are also listed on the following pages.

Australian bed and breakfasts (B&Bs), many in heritage-listed premises, also tend to be of a high standard. They range from farmstays to glamorous country house hotels.

BACKPACKER HOTELS AND YOUTH HOSTELS

One of the fastest growing areas of Australia's accommodation industry is hotels for the increasing number of young backpackers. Despite their budget prices and basic facilities, the majority are clean and comfortable, although standards can vary widely in different areas. The internationally renowned **Youth Hostel Association** also has its own chain of hostels across the country, in all the major cities, ski resorts and many of the national parks. These offer clean and comfortable accommodation, particularly for those travellers on a tight budget.

Backpackers' resort sign

While it is necessary to book in advance at some hostels, others do not take bookings and beds are on a first come, first served basis. Apartments, rooms and dormitories are all available, but dormitories may be mixed sex, so check, if necessary, before arriving.

The backpacker scene changes quickly, so it is often worth asking other travellers for the latest developments and for their recommendations, as well as gathering up-to-date information from the state tourist offices.

It is also worth remembering that, despite its name, the Youth Hostel Association also caters for senior citizens.

PUB ACCOMMODATION

Australian pubs are generally also referred to as hotels because historically they accommodated travellers. Many pubs still offer bed-and-breakfast accommodation. The quality can vary, but they are usually good value for money.

SELF-CATERING APARTMENTS

Self-Catering apartments are the latest accommodation trend in Australia. Full kitchen and laundry facilities are usually provided. Within cities, some apartments also cater for business travellers, complete with fax and other communications amenities.

Ornate Victorian Lenna of Hobart Hotel in Tasmania's capital *(see p516)*

Classic Australian pub accommodation at the Bellbird Hotel in the Hunter Valley *(see p482)*

Prices can vary, but they are generally on a par with the major chain motels.

FARM STAYS AND HOUSEBOATS

Many large sheep and cattle stations have now opened their doors to the public, and welcome visitors for farm stays. These offer a unique insight into rural Australian life. Many are situated near major cities, while others are located in the vast Outback *(see pp28–9)*. Accommodation may be in traditional shearers' or cattle herders' quarters, or within the homestead itself. A stay usually includes the opportunity to become involved in the daily working life of the station. State tourist offices will supply all necessary details.

Another interesting and very relaxing holiday can be had on a houseboat along the vast Murray River which crosses from New South Wales and Victoria to South Australia. An international driving licence is the only requirement to be your own riverboat captain.

CAMPING AND CARAVAN PARKS

Camp sites for both tents and caravans are found throughout the country, with the majority dotted along the vast coastline and in the many inland national parks. This form of accommodation offers a cheap and idyllic way of enjoying the natural beauty and wildlife of Australia.

Many camp sites allow "walk in" camping without the need for booking, provided space is available. However, some areas may require a camping permit, so it is always advisable to check with state or local tourist offices in advance.

The majority of caravan parks have on-site vans for rent at relatively low prices. Facilities usually include adequate laundry and shower blocks and often a small general store for basic food and drink supplies.

DIRECTORY

TOURIST OFFICES

Australian Tourist Commission UK
10–18 Putney Hill, London SW15 6AA.
Tel (020) 8780 2229.

United States
Suite 1920, 2049 Century Park East, Los Angeles, CA 90067.
Tel (310) 229 4870.

Tourism ACT
333 Northbourne Ave, ACT 2602. *Tel 6205 0044.*
www.visitcanberra.com.au

Tourism NSW
106 George St, Sydney, NSW 2000. *Tel 13 20 77.*

Queensland Travel Centre
The Mall, Brisbane, QLD 4001. *Tel 138 833.*

Tourism Top End
38 Mitchell St, Darwin NT 0801. *Tel (08) 8999 5511.*
www.ntholidays.com.au

Western Australia Tourist Centre
469 Wellington St, Perth, WA 6000.
Tel 1300 361 351.
www.westernaustralia.com

South Australian Travel Centre
1 King William St, Adelaide, SA 5000.
Tel 1300 655 276.
www.southaustralia.com

Tourism Victoria
55 Collins St, Melbourne, VIC 3000.
Tel 132 842.
www.visitvictoria.com.au

Tourism Tasmania
22 Elizabeth St, Hobart, Tasmania 7000. *Tel (03) 6230 8235.* **www**.discovertasmania.com

LUXURY HOTELS

Four Seasons
Tel 1800 222 200.

Hilton
Tel (02) 9287 0707.

Hyatt
Tel 131 234.

InterContinental
Tel 1300 363 300.

Sheraton
Tel 1800 073 535.

Westin
Tel 1800 656 535.

Regent Hotels
Tel (02) 9333 8669.

CHAIN HOTELS

Best Western
Tel 131 779.

Country Comfort
Tel 1800 065 064.

Choice Hotels
Tel 132 400.

Metro Inns
Tel 1800 004 321.

Travelodge
Tel 1300 728 628.

BACKPACKER HOTELS AND YOUTH HOSTELS

YHA Australia
422 Kent St, Sydney, NSW 2000.
Tel (02) 9261 1111.

Choosing a Hotel

The hotels in this guide have been selected for their good value, excellent facilities and location. The chart lists the hotels by region, starting with Sydney, in the same order as the rest of the guide. Within each region, entries are listed alphabetically within each price category, from the least to the most expensive.

PRICE CATEGORIES
For a standard double room per night inclusive of breakfast, service charges and additional taxes:
$ under A$100
$$ A$100–$150
$$$ A$150–$200
$$$$ A$200–$250
$$$$$ over A$250

SYDNEY

BONDI BEACH Ravesi's $$$$
Cnr Campbell Parade and Hall Street, NSW 2026 **Tel** *(02) 9365 4422* **Fax** *(02) 9365 1481* **Rooms** *12*

This lovely boutique hotel has recently been refurbished and epitomizes the relaxed style of beach life at Bondi. Split-level suites cost more but are gorgeous, opening onto private terraces with ocean views. There is also a restaurant downstairs and a popular bar *(see p524)*. **www.ravesis.com.au**

BONDI BEACH Swiss Grand Resort & Spa $$$$$
Cnr Campbell Parade and Beach Road, NSW 2026 **Tel** *(02) 9365 5666* **Fax** *(02) 9365 5330* **Rooms** *203*

This all-suite hotel is a kitsch take on the style of the French Riviera. Its exterior of terraces and balustrades looks a little like a giant wedding cake. Inside, marble adorns the lobby's every surface. Unbeatable location right on the beachfront, full resort and facilities, a rooftop pool, and two bars and restaurants. **www.swissgrand.com.au**

BONDI JUNCTION The Tiffany Serviced Apartments $$$$
95–97 Grafton Street, Bondi Junction, NSW 2022 **Tel** *(02) 9388 9700* **Fax** *(02) 9388 0391* **Rooms** *140*

Built above the Bondi Junction bus and train interchange, these two-bedroom apartments have views of Sydney Harbour or the ocean. Great features include full-sized kitchens and laundries, pools, tennis courts and virtual golf. **www.meritonapartments.com.au**

BOTANIC GARDENS AND THE DOMAIN Sydney Inter-Continental $$$$$
117 Macquarie Street, Sydney, NSW 2000 **Tel** *(02) 9253 9000* **Fax** *(02) 9240 1240* **Rooms** *509*   **Map** *1 C3*

The foyer and lower stories of this luxurious hotel are made up of part of the 1851 Treasury Building. Well-equipped rooms have window seats, chaise longues and views of the city or harbour and Botanic Gardens. High tea is served in the lobby for guests and visitors. **www.sydney.intercontinental.com**

BOTANIC GARDENS AND THE DOMAIN Sir Stamford at Circular Quay $$$$$
93 Macquarie Street, Sydney, NSW 2000 **Tel** *(02) 9252 4600* **Fax** *(02) 9252 4286* **Rooms** *105*   **Map** *1 C3*

The decor is built around the hotel's collection of 18th-century antiques and fine art. Paying a little extra per night allows guests access to the Executive Lounge, and with it a host of benefits including complimentary breakfast, snacks, drinks, garment pressing, faxes and cheap limos. **www.stamford.com.au**

CITY CENTRE Railway Square YHA $
8–10 Lee Street, Sydney, NSW 2000 **Tel** *(02) 9281 9666* **Fax** *(02) 9281 9688* **Rooms** *64*   **Map** *4 E5*

Located in a historic 1904 building, this YHA hostel adjoins Central Station's 'Platform Zero'. Some rooms are inside converted railway carriages, while others are in the main building. There's an internet café, over-sized spa pool, tour desk and 24-hour access. They do not accept Diners or American Express. **www.yha.com.au**

CITY CENTRE Y Hotel $$
5–11 Wentworth Avenue, Sydney, NSW 2000 **Tel** *(02) 9264 2451* **Fax** *(02) 9285 6288* **Rooms** *121*   **Map** *4 F3*

Expect less of the party crowd at this peaceful backpacker spot, since all dorm rooms have just four single beds and are single-sex. Standard double rooms are basic but clean and have shared toilets. Rooms with en suites and more luxurious amenities are still very reasonably priced. **www.yhotel.com.au**

CITY CENTRE Castlereagh Boutique Hotel $$$
169–171 Castlereagh Street, Sydney, NSW 2000 **Tel** *(02) 9284 1000, 1800 801 576* **Rooms** *82*   **Map** *1 B5*

Full of character, this hotel is great value. Don't miss the plush old-fashioned dining room, decorated with chandeliers and elaborate paint and plasterwork. The rooms, furnished with period pieces and patterned upholstery, offer essentials such as televisions, bars, fridges, and tea and coffee facilities. **www.thecastlereagh.net.au**

CITY CENTRE Hotel Mercure Sydney $$$
818–820 George Street, NSW 2000 **Tel** *(02) 9217 6666* **Fax** *(02) 9217 6888* **Rooms** *517*   **Map** *4 D5*

Close to trains and buses which depart from Central Station and Railway Square, this hotel is also a comfortable walking distance from Darling Harbour and Chinatown. It is a popular choice for families because two children are able to stay for free in their parents' room. **www.mecuresydney.com**

Key to Symbols *see back cover flap*

CITY CENTRE Waldorf Apartment Hotel $$$

57 Liverpool Street, NSW 2000 **Tel** *(02) 9261 5355* **Fax** *(02) 9261 3753* **Rooms** *40*   **Map** *4 E3*

From this handy hotel, it's a short stroll to the city shopping centres and cinemas and a slightly longer one to Darling Harbour's attractions. The apartments are spacious, with balconies overlooking the city. Facilities include a rooftop pool and complimentary in-house movies. **www.waldorf.com.au**

CITY CENTRE Central Park Hotel $$$$

185 Castlereagh Street, Sydney, NSW 2000 **Tel** *(02) 9283 5000* **Fax** *(02) 9283 2710* **Rooms** *35*   **Map** *1 B4*

Their "hip on a budget" slogan is a great description of this boutique hotel located above a popular bar and restaurant. It offers reasonably priced studio rooms, light and airy New York-style loft suites and smaller rooms with cable television, CD players and large granite bathrooms. **www.centralpark.com.au**

CITY CENTRE Meriton World Tower $$$$

91–95 Liverpool Street, Sydney, NSW 2000 **Tel** *(02) 8263 7500* **Fax** *(02) 9261 5722* **Rooms** *114*   **Map** *4 E3*

Some serviced apartments are available short term in this brand new vertical village, the tallest residential building in Sydney. Spacious two bedroom apartments can sleep up to five. Everything guests might need is just a short stroll away and facilities include a gym and child-minding centre. **www.meritonapartments.com.au**

CITY CENTRE Establishment Hotel $$$$$

5 Bridge Lane, Sydney, NSW 2000 **Tel** *(02) 9240 3100* **Fax** *(02) 9240 3101* **Rooms** *31*   **Map** *1 B3*

One of the most fashionable places in town. Two penthouses and 29 rooms offer a choice of lively or tranquil colour schemes, marble or stone bathrooms with separate baths and showers. Although there are eight bars, two restaurants and a nightclub in the building, sound-proofing ensures a peaceful stay. **www.establishmenthotel.com**

CITY CENTRE Hilton Sydney $$$$$

488 George Street, Sydney, NSW 2000 **Tel** *(02) 9266 2000* **Rooms** *577*   **Map** *1 B5*

An enormous renovation was carried out on this hotel, with the aim of setting new standards in luxury. The slick new design is immediately apparent and upgraded features include stylish interior design, quality furniture, LCD televisions and avant-garde internet phones. **www.hiltonsydney.com.au**

CITY CENTRE Sheraton on the Park $$$$$

161 Elizabeth Street, Sydney, NSW 2000 **Tel** *(02) 9286 6000* **Fax** *(02) 9286 6686* **Rooms** *557*   **Map** *1 B5*

Arriving at this hotel's very grand entrance, it's clear that no expense has been spared. Amenities include marble bathrooms, stylish furnishings, 24-hour room service, helpful concierges and lounges. Many rooms have views over Hyde Park. **www.sheraton.com/sydney**

CITY CENTRE Sofitel Wentworth $$$$$

61–101 Phillip Street, Sydney, NSW 2000 **Tel** *(02) 9230 0700* **Fax** *(02) 9228 9133* **Rooms** *436*   **Map** *1 B4*

Located in the heart of Sydney's Central Business District (CBD), this hotel is only minutes away from the Sydney Opera House, The Rocks, the Harbour Bridge and the Royal Botanic Gardens. It provides a luxury experience, successfully blending 21st-century design with the hotel's heritage-listed features. **www.accorhotels.com.au**

CITY CENTRE The York $$$$$

5 York Street, Sydney, NSW 2000 **Tel** *(02) 9210 5000* **Fax** *(02) 9290 1487* **Rooms** *130*   **Map** *1 A3*

There is an understated elegance throughout this centrally located hotel. Each of its apartments is individually designed and has a balcony, fully equipped modern kitchen and large bathroom. Apartments vary in size from studios to executive two-bedroom penthouses. **www.theyorkapartments.com.au**

COOGEE Dive Hotel $$$

234 Arden Street, Coogee, NSW 2034 **Tel** *(02) 9665 5538* **Fax** *(02) 9665 4347* **Rooms** *14*

A stylish hotel, its rooms have polished floorboards, high ceilings and designer bathrooms. This is a great sanctuary from the backpacker madness of Coogee Beach. The two front rooms have spectacular views. **www.divehotel.com.au**

DARLING HARBOUR Carlton Crest Hotel Sydney $$$

169–179 Thomas Street, Haymarket, NSW 2000 **Tel** *(02) 9281 6888* **Fax** *(02) 9281 6688* **Rooms** *251* **Map** *4 D5*

Located near Paddy's Market in Chinatown, this reasonable hotel is close to many city attractions. All rooms and suites are large. Guest facilities include a rooftop pool, barbecue area and garden. The hotel specializes in arranging theatre tickets and usually offers several packages. **www.carltonhotels.com.au/sydney**

DARLING HARBOUR Four Points By Sheraton $$$$

161 Sussex Street, Sydney, NSW 2000 **Tel** *(02) 9290 4000* **Fax** *(02) 9290 4040* **Rooms** *630*   **Map** *4 D2*

With 630 rooms, this is Australia's largest hotel. Located on the CBD side of Darling Harbour, it is close to restaurant and entertainment areas, including King Street and Cockle Bay wharfs. The hotel is also an easy walk from the Queen Victoria Building and Town Hall station. There is a great fitness centre. **www.fourpoints.com**

DARLING HARBOUR Holiday Inn Darling Harbour $$$$

68 Harbour Street, Darling Harbour, NSW 2000 **Tel** *(02) 9281 0400* **Fax** *(02) 9281 1212* **Rooms** *304*   **Map** *4 D3*

Perfectly located in the dynamic heart of Darling Harbour. The restaurant offers à la carte and casual dining plus a breakfast buffet, and guests can cook their own lunches on the stonegrill in the hotel's pub. Children eat for free. **www.holidayinndarlingharbour.com.au**

DARLING HARBOUR Novotel Sydney on Darling Harbour $$$$

100 Murray Street, Pyrmont, NSW 2009 **Tel** *(02) 9934 0000* **Fax** *(02) 9934 0099* **Rooms** *525*   **Map** *3 C2*

This modern superstructure towers above the Harbourside centre at Darling Harbour, close to the Powerhouse and Maritime museums. The rooms are four and a half-star quality and have views across the city. In cooler weather, guests can visit the Imax Theatre or play tennis instead. **www.noveldarlingharbour.com.au**

DOUBLE BAY Sir Stamford Plaza $$$$$

33 Cross Street, Double Bay, NSW 2028 **Tel** *(02) 9362 4455* **Fax** *(02) 9362 4744* **Rooms** *140*   **Map** *6 F1*

Guests can enjoy old-world style at this sumptuous hotel. The rooms are large and traditionally decorated, and the hotel's proximity to the classiest shopping precinct in Sydney is unbeatable. The central courtyard is in the style of a Mediterranean villa garden while the rooftop heated pool has fabulous views. **www.stamford.com.au**

KINGS CROSS AND DARLINGHURST The Chelsea $$

49 Womerah Avenue, Darlinghurst, NSW 2010 **Tel** *(02) 9380 5994* **Fax** *(02) 9332 2491* **Rooms** *13*   **Map** *5 C1*

This beautiful guesthouse is decorated in French Provincial and contemporary styles. Particularly popular with businesswomen, the establishment is gay and lesbian friendly. On-street parking is usually available nearby and it is a short walk to Oxford Street or the waterfront at Rushcutters Bay. **www.chelseaguesthouse.com.au**

KINGS CROSS AND DARLINGHURST Hotel Altamont $$

207 Darlinghurst Road, Sydney, NSW 2010 **Tel** *(02) 9360 6000, 1800 991 110* **Rooms** *14*   **Map** *5 A2*

At this fun budget hotel, formerly a Georgian mansion, all standard rooms have king- or queen-sized beds and solid, comfy wooden furniture. There are discount weekly rates and a few good quality backpacker rooms: they fill up quickly so book early. Even those rooms include cable television. **www.altamont.com.au**

KINGS CROSS AND DARLINGHURST L'otel $$

114 Darlinghurst Road, NSW 2010 **Tel** *(02) 9360 6868* **Fax** *(02) 9331 4536* **Rooms** *16*   **Map** *5 A2*

A large terrace house has been converted into a designer hotel with small but lovely rooms decorated in white on white French Provincial style with painted furniture and art pieces. There's a hip bar and restaurant downstairs, and the hotel is close to Oxford Street's cafés and bars. **www.lotel.com.au**

KINGS CROSS AND DARLINGHURST Medusa $$

267 Darlinghurst Road, Darlinghurst, NSW 2010 **Tel** *(02) 9331 1000* **Fax** *(02) 9380 6901* **Rooms** *18*   **Map** *5 B1*

Medusa makes its own rules as only a boutique hotel can. This old Victorian house has been transformed into a brightly coloured miracle of modernism, with inspiration from Caravaggio's *Medusa*. Lindt chocolates and Aveda toiletries are complimentary, as is use of a neighbouring gym. **www.medusa.com.au**

KINGS CROSS AND DARLINGHURST Morgan's Boutique Hotel $$

304 Victoria Street, Darlinghurst, NSW 2010 **Tel** *(02) 9360 7955* **Fax** *(02) 9360 9217* **Rooms** *26*   **Map** *2 E5*

This boutique Art Deco hotel is set in a leafy location in the café district and has a Japanese stone garden courtyard and fountain. It also has an upmarket restaurant serving breakfast, lunch and dinner. Rooms have cable and kitchens, and can accommodate a third person for a small extra charge. **www.morganshotel.com.au**

KINGS CROSS AND DARLINGHURST Simpsons of Potts Point $$$

8 Challis Avenue, Potts Point, 2011 **Tel** *(02) 9356 2199* **Fax** *(02) 9356 4476* **Rooms** *12*   **Map** *2 E4*

A charming B&B at the "Paris" end of Potts Point, where the complimentary breakfast is served in a glass-roofed conservatory. Built in 1892 as a family residence, the hotel has been exquisitely restored and boasts elegantly designed rooms. Guests staying in the romantic Cloud Suite enjoy a private spa bath. **www.simpsonshotel.com**

KINGS CROSS AND DARLINGHURST Regents Court $$$

18 Springfield Avenue, Potts Point, NSW 2011 **Tel** *(02) 9358 1533* **Fax** *(02) 9358 1833* **Rooms** *30*   **Map** *2 E5*

An innovative team transformed this Art Deco gentlemen's chambers into a stylish boutique hotel, favoured by artists, actors and writers. Each spacious and well-equipped studio sleeps two adults, in either twin or queen beds. A rooftop garden has great views over the city, particularly at sunset. **www.regentscourt.com.au**

KINGS CROSS AND DARLINGHURST W Sydney $$$$$

6 Cowper Wharf Road, Woolloomooloo, NSW 2011 **Tel** *(02) 9331 9000* **Fax** *(02) 9331 9031* **Rooms** *140*   **Map** *2 D5*

This hotel's glamour and reputation as the coolest in Sydney makes up for the far from spacious rooms. There is a fabulous cocktail bar and a row of great restaurants below on the fingerwharf. All rooms, including 36 loft rooms, are equipped with cutting-edge business technology and 27-inch television screens. **www.whotels.com**

MANLY Manly Pacific $$$$$

55 North Steyne, Manly, NSW 2095 **Tel** *(02) 9977 7666* **Fax** *(02) 9977 7822* **Rooms** *218*

Manly's ocean beach is one of Sydney's most famous, host to ironman competitions and triathalons, herds of surfers and plenty of people (tourists and locals) just after a sun tan. Situated right on the beach, this hotel has unbeatable views of sand and surf. All rooms are light and spacious with balconies. **www.accorhotels.com**

MANLY Periwinkle Manly Cove Guest House $$$$$

18–19 East Esplanade, Manly, NSW 2095 **Tel** *(02) 9977 4668* **Fax** *(02) 9977 6308* **Rooms** *18*

A striking Federation-era mansion has been converted into a B&B with antique furniture and tasteful colour schemes. Rooms with a view attract only a small premium. High ceilings, wrought-iron verandas and a leafy courtyard are features. There are private outdoor areas. **www.periwinkle.citysearch.com.au**

Key to Price Guide *see p478* **Key to Symbols** *see back cover flap*

NEWTOWN Rydges Camperdown $$$

*9 Missenden Road, Camperdown, NSW 2050 **Tel** (02) 9516 1522 **Fax** (02) 9519 4020 **Rooms** 144*

One of the few hotels in the gay and lesbian enclaves of Newtown and Camperdown. The hotel is also near Parramatta Road where buses leave for the city and Leichhardt. Relax in the pool, sauna or games room. The bar has a daily happy hour between 5:30 and 6:30pm. **www.rydges.com**

PADDINGTON Hughenden Boutique Hotel $$$

*14 Queen Street, Woollahra, NSW 2025 **Tel** (02) 9363 4863 **Fax** (02) 9362 0398 **Rooms** 36 Map 6 E4*

This rambling old building, once a 19th-century family home, has been restored to its original grandeur. Rooms are comfortably furnished and the restaurant is very good. Writers' groups meet and artists exhibit their work, providing a connection to the surrounding arty community. **www.hughendenhotel.com.au**

PADDINGTON Sullivans $$$$

*21 Oxford Street, Paddington, NSW 2021 **Tel** (02) 9361 0211 **Fax** (02) 9360 3735 **Rooms** 64 Map 5 B3*

Standard rooms at this family owned hotel face the bustle of Oxford Street. It's worth paying a tiny bit more for a garden room which overlooks the courtyard and swimming pool. The restaurant, with its large windows looking out onto Oxford Street, is a great place to people watch. **www.sullivans.com.au**

SURRY HILLS Medina on Crown $$$$$

*359 Crown Street, Surry Hills, NSW 2010 **Tel** (02) 8302 1000 **Fax** (02) 9361 5965 **Rooms** 85 Map 5 A1*

Close to the groovy Crown Street shops and restaurants, Sydney Cricket Ground and the Entertainment Quarter at Fox Studios, this hotel is a favourite with visiting rock bands. It is also right above the legendary restaurants, Bills 2, Marque and Billy Kwong. Apartments are spacious and have full kitchens. **www.medinaapartments.com.au**

THE ROCKS AND CIRCULAR QUAY Mercantile Hotel $$

*25 George Street, The Rocks, NSW 2000 **Tel** (02) 9247 3570 **Fax** (02) 9247 7047 **Rooms** 15 Map 1 B2*

This is a good choice for fans of pub accommodation, its George Street location means all of the Rocks attractions are nearby, including the Arglye Cut and Garrison Church. The hotel boasts spacious rooms containing period fittings and marble fireplaces. The basic rate is for a room with a shared bathroom (en suite costs a little more).

THE ROCKS AND CIRCULAR QUAY Lord Nelson Brewery Hotel $$$

*19 Kent Street, The Rocks, NSW 2000 **Tel** (02) 9251 4044 **Fax** (02) 9251 1532 **Rooms** 9 Map 1 A2*

The top floor of the celebrated pub, famous for its home brews, offers cosy bedrooms with stone walls and rustic furnishings. There are two basic rooms with shared bathrooms, for those not on a tight budget en suite rooms are available for $180 per night. It's an easy walk to Circular Quay. **www.lordnelson.com.au**

THE ROCKS AND CIRCULAR QUAY Rendezvous Stafford $$$$

*75 Harrington Street, The Rocks, NSW 2000 **Tel** (02) 9251 6711 **Fax** (02) 9251 3458 **Rooms** 61 Map 1 B2*

There really is something for everyone at this unusual boutique hotel. Most rooms are studio and one-bedroom apartments with good kitchen facilities. There are also more suites available in seven 1870 terrace houses nearby. There are excellent business services, a spa, pool and sauna. **www.rendezvoushotels.com**

THE ROCKS AND CIRCULAR QUAY The Observatory Hotel $$$$$

*89–113 Kent Street, Millers Point, NSW 2000 **Tel** (02) 9256 2222 **Fax** (02) 9256 2233 **Rooms** 99 Map 1 A2*

This luxury hotel is one of Sydney's most expensive, but there are often great internet deals. It is tastefully furnished, with original antiques and fine artwork. Excellent facilities for the business traveller don't end at the door, a limousine is on hand to chauffeur guests to morning meetings. **www.observatoryhotel.com.au**

THE ROCKS AND CIRCULAR QUAY Old Sydney Holiday Inn $$$$$

*55 George Street, The Rocks, NSW 2000 **Tel** (02) 9252 0524 **Fax** (02) 9251 2093 **Rooms** 175 Map 1 B2*

Big enough to offer all the facilities of a grand establishment, this hotel is also small enough to provide personal attention. Great location within the historic Rocks area and close to Circular Quay and the Sydney Opera House. The view from the sparkling blue rooftop pool is spectacular. **www.holidayinn.com.au**

THE ROCKS AND CIRCULAR QUAY Park Hyatt Sydney $$$$$

*7 Hickson Road, The Rocks, NSW 2000 **Tel** (02) 9241 1234 **Fax** (02) 9256 1555 **Rooms** 158 Map 1 B1*

Many rooms in this five-star hotel have views of the Opera House, as does the rooftop swimming pool. Walking up the road for a few minutes takes you to the small park beneath the Harbour Bridge, a few mintues in the other direction to Circular Quay. Well equipped for business travellers. **sydney.park.hyatt.com**

THE ROCKS AND CIRCULAR QUAY The Sebel Pier One Sydney $$$$$

*11 Hickson Road, Walsh Bay, NSW 2000 **Tel** (02) 8298 9999 **Fax** (02) 8298 9777 **Rooms** 161 Map 1 A2*

This is Sydney's first over-the-water hotel, built on a 1912 fingerwharf in the Walsh Bay World Heritage precinct, beside the Harbour Bridge. The hotel's luxurious rooms combine original features with contemporary design. Look right into the water through the lobby's glass floor. **www.mirvachotels.com.au**

THE ROCKS AND CIRCULAR QUAY Shangri-La $$$$$

*176 Cumberland Street, The Rocks, NSW 2000 **Tel** (02) 9250 6000 **Fax** (02) 9250 6250 **Rooms** 563 Map 1 A3*

This hotel has just spent A$31 million on a complete refurbishment and it shows. The spacious rooms are now decorated in neutral tones with rich gold brocade highlights. On the top floor, Altitude restaurant and the Blu Horizon bar are popular dining and night spots. **www.shangri-la.com**

THE BLUE MOUNTAINS AND BEYOND

ARMIDALE Abbotsleigh Motor Inn $$

76 Barney Street, Armidale, NSW 2350 **Tel** *(02) 6772 9488* **Fax** *(02) 6772 7066* **Rooms** *33*

Situated amongst the gorge country of Oxley Wild Rivers National Park and surrounded by native wilderness, this motor inn has a licensed restaurant open from Monday to Thursday. The staff at Abbotsleigh's tour desk can provide you with plenty of information, plus they offer guided tours. **www.armidaleabbotsleighmotorinn.com.au**

BALLINA Ballina Heritage Inn $$

229 River Street, Ballina, NSW 2478 **Tel** *(02) 6686 0505* **Fax** *(02) 6686 0788* **Rooms** *27*

Ballina got its name from an Aboriginal word meaning "place where oysters are plentiful", and this still rings true in this seafood-rich region. Close to seafood restaurants, this comfortable motel prides itself on service, offering babysitting facilities so parents can relax and enjoy the local offerings. **www.ballinaheritageinn.com.au**

BARRINGTON TOPS Barrington Guest House $$$$

2940 Salisbury Road, Salisbury via Dungog, NSW 2420 **Tel** *(02) 4995 3212* **Fax** *(02) 4995 3248* **Rooms** *40*

A venue offering a range of ecotourism-based escapes for all ages. Guests will enjoy interacting with native wildlife and accessing some of the finest natural freshwater swimming spots in Australia. The restaurant serves generous, country style meals. American express and Diners cards are not accepted. **www.barringtonguesthouse.com.au**

BLACKHEATH High Mountains Motor Inn $$

193 Great Western Highway, Blackheath, NSW 2785 **Tel** *(02) 4787 8216* **Fax** *(02) 4787 7802* **Rooms** *21*

The 21 ground-floor rooms are comfortable and affordable. But for guests preferring something larger, there are also two inter-connected cottages – ideal for a family or large group. The motel is conveniently located near the local village centre and also provides a home-made room service breakfast. **www.highmountainsmotel.com**

BLUE MOUNTAINS Lilianfels $$$$$

Lilianfels Avenue, Echo Point, Katoomba, NSW 2780 **Tel** *(02) 4780 1200* **Fax** *(02) 4780 1300* **Rooms** *85*

Following a multi-million dollar refurbishment, this historic country house, set amidst two acres of English-style gardens, continues to offer idyllic escapes for romantics, as well as for lovers of great food and stunning scenery. Both the house and its restaurant, Darley's, have won many prestigious awards. **www.lilianfels.com.au**

BYRON BAY The Oasis Resort $$$

24 Scott Street, Byron Bay, NSW 2481 **Tel** *(02) 66857390* **Fax** *(02) 6685 8290* **Rooms** *24*

A venue that allows guests to select their style of accommodation between spacious Mediterranean-style apartments and secluded tree-top vacation houses with private decks and outdoor spas. If stairs are a problem, try the cottage next door featuring modern Asian interior and design. **www.byronbayoasisresort.com.au**

COFFS HARBOUR Pelican Beach Resort $$$$$

Pacific Highway, Coffs Harbour, NSW 2450 **Tel** *(02) 6653 7000* **Fax** *(02) 6653 7066* **Rooms** *112*

This resort features a range of accommodation choices – from self-contained independence to 24-hr luxury service. Take advantage of the mini golf, tennis or volleyball on offer or enrol the children in the fun kids' club and and enjoy uninterrupted relaxation by the beautiful pool. **www.australishotels.com**

DUBBO Country Comfort Ashwood Resort $$

Cnr Newell Highway and East Street, Dubbo, NSW 2830 **Tel** *(02) 6881 8700* **Fax** *(02) 6881 8930* **Rooms** *39*

This family-friendly hotel is only ten minutes' walk from the famous Western Plains Zoo, and offers a range of interconnecting rooms as well as executive and honeymoon suites. Kids and adults alike will enjoy using the tennis court, swimming pool and spa, and good business facilities are also provided. **www.ashwoodresort.com.au**

FAULCONBRIDGE Rose Lindsay Cottage $$$$

113 Chapman Parade, Faulconbridge, NSW 2776 **Tel** *(02) 4751 4273* **Fax** *(02) 4751 9497* **Rooms** *3*

Rambling wildflowers surround this beautifully private sandstone cottage – designed by Rose, the wife of famed Australian artist Norman Lindsay. Take a seat amongst the fragrant, secluded garden, home to native birdlife and fauna. They do not accept American Express or Diners cards. **www.roselindsay.com.au**

HARTLEY VALE Collit's Inn $$$$$

Lot 101 Hartley Vale Road, Hartley Vale, NSW 2790 **Tel** *(02) 6355 2072* **Fax** *(02) 6355 2073* **Rooms** *4*

The rooms and larger stables cottage at Collit's Inn are not air conditioned. Instead, this 1823 double-brick building, built to serve the first explorers over the Blue Mountains, keeps perfectly cool all year round. There is also a French restaurant, which has won awards now too numerous to list since opening in 2002. **www.collitsinn.com.au**

HUNTER VALLEY The Bellbird Hotel $

388 Wollombi Road, Bellbird, NSW 2325 **Tel** *(02) 4990 1094* **Fax** *(02) 4991 5475* **Rooms** *15*

Within minutes of the valley's famous wineries *(see p174)* and golf courses, this historic pub built in 1914 offers bed-and-breakfast. A typical turn-of-the-century Australian country hotel it has a large beergarden and a reliable bistro. They have live music every Sunday afternoon.

Key to Price Guide *see p478* **Key to Symbols** *see back cover flap*

KATOOMBA Mercure Grand Hotel Hydro Majestic

Great Western Highway, Medlow Bath, NSW 2780 **Tel** *(02) 4788 1002* **Fax** *(02) 4788 1131* **Rooms** *84*

This fine establishment has long set the benchmark for impeccable accommodation in the Blue Mountains. Guests are treated like royalty from the moment they arrive, and indeed the views are equally majestic. The Hydro Majestic is the ultimate experience in luxury and indulgence. **www.hydromajestic.com.au**

LITHGOW Eagle View Escape

Lots 12 & 13 Sandalls Drive, Rydal via Lake Lyell, NSW 2790 **Tel/Fax** *(02) 6355 6311* **Rooms** *24*

Catering exclusively for couples, Eagle View provides all the ingredients for a truly romantic getaway. Three room styles are offered – wilderness spa cabins, studio spa suites or executive spa suites. There's no restaurant, but all kinds of meals can be arranged. They do not accept American Express or Diners cards. **www.eagleview.com.au**

MUDGEE Cobb & Co Court Boutique Hotel

97 Market Street, Mudgee, NSW 2850 **Tel** *(02) 6372 7245* **Fax** *(02) 6372 7525* **Rooms** *10*

Crisp, white linen sheets await guests at this delightful boutique hotel, close to the region's many wineries. Each room is stylishly decorated and features a spa, individually controlled air conditioning and much more. The hotel's Wineglass Restaurant and Patisserie Café serve loads of tasty local produce. **www.cobbandcocourt.com.au**

NEWCASTLE Crowne Plaza

Cnr Merewether Street and Wharf Rd, Newcastle, NSW 2300 **Tel** *(02) 4907 5000* **Fax** *(02) 4907 5055* **Rooms** *175*

This award-winning venue provides all you could ask for in a hotel. Situated in front of the foreshore promenade leading past the historic Nobby's Lighthouse and five kilometres of picturesque walking path, the Crowne Plaza features a 25-metre pool and gym. **www.crowneplaza.com.au**

NULKABA Hunter Valley YHA

100 Wine Country Drive, Nulkaba, NSW 2325 **Tel** *(02) 4991 32 78* **Fax** *(02) 4991 3278* **Rooms** *13*

In the heart of wine country, this hostel joined the YHA family in late 2005 and is well located at the gateway to the region's attractions. The lodge runs daily wine tours, and bikes are available for free. The outdoor eating area has a woodfired pizza oven for guests to use. American Express and Diners cards are not accepted. **www.yha.com.au**

POKOLBIN Tower Lodge

Halls Road, Pokolbin, NSW 2320 **Tel** *(02) 4998 7022* **Fax** *(02) 4998 7164* **Rooms** *12*

This stunning retreat offers a luxurious getaway for the most discerning of guests. Each of its 12 rooms has been individually styled, and one even features an outdoor plunge tub. Orlando Bloom and Kate Bosworth are among the many famous guests who have stayed here. The dining room serves breakfasts only. **www.towerlodge.com.au**

PORT STEPHENS Peppers Anchorage

Corlette Point Road, Corlette, Port Stephens, NSW 2315 **Tel** *(02) 4984 2555* **Fax** *(02) 4984 0300* **Rooms** *80*

Making the most of its water frontage, all rooms at Peppers have balconies which overlook the waters beneath the Anchorage Marina. Whether you opt for the cosy Loft Suite or supremely decadent Master Suite, you will experience absolute luxury. Be sure not to miss out on a meal at Merrett's restaurant. **www.peppers.com.au**

TAMWORTH Plumes on the Green

25 The Ringers Road, Tamworth, NSW 2340 **Tel** *(02) 6762 1140* **Fax** *(02) 6762 1165* **Rooms** *5*

Tamworth is more than just the nation's country music capital. Golfers in particular will love this boutique guesthouse, which sits alongside the picturesque Longyard Golf Course, designed by Greg Norman. Plumes also offers stunning bird-watching packages. **www.plumesonthegreen.com.au**

TERRIGAL Terrigal Pacific Motel

224–232 Terrigal Drive, Terrigal, NSW 2260 **Tel** *(02) 4385 1555* **Fax** *(02) 4385 1476* **Rooms** *35*

Just an hour's drive north of Sydney, beautiful Terrigal is home to some of the central coast's most stunning beaches and lagoons. Within walking distance of the water and close to local eateries, these spacious apartments have sleek polished floorboards and offer views of lush tropical gardens. **www.terrigalaccommodation.com**

TOUKLEY Beachcomber

200 Main Road, Toukley, NSW 2263 **Tel** *(02) 4397 1300* **Fax** *(02) 4396 1128* **Rooms** *61*

There's something for everyone at this resort, which prides itself on entertainment for all ages. Relax by the pool or take in the regular live acts, DJs or karaoke nights. Have a cocktail at the bar or milkshake at Beachie Bites Café. As they say at The Beachie: it's not a hotel, it's an experience! **www.beachcomber.net.au**

WAGGA WAGGA Country Comfort

Cnr Morgan and Tarcutta streets, Wagga Wagga, NSW 2650 **Tel** *(02) 6921 6444* **Fax** *(02) 6921 2922* **Rooms** *85*

Wagga Wagga sits on the highway between Sydney and Melbourne, and this hotel offers overnight respite for travellers as well as longer stays for guests enjoying the Riverina region. Situated opposite parkland, it boasts good conference facilities, with Capers Restaurant serving breakfast and dinner daily. **www.constellationhotels.com**

WINDSOR Macquarie Arms Hotel

99 George Street, Windsor, NSW 4577 **Tel** *(02) 4577 2206* **Fax** *(02) 4577 2206* **Rooms** *4*

Built in 1815 and regarded as the oldest continuously run inn in Australia, the Macquarie Arms is equally well known for its resident convict ghosts who haunt the premises, but don't worry, they're harmless. The hotel is now under new management and the bistro is as good as ever, with live acts playing regularly.

THE SOUTH COAST AND SNOWY MOUNTAINS

ADAMINABY Reynella Rides and Country Farmstay
$$$$

*699 Kingston Road, NSW 2629 **Tel** (02) 6454 2386, 1800 029 909 **Fax** (02) 6454 2530 **Rooms** 20*

Set in the foothills of the Snowy Mountains, this 2429-hectare (6000-acre) sheep and cattle farm offers lodge accommodation with spectacular views. From October to May there are horse treks and bush camping through the nearby ranges of the Kosciuszko National Park. Horse treks not included in price. **www.reynellarides.com.au**

BATEMANS BAY The Best Western Reef Motor Inn
$$

*27 Clyde Street, NSW 2536 **Tel** (02) 4472 6000 **Fax** (02) 4472 6059 **Rooms** 34*

Located beside the broad Clyde River, this motel is popular with flathead anglers. It is four hours south of Sydney and less than two hours from Canberra. It is close to the highway, shops, restaurants and the oceanfront. It offers car parking, good access for wheelchairs and room service. **http://reefmotorinn.bestwestern.com.au**

BATEMANS BAY Comfort Inn Lincoln Downs
$$

*Princes Highway, NSW 2536 **Tel** (02) 4478 9200 **Fax** (02) 4478 9299 **Rooms** 33*

This luxury country resort, which is set amidst pretty English country-style gardens with ornamental lake, is a peaceful retreat by the sea. Enjoy a hit of tennis or relax in the billiard room with a cocktail before enjoying a memorable evening of fine food and wine at the Briars Restaurant. **www.lincolndowns.com.au**

BERMAGUI Beachview Motel
$$

*12 Lamont Street, NSW 2546 **Tel** (02) 6493 4155 **Fax** (02) 6493 4879 **Rooms** 8*

This environmentally friendly motel faces the ocean beach. Some rooms have a balcony overlooking the ocean: perfect for whale watching in autumn and spring. Mimosa Rocks National Park is 15 minutes by car, and shops and restaurants are within walking distance. **www.beachview.thebegavalley.com**

BERRY Bunyip Inn Guesthouse
$$$$

*122 Queen Street, NSW 2535 **Tel** (02) 4464 2064 **Rooms** 12*

Housed in a heritage-listed 1885 Victorian-era bank building, this cosy guesthouse is a perfect base from which to explore Shoalhaven. The guesthouse is a smart and comfortable accommodation option, close to shops, restaurants and Shoalhaven. There is car parking and good wheelchair access.

BOWRAL Craigieburn Resort and Conference Centre
$$$$$

*Centennial Avenue, NSW 2576 **Tel** (02) 4861 1277 **Fax** (02) 4862 1690 **Rooms** 71*

Craigieburn is a large garden estate, boasting its own nine-hole golf course, two tennis courts, fly fishing lake, gym, snooker room and jogging track. Its old world charm has recently been refurbished with modern amenities. **www.craigieburnresort.com.au**

BOWRAL Milton Park Country House Hotel
$$$$$

*Horderns Road, NSW 2576 **Tel** (02) 4861 1522 **Fax** (02) 4861 7962 **Rooms** 47*

This early 20th-century mansion is located in tranquil parkland just east of Bowral, with nearby golf courses, horse-riding, bush picnics and tennis courts. The mansion is a fine example of the Federation Arts and Crafts architectural style. There is also a day spa, good wheelchair access, room service and views. **www.milton-park.com.au**

BUNDANOON Treetops Guesthouse Bundanoon
$$$

*101 Railway Avenue, NSW 2578 **Tel** (02) 4883 6372 **Fax** (02) 4883 6176 **Rooms** 22*

Enjoy the gardens of this quiet, Edwardian guesthouse furnished with four-poster beds, Persian rugs, artworks and roaring log fires. The tariff includes dinner, bed and breakfast. Four of the rooms offer spa baths. They do not accept American Express or Diners cards. **www.treetopsguesthouse.com.au**

CHARLOTTE PASS Kosciuszko Chalet
$$$$$

*Kosciuszko Road, NSW 2624 **Tel** (02) 6457 5254 1800 026 369 **Fax** 1800 802 687 **Rooms** 35*

This chalet was built in the 1930s Austrian style. At 1,760 metres (5,770 ft) above sea level, it is Australia's highest resort. Accordingly, it is snow bound for much of the ski season, so its position metres from the ski lift is a bonus. It also offers spectacular views and peace and quiet. Only open in winter. **www.charlottepass.com.au**

COOMA Kinross Inn
$$

*15 Sharp Street, NSW 2630 **Tel** (02) 6452 3577, 1800 223 229 **Fax** (02) 6452 4410 **Rooms** 17*

Historic Cooma's only four-star motel is tucked away, just back from the town's shops and restaurants. It is one hour from the Snowy Mountains and the southern ski slopes. It has free spa baths, BBQ facilities, undercover parking adjacent to every room, and free pay TV in every room. **www.kinrossinn.com.au**

CULBURRA BEACH Boyd's Beach House
$$$$$

*53 The Marina, NSW 2540 **Tel** (02) 9365 5552, 0411 890 532 **Rooms** 3 in one house*

This stylish and luxurious beach house, which once belonged to Australian artist Arthur Boyd, is perched on the sand dunes above Culburra Beach. It enjoys absolute ocean frontage, magnificent views, and is only minutes from shops, restaurants and the national parks at Jervis Bay. **wwwstonewalls.com.au/culburra**

Key to Price Guide *see p478* **Key to Symbols** *see back cover flap*

EDEN Wonboyn Lake Resort

204 Daunceys Road, NSW 2551 **Tel** *(02) 6496 9162* **Fax** *(02) 6496 9100* **Rooms** *15*

This resort is in an isolated location off the highway and surrounded by national park with abundant wildlife and birdlife. The self-contained cottages are ideal for a family beach and fishing holiday. Bream, flathead and salmon are commonly caught. Canoes and hire boats are available. **www.wonboynlakeresort.com.au**

EROWAL BAY Sea Shacks

6 Caulfield Parade, NSW 2540 **Tel** *(02) 4443 8912* **Fax** *(02) 4443 7422* **Rooms** *4*

These two two-bedroom shacks are set in landscaped gardens, planted with indigenous species, overlooking a saltwater lake. The shacks are a stylish take on the Australian beach shack vernacular and offer polished wooden floors, balconies overlooking the water and hand-crafted hardwood furniture. **www.jervisbay-getaways.com.au**

GOULBURN Pelican Sheep Station

Braidwood Road, NSW 2580 **Tel** *(02) 4821 4668* **Fax** *(02) 4822 1179* **Rooms** *23*

This family-owned sheep station is to the south of Goulburn. It offers bunkhouse accommodation with a shared common room, four self-contained cabins, a five-bedroom house and a three-bedroom cottage. They do not accept American Express or Diners cards. **www.pelicansheepstation.com.au**

KIAMA Kiama Cove Boutique Motel

10 Bong Bong Street, NSW 2533 **Tel** *(02) 4232 3000* **Fax** *(02) 4232 3911* **Rooms** *31*

This stylishly refurbished hotel offers all the mod cons as well as a pleasant garden, great views and good wheelchair access. It is located in central Kiama, close to shops and restaurants, overlooking the surfbeach and within walking distance of the harbour, blowhole, lighthouse and Pilot's Cottage Museum. **www.kiamacove.com.au**

MERIMBULA Albacore Apartments

Market Street, NSW 2548 **Tel** *(02) 6495 3187* **Fax** *(02) 6495 3439* **Rooms** *20*

Luxury accommodation offering self-contained one- and two-bedroom apartments with ocean views from private balconies. The apartments are located opposite Merimbula Lake and close to shops, restaurants and some of the Sapphire Coast's best surf beaches. The apartments have disabled facilities. **www.albacore.com.au**

NAROOMA Mystery Bay Cottages

121 Mystery Bay Road, NSW 2546 **Tel** *(02) 4473 7431* **Fax** *(02) 4473 7431* **Rooms** *12*

The six two-bedroom self-contained cottages at this peaceful location are light, airy and modern with cosy log fires. They are surrounded by countryside and are only a minute's walk from the beach. All of the cottages enjoy beautiful views. They do not accept American Express or Diners cards. **www.mysterybaycottages.com.au**

NORTH WOLLONGONG Novotel Northbeach Wollongong

2–14 Cliff Road, NSW 2500 **Tel** *(02) 4224 3111* **Fax** *(02) 4229 1705* **Rooms** *204*

An hour's drive south of Sydney and only minutes from the centre of Wollongong, this hotel is nestled between the spectacular Illawarra Escarpment and the sea. Some rooms have a balcony with great views overlooking the ocean. There are peaceful walking and cycle tracks nearby, a sauna and tennis courts. **www.novotelnorthbeach.com**

NOWRA Shoalhaven Lodge

480 Longreach Road, NSW 2541 **Tel** *(02) 4422 6686* **Fax** *(02) 4423 2638* **Rooms** *11 (4 lodges)*

The self-contained lodges, cottage and studio apartment enjoy peaceful surroundings and views over nearby mountains and the beautiful Shoalhaven River. The property is a beef cattle farm with 2 km (1 mile) of prime river frontage only ten minutes from Nowra. Disabled guests welcome. **www.shoalhavenlodge.com.au**

TATHRA Tathra Beach House Apartments

57 Andy Poole Drive, NSW 2550 **Tel** *(02) 6499 9900* **Fax** *(02) 6499 9950* **Rooms** *26*

Opposite the surf beach, these one-, two- and three-bedroom apartments are set in landscaped surrounds and feature private decks with spa. The apartments are walking distance from shops and the historic 150-year-old wharf, but are available only for weekly hire during the peak Christmas period. **www.tathrabeachhouse.com.au**

THREDBO Thredbo Alpine Hotel

Friday Drive, NSW 2625 **Tel** *(02) 6459 4200* **Fax** *(02) 6459 4201* **Rooms** *65*

This large complex in Thredbo Village is a favourite with skiers in the winter months as it is only a minute's walk from the ski lift. It is far cheaper, and quieter, in the summer months. Facilities include a sauna, spa and masseuse. There is plenty of chalet character, great views and room service. **www.thredbo.com.au**

THREDBO Novotel Lake Crackenback Resort

Lake Crackenback, Alpine Way via Jindabyne, NSW 2627 **Tel** *(02) 6451 3000* **Rooms** *48 apartments*

The self-contained apartments at this luxury resort are ideally located for skiers, with a courtesy bus running to and from the Skitube Alpine Rail Way. The resort is only 14 km (8 miles) from Kosciuszko National Park at Thredbo. One- and two-day guided tours of the park are available during the summer. **www.novotellakecrackenback.com.au**

TILBA TILBA The Two-Story Bed & Breakfast

Bate Street, Central Tilba, NSW 2546 **Tel** *(02) 4473 7290* **Fax** *(02) 4473 7290* **Rooms** *3*

Located in the National Trust village of Central Tilba, this 1894 building was once the post office. Close to the beach, open gardens, craft shops, bushwalks in the lush coastal hinterland and peaceful fishing spots. There is car parking and the lounge room features an open fire. Perfect for winter guests. **www.tilbatwostory.com**

CANBERRA AND ACT

BRINDABELLA Brindabella Station $$

Brindabella Valley, 2611 **Tel** *(02) 6236 2121* **Fax** *(02) 6236 2128* **Rooms** *4 (2 cabins)*

Bushwalking, bird-watching and trout fishing are on offer at this scenic and historic working farm. Miles Franklin, one of Australia's most famous authors, lived here as a child. The farm is bounded on three sides by national parks. Guests must provide their own food. **www.brindabellastation.com.au**

BUNGENDORE Carrington of Bungendore $$$$

21 Malbon Street, NSW 2621 **Tel** *(02) 6238 1044* **Fax** *(02) 6238 1036* **Rooms** *26*

Originally built in 1885 as a Cobb & Co inn, this lavishly restored Victorian house is a luxurious country retreat. The elegant restaurant with five dining rooms, the 200-year-old carved mahogany and etched glass bar, and the large gardens are highlights. **www.thecarrington.com**

CANBERRA Kingston Hotel $

73 Canberra Avenue, Griffith, NSW 2603 **Tel** *(02) 6295 0123* **Fax** *(02) 6295 7871* **Rooms** *36*

Low prices ensure that this lively country-style pub is popular with backpackers. Rooms and bathrooms are shared. Cooking facilities are available and the pub itself serves good-value counter meals. The heritage-listed building is a short walk from the city centre and close to shops and restaurants. Car parking is available.

CANBERRA Victor Lodge $

29 Dawes Street, Kingston, ACT 2604 **Tel** *(02) 6295 7777* **Fax** *(02) 6295 2466* **Rooms** *29*

A family run guesthouse within walking distance of the CBD and Manuka and Kingston pubs and restaurants. There is a free pick-up and drop-off service from Jolimont coach terminal during business hours. There is also mountain bike hire, off-street parking, a barbecue area and garden, TV room and internet. **www.victorlodge.com.au**

CANBERRA Blue and White and Canberran Lodges $$

524 & 528 Northbourne Avenue, Downer, ACT 2602 **Tel** *(02) 6248 0498* **Fax** *(02) 6248 8277* **Rooms** *19*

This establishment in Canberra's inner north is a friendly and comfortable bed-and-breakfast (reputedly Canberra's first B&B). It provides several budget and family accommodation options, and one room has a spa. It is five minutes' drive from the city centre and close to shops and several Asian and Italian restaurants.

CANBERRA Brassey Hotel $$

Belmore Gardens, Barton, ACT 2600 **Tel** *(02) 6273 3766, 1800 659 191* **Fax** *(02) 6273 2791* **Rooms** *81*

This 1927 heritage-listed building is set amid fine gardens. It enjoys a quiet location close to both Parliament House buildings, Lake Burley Griffin, the Press Club, the High Court of Australia and the National Gallery of Australia. It offers conference and internet facilities, and heritage and standard rooms. **www.brassey.net.au**

CANBERRA Last Stop Ambledown Brook $$

198 Brooklands Road, via Hall, ACT 2618 **Tel** *(02) 6230 2280* **Rooms** *6*

Sleep in a converted 1929 Melbourne tram or a 1935 Sydney train carriage at this rustic guesthouse, just 20 minutes from Canberra. Enjoy relaxing views of the nearby Brindabella Ranges, or hop in the car and visit nearby restaurants and cool climate vineyards. BBQ facilities and tennis courts are available. **www.laststop.com.au**

CANBERRA Miranda & Parkview Lodges $$

526 & 534 Northbourne Avenue, Downer, ACT 2602 **Tel** *(02) 6249 8038* **Fax** *(02) 6247 6166* **Rooms** *22*

These two lodges, only metres apart, are managed by the same owners. They are pleasant guesthouses in renovated two-storey duplexes, 4 km (2.5 miles) north of the GPO and within walking distance of the Yowani Country Club, Kamberra Winery, the Racecourse and 30 cafés and restaurants in nearby Dixon. **www.mirandalodge.com.au**

CANBERRA Olims Canberra Hotel $$

Cnr Ainslie & Limestone aves, Braddon, ACT 2612 **Tel** *(02) 6243 0000, 1800 475 337* **Rooms** *125*

This four-star 1927 Art Deco hotel, close to the War Memorial, the National Gallery of Australia and the city centre, is classified by the National Trust. It offers peaceful formal gardens, a cocktail bar, wheelchair access and a mixture of room styles and prices to suit most budgets, including heritage and de luxe rooms. **www.olimshotel.com**

CANBERRA University House $$

Cnr Balmain & Liversidge sts, ACT 2601 **Tel** *(02) 6125 5211* **Fax** *(02) 6125 5252* **Rooms** *106*

This hotel is situated in the peaceful gardens of the Australian National University. It offers conference facilities, internet access and two restaurants and bars. As well as spacious standard rooms and suites, there are several one- and two-bedroom apartments and a suite for disabled guests. **www.anu.edu.au/unihouse**

CANBERRA Belconnen Premier Inn $$$

110 Benjamin Way, Belconnen, ACT 2617 **Tel** *(02) 6253 3633, 1800 672 076* **Fax** *(02) 6253 3688* **Rooms** *74*

This stylish hotel offers the business traveller excellent convention facilities and a business centre. Rooms range from standard rooms (sleep two) to de luxe rooms to self-contained one- and two-bedroom apartments, some with spa. There is a gym, cocktail bar and three rooms with wheelchair access. **www.belconnenpremier.com**

Key to Price Guide *see p478* **Key to Symbols** *see back cover flap*

CANBERRA Hotel Kurrajong
$$$

8 National Circuit, Barton, ACT 2604 **Tel** *(02) 6234 4444* **Fax** *(02) 6234 4466* **Rooms** *26*

JS Murdoch, the architect who designed Canberra's first Parliament House, designed this 1926 Art Deco, pavilion-style hotel. Over the years it has welcomed several Australian prime ministers, and was home to Prime Minister Ben Chifley from 1940 to 1951. It offers conference and wheelchair access. **www.hotelkurrajong.com.au**

CANBERRA Canberra Rex Hotel
$$$$

150 Northbourne Avenue, Braddon, ACT 2601 **Tel** *(02) 6248 5311, 1800 026 103* **Rooms** *152*

This friendly up-market hotel, near the university and only 1 km (0.6 miles) north of the city centre, is a good option for disabled and corporate travellers. It offers free off-street parking, conference rooms, boardrooms, a games room, a sauna, a gym and room service. Some rooms have balconies with great views. **www.canberrarexhotel.com.au**

CANBERRA Crowne Plaza Canberra
$$$$$

1 Binara Street, ACT 2601 **Tel** *(02) 6247 8999, 1800 007 697* **Fax** *(02) 6247 3706* **Rooms** *295*

This modern four-and-a-half star hotel right in the heart of the city is offers a range of facilities, including sauna, internet access and secretarial services. It is particularly popular with visiting business people. It is close to shops and restaurants, the Australian War Memorial and the National Gallery of Australia. **www.crowneplaza.com.au**

CANBERRA Hyatt Hotel
$$$$$

Commonwealth Avenue, Yarralumla, ACT 2600 **Tel** *(02) 6270 1234* **Fax** *(02) 6281 5998* **Rooms** *249*

This centrally located heritage-listed Art Deco hotel, surrounded by manicured lawns and gardens, is Canberra's five-star showpiece. Its decor oozes 1920s sophistication, and the morning and afternoon teas in The Tea Lounge are a Canberra institution. It also offers first-class fitness and disabled facilities. **www.canberra.park.hyatt.com**

CANBERRA Pacific International Apartments Capital Tower
$$$$$

2 Marcus Clarke Street, ACT 2601 **Tel** *(02) 6276 3444* **Fax** *(02) 6247 0759* **Rooms** *40*

One-, two- and three-bedroom apartments and a quiet location make this an ideal option for travellers with children. The apartments enjoy views over Lake Burley Griffin, the mountains or the city. The lake is one minute's walk, and the city is an easy ten-minute walk. **www.pacificinthotels.com**

CANBERRA Pavilion on Northbourne
$$$$$

242 Northbourne Avenue, Dickson, ACT 2602 **Tel** *(02) 6247 6888* **Fax** *(02) 6248 7866* **Rooms** *156*

This refurbished hotel and serviced apartments, popular with business travellers, has recently gone up-market. It has excellent conference and internet facilities. There are several spa suites and there is an indoor tropical atrium. It is close to shops and restaurants and only 2 km (1 mile) from the city centre. **www.pavilioncanberra.com**

CANBERRA Rydges Lakeside Hotel Canberra
$$$$$

London Circuit, Canberra City, ACT 2600 **Tel** *(02) 6247 6244, 1800 026 169* **Rooms** *201*

Wonderful views over Lake Burley Griffin and the city distinguish this modern hotel, especially those from the 15th floor restaurant. The hotel is only ten minutes' walk from the city centre and 20 minutes' walk from the National Gallery of Australia. Car parking, wheelchair access and room service are available. **www.rydges.com**

MACGREGOR Ginninderry Homestead B&B
$$$

468 Parkwood Road, ACT 2615 **Tel** *(02) 6254 6464* **Fax** *(02) 6254 1945* **Rooms** *4*

This elegant guesthouse on a working farm offers pastoral views framed by the distant snow-capped Brindabella Ranges. The homestead has gracious formal gardens, verandas, a Victorian gazebo, a sunny courtyard, spa and BBQ area. Inside you'll find formal dining and lounge rooms and a charming billiards room. **www.ginninderry.com.au**

BRISBANE

BARDON The Bardon Centre
$$$

390 Simpsons Road, QLD 4065 **Tel** *(07) 3217 5333* **Fax** *(07) 3367 1350* **Rooms** *77*

Guest lodges set in the magnificent bushland of the Mount Cootha foothills make for a relaxing retreat. Delicious cuisine is served. In-room dining and mini bar is available on request. Perfect for the traveller looking for a meditative experience, yet on the bus route to the city and close to Paddington. **www.thevenues.com**

CITY CENTRE Explorers Inn Hotel
$

63 Turbot Street (cnr George Street), QLD 4000 **Tel** *(07) 3211 3488* **Fax** *(07) 3211 3499* **Rooms** *58*

Under its banner as Brisbane's cheapest three-star hotel, this comfortable inn offers accommodation for the budget conscious traveller. Testimonals boast "a friendly stay, clean rooms, well-prepared food, and a convenient location". Rooms include an en suite bathroom, designer decor, security, and a colour TV. **www.explorers.com.au**

CITY CENTRE Palace Backpackers Brisbane
$

Cnr Edward & Ann Streets, QLD 4000 **Tel** *(07) 3211 2433* **Fax** *(07) 3211 2466* **Rooms** *32*

Conveniently located backpacker hotel, the Palace offers dormitory rooms, single rooms and double rooms. Built in an historic hotel with laced wrought-iron balconies, renovated for modern travellers, this is a budget stay with historical value in a part of Brisbane's past. **www.palacebackpackers.com.au**

CITY CENTRE Eton Bed & Breakfast
436 Upper Roma Street, QLD 4000 **Tel** *(07) 3236 0115* **Fax** *(07) 3102 6120* **Rooms** *6*

This fully renovated, heritage-listed guesthouse is situated in a colonial Queenslander, built in 1877. Conveniently located on the edge of Brisbane's CBD, it is a 15-minute walk from the heart of the city and Brisbane's Exhibition and Convention Centre. A relaxed place, it is close to Caxton Street's nightlife and eateries. **www.babs.com.au/eton**

CITY CENTRE Hotel George Williams
317 George Street, QLD 4000 **Tel** *(07) 3308 0700* **Fax** *(07) 3308 0703* **Rooms** *81*

Hotel George Williams is located a short stroll from the city centre. It hosts one of the largest gyms in Australia – free for hotel guests. Other features include outdoor terrace rooms and free undercover parking. Alfresco dining is offered at Cerello's bar and restaurant. Located close to the Transit Centre. **www.hgw.com.au**

CITY CENTRE Hotel Ibis
27 Turbot Street, QLD 4000 **Tel** *(07) 3237 2333* **Fax** *(07) 3237 2444* **Rooms** *218*

Situated close to the banks of the busy Brisbane River, the Ibis Hotel offers spacious rooms with modern decor at a reasonable price. Child-minding is available at an extra cost. It is linked to its sister hotel, the Mecure Hotel Brisbane, situated next door and guests can enjoy the Mercure's bars and restaurants. **www.accorhotels.com.au**

CITY CENTRE Brisbane Hilton
190 Elizabeth Street, QLD 4000 **Tel** *(07) 3234 2000* **Fax** *3231 3199* **Rooms** *321*

The Brisbane Hilton is a modern hotel with a dramatic atrium soaring 20 floors above the lobby. The hotel was built in 1986 and has been renovated to include an Events floor and Atrium lounge. Features include a car park, wheel-chair access, room service, and a safety deposit box in all rooms. Excellent city views. **www.brisbane.hilton.com**

CITY CENTRE Clarion Rendezvous Hotel Brisbane
255 Ann Street, QLD 4000 **Tel** *(07) 3001 9888* **Fax** *(07) 3001 9700* **Rooms** *129*

Only a minute from the Queen Street Mall, this hotel offers private rooms and one- and two-bedroom self-contained apartments. The apartments have the added attraction of a separate bedroom, living/dining room and kitchen facilities. Bistro and wine bar open every evening. **www.rendezvoushotels.com**

CITY CENTRE Goodearth Hotel
345 Wickham Terrace, QLD 4000 **Tel** *(07) 3831 6177* **Fax** *(07) 3831 6363* **Rooms** *179*

A short stroll from Brisbane's CBD, shopping mall, nightlife and casino, the Goodearth Hotel is well located overlooking two of Brisbane's parklands and offers a view to the Western mountains. This reasonably priced accommodation provides guests with a "Food to Go" service. **www.goodearth.com.au**

CITY CENTRE Mercure Hotel
85 North Quay, QLD 4000 **Tel** *(07) 3237 2300* **Fax** *(07) 3236 1035* **Rooms** *194*

Check the prices daily for this luxury hotel as it offers dynamic pricing from A$120. The Mercure is situated on the banks of the Brisbane River and offers panoramic views over the Southbank Parklands, Victoria Bridge and the Cultural Centre. Parking is limited and can be arranged at an extra cost. **www.mercurebrisbane.com.au**

CITY CENTRE Quality Hotel The Inchcolm
73 Wickham Terrace, QLD 4000 **Tel** *(07) 3226 8888* **Fax** *(07) 3226 8899* **Rooms** *35*

This elegantly appointed, heritage hotel features handcrafted timber fittings and custom-built furniture. A cityscape pool provides stunning views. Tasteful refurbishing has retained the old caged lift and silky oak panelling. Downstairs is Armstrongs, an award-winning restaurant. **www.inchcolmhotel.com.au**

CITY CENTRE Brisbane Marriot Hotel
515 Queen Street, QLD 4000 **Tel** *(07) 3303 8000* **Fax** *(07) 3303 8088* **Rooms** *267*

With panoramic views of the city skyline and the river, the Marriot Hotel is well situated for business travellers and tourists. It features elegantly appointed rooms, exquisite timber veneers, marble bathrooms, a luxury spa, swimming pool, gym facilties and sauna. Alfresco dining is available. **www.marriot.com/bnedt**

CITY CENTRE Carlton Crest Hotel
Cnr Ann & Roma Street, QLD 4000 **Tel** *(07) 3229 9111* **Fax** *(07) 3229 9618* **Rooms** *438*

This elegantly appointed hotel offers two kinds of accommodation in two towers. The Carlton Tower offers de luxe rooms and suites; the Crest Tower has standard guest rooms. Special hotel features include a rooftop heated swimming pool, business centre, gym and sauna, and a selection of dining options. **www.carltonhotels.com**

CITY CENTRE Chifley at Lennons
66 Queen Street, QLD 4000 **Tel** *(07) 3222 3222* **Fax** *(07) 3221 9389* **Rooms** *154*

The Chifley at Lennons is located on the Queen Street Mall and close to shopping and the CBD. It is a short stroll away from the Botanical Gardens, Southbank Parklands and the Art Gallery. It has a variety of accommodation, including de luxe spa rooms. **www.chifleyhotels.com**

CITY CENTRE Conrad Treasury Brisbane
130 William Street, QLD 4000 **Tel** *(07) 3306 8888* **Fax** *(07) 3306 8823* **Rooms** *130*

Lit softly at night, this historic sandstone heritage building has a romantic ambience. The hotel offers two-service a day rooms, valet, laundry, easy access for wheelchairs and limousine services. The casino is open 24 hours and has a range of dining options. **www.conrad.com.au**

Key to Price Guide *see p478* **Key to Symbols** *see back cover flap*

CITY CENTRE Holiday Inn $$$$$

Roma Street, QLD 4000 **Tel** *(07) 3238 2222* **Fax** *(07) 32382288* **Rooms** *192*

Located next to the Brisbane Transit Centre and a short walk from the CBD and Queen Street Mall, this hotel is convenient for a City holiday and onward travel. It offers a comfortable stay with a great range of extra services. Staff speak English, Hindi, Spanish and Tagalog. The restaurant has a kids-eat-free deal. **www.holidayinn.com**

FORTITUDE VALLEY Tourist Guest House $

55 Gregory Terrace, QLD 4006 **Tel** *(07) 32524171* **Fax** *(07) 3252 2704* **Rooms** *46*

This country-style guesthouse with veranda and sundeck bar is situated in a quiet location, yet close to the Valley nightclubs, restaurants and shopping. It is budget priced, offering clean, comfortable rooms or dormitory stays. A communal kitchen and lounge make this a great spot to meet fellow travellers. **www.touristguesthouse.com**

KANGAROO POINT The Point Brisbane $$$

21 Lambert Street, QLD 4169 **Tel** *(07) 3240 0888* **Fax** *(07) 3392 1155* **Rooms** *104*

This hotel is situated at Kangaroo Point and has stunning views over the Story Bridge and Botanical Gardens and an impressive night skyline. A modern hotel, The Point hosts a courtesy shuttle bus to the CBD, a fully licensed bar and café, exercise and pool facilities and a 24-hour room service menu. **www.thepointbrisbane.com.au**

MILTON Cosmo on the Park Road $$$

60 Park Road, QLD 4064 **Tel** *(07) 3858 5999* **Fax** *(07) 3858 5988* **Rooms** *75*

A boutique hotel in the afresco dining, riverside precinct of Park Road, Cosmo on the Park Road is surrounded by trendy cafés, restaurants and is only a five-minute drive from the city. This is the ideal luxury stay for a weekend break, or a select stay for the business traveller. **www.centralgroup.com.au**

NEW FARM Cream Gables $$

70 Kent Street, QLD 4005 **Tel** *(07) 3358 2727* **Fax** *(07) 3358 2727* **Rooms** *3*

A stone's throw from New Farm's clubs, pubs, galleries, restaurants and shops, this guesthouse offers well-appointed guest rooms with their own courtyard, en suite and television. The king/twin room is disabled friendly. It is an easy walk to the city. **www.webminders.com.au/creamgables**

NEW FARM Willahra House $$

268 Harcourt Street, QLD 4005 **Tel** *(07) 3254 3485* **Fax** *(07) 3254 1325* **Rooms** *3*

This guesthouse in a restored inner-city home offers a comforatble, relaxed lounge, polished timber floors, old-world furniture and ornate pressed metal ceilings. Enjoy breakfast on the veranda. It is close to the river, the James Street Shopping precinct and public transport, cinemas, clubs and a range of dining options. **www.babs.com.au**

PADDINGTON Fern Cottage B&B $$

89 Fernberg Road, QLD 4064 **Tel** *(07) 3511 6685* **Fax** *(07) 3511 6685* **Rooms** *3*

This is a charming, refurbished 1930s Queenslander home in the upbeat Paddington/Rosalie area. Situated about 2 km (1 mile) from downtown Brisbane, this location is alive with small art galleries, boutiques, bistros, clothes shops, alfresco restaurants and cafés. Rooms are air conditioned with en suites. **www.ferncottage.net**

SOUTH BRISBANE La Torretta B&B $

8 Brereton Street, QLD 4101 **Tel** *(07) 3846 0846* **Fax** *(07) 3342 7863* **Rooms** *2*

Personalized service, relaxed atmosphere, and private leafy surrounds, this is budget accommodation at its Queensland best. This 100-year-old house has been carefully restored and offers a delightful holiday choice. Guest rooms have a private entrance. Sumptuous self-serve breakfast included in tariff. **www.latorretta.com.au**

SPRING HILL Metro Hotel Tower Mill $

239 Wickham Terrace, QLD 4000 **Tel** *(07) 3832 1421* **Fax** *(07) 3832 1421* **Rooms** *77*

This three-and-a-half star hotel is located opposite one of Brisbane's landmarks – the "Mill". The windmill is Brisbane's oldest building and is a relic from the penal settlement of 1824–42. The hotel overlooks Wickham Park and is conveniently close to the CBD and shopping areas. **www.MetroHospitalityGroup.com**

SPRING HILL Hotel Watermark $$

555 Wickham Terrace, QLD 4000 **Tel** *(07) 3831 3111* **Fax** *(07) 3832 1290* **Rooms** *95*

The Albert Park Hotel is a boutique hotel overlooking the Roma Street Parklands. The decor is modern. Rooms are well lit and spacious. Added features include 24-hour reception, secure undercover parking, wireless internet connection, hotel safe and an award-winning restaurant. **www.hotelwatermark.com.au**

SPRING HILL The Soho Motel $$

333 Wickham Terrace, QLD 4000 **Tel** *(07) 3831 7722* **Fax** *(07) 3831 8050* **Rooms** *50*

Located opposite the Roma Street parkland and just a short stroll from the city, this popular mid-range hotel offers a range of facilities. Every room opens onto its own private balcony. An extensive à la carte breakfast menu is available until 10am daily. **www.sohomotel.com.au**

SPRING HILL Hotel Grand Chancellor $$$$$

Cnr Leichhardt Street & Wickham Terrace, QLD 4000 **Tel** *(07) 3831 4055* **Fax** *(07) 3831 5031* **Rooms** *180*

Located on the highest point of the CBD, this hotel is situated on the main route to the airport and is a leisurely walk to the CBD down tree-lined stone steps and paths. The hotel features Frescos Restaurant, cocktail bar, garden courtyard, rooftop pool, conference facilities, and undercover parking. **www.ghihotels.com**

WEST END Somewhere to Stay

Cnr Brighton & Franklin streets, QLD 4101 **Tel** *1800 812398* **Fax** *(07) 3846 4584* **Rooms** *32*

For backpacker accommodation in Brisbane, this is an excellent choice. Single dorm rooms are priced from A$19 a night. A free shuttle-bus runs every day from 8am to 7:30pm to collect guests from Roma Street Transit Centre. It leaves every hour on the hour. A saltwater swimming pool makes this a fun stay. **www.somewheretostay.com.au**

WEST END Eskdale B&B

141 Vulture Street, QLD 4101 **Tel** *(07) 3255 2519* **Rooms** *4*

With only four guest bedrooms, there is an opportunity to meet other guests while relaxing in the lounge to read, talk or watch TV. The bathrooms are new, centrally located and airy. A stay in this authethic Queenslander (built in 1907) is reasonably priced and convenient for the Southbank. **www.eskdale.homestead.com**

SOUTH OF TOWNSVILLE

AGNES WATER Mango Tree Motel

7 Agnes Street, QLD 4677 **Tel** *(07) 4974 9132* **Fax** *(07) 4974 9132* **Rooms** *13*

Adjacent to the main surf beach in Agnes Water on the Discovery Coast, this budget motel is in one of Queensland's prettiest beach towns on southern end of the Great Barrier Reef. It is a short walk to shops, cafés and beach tracks. The popular beachside bar and restaurant adjoins the motel and is licensed. **www.mangotreemotel.com**

AIRLIE BEACH Club Crocodile Resort Airlie Beach

Shute Harbour Road, Airlie Beach, QLD 4802 **Tel** *(07) 4946 7155* **Fax** *(07) 4946 6007* **Rooms** *160*

This multi-award winning tropical resort overlooks the magnificent Whitsunday Islands. The resort features free-form pools and waterfalls. Tourists can go sailing, snorkelling, horse riding or fishing or yachting in the aquamarine waters surrounding the islands. The "Hard Croc Café" offers a delicious menu. **www.clubcroc.com.au**

AIRLIE BEACH Coral Sea Resort

25 Oceanview Avenue, QLD 4802 **Tel** *(07) 4946 6458* **Fax** *(07) 4946 6516* **Rooms** *78*

This resort has four styles of holiday suites, two-bedroom apartments, family apartments and one-, two- and three-bedroom penthouses. Decor is nautically themed with bright aqua and turquoise colours, deckside ornamentation, historic boat prints and yachting memorabillia. **www.coralsearesort.com**

BOREEN POINT Jetty Escape

1 Boreen Parade, QLD 4565 **Tel** *(07) 5485 3167* **Fax** *(07) 5486 3167* **Rooms** *2*

This three-level Mediterranean-style town house on Lake Cootharaba is ideal for a unique, relaxing holiday experience. Whether looking for a shady place to sit and read, or adventure boating on the Noosa River, this guesthouse is the genuine Australian encounter. It is a two-hour drive north of Brisbane. **www.jettyescape.com**

BUDERIM Aquila Retreat

21 Box Street, QLD 4556 **Tel** *(07) 5445 3681* **Fax** *(07) 5456 1140* **Rooms** *5*

This private bushland retreat is tucked away in the Sunshine Coast hinterland. It is just a five-minute drive from Mooloolaba's sandy white beaches and offers spectacular views of the Glass House Mountains. This retreat is ideal for couples but it does not accept children. **www.aquilaretreat.com.au**

CARNARVON GORGE Carnarvon Gorge Wilderness Lodge

PMB 1009 Rolleston, QLD 4702 **Tel** *(07) 4984 4503* **Fax** *(07) 4984 4500* **Rooms** *30*

This National Park has some of the best walking tracks in Australia. The lodge features a reference library, access to magnificent views, bird-watching, guided walks and the aboriginal rock art gallery. There is an abundance of flora and fauna to see. Safari cabins are inviting and airy. **www.carnarvon-gorge.com**

CURRUMBIN VALLEY Cottages on the Creek

1464 Currumbin Creek Road, Currumbin Valley, QLD 4223 **Tel** *(07) 5533 0449* **Fax** *(07) 5533 0449* **Rooms** *2*

Cottages on the Creek have been designed with minimal environmental impact. This is a eco-friendly stay in a wildlife haven. Black cockatoos, whipbirds and honey-eaters provide company for breakfast. It is a two-minute drive from the Currumbin rockpools and 15 minutes from the Coolongatta Airport. **www.cottagesonthecreek.com.au**

EUMUNDI Eumundi Country Cottage

47 Memorial Drive, QLD 4562 **Tel** *(07) 5442 7220* **Fax** *(07) 5442 7320* **Rooms** *3*

A luxury guesthouse in a tastefully restored historic Queensland house (built in 1911) with a guest cottage. Each room has its own en suite and private veranda, and is furnished with antiques and period china. This is Queensland hospitality at its best, close to the Eumundi markets and 15 minutes from Noosa. **www.babs.com.au**

FRASER ISLAND Eurong Beach Resort

Fraser Island, QLD 4655 **Tel** *(07) 4127 9122* **Fax** *(07) 4127 9178* **Rooms** *114*

This resort offers rooms for families and groups, units and apartments. Situated on the beachfront at Fraser Island's 123-km (76-mile) beach it is ideally suited to access the world heritage wilderness, including rainforest walks, freshwater lakes and creeks, coloured sands and the Maheno shipwreck. **www.eurong.com**

Key to Price Guide *see p478* **Key to Symbols** *see back cover flap*

FRASER ISLAND Kingfisher Bay Resort   🏊🏄🏋️🚗🚻🍽 $$$$

PMB 1 Urangan Hervey Bay, QLD 4655 **Tel** *(07) 4120 3333* **Fax** *(07) 4120 3326* **Rooms** *261*

A luxury resort on the edge of Fraser's wilderness, offering four-wheel drive eco tours and walks, canoeing and fishing. It has four return catamaran services each day from Hervey Bay. A vehicle barge runs three times a day from River Heads. Transfers are available from the airport and coach terminal. **www.kingfisherbay.com**

GLADSTONE Auckland Hill B&B   🏊🚻🍽 $$

15 Yarroon Street, QLD 4680 **Tel** *(07) 49724907* **Fax** *(07) 49727300* **Rooms** *6*

A refurbished guesthouse built in 1874, with de luxe rooms with balconies overlooking the harbour and marina. It has a guest lounge with a fireplace, choice of a luxury suite with spa bath and a large open deck for relaxing on while enjoying the sea air. **www.ahbb.com.au**

GOLD COAST Conrad Jupiters   🏊🏄🏊🚗🚻🍽 $$$$

Broadbeach Island, QLD 4218 **Tel** *(07) 5592 8100* **Fax** *(07) 5592 8219* **Rooms** *594*

An ideal location in the heart of the Gold Coast, this luxury hotel and casino offers sweeping views across the Pacific to the east, and across the hinterland and mountains to the west. There are four rooms with special facilities for disabled guests. The Coolongatta airport is a 20-minute drive away. **www.conrad.com.au**

GOLD COAST Palazzo Versace   🏊🏄🏊🚗🚻🍽 $$$$$

Seaworld Drive, Main Beach, QLD 4217 **Tel** *(07) 5509 8000* **Fax** *(07) 5509 8888* **Rooms** *205*

With a reputation for elegance, style and discerning taste, the Versace label has been translated to this stunningly designed hotel on the Gold Coast's broadwater. Rooms are decorous with warm timber tones and rich fabric colours. This is a stay for the senses. Try out the spa. **www.palazzoversace.com**

GOLD COAST Sheraton Mirage Resort & Spa   🏊🏄🏊🚗🚻🍽 $$$$$

Seaworld Drive, Main Beach, QLD 4217 **Tel** *(07) 5591 1488* **Fax** *(07) 5591 2299* **Rooms** *293*

Sheraton Mirage Resort & Spa is located 35 km (22 miles) from the Gold Coast Airport and 80 km (50 miles) from Brisbane Airport. Situated on the Broadwater Peninsula, the resort has an oceanfront position and views over the Gold Coast's broadwater. **www.sheraton.com/goldcoast**

GOLD COAST HINTERLAND Binna Burra Mountain Lodge   🏄🏋 $$$$

Lamington National Park, 4211 **Tel** *(07) 5533 3622* **Fax** *(07) 5533 3658* **Rooms** *40*

Binna Burra Lodge is an ecotourism retreat offering the peace and quiet of a natural rainforest setting with an educational adventure. Its rustic timber cabins are built from hand-cut tallow wood slabs. This is a modern stay, but the tranquillity is not interrupted by phones, clocks, radios or television. **www.binnaburralodge.com.au**

GOLD COAST HINTERLAND O'Reilly's Rainforest Retreat   🏄🏊🏋🚗 $$$$$

Lamington National Park, QLD 4275 **Tel** *(07) 5544 0644* **Fax** *(07) 5544 0638* **Rooms** *72*

O'Reilly's is situated in the lush rainforest covered mountains of the Lamington National Park, 119 km (74 miles) southwest of Brisbane – the largest world heritage listed sub-tropical rainforest in Australia. Modern rooms offer magnificent views of surrounding landscape, but have no phone, television or radios. **www.oreillys.com.au**

HERVEY BAY Mango Tourist Hostel $

110 Torquay Road, Scarness, QLD 4655 **Tel** *(07) 4124 2832* **Rooms** *3*

This friendly hostel caters for budget travellers and backpackers. Housed in a tastefully renovated Queenslander, it is situated a short distance from Hervey Bay's beach, esplanade and shops. This is a unique stay where homestyle atmosphere and good advice on Fraser Island's trails and Western beaches is offered. **www.mangohostel.com**

HERVEY BAY The Bay B&B   🏊 $$

180 Cypress Street, QLD 4655 **Tel** *(07) 4125 6919* **Fax** *(07) 4125 3658* **Rooms** *5*

Set in an idyllic tropical garden, this guesthouse is just one street from the esplanade, beach and shopping. Shady terraces, a saltwater pool and a sumptious breakfast make this stay a great stay. You can take a whale-watching tour or a catamaran to Fraser Island, fish, swim, hike or go for a bicycle ride. **www.hervey.com.au/bedandbreakfast**

HERVEY BAY Susan River Homestead   🏄🏊🏋🚗 $$

PO Box 516 Maryborough – off Hervey Bay Road, QLD 4650 **Tel** *(07) 4121 6846* **Fax** *(07) 4122 2675* **Rooms** *16*

Looking for an outback adventure not too far from the Coast, this friendly homestay farm is modern, well situated and offers horse riding, paragliding, waterskiing, absailing, a tennis court and swimming pool. This is the Queensland holiday of a lifetime. Backpackers and children are welcome. **www.susanriver.com**

HERVEY BAY Outrigger Hervey Bay   🏊🏄🏊🚗🚻🍽 $$$

Buccaneer Drive, Urangan, QLD 4655 **Tel** *(07) 4197 8200* **Fax** *(07) 4197 8222* **Rooms** *158*

Outrigger Hervey Bay is situated right on the Urangan marina. Small boats, idyllic weather, gentle water and relaxed shopping and restaurants make this one of Queensland's favourite holiday destinations. This is a choice spot whether you come to whale watch, trek through Fraser Island's wilderness or just lie on the beach. **www.outrigger.com**

HIGHFIELDS Oakleigh Country Cottage B&B $$$

Lot 10 Bowtell Drive, QLD 4352 **Tel** *(07) 4696 7021* **Fax** *(07) 4696 7284* **Rooms** *3*

Highfields is a ten-minute drive north of Toowoomba and a two-hour drive west of Brisbane. This comfortable guesthouse offers a hearty country breakfast and a cosy wood fire. The cottage and house is surrounded by extensive rose gardens. **www.members.ozemail.com.au**

MACKAY Cape Hillsborough Nature Resort $$

MS 895 Mackay, QLD 4740 **Tel** *(07) 4959 0152* **Fax** *(07) 4959 0500* **Rooms** *28*

Providing budget to mid-range accommodation, this unique nature stay offers a choice of motel rooms, huts, cabins or villas. The resort overlooks Causarina Beach and has nature reserve on three sides, creating a secluded environment for relaxing, fishing and hiking. **www.capehillsboroughresort.com**

MAGNETIC ISLAND Sails on Horseshoe $$$$

13–15 Pacific Drive, Horseshoe Bay, QLD 4819 **Tel** *(07) 4778 5117* **Fax** *(07) 4778 5104* **Rooms** *14*

Horseshoe Bay is the largest of Magnetic Island's 23 bays. "Sails on Horseshoe" features modern fully self-contained townhouse apartments and offers a relaxing island stay in the aquamarine waters of the Coral Coast. All townhouses have two bedrooms and will comfortably sleep a family of six. **www.sailsonhorseshoe.com.au**

NOOSA Sheraton Noosa Resort & Spa $$$$$

14–16 Hastings Street, QLD 4567 **Tel** *(07) 5449 4888* **Fax** *(07) 5449 2230* **Rooms** *175*

Located in Noosa's famous Hastings Street, this resort offers spacious rooms, each with a private balcony and spa. There are eight poolside villas which feature private courtyards. A comprehensive health club offers a full range of exercise options. **www.sheraton.com/noosa**

ROCKHAMPTON Myella Farm Stay $

Myella Baralaba, QLD 4702 **Tel** *(07) 4998 1290* **Fax** *(07) 4998 1104* **Rooms** *18*

This farm runs 400 head of cattle and offers a range of activity-filled packages including learning to ride a motorbike and horse riding. This is an authentic Queensland holiday experience. Overseas guests love the kangaroos and wallabies. **www.myella.com**

ROCKHAMPTON Country Comfort Rockhampton $$$

86 Victoria Parade, QLD 4700 **Tel** *(07) 4927 9933* **Fax** *(07) 4927 1615* **Rooms** *72*

International restaurant, cocktail bar, pool and luxury spa make this hotel the up-market choice in Rockhampton. Room options include penthouses, family and standard rooms. This coastline 40 km (25 miles) away boasts some of the best fishing spots in Queensland. Guests enjoy a variety of watersports. **www.countrycomforthotels.com**

STANTHORPE Amberley Edge Vineyard B&B $$

47 Clarke Lane, QLD 4380 **Tel** *(07) 4683 6203* **Fax** *(07) 4683 6203* **Rooms** *3*

This tastefully restored classic country homestead is in the heart of Queensland's wine country. Featuring stunning views of the countryside and Granite Belt, this winery stay is an eight-minute drive from Stanthorpe and offers wine sales and tasting at the cellar door. **www.amberleyedge.com.au**

STRADBROKE ISLAND Sunsets at Point Lookout B&B $$

6 Billa Street, Point Lookout, QLD 4183 **Tel** *(07) 3409 8823* **Fax** *(07) 3409 8873* **Rooms** *2*

This is a spectacularly appointed modern beach house overlooking the Pacific Ocean on one of Queensland's favourite Islands. For swimming, surfing, fishing, bird-watching, tennis or boating, this is the ideal stay, close to Brisbane and Moreton Bay. **www.babs.com.au**

SUNSHINE COAST Whale Watch Ocean Beach Resort $$$$$

Samarinda Drive, Point Lookout, QLD 4183 **Tel** *(07) 34098555* **Fax** *(07) 3409 8666* **Rooms** *40*

With breathtaking views of Stradbroke Island's beaches, this resort is the ideal spot to watch whales, dolphins, turtles and manta rays off Point Lookout. Located a short walk from Captain Cook's Lookout, the famous North Gorge Headlands walk and the Blowhole, it is also close to the Surf Club and cafés. **www.whalewatchresort.com.au**

SURFERS PARADISE Gold Coast International Backpackers Resort $

28 Hamilton Avenue, QLD 4217 **Tel** *(07) 5592 5888* **Fax** *(07) 5538 9310* **Rooms** *25*

Formerly known as Mardi Gras Backpackers, this budget accommodation is in the heart of Surfers Paradise. This is a great spot to stay during the Indy car races or for any action-packed holiday. There is a large self-contained kitchen, a games and recreation area, and a barbecue. **www.goldcoastbackpackers.com.au**

TOOWOOMBA Lauriston House Bed & Breakfast $$$

67 Margaret Street, QLD 4350 **Tel** *(07) 4632 4053* **Fax** *(07) 4639 5526* **Rooms** *3*

Heritage luxury in the heart of Toowoomba, this fabulous guesthouse is minutes from restaurants, galleries, parks and CBD. Built in 1920, this California bungalow reflects the charm of the region. It has an elegant guest lounge with a fireplace in winter, modern en suite facilities with spas, and gourmet breakfasts. **www.lauristonhouse.com**

TOWNSVILLE Seagulls Resort $$

74 The Esplanade, QLD 4810 **Tel** *(07) 4721 3111* **Fax** *(07) 4721 3133* **Rooms** *70*

This resort is set in tropical landscaped gardens, and offers a choice of hotel rooms and self-contained apartments. Extras include rooms with wheelchair access. The resort has a BBQ, tennis courts, playground and swimming pools and is located on the seafront, a five-minute drive from the airport. **www.seagulls.com.au**

TOWNSVILLE Jupiters Townsville $$$

Sir Leslie Thiess Drive, QLD 4810 **Tel** *(07) 4722 2333* **Fax** *(07) 4772 4741* **Rooms** *194*

Jupiters Townsville Hotel and Casino is situated on Queensland's tropical north coast. It overlooks Magnetic Island and provides access to the Great Barrier Reef for snorkelling, fishing and boating adventures. The hotel offers exceptional dining, bars, a swimming pool, sauna, spas, tennis courts and a gym. **www.jupiterstownsville.com.au**

Key to Price Guide *see p478* **Key to Symbols** *see back cover flap*

NORTHERN QUEENSLAND AND THE OUTBACK

ALEXANDER BAY Daintree Wilderness Lodge $$$$

83 Cape Tribulation Road, QLD 4873 **Tel** *(07) 4098 9105* **Fax** *(07) 4098 9258* **Rooms** *5*

This small lodge in the pristine wilderness of the Daintree National Park has won awards for ecotourism and donates A$1 of every stay to the local Cassoway Care Group. This is a unique holiday experience for nature lovers, bird lovers and travellers wanting to enjoy the lush rainforest of the Daintree. **www.daintreewildernesslodge.com.au**

ATHERTON TABLELAND: MALANDA Fur 'n' Feathers Rainforest Tree Houses $$$$$

247 Hogan Road, QLD 4885 **Tel** *(07) 4096 5364* **Fax** *(07) 4096 5380* **Rooms** *5*

Set in an ancient rainforest, perched on a riverbank, the Tree Houses provide the perfect balance of wilderness and luxury. There are fabulous views all round and this lush haven abounds with wildlife – platypuses can be spotted in the river. There is a restaurant nearby. **www.rainforesttreehouses.com.au**

BURKETOWN Savannah Lodge $$$$

Cnr Beames & Bowen streets, QLD 4830 **Tel** *(07) 4745 5177* **Fax** *(07) 47455211* **Rooms** *7*

This unique stay on the edge of the Gulf of Carpentaria offers roomy cabins and friendly service. This lodge is located in Burketown, close to facilities and the airport. Burketown sits on the Albert River between the Gulf wetlands and the savannah. Roads can become inaccessible in the monsoon season. **www.savannah-aviation.com**

CAIRNS Cairns Reef & Rainforest B&B $$

112 Mansfield Street, Earlville, QLD 4870 **Tel** *(07) 4033 5597* **Fax** *(07) 4033 5597* **Rooms** *3*

This guesthouse offers a tropical breakfast on the balcony overlooking the crystal clear rockpool and waterfall, a saltwater swimming pool, and a comprehensive tour desk which offers friendly advice and help to plan your ongoing trip. Situated in a pristine rainforest environment. **www.cairnsreefbnb.com.au**

CAIRNS Hotel Sofitel Reef Casino Cairns $$$$$

35–41 Wharf Street, QLD 4870 **Tel** *(07) 4030 8888* **Fax** *(07) 4030 8777* **Rooms** *128*

A stylish hotel experience, offering elegance and fun. The Sofitel Reef Casino is incorporated into the uniquely designed building, with the Cairns Rainforest Dome situated on top. There are Jacuzzi-style baths in every room, a selection of dining options and a rooftop pool. **www.reefcasino.com.au**

CAIRNS Mecure Hotel Harbourside $$$$$

209–217 The Esplanade, QLD 4870 **Tel** *(07) 4051 8999* **Fax** *(07) 4051 0317* **Rooms** *173*

A tropical theme runs through the decor of this up-market stay. Each room has a private balcony with spectacular views to Trinity Bay. Teshi's Restaurant is open from 6:30am until 10:30pm, offering a fusion of Eastern and Western cuisine and featuring local tropical produce and fresh seafood. **www.mecure-harbourside.com.au**

CAIRNS The Oasis Resort – Cairns $$$$$

122 Lake Street, QLD 4870 **Tel** *(07) 4080 1888* **Fax** *(07) 4080 1889* **Rooms** *314*

Stunning views of the Coral Coast and the Cairns hinterland make this the ideal luxury vacation choice. Set in landscaped tropical gardens, this resort has every modern facility plus a few extras. It has several rooms for disabled guests, a fully equipped gym, a lagoon, valet parking, laundry services and babysitting. **www.oasis-cairns.com.au**

CAIRNS Shangri-La Hotel (formerly Radisson Plaza at the Pier) $$$$$

Pierpoint Road, QLD 4870 **Tel** *(07) 4031 1411* **Fax** *(07) 4031 3226* **Rooms** *255*

The location of this hotel is breathtaking, situated on the marina at the pier. The marina serves as a gateway to the Great Barrier Reef. Enjoy the fishing, the view of Trinity Bay, rainforest gardens, or a safe swim in the hotel pool. Cairns lagoon is a short stroll away. **www.shangri-la.com**

CAPE TRIBULATION Coconut Beach Rainforest Resort $$$$$

Lot 10, Cape Tribulation Road, QLD 4873 **Tel** *1 300 134 044* **Fax** *(02) 9299 2103* **Rooms** *66*

A luxury stay on the edge of the lush rainforest of the Daintree. This resort offers a tropical holiday in a pristine natural setting with every modern convenience, including babysitting. Close to the Great Barrier Reef, this is an ideal stay for snorkelling, kayaking and 4WD trips. **www.coconutbeach.com.au**

COOKTOWN Pam's Place Motel Hostel $

Cnr Boundary & Charlotte streets, QLD 4895 **Tel** *(07) 4069 5166* **Fax** *(07) 4069 5964* **Rooms** *32*

Cooktown is an exotic, relaxed coastal town with a rich history including its Aboriginal cultural heritage. It is located only five nautical miles from the Great Barrier Reef and offers scenic flights and day trip charters to Lizard Island. The hostel has single and double rooms and dorms. **www.cooktownhostel.com**

CUNNAMULLA Nardoo Station Tourist Retreat $

"Nardoo", Cunnamulla, QLD 4490 **Tel** *(07) 4655 4833* **Fax** *(07) 4655 4835* **Rooms** *13*

This is the genuine Australian outback adventure. Lie back in the hot artesian spas or feed-up on good Australian cooking. Stays are catered to suit the individual traveller and whether you prefer to view the abundant wildlife or feed the farm animals, or go yabbying or fishing, this stay is friendly and unique. **www.nardoo.com.au**

DAINTREE Red Mill House

Red Mill House, Daintree Village, QLD 4873 **Tel** *(07) 4098 6233* **Fax** *(07) 4098 6233* **Rooms** *6*

This spacious, old home renovated in a tasteful modern design is situated in the Daintree and offers amazing bird-watching – seven of Australia's kingfishers have been spotted in the Red Mill House garden. Full breakfast with fresh seasonal fruit is included. **www.redmillhouse.com.au**

LONGREACH Aussie Betta Cabins

63 Sir Hudson Fysh Drive, QLD 4730 **Tel** *(07) 4658 3811* **Fax** *(07) 4658 3812* **Rooms** *22*

Longreach, in the heart of Queensland's outback, offers the tourist a chance to visit a famous Australian landmark – the Stockman's Hall of Fame. The cabins are conveniently located in walking distance of both these attractions. Extras include an outdoor pool and barbecue area. **www.queenslandholidays.com.au/outback/**

LONGREACH Albert Park Motor Inn

Sir Hudson Fysh Drive, QLD 4730 **Tel** *(07) 4658 2411* **Fax** *(07) 4658 3181* **Rooms** *56*

The Albert Park Motor Inn has extensive landscaped surrounds exhibiting local trees and shrubs; and is home to local wildlife. There is a resort-style swimming pool, Oasis restaurant and bar, and a playground for children. Longreach is a good base to explore the local area's attraction. **www.destinationlongreach.com.au**

MOSSMAN Silky Oaks Lodge & Healing Waters Spa

Mossman River Gorge, QLD 4873 **Tel** *1300 134 044* **Fax** *(07) 9299 2103* **Rooms** *50*

On the edge of Mossman Gorge, this luxury retreat has spectacular views of the Daintree. Buildings are designed to blend into the treetops and draw the visitor deep into the rainforest magic. Take a walk through the Mossman Gorge National Park or a trip to the Great Barrier Reef. **www.silkyoakslodge.com.au**

MOUNT ISA Travellers Haven Backpackers

75–77 Spence Street, QLD 4825 **Tel** *(07) 4743 0313* **Fax** *(07) 4743 4007* **Rooms** *21*

This backpackers' place offers a free pick up and drop off from the bus or train, and has a relaxed atmosphere. If you want to explore the region take the underground tour of the Mount Isa mine or visit the Riversleigh Fossil Centre. The Mount Isa Rodeo is between late July and early August. **www.users.bigpond.com.au/travellershaven**

MOUNT ISA All Seasons Burke & Wills

Cnr Grace & Camooweal Drive, QLD 4825 **Tel** *(07) 4743 8000* **Fax** *(07) 4743 8424* **Rooms** *56*

This Inn offers comfortable, air-conditioned rooms to cater for Mount Isa's climate. It is centrally located a short walk from the CBD, shops and cinemas. This hotel has some uniquely designed rooms which feature popular old-time frontshop façades. It also has off-street parking. **www.accorhotels.com.au**

NORMANTON The Gulfland Motel

PO Box 30, Normanton, QLD 4890 **Tel** *(07) 4745 1290* **Fax** *(07) 4745 1138* **Rooms** *28*

A motel with all the conveniences that a traveller to the Gulf expects, including a shaded garden setting and licensed restaurant. Each room has a television, coffee- and tea-making facilities and ironing facilities. Pre-dinner drinks are available in the licensed restaurant. **www.gulflandmotel.com.au**

PORT DOUGLAS Breakfree Portsea

76 Davidson Street, QLD 4877 **Tel** *(07) 4087 2000* **Fax** *(07) 4087 2001* **Rooms** *145*

A Mediterranean-style resort in the tropics, with lagoon pools and waterways, shady palms and open verandas. Classicaly furnished air-conditioned apartments with balconies overlooking the pools and gardens, this resort offers privacy and fun. Tone up in the gym or take a short stroll into Port Douglas. **www.breakfree.com.au**

PORT DOUGLAS Radisson Tree Tops Resort & Spa

316 Port Douglas Road, QLD 4871 **Tel** *(07) 4030 4333* **Fax** *(07) 4030 4323* **Rooms** *303*

Less than an hour's drive north of Cairns Airport, this luxury resort, set in the tropical rainforest of the Daintree, offers a sensual, serene environment. There is a range of room options, a spacious open-air restaurant and several bars built around the lagoon pool – opulent and fun. **www.radisson.com**

TORRES STRAIT ISLANDS: HORN ISLAND Gateway Torres Strait Resort

24 Outie Street, QLD 4875 **Tel** *(07) 40691902* **Fax** *(07) 40692211* **Rooms** *22*

Only a two-minute walk from the wharf on Horn Island, this resort offers a saltwater pool, an outdoor entertainment area and is home to the largest collection of Torres Strait history. It houses the Torres Strait Heritage Museum. The licensed restaurant boasts its differently themed nights and a "well-stocked bar". **www.torresstrait.com.au**

TORRES STRAIT ISLANDS: THURSDAY ISLAND Jardine Motel

Cnr Normanby Street & Victoria Parade, QLD 4875 **Tel** *(07) 4069 1555* **Fax** *(07) 4069 1470* **Rooms** *61*

Set in tropical landscaped gardens, this motel is decorated with local indigenous artwork and offers views of Prince Wales and Horn Islands. Disabled guests are catered for and trips organized, such as to the marine museum, fishing trips, island cruises and day trips to the Cape, or a visit to the historical cemetry. **www.jardinemotel.com.au**

WEIPA Heritage Resort

Commercial Avenue, QLD 4874 **Tel** *(07) 4069 8000* **Fax** *(07) 4069 8011* **Rooms** *30*

Located in the town centre adjacent to the Heritage Shopping Village, this resort features a licensed à la carte restaurant and bar and a landscaped tropical pool and barbecue area. Rooms are clean and comfortable with a homestyle touch. This is a great spot for fishing. **www.heritageresort.com.au**

Key to Price Guide *see p478* **Key to Symbols** *see back cover flap*

DARWIN AND THE TOP END

DARWIN Frogshollow Backpackers

27 Lindsay Street, NT 0800 **Tel** *(08) 8941 2600* **Fax** *(08) 8941 0758* **Rooms** *25*

Located opposite historic Frog's Hollow Park, this is one of Darwin's most popular backpacker hostels. It features an open-air saltwater plunge pool and two spas. As a licensed travel agent the hostelry offers the extra service of helping travellers with plans and bookings. **www.frogs-hollow.com.au**

DARWIN Crowne Plaza

32 Mitchell Street, NT 0800 **Tel** *(08) 89820000* **Fax** *(08) 89811765* **Rooms** *233*

Located in the heart of Darwin's CBD, Darwin's Crowne Plaza is a 15-minute drive from Darwin's International Airport. The hotel has an exciting cosmopolitan atmosphere and looks out over the Timor Sea, and is just a stroll from major shopping spots, cafés and Darwin's nightlife. **www.crowneplaza.com.au**

DARWIN Mirambeena Resort Darwin

64 Cavenaugh Street, NT 0800 **Tel** *(08) 8981 0100* **Fax** *(08) 8981 5116* **Rooms** *225*

Mirambeena means "welcome" and this tourist resort offers two swimming pools, two spas, a licensed restaurant, games room and fitness room. This hotel is conveniently located for the golf course and the Port of Darwin. The choice of accommodation includes town houses, de luxe or standard rooms. **www.mirambeena.com.au**

DARWIN Skycity

Gilruth Avenue The Gardens, NT 0800 **Tel** *(08) 8943 8888* **Fax** *(08) 8946 8999* **Rooms** *117*

This multi-award winning hotel is uniquely designed to blend into the landscape of the golf links. This hotel and casino offers world-class dining facilities and 24-hour entertainment and gambling. Close to the Mindil Beach markets, the grounds are home to goannas, colourful birds and green tree-frogs. **www.skycitydarwin.com.au**

DARWIN Saville Park Suites

88 The Esplanade, NT 0800 **Tel** *(08) 8943 4333* **Fax** *(08) 8943 4388* **Rooms** *204*

Overlooking Darwin's harbour with views to the Arafura Sea, this Australian luxury stay offers a licensed restaurant, bar, swimming pool and spa. Apartments have large private balconies, 24-hour room service and laundry facilities. Features include spacious rooms, lounge and dining areas. **www.savillesuites.com.au**

DARWIN:LUDMILLA Bremer B&B

27 Bremer Street, Ludmilla, NT 820 **Tel** *(08) 8981 3900* **Rooms** *2*

This guesthouse offers the visitor to Darwin quality accommodation at a budget price. Situated in a quiet, leafy street with a park across the road, it is located just a ten-minute walk from the Ludmilla Saturday markets and a short bus ride to the Thursday night markets. **www.bremerbnb.com.au**

HOWARD SPRINGS Melaleuca Homestead

163 Melaleuca Road, NT 0820 **Tel** *(08) 8983 2736* **Fax** *(08) 8983 3314* **Rooms** *2*

The Frangipani and Hibiscus Cottages are named in keeping with the tropical theme of this homestead. Both tastefully designed cottages are built in the style of the settlers' cottages of the late 19th century, and are raised for ventilation and feature wide verandas. **www.melaleucahomestead.com.au**

HUMPTY DOO Humpty Doo Hotel

Arnhem Highway, NT 0836 **Tel** *(08) 89881372* **Fax** *(08) 8988 2470* **Rooms** *16*

Humpty Doo is a small town on the Arnhem Highway between Darwin and Kakadu. It is an exceptional outback hotel for the visitor seeking to experience the true character of the Northern Territory. It offers ten cabins at the back of the hotel.

HUMPTY DOO Mango Meadows Homestay

2759 Bridgemary Crescent, NT 0836 **Tel** *(08) 8988 4417* **Fax** *(08) 8988 2883* **Rooms** *4*

This is an oasis in the bush, a stylish, relaxing guesthouse with wide verandas and attractive gardens. Mango Meadows is situated 45 km (28 miles) from Darwin CBD, 17 km (10 miles) from Palmerston City and 7 km (4 miles) from Humpty Doo Village. Tariff includes a full continental breakfast. **www.mangomeadows.com**

KAKADU NATIONAL PARK Gagudju Lodge Cooinda

Kakadu National Park, Kakadu Highway, Jim Jim, NT 0886 **Tel** *(08) 8979 0145* **Fax** *(08) 8979 0148* **Rooms** *48*

Picturesque and awe inspiring, this lodge is situated on Yellow Water Billabong in Kakadu National Park. Kakadu is home to one third of Australia's birdlife. Gagudju Lodge features two restaurants, a swimming pool, general store, airport and tour desk. **www.gagudjulodgecooinda.com.au**

KATHERINE Kookaburra Backpackers

Cnr Third & Lindsay streets, NT 0850 **Tel** *(08) 8971 0257* **Fax** *(08) 8972 1567* **Rooms** *26*

This unique backpackers offers free transfers to and from the Ghan train. Free breakfast, tea and coffee and 20 minutes of internet access are part of the deal. There is a large garden with swimming pool and barbecue. Offering four- and eight-bedroom dormitories and single or double rooms. **www.kookaburrabackpackers.com.au**

KATHERINE Knotts Crossing Resort

⬛⬛⬛⬛ $$$$$

NT 0850 **Tel** *(08) 8972 22511* **Fax** *(08) 8972 2628* **Rooms** *56*

This five times winner of the Brolga Award for accommodation offers family suites for up to six guests; executive suites with mini-bar and fax; and de luxe and standard rooms with tea- and coffee-making facilities. Each private cabin has its own outside en suite. **www.knottscrossing.com.au**

MARY RIVER The Bark Hut Tourism Centre

⬛⬛⬛ $$

Arnhem Highway, Annaburroo, NT 0850 **Tel** *(08) 8978 8988* **Fax** *(08) 8978 8932* **Rooms** *32*

The Bark Hut Tourism Centre is a historic icon in the Northern Territory. It was built in the era of crocodile and buffalo hunting, and is a hub of activity for visitors in Mary River and Kakadu National Park. The property features powered caravan sites, grassed camp sites and air-conditioned rooms. **www.barkhut.com.au**

THE RED CENTRE

ALICE SPRINGS Alice Motor Inn

⬛⬛⬛ $$

27 Undoolya Road, NT 870 **Tel** *(08) 8952 2322* **Fax** *(08) 8953 2309* **Rooms** *20*

A friendly and inexpensive motel, only a short distance from the centre of town in the quiet eastside of Alice Springs. A clean, comfortable, family-orientated environment with a lovely barbecue area by the outdoor swimming pool. Breakfast upon request and transport to and from the airport is also available. **www.alicemotorinn.com.au**

ALICE SPRINGS The All Seasons Diplomat

⬛⬛⬛⬛ $$

Cnr Gregory Terrace and Hartley Street, NT 870 **Tel** *(08) 8952 8977* **Fax** *(08) 8953 0225* **Rooms** *81*

The All Seasons Diplomat is located in the city centre. The hotel features two restaurants and bars, barbecue and a swimming pool. It's a handy base from which to explore Flynn's memorial, the Old Ghan train, Desert Park and the Botanical Gardens, and it's close to several art galleries and museums. **www.accorhotels.com**

ALICE SPRINGS All Seasons Oasis

⬛⬛⬛⬛⬛ $$

10 Gap Road, NT 870 **Tel** *(08) 8952 1444* **Fax** *(08) 8952 3776* **Rooms** *102*

Set amongst lush green gardens, this affordable hotel is a handy place to base yourself while you explore the variety of activities on offer, including Aboriginal Dreamtime tours, camel rides, hot-air balloon trips, bush restaurants, 4WD safaris, a desert golf course and a visit to Central Australia's only winery. **www.accorhotels.com.au**

ALICE SPRINGS Desert Palms Resort

⬛⬛⬛ $$

74 Barrett Drive, NT 870 **Tel** *(08) 8952 5977* **Fax** *(08) 8953 4176* **Rooms** *80*

This resort offers air-conditioned villa accommodation with private verandas set in a tropical paradise. Check out the stunning pool with its own island, footbridge and waterfall. A short distance from Lasseter's casino and close to the town centre. An ideal family destination. **www.desertpalms.com.au**

ALICE SPRINGS Heavitree Gap Outback Lodge

⬛⬛⬛⬛⬛ $$

1 Palm Circuit, NT 870 **Tel** *(08) 8950 4444* **Fax** *(08) 8952 9394* **Rooms** *78*

This lodge nestles amongst eucalypts at the base of the spectacular MacDonnell Ranges. Every night, wild black-footed rock wallabies come down from the mountains, and guests are able to feed them specially prepared food. The rooms have all the standard amenities and there is also a swimming pool. **www.auroraresorts.com.au**

ALICE SPRINGS MacDonnell Range Holiday Park

⬛⬛⬛ $$

Palm Circuit, NT 870 **Tel** *(08) 8952 6111* **Fax** *(08) 8952 5236* **Rooms** *48*

This multi-award-winning holiday park in the picturesque surroundings of the MacDonnell Ranges has a lot to offer the keen traveller. There are nightly talks on stars, bush tucker and 4WD preparation. There is music a couple of times a week. There's also a BMX track and two pools. Pets are not allowed. **www.macrange.com.au**

ALICE SPRINGS Novotel Outback Alice Springs

⬛⬛⬛⬛⬛⬛ $$

46 Stephens Road, NT 870 **Tel** *(08) 8952 6100* **Fax** *(08) 8952 1988* **Rooms** *138*

This resort-style complex is adjacent to the convention centre and golf course, it also has outstanding views of the nearby MacDonnell Ranges. It's an ideal base for travellers taking day trips to Ayers Rock, Stanley Chasm, Ormiston Gorge and the Alice Springs Desert Park. **www.accorhotels.com.au**

ALICE SPRINGS Aurora Alice Springs

⬛⬛⬛⬛⬛⬛ $$$

11 Leichhardt Terrace, NT 870 **Tel** *(08) 8950 6666* **Fax** *(08) 8952 7829* **Rooms** *108*

Aurora Alice Springs is the only hotel situated on the bustling Todd Mall – the town's main shopping, restaurant and entertainment precinct. It's also home to the famous Red Ochre Grill Café Restaurant, on whose walls hang one of the finest collections of Central Australian panoramic photography in the world. **www.auroraresorts.com.au**

ALICE SPRINGS Desert Rose Inn

⬛⬛⬛ $$$

15 Railway Terrace, NT 870 **Tel** *(08) 8952 1411* **Fax** *(08) 8952 3232* **Rooms** *35*

This inexpensive hotel has rooms overlooking the MacDonnell Ranges. Rooms are ideally suited to the budget traveller looking for a quiet location that is close to just about everything. The rooms are what you'd expect for the price. All have standard facilities, some have a private balcony as well. **www.desertroseinn.com.au**

Key to Price Guide *see p478* **Key to Symbols** *see back cover flap*

ALICE SPRINGS Voyages Alice Springs Resort
$$$

34 Stott Terrace, NT 870 **Tel** *(08) 8951 4545* **Fax** *(08) 8953 0995* **Rooms** *139*

Situated on the banks of the Todd River with its magnificent river red gums, this award-winning resort combines efficient and friendly Outback service with modern, comfortable facilities. Low-rise architecture and lush green lawns contribute to the relaxed atmosphere, and the bustling city centre is only five minutes away. **www.voyages.com.au**

ALICE SPRINGS Alice Springs Plaza Hotel
$$$$

94 Todd Street, NT 870 **Tel** *(08) 8952 2233* **Fax** *(08) 8952 7829* **Rooms** *50*

Close to the Royal Flying Doctors Service Museum, the Alice Springs Reptile Centre and Todd Mall, this hotel is affordable and convenient. There's a cocktail bar and restaurant on site, as well as a games and recreation room and a fantastic pool and relaxation area. **www.alicespringsplazahotel.com.au**

ALICE SPRINGS Crowne Plaza Hotel
$$$$

89 Barrett Drive, NT 870 **Tel** *(08) 8950 8000* **Fax** *(08) 8952 3822* **Rooms** *235*

Recently renovated to add a more contemporary feel, this hotel offers a wide range of services for the leisure and business traveller in a relaxed and stylish environment. Alice Springs Golf Course lies immediately behind it, and it's close to most of the town's main attractions. Breakfast is not included in the standard fare. **www.crowneplaza.com**

ERLDUNDA Desert Oaks Resort
$

Cnr Stuart Highway and Lasseters Highway, NT 872 **Tel** *(08) 8956 0984* **Fax** *(08) 8956 0942* **Rooms** *48*

Located 200 km (124 miles) from Alice Springs, this is a fine affordable place to stay, especially if you are planning on visiting Uluru or Kata Tjuta. Suited to families, there is a swimming pool and tennis court available for use. There's also a restaurant and tavern on site. Enjoy the old-fashioned country hospitality. **www.desertoaks.com**

TENNANT CREEK Eldorado Motor Inn
$$

195 Paterson Street, NT 860 **Tel** *(08) 8962 2402* **Fax** *(08) 8962 3034* **Rooms** *78*

This friendly motel is situated at the northern end of town. Wander around the grounds and marvel at the intricate work in the large termite hills, the fine detail of the swallow nests or just sit back and view the most stunning sunsets across unspoilt native lands and on to the MacDonnell Ranges. **www.eldoradomotorinn.com.au**

WATARRKA NATIONAL PARK Voyages Kings Canyon Resort
$$$

Luritja Road, NT 872 **Tel** *(08) 8956 7442* **Fax** *(08) 8956 7410* **Rooms** *128*

This sensitively designed resort is just 7 km (4 miles) from Watarrka National Park, the home of the magical sandstone formation of Kings Canyon. For those keen to enjoy a romantic evening, try the Sounds of Firelight four-course dinner for two, served under a canopy of stars. **www.voyages.com.au**

YULARA Outback Pioneer Hotel
$$

Yulara Drive, NT 870 **Tel** *(08) 8957 7605* **Fax** *(08) 8957 7615* **Rooms** *167*

There's a good friendly atmosphere around this place, with its huge cook-your-own communal barbecue area and nightly live entertainment. It's a good hotel to meet other travellers who like a beer and a fun time. There are plenty of budget rooms available, although in some cases this means sharing bathroom facilities. **www.voyages.com.au**

YULARA Desert Gardens Hotel
$$$

Yulara Drive, NT 872 **Tel** *(08) 8957 7888* **Fax** *(08) 8957 7716* **Rooms** *218*

This luxury hotel caters well for those who like to travel in style. A short walk to one of its many lookouts and you can view what is arguably one of Australia's greatest sunsets with a spectacular display of colours stretching across the face of Uluru and the surrounding desert. **www.voyages.com.au**

YULARA The Lost Camel Hotel
$$$

Yulara Drive, NT 872 **Tel** *(08) 8957 7650* **Fax** *(08) 8957 7657* **Rooms** *99*

This boutique hotel has apartment-style studios furnished in vibrant colours, mixing urban chic with traditional Aboriginal artifacts. The studio rooms are located around a sparkling pool and garden courtyard. It's one for those who would like a funky, contemporary feel to their Outback experience. **www.voyages.com.au**

YULARA Sails in the Desert
$$$$

Yulara Drive, NT 872 **Tel** *(08) 8957 7888* **Fax** *(08) 8957 7474* **Rooms** *224*

Named after the soaring white sails that crown its roof, this is Ayers Rock Resort's premier five-star hotel. Exquisitely furnished and designed, the interior decor focuses on Aboriginal heritage and culture, with a gallery in the lobby and significant artworks featured throughout the public areas and in the private rooms. **www.voyages.com.au**

PERTH AND THE SOUTHWEST

ALBANY Ace Motor Inn
$$$

314 Albany Highway, Albany, WA 6330 **Tel** *(08) 9841 2900/1800 625 900* **Fax** *(08) 9841 4443* **Rooms** *56*

Good, clean affordable lodging. All rooms have ground floor access and include satellite TV, free movies, electric blankets, hairdryer, tea and coffee facilities, iron and ironing board. Family rooms and spa suites are also available. Nestled in a peaceful garden a short distance from the town's main thoroughfare. **www.acemotorinn.com.au**

BRIDGETOWN Nelson's of Bridgetown

38 Hampton Street, Bridgetown, WA 6255 **Tel** *(08) 9761 1641/1800 635 565* **Fax** *(08) 9761 2372* **Rooms** *35*

Self-described as "olde worlde" lodging, this triple Tourism Award winner has extras like a large hot tub spa. A pretty courtyard is nestled beside the 1898 hotel building. In keeping with tradition, the rooms have antique decor and Baltic federation furniture. **www.nelsonsofbridgetown.com.au**

BUNBURY The Rose Hotel

Victoria Street, Bunbury, WA 6230 **Tel** *(08) 9721 4533* **Fax** *(08) 9721 8285* **Rooms** *25*

One of the best-preserved historic buildings in the city centre, this Victorian hotel retains the opulence and extravagant details of the glory days of the 19th century. The architectural highlights are the intricate ironwork and the ornate first-floor veranda. Some of the ground-floor units are accessible for wheelchair-users.

BUSSELTON Mandalay Holiday Resort

652 Geographe Bay Road, Busselton, WA 6280 **Tel** *(08) 9752 1328, 1800 248 231* **Rooms** *56*

Accommodation options at this budget resort complex include villas, chalets, cabins, cottages and onsite caravans. Standard en suite cabins include fully equipped kitchens. Resort facilities include barbecues, games rooms, adventure playgrounds, bicycle hire and a communal TV lounge. **www.mandalayresort.com.au**

DENMARK Karri Mia Resort

Mount Shadforth Road, Denmark, WA 6333 **Tel** *(08) 9848 2233* **Fax** *(08) 9848 1133* **Rooms** *25*

A beautiful, relaxed setting beside the southern ocean, national park and vineyard. Choose from motel suites, bungalows and studios. De luxe bungalows are split level with a double-shower and spa bath en suite. Guests can cook on the barbecue outside and play in the games room. **www.karrimia.com.au**

ESPERANCE Hospitality Inn Esperance

The Esplanade, Esperance, WA 6450 **Tel** *(08) 9071 1999* **Fax** *(08) 9071 3915* **Rooms** *50*

All standard rooms are light and roomy with quality, queen-size beds, TV, mini bar and tea- and coffee-making facilities. Set on the shores of the Great Southern Ocean in Esperance Bay, the hotel is only a two-minute walk to the heart of the township. Caters for the disabled. **www.hinnesperance.bestwestern.com.au**

FREMANTLE Backpackers Inn

11 Pakenham Street, Fremantle, WA 6160 **Tel** *(08) 9431 7065* **Fax** *(08) 9336 7106* **Rooms** *40*

This well-managed youth hostel comes with an excellent reputation for comfortable, budget accommodation. Set in the heart of Fremantle, it has a lounge area, open fireplace and reading room, pool table and table tennis. internet bookings are recommended ahead of time. Reception open from 7am to 10pm. **www.yha.com.au**

FREMANTLE Old Firestation Backpackers

18 Phillimore Street, Fremantle, WA 6160 **Tel** *(08) 9430 5454* **Rooms** *6*

Budget-style accommodation in this heritage-listed building close to the railway station. Dormitory style sleeping arrangements plus six double rooms. Facilities include free parking, sun lounge and barbecue area, 24-hour internet access, TV and fridge, playstation, DVDs and games room. **www.old-firestation.net**

FREMANTLE Harbour Village Quest Apartments

Mews Road, Fremantle, WA 6160 **Tel** *(08) 94303888* **Fax** *(08) 94303800* **Rooms** *56*

This modern apartment hotel on the quay in Challenger Harbour offers a spa, barbecue area, in-house movies, internet access and laundry. The smart, functional rooms have fully equipped kitchens and excellent views. **www.harbourvillage.property.questwa.com.au**

FREMANTLE Esplanade Hotel Fremantle

Cnr Marine Terrace & Essex Street, Fremantle, WA 6160 **Tel** *(08) 94324000* **Fax** *(08) 94304539* **Rooms** *300*

A famous building in the heart of Fremantle, this grand hotel has homely rooms, most with private balconies. Standard rooms include mini bar, hairdryer, voice mail messaging, radio alarm and satellite TV. Facilities include sauna, three outdoor spas and bicycle hire. **www.esplanadehotelfremantle.com.au**

HYDEN Wave Rock Motel

2 Lynch Street, Hyden, WA 6359 **Tel** *(08) 9880 5052* **Fax** *(08) 9880 5041* **Rooms** *54*

Surrounded by Australian bushland, this Outback motel has excellent facilities, including three restaurants. It's a good base for visitors to nearby Wave Rock (*see p318*), the bizarre granite rock formation. The hotel rooms are basic but they are clean and comfortable enough. **www.waverock.com.au**

KALGOORLIE York Hotel

259 Hannan Street, Kalgoorlie, WA 6430 **Tel** *(08) 9021 2337* **Fax** *(08) 9021 2337* **Rooms** *20*

A air of grace and elegance to this magnificently preserved Kalgoorlie iconic building. It was built during the gold rush in 1896 and the Victorian architecture features an ornate facade and domed roof (*see p319*). Rooms are simple and snug, and some have balconies. It is ideally situated in the centre of town.

MARGARET RIVER Surfpoint Resort

12 Riedle Drive, Margaret River, WA 6285 **Tel** *(08) 9757 1777* **Fax** *(08) 9757 1077* **Rooms** *16*

This budget beachside lodging won the WA Tourism Award in 2003. The 16 double rooms and nine dorms are clean and comfortable. There is also a lounge, dining area, kitchen, barbecue, laundry and internet access. Guests can hire boogie boards, surf boards and mountain bikes from the hotel. Fully wheelchair accessible. **www.surfpoint.com.au**

Key to Price Guide *see p478* **Key to Symbols** *see back cover flap*

MARGARET RIVER Grange on Farrelly $$$$$

18 Farrelly Street, Margaret River, WA 6285 **Tel** *1800 650 100* **Fax** *(08) 9757 3076* **Rooms** *29*

A tranquil location close to the centre of town. Rooms are cosy and offer a choice of four-poster beds or canopy beds, and have ground-floor access. Outside are native gardens, a barbecue area and half-court tennis court. A spa and free in-house movies are also available. **www.grangeonfarrelly.com.au**

NORTHAM Shamrock Hotel $$

112 Fitzgerald Street, Northam, WA 6401 **Tel** *(08) 9622 1092* **Fax** *(08) 9622 5707* **Rooms** *14*

This historic colonial building dates back to 1866. It has been restored and contains memorabilia documenting the history of the town. The beautiful bedrooms all come with king-size bed, en suite, TV, fridge and hot-drink facilities while de luxe suites have personal spas.

PEMBERTON Karri Valley Resort $$$$

Vasse Highway, Pemberton, WA 6260 **Tel** *(08) 9776 2020/1800 245 757* **Fax** *(08) 9776 2012* **Rooms** *62*

Nestled in the heart of the Karri Valley overlooking Lake Beedelup, these cosy chalets are fully equipped for self-catering visitors. Many chalets have lake views and a private balcony and the resort feaures mini golf and two tennis courts. A general store is on site for basic food and souvenirs. **www.karrivalleyresort.com.au**

PERTH Criterion Hotel $

560 Hay Street, Perth, WA 6000 **Tel** *(08) 9325 5155, 1800 245 155* **Rooms** *69*

This dependable, good-value hotel has an impressive Art Deco façade. It is well positioned in the centre of Perth, within walking distance of most of the city's notable sights. The rooms are spacious, have en suite bathrooms and are well appointed with all the usual modern facilities. **www.criterion-hotel-perth.com.au**

PERTH Miss Maud Swedish Hotel $$

97 Murray Street, Perth, WA 6000 **Tel** *(08) 9325 3900/1800 998022* **Fax** *(08) 92213225* **Rooms** *52*

Self-dubbed "our little bit of Sweden in the heart of the city". Awarded Best Mid-range Accommodation in Australia for two years running. Uniquely designed Nordic and Scandinavian rooms. Some rooms have internet access. Smorgasbord breakfasts available in the downstairs restaurant. **www.missmaud.com.au**

PERTH Acacia Hotel $$$

15 Robinson Avenue, Northbridge, WA 6003 **Tel** *(08) 93280000* **Fax** *(08) 93280100* **Rooms** *96*

Bright, modern rooms feature mini bar, satellite TV, long bathtub and hairdryer. Excellent location in the nightlife and restaurant zone. Other features include 24-hour reception, free undercover parking and room access for the disabled. Various package deals also available. **www.acaciahotel.com.au**

PERTH Scarborough Indian Ocean Hotel $$$

23 Hastings Street, Scarborough, WA 6019 **Tel** *(08) 9341 1122* **Fax** *(08) 9341 1899* **Rooms** *59*

This good value accommodation is very popular in summer, so be sure to book ahead. The basic, neat and tidy rooms come as economy, de luxe or poolside. There is a games room, internet access and free in-house movies. The hotel also offers baby-sitting and an airport shuttle service. **www.ioh.com.au**

PERTH Intercontinental Burswood Resort $$$$$

Corner Bolton Avenue & Great Eastern Highway, Burswood, WA 6100 **Tel** *(08) 9362 7777* **Rooms** *413*

A large stylish resort with nine restaurants, six bars, a nightclub, a 24-hour casino, gift stores, tennis courts and a golf course. It's only a five-minute drive to the city centre and 15 minutes from the airport, and the modern rooms come with bathtub, satellite TV and internet access. **www.intercontinental.com**

PERTH Rendezvous Observation City Hotel $$$$$

The Esplanade, Scarborough, WA 6019 **Tel** *(08) 92451000* **Fax** *(08) 92451345* **Rooms** *333*

This high-rise luxury hotel is a landmark in Perth. Smartly furnished rooms include big-screen TV and in-house movies. Many rooms have a spa and superb ocean views. The heated pool, sun lounge, children's wading pool and spa occupy the tenth floor. The poolside bar features a tropical garden. **www.rendezvoushotels.com**

PERTH Sheraton Perth Hotel $$$$$

207 Adelaide Terrace, Perth, WA 6000 **Tel** *(08) 9224 7777* **Fax** *(08) 9224 7788* **Rooms** *390*

Everything you expect from a genuine five-star luxury hotel. Located in Perth's Central Business District and a few minutes walk from the main shopping and dining district. Most rooms have panoramic views of the Swan River, 24-hour room service, safety deposit boxes and internet access. **www.sheraton.com/perth**

ROTTNEST ISLAND The Rottnest Hotel – Quokka Arms $$$

Bedford Avenue, Rottnest Island, WA 6161 **Tel** *(08) 92925011* **Fax** *(08) 92925188* **Rooms** *18*

Built in 1864, this was originally the summer residence of the governors of Western Australia. It underwent a major renovation in 2004 when it was officially renamed as the Quokka Arms. Its motel-style rooms are comfortable and clean, and there is a great beer garden with superb ocean views. **www.axismgt.com.au/rottnesthotel**

ROTTNEST ISLAND Rottnest Lodge $$$$

Rottnest Island, WA 6161 **Tel** *(08) 92925161* **Fax** *(08) 92925158* **Rooms** *80*

Popular with families, this hotel has five styles of accommodation from budget rooms to premium suites. Standard rooms have plain decor, ceiling fans, private bathroom, fridge, satellite TV with pay-to-view movies and shared veranda. An idyllic setting by the water's edge. **www.rottnestlodge.com.au**

WALPOLE Tree Top Walk Motel
Nockolds Street, Walpole, WA 6398   **Tel** *(08) 9840 1444/1800 420 777*   **Fax** *(08) 9840 1555*   **Rooms** *37*

A top location in the Walpole wilderness area. Close to Conspicuous Beach and the impressive Valley of the Giants *(see p313)* to the east of Walpole, where a treetop walk takes visitors through the high canopy of massive tingle trees. The hotel has en suite standard rooms and two two-bedroom family units. **www.treetopwalkmotel.com.au**

YORK Settlers House
125 Avon Terrace, York, WA 6302   **Tel** *(08) 9641 1096*   **Fax** *(08) 9641 1093*   **Rooms** *18*

Situated in York's main street, this historic local landmark was built in 1845 and is classified by the National Trust. Recently refurbished, the classic furniture and colonial decor match the hotel's yesteryear style. Log fires, lace table clothes, lamp-lit passages, cobbled courtyards and country hospitality. **www.settlershouse.com.au**

NORTH OF PERTH AND THE KIMBERLEY

BROOME Courthouse B&B
10 Stewart Street, Broome, WA 6725   **Tel** *(08) 9192 2733*   **Fax** *(08) 9192 2956*   **Rooms** *3*

A huge two-storey family home which has three luxurious rooms: the pearling masters room; the Broome room; and the Oriental room. Cooked, tropical breakfasts can be enjoyed beside the pool or on the balcony. Centrally located across from Broome's Saturday markets and a three-minute walk from Chinatown. **www.thecourthouse.com.au**

BROOME Tropicana Inn Broome
Cnr Saville Street and Robinson Street, Broome, WA 6725   **Tel** *(08) 9192 2583*   **Fax** *(08) 9192 2583*   **Rooms** *90*

A quality, mid-range hotel with economy, standard and superior rooms. Rooms feature include TV and hot beverage making facilities, and all rooms are non-smoking. Outdoor entertaining includes a barbecue and tropical gardens. Located a short stroll from the town beach. **www.tropicanainnbroome.com.au**

BROOME Cable Beach Club Resort
Cable Beach Road, Broome, WA 6725   **Tel** *(08) 9192 0400*   **Fax** *(08) 9192 2249*   **Rooms** *280*

A prominent, recently renovated resort hotel on the edge of famous Cable Beach *(see p296)*. Western-Oriental fusion of architectural styles includes eastern artifacts and a Buddha sanctuary. Beautifully landscaped gardens and ocean views. Studio rooms have polished timber floors and private veranda. **www.cablebeachclub.com**

CARNARVON Fascine Lodge
David Brand Drive, Carnarvon, WA 6701   **Tel** *(08) 9941 2411*   **Fax** *(08) 9941 2491*   **Rooms** *60*

Conveniently located right in the heart of town with the waterfront and a shopping centre both nearby. The lodge offers respectable en-suite rooms with their own fridges. Guests can kick back and relax in the evening at the informal cocktail bar beside the swimming pool.

CORAL BAY Ningaloo Reef Resort
1 Robinson Street, Coral Bay, WA 6701   **Tel** *(08) 9942 5934*   **Fax** *(08) 9942 5953*   **Rooms** *36*

Superbly located accommodation beside the shores of stunning Coral Bay and the outer reef, the perfect spot for snorkelling trips in crystal turquoise sea. Standard rooms are en suite with pool and ocean views. The resort also has self-contained apartments has a bar, games room and barbecue in the garden. **www.coralbay.org/resort.htm**

DAMPIER Dampier Mermaid Hotel & Motel
The Esplanade, Dampier, WA 6713   **Tel** *(08) 9183 1222*   **Fax** *(08) 9183 1028*   **Rooms** *63*

This hotel overlooking King Bay has tropical gardens, a spa and an outdoor barbecue, where guests can make the most of the balmy evenings. There is also a cocktail bar, pool table and billiards tables. All rooms are en suite and have satellite TV. The hotel caters for families and cots provided upon request. **www.dampiermermaid.com.au**

DENHAM Bay Lodge
113 Knight Terrace, Denham, WA 6537   **Tel** *(08) 9948 1278 / 1800812780*   **Fax** *(08) 9948 1031*   **Rooms** *17*

Cheap accommodation in a great spot for reaching some of the loveliest attractions of Shark Bay, one of the highlights of the West Coast, such as the bright white Shell Beach, the dolphins of Monkey Mia and the bizarre Stromatolites *(see pp326-7)*. The lodge has a swimming pool. **www.baylodge.info**

DENHAM Heritage Resort Shark Bay
73 Knight Terrace, Denham, WA 6537   **Tel** *(08) 9948 1133*   **Fax** *(08) 9948 1134*   **Rooms** *27*

First-class service in this oceanside lodging in Denham's main street. Contemporary, spacious rooms each with king-size bed, en suite, fridge, TV and in-room movies. The hotel has a cocktail lounge, saloon bar, liquor store and fresh local seafood menu. **www.heritageresort.net.au**

DERBY King Sound Resort Hotel
Loch Street, Derby, WA 6728   **Tel** *(08) 9193 1044*   **Fax** *(08) 9191 1649*   **Rooms** *75*

This established resort hotel is a good base for arranging trips to the magnificent Kimberley *(see p296-7)*. The hotel has a cocktail bar and an outdoor barbecue, and rooms are cosy, modern and fully equipped with queen-size beds, en suite bathrooms and free in-house films. **www.kingsoundresort.com.au**

Key to Price Guide *see p478*   **Key to Symbols** *see back cover flap*

EXMOUTH Exmouth Cape Tourist Village

Cnr Murat Road & Truscott Crescent, Exmouth, WA 6707 **Tel** *(08) 9949 1101* **Fax** *(08) 9949 1402* **Rooms** *12*

Budget accommodation popular with backpackers. Exmouth is a great place for learning to dive. The nearest beach is a four-minute drive away and idyllic Turquoise Bay, where the Ningaloo Reef comes right into the shore, is also not far off. The resort runs a free beach bus and rents out mountain bikes. **www.exmouthvillage.com**

HALLS CREEK Kimberley Hotel

Roberta Avenue, Halls Creek, WA 6770 **Tel** *(08) 9168 6101* **Rooms** *63*

Halls Creek is in the heart of the Kimberley and close to the remarkable Bungle Bungles. The hotel contains 42 well-appointed units built in the design of small station homesteads. Standard rooms are self-contained with high roofs and wide verandas. There is a spa and airport shuttle service. **www.kh.kimberley-accom.com.au**

KALBARRI Kalbarri Palm Resort

8 Porter Street, Kalbarri, WA 6536 **Tel** *(08) 9937 2333/1800 819 029* **Fax** *(08) 9937 1324* **Rooms** *78*

A popular, family-style lodging in beautiful Kalbarri. The spectacular estuary is the perfect place for swiming or horse-riding at sunset. The resort accommodates its active guests by offering indoor cricket, lawn bowls and tennis courts. There is also a heated outdoor spa for those who just want to relax. **www.kalbarri.bestwestern.com.au**

KARRATHA Mercure Inn Hotel

Searipple Road, Karratha, WA 6714 **Tel** *(08) 9185 1155* **Rooms** *60*

All standard rooms in this centrally located hotel are en suite. Business suites and family rooms are also available. There is a 24-hour reception, spa, internet access, three bars, dry-cleaning and laundry service. Outside the hotel are barbecue facilities in a tropical courtyard. **www.accorhotels.com.au**

KUNUNURRA Best Western Country Club Hotel

47 Coolibah Drive, Kununurra, WA 6743 **Tel** *(08) 9168 1024* **Fax** *(08) 9168 1189* **Rooms** *88*

Lovely tropical gardens surround this pleasant lodging. Choose from 40 ground-floor units and 48 rooms in eight sets of two-storey buildings. Standard rooms include en suite bathroom, satellite TV and in-room movies. The hotel has a bar-side pool, cocktail bar, guest laundry and shared veranda. **www.countryclubhotel.com.au**

MONKEY MIA Monkey Mia Dolphin Resort

Monkey Mia, Denham, WA 6537 **Tel** *(08) 9948 1320* **Fax** *(08) 9948 1034* **Rooms** *90*

Superb seaside spot with beach front, garden and limestone villas, which are very popular. People come in droves to see the dolphins *(see p327)*. There are also hot tubs, three eateries, two bars and a tennis court at the resort. Standard beachside units have king-size beds and are en suite. **www.monkeymia.com.au**

NEW NORCIA New Norcia Hotel

Great Northern Highway, New Norcia, WA 6509 **Tel** *(08) 9654 8034* **Fax** *(08) 9654 8011* **Rooms** *16*

This hotel located beside a monastery offers plain, simple, tidy rooms run by friendly management. Rooms have overhead fans, fridge, plus shared bathroom and toilet. Also available is one en suite room with a queen-size bed and two bunks. The bar is open from 10am to midnight. **www.newnorcia.wa.edu.au/hotel.htm**

ADELAIDE AND THE SOUTHEAST

ADELAIDE Plaza Hotel

85 Hindley Street, SA 5000 **Tel** *(08) 8231 6371* **Fax** *(08) 8231 2005* **Rooms** *20*

This very central hotel is situated on one of Adelaide's busiest and most famous streets. It shares a colonial estate building with a hairdressers, coffee/café bar, trendy clothes shop and art studio. There is a magnificent palm tree garden in the centre of the hotel, featuring one of the oldest palm trees in Adelaide. **www.plazahotel.com.au**

ADELAIDE Majestic Roof Garden Hotel

55 Frome Street, SA 5000 **Tel** *(08) 8100 4400* **Fax** *(08) 8100 4488* **Rooms** *120*

This new and unique hotel has a landscaped garden on the roof that will make your jaw drop. Designed by award-winning architect David Baptiste and with views of the Adelaide Hills and CBD, it makes for an inspiring haven. The rest of the place is modern and welcoming and the staff are attentive and friendly. **www.majestichotels.com.au**

ADELAIDE Mercure Grosvenor

125 North Terrace, SA 5000 **Tel** *(08) 8407 8888* **Fax** *(08) 8407 8866* **Rooms** *243*

This hotel has a reputation for friendly, unobtrusive and attentive service. Opposite Adelaide Casino, Adelaide Convention Centre and the Festival Theatre, it's an ideal base for exploring Adelaide's plethora of cultural offerings. **www.mercuregrosvenorhotel.com.au**

ADELAIDE Holiday Inn Adelaide

65 Hindley Street, SA 5000 **Tel** *(08) 8231 5552* **Fax** *(08) 8237 3800* **Rooms** *181*

This well run and modern hotel is conveniently located right in the middle of Adelaide's main nightlife strip. The stylish rooms have superb city views and modern facilities. There are several rooms that cater for people with disabilities. The staff are wonderful. **www.ichotelsgroup.com**

ADELAIDE Hotel Richmond $$$$

128 Rundle Mall, SA 5000 **Tel** *(08) 8223 4044* **Fax** *(08) 8232 2290* **Rooms** *30*

Located in the heart of Adelaide's Rundle Mall, this hotel has an ultra modern feel about it. The decor is classy and contemporary. The rooms are stunningly presented, some with flatscreen TVs and marble en suite bathrooms with separate bath and shower. The staff are friendly and professional. **www.hotelrichmond.com.au**

ADELAIDE Rockford Adelaide $$$$

164 Hindley Street, SA 5000 **Tel** *(08) 8211 8255* **Fax** *(08) 8231 1179* **Rooms** *68*

The modern rooms are extremely satisfying in this quality hotel. Situated right in the heart of Adelaide's hip West End, on the corner of Hindley Street and Morphett Street it's merely minutes from most of the city's attractions. **www.rockfordhotels.com.au**

ADELAIDE Rydges South Park Hotel $$$$

1 South Terrace, SA 5000 **Tel** *(08) 8212 1277* **Fax** *(08) 8212 3040* **Rooms** *97*

The Rydges at South Park has impressive views of Adelaide's parklands and the Adelaide Hills. It's very reasonably priced for its location and is the closest hotel to the Adelaide Showgrounds. All rooms come with full amenities and are spacious, attractive and comfortable. **www.rydges.com/southpark**

ADELAIDE Chifley on South Terrace $$$$$

226 South Terrace, SA 5000 **Tel** *(08) 8223 4355* **Fax** *(08) 8232 5997* **Rooms** *93*

Homely decor, earthy red colours, couches and a fireplace in the foyer make this hotel seem all the more welcoming. The rooms overlook the South Parklands and the hotel itself is close to the city and the airport. It also has convenient public transport – the nearby tram will take you all the way to Glenelg. **www.chifleyhotels.com**

ADELAIDE Hilton Adelaide $$$$$

233 Victoria Square, SA 5000 **Tel** *(08) 8217 2000* **Fax** *(08) 8217 2001* **Rooms** *380*

It has everything you would expect from a Hilton hotel and is located near to Adelaide's famous bustling Central Markets and around the corner from one of the city's best restaurant strips, Gouger Street. The views across the city are spectacular and Adelaide's main shopping precinct is only a few minutes walk away. **www.hilton.com**

ADELAIDE Hotel Grand Chancellor Adelaide $$$$$

18 Currie Street, SA 5000 **Tel** *1800 801 849* **Fax** *(08) 8112 8899* **Rooms** *60*

Ideally positioned in the Central Business District, this hotel is within walking distance of the major cultural attractions, shopping precincts and entertainment centres. The interior is extremely pleasing to the eye, with Art Nouveau-style decor and rich vibrant colours throughout. Breakfast is included in the standard room price. **www.ghihotels.com**

ADELAIDE Hyatt Regency $$$$$

North Terrace, SA 5000 **Tel** *(08) 8231 1234* **Fax** *(08) 8231 1120* **Rooms** *367*

Next to the Adelaide Casino, this hotel is typical of the Hyatt hotel chain. Most of the rooms have spectacular views of the city. The service and facilities are top class. The Adelaide Convention Centre is next door, the Festival Theatre is a minute's walk away and the hustle and bustle of Hindley Street is one block over. **www.adelaide.hyatt.com**

ANGASTON Collingrove Homestead $$$$$

Eden Valley Road, SA 5353 **Tel** *(08) 8564 2061* **Fax** *(08) 8564 3600* **Rooms** *6*

This stunning heritage-listed 1800s homestead is one of the most beautiful buildings in South Australia. Its seven uncluttered, luxurious, private rooms have all the modern facilities you would expect. Breakfasts are an absolute highlight, including home-made jams, muffins and croissants. **www.collingrovehomestead.com.au**

COONAWARRA Chardonnay Lodge Coonawarra Wine Resort $$$

Riddoch Highway, SA 5263 **Tel** *(08) 8736 3309* **Fax** *(08) 8736 3383* **Rooms** *38*

Located in the heart of the Coonawarra Vineyards on beautifully landscaped grounds, this lodge is perfect for travellers who appreciate some fine wine – it has its own wine label. Light breakfasts are provided free of charge but there is a small extra fee for those requiring a cooked meal. **www.chardonnaylodge.com.au**

CRAFERS Grand Mercure Mount Lofty House $$$$

74 Mount Lofty Summit Road, SA 5152 **Tel** *(08) 8339 6777* **Fax** *(08) 8339 5656* **Rooms** *29*

This historic country house has been made into an award-winning boutique hotel. Most of the comfortable, well-equipped guestrooms have fantastic views of the Adelaide Hills. It has a relaxed atmosphere but there's plenty to do if you feel like it, with tennis, volleyball and swimming facilities all available. **www.mtloftyhouse.com.au**

GLENELG Norfolk Motor Inn $

71 Broadway, SA 5045 **Tel** *(08) 8295 6354* **Fax** *(08) 8295 6866* **Rooms** *20*

This small peaceful motel is in one of the nicest old suburbs of Adelaide. It's only five minutes walk from the beach and two minutes from the hustle and bustle of Glenelg's trendy Jetty Road. It's very affordable, the rooms are small but comfortable and a continental breakfast is available upon request. **www.norfolkmotorinn.com**

GLENELG Oaks Plaza Pier $$$

16 Holdfast Promenade, SA 5045 **Tel** *(08) 8350 6688* **Fax** *(08) 8350 6699* **Rooms** *180*

This five-star hotel is right on the beachfront in Glenelg, close to Jetty Road and only ten minutes drive from the city. It has outstanding facilities, including a lap pool, spa, plunge pool and sauna. It was the winner of the 2004 AHA Award for Excellence as Best Superior Accommodation. All rooms have balconies. **www.theoaksgroup.com.au**

Key to Price Guide *see p478* **Key to Symbols** *see back cover flap*

GLENELG Stamford Grand Hotel $$$

Moseley Square, SA 5045 **Tel** *(08) 8376 1222* **Fax** *(08) 8376 1111* **Rooms** *241*

Plum in the middle of the most vibrant area of Glenelg, the Stamford Grand is a luxury hotel boasting magnificent views of the ocean, the city and the Adelaide Hills. The rooms are ultra modern and have top-class facilities. The hotel is just minutes from the airport. **www.stamford.com.au**

HAHNDORF The Hahndorf Old Mill $$$

98 Main Street, SA 5245 **Tel** *(08) 8388 7888* **Fax** *(08) 8388 7242* **Rooms** *22*

Part of an 1854 flour mill has been incorporated into this complex in Australia's oldest German town. Located in the heart of Hahndorf's bustling main street, it offers a range of accommodation from motel rooms to spa chalets. The service is friendly and there are art galleries and craft shops just minutes from the front door.

KANGAROO ISLAND Comfort Inn Wysteria Lodge $$$$

7 Cygnet Road, Kingscote, SA 5223 **Tel** *(08) 8553 2011* **Fax** *(08) 8553 2200* **Rooms** *20*

All of the units in this quiet seafront lodge have lovely panoramic views of the ocean. They are perfect for those who want to escape the rat race for a little while and maybe just watch a yacht race instead. Modern facilities throughout and a few extras such as private spa baths in the de luxe suites.

KANGAROO ISLAND Wanderers Rest $$$$

Bayview Road, American River, SA 5221 **Tel** *(08) 8553 7140* **Fax** *(08) 8553 7282* **Rooms** *9*

Set high on the island hillside, this intimate classy guesthouse has marvellous views across the ocean to the far-off mainland. It's surrounded by native bush and wildlife, including wallabies and a myriad of bird species. The emphasis on intimacy and peacefulness means it is unsuitable for children. **www.wanderersrest.com.au**

KANGAROO ISLAND Ozone Seafront Hotel $$$$$

The Foreshore, Kingscote, SA 5223 **Tel** *(08) 8553 2011* **Fax** *(08) 8553 2249* **Rooms** *37*

First opened in 1907 and situated on the shores of Nepean Bay, this affordable family retreat blends country style charm with modern facilities. There is an outdoor solar-heated pool, internet access, extensive conference facilities and plenty more. It's also only a two-minute walk to the beach. **www.ozonehotel.com**

LYNDOCH Chateau Barrosa Motel $$$

Barossa Valley Highway, SA 5351 **Tel** *(08) 8524 4268* **Fax** *(08) 8524 4725* **Rooms** *34*

This motel, set in a stunning garden of 30,000 roses, is situated at the gateway to the Barossa Valley. There are daily tours of the nearby chateau which houses one of the world's great collections of Meissen porcelain, antique furniture, tapestries and paintings. **www.chateaubarrosa.com.au**

MOUNT GAMBIER Lakes Resort $$$$

17 Lakes Terrace West, SA 5290 **Tel** *(08) 8725 5755* **Fax** *(08) 8723 2710* **Rooms** *40*

This four-star resort suits people who are after somewhere quiet to stay, as it is the only one that isn't built along the highway. Also, it's the only resort with views over the town of Mount Gambier. Built on the slopes of an extinct volcano it offers a variety of options from budget accommodation to executive suites. **www.lakesresort.com.au**

NORTH ADELAIDE Princes Lodge Motel $

73 Lefevre Terrace, SA 5006 **Tel** *(08) 8267 5566* **Fax** *(08) 8239 0787* **Rooms** *22*

Just 2 kilometres (1 mile) from Adelaide's Central Business District, this delightful old mansion is both affordable and comfortable. Built in 1913, it's a stately manor with old wooden panels, leadlight windows and architraves throughout. There are magnificent views across the adjacent parklands. **www.princeslodge.com.au**

PADTHAWAY Padthaway Estate Homestead $$$

Riddoch Highway, SA 5271 **Tel** *(08) 8765 5555* **Fax** *(08) 8765 5554* **Rooms** *6*

Surrounded by vineyards, this historic homestead is a lovely quiet spot to spend the weekend. Built from local limestone in 1882, it consists of a two-storey Victorian mansion and renovated shearers' quarters beautifully set in the Padthaway Estate among the vines and towering red gums. **www.padthawayestate.com**

PARKSIDE Tiffins on the Park $$$$

176 Greenhill Road, SA 5063 **Tel** *(08) 8271 0444* **Fax** *(08) 8272 8675* **Rooms** *54*

Adjacent to the city, nestled in tranquil parklands, this spacious and elegant boutique style hotel underwent a full refurbishment in 2004. It's only a short distance from two major shopping precincts. The enthusiastic and attentive staff are bound to make an impression and the poolside bar/restaurant is a winner. **www.tiffinsonthepark.com.au**

ROBE Robe House $$$

Hagen Street, SA 5276 **Tel** *(08) 8768 2770* **Fax** *(08) 8768 2770* **Rooms** *4*

Built in 1847 from locally quarried sandstone, this charming building is only a short walk from fine art galleries and restaurants. The four self-contained guesthouse units feature local artworks and Australian furnishings. It's a handy place to stay if you are travelling along the Great Ocean Road. **www.robehouse.com.au**

STIRLING Thorngrove Manor Hotel $$$$$

2 Glenside Lane, SA 5152 **Tel** *(08) 8339 6748* **Fax** *(08) 8370 9950* **Rooms** *6*

This is an extraordinary hotel with an international reputation for its luxury, striking originality and attention to aesthetic detail – the pinnacle of hotel experiences. Privacy is absolute and you may never even see the other guests. The dining and comfort levels surpass all five-star ratings. **www.slh.com/thorngrove**

TANUNDA Barossa Weintal Resort
Murray Street, SA 5352 **Tel** *(08) 8563 2303* **Fax** *(08) 8563 2279* **Rooms** *40*

Centrally located at Tanunda, the largest of the Barossa Valley towns, this resort is a great place from which to access all the local wineries. The rooms are clean and comfortable. Tea/coffee facilities, hair dryers and direct-dial telephone and internet access are complimentary with all accommodation suites. **www.barossa-weintal.com**

VICTOR HARBOR Whaler's Inn Resort
121 Franklin Parade, The Bluff, SA 5211 **Tel** *(08) 8552 4400* **Fax** *(08) 8552 4240* **Rooms** *47*

Nestled at the base of the Bluff, the Whalers Inn Resort is one of South Australia's best-kept secrets. Most rooms have views across Encounter Bay and of nearby Granite Island. There is a swimming pool, tennis court and barbecue facilities and you can also get access to mountain bikes, games and videos. **www.whalersinnresort.com.au**

THE YORKE AND EYRE PENINSULAS AND THE FAR NORTH

ARDROSSAN Ardrossan Hotel/Motel
36 First Street, SA 5571 **Tel** *(08) 8837 3008* **Fax** *(08) 8837 3468* **Rooms** *11*

This family run hotel is within walking distance of shops, a museum, walking trails, a playground and, of course, the beach – a great place for fishing or catching the renowned Blue Swimmer Crabs. Each room has its own en suite bathroom, air conditioning and TV. There is also a family room available, which sleeps five.

ARKAROOLA Arkaroola Wilderness Sanctuary
North Flinders Ranges, SA 5732 **Tel** *(08) 8648 4848* **Fax** *(08) 8648 4846* **Rooms** *50*

The largest resort in the Flinders Ranges offers a range of accommodation. The rooms are comfortable and functional. Scenic flights and 4WD tours are available. The resort itself is widely recognized as being one of Australia's premier eco-tourist destinations. **www.arkaroola.com.au**

ARNO BAY Hotel Arno
Government Road, SA 5603 **Tel** *(08) 8628 0001* **Fax** *(08) 8628 0150* **Rooms** *75*

Across the road from the beach and a caravan park, Hotel Arno is a friendly place to stay. Rooms are cheap and fairly simple, but they are air conditioned and children are welcome. Arno bay itself is a sleepy little village. It is an ideal place for people who really do want to get away from it all.

AUBURN Rising Sun Hotel and Mews
Main North Road, SA 5451 **Tel** *(08) 8849 2015* **Fax** *(08) 8849 2266* **Rooms** *10*

This classic 1850s building was actually the very first business in Auburn. Considerably renovated since those days, it now houses ten comfy spacious rooms, all with en suites. A continental breakfast is included in the standard room price and dinner can be enjoyed in the adjacent restaurant.

BLINMAN Blinman Hotel
Main Street, SA 5730 **Tel** *(08) 8648 4867* **Fax** *(08) 8648 4621* **Rooms** *17*

It's the centre of the Flinders Ranges, so it's an easy drive to all the attractions. Just at the end of Main Street is a miner's cottage that dates back to 1862, or, if you feel like a longer journey, the stunning Chambers Gorge is 80 km (50 miles) away. The hotel itself is pretty standard. Breakfast is not included in price. **www.blinmanhotel.com.au**

BURRA Burra Heritage Cottages
Tivers Row, 8–18 Truro Street, SA 5417 **Tel** *(08) 8892 2461* **Fax** *(08) 8892 2948* **Rooms** *6 (cottages)*

These spacious bluestone cottages date back to 1856. Generous breakfast provisions are included in the tariff so that you can cook a country-style breakfast and enjoy it in the privacy of your cottage garden. Open fires add a special touch indoors. It's a real journey to the past, travelling first class. **www.burraheritagecottages.com.au**

CLARE Thorn Park Country House
College Road, Sevenhill, SA 5453 **Tel** *(08) 8843 4304* **Fax** *(08) 8843 4296* **Rooms** *6*

Situated close to wineries and the famous Riesling Trail walk, this gourmet retreat has earned a reputation for being the best place to stay in South Australia. In 1997 it was inducted into the South Australian Tourism hall of fame. Rooms are marvellously decorated with quality art and antiques. **www.thornpark.com.au**

COOBER PEDY The Underground Motel
Catacomb Road, SA 5723 **Tel** *(08) 8672 5324* **Fax** *(08) 8672 5911* **Rooms** *8*

The world's first underground guesthouse has a spectacular view of the desert sunsets from its veranda. All guest rooms are underground and equipped with en suites and fans, and are perfect for escaping the fierce summer heat of this Outback town. It's very family friendly: there's a children's play area and pets are welcome.

COOBER PEDY Desert Cave Hotel
Hutchison Street, SA 5723 **Tel** *(08) 8672 5688* **Fax** *(08) 8672 5198* **Rooms** *50*

This award-winning hotel provides underground shops, bar and opal display areas – all within sandstone surrounds in the heart of Coober Pedy. You can stay either above ground or underground, and there are excellent dining and convention facilities. It's the world's only truly international underground hotel. **www.desertcave.com.au**

Key to Price Guide *see p478* **Key to Symbols** *see back cover flap*

EDITHBURGH Edithburgh House

7 Edith Street, SA 5583 **Tel** *(08) 8852 6373* **Fax** *(08) 8852 6373* **Rooms** *6*

This delightful building has been used as a guesthouse since the 1890s. Just a minute's walk from the seashore and across the road from the local museum, and is an ideal base from which to explore Edithburgh, a town steeped in maritime history. All the rooms are en suite. **www.edithburghhouse.com.au**

EDITHBURGH The Anchorage Motel

25 O'Halloran Parade, SA 5583 **Tel** *(08) 8852 6262* **Fax** *(08) 8852 6147* **Rooms** *9*

Located on the foreshore near the jetty, these hotel units offer all the amenities needed for self-contained relaxation. Fish-cleaning tables, a freezer for bait and boat-washing facilities are all on hand. For a small extra charge, guests can enjoy a home cooked breakfast delivered to their rooms. **www.anchorage-edithburgh.net**

MINTARO Martindale Hall

Manoora Road, SA 5145 **Tel** *(08) 8843 9088* **Fax** *(08) 8843 9082* **Rooms** *9*

This authentic luxurious 19th-century Georgian mansion was featured in the famous Australian film *Picnic at Hanging Rock*. You can enjoy a formal dinner served by a butler and maid, browse through the extensive private library or simply have a lazy game of pool on the 125-year-old billiard table. **www.martindalehall.com**

PORT LINCOLN Lincoln Cove Villas

42 Parnkalla Avenue, SA 5606 **Tel** *(08) 8683 0657* **Fax** *(08) 8683 3165* **Rooms** *3 (villas)*

These four-star villas are located at the marina. They are also right on the breathtakingly scenic Parnkalla walking trail. The yards have childproof fencing and the bedrooms are all decorated in a marine sea theme. Cook your own breakfast in the fully equipped kitchens. **www.lincolncovevillas.com**

PORT LINCOLN Blue Seas Motel

7 Gloucester Terrace, SA 5606 **Tel** *(08) 8682 3022* **Fax** *(08) 8682 6932* **Rooms** *15*

This family owned and operated motel overlooks the beautiful Boston Bay, one of the largest protected natural harbours in the world. All rooms have queen-size beds, electric blankets, TVs and air conditioning. The motel is literally across the road from the beach and a short walk from the Port Lincoln CBD. **www.blueseasmotel.com**

RAWNSLEY PARK Rawnsley Park Station

Hawker-Wilpena Road, SA 5434 **Tel** *(08) 8648 0030* **Fax** *(08) 8648 0013* **Rooms** *28 (cabins)*

Rawnsley Park Station won the Hall of Fame Award for standard accommodation at the South Australian Tourism Awards in 2004. The de luxe cabins are self-contained and serviced every second day. The staff can help travellers with a range of activities such as horse riding, cycling and sheep-shearing. **www.rawnsleypark.com.au**

WHYALLA Alexander Motor Inn

99 Playford Avenue, SA 5600 **Tel** *(08) 8645 9488* **Fax** *(08) 8645 2211* **Rooms** *40*

This comfortable motel has single and two-bedroom suites available. Children are most welcome. There is a nice walking path through the adjacent wetlands. The inn has good facilities but breakfast is not included in the standard room price. **www.alexandermotel.com.au**

WILPENA Wilpena Pound Resort

Hawker-Wilpena Road, SA 5434 **Tel** *(08) 8648 0004* **Fax** *(08) 8648 0028* **Rooms** *60*

The sheer range of available accommodation makes this resort suitable for families, couples, groups and backpackers alike. The staff at the Visitor Information Centre can help you organize 4WD tours and scenic flights, or assist you with planning a walk through the vast landscapes of the Flinders Ranges. **www.wilpenapound.com.au**

WUDINNA Gawler Ranges Motel

72 Eyre Highway, SA 5652 **Tel** *(08) 8680 2090* **Fax** *(08) 8680 2184* **Rooms** *23*

Less than an hour's drive from the Gawler Ranges, this motel offers pleasant accommodation for the whole family. There's an indoor heated pool and spa, an onsite conference room and all basic amenities are supplied. Breakfast is available for a small extra fee. **www.gawlerrangesmotel.com**

MELBOURNE

ALBERT PARK Carlton Crest Hotel Melbourne

65 Queens Road, VIC 3004 **Tel** *(03) 9529 4300* **Fax** *(03) 9521 3111* **Rooms** *374*   **Map** *3 B5*

This popular option for business travellers offers generous rooms, some with views of Albert Park Lake and golf course. The hotel is convenient for city transport, the Botanic Gardens and Shrine of Remembrance, South Yarra's shops and restaurants, St Kilda and the Sports and Aquatic Centre. **www.carltonhotels.com.au**

CARLTON Comfort Hotel Elizabeth Tower

792 Elizabeth Street, VIC 3000 **Tel** *(03) 9347 9211* **Fax** *(03) 9347 0396* **Rooms** *100*

This eight-storey hotel, opposite the Royal Melbourne Hospital and Melbourne University, is just up the road from the Queen Victoria Market and CBD. It's also within walking distance of Lygon Street's Italian restaurants. Its glazed corner spiral staircase would make an ideal set for an action movie chase scene. **www.elizabethtower.com.au**

CARLTON Downtowner on Lygon
⚂⓫🔲📧   ⓢⓢ

66 Lygon Street, VIC 3053 **Tel** *(03) 9663 5555* **Fax** *(03) 9662 3308* **Rooms** *98*   **Map** *1 C1*

This quality motel accommodation is conveniently located at the CBD end of the bustling Lygon Street restaurant strip and just up the road from the historic Trades Hall building. It offers a range of rooms, some with kitchens and spas. It is suitable for disabled travellers and offers room service. **www.downtowner.com.au**

CARLTON Rydges Carlton
⚂⓫⛳📺🔲📧   ⓢⓢⓢⓢ

701 Swanston Street, VIC 3053 **Tel** *(03) 9347 7811, 1800 333, 001* **Fax** *(03) 9347 8225* **Rooms** *107*

Within a stone's throw of Melbourne University and only two blocks from Lygon Street, this refurbished hotel is a good option for visiting academics. It is also popular with country and business travellers. Fitness facilities include a spa and sauna and for the business traveller there is a corporate shuttle bus service. **www.rydges.com**

CITY CENTRE The Friendly Backpacker
📧   ⓢ

197 King Street, VIC 3000 **Tel** *(03) 9670 1111, 1800 671 115* **Fax** *(03) 9670 9911* **Rooms** *40*   **Map** *1 A3*

Close to Spencer Street Station and more intimate than its Flinders Lane cousin, this friendly option is popular with international travellers. Rooms and facilities are clean and airy, the self-catering kitchen is excellent, one room is wheelchair accessible, and the price includes 30 minutes of internet access. **www.friendlygroup.com.au**

CITY CENTRE The Greenhouse
⚂📧   ⓢ

228 Flinders Lane, VIC 3000 **Tel** *(03) 9639 6400, 1800 249 207* **Fax** *(03) 9639 6900* **Rooms** *63*   **Map** *1 C3*

This is an excellent central choice for those on a budget. Rooms are pleasant, there is a games room, self-contained kitchen, TV room and free pancake brunches on Sundays. The relaxing rooftop terrace is upstairs, and downstairs is the slick 6 Links bar and internet café, sometimes featuring live music. **www.friendlygroup.com.au**

CITY CENTRE Hotel Enterprize Melbourne
⚂⓫📧   ⓢ

44 Spencer Street, VIC 3000 **Tel** *(03) 9629 6991* **Fax** *(03) 9614 7963* **Rooms** *200*   **Map** *1 B4*

Another well-located option for budget travellers, especially if arriving at Spencer Street Station by train or bus. There is an Asian restaurant and pizza café, and rooms range from budget options to luxury suites. It is also close to Telstra Dome, but can get noisy when the "footy" crowds descend. **www.hotelenterprize.com.au**

CITY CENTRE Atlantis Hotel
⚂🔲📧   ⓢⓢ

300 Spencer Street, VIC 3000 **Tel** *(03) 9600 2900* **Fax** *(03) 9600 2700* **Rooms** *72*   **Map** *1 A3*

Opened in 2002, this hotel is well positioned for visitors arriving via train or bus at Spencer Street Station. It offers comfortable and spacious rooms, some overlooking the Telstra Dome and the emerging Docklands precinct. It is within walking distance of the Casino, Melbourne Convention Centre and Southbank. **www.atlantishotel.com.au**

CITY CENTRE Hotel Y
⚂⓫🔲📧   ⓢⓢ

489 Elizabeth Street, VIC 3000 **Tel** *(03) 8327 2777, 1800 468 359* **Fax** *(03) 8327 2777* **Rooms** *60*   **Map** *1 B2*

The old YWCA has never looked so good. Within a bagel's throw of the Queen Victoria Market, this refurbished option offers light and pleasant, if unremarkable, rooms. It also provides a helpful tour desk, off-site parking, café, 24-hour reception, a business centre and access to local gym and swimming facilities. **www.hotely.com.au**

CITY CENTRE Nova Stargate
⚂⓫📺🔲📧   ⓢⓢ

118 Franklin Street, VIC 3000 **Tel** *(03) 9321 0300* **Fax** *(03) 9321 0301* **Rooms** *120*   **Map** *1 B2*

This hotel at the northern end of the CBD is close by Queen Victoria Market, Melbourne Central and the Royal Melbourne Institute of Technology (RMIT). It offers several one- and two-bedroom apartment options. The restaurant is licensed and the fitness facilities include a spa and sauna. **www.novastargate.com.au**

CITY CENTRE Rendezvous Hotel
⚂⓫📺🔲📧   ⓢⓢⓢ

328 Flinders Street, VIC 3000 **Tel** *(03) 9250 1888* **Fax** *(03) 9250 1877* **Rooms** *338*   **Map** *1 C4*

Originally built in 1913 as the Commercial Travellers Club, this renovated heritage-listed building at the southern end of the CBD blends historic detailing with contemporary decor. It offers valet parking, attentive room service and business facilities. The Club Lounge and Bar overlook the grand foyer. **www.rendezvoushotels.com.au**

CITY CENTRE Victoria Hotel
⚂⓫🏊📺📧   ⓢⓢⓢ

215 Little Collins Street, VIC 3000 **Tel** *(03) 9653 0441* **Fax** *(03) 9650 9678* **Rooms** *464*   **Map** *1 C3*

Built in 1880, this centrally located hotel is close to theatres, department stores, restaurants and boutiques. For years it has been the hotel of choice for country guests who enjoy its no fuss hospitality and reasonable tariffs. It now boasts an indoor pool, gym, sauna, spa, internet café and conference facilities. **www.victoriahotel.com.au**

CITY CENTRE The Crossley Hotel managed by Mercure
⚂⓫🔲📧   ⓢⓢⓢⓢ

51 Little Bourke Street, VIC 3000 **Tel** *(03) 9639 1639* **Fax** *(03) 9639 0566* **Rooms** *88*   **Map** *2 D2*

Located at the top end of Chinatown and the theatre district, this comfortable hotel is also close to some of Melbourne's finest eateries, including Grossi Florentino, Becco and Madam Fang. It offers exceptional service and the rooms are large. **www.crossleyhotel.com.au**

CITY CENTRE The Grand Hotel Melbourne
⚂⓫🏊📺🔲📧   ⓢⓢⓢⓢ

33 Spencer Street, VIC 3000 **Tel** *(03) 9611 4567 1300 361 455* **Fax** *(03) 9611 4655* **Rooms** *114*   **Map** *1 B4*

This luxury all-suite boutique hotel occupies a heritage-listed former railways building at the western end of the CBD. Facilities include spa, sauna, gym and rooftop pool (which features a retractable roof, not unlike the nearby Telstra Dome). All suites have a fully equipped kitchenette and Victorian features. **www.grandhotelsofitel.com.au**

Key to Price Guide *see p478* **Key to Symbols** *see back cover flap*

CITY CENTRE Hotel Causeway ⌖⏱🛏🏠 $$$$

275 Little Collins Street, VIC 3000 **Tel** *9660 8888, 1800 660 188* **Fax** *(03) 9660 8880* **Rooms** *45* **Map** *1 C3*

Tucked away in Little Collins Street, this boutique hotel occupies a 1920s building in the heart of the city. It is perfectly located for those who want to savour Melbourne's bars, laneways and arcades. It has a rooftop terrace, excellent fitness facilities (including a steam room) and stylish, contemporary decor. **www.causeway.com.au**

CITY CENTRE Hotel Lindrum ⌖⏱🛏🏠 $$$$

26 Flinders Street, VIC 3000 **Tel** *(03) 9668 1111* **Fax** *(03) 9668 1199* **Rooms** *59* **Map** *2 D3*

This chic boutique hotel occupies a heritage-listed building at the eastern edge of the CBD. It overlooks the historic Jolimont Railyards, the Yarra River and Botanic Gardens. The rooms are contemporary, with minimalist decor and home comforts. It is within walking distance of Federation Square and Birrarung Marr. **www.hotellindrum.com.au**

CITY CENTRE Novotel Melbourne on Collins ⌖⏱≋🛏⏱🛏🏠 $$$$

270 Collins Street, VIC 3000 **Tel** *(03) 9667 5800* **Fax** *(03) 9667 5805* **Rooms** *324* **Map** *1 C3*

Melbourne's most central hotel overlooks Collins Street and the Australia on Collins shopping centre. Rooms are spacious and comfortable. It caters to mainly corporate clients, and offers conference rooms, a business centre, car parking, room service and fitness facilities, including spa, sauna, pool and gym. **www.novotelmelbourne.com.au**

CITY CENTRE Rydges Melbourne ⌖⏱≋🛏🏠 $$$$

186 Exhibition Street, VIC 3000 **Tel** *(03) 9662 0511* **Fax** *(03) 9663 6988* **Rooms** *363* **Map** *2 D2*

This stylish hotel is located in the heart of the theatre district, just uphill from Chinatown and just downhill from the 19th-century state parliament and treasury buildings. It offers luxury suites and the overall decor is contemporary. The hotel's Events Centre is well suited to business travellers. **www.rydges.com/melbourne**

CITY CENTRE Sofitel Melbourne ⌖⏱🛏🏠 $$$$

25 Collins Street, VIC 3000 **Tel** *(03) 9653 0000* **Fax** *(03) 9650 4231* **Rooms** *362* **Map** *2 D3*

The hotel occupies the top floors of an old building at the "Paris End" of Collins Street. There are several room types, but all feature floor-to-ceiling windows and panoramic views over the CBD, the Bay or Yarra River. The fitness facilities are excellent and the service is first class. **www.sofitelmelbourne.com.au**

CITY CENTRE Stamford Plaza Melbourne ⌖⏱≋🛏🏠 $$$$

111 Little Collins Street, VIC 3000 **Tel** *(03) 9659 1000, 1800 035 377* **Rooms** *283* **Map** *2 D3*

At the "Paris End" of Collins Street, the Stamford is Melbourne's only five-star all-suite hotel. Its stylish one-, two- and three-bedroom suites have fully equipped kitchens and lounges. There is a business centre, private offices, conference rooms and a gym, spa, sauna and pleasant rooftop pool. **www.stamford.com.au**

CITY CENTRE Adelphi ⌖⏱≋🛏🏠 $$$$$

187 Flinders Lane, VIC 3000 **Tel** *(03) 9650 7555* **Fax** *(03) 9650 2710* **Rooms** *34* **Map** *2 D3*

This small and groovy luxury hotel is known for both its innovative architecture (especially the glass-bottomed rooftop swimming pool, which partially overhangs the street below) and its classy restaurant in the hotel basement. It is right in the middle of the CBD, just around the corner from Federation Square. **www.adelphi.com.au**

CITY CENTRE Golden Tulip Melbourne ⌖⏱≋🛏🏠 $$$$$

60 Market Street, VIC 3000 **Tel** *(03) 9602 3644* **Fax** *(03) 8631 1188* **Rooms** *280* **Map** *1 B4*

This 28-storey hotel was opened in late 2005. It provides serviced apartment accommodation combined with fitness and business facilities. All rooms feature modern decor and a well-equipped kitchenette, and overlook either the Yarra River, Botanic Gardens and Southbank or the CBD. **www.goldentulipmelbourne.com**

CITY CENTRE Grand Hyatt ⌖⏱≋🛏🏠 $$$$$

123 Collins Street, VIC 3000 **Tel** *(03) 9657 1234* **Fax** *(03) 8843 1300* **Rooms** *550* **Map** *2 D3*

A member of the Hyatt hotel chain, this five-star hotel is within walking distance of some of Melbourne's best boutiques, galleries, theatres, restaurants and bars. Its own cocktail bar has an enviable reputation, and views from the upper floors include sweeping views of Port Phillip Bay and the CBD. **www.melbourne.grand.hyatt.com**

CITY CENTRE Holiday Inn Melbourne ⌖⏱≋🛏🏠 $$$$$

Cnr Flinders & Spencer sts, VIC 3005 **Tel** *(03) 9648 2777, 1300 666 747* **Rooms** *385* **Map** *1 B4*

On the bank of the Yarra River opposite the Melbourne Exhibition Centre and the Polly Woodside Maritime Museum, this modern hotel is close to Docklands, the Telstra Dome, the Melbourne Aquarium, Southbank, the Casino and the Arts Centre. Rooms offer views of Port Phillip Bay and the CBD. **www.holidayinn.com.au**

CITY CENTRE Melbourne Marriott Hotel ⌖⏱≋🛏🏠 $$$$$

Cnr Exhibition & Lonsdale sts, VIC 3000 **Tel** *(03) 9662 3900* **Fax** *(03) 9663 4297* **Rooms** *185* **Map** *2 D2*

A favourite of Melbourne's theatre crowd, with elegant rooms and grand suites, this hotel is adjacent to Chinatown and the theatre district and within walking distance of the Melbourne Museum and historic Exhibition Buildings. Fitness facilities include spa, sauna and gym, and the business facilities are first rate. **www.marriott.com.au**

CITY CENTRE Saville Park Suites Melbourne ⌖⏱≋🛏🏠 $$$$$

333 Exhibition Street, VIC 3000 **Tel** *(03) 9668 2500* **Fax** *(03) 9668 2599* **Rooms** *144* **Map** *2 D2*

One- and two-bedroom suites are available in this modern hotel close to the theatre district and Chinatown. All apartments feature full-size kitchens, lounge, bathrooms and balconies. Perfect for families and in a great location on the free City Circle tram route and within walking distance of Carlton Gardens. **www.savillesuites.com.au**

CITY CENTRE Somerset Gordon Place $$$$$

24 Little Bourke Street, VIC 3000 **Tel** *(03) 9663 2888, 1800 766 377* **Fax** *(03) 9639 1537* **Rooms** *64*   **Map** *2 D2*

These self-contained serviced apartments occupy a National Trust listed former doss house, built in 1884 at the top end of Chinatown. The apartments are set around an attractive courtyard, and all feature well-equipped kitchens and stylish decor. It is a good option for families or those planning an extended stay. **www.the-ascott.com**

CITY CENTRE The Westin Melbourne $$$$$

205 Collins Street, VIC 3000 **Tel** *(03) 9635 2222* **Fax** *(03) 9635 2333* **Rooms** *262*   **Map** *1 C3*

This hotel is Number One for travellers with children. It is a stylish and award-winning hotel, opposite the Town Hall and down the road from Federation Square. It also offers a wellness centre, business facilities and elegant rooms overlooking the City Square, some with balconies. **www.westin.com/melbourne**

CITY CENTRE The Windsor Hotel $$$$$

103 Spring Street, VIC 3000 **Tel** *(03) 9633 6002* **Fax** *(03) 9633 6005* **Rooms** *180*   **Map** *2 D2*

This grand Victorian hotel, built in 1883, is a stunning reminder of Marvellous Melbourne's gold rush era. Rooms provide five-star luxury and charm, and many enjoy views of the state parliament and treasury buildings. Don't miss Afternoon Tea downstairs – a Melbourne institution in an Merchant Ivory setting. **www.thewindsor.com.au**

EAST MELBOURNE Georgian Court Bed & Breakfast $$

21–25 George Street, VIC 3002 **Tel** *(03) 9419 6353* **Fax** *(03) 9416 0895* **Rooms** *31*   **Map** *2 F3*

This traditional guesthouse in a large Georgian house in historic East Melbourne enjoys a peaceful location. However, it is only a short stroll through the Fitzroy Gardens before you find yourself at the eastern edge of the city centre. It is within walking distance of the MCG. **www.georgiancourt.com.au**

EAST MELBOURNE Magnolia Court Boutique Hotel $$$

101 Powlett Street, VIC 3002 **Tel** *(03) 9419 4222* **Fax** *(03) 9416 0841* **Rooms** *25*   **Map** *2 F2*

This family owned boutique hotel, established in the 1880s and only one block back from the Fitzroy Gardens, occupies a charming Victorian terrace house. Several rooms have their own balconies and there are luxury suites and single units. The downstairs terrace café has outdoor seating. **www.magnolia-court.com.au**

FITZROY The Nunnery $

116 Nicholson Street, VIC 3065 **Tel** *(03) 9419 8637, 1800 032 635* **Fax** *(03) 9417 7736* **Rooms** *35*

There are three accommodation options here with prices to match: Guesthouse, Townhouse and Budget. The clean, comfortable budget option, opposite Melbourne Museum, is the former residence of the Daughters of Charity. It features a grand staircase, stained-glass windows and 1880s Georgian decor. **www.nunnery.com.au**

FITZROY The Chifley at Metropole, Melbourne $$$

44 Brunswick Street, VIC 3065 **Tel** *(03) 9411 8100, 1800 061 441* **Fax** *(03) 9411 8200* **Rooms** *60*   **Map** *2 E1*

At the southern end of Brunswick Street and opposite a historic row of terrace houses, these modern hotel rooms and apartments are perfectly situated for those who enjoy restaurants, bars and nightlife. Trams run past the front door into town every few minutes, although the city centre is an easy ten-minute walk. **www.chifleyhotels.com**

FITZROY Quest Royal Gardens Apartments $$$$$

8 Royal Lane, VIC 3065 **Tel** *(03) 9419 9888, 1800 334 033* **Fax** *(03) 9416 0451* **Rooms** *70*   **Map** *2 D1*

Tucked away in a back alley off Gertrude Street, these spacious self-contained one-, two- and three-bedroom apartments are within a stone's throw of the Carlton Gardens, Royal Exhibition Buildings and Melbourne Museum, and within easy walking distance of the CBD and Brunswick Street. **www.questroyalgardens.com.au**

NORTH MELBOURNE Melbourne Metro YHA $

78 Howard Street, VIC 3051 **Tel** *(03) 9329 8599* **Fax** *(03) 9326 8427* **Rooms** *81*   **Map** *1 A1*

A five-minute walk to Queen Victoria Market and just down the road from Errol Street, North Melbourne's pubs and cafés, this is an excellent budget option. The rooftop terrace offers 360° views of the CBD, there are bicycles for hire, guided walking tours and clean, comfortable rooms. **www.yha.org.au**

RICHMOND Richmond Hill Hotel $$$

353 Church Street, VIC 3121 **Tel** *(03) 9428 6501* **Fax** *(03) 9427 0128* **Rooms** *60*   **Map** *4 E2*

A little farther out, but only minutes from town by tram, this boutique hotel and guesthouse in a heritage-listed Victorian terrace offers pleasant rooms and relaxing courtyards and gardens. There is a guest lounge, bar, off-street parking, family rooms and apartments. **www.richmondhillhotel.com.au**

RICHMOND Rydges Riverwalk $$$$$

649 Bridge Road, VIC 3121 **Tel** *(03) 9246 1200* **Fax** *(03) 9246 1222* **Rooms** *94*

With self-contained apartments and clean, modern hotel rooms offering views over the Yarra River, this is a pleasant option for those wanting something quieter than the city centre. A lovely walking and cycle path meanders beside the Yarra, and Bridge Road's restaurants and shops are within easy walking distance. **www.rydges.com/riverwalk**

SOUTH YARRA The Albany $$$$$

Cnr Toorak Road and Millswyn Street, VIC 3141 **Tel** *1800 338 877* **Fax** *(03) 9820 9419* **Rooms** *70*   **Map** *3 B5*

Tastefully renovated in the style of the 1960s, this attractive Victorian mansion has large rooms which are suitable for families or those planning a long stay. Added extras include parking, laundry service and alfresco breakfasts. Great value accommodation. **www.thealbany.com.au**

Key to Price Guide *see p478* **Key to Symbols** *see back cover flap*

SOUTH YARRA The Como Melbourne [$][$][$][$][$]

630 Chapel Street, VIC 3141 ***Tel*** *(03) 9825 2222, 1800 033 400* ***Fax*** *(03) 9824 1263* ***Rooms*** *106* ***Map*** *4 E5*

Just down from the intersection of Chapel Street's stylish café and fashion strip and trendy Toorak Road, this hotel is a favourite with entertainers and sports people. Expect valet parking, 24-hour room service, first-class business facilities, contemporary decor and a free daily limousine service to the city centre. **www.mirvachotels.com.au**

SOUTHBANK Crown Promenade Hotel [$][$][$][$][$]

8 Whiteman Street, VIC 3006 ***Tel*** *(03) 9292 6688, 1800 776 612* ***Fax*** *(03) 9292 6600* ***Rooms*** *465* ***Map*** *1 C5*

Stylish contemporary luxury on 23 levels, just behind the Crown Casino, with views of the CBD and Port Phillip Bay. If you really need to unwind, the leisure facilities here are first class, including male and female sauna and steam rooms, gym, two outdoor decks, heated spas and an infinity lap pool. **www.crownpromenade.com.au**

SOUTHBANK Langham Hotel [$][$][$][$][$]

1 Southgate Avenue, VIC 3006 ***Tel*** *1800 858 662* ***Fax*** *(03) 8696 8110* ***Rooms*** *387* ***Map*** *1 C4*

Overlooking the Yarra River and CBD, and close to Federation Square, the Casino and the Arts precinct, this luxury hotel lays it on thick with chandeliers, sweeping staircases and marble bathrooms. The business centre is well equipped and the spa and fitness facilities are perfect for gym junkies. **www.langhamhotels.com**

ST KILDA Jackson's Manor [$][$]

53 Jackson Street, VIC 3182 ***Tel*** *(03) 9534 1877* ***Rooms*** *30* ***Map*** *5 B4*

This renovated former homestead is located in a quiet back street just behind hectic Fitzroy Street, a two-minute walk to Acland Street and a five-minute walk to St Kilda Beach. It is a pleasant budget option offering cable TV, a barbecue area, car parking, internet access, laundry and kitchen facilities. **www.jacksonsmanor.com.au**

ST KILDA Base Backpackers [$][$][$][$]

17 Carlisle Street, VIC 3182 ***Tel*** *(03) 8598 6200* ***Fax*** *(03) 8598 6222* ***Rooms*** *43* ***Map*** *5 C5*

Gone are the days of grungy accommodation for budget travellers. This modern establishment in a central St Kilda location rightly assumes that even those travelling on a budget appreciate a little bit of style now and again. There is a girls-only "Sanctuary" level, a bar and speedy internet facilities. **www.basebackpackers.com.au**

ST KILDA Boutique Hotel Tolarno [$][$][$][$][$]

42 Fitzroy Street, VIC 3182 ***Tel*** *(03) 9537 0200* ***Fax*** *(03) 9534 7800* ***Rooms*** *34* ***Map*** *5 B4*

In the heart of St Kilda's café scene, this modernized hotel features contemporary artworks by local artists and original works by noted Melbourne artist Mirka Mora, which adorn the restaurant walls. Rooms are clean and comfortable and some have views over Fitzroy Street. **www.hoteltolarno.com.au**

ST KILDA Fountain Terrace [$][$][$][$][$]

28 Mary Street, West St Kilda, VIC 3182 ***Tel*** *(03) 9593 8123* ***Fax*** *(03) 9593 8696* ***Rooms*** *7* ***Map*** *5 B4*

A well-located guesthouse in a charmingly restored and refurbished 1880s Victorian terrace residence, close to Fitzroy Street's bustling cafés and restaurants, yet surprisingly quiet. All rooms are individually styled and beautifully furnished. There is also a shady courtyard, a guest dining and sitting room. **www.fountainterrace.com.au**

ST KILDA The Prince [$][$][$][$][$]

2 Acland Street, VIC 3182 ***Tel*** *(03) 9536 1111* ***Fax*** *(03) 9536 1100* ***Rooms*** *40* ***Map*** *5 B5*

In the 1980s and 1990s, The Prince was one of St Kilda's grungiest pubs. Now, nothing could be further from the truth. Slick, minimalist interior design and understated luxury is the order of the day at this boutique hotel. Call into the day spa and retreat for a little pampering, before enjoying dinner at Circe, The Prince. **www.theprince.com.au**

ST KILDA PRECINCT Albert Park Manor Hotel [$][$]

405 St Kilda Road, VIC 3004 ***Tel*** *(03) 9821 4486* ***Fax*** *(03) 9821 4496* ***Rooms*** *20* ***Map*** *3 B5*

Situated opposite the Royal Botanic Gardens and within easy reach of the city centre, this 98-year-old family run Victorian hotel has Old World style. Trams pass by the front door every three minutes during normal business hours. Family rooms, spa rooms and budget rooms with shared bathrooms are available. **www.albertparkmanor.com.au**

ST KILDA PRECINCT Royce Hotel [$][$][$]

379 Street Kilda Road, VIC 3004 ***Tel*** *1800 820 909* ***Fax*** *(03) 9677 9922* ***Rooms*** *71* ***Map*** *3 B4*

This boutique option on leafy St Kilda Road occupies a National Trust listed 1920s former Rolls Royce showroom. The rooms feature contemporary styling and the hotel is within easy walking distance of the Royal Botanic Gardens, Albert Park Lake and up-market Toorak Road, South Yarra. **www.roycehotels.com.au**

ST KILDA PRECINCT St Kilda Road Parkview Hotel [$][$][$]

562 St Kilda Road, VIC 3004 ***Tel*** *1300 785 453* ***Fax*** *(03) 9525 1242* ***Rooms*** *220* ***Map*** *2 D5*

St Kilda Road is a grand boulevard linking the city with the beach. Some rooms at this hotel have city or park views. The hotel is only 3 km (2 miles) from town and is popular with those attending the Australian Grand Prix, although the race cars and media helicopters can be deafening. **www.viewhotels.com.au**

ST KILDA PRECINCT The Hotel Charsfield [$][$][$][$][$]

478 St Kilda Road, VIC 3004 ***Tel*** *1300 301 830* ***Fax*** *(03) 9867 2277* ***Rooms*** *41* ***Map*** *5 B1*

A private dining room, reading room and billiards room; massage, reflexology and beauty treatment; dinners served on the lawn in summer; easy access to the St Kilda Road Arts precinct – these are just some of the treats on offer at this boutique hotel, occupying an 1889 heritage-listed mansion on a tree-lined boulevard. **www.charsfield.com**

WESTERN VICTORIA

AIREY'S INLET Airey's Overboard Seaside Cottage 📋 $$$$$

1 Barton Street, VIC 3231 **Tel** *(03) 5289 7424* **Fax** *(03) 5289 7424* **Rooms** *2*

This environmentally friendly cottage, clad with radial-sawn timber, is nestled amongst native trees on the beach side of the Great Ocean Road. The decor is nautical and the cottage is within walking distance of the lighthouse and several beaches. The outdoor shower is perfect after a day at the beach. **www.aireysoverboard.com.au**

APOLLO BAY Chris's Beacon Point Restaurant & Villas 🍴📋 $$$$$

280 Skenes Road, VIC 3233 **Tel** *(03) 5237 6411* **Fax** *(03) 5237 6930* **Rooms** *8*

Panoramic ocean views are the main selling point for these self-contained mountaintop villas. It is only a ten-minute drive down the hill to Apollo Bay, however, most guests see no need to leave as the adjoining Greek restaurant enjoys a reputation as one of the coast's best. **www.beaconpoint.com.au**

APOLLO BAY Claerwen Retreat 🏊🏇🎾📺🍴 $$$$$

480 Tuxian Road, VIC 3233 **Tel** *(03) 5237 7064* **Fax** *(03) 5237 7054* **Rooms** *8*

Every room at this hilltop retreat offers views over the ocean and Otway Ranges. There is modern, architect-designed guesthouse accommodation and two self-contained cottages, as well as an outdoor saltwater pool, tennis court and horses. Bushwalking in the Otway Ranges is just as popular as days spent on the beach. **www.claerwen.com.au**

APOLLO BAY Whitecrest Holiday Retreat 🏊🏇🎾📺📋 $$$$$

5230 Great Ocean Road, VIC 3221 **Tel** *(03) 5237 0228* **Fax** *(03) 5237 0245* **Rooms** *14*

Each of these modern one-, two- and three-bedroom self-contained split-level apartments offers an en suite spa bath and a private balcony with stunning ocean views. Single rooms also available. As well as the swimming pool, there is a tennis court, billiards room, table tennis and barbecue facilities. **www.whitecrestonline.com.au**

BALLARAT Ansonia 🍴🏇📋 $$$$$

32 Lydiard Street South, VIC 3350 **Tel** *(03) 5332 4678* **Fax** *(03) 5332 4698* **Rooms** *19*

This recently restored 1870s building is centrally located in one of Australia's best-preserved 19th-century streetcapes. It offers comfortable, modern rooms that look out onto the central atrium with its potted ferns and rattan seating. There is a guest library and lounge room, and the sunny courtyard restaurant is popular. **www.ansonia.com.au**

BALLARAT Ballarat Heritage Homestay 🏇📋 $$$$$

PO Box 1360, Ballarat Mail Centre, VIC 3354 **Tel** *(03) 5332 8296* **Fax** *(03) 5331 3358* **Rooms** *6*

This accommodation service offers six self-contained Victorian and Federation cottages and one B&B. All feature modern amenities, pleasant cottage gardens and convenient central locations in Ballarat and Creswick. They are suitable for travellers with children and some are suitable for disabled travellers. **www.heritagehomestay.com**

BALLARAT Craig's Royal Hotel 📶🍴🏇📋 $$$$$

10 Lydiard Street South, VIC 3350 **Tel** *(03) 5331 1377* **Fax** *(03) 5331 7103* **Rooms** *41*

This classic old hotel in the historic heart of this gold-rush era city has undergone a major renovation in recent years. It now offers some of Ballarat's grandest accommodation. All suites have en suite spa baths, and there is a magnificent downstairs public bar, banquet rooms and a private dining cellar. **www.craigsroyal.com**

BENDIGO Greystanes Manor 🍴🏇📋 $$$$$

57 Queen Street, VIC 3550 **Tel** *(03) 5442 2466* **Fax** *(03) 5442 2447* **Rooms** *6*

A two-minute walk from Bendigo's CBD, this Georgian-style mansion was built in 1882 by a local architect for his family. It's now a boutique hotel surrounded by pleasant century-old gardens. Each suite has antique furnishings and en suite facilities. Children are not welcome. **www.greystanesmanor.com.au**

BENDIGO Shamrock Hotel 📶🍴🏇📋 $$$$$

Cnr Pall Mall & Williamson Street, VIC 3550 **Tel** *(03) 5443 0333* **Fax** *(03) 5442 4494* **Rooms** *28*

This ornate 1855 Victorian hotel with upper floor verandas is perfectly located opposite Roslyn Park and Law Courts precinct and just down the hill from Bendigo's impressive art gallery. Some rooms have access to the veranda, which is the perfect spot to enjoy a cold beer on a hot afternoon. **www.shamrockbendigo.com.au**

CASTLEMAINE The Empyre Boutique Hotel 🍴🏇📋 $$$$$

68 Mostyn Street, VIC 3450 **Tel** *(03) 5472 5166* **Fax** *(03) 5472 3204* **Rooms** *6*

This new boutique hotel delivers contemporary but understated luxury. Two rooms have balcony access overlooking one of Castlemaine's historic main streets. Two suites open onto the walled private garden at the rear. The restaurant serves Mod Oz cuisine and the lounge area is a pleasant place to unwind before dinner. **www.empyre.com.au**

DAYLESFORD Central Springs Inn 🍴🏇📋 $$$$$

Cnr Camp & Howe sts, VIC 3350 **Tel** *(03) 5348 3134* **Fax** *(03) 5348 3967* **Rooms** *26*

The inn has three buildings located just back from Daylesford's lively Vincent Street, and only a ten-minute walk from the scenic lake or botanic gardens. One of the buildings, built in 1875, is listed by the National Trust. It comprises 16 suites, with period decor, mezzanine sleeping lofts and open fireplaces. **www.centralspringsinn.com.au**

Key to Price Guide *see p478* **Key to Symbols** *see back cover flap*

DAYLESFORD Lake House

3 King Street, VIC 3460 **Tel** *(03) 5348 3329* **Fax** *(03) 5348 3995* **Rooms** *33*

This boutique hotel surrounded by 3 hectares (7 acres) of manicured gardens complements the award-winning restaurant, cellar and day spa (offering mineral spas and treatments) and delivers a memorable package. There are several room options, most overlooking the picturesque lake, including waterfront rooms. **www.lakehouse.com.au**

DUNKELD Southern Grampians Cottages

33–35 Victoria Valley Road, VIC 3294 **Tel** *(03) 5577 2457* **Fax** *(03) 5577 2489* **Rooms** *9*

Tucked beneath Mount Sturgeon and offering spectacular views of the Grampians, these log cabins combine modern amenities with rustic features such as log fires and open verandas. Some cabins also have spas. It is a great option for travellers with children. **www.grampianscottages.com.au**

ECHUCA Etan House Bed & Breakfast

11 Connelly Street, VIC 3564 **Tel** *(03) 5480 7477* **Fax** *(03) 5480 7466* **Rooms** *4*

A pleasant guesthouse set in large cottage gardens and only minutes from the centre of town, the Murray River and the historic port district. The 1864 restored heritage building features period furnishings and decor, open fires in the guest lounge and formal dining room, tennis court, veranda and private courtyard. **www.etanhouse.com.au**

GEELONG Four Points by Sheraton Geelong

10–14 Eastern Beach Road, VIC 3220 **Tel** *(03) 5223 1377* **Fax** *(03) 5223 3417* **Rooms** *109*

On the waterfront overlooking the marina and Corio Bay, but only a few minutes' walk from Geelong's main shopping area, this resort-style hotel offers a bar, café, steam room, fitness centre, indoor heated pool, conference centre, undercover parking, good disability access and 24-hour reception. **www.fourpoints.com/geelong**

HALLS GAP YHA Eco-Hostel

Cnr Buckler Street and Grampians Road, VIC 3381 **Tel** *(03) 5356 4544* **Fax** *(03) 5536 4543* **Rooms** *20*

This environmentally friendly YHA hostel offers dorm, single, double and family rooms. They also offer bicycle hire and organize abseiling, rock climbing, horse riding, canoeing, cycling and wine-tasting tours. There is a self-contained kitchen and a coach service to and from Melbourne three times a week. **www.yha.org.au**

KYNETON Gainsborough Guesthouse B&B

66 Jennings Street, VIC 3444 **Tel** *(03) 5422 3999* **Fax** *(03) 5422 1963* **Rooms** *4*

An 1860 two-storey brick residence set in English-style gardens just up from the Campaspe River, the Botanic Gardens and Kyneton's town centre. It is a peaceful retreat with light and airy period-style rooms, and a wisteria-draped veranda perfect for enjoying a glass or two of the local red. **www.babs.com.au/gainsborourgh**

LORNE Stanmorr Bed & Breakfast

64 Otway Street, VIC 3232 **Tel** *(03) 9289 1530* **Fax** *(03) 5289 2805* **Rooms** *5*

For something different, stay at this elegant 1920s Queenslander-style residence set within 0.8 hectares (2 acres) of gardens abutting the Angahook-Lorne State Park forest. There are great views of Loutitt Bay and the beach from the veranda, and all rooms are en suite. It is only five minutes' walk into town. **www.stanmorr.com**

LORNE Cumberland Lorne Resort

150–178 Mountjoy Parade, VIC 3232 **Tel** *(03) 5289 2400, 1800 037 010* **Fax** *(03) 5289 2256* **Rooms** *99*

Overlooking (some would say overshadowing) this upmarket township is a resort-style complex with a range of modern and recently refurbished apartments, most with ocean views. There is a Kid's Club, toddler pool and games area, and also free use of surfboards, tennis racquets and mountain bikes. **www.cumberland.com.au**

MALDON Heritage Cottages of Maldon

41 Main Street, VIC 3463 **Tel** *(03) 5475 1094* **Fax** *(03) 5475 1094* **Rooms** *8*

Each of these eight self-contained properties has a pleasant garden and is within a few minutes of Australia's first "Notable Township". Some of the properties are Victorian homes, some are renovated miner's cottages, and one is an octagonal stone house with a resident magpie that guards the stairwell. **www.heritagecottages.com.au**

MILDURA Mildura Grand Hotel

Cnr Deakin Avenue & Seventh Street, VIC 3502 **Tel** *(03) 5023 0511* **Fax** *(03) 5002 1801* **Rooms** *120*

A former bellboy and his extended Italian family has transformed this 1891 coffee palace into a luxury hotel offering a range of modern rooms and guest facilities, including two cafés, bars, grill room, boutique brewery, wine room, ballrooms, produce store and Victoria's only three-hat restaurant outside Melbourne. **www.milduragrandhotel.com**

NHILL Little Desert Nature Lodge

Nhill-Harrow Road, VIC 3418 **Tel** *(03) 5391 5232* **Fax** *(03) 5391 5217* **Rooms** *40*

There are 23 rooms with en suite facilities, 16 bunk rooms which share amenities, and powered and unpowered camp sites on this 117-hectare (288-acre) natural bushland property outside Nhill and adjacent to the Little Desert National Park. The lodge organizes wildlife tours. **www.littledesertlodge.com.au**

OCEAN GROVE Ti-Tree Village

34 Orton Street, VIC 3226 **Tel** *(03) 5255 4433* **Fax** *(03) 5225 5700* **Rooms** *23*

These 23 self-contained one- and two-bedroom log cabins, which feature modern interiors and amenities, are only five minutes' walk from town and two minutes' walk from the beach. Some offer spas and open fireplaces. The grounds are pleasant and have barbecue areas. **www.ti-treevillage.com.au**

PORT FAIRY Oscars Waterfront Boutique Hotel ✱ ▤ $$$$$

41B Gipps Street, VIC 3284 ***Tel*** *(03) 5568 3022* ***Fax*** *(03) 5566 3042* ***Rooms*** *7*

Some might say there is no better place to enjoy breakfast in Port Fairy than on the veranda of this "French Provincial" hotel overlooking the Moyne River marina. Or no better place for a stylish dinner than in its grand dining room. All suites have views of the water or the garden. Children are not permitted. **www.oscarswaterfront.com**

PORTLAND Victoria House 🅿 $$$

5–7 Tyers Street, VIC 3305 ***Tel*** *(03) 5521 7577* ***Fax*** *(03) 5523 6300* ***Rooms*** *8*

This Georgian-style, 1850s double-storey bluestone mansion first operated as a hotel in 1856. It enjoys a central location close to the beach, shops, restaurants and harbour. The rooms are large and tastefully decorated with en suite facilities. There is a guest lounge, dining room and sitting room with open fire. **www.babs.com.au/vichouse**

QUEENSCLIFF Queenscliff Hotel 🍴 🅿 $$$$$

16 Gellibrand Street, VIC 3225 ***Tel*** *(03) 5258 1066* ***Fax*** *(03) 5258 1899* ***Rooms*** *18*

One of the world's grand 19th-century seaside hotels, this elegant 1887 Victorian mansion, across the road from the beach and jetty, is furnished with period decor throughout. All rooms have en suites, but in keeping with the historic atmosphere and emphasis on relaxation, no rooms have a TV, telephone or radio. **www.queenscliffhotel.com.au**

QUEENSCLIFF Vue Grand 🍴 🅿 ≋ 🍸 ▤ $$$$$

46 Hesse Street, VIC 3225 ***Tel*** *(03) 5258 1544* ***Fax*** *(03) 5258 3471* ***Rooms*** *32*

Rooms at this opulent, restored 19th-century hotel are designed to pamper with Old-World style and creature comforts. There is also a grand dining room, spa, club lounge, billiards room, indoor heated pool, gymnasium, conservatory and courtyard. It has spectacular views across Port Phillip Bay. **www.vuegrand.com.au**

SWAN HILL Sundowner Swan Hill Resort 🍴 ≋ ✱ 🍸 🅿 ▤ $$

405–415 Campbell Street, VIC 3585 ***Tel*** *(03) 5032 2726, 1800 034 220* ***Fax*** *(03) 5032 9109* ***Rooms*** *60*

You have the choice of an indoor heated pool or an outdoor saltwater swimming pool with spa at this tropical-themed motel-style resort. Also a tennis court, games room, mini golf, squash court and bicycle hire. The resort is a ten-minute walk from the Murray River and a five-minute walk from town. **www.sundownermotorinns.com.au**

WARRNAMBOOL Manor Gums 🍸 🅿 ▤ $$$$

Shady's Lane, Mailors Flat, VIC 3275 ***Tel*** *(03) 5565 4410* ***Fax*** *(03) 5565 4409* ***Rooms*** *4*

This modern, architect-designed retreat offers four private self-contained suites set in native bushland a ten-minute walk from the beach. Each suite offers something different in terms of style and amenities, but all deliver relaxing views and numerous encounters with the abundant local birdlife. **www.travel.to/manorgums**

WOODEND Campaspe Country House Hotel & Restaurant 🍴 ≋ 🅿 ▤ $$$$$

10 Goldies Lane, VIC 3442 ***Tel*** *(03) 5427 2273* ***Fax*** *(03) 5429 1049* ***Rooms*** *20*

This property is set within 13 hectares (32 acres) of historic Edna Walling gardens and native bushland. It offers 16 courtyard rooms, a two-bedroom cottage, and two manor rooms in the main residence. There is also a purpose-built conference facility, croquet lawns and an award-winning restaurant. **www.campaspehouse.com.au**

EASTERN VICTORIA

BAIRNSDALE Riversleigh Country Hotel 🍴 🅿 ▤ $$$

1 Nicholson Street, VIC 3875 ***Tel*** *(03) 5152 6966* ***Fax*** *(03) 5152 4413* ***Rooms*** *20*

Sit back and enjoy relaxing views of the Mitchell River, mountains and farmland from the balconies of these grand, 1886, National Trust-listed Victorian terraces. All rooms are en suite and there is a ground-floor suite for disabled guests in one terrace. The restaurant is open for breakfast, lunch and dinner. **www.riversleigh.info**

BEECHWORTH Finches of Beechworth ▤ $$$$$

3 Finch Street, VIC 3747 ***Tel*** *(03) 5728 2655* ***Fax*** *(03) 5728 2656* ***Rooms*** *6*

This restored Victorian residence in a peaceful location two blocks from the main street features antique furniture and period fittings, a delightful wisteria-clad veranda and English-style gardens. The six rooms all have their own bathroom, and there is a guest sitting room. **www.beechworth.com/finches**

BRIGHT Ashwood House Cottage ▤ $$$

22A Ashwood Avenue, VIC 3741 ***Tel*** *(03) 5755 1081* ***Fax*** *(03) 5755 1115* ***Rooms*** *3*

For absolute peace and quiet, and complete privacy, these three architect-designed and self-contained one-bedroom cottages are perfect. They share native bushland with abundant wildlife beside the Ovens River. It is an easy and pleasant 20-minute riverside walk into the centre of Bright. **www.ashwoodcottages.com.au**

DANDENONG RANGES Cottages of Mount Dandenong ▤ $$$$

1411–1413 Mount Dandenong Tourist Road, VIC 3767 ***Tel*** *(03) 9751 2447* ***Fax*** *(03) 9751 2391* ***Rooms*** *3*

Nestled into the forest are a charming two-bedroom 100-year-old farmhouse and a one-bedroom Bavarian-style log cabin (an odd, but common architectural theme in the Dandenongs). If you have spent a long day bushwalking through the National Park, there are 20 restaurants within 2 km (1 mile) of the cottages to choose from.

Key to Price Guide *see p478* **Key to Symbols** *see back cover flap*

DINNER PLAIN Crystal Creek Resort 🏋️🛏️🎿🗐 $$$

Big Muster Drive, VIC 3898 **Tel** *(03) 5159 6422* **Fax** *(03) 5159 6500* **Rooms** *15*

Open year round, this resort offers spas, saunas and tennis courts, and can organize horse and mountain bike treks. They also provide ski equipment and free transfers to Mount Hotham. Rooms accommodate six people, the à la carte restaurant serves breakfast, lunch and dinner, and the bar presents live bands. **www.crystalcreekresort.com.au**

EILDON RobynsNest Bed and Breakfast 🏋️🗐 $$$

13 High Street, VIC 3713 **Tel** *(03) 5774 2525, 0409 932 724* **Fax** *(03) 5774 2525* **Rooms** *2*

After a hard day's trout fishing on the Goulburn River or Eildon Pondage, water skiing on Lake Eildon, or mountain biking in the nearby hills, you and your partner can retire to this award-winning guesthouse and relax with an in-room Shiatsu or aromatherapy massage. **www.visitvictoria.com/robynsnest**

FALLS CREEK The Falls Creek Hotel 🏋️🎿🛏️🗐 $$$$

23 Falls Creek Road, VIC 3699 **Tel** *(03) 5758 3282* **Fax** *(03) 5758 3296* **Rooms** *24*

The main attraction at this chalet-style hotel is the "Ski In, Ski Out" facility. There are three lifts to choose from within a ski boot's throw of the front door. All rooms have views of the slopes and can accommodate up to five guests. There is an excellent Kid's Club and the tariff is per person and inclusive of dinner. **www.fallscreekhotel.com.au**

GIPPSLAND LAKES The Moorings at Metung 🏊🎿🏋️🛏️🗐 $$$$$

44 Metung Road, VIC 3904 **Tel** *(03) 5156 2750* **Fax** *(03) 5156 2755* **Rooms** *39*

These one-, two- and three-bedroom apartments (and penthouse) enjoy waterfront views over Bancroft Bay. Located in the centre of Metung village, this complex offers water frontage and private boat berthing. There is a tennis court, barbecue area, boat and kayak hire. The friendly local pub is a two-minute walk. **www.themoorings.com.au**

GIPPSLAND LAKES Wattle Point Waterfront Retreat 🏊🎿🏋️🗐 $$$$$

200 Wattle Point Road, Wattle Point, VIC 3875 **Tel** *(03) 5157 7517* **Fax** *(03) 5157 7677* **Rooms** *16*

This peaceful retreat 15 km (9 miles) from Bairnsdale offers private self-contained one- to four-bedroom cedar lodges nestled within 8 hectares (20 acres) of native bushland on the edge of Lake Victoria. There is an indoor pool, mineral spa, tennis court, sauna, fishing jetty and canoe and mountain bike hire. **www.wattlepointholiday.com.au**

KING VALLEY Casa Luna Gourmet Accommodation 🏋️🛏️🎿🗐 $$$

1569 Boggy Creek Road, Myrrhee, VIC 3732 **Tel** *(03) 5729 7650* **Rooms** *2*

Close to some of Victoria's best wineries and gourmet cheese producers, the rooms at this stylish retreat overlook a peaceful valley and vineyards. The restaurant specializes in regional Italian cuisine and can provide guests with breakfast and dinner hampers. There is a petanque court and private dining room. **www.casaluna.com.au**

LAKES ENTRANCE Comfort Inn & Suites Emmanuel 🏋️🎿🛏️🗐 $$$

151 Esplanade, VIC 3909 **Tel** *(03) 5155 1444* **Fax** *(03) 5155 2401* **Rooms** *32*

A good option for travellers with children, these modern self-contained two-bedroom suites, which sleep up to seven, have access to adult and toddler pools, spa, landscaped gardens, barbecue areas and playground. Some rooms are suitable for disabled travellers. **www.comfortinnemmanuel.com.au**

MALLACOOTA Melaleuca Grove Holiday Units 🎿🛏️🎿 $$$

178 Mirrabooka Road, VIC 3892 **Tel** *(03) 5158 0407* **Fax** *(03) 5158 0407* **Rooms** *12*

Six modern and self-contained two-bedroom units with private courtyards are set within 1 hectares (2.5 acres) of bushland and surrounded by a National Park. There is a playground and barbecue facilities, and pets are welcome. The shops, beach and lake are a five-minute drive, and boat and bicycle hire is available.

MANSFIELD Howqua Dale Gourmet Retreat 🏋️🎿🏊🛏️🗐 $$$$$

Howqua River Road, VIC 3722 **Tel** *(03) 5777 3503* **Fax** *(03) 5777 3896* **Rooms** *6*

A chef and a wine expert run this cooking school and gourmet retreat hidden away in the mountains. The accommodation is modern and surrounded by a large garden with river frontage. The cooking course must be booked in advance. Children not welcome. **www.gtoa.com.au/howqua_dale_retreats**

MANSFIELD Mansfield Valley Motor Inn 🎿🗐 $$$$$

Maroondah Highway, VIC 3722 **Tel** *(03) 5775 1300* **Fax** *(03) 5775 1693* **Rooms** *23*

This motel offers a straightforward range of two-bedroom and motel-style units at the edge of town, a 40-minute drive from Mount Buller. The motel has big gardens, barbecue facilities and views of Mount Buller. All rooms are en suite and look out onto the gardens, bushland or horse paddocks. **www.mansfieldvalley.com.au**

MARYSVILLE Lyell Guest Cottages 🎿🗐 $$$$

30 Lyell Street, VIC 3779 **Tel** *(03) 5963 3383* **Fax** *(03) 5963 3383* **Rooms** *9*

A five-minute walk from the centre of this small township nestled in the mountains are four contemporary and well-appointed two- and three-bedroom self-contained cottages. Relax on the front deck or enjoy local bushwalking and mountain bike opportunities. It is only a 25-minute drive to Lake Mountain. **www.lyell.com.au**

MORNINGTON PENINSULA Bayplay Adventure Lodge 🏋️🎿🛏️🎿 $$$$

46 Canterbury Jetty Road, Blairgowrie, VIC 3942 **Tel** *(03) 5988 0188* **Fax** *(03) 5988 8032* **Rooms** *8*

This inexpensive lodge, a short walk from the beach, provides accommodation options ranging from bunkrooms to family rooms. There is a licensed café and communal kitchen, bus transfers to and from Melbourne, and free bicycle hire for guests. The lodge can also organize kayaking, scuba diving, surfing and horse riding. **www.bayplay.com.au**

MORNINGTON PENINSULA Carmel of Sorrento

$$$$$

142 Ocean Beach Road, Sorrento, VIC 3943 **Tel** *(03) 5984 3512* **Fax** *(03) 5984 0094* **Rooms** *10*

There are several options here, including traditional guesthouse accommodation in an original Federation guesthouse, self-contained units and a heritage beach cottage that sleeps six. The property is halfway between the front beach and the back beach of Sorrento. **www.carmelofsorrento.com.au**

MOUNT BAW BAW Kelly's Lodge

$$$

11 Frostii Lane, VIC 3068 **Tel** *(03) 5165 1129* **Fax** *(03) 5165 1159* **Rooms** *4*

A major attraction of this lodge is its central location within the Baw Baw Alpine Resort. The toboggan run is just outside the front door and it is only metres to the ski lift, and for those whose equipment needs upgrading or who need to purchase the latest in ski wear, there is an excellent ski shop right next door. **www.kellyslodge.com.au**

MOUNT BEAUTY Harrietville Hotel/Motel

$$$$

169 Great Alpine Road, Harrietville, VIC 3698 **Tel** *(03) 5759 2525* **Fax** *(03) 5759 2766* **Rooms** *24*

These motel-style family rooms in a quiet township below Mount Hotham offer ski and chain hire, and drying rooms. There is also a licensed restaurant, bar and beer garden. And an outdoor pool and mountain bike hire for those guests who enjoy the area's summer attractions. **www.harrietvillehotelmotel.com**

MOUNT BUFFALO Mount Buffalo Chalet

$$$$$

Mount Buffalo National Park, VIC 3740 **Tel** *(03) 5755 1500, 1800 037 038* **Fax** *(03) 5755 1892* **Rooms**

Built in 1910, this atmospheric chalet (once a retreat for Victorian Railways employees) makes the most of its spectacular mountaintop setting. There is a range of rooms, a kid's club and activities ranging from abseiling and canoeing, to croquet and petanque. The price includes dinner, bed and breakfast. **www.mtbuffalochalet.com.au**

MOUNT BULLER Grand Mercure Chalet

$$$

Mount Buller Village, VIC 3723 **Tel** *(03) 5777 6566* **Fax** *(03) 5777 6455* **Rooms** *65*

This luxurious hotel, only metres from the ski lift, offers single and twin rooms (all en suite) and first-class fitness facilities, including an indoor heated pool, sauna, gym and squash court. There is also a library for the less frenetic, and the chalet is child friendly. **www.mtbullerchalet.com.au**

MOUNT HOTHAM Snowbird Inn

$$$$$

Great Alpine Road, VIC 3741 **Tel** *(03) 5759 3503, 1800 659 009* **Fax** *(03) 5759 3172* **Rooms** *24*

Ski in, Ski out. This central, no-frills lodge opposite the ski lift offers backpacker-style accommodation with 24 bunkrooms sleeping from four to eight guests. There is a guest lounge with open fire, a bistro, a bar, a ski-wear boutique and equipment hire and good balcony views. Closed during summer. **www.snowbirdinn.com.au**

PHILLIP ISLAND Cowes Eco Cottages

$$$

Cnr Justice & Ventnor Road, Cowes, VIC 3922 **Tel** *(03) 5952 6466* **Fax** *(03) 5952 3950* **Rooms** *4*

Surrounded by large coastal gardens, these environmentally sustainable, self-contained cottages deserve their four-star AAA tourist rating. The two one-bedroom cottages (Banksia and Melaleuca) feature spas and wood heaters. The third cottage (Acacia) has two bedrooms. **www.cowesecocottages.com.au**

PHILLIP ISLAND The Gatehouse Cottage

$$$$$

32–34 Walton Street, Rhyll, VIC 3923 **Tel** *(03) 5956 9090* **Fax** *(03) 5956 9008* **Rooms** *2*

Within earshot of the beach, these two self-contained one-bedroom cottages are surrounded by English-style gardens. The Gatehouse Cottage looks over the garden, while the split-level Edgewater Studio offers a spa and bay views. Children are not welcome. **www.phillipisland.net.au**

RUTHERGLEN Mount Ophir Estate

$$$$$

Stillards Lane, VIC 3685 **Tel** *(03) 6032 8920* **Fax** *(03) 6032 9911* **Rooms** *15*

The 1891 French Provincial tower set in a vineyard and organic olive farm seems incongruous, but this accommodation complex does not disappoint. Options include a 1902 homestead guesthouse, a self-contained farmhouse, and three floors of four-star luxury in the tower. Children are welcome. **www.mount-ophir.com**

SOUTH GIPPSLAND Waratah Park Country House

$$$

Thomson Road, Waratah Bay, VIC 3959 **Tel** *(03) 5683 2575* **Fax** *(03) 5683 2275* **Rooms** *6*

This four-star accommodation is located in a bushland setting overlooking Wilson's Promontory and Bass Strait. The views are spectacular and the restaurant enjoys a well-deserved reputation. It is only a short drive to nearby beaches and a 20-minute drive to Wilson's Promontory. **www.wpe.com.au**

WALHALLA Windsor House B&B

$$$

Lot 66 Right hand Branch Road, VIC 3825 **Tel** *(03) 5165 6237* **Rooms** *6*

This guesthouse's website boasts it hasn't seen a ghost in weeks. The two-storey, fully restored 1878 Georgian guesthouse is Walhalla's original accommodation. There are six rooms – one is reserved for those who snore, and one is named after a well-known local poacher. **www.windsorhouse.com.au**

WILSONS PROMONTORY Tidal River Cottages

$$

National Parks Service, Tidal River, VIC 3690 **Tel** *(03) 5680 9555, 1800 350 552* **Fax** *(03) 5680 9516* **Rooms**

A favourite destination for Melbournians, so book well ahead. It is the only accommodation service in the National Park, but it offers everything from unpowered camp sites to the eco-friendly Smart Shax. There is only a general store, post office and takeaway food in Tidal River, so bring your own luxuries. **www.parkweb.vic.gov.au**

Key to Price Guide *see p478* **Key to Symbols** *see back cover flap*

YARRA VALLEY Sanctuary House Motel $$

326 Badger Creek Road, Healesville, VIC 3777 **Tel** *(03) 5962 5148* **Fax** *(03) 5962 5392* **Rooms** *25*

On the same road as the Healesville Sanctuary and surrounded by native bush and gardens, this recently renovated resort-style motel offers several room types and self-contained cabins, barbecue areas, a guest lounge, billiards room, pool, sauna, spa, adventure playground, live entertainment and a Spanish tapas bar. **www.sanctuaryhouse.com.au**

YARRA VALLEY The Yarra Glen Grand Hotel $$$$$

19 Bell Street, Yarra Glen, VIC 3775 **Tel** *(03) 9730 1230* **Fax** *(03) 9730 1124* **Rooms** *10 (4 suites)*

This 1888 National Trust classified hotel in the centre of the Yarra Valley comes with all the trimmings: four-poster beds, lashings of antique furniture, à la carte dining in three venues, winery tours and hot-air balloon flights with champagne breakfast packages. Price includes dinner and breakfast. **www.yarraglengrand.com.au**

TASMANIA

BICHENO Bicheno Gaol Cottages $$$

Cnr James & Burgess sts, TAS 7215 **Tel** *(03) 6375 1430* **Rooms** *3*

The National Trust listed gaol house is the oldest building in this seaside holiday town and has been converted into a charming and comfortable guesthouse. Also on the site is the Old School House, providing self-contained accommodation ideal for families. **www.bichenogaolcottages.com**

BINALONG BAY Bay of Fires Character Cottages $$$

64–74 Main Road, Binalong Bay, TAS 7216 **Tel** *(03) 6376 8262* **Fax** *(03) 6376 8261* **Rooms** *8*

Overlooking the breathtaking Binalong Bay and the Bay of Fires, these cottages are a short distance from the beach and nestled in the seaside village. Dine in the onsite restaurant or make the most of the self-contained kitchen (breakfast not included). **www.bayoffirescottages.com.au**

BRIDPORT Platypus Park Country Retreat $$

20 Ada Street, Bridport, TAS 7262 **Tel** *(03) 6356 1873* **Rooms** *7*

Country hospitality by the seaside can be found at Platypus Park. Located in the holiday town of Bridport in the state's northeast, the retreat is just a short drive from the spectacular Barnbougle Dunes golf links course, a lavender farm and a number of wineries. **www.platypuspark.com.au**

BRUNY ISLAND Morella Island Retreats $$$$

46 Adventure Bay Road, Adventure Bay, TAS 7150 **Tel** *(03) 6293 1131* **Fax** *(03) 6293 1137* **Rooms** *5*

The hosts of Morella Island Retreats invite you to escape from the real world in one of their five themed cottages. Boasting incredible views over the "neck", an onsite art gallery, café, landscaped gardens, the retreat is suitable for families or those seeking a private island retreat. Breakfast not included. **www.morella-island.com.au**

BURINE The Duck House $$

26 Queen Street, TAS 7320 **Tel** *(03) 6431 1712* **Fax** *(03) 6431 1712* **Rooms** *3*

Early last century the Duck family called this Federation cottage home. Now it is a comfortable, centrally located guesthouse with a pleasant veranda, antique furniture and modern amenities. Rooms come with provisions for a self-catered full English breakfast. There are concessions for children and longer stays. **www.ozpal.com/duck**

COLES BAY Iluka Holiday Centre $$

Esplanade, Coles Bay, TAS 7215 **Tel** *(03) 6257 0115* **Fax** *(03) 6257 0384* **Rooms** *15*

The Iluka Holiday Centre is in the centre of Coles Bay village, across the road from Muirs Beach. The self-contained two-bedroom cabins come with television, covered deck and carport. The centre also incorporates a YHA Backpackers lodge, powered caravan sites and camping ground. **www.ilukaholidaycentre.com.au**

COLES BAY Edge of the Bay Resort $$$$

2308 Coles Bay Road, Coles Bay, TAS 7215 **Tel** *(03) 6257 0102* **Fax** *(03) 6257 0437* **Rooms** *22*

This private resort retreat is positioned on the edge of Great Oyster Bay with stunning views to the Hazards Mountain Range and Freycinet National Park. Offering waterfront suites and self-contained cottages, there is a restaurant on site and no shortage of activities. Breakfast baskets are available. **www.edgeofthebay.com.au**

COLES BAY Freycinet Lodge $$$$$

Freycinet National Park, TAS 7215 **Tel** *(03) 6257 0101* **Fax** *(03) 6225 3909* **Rooms** *60*

Award-winning, ecologically friendly lodge overlooking Great Oyster Bay backed by the Hazards Mountains. The ideal base for exploring the World Heritage listed Wineglass Bay and the glorious coast of the Tasmanian east coast. Wooden cabins and boardwalks complement the lodge's setting. **www.puretasmania.com.au**

CRADLE MOUNTAIN Cradle Mountain Lodge $$$$$

Cradle Mountain Road, National Park, TAS 7306 **Tel** *(03) 6492 1303* **Fax** *(03) 6492 1309* **Rooms** *86*

This rustic alpine retreat is located on the edge of the World Heritage listed Cradle Mountain/Lake St Clair National Park. Featuring cosy log cabins (some with spas), guided tours, lodge-style restaurant and guest lounge with stone fireplace. The Waldheim Spa onsite offers spa treatment. **www.cradlemountainlodge.com.au**

DEVONPORT Birchmore Bed and Breakfast 🚶🛏 $$$$$

8–10 Oldaker Street, TAS 7310 **Tel** *(03) 6423 1336* **Fax** *(03) 6423 1338* **Rooms** *7*

Birchmore offers guests outstanding accommodation and personal service in the heart of Devonport. Only a minute from the city centre, Birchmore is ideally located for restaurants, shopping and business. Rooms are designed with the business guest in mind. Hearty breakfast included. **www.bedsandbreakfasts.com.au/Birchmore**

HOBART Motel 429 📶📺🍴📋 $$

429 Sandy Bay Road, Sandy Bay, TAS 7005 **Tel** *(03) 6225 2511* **Fax** *(03) 6225 4354* **Rooms** *33*

Conveniently located in Sandy Bay with views of the River Derwent, close to Wrest Point Casino and the Sandy Bay shopping village. The motel is well served by public transport direct to the city centre. Some rooms have been recently renovated and have air conditioning. The motel has a spa and sauna. **www.motel429.com.au**

HOBART Avon Court Apartments 🚶 $$$

4 Colville Street, Battery Point, TAS 7004 **Tel** *(03) 6223 4837* **Fax** *(03) 6223 7207* **Rooms** *8*

Situated within the historic village of Battery Point, just a short walk to Salamanca Place, Hobart's waterfront and the city centre, these one- and two-bedroom apartments are fully self-contained and are an ideal base for exploring Hobart and its surrounds. There is off-street parking available and cafés, restaurants and services are a stroll away.

HOBART Battery Point Manor 📋 $$$$

13–15 Cromwell Street, TAS 7004 **Tel** *(03) 6224 0888* **Fax** *(03) 6224 2254* **Rooms** *8*

This grand Georgian home was built in 1834 and is now a European-style guesthouse, with commanding views across the River Derwent. Choose from the seven en suite rooms, or the privacy of the two-bedroom self-contained cottage. Take advantage of the historic village's restaurants, cafés and shops. **www.batterypointmanor.com.au**

HOBART Henry Jones Art Hotel 📶🍴🚶🛏📋 $$$$$

25 Hunter Street, Hobart, TAS 7000 **Tel** *(03) 6210 7700* **Fax** *(03) 6210 7755* **Rooms** *50*

Winner of the Australian Hotel Association Best Overall Hotel in 2005, this is a stylish, first-class hotel with a strong focus on Tasmanian art and design. Formerly the site of the Jones & Co. IXL jam factory, it is part of a sympathetic redevelopment of this historic area of Hobart into an art and cultural centre. **www.thehenryjones.com**

HOBART Hotel Grand Chancellor 📶🍴🏊🛏📺📋 $$$$$

1 Davey Street, Hobart, TAS 7000 **Tel** *(03) 6235 4535* **Fax** *(03) 6223 8175* **Rooms** *240*

Located right on the waterfront, adjacent to the Federation Concert Hall, the Hotel Grand Chancellor offers rooms with waterfront, city and mountain aspects. There is a range of facilities and services including a fully equipped gym, indoor swimming pool, restaurant and comprehensive business and conference facilities. **www.ghihotels.com**

HOBART Kinvara House 🛏📋 $$$$$

86 Forest Road, West Hobart, TAS 7000 **Tel** *(03) 6278 8232* **Fax** *(03) 6278 8276* **Rooms** *1 Apartment*

Built in the 1890s, Kinvara House provides ultra-modern, luxury self-contained accommodation for up to six people. It boasts spectacular views of the city and River Derwent and is located within walking distance of the city centre and Salamanca Place. Continental breakfast provisions on day of arrival. **www.tasmanianindulgence.com.au**

HOBART Lenna of Hobart 📶🍴🚶🛏 $$$$$

20 Runnymede Street, Battery Point, TAS 7004 **Tel** *(03) 6232 3900* **Fax** *(03) 6224 0112* **Rooms** *50*

The heritage-listed Lenna – formerly the residence of Scottish merchant Alexander McGregor – is now a gracious boutique hotel just around the corner from Salamanca Place. It offers spacious en-suite rooms adjoining the original mansion, well-equipped function venues and the award-winning Alexander's restaurant. **www.lenna.com.au**

LAUNCESTON Peppers Seaport Hotel 📶🍴🚶📺🛏📋 $$$$

28 Seaport Boulevard, TAS 7250 **Tel** *(03) 6345 3333* **Fax** *(03) 6345 3300* **Rooms** *60*

Peppers Seaport Hotel is the centre of Launceston's newest lifestyle precinct on the North Esk River. This sleek and very modern hotel comprises en-suite rooms and fully self-contained apartments. There are several restaurants and bars on site, a marina, boardwalk and the city's first-class sports stadium is just a short walk away. **www.peppers.com.au**

LAUNCESTON Ashton Gate 🚶📋 $$$$$

32 High Street, Launceston, TAS 7250 **Tel** *(03) 6331 6180* **Fax** *(03) 6334 2232* **Rooms** *8*

Ashton Gate (c.1880) was built by Mr AW Birchall, the owner of Australia's oldest bookshop. The home became a guesthouse after World War II and today the accommodation includes de luxe suites and a self-contained apartment. Breakfast is included and can be enjoyed on the new outdoor deck. **www.ashtongate.com.au**

LAUNCESTON Hatherley House 🛏📋 $$$$$

43 High Street, Launceston, TAS 7250 **Tel** *(03) 6334 7727* **Fax** *(03) 6334 7728* **Rooms** *9*

The outstanding Hatherley House was voted Australia's best guesthouse by Australian *Gourmet Traveller* magazine in 2004. Each themed suite is impeccably decorated with the highest quailty fittings and furnishings. There is high speed ADSL internet access available in each room. **www.hatherleyhouse.com.au**

NEW NORFOLK Tynwald Willow Bend Estate 🍴🏊🚶🛏 $$$

Hobart Road, New Norfolk, TAS 7140 **Tel** *(03) 6261 2667* **Fax** *(03) 6261 2040* **Rooms** *7*

This gracious 1830s mansion overlooking the River Derwent was once a part of an old flour mill. Set in 16 hectares (39 acres) featuring garden walks, a solar-heated outdoor swimming pool and tennis court. There are six rooms within the mansion and a self-contained stone cottage known as 'The Granary'. **www.tynwaldtasmania.com**

Key to Price Guide *see p478* **Key to Symbols** *see back cover flap*

RICHMOND Hatchers Richmond Manor
73 Prossers Road, Richmond, TAS 7025 **Tel** *(03) 6260 2622* **Fax** *(03) 6260 2744* **Rooms** *8*

A luxury rural getaway for couples and families, set among gardens, orchards and a private lake. Start the day with a full country breakfast before exploring the quaint historic township of Richmond. Rooms are very well equipped, including internet access. **www.hatchersmanor.com.au**

ROSS Man-O-Ross Hotel
35 Church Street, TAS 7209 **Tel** *(03) 6381 5445* **Fax** *(03) 6381 5440* **Rooms** *7*

This attractive sandstone building, situated on the highway coming into Ross, was constructed in 1835 and has been carefully refurbished. The traditional elegance of the interior is complemented by the friendly, homey decor of the rooms. **www.manoross.com.au**

ROSS Colonial Cottages and Ross Bed & Breakfast
12 Church Street, TAS 7209 **Tel** *(03) 6381 5354* **Fax** *(03) 6331 1895* **Rooms** *7*

These charming cottages in the historic town of Ross date from the 1840s and are situated in the town centre. Each cottage has been affectionately restored and features antiques, thick sandstone walls and wooden four-poster beds. **www.rossaccommodation.com.au**

SHEFFIELD Wild Gowrie Park
1447 Claude Road, Gowrie, TAS 7306 **Tel** *(03) 6491 1385* **Fax** *(03) 6491 1848* **Rooms** *4*

Tucked away within ancient forests, beneath the rugged Mount Roland, these cosy well-equipped cabins provide the perfect base for exploring the magnificent wilderness of the Walls of Jerusalem and Cradle Mountain-Lake St Clair National Parks. Self-cater or take advantage of the on-site restaurant. **www.gowriepark.com.au**

STANLEY Beachside Retreat West Inlet
253 Stanley Highway, TAS 7331 **Tel** *(03) 6458 1350* **Fax** *(03) 6458 1350* **Rooms** *6*

Waterfront nature retreat and haven for wildlife and cattle, across from a secluded beach and close to the historic township of Stanley. Offering three types of contemporary self-contained accommodation: a spacious spa lodge, contemporary ecocabins and a luxury nature cabin. **www.beachsideretreat.com**

STRAHAN Aldermere Estate
27 Harvey Street Strahan, TAS 7468 **Tel** *(03) 6471 7418* **Fax** *3 6471 7418* **Rooms** *8*

Aldermere Estate is a modern establishment designed with an eye to Tasmania's colonial past. The fully self-contained two-storey apartments have been tastefully decorated in period style with all the modern conveniences and continental breakfast provisions. **www.aldermere.com.au**

STRAHAN Franklin Manor
The Esplanade, Strahan, TAS 7468 **Tel** *(03) 6471 7311* **Fax** *(03) 6471 7267* **Rooms** *18*

Overlooking the vast Macquarie Harbour at the gateway to the rugged west coast, Franklin Manor is steeped in history and charm. The grand old home is now a haven for those seeking to experience the pristine wilderness and savour the delicious food and wine in Franklin Manor's first-class restaurant. **www.franklinmanor.com.au**

SWANSEA Swansea Holiday Park at Jubilee Beach
27 Shaw Street, Swansea, TAS 7190 **Tel** *(03) 6257 8177* **Fax** *(03) 6257 8511* **Rooms** *14*

One of the two locations of the Swansea Holiday Park, situated at Jubilee Beach, within the heritage township of Swansea. There are a range of self-contained cabins plus powered sites for caravans. There is an outdoor swimming pool and games room, as well as a barbecue. **www.swansea-holiday.com.au**

SWANSEA Kabuki By the Sea
Rocky Hills, Tasman Highway, Swansea, TAS 7190 **Tel** *(03) 6257 8588* **Fax** *(03) 6257 8588* **Rooms** *7*

These Japanese-inspired cottages are perched on a clifftop and boast spectacular views of the Freycinet Peninsula. There are five one-bedroom cottages, each with bathroom, sitting/dining room and kitchen facilities. The on-site restaurant uses the local produce to create exquisite Japanese and oriental cuisine. **www.kabukibythesea.com.au**

SWANSEA Schouten House
1 Waterloo Road, TAS 7190 **Tel** *(03) 6257 8564* **Fax** *(03) 6257 8564* **Rooms** *6*

This is a beautifully restored Georgian house (c.1846) on Tasmania's stunning east coast. It provides bed-and-breakfast accommodation and each room features antique heritage furniture, mini bar and en-suite bathroom. Adding to the welcome is a log fire. **www.schoutenhouse.com.au**

TASMAN PENINSULA Norfolk Bay Convict Station
5862 Arthur Highway, Taranna, TAS 7180 **Tel** *(03) 6250 3487* **Fax** *(03) 6250 3701* **Rooms** *5*

Built with convict labour in 1838, this was once the site of Australia's first railway station, linking Hobart with the penal settlement of Port Arthur. Today the commissariat store has been transformed into a haven of comfort with log fires and bay views, and five themed suites. **www.convictstation.com**

WOODBRIDGE Old Woodbridge Rectory
15 Woodbridge Hill Road, Woodbridge, TAS 7162 **Tel** *(03) 6267 4742* **Fax** *(03) 6267 4746* **Rooms** *2*

Just a 30-minute drive from Hobart along the scenic Channel Highway, this boutique bed-and-breakfast is perfectly positioned for those wanting to explore the Huon Valley, Bruny Island and local wineries. The Old Rectory has been tastefully restored and comprises two en suite rooms. **www.rectory.alltasmanian.com**

WHERE TO EAT

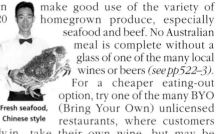

Fresh seafood, Chinese style

A ustralia has developed its own culinary identity in the past 20 years or so and modern Australian food, often with a Mediterranean or Asian twist, is now widely available. Reflecting the country's multicultural population, there is also a wealth of ethnic restaurants. Every cuisine, from Algerian to Zambian, is on a menu somewhere in Australia, particularly in the major cities. Australian restaurants make good use of the variety of homegrown produce, especially seafood and beef. No Australian meal is complete without a glass of one of the many local wines or beers *(see pp522–3)*. For a cheaper eating-out option, try one of the many BYO (Bring Your Own) unlicensed restaurants, where customers take their own wine, but may be charged a minimal corkage fee.

Marco Polo Restaurant at the Conrad in Brisbane *(see p536)*

TYPES OF RESTAURANTS

All major Australian cities offer a wide choice of restaurants. Formal dining establishments, bistros, stylish cafés and pubs are all readily available to suit any budget. Food on offer ranges from haute cuisine to informal snacks. Outside the main cities, some of the best restaurants can be found in the many wine regions and often in the wineries themselves *(see pp36–7)*.

Prices, however, vary widely. They tend to be highest in Sydney, Melbourne and other major tourist resorts, although prices are usually lower than in comparable places in Europe and the United States. As a general guideline, the bill at a showcase Melbourne or Sydney restaurant featuring a celebrity chef will be at least A$150 per head, including a shared bottle of wine. At a Bring Your Own (BYO) or an unpretentious Asian or Italian restaurant it may only be A$30–40 per head. A counter meal at a pub, café or at a snack bar should generally cost around A$15–20 per head, if you include the cost of a drink.

A welcome new trend in Australia is the increasing emphasis on courtyard, garden, boulevard and other outdoor eating facilities, making the most of the country's benevolent climate.

EATING HOURS AND RESERVATIONS

Most restaurants serve lunch between 12:30pm and 3pm; dinner is served from 6:30 to 10:30pm. Many establishments, however, particularly the big city bistros and cafés, have become more flexible, opening for breakfast and closing late. Most budget and ethnic restaurants often close a little earlier, at around 9:30pm, depending on the demand. Most establishments are also open seven days a week, 365 days a year. However, it is advisable to check in advance with individual restaurants, particularly those outside the capital cities. To avoid disappointment, advance telephone bookings are generally recommended.

PAYING AND TIPPING

Major credit cards are accepted in the majority of Australian restaurants, although it is a good idea to confirm this in advance or on arrival. A General Service Tax (GST) is added to restaurant bills in Australia, but tipping is not compulsory. In recognition of outstanding service or a particularly fine meal, a small gratuity is always appreciated. How much to leave is the prerogative of the customer,

Skillogalee Winery and Restaurant in the Clare Valley *(see p552)*

Doyle's On the Beach in Watsons Bay, Sydney *(see p528)*

but 10 per cent of the total bill would generally be regarded as generous. This can be left either as a cash tip on the table when you are ready to leave or by adding it to the total if paying your bill by cheque or credit card.

Ravesi's, one of the many eateries at Bondi Beach, Sydney *(see p524)*

CHILDREN

Few restaurateurs will refuse admission to children as long as they are well behaved. Many restaurants also provide high chairs and a children's menu. The best budget options for families are hamburger chains or Italian or Asian eateries.

WHEELCHAIR ACCESS

Spurred by legislation in the various states, most restaurants now provide special wheelchair access and toilet facilities for the disabled.

However, it is still advisable to check in advance on the facilities available.

VEGETARIANS

It is rare for a restaurant not to feature at least one dish for vegetarians, and a variety of choices is the norm, particularly in regions where there is an abundance of homegrown produce. There are also specialist vegetarian restaurants and cafés in the major cities. If you have special dietary requirements, it is sensible to call the restaurant in advance, especially in more rural areas.

ALCOHOL AND OTHER DRINKS

If a restaurant is described as licensed, it refers to its licence to sell alcohol. Australian wine lists are outstanding and generally highlight the wines of the particular state or district *(see pp32–3)*. Wine is sold by the bottle, carafe or glass. There is usually a good choice of beers, ales, ciders and spirits as well.

BYO restaurants, which are not licensed to sell alcohol, are extremely popular in Australia and offer diners the opportunity to bring the wines they wish to drink with their meal, although beer is not usually permitted. For non-alcohol drinkers, tap water is entirely safe, but many people prefer to drink bottled still or sparkling water. Fresh fruit juices are also very popular *(see pp522–3)*.

DRESS

Dress codes are virtually non-existent in Australian restaurants, although a handful of the more up-market establishments may ask men to wear a tie in the evenings. Most establishments, however, including beachside cafés, frown on scant beachwear and flip flops or sandals.

For most situations, the phrase "smart casual" sums up the Australian approach to eating out.

SMOKING

Smoking is now banned inside restaurants and cafés, although smoking is permitted at outside tables. Fines may be levied if these regulations are disregarded. Smoking restrictions, however, are rarely applied in traditional pubs.

Café Provincial in the heart of Fitzroy in Melbourne *(see p555)*

The Flavours of Australia

Modern Australian cuisine has been evolving from traditional British since World War II. An influx of people from Italy, Greece, Turkey, Lebanon, Thailand, China, Malaysia, Indonesia and Vietnam (to name but a few) have contributed influences to what is now known as Mod-Oz cuisine. However, a lot of Aussies will still sit down to a Sunday roast and swelter over turkey on a midsummer Christmas day. Dramatically varying climates over such a large country mean an abundance and diversity of local produce, so it's no surprise that some of the world's best chefs hail from this rich and exciting culinary playground.

Wattleseed, pepperberry and lemon myrtle

Chef filleting snapper, one of Australia's finest fish

NATIVE INGREDIENTS

There are many native foods in Australia that have been used by aborigines for thousands of years, and which are now becoming widely popular. Quandong, munthari, bush tomato, wild limes and rosellas are native fruits with distinctive colours, flavours and textures, while warrigal greens are a spinach-like herb. All of them are still primarily wild-harvested by aboriginal communities. Although native Australians never used seasonings in their campfire cooking, modern Australians have discovered the exciting flavours of such indigenous herbs and spices as lemon myrtle, wattleseed, mountain pepperleaf, pepperberry, forest berry and akudjura. Native meats such as kangaroo and emu are also being used more frequently, although don't expect to see witchity grubs on many menus. These native meats sit alongside a vast and impressive array of beef, lamb and, of course, seafood. Fish native to Australia include barramundi, trevally and blue-eye cod. The popular native shellfish, yabbies and Moreton Bay bugs, are similar to, but smaller than, lobster. Also worth a mention is the lovely fragrant honey produced out of native Australian forests.

Samphire   Snapper   Lobster
Scallops   Red mullet   Oysters
Selection of seafood to be found in the oceans around Australia

AUSTRALIAN DISHES AND SPECIALITIES

Australians love a barbecue, as a social and culinary hub, and you will find a wide variety of meats and cuisines on the grill. Major cities offer a huge choice of foods, from high end French-style fare to fish and chips or cheap and cheerful noodle bars. Melbourne, in particular, has a strong Greek and Italian influence and prides itself on a vibrant café culture, serving unbeatable coffee. Meat pies are a staple in the Aussie diet with the annual Meat Pie Competition attracting great interest, and you will see pies inspired by different cuisines such as Thai, Indian and Moroccan.

For those with a sweet tooth, pumpkin scones are a traditional Australian favourite, alongside passionfruit tart, Lamingtons, Pavlova, and oat and coconut Anzac biscuits.

Anzac biscuits

Kangaroo pizza *This Italian classic is given a modern Australian spin with the addition of seared lean fillet.*

Vegetable stall at Queen Victoria Market, Melbourne *(see p386)*

THE WORLD ON A PLATE

Having one of the most eclectic populations on earth means great things for food (or "tucker"). Australians are as happy exporting their wealth of homegrown produce as they are embracing international cuisine.

Farming plays a very important role in Australia, the world's largest producer of beef. The lush pastures on the coast are particularly good for farming, and the milk-fed lamb from New South Wales is as wonderful as the brie produced in South Australia. King Island, off the coast of Victoria, is dedicated to dairy produce, whose farmers sell their amazing cheese and creams all around the country. Alongside the rapidly growing wine industry is olive oil and balsamic vinegar production, examples of which you are likely to find at the cellar door of many vineyards.

Australia has one of the most diverse marine faunas in the world, due to its range of

Wooden crate of sweet, juicy apples from Tasmania

habitats, from the warm tropical northern waters to the sub-Antarctic Tasman sea, as well as its geographical isolation. A total of 600 marine and freshwater species are caught in Australian waters, providing chefs with plenty of inspiration.

Every kind of fruit and vegetable is produced in Australia. Pineapples and mangoes are widely grown in Queensland, apples in Victoria, strawberries in New South Wales and rambutans in the Northern Territory. Exotic and notoriously hard to farm, truffles have recently been cultivated in Tasmania, highlighting just how versatile Australia's land is.

FOOD ON THE RUN

Sushi Major cities are dotted with tiny counters offering fresh sushi to grab on the go.

Juice bars This booming industry is found on most city streets, serving delicious, cool blends of fruit.

Milk bars As well as milkshakes, ice creams and salads, these sell a wide range of deep-fried foods.

Coffee & cake Little cafés everywhere also sell Italian-style cakes and pastries.

Pubs Most pubs serve a decent steak sandwich.

Pies An Aussie institution, pies are readily available. Look out for gourmet versions.

Grilled barramundi *Served on ginger and bok choy risotto, this is a great mix of local seafood and Asian flavours.*

Prawn Laksa *This spicy coconut noodle soup can be found all over the country in noodle bars, cafés and pubs.*

Lamingtons *These little Victoria sponge cakes are coated in chocolate icing and shredded coconut.*

What to Drink in Australia

Semillon Chardonnay

Australia has one of the world's finest cuisines and part of its enjoyment is the marriage of the country's wine with great food. Australians have a very relaxed attitude to food and wine mixes, so red wine with fish and a cold, dry Riesling as an aperitif can easily be the order of the day. Also, many of the restuarants in the wine regions offer exclusive brands, or offer rare wines so these are worth seeking out. Australians also enjoy some of the best good-value wine in the world *(see pp36–7)*. It is estimated that there are 10,000 different Australian wines on the market at any one time. Australians do love their beer, and it remains a popular drink, with a wide range of choices available. While the health-conscious can choose from a variety of bottled waters and select-your-own, freshly-squeezed fruit juices. Imported wines, beers and spirits are also readily available.

SPARKLING WINE

Domaine Chandon in the Yarra Valley *(see p433)* in Eastern Victoria

Australia is justly famous for its sparkling wines, from Yalumba's Angas Brut to Seppelts Salinger. Most recently, Tasmania has showed considerable promise in producing some high quality sparkling wines, particularly Pirie from Pipers Brook. However, the real hidden gems are the sparkling red wines – the best are made using the French *Méthode Champenois*, matured over a number of years and helped by a small drop of vintage port. The best producers of red sparkling wines are Rockford and Seppelts. These sparkling wines are available throughout the country from "bottle shops".

Angus Brut premium

WHITE WINE

Rhine Riesling   Botrytis Semillon

The revolution in wine making in the 1970s firmly established dry wines made from international grape varieties on the Australian table. Chardonnay, Sauvignon Blanc, and more recently Viognier and Pinot Gris are all popular. However, in recent years there has also been a renaissance and growing appreciation for Riesling, Marsanne and Semillon, which age very gracefully. Australia's other great wines are their fortified and desert wines. Australian winemakers use *botrytis cinera*, or noble rot, to make luscious dessert wines such as Muscats and Tokays.

Some of the vines in Australia are the oldest in the world

GRAPE TYPE	STATE	BEST REGIONS	BEST PRODUCERS
Chardonnay	VIC	Geelong, Beechworth	Bannockburn, Giaconda, Stoniers
	NSW	Hunter Valley	Lakes Folly, Rosemount, Tyrrell's
	WA	Margaret River	Leeuwin Estate, Pierro, Cullen
	SA	Barossa Valley, Eden Valley	Penfolds, Mountadam
Semillon	NSW	Hunter Valley	Brokenwood, McWilliams, Tyrrell
	SA	Barossa Valley	Peter Lehmann, Willows, Penfolds
	WA	Margaret River	Moss Wood, Voyager, Evans & Tate
Riesling	SA	Clare Valley and Adelaide Hills	Grosset, Pikes, Petaluma, Mitchells
	SA	Barossa Valley	Richmond Grove, Leo Buring, Yalumba
	TAS	Tasmania	Piper's Brook
Marsanne	VIC	Goulburn Valley	Chateau Tahbilk, Mitchelton

RED WINE

Vineyards of Leeuwin Estate, Margaret River

Australia's benchmark red is Grange Hermitage, the creation of the late vintner Max Schubert in the 1950s and 1960s. Due to his work, Shiraz has established itself as Australia's premium red variety. However, there is also plenty of diversity with the acknowledged quality of Cabernet Sauvignon produced in the Coonawarra. Recently, there has also been a re-appraisal of traditional "old vine" Grenache and Mourvedre varieties in the Barossa Valley and McLaren Vale.

Shiraz   Pinot Noir

GRAPE TYPE	BEST REGIONS	BEST PRODUCERS
Shiraz	Hunter Valley (NSW)	Brokenwood, Lindmans, Tyrrells
	Great Western, Sunbury (VIC)	Bests, Seppelts, Craiglee
	Barossa Valley (SA)	Henschke, Penfolds, Rockford, Torbreck
	McLaren Vale (SA)	Hardys, Coriole, Chapel Hill
	Margaret River, Great Southern(WA)	Cape Mentelle, Plantagenet
Cabernet Sauvignon	Margaret River (WA)	Cape Mentelle, Cullen, Moss Wood
	Coonawarra (SA)	Wynns, Lindemans, Bowen Estate
	Barossa, Adelaide Hills (SA)	Penfolds, Henschke, Petaluma
	Yarra Valley, Great Western (VIC)	Yarra Yering, Yerinberg, Bests
Merlot	Yarra Valley, Great Western (VIC)	Bests, Yara Yering
	Adelaide Hills, Clare Valley (SA)	Petaluma, Pikes
Pinot Noir	Yarra Valley (VIC)	Coldstream Hills, Tarrawarra
	Gippsland, Geelong (VIC)	Bass Philip, Bannockburn, Shadowfax

BEER

Tooheys Red Bitter   Cascade Premium Lager

Most Australian beer is vat fermented real ale or lager, both consumed chilled. Full-strength beer has an alcohol content of around 4.8 per cent, mid-strength beers have around 3.5 per cent, while "light" beers have less than 3 per cent. Traditionally heat sterilized, cold filtration is now becoming increasingly popular. Among the hundreds of fine lagers and stouts are James Boag and Cascade from Tasmania, Castlemaine XXXX from Queensland, Fosters and Melbourne Bitter from Victoria, Toohey's red and blue labels from New South Wales and Cooper's Sparkling Ale from South Australia. Aficionados of real ale should seek out a pub brewery. Beer is ordered by glass size: a schooner is a 426 ml (15 fl oz) glass and a middy is 284 ml (10 fl oz).

SPIRITS

Australian distillers produce fine dark and white rums from Queensland's sugar cane plantations (see p246). The more notable labels include Bundaberg, from the town of that name, and Beenleigh. Australia's grape vintage is also the basis of good-value domestic brandies. Popular labels are St Agnes and Hardy's.

Bundaberg rum

OTHER DRINKS

With a climate ranging from tropical to alpine, Australia has year-round fresh fruit for juicing. Its apples are also used to make cider. Scores of still and sparkling mineral and other bottled waters now supply an annual market of nearly 200 million litres. Hepburn Spa, Deep Spring and Mount Franklin have national distribution. Coffee, prepared in a wide variety of ways, is another popular drink with Australians.

White coffee

Pear and kiwi frappé

Banana smoothie

Strawberry juice

Caffe latte

Choosing a Restaurant

The restaurants in this guide have been selected for their exceptional food, good value and interesting location. They are listed by region, starting with Sydney, in the same order as the rest of the guide. Within each region, entries are listed alphabetically by price category, from the least to the most expensive.

PRICE CATEGORIES
For a three-course meal for one, including half a bottle of house wine and service charges:

$ A$0–A$35
$$ A$35–A$60
$$$ A$60–A$85
$$$$ A$85–A$120
$$$$$ over A$120

SYDNEY

BONDI BEACH Ravesi's on Bondi Beach　　$$$
118 Campbell Parade, Bondi Beach, NSW 2026 **Tel** *(02) 9365 4422*

Sit on the balcony to catch the sea breeze and enjoy fish and chips with house tartare or barramundi fillet steamed in coconut with sweet potato and watercress salad. Finish with delicious Amaretto and bitter chocolate or cheese plate with lavosh and glazed fruits. The two- and three-course set menus are excellent, and brunch is served on Sundays.

BONDI BEACH Hugo's　　$$$$
70 Campbell Parade, Bondi Beach, NSW 2026 **Tel** *(02) 9300 0900*

Perenially popular, this beachfront fine diner manages to be relaxed and glamorous simultaneously. It's a great place for a romantic dinner and has spawned other equally glam venues: Hugo's Lounge and Hugo's Bar Pizza, both in Kings Cross. Here at the original, the best tables are outside, with cushioned banquettes overlooking the beach.

BONDI BEACH Icebergs Dining Room　　$$$$
1 Notts Avenue, Bondi Beach, NSW 2026 **Tel** *(02) 9365 9000*

The first really swish restaurant to hit the surf at Bondi is this dining room above the famous swimming pool. The decor gives a glamourous beach feel with a palette of ocean blues, giant rustic chandeliers and a scattering of silk cushions. Food is simple, modern Italian, such as *cacciucco alla Livornese*.

BONDI BEACH mu shu　　$$$$
108 Campbell Parade, Bondi Beach, NSW 2026 **Tel** *(02) 9130 5400*

This is the hippest place at the beach. Kick off your shoes and jump onto a day bed, but don't be put off by signs prohibiting hanky-panky. There's a great range of cocktails and modern Asian food designed to be shared among friends. Try a selection of Yum Cha as appetizers, followed by the signature roast duck pancakes.

BOTANIC GARDENS AND THE DOMAIN Botanic Gardens Restaurant　　$$$
Royal Botanic Gardens, Mrs Macquaries Road, NSW 2000 **Tel** *(02) 9241 2419*　　**Map** *2 D4*

Set among the lush greenery this excellent value lunch venue opens on to a terrace, letting in the sounds of the gardens, even the squawks of the famous bats. Serious gourmets might try the grilled beef tenderloin with potato rosti, foie gras and cabernet sauvignon jus. Weekend brunch is lovely too and there's a café below.

BOTANIC GARDENS AND THE DOMAIN Pavilion on the Park　　$$$
1 Art Gallery Road, The Domain, NSW 2000 **Tel** *(02) 9232 1322*　　**Map** *2 D4*

A fabulous location in sunny weather, the Pavilion is open for lunch only. A classy menu and wine list make for a luxurious meal, which might begin with lobster pannacotta, followed by a duck and foie gras pie and topped off by honey parfait with pecans and macadamias. A matching wine, available by glass or bottle, is suggested for each dish.

BOTANIC GARDENS AND THE DOMAIN The Art Gallery Restaurant　　$$$
The Art Gallery of New South Wales, Art Gallery Road, The Domain, NSW 2000 **Tel** *(02) 9225 1819*　　**Map** *2 D4*

Open for lunch daily and also for brunch on weekends, this restaurant provides a sophisticated place to discuss the latest exhibition. The menu is small but should please most. There's also a more casual café on the lower level, which is great for kids, offering little cardboard boxes with sandwiches, a drink and a chocolate.

CITY CENTRE Mother Chu's Vegetarian Kitchen　　$
367 Pitt Street, Sydney, NSW 2000 **Tel** *(02) 9283 2828*　　**Map** *4 E3*

A cheap and cheerful restaurant that offers large portions of hearty food, blending the flavours of Taiwan, China and Japan. Often full of students and arty types, enjoying the warm Buddhist hospitality, and delicious stir-fries and curries you can trust are trully vegetarian. Don't be put off by the canteen decor.

CITY CENTRE Bodhi Restaurant Bar　　$$
Cook & Phillip Park, 2-4 College Street, Sydney, NSW 2000 **Tel** *(02) 9360 2523*　　**Map** *1 C5*

This is a wonderful place to come for lunch on a sunny day, or for dinner on a summer's night, when you can take an outside table under the trees. You'll be amazed by the realistic vegan versions of fish and chicken. The not-pork sang choy bau is excellent, as is the signature dish, a skin-and-all vegan Peking duck. A good wine list.

Key to Symbols *see back cover flap*

CITY CENTRE Diethnes $$

336 Pitt Street, Sydney, NSW 2000 **Tel** *(02) 9267 8956*   **Map** *1 B5*

A Sydney institution, Diethnes has been in the same basement spot for 35 years, and you can tell. But get past the kitsch decor, and you'll find healthy portions of hearty meals. With dozens of meaty dishes, pasta, rice, salads and traditional Greek dishes like *tzaziki* and *spanakopita*, there's something for everyone.

CITY CENTRE Slip Inn $$

111 Sussex Street, Sydney, NSW 2000 **Tel** *(02) 9299 4777*   **Map** *1 A4*

This is the gentrified pub where Australia's Mary Donaldson met her husband, Crown Prince Frederik of Denmark. During the day, two menus offer Mod Oz and Thai fare, best devoured in the sunny courtyard to eat it in. At night, a short and sweet selection of pizzas keeps the punters happy.

CITY CENTRE sushi-e $$

Level 4, Establishment, 252 George Street, Sydney, NSW 2000 **Tel** *(02) 9240 3041*   **Map** *1 B3*

Located inside the exclusive Hemmeshere bar, there are so many magnificent sushi and sashimi dishes on offer here, it is impossible to list them. You might follow this with a *nigiri* sushi set or test your tastebuds with a chilli-loaded dynamite sushi roll.

CITY CENTRE est. $$$$

Level 1, 252 George Street, Sydney, NSW 2000 **Tel** *(02) 9240 3010*   **Map** *1 B3*

Bookings are essential if you wish to dine in this exclusive restaurant. The Establishment complex houses a lively ground level bar and a more restrained lounge above. In between, this dining room provides the setting for a luxurious meal. Don't miss the famous soufflé dessert.

CITY CENTRE Industrie – South of France $$$$

107 Pitt Street, Sydney, NSW 2000 **Tel** *(02) 9221 8001*   **Map** *1 B4*

It's a café, bar, restaurant, club – anything you want it to be really, from breakfast through to dinner, drinks and dancing; all infused with the flavour and spirit of the French Riviera. They run vodka appreciation courses on Tuesday and Wednesday nights and have DJs Wednesday to Saturday.

CITY CENTRE Omega $$$$

161 King Street, Sydney, NSW 2000 **Tel** *(02) 9223 0242*   **Map** *1 B5*

The menu at this snazzy modern Greek fine diner reads like a recipe for exotica. Mains include duck pie with celeriac skordalia and black olive sauce; and herb-crusted whiting in *kataifi* pastry with crab, *cavalo nero* and *savoro* sauce. For dessert, a baked nougat tart is served with orange blossom custard, candied sour cherries and Iranian fairy floss.

CITY CENTRE Forty One $$$$$

Level 42, Chifley Tower, 2 Chifley Square, Sydney, NSW 2000 **Tel** *(02) 9221 2500*   **Map** *1 B4*

The old Sydney favourite offers impressive views of the city and harbour. Chef Dietmar Sawyere's blend of European and Asian flavours is a winning combination. Specialities include roast wild hare with sauteed chestnuts and brussel sprout leaves, sweet potato purée and a shallot jus. A vegetarian menu is available.

CITY CENTRE Tetsuya's $$$$$

529 Kent Street, Sydney, NSW 2000 **Tel** *(02) 9267 2900*   **Map** *4 E3*

Internationally revered and widely considered Australia's best restaurant, Tetsuya's serene space puts the emphasis on the food and wine. The dégustation (only) menus fuse Japanese flavours with French technique. Wines can be matched to each course and vegetarian dégustations are available on request. Ask to meet the chef and for a tour.

DARLING HARBOUR Pasteur $

709 George Street, Haymarket, NSW 2000 **Tel** *(02) 9212 5622*   **Map** *4 E4*

Finish your A$9-bowl of beef and rice noodle soup and you may not need dinner. *Pho* is a Vietnamese speciality, which may come with chicken or beef. These float in fragrant broth, served with a pile of mint and basil leaves, chilli and fish sauce. Fresh spring rolls are another delicious snack, filled with pork and prawns.

DARLING HARBOUR Chinta Ria… The Temple of Love $$

The Roof Terrace, Cockle Bay Wharf, 201 Sussex Street, Darling Harbour, NSW 2000 **Tel** *(02) 9264 3211* **Map** *4 D2*

Feelings of happiness are brought into this restaurant by the giant Buddha that takes centre stage. Its reasonable prices and fun atmosphere make it popular with a young crowd. The fresh and spicy Malaysian food is great for sharing. No bookings are taken for dinner, so be prepared to have a drink while you wait for a table.

DARLING HARBOUR Golden Century $$

393–399 Sussex Street, Sydney, NSW 2000 **Tel** *(02) 9212 3901*   **Map** *4 E4*

The menu is huge, the staff are friendly and the selection of live seafood, including crab, abalone, lobster, parrot fish, barramundi and coral trout, is enormous. But what's truly amazing about this restaurant, in a city that catches plenty of sleep, is that its kitchen stays open until 3:30am. It's not unusual to find other chefs relaxing here after work.

DARLING HARBOUR The Regal $$

347–353 Sussex Street, Sydney, NSW 2000 **Tel** *(02) 9261 8988*   **Map** *4 E3*

Away from the bustle of Dixon and Hay Streets, the Regal is decked out with glittering chandeliers and private rooms. Waiters pushing dim sum-laden trolleys make it reminiscent of the yum cha places of Hong Kong. Cantonese seafood is popular, as well as plenty of hearty roast suckling pig and steamed fish chosen from the tank.

DARLING HARBOUR Zaaffran

Level 2, 345 Harbourside Shopping Centre, Darling Harbour, NSW 2000 **Tel** *(02) 9211 8900*   **Map** *3 C2*

The pick of Darling Harbour's eateries, this Indian restaurant is heaven for vegetarians. The food goes beyond the standards, to offer spicy mixed vegetable in a tomato and coconut sauce. Carnivores will be satisfied by an aromatic lamb shank stew or chicken biryani. The best tables are outside and there are good value set menus.

DARLING HARBOUR Zibar

49a Druitt Street, Sydney, NSW 2000 **Tel** *(02) 9268 0222*   **Map** *4 E2*

A small restaurant/café conveniently situated between the city centre and Darling Harbour. The food is consistently good and the coffee is arguably the best to be found in the whole area. A busy and friendly place often filled with hotel guests from next door and "journos" from Fairfax down the road.

DARLING HARBOUR Jordan's Seafood Restaurant

197 Harbourside, Darling Harbour, NSW 2000 **Tel** *(02) 9281 3711*   **Map** *3 C2*

This restaurant overlooks Darling Harbour and offers quality fresh seafood. Sushi, sashimi, char-grilled baby octopus, salmon, deep-fried snapper and calamari are available. Splashing out on a de luxe platter for two, will see you served a hot and cold selection of the market's best, including lobster.

DARLING HARBOUR Coast

The Roof Terrace, Cockle Bay Wharf, 201 Sussex Street, Sydney, NSW 2000 **Tel** *(02) 9267 6700*   **Map** *4 D2*

Eating fresh local seafood by the water is a quintessential Sydney experience. Renowned chef Stefano Manfredi is at the helm, producing a unique and celebrated style of Italian cuisine. The dining room and views are spectacular, and there is also a beautiful outdoor terrace as well as a private dining room.

KINGS CROSS AND DARLINGHURST Bill and Toni's

74 Stanley Street, East Sydney, NSW 2010 **Tel** *(02) 9360 4702*   **Map** *5 A1*

A Sydney stalwart, loved for its strong coffee, old-fashioned free cordial and checked tablecloths. Upstairs you'll find basic but delicious home-style Italian, like spaghetti bolognese and *bistecca*, and fast, friendly service. Afterwards, head downstairs for *macchiato* and *gelato*. Good place to bring kids, with its pinball and racing games.

KINGS CROSS AND DARLINGHURST Fu Manchu

249 Victoria Street, Darlinghurst, NSW 2010 **Tel** *(02) 9360 9424*   **Map** *5 B2*

A small, hip Chinese noodle bar, serving Northern Chinese and Southeast Asian hawker-style and home-cooked dishes. This is a fun place for a quick dinner at a communal table. The menu offers fresh and tasty dumplings, soups and stir-fries and good vegetarian choices. You'll want to take the red vinyl stools home. Open for dinner.

KINGS CROSS AND DARLINGHURST Govindas

112 Darlinghurst Road, Darlinghurst, NSW 2010 **Tel** *(02) 9380 5155*   **Map** *5 B1*

Dining at this vegetarian Hindu restaurant means piling up a plate of delicious curries, breads and salads from the all you can eat buffet. Many of the dishes are Indian, but pastas and casseroles are often available too. For a little extra you can see a film in the upstairs movie room, and it's best to eat afterwards to avoid drifting off in the couches.

KINGS CROSS AND DARLINGHURST Mahjong Room

312 Crown Street, Surry Hills, NSW 2010 **Tel** *(02) 9361 3985*   **Map** *5 A2*

This modern Chinese, packed with a young crowd, restaurant is very different from the big Chinatown diners. Instead, dishes such as bang bang chicken with century eggs and stir-fried prawns and snow peas are served at mahjong tables in a series of small rooms. Double the experience for your tastebuds by sharing the reasonably priced dishes.

KINGS CROSS AND DARLINGHURST Fish Face

132 Darlinghurst Road, Darlinghurst, NSW 2010 **Tel** *(02) 9332 4803*   **Map** *5 B2*

In a tiny space which seats just 26, this restaurant may look humble, but it offers the best value, superb fish in town. The beer-battered fish and handcut chips are famous, and there's also a sushi bar and a menu full of appealing choices including the signature dish of blue-eye cod topped with thin rounds of potato shaped into scales.

KINGS CROSS AND DARLINGHURST Lotus

22 Challis Avenue, Potts Point, NSW 2010 **Tel** *(02) 9326 9000*   **Map** *2 E4*

A bistro full of clean lines, blond wood and designer wallpaper – a favourite haunt of the Potts Point glamour set. Chef Lauren Murdoch produces heart-warming French bistro fare with a contemporary Australian twist. The intimate cocktail bar is a perfect place to relax.

KINGS CROSS AND DARLINGHURST Oh! Calcutta!

251 Victoria Street, Darlinghurst, NSW 2010 **Tel** *(02) 9360 3650*   **Map** *5 B2*

Serving fabulous, modern Indian food with remarkable complexity of flavour, this small, stylish restaurant manages to offer the cuisine of a fine diner at almost café prices. The tasting menu is particularly good value, allowing you to try three entrées and three mains, plus rice, accompaniments and bread for A$48. There are also pre-theatre deals.

KINGS CROSS AND DARLINGHURST Tilbury Hotel

12–18 Nicholson Street, Woolloomooloo, NSW 2010 **Tel** *(02) 9368 1041*   **Map** *2 D5*

The Tilbury Hotel was refurbished recently, resulting in its transformation into one of the sexiest pubs in Sydney. The restaurant offers excellent, hearty Italian fare, and the daily menu might include gnocchi with chicken, sausage, borlotti beans and fennel. There's also a café serving wraps, melts and coffees. Jazz on Sunday afternoons.

Key to Price Guide *see p524* **Key to Symbols** *see back cover flap*

KINGS CROSS AND DARLINGHURST Yellow Bistro & Food Store
57 Macleay Street, Potts Point, NSW 2011 **Tel** *(02) 9357 3400*
$$$ | Map 2 E4

Van Gogh yellow walls make this, one of the most famous buildings in the Cross, stand out. In the 1970s it was an artists' commune which housed Brett Whiteley. Today creative genius is obvious in the food. The brunch menu is lovely but nothing beats the celebrated date tart created by pastry chef Lorraine Godsmark. Excellent food store too.

KINGS CROSS AND DARLINGHURST Otto
Area 8, The Wharf, 6 Cowper Wharf Road, Woolloomooloo, NSW 2011 **Tel** *(02) 9368 7488*
$$$$ | Map 2 D4

It's a piece of Melbourne brought to Sydney's waterfront and so appreciated that it often draws celebrities to its handsome surrounds, from Kylie Minogue to footballers. Italian fare is jazzed up with great local ingredients, such as in winter fillet of Mandagery Creek venison with celeriac parsnip purée, pancetta, green beans and juniper jus.

MANLY Alhambra
1/54 West Esplanade, Manly, Sydney, NSW 2095 **Tel** *(02) 9976 2975*
$$$

Hugely popular on Friday and Saturday nights, when flamenco dancers add to the din, this casual restaurant has views of the Manly wharf. The Morrocan chef cooks Moorish and Spanish food. A meal might begin with tapas, followed by a Moroccan *tagine* of chicken and preserved lemon or lamb and date.

MANLY The Manly Wharf Hotel
Manly Wharf East Esplanade, Manly, NSW 2095 **Tel** *(02) 9977 1266*
$$$

Not much beats sharing a seafood platter packed with oysters, prawns, crab, salt-and-pepper squid, octopus, scallops and fish, while looking out over Sydney Harbour. Even better, this is a pub you can bring your kids to, keeping them happy with one of the well-priced offerings from the kids' menu.

PADDINGTON Paddington Inn
338 Oxford Street, Paddington, NSW 2010 **Tel** *(02) 9380 5913*
$$ | Map 6 D4

This perenially popular pub in the heart of the Paddington strip is especially busy on weekend afternoons, when hip locals meet over beers and tapas-style plates. Pub classics like bangers and mash and fish and chips are given a restaurant touch. There are also plenty of lighter meals, such as salads and seafood. No bookings.

PADDINGTON Buzo
3 Jersey Road, Woollahra, NSW 2025 **Tel** *(02) 9328 1600*
$$$ | Map 6 D4

Buzo is another piece of evidence showing that bistro food is booming in Sydney. Bookings are essential at this restaurant, just off Oxford Street. A great meaty menu, offering roast lamb, char-grilled steak and even various offal dishes. You'll need to order some side dishes to accompany your main, preventing meals here from being great value.

PADDINGTON Lucio's Italian Restaurant
47 Windsor Street, Paddington, NSW 2021 **Tel** *(02) 9380 5996*
$$$$ | Map 6 D3

Lucio's is right in the middle of the area of Sydney densest with art galleries and the walls of the restaurant display a large collection of contemporary Australian artists, such as John Olsen, John Coburn, Gary Shead and Tim Storrier. There's art on the plate, too; the expertly cooked Italian food varies according to what's in season.

PADDINGTON Buon Ricordo
108 Boundary Street, Paddington, NSW 2021 **Tel** *(02) 9360 6729*
$$$$$ | Map 5 C2

Ask a Sydney chef where he goes on nights off and the answer is likely to be this small restaurant. The decor is old fashioned and the food is often Old World. So, too, is the great service, which sees the signature dish of fettuccine with parmesan, cream and truffled egg tossed at table. Bookings essential.

PADDINGTON Claude's
10 Oxford Street, Woollahra, NSW 2025 **Tel** *(02) 9331 2325*
$$$$$ | Map 6 D4

A Sydney icon for nearly 30 years, this special, intimate restaurant in a converted terrace house seats just 45 people. In season, the set-price menu features fresh Tasmanian truffles. Dishes sound simple on paper but are actually as close to works of art as food can get. Bookings are essential. Ring the doorbell when you arrive.

ROSE BAY Catalina
1 Sutherland Avenue, Rose Bay, NSW 2029 **Tel** *(02) 9371 0555*
$$$$

A long-established restaurant where the executive chef Paul McMahon concentrates on Italian and Spanish flavours in a contemporary Oz fashion. With floor-to-ceiling glass sliding doors the full length of the building, every table in the minimalist interior has views across Rose Bay.

ROSE BAY Pier
594 New South Head Road, Rose Bay, NSW 2029 **Tel** *(02) 9327 6561*
$$$$

This restaurant is one long, light room which runs the length of a small pier and juts out into the harbour. Yachts moored in the marina float all around and make you feel like you are on one. Wonderful quality fish is treated with care and cooked to perfection in dishes such as carpaccio of tuna and roasted barramundi.

SURRY HILLS Café Mint
579 Crown Street, Surry Hills, NSW 2010 **Tel** *(02) 9319 0848*
$

Mint's precursor, Fez, was a top breakfast venue, often with long queues. This café is tiny and can seem equally crammed. The coffee is excellent and food is fabulous value, particularly at lunch. For a rainbow of dips and pickles, try the large *meze* plate, which easily fills two. The Lebanese *fattoush* salad with garlicy, crunchy pitta is great too.

THE ROCKS AND CIRCULAR QUAY Vintage Café on the Rocks 🧒 ♫ ▤ ⛱ $

Shop R2, Nurses Walk, The Rocks, NSW 2000 ***Tel*** *(02) 9252 2055* ***Map*** *1 B2*

Tucked away in a little cobble-stoned courtyard, in this earliest-settled part of Sydney, this sweet diner is a great place for a quick lunch or afternoon pit stop. Pierce Brosnan and Princess Anne were both spotted here when in town, though it's unknown whether they were dining on sandwiches or Devonshire tea. Excellent, big all-day breakfasts.

THE ROCKS AND CIRCULAR QUAY Heritage Belgium Beer Café 🧒 ▤ ♿ $$$

135 Harrington Street, The Rocks, NSW 2000 ***Tel*** *(02) 9241 1775* ***Map*** *1 A3*

There are other options listed on the menu but for anyone in the know, mussels provide the only authentic Belgian experience, cooked one of eight ways and served in a pot. Use the shell of the first mussel you eat as a pincher to draw out the rest. Of course, there are Belgian beers on tap and an amazing range of artisan brews.

THE ROCKS AND CIRCULAR QUAY MCA Cafe 🧒 ▤ ♿ ⛱ $$$

Museum of Contemporary Art, 140 George Street, The Rocks, NSW 2000 ***Tel*** *(02) 9241 4253* ***Map*** *1 B2*

A menu full of Sydney favourites like pan-fried Atlantic salmon, and its fabulous location on the Circular Quay side of the MCA building make this restaurant a good pick. After satisfying sweet teeth with a fabulous dessert, diners head upstairs to absorb the art.

THE ROCKS AND CIRCULAR QUAY Sailors' Thai ▤ ⛱ $$$

106 George Street, The Rocks, NSW 2000 ***Tel*** *(02) 9251 2466* ***Map*** *1 B3*

While chef and Thai food expert David Thompson is now earning acclaim at his London restaurant, he continues to oversee the menu at this restaurant in the historic Sailors' Home. The food is far removed from the neighbourhood Thai you'll find in every Sydney suburb. The cheaper canteen, upstairs, is open for lunch and dinner too.

THE ROCKS AND CIRCULAR QUAY The Wharf Restaurant 🧒 ♿ ⛱ $$$

Sydney Theatre Company, harbour end of Pier 4, Hickson Road, Walsh Bay, NSW 2000 ***Tel*** *(02) 9250 1761* ***Map*** *1 A1*

A wonderful setting in a restored fingerwharf also offers an unusual view of the Harbour Bridge. In the winter truffle season, special dishes such as truffle-infused Brie are added to the menu. Plan to dine after 8pm to avoid the theatre crowd. Disabled access should be arranged in advance.

THE ROCKS AND CIRCULAR QUAY Café Sydney 🧒 ▤ ♿ ♫ ⛱ $$$$

Level 5, Customs House, 31 Alfred Street, Circular Quay, NSW 2000 ***Tel*** *(02) 9251 8683* ***Map*** *1 B3*

This buzzy restaurant, on the top floor of historic Customs House, has dress circle views. Sitting on the terrace is wonderful, in winter gas heaters keep diners warm and special resin lamps make each table glow. The kitchen's tandoor oven, wood-fired grill, wok and rotisserie turn out a great variety of food. Live jazz on Sunday afternoons.

THE ROCKS AND CIRCULAR QUAY Guillaume at Bennelong ▤ $$$$

Sydney Opera House, Bennelong Point, NSW 2000 ***Tel*** *(02) 9241 1999* ***Map*** *1 C2*

You can't beat the excitement of dining in the Opera House, especially in such a romantic, elegant space. An emphasis on seafood produces dishes like the signature basil-infused tuna with mustard seed and soy vinaigrette. A cheaper way to taste chef Guillaume Brahimi's marvellous food is by ordering tapas-style dishes from the cocktail bar.

THE ROCKS AND CIRCULAR QUAY harbourkitchen&bar ▤ ♿ $$$$

Park Hyatt Sydney, 7 Hickson Road, The Rocks, NSW 2000 ***Tel*** *(02) 9256 1661* ***Map*** *1 B1*

Especially lovely by day, when the bustle of Circular Quay can be fully appreciated and ferries pass close by the wall of windows. Good value lunch and pre-theatre deals allow Chef Danny Drinkwater's signature duck and beetroot tart to be tasted for less. Modern high tea is served in the more casual little kitchen, which is a better choice for children.

THE ROCKS AND CIRCULAR QUAY Quay ▤ ♿ ⛱ $$$$$

Upper Level, Overseas Passenger Terminal, The Rocks, NSW 2000 ***Tel*** *(02) 9251 5600* ***Map*** *1 B2*

Another spectacular view, and food to match, with star chef Peter Gilmore making magic out of the best and freshest produce and combining ingredients in suprising ways. Try the suckling pig, prunes, Pedro Ximenez vinegar, black pudding, cauliflower cream and the famous five-textured chocolate cake made from the finest couverture.

THE ROCKS AND CIRCULAR QUAY Rockpool 🧒 ♿ $$$$$

107 George Street, The Rocks, NSW 2000 ***Tel*** *(02) 9252 1888* ***Map*** *1 B3*

Neil Perry opened his Sydney fine-dining institution in 1989 and invented Modern Australian cuisine with his fusion of European and Asian techniques and flavours. Recent renovations spruced the place up and added a seafood bar. For complete indulgence, book the tasting menu. Bookings advised. Wheelchair accessible but call first.

THE ROCKS AND CIRCULAR QUAY Yoshi $$$$$

115 Harrington Street, The Rocks, NSW 2000 ***Tel*** *(02) 9247 2566* ***Map*** *1 A3*

Ryuichi Yoshi is one of Sydney's top sushi chefs and the author of a sushi cookbook. His restaurant serves dinner in the *kaiseki* style, a series of unique small dishes that gradually warm the stomach like a small stone (a Japanese precursor to the hot water bottle). Though pricey, this is excellent value. Lunchtime bento boxes are cheaper.

WATSON'S BAY Doyles on the Beach ♿ ⛱ [V] $$

11 Marine Parade, Watson's Bay ***Tel*** *(02) 9337 2007* ***Map*** *1 C2*

Five generations on, the Doyles are still serving great fish and chips. Eat at a table outside and admire the stunning view of the CBD across the harbour. The menu offers an array of fish and seafood dishes, including wild barramundi fillets and live lobster mornay. Open daily. There are two branches at Watson's Bay wharf and Circular Quay.

Key to Price Guide *see p524* **Key to Symbols** *see back cover flap*

THE BLUE MOUNTAINS AND BEYOND

ARMIDALE Jitterbug Mood
Upstairs, 115 Rusden Road, Armidale, NSW 2350 **Tel** *(02) 6772 3022*

Two words to sum up this long-time Armidale favourite are unpretentious and delicious. This quaint eatery is always busy, appealing to a varied clientele, so it's best to book. Suggestions from their wine list are matched to each dish, and the vegetarian options are mouthwatering.

BYRON BAY Belongilbeachcafé
Byron Beach House, 25 Childe Street, Byron Bay NSW 2481 **Tel** *(02) 6685 6868*

This adorable place is where the locals go to escape the bustle of Byron Bay. Situated amongst lush subtropical gardens and serving a range of meals and tapas featuring local produce and organic meats, this café offers everything from light snacks to substantial meals. And the coffee is always fantastic.

BYRON BAY Fins
Beach Hotel, Cnr Jonson Street and Bay Lane, Byron Bay NSW 2481 **Tel** *(02) 6685 5029*

Fins is a unique place where only the freshest produce is used – often from the chef's own garden – and the fish is line-caught where possible, sometimes only hours before eating. Fins also has one of the most extensive wine lists to be found, including local varieties and overseas gems.

COFFS HARBOUR Maria's Italian Restaurant
368 Harbour Drive, Coffs Harbour, NSW 2450 **Tel** *(02) 6651 3000*

It has been around for a decade and is quite a local icon, but there's something new to discover each time you dine at Maria's. The chefs are flexible and will prepare almost anything, with particular attention paid to food allergies. This is basic, quality Italian food, and the pizzas are the best in town.

COFFS HARBOUR Shearwater
321 Harbour Drive, Coffs Harbour, NSW 2450 **Tel** *(02) 6651 6053*

Enjoy fresh local seafood in the relaxed atmosphere of this great restaurant in the heart of Coffs Harbour looking out over Coffs Creek. The Shearwater is open for breakfast, lunch and dinner, seven days a week, and is suitable for a quick working lunch or a leisurely dinner.

COOKS HILL One O Three
103 Darby Street, Cooks Hill, NSW 2300 **Tel** *(02) 4925 2522*

While One O Three serves a range of food for all occasions, it really shines with its 'Global Morning' breakfast options. Work your way around the world from the "New York" dish of buttermilk pancakes served with praline cream to the health-conscious "Nimbin" plate of vegetarian, gluten-free, dairy-free delights.

EAST GOSFORD Caroline Bay Brasserie
36 Webb Street, Gosford East, NSW 2250 **Tel** *(02) 4324 8099*

Tasty, fuss-free food is the order of the day at Caroline Bay Brasserie. Open for breakfast, lunch and morning and afternoon teas, it's the place to go to indulge in a classic Devonshire tea. Lunches include a range of salads, burgers, melts and more, and the picturesque grounds are simply stunning.

GOSFORD Upper Deck
61 Masons Parade, Gosford, NSW 2250 **Tel** *(02) 4324 6705*

Perfectly positioned with breathtaking views over the water, Upper Deck has been serving the locals of Gosford for many years now. Specializing in oysters and steak cooked to perfection, the restaurant offers great value set menus and a private dining room for special intimate gatherings.

JUNEE Betty & Muriel's at The Loftus Comlex
6 Humphrys Street, Junee, 2663 **Tel** *(02) 6924 2555*

Everyone will feel instantly at home in this Hollywood-inspired café. All dishes are named after celebrities – from the Judi Dench entrée of avocado draped in smoked salmon, to the Jennifer Lopez burger of Mexican chicken, cheese, salsa, guacamole and sour cream. This cute café is part of a hotel too.

KATOOMBA Swiss Cottage
132 Lurline Street, Katoomba, NSW 2780 **Tel** *(02) 4782 2281*

Remember to visit the bank before dining at the Swiss Cottage as they only accept cash, but don't let that keep you away from this culinary gem! Housed in a cottage built in 1898, the Swiss Cottage serves what some call the best fondue in Australia as well as a sumptuous Lindt hot chocolate in a mug.

KATOOMBA The Rooster
48 Meriwa Street, Katoomba, NSW 2780 **Tel** *(02) 4782 1206*

Sit near the fireplace in this gorgeous federation-style building and experience utterly delicious French cuisine. The view from the clifftops overlooking the Jamison Valley is stunning, but it's near impossible to see anything at night, so outside dining is offered only during the day.

KATOOMBA Darley's   ⬛⬛ $$$$
Lilianfels, Lilianfels Avenue, Katoomba, NSW 2780 **Tel** *(02) 4780 1200*

The building housing this beautiful restaurant is over a century old. Well known for serving local venison, Darley's also boasts a delicious range of cheeses and an enviable wine list. Dine on the balcony with magnificent views or sit indoors to experience the ambience of open fireplaces.

LAKE MACQUARIE Milano's On The Lake   ⬛⬛⬛⬛ $$$
89 Soldier's Road, Pelican, NSW 2281 **Tel** *(02) 4972 0550*

The chef at this innovative lakeside restaurant is happy to adapt dishes to suit vegetarian diners. Adding to the culinary feel is the neighbouring cooking school, and if its students manage to create anything as delicious as Milano's seafood *mezze* plate served with olive crisp bread, they will have spent their money wisely.

LENNOX HEAD Mi Thai Restaurant   ⬛⬛⬛ $$
76 Ballina Street, Lennox Head, NSW 2478 **Tel** *(02) 6687 5820*

Serving a mixture of modern and classic Asian cuisine in an area known to many as the "Surf Capital of the Far North Coast", this intimate restaurant is a favourite with locals after a quick, satisfying meal. And they return again and again for the changing daily specials and mouthwatering Choo Chee Curry.

LEURA Silks Brasserie   ⬛⬛⬛ $$$
128 'The Mall', Leura, NSW 2780 **Tel** *(02) 4784 2534*

It's refreshing to find a fine dining restaurant that welcomes children – Silk's even provides coloured pencils for kids to use on the table-top butcher's paper. Adults, meanwhile, will enjoy the delicious dishes and comprehensive wine list. Do not leave the region without experiencing this Leura legend.

MCGRATH'S HILL Valentino's Italian Restaurant   ⬛⬛⬛⬛ $$$
11 Groves Avenue McGrath's Hill NSW 2756 **Tel** *(02) 4577 9797*

Valentino's serves Italy up on a plate. The menu at this excellent restaurant is a combination of traditional food with contemporary flair. For instance, weekly specials could include pan-fried barramundi on traditional ratatouille with black mussels and lemon butter broth.

MEGALONG VALLEY Megalong Tea Room   ⬛⬛⬛⬛ $
Megalong Road, Megalong Valley, NSW 2785 **Tel** *(02) 4787 9181*

Those looking for a place where the food is home-made need go no further than the Megalong Tea Room. There's no need to rush here – linger over a classic morning tea with scones or stop for one of their hearty pies for lunch and enjoy the idyllic beaty of the surrounding Megalong Valley.

NELSON BAY Zest Restaurant   ⬛⬛⬛⬛ $$$
16 Stockton Street, Nelson Bay, NSW 2315 **Tel** *(02) 4984 2211*

In an area renowned for quality seafood restaurants, the award-winning Zest goes far beyond the rest. The walls feature a stunning display of local artworks, while the menu offers an equally stunning selection of European-inspired dishes with local seafood, meat and game on offer. BYO Tue–Thu.

NEWCASTLE Scratchley's On The Wharf   ⬛⬛ $$
200 Wharf Road, Newcastle, NSW 2300 **Tel** *(02) 4929 1111*

Scratchley's On The Wharf proudly boasts eco-friendly architecture and utilizes environmentally-friendly practices wherever possible. This is a terrific place to eat before attending the nearby cinema, as the friendly, helpful staff will ensure you're in and out before the previews begin.

NEWCASTLE Sesame's A Taste Of Asia   ⬛⬛⬛⬛⬛ $$
52 Glebe Road, The Junction, Newcastle, NSW 2291 **Tel** *(02) 4969 2033*

This great eatery recently won the "best Asian restaurant" category of the 2005 Hunter Awards for Excellence. Cambodian, Thai, Vietnamese and Malaysian cuisine grace the menu at Sesame's, and there is a separate vegan/vegetarian menu too. Don't miss their signature twice-cooked duck.

NEWCASTLE Customs House Hotel   ⬛⬛⬛ $$$
1 Bond Street, Newcastle, NSW 2300 **Tel** *(02) 4925 2585*

Want to know where to find great food accompanied by pub-priced drinks? Right here. From a light salad of prawns, witlof, blue cheese, shaved hazelnuts and sauce *vierge* to a hearty grain-fed beef fillet with potato mash and red wine jus, there's a dish to suit your appetite and budget.

NEWCASTLE Lime Bar & Restaurant   ⬛⬛⬛ $$$
52 Glebe Road, The Junction, Newcastle, NSW 2291 **Tel** *(02) 4969 2060*

Serving breakfast, lunch and tapas throughout the day, Lime really comes into its own when night falls. The dinner menu boasts fresh, vibrant Modern Australian flavours – easy to match with over 30 wines available by the glass. Or enjoy a cocktail and people-watch through the floor to ceiling windows. BYO Mon–Thu.

POKOLBIN Chez Pok at Peppers   ⬛⬛⬛⬛⬛ $$$
Peppers Guesthouse, Hunter Valley, Ekerts Road, Pokolbin, NSW 2320 **Tel** *(02) 4993 8999*

A long-time favourite of gourmets and critics alike, Chez Pok blends fine dining with local produce – indeed, the herbs are grown in the guesthouse's garden! Staff advise which wines best suit your meal, and considering the award-winning wine list, you're in for a treat. Bookings essential.

Key to Price Guide *see p524* **Key to Symbols** *see back cover flap*

POKOLBIN Esca Bimbadgen 🥗♿🍸 $$$

Bimbadgen Estate, 790 McDonald's Road, Pokolbin, NSW 2320 ***Tel*** *(02) 4998 4666*

A part of the respected Bimbadgen Estate Winery, Esca Bimbadgen is positioned overlooking the superb views of the Estate's vineyards. The dessert-tasting plate, served with a glass of botrytis semillon, is great value. Be sure to book at this popular eatery to avoid disappointment.

POKOLBIN San Martino Restaurant ☂🥗♿🍸 $$$

Hunter Resort, Hermitage Road, Pokolbin NSW 2320 ***Tel*** *(02) 4998 7777*

San Martino, or Saint Martin, is the patron saint of churchgoers, wine-makers and the protector of all drinkers. And considering that this restaurant sits alongside the brewery and winery at the Hunter Resort, that's a good thing! A must for fans of innovative modern Australian cuisine.

POKOLBIN Terroir Restaurant And Wine Bar Hungerford Hill 🥗♿🍸 $$$

1 Broke Road Pokolbin NSW 2320 ***Tel*** *(02) 4990 0711*

This classy venue has just undergone renovations, producing a new entrance and outside dining area on the eastern terrace. Catering for all tastes, Terroir has separate children's and vegetarian menus, as well as a tempting tasting menu. Don't miss the solo guitarist on Friday and Saturday nights.

POKOLBIN Robert's Restaurant 👪🥗♿🍸 $$$$

Halls Road Pokolbin, NSW 2325 ***Tel*** *(02) 4998 7330*

Set in an early settler's slab cottage, Robert's at Pepper Tree doesn't just serve fine food, it delivers a complete gastronomical experience. The delicious French-inspired dishes from the talented owner/chef are carefully matched with perfectly complementary wines, ensuring that at Robert's, you won't be disappointed.

PORT STEPHENS Merretts at Peppers Anchorage 👪🥗♿🍸 $$$$

Corlette Point Road, Corlette, NSW 2315 ***Tel*** *(02) 4984 2555*

This renowned restaurant continues to serve up top quality meals boasting French, Mediterranean and Asian influences. Dining here is an utterly decadent experience, and dishes like the Chocolate Trio – a milk chocolate tart served with white and dark chocolate mousse and choc hazelnut parfait – are to die for.

SINGLETON Fusions 👪♿🥗 $$$

Mid City Motor Inn, 180 John Street, Singleton, NSW 2330 ***Tel*** *(02) 6572 2011*

Comfortable, bright purple chairs complement the decor at this intimate restaurant which is part of the Best Western hotel. Singleton, known largely for its army base, is also home to several vineyards, and the produce of many is offered here. As well as serving daily meals, Fusions will also arrange packed lunches for patrons to take with them.

SOLDIERS POINT The Point Restaurant 👪☂🥗🍸 $$$

Ridgeway Avenue, Soldiers Point, NSW 2317 ***Tel*** *(02) 4984 7111*

This waterfront restaurant offers specials that vary according to the freshest catch and might include dishes like wok-tossed squid and scallops with a Vietnamese soy glaze. Even if you're out on a boat, you needn't miss out. The Point will prepare a delicious platter for you to enjoy aboard your vessel.

WAGGA WAGGA Indian Tavern Tandoori Restaurant 👪☂🥗♿ $$

81 Peter Street, Wagga Wagga, NSW 2650 ***Tel*** *(02) 6921 3121*

The owners boast that patrons can "visit India in an hour" with their menu, and they're right. The restaurant's cuisine originates from all regions of India, and ranges in spiciness from super-hot to mild. The butter chicken flavoured with cashew nut butter remains a favourite with locals. Fully licensed and BYOB.

THE SOUTH COAST AND SNOWY MOUNTAINS

BATEMANS BAY On the Pier 👪☂🥗♿🍸 $$

Old Punt Road, NSW 2536 ***Tel*** *(02) 4472 6405*

If you fancy seafood with a waterside view for lunch or dinner, and who could resist after a few hours in Bateman's Bay, then On the Pier is a prize catch. They offer dishes such as chargrilled tuna with spiced watermelon and green olive crème fraîche. BYO at lunchtime.

BATEMANS BAY Starfish Deli ♿🥗🍸 $$

Shop 1 Promenade Plaza, Clyde Street, NSW 2536 ***Tel*** *(02) 4472 4880*

This up-market bistro and function centre, next to a boatshed and overlooking the Clyde River, offers a fine Mod Oz menu. It also serves up excellent wood-fired pizzas, local seafood and Clyde River oysters. It is open for breakfast, lunch and dinner and if you're lucky enough to secure an outside table, you might spy a dolphin cruising past.

BERMAGUI Salt Water at Bermagui 👪☂♿🍸 $$

75 Lamont Street, NSW 2546 ***Tel*** *(02) 6493 4328*

You can enjoy fresh seafood straight off the trawlers in the pleasant and comfortable restaurant on the wharf, or simply grab takeaway fish and chips and enjoy them on the waterfront of Bermagui Harbour, now famous as the setting for the Billy Connelly and Judy Davis movie, *The Man Who Sued God*.

BERRIMA The White Horse Inn 🧒 🍷 $

Market Place, NSW 2577 ***Tel*** *(02) 4877 1204*

Originally built in 1832 by convict labour, this Georgian inn is not only old, but also old fashioned, with specialties such as steak-and-kidney pudding and high teas served in the Georgian dining room. The odd goings-on that are said to have occurred are credited to "Jimmy", the ghost of a convict who drowned in the cellar during a flood.

BOWRAL Briar's Inn 🧒 📋 ♿ 🍷 $$

653 Moss Vale Road, NSW 1734 ***Tel*** *(02) 4868 1724*

This Georgian, wisteria-draped inn has been sustaining travellers since 1845, although nowadays it also offers boutique beers on tap and a generous wine list. You can cook your own steak, chicken or fish on the barbecue. Or tuck into something hearty like lamb shanks with tomato and onion. There is also a kid's menu and playground.

EDEN Wheelhouse Restaurant 🧒 📋 🍷 $$$

Main Wharf, NSW 2551 ***Tel*** *(02) 6496 3392*

Seafood is all the rage at this award-winning restaurant on the wharf overlooking Eden Harbour. It's popular with the locals as much for the fact that it is reasonably priced as for its generous servings of fresh local seafood. The wine list is quite acceptable and it's a pleasant venue with friendly service.

GOULBURN The Rimbolin 🧒 🌳 🍷 $$

380 Auburn Street, NSW 2580 ***Tel*** *(02) 4821 7633*

Start the day with banana pancakes and maple syrup in the cafe. Lunches in the pleasant garden out the back range from salads to pastas and sandwiches. Dinners in the more formal restaurant are hearty and heavy on the meat, with mains such as lamb shanks, parsnip mash and Italian tomato sauce. There is a good kid's menu.

GOULBURN Willow Vale Mill Restaurant and Guesthouse 🧒 📋 ♿ 🍷 $$

Willow Vale Mill, Laggan via Crookwell, NSW 2583 ***Tel*** *(02) 4837 3319*

Slightly off the beaten track in an old mill house, potato farmer-cum-chef Graham Liney serves up hearty good-value meals to suit the season, using local produce, including game and fish, and organic vegetables from the garden. Guestrooms are also available and the licensed restaurant is open for lunch and dinner.

KIAMA Zumo Restaurant 🧒 🌳 ♿ 🍷 $$

127 Terralong Street, NSW 2533 ***Tel*** *(02) 4232 2222*

This new fully licensed, Italian-style restaurant in a heritage-listed building in Kiama's main street serves pizzas, a reasonable range of pastas and hearty provincial à la carte meals in a casual atmosphere. It is also possible to dine out on the veranda, and takeaway pizzas are available. Closed weekends.

MOLLYMOOK Bannister's 📋 🍷 $$$

191 Michell Parade, NSW 2539 ***Tel*** *(02) 4455 3044*

A classy and award-winning resort restaurant with sweeping ocean views from every table. The Mod Oz menu changes with the seasons, but expect dishes such as soy lacquered duck with noodles and bok choy, and desserts such as chocolate tart with marinated strawberries and espresso ice cream.

NAROOMA Quarterdeck Cafe 🧒 🌳 ♿ $

Riverside Drive, NSW 2546 ***Tel*** *(02) 4476 2723*

Well known as a child-friendly local café overlooking Wagonga Inlet, the Quarterdeck serves up quick, cheap seafood favourites such as fish and chips, salt and chilli squid, bouillabaisse and local Narooma oysters. They are open every day for breakfast and lunch.

SNOWY MOUNTAINS The Credo Restaurant 🧒 ♿ 🍷 $$$

Riverside Cabins, Thredbo Alpine Village, NSW 2625 ***Tel*** *(02) 6457 6844*

Award-winning Australian cuisine, an extensive, award-winning wine list, a large cocktail bar, a relaxed atmosphere and views over the Thredbo River and snow-capped mountains make for a fine night's dining. The Credo prides itself on the double-roasted duck and deboned and stuffed Snowy River trout.

SNOWY MOUNTAINS Cuisine on Lake Crackenback 📋 ♿ 🍷 $$$

Lake Crackenback, Alpine Way via Jindabyne, NSW 2627 ***Tel*** *(02) 6451 3000*

The fine cuisine at this resort restaurant comes with amazing views over the lake and nearby hills. There is a kid's menu, but for adults the options are seasonal with an emphasis on local produce such as smoked mountain trout and poached rabbit. It is also open for a buffet breakfast, and picnic and bushwalking hampers can be arranged.

SOUTHERN HIGHLANDS Blue Cockerel Café/Restaurant 🧒 🌳 📋 ♿ $$

95 Hume Highway, Mittagong, NSW 2575 ***Tel*** *(02) 4872 1677*

This establishment specializes in locally sourced produce. Lunches are casual, but for dinner the Mod Oz cuisine is served in a cosy but more formal atmosphere, with white linen table settings, wood fire and attentive professional service. Open for breakfast, lunch and dinner, except Monday and Tuesday.

SOUTHERN HIGHLANDS Eling Forest Winery Restaurant 🧒 📋 ♿ 🍷 $$

Hume Highway, Sutton Forest, NSW 2577 ***Tel*** *(02) 4878 9499*

This relative newcomer just south of Berrima has already won a regional award for its Italian-influenced menu, with an occasional Asian twist. The wine list features their own vintage as well as other Southern Highlands cool climate wines. There is a sunny courtyard and reasonably priced kid's menu.

Key to Price Guide *see p524* **Key to Symbols** *see back cover flap*

SOUTHERN HIGHLANDS Horderns 📋♿ $$$

Hordern's Road, Bowral, NSW 2576 ***Tel*** *(02) 4861 1522*

Modern Australian food with European and Asian influences is served in this elegant country hotel with two dining rooms, high-backed chairs and sumptuous fabrics. Bookings are advised and accommodation is also available. The restaurant offers an extensive wine list and views out over the lovely garden.

ULLADULLA Carmelo Italian Restaurant 🚸☀♿🍷 $$

Shop 2, 10 Watson Street, NSW 2539 ***Tel*** *(02) 4454 1443*

Settle down at an outside table at this casual restaurant-cum-café near the harbour and enjoy the water views and straightforward Italian seafood cuisine, including lobsters, seafood platters and pastas. Takeaway food is also an option if you want to sit by the waterfront, and it is child friendly. Closed Tuesdays.

WOLLONGONG Lorenzo's Diner 📋 $$

119 Keira Street, NSW 2500 ***Tel*** *(02) 4229 5633*

This award-winning and well-priced restaurant (regarded by many as one of the best on the south coast) serves modern Italian cuisine with a central and northern Italian bent. For example, fried calves' liver, lamb stew with spices and tiramisu. The setting is smart-casual with friendly waiters. BYO on Tue and Wed.

WOLLONGONG Caveau 🚸📋 $$$

122–124 Keira Street, NSW 2500 ***Tel*** *(02) 4226 4855*

This modern French restaurant in a heritage building across the road from Lorenzo's offers seasonal produce and formal dining. The co-owner and chef, Peter Sheppard, hails from one of Sydney's finest restaurants, Banc. The reviews are consistently favourable and there is a lounge bar upstairs.

WOMBARRA Black Duck Kitchen 🚸📄 $

578 Lawrence Hargrave Drive, NSW 2515 ***Tel*** *(02) 4267 2139*

A hidden gem where the emphasis is on slow cooking. This newcomer has revitalized the lounge of the local bowling club, which enjoys spectacular views over the ocean. The friendly service has made it popular with locals, who can duck into the bar next door to replenish their glass. Great food in a retro atmosphere.

CANBERRA AND ACT

CANBERRA The High Court Café 🚸☀📋♿ $

High Court of Australia, Parkes Place, Parkes, ACT 2600 ***Tel*** *(02) 6270 6828*

Situated in the imposing glass edifice of the High Court of Australia (the highest court in the land), this restaurant serves up elegant breakfasts and light lunches, such as foccacias and salads, not to mention panoramic views of Lake Burley Griffin. Canberra's regional wines feature in the wine list. It is closed on weekends.

CANBERRA Ruby Chinese Restaurant 🚸📋♿ $

Ground Floor, 18-20 Wooley Street, Dickson, ACT 2602 ***Tel*** *(02) 6249 8849*

Ruby's has a fascinating reputation as being the place where spies of all nationalities rendezvous while enjoying honey prawns and classic Australian Chinese restaurant decor. It is also a favourite with visiting celebrities. Specializing in live seafood, it is in the heart of Canberra's only "Chinatown" street.

CANBERRA Benchmark Wine Bar 📋♿🍷 $$

65 Northbourne Avenue, ACT 2600 ***Tel*** *(02) 6262 6522*

If you love your wine, don't miss Benchmark, which has more than 100 wines by the glass and another 600 bottles lurking in the cellar. This lively venue, where the service is friendly without being intrusive, is perfect for business meetings and quiet civilized conversations. It offers a stylish atmosphere and a European bistro menu.

CANBERRA The Republic 🚸☀📋♿🍷 $$

20 Allara Street, Canberra City, ACT 2600 ***Tel*** *(02) 6247 1717*

The atmosphere here is noisy and the decor colourful and inviting. The Modern Australian menu is light, elegant and interesting, often with an emphasis on fresh seafood. It is open for breakfast and lunch only, and the wine list is consistently praised. A well-deserving Canberra favourite. It is closed on weekends.

CANBERRA Taj Mahal ☀📋 $$

39 Northbourne Avenue, ACT 2601 ***Tel*** *(02) 6247 6528, 0418 633436*

This bustling licensed restaurant, upstairs in the Melbourne Building, has been serving good, cheap North Indian cuisine since the early 1970s. For many Canberrans it is a comforting tradition. The tandoori chicken and lamb curries are particularly recommended, and vegetarians are well catered for.

CANBERRA Timmy's Kitchen 🚸☀📋♿🍷 $$

Manuka Village Centre, Furneaux Street, Manuka, ACT 2603 ***Tel*** *(02) 6295 6537*

This Chinese and Malaysian restaurant and takeaway has moved into these large premises in Manuka. It is a true Canberra experience and popular with the locals, who love its good cheap Southeast Asian food and speedy service. The Malaysian menu items are particularly recommended, including the curry laksas.

CANBERRA Tosolini's

$$$ ⑂

Baileys Corner, Cnr London Circuit and East Row, Canberra City, ACT 2600 **Tel** *(02) 6247 4317*

Open for breakfast, lunch and dinner, this cosy licensed Canberra institution is well known as a place to be seen. The food is inexpensive, and some say the coffee is the best in town, but the service gets mixed reviews, although they have been known to provide blankets for those mad enough to dine alfresco in winter.

CANBERRA Anise

$$$$

20 West Row, Melbourne Building, Civic, ACT 2600 **Tel** *(02) 6257 0700*

Combine quality Mod Oz cuisine with an award-winning wine list, attentive and knowledgable floor staff and management, comfortable seating and a stylish but no-nonsense setting in one of Canberra's best foodie neighbourhoods and you're sure to enjoy one of the city's best dining experiences.

CANBERRA Artespresso

$$$$

31 Giles Street, Kingston, ACT 2600 **Tel** *(02) 6295 8055*

Critics were enthusiastic when they heard that former members of Canberra's Atlantic and Sydney's Arena restaurants were setting up shop in Kingston, and they have not been disappointed. The menu and atmosphere is easygoing brasserie style, with bare floorboards and temporary artworks adorning the walls.

CANBERRA Axis Restaurant

$$$$

National Museum of Australia, Acton Peninsula, Acton, ACT 2601 **Tel** *(02) 6208 5176*

Open for breakfast, lunch and dinner, this award-winning and up-market restaurant is one of three cafés and restaurants located in the National Museum. It has spectacular views over Lake Burley Griffin, a seasonal Mediterranean and Asian-inspired menu and grill, and a terrific boutique wine list. Book ahead.

CANBERRA The Chairman and Yip

$$$$

108 Bunda Street, Canberra City, ACT 2601 **Tel** *(02) 6248 7109*

This Asian restaurant has all the local food critics raving. Not to mention international scribes from the likes of *Gourmet Traveller*. Its wine list is recommended, the service is friendly and professional, and the menu is light and inventive. How does char-grilled mushroom with coriander and cashew pesto sound?

CANBERRA Hill Station Restaurant

$$$$

51 Sheppard Street, Hume, ACT 2620 **Tel** *(02) 6260 1393*

This once isolated 1909 homestead and sheep farm has been converted into a charming restaurant and function centre with pleasant formal gardens and period decor and furnishings. It serves sophisticated and award-winning country cuisine. Book ahead as it is only open Friday and Saturday night.

CANBERRA The Lobby Restaurant

$$$$

King George Terrace, Parkes, ACT 2600 **Tel** *(02) 6273 1563*

Set within the National Rose Gardens opposite old Parliament House, The Lobby has long been a favourite with politicians, journalists and diplomats. The cuisine is seasonal Mod Oz and the setting smart modern with discreet seating and wraparound windows. Choose from a quality set menu or dine à la carte.

CANBERRA Mitzi's Carousel

$$$$

Red Hill Lookout, Red Hill, ACT 2603 **Tel** *(02) 6273 1808*

Overlooking Parliament House, this licensed restaurant offers contemporary Central European and Australian cuisine. There is alfresco dining downstairs in the café, while upstairs the atmosphere is more formal. It is open for breakfast, lunch and dinner. Some critics think it's overpriced. Bookings required.

CANBERRA Rosso Restaurant

$$$$

Palmerston Lane, Manuka, ACT 2603 **Tel** *(02) 6295 6703*

You'll find this classy and architecturally stylish licensed restaurant down a back alley in Manuka. Many claim it is one of Canberra's best, offering simple meals well done, with professional and attentive service. There are two dining rooms and the cuisine is Modern Australian with a good wine list. Closed Sunday and Monday.

CANBERRA The Boat House by the Lake

$$$$$

Grevillea Park, Menindee Drive, Barton, ACT 2600 **Tel** *(02) 6273 5500*

Situated on the northern edge of Lake Burley Griffin, this restaurant is prized for its views of Canberra's main attractions. Aim for lunch and be sure to book an outside table if the weather is fine. The menu is Mod Oz with limited (but quality) options, such as cider-glazed pork loin, with apple and Szechuan pepper relish.

CANBERRA Water's Edge

$$$$$

40 Parkes Place, Parkes, ACT 2600 **Tel** *(02) 6273 5066*

Subdued lighting and a stylish setting, sweeping views across Lake Burley Griffin, and an established reputation for excellent cuisine and professional service are your guarantee of a fine dining experience. The menu (ambitious modern European) is complemented by the wine list's quality French, Italian and Australian options.

QUEANBEYAN Basil at Byrne's Mill

$$$$

55 Collett Street, Queanbeyan, NSW 2620 **Tel** *(02) 6297 8283*

This rustic yet elegant restaurant is set in a 120-year-old, heritage-listed sandstone mill, 20 minutes' drive from the centre of Canberra. It consistently reaps culinary awards and praise for its adventurous cuisine, which often features game such as quail and duck. Its desserts are regularly cited as the highlight of the meal.

Key to Price Guide *see p524* **Key to Symbols** *see back cover flap*

BRISBANE

ALBION Breakfast Creek Hotel ≡ ♿ ♫ ⛱ $

2 Kingsford Smith Drive, QLD 4010 ***Tel*** *(07) 3262 5988*

This famous Brisbane icon is noted for its steaks. Part of the experience is to choose your own steak before it is cooked. A Queensland favourite since its construction in 1889, it is situated a short drive from the city, en route to the airport. The menu also offers chicken and fish dishes.

BULIMBA Riverbend Books & Teahouse ♿ ⛱ $

193 Oxford Street, QLD 4171 ***Tel*** *(07) 3899 8555*

This is a small bookshop restaurant with outdoor dining, perfect for a warm Brisbane night or a sunny day. Now featuring a full sushi menu and offering meals for vegetarians, this eating place is in the trendy Oxford Street district of Bulimba. It is a ten-minute walk past shops, cinemas and galleries to the CityCat.

BULIMBA Oxford 152 ≡ ♿ ⛱ $$

152 Oxford Street, 4171 ***Tel*** *(07) 3899 2026*

The uniqueness of this dining experience comes from the microbrewery. Experiment with Bee-sting seasonal honey beer or an aromatic lager. The Oxford Brewing Co. was the most awarded small brewery at the Australian International Beer Awards. The Oxford Premium Battered Barramundi is featured on the modern menu.

CAMP HILL Restaurant Rapide ♿ ≡ ⛱ $$$

Shop 1/4 Martha Street, QLD 4152 ***Tel*** *(07) 3843 5755*

This small suburban restaurant is hidden away in a sidewalk of Camphill but worth the ten-minute drive out of the city. This bistro run by chef Paul McGivern and his wife Prue boasts modern Australian food and inspirational variations to Italian favourites, including grilled whitefish with sweet corn and crab pancake.

CITY CENTRE Vil'laggio 🔨 ≡ ⛱ $

695 Brunswick Street, New Farm, QLD 4000 ***Tel*** *(07) 3254 0275*

Award-winning pizzas, mouth-watering calzone, authentic Italian oxtail risotto, this menu is the reason for Augello's reputation for taste. There is an outdoor courtyard, a children's menu and gluten-free, fat-free options for vegetarians or those on a special diet. Don't forget to leave room for the dessert menu.

CITY CENTRE Gilhooley's Irish Pub and Restaurant ≡ ♫ ⛱ $$

Cnr Albert & Charlotte Streets, QLD 4000 ***Tel*** *(07) 3229 0672*

This is Brisbane's original Irish restaurant, a great spot in the city for food and entertainment. The menu offers succulent steaks, traditional beef and Guiness, or braised steak served with salad and chips and a range of other Australian and Irish meals. A friendly place to sit with a drink while the Irish musicians rehearse.

CITY CENTRE Cha Cha Char ≡ ♿ $$$

Shop 5 Eagle Street Pier Eagle Street, QLD 4000 ***Tel*** *(07) 3211 9944*

Specializing in Wagyu grain- and grass-fed beef, this restaurant is in a stunning location with sweeping views of the Brisbane River. It features a separate bar and cocktail area. Try the roasted duck, the fish of the day or the extensive vegetarian menu, while for dessert, chocolate tart.

CITY CENTRE Custom's House ≡ ♿ $$$

399 Queen Street, QLD 4001 ***Tel*** *(07) 3365 8999*

Custom's House, a heritage icon in Brisbane situated close to the CBD operates a fully licensed restaurant. Alfresco dining is also available, overlooking the river and the Story Bridge. Excellent innovative international cuisine, fantastic river views and friendly professional service. The wine list has quality wines at competitive prices.

CITY CENTRE Il Centro Restaurant and Bar ≡ ♿ ⛱ $$$

Eagle Street Pier, QLD 4000 ***Tel*** *(07) 3221 6090*

Located at the Eagle Street Pier in the city, this restaurant has photographic views of the Brisbane River and Story Bridge. The menu is modern Italian but the flavours are unique to Queensland – fresh seafood, prime cuts of meat, tropical fruit, seasonal vegetables and delicate garden herbs. Try the sandcrab lasagne and the vanilla pannacotta.

CITY CENTRE Lat 27 Brisbane ≡ ♿ $$$

471 Adelaide Street, QLD 4000 ***Tel*** *(07) 3839 2727*

A stylish modern restaurant with views of the Brisbane River, named Lat 27 Brisbane because of the city's latitudinal location. Try the spatchcock with mushrooms, or the seared barramundi with a side of creamy mash with truffle oil. For dessert the vanilla brulée with berry ice cream or the hot chocolate marbre.

CITY CENTRE Pier Nine ≡ ♿ ⛱ $$$

Eagle Street Pier, QLD 4000 ***Tel*** *(07) 3228 2100*

The menu at Pier Nine is updated on a seasonal basis and uses fresh local produce. This open-plan restaurant with a floor-to-ceiling glass wall has 180-degree views, taking in the Story Bridge on the left, Brisbane River right in front and Kangaroo Point cliffs to the right.

CITY CENTRE Urbane

🖼 $$$

179 Mary Street, QLD 4000 **Tel** *(07) 3229 2271*

The chef here is Ryan Alexander Squires, who has worked at French Laundry, Nappa Valley, and Per Se, New York. The innovative concept behind Urbane's menu is aimed at allowing diners to experience more flavours by having several smaller dishes. For instance, the first two courses are half the size of a regular entrée.

CITY CENTRE E'cco

🖼 $$$$

100 Boundary Street (cnr Adelaide Street), QLD 4000 **Tel** *(07) 3831 8344*

This award-winning bistro is simple and welcoming. Run by chef Phillip Johnson, it boasts a menu based on fresh seasonal food "that hasn't been fussed over". Main courses include porcini-dusted lamb loin with potato gnocchi or Sichuan spiced duck breast with Asian greens. Give in to the poached gooseberry and almond biscotti for dessert.

CITY CENTRE Gianni Vintage Cellar Bar Restaurant

🖼&📶 $$$$

12 Edward Street, QLD 4000 **Tel** *(07) 3221 7655*

Modern elegance and fine cuisine made this the Queensland restaurant of the year in 2004. To begin try the avocado and crab *rillette*. For a main meal, the suckling piglet or Darling Downs Wagyu beef sirloin. To finish experience the chocolate and vanilla bean ice cream.

CITY CENTRE Marco Polo

🖼& $$$$

Level 2 Treasury Casino Queen Street, QLD 4000 **Tel** *(07) 3306 8744*

This heritage restaurant in the elegantly appointed riverscape dining room of the Conrad Treasury has an opulent and sophisticated atmosphere. Themed around Marco Polo's journey, the decor and menu reflects his travels. Choose from lamb, duck, chicken or seafood dishes on a sumptious menu. What about pistachio ice cream to finish?

CITY CENTRE Siggi's at the Port Office – Restaurant and Wine Bar

🖼& $$$$$

Stamford Plaza Cnr Edward and Margaret Streets, QLD 4000 **Tel** *(07) 3221 4555*

Offering world-class dining in a sophisticated 19th-century setting, Siggi's menu serves classical and contemporary Australian cuisine. Fine wines and a superb tapas bar make this one of Queensland's premier dining choices. Try the *feuillete* salad of crayfish, with crayfish tail. For dessert try Siggi's crepes for two.

COORPAROO The Curry Hut

📶🖼&📶 $

Cnr Cavendish Road & Holdsworth Street, QLD 4151 **Tel** *(07) 3397 5545*

A long established favourite in Coorparoo, this authentic Indian restaurant offers superb butter chicken and an excellent beef vindaloo. It is a 12-minute drive from the city to find this gem, hidden behind the main shopping complex, but it is worth it. The atmosphere is inviting and subdued with soft candle lighting.

COOPAROO Belesis

📶🖼&📶 $$

198 Old Cleveland Road, QLD 4158 **Tel** *(07) 3324 2446*

This fabulous Mediterannean café in Cooparoo is worth the short drive out of the city. The meals are crafted with fresh ingredients and include seafood pastas, roasted vegetables, ravioli and a rack of lamb with rosemary worthy of the wait. Desserts include a range of Greek cakes and pastries. Great coffee and an intimate atmosphere for a liqueur.

EAST BRISBANE Green Papaya Vietnamese Restaurant

🖼& $$$

898 Stanley Street, QLD 4169 **Tel** *(07) 3217 3599*

A short drive out of the city, this authentic North Vietnamese restaurant is run by Lien Yeomans. The emphasis in Lien's cooking is on the perfect balance of flavours. Dishes include turmeric fish, grilled lemon myrtle prawns and curried duck Vietnamese style. For a side dish try a lotus salad and to finish, the black rice pudding or a sorbet.

FORTITUDE VALLEY Asian Fusion

📶🖼& $$

149 Wickham Street, QLD 4006 **Tel** *(07) 3852 1144*

Specializing in Vietnamese and Chinese dishes, Asian Fusion cooks great Asian meals with fresh local ingredients while you wait, or sit down and enjoy. The menu includes such favourites as chicken and cashew or barbecue pork noodle dishes. Vietnamese rice paper rolls are made in the kitchen.

MILTON La Dolce Vita

📶🖼&📶 $

20 Park Road Savoir Faire, QLD 4064 **Tel** *(07) 3368 3805*

Sit out in the morning sun or under the Brisbane stars on a warm night and smell the Italian food of La Dolce Vita. Feel the buzzy atmosphere of busy Park Road while you relax for breakfast, lunch or dinner and enjoy authentic pastas, coffee, pastries, fresh salads, cakes and ice creams.

MILTON Oxley's on the River

🖼&📶 $$

330 Coronation Drive, QLD 4064 **Tel** *(07) 3368 1866*

Located on the riverbank, this dining experience is unique. Eating at Oxley's on the River gives the sensation of dining on a cruise ship. An à la carte menu offers steamed Moreton Bay bugs and rosemary-scented prawns, or stay with the set menu for a choice of steak, seafood, chicken or veal. For dessert try the citrus and passionfruit torte.

MOUNT COOT-THA Kuta Cafe

🖼&📶 $

Sir Samuel Griffith Drive, QLD 4066 **Tel** *(07) 3369 9922*

Situated adjacent to Mount Coot-tha Lookout, Kuta Cafe offers a varied menu as well as an array of self-select food complemented by a wide choice of coffees and alcoholic beverages. This small café is open from 7am to 11pm with indoor and outdoor dining with excellent views of Brisbane and the surrounding countryside.

Key to Price Guide *see p524* **Key to Symbols** *see back cover flap*

NEW FARM The Purple Olive 🖼️📋♿🔲 $$
79 James Street, QLD 4005 **Tel** *(07) 3254 0097*

This Mediterranean-style restaurant is situated in trendy James Street, close to shops, galleries and cinemas. Having all the charms of the classic alfresco cafés of Europe, this popular BYO captures the modern gourmet dining experience. The menu offers the authentic flavours of southern Europe, while catering to modern Australian tastes.

NEW MARKET Squirrels 🖼️📋🔲 $$
184 Enoggera Road, QLD 4051 **Tel** *(07) 3856 0966*

This vegetarian restaurant receives good reviews from vegetarians and non-vegetarians alike. It offers a range of vegan and vegetarian dishes, including the favourite Cajun tofu. Choose from fresh salads, juices and scrumptious cakes and breads or try the set menu. For dessert, try the vegan mudcake. About a seven-minute drive out of the city.

PADDINGTON Kookaburra Cafe 📋♿🔲 $
280 Given Terrace, QLD 4064 **Tel** *(07) 3369 2400*

This is a popular Brisbane spot to meet friends. It is famous for its pizzas, which include the spicy chicken or chicken satay, the gorgonzola special, and the Aussie with sizzling bacon, egg and onion. A favourite pasta dish is the Ravioli Alaskan – ricotta-filled ravioli with a delicious wine sauce and smoked salmon.

RED HILL Olivetto's 🖼️📋🔲 $$$
5 Enoggera Terrace, QLD 4059 **Tel** *(07) 3369 0610*

Internationally acclaimed chef Paul Newsham runs the kitchen at this Red Hill favourite and presents a unique menu. For a main meal with a difference, try the Bo-Kapp, a South-African chicken and prawn curry. Desserts include baked apple tart with gingerbread ice cream.

ROSALIE Indian Aroma 🖼️📋♿🔲 $
1/155 Baroona Road, QLD 4064 **Tel** *(07) 3369 3544*

This small restaurant offers an "eat until you drop" smorgasbord at the budget price of A$16.95 per person. The menu is Indian and there is a range of tasty meals on offer. Situated in a quiet part of Brisbane, not far from the city centre or the trendy shops and galleries of Paddington.

SOUTH BRISBANE River Canteen ♿🔲 $$$
The Boardwalk Southbank, QLD 4101 **Tel** *(07) 3846 1880*

Sophisticated yet relaxed decor with crisp white tablecloths, this restaurant overlooking the river offers exciting dishes. The main menu includes braised oxtail with potato gnocchi, roast parsnips and caramelized shallots, or seared fillet of kangaroo, onion relish, French lentils, buffalo mozzarella and Swiss chard.

TENERIFFE Beccofino 📋♿🔲 $$
10 Vernon Terrace, QLD 4005 **Tel** *(07) 3666 0207*

In the mood for a wood-fired pizza with a glass of wine while you wait for a table? The short wait is worth it, as the menu is tantalizing. Try the *calamari fritti con rucola e balsamico* (baby calamari) for an entrée or a Scotch fillet of steak for a main course; or perhaps a shellfish and fish stew on a cool night.

TOOWONG Boatshed at Regatta 📋♿🎵🔲 $$
543 Coronation Drive, Toowong, QLD 4064 **Tel** *(07) 3871 9533*

This is just for starters – oysters, Moreton Bay bugs, fresh ocean king prawns, smoked salmon on fried caper potato salad, or barramundi spring rolls. This hotel restaurant has been a local favourite for decades. It is situated close to the river, university and train station at Toowong.

TOOWONG Brent's, The Dining Experience 📋 $$$
85 Miskin Street, QLD 4066 **Tel** *(07) 3371 4558*

An excellent restaurant that offers a perfect romantic dinner menu for two. Alternatively, try the speciality menu of chef Brent Farrell. All the dishes on this menu are created using only fresh local produce and are changed daily. This restaurant has developed and maintains a reputation for fine dining.

WEST END Bombay Dhaba 🖼️📋♿🔲 $$
5/220 Melbourne Street, QLD 4101 **Tel** *(07) 3846 6662*

For lamb, beef, chicken, seafood or vegetarian curries, it is difficult to beat the Bombay Dhaba. This authentic Indian restaurant in Brisbane's ethnic West End offers great food and a warm atmosphere. Try the Kashmiri naan or the *aloo paratha* (bread stuffed with potatoes). There is an adequate car park underneath the restaurant.

WEST END The Gun Shop Cafe 🖼️🔲 $$
53 Mollison Street, QLD 4101 **Tel** *(07) 3844 2241*

A hit with locals, the menu is inlcudes spiced crusted salmon, fantastic seafood or linguine with a range of vegetable dishes, such as sweet potato curls, wild mushrooms or Asian greens. This little café is all about taste sensation – ginger and lime, chilli and garlic, hot greens with garlic butter.

WEST END Mondo Organics 📋♿🔲 $$$
166 Hardgrave Road, West End, QLD 4101 **Tel** *(07) 3844 1132*

Offering vegetarian and organic dishes, this venue in Brisbane's bohemian centre is a favourite with the locals. An antipasti of roast pepper *harissa*, *baccala*, and almond verjuice pesto is indicative of the menu. Entrées include grilled almond-encrusted scallops with accompaniments. Try the braised duck with caramelized radicchio.

SOUTH OF TOWNSVILLE

AIRLEE BEACH Mangrove Jack's Cafe Bar ▤ ♿ 🍷 $$

Cnr The Esplanade & Coconut Grove, QLD 4802 ***Tel*** *(07) 4964 1999*

Combining an alfresco café with an excitiing entertainment venue, Mangrove Jack's, in the Airlie Beach Hotel, offers dinner, music and a wine bar, which sells over 35 wines and champagnes by the glass. This hotel is located on the busy Shute Harbour Road and has a reputation for wood-fired pizzas and a superb bistro menu.

BROADBEACH Giulio's on Broadbeach ▤ ♿ 🍷 $$

The Phoenician Resort Surf Parade, QLD 4218 ***Tel*** *(07) 5539 0169*

This is a popular spot for locals. Sit in, or outside on the sidewalk and enjoy the Queensland beach atmosphere while being spoilt by the authentic European flavours. The breads and pastas are cooked on the premises. Try the risotto or the smoked salmon penne for a main meal, or a spaghetti with Tuscan spicy sausage. The desserts are to die for.

BUDDINA The Curry Bowl 🌳 ▤ ♿ $

7/115 Point Cartwright Drive, QLD 4575 ***Tel*** *(07) 5478 0800*

This Indian restaurant is situated on the Sunshine Coast close to Caloundra. It has a repuation with the locals for friendly service and tasty Indian meals made with fresh ingredients. The menu includes all the favourites, including samosas, curry puffs and great naan breads. Try the Madras curry or the superb chicken curry.

BUNDABERG Pier One Bistro (Across the Waves) ▤ ♿ ♫ 🍷 $

1 Miller Street, QLD 4670 ***Tel*** *(07) 4152 1531*

Offering a range of Australian club-style meals including seafood, steak, Chinese, Irish and Italian meals, this restaurant situated in the Sports Club has a great reputation with the locals. Waves buffet operates weekly. If you wait more than 30 minutes after you place your order – your meal is free!

CALOUNDRA Cafe by the Beach 🌳 🍷 $$

Seaview Terrace, Moffat Beach, QLD 4551 ***Tel*** *(07) 5491 9505*

This small, busy café is popular with the locals for an evening meal or for lunch or snacks. The menu offers pancakes, burgers with chips and salad, succulent steaks, pizzas with a range of fresh toppings, pastas, fresh fish and all-day breakfast. Specials are offered every night and there is a children's meal.

GLADSTONE Chattin Cafe ▤ ♿ 🍷 $$

Shop 5/100 Goondoon Street, QLD 4680 ***Tel*** *(07) 4972 4912*

This café-restaurant, a short walk from the marina, is open for breakfast and lunch every day, and dinner on Thursday, Friday and Saturday nights. The evening menu offers modern Australian meals with an Asian influence using fresh produce and seafood. Try the pan-fried Atlantic salmon.

GOLD COAST The Burleigh Bluff Cafe 🌳 ♿ 🍷 $

The Old Burleigh Theatre Arcade, QLD 4220 ***Tel*** *(07) 5576 6333*

This café is a favourite with locals. Situated opposite the beach in Burleigh with tables in the sun, or sit inside. It is a lively spot for breakfast – open every morning. It offers reasonably priced food with friendly service. Try the apple pancakes with cream or a burger and chips. A beautiful spot in the evening.

GOLD COAST Shogun Japanese Karaoke Restaurant ▤ ♿ ♫ $

90 Bundall Road, Surfers Paradise, QLD 4217 ***Tel*** *(07) 5538 2872*

Offering Japanese and à la carte menus, this karaoke restaurant is a popular spot for tourists and visitors to Surfers Paradise and features an authentic Japanese water garden. Vegetarian food is also available. Dress is smart-casual – no bare arms. This restaurant is licensed and does not allow BYO. Children require strict parental supervision.

GOLD COAST Elevations 🌳 ▤ ♿ ♫ 🍷 $$

1705 Gold Coast Highway, Burleigh Heads, QLD 4220 ***Tel*** *(07) 5568 7644*

This Gold Coast hilltop restaurant provides stunning views of the countryside and coastline. The elevated cocktail bar has 360-degree views. The chef Jeff Hawkes provides a modern Australian menu, including seafood, steak, pizza and pasta dishes. Try the fish of the day or the veal for a main course.

GOLD COAST Conrad Jupiters Charters Towers ▤ ♿ $$$

Broadbeach Island, Broadbeach, QLD 4218 ***Tel*** *(07) 5592 8443*

Mouthwatering entrée suggestions on this menu include Moorish spiced veal or Tas salmon sashimi. It is difficult to ignore the Black Angus tenderloin, or try the terrine of poached chicken and grilled quail. An excellent wine list includes a fine Margaret River white wine by the glass.

GOLD COAST Palazzo Versace Vanitos Restaurant ▤ ♿ $$$$

94 Seaworld Drive, Surfers Paradise, QLD 4217 ***Tel*** *(07) 5509 8000*

This sensational venue, overlooking the lagoon, attracts tourists and dining enthusiasts alike. The atmosphere and decor are indicative of Versace, elegant and tasteful with original art and fine quality furnishings. The food is equally superb. Try the Moreton Bay bugs and don't miss the fabulous wine list.

Key to Price Guide *see p524* **Key to Symbols** *see back cover flap*

MOUNT MEE Birches $$

1350 Mount Mee Road, QLD 4521 Tel (07) 5498 2244

Situated near the Glass House Mountains in the Caboolture Shire, this modern restaurant offers a range of dishes including special meals for coeliacs and vegetarians. The superb country atmosphere is welcoming to the traveller and the timber decor is enhanced by a fireplace in the winter.

NOOSA Jasper $$$

The Emerald Hastings Street, QLD 4567 Tel (07) 5474 9600

Would you like to be seen dining out on Noosa's famous Hastings Street? Here is the opportunity to do so and have good food in a relaxed garden atmosphere at the same time. Enjoy local seafood and a fine wine selection. Dinner is served by candlelight and the bar provides a trendy, relaxed spot to sit and watch the passing people.

NOOSAVILLE Magic of India $$

Islander Resort Thomas Street, QLD 4566 Tel (07) 5449 7788

Customers travel from Brisbane to eat at this delightful Indian restaurant in Noosaville. The pride of the kitchen is the boneless butter chicken. Situated a short distance from the river, this is a relaxed place to eat an evening meal. It has a friendly atmosphere and is highly recommended by the locals.

ROCKHAMPTON Hog's Breath Cafe $$

1 Aquatic Place North Rockhampton, QLD 4702 Tel (07) 4926 3646

This franchise is well known in Rockhampton for offering inventive entrées, such as fried chicken tenders, or crumbed calamari. Mains include the favourite prime rib, a New York grill or fish of the day. For snacks, try the burgers or salads.

SAMFORD Samford Valley Hotel $$

Main Street, QLD 4520 Tel (07) 3289 1212

For entrée the home-made fishcakes are delicious. The oysters are Queensland favourites and the Moreton Bay prawns are succulent. This hotel, a 30-minute drive from Brisbane city has been an icon for decades for locals, tourists and those en route to Mount Glorious. Try the rosemary-infused lamb rump or the grilled Atlantic salmon.

SOUTH TOWNSVILLE Scirocco cafe Bar & Grill $$

Palmer Street, QLD 4810 Tel (07) 4724 4508

Offering an interesting combination of Italian and Thai foods, this Townsville restaurant is popular with the locals. The restaurant caters for 100 people inside and has a small garden section with sails and umbrellas, which seats 40 people outside. It attracts mature diners interested in the tasty menu and relaxed atmosphere.

TOOWOOMBA Weis Restaurant $$

2 Margaret Street, QLD 4350 Tel (07) 4632 7666

This homestyle restaurant offers both steak and seafood smorgasbord, an array of delicious hot dishes, fresh garden salads and home-baked desserts. Loved by locals and travellers for many years, it is situated in the historic family home "Alameda" built in 1925. It offers a unique setting and pleasant ambience.

TOWNSVILLE Seagulls Resort on the Seafront $$

74 The Esplanade, QLD 4810 Tel (07) 4721 3111

Seagulls offers à la carte dining in either air-conditioned comfort or on the deck overlooking the swimming pool and gardens. This beautiful venue provides a superb menu, friendly service and attention to detail. Choose from one of the delicious seafood dishes or juicy steaks.

NORTHERN QUEENSLAND AND THE OUTBACK

BARCALDINE Lee's Garden Motel and Chinese Restaurant $

1 Box Street, QLD 4725 Tel (07) 4651 1451

This 20-room motel in Barcaldine has its own licensed Chinese restaurant, which offers excellent meals for the Outback traveller. Barcaldine is located 1,080 km (670 miles) northwest of Brisbane and is a sleepy town of 1,700 people with plenty of pubs and a wealth of historic buildings. It has an interesting political history.

BLACKALL Acacia Motor Inn $$

Cnr Short Street & Shamrock Street, QLD 4472 Tel (07) 4657 6022

This is a modern restaurant noted for its homestyle cooking. It is spacious with friendly service. Blackall is famous for its woolscour – the last remaining steam-driven wool-washing plant in Australia. It is also home of the original Black Stump which is the exact centre of a meridian square used by surveyors to align the borders of Queensland in 1887.

BURKETOWN Savannah Lodge $$

Cnr Beames & Bowen Streets, QLD 4830 Tel (07) 4745 5177

This lodge provides friendly service and meals and is situated in Burketown on the Gulf of Carpentaria. It offers sunset drinks on the salt flats, bird-watching and fishing expeditions, or the lodge can arrange a small flight over the Gulf country. Travel to Lawn Hill Gorge to see the saltwater crocodile and skink.

CAIRNS Barnacle Bill's Seafood Inn 📋 ♿ ⛱ $$

103 The Esplanade, QLD 4870 ***Tel*** *(07) 4051 2241*

Situated on the esplanade in Cairns, this popular seafood restaurant has been a favourite for over two decades. It offers fresh dishes of oysters, calamari, mussels, scallops, prawns, bugs and fish of the day. The house favourites include the seafood jambalaya – prawns, fish and scallops served in a hot, spicy tomato-based sauce.

CAIRNS Cafe China 📋 ♿ $$

Grafton Street, QLD 4870 ***Tel*** *(07) 4041 2828*

This large and busy restaurant offers Oriental delicacies served by friendly and professional staff. The mouthwatering coral trout fillet with snow peas and ginger is superb for a main course. For dessert, try the black sesame pudding with Kahlua-flavoured strawberries. The wine list is extensive and will please any wine enthusiast.

CAIRNS Kanis Seafood & Steak Restaurant 🧒 📋 ⛱ $$$

59 The Esplanade, QLD 4870 ***Tel*** *(07) 4051 1331*

Enjoy the water views at this large, wonderful restaurant with its nautical decor. The vast menu has dishes that will please just about every taste, with its seafood, steak, vegetarian and international selections. Kanis is open every day for dinner and has two levels as well as outdoor tables.

CAIRNS Red Ochre Grill 📋 ♿ ⛱ $$$

43 Shields Street, QLD 4870 ***Tel*** *(07) 4051 0100*

This unique menu is based on Australian native foods. Dishes such as lemon aspen cured ocean trout, twice-cooked Mareeba pork shoulder and blackened yellow-fin tuna fillet entice the tastebuds; or try the Australian game platter for two. For dessert the wattle-seed pavlova is a treat; or experiment with the Quandong brûlée.

CHARLEVILLE Hotel Corones 📋 $

Wills Street, QLD 4470 ***Tel*** *(07) 4654 1022*

Marvel at the grandeur of this historic hotel while enjoying an evening meal. Charleville is situated in the heart of Queensland's mulga country. It is the largest town in the southwest Outback of Queensland and has a direct rail link to Brisbane. The Charleville heritage trail guides visitors through the historic sights.

CHARLEVILLE Cattle Camp Hotel 📋 $$

149 Alfred Street, QLD 4470 ***Tel*** *(07) 4654 3473*

This popular pub offers meals for guests and travellers. While in town visit the historic house located in Alfred Street. The Queensland National Parks and Wildlife Service office on Park Street has a bird aviary. To the south of town is the Steiger Gun, one of ten, used by meteorologist Professor Clement Wragge to break the 1902 drought.

CLONCURRY The Gidgee Grill 📋 ♿ $$

Matilda Highway, QLD 4824 ***Tel*** *(07) 4742 1599*

This à la carte restaurant offers a choice of specially created meals. The menu features top quality fish from the gulf and beef from the surrounding area. Seafood meals include mouthwatering choices of oysters, prawns or barramundi. The char-grilled grain and grass-fed steaks are succulent.

CUNNAMULLA Club Hotel 🧒 📋 ♿ ⛱ $$

15 Louise Street, QLD 4490 ***Tel*** *(07) 4655 1209*

A relaxing atmosphere, sparely furnished and simple decor, with artwork brought back from Thailand giving the dining room an attractive, Oriental feel. The specialities of the house are Chinese dishes and pizzas. A good value, reliable restaurant if you're looking for a quick meal.

CUNNAMULLA The Woolshed Restaurant 📋 ♿ $$

9 Louise Street, QLD 4490 ***Tel*** *(07) 4655 1737*

The Woolshed Restaurant at the Warrego Hotel provides the traveller with an excellent choice of fine pub meals. In particular, try the roast lamb or chicken with vegetables accompanied with a bottle of Australian wine, perhaps a nice Jacob's Creek.

DAINTREE Crossroads Cafe Bar & Grill 🍷 ♿ ⛱ $$

Daintree Road, Lower Daintree, QLD 4873 ***Tel*** *(07) 4098 7658*

Enjoy a burger or a sit-down dinner and friendly conversation at the Daintree Crossroads Cafe Bar & Grill. Glazed grilled chicken breast supreme filled with fresh mango and crushed macadamia nuts is tempting, or try the fresh local seafood platter of crumbed prawns, reef fish, oysters, scallops and calamari.The Queenslander eye fillet is superb.

DAINTREE Mangroves 🍷 ♿ ⛱ $$

2054 Mossman Daintree Road, QLD 4873 ***Tel*** *(07) 4098 7272*

Beer-battered local fish, a rump steak with chips or a chicken curry – whatever you choose from this menu is prepared with care and fresh local ingredients. Try the Kuranda home-made ice cream or fresh fruit salad. For vegetarians, the ricotta and spinach pasta is tasty or choose from a fresh salad, Greek style or caesar.

DAINTREE Julaymba ♿ ⛱ $$$

20 Daintree Road, QLD 4873 ***Tel*** *(07) 4098 6100*

Internationally trained chefs prepare Australian gourmet tropical cuisine in this tantalizing environment. The menu has been designed to balance the multicultural tastes of modern Australia, combining many exotic Queensland fruits, tropical reef fish and local produce with native and indigenous nuts, berries, flowers, leaves and seeds.

Key to Price Guide *see p524* **Key to Symbols** *see back cover flap*

LONGREACH Oasis Restaurant & Coolibah Bar

Cnr Landsborough Highway & Stork Road, QLD 4730 **Tel** *(07) 4658 2411*

Magnificent setting and excellent cuisine in this Outback town of Longreach makes the Oasis Restaurant an ideal dining location after a long drive. Sit by the campfire and enjoy a conversation. The poolside bar is an ideal setting to share a wine on a starry night. Dine inside or out. Enjoy the country-style menu, local produce and friendly service.

PORT DOUGLAS Cactus Bar & Grill

38 Macrossan Street, QLD 4877 **Tel** *(07) 4099 6666*

This is an internet café and restaurant right in the centre of Port Douglas. The traveller can sip a margarita and munch on potato wedges, have a game of pool, meet with friends or dine alfresco in this popular little street café and bar. Try one of the great lunches or stay for dinner and enjoy fresh seafood, including oysters, bugs and scallops.

PORT DOUGLAS The Funky Cow

123 Davidson Street, QLD 4877 **Tel** *(07) 4099 6585*

This place lives up to its name – funky by name, definitely funky by nature, with loads of colours, cushions and a great eclectic mix of music. A restaurant with a fun atmosphere. The menu boasts steaks of all types, including camel, as well as all kinds of seafood.

PORT DOUGLAS Pepperazzi Pizzeria

Shop 6/79 Davidson Street, QLD 4877 **Tel** *(07) 4099 4054*

All dining is outdoors at this small, bright red restaurant with its comfortable cane chairs under umbrellas – a great place to watch the world go by. The extensive menu is of traditional Italian food (they do takeaway as well). It is also very handy for the beach, which is only a couple of minutes' walk away.

PORT DOUGLAS On the Inlet

3 Inlet Street, 4871 QLD **Tel** *(07) 4099 5255*

Located on the waterfront of Dickson Inlet, this stylish restaurant offers views across the Coral Sea to Mossman and the Daintree. For starters try the oysters with some house-baked bread, then the Coral trout or the whole char-grilled baby barramundi with a sauvignon blanc from the Adelaide Hills.

TAMBO Fanny Mae's Roadhouse

15 Arthur Street, QLD 4478 **Tel** *(07) 4654 6137*

Fanny Mae's Roadhouse is in the lovely Matilda Highway town of Tambo. Sit out on the peaceful deck and enjoy the home-cooked meals. They offer roadhouse fare of fish or steak with salad and chips, or try one of the great burgers, which are generous in size and made with fresh salad and served with chips.

THURSDAY ISLAND Pearl Lugger Restaurant

Cnr Victoria Parade & Jardine Street, QLD 4875 **Tel** *(07) 4069 1569*

The chef's speciality is local seafood, featuring mudcrab and tropical crayfish. This is a historic hotel built about 1901. It offers popular counter meals in the beer garden from 12pm to 2pm and 6pm to 7:30pm daily, or for a more sophisticated menu indulge in the seafood at the Pearl Lugger. The garlic prawns are succulent and fresh.

WINTON North Gregory Hotel

67 Elderslie Street, QLD 4735 **Tel** *(07) 4657 1375*

Situated in the heart of the Outback the North Gregory Hotel lays claim to hosting the first live performance of "Waltzing Matilda" in 1895. While you're in town, be sure to visit the Waltzing Matilda Centre opened in 1998. The North Gregory offers a good range of pub fare.

DARWIN AND THE TOP END

CULLEN BAY Buzz Cafe

The Slipway Larrakeyah, NT 0801 **Tel** *(08) 8941 1141*

This unique café provides a beautiful outlook over the marina and waters of Cullen Bay. The pleasant atmosphere is enhanced by the interesting Javanese decor with handmade Indonesian furnishings. It is only a five-minute drive from Darwin's CBD. The menu has a reputation for tasty food. Try the wild barramundi or the salt-and-pepper chilli squid.

CULLEN BAY Bella Amore

Unit 2/52 Marina Boulevard, NT 0820 **Tel** *(08) 8981 4988*

The decor's fresh autumn colours and simple furnishings create a pleasant, relaxed atmosphere. The menu is not exclusively Italian and includes steak, seafood, game and even live red claw in the dry season. Try the popular cowboy shooter cheesecake speciality.

DARWIN Cafe Kashmir

2 Pavonia Place, Nightcliffe, NT 0810 **Tel** *(08) 8948 0688*

This restaurant offers a mouthwatering menu of authentic Indian Mughlai and Punjabi dishes. The rice dishes include biryani served with raita and pappadum. The alu baigan is a wonderful vegetarian dish with eggplant and potato. Try a lamb or chicken vindaloo or a prawn masala in a creamy sauce. Exotic and sensational. Great service.

DARWIN Cafe Olio @ The Cavenagh ▤ ♿ ♫ ☂ $

12 Cavenagh Street, NT 800 ***Tel** (08) 8981 2600*

Offering pizzas, pastas, fish and chips and grills, this café has a courtyard, a bar, indoor eating and outdoor tables on the pavement. It is open 5:30pm until late seven days a week. On Sunday from 4pm until 8pm there is live music on the deck. There are large timber tables for families or more intimate settings for couples.

DARWIN Hanuman ✦ ▤ ♿ ☂ $$

Shop 1, Mitchell Plaza, NT 0800 ***Tel** (08) 8941 3500*

This long-established Darwin favourite offers Asian food, predominantly Thai. The menu has authentic tandoori, Thai and Nonya dishes prepared with wonderful exotic spices. The fish dishes are prepared with fresh local seafood and the vegetable dishes also use tropical ingredients. The owner Jimmy Shu is passionate about Asian influences.

DARWIN Moorish Cafe ▤ ♿ $$

37 Knuckey Street, NT 0800 ***Tel** (08) 8981 0010*

This is a Moroccan meets Spanish-style café with comfy corner lounges and candles.The tapas are tasty and the paella is a favourite; or try the warm chick pea and chiroza salad. Meals are cooked with authentic North African and Spanish seasonings and are delicious and flavoursome.

DARWIN Shenannigan's Irish Pub ▤ ♿ ♫ ☂ $$

69 Mitchell Street, NT 0800 ***Tel** (08) 8981 2100*

Offering alfresco dining with full table service, this Irish pub has a plasma-screen TV that can be watched from the dining area. If you are not so interested in local sports, watch the passers-by on Mitchell Street. Entertainment is provided seven nights a week. The food is excellent – try the catch of the day or a rich Irish stew.

DARWIN Crustaceans on the Wharf ▤ ♿ ☂ $$$

Stoke Hill Wharf, NT 0800 ***Tel** (08) 8981 8658*

Situated in Darwin's wharf precinct, this restaurant offers a fabulous menu. The oysters are a must for starters. The barramundi fritters coated in spring onion, garlic and mild chilli egg wash, pan-fried and served with pappadum are a favourite. If you would prefer a meat meal, the double-boned lamb cutlets have plenty of flavour.

DARWIN Ducks Nuts ▤ ♿ ☂ $$$

76 Mitchell Street, NT 0800 ***Tel** (08) 8942 2122*

Stylish setting, good service and a relaxed atmosphere are offered by this popular Darwin venue. The bar and grill alfresco restaurant serves hearty breakfasts until 11am, tasty lunches from 12pm until 3pm, and dinner through until 10pm, Monday to Sunday. Cocktails served on Sundays.

DARWIN Evoo ▤ ♿ ♫ ☂ $$$

Skycity, Gilruth Avenue, NT 0800 ***Tel** (08) 8943 8888*

Skycity Darwin is set in lush tropical gardens. Offering ocean views from an elegant private dining room, this casino restaurant has a fine wine list offering Australian and French wines. Try the pan-seared Evoo king prawns on lobster risotto with sautéd asparagus or maybe the chocolate lava pudding with strawberries for dessert.

DARWIN Rooftop Restaurant ▤ ♿ $$$

7th Floor, Quality Hotel Frontier Darwin, 3 Buffalo Court, NT 0800 ***Tel** (08) 8981 5333*

Situated in the Quality Hotel Frontier Darwin, this rooftop restaurant offers great views of the city and ocean. The à la carte menu offers modern Australian cuisine accompanied by a comprehensive wine list. It is open daily for breakfast and dinner. The hotel, which was refurbished in 2000, is moderately priced.

FANNY BAY Pee Wee's ▤ ♿ ☂ $$$

Alec Fong Lim Drive, East Point Reserve, Fanny Bay, NT 0801 ***Tel** (08) 8981 6868*

This premier Darwin restaurant is situated in the East Point Nature Reserve only five minutes from Darwin's CBD. Pee Wee's offers spectacular views across the bay and has a reputation for fine dining. Try the fresh local saltwater barramundi and indulge in the white chocolate and orange-oil mascarpone cheesecake for dessert.

JABIRU Jabiru Sports and Social Club ▤ ♿ ☂ $

Lakeside Drive, NT 0886 ***Tel** (08) 8979 2326*

Jabiru is a pocket of modern life in an ancient landscape. The Sports and Social Club is a community hub offering meals. It welcomes visitors for a meal and a drink for lunch and dinner from Wednesday through to Saturday, lunch on Sunday, but no takeaway alcohol is permitted. The Jabiru Tourist Centre can be found at Jabiru Town Plaza.

JABIRU Aurora Kakadu ▤ ♿ ☂ $$

Arnhem Highway, South Alligator, Kakadu National Park, NT 0886 ***Tel** (08) 8979 0166*

Dinner is served buffet style at this tropical restaurant situated in this wetlands lodge. The menu includes fish dishes, cold meats, chicken, stir-fries and roasts. There is a salad bar and a range of desserts. The price is inclusive of tea and coffee. Enjoy this convenient, sumptious buffet or have a snack at the bistro which offers burgers and sandwiches.

JABIRU Gagudju Crocodile Holiday Inn Escarpment Restaurant ▤ ♿ $$$

Flinders Street, NT 0886 ***Tel** (08) 8979 9000*

This unique hotel is shaped like a crocodile. It is located in the heart of the world heritage listed Kakadu National Park. The restaurant is open all day and offers a full breakfast, a snack lunch menu and both buffet and à la carte dinner menus. A cocktail bar adjoins the restaurant.

Key to Price Guide *see p524* **Key to Symbols** *see back cover flap*

KATHERINE All Seasons Katherine ⬛♿🖨 Ⓢ
*Stuart Highway, NT 0850 **Tel** (08) 8972 1744*

This beautiful garden restaurant and bar is situated in the All Seasons Katherine, which is an Accor Hotel with a swimming pool, tropical environs. The restaurant offers alfresco dining for guests and visitors. It is conveniently located close to the Katherine Gorge, the Cuta Cuta Caves and the Mataranka thermal pool.

KATHERINE Kumbidgee Lodge 🏞♿🖨 Ⓢ
*Gorge Road, NT 0850 **Tel** (08) 8971 0699*

On the way to Nitmiluk, the traveller can stop here for breakfast or a Devonshire tea. The "bush breakfast" is a favourite with locals and travellers. It is generous and includes cereal, bacon and eggs, mushrooms, toast and tea or coffee. Try the barramundi for lunch or dinner. The pub menu offers steaks, lasagne, fish and chips and dessert.

KATHERINE Shanghai Chinese Restaurant 🏞⬛♿ Ⓢ
*Katherine Terrace, NT 0850 **Tel** (08) 8972 3170*

This corner café serves reasonably priced Chinese meals. It offers traditional Chinese cooking with an Australian influence. Katherine is famous for the rugged beauty of its surrounding countryside. The Nitmiluk Katherine Gorge is spectacular and the wetlands of Kakadu are alive with wildlife.

TENNANT CREEK Margo Miles Steakhouse ⬛♿ ⓈⓈ
*146 Patterson Street, NT 0860 **Tel** (08) 8962 2006*

This award-winning steakhouse offers great food, wine and atmosphere. Steaks include rump, rib, scotch fillet and T-bone, all done to the customer's preference and served with chips and salad. The menu also offers a range of seafood dishes, including grilled or battered barramundi. There is a comprehensive list of Australian wines.

THE RED CENTRE

ALICE SPRINGS Annie's Place ⬛♿🖨 Ⓢ
*4 Traeger Avenue, NT 870 **Tel** (08) 8952 1545*

One for the budget-conscious traveller who feels the need for a hearty feed. It's the sort of place you can take a load off, relax to some groovy tunes and chat with the friendly staff. The home-made pizzas for one are pretty popular while the pick of the menu is probably the spicy kangaroo curry. A cosy café atmosphere.

ALICE SPRINGS Bar Doppio 🍴🏞⬛♿🖨 Ⓢ
*Shop 2, Fan Arcade, Todd Mall, NT 870 **Tel** (08) 8952 6525*

One for the health-conscious snackers. Although not exclusively, Bar Doppio caters well for vegetarians and vegans, and has a variety of wholesome foccacias and soups available. It has funky fresh food and a friendly atmosphere. Patrons easily distracted by kitchen clatter might want to sit outside under the shade covers.

ALICE SPRINGS Casa Nostra Pizza and Spaghetti House 🏞⬛ Ⓢ
*Shop 2, Undoolya Road, NT 870 **Tel** (08) 8952 6749*

This is traditional Italian dining right down to the red-and-white chequered tablecloths. Family owned and operated, it's affordable, hearty Italian cuisine. The pasta sizes are generous, as is the service. Garlic bread aficionados have something to write home about. Admirers of authentic Italian decor and relaxed family atmosphere will too.

ALICE SPRINGS Outback Bar & Grill ⬛♿🎵🖨 Ⓢ
*75 Todd Mall, NT 870 **Tel** (08) 8952 7131*

Recently renovated to create more of a modern feel, this casual eatery is reputedly home to some of the coldest beer in the Red Centre, thanks to specially chilled tap handles. As you drink your ice-cold beer, you can watch the chefs grill your steak right in front of you to make sure it's done just right! Remember, too many cooks...

ALICE SPRINGS Red Dog Australiana Café 🍴🏞⬛♿🖨 Ⓢ
*64 Todd Mall, NT 870 **Tel** (08) 8953 1353*

Good food and good value for money. A hearty bushman's breakfast or a lazy light lunch here won't set you back too much. Choose from the whole bacon and egg shebang or tuck into fresh sandwiches and coffee. It's a cosy café, with saddles and bridles and other horsey things all around.

ALICE SPRINGS Alfresco Café Bar and Restaurant ⬛🖨 ⓈⓈ
*Cinema Complex, Todd Street, NT 870 **Tel** (08) 8953 4944*

A lovely place to stop by for breakfast, lunch or dinner on any day of the week. The food is simple yet satisfying. It's mostly standard café fare with an Italian influence. Expect good soups, crunchy bruschetta and a variety of tasty pastas. This place is perhaps best known for its quality pastries, great coffee and friendly relaxed atmosphere.

ALICE SPRINGS Barra on Todd Restaurant ⬛♿🎵🖨 ⓈⓈ
*34 Stott Terrace, NT 870 **Tel** (08) 8951 4545*

While the menu does try to cater for most tastes, the emphasis is definitely on seafood. Some of these dishes are simply mouthwatering. Try the char-grilled barramundi with lemon and dill risotto topped with a Moreton Bay bugtail and champagne caviar butter. It's a relaxed setting. You can dine by the pool or tuck yourself away in a quiet corner.

ALICE SPRINGS Keller's Restaurant
20 Gregory Terrace, NT 870 **Tel** *(08) 8952 3188*

A genuinely eclectic menu created by an original personality. Swiss-trained chef Beat Keller can serve anything from camel spring rolls to home-made roasted wattleseed ice cream with everything Swiss and Indian in between. An award-winning restaurant for restaurant lovers.

ALICE SPRINGS Oriental Gourmet Chinese Restaurant
80 Hartley Street, NT 870 **Tel** *(08) 8953 0888*

For locals and tourists alike, this is the Asian restaurant of choice in town. Its affordable Cantonese cuisine is served in a buzzing friendly atmosphere. The signature dish is probably the honey prawns: battered prawns coated with honey and topped with sesame seeds. For a dessert with a difference, try the Galliano fried ice cream.

ALICE SPRINGS Oscar's Café and Restaurant
Cinema Complex, Todd Mall, NT 870 **Tel** *(08) 8953 0930*

Winner of the 2004 Gold Plate award for Best Northern Territory Café. The menu is Mediterranean influenced, with seafood being a speciality. Try the baked barramundi fillet with lemon butter and herb/garlic glaze. The superb food is served by staff with a great attitude in a comfortable clean environment. Bookings are recommended.

ALICE SPRINGS Seasons Restaurant
10 Gap Road, NT 870 **Tel** *(08) 8952 1444*

A truly international menu and a relaxed setting make this a place worth visiting. Choose from a wide variety of dishes, including European, Asian, Mediterranean and, of course, Australian. A children's menu is available, but you don't need to be young to enjoy the dessert speciality: a chocolate soufflé with locally made rum-and-raisin ice cream.

ALICE SPRINGS Ainslie's Restaurant
46 Stephens Road, NT 870 **Tel** *(08) 8952 6100*

Local wonderchef Craig Lovewell takes care of all things food here. The à la carte menu is predominantly modern Australian cuisine with an international influence and an emphasis on quality produce. It's elegant yet affordable dining for the family in a relaxed atmosphere.

ALICE SPRINGS Bojangles Saloon and Restaurant
80 Todd Street, NT 870 **Tel** *(08) 8952 2873*

The food is quality and about as Outback as it gets, but with an international twist. Try a home-made camel and Guinness pie, or perhaps a Thai-style crocodile salad. At night there is a live radio show broadcast from the bar, which just adds to the already vibrant atmosphere.

ALICE SPRINGS Samphire Restaurant
93 Barrett Drive, NT 870 **Tel** *(08) 8950 7777*

Named after an edible herb found in the salt marches, this restaurant is well known for its quality contemporary Australian cuisine. Emu steak and tempura crocodile are just two of the delicious native delicacies on offer. Families are well catered for, poolside dining is an option and there is a special menu for children.

WATARRKA Carmichael's
Kings Canyon Resort, Luritja Road, Watarrka National Park, NT 872 **Tel** *(08) 8956 7442*

With outstanding views of Kings Canyon, this restaurant is a good one for families. Every paying adult allows an accompanying child under the age of 15 to eat for free. Choose from a huge buffet of seafoods, roast meats, salads and desserts. There's even some camel and buffalo for those with adventurous tastes. Bookings are essential.

YULARA Bough House Restaurant
Outback Pioneer Hotel, Yulara Drive, NT 872 **Tel** *(08) 8957 7888*

This is a good place for families. Meals are free for children under the age of 15. There is an extensive buffet including a mouthwatering roast meat carvery, fresh seafoods, crispy salads and desserts. The rustic homestead-style decor only adds to the Outback experience, as does the restaurant's famous kangaroo pie.

PERTH AND THE SOUTHWEST

ALBANY Hands-on Restaurant
42 Stirling Terrace, Albany, WA 6330 **Tel** *(08) 9842 9696*

Australian cuisine and a recent addition to Albany's dining scene, Hands-on has a mainly traditional menu plus some more adventurous creations. Non-carnivores should tuck into the scrumptious vegetarian parcels while fish-lovers will appreciate the fresh roast trout. The restaurant is regularly fully booked on Saturdays.

AUGUSTA August Moon Chinese Restaurant
3 Matthew Flinders Shopping Centre, Allnutt Street, Augusta, WA 6290 **Tel** *(08) 9758 1322*

Authentic Chinese cuisine and a massive menu, this is the town's only Asian restaurant. The accommodating staff serve a large choice of Chinese dishes in a warm, inviting ambience. Popular and regular favourites include chow mein, chicken and cashew nuts and special fried rice. Ideally located in the centre of the township. BYO.

Key to Price Guide *see p524* **Key to Symbols** *see back cover flap*

BRIDGETOWN Tongue and Groove Café $$

Ford House Retreat, Eedle Terrace, Bridgetown, WA 6255 **Tel** *(08) 9761 1816*

This boutique café doubles up as a restaurant from Fridays to Sundays, serving contemporary Australian cuisine. They produce well-presented light meals, including many vegetarian choices and a range of desserts and cakes. The boysenberry and strawberry crepes are a big draw. Reservations are required.

BUNBURY VAT 2 $$$

2 Jetty Road, Bunbury, WA 6230 **Tel** *(08) 9791 8833*

Bunbury dining at its best with vistas across the harbour and Jetty Baths. Modern Australian cuisine including the chef's grazing plate or the daily ocean catch. Other highlights are the French and Spanish cheese platters and the tempting dessert menu (try warm chocolate pudding or raspberry risotto).

BUSSELTON Esplanade Hotel $

Lot 1, Marine Terrace, Busselton, WA 6280 **Tel** *(08) 9752 1078*

Affectionately known by locals as the Nard, The Esplanade is touted as Busselton's most popular pub-restaurant, offering hearty meals at reasonable prices. They have a regular menu plus daily specials on the blackboard and a children's menu. Sit in the big open dining area or the beer garden and enjoy the amiable, informal atmosphere.

BUSSELTON Equinox Café $$

Queen Street, Busselton, WA 6280 **Tel** *(08) 9752 4641*

Prominently located beside Busselton's famous jetty *(see p314)*, the venue has three main dining areas and genuinely friendly service. The menu is contemporary and varied, with everything from silken tofu, tandoori chicken, chilli mussels, steak sandwiches and house-baked cakes. Popular with locals and tourists and open for three meals a day.

COWARAMUP Vasse Felix Winery and Restaurant $$$

Caves Road (cnr Harmans Road South), Cowaramup, WA 6284 **Tel** *(08) 9755 5242*

Contemporary Australian cuisine combining fresh, regional ingredients with European and Asian influences. The winter and summer menus and excellent wines are well worth the steep prices. It has sweeping views of the vineyards. Open for lunch only. Later you can visit the permanent art collection.

DENMARK Mary Rose Restaurant $

11 North Street, Denmark, WA 6333 **Tel** *(08)9848 2899 / 9848 1260*

This easygoing establishment serves good, wholesome country food at exceptionally fair prices. Plates are varied and include the contemporary favourite Morroccan lamb tagine. The restaurant has a seating area under a grand old veranda and is nestled beside the Old Butter Factory Gallery. BYO.

ESPERANCE Ollies Café $

51 The Esplanade, Esperance, WA 6450 **Tel** *(08) 9071 5268*

Café-style eating surrounded by plain and simple decor, this is a well-liked local dining haunt. They offer hot and cold meals with a minimum of fuss. The retro eating booths are under-rated and the juicy steaks very well regarded. The café is part of Bonaparte Seafood Restaurant located above Ollie's. BYO and closed Mondays.

HYDEN Sandalwood Restaurant $

2 Lynch Street, Hyden, WA 6359 **Tel** *(08) 9880 5052*

Buffet-style breakfasts and dinners in an informal setting at the Wave Rock Motel Homestead. It closes on some nights, when the homestead's sister, The Bush Bistro, serves grill-and-salad-style meals, otherwise it's seven days a week dining for breakfast, lunch and dinner.

KALGOORLIE Top End Thai Restaurant $

71 Hannan Street, Kalgoorlie, WA 6430 **Tel** *(08) 9021 4286*

Great Thai cooking set in an historic 1897 building, which is one of the oldest in town. It has three open dining areas in the garden and indoors. The menu's emphasis is on authentic Thai food and the wide selection of dishes include a vegetarian menu and a chef's speciality menu. BYO.

KALGOORLIE Saltimbocca $$

90 Egan Street, Kalgoorlie, WA 6430 **Tel** *(08) 9022 8028*

Centrally located and easily accessible, this eatery opened in 2003 and offers standard Italian meals and speedy service. Not surprisingly, the dish saltimbocca (a Roman speciality made with veal and prosciutto) is on the menu. Relaxed, casual atmosphere and a roaring tourist trade. Only open for dinner and closed on Sundays.

MANDURAH Jolly Frog Restaurant $$$

8 Rod Court, Mandurah, WA 6210 **Tel** *(08) 9534 4144*

Jolly Frog boasts an international menu with some highly original dishes, such as rack of lamb with crushed macadamia nuts or marinated kangaroo with redcurrants. Vegetarian choices are included in the menu and the seafood is guaranteed fresh. Superb views over the Dawesville Channel are another attraction.

MARGARET RIVER Arc of Iris $

1/151 Bussell Highway, Margaret River, WA 6285 **Tel** *(08) 9757 3112*

Modern café cuisine in a somewhat eccentric, sometimes hippie and always fun atmosphere. An à la carte menu with a touch of France come thanks to the proud French proprietor. Popular with both locals and visitors, this funky eatery includes a room at the back with communal tables and armchairs. BYO.

MARGARET RIVER The Berry Farm Tea Rooms $

Bessell Road, Margaret River, WA 6285 **Tel** *(08) 9757 5054*

A café-style eatery located 15 km (9 miles) from the centre of Margaret River. This picturesque garden café has regular menu changes to reflect the seasons. A staple home-made favourite is beef and red wine pie. Wander around the farm to help burn off the delicious boysenberry pie. Strictly BYO and country hospitality.

MARGARET RIVER The 1885 at The Grange on Farrelly $$

Farrelly Street, Margaret River, WA 6285 **Tel** *(08) 9757 3177*

Located in a grand, 1885 building, this is a top-notch restaurant and hotel. The menu changes daily and boasts an exciting fusion of local and Asian ingredients and ideas. There is a good range of local wines and a warm, friendly ambience. They serve dinners daily except Sunday.

MARGARET RIVER Leeuwin Estate Winery Restaurant $$$

Stevens Road, Margaret River, WA 6825 **Tel** *(08) 9759 0000*

Classic European fare at the most prestigious restaurant in the Margaret River area. Honours include Prix d'Honneur, so not surprisingly this triple Gold Plate Award winner is formal and expensive. The menu reflects seasonal produce and intelligent wine selections. They only open for lunch plus Saturday for dinner (bookings are essential).

MARGARET RIVER VAT 107 $$$

107 Bussell Highway, Margaret River, WA 6285 **Tel** *(08) 9758 8877*

This is a fresh, feel-good venue where the philosophy of the menu is "clean and simple". The focus is on fresh, organic products (the cloverdene lamb is a treat). Interior features include polished floorboards, marble counters and classy decor. VAT 107 serves breakfast, lunch and dinner, and is right in the centre of Margaret River.

PEMBERTON Gloucester Ridge Café $$

Burma Road, Pemberton, WA 6260 **Tel** *(08) 9776 1035*

A relaxed, contemporary setting at the Gloucester Ridge Vineyard and the perfect stop on the way to the Gloucester Tree Top. There is a great decking area with tremendous views of the Karri Forest. The chef focuses on local products, such as grilled Pemberton marron. Popular for lunch and only open for dinner on Saturdays.

WILYABRUP Flutes Restaurant $$$

Caves Road, Wilyabrup, WA 6284 **Tel** *(08) 9755 6250*

Flutes is part of Brookland Valley Winery and overlooks Willyabrup Brook and the estate gardens. The magical setting is matched by exquisite, contemporary European cuisine strongly influenced by the chef's French roots. There is also a fine dessert menu. Soak up the ambience and later browse the range of gourmet products on sale.

NORTH OF PERTH AND THE KIMBERLEY

BROOME Frangipanis Café Restaurant $

5 Napier Terrace, Broome, WA 6725 **Tel** *(08) 9193 6766*

Opened in 2003, Frangipanis has fast gained a "good food good prices" reputation. The menu has a Mediterranean influence and there is a garden area to enjoy Kimberley-style carefree dining under the stars. They serve food throughout the day and the evening.

BROOME Wing's Chinese Restaurant $

Lot 18, Napier Terrace, Broome, WA 6725 **Tel** *(08) 9192 1072*

A very popular place with locals and visitors who fancy genuine Chinese cuisine. Located in the heart of Chinatown, diners can expect fresh meats and vegetables stir-fried with delicious Chinese sauces. Beef chop suey and vegetable spring rolls dipped in sweet chilli sauce are big favourites. BYO.

BROOME Cable Beach Sand Bar & Grill $$

Cable Beach Road, Broome, WA 6726 **Tel** *(08) 9193 5090*

Tourists come to watch the sunset over an outdoor dinner at this popular Cable Beach restaurant. A massive Oz-classic menu includes everything from fish, poultry, red meat, vegetarian, pasta, and bakery food. The prepay at the counter ordering system works well at peak eating times during breakfast, lunch and dinner.

BROOME Matso's $$

60 Hammersley Street, Broome, WA 6725 **Tel** *(08) 9193 5811*

A unique Australian-Asian themed restaurant situated in Matso's Brewery with views of Roebuck Bay. It serves delicious dishes, including a superb Indian curry, or for something different try crocodile shanks with spices, herbs and mango. Cold boutique beers are brewed on site.

CARNARVON Water's Edge $

28 Olivia Terrace, Carnarvon, WA 6701 **Tel** *(08) 9941 1181*

Standard pub meals served in the large indoor dining area or the small outdoor setting overlooking the sea. The food is excellent given the budget prices, with decent portions served in an informal and friendly atmosphere. The restaurant is part of the Carnarvon Hotel, which is popular with the town's residents.

Key to Price Guide *see p524* **Key to Symbols** *see back cover flap*

CERVANTES Sea Breeze Café 📋⛱ $

10 Cadiz Street, Cervantes, WA 6311 ***Tel*** *(08) 9652 7233*

A small, standard country café serving basic meals, fast-food takeaway and made-to-order sandwiches and rolls. They also serve tasty pizzas plus fizzy drinks and juices. The owner is very welcoming and used to visitors using the café as convenient pit stop for visits to the Pinnacles and Nambung National Park *(see p324)*.

CORAL BAY Ningaloo Reef Café ♿🧒 $

Lot 1, Robinson Street, Coral Bay, WA 6701 ***Tel*** *(08) 9942 5882*

This place has something for everyone, including fish, steak, chicken and vegetarian dishes. It is also particularly famous for its made-to-order pizzas. Cheerful service and a happy to please attitude makes for a leisurely meal. The café has indoor and outdoor dining areas and also does takeaways.

DAMPIER Barnacle Bob's Restaurant ⛱📋♿🧒 $

The Esplanade, Dampier, WA 6713 ***Tel*** *(08) 9183 1053*

A standard seafood restaurant with outstanding waterfront views. They use only fresh fish and cook it the way the customer prefers: grilled, battered, deep-fried or pan-fried. Try the grilled northwest snapper with chips and salad. An ideal location for sunset watchers to enjoy the balmy evenings in the casual outdoor dining setting. BYO.

DENHAM Old Pearler Restaurant 📋♿🧒 $$

Knight Terrace, Denham, WA 6537 ***Tel*** *(08) 9948 1373*

Its claim to fame is that it is the only restaurant in the world made of coquina shell. It is also full of character and uses quality local seafood for many dishes. Apart from choice ingredients, the philosophy reflected in the menu is to emphasize healthy cooking (hence nothing is deep-fried). Bookings are recommended.

DERBY Wharf Restaurant ⛱📋♿🧒 $

1 Jetty Road, Derby, WA 6728 ***Tel*** *(08) 9191 1195*

With a massive outdoor setting overlooking King Sound, Wharf specializes in fresh seafood dishes. The menu also includes chicken, beef and a variety of other options. Prices are more than fair and the service is relaxed and cheerful. They are open from Tuesday to Saturday and be sure to book ahead. BYO.

EXMOUTH Whalers Licensed Restaurant 📋♿🧒 $$

5 Kennedy Street, Exmouth, WA 6707 ***Tel*** *(08) 9949 2416*

Whalers has the reputation of informal dining and quality food, with the speciality being Kailis prawns. It also presents other seafood dishes and tender steaks and are genuinely happy to accommodate vegetarian requests. It has an outdoor dining area and friendly country service. Open for breakfast, lunch and dinner.

GERALDTON Tanti's Restaurant ⛱📋♿ $

174 Marine Terrace, Geraldton, WA 6530 ***Tel*** *(08) 9964 2311*

The reputation of this Thai restaurant has spread, so much so that the Thai ambassador to Australia went out of his way to eat there in 2002. The decor may be simple but the food is exquisite. The main ingredients are mostly locally grown or caught, including fresh crustaceans and herbs. BYO.

HALLS CREEK Gabi's Restaurant 📋♿ $$

Roberta Avenue, Halls Creek, WA 6770 ***Tel*** *(08) 9168 6101*

Gabi's is part of the Kimberley Hotel and offers Mediterranean and international dishes. Open for breakfast, lunch and dinner, vegetarians will be pleased to know they are also catered for in the mainly carnivorous-orientated menu. There is a surprisingly good wine list and children's meals are available.

KALBARRI Finlays Fresh Fish BBQ ⛱♿🎵🧒 $

McGee Crescent, Kalbarri, WA 6536 ***Tel*** *(08) 9937 1260*

Situated on the old iceworks site, this seafood eatery is well frequented and recommended by most of the locals. Specializing in seafood barbecue-style cooking, it has outdoor seating and a great atmosphere. The barramundi and prawns with fresh damper and salad is excellent. Fish-free dishes are also on the menu. Closed Mondays. BYO.

KALBARRI Black Rock Café 📋♿🧒 $$

80 Grey Street, Kalbarri, WA 6536 ***Tel*** *(08) 9937 1062*

This self-described "fine food restaurant and alfresco café" looks out onto the Murchison River. The international menu includes local ingredients with original results. Examples include kangaroo with half lobster mornay, local prawn and scallop mornay. Seafood platter for two is a popular choice. Closed Sunday nights and all day Mondays.

KARRATHA Etcetera Brasserie 📋♿ $$

Dampier Road (Cnr Hillview Road), Karratha, WA 6714 ***Tel*** *(08) 9185 3111/1800 099 801*

This pavilion restaurant located at Karratha International Hotel offers fine dining with both classic and contemporary cuisine. Choose from the elegant interior tables or the poolside alfresco area surrounded by tropical gardens. There is also luxury lounge seating and a bar. A popular Pilbara mingling place for tourists and locals.

KUNUNURRA Kelly's Bar & Grill 📋♿ $

76 Coolibah Drive, Kununurra, WA 6743 ***Tel*** *(08) 9168 1024*

Classic Australian food served with bush hospitality. Run by the Country Club hotel, it is open for breakfast, morning tea, lunch and dinner. Evening meals specialize in steaks and seafood. Dine inside in air-conditioned comfort or outdoors in the exotic garden. The bar is a quiet drinking place popular with locals.

NEW NORCIA Salvado's Restaurant ☀ 📋 ♿ $

Monastery Roadhouse, Great Northern Highway, WA 6509 ***Tel*** *(08) 9654 8020*

Named after the town's founder, Salvado's is a no-frills roundhouse sit-down restaurant with budget meals at reasonable prices. A stand-out choice is New Norcia focaccia toasted with ham, cheese, tomato and pesto. New Norcia's famous bread is available, freshly baked in the monastary bakery. BYO.

SHARK BAY The Bough Shed ♿ 🪑 $$

Monkey Mia Dolphin Resort, WA 6537 ***Tel*** *(08) 9948 1171*

This beachfront restaurant has the privilege of being a stone's throw away from where the Monkey Mia dolphins come in to greet tourists *(see p327)*. Meals are served throughout the day, including an excellent range of cooked breakfasts. Grilled Shark Bay pink snapper will please seafood lovers. The bar stays open until midnight.

ADELAIDE AND THE SOUTHEAST

ADELAIDE Goodlife Modern Organic Pizza ☀ 📋 ♿ 🪑 $

170 Hutt Street, SA 5000 ***Tel*** *(08) 8223 2618*

This is delicious, healthy pizza with a difference from the only fully certified organic restaurant in Adelaide. There are heaps to try but perhaps the pick of the bunch is the free-range roast duck pizza with shiitake mushrooms, spring onions and home-made ginger jam. It's tasty, affordable stuff in a relaxed environment with friendly, efficient staff.

ADELAIDE Jerusalem Sheshkebab House 🍷 ☀ 📋 ♿ $

131B Hindley Street, SA 5000 ***Tel*** *(08) 8212 6185*

You'd be hard pressed to get a better meal in Adelaide at this price. This family owned and operated restaurant is one of the best kept secrets in the city's vibrant West End. The *kafta* with spicy yoghurt sauce is divine and the home-made hummus dip is to die for. It is BYO only and bills must be paid in cash but it's definitely worth the extra effort.

ADELAIDE Mandarin House Restaurant ☀ 📋 $

47A Gouger Street, SA 5000 ***Tel*** *(08) 8231 3833*

This family restaurant specializes in delicious Northern Chinese dishes. It's affordable and scrumptious fare. There is an almost overwhelming choice of dishes. The sizzling beef with snow peas has a nice bit of zing, and the vegetarian dumplings, either steamed or fried and served with a chilli sauce must be tried.

ADELAIDE Worldsend Hotel ☀ 📋 ♿ 🪑 $

208 Hindley Street, SA 5000 ***Tel*** *(08) 8231 9137*

Excellent staff and an artistically hip interior make this a fine place to kickback for a beer and a decent meal. The restaurant prides itself on its quality pub food with an original twist. It has a constantly changing menu with Asian and Italian influences. Stick around after dinner and there's a good chance of hearing some live jazz or a DJ.

ADELAIDE Ying Chow ☀ 📋 🪑 $

114 Gouger Street, SA 5000 ***Tel*** *(08) 8221 7998*

Delicious affordable Chinese food is the order of the day at Ying Chow. It's a great place to grab a quick lunch or to share a few tasty dinner courses with friends. There is a huge range of dishes to choose from but you shouldn't miss the broad bean curd with Chinese chutney. The salt-and-pepper tofu is also very good.

ADELAIDE Botanic Café ☀ 📋 ♿ 🪑 $$

4 East Terrace, SA 5000 ***Tel*** *(08) 8232 0626*

Great for drinks and suppers, this ultra-hip restaurant is situated nicely on the fringe of Adelaide's bustling East End. The cuisine is modern Italian, with organic and fresh South Australian produce a speciality. There is a huge communal, marble table as the centrepiece of the striking interior design.

ADELAIDE Crown & Sceptre ☀ 📋 ♿ ♫ 🪑 $$

308 King William Street, SA 5000 ***Tel*** *(08) 8212 4159*

Dining at the Crown & Sceptre can mean anything from an informal meal in the bar, beer garden or al fresco outdoor eating areas, through to an à la carte dining experience with all the trimmings. The staff are noticeably friendly and efficient, and the extensive and balanced wine list has been recognized nationally.

ADELAIDE House of Chow ☀ 📋 ♿ $$

82 Hutt Street, SA 5000 ***Tel*** *(08) 8223 6181*

David and Roz Chow have gone to great lengths to create not only an aesthetically pleasing ambience but also the best in Asian gourmet cuisine. The restaurant prides itself on its consistency and has won numerous awards for excellence. An indoor aquarium with live coral makes a impressive restaurant centrepiece.

ADELAIDE Jasmin Restaurant 📋 🪑 $$

31 Hindmarsh Square, SA 5000 ***Tel*** *(08) 8223 7837*

It's the restaurant of choice for the South Australian Premier and with good cause. It's an exquisite dining environment with mahogany tables and chairs, flowers aplenty and art on the walls. The quality Northern Indian style food is heaven for the senses. The head chef has been there for nearly 26 years and deserves his outstanding reputation.

ADELAIDE Pranzo

⚑🍽️♿🎵 $$

5 Exchange Place, SA 5000 **Tel** (08) 8231 0661

Situated in the heart of Adelaide's business and judicial district, this slick city restaurant buzzes all day long with the sound of lawyers, politicians and stockbrokers tucking into some of the tastiest southern Italian food around. Try the poached baby chicken, ox tongue and cottechino sausage with salsa verde. Dress sharp and eat well.

ADELAIDE Prince Albert Hotel

⚑🍽️♿🎵🚻 $$

254 Wright Street, SA 5000 **Tel** (08) 8212 7912

This friendly relaxed inner-city pub has a great atmosphere and food to match. It's traditional pub fare and good value for money. Pride in preparation, presentation and service is a priority for the staff at the Prince Albert, and it shows. There's regular live acoustic shows to keep things ticking along and the interior is clean and warm.

ADELAIDE Sprouts Vegetarian Cuisine

⚑🍽️🚻 $$

9 Hindmarsh Square, SA 5000 **Tel** (08) 8232 6977

This relatively new, award-winning restaurant gives a uniquely European twist to it's vegetarian dishes. The menu changes regularly but the meals are consistently as tasty as they are original. The vege burger de luxe lives up to its name magnificently, and for those with a sweet tooth, the chocolate lasagne is a must.

ADELAIDE Stanley's Great Aussie Fish Café

⚑🍽️♿🚻 $$

76 Gouger Street, SA 5000 **Tel** (08) 8410 0909

This bustling restaurant specializes in fresh seafood, simply prepared. Friendly staff and good service make any visit well worth while. The grilled octopus and the Moreton Bay bugs are superb, while the chips are good enough to eat just on their own. It's affordable enjoyable South Aussie seafood in a relaxed family environment.

ADELAIDE Universal Wine Bar

⚑🍽️♿🎵🚻 $$

285 Rundle Street, SA 5000 **Tel** (08) 8232 5000

Situated in the heart of Adelaide's East End, the Universal Wine Bar sets a dining standard all of its own. The menu is modern Australian with a French twist. The warm duck salad tossed with shiitake mushrooms is a favourite, and with more than 300 different wines to choose from, you are guaranteed to find the perfect match to any meal.

ADELAIDE Alphutte

🍽️♿🚻 $$$

242 Pultney Street, SA 5000 **Tel** (08) 8223 4717

With an emphasis on quality Swiss-European style cuisine, this landmark Adelaide restaurant has won a swag of national and international awards over the years. It's renowned for its authentic Swiss Roschti, a melt-in-the-mouth potato and onion cake that makes a delicious accompaniment to any of the tantalizing meals on offer.

ADELAIDE Auge

⚑🍽️♿ $$$

22 Grote Street, SA 5000 **Tel** (08) 8410 9332

Minimalistic decor and a stunning water feature provide a cool and modern setting in which Adelaide cultural movers and shakers come to enjoy this expertly prepared quality Italian cuisine. The friendly, smartly dressed staff are knowledgeable and highly efficient. The food is immensely satisfying. The experience is worth savouring.

ADELAIDE Gaucho's

⚑🍽️♿🚻 $$$

91 Gouger Street, SA 5000 **Tel** (08) 8231 2299

Australia's first Argentinean restaurant has a heavy emphasis on char-grilled meat – the beef is even butchered and aged on the premises. Watch out for their spicy chimmichurri sauce, a combination of olive oil, lemon juice, garlic, herbs, spices and fennel. It's a taste sensation not to be forgotten. Gaucho's is always busy, so bookings are essential.

ADELAIDE Jolleys Boathouse

⚑🍽️♿🚻 $$$$

Jolleys Lane, SA 5000 **Tel** (08) 8223 2891

Situated on the bank of Adelaide's Torrens River, this is a lovely place to enjoy fine dining at its best. The menu is contemporary with a hint of Mediterranean and Asian influence. The wine list is extensive, the decor relaxed and the service second to none. It's an ideal place for a quiet business lunch or an enjoyable evening with friends.

ADELAIDE Night Train Theatre Restaurant

🍽️♿🎵 $$$$

2A Light Square, SA 5000 **Tel** (08) 8231 2252

If you feel like something exciting and different, you should spend a Saturday night with the award-winning Night Train crew. The price of a meal includes three courses and a show. Fun and laughter are guaranteed as are quality large platters of delectable cuisine. Take a walk through the infamous Night Train tunnel and see where it leads you...

ANGASTON barr-Vinum

⚑🍽️♿🚻 $$$

Washington Street, SA 5353 **Tel** (08) 8564 3688

Co-owner Bob McLean swears that he started up this restaurant just to keep highly respected chef Sandor Palmai in the Barossa Valley. Whatever the case, Bob, fellow winemaker Chris Ringland and chef Palmai have applied their various expertise to make this one of the finest dining venues in the area. The barr-eden lamb is a menu highlight.

ARMERA Bonneyview Winery Restaurant

🍽️♿🎵🚻 $$

Sturt Highway, SA 5345 **Tel** (08) 8588 2279

Like many restaurants attached to wineries, this is a family owned establishment set in attractive surroundings. Summer is a great time to dine under the vines in the delightful Tuscan garden, while winter meals are best enjoyed inside by the open fires. Food is high quality traditional Australian cuisine with an emphasis on using local produce.

BRIDGEWATER Bridgewater Mill

$$$

Mount Barker Road, SA 5155 **Tel** *(08) 8339 9200*

Set amongst a grove of colourful trees in the beautiful Adelaide Hills, the Bridgewater Mill provides the absolute finest of dining experiences. The exquisite food in this multi-award-winning restaurant is in the gloriously capable hands of one of the country's most respected chefs, Le Tu Thai. Food and service rarely come better than this.

CLARENDON Royal Oak Hotel Clarendon

$$

47 Grants Gully Road, SA 5157 **Tel** *(08) 8383 6113*

Set in the picturesque Adelaide Hills, this old-style country pub restaurant is only a short but scenic drive from the city centre. The food is traditional modern Australian with an emphasis on quality seafood and steaks. It's a great place to sit out on a sunny veranda with a quiet beer and a hearty meal and watch the rest of the world go by.

COONAWARRA The Poplars at Chardonnay Lodge

$$

Riddoch Highway, SA 5263 **Tel** *(08) 8736 3309*

This is a restaurant that has not closed for one day in the past 21 years. Business must be good, and it's not surprising when you consider they are serving mouthwatering dishes such as pan-fried kangaroo fillet with quandong relish and Spanish onion glaze served on wild rocket.

COONAWARRA Upstairs at Hollick

$$$

Ravenswood Lane, SA 5152 **Tel** *(08) 8737 2752*

Set amid the Coonawarra vineyards, this was the first winery restaurant in the area. The dining room features floor to ceiling windows that ensure uninterrupted views over the Hollick "Neilson's Block" vineyard and beyond to the broader Coonawarra region. The menu presents modern Australian cuisine using fresh quality local produce.

CRAFERS Jimmies Café

$$

6 Main Street, SA 5152 **Tel** *(08) 8339 1534*

Half the menu changes on almost a weekly basis in this softly lit, wooden floored Adelaide Hills café. Best known for its delicious wood-oven pizzas and relaxed atmosphere, it's the sort of place you will drive a long way out of your way to visit. The food is an adventure to be enjoyed.

GLENELG Esca Restaurant and Espresso Bar

$$

Shop 13–15, Marina Pier, Holdfast Shores, SA 5045 **Tel** *(08) 8376 6944*

This beachfront eatery and espresso bar has couches and fireplaces throughout. Relax, warm and toasty, with a perfect coffee. Or alternatively, move outside and enjoy ocean views while eating quality European cuisine such as the seafood *cataplana*: local seafood infused with a Portuguese broth of exotic spices, garlic, wine and tomato.

GOODWOOD Brown Dog Café

$

143 Goodwood Road, SA 5034 **Tel** *(08) 8172 1752*

If you are looking for home-cooked comfort food with a gourmet twist, look no further. With a menu drawing on Asian, Indian and Cajun influences, Brown Dog is a comfortable café reminiscent of the Brunswick Street haunts in Melbourne. Hip and inviting, it's a great place to enjoy a tasty salt-and-pepper squid and a nice glass of wine.

HAZELWOOD PARK The Food Business

$$

4 Lenden Avenue, SA 5066 **Tel** *(08) 8379 8699*

Owners John Gabel and Cindy McFarlane have a passion for food and it shows. Their modern, clean restaurant is open daily for breakfast and lunch, and dinner on the last Friday of the month. Try the little oyster and leek pies: rich, petite delicacies in buttery coats topped with a sweet and sour shred of spinach with a hint of spice.

HINDMARSH The Governor Hindmarsh Hotel

$

59 Port Road, SA 5007 **Tel** *(08) 8340 0744*

This landmark live music venue has a spacious yet cosy feel to the main eating area. The food is high quality pub food prepared with care. The prime grain-fed Scotch fillet is served on potato and parsnip mash and topped with roasted field mushrooms and a rich shiraz glaze.

HYDE PARK The Melting Pot Restaurant

$$$$

160 King William Road, SA 5062 **Tel** *(08) 8373 2044*

An extremely classy and yet comfortably cosy venue, this restaurant specializes in excellent modern European cuisine. The aptly named "4 P's" makes for an inviting entrée: pigeon, porcini, polenta and parmesan. Main courses are just as tastefully intriguing. Desserts have to be experienced to be believed.

KENT TOWN Tincat Café Restaurant and Gallery

$$

107 Rundle Street, SA 5067 **Tel** *(08) 8362 4748*

Dine amongst an ever-changing display of local art. Stick around after dinner and enjoy some fine wine with a poetry reading. You never know quite what cultural treat is going to crop up at this marvellously bohemian retro hub of artistic activity. One thing is for sure, you are guaranteed fine food, excellent wine and superb service.

NORTH ADELAIDE The Wellington Tap & Grill

$

36 Wellington Square, SA 5006 **Tel** *(08) 8267 1322*

There is a range of quality dishes on offer but the speciality is Premium MSA grade steaks. It would be hard to find a better steak sandwich in all of North Adelaide. With 32 different beers on tap in the adjoining bar, a few hours at the Welly Tap & Grill can be every steak-and-beer lovers dream.

Key to Price Guide *see p524* **Key to Symbols** *see back cover flap*

NORTH ADELAIDE The British Hotel
$$

58 Finniss Street, SA 5006 **Tel** *(08) 8267 2188*

There is always a buzz around lunchtime in the beer garden at The British Hotel. Choose from the range of quality modern Australian dishes, or if you prefer, you can select a prime cut of meat from the kitchen and cook it yourself on the communal barbecue. Whatever the case, the food is easy to enjoy and the atmosphere even easier.

NORTH ADELAIDE The Greedy Goose
$$$

153–155 Melbourne Street, SA 5006 **Tel** *(08) 8267 2385*

They may have become minor celebrities after winning a reality television show but for the owners of this restaurant, it's always been about the food. Forget the hype. Instead, remember the Blue Lake beef fillet wrapped in prosciutto with warm confit potato and mushroom fricassee.

NORWOOD Martini Café
$$

59A The Parade, SA 5067 **Tel** *(08) 8362 7822*

This fine Italian restaurant is an integral part of Norwood's main culinary strip. It's chic: the walls are adorned with posters of 1950s film stars. The dishes are superb. Try the rabbit baked in a clay pot with potato, tarragon, wine and spices, or the taglierini with Port Lincoln blue swimmer crab meat, roma tomatoes, basil, chilli and mascarpone.

TANUNDA 1918 Bistro & Grill
$$$

94 Murray Street, SA 5352 **Tel** *(08) 8563 0405*

This restaurant gets its name from the foundation stone of the old villa in which it is housed. The interior has been tastefully modernized, the walls adorned with local art and pictures of vineyards. Open fires at each side of the main dining room provide a warm and cosy atmosphere in which to enjoy the excellent modern Australian cuisine on offer.

WEST BEACH Café Salsa
$$

5 West Beach Road, SA 5024 **Tel** *(08) 8235 1991*

This family run restaurant serves authentic mid-northern Italian cuisine. The interior is retro, with laminex-topped tables and chairs. There's a full range of tasty pastas available and some excellent vegetarian options, such as the eggplant parmigiana. The service is quite relaxed and the overall atmosphere is comfortable.

THE YORKE AND EYRE PENINSULAS AND THE FAR NORTH

ARDROSSAN The Ardrossan Top Pub Restaurant
$

36 First Street, SA 5571 **Tel** *(08) 8837 3008*

If it's a good ice-cold beer and a decent meal that you seek, then this is the place to go. Family owned and operated, the restaurant caters for those wanting a simple pub meal as well as those who prefer à la carte. The chef has over 30 years experience and there is an extensive dessert and coffee menu to work through.

AUBURN Rising Sun Hotel Restaurant
$$

Main North Road, SA 5451 **Tel** *(08) 8849 2015*

Traditional family fare and a friendly atmosphere are staples of this lively eatery. Choose from a variety of quality meat and fish dishes, or perhaps venture into the "stables steakhouse" and cook your own barbecue. Either way, it's all about relaxing and enjoying the quality food and wine.

AUBURN Tatehams
$$$$

Main North Road, SA 5451 **Tel** *(08) 8849 2030*

A fine dining experience not to be missed and a contemporary European menu to be applauded. The highlight of this exquisitely delicious food would have to be the marinated beef served with taro and stuffed with blue cheese. Sit comfortably at the country-style long tables and indulge in excellent food and an extensive wine list.

BLINMAN Blinman Hotel Restaurant
$

Main Street, SA 5730 **Tel** *(08) 8648 4867*

Relax on the veranda and enjoy quality modern Australian cuisine in picturesque surroundings. Try the baked pork fillet with honey or the native pepper leaf kangaroo. Sip some of South Australia's best wine by a Flinders Ranges sunset, then head back into the bar, where a roaring open fire makes it the place to be after a good meal.

CLARE Salt'n'Vines Bar and Bistro
$$$

Wendouree Road, SA 5453 **Tel** *(08) 8842 1796*

The balcony tables overlook the local vineyards and hills of the Clare Valley. It's an extremely pleasant spot in which to savour fresh seafood, steak and fine wine. There is also a special menu for kids, and a range of mouthwatering desserts, such as home-made ice cream flavoured with Bailey's. Live music on Fridays.

COOBER PEDY Umberto's
$$$

Desert Cave Hotel, 20 Hutchison Street, SA 5723 **Tel** *(08) 8672 5688*

It's the flagship restaurant of the world's only international underground hotel and there's something for everyone on the menu. Try the French onion soup with melted cheese and garlic croutons for starters. The Atlantic salmon fillet on roasted macadamia nuts, baked in paper bark and topped with Spanish onion salsa is also well worth a taste.

EDITHBURGH Sails Seafood and Steak Restaurant

Troubridge Hotel, Blanche Street, SA 5583 **Tel** *(08) 8852 6013*

As the name suggests, these guys like to keep the menu pretty simple. It's traditional pub fare with an emphasis on quality and local ingredients. Their signature dish is the Troubridge Rump, a nice thick piece of beef served with prawns on top and a wholegrain mustard sauce. Seafood and steak – not complicated, but delicious.

EDITHBURGH Faversham's

7 Edith Street, Edithburgh, SA 5583 **Tel** *(08) 8852 6373*

There's a comfortable Old World feel to this place, with its open fires and numerous antiques throughout. The owners won the 2004 SA Great Regional Award for best family business and it shows in the attitude of the service. It's affordable fine dining with a menu that stresses using local produce. Quality modern Australian cuisine.

MINTARO Mintaro Mews

Burra Street, SA 5415 **Tel** *(08) 8843 9001*

This restaurant caters beautifully for adults wanting a first-class meal in a warm, tranquil environment. The pot-belly stove and the flagstone floors help provide the perfect setting in which to enjoy a double-roasted duck or smoked rack of lamb. Up there with the best in modern Australian fine dining.

QUORN Old Willows Brewery Restaurant

Port Augusta Road, Pichi Richi Pass, SA 5433 **Tel** *(08) 8468 6391*

Built upon the remains of a burntout brewery, this award-winning restaurant is notable for its friendly country feel and tasty Australian cuisine. You can feast on smoked kangaroo, barramundi and quandong pie, while the Pichi Richi steam train rumbles past just metres from the restaurant. Bookings are essential.

RAWNSLEY PARK Woolshed Restaurant

Rawnsley Park Station, Hawker-Wilpena Road, SA 5434 **Tel** *(08) 8648 1026*

The view of the sunset upon the Chace Range is stunning. The food here is high quality and distinctly Australian. Try the Drover's Mix: a collage of steak, sausages, lamb, bacon and egg. Good stuff for the stomach and soul. The Woolshed is often full of song, from casual patron sing-alongs to organized operatic events.

SEVENHILL Skillogalee Winery and Restaurant

Trevarrick Road, via Clare, SA 5453 **Tel** *(08) 8843 4311*

Open fires in winter and the veranda in spring make this an idyllic dining setting. It was the first full-time professional winery restaurant in the Clare Valley and the building itself is over 150 years old. The menu is seasonal and while internationally influenced, relies on the best local fresh produce. Simple yet superb.

WALLAROO The Boat Shed Restaurant

Jetty Road, SA 5556 **Tel** *(08) 8823 3455*

It's so close to the beach that a lot of the seafood on offer comes straight off the boats, and you can't get fresher than that. The menu is heavily seafood oriented, even the wood-fire oven pizzas have a predominant ocean twist. The sea views and the affordable tasty dishes make this coastal eatery a place well worth visiting.

WHYALLA Alexander Motor Inn Restaurant

99 Playford Avenue, SA 5600 **Tel** *(08) 8645 9488*

This restaurant combines seafood caught along the Eyre Peninsula Coastline with the best locally farmed produce to create a menu that is consistently fresh and appetizing. Specialties are seafood, vegetarian fare and curries. For those who like a bit of family fun with their food, keep an eye out for the regular theme nights.

WILPENA Captain Starlight Bistro

Wilpena Pound Resort, Hawker-Wilpena Road, SA 5434 **Tel** *(08) 8648 0004*

This casual family orientated restaurant has a strong emphasis on food with an Australian twist. There's a kangaroo fillet served with roasted yam and native bush tomato salsa, and a Wilpena Pounder beefburger with home-made quandong and chilli sauce. Open wood fires in winter add a cosy touch.

WUDINNA Gawler Ranges Motel Restaurant

72 Eyre Highway, SA 5652 **Tel** *(08) 8680 2090*

It's all about the fresh air in Wudinna and, of course, the Fresh Eyre Lamb Pot. This signature dish is a simmering pot of succulent lamb and bacon, braised in red wine and herbs and topped with a layer of golden pastry. It's country cooking at its best, and just the thing to tuck into after a long day's sightseeing.

MELBOURNE

CENTRAL MELBOURNE Lebanese House Restuarant

264 Russell Street, VIC 3000 **Tel** *(03) 9662 2230*

Map *1 C2*

The dated travel posters haven't been updated since this restaurant opened in 1959. It's cheap, unpretentious and welcoming. The waiters have a wry sense of humour and there is an odd selection of left-wing cartoons taped to the wall beside the cash register. Great dips, kebabs and cardamom-infused coffee.

Key to Price Guide *see p524* **Key to Symbols** *see back cover flap*

CENTRAL MELBOURNE Pellegrini's 📋 ♿ $

66 Bourke Street, VIC 3000 ***Tel*** *(03) 9662 1885* ***Map*** *2 D2*

Noisy, fast, Italian and retro before its time. For many Melbourne baby boomers, this institution is the site of their first encounter with "spag bol", lasagne and espresso. It's still the benchmark for standard Italian food, and it's always a pleasure to pull up a stool at the bar. Lively conversation is mandatory.

CENTRAL MELBOURNE Supper Inn ⚑ 📋 $

15 Celestial Avenue, VIC 3000 ***Tel*** *(03) 9663 4759* ***Map*** *1 C2*

After ascending the flight of stairs leading from Chinatown's seedy Celestial Avenue, you may be disappointed at the lacklustre decor, but don't be deterred. The food here is as good and cheap as you're likely to find anywhere, with some oddities that are sure to challenge.

CARLTON Abla's ⚑ 📋 ♿ $$

109 Elgin Street, VIC 3053 ***Tel*** *(03) 9347 0006*

Abla's has staked a claim with many Melbournians as the spark that ignited an abiding love affair with Middle-Eastern (particularly traditional Lebanese) cuisine. Its location in a Victorian terrace on a busy Carlton thoroughfare seems odd, but any misgivings soon dissipate as hearty classics and welcoming service take over.

CARLTON Brunetti ⚑ 📋 ♿ ☂ $$

194 Faraday Street, VIC 3053 ***Tel*** *(03) 9347 2801*

This classy Italian venue with covered outdoor seating serves wonderful cakes, pastries, gelato, chocolates, nougat and biscuits, as well as club sandwiches, foccacia, calzone, bruschetta and java. The restaurant serves regional Italian cuisine. In 2005 they opened an outlet in the Melbourne City Square.

CENTRAL MELBOURNE Hanabishi 📋 ♿ $$

187 King Street, VIC 3000 ***Tel*** *(03) 9670 1167* ***Map*** *1 B3*

Often voted Melbourne's best Japanese restaurant (with very good reason), this is the place for sashimi, steaming hotpots and melt-in-your-mouth tempura. The lunchtime menu and atmosphere is less formal than at night, and popular with the denizens of Melbourne's nearby legal and financial districts.

CARLTON Hotel Lincoln 📋 ♿ $$

91 Cardigan Street, VIC 3053 ***Tel*** *(03) 9347 4666* ***Map*** *1 C1*

The management of this once-neglected corner pub, one street back from Lygon Street's hectic Italian restaurant strip, is keen to ensure that a revitalized venue and menu does not put off the locals. It's inexpensive, quality gastropub cuisine that's not afraid to present unlikely sounding restaurant menu items, such as meatloaf.

CARLTON Shakahari 📋 ♿ ☂ $$

201-203 Faraday Street, VIC 3053 ***Tel*** *(03) 9347 3848*

This vegetarian stalwart has a reputation for good value, inventive menus with a mainly Asian feel. Gone are the days of stodgy lentil bakes served in an earnest but dreary setting. Here the food is fresh and light, served in simple surroundings highlighted by two magnificent 19th-century Indian cloth paintings.

CARLTON University Cafe ⚑ 📋 ♿ ☂ $$

257 Lygon Street, VIC 3053 ***Tel*** *(03) 9347 2142*

This homely Lygon Street institution with on-street covered seating (a second home to generations of Melbourne University academics) has been serving up fine Italian pastas, seafood and foccacias since 1952. It's a great venue for people-watching, so be sure to secure an outside table early on sunny days.

CARLTON Toofey's Seafood Restaurant 📋 ♿ $$$

162 Elgin Street, VIC 3053 ***Tel*** *(03) 9347 9838*

If you take your seafood seriously and fancy a step up from fish and chips, this licensed restaurant (with a worthwhile wine list) shouldn't be missed. Its casual but smart atmosphere wins praise, as does its menu which aims to do the simple things well, like crab and fennel soup, and beer-battered King George whiting.

CENTRAL MELBOURNE Cafe Segovia 📋 ♿ ☂ $$

33 Block Place, VIC 3000 ***Tel*** *(03) 9650 2373* ***Map*** *1 C3*

Cafe Segovia was quick to stake a claim when Melbourne's CBD alleys and arcades renaissance took off in the 1980s and 1990s. It was the first café in Block Place, and is still one of the best. Its great coffee, cramped indoor and outdoor seating, youthful vibe and Spanish inspired café menu ensure it's always hectic.

CENTRAL MELBOURNE Funkfish 📋 ♿ ☂ $$

Federation Square, Cnr Flinders & Swanston sts, VIC 3000 ***Tel*** *(03) 9650 7011* ***Map*** *2 D4*

You can dine inside at this cool Federation Square option, or grab an outdoor table overlooking the Yarra, or simply take your beer-battered seafood of choice with you. The food ranges from simple fish soup with barley and truffle oil, to more exotic items such as steamed fillet of barramundi with coconut and tamarind sauce.

CENTRAL MELBOURNE Yu-u 📋 $$

137 Flinders Lane, VIC 3000 ***Tel*** *(03) 9639 7073* ***Map*** *2 D3*

Don't be mistaken in thinking you have been given the wrong address; this kooky little restaurant, entered from seedy Oliver Lane, serves good quality and reasonably priced Japanese classics. For anyone who has dined in Tokyo's Shibuya district, the smells here will take you back. Book ahead.

CENTRAL MELBOURNE Becco
📇 ♿ ⓈⓈⓈ

11–25 Crossley Street, VIC 3000 **Tel** *(03) 9663 3000* **Map** *2 D2*

Cool, inspired and modern Italian with casual but professional service. Although a relative newcomer, Becco has rightly staked a claim as one of Melbourne's finest. The restaurant serves up winners like roast duck with muscatel and grappa sauce, while the cheaper bar menu offers the likes of chilli flour-dusted calamari.

CENTRAL MELBOURNE Il Solito Posto
📇 ♿ ⓈⓈⓈ

Basement, 113 Collins Street, VIC 3000 **Tel** *(03) 9654 4466* **Map** *2 D3*

This restaurant is a popular lunchtime venue, although it also serves breakfasts and dinner. It is a welcoming, cosy and stylish basement trattoria, entered from George Parade, with slate floors, a bar and wooden tables. The menu is seasonal Italian, with an excellent wine list that offers local and Italian selections.

CENTRAL MELBOURNE Mask of China
📇 ♿ ⓈⓈⓈ

115–117 Little Bourke Street, VIC 3000 **Tel** *(03) 9662 2116* **Map** *2 D2*

An often-cited contender for Flower Drum's title as Melbourne's premier Chinese restaurant, and with good reason. As well as Cantonese dishes, this distinguished restaurant specializes in southern Chinese Chiu Chow cuisine. Its menu is as delicate as its table settings and the service is excellent.

CENTRAL MELBOURNE Shah's Madam Fang
🏠📇 ⓈⓈⓈ

27–29 Crossley Street, VIC 3000 **Tel** *(03) 9663 3199* **Map** *2 D2*

This romantic restaurant, named after a famous courtesan and tucked down a sidestreet, serves Modern Asian cuisine and inventive dishes, such as black-skinned chicken, in an intimate and sensuous Oriental atmosphere. Its wine list is always well considered and the staff attentive without being omnipresent.

CENTRAL MELBOURNE The European
📇 ♿ 🍴 ⓈⓈⓈ

161 Spring Street, VIC 3000 **Tel** *(03) 9654 0811* **Map** *2 D2*

One of Melbourne's best European wine lists is just the beginning at this top-end-of-town Parisian-styled bistro. It's smart and sophisticated and attracts the pre-theatre crowd. Politicians also duck in following question time at the state parliament across the road to enjoy the mainly French and Italian culinary repertoire.

CENTRAL MELBOURNE ezard
📇 ♿ ⓈⓈⓈⓈ

187 Flinders Lane, VIC 3000 **Tel** *(03) 9639 6811* **Map** *2 D3*

Chef Teage Ezard explores the possibilities and complexities of Modern Australian cuisine's love affair with Asia in an ultra-modern (and often noisy) setting. The menu is flavour packed and the wine list and staff are excellent. You can dine à la carte or enjoy the eight-course degustation or express lunch menus.

CENTRAL MELBOURNE Flower Drum
📇 ♿ ⓈⓈⓈⓈ

17 Market Lane, VIC 3000 **Tel** *(03) 9662 3655* **Map** *2 D2*

This Cantonese restaurant is often rated the best in Australia, let alone food-mad Melbourne. Although its regular clientele of media and sporting celebrities rubs shoulders with the Big End of Town, it's suprisingly relaxed and just as happy to accommodate a family celebration as a power lunch.

CENTRAL MELBOURNE Grossi Florentino
📇 ♿ ⓈⓈⓈⓈ

80 Bourke Street, VIC 3000 **Tel** *(03) 9662 1811* **Map** *2 D2*

Definitely one for that special occasion: the rich modern Italian food served by attentive staff in the fin-de-siècle Mural Room is memorable. The Cellar Bar and Grill are cheaper and less subdued, but equally pleasing. The wine list is always a talking point, with several top French and Italian producers to choose from.

CENTRAL MELBOURNE Langton's Restaurant and Wine Bar
📇 ⓈⓈⓈⓈ

61 Flinders Lane, VIC 3000 **Tel** *(03) 9663 0222* **Map** *2 D3*

Langton's is an established name in the Australian wine business and its basement wine bar and restaurant doesn't disappoint. Entrées include fried oysters with leek, tartare sauce and grilled Toulouse sausage while the rich and hearty main courses offer up rabbit, bouillabaisse and quince glazed duck breast. BYO Tuesday only.

CENTRAL MELBOURNE Mo Mo
📇 ⓈⓈⓈⓈ

Basement, 115 Collins Street, VIC 3000 **Tel** *(03) 9650 0660* **Map** *2 D3*

Chef and author Greg Malouf has pioneered modern Middle-Eastern cuisine in Australia, and Mo Mo is his stylish basement home away from home. The food is always aromatic and well conceived, with subtle and intriguing contrasts, such as spicy pigeon pie cooked with almonds, eggs and cabbage, or sticky fig and chocolate pudding.

CENTRAL MELBOURNE Taxi
📇 ♿ 🍴 ⓈⓈⓈⓈ

Level 1, Transport Hotel, Federation Square, Cnr Flinders & Swanston sts, VIC 3000 **Tel** *(03) 9654 8808* **Map** *2 D4*

In 2005 Taxi won Melbourne's most prestigious Restaurant of the Year award. Not bad going for Federation Square's new kid on the block. Modern Australian and Japanese cuisine combine with futuristic architecture and lighting and views over St Kilda Road, Southbank and Federation Square to deliver something truly special.

CENTRAL MELBOURNE Vue de monde
📇 ♿ ⓈⓈⓈⓈ

430 Little Collins Street, VIC 3000 **Tel** *(03) 9691 3888* **Map** *1 B3*

How does braised scallop with twice-cooked pork belly finished with spiced pumpkin purée sound? Melbourne's answer to Jamie Oliver, the youthful and European-trained chef-cum-author Shannon Bennett serves up exquisite modern French cuisine in his new CBD premises in the historic Normanby Chambers.

Key to Price Guide *see p524* **Key to Symbols** *see back cover flap*

COLLINGWOOD Jim's Greek Tavern ☀📋 $$

32 Johnston Street, VIC 3066 ***Tel*** *(03) 9419 3827*

Melbourne has the largest Greek population of any city except Athens, and this is one of the best classic tavernas in the city. It has everything you could wish for in a Greek restaurant, including generous seafood platters, fried saganaki, metzes and charcoal-grilled lamb. And it's good value.

FITZROY Babka ☀📋👶 $

358 Brunswick Street, VIC 3000 ***Tel*** *(03) 9416 0091*

This cramped but friendly café-cum-bakery made Brunswick Street sit up and beg when it opened several years ago. It serves light meals, many with a Russian flavour, although its meat pies and salad are a good value lunch option. Join the scene and grab an outdoor seat. The shoo-fly buns are also recommended.

FITZROY Ladro 📋♿ $$

224 Gertrude Street, VIC 3065 ***Tel*** *(03) 9415 7575*

An award-winning restaurant located in cosmopolitan Fitzroy, this new kid on the block offers an intimate setting with daily specials, crispy wood-fired pizzas and reasonably priced wine list. There is even a roast of the day. It's breezy and hugely popular, so book ahead.

FITZROY Mario's 📋👶 $$

303 Brunswick Street, VIC 3065 ***Tel*** *(03) 9417 3343*

Crisp white linen tablecloths, benchtop seats facing Brunswick Street and a couple on the street, classic café food (antipasto, pastas and specials) and slick waiting staff have made this bustling joint a favourite with the local art crowd. It's cramped and usually noisy inside, but well worth a visit. A Fitzroy favourite.

FITZROY Café Provincial ♿👶 $$$

299 Brunswick Street, VIC 3065 ***Tel*** *(03) 9417 2228*

A bustling, bohemian-type café which has undergone several changes of management but remains a Melbourne institution. They serve inexpensive French and Italian fare. It attracts a mixed crowd – backpackers to suits – and is a popular place with the locals at the end of a long night.

FITZROY Interlude 📋♿ $$$$

211 Brunswick Street, VIC 3065 ***Tel*** *(03) 9415 7300*

When the French-trained but English-born chef has won a major Young Chef of the Year award, you can rest assured you're in for something special. Both the limited à la carte and the seven-course degustation menus rely on fresh seasonal produce. Expect delights such as wild asparagus, chorizo and fried quail egg.

NORTH MELBOURNE The Court House ☀♿📋 $$$

86–90 Errol Street, VIC 3051 ***Tel*** *(03) 9329 5394*

In a neck of the woods not known for its fine dining, this former corner pub now serves reasonably priced gastropub cuisine. It also offers a decent wine list and an intimate dining room with open fire. Although the menu is never extensive, it knows how to impress with attention to detail and a careful choice of seasonal produce.

PRAHAN Jacques Reymond Restaurant 📋♿ $$$$

78 Williams Road, VIC 3181 ***Tel*** *(03) 9525 2178* ***Map*** *6 F3*

Jacques Reymond's exacting standards, devotion to seasonal produce and determination to challenge modern Australian cuisine delivers a flamboyant yet accessible menu in a magnificent setting. The two-storey former Victorian residence is a mecca for those seeking the perfect setting for a big occasion.

RICHMOND Richmond Hill Cafe and Larder ☀📋♿👶 $$

48–50 Bridge Road, VIC 3121 ***Tel*** *(03) 9421 2808* ***Map*** *4 D2*

Stephanie Alexander, doyenne of Australian cuisine, opened this light and airy venue, which serves great coffee and light breakfasts, brunches and lunches. The treasures in its cheese room are to die for, and they even have a Cheese Club. Such is its popularity that evenings are reserved for private functions.

RICHMOND Pearl 📋♿👶 $$$

631–633 Church Street, VIC 3121 ***Tel*** *(03) 9421 4599* ***Map*** *4 E3*

A pleasing blend of Asian influences continues to draw the crowds, many of them seasoned regulars. The staff is professional, the decor sleek and inviting, and you can dine in the restaurant or the bar. Offerings range from bacon and egg sandwiches to green peppercorn rubbed Jewfish and red duck curry.

SOUTH MELBOURNE O'Connell's 📋♿👶 $$

407 Coventry Street, VIC 3205 ***Tel*** *(03) 9699 9600*

This convivial corner pub's menu delivers reasonably priced and pleasing takes on Anglo pub grub standards like beef and Guiness pie, beer-battered flathead and burgers and chips. But it's not afraid to toss something different into the mix, such as smoked trout caesar salad with poached egg, wild onions and parmesan.

SOUTH MELBOURNE The Isthmus of Kra 📋👶 $$$

50 Park Street, VIC 3205 ***Tel*** *(03) 9690 3688* ***Map*** *3 A4*

A consistent and deserving award winner for its exotic decor, well-planned wine list and exquisitely presented Thai Nonya cuisine, including favourites such as red roast duck curry, king prawns in coconut crepe, and baked whole barramundi stuffed with lemongrass and chilli rempah and wrapped in bamboo leaves.

SOUTH YARRA Lynch's 　　　　　　　　　　　　　　　□🚼　　$$

133 Domain Road, VIC 3141 **Tel** *(03) 9866 5627* **Map** *3 B4*

Lynch's almost prides itself on keeping out the hoi polloi (especially kids), yet its menu dares to present simple offerings, such as King George whiting fillets with classic coleslaw, French fries and tartare, and corned beef (albeit on "braised cabbage with crispy lardons, mashed potato and mustard cream").

SOUTH YARRA Botanical 　　　　　　　　　　　　　□🚼🏠　　$$$

169 Domain Road, VIC 3141 **Tel** *(03) 9820 7888* **Map** *3 B4*

Named after the Botanic Gardens across the road, this restaurant is a favourite with South Yarra's well-healed set. The decor is hard-edged contemporary and the atmosphere unsuited to a romantic tête-à-tête. Nonetheless, the Mod Oz cuisine and wine list consistently score praise from Melbourne's food critics.

SOUTH YARRA Caffè e Cucina 　　　　　　　　　　　　　□🏠　　$$$

581 Chapel Street, VIC 3141 **Tel** *(03) 9827 4139* **Map** *4 E5*

This bustling Italian café and restaurant, with style and attitude aplenty, is a perennial favourite with Melbourne's younger celebrities and beautiful people. Inside it's dark and cramped. Outside, the Chapel Street tables and pocket-handkerchief balcony are perfect for people-watchers, and those keen to be seen.

SOUTH YARRA France-Soir 　　　　　　　　　　　🚼□🚼　　$$$$

11 Toorak Road, VIC 3141 **Tel** *(03) 9866 8569* **Map** *4 D5*

This energetic Traditional French bistro serves up "Plats de Résistance" such as filet de boeuf béarnaise, poissons du jour and boeuf bourguignon. Some claim it also serves Melbourne's best crème brûlée. The wine list and cellar are winners, and its French waiters play the part. Good fun and good value.

SOUTHBANK Cecconi's 　　　　　　　　　　　　　　□🚼🏠　　$$$

Ground Level, Crown Entertainment Complex, Southbank, VIC 3006 **Tel** *(03) 9686 8648* **Map** *1 B5*

Another award-winning favourite. Olimpia Bortolotto's restaurant, with views across the Yarra to the CBD, serves exquisite Modern Italian cuisine and classics, such as osso buco and risotto Milanese. For many well-healed Melbournians, this is quintessential Italian cooking. The wine list is heartily recommended.

SOUTHBANK Walter's Wine Bar 　　　　　　　　　　　□🚼🏠　　$$$

Upper Level, Southgate, Southbank, VIC 3006 **Tel** *(03) 9690 9211* **Map** *1 C4*

Offering views of the city, Flinders Street Station and the most lively stretch of the Yarra River, Walter's come up trumps for fine dining, and its wine list is up there with the very best. The setting is understated, the service impeccable, and the Mod Oz menu guaranteed to satisfy with offerings such as char-grilled kangaroo.

ST KILDA Cicciolina 　　　　　　　　　　　　　　　□🚼🏠　　$$

130 Acland Street, VIC 3182 **Tel** *(03) 9525 3333*

Earthy, full-bodied comfort food with a Modern Italian sensibility is the order of the day at this cosy Acland Street favourite (the eye fillet is always a winner). They don't take bookings, but you can wait for a spare restaurant seat to materialize while sampling the wine list and a fine antipasto out in the back bar.

ST KILDA Il Fornaio 　　　　　　　　　　　　　　　□🏠　　$$

2 Acland Street, VIC 3182 **Tel** *(03) 9534 2922* **Map** *5 B5*

One part industrial bakery, one part groovy cafe. Locals cruise through from breakfast till dark. It's a good place to enjoy a light lunch, or to find a healthy takeaway option in St Kilda. Try the filling ciabatta rolls with roasted vegetables. The coffee is always strong and the clientele makes it a place to be seen.

ST KILDA Café di Stasio 　　　　　　　　　　　　　　□🏠　　$$$

31 Fitzroy Street, VIC 3182 **Tel** *(03) 9525 3999* **Map** *5 B4*

Muted lighting, views onto Fitzroy Street, impeccable and friendly service in a small and cosy dining room, and a menu that takes homely Italian fare to another dimension sets this classy St Kilda establishment apart. The two-course set lunch menu, which includes a glass of wine, is recommended for diners on the run.

ST KILDA Donovans 　　　　　　　　　　　　　　🚼□🚼　　$$$

40 Jacka Boulevard, VIC 3182 **Tel** *(03) 9534 8221*

Views over the beach, the foreshore's cycle path, and Port Phillip Bay are just the beginning at Donovan's. Its beach-house inspired decor and self-assured Mediterranean menu can always be counted on to deliver finely rendered seafood dishes with ingredients such as Western Australian scampi and Balmain Bug.

ST KILDA The Stokehouse 　　　　　　　　　　　　□🚼🏠　　$$$

30 Jacka Boulevard, VIC 3182 **Tel** *(03) 9525 5555*

Upstairs you'll find a casual restaurant with polished boards, floor-to-ceiling windows and fantastic bay views. Downstairs you'll find outside tables where the menu items are generally cheaper. Seafood is not the only drawcard, but it's hard to pass up offerings such as calamari salad with Asian herbs and a mint lime dressing.

ST KILDA Circa, the Prince 　　　　　　　　　　　　□🚼　　$$$$

2 Acland Street, VIC 3182 **Tel** *(03) 9536 1122* **Map** *5 B5*

Subtle yet unexpected combinations define this modern European menu. The bill comes as a pleasant surprise after having enjoyed one of Melbourne's finest meals in a low-key but stylish setting. The wine list is befitting of Aladdin's Cave and the service is unobtrusive. Recommended treat for budget travellers.

Key to Price Guide *see p524* **Key to Symbols** *see back cover flap*

WESTERN VICTORIA

APOLLO BAY Bay Leaf Cafe

$$

131 Great Ocean Road, VIC 3233 **Tel** *(03) 5237 6470*

A laidback and friendly licensed café and local favourite, with beach views and inexpensive excellent breakfasts, lunches and dinners. At dinnertime the menu and atmosphere is a little more formal, but in Apollo Bay that simply means leave your shorts and surfboard at home.

APOLLO BAY Buff's Bistro

$$

51–53 Great Ocean Road, VIC 3233 **Tel** *(03) 5237 6403*

Just down the road from the Great Ocean Hotel and across the road from the beach, this fully licensed and comfortable tavern-style bistro offers Mediterranean dishes with an emphasis on local seafood. There is also an inexpensive children's menu and a cake cabinet to tempt you.

APOLLO BAY The Blue Olive

$$

311 Great Ocean Road, VIC 3233 **Tel** *(03) 5237 7118*

A busy café on the main street, especially during the Apollo Bay Music Festival (April). It has a bar, elevated views, and specializes in local produce. Vegetarians and vegans are well catered for, as are seafood and coffee lovers. It's BYO musical instruments between 3pm and 6pm on the first Sunday of each month.

APOLLO BAY Chris's Beacon Point Restaurant & Villas

$$$

280 Skenes Road, VIC 3233 **Tel** *(03) 5237 6411*

Chef Chris Talihmanidis, who has owned this Greek restaurant since the 1970s, blends Mediterranean flavours with local produce, especially seafood. The restaurant was recently rebuilt and now has floor-to-ceiling windows to maximize the dramatic coastal views from this hilltop location. The wine list is excellent.

BALLARAT AnsoniA

$$

32 Lydiard Street South, VIC 3350 **Tel** *(03) 5332 4678*

This warm and sophisticated restaurant at the rear of a boutique hotel offers a Mod Oz menu with a Mediterranean influence. It's open for breakfast, lunch and dinner, and despite a fire in the kitchen in 2005, the restaurant has managed to soldier on to ensure it provides one of Ballarat's best dining experiences.

BALLARAT Europa Café

$$

411 Sturt Street, VIC 3350 **Tel** *(03) 5331 2486*

Europa is a smart and inexpensive family friendly bistro, offering a traditional café menu spiced up with Middle-Eastern and Asian dishes. All-day breakfasts are popular and the wine list is one of the best in Ballarat. Lunches include burgers, pizzas, soups, pastas etc. Dinner could be tandoori chicken or lamb and prune tagine.

BALLARAT L'espresso

$$

417 Sturt Street, VIC 3350 **Tel** *(03) 5333 1789*

This popular restaurant serves Mod Oz cuisine with an Italian influence. It's open for breakfast, lunch and dinner, and offers good quality coffee, cakes and gelati. For lunch there are the usual Italian menu items: pasta, risotto etc. For dinner you might like to try the oven-baked Tasmanian salmon or char-grilled kangaroo fillet.

BENDIGO Bazzani

$$$

Howard Place, VIC 3550 **Tel** *(03) 5441 3777*

This smart restaurant, housed in an 1880s heritage-listed building opposite Rosalind Park, serves Mod Oz cuisine with an emphasis on local specialties, such as Holy Goat cheese and aged Kyneton Black Angus beef. It is the place for a grand night out in Bendigo, although lunches are a more casual affair.

BENDIGO Whirrakee

$$$

17 View Point, VIC 3550 **Tel** *(03) 5441 5557*

At this warm and inviting restaurant in Bendigo's historic Royal Bank Building, the Mod Oz menu samples the world's great cuisines, including French, Indian, Indonesian, Mediterranean and Vietnamese. The wine list features several local wines, including the fine Blackjack Shiraz and Passing Clouds Sauvignon Blanc.

CASTLEMAINE Templeton Cafe and Accommodation

$$

31 Templeton Street, VIC 3450 **Tel** *(03) 5472 5311*

This modest but smart café-restaurant in a small gold-rush era terrace enjoys a reputation with locals for quality dining in a relaxed atmosphere. The rear, north-facing courtyard is particularly popular on a sunny afternoon. Vegetarians are well catered for, as are those popping in for coffee and cake. Open Thu–Sun.

CASTLEMAINE Tog's Place

$$

58 Lyttleton Street, VIC 3450 **Tel** *(03) 5470 5090*

A cosy Castlemaine favourite. The food is hearty Mod Oz with Mediterranean and Asian tendencies. There is outdoor seating under the broad veranda at the front, and upstairs on the rooftop deck. The owners also operate the excellent delicatessen next door, which supplies local gourmet produce, quiche, bread and cheese.

DAYLESFORD Cliffy's   ⓢⓢ

30 Raglan Street, VIC 3460 **Tel** *(03) 5348 3279*

Down the hill from the Botanic Gardens and a few minutes' walk from the lively Sunday Market, this light and airy old shop is now a relaxed and mega-friendly café and produce store. It's perfect for a hearty slow-paced breakfast or a quick lunch, especially if you've managed to get an outside table on a sunny day.

DAYLESFORD Koukla   ⓢⓢ

82 Vincent Street, VIC 3460 **Tel** *(03) 5348 2363*

Frangos & Frangos' younger offshoot next door is a more humble affair, serving inexpensive Italian options such as pasta, risotto and pizza. It is open for breakfast, lunch and dinner, and its bi-fold doors, which open out onto Vincent Street, ensure that the atmosphere is relaxed and casual. Very pleasant on a sunny afternoon.

DAYLESFORD Frangos & Frangos   ⓢⓢⓢ

82 Vincent Street, VIC 3460 **Tel** *(03) 5348 2363*

This fine-dining option in a former pub on Daylesford's main street delivers Mediterranean (essentially Greek) cuisine in a romantic setting. It's popular with weekenders and Melbourne tourists who gravitate towards its sophisticated Melbourne ambience and quality wine list. Hence, it's quite a scene.

DAYLESFORD Lake House   ⓢⓢⓢ

King Street, VIC 3460 **Tel** *(03) 5348 3329*

Seasonal local produce works with a light and airy setting and service par excellence to deliver an award-winning Mod Oz dining experience. Dine beside the open fire or take a seat outside under a market umbrella and overlooking the picturesque lake. Regarded by critics as one of Australia's top restaurants.

DUNKELD Royal Mail Hotel Bistro   ⓢⓢ

Glenelg Highway, VIC 3294 **Tel** *(03) 5577 2241*

This 1850s pub on a lonely stretch of highway at the southern end of the Grampians mountain range was completely overhauled and modernized several years ago. It now offers fine Mod Oz cuisine in a sophisticated setting, complemented by an award-winning cellar and wine list, and great views of Mount Sturgeon.

ECHUCA Oscar W's Wharfside   ⓢⓢⓢ

101 Murray Esplanade, VIC 3564 **Tel** *(03) 5482 5133*

Overlooking the Murray River, Oscar W's takes the cake for perfect settings. Its Mod Oz menu sources local produce to create memorable dishes such as fettucine with yabbies, twice-cooked duck with cinnamon pearl couscous, and pavlova with dark chocolate sauce, passionfruit, fresh mint and double cream.

GEELONG Go Food   ⓢ

37 Bellarine Street, VIC 3220 **Tel** *(03) 5229 4752*

Great for all-day breakfasts, lunchtime burgers and foccacia, and inexpensive and casual dinners. A popular option with Geelong's smart young set, this licensed café serves great coffee and cakes. The sunny courtyard is popular and the retro interior decor and laidback service makes folks feel like settling in.

GEELONG Le Parisien   ⓢⓢⓢⓢ

15 Eastern Beach Road, VIC 3218 **Tel** *(03) 5229 3110*

For that Big Night Out in Geelong, most locals head to this classic French restaurant in a boatshed overlooking Corio Bay. The menu delivers classic Gallic favourites and standards such as French onion soup, bouillabaisse and soufflé au chocolat. For a French-Australian culinary detour, try the marinated kangaroo fillet.

LORNE Kosta's Taverna   ⓢⓢⓢ

48 Mountjoy Parade, VIC 3232 **Tel** *(03) 5289 1883*

Kosta's eponymous owner and his wife sold the business a few years ago, but this lively Greek seafood restaurant is still a great spot to tuck into calamari, grilled whiting or haloumi. The setting is light with white tablecloths and bentwood chairs right on Lorne's main strip and across from the beach. It's packed in summer.

MALMSBURY The Stables Pizzeria   ⓢⓢ

75 Mollison Street, VIC 3446 **Tel** *(03) 5423 2369*

On Friday and Saturday nights only, locals round up their kids and head to the small township of Malmsbury on the Calder Highway for the best gourmet pizzas for miles. The bluestone courtyard behind the jointly owned bakery is a relaxed setting and the pizzas, which include dessert options, are excellent.

MILDURA Ziggy's Café   ⓢ

145 Eighth Street, VIC 3500 **Tel** *(03) 5023 2626*

A popular family owned and operated licensed café that serves up Mediterranean inspired breakfasts, brunches and lunch. The food is more up-market than its prices would suggest, with daily specials such as king prawn and asparagus risotto. There is a children's menu and they do a brisk trade in coffee and cake.

MILDURA Stefano's Restaurant   ⓢⓢⓢⓢ

Cnr Deakin & Seventh sts, VIC 3502 **Tel** *(03) 5023 0511*

Located in the Grand Hotel's cellar, Stefano di Pieri's eponymous Italian restaurant is classic three-hat quality. Well known as the host of a successful TV cooking series (*A Gondola on the Murray*), Stefano is a dynamic advocate of local produce. His signature restaurant is a testament to his passion. Bookings advised.

Key to Price Guide *see p524* **Key to Symbols** *see back cover flap*

MOONAMBEL Warrenmang Vineyard Resort

🔳♿🏠 $$$

Mountain Creek Road, VIC 3478 **Tel** *(03) 5467 2233*

Lunches at this vineyard restaurant in Victoria's Pyrenees-style Ranges are a casual affair, while dinner is more formal. The Modern European cuisine offers light lunch specials such as warm potato and asparagus salad. For dinner you could expect wild hare and pork trotter with prunes, hickory nuts and truffle cream sauce.

PORT FAIRY Victoria Hotel

🛏🔳♿🎵🏠 $$

42 Bank Street, VIC 3284 **Tel** *(03) 5568 2891*

Chef Yazan Akeel's European and Middle-Eastern training is apparent when you peruse the Mod Oz menu at this pleasantly renovated 1850s pub in the centre of historic Port Fairy. You can dine simply in the café/courtyard (a popular music venue) or splurge at night when the café is transformed into Port Fairy's fine dining Mecca.

QUEENSCLIFF Queenscliff Hotel

🔳♿🏠 $$$$

16 Gellibrand Street, VIC 3225 **Tel** *(03) 5258 1066*

If you've ducked down to Queenscliff for a romantic weekend, and your bank account is flush, don't leave town without dining in this grand 19th-century seaside hotel's award-winning formal dining room. Meals in the bistro are a cheaper option for the budget-conscious. The cuisine is Mod Oz and highly recommended.

QUEENSCLIFF Vue Grand Dining Room

🔳♿🏠 $$$$

46 Hesse Street, VIC 3225 **Tel** *(03) 5258 1544*

Another grand Queenscliff experience with a menu to match. The main courses swing from Asian dishes such as drunken chicken (marinated in sake) to European flavours like sebago potatoes served with caramelized chicory and almond and beetroot jus. The desserts are visually spectacular and the wine list impressive.

WARRNAMBOOL Frenchy on Liebig

🔳🏠 $$

78 Liebig Street, VIC 3280 **Tel** *(03) 5561 3188*

Warrnambool's newest restaurant delivers classic Gallic cuisine, from snails with garlic butter all the way through to eye fillet with forest mushroom sauce and crème brûlée. The decor is rustic French Provincial. Open for dinner nightly except Sunday, and open for lunch and dinner in summer with outside tables.

WOODEND Holgate's Bar & Restaurant

🔳♿🎵🏠 $$

79 High Street, VIC 3442 **Tel** *(03) 5427 2510*

This revamped 1902 pub's bar, lounge, restaurant and beer garden are the hospitable arm of the family owned Holgate micro-brewery enterprise. The menu is designed to complement the beers on offer, but wine lovers need not despair with local tipples on offer for lunch and dinner. Bookings are advisable at weekends.

WOODEND Campaspe Country House

🔳♿🏠 $$$

10 Goldies Lane, VIC 3442 **Tel** *(03) 5427 2273*

Chef Brad Lobb (ex Frangos & Frangos and Warrenmang) creates exquisite modern European menus based on seasonal produce sourced from local suppliers, such as the Tuki Trout Farm and Harcourt apple orchards. The elegant restaurant is an easy day trip from Melbourne and overlooks the pool. Bookings advisable.

EASTERN VICTORIA

ALEXANDRA Stonelea Country Estate

🔳♿🏠 $$$

Connelly's Creek Road, VIC 3714 **Tel** *(03) 5772 2222*

It would be just so easy to settle in here and never leave. A major restaurant guide awarded the restaurant its first chef's hat in 2006, and with good reason. You might start the meal with a duck, ginger and udon noodle broth and end with a trio of home-made sorbets with vanilla and hazelnut biscotti.

AVENEL Harvest Home Country House Hotel

🔳🏠 $$

1–9 Bank Street, VIC 3664 **Tel** *(03) 5796 2339*

This 1860s pub in a small town best known as a childhood home to bushranger Ned Kelly has been converted into a hospitable restaurant, bar and hotel with lovely gardens and a happy inclination towards rustic European cuisine combined with convivial conversation. Well worth staying the night.

BAIRNSDALE Riversleigh Country Hotel

🔳🏠 $$$

1 Nicholson Street, VIC 3875 **Tel** *(03) 5152 6966*

Enjoy modern European cuisine in the formal dining room, or sample a casual brunch or dinner in the conservatory bistro. If you've stayed overnight and the weather is fine, you'll find the courtyard a pleasant setting for a traditional buffet-style breakfast. The wine list highlights Gippsland wineries.

BEECHWORTH Gigi's of Beechworth

🛏🔳🏠 $$

69 Ford Street, VIC 3747 **Tel** *(03) 5728 2575*

Open for breakfast, lunch and dinner, Gigi's regular clientele love the regional Italian cuisine, the extensive wine list (which features some of Italy's and northeast Victoria's best wines) and the imported Italian produce. The food is homely and filling, the coffee strong and inviting, and the service amiable. Closed Wednesdays.

BEECHWORTH The Bank Restaurant & Mews — 🍴 ♿ 🏠 $$

86 Ford Street, VIC 3747 ***Tel*** *(03) 5728 2223*

A stately 1856 bank building with shady courtyard (and an adjoining guesthouse in converted stables and coach house if you need to linger), makes for an ideal culinary setting in this historic gold rush-era township. The food is Mod Oz and there's a cellar in the old gold vault that is home to some fine Australian wine.

BRIGHT Sasha's of Bright — ⛱ 🍴 ♿ 🏠 $$

2d Anderson Street, VIC 3741 ***Tel*** *(03) 5750 1711*

The eponymous Sasha serves up Middle-European cuisine in this intimate, bistro-style restaurant. Roast duck with red cabbage and rösti is his signature dish (often preceded by a "duck call" from the kitchen). There are usually three children's specials on the menu. From November to May, book ahead.

BRIGHT Simone's of Bright — ⛱ 🍴 ♿ $$$

98 Gavan Street, VIC 3741 ***Tel*** *(03) 5755 2266*

Critics rave about the regional Italian cuisine served at Patrizia Simone's, where the emphasis is always on local seasonal produce. Signature dishes in this renovated heritage building on the main street include home-made pasta, pigeon, trout and goat, enhanced by local produce such as wild spinach.

DANDENONG RANGES ripe — 🍴 ♿ 🏠 $$

376 Mount Dandenong Tourist Road, Sassafras, VIC 3787 ***Tel*** *(03) 9755 2100*

This cosy weatherboard cottage is another eatery giving the Dandenongs an overdue culinary fillip. The menu shines with heartwarming favourites such as osso bucco, rabbit pie and lentil soup. On the lighter side there are baguettes and cakes. There's a deck out the back for summer dining and a corner fireplace in winter.

DANDENONG RANGES Wild Oak Café — ⛱ 🍴 ♿ ♫ 🏠 $$

232 Ridge Road, Olinda, VIC 3788 ***Tel*** *(03) 9751 2033*

Wild Oak's award-winning formula is simple: deliver well-presented Mod Oz cuisine and fine wines in a relaxed contemporary setting. The menu features specials such as seared kangaroo, slow-braised pork belly and ginger infused crème brûlée with citrus granita. There is live jazz on the last Friday of the month.

FALLS CREEK Astra Lodge Restaurant — ♿ ♫ $$$

5 Sitzmark Street, VIC 3699 ***Tel*** *(03) 5758 3496*

Astra Lodge's restaurant starts the day with cooked and buffet breakfasts and ends with à la carte dining in the dining room. The menu is Mod Oz, specializing in local produce, for example, bush tomatoes and wild berries. There is an extensive wine list and the ambient Vodka Bar has almost 80 vodkas in stock.

LAKES ENTRANCE Nautilus Floating Dockside Restaurant — ⛱ 🍴 ♿ $$$

Western Boat Harbour, The Esplanade, VIC 3909 ***Tel*** *(03) 5155 1400*

Unlike its Jules Verne's namesake, this floating restaurant keeps its head above water. It specializes in Gippsland wines, and given its position berthed alongside fishing craft, it couldn't help but offer Lakes Entrance scallops, Eden mussels and the catch of the day. Some say it's the best seafood in Gippsland.

MILAWA Milawa Factory Bakery & Restaurant — ⛱ 🍴 ♿ 🏠 $$

Factory Road, VIC 3678 ***Tel*** *(03) 5727 3588*

You can't blame the chef for insinuating Milawa cheeses into almost every menu item; it's one of Australia's best farmhouse cheesemakers. With relaxing views over the nearby ranges, the café menu has an Italian flavour, with inexpensive items such as polenta and grilled prosciutto with aged Milawa blue cheese sauce.

MILAWA The Epicurean Centre — ♿ 🏠 $$

Brown Brothers Winery, 239 Milawa, Bobinawarrah Road, VIC 3678 ***Tel*** *(03) 5720 5540*

The trick here is the attention paid to matching wine with local produce. Each dish is created to a balance with the flavours and textures of the wine. The menu is contemporary Asian and Mediterranean with locally sourced trout, nuts, mushrooms, beef, lamb, turkey, venison, berries and cheese. BYO wine only.

MORNINGTON PENINSULA Coast 2827 — ♿ 🏠 $$

2827 Point Nepean Road, Blairgowrie, VIC 3942 ***Tel*** *(03) 5988 0700*

The staff here manage to keep everybody happy. Whether it's delivering a quick and satisfying brunch for the older customers, or keeping the little ones happy with a crayon and chips. At night the menu is likely to feature Asian-inspired seafood dishes. The decor is beach-shack chic and the atmosphere casual.

MORNINGTON PENINSULA Montalto Vineyard & Olive Grove — 🍴 ♿ 🏠 $$$$

33 Shoreham Road, Red Hill South, VIC 3937 ***Tel*** *(03) 5989 8412*

Combine contemporary architecture with French-inspired cuisine and views over the olive grove, vineyard and gardens and you have a winning formula. You can dine à la carte, or enjoy a casual meal at the café. They also cater for private picnics, which is an option worth considering in this picturesque neck of the woods.

MOUNT BULLER Breathtaker Signature Restaurant — 🍴 ♿ $$$

Breathtake All Suite Hotel, 8 Breathtaker Road, VIC 3723 ***Tel*** *(03) 5777 6377*

Open year-round, this smart restaurant offers views over Mount Buller Village and a Mod Oz menu with specials ranging from crisp, oven-baked barramundi on spicy turmeric potatoes with tzatziki rocket salad and dill and lime butter sauce, to simple pleasures such as South Australian oysters served Kilpatrick. Try the chocolate mud truffle cake.

Key to Price Guide *see p524* **Key to Symbols** *see back cover flap*

MOUNT HOTHAM Zirky's

Great Alpine Road, VIC 3741 **Tel** *(03) 5759 3518*

Zirky's offers à la carte dining in the restaurant, and breakfasts and lunches in the café and bar/bistro. The café serves cooked breakfasts, foccacias, hot chocolate and schnapps, while the Euro-centric menus in the restaurant and bistro/bar deliver hearty fillers such as lasagne and goulash. Open June to October.

NOOJEE The Outpost Retreat

38 Loch Valley Road, VIC 3833 **Tel** *(03) 5628 9669*

This rustic restaurant with wide verandahs is set beside the LaTrobe River en route to Mount Baw Baw. Chef John Snelling (ex Di Stasio) knows a thing or two about fine Italian food and his menu benefits from local produce, including Noojee trout. Open Friday nights and weekends only. The adjoining Toolshed Bistro offers cheaper fare.

OXLEY King River Cafe

Snow Road, VIC 3678 **Tel** *(03) 5727 3461*

If you're en route to Mount Buffalo, Falls Creek or Mount Hotham, the King River Cafe is a great halfway stop. The café occupies the town's charming 1860s post office and general store. The menu favours local King Valley wines and produce, and delivers fresh and ever-changing Mediterranean and Asian flavours.

PHILLIP ISLAND Harry's on the Esplanade

17 The Esplanade, Cowes, VIC 3922 **Tel** *(03) 5952 6226*

The cuisine is middle-European, with seafood delights such as crayfish thrown in for good measure. Close your eyes and tuck into veal with dumplings and you could be back in Budapest. Open them again and enjoy the ocean views from the balcony. The chef also prepares his own bread, pastries and ice cream.

PHILLIP ISLAND The Jetty Restaurant

11–13 The Esplanade, Cowes, VIC 3922 **Tel** *(03) 5952 2060*

With beach frontage and views to match, it's understandable that this old-timer's menu is heavy on the seafood, offering classics such as whole baby snapper and that 1970s throwback, the "surf and turf". Although char-grilled kangaroo with plum sauce might be more to your liking. The decor is rustic and homey.

YARRA VALLEY De Bortoli Winery and Restaurant

Pinnacle Lane, Dixons Creek, VIC 3775 **Tel** *(03) 5965 2271*

The Wow Factor is big at this award-winning vineyard restaurant. The De Bortoli family are winemaking legends and the North Italian menu at their Yarra Valley restaurant sparkles with gems such as braised ox tongue with fennel, borlotti beans and salsa. Try the poached quince with star anise and honey for dessert.

YARRA VALLEY Eleonore's at Chateau Yering

42 Melba Highway, Yering, VIC 3770 **Tel** *(03) 9237 3333*

It's best not to ponder the menu too long. Just dive in and drift from poached oysters to braised squab with chestnuts to prune and Armagnac soufflé. The 26-year-old chef, Shane Delia, will guarantee you won't be disappointed. The setting is elegant with views over the gardens. The adjoining Sweetwater Cafe is marginally cheaper.

YARRA VALLEY Healesville Hotel

256 Maroondah Highway, VIC 3777 **Tel** *(03) 5962 4002*

As if two Tucker Seabrook awards for their wine list weren't enough, this 1910 pub won *The Age*'s 2006 gong for Best Country Restaurant. The laidback bistro and stylish dining room menu rely on quality local produce, including Buxton salmon, Yarra Valley dairy cheeses and homegrown herbs, salad greens and venison.

TASMANIA

BATTERY POINT Da Angelo Ristorante

47 Hampden Road, Battery Point, TAS 7004 **Tel** *(03) 6223 7011*

This little piece of Italy located in historic Battery Point serves home-made pasta, pizza and ice cream. Much loved by locals for its excellent value for money and legendary pizzas, meals are presented with true Italian style and hospitality. A Hobart institution for over a decade, it is packed seven nights a week, so be sure to book ahead.

BATTERY POINT/HOBART Restaurant Gondwana

22 Francis Street, Battery Point, TAS 7004 **Tel** *(03) 6224 9900*

Signature contemporary dishes prepared with the finest Tasmanian produce have made Restaurant Gondwana a Hobart legend. Be tempted by dishes such as gin-cured ocean trout, pepperberry marinated venison and the world-renowned Tasmanian salmon. The knowledgable staff will help you choose the perfect wine to accompany your meal.

CAMPBELL TOWN Zeps Café

92–94 High Street, TAS 7210 **Tel** *(03) 6381 1344*

Definitely the best food stop on the Heritage Highway between Hobart and Launceston. This licensed cafe serves an all-day breakfast, great pizzas, toasted panini, pasta and more. There's a great range of sweets available, hot and cold drinks, plus excellent coffee to prepare you for the journey ahead.

COLES BAY Freycinet Lodge

Freycinet National Park, TAS 7215 **Tel** *(03) 6257 0101*

Set amidst the Freycinet National Park and the stunning Great Oyster Bay, this low-key but luxurious holiday lodge offers both formal and casual dining options. Richardson Bistro opens from 10am while the more formal Bay Restaurant serves breakfast and dinner, and offers a comprehensive wine list.

CRADLE MOUNTAIN Highland Restaurant

Cradle Mountain Lodge, TAS 7306 **Tel** *(03) 6492 1303*

Excellent Tasmanian wines (if a little high-priced) and modern Australian cuisine are the specialities of this sophisticated restaurant located on the edge of Tasmania's World Heritage wilderness area. The restaurant also offers an enormous buffet breakfast for guests wanting to make a solid start to a day of wilderness exploration.

CRADLE VALLEY Lemonthyme Lodge

Dolcoath Road, Moina, TAS 7306 **Tel** *(03) 6492 1112*

Award-winning restaurant offering fine food and wine. The dinner menu features Tasmanian produce, including game, local meat and seafood. The wine cellar has an extensive range of fine Australian and Tasmanian wines. After dinner warmth is provided around the huge open fire in the lounge.

HOBART Fish Frenzy

Elizabeth Street Pier, TAS 7000 **Tel** *(03) 6231 2134*

Map

One of the best value eateries on the Hobart waterfront, serving big paper cones of excellent fish and chips in different incarnations, plus enormous seafood platters and other creations. Fish Frenzy caters for children and there are plenty of outside tables right on the water of Victoria Dock.

HOBART Marti Zucco's

364 Elizabeth Street, North Hobart, TAS 7000 **Tel** *(03) 6234 9611*

Marti Zuccos was one of the first restaurants in Hobart to serve "international" food. As popular as ever, Marti's is a eat-in or takeaway pizza and pasta restaurant, with a range of traditional Italian meat dishes and home-made gelato. Great prices, casual dining, BYO and fully licensed.

HOBART Siam Garden Restaurant

81a Bathurst Street, TAS 7000 **Tel** *(03) 6234 4327*

Tucked away upstairs off Bathurst Street in Hobart's CBD, Siam Garden could be easily missed as it is out of the main restaurant precincts. Serving really good Thai food that is excellent value for money in a relaxed and casual atmosphere. If you like your Thai extra-hot then ask the cheerful staff and the chef will gladly oblige.

HOBART Sirens

6 Victoria Street, Hobart, TAS 7000 **Tel** *(03) 6234 2634*

Sirens is a lusciously decorated, Persian harem-style restaurant in Hobart's CBD. Serving exquisite vegetarian dishes with vegan and gluten-free options, the menu at Sirens lends itself to the sharing of lots of small to medium-size dishes. Be sure to leave room for divine desserts, such as the decadent chocolate Cointreau tart.

HOBART Drunken Admiral

17–19 Hunter Street, Old Wharf, TAS 7000 **Tel** *(03) 6234 1903*

Tasmania's most distinctive seafarer's restaurant serves fresh fish in both traditional and international styles. The Drunken Admiral offers a lot more than just seafood and there are a number of set menus to choose from, plus a children's menu. The nautical decor adds to the atmosphere.

HOBART Prossers on the Beach

Beach Road, Sandy Bay, TAS 7005 **Tel** *(03) 6225 2276*

Set in the Sandy Bay Regatta Pavilion just metres from the popular Nutgrove Beach, Prossers has great views and a reputation for excellence. Its speciality is seafood and incorporating the finest Tasmanian produce into its quality dishes. Prossers was awarded Tasmania's best seafood restaurant in 2002, 2003 and 2004.

HOBART The Point Revolving Restaurant

410 Sandy Bay Road, Sandy Bay, TAS 7005 **Tel** *1800 030 611*

Superb 360-degree views are a feature of this revolving restaurant in Australia's longest-running casino. The Point's international/modern Australian menu caters to a broad clientele. There is a lounge and cocktail bar for those just wanting to take in the ever-changing mountain, city and river vistas.

LAUDERDALE Eating on the Edge

13 North Terrace, TAS 7021 **Tel** *(03) 6248 7707*

With a loyal following of regulars, both local and from across town, this beachside restaurant serves well-priced fine Italian food and seafood. Eating on the Edge boasts stunning views and a relaxed atmosphere. The servings are generous and the service friendly – excellent value for money.

LAUNCESTON Pierre's on George

88 George Street Launceston, TAS 7250 **Tel** *(03) 6331 6835*

Pierre's is a Launceston institution. The city's oldest café/restaurant was the birthplace of Launceston's café culture. Today, Pierre's stretches a block in the CBD, from street to rear courtyard. Offering quiet nooks for coffee contemplation plus plenty of people-watching opportunities.

Key to Price Guide *see p524* **Key to Symbols** *see back cover flap*

LAUNCESTON The Metz
119 St John Street, Launceston, TAS 7250 **Tel** *(03) 6331 7277*

The Metz is a popular café/wine bar in central Launceston, offering casual dining in an often lively atmosphere. Their wood-fired pizza is very popular with locals and they also serve pasta, salads and traditional pub food plus an extensive wine list and beers on tap. The Metz has opened a sister café in the Hobart suburb of Sandy Bay.

LAUNCESTON Fee and Me
190 Charles Street, Launceston, TAS 7250 **Tel** *(03) 6331 3195*

Truly outstanding, multi-award-winning restaurant in a gracious 1835 town house. The food at Fee and Me is impeccable, the service is seamless and the atmosphere elegant and intimate. Chef Fiona Hoskin's unique degustation menu and expertly chosen wine list provide the ultimate fine dining experience.

LAUNCESTON Jailhouse Grill
32 Wellington Street, Launceston, TAS 7250 **Tel** *(03) 6331 0466*

Located in a heritage-listed, convict-built building, the Jailhouse Grill specializes in Tasmanian steak dishes, cooked how you like it with a myriad of sauces. Open 365 days a year, this family friendly restaurant is fully licensed, featuring a comprehensive wine list and is open for lunch Thu–Sun.

LAUNCESTON Synergy
135 George Street, Launceston, TAS 7250 **Tel** *(03) 6331 0110*

This award-winning small restaurant feels more like a private dining room, but there is no mistaking the professionalism and quality of Synergy's exceptional modern cuisine. With a focus on local seasonal produce, with international influences, this restaurant now appears on everyone's list.

LAUNCESTON Stillwater
Ritchies Mill, 2 Bridge Road, TAS 7250 **Tel** *(03) 6331 4153*

Offering a casual café atmosphere by day, it is Stillwater's evening dinner menu by chef Don Cameron that has won it acclaim. Situated in the old Ritchies Mill historic site, with views across the river, the Stillwater complex incorporates a providore and craft store upstairs and an amazing stone wine cellar below.

NORTH HOBART Annapurna
Elizabeth Street, North Hobart **Tel** *(03) 6236 9500*

Located in Hobart's multicultural food district, Elizabeth Street, North Hobart, Annapurna serves great value Indian cuisine, using traditional recipes and cooking techniques. They offer great vegetarian options and a legendary Masala Dosa. This place is often packed to the rafters, so be sure to book. The banquets are exceptional value for money.

NORTH HOBART Raincheck Lounge
392 Elizabeth Street, North Hobart **Tel** *(03) 6234 5975*

Groovy, retro-inspired decor and well-priced favourites have made this Hobart newcomer an instant hit. Café-style eatery by day, the Raincheck Lounge also boasts an impressive cocktail list making it ideal for those in for the long haul. Located on the cosmopolitan restaurant strip of Elizabeth Street, north of the CBD.

SALAMANCA Maldini
47 Salamanca Place, Hobart, TAS 7004 **Tel** *(03) 6223 4460*

Crown Prince Frederick of Denmark dined here; so did swim star Ian Thorpe. Hobart's famous visitors are discovering what locals have known for years – Maldini serves fabulous Italian food. Located on historic Salamanca Place, this sleek café/restaurant also boasts great coffee and home-made cakes that keep it thriving all day long.

SHEFFIELD Weindorfers
Wellington Street, Gowrie Park, TAS 7306 **Tel** *(03) 6491 1385*

In memory of Gustav Weindorfer (founder of Cradle Mountain National Park) and his wife, Kate, Weindorfer's serves generous portions of home-cooked country fare. Located in a rustic, shingled building beneath the mystical beauty of Mount Roland, Weindorfer's is a licensed restaurant seating up to 60 plus a private room for 100.

STRAHAN Risby Cove
The Esplanade, Strahan, TAS 7486 **Tel** *(03) 6471 7572*

This eco-tourism centre is situated right on the water's edge, overlooking Strahan's harbour. At Risby Cove the emphasis is on seasonal, fresh ingredients, complementary flavours and impeccable presentation. The knowledgable staff and harbourside ambience create a wonderful dining experience.

STRAHAN Franklin Manor
The Esplanade, Strahan, TAS 7468 **Tel** *(03) 6471 7311*

Strahan's most gracious mansion provides quality accommodation and a first-class dining experience. Admire the superb 19th-century garden from the dining room or the veranda. There is a strong emphasis on Tasmanian produce and there is a great selection of premium Tasmanian wines.

WOODBRIDGE Peppermint Bay
3435 Channel Highway, Woodbridge, TAS 7162 **Tel** *(03) 6267 4088*

Cruise from the Hobart docks or drive the scenic route to this world-class establishment incorporating a fine-dining restaurant, casual local bar serving quality pub food, and a craft and produce centre. Peppermint Bay supports local suppliers by sourcing produce from the surrounding region. The views are magnificent.

SHOPPING IN AUSTRALIA

Australia has much to offer the visiting shopper beyond the standard tourist fare of koala bear purses and plastic boomerangs. The tourist shops can be worth exploring, some stock being of a high standard and including goods not available in other countries. In each state capital, especially Sydney *(see pp132–5)* and Melbourne *(see pp406–9)*, there are precincts and open-air markets with a range of shops, stalls and cafés to

Colourful craft shop sign in Margaret River

explore. Wine and gourmet food products are a major attraction, and a wide range of reasonably priced world-class goods is available. Australian contemporary design has a refreshing irreverence for convention – look out for homewares and fashion in the inner-city precincts. In country areas, unusual items made by local craftspeople make good buys. Australia recently introduced a goods and services tax (GST), adding 10 per cent to the cost of most items.

Browsers at a stall in Mindil Beach Sunset Markets, Darwin *(see p272)*

SHOPPING HOURS

Standard weekday opening times are 9am–5:30pm, Monday to Friday. Late night shopping is usually available on Thursdays or Fridays, when stores stay open until 9pm. Weekend hours vary greatly. Deregulation has meant that many stores, particularly in city locations, open on both Saturday and Sunday. In most country areas, however, stores will open only until 1pm on Saturday. Many supermarkets in city and suburban areas now operate 24 hours. Bookshops and other specialist shops stay open late – until around 10pm – in downtown areas.

HOW TO PAY

Major credit cards are accepted by most stores, generally with a minimum purchase limit. Identification, such as a valid passport or

driver's licence, is required when using traveller's cheques. Personal cheques are also accepted at the majority of larger stores, with identification, but a telephone check on your account may be made. Payment by cash is the preferred method for traders and can be used to negotiate a lower price for your goods in some instances.

RIGHTS AND REFUNDS

The laws on consumer rights in Australia vary slightly from state to state. If you have a complaint or query, look under "Consumer" in the government section at the front of the White Pages telephone directory. If the goods purchased are defective in any way, customers are entitled to a full refund. If you decide you don't like an item, try to get a refund, but you will probably have to

settle for a credit note or exchange. As a general rule, the larger the store, the more protected you are – you can always ask to speak to a manager or customer relations officer if you are unhappy with the service you receive.

ESSENTIALLY AUSTRALIAN

Aboriginal art is available for purchase from community-owned or managed galleries in the Northern Territory and good specialist galleries in the cities. Take the time to discuss the work with the painter or gallery staff: spiritual and cultural meanings are inextricably linked with aesthetic properties, and the painting or artifact that you choose will be all the more valuable with a little knowledge. These

Shoppers in London Court, Perth's Tudor-style street *(see p304)*

A colourful arts and crafts stall in one of Australia's many markets

artworks are by their nature expensive, so do not be beguiled by cheaper imitations.

Australia produces 95 per cent of the world's opals. Their quality varies greatly, so when considering a purchase a little research will go a long way. Opals are widely available at duty-free stores. Many other places will deduct the luxury excise tax from the price if you produce your passport.

Outback clothing is a specialist industry in Australia. Look for Akubra hats, boots by RM Williams and Driza-bone overcoats in camping and army stores. Surf clothing has become highly desirable among tourists, as it can be a lot cheaper to buy in Australia than abroad. Board shorts and bikinis are popular purchases.

Fresh fish on display at Wollongong Fish Market (see p186)

MARKETS

Most Australian cities have a large central produce market and a range of small community markets that operate at the weekend. The bustling city food markets are as sensational for their vibrant multicultural atmosphere as they are for the extraordinary range of fresh, cheap produce available. Look out for local specialities such as cheeses, olives and unusual fruits. Melbourne's Queen Victoria Market (see p386) and the Adelaide Central Market (see p346) are particularly good and well worth visiting. Community markets, such as those in Paddington, Sydney (see p125), and Salamanca Place, Hobart (see p466), offer an interesting and eclectic range of locally designed clothing and crafts. In a class of their own, the Mindil Beach Sunset Markets in Darwin combine eating, shopping and entertainment in a spectacular tropical setting (see p272).

DEPARTMENT STORES

Department stores occupy the up-market end of the chain-store scale and sell quality merchandise. They include names such as Myer, David Jones and Grace Brothers (see p406) and some of the top stores are sumptuously decorated. Local and overseas designer fashions, top-brand cosmetics and all manner of household goods and furnishings can be purchased. These stores are competitive and will often match prices on identical items found at more down-market stores. Their shopper facilities and standards for customer service are excellent.

SHOPPING PRECINCTS

Because the city centres have been colonized by the retail giants in Australia, many small and interesting shops have moved out to the lively precincts that lie somewhere between the city centre and suburbia. These precincts represent some of the best and most interesting shopping in the country. Young designer outlets, specialist book stores, craft studios and galleries sit next to food stores, cafés, restaurants and bars. Some of these precincts are decidedly up-market, while others relish their bohemian roots. There is nearly always a strong mix of cultural influences – Jewish, Italian, Lebanese, Vietnamese, for example – depending on the area and the city. Ask at tourist information centres for the best precincts in each city.

Herbal infusions on sale in Brisbane's Chinatown (see p218)

OUT OF TOWN

Shopping in Australian country areas can be a mixed experience. In some areas the range of standard items is limited and prices can be much higher than you would expect to pay in the city. However, there are always unexpected surprises such as dusty second-hand shops with rare knick-knacks at absurdly low prices and small craft outlets and galleries with unusual items that make great gifts.

The attractive tiled interior of a shopping arcade in Adelaide

SPECIALIST HOLIDAYS AND OUTDOOR ACTIVITIES

To make the most of a trip to a country as vast and geographically diverse as Australia, a specialist holiday is an excellent idea. Whether you're pursuing an interest, acquiring a new skill or learning about the environment, such holidays can be very rewarding experiences. There is a wide range of specialist operators to choose

Sign for glass-bottom boat tour in Western Australia

from. If travelling to Australia from abroad, the best starting points are the local Australian Tourism Commission offices or your local travel agent. Once in the country, the state tourism associations *(see p575)* can offer expert advice, make bookings with reputable companies and contact local activity associations for information.

Bushwalking in Namadgi National Park in the ACT *(see p207)*

BUSHWALKING

National Parks are without doubt the best places for bushwalking in Australia. Not only do they preserve the best of the country's natural heritage, but they also offer expert advice and well-marked trails for bushwalkers. These parks are state-managed and each state has a central information service. Look under "National Parks" in the government listings at the front of the telephone directory.

Equipment, including backpacks, boots and tents, is available for hire from camping stores in city and country areas. Joining up with a tour is a good alternative for those planning long bushwalking trips, as tour members will benefit from a guide's expertise on local flora and fauna, and access to remote wilderness areas. Exceptional bushwalking regions in Australia include Cradle Mountain in Tasmania

(see p467), the MacDonnell Ranges in the Northern Territory *(see p284)* and the Blue Mountains in New South Wales *(see pp170–73)*.

CYCLING

With its vast stretches of near-empty roads, many of them without a hill in sight, it is no wonder that Australia is becoming increasingly popular as a long-distance cycling destination. Visitors can bring their own bicycles, but are advised to check first whether this is acceptable with the airlines. Trains and buses will usually carry bikes provided they are dismantled. To hire a bike in Australia, look under "Bicycles" in the Yellow Pages. Bike helmets are a legal

requirement throughout Australia and can be bought cheaply or hired.

Many cyclists spend several days on the road camping along the way, while others will arrange an itinerary that allows them to stop for the comfort of a bed and meal in a town. The wine-growing areas of South Australia *(see pp338–9)*, the Great Ocean Road in Victoria *(see pp428–9)* and almost anywhere in Tasmania *(see pp456–71)* are terrific cycling destinations.

Bicycling associations in Australia also arrange regular cycling tours that anyone can join. These include accommodation, food and vehicle back-up; most of the organizations are non-profit-making, so the costs are generally low. Contact **Bicycle New South Wales** for a catalogue specializing in Australian cycling publications. They will also provide information on their sister associations in other states.

Cycling around Canberra's lake *(see pp194–5)*

ADVENTURE SPORTS

Appropriate training is a component of adventure sports in Australia, so novices are always welcome alongside more expert adventurers. Contact specialist tour operators or national associations *(see p569)* for information about anything from a one-day class to a two-week tour.

Abseiling, canyoning, rock climbing and caving are all popular in Australia, which has some fantastic natural landscapes ideally suited to these pursuits. The Blue Mountains are something of a mecca for enthusiasts of all the above. Naracoorte in South Australia *(see p355)* is a great location for caving, while the Grampians National Park in Victoria *(see p427)* attracts a large share of abseilers and climbers.

Climbing on Wilsons Promontory in Victoria *(see p444)*

GOLF

There are 1,450 golf courses in Australia and 1,580 golf clubs. Many clubs have affiliations with clubs overseas and offer reciprocal membership rights, so members should check with their own club. There are also public municipal golf courses in many towns.

Australian courses are of a high standard, and Melbourne is home to two of the top 30 courses in the world, the Royal Melbourne and Kingston Heath. A round of golf will cost anything from A$20–$250. The **Australian Golf Union** has a handbook that lists all of the golf courses in Australia.

Camel trekking along Cable Beach, Broome *(see p330)*

ABORIGINAL HERITAGE TOURS

Aboriginal heritage tours can range from a visit to an Aboriginal art gallery to days spent with an Aboriginal guide touring Arnhem Land or Kakadu National Park in the Northern Territory *(see pp276–7)*. With the highest percentage of Aboriginal land and people in the country, the Northern Territory has the greatest number of activities, but there are sights and operators all over Australia. The focus of activities varies and may encompass a number of themes, including traditional bush food, hunting, rock art and Aboriginal culture.

Perhaps the best aspect of many of these tours is the chance to see the remarkable Australian landscape from a different perspective; Aboriginal spirituality is closely linked with the land. In addition, some tours will journey to Australia's most remote areas and travel through Aboriginal lands that are usually closed to all but members of the local Aboriginal communities.

CAMEL TREKKING

Camels have been an invaluable form of transport in Australia's Outback since Afghan-run camel trains were used to carry goods across the Australian desert from the 1840s until the coming of the railway. Joining a camel trek today is still an adventure, and activities range from a one-hour jaunt to a two-week trek. Food and accommodation (usually camping) are provided by tour operators. Alice Springs *(see pp282–3)* is the most popular starting point, but tours are available country-wide.

AERIAL TOURS

Aerial Tours can provide an exhilarating overview of an area and are a good option for time-restricted travellers who want to see some of the more far-flung attractions. Aerial safaris, stopping at major sights, are popular in the Outback. For charter flights to Australia's furthest flung territory, Antarctica, contact **Croydon Travel**.

Seaplane moored at Rose Bay in Sydney, ready for a scenic flight

FISHING

Australia has around four million fishing enthusiasts and, given the country's natural advantages, it's not difficult to see why. Vast oceans, a 12,000-km (7,500-mile) shoreline and a large inland river system, all combined with a terrific climate, make Australia a haven for local and visiting anglers alike.

Fishing for barramundi in the remote inland waters of the Northern Territory and game fishing off Australia's tropical coastline for species such as black marlin and yellowfin tuna are among the world's best fishing experiences. You will need to join a charter as these activities require a great deal of local expertise. Most operators will provide equipment.

The inland waters of Tasmania are famed for their excellent trout fishing prospects. The estuaries and beaches in the southern states, such as the Fleurieu Peninsula in South Australia (*see pp350–51*), are full of species such as bream, salmon and flathead.

Canoeing on the Roper River in the Northern Territory *(see pp268–9)*

Small boats are readily available for hire and fishing tackle can be purchased and occasionally hired at most of the popular fishing destinations around the country. Each state has a government department with a special fisheries section. Staff provide excellent information on locations, restrictions and safety issues. Check the weather forecast and heed warnings about dangerous spots, particularly rock platforms.

Mural advertising the services of a boat charter company

ECOTOURISM

This relatively new tourism concept has its roots in activities as old as bird watching and wildflower identification. It incorporates many of the activities mentioned in this section, but is generally distinguished by its emphasis on issues concerning the appreciation and conservation of the natural heritage. Given Australia's enormous natural bounty, it is hardly surprising that the market is now flooded with operators offering an astonishing range of nature-based activities. These encompass wildlife watching (including whales, birds and dolphins), nature walks, and trekking and rafting expeditions to remote wilderness areas. Visitors can also stay at resorts which are operated along strictly "green" guidelines. These are eco-friendly and are usually located within some of the most environmentally valuable regions in the country. The **Ecotourism Association of Australia** can provide information on tour operators and publications.

WATER SPORTS

Australia is one of the world's great diving destinations, and the Great Barrier Reef is the centre of most of the diving activity (*see pp212–17*). Visitors can combine a holiday on the reef with a few days of diving instruction from one of the many excellent schools in the area. There are opportunities for diving all around Australia, however, and other popular locations include Rottnest Island (*see pp308–9*) and Esperance (*see p319*) in Western Australia and the beautiful World Heritage Area of Lord Howe Island off the coast of New South Wales.

Canoeing in Australia can mean a quiet paddle in a hire-boat on a city lake, or an exciting adventure in a kayak on the high seas. It is a reasonably priced sport and is widely available throughout the country. Popular spots include the Murray River (*see p355*), Sydney Harbour (*see pp144–5*) and the rivers of national parks nationwide.

Whitewater rafting is another favourite sport in this land of outdoor enthusiasts and there are many opportunities for people of all abilities to have a go. The inexperienced can try a day with an instructor on an easy run; the confident can tackle a two-week tour on the rafter's mecca, the Franklin-Gordon River system in Tasmania (*see p468*).

Sailing in Gippsland Lakes Coastal Park, Eastern Victoria (*see p444*)

Long stretches of unspoilt coastline, remote bays and harbours, tropical reefs and uninhabited islands make Australia an excellent destination for sailing enthusiasts. Skippered cruises are the most usual kind of holiday, but some visitors will want to hire a vessel and set off for themselves – a practice known as bareboating. To do this you will need to prove to the operator that you are an experienced sailor. It is difficult to beat the tropical splendours of the Whitsunday Islands in Queensland *(see p216)* as a location. Other popular sailing areas include Pittwater in New South Wales and Queensland's Gold Coast *(see pp238–9)*.

Australia is also world-renowned for its abundance of outstanding surfing beaches. For more information about the country's best places to surf, see pages 38–9.

SKIING

The Ski season in Australia extends from June to September. Downhill skiing is restricted to the Victorian Alps *(see p446-9)*, the New South Wales mountains and two small resorts in Tasmania *(see p469)*. The ski villages have excellent facilities, but the fields can get crowded during school holidays and long weekends, and prices for ski-lifts and equipment hire can be high.

Upland areas around these resorts are superb for cross-country skiing. Traversing gentle slopes and rounded

Skiing Eagle Ridge on Mount Hotham in the Victoria Alps

peaks, skiers will be treated to glimpses of Australia's rare alpine flora and fauna, and spectacular sweeping scenery.

SPECTATOR SPORTS

Most sports enthusiasts will enjoy taking in a fixture during their trip, while a few visitors come to Australia especially for a sporting event, such as yacht races, cricket or tennis events. Early booking is advisable as competition for tickets can be fierce. Regular highlights include the Australian Tennis Open, Melbourne Cup and the Grand Prix, all Melbourne events, and international Test cricket and the Australian Open golf that moves from state to state each year *(see pp40–43)*. Rugby League and Australian Rules football are the most popular spectator sports. The finals are the main event, but excitement is high at almost any match.

AFL Australian Rules football grand final in Melbourne

SURVIVAL GUIDE

PRACTICAL INFORMATION 572–581

TRAVEL INFORMATION 582–591

PRACTICAL INFORMATION

Australia has surged ahead as a major tourist destination in recent years, and the facilities for travellers have kept pace with this rapid development. Visitors should encounter few problems in this safe and friendly destination. Accommodation and restaurants *(see pp474–563)* are of international standard, public transport is readily available *(see pp584–91)* and

Aquarium sign in Queensland

tourist information centres are everywhere. The following pages contain useful information for all visitors. Personal Security and Health *(see pp576–7)* details a number of recommended precautions, while Banking and Currency *(see pp578–9)* answers all the essential financial queries. There is also a section detailing the Australian telephone and postal systems *(see pp580–81)*.

Skiers enjoying the slopes at Falls Creek in Eastern Victoria (see pp448-9)

WHEN TO GO

The northern half of the country lies in a tropical zone and is subject to "wet" and "dry" seasons *(see pp44–5)*. The dry season falls between May and October, and is regarded as the best time to visit this area. During the wet season, conditions are hot and humid, and many areas are inaccessible because of flooding. For those with an interest in wildlife, however, there are areas such as Kakadu National Park *(see pp276–7)* which are particularly spectacular at this time of year.

The southern half of the continent is temperate and the seasons are the exact opposite to those in Europe and North America. Victoria and Tasmania can be a little cloudy and wet in winter, but they are very colourful and quite balmy in autumn. The vast southern coastline is a popular touring destination during the summer months – the climate is warm, with a gentle breeze. Avoid the

Outback areas during the summer, however, as the temperatures can be extreme. The popular ski season in the Victoria Alps takes place between June and September *(see p446)*. In the states of South Australia and Western Australia, there are spectacular wildflower displays between September and December.

ENTRY REQUIREMENTS

Visitors to Australia must have a passport valid for longer than the intended period of stay. All visitors other than New Zealand passport holders must also have a visa issued in their own country. Apply either through some travel agents or airlines, at the Australian Embassy or by post – allow at least four weeks for postal applications. Visitors will be asked for proof of a return ticket and of sufficient funds for the duration of their stay. Once in Australia, you

can extend your visa by applying to the **Department of Immigration**, but tourist visas are rarely extended beyond a year.

TOURIST INFORMATION

The **Australian Tourist Commission** is the central tourism body, but each state and territory has its own tourism authority. Travel centres in the capital cities provide abundant information and these are often the best places to seek advice on specialist tours and to make bookings. Information booths can also be found at airports, tourist sites and in shopping centres. Smaller towns often have tourist offices located in general stores, galleries or petrol stations – look for the blue and white information symbol. In remoter areas, national park visitors' centres will provide useful information on bushwalks and the local terrain.

International tourist information sign

Visitor information kiosk inside Central Railway Station in Sydney

◁ **Caravan driving through The Olgas (Kata Tjuṭa) in the Northern Territory**

Corkscrew roller coaster at Sea World Theme Park on Queensland's Gold Coast *(see p238)*

OPENING HOURS AND ADMISSION PRICES

Most major tourist sites are open seven days a week, but it is always advisable to check first. In smaller centres, galleries and other sites are often closed during the early part of the week. Compared to Europe, admission prices are generally moderate and, in some cases, admission is free. Exceptions are major touring exhibitions at art galleries, zoos, theme parks and specialist attractions such as Sovereign Hill in Ballarat *(see p433)*. Make the most of weekdays – locals will be competing for viewing space at weekends.

ETIQUETTE

While Australian society is generally laid-back, there are a few unwritten rules which visitors should follow. Eating and drinking is frowned upon while travelling on public transport, in taxis and also in many shops and galleries. Dress codes are casual, particularly in summer when the weather is hot, but some bars and restaurants may require men to wear shirts and have a ban on jeans and sports shoes. Topless bathing is accepted on many beaches, but it is advisable to see what the locals are doing.

Tipping is optional in Australia; however, 10 per cent of the final bill for good service in a restaurant is customary, as is a couple of dollars for taxi drivers, hotel porters and bar tenders.

Smoking is prohibited in all public buildings, on public transport, in taxis, in cafés and restaurants, and in most stores. Ask about smoking policies when booking hotels.

DISABLED TRAVELLERS

Disabled travellers can generally expect the best in Australia in terms of facilities. Many hotels, restaurants, tourist sites, cinemas, theatres, airports and shopping centres have wheelchair facilities, and guide dogs for the blind are always welcomed.

Traditionally, public transport is a problem for wheelchair users, although most states are now making their systems more accessible to disabled travellers. Contact the transport authority state by state for more detailed information. Tourist information centres and council offices can provide maps that show sites with wheelchair access.

One of the most useful organizations for disabled travellers is the **National Information Communication Awareness Network (NICAN)** in Canberra. This nationwide database provides information on disabled facilities in different parts of the country and, if they don't have the appropriate information at hand, they will do their best to seek it out. They also have details of many publications specifically written for disabled travellers in Australia.

Circular Quay Station, Sydney, accessible to disabled travellers

AUSTRALIAN TIME ZONES

Australia is divided into three separate time zones: Western Standard Time, Central Standard Time and Eastern Standard Time. Eastern Australia is two hours ahead of Western Australia; Central Australia is one-and-a-half hours ahead. Daylight saving is observed in New South Wales, the ACT, Victoria and South Australia, from October to March, which adds an hour to the time differences.

City and State	Hours + GMT
Adelaide (SA)	+9.5
Brisbane (QLD)	+10
Canberra (ACT)	+10
Darwin (NT)	+9.5
Hobart (TAS)	+10
Melbourne (VIC)	+10
Perth (WA)	+9
Sydney (NSW)	+10

Student travellers exploring Australia's landscape

TRAVELLING WITH CHILDREN

Australia, with its beautiful sandy beaches, abundant wildlife and open spaces and opportunity for adventure, is an ideal destination for children. Most hotels welcome children as guests and can usually provide all the necessary facilities, such as cots, highchairs and, in some cases, babysitting services. However, some of the smaller bed-and-breakfasts advertise themselves as child-free zones.

Restaurants are also generally welcoming to children and offer children's portions, although it is advisable to check first with the more up-market establishments. City department stores and most major tourist sites have feeding and nappy-changing rooms as standard features.

Parents travelling with young children are also encouraged through the range of discounts on air, coach, train and boat travel to which children are entitled *(see pp542–51)*.

Children less than four years of age travelling in cars must be restrained in infant seats according to Australian guidelines. As many cars do not have these restraints as standard fixtures, it is essential that prior arrangements must be made. **Gillespies Hire and Sales Service** leases restraints, pushchairs, baby carriers and travel cots; deliveries can be made to Sydney hotels. Car hire firms in the larger cities will generally supply car restraints on behalf of clients for a small extra charge.

International student ISIC card

STUDENT TRAVELLERS

The International Student Identity Card (ISIC) is available to all students worldwide in full-time study. The ISIC card should be purchased in the student's own country at a Student Travel Association (STA) office. The card can be purchased in Australia only by students enrolled at an Australian educational institution.

Card-holders are entitled to substantial discounts on overseas air travel and a 25 per cent reduction on domestic flights within Australia *(see pp582–5)*. There is also a 15 per cent reduction on private coach travel *(see p587)* and discounts on admission prices to cinemas, galleries, museums and the majority of other tourist sites.

GUIDED TOURS AND EXCURSIONS

Tours and excursions offer the visitor different ways of exploring cities and their surroundings – from bus tours, jaunts on a Harley Davidson, guided nature walks, harbour cruises and river runs, to aerial adventures by hot-air balloon, seaplane or helicopter. As well as an easy way to take in sights, it helps you get a feel for new surroundings.

Mother and child feeding some of Australia's famous marsupials

NEWSPAPERS, TELEVISION AND RADIO

Australia has two national newspapers, *The Australian*, a well-respected broadsheet with excellent national and overseas news coverage, and the *Australian Financial Review*, which largely reports on international monetary matters. *Time* magazine is Australia's leading weekly international news magazine, though many stories are taken from the American version of the magazine. All major foreign newspapers and magazines are readily available in the state capitals and in some of the larger towns. Each state capital also has its own broadsheet and usually a tabloid newspaper as well.

The Australian Broadcasting Corporation (ABC) is a nationwide television station which provides excellent news and current affairs coverage, children's programmes and high-quality local and international drama. In addition, the corporation has its own AM and FM radio stations which offer a wide

Logo for the ABC television network

range of services, including news, rural information for farmers, arts commentary, modern and classical music, magazine-style women's programmes and an acclaimed nationwide channel for the under thirties called Triple J. SBS (Special Broadcasting Service) is Australia's other state-run television network and caters to Australia's many cultures with foreign language programmes for both television and radio. There are also three commercial television stations in Australia, Channels 7, 9 and 10, all of which offer a range of soap operas, news, sports, game shows and other light entertainment.

In all state capitals there is an enormous variety of local FM and AM radio stations. Details of current programming are available in local newspapers. Of interest also are the community radio stations which cater to local cultural and social interests.

The standard of all Australian broadcasting is generally considered to be high.

ELECTRICAL APPLIANCES

Australia's electrical current is 240–250 volts AC. Electrical plugs have either two or three pins. Most good hotels will provide 110-volt shaver sockets and hair dryers, but a flat, two- or three-pin adaptor will be necessary for other appliances. Buy these from electrical stores.

Standard Australian three-pin plug

CONVERSION CHART

Imperial to Metric
1 inch = 2.54 centimetres
1 foot = 30 centimetres
1 mile = 1.6 kilometres
1 ounce = 28 grams
1 pound = 454 grams
1 pint = 0.6 litres
1 gallon = 4.6 litres

Metric to Imperial
1 centimetre = 0.4 inches
1 metre = 3 feet, 3 inches
1 kilometre = 0.6 miles
1 gram = 0.04 ounces
1 kilogram = 2.2 pounds
1 litre = 1.8 pints

DIRECTORY

IMMIGRATION

Department of Immigration
6 Chan St, Belconnen, ACT 2616. *Tel (02) 6264 1111.*

DISABLED TRAVELLERS

NICAN
PO Box 407, Curtin, ACT 2605. *Tel 1800 806 769.*

CHILDREN'S FACILITIES

Gillespie's Hire & Sales Service
13 Elizabeth St, Artarmon, NSW 2064.
Tel (02) 9419 2081.
www.ghss.com.au or
www.sydneyschild.com.au

TOURIST COMMISSION OFFICES

United Kingdom
Australia House, 6th Floor, The Strand, London WC2B 4LG.
Tel (020) 8780 2229.

USA and Canada
6100 Center Drive, Suite 1150, Los Angeles, CA 90045.
Tel (310) 695 3200.

STATE TOURIST OFFICES

ACT
330 Northbourne Ave, Dickson, ACT 2602.
Tel (02) 6205 0044.
www.visitcanberra.com.au

New South Wales
106 George St, Sydney, NSW 2000. *Tel 132 077*
www.visitnsw.com.au.

Northern Territory
38 Mitchell St, Darwin, NT 0800.
Tel (08) 8999 3900.

also at:

67 Stuart Hwy, Alice Springs, NT 0870.
Tel (08) 8999 8555.
www.ntholidays.com.au

Queensland
The Mall, Brisbane, QLD 4001. *Tel (07) 3006 6290.*
also at:
Pier Market Place, Pierpoint Road, Cairns, QLD 4870.
Tel (07) 4051 3588.
www.queensland holidays.com.au

South Australia
18 King William St, Adelaide, SA 5000.
Tel 1300 655 276.
www.southaustralia.com

Tasmania
22 Elizabeth St, Hobart, TAS 7000.
Tel (03) 6230 8235.
www.discover tasmania.com.au

Western Australia
Albert Facey House, cnr Forrest Place & Wellington St, Perth, WA 6000.
Tel 1300 361 351.
www.westernaustralia.com

Victoria
Federation Square, cnr Swanston & Flinders sts, Melbourne, VIC 3000.
Tel 132 842. **www**.visitvictoria.com.au

Personal Security and Health

National park sign

Australia has a low crime rate and is generally regarded as a safe tourist destination. There is a strong police presence in all the state capitals, and even small towns will have at least one officer. In terms of climate and environment, however, Australia is a tough country, and visitors must observe safety procedures whether travelling to remote areas or merely planning a day at the beach. If you get into trouble, contact one of the national emergency numbers in the telephone directory.

Police vehicle

Fire engine

Intensive care ambulance

LOOKING AFTER YOUR PROPERTY

Leave valuables and important documents in your hotel safe, and don't carry large sums of cash with you. Traveller's cheques are generally regarded as the safest way to carry large sums of money. It is also worth photocopying vital documents in case of loss or theft.

Be on guard against pickpockets in places where big crowds gather. Prime areas for petty theft are popular tourist attractions, beaches, markets, sporting venues and on peak-hour public transport.

Never carry your wallet in an outside pocket where it is an easy target for a thief. Wear shoulder bags and cameras with the strap across your body and with

any clasps fastened. If you have a car, always try to park in well-lit, reasonably busy streets. Lock the vehicle securely and don't leave any valuables or property visible that might attract a thief.

PERSONAL SAFETY

There are few, if any, off-limit areas in Australian cities. Red-light districts may be a little seedy, but the fact that they are often busy and well policed probably makes them safer than the average suburban street at night. Avoid poorly lit areas and parks at night. Buses (and trams in Melbourne) are regarded as a safe means of travel at night. However, when travelling by train it is worth remembering that many stations are not

Ambulance paramedic

staffed after hours, particularly in suburban areas. Travel in the train carriage nearest the driver or those marked as being safe for night travel. Taxis are a safe and efficient way of getting around late at night. Hitch-hiking is not an advisable option for any visitor to Australia, and for women it can be particularly dangerous.

Country towns can shut down fairly early in Australia, which is often a surprise to many visitors. It is advisable to reach a destination before nightfall and avoid wandering around looking for accommodation or a meal after dark. The majority of places are extremely friendly to travellers. However, in remote areas, visitors do stand out and as such are potential targets if a threat exists.

MEDICAL MATTERS

Australia's medical services are among the best in the world. Under reciprocal arrangements visitors from the UK, New Zealand, Malta, Italy, Finland, Sweden and Holland are entitled to free hospital and medical treatment provided by Australia's national insurance scheme, Medicare. Medicare does not, however, cover dental work, so dental insurance is worth considering. Visitors from countries other than those mentioned will face prohibitive medical bills if uninsured.

Park ranger   **Policeman**   **Fire officer**

Arrangements for adequate medical cover should be made before leaving home.

Dial 000 in any part of the country for ambulance assistance. Most public hospitals have a casualty department. For less urgent treatment, however, queues can be very long. There are 24-hour medical centres in the major cities and doctors in or nearby most country towns. Look in the local Yellow Pages under "Medical Practitioners".

There are dental hospitals in the state capitals that provide emergency treatment. Call the **Australian Dental Association** for emergency advice on treatment and a list of appropriate dentists practising in your area.

Chemist shop in Sydney

PHARMACIES

Pharmacies (or chemist shops as they are known in Australia) are liberally scattered throughout cities and suburbs, but can be thin on the ground in remote areas, so it is advisable to stock up before heading off. Unrestricted drugs such as painkillers and other goods such as cosmetics, toiletries, suncreams and baby products are standard stock items available in all chemist

shops. Most pharmacies will provide free advice on minor ailments, but foreign prescriptions can only be met if they are endorsed by a local medical practitioner.

Hotel staff and hospitals will direct you to after-hours pharmacies in major cities.

ENVIRONMENTAL HAZARDS

Take care when going out in the sun – the ultraviolet rays are very intense in Australia, even on cloudy days. Wear an SPF 15+ sunblock at all times if your skin is exposed to direct and sustained sunlight. Sunglasses and hats are recommended, and stay out of the sun between 10am and 2pm.

Tasmania parks logo

Lifesavers patrol many beaches in populated areas, and red and yellow flags indicate safe swimming areas. However, it is vital to remember that there are vast stretches of unpatrolled beaches in Australia and many of these are subject to dangerous rips. Certain rips can be so strong that even wading can pose a threat, especially for elderly people and children. Follow local advice and, if in any doubt, do not swim.

Never underestimate the Australian bush. Even in well-trodden areas, hikers can lose their way. Always ask advice and inform someone of your route. Staff at national parks can offer expert advice along with maps, and will keep a note of your intended trip.

Take a basic first aid kit, food and water, and extra clothing. In many regions, temperatures plummet when the sun sets.

Australia shelters some of the most venomous creatures on earth. While it is highly unlikely that you will be bitten, basic precautions such as good boots and a wary eye are necessary. Snake-bite victims should be kept calm while emergency help is sought. Try to identify the creature by size and colour so that the appropriate anti-venom can be administered.

Crocodiles are fascinating but dangerous creatures. In the northern regions of the continent, heed the warning signs and make enquiries if you intend to swim in remote, unpatrolled areas. Box jellyfish patrol tropical waters between October and May. They are hard to see and their sting is extremely dangerous. Again, observe the signs.

Bush fires are a fact of life in Australia. When planning a camping trip, ring the **Rural Fire Service** to check on restrictions. Total fire bans are not uncommon during warm, dry seasons. Avoid high-risk areas and dial 000 if in immediate danger from fire.

DIRECTORY

EMERGENCY SERVICES

Police, Fire and Ambulance
Tel 000 from any telephone.
Service operates 24 hours and calls are free.

NATIONAL HELPLINES

Australian Dental Association (Federal)
Tel (02) 9906 4412.

Rural Fire Service
Tel (02) 8741 5555.
www.rfs.nsw.gov.au

Lifeline
Tel 131 114.

Poisons Information
Tel 131 126.

Surf lifesaving sign indicating a dangerous undertow or "rip"

Banking and Local Currency

Branches of national, state and some foreign banks can be found in the central business districts of Australia's state capitals. Suburban shopping centres and country towns will often have at least one branch of a major Australian bank. If travelling to remote areas, find out what banking facilities are available in advance. Banks generally offer the best exchange rates; money can also be changed at bureaux de change, large department stores and hotels. There is no limit to the amount of personal funds that can be taken in or out of Australia, although cash amounts of A$10,000 or more must be declared to customs on arrival or prior to departure.

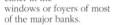

High street bank logos

BANKING

Bank trading hours are generally from 9:30am to 4pm Monday to Thursday and 9:30am to 5pm on Fridays. Outside banking hours, many transactions can be handled through automatic teller machines. All the current exchange rates are displayed either in the windows or foyers of most of the major banks.

Automatic cash dispenser

TRAVELLER'S CHEQUES

Australian dollar traveller's cheques issued by major names such as Thomas Cook and American Express are usually accepted (with a passport) in large shops. You may have problems, however, cashing these in smaller outlets. Foreign currency cheques can be cashed at all major banks, bureaux de change and established hotels in the main cities.

Banks are generally the best places to go to cash traveller's cheques as their fees are lower.

Westpac Bank will cash traveller's cheques in Australian dollars without charge. ANZ, the National and Commonwealth banks charge a small fee for this service. A passport or another form of photo ID is usually needed to cash traveller's cheques at a bank.

CREDIT CARDS

All well-known international credit cards are widely accepted in Australia. Major credit cards such as VISA, MasterCard, Diners Club and American Express can be used to book and pay for hotel rooms, airline tickets, car hire, tours and concert and theatre tickets. Credit cards are accepted in most restaurants and shops, where the logos of all recognized cards are usually shown on doors and counter tops. You can also use credit cards in automatic teller machines at most banks to withdraw cash.

Credit cards are also a very convenient way to make telephone bookings and avoid the need to carry large sums of cash. They can be particularly useful in emergencies or if you need to return home at short notice.

You should always carry an emergency cash amount, however, if travelling to remote areas, particularly the Outback. Credit cards may not be accepted at small stores and cafés, and alternatives may not always be available.

AUTOMATIC TELLER MACHINES AND ELECTRONIC TRANSFER

Automatic teller machines can be found in most banks, as well as in shopping and tourist areas. In most cases it is possible to access foreign accounts from ATMs by using a linked credit card. Ask your bank about making your card valid for this kind of use.

Linking credit and other bank accounts in this way will also give you access to EFTPOS (Electronic Funds Transfer at Point Of Sale). Pay for goods using a card, and funds are automatically debited from your chosen bank account. In many stores customers will also be allowed to withdraw cash, providing a purchase has been made. This is a useful facility if the town you are in doesn't have an appropriate ATM. It is also a good alternative to using credit in every instance.

BUREAUX DE CHANGE

Australian cities and larger towns, particularly those popular with tourists, have many bureaux de change. These are usually open Monday to Saturday from 9am to 5:30pm. Some branches also operate on Sundays.

While the opening hours of bureaux de change make them a convenient alternative to a bank, their commissions and fees are generally higher.

DIRECTORY

FOREIGN CURRENCY EXCHANGE

American Express
Tel 1300 136 060.
www.americanexpress.com.au

Commonwealth Bank
Tel 13 22 21.
www.commbank.com.au

Travelex
Tel 1800 637 642.
www.travelex.com.au

Westpac
Tel 13 20 32.
www.westpac.com.au

LOCAL CURRENCY

The Australian currency is the Australian dollar (A$), which breaks down into 100 cents (c). The decimal currency system now in place has been in operation since 1966.

Single cents may still be used for some prices, but as the Australian 1c and 2c coins are no longer in circulation, the total amount to be paid will be rounded up or down to the nearest five cents.

It can be difficult to change A$50 and A$100 notes, so avoid using them in smaller shops and cafés and, more particularly, when paying for taxi fares. If you do not have change, it is always wise to tell the taxi driver before you start your journey to avoid any misunderstandings. Otherwise, when you arrive at your destination, you may have to find change at the nearest shop or ATM.

To improve security, as well as increase their lifespan, all Australian bank notes have now been plasticized.

Bank Notes

Australian bank notes are produced in denominations of A$5, A$10, A$20, A$50 and A$100. All bank notes are made of plastic. Paper notes have been phased out and are no longer legal tender.

A$100 note

A$50 note

A$20 note

A$10 note

A$5 note

5 cents (5c)   **10 cents (10c)**

20 cents (20c)   **50 cents (50c)**

1 dollar (A$1)   **2 dollars (A$2)**

Coins

Coins currently in use in Australia are 5c, 10c, 20c, 50c, A$1 and A$2. There are several different 50c coins in circulation; all are the same size and shape, but have different commemorative images on the face. The 10c and 20c coins are useful for local telephone calls (see pp580–81).

Using Australia's Telephones

Australia's public payphones are generally maintained in good working order. They are widely available on streets throughout cities and in country towns, as well as in cafés, shops, post offices, public buildings, railway and service stations. It is wise to invest in a phonecard to avoid the annoyance of looking for change. Also avoid making calls from hotel rooms as hotels set their own rates. Use the hotel foyer payphone instead.

Using a mobile phone at Bondi

Telstra Corporation logo

PUBLIC TELEPHONES

Most payphones accept both coins and phone-cards, although some operate solely on phonecards or major credit cards. Phonecards can be bought from selected newsagents and news kiosks, as well as from the many other outlets displaying the blue and orange Telstra sign.

Although slightly varied in shape and colour, all public telephones have a hand-held receiver and a 12-button key pad, as well as clear instructions (in English only), a list of useful phone numbers and telephone directories.

Telstra payphones

PAYPHONE CHARGES

Local calls are untimed and cost 40 cents. Depending on where you are, "local" means the city and its suburbs, or outside the city, a defined country region. **Telstra** can provide information on exact costs. Dial freephone 1800 113 011 for an estimate of the cost of long-distance and international calls. Phonecard and credit card phones all have a A$1.20 minimum fee. Long-distance calls are less expensive if you dial without the help of an operator. You can also save money on all calls by phoning during off-peak periods. Peak and discount calling times fall into three periods. Peak times are between 7am–7pm Monday

to Friday. There are capped call rates between 7pm and midnight Sunday to Friday and between 4pm and midnight on Saturday. All other times are economy rate.

MOBILE TELEPHONES

Mobile telephones are used widely in Australia. Short-term rentals are available to visitors, but mobile calls are costly – even local calls are billed at an STD rate.

Making calls while driving is illegal and carries a stiff fine. Many places in remote Australia are not on the mobile net.

FAX SERVICES

Many Australian post offices offer a fax service. There are also many copy shops that will send or receive faxes on your behalf. Look under the heading "Facsimile and Telex Communication Services" in the Yellow Pages.

Post offices charge per-page fees to send a fax within Australia. The cost per page is reduced if you are sending more than one page. If you are not sure of a correct fax number, you can fax a document to the nearest post office, who will then deliver it to the right address by mail. There is an additional small delivery fee for this service.

USING A COIN/PHONECARD OPERATED PHONE

1 Lift the receiver and wait for the dialling tone.

2 Insert the coins required or a Telstra phonecard.

3 Dial the number and wait to be connected.

5 Replace the receiver at the end of the call and withdraw your card or collect any unused coins.

6 When you finish your call, the phonecard is returned to you with a hole punched in it showing the approximate remaining value.

4 The display shows you how much value is left on your phonecard or coins. When your money runs out you will hear a warning beep. Insert more coins or a new phonecard.

Phonecards
These are available in A$5, A$10, A$20 and A$50 denominations.

TELEPHONE DIRECTORIES

Each city and region in Australia has two telephone directories: the White Pages and the Yellow Pages. The White Pages list private and business numbers in alphabetical order. They also have a guide to emergency services and government departments. The Yellow Pages list businesses under relevant headings such as Dentists, Car Hire and so on.

USEFUL INFORMATION

Telstra Mobile Sales
Tel 12 51 11.

REACHING THE RIGHT NUMBER

• To ring Australia from the UK dial 0061, then the area code, then the local number.
• To ring Australia from the USA or Canada dial 011 61, then the area code, then the local number.
• For long-distance direct-dial calls outside your local area code, but within Australia (STD calls), dial the appropriate area code, then the number.
• For international direct-dial calls (IDD calls): dial **0011**, followed by the country code (USA and Canada: 1; UK: 44; New Zealand: 64), then the city or area code (omit initial 0) and then the local number.
• Directory information with automatic connection to local and national destinations: dial **12455**.
• Local and national directory enquiries: dial **12455**.
• Reverse charge or third party charge calls: dial **12550**.
• National and international operator assisted calls: dial **1234** or **12550**.
• National and international call-cost enquiries: dial **1800 113 011**.
• Numbers beginning with **1 800** are usually toll-free numbers, but not always.
• Numbers beginning with **13** are charged at a rate that is slightly higher than the local call rate.
• Numbers with the prefix **014**, **015**, **018**, **019**, **040**, **041** or **042** are mobile or car phones.
• See also Emergency Numbers, *p577*.

Postal Services

Post offices are open 9am–5pm weekdays, and some branches are open on Saturday mornings. Telephone **Australia Post Customer Service** for details of opening times. Many post offices offer a wide range of services, including poste restante and electronic post. In country towns, the local general store is often also a post office. Look for the red and white postal sign.

Australian Post logo

Australian postman

DOMESTIC AND INTERNATIONAL MAIL

All domestic mail is first class and usually arrives within one to five days, depending on distance. Be sure to include postcodes on mailing addresses to avoid delays in delivery.

Express Post, for which you need to buy the special yellow and white envelopes sold in post offices, guarantees next-day delivery in certain areas of Australia. Air mail will take from five to ten days to reach most countries. There are two types of international express mail. EMS International Courier will reach nearly all overseas destinations within two to three days, whereas Express Post International takes four to five days.

Labels used for overseas mail

Typical stamps used for local mail

Stamp from a scenic series issue

Standard and express postboxes

POSTBOXES

Australia has both red and yellow postboxes. The red boxes are for normal postal service; yellow boxes are used exclusively for Express Post. Both types of postbox can be found on most street corners as well as outside post offices. If a yellow postbox is not to be seen, go to a post office and deliver your express mail over the counter.

POSTE RESTANTE

Poste restante can be sent to any post office in Australia. Mail should be addressed clearly and marked "poste restante". Visitors picking up mail will need to produce a passport or other proof of identity.

USEFUL INFORMATION

Australia Post Customer Service Centre
Tel 13 13 18.

TRAVEL INFORMATION

While some visitors to Australia may choose to arrive by sea ship, the vast majority arrive by air. Once here, flying between locations is also the most popular form of long-distance travel, but there are some other choices, all of which offer the chance to see something of the country along the way. The national rail network links all major

Airport Express bus into central Sydney

cities, while coach routes provide regular services to most provincial and country areas. If you have the time, driving in Australia is an excellent option. Boat travel is best for those wanting to visit Australia's islands, principally Tasmania, but regular services run to other island destinations such as Rottnest Island off the coast of Western Australia *(see pp308–9)*.

International Qantas flight arriving in Sydney

ARRIVING BY AIR

Australia is served by around 50 international airlines. The Australian airline **Qantas** has a worldwide network and offers the most flights in and out of Australia every week. Qantas is also the main domestic carrier in Australia *(see p584)*. **Air New Zealand**, Qantas and **United Airlines** have regular flights from the USA, with a range of stopovers available. The large Asian and European carriers, **British Airways**, **Singapore Airlines**, **Cathay Pacific** and **Japan Airlines**, offer many routes and stopovers on the Europe-Asia-Australia run. Canadian travellers can fly **Air Canada**, which connects with Qantas flights in Hawai'i.

INTERNATIONAL FLIGHTS

Flights between Australia and Europe take upwards of 22 hours, and with delays you may be in transit for more than 30 hours. A stopover in Asia is worth considering for

the sake of comfort, especially if travelling with children, as is one in Hawai'i or the Pacific islands for visitors from the USA. Also, consider arranging flights so that they account for international time differences. Arriving in the afternoon, spending the rest of the day

awake, then going to sleep in accordance with local time will help to counteract jet lag.

Australia has several international air terminals, so visitors can choose different arrival and departure points. Sydney and Melbourne have major airports servicing flights from all over the world. Sydney's Kingsford Smith Airport is the busiest and can be congested. Melbourne is consistently voted one of the world's best airports by travellers. Hobart has flights from New Zealand in the summer months, while Adelaide has direct flights to Singapore and and flights to Europe via Sydney or Melbourne. Visitors to the west coast can arrive in Perth from Africa, Asia and the UK. Darwin, Brisbane and Cairns mostly service Asia, but there are a few possibilities for connections from Europe.

AIRPORT	ℹ️ INFORMATION
Sydney	*(02) 9667 9 111* **www.sydneyairport.com.au**
Melbourne	*(03) 9297 1600* **www.melair.com.au**
Brisbane	*(07) 3406 3000* **www.bne.com.au**
Cairns	*(07) 4052 3888* **www.cairnsport.net.au**
Perth	*(08) 9478 8888* **www.perthairport.net.au**
Adelaide	*(08) 8308 9211* **www.aal.com.au**
Darwin	*(08) 8920 1811* **www.darwinairport.com.au**
Hobart	*(03) 6216 1600*

Singapore Airlines 747 taking off at Perth Airport

AIR FARES

Flights to Australia can be expensive, especially during December, the peak season. January to April is slightly cheaper. During the off-peak season, airlines offer Apex fares that are often 30–40 per cent below economy fares (see p584). Many stipulate arrival and departure times and carry cancellation penalties. Round-the-world fares are good value and increasingly popular.

Check with discount travel agents if you can fly at short notice, as they regularly receive unsold tickets from the airlines. In these cases, flexibility isn't usually a feature.

ON ARRIVAL

Just before setting down in Australia you will be given custom documents to fill in. On arrival you will be asked to present your documents, including passport, at the Entry Control Point (see p572). You will also be asked to throw away any food items. You can then collect your baggage and, if you have nothing to declare, proceed straight into the main area of the airport.

Larger airports have better services, but most have good shopping, postal and medical facilities. You can hire cars and change money at all airports. Taxis and buses are available for transport into city centres.

Arrangements for domestic flight connections are usually made when purchasing your

Check-in information board at Sydney Airport

original ticket. Airline staff will advise you how to proceed. In Melbourne, the domestic and international services are in the same terminal. In many places the terminals are separate and distances can be long – 10 km (6 miles) in the case of Perth. Free shuttle buses transfer passengers between terminals.

DIRECTORY

AIRLINE CARRIERS

Air New Zealand
Tel 132 476.

British Airways
Sydney **Tel** 1300 767 177.
Melbourne **Tel** 1300 767 177.
Perth **Tel** 1300 767 177.

Air Canada
Tel 1300 655 767.

Cathay Pacific
Tel 131 747.

Japan Airlines
Sydney **Tel** (02) 9272 1111.
Melbourne **Tel** (02) 8662 8333.
Brisbane **Tel** (07) 3229 9916.

Qantas
Tel 13 13 13.

Singapore Airlines
Tel 131 011.

United Airlines
Tel 131 777.

DISTANCE FROM CITY	TAXI FARE TO CITY	BUS TRANSFER TO CITY
9 km (6 miles)	A$25	30 mins
22 km (14 miles)	A$50	30–40 mins
15 km (9 miles)	A$30	30 mins
6 km (4 miles)	A$10	10 mins
15 km (9 miles)	A$26	25 mins
6 km (4 miles)	A$17	20 mins
6 km (4 miles)	A$15	15 mins
22 km (14 miles)	A$25	20–30 mins

Domestic Air Travel

Air travel accounts for a large proportion of long-distance journeys in Australia and is by far the most practical way of taking in a country of this size, particularly for those with time constraints. The main domestic air carriers in Australia, **Qantas**, **Virgin Blue** and **Jetstar**, concentrate on the high-volume interstate routes, while a host of small operators handle air travel within states and to remote locations. Fares can be expensive, but with the range of discounts available in this deregulated and aggressively competitive industry, it is unlikely that you will ever have to pay the full fare, providing you plan your air trips in advance. Spectacular speciality aerial tours of distant or hard-to-reach landmarks are also available *(see p567)*.

Cut-price domestic flight operated by Virgin Blue

Tiny domestic terminal in Birdsville, Queensland

AIR ROUTES AND AIRLINES

Australia's air network is vast, but reasonably streamlined, so arranging flights to even the most remote spots should never be a problem. It is possible to fly direct between most major destinations such as Sydney–Darwin or Melbourne–Perth. However, for smaller centres, you will invariably have to fly first to the capital city in the state, and then on to your destination. The small airlines that cover out-of-the-way routes are, in most cases, affiliated with Qantas, which means bookings can be made through Qantas' centralized booking services.

DISCOUNTS FOR OVERSEAS VISITORS

Discounted domestic air travel is often offered as part of an international package, so check with your travel agent about booking domestic trips before leaving home.

Once in Australia, Qantas offers immediate discounts to overseas travellers, which range from 25–40 per cent; proof of overseas residence is required when booking these tickets. Various air passes are available from Qantas which allow you to make a number of single flights for a set price. You can then move from leg to leg around the country rather than having to make return flights, which are normally expensive. When buying these passes abroad, you are sometimes required to pay half the cost before leaving home and half when booking the flights. In these cases, avoid buying too many flights in case your plans change. The passes are flexible, but restrictions do apply.

APEX FARES

Advance Purchase Excursion fares (Apex) are widely available for round-trip travel in Australia, and offer as much as 55 per cent off the full economy fare. There is usually no refund on these tickets, but flight times can often be altered. The general rule is that the further in advance you book your ticket, the better the discount. A 14-day advance booking will give you the best discount, then seven days, five days and so on. In most cases, you will be required to stay a Saturday night. Keep an eye out for very cheap, one-off fares advertised during quiet periods of the year, usually on popular routes such as Melbourne to Sydney. There is very little flight flexibility on these tickets and passengers are strictly required to fly within a set period of time. Cheap, no-frills flights are

Plane on the harbourside runway, Hamilton Island *(see p208)*

operated by Jetstar and Virgin Blue. These are best booked well in advance on the internet – the cheapest seats sell first.

FLY-DRIVE DEALS

A great way to see Australia is to fly to a destination and then continue on by car. Arrangements can be made for different pick-up and drop-off points for hire vehicles. For example, you could pick up a car in Sydney, drive to Brisbane, fly to Alice Springs and then pick up a car there. Virgin Blue and Qantas have deals with car hire companies, and they offer discounts to passengers who are travelling on those airlines (see p588).

BAGGAGE RESTRICTIONS

Passengers travelling economy on domestic flights may check in one piece of baggage weighing no more than 32 kg (70 lbs). For children under

Queueing for taxis at Sydney Airport domestic terminal

three who are travelling free, Virgin Blue and Jetstar allow one piece of baggage. Qantas has a policy of charging A\$10 per extra item; however, in many instances if there is no excess baggage on the flight, the charge is not applied. The cabin baggage weight and item allowance is strictly enforced. Personal items such as walking sticks, cameras, hand-bags, briefcases, overcoats and duty free items are all classified and weighed as part of the hand luggage allowance.

QANTAS
Qantas logo

CHECKING IN

Airlines request that you check in at least 30 minutes before your flight time. While it is not necessary to confirm flights, it is a good idea to call the airline to ensure that the flight is on time. Make sure you alight at the right terminal as many domestic and international terminals are at separate locations.

DIRECTORY

DOMESTIC AIRLINES

Qantas
Tel 131 313.
www.qantas.com.au

Virgin Blue
Tel 136 789 or
(61 7) 3295 2296.
www.virginblue.com.au

Jetstar
Tel 131 358.
www.jetstar.com.au

PRINCIPAL DOMESTIC AIR ROUTES

Domestic flights cover vast distances. Sydney to Perth, for example, is 3,400 km (2,225 miles) and a flight of 5 hours; the 2,600-km (1,615-mile) flight from Adelaide to Darwin is 3.5 hours.

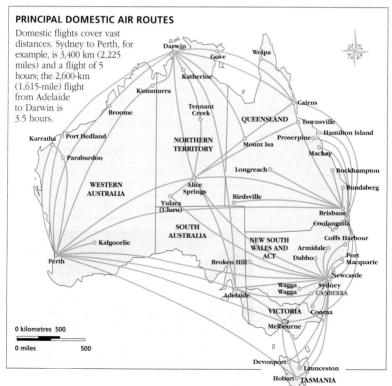

Travelling by Train and Coach

Rail Australia logo

The Australian continent does not have a comprehensive rail network. With its small population, the country has never been able to support an extensive system of railways and, in fact, services have declined in number over recent decades. However, there are several opportunities for rail enthusiasts: Australia still offers some of the world's great train trips, as well as regular services linking the cities of the east coast. Train journeys should also be considered for quick trips away from the city centres. Coach trips fill any gaps in overland travel in Australia, servicing major centres and remote outposts alike.

Mass Transit Railway Station in Perth

THE AUSTRALIAN RAIL NETWORK

Railways in Australia are state-operated. **Countrylink**, the federal body, oversees the various services. A staff change at state borders is the only indication most passengers get of a state-by-state system at work.

Train travel is cheaper than flying, but journey times are long. The Sydney–Brisbane trip takes 13.5 hours and Sydney–Melbourne takes 10.5 hours.

The prospects for rail travel within state boundaries vary. An increasingly common way of coping with the expense of maintaining rail systems is to substitute state-run coach services on under-used lines.

State governments accept responsibility for providing access to most areas, so where there is no rail network, such as in Tasmania, there will be an efficient, cheap coach network instead. Queensland, however, has increased its rail services, most of which are aimed at the tourist market.

SPECIALITY TRIPS

The chance to take in some of the country's extraordinary landscapes are what makes rail journeys in Australia so special. Standards are high, often with a level of luxury reminiscent of the grand old days of rail travel.

The Indian Pacific route takes three days to cover the 4,352 km (2,700 miles) from Sydney to Perth. The 478-km (300-mile) crossing of the Nullarbor Plain *(see p319)* is on the world's longest length of straight railway track.

The fabled Ghan railway runs between Adelaide and Alice Springs where there is a museum recounting its history *(see p283)*. The 1,559-km (970-mile) trip offers amazing desert scenery and takes two days.

Three different lines run the 1,681 km (1,045 miles) between Brisbane and Cairns: the Queenslander, the Sunlander and the Spirit of the Tropics. Another Queensland journey is aboard the Gulflander, a 152-km (95-mile) trip through some of Australia's most remote country.

The Overland (Melbourne–Adelaide) and the fast XPT trains (Brisbane–Sydney–Melbourne) have a more utilitarian approach to train travel.

TRAVEL CLASSES

There are three types of travel available on most interstate trains. Overnight services, such as Melbourne–Adelaide, offer first-class sleeper, first-class sit-up and economy sit-up. In addition, the Indian Pacific, the Ghan and various Queensland trains offer economy sleepers. All long-distance trains have dining facilities. First-class travel includes meals in the price of your ticket.

Motorail means you can travel with your car. The service is expensive, however, and you are better off hiring a car at your destination.

TICKETS AND BOOKINGS

Bookings for rail travel can be made with travel agents and at railway stations. Rail Australia provides support for the state operators. Further booking

Indian Pacific Railway, running from Sydney to Perth

Greyhound coach station in Sydney

DIRECTORY

RAIL COMPANIES

Countrylink
Info. and reservations. *Tel 132 232.* www.countrylink.info

COACH COMPANIES

Greyhound Australia
Tel 132 030 or 131 499.
www.greyhound.com.au

Premier Motor Service
Tel 133 410.
www.premierms.com.au

information is on their website (www.railaustralia.com).

There are a number of passes available to overseas visitors. The Austrail Pass allows travel anywhere in Australia, including metropolitan services, for 14-, 21- or 30-days. The Austrail Flexi-pass offers between 8 and 29 days of travel which can be taken any time over a six-month period.

Standard rail fares are high in Australia. However, there is a good range of rail fare discounts with up to 40 per cent off advance bookings.

COACH TRAVEL

Coach travel in Australia is cheap, efficient and generally safe. The two main operators are **Greyhound Australia** and **Premier Motor Service**.

There are a range of passes that reduce the cost of any extended travel. The Greyhound Aussie Explorer Pass is available on 12 pre-set routes, while the Aussie Kilometre pass offers greater flexibility; McCafferty's Coast and Centre pass will take you from Cairns, down the east coast and then up to Uluru and Alice Springs. However, it is worth remembering that this kind of travel can mean day after day on the road and nights spent sleeping upright. There are a range of other companies operating at a local level. These are good for trips to particular sights or national parks. Tourist information bodies in each state will give you advice on which company services which route *(see p575)*.

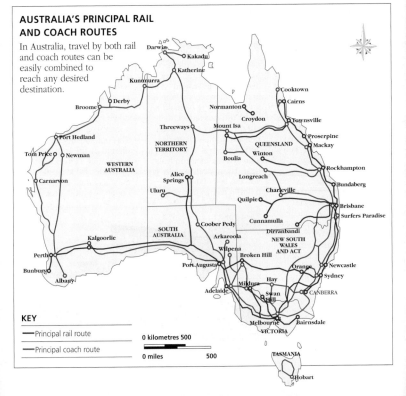

AUSTRALIA'S PRINCIPAL RAIL AND COACH ROUTES

In Australia, travel by both rail and coach routes can be easily combined to reach any desired destination.

KEY

—— Principal rail route

—— Principal coach route

0 kilometres 500

0 miles 500

Travelling by Car and Four-Wheel Drive

Great Ocean Road sign

It is well worth considering hiring a car when visiting Australia. Other modes of transport will get you around the cities and from one country town to another, but, once you arrive in a rural area or a small town, you may find it impossible to explore the area other than on foot or with a tour.

Australia offers the motorist the chance to meander through areas such as the vineyard regions of South Australia *(see pp338–9)*, the Southern Highlands of New South Wales *(see pp186–7)* and the Great Ocean Road of Victoria *(see pp428–9)*, as well as the experience of Outback travel on near-empty roads.

Driving through the Pinnacles in Nambung National Park *(see p316)*

DRIVING LICENCES

Providing your driving licence is in English and you have proof that you are a tourist, there is no need for an additional permit when driving in Australia. If the licence is not in English, you must carry a translation. It is a legal requirement that you have your licence with you at all times when driving.

CAR HIRE

Rental cars are available just about anywhere in Australia. They can be picked up at the airport on arrival, or arrangements can be made for delivery to your hotel. The big car rental firms **Avis**, **Budget**, **Hertz** and **Thrifty** have nationwide networks – an advantage if you are considering making several different trips across the continent. Check with your travel agent before leaving home about discounts or special fly-drive offers.

Rates vary from around A$55 a day for a small car to A$100 a day for larger vehicles. It is invariably more expensive to hire a 4WD vehicle; rates average out at around A$120 and are more costly in remote areas where the demand is high. You can reduce daily rates by hiring over longer periods (usually three days and over), or if you accept a limited kilometre/mileage deal. These deals usually give you the first 100 km (60 miles) a day as part of the

daily charge, and a per kilometre rate after that. This is well worth considering for inner-city driving, but not good value beyond the city limits where distances can add up very quickly. The smaller local operators offer very competitive rates, sometimes as low as A$25 a day, but read the small print carefully. Often the quote does not include the extras that the larger companies consider standard. If travelling with children, make sure the car is equipped with restraints according to Australian guidelines *(see p574)*.

Credit cards are the preferred method of payment when hiring a car. If paying with cash you will usually be required to pay the full cost of the rental, plus a deposit, when you pick up the car.

INSURANCE

For peace of mind it is a good idea to have comprehensive insurance when hiring a car. "Third party fire and theft" insurance is standard and included in the cost of the hire, as is insurance against accidental damage to the hire car. However, you will have to pay extra to reduce the excess payment. From upwards of A$7 a day, you can bring the excess down from around A$2,000 to a more comfortable A$100. This option is usually only offered by the larger car hire companies. Personal accident plans are also available, but they may not be necessary, depending on the cover

Car and van rental company in Sydney

offered with your own travel insurance. Four-wheel drive vehicles attract an excess rate of around A$4,000. For A$20 a day this can be reduced to a A$1,000, but never lower than this figure. Car hire companies will not offer insurance on any off-road driving, regardless of the vehicle type. Higher rates of insurance apply to drivers under the age of 25. Car hire in Australia is often not available to drivers under the age of 21.

Petrol station in Sydney

PETROL

Petrol is relatively cheap in urban areas compared to prices in Europe (though this may change), but in remote regions of the country prices rise considerably. It is dispensed by the litre and can be purchased in leaded, regular unleaded, premium unleaded and diesel grades. Many petrol stations are self-service and most accept major credit cards and have an EFTPOS facility *(see pp 578–9)*.

RULES OF THE ROAD

Australians drive on the left-hand side of the road and give way to the right in all circumstances unless otherwise indicated. Drivers must also give way to emergency vehicles – if possible, pull over to the side of the road when you hear a siren. The speed limit is 60 km/h (37 mph) in cities, towns and suburban areas and 100–110 km/h (62–68 mph) on major highways. The wearing of seat belts is compulsory for drivers and passengers.

Drink-driving laws are strictly enforced in Australia. The legal blood alcohol level is 0.05 per cent maximum. Should you be involved in an accident while over the alcohol limit, your vehicle insurance may be invalidated. Police in country areas are just as vigilant as their counterparts in the city, and it is not unusual to see a random breath-test taking place on an otherwise deserted road.

Beware of kangaroos sign

Any accident involving injury in Australia must be reported to the police within 24 hours. In Western Australia all accidents must be reported and in other states it is advisable to do so if there is considerable property damage. Always get insurance details from the other motorist. Do not admit fault – it is better to tell the police your version of events and let them decide.

The city of Melbourne has two road laws worth noting. First, motorists must stop behind a stationary tram to allow passengers to alight. Second, at certain city intersections, motorists who intend to turn right must pull over to the left of the intersection *(see pp 412–13)*. Called hook turns, they are clearly indicated and are designed to prevent traffic queuing across tram tracks.

ROAD CONDITIONS

Australia's road network is quite remarkable considering the distances it has to cover. Stretches of multi-lane highways are to be found on most of the major routes. The majority of other routes are covered by two-lane highways, which are generally well sealed and signposted. Unsealed dirt roads can always be found in country regions, but are rarely the only means of getting to a destination unless you are travelling through particularly remote country. Tollways are restricted to areas in the immediate vicinity of the large cities, such as the Western Motorway that covers part of the Sydney–Blue Mountains route. Melbourne has an intricate tollway system which is currently under construction. Service stations are plentiful along all the well-travelled routes, but they can be few and far between in the Outback. A particularly Australian and very dangerous road hazard is the prevalence of wildlife crossing country highways. This danger increases greatly at dusk and after dark when the nocturnal mammals, such as kangaroos and wallabies, surface to feed, but are often hard to see by the motorist.

ROADSIDE ASSISTANCE

Car hire companies will look after breakdowns of their rental cars and, if necessary, arrange for vehicle replacements. State-based motoring organizations provide roadside assistance for members around the country. The organizations also sell maps and guides in their central branches, and are a great source of information on road rules, road conditions and Outback driving. Members of motoring organizations in Great Britain, Canada and the United States usually have reciprocal membership rights with Australian organizations.

Royal Automobile Association vehicle in Adelaide

South approach to the Harbour Bridge in Sydney

INNER CITY DRIVING

If you are planning to drive within any city, a good street directory will be essential. If possible, avoid peak-hour traffic (7:30–9:30am and 4:30–7:30pm). Traffic reports are broadcast on radio stations.

The larger the city, the more difficult it will be to park in the city centre. Parking restrictions are clearly signposted and usually specify an hour or two of metered parking during business hours. Make sure you carry coins for the meters. Many cities have clearway zones that apply at certain times of the day and vehicles will be towed away if they are found parked here during these times. If this happens, telephone the local traffic authority or the police to find out where your vehicle has been impounded. Car parks are also to be found in and around city centres. Make sure you are clear about the cost before you park.

OUTBACK DRIVING

For any Outback travel, it is important to first check your route to see if a 4WD is required. Although some Outback areas now have roads of a high enough standard to carry conventional cars, a 4WD will be essential to travel to some wild and remote areas. Motoring organizations and tourist information centres can provide information that will enable you to assess your journey properly.

There are a number of basic points of safety that should be observed on any trip of this kind. Plan your route and carry up-to-date maps. If you are travelling between remote destinations, inform the local police of your departure and expected arrival times. Check road conditions before you start and carry plenty of food and water. Make sure you know where you can get petrol and carry extra supplies if necessary. If you run out of petrol or break down, remain with your vehicle. It offers some protection from the elements and, if you fail to arrive at the expected time, a search party will be sent out to look for you.

The **Australian Council of the Royal Flying Doctor Service (RFDS)** can offer safety advice to Outback tourists. You can also hire radio sets that have an emergency call button to the RFDS from **McKays Communication**. You should also observe important guidelines to protect the land. Native flora and fauna should not be removed or damaged. Stick to vehicle tracks, carry a stove and fuel

to avoid lighting fires, and take all rubbish with you. Be aware of Aboriginal land boundaries and national parks and leave gates as you find them: either open or shut.

DIRECTORY

CAR HIRE COMPANIES

Avis
Tel 136 333. www.avis.com.au

Budget
Tel 13 27 27.
www.budget.com.au

Hertz
Tel 133 039.
www.hertz.com.au

Thrifty
Tel 13 61 39.
www.thrifty.com.au

MOTORING ORGANIZATIONS

National Roadside Assistance
Australia-wide breakdown service.
Tel 131 111

New South Wales and ACT
National Road and Motorist's Association (NRMA). *Tel 131 111.*
www.nrma.com.au

Northern Territory
Automobile Association of NT Inc (AANT). *Tel (08) 8981 3837.*
www.aant.com.au

Queensland
Royal Automobile Club of Queensland (RACQ). Tel *13 19 05.*
www.racq.com.au

South Australia
Royal Automobile Association of SA Inc (RAA). *Tel (08) 8202 4600.*

Tasmania
Royal Automobile Club of Tasmania (RACT). *Tel (03) 6232 6300.*

Victoria
Royal Automobile Club of Victoria (RACV). *Tel 13 19 55.*

Western Australia
Royal Automobile Club of WA Inc (RACWA). *Tel 13 17 03.*

OUTBACK DRIVING

Royal Flying Doctor Service of Australia
Tel (02) 9241 2411 or (08) 8080 1777. www.flyingdoctors.net

McKays Communication
Tel 1300 656 186. www.mackayscommunications.com.au

Driving a 4WD along the Gibb River Road in the Kimberley

Travelling by Ferry and Cruise Boat

For an island continent, Australia has surprisingly few tourist cruises on offer. The most important route is that between Melbourne and Tasmania. Elsewhere ferries run between the mainland and island destinations such as Rottnest Island, Western Australia *(see pp308–9)*, and Fraser Island, off the Queensland coast *(see p242)*. There are, however, plenty of cruises of local waterways. Large cruise ships concentrate on the local Pacific area and in most cases sail in and out of Sydney.

The *QEII* passenger ship berthed at Circular Quay, Sydney *(see p75-85)*

ARRIVING BY BOAT

There is probably no better way of arriving in Australia than to sail into Sydney Harbour aboard a cruise ship. Cruising is expensive, however, and the services to Australia are very limited. In terms of getting to Australia from the USA or Europe, you may have to wait for the next world cruise on **P&O** or **Cunard Line** vessels. Another option is to fly to an Asian city such as Hong Kong and join up with **Princess Cruises**. Sydney is the main port of call for most cruise ships, and its two passenger terminals have excellent facilities.

FERRIES TO TASMANIA

The *Spirit of Tasmania* takes just over 14 hours to cross the Bass Strait from Melbourne to the island state of Tasmania. It runs at 6pm, Monday to Saturday, departing alternately from Port Melbourne and Devonport. The ship has every level of accommodation ranging from reclining cruise seats and backpacker berths to fully equipped suites. There are several restaurants, shops, and entertainment for children. The fares are reasonable considering the experience – a double cabin will cost around A$450 return for a couple in off-peak season, less if you book during a special offer period.

ISLAND CRUISES AND FERRIES

A sealink ferry departs from Cape Jervis, south of Adelaide, for Kangaroo Island *(see p354)*. In Western Australia, regular ferries run to Rottnest Island from Perth. There are many services between the mainland and the Barrier Reef islands *(see p216)*. A boat also runs between Seisia, Cape York, and Thursday Island, *(see p252)*. Contact the **Queensland Government Travel Centre** for more information.

RIVERS AND HARBOURS

Hiring a houseboat is an excellent way of seeing some of Australia's spectacular river scenery. Popular spots include the Hawkesbury River, New South Wales, and the Murray River which runs through New South Wales, Victoria and South Australia. There are tours of Darwin and Sydney harbours, cruises of the Swan River in Perth and the Yarra River in Melbourne. State tourist authorities can provide details *(see p575)*.

DIRECTORY

SHIPPING COMPANIES

P & O
Sydney. *Tel 1800 076 276.*
www.poaustralia.com.au

Southampton, UK.
Tel (0845) 358 5585.

Princess Cruises
California, USA.
Tel 1 800 PRINCESS or (661) 753 0000. www.princess.com

Cunard Line
New York, USA. *Tel (1 800) 254 5067.* www.cunard.com

Southampton, UK.
Tel (0845) 071 0300.

Sealink
Kangaroo Island. *Tel 131 301.*
www.sealink.com.au

Spirit of Tasmania
Hobart. *Tel 1800 634 006.*
www.spiritoftasmania.com.au

TOURIST INFORMATION

Queensland Travel Centre
Tel 1300 730 039.
www.queenslandtravel.com

Taking the ferry to Rottnest Island *(see pp308-9)*

General Index

Page numbers in **bold** type refer to main entries

A

Abbey's Bookshop (Sydney) 135
Aboriginal and Pacific Art (Sydney) 135
Aborigines **18–19**
  Aboriginal art **32–3**
  Aboriginal culture **30–31**
  Aboriginal Dreamtime Cultural Centre (Rockhampton) 244
  Aboriginal heritage tours 567
  Aboriginal Lands **262–3**
  Art Gallery of New South Wales (Sydney) 112
  Australian Museum (Sydney) 94
  Brisbane Waters National Park 169
  Burrup Peninsula 328
  Carnarvon National Park 245
  colonization of Australia 50
  Darwin and the Top End 267
  Dreamtime 18–19
  history 47–8
  Kakadu National Park 11, 276
  The Kimberley **297**
  Ku-ring-gai Chase National Park 126
  land rights 31, 58, 59
  Laura 252
  Moochalabra Dam 331
  Mulka's Cave 318
  Multicultural Northern Territory 265
  Mungo World Heritage Area 181
  Museum and Art Gallery of the Northern Territory (Darwin) 273
  Namadgi National Park 207
  National Gallery of Australia (Canberra) 202, 203
  poets 35
  Red Centre 279
  shops **134**, 135, 564–5
  Tasmania 457, 465, 466, 469
  Tiwi Aborigines 260, 274
  Ubirr Rock 263
  Uluru-Kata Tjuta National Park 286, 288–9
Abrolhos Islands 324, 325
Accessory shops 137
Accidents 589
ACT *see* Canberra and Australian Capital Territory
Adelaide and the Southeast **341–57**
  Adelaide 12, 335, **344–9**
  airport 582–3
  Ayers House **348–9**
  Barossa Valley Tour **356–7**
  climate 44
  discovering Australia 12
  history 341
  hotels 501–4
  map 342–3, 347
  restaurants 548–51
  Southeast Coastline **350–51**
  Street-by-Street map 344–5
  time zone 574
Adelaide Fringe 41
Adelaide Hills 338
Adelaide House (Alice Springs) 282
Adelaide Town Hall **346**
Administration Centre (Brisbane) 233
Adventure Associates 569

Adventure sports 567
  Sydney 147
Aerial tours 567
Agnes Waters 243
Air Canada 583
Air New Zealand 583
Air travel **582–5**
  Australian Aviation Heritage Centre (Darwin) 272
  domestic 584–5
  international 582–3
Aireys Inlet 429
Airports 582–3
Akira Isogawa (Sydney) 137
El Alamein Fountain (Sydney) **120**
Alannah Hill (Melbourne) 409
Albany 312, **316**
Albert, Prince Consort
  statue of 115
Albert Park (Melbourne) **403**
Alcohol
  driving laws 589
  in restaurants 519
  see also Wines
Alexandra Gardens (Melbourne) 375
Alice Springs 12, 261, 279, 281, **282–3**
  festivals 40, 43
  map 283
Alice Springs Show 43
Alligator Creek 246
Allom, Lake 243
Almond Blossom Festival (Mount Lofty) 43
Almonta Beach 366, 367
Alpine National Park 13, 446, 447, **448–9**
Alpine Way 160
Ambulances 576, 577
American Express 578
America's Cup 59, 310
AMP Tower *see* Sydney Tower
Anangu people 286, 287, 288, **289**
Andrew (Boy) Charlton Pool (Sydney) 71
Andrew McDonald (Sydney) 137
Angas family 357
Angus & Robertson's Bookworld (Sydney) 135
Animals *see* Wildlife; Zoos
Annandale Hotel (Sydney) 143
Anthem Records (Sydney) 135
Antipodeans **34**
Anzac Day 42, 43, 56–7
  Martin Place (Sydney) 90
Anzac Memorial (Sydney) 66, 93
Anzac Parade (Canberra) 195
Anzac Square (Brisbane) 220, **226**
ANZUS treaty 58
Apex fares
  domestic air travel 584–5
  international air travel 583
Apollo Bay 429
Aquariums
  Aquascene (Darwin) 272
  AQWA, Aquarium of Western Australia (Perth) 306
  Melbourne Aquarium **402**
  National Zoo and Aquarium (Canberra) **204**
  Oceanworld (Manly) 126
  Reef HQ (Townsville) 247
  Sydney Aquarium 97, **98**
Arakoon 178
Aranda people 284, 285

Arcades, shopping
  Melbourne 406–7
  Sydney 132–3
Archer, John Lee 460
Archibald, JF 93
Architecture
  Melbourne's Best **376–7**
  Sydney's Best **66–7**
Arid Lands Botanic Garden (Port Augusta) 365
Arid regions 24
Ariel (Sydney) 135
Arkaroola 369
Armani (Sydney) 137
Armidale **175**
Armstrong, Bruce 388
Armytage, Caroline 405
Armytage, Charles Henry 405
Armytage family 405
Arnhem Land 267
  rock art 33
ARQ (Sydney) 143
Art 21
  Aboriginal art **32–3**
  see also Museums and galleries
Art Gallery of New South Wales (Sydney) 63, 65, **110–13**
  Asian art 113
  Australian art 112
  contemporary art 113
  European art 112
  floorplan 110–11
  photography 112
  prints and drawings 113
  Visitors' Checklist 111
Art Gallery of South Australia (Adelaide) 345
Arthur's Seat 442
Artists **34**
The Ashes **436**
Athenaeum Theatre (Melbourne) 411
Atherton 255
Atherton, John 255
Atherton, Kate 255
Atherton Tableland **255**
The Atrium (Melbourne) 385
Augusta 312
Augustine, St 48
Ausfurs (Sydney) 135
Australia Act (1986) 59
Australia Day 43
Australia Day Concert (Sydney) 41
Australia Ensemble (Sydney) 141
Australia on Collins (Melbourne) 407
Australia Post Customer Service Centre 581
Australian Alps Walking Track 448
Australian-American Memorial (Canberra) 195
Australian Aviation Heritage Centre (Darwin) 272
Australian Ballet 21, 141
Australian Beach Pattern (Meere) 65
Australian Capital Territory (ACT) *see* Canberra and Australian Capital Territory
Australian Celtic Festival (Glen Innes) 42
Australian Centre for the Moving Image (ACMI, Melbourne) 402
Australian Chamber Orchestra (Sydney) 141
Australian Dental Association 577

Australian Football League Grand
  Final 40
Australian Formula One Grand Prix
  (Melbourne) 42
Australian Gallery of Sport and
  Olympic Museum (Melbourne)
  396
Australian Gold Diggings
  (Stocqueler) 54
Australian Golf Union 569
Australian Institute of Sport
  (Canberra) **204**
Australian Museum (Sydney) 65,
  94–5
Australian Museum Shop (Sydney)
  135
Australian National Botanic Gardens
  (Canberra) **204**
Australian National Maritime
  Museum (Sydney) 64, 66,
  100–101
  Street-by-Street map 97
Australian Open (tennis) 41
Australian Parachute Federation 569
Australian Rainforest Sanctuary
  168–9
Australian Reptile Park (Gosford)
  169
Australian Rugby League Grand
  Final 40
Australian Rules football
  Melbourne 13
  Sydney 146
Australian Stockman's Hall of Fame
  (Longreach) 257
Australian Tourist Commission 477,
  575
Australian Travel Specialists
  (Sydney) 131
Australian War Memorial (Canberra)
  195, **200–201**
Australian Woolshed (Brisbane) 219,
  231
Australian Yachting Federation 569
Australian Youth Choir (Sydney)
  141
Australiana shops **134**, 135, 564–5
Authors **35**
Automatic teller machines (ATMs)
  578
Autumn in Australia 42
Avalon 145
Avis 590
Avon River 317
Ayers, Sir Henry 348–9
Ayers House (Adelaide) **348–9**
Ayers Rock *see* Uluru-Kata Tjuta
  National Park
Ayers Rock Resort 289
Ayr **246**

B

Babinda and the Boulders **255**
Backhouse, Benjamin 224
Backpacker hotels and youth
  hostels **476**, 477
Bacon, Francis
  Study for Self Portrait 112
Baggage restrictions 585
Bairnsdale 445
The Balcony (2) (Whiteley) 112
Bald Rock 176
Baldessin, George 202
Ballarat 372, **434–5**
  festivals 42
  map 435

Ballarat Fine Art Gallery 434
Bally (Sydney) 137
Balmain Market (Sydney) 133
Balmoral 145
Balmoral House 37
Balmoral Windsurfing and
  Kitesurfing School (Sydney) 144
Banfield, EJ 255
Bangarra Dance Theatre (Sydney)
  141
Bank Hotel (Sydney) 143
Bank notes 579
Banking **578**
Banks, Sir Joseph
  Botany Bay 50, 51
  statue of 92
Barcaldine 249
Barmah Forest 431
Barnet, James
  Australian Museum (Sydney) 94
  Customs House (Sydney) 83
  General Post Office (Sydney) 90
  Justice and Police Museum
    (Sydney) 83
  Lands Department Building
    (Sydney) 92
Barney, Lt Colonel George 124
Barossa Valley 12, 19, 341
  Barossa Valley tour **356–7**
  Barossa wine region 335
Barracks Archway (Perth) 304
Barrington Tops World Heritage
  Area **175**
The Basement (Sydney) 143
The Basin (Rottnest Island) 309
The Basin (Sydney) 145
Basketball
  Sydney 146–7
Bass, George 52
  statue of 92
Bass, Tom 201
Bass Strait 465, 466, 467
  ferries 591
Batemans Bay 189
Bathers (Bunny) 228
Bathurst Island 11, 260, 267, **274**
Batman, John 52, 381
Battery Point (Hobart) 457, **461**
Baxters Cliff 319
Bayliss, Charles 112
Beach Watch Info Line (Sydney)
  144
Beaches
  Beach culture **38–9**
  Bondi Beach **126–7**
  Eastern Victoria's coastline **444–5**
  Great Ocean Road coastline
    428–9
  Northern New South Wales
    coastline **178–9**
  safety 577
  Southeast Coastline **350–51**
  Southern Coastline (Western
    Australia) **312–13**
  Southern Queensland coastline
    238–9
  Sunset Coast 306–7
  Sydney **144–5**
Beachport 351
Beagle, HMS 267
Beare Park (Sydney) **120**
Beatus 48
Beccafumi, Domenico
  *Madonna and Child with Infant
    St John the Baptist* 110
Bedarra Island 217

Beechworth 440, **450**
Beedelup National Park 315
Beer 523
Begonia Festival (Ballarat) 42
Belair National Park **352**
Belinda (Sydney) 137
Belinda Shoe Salon (Sydney) 137
Bell Shakespeare Company
  (Sydney) 141
Bellarine Peninsula **426**
La Belle Hollandaise (Picasso) 228
Bellenden Ker National Park **255**
Bellini, Mario 377
Bells Beach 429
  festivals 42
Belvoir St Theatre (Sydney) 141
Ben Boyd National Park 184, 189
Ben Lomond National Park **464**
Ben Sherman (Melbourne) 409
Benalla **451**
Benalla Art Gallery 451
Bendigo **432**
  Gold Rush 55
Bendigo Art Gallery 432
Benedictines 321, 324
Bennelong 51
Bent, Sir Thomas 404
Bentley, Peter 434
Berkelouw Books (Sydney) 135
Berri 355
Berri Renmano winery 339
Berrima 186
Berry Springs 272
Best's Wines 378
Bettina Liano (Melbourne) 409
Bicentennial Park (Darwin) 270
Bicentennial Park (Sydney) 68
Bicheno **463**
Bicycle New South Wales 128, 569
Bicycle Victoria (Melbourne) 413
Bicycles
  in Melbourne **412**, 413
  specialist holidays 566
  in Sydney 128, 147
Big Brother movement 56
Big Desert Wilderness Park **430**
Big Pineapple 238
The Big Swim (Sydney) 137
Bilgola 145
Birdland (Sydney) 135
Birds
  Birds of South Australia **336–7**
  Bool Lagoon 355
  Eagles Heritage Raptor Wildlife
    Centre (Margaret River) 314–15
  emus 337
  Flora and fauna **24–5**
  Great Barrier Reef 215
  Kakadu National Park 276
  Phillip Island 442
Birdsville Races 29
Birdwood **353**
Black Mountain National Park 252
Blackall Mountain Range 240
Blackdown Tableland National Park
  244
Blacket, Edmund
  Justice and Police Museum 83
  St Andrew's Cathedral (Sydney) 93
  St Philip's Church (Sydney) 82
Blackheath **173**
Blackman, Charles 34
Blackwood River 315
Blake, William 113
Blaxland, Gregory 52, 172
  statue of 92

Blechynden, John 315
Bligh, Ivo 436
Bligh, William 53
Block Arcade (Melbourne) **389**
The Blowholes 325
Blue Lake 160, 335, 354
Blue Mountains and Beyond
   165–81
   climate 45
   discovering Australia 10
   festivals 43
   hotels 482–3
   map 166–7
   restaurants 529–31
Blue Mountains Adventure
   Company (Sydney) 147
Blue Mountains National Park 10,
   170–73
Blue Poles (Pollock) 203
Blues music
   Sydney **142**, 143
Bluff Knoll 316–17
Blundell, George 196
Blundell's Cottage (Canberra) 194,
   196
Boats
   America's Cup 59, 310
   Australian National Maritime
     Museum (Sydney) 66, **100–101**
   ferries and cruise boats 131, **591**
   Great Barrier Reef 216
   houseboats 477, 591
   Maritime Museum (Hobart) **461**
   Melbourne Maritime Museum
     401, **402**
   Murray River Paddlesteamers
     430
   Queensland Maritime Museum
     (Brisbane) **227**
   river cruises (Melbourne) 413
   sailing 144, 569
   Sydney Harbour cruises 72
   Sydney to Hobart Yacht Race 41
   water taxis 131
   Western Australian Maritime
     Museum (Fremantle) 310
   Whyalla Maritime Museum
     (Whyalla) 365
Bogong High Plains 447
La Boite Theatre (Brisbane) 233
Boldrewood, Rolf 34, 180
Bond, Albert 93
Bondi Beach **126–7**, 145
   festivals 39, 40, 41
Bondi Beach Market (Sydney) 133
Bondi Surf Co. (Sydney) 137
Bondietto, Basilio 394
Bonner, Neville 58
Boodjidup Beach 312
Book shops **134**, 135, 409
The Bookshop Darlinghurst
   (Sydney) 135
Bool Lagoon 342, 355
Boomalli Aboriginal Artists'
   Cooperative (Sydney) 135
Boomerangs **30**
Boonoo Boonoo Falls 176
Borders (Melbourne) 409
Boston Bay 366
Botanic Gardens (Adelaide)
   Street-by-Street map 345
Botanic Gardens and the Domain
   (Sydney) **105–15**
   area map 105
   The Domain 69, **109**
Botanical Gardens (Ballarat) 435

Botany Bay 50
Bothwell **462–3**
Boulder *see* Kalgoorlie-Boulder
Bounty 53
Bourke 158, **181**
"Boutique" hotels 476
Bowali Visitor Centre 277
Bowling Green Bay National Park
   246
Bowral 186
Boxing Day 43
Boxing Day Test Match 41
Boyd, Arthur 34, 169
   Art Gallery of New South Wales
     (Sydney) 112
   National Gallery of Australia
     (Canberra) 202
   Parliament House (Canberra)
     tapestry 198
Boyd, David 34
Brack, John 34
Bradbridge brothers 93
Bradfield, Dr John 81
Bradleys Head (Sydney) 69
Bradman, Sir Donald 396
   Bradman Museum (Bowral) **186**,
     187
Brambuk National Park 427
Brampton Island 217
Brass Monkey Festival (Stanthorpe)
   43
Bridal Falls 173
Bridge Hotel (Sydney) 141
BridgeClimb (Sydney) 81
Bridges
   Pyrmont Bridge (Sydney) 97
   Sydney Harbour Bridge **80–81**
Bridgetown **315**
Bridgewater Mill winery 338
Bright **447**
Bright Autumn Festival 42
Brisbane 211, **219–33**
   airport 582–3
   climate 45
   discovering Australia 11
   entertainment 232–3
   hotels 487–90
   map 220–21
   practical information **232–3**
   Queensland Cultural Centre
     228–9
   restaurants 535–7
   shopping **232**, 233
   Street-by-Street map 222–3
   time zone 574
   travel 233
Brisbane, Sir Thomas 219
Brisbane Arcade (Brisbane) 233
Brisbane Botanic Gardens 220, **230**
Brisbane City Botanic Gardens
   (Brisbane) 11, **224–5**
Brisbane Forest Park **230–31**
Brisbane Marketing 233
Brisbane Ranges National Park 427
Brisbane River 219, 226, 227, 231
Brisbane Waters National Park 169
British Airways 583
British East India Company 79
Broken Bay 126
Broken Hill 158, **181**
Brokenwood
   Hunter Valley tour 174
Bronte 145
Broome 12, **330**
   festivals 43
Brown, Ford Madox 112

Brown Brothers 379
Brunswick Street (Melbourne) **396**
Brunswick Street Bookstore
   (Melbourne) 409
Bruny Island **469**
Buda Historic Home and Gardens
   (Castlemaine) 433
Budget (car hire) 590
Buffalo River 447
Builders Labourers' Federation 78
Building 8, RMIT (Melbourne) 384,
   385
Bulcock Beach (Caloundra) 238
Bunbury **314**
Bundaberg 235, 241
Bundaberg and District Historical
   Museum (Bundaberg) 241
Bungalow 8 (Sydney) 143
Bungaree Station 364
Bungle Bungles **296–7**, 321, 330,
   331
Bunker Bay 312
Bunning, Walter 197
Bunny, Rupert
   Bathers 228
Burdekin River Delta 235, 246
Bureaux de change **578**
Burge, Grant
   Barossa Valley tour 356
Burge, Helen 356
Burke, Robert O'Hara 29, 53
Burketown **257**
Burleigh Heads National Park 238
Burley Griffin, Lake 191, 195, 196
Burley Griffin, Walter 56, **197**
   Canberra 11, 159, 191, 197, 198,
     201
   General Post Office (Melbourne)
     388
   Parliamentary Triangle
     (Canberra) 194, 195
Burnett, Beni Carr Glynn 271
Burnie **466**
Burra Mine 364
Burrup Peninsula 328
Busby, James **36**
Buses
   Melbourne 412–13
   Sydney 129
Bush fires 577
Bush Plum Dreaming (Tjapaltjarri)
   33
Bush Tucker Dreaming
   (Napanangka) 263
Bushfire (Drysdale) 228
Bushwalking 566
Bussell, Alfred 315
Busselton **314**
Butler, Captain Harry 362
Butterfield, William 384, 389
Bvlgari (Melbourne) 409
BYO (Bring Your Own) 518, 519
Byron Bay 167, 178

C

Cable Beach 296, 330
Cadigal people 92
Cadman, Elizabeth 77, 78
Cadman, John 77, 78
Cadman's Cottage (Sydney) 66, **78**
   Street-by-Street map 77
Cairns 11, 210, 250, **254**
   airport 582–3
   map 254
Cairns Show 43
Calibre (Melbourne) 409

Caloundra 238
Camberwell Market (Melbourne) 407
Camel Cup (Alice Springs) 43
Camels 28
  camel trekking 567
Camp Cove 145
Campbell, Robert 79
Campbell family 196
Campbell's Storehouses (Sydney) **79**
Camping 477
  Outback 28
Canberra and Australian Capital Territory 20, 159, **191–207**
  Australian War Memorial **200–201**
  climate 45
  discovering Australia 11
  festivals 41
  Further afield in the ACT **206–7**
  hotels 486–7
  map 192–3
  Namadgi National Park **207**
  National Gallery of Australia **202–3**
  Parliament House **198–9**
  Parliamentary Triangle 194–5
  restaurants 533–4
  State tourist office 575
  time zone 574
Canberra Space Centre **206**
Candy's Apartment (Sydney) 143
Canoeing 568
Cape Barren Island 465
Cape Byron 165, 167
Cape Inscription 326
Cape Jervis 350
Cape Leeuwin 312
Cape Range National Park 328
Cape Tribulation 253
Cape Vlamingh Lookout 308
Cape Woolamai 442
Cape York
  festivals 43
Capital L (Sydney) 137
Capitol Theatre (Sydney) 141
Caravan parks 477
Cardin, Pierre 90
Carey, Peter 83
Carlton Gardens (Melbourne) 374
Carnarvon **325**
Carnarvon National Park 235, **245**
Carnival of Flowers 40
Carols by Candlelight (Melbourne) 41
Carrington Falls 186
Cars **588–90**
  driving in Melbourne **412**, 413
  driving in Sydney 128
  hiring 588, 590
  inner city driving 590
  insurance 588–9
  National Motor Museum (Birdwood) 353
  Outback driving 590
  parking 590
  petrol 589
  road conditions 589
  roadside assistance 589
  rules of the road 589
  safety 576
  York Motor Museum 317
  see also Tours by car
Castlemaine **432–3**
Castray Esplanade (Hobart) **461**

Cat & Fiddle Hotel (Sydney) 143
Catani, Lake 447
Cataract Gorge Reserve (Launceston) 465
Cathay Pacific 583
Cathedral of Ferns 170
Cathedral Ranges 446
Cathedrals
  Cathedral of St Stephen (Brisbane) 222, **224**
  St Andrew's Cathedral (Sydney) 93
  St Francis Xavier Cathedral (Geraldton) 322, 324
  St Francis Xavier Catholic Cathedral (Adelaide) **346**
  St George's Anglican Cathedral (Perth) 302, 304–5
  St James' Old Cathedral (Melbourne) **387**
  St John's Anglican Cathedral (Brisbane) **226**
  St Mary's Cathedral (Sydney) **92**
  St Mary's Roman Catholic Cathedral (Perth) 303
  St Patrick's Cathedral (Melbourne) 393
  St Paul's Cathedral (Melbourne) 381, 384, **389**
  St Peter's Anglican Cathedral (Adelaide) 341, 342
The Cathedrals (Fraser Island) 242
Catherine Manuell (Melbourne) 409
Cave (Sydney) 143
Caves
  Carnarvon National Park 245
  Cutta Cutta 275
  Engelbrecht Cave 354
  Jenolan Caves 170, **173**
  Lake Cave 313
  Maternity Cave 355
  Mount Etna National Park 244
  Mulka's Cave 318
  Naracoorte Caves Conservation Park **355**
  Nullarbor Plain 367
  Victoria Cave 355
  Wombeyan Caves 186–7
  Yarrangobilly Caves 161
Cazneaux, Harold 112
Ceduna **367**
Centennial Park (Sydney) 69, **125**
Centennial Park Cycles (Sydney) 147
Centennial Parklands Equestrian Centre (Sydney) 147
Central Deborah Goldmine (Bendigo) 432
Central Land Council 262
Central Market (Adelaide) **346**
Central Plateau Conservation Area 463
Central Station (Fraser Island) 242
Central Station Records and Tapes (Sydney) 135
Central Tilba 188
Chaffey, George 430
Chaffey, William 430, 431
Chain hotels **475**, 477
Challis Avenue (Sydney)
  Street-by-Street map 119
Chambers Pillar Historical Reserve 261, **284**
Champion Bay 324
Champions – Australian Racing Museum and Hall of Fame (Melbourne) 402

Chan, Harry 264
Chanel (Sydney) 137
Chapel Street (Melbourne) **403**
Charles Sturt University Winery 162
Charlottes Pass 160
Charters Towers 235, **247**
Chemist shops 577
Cheques, in shops 564
Chifley Plaza (Sydney) 133
Children **574**, 575
  clothes shops 136–7, 408
  in hotels 474–5
  in restaurants 519
Chiltern **450**
Chinatown (Brisbane) **226–7**
Chinatown (Melbourne) **391**
Chinatown (Sydney) **99**
Chinese community
  The Chinese in the Top End **264**
  The Chinese on the Gold Fields **433**, 450
  Museum of Chinese Australian History (Melbourne) **391**
Chinese Garden (Sydney) **98–9**
  Street-by-Street map 96
Chinese Laundry (Sydney) 143
Chinese New Year 41
Chirnside family 426
Christmas 41, 43
Christo 78
Churches *see* Cathedrals *and individual towns and cities*
Cinema 21
  Australian Centre for the Moving Image (ACMI, Melbourne) 402
  Melbourne International Film Festival 43
  Outback 29
  Powerhouse Museum (Sydney) 64
  Sydney 141
  Sydney Film Festival 43
Cinema Paris (Sydney) 141
Circular Quay (Sydney) *see* The Rocks and Circular Quay
Cities, driving in 590
City Baths (Melbourne) 384, 415
City Centre and Darling Harbour (Sydney) **87–103**
  area map 87
  Street-by-Street map 88–9
City Hall (Brisbane) **225**
City Museum (Melbourne) **396**
City of York Bay 308
City Recital Hall (Sydney) 141
City Sights Bus Tour (Brisbane) 233
City to Surf Race 43
CityLink (Melbourne) 412, 413
CityRail (Sydney) 130
Civic Square (Canberra) **201**
Clare Valley 12, 360, **364**
Clarence, Duke of 434
Clark, John James 392, 396
Clarke, Lady 436
Clarke, Sir William John 436
Clarke Ranges 246
Classical music **140**, 141
Cleland Wildlife Park (Mount Lofty) 353
Clifton Gardens 145
Climate **44–5**
  when to go 572
Cloncurry 257
Clothes
  dress codes 573
  Outback clothing 565

Clothes (cont.)
in restaurants 519
shops **136**, 137, 408
size chart 136
Clovelly 145
Club Kooky (Sydney) 143
Clyde River 462
Coach travel 413, **587**
Coal Board building (Brisbane)
Street-by-Street map 223
Coastlines *see* Beaches
Cobourg Peninsula **274**
Cockburn Ranges 297
Cockle Bay Wharf (Sydney)
Street-by-Street map 97
Cocklebiddy 319
Coffin Bay 359
Coffin Bay National Park **366–7**
Coffs Harbour 178
Coins 579
Coles Bay 463
Collect (Sydney) 137
Collette Dinnigan (Sydney) 137
Collingwood Homestead
(Angaston)
Barossa Valley tour 357
Collins Street (Melbourne), No.120
390–91
Colombian (Sydney) 143
Colonization of Australia **50–51**
Combes, James 75
Comedy
Comedy Store (Sydney) 141
Comedy Theatre (Melbourne)
411
Sydney **140**, 141
Commissariat Store Museum
(Brisbane) **224**
Street-by-Street map 222
Commonwealth Bank 578
Commonwealth Games 59, 219
Commonwealth Park (Canberra)
195
Commonwealth of Australia 56
Como Centre (Melbourne) 407
Como Historic House and Garden
(Melbourne) **405**
Conder, Charles 34, 112
Conjola, Lake 189
Conrad, Joseph 83
Conrad Treasury (Brisbane) 233
Conservatorium of Music (Sydney)
108
Conspicuous Beach 313
Constable, John 113
Constitution Dock (Hobart) 458,
460
Consumer rights, shopping 564
Continent, Australian 23
Conversion chart 575
Convicts
colonization of Australia 19–20,
50–51
Hyde Park Barracks (Sydney) 65
Port Arthur 470–71
Coo-Ee Aboriginal Art Gallery
(Sydney) 135
Coober Pedy 12, 334, **368**
Coogee 145
Cook, Captain James 50, 51
Cape Tribulation 253
Captain Cook Memorial Jet
(Canberra) 195, 196–7
Cook's Cottage (Melbourne) 392
Cooktown 252
Endeavour 101

Cook, Captain James (cont.)
Gladstone 243
Glasshouse Mountains 230, 241
Indian Head 242
James Cook Memorial Museum
(Cooktown) 252
journals 195, 197
Magnetic Island 247
Moreton Bay 219
New South Wales 165
Northern and Outback
Queensland 249
Point Hicks 445
Cook's Cottage (Melbourne) 376
Street-by-Street map 392
Cooktown **252**
Coolangatta 238
Cooloola National Park 239
Cooma 185, **187**
Coonawarra 334
Cooper, Robert 124
Cooper, Sarah 124
Cooper Park Tennis Courts
(Sydney) 147
Cooraminta Estate 162
Coorong National Park 12, 341, 351
"Copper Coast" 363
Coral
Great Barrier Reef **212–17**
Houtman Abrolhos Islands 325
Ningaloo Reef Marine Park 328
Corin Dam 207
Corner Inlet 444
Corrigan, Peter 377
Corroboree Rock 284, 285
Cosmopolitan Shoes (Sydney) 137
Cossack Historical Town **329**
Cossington Smith, Grace
Interior with Wardrobe Mirror
112
Cotter River 206
Cottesloe Beach 306
Country house hotels 475
Country Music Festival (Tamworth)
41
Countrylink **587**
CountryLink (Victoria) 412, 413
Countrylink Travel Centres 130
Cowan, Edith 56, 317
Cowan, Walkinshaw 317
Cowes 442
Cox, Philip 100, 377
Cox River 172
Cradle Mountain Lake St Clair
National Park 13, 22, 454, **467**
Cranbourne Botanic Gardens **442**
Credit cards **578**
in restaurants 518
in shops 132, 564
Crescent Head 179
Cricket
Bradman Museum (Bowral) **186**,
187
Melbourne Cricket Ground 13,
397
Rupertswood and the Ashes **436**
Sydney 146
Test Match (Sydney) 41
Crime 576
Criminal Courts and Penitentiary
Chapel (Hobart) **460**
Croajingolong National Park 439, 445
Crocodiles
Broome Crocodile Park 330
safety 577
Wyndham Crocodile Park 331

Crowdy Bay 178
Crown Entertainment Centre
(Melbourne) 401
Croydon Travel 569
Cruise boats **591**
Crumpler (Melbourne) 409
Crumpler (Sydney) 137
CUB Malthouse (Melbourne) 411
Cunard Line 591
Curl Curl 145
Currency 579
Customs and excise 583
Customs House (Brisbane) **226**
Customs House (Sydney) **83**
Cutta Cutta caves 275
Cycling
in Melbourne **412**, 413
specialist holidays 566
in Sydney 128, 147
Cyclone Tracy **272**

D

Daintree National Park 11, 250, **253**
Dampier **328–9**
Dampier, William 49, 321
Dampier Archipelago 329
Dance
Aboriginal 31
Sydney **140**, 141
Dandenong Ranges **443**
Darling Downs 240
Darling Harbour (Sydney) 87
Street-by-Street map 96–7
Darling Harbour Jazz Festival
(Sydney) 43
Darling River 181
Darlinghurst (Sydney) *see* Kings
Cross, Darlinghurst and
Paddington
Darlinghurst Court House (Sydney)
67, **121**
Darwin, Charles 83, 267
Darwin and the Top End **267–77**
airport 582–3
climate 44
Darwin 260, **270–73**
discovering Australia 11
Greater Darwin **272**
history 267
hotels 495–6
map 268–9, 271
Multicultural Northern Territory
264–5
Museum and Art Gallery of the
Northern Territory **273**
restaurants 541–3
time zone 574
Dauphin Chart 48
David Jones (Melbourne) 407
David Jones (Sydney) 133, 137
Dawson, Alexander 83
Dayes, Edward
A View of Sydney Cove 50–51
De Bortoli winery 162
De Groot, Francis 80
Dead Horse Gap 160
The Deanery (Perth)
Street-by-Street map 302
Déclic (Melbourne) 409
Dee Why 145
Dehydration in deserts 287
Del Rio (Sydney)
Street-by-Street map 119
Dendy Cinema (Sydney) 141
Denham 326

Denmark 313, **316**
Dentists 577
D'Entrecasteaux National Park 313
Department of Immigration 575
Department stores 565
  Melbourne **406**, 407
  Sydney 133
Derby **331**
Derwent River 460, 462
Deserts
  dehydration 287
  Kimberley and the Deserts **330**
Desmond, A New South Wales Chief
  (Earle) 47
Devil's Marbles Conservation
  Reserve 261, **285**
Devonian Reef National Parks 331
Devonport **466**
Dialling codes 581
Dickerson, Robert 34
Diesel (Sydney) 137
Dinosaur Designs (Melbourne) 409
Dinosaur Designs (Sydney) 135
Disabled travellers **573**, 575
  entertainments 139, 411
  hotels 475
  Melbourne 413
  restaurants 519
Discounts
  domestic air travel 584
  entertainment tickets 139, 411
Discurio (Melbourne) 409
Dive Centre Manly (Sydney) 144
Diving 568
  Fishing and Diving on the Yorke
    Peninsula **363**
  Great Barrier Reef 216
  Sydney 144
Dobell, William 34, 112
  Darlinghurst Art School 121
  Dobell House (Wangi Wangi) 169
  Dobell Memorial Sculpture
    (Sydney) 90
Docklands (Melbourne) **388**
Doctors 576–7
Dolphin Discovery Centre
  (Bunbury) 314
The Domain (Sydney) *see* Botanic
  Gardens and the Domain
Domaine Chandon vineyard 443
Done, Ken 34
  Toberua 34
Done Art and Design (Sydney) 135
Donnelly River 315
Douglas Apsley National Park 463
Dowie, John 346
Downe, William Benyon 432–3
Dragstar (Sydney) 137
Drake, Sir Francis 48, 49
Dreamtime 18–19, **30–31**
Drinking Fountains (Healey) 345
Drinks *see* Food and drink
Driving licences 588
Drysdale, Sir Russell 34, 112
  Bushfire 228
  Sofala 110
Dubbo **180**
Ducker, Andy 316
Dunk Island 217, 251, **255**
Dunsborough 312
Dupain, Max
  Sunbaker 110
Duty-free shops 132
Duxford Street (Sydney)
  Street-by-Street map 122
Dymocks (Sydney) 135

E
Eagle Bluff 326
Eagle Point 445
Eagles Heritage Raptor Wildlife
  Centre (Margaret River) 314–15
Earle, Augustus
  *Desmond, A New South Wales
    Chief* 47
East Sail 144
East Timor 265
Easter 42, 43
Easter Fair (Maldon) 42
Eastern Victoria **439–51**
  climate 45
  coastline **444–5**
  discovering Australia 13
  hotels 512–15
  map 440–41
  restaurants 559–61
Echo Point 165
Echuca **431**
Ecotourism 568
Ecotourism Association of Australia
  569
Eden 188
Eden Valley 335
Edinburgh, Prince Alfred, Duke of
  434
Edith Falls 275
Edmund Wright House (Adelaide)
  346
Eildon, Lake 441, **446**
Eildon National Park 446
Electrical appliances 575
Electronic transfer of money **578**
Eli Creek 242
Elizabeth II, Queen of England
  High Court of Australia
    (Canberra) 197
  Sandringham Garden (Sydney) 93
Elizabeth Arcade (Brisbane)
  Street-by-Street map 222
Elizabeth Bay (Sydney) 63
  Street-by-Street map 119
Elizabeth Bay House (Sydney) 65,
  67, **120**
  Street-by-Street map 119
Elizabeth Farm (Parramatta) 127
Ellensbrook 315
Elsey Homestead 261
Elsey National Park 275
Emerald 244
Emergency services 577
Emma Gorge 297
Empire Hotel (Sydney) 143
Emus 337
Endeavour, HMS 50, 249, 252
  Australian National Maritime
    Museum (Sydney) 64
  replica 101
Engelbrecht Cave 354
Enmore Theatre (Sydney) 143
Enright, Nick 35
Ensemble Theatre (Sydney) 141
Entally House (Hadspen) 466
Entertainment
  booking agencies 139, 410–11
  Brisbane 232–3
  buying tickets 138
  choosing the best seats 139, 411
  cinema 141
  classical music **140**, 141
  comedy **140**, 141
  dance **140**, 141
  disabled visitors 139, 411

Entertainment (cont.)
  discount tickets 139, 411
  information 138
  Melbourne **410–11**
  music venues and nightclubs
    142–3
  opera **140**, 141
  outdoor and street entertainment
    411
  Sydney **138–43**
  theatre **140**, 141
Environmental hazards 577
Esperance **319**
Etiquette 573
Eucalypts 17
Eucla National Park 319
Eungella National Park **246**
Eureka Centre (Ballarat) 434–5
Eureka Stockade 54, **434**
Eureka Tower 376
Eurobodalla Coast 188
Evans, Len 174
Everglades House (Leura) 172
Exmouth **328**
Explorers 29
  Northern and Outback
    Queensland 249
Eyre, Edward John 29, 52, 53
Eyre, Lake 369
Eyre Highway 318, 319, 367
Eyre Peninsula *see* Yorke and Eyre
  Peninsulas

F
Fairfax & Roberts (Sydney) 135
Fairy Bower 145
Falls Creek 447
  Skiing in the Victorian Alps 448
Famous Grapevine Attraction
  (Chiltern) 450
Far North (South Australia) **368**
  map 368
Farage Man & Farage Women
  (Sydney) 137
Farm Cove (Sydney) 71
Farm stays 477
Farmshed Museum and Tourism
  Centre (Kadina) 363
Fashion **136**, 137
Fat (Melbourne) 409
Fat (Sydney) 137
Fawcett & Ashworth 402
Fawkner, John 375
Fawkner Park (Melbourne) 375
Fax services 580
Federation 56
Federation Square (Melbourne) 385,
  402
Felipe III, King of Spain 49
Felton, Alfred 403
Ferries **591**
  Sydney 131
Festival Centre (Adelaide)
  Street-by-Street map 344
Festival of Perth 41
Festival of Sydney 41, 141
Festival of the Winds (Bondi Beach)
  39, 40
Festivals **40–43**
Film *see* Cinema
Finke Gorge National Park 284–5
Fire
  bush fires 577
  fire services 576, 577
Fire Brigade Museum (Perth) 305
  Street-by-Street map 303

Fireworks Gallery (Brisbane) 233
First Fleet 50, 75
First Fleet Ship (Holman) 51
Fish
　fishing 145, 568
　Fishing and Diving on the Yorke
　　Peninsula **363**
　Great Barrier Reef **214–15**
　Sydney Fish Market 133
　see also Aquariums
Fish Records (Sydney) 135
Fisher, Andrew 197
Fishermans Beach 145
Fitzroy Gardens (Melbourne) 374
　Street-by-Street map 393
Fitzroy (Melbourne) **396**
Fitzroy Falls 186
Fitzroy Island 217
Fitzroy River 244
Fitzroy Street (Melbourne) **403**
Five Ways (Sydney) **124**
　Street-by-Street map 122
Flagpole (Cockle Bay, Sydney) 82
Flagstaff Gardens (Melbourne) 375
Flame Opals (Sydney) 135
Flecker Botanic Gardens (Cairns)
　254
Fleurieu Peninsula 341
Flickerfest (Sydney) 141
Flinders 442
Flinders, Matthew 52
　statue of 92, 109
Flinders Bay 312
Flinders Chase National Park 350,
　354
Flinders Island **465**
Flinders Ranges 12, 335, **369**
　Birds of South Australia 336
Flinders Ranges National Park 359,
　369
Flinders Street Station (Melbourne)
　373, 381, 385, 400, **402**
Flora and fauna **24–5**
Floriade (Canberra) 41
Flowers
　Flora and fauna **24–5**
　International Flower and Garden
　　Show (Melbourne) 42
　Jacaranda Festival (Grafton) 41
　Wildflowers of Western Australia
　　294–5
　see also Parks and gardens
Flugelman, Bert 90, 202
Fly-drive deals 585
Flying Doctors *see* Royal Flying
　Doctor Service
Flynn, Rev John 257, 282
　John Flynn's Memorial Grave 284
Folk music
　Maldon Folk Festival 41
　Sydney **142**, 143
Folkways (Sydney) 135
Food and drink
　beach snack food 39
　The Flavours of Australia
　　520–21
　What to Drink in Australia **522–3**
　Wines of Australia **36–7**
　Wines of New South Wales and
　　ACT **162–3**
　Wines of South Australia **338–9**
　Wines of Victoria **378–9**
　see also Restaurants
Football (Sydney) 146
Fort Denison (Sydney) **108**
Fort Stratchley (Newcastle) 169

Fortitude Valley (Brisbane) **226–7**
Forum Theatre (Melbourne) 411
The Founding of Australia
　(Talmage) **82**
Four Sisters 378
Fox Studios Entertainment Quarter
　125
François Peron National Park 326
Franklin, Miles 35, 83
Franklin-Gordon Wild Rivers
　National Park 13, 455, 458,
　468–9
Franklin River 455, **468–9**
Fraser, Elizabeth 242
Fraser, James 242
Fraser, Malcolm 59
Fraser Island 237, **242**
Fraser National Park 446
Free Traders 56
Fremantle 12, 292, **310–11**
　map 311
Fremantle Museum and Arts Centre
　(Fremantle) 311
French, Leonard 197, 377
French Island 442
Frenchmans Cap 468, 469
Freshwater 145
Freycinet National Park 459, **463**
Freycinet Reach 326
Friend, Donald 120
Furneaux Island Group 465
Fysh, Hudson 257

G

The Gaelic Club (Sydney) 143
Galeries Victoria (Sydney) 133
Galleria Shopping Plaza
　(Melbourne) 407
Gammon Ranges National Park 369
Garden Island (Sydney) 70
Garden of Joy (Bendigo) 432
Gardens *see* Parks and gardens
Garigal National Park 68
Garrison Church (Sydney) **82**
　Street-by-Street map 76
Gascoyne River 325
Gaslight Records (Melbourne) 409
Gaunt, Thomas 389
Gawler
　festivals 43
Gay and Lesbian Mardi Gras
　Festival (Sydney) 41
Gay and lesbian pubs and clubs,
　Sydney 143
Geelong **426–7**
Gemstones
　opals 29, **134**, 135, 180, 368, 565
　sapphires 176, 177, 244
General Pants (Sydney) 137
General Post Office (Brisbane)
　224
General Post Office (Melbourne)
　388
Genki (Melbourne) 409
George III, King of England 50, 51
George V, King of England 93, 434
George VI, King of England 93
George Brown Darwin Botanic
　Gardens 272
Geraldton 322, **324–5**
Gerlinki Junior (Melbourne) 409
Gibb River Road 297
Gibraltar Range National Park **176**
Gibson Desert 330
Gill, ST
　Might versus Right 55

"Gingerbread houses" (Sydney)
　Street-by-Street map 122
Ginn, Henry 82
Gippsland 439
　Eastern Victoria's coastline
　　444–5
Gippsland Lakes 444, 445
Gipsy Point 445
Giulian's (Sydney) 135
Gladstone **243**
Glasser, Neil 90
Glasshouse Mountains 230, 241
Glebe Market (Sydney) 133
Gleebooks (Sydney) 135
Glen Innes 176
　festivals 42
Glenoran Pool 315
Glenrowan **451**
Gliding Federation of Australia 569
Gloucester National Park 315
Glover, John 112
Gold Coast 211, 235, 238
Gold Rush **54–5**
　Ballarat 434
　Beechworth 450
　Bendigo 432
　Central Deborah Goldmine
　　(Bendigo) 432
　Charters Towers 247
　The Chinese on the Gold Fields
　　433, 450
　Gold Fields and Nullarbor Plain
　　12, **318**
　Halls Creek 331
　Kalgoorlie-Boulder **318–19**
　　map 318
　Mudgee 177
　Norseman 319
　Sovereign Hill **433**
　"Welcome Stranger" gold nugget
　　95
Golden Beach (90 Mile Beach) 444
Golden Dragon Museum (Bendigo)
　432
The Golden Fleece (Roberts) 111,
　112
Golf 567
　Sydney 146
Gondwanaland 23, 47
Good Friday 43
Good Living Growers' Market
　(Sydney) 133
Goodbar (Sydney) 143
Goona Warra 437
Gordon River 468
Gordons Bay 145
Gosford **168–9**
Goulburn **187**
Goulburn River 446, 451
Government 20–21
Government House (Canberra) **199**
Government House (Melbourne)
　399
Government House (Perth)
　Street-by-Street map 302
Government House (Sydney) 72
Governor Phillip Tower (Sydney)
　66
Governor Phillip's House (Sydney)
　51
Gow, Charles 348
Gowings (Sydney) 133
Grafton 178
　festivals 41
Grampians 13, 423
　Flora and Fauna **427**

Grampians National Park 372, 425, **427**
Grapes
red wine 523
white wine 522
Wines of New South Wales and ACT 163
Wines of South Australia 339
Wines of Victoria 378, 379
Great Australian Bight 318, 360, 367
Great Barrier Reef 11, 23, 38, 211, **212–17**
islands 243, **246**, 255
Great Depression 57
Great Dividing Range 17, 22
Great Keppel Island 217
Great Mountain Race of Victoria (Mansfield) 41
Great Northern Highway 296
Great Ocean Road 13, 425, 426
Great Ocean Road coastline **428–9**
Great Sandy Desert 330
Great Synagogue (Sydney) **93**
Greater Union Hoyts Village Complex (Sydney) 141
Green, Alexander "The Strangler" 121
Green Island 217, 249, **253**
Greenway, Francis 66, **169**
Conservatorium of Music (Sydney) 108
Hyde Park Barracks (Sydney) 114
Macquarie Place (Sydney) 83
Old Government House (Parramatta) 127
St James' Church (Sydney) 66, 115
St Matthew's Church (Windsor) 168
Greer, Germaine 83
Gregory National Park **275**
Grey, Zane 188
Greyhound Australia 587
Griffin, Walter Burley see Burley Griffin, Walter
Grollo, Bruno 387
Grose River 172, 173
Grotto Point (Sydney) 69
Grounds, Sir Roy 377
Group Hassell 390
Guerard, Eugene von 434
Guided tours 574
Guilfoyle, William 374–5, 398, 399
Gucci (Sydney) 137
Guluyambi Cultural Cruises 277
"Gum trees" 17
Gundagai 181
Gunlom Waterhole 276
Gunn, Jeannie 261, 275
Gurig National Park 274
Guston, Philip 113
Guth, Hendrik
Panorama Guth (Alice Springs) 282

H
Hadspen **466**
Hahn, Captain Dirk 352
Hahndorf 341, **352–3**
Half Tix (Melbourne) 411
Halls Creek **331**
Halls Gap 372
Halpern, Deborah 414
Hamelin Bay 312

Hamelin Pool Stromatolites 327
Hamilton Island 217
Hanging Rock
Macedon Ranges and Spa Country tour 437
Hanging Rock Picnic Races 41
Hannan, Paddy 319
Harbourside Complex (Sydney) 133
Street-by-Street map 96
Hardy Brothers (Sydney) 135
Hargraves, Edward 54
Harry's Café de Wheels (Sydney) 71
Hartog, Dirk 49, 326
Hattah-Kulkyne National Park **430**
Hawke, Bob 59
Hawkesbury Museum (Windsor) 168
Hawkesbury River 126, 168
Hawks Head 325
Hayman Island 217
Hazards Mountains 463
Head of Bight 367
The Heads 442
Healesville Sanctuary 443
Healey, Christopher
Drinking Fountains 345
Health **576–7**
Royal Flying Doctor Service 57, **257**, 590
Heat exhaustion 287
Heidelberg School 34, 112
Helen Kaminski (Sydney) 137
Helplines 577
Henbury Meteorites Conservation Reserve **284**
Henley-on-Todd Regatta (Alice Springs) 40
Henrietta Rocks 309
Henry the Navigator 48
Henschke Winery
Barossa Valley tour 357
Hepburn Springs
Macedon Ranges and Spa Country tour 436
Her Majesty's Theatre (Melbourne) 411
Herbert, Daniel 464
Heritage and Nautical Museum (Wallaroo) 363
Hermannsburg Historic Precinct **284**, 285
Hero of Waterloo (Sydney) **79**
Street-by-Street map 76
Heron Island 217, 243
Hertz 590
Hervey Bay **241**
Heysen, Sir Hans 34, 353
High Court of Australia (Canberra) 194, **197**
Highfield House (Stanley) 466–7
Hill, Walter 225
Hills Forest 307
Hinchinbrook Island **255**
Hindmarsh, John 341
Hindmarsh Island 350
Hinkler, Bert 241
Hip hop music
Sydney **142**, 143
Hiring cars 588, 590
History **47–59**
Hitch-hiking 576
Hitler, Adolf 121
Hobart 13, 53, 458, **460–61**
airport 582–3

Hobart (cont.)
map 461
time zone 574
Hockney, David 78
Hoddle, Robert 177, 388
Hodgkinson, Frank 121
Hogarth Galleries Aboriginal Art Centre (Sydney) 135
Holden 57
Holidays, public 43
Holman, Francis
First Fleet Ship 51
Holt, Harold 196, 442
Home Sydney (Sydney) 143
Homebush Bay 127
Honeymoon Cove 329
Hopetoun Hotel (Sydney) 143
Hopwood, Henry 431
Hordern Pavilion (Sydney) 143
Horses
Great Mountain Race of Victoria (Mansfield) 41
Hanging Rock Picnic Races 41
Melbourne Cup 41
riding (Sydney) 147
Three-day equestrian event (Gawler) 43
Horseshoe Bay Beach (Bermagui) 188
Hospitals 576–7
Hotels **474–517**
Adelaide and the Southeast 501–4
backpacker hotels and youth hostels **476**, 477
Blue Mountains 482–3
bookings 474
boutique hotels 476
Brisbane 487–90
camping and caravan parks 477
Canberra and ACT 486–7
chain hotels **475**, 477
children in 474–5
country house hotels 475
Darwin and the Top End 495–6
disabled travellers 475
Eastern Victoria 512–15
farm stays and houseboats 477
gradings and facilities 474
luxury hotels and resorts **475**, 477
Melbourne 505–9
North of Perth 500–501
Northern Queensland 493–4
Outback 29
Perth and the Southwest 497–500
prices 474
pub accommodation 476
Red Centre 496–7
self-catering apartments 476–7
South Coast and Snowy Mountains 484–5
South of Townsville 490–92
Sydney 478–81
Tasmania 515–17
Western Victoria 510–11
Yorke and Eyre Peninsulas 504–5
The Hour Glass (Sydney) 135
House music
Sydney **142**, 143
Houseboats 477, 591
Houtman Abrolhos 324, **325**
Hovell, William 52
statue of 92
Howard, John 59
Howard Springs Nature Park 272

Howqua Mountain Ranges 446
Hume, Hamilton 52
   statue of 92
Humphries, Barry 83
Hunter, Henry 460
Hunter Valley 10
   Hunter Valley tour 174–5
   vineyards 36, 167
   wines 163
Hunter Valley Wine Society
   Hunter Valley tour 175
Hyde Park (Sydney) 68, **93**
Hyde Park Barracks Museum
   (Sydney) 65, 67, **114**, 115
Hype DC (Sydney) 137

I

Ian Potter Centre – NGV: Australia
   (Melbourne) 402
Ideas Incorporated (Sydney) 139
IMAX Theatre (Sydney) 141
Immigration 57
   Department of Immigration 575
   Immigration Restriction Act 56
   Migration Museum (Adelaide)
      344, **347**
   postwar immigration 20, 58
Imperial Hotel (Sydney) 143
In a Corner on the MacIntyre
   (Roberts) 202
Indian Head 242
Inline skating, Sydney 147
Innes National Park 362
Insurance, car 588–9
Interior with Wardrobe Mirror
   (Cossington Smith) 112
International Flower and Garden
   Show (Melbourne) 42
Inverell **177**
Islands
   cruises and ferries 591
   Great Barrier Reef 217
Issey Miyake (Melbourne) 409

J

Jabiru 277
Jacaranda Festival (Grafton) 41
Jackson, Daryl 390
James, Clive 83
James Street Precinct (Brisbane)
   233
Jamison Valley 172
Jan Logan (Sydney) 135, 137
Jansz, Willem 49
Japan Airlines 583
Jaru people 331
Jazz
   Darling Harbour Jazz Festival
      (Sydney) 43
   Sydney **142**, 143
Jekyll, Gertrude 399
Jellyfish 38, 577
Jenolan Caves 170, **173**
Jervis Bay 189
Jet lag 582
Jetstar 585
Jewellery shops **134**, 135, 408
Jews
   Great Synagogue (Sydney) **93**
   Sydney Jewish Museum (Sydney)
      65, **121**
Jim Jim Falls 268
Jindabyne 187
Johanna Beach 429
John Forrest National Park 307
Johnson, Lyndon B 59

Johnston, Major George 52, 53
Jondaryan Woolshed (Darling
   Downs) 240
Jones, Louisa 404, 405
Jukes, F 50
Juniper Hall (Sydney) **124**
Just Jeans (Sydney) 137
Justice and Police Museum
   (Sydney) 64, **83**

K

Kadina 363
Kakadu National Park 11, 26, 33,
   260, 267, 268, **276–7**
Kalbarri National Park **325**
Kalgoorlie-Boulder 293, **318–19**
Kanakas 235, 241, 247
Kangaroo Island 12, 334, 341, 350,
   354
Kangaroos 18
Kantju Gorge 287
Karijini National Park 293, 323, **329**
Karri Forest Discovery Centre 315
Kata Tjuta (The Olgas) *see* Uluru-
   Kata Tjuta National Park
Katherine **274–5**
Katherine Gorge *see* Nitmiluk
   National Park
Katoomba 170, **172–3**
Keating, Paul 59
Keep River National Park **275**
Kelly, Archbishop
   statue of 92
Kelly, Ellen 394
Kelly, Ned **394**
   Beechworth 450
   Benalla 451
   capture 439, 451
   death mask 53
   Glenrowan 451
   Sidney Nolan's paintings 34, 206
   Stringybark Creek 446–7
Kelly in Spring (Nolan) 34
Kemp, JE 124
Keneally, Thomas 35
Kennedy, Edmund 249
Kernewek Lowender Cornish
   Festival (Little Cornwall) 42
Kerr, Sir John 196
Kerry, Charles 112
Kiandra 187
Kiewa River 439, 447
Kija people 331
The Kimberley 12, **296–7**, **330**
   map 330
King Cottage Museum (Bunbury)
   314
King Island **467**
   map 458
King Street Wharf (Sydney) **98**
Kings Canyon **285**
Kings Cross, Darlinghurst and
   Paddington (Sydney) **116–25**
   map 117
Kings Domain (Melbourne) 374,
   398–9
Kings Park (Perth) 306
Kingscote 350
Kingston, Sir George Strickland
   348
Kinki Gerlinki (Melbourne) 409
Kites 39
Klein, Yves 113
Knappstein winery 338
Kngwarreye, Emily Kame 31, 112
Knorr, Frances 394–5

Koalas
   Lone Pine Koala Sanctuary
      (Brisbane) 11, **230**
Koorie tribe 30
Koppio Smithy Museum (Port
   Lincoln) 366
Kosciuszko National Park 187
Kozminsky (Melbourne) 409
Ku-ring-gai Chase National Park
   126
Kuranda 254
Kyneton
   Macedon Ranges and Spa
      Country tour 437

L

La Trobe, Charles 399
La Trobe Bateman, Edward 374
La Trobe's Cottage (Melbourne)
   376, 399
Labor Party 56, 59, 249
Labyrinth (Sydney) 137
Lachlan River 181
Lady Elliot Island 217
Lake, Max 174
Lake Cave 313
Lake Eyre National Park **369**
Lake Mountain 446
   Skiing in the Victorian Alps 448
Lakefield National Park **252**
Lakes Entrance 444
Lake's Folly
   Hunter Valley tour 174
Lalor, Peter 434
Lambing Flag gold fields 55
Lamington National Park **240**
Land Titles Office (Sydney) 115
Lands Department Building
   (Sydney) **92**
Landscape **22–3**
Lane Cove National Park 68
Lanyon Homestead 206
Launceston **464–5**
Laura 252
Laura Dance & Cultural Festival 43
Laurasia 23
Lawler, Ray 35
Laws, Aboriginal 263
Lawson, Henry 35
   Henry Lawson Centre (Gulgong)
      177
Lawson, Louisa 35
Lawson, William 52, 172, 177
   statue of 92
Layman, George 314
Leeuwin Estate Winery 36
Leeuwin Estate Winery Music
   Concert 41
Leeuwin Naturaliste National Park
   300, 313
Legs on the Wall (Sydney) 141
Lehmann, Peter
   Barossa Valley tour 356
Leichhardt, Ludwig 35, 244, 249
   statue of 92
Lesley Mackay's Bookshop
   (Sydney) 135
Leslie, Patrick 230
Lets Go Surfing (Sydney) 144
Letts Beach (90 Mile Beach) 444
Leura 171, **172**
Leura Garden Festival 41
Leviny, Ernest 433
Lewis, Mortimer 96, 121
Lewis, TC & Co. 389
Liberal Party 56

Libraries
Mitchell Library (Sydney) 109, 114
National Library of Australia (Canberra) 191, 195, **197**
State Library (Brisbane) **229**
State Library (Melbourne) 385
State Library of New South Wales (Sydney) **109**, 114
Lichtenstein, Roy 78
Licola **446**
Lifeline 577
Lifesavers 39, 577
Light, William 341
Lightning Ridge **180**
Lincoln National Park **366–7**
Lindemans
Hunter Valley tour 174
Lindsay, Lionel 113
Lindsay, Norman 113, 175
Norman Lindsay Gallery and Museum **172**
Lisa Ho (Sydney) 137
Litchfield National Park 267, 269, **274**
Literature **35**
Little Cornwall **363**
festivals 42
Little Desert National Park 430
Little Parakeet Bay 309
"Living Lagoon" sculptures (Walker) 246
Lizard Island 217
Loch Ard Gorge 425, 429
London Tavern (Sydney)
Street-by-Street map 122
Lone Pine Koala Sanctuary (Brisbane) 11, **230**
Long Island 217
Long Reef 145
Longford 465
Longreach 11, 210, **257**
The Looking Glass (Sydney) 135
Lord Howe Island 27
Lord Nelson Hotel (Sydney) 62
Lorne 429
Lost City 269, 274
Louis Vuitton (Sydney) 137
Le Louvre (Melbourne) 409
Love & Hatred (Sydney) 135
Low Isles 217
Ludlow Tuart Forest National Park 314
Lutherans 356
Luxury hotels and resorts **475**, 477
Lydiard Street (Ballarat) 434
Lygon Street (Melbourne) **395**
Lygon Street Festa (Melbourne) 40

M
Mabo, Edward Koiki (Eddie) 58, 252
Macalister River 446
Macarthur, Elizabeth 36
Macarthur, John
Elizabeth Farm (Parramatta) 127
merino sheep 51
Rum Rebellion 53
wine 36
McCarthy, Matthew 388
McCubbin, Frederick 34, 112
MacDonnell Ranges **284–5**
Macedon Ranges
Macedon Ranges and Spa Country tour **436–7**

McElhone Stairs (Sydney)
Street-by-Street map 118
McGill, Walter 107
Mackay 236, 246
McKay, Hugh Victor 257
MacKennal, Bertram 90, 92
McKenzie, Lake 242
MacKenzie Falls 427
McLaren Vale 351
Macleay, Alexander 65
Elizabeth Bay (Sydney) 119
Elizabeth Bay House (Sydney) 120
McNiven, Marie
Portrait of Miles Franklin 35
McPherson Mountain Range 240
Macquarie, Elizabeth
Mrs Macquarie's Chair 107, **108**
Macquarie, Governor Lachlan 82
Conservatorium of Music (Sydney) 108
and Francis Greenway 169
Hyde Park (Sydney) 93
Macquarie Place (Sydney) 83
Oatlands 463
Rum Rebellion 53
St Mary's Cathedral (Sydney) 92
Windsor 168
Macquarie, Lake 169
Macquarie Harbour **468**
Macquarie Place (Sydney) **83**
Macquarie River 180, 464
Macquarie Street (Sydney) **114–15**
Macquarie Trio (Sydney) 141
McRae, George 90
Macrobius 48
McWilliams Mount Pleasant Winery
Hunter Valley tour 174
Madonna and Child with Infant St John the Baptist (Beccafumi) 110
Magellan, Ferdinand 48
Magnetic Island 11, 217, **247**
Maheno 237
Maillol, Aristide
The Mountain 202
Maitland **362–3**
Maker's Mark (Melbourne) 409
Makers Mark (Sydney) 135, 137
Maldon **432**
Easter Fair 42
Maldon Folk Festival 41
Maleny 241
Mallacoota 445
Mallacoota Inlet 445
Mallee scrub habitat
Birds of South Australia 336
Malls, shopping 132–3, 406–7
Malmsbury
Macedon Ranges and Spa Country tour 436
Malouf, David 35
Mambo Friendship Store (Sydney) 137
Mammals 25
Manjimup **315**
Manly **126**
Manly Beach 145
Manly Surf School (Sydney) 144
Mansfield **446–7**
festivals 41
The Mansions (Brisbane)
Street-by-Street map 223
Mapplethorpe, Robert 112
Maps
Aboriginal art 32–3
Aboriginal lands 262

Maps (cont.)
Adelaide 344–5, 347
Adelaide and the Southeast 342–3
Alice Springs 283
Australasia and the Pacific Rim 14
Australia 14–15
Ballarat 435
Barossa Valley tour 356–7
Blue Mountains and Beyond 166–7
Blue Mountains National Park 170–73
Brisbane 220–21, 222–3
Cairns 254
Canberra: Parliamentary Triangle 194–5
Canberra and ACT 192–3
Carnarvon National Park 245
Darwin 271
Darwin and the Top End 268–9
domestic air travel 585
Fraser Island 242
Fremantle 311
Gold Fields and Nullarbor Plain 318
Great Barrier Reef 216
Great Ocean Road coastline 428–9
Greater Sydney 63
Hobart 461
Hunter Valley tour 174–5
Kakadu National Park 276–7
The Kimberley 296–7
Kimberley and the Deserts 330
King Island 458
Macedon Ranges and Spa Country tour 436–7
Melbourne 382–3
Melbourne: Parliament Area 392–3
Melbourne: Street Finder 414–21
Melbourne: Swanston Street Precinct 384–5
Melbourne: tram routes 412–13
Namadgi National Park 207
New South Wales and ACT 158–9
Northern New South Wales coastline 178–9
Northern Territory 260–61
Paddington (Sydney) 122–3
Perth 302–3, 305
Perth: Greater Perth 306
Perth: North of Perth 322–3
Perth and the Southwest 300–301
Port Arthur 470–71
Queensland 210–11
Queensland: Northern Queensland 250–51
Queensland: Southern Queensland coastline 238–9
Queensland's Outback 256
rail and coach routes 587
Red Centre 280–81
Rottnest Island 308–9
Shark Bay World Heritage and Marine Park 326–7
Skiing in the Victorian Alps 448–9
Snowy Mountains 160–61
South Australia 334–5
South Australia: Far North 368
South Coast and Snowy Mountains 184–5, 188–9
South of Townsville 236–7

Maps (cont.)
Southeast Coastline 350–51
Sydney: Botanic Gardens and
the Domain 105
Sydney: Central Sydney 62–3
Sydney: City Centre and Darling
Harbour 87, 88–9
Sydney: Darling Harbour 96–7
Sydney: Garden Island to Farm
Cove 70–71
Sydney: Greater Sydney 126
Sydney: Kings Cross,
Darlinghurst and Paddington
117
Sydney: Potts Point 118–19
Sydney: The Rocks and Circular
Quay 75, 76–7
Sydney: Street Finder 148–55
Sydney: Sydney Cove to Walsh
Bay 72–3
Sydney: Sydney Harbour 70–73
Sydney's beaches 145
Sydney's Best: Architecture 66–7
Sydney's Best: Museums and
Galleries 64–5
Sydney's Best: Parks and
Reserves 68–9
Tasmania 458–9
Uluru-Kata Tjuta National Park
286
Victoria 372–3
Victoria: Eastern coastline 444–5
Victoria: Eastern Victoria 440–41
Victoria: Western Victoria 424–5
West of the Divide 180
Western Australia 292–3
Western Australia: Southern
Coastline 312–13
Where to Surf 38
Wines of Australia 36–7
Wines of New South Wales and
ACT 162–3
Wines of South Australia 338–9
Wines of Victoria 378–9
World Heritage Areas 26–7
Yorke and Eyre Peninsulas
360–61
Marble Bar (Sydney)
Street-by-Street map 88
Marcs (Melbourne) 409
Margaret River 12, 312, **314–15**
Maritime Museum (Hobart) **461**
Maritime Museum (Melbourne) 401,
402
Maritime Museum (Port Victoria)
362
Maritime Museum, Australian
National (Sydney) 64, 66,
100–101
Maritime Museum, Western
Australian (Fremantle) 310
Markets 565
Central Market (Adelaide) **346**
Fremantle Markets 310
Melbourne 407
Mindil Beach Sunset Markets
(Darwin) 264, 272
Paddington Markets (Sydney)
124–5
Paddy's Markets (Sydney) **99**
Queen Victoria Market
(Melbourne) **386**
Salamanca Market (Hobart)
460–61
Sydney 133
The Rocks Market (Sydney) 77

Marlo 445
Maroochydore Beach 238
Maroubra 145
Mars Lounge (Sydney) 143
Martens, Conrad 34, 82
Martin, Emil 282
Martin Place (Sydney) **90**
Street-by-Street map 89
Martindale Hall (Mintaro) 364
Maruku Gallery 286
Mary River 241
Maryborough 211, **241**
Marylebone Cricket Club (MCC) 436
Marysville **446**
Mast, Trevor 378
Mataranka 275
Mategot, Mathieu 197
Maternity Cave 355
Meale, Richard 35
Medical care 576–7
Royal Flying Doctor Service 57,
257, 590
Meere, Charles
Australian Beach Pattern 65
Megalong Australian Heritage
Centre (Sydney) 147
Melba, Dame Nellie 21, 426
Melbourne **381–421**
airport 582–3
architecture **376–7**
climate 45
Commonwealth Games 59
discovering Australia 13
entertainment **410–11**
festivals 40–43
hotels 505–9
map 382–3
parks and gardens **374–5**
practical information **412–13**
restaurants 552–6
Rippon Lea **404–5**, 415
Royal Botanic Gardens and Kings
Domain **398–9**
rules of the road 589
shopping **406–9**
Street Finder 414–21
Street-by-Street map: Parliament
Area 392–3
Swanston Street Precinct **384–5**
time zone 574
travel **412–13**
Yarra River **400–401**
Melbourne Aquarium **402**
Melbourne Central 407
Melbourne Contemporary Art Fair
43
Melbourne Convention Centre 401
Melbourne Cricket Ground 13, **397**
Melbourne Cup 41
Melbourne Exhibition Centre 401
Melbourne Fringe Festival 40
Melbourne International Arts
Festival 40
Melbourne International Comedy
Festival 42
Melbourne International Film
Festival 43
Melbourne Marathon 40
Melbourne Maritime Museum 401,
402
Melbourne Museum **395**
Melbourne Park 13, 377, **397**
Melbourne Town Hall 384, **389**,
411
Melbourne Water Taxis 413
Melville Island 260, 267, **274**

Menzies, Robert 58–9
Merimbula Beach 188
Merimbula Wharf 183
The Mermaid Coffin (Peaty) 205
Mersey Bluff 466
Mersey River 466
The Met (Melbourne) 412–13
Meteorites
Henbury Meteorites
Conservation Reserve **284**
Wolfe Creek Crater National Park
331
Metlink (Melbourne) 412, 413
Metro Light Rail (MLR, Sydney) 130
Metro Theatre (Sydney) 143
Metung 445
Michael's Music Room (Sydney) 135
Mid City Centre (Sydney) 133
Middle Head (Sydney) 69
Middleton Beach 312
Midnight Shift (Sydney) 143
Midsumma Festival (Melbourne) 41
Might versus Right (Gill) 55
Migration Museum (Adelaide) **347**
Street-by-Street map 344
Mikkira Station (Port Lincoln) 366
Milawa 451
Mildura **430–31**
Miles, John Campbell 257
Millstream-Chichester National Park
329
Mimosa Rocks 189
Mindil Beach Sunset Markets
(Darwin) 264, 272
Minlaton **362**
The Mint (Sydney) **113**, 114
Mintaro 364
Miss Louise (Melbourne) 409
Mrs Macquarie's Chair (Sydney) 70,
107, **108**
Mitchell, Major Thomas 431
statue of 92
Mitchell Library (Sydney) 109, 114
MLC Centre (Sydney) 133
MLR (Metro Light Rail, Sydney) 130
Mobile telephones 580
Molonglo River 191
Molvig, Jon 121
Mon Repos Conservation Park **243**
Monet, Claude 112
Money **578–9**
Monkey Mia 12, 321, 327
Monorail, Sydney 130
Moochalabra Dam 331
Mooloolaba Wharf 238
Moomba Festival (Melbourne) 42
Moonarie 359
Moonee Beach 178
Moonlight Head 429
Moonta Mines State Heritage Area
363
Moore, Henry
Reclining Figure: Angles 112
Moore Park (Sydney) 69
Moore Park Golf Club (Sydney) 147
Moran, Cardinal
statue of 92
Moreton Bay 219, 238
Morgan 355
Morgan, Francis 108
Morgan, Sally 35
Mornington Peninsula **442**
Morris, Mick 379
Mort, Thomas
statue of 83
Morton National Park 184, **187**, 188

Moshtix (Sydney) 143
Motor racing
    Australian Formula One Grand
        Prix (Melbourne) 42
Motoring organizations 589, 590
Motorways 589
Mount Ainslie 192
Mount Baw Baw
    Skiing in the Victorian Alps 448
Mount Beauty **447**
Mount Bogong 447
Mount Buffalo 447
    Skiing in the Victorian Alps 448
Mount Buffalo National Park 447
Mount Buller 447
    Skiing in the Victorian Alps 448
Mount Buller Alpine Village 439
Mount Clear 207
Mount Coot-tha Forest Park
    (Brisbane) 220, 230
Mount Etna National Park 244
Mount Feathertop 447
Mount Field National Park 454, **469**
Mount Gambier 335, **354**
Mount Gibraltar 186
Mount Hotham 447
    Skiing in the Victorian Alps 449
Mount Hurtle winery 36
Mount Hypipamee Crater 255
Mount Isa 210, **257**
Mount Isa Rodeo 43
Mount Kosciuszko 158, 160
Mount Lofty **353**
    festivals 43
Mount Lofty Botanic Gardens 353
Mount Macedon
    Macedon Ranges and Spa
        Country tour 437
Mount Morgan 244
Mount Ossa 467
Mount Remarkable National Park
    369
Mount Stirling 447
Mount Stromlo Observatory **206**
Mount Tamboritha 446
Mount Tomah Botanic Gardens 171,
    173
Mount Townsend 160
Mount Warning 179
Mount Wilson 170
The Mountain (Maillol) 202
Mrs Macquarie's Chair (Sydney) 70,
    107, **108**
Mud Crabs (Nyoka) 64
Mudgee **177**
    wines 163
Mudgee Wine Festival 40
Mueller, Baron von 374
Mulka's Cave 318
Multicultural Northern Territory
    264–5
Munch, Edvard 113
Mungo, Lake 47, 48, 181
Mungo World Heritage Area 10, **181**
Murchison River 325
Murramarang National Park 189
Murray Island 252
Murray River 13, 341, 343, **355**
    Adelaide 346
    Echuca 431
    Hattah-Kulkyne National Park
        430
    Paddlesteamers **430**
    Swan Hill Pioneer Settlement 423
Murray-Sunset Country **430**
Murrumbidgee River **206**

Museums and galleries (general)
    admission prices 573
    opening hours 573
Museums and galleries (individual)
    Aboriginal Dreamtime Cultural
        Centre (Rockhampton) 244
    Adelaide House (Alice Springs)
        282
    Art Gallery of New South Wales
        (Sydney) 63, 65, **110–13**
    Art Gallery of South Australia
        (Adelaide) 345
    Australian Aviation Heritage
        Centre (Darwin) 272
    Australian Centre for the Moving
        Image (ACMI, Melbourne) 402
    Australian Gallery of Sport and
        Olympic Museum (Melbourne)
        396
    Australian Museum (Sydney) 65,
        94–5
    Australian National Maritime
        Museum (Sydney) 64, 66, 97,
        100–101
    Ballarat Fine Art Gallery
        (Ballarat) 434
    Battery Hill Mining Centre
        (Tennant Creek) 285
    Benalla Art Gallery (Benalla) 451
    Bendigo Art Gallery (Bendigo)
        432
    Bradman Museum (Bowral) **186**,
        187
    Bundaberg and District
        Historical Museum 241
    Cairns Museum (Cairns) 254
    Champions – Australian Racing
        Museum and Hall of Fame
        (Melbourne) 402
    City Museum (Melbourne) **396**
    Commissariat Store Museum
        (Brisbane) 222, **224**
    East Point Military Museum 272
    Elizabeth Bay House (Sydney)
        65, **120**
    Elizabeth Farm (Parramatta) 127
    Eureka Centre (Ballarat) 434–5
    Famous Grapevine Attraction
        (Chiltern) 450
    Fannie Bay Gaol 272
    Farmshed Museum and Tourism
        Centre (Kadina) 363
    Fire Brigade Museum (Perth)
        303, 305
    Fremantle Museum and Arts
        Centre (Fremantle) 311
    Geraldton Art Gallery
        (Geraldton) **324**, 325
    Golden Dragon Museum
        (Bendigo) 432
    Hawkesbury Museum (Windsor)
        168
    Henry Lawson Centre (Gulgong)
        177
    Hermannsburg Historic Precinct
        284, 285
    Hyde Park Barracks Museum
        (Sydney) 65, **114**, 115
    Ian Potter Centre – NGV:
        Australia (Melbourne) 402
    James Cook Memorial Museum
        (Cooktown) 252
    Jondaryan Woolshed (Darling
        Downs) 240
    Justice and Police Museum
        (Sydney) 64, **83**

Museums and galleries (cont.)
    Karri Forest Discovery Centre
        (Pemberton) 315
    King Cottage Museum (Bunbury)
        314
    Koppio Smithy Museum (Port
        Lincoln) 366
    Maitland Museum (Maitland) 363
    Manjimup Timber Park
        (Manjimup) 315
    Margaret River Museum
        (Margaret River) **314**, 315
    Maritime Museum (Hobart) **461**
    Maritime Museum (Port Victoria)
        362
    Melbourne Maritime Museum
        401, **402**
    Melbourne Museum **395**
    Migration Museum (Adelaide)
        344, **347**
    Mikkira Station (Port Lincoln)
        366
    Museum and Art Gallery of the
        Northern Territory (Darwin) **273**
    Museum of Central Australia
        (Alice Springs) 282
    Museum of Childhood (Perth)
        306
    Museum of Chinese Australian
        History (Melbourne) **391**
    Museum of Contemporary Art
        (Sydney) 64, 76, **78**
    Museum of Sydney (Sydney) 64,
        92
    Museum of Tropical Queensland
        (Townsville) 247
    Narryna Heritage Museum
        (Hobart) **461**
    National Capital Exhibition
        (Canberra) **196–7**
    National Design Centre
        (Melbourne) 402
    National Gallery of Australia
        (Canberra) 11, 194, **202–3**
    National Gallery of Victoria
        (Melbourne) 377, 400, **403**
    National Motor Museum
        (Birdwood) 353
    National Museum of Australia
        (Canberra) 11, **205**
    National Trust Centre (Sydney)
        82
    National Trust Museum (Port
        Pirie) 364
    National Wool Museum
        (Geelong) 427
    New England Regional Art
        Museum (Armidale) 175
    New Norcia Museum and Art
        Gallery (New Norcia) 324
    Newcastle Region Art Gallery
        (Newcastle) 169
    Norman Lindsay Gallery and
        Museum (Faulconbridge) **172**
    Norseman Historical and
        Geological Museum (Norseman)
        319
    Old Ghan Train Museum (Alice
        Springs) 283
    Old Melbourne Gaol
        (Melbourne) **394–5**
    Old Schoolhouse National Trust
        Museum (Ceduna) 367
    Outback at Isa (Mount Isa) 257
    Panorama Guth (Alice Springs)
        282

Museums and galleries (cont.)
Penny Royal World (Launceston) 465
Perth Cultural Centre (Perth) 304
Pioneer Settlement Museum (Victoria) 431
Port of Morgan Museum (Morgan) 355
Powerhouse Museum (Sydney) 64, **102–3**
Queen Victoria Museum and Art Gallery (Launceston) 465
Queensland Cultural Centre (Brisbane) 11, **228–9**
Queensland Maritime Museum (Brisbane) **227**
Queensland Museum (Brisbane) **229**
Questacon (Canberra) 194, **197**
The Rocks Discovery Museum (Sydney) 77, **79**
Rottnest Museum (Rottnest Island) 309
Royal Flying Doctor Service Visitor Centre (Alice Springs) 283
Sidney Nolan Gallery (Lanyon Homestead) 206
South Australian Museum (Adelaide) 345, **347**
Sovereign Hill **433**
State Library (Brisbane) **229**
Stockman's Hall of Fame (Longreach) 11, 257
Susannah Place (Sydney) **78**
Sydney Jewish Museum 65, **121**
Sydney's Best **64–5**
Tandanya (Adelaide) **347**
Tasmanian Museum and Art Gallery (Hobart) **460**
Telegraph Station (Tennant Creek) 285
Tiagarra (Devonport) 466
Uluru-Kata Tjuta Cultural Centre 289
Underground Art Gallery (Coober Pedy) 368
WA Museum Geraldton **324**, 325
WA Museum Kalgoorlie-Boulder 319
Wadlata Outback Centre (Port Augusta) 365
Wallaroo Heritage and Nautical Museum 363
Western Australian Maritime Museum (Fremantle) 310
Western Australian Museum (Perth) 304
Whale World (Albany) 316
Whyalla Maritime Museum (Whyalla) 365
York Motor Museum (York) 317
York Residency Museum (York) 317
Music
Aboriginal 31
Australia Day Concert (Sydney) 41
classical **140**, 141
Conservatorium of Music (Sydney) **108**
Country Music Festival (Tamworth) 41
Darling Harbour Jazz Festival (Sydney) 43
house, breakbeats and techno **142**, 143

Music (cont.)
jazz, folk and blues **142**, 143
Leeuwin Estate Winery Music Concert (Margaret River) 41
Maldon Folk Festival 41
opera **140**, 141
rock, pop and hip hop **142**, 143
shops **134**, 135, 409
venues (Sydney) **142–3**
Musica Viva (Sydney) 141
Muybridge, Eadweard 112
Myall Beach 253
Myer (Sydney) 133, 137
Myer Melbourne 407
Mythology, Aboriginal 297

N

Namadgi National Park 11, **207**
Namatjira, Albert 284
Nambucca Heads 179
Nambung National Park 322, **324**
Napanangka, Gladys
Bush Tucker Dreaming 263
Napoleon Perdis Cosmetics (Sydney) 135
Naracoorte 26
Naracoorte Caves Conservation Park 342, **355**
Narrabeen 145
Narryna Heritage Museum (Hobart) **461**
Nathan, Benjamin 404
Nathan family 404
National Capital Exhibition (Canberra) **196–7**
National Design Centre (Melbourne) 402
National Gallery of Australia (Canberra) 11, 194, **202–3**
National Gallery of Victoria (Melbourne) 377, 400, **403**
National Herbarium of New South Wales (Sydney) 107
National Library of Australia (Canberra) 191, 195, **197**
National Maritime Museum (Sydney) 64, 66, 97, **100–101**
National Motor Museum (Birdwood) 353
National Museum of Australia (Canberra) 11, **205**
National parks (general)
bushwalking 566
National parks (individual)
Alpine 13, 446, 447
Barrington Tops **175**
Beedelup 315
Belair **352**
Bellenden Ker **255**
Ben Boyd 184, 189
Ben Lomond **464**
Black Mountain 252
Blackdown Tableland **244**
Blue Mountains 10, **170–73**
Bowling Green Bay 246
Brambuk 427
Brisbane Ranges 427
Brisbane Waters 169
Burleigh Heads 238
Cape Range 328
Carnarvon 235, **245**
Coffin Bay **366–7**
Cooloola 239
Coorong 12, 341, 351
Cradle Mountain Lake St Clair 13, 22, 454, **467**

National parks (individual) (cont.)
Croajingolong 439, 445
Daintree 11, 250, **253**
D'Entrecasteaux 313
Devonian Reef 331
Douglas Apsley 463
Eildon 446
Elsey 275
Eucla 319
Eungella **246**
Finke Gorge 284–5
Flinders Chase 350, 354
Flinders Ranges 359, 369
François Peron 326
Franklin-Gordon Wild Rivers 13, 455, 458, **468–9**
Fraser 446
Freycinet 459, **463**
Gammon Ranges 369
Garigal 68
Geikie Gorge 331
Gibraltar Range **176**
Gloucester 315
Grampians 372, 425, **427**
Gregory **275**
Gurig 274
Hattah-Kulkyne **430**
Hinchinbrook Island **255**
Innes 362
John Forrest 307
Kakadu 11, 26, 33, 260, 267, 268, **276–7**
Kalbarri **325**
Karijini 293, 323, **329**
Keep River **275**
Kosciuszko 187
Ku-ring-gai Chase **126**
Lake Eyre **369**
Lakefield **252**
Lamington **240**
Lane Cove 68
Leeuwin Naturaliste 300, 313
Lincoln **366–7**
Litchfield 267, 269, **274**
Little Desert 430
Ludlow Tuart Forest 314
Millstream-Chichester 329
Mornington Peninsula 442
Morton 184, **187**, 188
Mount Buffalo 447
Mount Etna 244
Mount Field 454, **469**
Mount Remarkable 369
Murramarang 189
Namadgi 11, **207**
Nambung 322, **324**
Nitmiluk (Katherine Gorge) 267, 274–5
Noosa 239
Nullarbor 367
Otway 429
Oxley Wild Rivers 175
Port Campbell 423
Purnululu (Bungle Bungle) 293, 321, **331**
Queen Mary Falls 240
Royal 10, **186**
Stirling Range 299, **316–17**
Strezelecki 465
Sydney's Best **68–9**
Tunnel Creek 331
Uluru-Kata Tjuta 12, 26, 260, 280, **286–9**
Walls of Jerusalem 457
Warren 315
Washpool 176

National parks (individual) (cont.)
Watarrka 285
Willandra 181
Wilsons Promontory 13, 439, 444
Windjana Gorge 296, 331
Witjira 369
Wolfe Creek Crater 331
Wyperfield 430
National Roadside Assistance 590
National Trust Centre (Sydney) 82
National Trust Museum (Port Pirie)
364
National Wool Museum (Geelong)
427
National Zoo and Aquarium
(Canberra) 204
Native Fuchsia (Preston) 202
Nelson, Michael Tjakamarra
The Possum Dreaming 84
Nelson Falls 458
Nepean River 47
New England Regional Art Museum
(Armidale) 175
New Mardi Gras Festival (Sydney)
141
New Norcia 324
New Norfolk 462
New South Wales and ACT
157–207
Blue Mountains and Beyond
165–81
Canberra and ACT 191–207
hotels 478–85
map 158–9
motoring organizations 590
Northern New South Wales
coastline 178–9
restaurants 524–33
Snowy Mountains 160–61
South Coast and Snowy
Mountains 183–9
state tourist office 575
Sydney 61–155
Wines of New South Wales and
ACT 162–3
New South Wales Snow Sports
Association 569
New Year's Day 43
New Year's Eve 41
Newcastle 169
Newcastle Region Art Gallery 169
Newport Beach 145
Newspapers 138, 575
Newstead House (Brisbane) 230
Newtown Hotel (Sydney) 143
@Newtown (Sydney) 143
Nielsen, Juanita 120
Nielsen Park (Sydney) 69
Nightclubs
Sydney 142–3
Nightingale, Florence 113
90 Mile Beach 13, 444
Ningaloo Reef Marine Park 12, 328
Nitmiluk (Katherine Gorge)
National Park 267, 274–5
Nolan, Sir Sidney 34
Art Gallery of New South Wales
(Sydney) 112
Kelly in Spring 34
National Gallery of Australia
(Canberra) 202
Queensland Cultural Centre
(Brisbane) 228
Sidney Nolan Gallery (Lanyon
Homestead) 206
Noonuccal, Oodgeroo 35, 83

Noosa Heads 239
Noosa National Park 239
Norfolk Plains 465
Norman Lindsay Gallery and
Museum (Faulconbridge) 172
Norman River 256
Normanton 256
Norrie, Susan 113
Norseman 319
North Arm Walk (Sydney) 68
North Head (Sydney) 69
North of Perth and the Kimberley
321–31
climate 44
discovering Australia 12
hotels 500–501
The Kimberley and the Deserts
330
map 322–3
restaurants 546–8
Shark Bay World Heritage and
Marine Park 326–7
Northam 317
Northeastern Wineries 450–51
Northern and Outback Queensland
249–57
climate 44
discovering Australia 11
hotels 493–4
map 250–51
Outback 256
restaurants 539–41
Northern Land Council 262
Northern Territory 259–89
Aboriginal Lands 262–3
Darwin and the Top End
267–77
hotels 495–7
map 260–61
motoring organizations 590
Multicultural Northern Territory
264–5
Red Centre 279–89
restaurants 541–4
state tourist office 575
Northern Territory Parks and
Wildlife Commission 262
Nourlangie rock 262, 277
Nowra 188
Nowra, Louis 35
Nullarbor Plain 12, 23, 318, 319, 367
map 318
No. 120 Collins Street (Melbourne)
390–91
Nyoka, Tony Dhanyula
Mud Crabs 64

O
Oatlands 463
Obelisk Bay (Sydney) 69, 145
Observatories
Mount Stromlo 206
Sydney 76, 82
Ocean Beach 313, 316
Oceanworld (Manly) 126
Oenpelli 277
Old Fire Station (Perth) see Fire
Brigade Museum
Old Gaol, Darlinghurst (Sydney)
121
Old Ghan Train Museum (Alice
Springs) 283
Old Government House (Brisbane)
225
Old Government House
(Parramatta) 127

Old Magistrate's Court (Melbourne)
383, 394
Old Manly Boatshed (Sydney) 141
Old Melbourne Gaol (Melbourne)
394–5
Old Parliament House (Canberra)
194, 196
Old Schoolhouse National Trust
Museum (Ceduna) 367
Old Windmill (Brisbane) 226
Olga Gorge 280, 287, 289
The Olgas see Uluru-Kata Tjuta
National Park
Oliver Hill 309
Olympic Games
Melbourne (1956) 58, 381
Sydney (2000) 59, 127
Opal Fields (Sydney) 135
Opals
Coober Pedy 368
Lightning Ridge 180
mines 29
shops 134, 135, 565
Open Garden Scheme (Victoria) 40
Opening hours 573
banks 578
bureaux de change 578
restaurants 518
shops 132, 406, 564
Opera
Opera Australia 21, 141
Sydney 140, 141
Sydney Opera House 84–5, 139
Organ Pipes
Macedon Ranges and Spa
Country tour 437
Orlando
Barossa Valley tour 356
Ormiston Gorge 284
Orpheus Island 217
Orroral Bush Camp Site 207
Orson & Blake (Sydney) 135
Otway National Park 429
Out of the Closet (Melbourne) 409
Outback 17–18, 28–9
Birds of South Australia 336
bushwalking 566
clothing 565
driving in 590
Queensland 256
safety 577
South Australia 368
Wadlata Outback Centre (Port
Augusta) 365
West of the Divide 180
Outback at Isa (Mount Isa) 257
Outdoor gear shops 408
Ovens River Valley 447
Overland Track 467
Overseas Passenger Terminal
(Sydney)
Street-by-Street map 77
Oxford Hotel (Sydney) 143
Oxley, John 180, 219
Oxley Wild Rivers National Park
175

P
P&O 591
Paddington (Sydney) 117
Street-by-Street map 122–3
Paddington Markets (Sydney)
124–5
Paddington Street (Sydney) 125
Paddington Town Hall (Sydney)
124

Paddington Village (Sydney) **124**
Paddlesteamers **430**
Paddy Pallin (Melbourne) 409
Paddy's Markets (Sydney) **99**
Palace Cinemas (Sydney) 141
Palais Theatre (Melbourne) 411
Palm Beach 145
Panorama Guth (Alice Springs) 282
Parade Theatre (Sydney) 141
Park, Ruth 35
Parkes, Sir Henry 176
Parking 590
Parkland Sports (Sydney) 147
Parks and gardens
   Albert Park (Melbourne) **403**
   Alexandra Gardens (Melbourne)
      375
   Arid Lands Botanic Garden (Port
      Augusta) 365
   Australian National Botanic
      Gardens (Canberra) **204**
   Beare Park (Sydney) **120**
   Bicentennial Park (Darwin) 270
   Bicentennial Park (Sydney) 68
   Botanic Gardens (Adelaide) 345
   Botanic Gardens (Darwin) 272
   Botanic Gardens (Rockhampton)
      244
   Botanical Gardens (Ballarat) 435
   Brisbane Botanic Gardens 220,
      230
   Brisbane City Botanic Gardens
      (Brisbane) 11, **224–5**
   Brisbane Forest Park (Brisbane)
      230–31
   Carlton Gardens (Melbourne)
      374
   Centennial Park (Sydney) 69,
      125
   Chinese Garden (Sydney) 96,
      98–9
   Commonwealth Park (Canberra)
      195
   Dandenong Ranges 443
   The Domain (Sydney) **109**
   Everglades House (Leura) 172
   Fawkner Park (Melbourne) 375
   Fitzroy Gardens (Melbourne)
      374, 393
   Flagstaff Gardens (Melbourne)
      375
   Flecker Botanic Gardens (Cairns)
      254
   Garden of Joy (Bendigo) 432
   Hyde Park (Sydney) 68, **93**
   International Flower and Garden
      Show (Melbourne) 42
   Kings Domain (Melbourne) 374,
      398–9
   Kings Park (Perth) 306
   Leura Garden Festival (Blue
      Mountains) 41
   Macquarie Place (Sydney) 83
   Melbourne's Best **374–5**
   Moore Park (Sydney) 69
   Mount Lofty Botanic Gardens
      353
   Mount Tomah Botanic Gardens
      171, **173**
   Open Garden Scheme (Victoria)
      40
   Pioneer Women's Garden
      (Melbourne) 398
   Princes Park (Melbourne) 375
   Queen Victoria Gardens
      (Melbourne) 374

Parks and gardens (cont.)
   Rippon Lea 373
   Royal Botanic Gardens
      (Cranbourne) **442**
   Royal Botanic Gardens
      (Melbourne) 13, 374–5, **398–9**
   Royal Botanic Gardens (Sydney)
      71, 105, **106–7**
   South Bank Precinct (Brisbane)
      227
   Sydney's Best **68–9**
   Treasury Gardens (Melbourne) 375
   Victoria State Rose Garden
      (Werribee) 426
   Whiteman Park (Perth) 307
   Yarra Park (Melbourne) 375
   see also National parks
Parliament Area (Melbourne)
   Street-by-Street map 392–3
Parliament House (Adelaide)
   Street-by-Street map 344
Parliament House (Brisbane) **224**
   Street-by-Street map 223
Parliament House (Canberra) 191,
   194, **198–9**
Parliament House (Darwin) 270
Parliament House (Hobart) **460**
Parliament House (Melbourne) 373,
   376
   Street-by-Street map 393
Parliament House (Sydney) **109**,
   114–15
Parliamentary Triangle (Canberra)
   194–5
   map 194–5
Parramatta **127**
Parsley Bay 145
Paspaley Pearls (Darwin) 265
Paspaley Pearls (Sydney) 135
Passports 572
Paterson, AB "Banjo" 35, 249, 447
Peaceful Bay 312
Pearls
   Broome 330
   Cossack Historical Town 329
   Darwin 265
Peaty, Gaynor
   The Mermaid Coffin 205
Pebbly Beach 189
Pedder, Lake 455
Pemberton **315**
Penfolds
   Barossa Valley tour 357
Penguins
   Phillip Island 442
Penny Royal World (Launceston)
   465
Penola **355**
Perceval, John 34
Percy Marks (Sydney) 135
Performing arts
   Sydney **140–1**
Peron Homestead 326
Perry, Charles, Bishop of
   Melbourne 387
Personal security 576
Perth and the Southwest 292,
   299–319
   airport 582–3
   Central Perth 12, **304–5**
   climate 44
   discovering Australia 12
   festivals 41
   Fremantle **310–11**
   Gold Fields and Nullarbor Plain
      12, **318**

Perth and the Southwest (cont.)
   Greater Perth **306–7**
   hotels 497–500
   map 300–301, 305
   restaurants 544–6
   Rottnest Island **308–9**
   Southern Coastline **312–13**
   Street-by-Street map 302–3
   time zone 574
Perth Cultural Centre 304
Perth Mint 305
   Street-by-Street map 303
Perth Zoo 307
Peterborough 429
Petersons Winery
   Hunter Valley tour 174
Petrie, Andrew 225
Petrol 589
Pharmacies 577
Philippines 265
Phillip, Captain Arthur 10, 76, 82,
   126
Phillip Island 13, 439, **442**
Phonecards 580
Picasso, Pablo 112
   La Belle Hollandaise 228
Pickpockets 576
Pigeon House 187
Pike, Jimmy 102
Pilbara 47
Pineapples
   Sunshine Plantation 230
The Pinnacles 322, 324
Pioneer Settlement Museum
   (Victoria) 423, 431
Pioneer Women's Garden
   (Melbourne) 398
Pioneers and explorers 29
Pipers Brook 37
Pissarro, Camille 112
Pitjantjatjara tribe 30
Plants
   Snowy Mountains **161**
   Wildflowers of Western Australia
      294–5
   see also Parks and gardens
Playwrights **35**
Poets **35**
Point Addis 429
Point Hicks 445
Point Lonsdale 426
Point Moore Lighthouse
   (Geraldton) 324
Point Nepean 442
Point Samson **329**
Poisons Information 577
Police 576, 577
Politics 20–21
Pollock, Jackson
   Blue Poles 203
Polly Woodside Maritime Museum
   see Melbourne Maritime Museum
Polo, Marco 49
Pomodoro, Arnaldo 225
Pop music
   Sydney **142**, 143
Port Albert 444
Port Arthur 13, **470–71**
   map 470–71
Port Augusta 334, **365**
Port Campbell 429
Port Campbell National Park 423
Port Douglas **253**
Port Elliot 350
Port Fairy 428
Port Jackson 70

Port Lincoln 360, **366**
　festivals 41
Port Macquarie 179
Port of Morgan Museum (Morgan)
　355
Port Noarlunga 350
Port Phillip 426
Port Pirie **364**
Port Victoria **362**
Portarlington 426
Portland 428
Portsea 442
The Possum Dreaming (Nelson)
　84
Postal services **581**
Poste restante 581
Potts Point (Sydney)
　Street-by-Street map 118–19
Power, John 78
Powerhouse Museum (Sydney) 64,
　102–3
Prada (Sydney) 137
Prahran Market (Melbourne) 407
Premier Motor Service 587
Preston, Margaret 82, 112, 228
　Native Fuchsia 202
Princes Park (Melbourne) 375
Princess Cruises 591
Princess Theatre (Melbourne) 411
Prisons
　Port Arthur 470–71
Pro Dive Coogee (Sydney) 144
Proctor, Thea 113
Protectionists 56
Ptolemy of Alexandria 48
Pub accommodation 476
Public holidays 43
Pubs, Gay and lesbian 143
Puffing Billy 443
Pugh, Clifton 34
Pugin, AW 224
Purnululu (Bungle Bungle) National
　Park 293, 321, **331**
Pyrmont Bridge (Sydney)
　Street-by-Street map 97
Pythagoras 48

Q

Q Bar (Sydney) 143
Qantas
　Cloncurry 257
　domestic air travel 585
　history 56, 57
　international air travel 583
Queen Mary Falls National Park
　240
Queen Street Mall (Brisbane) 233
Queen Victoria Building (Sydney)
　62, 66, **90**
　Street-by-Street map 88
Queen Victoria Gardens
　(Melbourne) 374
Queen Victoria Market (Melbourne)
　386
Queen Victoria Museum and Art
　Gallery (Launceston) 465
Queen Victoria Statue (Sydney)
　Street-by-Street map 88
Queen's Birthday 43
Queenscliff 426, 442
Queensland **209–57**
　Brisbane **219–33**
　Great Barrier Reef **212–17**
　history 52
　hotels 487–94
　map 210–11

Queensland (cont.)
　motoring organizations 590
　Northern and Outback
　Queensland **249–57**
　Outback **256**
　restaurants 535–41
　South of Townsville **235–47**
　Southern Queensland coastline
　238–9
　state tourist office 575
　World Heritage Area 27
Queensland Club (Brisbane)
　Street-by-Street map 223
Queensland Cultural Centre
　(Brisbane) 11, **228–9**
Queensland Maritime Museum
　(Brisbane) **227**
Queensland Museum (Brisbane)
　229
Queensland Performing Arts Centre
　(Brisbane) 229, 233
Queensland Travel Centre
　(Brisbane) 477, 591
Questacon (Canberra) 194, **197**
Quokkas **309**
Quorn 335, 369
QV (Melbourne) 407

R

Radio 575
Rafting 568
Railways *see* Trains
Rainfall 44–5
Rainforests 24, 213
Ranger Uranium Mine 277
Ravenswood 235
Ray, Man 112
Reading Cinema (Sydney) 141
Readings (Melbourne) 409
Recherche Archipelago 319
Reclining Figure: Angles (Moore)
　112
Red Centre **279–89**
　Alice Springs **282–3**
　climate 44
　discovering Australia 12
　hotels 496–7
　map 280–81
　restaurants 543–4
　Uluru-Kata Tjuta National Park
　286–9
Red Cliff Beach 178
Red Eye Records (Sydney) 135
Red Hill (Canberra) **198**
Red Hill wineries 442
Red wine 523
Reed, Joseph
　Melbourne Town Hall 389
　Rippon Lea (Melbourne) 404–5
　Royal Exhibition Building
　(Melbourne) 395
　St Paul's Cathedral (Melbourne)
　389
　Scots' Church (Melbourne)
　390
　State Library (Melbourne) 385
Reed & Barnes 389
Reef Fleet Terminal (Cairns) 254
Reef HQ (Townsville) 247
Rees, Lloyd 113
Refunds, shopping 564
Regent Theatre (Melbourne) 390,
　411
Remarkable Rocks 354
Rembrandt 113
Renmark 355

Reptiles
　Australian Reptile Park (Gosford)
　169
　Broome Crocodile Park 330
　safety 577
　Wyndham Crocodile Park 331
Restaurants **518–63**
　Adelaide and the Southeast
　548–51
　alcohol and other drinks 519
　Blue Mountains and Beyond
　529–31
　Bring Your Own 518, 519
　Brisbane 535–7
　Canberra and ACT 533–4
　children in 519
　Darwin and the Top End 541–3
　disabled travellers 519
　dress 519
　Eastern Victoria 559–61
　eating hours and reservations
　518
　The Flavours of Australia **520–21**
　Melbourne 552–6
　North of Perth 546–8
　Northern Queensland 539–41
　paying and tipping 518–19
　Perth and the Southeast 544–6
　Red Centre 543–4
　smoking 519
　South Coast and Snowy
　Mountains 531–3
　South of Townsville 538–9
　Sydney 524–8
　Tasmania 561–3
　types of restaurant 518
　vegetarian meals 519
　Western Victoria 557–9
　What to Drink in Australia **522–3**
　Yorke and Eyre Peninsula 551–2
Rialto Towers (Melbourne) **387**
Richardson, Henry Handel 35, 450
Richmond 168, **462**
Riley, Edward and Mary 78
Rio Vista (Mildura) **430**, 431
Rip Curl (Sydney) 137
Rip Curl Pro Surfing Competition
　(Bells Beach) 42
Rippon Lea (Melbourne) 373,
　404–5, 415
Rivers
　cruises in Melbourne 413
　houseboats 591
　Tasmania 455
Rivers, R. Godfrey
　Under the Jacaranda 228
Riverside Markets (Brisbane) 233
Riversleigh 26
RMIT Building (Melbourne) 384,
　385
Road transport 588–9
Robby Ingham Stores (Sydney) 137
Robe 351
Roberts, Tom 34, 175
　The Golden Fleece 111, 112
　In a Corner on the MacIntyre
　202
Robertson, Ethel 35, 450
Robinson, Rev George Augustus
　465, 469
Robinson, William
　*William and Shirley, Flora and
　Fauna* 229
Rock art *see* Aborigines
Rock music
　Sydney **142**, 143

Rockford
  Barossa Valley tour 356
Rockhampton **244**
The Rocks and Circular Quay
  (Sydney) 10, 73, **75–85**
  area map 75
  Circular Quay 73
  Street-by-Street map 76–7
  Sydney Harbour Bridge **80–81**
The Rocks Discovery Museum
  (Sydney) 77, **79**
Rocks Market (Sydney) 133
  Street-by-Street map 77
Rockwall (Sydney)
  Street-by-Street map 119
Rocky Bay (Rottnest Island) 308
Rocky Valley Dam 447
Rodeo
  Mount Isa Rodeo 43
  Rose and Rodeo Festival
  (Warwick) 41
Roebourne **329**
Rollerblading.com (Sydney) 147
Roper River 568
Rose and Rodeo Festival (Warwick)
  41
Ross **464**
Ross, John 284
Rothbury
  Hunter Valley tour 175
Rothbury Estate
  Hunter Valley tour 174
Rottnest Island **308–9**
Rottnest Museum 309
Route 66 (Melbourne) 409
Rowe, Thomas 93
Royal Arcade (Melbourne) **388–9**
Royal Australian Mint (Canberra)
  198–9
Royal Australian Navy 101
Royal Automobile Club of Victoria
  413
Royal Botanic Gardens
  (Cranbourne) **442**
Royal Botanic Gardens (Melbourne)
  13, 374–5, **398–9**
Royal Botanic Gardens (Sydney) 71,
  105, **106–7**
Royal Easter Show (Sydney) 42
Royal Exhibition Building
  (Melbourne) 395
Royal Flying Doctor Service 57,
  257, 590
Royal Flying Doctor Service Visitor
  Centre (Alice Springs) 283
Royal Melbourne Institute of
  Technology 377
Royal Melbourne Show 40
Royal Mint (Melbourne) **387**
Royal National Park 10, **186**
Rugby League, Sydney 146
Rugby Union, Sydney 146
Rum Rebellion (1808) **53**
Rundle Mall (Adelaide) **347**
Rupertswood 424
  Macedon Ranges and Spa
  Country tour 437
  Rupertswood and the Ashes **436**
Rural Fire Service 577
Russell Falls 454, 469
Rutherglen 450–51
Ryan, Phil 174

S

Sabi (Melbourne) 409
Safety 576

Safety (cont.)
  beaches 39
  Outback driving 590
Sailing 569
  America's Cup 59, 310
  Sydney 144
  Sydney to Hobart Yacht Race 41
Sailors' Home (Sydney) 75, **79**
St Andrew's Cathedral (Sydney) **93**
St Clair, Lake 13, 467
St Francis' Church (Melbourne) **386**
St Francis Xavier Cathedral
  (Geraldton) 322, 324
St Francis Xavier Catholic Cathedral
  (Adelaide) **346**
St George's Anglican Cathedral
  (Perth) 304–5
  Street-by-Street map 302
St James' Church (Sydney) 66, **115**
St James' Old Cathedral
  (Melbourne) **387**
St John the Baptist Church and
  Schoolhouse (Canberra) 195
St John's Anglican Cathedral
  (Brisbane) **226**
St John's Cemetery (Parramatta) 127
St Kilda (Melbourne) 403
St Kilda Market (Melbourne) 407
St Leonards 426
St Mary's Cathedral (Sydney) **92**
St Mary's Roman Catholic Cathedral
  (Perth)
  Street-by-Street map 303
St Michael's Golf Club (Sydney) 147
St Patrick's Cathedral (Melbourne)
  Street-by-Street map 393
St Patrick's Day Parade (Sydney) 42
St Paul's Cathedral (Melbourne)
  381, 384, **389**
St Peter's Anglican Cathedral
  (Adelaide) 341, 342
St Philip's Church (Sydney) **82**
Salamanca Place (Hobart) **460–61**
Saltram
  Barossa Valley tour 357
Samarai Park Riding School
  (Sydney) 147
Sanctuary Cove 239
Sands Hill Vineyard 162
Sandstone Bluff 235
Sandy Cape 242
Sangster, William 405
Sapphire Coast 183, 188
Sapphires 176, 177, 244
Sarah Island 468
Sargood, Frederick 404, 405
Sargood family 404
Sass & Bide (Sydney) 137
Save Time Services (Melbourne)
  411
Scanlan & Theodore (Sydney) 137
Scanlon & Theodore (Melbourne)
  409
Scarborough Beach 307
Schiele, Egon 113
  Poster for the Vienna Secession
  113
Scobie, James 434
Scots' Church (Melbourne) **390**
Scuba diving
  Sydney 144
Sculpture by the Sea (Sydney) 41
Seal Rocks 442
Sealife 25
Sealink 591
Seaman's Hut 160

Self-catering apartments 476–7
Sensbergs, Jan 197
Seppelt
  Barossa Valley tour 356
Seven Shillings Beach 145
Sevenhill Cellars 338, 364
Seventy-Five Mile Beach 242
Sewell, Stephen 35
Seymour Theatre Centre (Sydney)
  143
Shakespeare by the Sea (Sydney)
  141
Shark Bay 26, 145
Shark Bay World Heritage and
  Marine Park 321, **326–7**
Sharp, William 120
Sheep
  Australian Woolshed (Brisbane)
  219, **231**
  Jondaryan Woolshed (Darling
  Downs) 240
  National Wool Museum
  (Geelong) 427
Shell Beach 327
Shelly Beach 145
Shepparton **451**
Sherman, Cindy 113
Sherman Gallery (Sydney)
  Street-by-Street map 123
Shinju Matsuri Festival (Broome) 43
Shoalhaven Coast 188
Shoalhaven Heads 189
Shoe shops 408
Shopping **564–5**
  Aboriginal art **134**, 135
  accessories 137
  arcades, malls and shopping
  centres **132–3**, **406–7**, 565
  Australian fashion **136**, 137
  Australiana **134**, 135, 564–5
  books **134**, 135, 409
  Brisbane **232**, 233
  department stores 133, **406**, 407,
  565
  how to pay 132, 564
  international labels **136**, 137
  jewellery **134**, 135, 408
  luxury brands **136**, 137
  markets 133, 407, 565
  Melbourne **406–9**
  music **134**, 135, 409
  one-offs **134**, 135
  opals **134**, 135
  opening hours 132, 406, 564
  out of town 565
  outdoor gear 408
  rights and refunds 564
  sales 132
  shoes 408
  surf shops **136**, 137
  Sydney **132–7**
  tax-free sales 132
Shrine of Remembrance
  (Melbourne) 382, 398
Shute, Neville 257
Sicard, François 93
Sidney Myer Music Bowl
  (Melbourne) 398
Silverton 19, 181
Simpson (stretcher bearer)
  statue of 374
Simpson Desert Conservation Park
  369
Simpsons Gap 281, 284
Sinclair, James 374, 393
Singapore Airlines 583

Skating, inline 147
Skiing 569
  Skiing in the Victorian Alps
    448–9
Skybus Information Service
  (Melbourne) 413
Skygarden (Sydney)
  Street-by-Street map 89
Smellie & Co (Brisbane)
  Street-by-Street map 223
Smith, Joshua 34
Smiths Beach 312
Smitten Kitten (Melbourne) 409
Smoking 573
  in restaurants 519
Snake bites 577
Snorkelling
  Great Barrier Reef 216
Snowgum (Melbourne) 409
Snowy Mountain Scheme 183, 187
Snowy Mountains 10, **160–61**, **187**
  Flora and Fauna **161**
  map 160–61
  see also South Coast and Snowy
    Mountains
Snowy River 160
Sofala (Drysdale) 110
Songlines 31
Songs, Aboriginal 31
Sorrento 442
Sorrento Beach 306
Soup Plus (Sydney) 143
South Alligator River 276
South Australia **333–69**
  Adelaide and the Southeast
    341–57
  Birds of South Australia **336–7**
  history 53
  hotels 501–5
  map 334–5
  motoring organizations 590
  restaurants 548–52
  state tourist office 575
  Wines of South Australia **338–9**
  Yorke and Eyre Peninsulas and
    the Far North **359–69**
South Australian Museum
  (Adelaide) **347**
  Street-by-Street map 345
South Australian Tourist Centre
  (Adelaide) 477
South Bank Precinct (Brisbane) 11,
  227
South Coast and Snowy Mountains
  183–9
  climate 45
  discovering Australia 10
  hotels 484–5
  map 184–5, 188–9
  restaurants 531–3
South Head (Sydney) 69
South Melbourne Market
  (Melbourne) 407
South Molle Island 217
South Stradbroke Island Beach
  239
South of Townsville **235–47**
  climate 45
  discovering Australia 11
  hotels 490–92
  map 236–7
  restaurants 538–9
Southbank Markets (Brisbane) 233
Southeast Coastline **350–51**
Southern Coastline (Western
  Australia) **312–13**

Southern Highlands 10, **186**
Southgate Complex (Melbourne)
  407
Sovereign Hill **433**
Spa Country
  Macedon Ranges and Spa
    Country tour **436–7**
Space Centre (Canberra) **206**
Sparkling wine 522
Specialist holidays and activities
  566–9
Spectator sports 569
Spectrum (Sydney) 143
Speed limits 589
Spencer, John 90
Spielberg, Steven 35
Spirit of Tasmania 591
Spirits
  What to Drink in Australia 523
Sport
  adventure sports 567
  Australian Gallery of Sport and
    Olympic Museum (Melbourne)
    396
  Australian Institute of Sport
    (Canberra) **204**
  Melbourne Park **397**
  Olympic Games
    Melbourne (1956) 58, 381
    Sydney (2000) 59, 127
  surfing and beach culture **38–9**
  Sydney **146–7**
Sportsgirl (Sydney) 137
Spring in Australia 40–41
Squeaky Beach 444
STA Travel 569
Stables Theatre (Sydney) 141
Standley Chasm 284
Stanford, William 392
Stanford Fountain (Melbourne)
  Street-by-Street map 392
Stanley **466–7**
Stanthorpe 240
  festivals 43
Star City (Sydney) 141
State Library (Melbourne) 385
State Library of New South Wales
  (Sydney) **109**, 114
State Library of NSW Shop
  (Sydney) 135
State Library of Queensland
  (Brisbane) **229**
State Theatre (Sydney) **90**, 141, 143
  Street-by-Street map 88
State tourist offices 575
Steavenson Falls 446
Steep Point 326
Steiglitz 427
Stephenson, Robert 103
Stirling Range National Park 299,
  316–17
Stockman's Hall of Fame
  (Longreach) 11
Stocqueler, Edwin
  Australian Gold Diggings 54
Stokes, John Lort 267
Stonewall (Sydney) 143
Storey Hall (Melbourne) 384
Strahan 468
Strand Arcade (Sydney) **90**
  Street-by-Street map 89
Strathalbyn **353**
Street entertainment
  Melbourne 411
Streeton, Arthur 34, 112
Strezelecki National Park 465

Strickland, Sir Gerald 308
Strickland Bay 308
Stuart, John McDouall 29, 53
Student travellers 574
Study for Self Portrait (Bacon) 112
Sturt, Charles 52
Summer in Australia 41
Sun protection 577
Sunbaker (Dupain) 110
Sunset Coast (Perth) 306–7
Sunshine 44–5
Sunshine Coast 11, 238
Sunshine Coast Hinterland **240–41**
Supreme Court (Melbourne)
  386–7
Surf Life Saving NSW (Sydney) 144
Surfers Paradise 211, 235, 239
Surfing **38–9**, 569
  International Surfing Competition
    (Bells Beach) 42
  Rip Curl Pro Surfing Competition
    (Bells Beach) 42
  shops **136**, 137
  Surf Schools (Sydney) 144
  Sydney 144
Susannah Place (Sydney) **78**
Sutherland, Dame Joan 21
Swan Bells Tower (Perth) 305
Swan Hill **431**
Swan Reach 343
Swan River 310
Swanbourne Beach 307
Swanston Street Precinct
  (Melbourne) **384–5**
Swimming 39
  safety 577
  Sydney 144
Sydney **61–155**
  airport 582–3
  architecture **66–7**
  Art Gallery of New South Wales
    110–13
  Australian Museum **94–5**
  Australian National Maritime
    Museum **100–101**
  beaches **144–5**
  Botanic Gardens and the Domain
    105–15
  City Centre and Darling Harbour
    87–103
  climate 45
  discovering Australia 10
  entertainment **138–43**
  festivals 40, 41, 42, 43
  fishing 145
  Further afield **126–7**
  Garden Island to Farm Cove
    70–71
  harbour **70–73**
  hotels 478–81
  Kings Cross, Darlinghurst and
    Paddington **116–25**
  Macquarie Street **114–15**
  map 62–3
  Metro Light Rail (MLR) 130
  museums and galleries **64–5**
  Olympic Games (2000) 59, 127
  parks and reserves **68–9**
  performing arts and film **140–41**
  Powerhouse Museum **102–3**
  restaurants 524–8
  The Rocks and Circular Quay
    75–85
  Royal Botanic Gardens **106–7**
  shopping **132–7**
  sport **146–7**

Sydney (cont.)
Street-by-Street map: City Centre 88–9
Street-by-Street map: Darling Harbour 96–7
Street-by-Street map: Paddington 122–3
Street-by-Street map: Potts Point 118–19
Street Finder 148–55
Sydney Cove to Walsh Bay 72–3
time zone 574
travel 128–31
Sydney Aquarium **98**
Street-by-Street map 97
Sydney Buses Transit Shop 128
Sydney Central Plaza 133
Sydney Convention and Exhibition Centre
Street-by-Street Map 96
Sydney Cove 50, 75
Flagpole 82
Sydney Dance Company 141
Sydney Entertainment Centre (Sydney) 143
Sydney Ferries 131
Sydney Ferries Lost Property 131
Sydney Film Festival 43
Sydney Fish Market 133
Sydney Harbour 10
ferries and water taxis 131
Garden Island to Farm Cove **70–71**
Sydney Cove to Walsh Bay 72–3
Sydney Harbour Bridge 57, 72, **80–81**
Sydney Harbour Tunnel 81
Sydney Hospital **113**, 115
Sydney Jewish Museum 65, **121**
Sydney Modernist movement 34
Sydney Observatory **82**
Street-by-Street map 76
Sydney Olympic Park **127**, 143
Sydney Opera House 10, 17, 21, 58, 66, 67, 72, **84–5**
Information desk 139
Sydney Opera House Market 133
Sydney Philharmonia Choirs 141
Sydney Symphony Orchestra 141
Sydney Theatre Co. 141
Sydney to Hobart Yacht Race 41
Sydney Tower **91**
Street-by-Street map 89
Sydney Town Hall **93**, 141
Sydney Transport Management Centre (Traffic Control) 128
Sydney Visitor Centre 139
Sydney Youth Orchestra 141
Synagogues
Great Synagogue (Sydney) **93**
Synergy (Sydney) 141

T

Tahbilk Wines 373, 379
Tallows Beach 179
Talmage, Algernon
The Founding of Australia **82**
Tamar River 464
Tamarama 145
Tamburlaine
Hunter Valley tour 174
Tamworth 159, **177**
festivals 41
Tandanya (Adelaide) **347**
Tank (Sydney) 143
Tank Stream (Sydney) 73

Target (Melbourne) 407
Tasma Terrace (Melbourne) 376
Street-by-Street map 393
Tasman, Abel 49, 109
Tasmania **453–71**
climate 45
discovering Australia 13
ferries 591
history 49, 52
Hobart **460–61**
hotels 515–17
map 458–9
motoring organizations 590
Port Arthur **470–71**
restaurants 561–3
state tourist office 575
Wildlife and Wilderness **454–5**
World Heritage Area 27
Tasmanian Museum and Art Gallery (Hobart) **460**
Tathra Beach 189
Tax-free sales 132
Taxis
Sydney 128
water taxis 131
Telephones **580–81**
Television 575
Telstra Mobile Communications 581
Telstra Tower (Canberra) **204**
Temperatures 44–5
Tennant Creek 279, **285**
Tennis
Australian Open 41
Sydney 146
Tenterfield 159, **176**
Territory Wildlife Park (Berry Springs) 272
Terry, Leonard 434
Tewantin 238
Theatre
Sydney **140**, 141
Theatre Royal (Hobart) **460**
Theatre Royal (Sydney) 141
Theft 576
Third Headland Beach 178
Thredbo River 161
Thredbo Village 185, 187
Three-day equestrian event (Gawler) 43
Three Sisters 159, 165, 166, 171
Thrifty 590
Thursday Island 252
festivals 42
Tiagarra (Devonport) 466
Ticketek (Brisbane) 233
Ticketek (Melbourne) 411
Ticketek (Sydney) 139, 147
Ticketmaster (Melbourne) 411
Ticketmaster (Sydney) 139
Tidal Cascades (Sydney)
Street-by-Street map 96
Tidbinbilla Nature Reserve **206**
Tiffin, Charles 224, 225
Tillers, Imants 113
Time zones 574
Tipping 573
in restaurants 518–19
Tirari Desert 369
Tiwi Aborigines 30, 111, 260, 274
Tiwi Islands 274
Tiwi Land Council 262
Tjapaltjarri, Clifford Possum
Bush Plum Dreaming 33
Toberua (Done) 34
Todd, Alice 282
Todd River 282

Toowoomba 240
Top End *see* Darwin and the Top End
Torrens, River 344, 346
Torres, Luis Vaez de **49**
Torres Strait Cultural Festival (Thursday Island) 42
Torres Strait Islands 11, 58, **252**
Total Skate (Sydney) 147
Tour operators 569
Tourism
Aboriginal lands 263
Tourism ACT 477
Tourism NSW (Sydney) 139, 477
Tourism Tasmania (Hobart) 477
Tourism Top End (Darwin) 477
Tourism Victoria (Melbourne) 477
Tourist information offices 477, 572, 575
Brisbane 233
Melbourne 413
Sydney 575
Tours by car
Barossa Valley **356–7**
Hunter Valley 174–5
Macedon Ranges and Spa Country **436–7**
Tower Hill Game Reserve 428
Towns, Robert 247
Townsville 11, **247**
Traeger, Alfred 257
Trains **586–7**
Melbourne 412
Puffing Billy 443
Sydney 130
Trams
Melbourne 412–13
Sydney 128
Trans-Australian Railway 367
Transinfo (Brisbane) 233
Transport Infoline (Sydney) 129
Transport Information Line (Melbourne) 413
Transport Management Centre (Sydney) 128
Travel **582–91**
Adelaide and the Southeast 343
aerial tours 567
air **582–5**
bicycles 128
Blue Mountains and Beyond 167
Brisbane 221, 233
buses 129, 412–13
Canberra and ACT 193
cars and four-wheel drive 412, 588–90
coaches 413, **587**
cycling 412
Darwin and the Top End 268
ferries and cruise boats 131, **591**
Melbourne 383, **412–13**
monorail 130
North of Perth 323
Northern Queensland 250
Perth and the Southwest 300
Red Centre 281
safety 576
South Coast and Snowy Mountains 184
South of Townsville 237
Sydney **128–31**
Tasmania 459
taxis 128
trains 130, 412, **586–7**
trams 128, 412–13
Victoria: Eastern Victoria 441

Travel (cont.)
Victoria: Western Victoria 424
water taxis 131
Yorke and Eyre Peninsulas 360
Travel Coach Australia (Melbourne) 413
Travelex 578
Traveller's cheques **578**
safety 576
in shops 132
Treasury Building (Melbourne)
Street-by-Street map 392
Treasury Gardens (Melbourne) 375
Tree of Knowledge (Barcaldine) 249
Trees
Western Australia 295
Trentham Falls
Macedon Ranges and Spa Country tour 436
Trentham family 471
Trigg Beach 307
Trollope, Anthony 346
Tropfest (Sydney) 141
Truganini 53, 469
Tsubi (Sydney) 137
Tulip Festival 40
Tunarama Festival (Port Lincoln) 41
Turquoise Bay 328
Turtles
Mon Repos Conservation Park **243**
Tusculum Villa (Sydney)
Street-by-Street map 118
Twain, Mark 83
The Twelve Apostles 372, 423
Twin Falls 277
Tyrrells' Vineyards
Hunter Valley tour 174

U

Ubirr 263, 277
Ulladulla 188
Uluru-Kata Tjuta National Park 260, **286–9**
map 280
The Olgas 22
rock art 33
sacred sites 263
Uluru (Ayers Rock) 12, 279, 286–7, **288**
World Heritage Areas of Australia 26
Under the Jacaranda (Rivers) 228
Underground Art Gallery (Coober Pedy) 368
Underwood, Jacky 180
UNESCO 26, 355
United Airlines 583
Unsworth, Ken 113
Upper Murray Valley 441
Urunga 178
Usher, Pat 314
Utopia Records (Sydney) 135
Utzon, Jørn
Sydney Opera House 66, 67, 85

V

Vampire (Sydney)
Street-by-Street map 97
Valley of the Giants 313
Van Diemen's Land 49
Vancouver, Captain 316
The Vanguard (Sydney) 143
Vegetarian menus, restaurants 519
The Venus Room (Sydney) 143

Verge, John
Elizabeth Bay House (Sydney) 67, 120
Rockwall (Sydney) 119
St James' Church (Sydney) 115
Vernon, WL 110, 115
Versace (Sydney) 137
Vespucci, Amerigo 48
Victor Harbor 350
Victoria **371–451**
Eastern Victoria **439–51**
Eastern Victoria's coastline **444–5**
Great Ocean Road coastline **428–9**
history 52
hotels 505–15
map 372–3
Melbourne **381–421**
motoring organizations 590
restaurants 552–61
state tourist office 575
Skiing in the Victorian Alps **448–9**
Western Victoria **423–51**
Wines of Victoria **378–9**
Victoria, Queen of England 223
statues of 88, 90, 374
Victoria Barracks (Sydney) 67, **124**
Victoria Cave 355
Victoria River 275
Victoria Spring Designs (Sydney) 135
Victoria Square (Adelaide) **346**
Victoria State Rose Garden (Werribee) 426
Victoria Street (Sydney) **120**
Street-by-Street map 118
Victorian Alps 373, 439, 441, 447
Skiing in the Victorian Alps **448–9**
Victorian Arts Centre (Melbourne) 400, 411
Victorian Tourism Information Service (Melbourne) 413
Victoria's Open Range Zoo 426
Vietnam War 58, 59
A View of Sydney Cove (Dayes) 50–51
Vineyards
Hunter Valley tour 174–5
see also Wines
Violet Gorge 235
Virgin Blue 585
Visas 572
Vlamingh, Willem de 308, 309
Volleyball, beach 39

W

WA Museum Geraldton **324**, 325
WA Museum Kalgoorlie-Boulder 319
Wadlata Outback Centre (Port Augusta) 365
Wagbara, Samuel 112
Wagga Wagga **181**
Waikerie 355
Waitpinga Beach 350
The Walk Arcade (Melbourne) 407
Walkabout Creek Wildlife Centre (Brisbane) 231
Walker, Stephen 225
"Living Lagoon" sculptures 246
Walker Flat 343
Walking (bushwalking) 566

Wallabies 309
Wallaroo 363
Wallaroo Heritage and Nautical Museum 363
Walls of Jerusalem National Park 457
Walsh Bay (Sydney) 72
Wardang Island 362
Wardell, William 92
Warhol, Andy 78
Warrawong Sanctuary **352**
Warren National Park 315
Warringah Golf Club (Sydney) 147
Warrnambool 428
Warwick (Queensland) 240
festivals 41
Warwick (Sydney)
Street-by-Street map 123
Washpool National Park 176
Watarrka National Park 285
Water sports 568–9
Water taxis (Sydney) 131
Waterfalls
Atherton Tableland 255
Boonoo Boonoo Falls 176
Bridal Falls 173
Carrington Falls 186
Edith Falls 275
Fitzroy Falls 186
Jim Jim Falls 268
MacKenzie Falls 427
Nelson Falls 458
Queen Mary Falls National Park 240
Russell Falls 454, 469
Steavenson Falls 446
Trentham Falls 436
Twin Falls 277
Wentworth Falls 171
Wollomombi Gorge 175
Waterfront (Sydney) 135
Watson, GW 432
Watson, Judy 395
Watsons Bay 147
Wave Rock 293, **318**
Weather **44–5**
when to go 572
Webb, Charles 388
Weindorfer, Gustav 467
Weiss Art (Sydney) 135
Welch, Dr Kenyon St Vincent 257
"Welcome Stranger" gold nugget 95
Weld, Governor 329
Wentworth, William Charles 52, 172
statue of 92
Wentworth Falls **171**
Werribee Park **426**
Werrington (Sydney)
Street-by-Street map 118
Western Australia **291–331**
history 52
hotels 497–501
The Kimberley **296–7**
map 292–3
motoring organizations 590
North of Perth and the Kimberley **321–31**
Perth and the Southwest **299–319**
restaurants 544–8
Southern Coastline **312–13**
state tourist office 575
Wildflowers of Western Australia **294–5**
Western Australia Tourist Centre (Perth) 477

Western Australian Maritime
  Museum (Fremantle) 310
Western Australian Museum (Perth)
  304
Western Plains Zoo (Dubbo) 180
Western Victoria **423–51**
  Ballarat **434–5**
  climate 45
  discovering Australia 13
  Great Ocean Road coastline
    428–9
  hotels 510–11
  Macedon Ranges and Spa
    Country tour **436–7**
  map 424–5
  restaurants 557–9
Westpac 578
Westwood, Vivienne 103
Wetland habitat
  Birds of South Australia 337
Whale Beach 145
Whales
  Ceduna 367
  Hervey Bay 241
  Whale World (Albany) 316
Wharf Theatre (Sydney) 73, 141
Wheelchair access *see* Disabled
  travellers
Wheels & Doll Baby (Sydney) 135
White, Patrick 35, 242
White Australia Policy 56
Whiteley, Brett 34, 169
  The Balcony (2) 112
Whiteman Park (Perth) 307
Whitewater rafting 568
Whitlam, Edward Gough 59
  dismissal 196
Whitsunday Islands **246**
Whyalla **365**
Whyalla Maritime Museum
  (Whyalla) 365
Whyalla Wildlife and Reptile
  Sanctuary (Whyalla) 365
Wickham, Captain John 230
Wilderness
  Tasmania **454–5**
Wildlife 17
  Alice Springs Desert Park 283
  Arkaroola 369
  Birds of South Australia **336–7**
  Blue Mountains 170
  Broome Crocodile Park 330
  Cataract Gorge Reserve
    (Launceston) 465
  Cleland Wildlife Park (Mt Lofty)
    353
  Dampier Archipelago 329
  Dolphin Discovery Centre
    (Bunbury) 314
  Eagles Heritage Raptor Wildlife
    Centre (Margaret River) 314–15
  Flora and fauna **24–5**
    of the Grampians **427**
  Great Barrier Reef **212–17**
  Healesville Sanctuary 443
  Howard Springs Nature Park 272
  Kangaroo Island 354
  King Island 467
  Lone Pine Koala Sanctuary
    (Brisbane) 11, **230**
  Mon Repos Conservation Park
    243
  Ningaloo Reef Marine Park 12,
    328
  Phillip Island 442
  quokkas **309**

Wildlife (cont.)
  Shark Bay World Heritage and
    Marine Park 292, 321, **326–7**
  Simpson Desert Conservation
    Park 369
  Snowy Mountains **161**
  Tasmania's Wildlife and
    Wilderness **454–5**
  Territory Wildlife Park (Berry
    Springs) 272
  Tidbinbilla Nature Reserve **206**
  Walkabout Creek Wildlife Centre
    (Brisbane) 231
  Warrawong Sanctuary **352**
  Whyalla Wildlife and Reptile
    Sanctuary (Whyalla) 365
  Wildlife of the Eyre Peninsula
    366
  Wyndham Crocodile Park 331
  see also Aquariums; Birds;
    National parks; Reptiles; Zoos
Willandra Lakes 27
Willandra National Park **181**
*William and Shirley, Flora and
  Fauna* (Robinson) 229
Williams, Edward Eyre 405
Williamson, David 35
Williamson, JC 120
Williamstown Bay and River Cruises
  (Melbourne) 413
Wills, William 53
Wilson, JH 93
Wilson Inlet 313
Wilsons Promontory National Park
  13, 439, 444
Windjana Gorge National Park 296,
  331
Windsor 159, **168**
Windsor Hotel (Melbourne)
  Street-by-Street map 392
Windsor Street (Sydney)
  Street-by-Street map 123
Windsurfing (Sydney) 144
Wine Banq (Sydney) 143
Wineglass Bay 459, 463
Wines **36–7**
  Barossa Valley tour **356–7**
  Northeastern Wineries (Victoria)
    450–51
  What to Drink in Australia **522–3**
  Wines of New South Wales and
    ACT **162–3**
  Wines of South Australia **338–9**
  Wines of Victoria **378–9**
  Yarra Valley 443
Winter in Australia 43
Winton 249
Witchery (Sydney) 137
Witjira National Park **369**
Wivenhoe, Lake 231
Wolf Blass 338
  Barossa Valley tour 357
Wolfe Creek Crater National Park
  331
Wollomombi Gorge 175
Wollongong **186**
Wombeyan Caves 186–7
Wonnerup House (Busselton) 314
Woodend
  Macedon Ranges and Spa
    Country tour 437
Woodland habitat 25
  Birds of South Australia 337
Woodside Beach 445
Woodward, Robert 96
Woody Bay Beach 179

Woody Island 319
Wool
  Australian Woolshed (Brisbane)
    219, **231**
  Jondaryan Woolshed (Darling
    Downs) 240
  National Wool Museum
    (Geelong) 427
Woolloomooloo Finger Wharf
  (Sydney) 71
Woolnorth **467**
World Expeditions 569
World Heritage Areas **26–7**
World War I 56–7
World War II 57–8, 270
World Wide Wear (Melbourne) 409
Wreck Bay 189
Wright, Edmund 346
Wright, Judith 35, 83
Writers 35
Writers' Walk (Sydney) **83**
Wyndham **331**
Wynns Winery 339
Wyperfield National Park 430

Y
Yallingup 312
Yalumba Vineyard 339
Yamba 179
Yapurrara Aborigines 328
Yardie Creek Gorge 328
Yarra Park (Melbourne) 375
Yarra River 375, 388, **400–401**
Yarra Valley 13, **443**
Yarra Valley Grape Grazing 42
Yarralumla (Canberra) **200–201**
Yarrangobilly Caves 161
Yass 187
Yellow Water 276
York **317**
Yorke and Eyre Peninsulas and the
  Far North **359–69**
  climate 44
  discovering Australia 12
  The Far North **368**
  Fishing and Diving on the Yorke
    Peninsula **363**
  hotels 504–5
  map 360–61
  restaurants 551–2
  Wildlife of the Eyre Peninsula
    366
Yorketown 362
Young and Jackson's (Melbourne)
  385
Youth hostels **476**, 477
Yulara 286, 289
Yulefest (Blue Mountains) 43
Yungaburra 255

Z
Zambesi (Sydney) 137
Zimmermann (Sydney) 137
Zoo Emporium (Sydney) 137
Zoos
  Australian Reptile Park (Gosford)
    169
  Lone Pine Koala Sanctuary
    (Brisbane) 11, **230**
  National Zoo and Aquarium
    (Canberra) **204**
  Perth Zoo 307
  Victoria's Open Range Zoo 426
  Western Plains Zoo (Dubbo) 180
  see also Wildlife
Zuytdorp Cliffs 326

Acknowledgments

Dorling Kindersley would like to thank the following people whose contributions and assistance have made the preparation of this book possible.

Consultant
Helen Duffy is an editor and writer. Since 1992 she has managed and contributed to a range of tourist publications on Australia.

Main Contributors
Louise Bostock Lang has worked on a number of Dorling Kindersley Travel Guides.
Jan Bowen is a travel broadcaster and writer. Her travel books include *The Queensland Experience*.
Paul Kloeden lives in Adelaide. A freelance writer and historian, his work ranges from travel articles to government-sponsored heritage surveys.
Jacinta le Plaistrier is a Melbourne-based journalist, poet and librettist.
Sue Neales is a multi-award winning Australian journalist. Her travel articles have appeared in major Australian newspapers and magazines.
Ingrid Ohlsson is a Melbourne-based writer who has contributed to many travel publications.
Tamara Thiessen is a Tasmanian freelance travel writer and photographer.

Additional Contributors
Tony Baker, Libby Lester.

Additional Photography
Simon Blackall, DK Studio, Geoff Dunn, Jean-Paul Ferrero, Esther Labi, Jean-Marc La Roque, Michael Nicholson, Ian O'Leary, Rob Reichenfeld, Carol Wiley, Alan Williams.

Cartography
Lovell Johns Ltd, Oxford, UK; ERA-Maptec Ltd, Dublin, Ireland.

Indexer
Hilary Bird.

Senior Revisions Editor
Esther Labi.

Design and Editorial
Duncan Baird Limited
PICTURE RESEARCH Victoria Peel
DTP DESIGNER Rhona Green
Dorling Kindersley Limited
SENIOR MANAGING EDITOR Vivien Crump
MANAGING EDITOR Helen Partington
PROJECT EDITOR Rosalyn Thiro
DEPUTY ART DIRECTOR Gillian Allan
ART EDITOR Stephen Bere
MAP CO-ORDINATORS Emily Green, David Pugh
PRODUCTION David Proffit
Ross Adams, Rosemary Bailey, Uma Bhattacharya, Hilary Bird, Hanna Bolus, Debbie Brand, Sue Callister, Wendy Canning, Sherry Collins, Laura Cook, Lucinda Cooke, Bronwen Davies, Stephanie Driver, Jonathan Elphick, Fay Franklin, Anna Freiberger, Vinod Harish, Gail Jones, Christine Keilty, Esther Labi, Maite Lantaron, Stefan Laszczuk, Maria Leonardis, Ciaran McIntyre, Siobhan Mackay, Claudine Meissner, Sam Merrell, John Miles, Tania Monkton, Michael Palmer, Manisha Patel, Sangita Patel, Alok Pathak, Giles Pickard, Rachel Power, Garry Ramler, Louise Roberts, Lamya Sadi, Mark Sayers, Shailesh Sharma, Azeem Siddiqui, Kunal Singh, Adrian Tristram, Lynda Tyson, Carol Wiley, Ros Walford, Steve Womersley.

Special Assistance
Sue Bickers, Perth; Craig Ebbett, Perth; Peter Edge, Met. Office, London; Chrissie Goldrick, The Image Library, State Library of NSW; Cathy Goodwin, Queensland Art Gallery; Megan Howat, International Media & Trade Visits Coordinator, WA Tourist Commission; John Hunter and Fiona Marr, CALM, Perth; Vere Kenny, Auscape International; Selena MacLaren, SOCOG; Greg Miles, Kakadu National Park; Ian Miller, Auslig; Gary Newton, Perth; Murray Robbins, Perth; Ron Ryan, Coo-ee Historical Picture Library; Craig Sambell and Jill Jones, GBRMPA; Norma Scott, Australian Picture Library; Andrew Watts, QASCO; and all state tourist authorities and national park services.

Photography Permissions
Dorling Kindersley would like to thank the following for their kind assistance and permission to photograph at their establishments: Art Gallery of WA; Australian Museum; National Gallery of Australia; Australian War Memorial; Ayers House; Department of Conservation and Land Management (WA); Department of Environment and Natural Resources (Adelaide); Department of Environment (Queensland); Government House (Melbourne); Hermannsburg Historic Precinct; Jondaryan Woolshed Historical Museum; Museum and Art Gallery of NT; Museum of WA; National Gallery of Victoria; National Maritime Museum; National Museum of Australia; National Parks and Wildlife Services (all states); National Trust of Australia (all states); Parliament House (Melbourne); Port Arthur Historic Site; Powerhouse Museum; Rottnest Island Authority; Royal Flying Doctor Service of NT; Shrine of Remembrance Trustees (Victoria); South Australian Museum; *Spirit of Tasmania*; Supreme Court (Melbourne), Tandanya National Aboriginal Cultural Institute Inc; Victoria Arts Centre Trust; WA Maritime Museum; and all the other sights too numerous to thank individually.

Picture Credits
t = top; tl = top left; tlc = top left centre; tc = top centre; trc = top right centre; tr = top right; cla = centre left above; ca = centre above; cra = centre right above; cl = centre left; c = centre; cr = centre right; clb = centre left below; crb = centre right

below; cb = centre below; bl = bottom left; br = bottom right; b = bottom; bc = bottom centre; bcl = bottom centre left; bcr = bottom centre right; (d) detail.

Works of art have been reproduced with the permission of the following copyright holders: Francois Gohier 455t; *Ngalyod and Ngalkunburriyaymi*, Namerredje Guymala, c.1975, Natural pigments on bark, The National Museum (Canberra) ©1978 Aboriginal Artists Agency Limited 13c,

The publisher would like to thank the following individuals, companies and picture libraries for their kind permission to reproduce their photographs: ALAMY IMAGES: Bill Bachman 12bc, 13tr, 388bl, 407tl; Cephas Picture Library / Mick Rock 10bl; Foodpix 520cl; Chris McLennan 246tl; Doug Stely 521t, 521tl; David Wall 406cl; Rob Walls 521c; ALLSPORT: 539b, 42t; ARDEA LONDON LTD: © D Parer & E Parer Cook 216tr; Davo Blair 446tl; © Francois Gohier 455t; Jean-Marc La Roque 448cla; Peter Steyn 13ca; © Ron and Valerie Taylor 216cla; ART GALLERY OF NSW: © Ms Stephenson-Meere 1996, *Australian Beach Pattern* 1940, Charles Meere (1890–1961) oil on canvas, 91.5 x 122cm, 65tl; *Bridge Pattern*, Harold Cazneaux (1878–1953), gelatin silver photography, 29.6 x 21.4cm, gift of the Cazneaux family, 1975, 72bc(d); © Art Gallery of NSW *Sofala* 1947 Russell Drysdale (1912-81), oil on canvas on hardboard, 71.7 x 93.1cm 110cla; *Sunbaker* 1937, Max Dupain, gelatin silver photograph, 38.3 x 43.7cm 110ca; *Madonna and Child With Infant St John The Baptist* c. 1541, Domenico Beccafumi, oil on wooden panel 92 x 69cm Art Gallery of NSW Foundation Purchase 1992 110clb; © Tiwi Design Executive 1996, *Pukumnai Grave Posts, Melville Island* 1958, various artists, natural pigments on wood, 165.1 x 29.2cm, gift of Dr Stuart Scougall 1959, 111t; *Sheild*, collected 1969, Unknown Lake Kopiago, Southern Highlands, Papua New Guinea, wood, bark, split bamboo, dark brown, white and red natural pigments, 17 x 35.6 cm, Gift of Stan Moriarty 1978 111ca; Art Gallery of NSW Foundation purchase 1990, *A Pair of Tomb Guardian Figures*, late 6th century AD Early, Unknown (China), sculpture earthenware with traces of red and orange pigment, 93 x 82cm, Art Gallery of NSW Foundation Purchase 1990 111crb; *The Golden Fleece – Shearing at Newstead* 1894, Tom Roberts, oil on canvas 104 x 158.7cm 111b; © Estate of Francis Bacon, *Study for Self Portrait* 1976, Francis Bacon (1901–92), oil and pastel on canvas, 198 x 147.5cm, 112tr;© Art Gallery of NSW *Interior With Wardrobe Mirror* 1955, Grace Cossington Smith oil on canvas on paperboard 91.4 x 73.7cm 112cla; © Wendy Whitely 1996, *The Balcony 2* 1975, Brett Whitely (1939–92), oil on canvas, 203.5 x 364.5cm 112b; © ASSOCIATED PRESS, LONDON: 59t; AUSCAPE INTERNATIONAL: 39cr; © Kathie Atkinson 26clb; © Nicholas Birks 344bl; © Donna Browning 268br; © John Cancalosi 25clb, 245bl; © Kevin Deacon 25cr; © Jean-Paul Ferrero 2–3, 23b, 24t, 26cla, 159crb, 161trb, ba, 237, 242cl, 258–9, 260cb, 263t, 288cl, 455t, bra,

472–3; © Jeff & Sandra Foott 25br; © Brett Gregory 170b, 454bl; © Dennis Harding 27b, 452–3, 456; © Andrew Henley 40ra; © Matt Jones 277cra, b; © Mike Langford 27crb; © Wayne Lawler 161cr; © Geoffrey Lea 457b; © Darren Leal 24br, 243t, 244t, 245cr; © Reg Morrison 24bca, 242cr, 454tr, 455cl; © Jean-Marc La Roque 18t, 24cr, 27cr, 28-9c, 181t, 238cla, 239cb, 261br, 280l, 370-71, 376t, 377t, cb, 385cla, 426cr, 428t, cl, 430t, 572cl; © Jamie Plaza Van Roon 24bl, 25cl, 161t, cb, 234; © Becca Saunders 25cb; © Gary Steer 28tl; AUSTRALIAN BROADCASTING CORPORATION: 575t; AUSTRALIAN MUSEUM www.austmus.gov.au: 30cl, 94cla, 94clb, 95cra, 95crb; Nature Focus/John N Cornish; AUSTRALIAN PICTURE LIBRARY: 18c, 158clb, 588cl, 586b, 587t; Adelaide Freelance 367b; Douglas Baglin 47ca; John Baker 20b, 21tr, 173t, 178ba, 249t, 415b, 431tr; JP & ES Baker 160b, 184, 471cra; John Carnemolla 15t, 29crb, 38l, 39cra, 40clb, 41t, l, 43cr, 142b, 158cl, 184t, 210cla, 262tr, 264cl, 334cb, 351t, 365t, 366bl, 372cl, 573c, 574b; Sean Davey 38–9c; R. Eastwood 470tr; Flying Photos 574b; Evan Gillis 367t; Owen Hughes 253b; S & B Kendrick 335b, 354t; Ian Kenins 397t; Craig La Motte 211b; Michael Lees 427b; Gary Lewis 40t; Lightstorm 188b, 360b, 361c, 465cb; Johnathan Marks 185cr, 428crb; Aureo Martelli 171cra; Leo Meier 27t, 250cl, 252t, 263clb; PhotoIndex 257b; Fritz Prenzel 428b, 442b; Dereck Roff 40b; Stephen Sanders 352b; Peter Solness 38tr; Oliver Strewe 32cl, 33tr; Neale Winter 368b; Gerry Withom 171t; AUSTRALIAN WAR MEMORIAL: 201c.

GREG BARRETT, THE AUSTRALIAN CHAMBER ORCHESTRA: 133b; BARTEL PHOTO LIBRARY: 175b; BILL BACHMAN: 26t, 28cl, 29c, 33tl, 43t, b, 165b, 167t, 210clb, 245br, 256b, 274t, 275c, b, 276bl, 287b, 296b, 327crb, 335bra, 438, 446tr; BERINGER BLASS WINE ESTATES: 338br; 357cr; BEST'S WINES: 378ca; © MERVYN BISHOP: 59cb; BRIDGECLIMB SYDNEY: 81tl; BRIDGEMAN ART LIBRARY London/ New York: *Kangaroo Dreaming with Rainbow Serpent*, 1992 (acrylic) Michael Nelson Tjakamarra (b.c.1949), Corbally Stourton Contemporary Art, London © Aboriginal Artists Agency Ltd 8–9; *Bush Plum Dreaming* 1991 (acrylic) by Clifford Possum Tjapaltjarri (b.c.1932), Corbally Stourton Contemporary Art, London © Aboriginal Artists Agency Ltd 33cr; *Men's Dreaming* 1990 (acrylic) by Clifford Possum Tjapaltjarri (b.c.1932), Corbally Stourton Contemporary Art, London © Aboriginal Artists Agency Ltd 30c; *Kelly in Spring*, 1956 (ripolin on board) by Sidney Nolan (1917–92), Arts Council, London © Lady Mary Nolan 34bl; National Maritime Museum, London 49bla(d); British Museum 51cra; Mitchell Library, State Library of NSW 54tr, bl, 55tl; National Library of Australia 50tr(d), 53tl, cb, 54–5c; *Bush Tucker Dreaming*, 1991 (acrylic) by Gladys Napanangka (b.c.1920) Corbally Stourton Contemporary Art, London, © Aboriginal Artists Agency Ltd 253cr; *The Ashes*, 1883 (The Urn) Marylebone Cricket Club, London, 436b; Photo reproduced courtesy of BRISBANE CITY COUNCIL: 233b; BRITSTOCK-IFA/ GOTTSCHALK: 260ca; GRANT BURGE WINES PTY LTD: 356b.

CANBERRA TOURISM: 191b, 566c; CENTREPOINT

MANAGEMENT: 91br; CEPHAS PICTURE LIBRARY: Andy Christodolo 163t, 332-3, 338bla, 339c, 378cla; Chris Davis 334cl; Mick Rock 19t, 36cl, 37cr; 162tl, cl, 163cr, 174tr, cla, 37br, 339c, 341b, 356cla, 357tr, 369t, ca; PETER CLARKE: 402br; BRUCE COLEMAN LTD: John Cancalosi 69b; Alain Compost 337tl; Francisco Futil 68tr; Hans Reinhard 336bcl; Rod Williams 337bl; COLORIFIC: 31t; Bill Angove 263b, 293c; Bill Bachman 257t, 266, 359, 397b; Penny Tweedie 265t, 267b; Patrick Ward 235b; COO-EE HISTORICAL PICTURE LIBRARY: 9c, 32-3c, 33b, 34tl, 35cr, 49t, 50b, 51ba, 52bra, 56cr, 57clb, 157c, 209c, 259c, 291c, 333c, 433cr, 434b, 453c, 455bl, 469c, 473c, 571c; CORBIS: Free Agents Limited 449bc; Royalty Free 12tr; Kevin Schafer 11cl; Zefa/Stock Photos/R.Wallace 10c; SYLVIA CORDAIY PHOTO LIBRARY LTD: © John Farmer 334bl; Nick Rains 296c, 369t.

RUPERT DEAN: 36br, 356clb, bc, 357b, 379b, 522cla, 522crb; DINOSAUR DESIGNS: 406tc; DIXON GALLERIES, STATE LIBRARY OF NSW: 80tl; © DOMAINE CHANDON, AUSTRALIA: 443c; © KEN DONE: Drunken Admiral, Hobart: 460tl; © DW STOCK PICTURE LIBRARY: 188tr; P Brunotte 589b; M French 588b; ENVIRONMENTAL PROTECTION AGENCY, Queensland: 240c; MARY EVANS PICTURE LIBRARY: 61ca; FAIRFAX PHOTO LIBRARY: 58clb, bcb, 81bra, 146 cla, 169br(d), 272br; Ken James: 133tr; McNeil 120b; FALLS CREEK ALPINE RESORT: 448tl, 449t.

RONALD GRANT ARCHIVE: Buena Vista 21b; Universal 35b; © GREAT BARRIER REEF MARINE PARK AUTHORITY: 215t, 217t, cr; Photo: S Browne 215bl; Photo: W Craik 212b; Photo: N Collins 212cla; Photo: L Zell 213b, 214ca; ROBERT HARDING PICTURE LIBRARY: 290-91, 375t, 583c; © Rolf Richardson 298; © Nick Servian 340, 590t; C Moore Hardy: 132br; HISTORIC HOUSES TRUST: 64cla; HOOD COLLECTION, STATE LIBRARY OF NSW: 81bl; HORIZON: © Andris Apse 279b; HUTCHISON LIBRARY: © R. Ian Lloyd 12, 570-71; © Sarah Murray 586c.

IMAGES COLOUR LIBRARY: 26b, 211ca, 287t, 289b; THE IMAGE LIBRARY, STATE LIBRARY OF NSW: 34tr, 36bl, 48tl, cb, 49c, 52bla, 55crb, 58t, 349br; ALI KAYN: 392cla; © DR RUTH KERR (Commissariat Stores, Brisbane) 222bl.

FRANK LANE PICTURE LIBRARY – Images of Nature: 24clb, 215br, 336tl; © Tom & Pam Gardner 25bc, 337bcr; © David Hosking 337tr, cb; © E & D Hosking 337crb, 455cra, cb; © M Hollings 336crb; © Gerard Lacz 161br; © Silvestris 216tl, 454tl; © Martin Withers 170cl, 336bcl; LEISURE RAIL, RAIL AUSTRALIA: 586tl; LIBERTY WINES: 378br; LOCHMAN TRANSPARENCIES: © Bill Belson 323r; © Wade Hughes 296t; © Jiri Lochman 307t, 307cl; © Marie Lochman 293tc, 309 t; © Dennis Sarson 303cr; © Len Stewart 303b; LONELY PLANET IMAGES: Glenn Beanland 388tl.

MAMBO: 134br; LINDSAY MAY PR: 338ca, 338cl; © GREG MILES (ENVIRONMENTAL MEDIA): 276br; © MIRROR AUSTRALIAN TELEGRAPH PUBLICATIONS: 58cr; MITCHELL LIBRARY, STATE LIBRARY OF NSW: 48blb; 50-51c, 52b, 68tl, 81cra, 108c, 109t; MOUNT BAW BAW ALPINE RESORT: James

Lauritz 448clb; MUSEUM & ART GALLERY OF THE NORTHERN TERRITORY: 265ca; MULTIPLEX PROPERTY SERVICES: 98tr; MUSEUM OF CONTEMPORARY ART, SYDNEY: Tony Dhanyula, Nyoka (Mud Crabs) circa 1984, ochres and synthetic polymer on bark, JW Power Bequest, purchased 1984, Ramingining Collection, 64cl.

COLLECTION OF THE NATIONAL GALLERY OF AUSTRALIA, CANBERRA: Tom Roberts, In a corner in a Macintyre 1895, oil on canvas, 73.4 x 88.00cm, 202cl; Margaret Preston, The Native Fuscia 1925, woodblock print on paper, 44.8 x 28.2cm, 202cb; Aristide Maillol, The Mountain (La Montagne) 1937, lead, 167,4 (h) x 193.0 (w) x 82.3 (d)cm 202b; Artist Unknown Kamakura period, Japan, Prince Shotoku praying to the Buddha c. 1300, wood, gesso and lacquer, height 48.2cm, 203tl; © ARS, NY and DACS, London 1997, Jackson Pollock, Blue Poles 1952, oil enamel and aluminium paint on canvas, 212.0 x 489.00cm, 203cra; © Bula'bula Arts, Ramingining Artists, Raminginging, Central Arnhem Land, NT, The Aboriginal Memorial 1998, natural pigments on wood: an installation of 200 hollow log coffins, height 40.0 to 327.00cm, purchased with the assistance of funds from gallery admission charges and commissioned in 1987, 203cr; NATIONAL GALLERY OF VICTORIA, MELBOURNE: 400cla; NATIONAL LIBRARY OF AUSTRALIA: 35t, 46, 49bra (original in possession of the WA Museum), 52ca, 53cra 55cra, 56tl, 197br; Rex nan Kivell Collection 49crb, b, 51crb; ES Theodore, Campaign Director, ALP State of NSW, Trades Hall 56clb; NATIONAL MARITIME MUSEUM, SYDNEY: 51tl, 97cra, 100tl, clb, 101cra, 101tl, bc; NATURE FOCUS: H & J Bestel 454cl; Rob Blakers 454br; John Fields 68b; Dave Watts 454cr; Babs & Bert Wells 287cra, 336br; © Australian Museum 30tl, 32tr, Carl Bento 64cla; NATIONAL MUSEUM OF AUSTRALIA: © Australia-China Friendship Society, The Harvest of Endurance Scroll. The scroll is of 18 segments, ink and colour on paper, mounted on silk and paper 205t, Untitled by Charlie Alyungurra, 1970 pigment on composite board 205c, The Mermaid Coffin by Gaynor Peaty, 205b; NATIONAL TRUST OF AUSTRALIA: © Christopher Groenhout 404cl, 405tl, b; NATURAL HISTORY PHOTOGRAPHIC AGENCY: © A.N.T 24cl, 161ca, 213t, 295bl, br, 336tr, cr, 454cra, cb, 458t; © Patrick Faggot 248; © Pavel German 286tl; © Martin Harvey 25ca; © Ralph & Daphne Keller 294bca; © Norbert Wu 214tl; PETER NEWARK'S HISTORICAL PICTURES: 29cr, 50clb, 371ca; TOURISM NSW: 178cl, cb; NORTHERN TERRITORY LIBRARY: 264-5c, 265crb; Percy Brown Collection 264br; N Gleeson Collection 264tr; NUCOLORVUE PRODUCTIONS PTY LTD: 53b.

Photography courtesy of the Olympic Co-ordination Authority: 143 cla; Photo: Karl Carlstrom 143 clb; © OPEN SPACES PHOTOGRAPHY: Photo: Andrew Barnes 439b; Photo: Glen Tempest 358, 567cl, 569t; © OUTBACK PHOTOGRAPHICS, NT: Steve Strike 1994 288tr; Steve Strike 1995 289c; OXFORD SCIENTIFIC FILMS: © Mantis Wildlife Films 294cl; © Babs & Bert Wells 294clb; PARLIAMENT HOUSE: The Hon Max Willis, RFD, ED, LLB, MLC, President, Legislative Council, Parliament of NSW. The Hon J Murray, MP, Speaker, Legislative Assembly, Parliament of NSW. Artist's original sketch of the

Sydney Transport Map

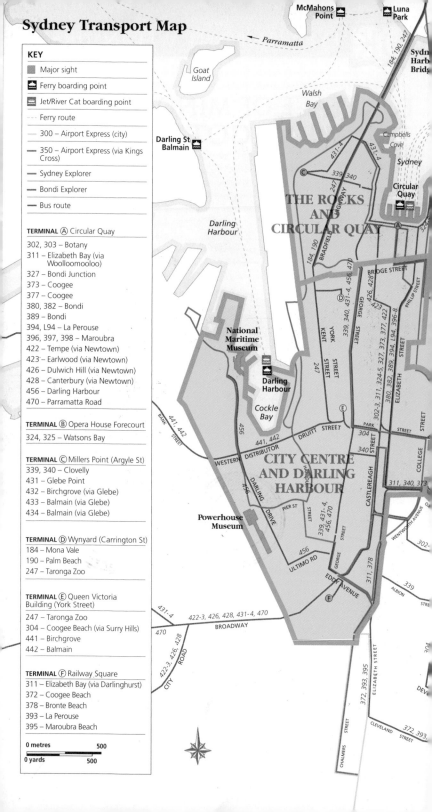

KEY

- ▪ Major sight
- ⛴ Ferry boarding point
- ⛴ Jet/River Cat boarding point
- ---- Ferry route
- —— 300 – Airport Express (city)
- —— 350 – Airport Express (via Kings Cross)
- —— Sydney Explorer
- —— Bondi Explorer
- —— Bus route

TERMINAL Ⓐ Circular Quay

302, 303 – Botany
311 – Elizabeth Bay (via Woolloomooloo)
327 – Bondi Junction
373 – Coogee
377 – Coogee
380, 382 – Bondi
389 – Bondi
394, L94 – La Perouse
396, 397, 398 – Maroubra
422 – Tempe (via Newtown)
423 – Earlwood (via Newtown)
426 – Dulwich Hill (via Newtown)
428 – Canterbury (via Newtown)
456 – Darling Harbour
470 – Parramatta Road

TERMINAL Ⓑ Opera House Forecourt

324, 325 – Watsons Bay

TERMINAL Ⓒ Millers Point (Argyle St)

339, 340 – Clovelly
431 – Glebe Point
432 – Birchgrove (via Glebe)
433 – Balmain (via Glebe)
434 – Balmain (via Glebe)

TERMINAL Ⓓ Wynyard (Carrington St)

184 – Mona Vale
190 – Palm Beach
247 – Taronga Zoo

TERMINAL Ⓔ Queen Victoria Building (York Street)

247 – Taronga Zoo
304 – Coogee Beach (via Surry Hills)
441 – Birchgrove
442 – Balmain

TERMINAL Ⓕ Railway Square

311 – Elizabeth Bay (via Darlinghurst)
372 – Coogee Beach
378 – Bronte Beach
393 – La Perouse
395 – Maroubra Beach

0 metres 500
0 yards 500